Students'
DICTIONARY

Editors
Sandra Anderson
Kay Cullen

Chambers Martins Fontes

CHAMBERS – MARTINS FONTES
Published by arrangement with Chambers Harrap Publishers Ltd
Copyright © Chambers Harrap Publishers Ltd 1998

1ª edition
august, 1999

All rights reserved. No part of this publication may be reproduced, stored or transmitted by any means, electronic, mechanical, photocopying or otherwise, without prior permission of the publisher.

A CIP catalogue record for this book is available from the British Library.

ISBN 85-336-1078-5

We have made every effort to mark as such all words which we believe to be trademarks. We should also like to make it clear that the presence of a word in the dictionary, whether marked or unmarked, in no way affects its legal status as a trademark.

The British National Corpus is a collaborative initiative carried out by Oxford University Press, Longman, Chambers Harrap, Oxford University Computing Services, Lancaster University's Unit for Computer Research in the English language, and the British Library. The project received funding from the UK Department of Trade and Industry and was supported by additional research grants from the British Academy and the British Library.

Typeset in Great Britain by Chambers Harrap Publishers Ltd, Edinburgh
Printed in Brazil by Cromosete, São Paulo, S.P.

Todos os direitos para o Brasil, desta edição, reservados à
Livraria Martins Fontes Editora Ltda.
Rua Conselheiro Ramalho, 330/340
01325-000 São Paulo SP Brasil
Tel. (011) 239-3677 Fax (011) 3105-6867
e-mail: info@martinsfontes.com
http://www.martinsfontes.com

CONTENTS

Contributors iv

Introduction v

Pronunciation guide vii

The dictionary **1**

Appendix 603

CONTRIBUTORS

Publishing Director
Robert Allen

Managing Editor
Elaine Higgleton

Senior Editor
Anne Seaton

Editors
Sandra Anderson
Kay Cullen

Computer Officer
Ilona Morison

INTRODUCTION

Chambers Students' Dictionary is a dictionary for lower intermediate students who have already started to learn English and who need help in widening their English vocabulary and their knowledge of how to use the English language.

It is the aim of this dictionary actively to teach and guide, as well as to be an accurate reference for words and their meanings. Special help in avoiding common errors and pitfalls is given in tinted boxes, and extra help – with grammar, spelling rules and several other topics – is given in the appendix section at the back of the book.

The following guide shows how an entry in this dictionary is arranged.

Pronunciation is shown for each headword using the International Phonetic Alphabet.

Words connected with the headword
The part that you put the heavy 'stress' or 'accent' on has the mark ' before it.

allergy /ˈalədʒɪ/ *n* something in your body or skin that makes certain foods or materials disagree with you: *She has an allergy to fish.* **alˈlergic** *adj* affected in a bad way by certain things: *He is allergic to milk*

If the pronunciation of a word is in any way difficult, then pronunciation is given using the International Phonetic Alphabet.

allege /əˈlɛdʒ/ *v* to say something without proof: *The lady alleged that he had stolen her handbag.* **allegation** /alə'geɪʃən/ *n*.

Grammatical use or part of speech
The way a word is used is shown by a label:
n = noun   *v* = verb
ns = nouns   *prep* = preposition
adj = adjective   *pron* = pronoun
adv = adverb

alike /əˈlaɪk/ *adj* like one another; similar: *Twins are often very alike.* — *adv* in the same way: *He treated all his children alike.*

Plurals The plural of a word is given if it is formed in an unusual way, or is difficult to remember.

basis /ˈbeɪsɪs/, *plural* **bases** /ˈbeɪsiːz/, *n* **1** something on which a thing rests or depends: *This idea is the basis of my argument.* **2** the

---

Meanings If a word has several meanings, these are separately numbered.

Examples To make the meaning clearer, there is very often an example showing the word being used. Examples are supported by the British National Corpus, a 100-million-word database of current English.

all /ɔːl/ *adj, pron* **1** the whole: *He ate all the cake; Did you eat it all?* **2** every one: *They were all present; All men are equal.* **3** everything; the only thing: *She told me all she knew; All I want is a bit of peace.* — *adv* **1** completely: *all alone; dressed all in white.* **2** much; even: *I feel all the better for a shower.* **3** for each side: *The score is five all.*

v

Arrangement of words In many cases a headword is followed by a group of words and phrases that are connected with it.	**alert** /ə'lɜːt/ *adj* **1** quick-thinking: *She's old but still very alert.* **2** watchful and aware: *You must be alert to danger.* — *n* a signal to be ready for action. — *v* to make someone alert; to warn: *The alarm alerted us to the fire.* **a'lertly** *adv.* **a'lertness** *n.* **on the alert** watchful: *He was on the alert for any strange sound.*
Some words are given without definitions or examples, if their meaning is clear.	**accurate** /'akjʊrət/ *adj* **1** exactly right: *an accurate drawing.* **2** making no mistakes: *an accurate memory.* **'accuracy** *n.* **'accurately** *adv.*
Some words are shown only in a particular phrase, because this is the way they are normally used.	**aback** /ə'bak/: **taken aback** surprised and rather upset: *She was clearly taken aback at the suggestion.*
When two or more words have the same spelling, they are numbered.	**bay**¹ /beɪ/ *n* a wide inward bend in the coast: *Ships were anchored in the bay.* **bay**² /beɪ/ *n* an area which has a particular purpose in a building: *a factory loading bay; a parking bay.*
Tinted boxes give extra help with words that are especially difficult to use, extra information, the parts of irregular verbs, and opposites.	A **battle** is a fight between armies, lasting a short time. A **war** is a period of armed fighting between nations, that can last several years.
The words 'see' and 'see also' tell you to look at another word in the dictionary where more information is given.	See **disembark**.

vi

PRONUNCIATION GUIDE

Key to the phonetic symbols used in the dictionary:

Consonants

p	/piː/	**p**ea
t	/tiː/	**t**ea
k	/kiː/	**k**ey
b	/biː/	**b**ee
d	/daɪ/	**d**ye
g	/gaɪ/	**g**uy
m	/miː/	**m**e
n	/njuː/	**n**ew
ŋ	/sɒŋ/	so**ng**
θ	/θɪn/	**th**in
ð	/ðɛn/	**th**en
f	/fan/	**f**an
v	/van/	**v**an
s	/siː/	**s**ee
z	/zuːm/	**z**oom
ʃ	/ʃiː/	**sh**e
ʒ	/beɪʒ/	bei**ge**
tʃ	/iːtʃ/	ea**ch**
dʒ	/ɛdʒ/	e**dge**
h	/hat/	**h**at
l	/leɪ/	**l**ay
r	/reɪ/	**r**ay
j	/jɛs/	**y**es
w	/weɪ/	**w**ay

Vowels

Short vowels

ɪ	/bɪd/	b**i**d
ɛ	/bɛd/	b**e**d
a	/bad/	b**a**d
ʌ	/bʌd/	b**u**d
ɒ	/pɒt/	p**o**t
ʊ	/pʊt/	p**u**t
ə	/əˈbaʊt/	**a**bout

Long vowels

iː	/biːd/	b**ea**d
ɑː	/hɑːm/	h**ar**m
ɔː	/ɔːl/	**a**ll
uː	/buːt/	b**oo**t
ɜː	/bɜːd/	b**ir**d

Diphthongs

eɪ	/beɪ/	b**ay**
aɪ	/baɪ/	b**uy**
ɔɪ	/bɔɪ/	b**oy**
aʊ	/haʊ/	h**ow**
oʊ	/goʊ/	g**o**
ɪə	/bɪə(r)/	b**eer**
ɛə	/bɛə(r)/	b**are**
ʊə	/pʊə(r)/	p**oor**

Notes

1. The stress mark (ˈ) is placed before the stressed syllable on both phonetics and nested bold items (*eg* **bonnet** /ˈbɒnɪt/ and ˈ**bookcase**).

2. The symbol '(r)' is used to represent *r* when it comes at the end of a word, to indicate that it is pronounced when followed by a vowel (as in the phrase *four or five* /fɔːr ɔː ˈfaɪv/).

A

A or **a** /eɪ/, *plural* **As** or **a's**, *n* the best grade that can be given for an essay or exam: *She got three As in history last term.*

a /eɪ/ or /ə/ or **an** /an/ or /ən/ *adj* **1** one: *a cup of coffee and two teas, please*; *a million dollars.* **2** any; every: *An owl can see in the dark.* **3** one of a group or class of people or things: *She wants to be a doctor.* **4** for each: *We earn £6 an hour.*

> **an** is used before words beginning with **a, e, i, o, u**: *an apron*; *an officer*; also before **h** when **h** is not sounded: *an hour*. **a** is used before all other letters: *a book*; *a house*; also before **u** when its sound is /juː/ *a union.*

aback /əˈbak/: **taken aback** surprised and rather upset: *She was clearly taken aback at the suggestion.*

abacus /ˈabəkəs/, *plural* **ˈabacuses**, *n* a frame with rows of sliding beads that are used for counting: *The teacher is showing the children how to count with an abacus.*

abandon /əˈbandən/ *v* **1** to leave something behind on purpose: *They abandoned the stolen car.* **2** to give up an idea *etc*: *They abandoned the plan.* **aˈbandonment** *n*.

abashed /əˈbaʃt/ *adj* shy; embarrassed.

abate /əˈbeɪt/ *v* to become less: *The storm abated.*

abattoir /ˈabətwɑː(r)/ *n* a place where animals are killed for food.

abbess /ˈabɛs/ *n* the female head of an abbey.

abbey /ˈabɪ/ *n* **1** the building in which a Christian group of monks or nuns lives. **2** the church belonging to it.

abbot /ˈabət/ *n* the male head of an abbey.

abbreviate /əˈbriːvɪeɪt/ *v* to shorten a word, name *etc*.

abbreviˈation *n* a shortened form of a word *etc*: *Maths is an abbreviation of mathematics.*

abdicate /ˈabdɪkeɪt/ *v* to give up the position of king or queen: *The king abdicated (the throne) in favour of his son.* **abdiˈcation** *n*.

abdomen /ˈabdəmən/ *n* the part of the body between the chest and the hips. **abdominal** /abˈdɒmɪnəl/ *adj*.

abduct /əbˈdʌkt/ *v* to take someone away against their will by trickery or violence. **abˈduction** *n*.

abhor /əbˈhɔː(r)/ *v* to hate very much. **abhorrence** /əbˈhɒrəns/ *n*.
abhorrent /əbˈhɒrənt/ *adj* horrible.

abide /əˈbaɪd/ *v* to put up with; to bear: *I can't abide noise.*
abide by to obey: *You must abide by the rules.*

ability /əˈbɪlɪtɪ/ *n* **1** the power, strength or knowledge to do something: *Small babies don't have the ability to walk.* **2** a skill or talent: *She showed remarkable ability as an organizer. a person of unusual abilities.*

ablaze /əˈbleɪz/ *adj* on fire: *The building was ablaze.*

able /ˈeɪbəl/ *adj* **1** having enough strength or knowledge or time to do something: *He was able to open the door*; *He will come if he is able.* **2** clever and skilful; good at your job: *a very able government minister.* **ably** /ˈeɪblɪ/ *adv*.

abnormal /abˈnɔːməl/ *adj* strange; not normal: *Rainfall of more than 100 inches per year isn't abnormal in this part of Scotland.*
abnorˈmality *n*. **abˈnormally** *adv*.

aboard /əˈbɔːd/ *adv, prep* on or onto, in or into a ship, train, bus or aircraft: *He went aboard the aeroplane*; *We remained aboard after the ship docked.*

abode /əˈboʊd/ *n* an old word for a house or the place where someone lives: *The poor old man had no fixed abode and lived on the streets.*

abolish /əˈbɒlɪʃ/ *v* to put an end to a custom, law *etc*. **abolition** *n*.

aboriginal /abəˈrɪdʒɪnəl/ *n* a native of a country, especially of Australia. — *adj*.

abort /əˈbɔːt/ *v* to lose a baby before birth, or stop a baby being born.
aˈbortion *n* an operation to stop a baby being born.
aˈbortive *adj* unsuccessful.

abound /əˈbaʊnd/ *v* to be very plentiful.

about /əˈbaʊt/ *prep* **1** on the subject of: *We talked about our plans*; *What is the book about?* **2** around; in: *Toys were lying about the room*; *She is somewhere about the house.* **3** connected with an activity, a place or a person's character: *What do you like best about school?*; *There's something very strange about her.* — *adv* **1** nearly; roughly; around: *about five miles away*; *about six* *o'clock; just about big enough.* **2** in different directions; here and there: *The children ran about; Clothes were scattered about.* **3** present in a place: *It was dark and there was nobody about.*

about to going to: *I am about to leave.*

about turn or **about face** a command to turn to face in the opposite direction.

above /əˈbʌv/ *prep* **1** over; higher up than: *a picture above the fireplace.* **2** greater than: *The rainfall is above average.* — *adv* **1** higher up: *The noise seemed to be coming from above; a student in the year above.* **2** earlier in a text: *Study the questions above carefully before writing your answers.*

> See **over**.

above all most importantly: *He is strong, brave and, above all, honest.*

above-board /əbʌvˈbɔːd/ *adj* open and honest.

abrasion /əˈbreɪʒən/ *n* a scrape or scratch, especially on the skin.

aˈbrasive *adj* **1** very unpleasant and annoying: *I don't like the way he talks to me — he is always so abrasive.* **2** making surfaces rough when rubbed on them: *An abrasive cleaner will damage the polished table top.*

abreast /əˈbrɛst/ *adv* side by side: *They walked along the road three abreast.*

keep abreast of to keep up with.

abridge /əˈbrɪdʒ/ *v* to make a book *etc* shorter. **aˈbridged** *adj.* **aˈbridgement** *n*.

abroad /əˈbrɔːd/ *adv* in or to another country: *He lived abroad for many years.*

abrupt /əˈbrʌpt/ *adj* **1** sudden; unexpected: *The arrival of the police brought the party to an abrupt end.* **2** rude or sharp in the way you speak: *an abrupt manner.* **aˈbruptly** *adv.* **aˈbruptness** *n*.

abscess /ˈabsɛs/ or /ˈabsəs/ *n* a painful swelling, containing pus.

abscond /əbˈskɒnd/ *v* to escape or run away: *He absconded from police custody.*

absent /ˈabsənt/ *adj* away; not present: *Johnny was absent from school with a cold.*

> The opposite of **absent** is **present**.

ˈabsence *n* being away: *He returned home after an absence of two years; Nobody noticed her absence.*

absentee /absənˈtiː/ *n* a person who is absent.

absent-ˈminded *adj* forgetful: *an absent-minded professor.*

absolute /ˈabsəluːt/ or /ˈabsəljuːt/ *adj* complete: *absolute honesty.*

ˈabsolutely *adv* **1** completely: *It is absolutely impossible for me to go.* **2** a word used to agree completely: *'It was a wonderful film, wasn't it?' 'Absolutely!'*

absolution /absəˈluːʃən/ *n* forgiveness.

absolve /əbˈzɒlv/ *v* to forgive; to pardon.

absorb /əbˈzɔːb/ *v* **1** to soak up: *The earth absorbs the rain.* **2** to take up a person's attention.

abˈsorbent *adj* able to soak up: *absorbent paper.*

absorption /əbˈzɔːpʃən/ *n*.

> The noun **absorption** is spelt with a **p**.

abstain /əbˈsteɪn/ *v* **1** to decide not to vote in an election *etc.* **2** to keep away from, or not do something, especially something you want to do: *to abstain from alcohol.*

abstention /əbˈstɛnʃən/ *n* not voting for or against something: *There were six votes for the motion, four against it and two abstentions.*

abstract /ˈabstrakt/ *adj* existing only as an idea, not as a real thing. — *n* a summary of a book *etc*.

in the abstract in theory and not in practice: *She understands how to drive a car in the abstract but still needs lots of practice before she takes her test.*

absurd /əbˈsɜːd/ *adj* very silly. **abˈsurdity**, **abˈsurdness** *ns*. **abˈsurdly** *adv*.

abundance /əˈbʌndəns/ *n* a large amount: *an abundance of food; There was food in abundance.*

aˈbundant *adj* plentiful. **aˈbundantly** *adv*.

abuse *v* /əˈbjuːz/ **1** to use wrongly: *He was accused of abusing his power.* **2** to insult or speak roughly to: *She was abused by a hostile crowd.* **3** to treat cruelly: *They had been beaten and abused.* — *n* /əˈbjuːs/ **1** insults: *verbal abuse; to shout abuse at someone.* **2** cruelty: *She suffered years of abuse from her husband.* **3** the wrong use of something: *drug abuse.*

aˈbusive *adj* using insulting words.

abysmal /əˈbɪzməl/ *adj* very bad: *For them, it was an abysmal result.* **aˈbysmally** *adv*.

abyss /əˈbɪs/ *n* a very deep or bottomless hole.

academy /əˈkadəmɪ/ *n* a college for special study.

academic /akəˈdɛmɪk/ *adj* **1** having to do with study in schools, colleges *etc*: *the academic year.* **2** connected with study and thinking, not practical skills: *He enjoyed drawing and painting more than the academic subjects.* — **acaˈdemically** *adv*.

accede /ək'siːd/: **accede to** to agree to.
  accede to the throne to become king or queen: *She acceded to the throne in 1952.*
accelerate /ək'sɛləreɪt/ *v* to increase speed. **acceleˈration** *n*.
  acˈcelerator *n* a pedal, lever *etc* by which speed is increased.
accent *n* /'aksənt/ **1** the sounding of part of a word extra strongly: *In 'banana', the accent is on the second syllable.* **2** a mark used to show the pronunciation of a letter: *You can put an accent on the e in début.* **3** a special way of pronouncing words in a particular area *etc*: *an American accent.* — *v* /ak'sɛnt/ to pronounce with stress or emphasis.
  accentuate /ək'sɛntʃʊeɪt/ *v* to emphasize: *This colour accentuates her blue eyes.* **accentuˈation** *n*.
accept /ək'sɛpt/ *v* **1** to take something offered: *He accepted the gift.* **2** to believe in or agree to: *We accept your explanation of what happened*; *Their proposal was accepted.* **3** to say 'yes' to an invitation: *She invited me to tea and I accepted.* **4** to decide that a person is suitable for a course: *She has been accepted by the university to study English.*

> Please **accept** (not **except**) this gift.

  acˈceptable *adj* **1** satisfactory. **2** pleasing. **acˈceptably** *adv*.

> The opposite of **acceptable** is **unacceptable**.

  acˈceptance *n*.
access /'aksɛs/ *n* way of entry: *We gained access to the house through a window.*
  acˈcessible *adj* able to be reached easily.
accession /ək'sɛʃən/ *n* coming to the position of king or queen: *the Queen's accession to the throne.*
accessory /ək'sɛsərɪ/ *n* something additional or extra.
accident /'aksɪdənt/ *n* **1** an unexpected happening, especially an unpleasant one in which people are hurt: *There has been a road accident.* **2** chance: *I met her by accident.*
  acciˈdental *adj* happening by chance.
  acciˈdentally *adv*.
acclaim /ə'kleɪm/ *v* to praise or welcome: *The footballer was acclaimed by the fans.* — *n* praise.
  acclamation /aklə'meɪʃən/ *n* noisy agreement or praise.
acclimatize /ə'klaɪmətaɪz/ *v* to make or become accustomed to a place or thing: *You'll be able to find your way around once you've acclimatized.* **acˈclimatization** *n*.
accommodate /ə'kɒmədeɪt/ *v* **1** to provide a person with a place to stay: *The conference delegates will be accommodated in hotels.* **2** to be big enough for: *The house will accommodate two families.*

> **accommodate** has two **c**s and two **m**s.

  acˈcommodating *adj* helpful.
  accommoˈdation *n* rooms in a house or hotel in which to stay.

> **accommodation** has no plural.

accompany /ə'kʌmpənɪ/ *v* **1** to go with someone or something: *He accompanied her to school.* **2** to play music for a singer or solo instrument *etc*: *He accompanied her on the piano.* **aˈccompaniment** *n*.
aˈccomplice /ə'kʌmplɪs/ or /ə'kɒmplɪs/ *n* a person who helps another, especially in crime.
accomplish /ə'kʌmplɪʃ/ or /ə'kɒmplɪʃ/ *v* to complete something successfully: *Have you accomplished your task?*
  acˈcomplished *adj* good at something: *an accomplished singer.*
  acˈcomplishment *n* **1** completing; finishing. **2** a special skill.
accord /ə'kɔːd/ *v* **1** to agree with. **2** to give.
  acˈcordance: **in accordance with** in agreement with; according to.
  acˈcordingly *adv* **1** in a suitable way. **2** therefore.
  according to 1 as said or told by someone: *According to John, the bank closes at 3 p.m.* **2** in agreement with something: *He acted according to his promise.* **3** in the order of: *books arranged according to their subjects.* **4** as is right for: *You will be paid according to the amount of work you have done.*
  of your own accord of your own free will: *He did it of his own accord, without being forced to.*
accordion /ə'kɔːdɪən/ *n* a musical instrument with keys like a piano, that you play by squeezing.
accost /ə'kɒst/ *v* to stop someone and speak to them: *He accosted me in the street.*
account /ə'kaʊnt/ *n* **1** a description or explanation of something that has happened: *He wrote an interesting account of his holiday in New Zealand.* **2** an arrangement by which a person keeps his money in a bank; the amount of money he has in the bank: *she has only £50 left in her account.* **3** an arrange-

accumulate

ment with a shop *etc* by which a person can pay at the end of each month for all the things he buys during the month. **4** a statement of money that is owed; a bill.

> See **bank**².

ac'countable *adj* responsible.
ac'countancy *n* the work of an accountant.
ac'countant *n* someone whose job is to look after money accounts.
ac'counts *n* written records of money received and spent.
account for to give a reason for; to explain: *I cannot account for the mistake.*
by all accounts according to what everyone says.
on account of because of: *She stayed indoors on account of the bad weather.*
on no account or **not on any account** not for any reason: *You must not on any account, go out alone at night*; *On no account should you enter the room without knocking.*
take into account or **take account of** consider something when making a decision.
accumulate /əˈkjuːmjʊleɪt/ *v* to gather or be gathered together in a large quantity: *Rubbish accumulates very quickly in our house.* **ac'cumulation** *n*.
accurate /ˈakjʊrət/ *adj* **1** exactly right: *an accurate drawing.* **2** making no mistakes: *an accurate memory.* **'accuracy** *n*. **'accurately** *adv*.

> The opposite of **accurate** is **inaccurate**.

accuse /əˈkjuːz/ *v* to tell someone that you know or think they have done something wrong: *They accused him of stealing the car.* **accu'sation** *n*.
the accused the person or people accused in a court of law.
accustom /əˈkʌstəm/ *v* to make someone used to something: *He soon accustomed himself to his new life.*
ac'customed *adj* usual: *his accustomed seat.*
accustomed to used to: *I am not accustomed to being treated like this.*
ace /eɪs/ *n* **1** the one in playing-cards: *the ace of spades.* **2** a person who is expert at anything: *He's an ace at shooting with a rifle.* **3** a serve in tennis that the other player cannot hit back.
ache /eɪk/ *n* a continuous pain: *I have an ache in my stomach.* — *v* to be in continuous pain: *My tooth aches.*
achieve /əˈtʃiːv/ *v* to gain; to reach suc-

cessfully: *He has achieved his ambition.* **a'chievement** *n*.
acid /ˈasɪd/ *adj* **1** sharp or sour in taste: *Lemons and limes are acid fruits.* **2** rather sharp or unkind in the way you speak. — *n* a sour substance that can burn the skin.
acid house a style of dance music with a repetitive beat.
acid rain rain that contains harmful acids released into the air by cars and factories: *Acid rain is responsible for the destruction of many acres of forest land.*
a'cidity *n* sourness.
acknowledge /əkˈnɒlɪdʒ/ *v* **1** to admit; to agree that something is true: *He acknowledged that I was right.* **2** to say thank-you to someone for something, or to let them know you have received it: *He acknowledged my letter.* **ac'knowledgement** *n*.
acne /ˈakni/ *n* a skin disease with spots and pimples on the face, chest and back: *Acne is common among teenagers.*
acoustics /əˈkuːstɪks/ *n plural* the qualities of a room or hall that make hearing in it good or bad: *The acoustics of the new concert hall are very good.* **a'coustic** *adj*.
acquaint /əˈkweɪnt/ *v* to make someone know something well: *to acquaint yourself with the rules.*
ac'quaintance *n* **1** a person whom you know. **2** knowledge. **3** a friendship.
acquainted with friendly or familiar with: *I'm not acquainted with her father.*
acquire /əˈkwaɪə(r)/ *v* to get: *He acquired a knowledge of English.*
acquisition /akwɪˈzɪʃən/ *n* **1** getting: *Some people are only interested in the acquisition of wealth.* **2** something got; a new possession.
acquit /əˈkwɪt/ *v* to declare innocent: *The judge acquitted her of murder.* **ac'quittal** *n*.

> **acquitting** and **acquitted** are spelt with two **t**s.

acre /ˈeɪkə(r)/ *n* a measure of land equal to 4840 square yards or 4047 square metres: *24 acres of forest.*
acrobat /ˈakrəbat/ *n* a person in a circus *etc* who performs gymnastics. **acro'batic** *adj*.
acro'batics *n* gymnastics.
across /əˈkrɒs/ *prep* **1** to the other side of something; from one side to the other side of something: *He took her across the road.* **2** at the other side of something: *The butcher's shop is across the street.* — *adv* to the other side: *If the road is busy, don't run across.*

use **across** or **over** for moving to the other side of something flat: *walk across the road.*

use **over** when something is high: *climb over the wall.*

acrylic /ə'krılık/ *n* a man-made material often used instead of wool. — *adj*: *an acrylic sweater.*

act /akt/ *v* **1** to do something: *Don't wait — act now!* **2** to behave: *He acted foolishly.* **3** to perform a part in a play: *Would you like to act the part of the witch?* — *n* **1** something done: *Running away is a cowardly act.* **2** a section of a play: *a play with two acts.* **3** an entertainment: *a comedy act.*

a stupid **act** or a stupid **action**, but only an **act** (not **action**) of stupidity.

act as to do the work or duties of: *Mrs Brown will act as headmistress till I return.*

act for to take the place of someone else and do their duties: *She is acting for the headmaster in his absence.*

act on 1 to obey: *I acted on his instructions.* **2** to have an effect on something.

in the act at the exact moment of doing something: *He was caught in the act of stealing my car.*

put on an act to pretend: *I thought she had hurt herself but she was only putting on an act.*

acting /'aktıŋ/ *n* performing in plays and films. — *adj* temporary: *I am the acting manager while Mr. Ross is on holiday.*

action /'akʃən/ *n* **1** something done: *a foolish action; Take action immediately; The firemen are ready to go into action.* **2** movement: *Tennis needs a good wrist action.* **3** a battle; fighting: *He was killed in action.* **4** the events in a story: *Most of the action takes place in India.*

in action working: *Is your machine still in action?*

out of action not working: *My car's out of action this week.*

active /'aktıv/ *adj* **1** lively; able to work *etc*: *At seventy, he's no longer very active.* **2** busy: *She is an active member of the club.* **3** causing an effect: *an active force.* **4** likely to erupt: *active volcanoes.* **5** a verb is called **active** when its subject performs the action of the verb: *The dog bit the man.*

See **passive**.

activate /'aktıveıt/ *v* to make something start working: *The smoke activated the fire alarm.*

ac'tivity *n* **1** the state of being active or lively: *The school is full of activity this morning.*

The opposite of **activity**¹ is **inactivity**.

2 something you do as a hobby or as part of your job: *His activities include fishing and golf.*

actor /'aktə(r)/ *n* a performer in a play or film: *He wanted to go on the stage, so he joined a troupe of actors.*

actress /'aktrıs/ *n* a female performer in a play or film.

actual /'aktʃʊəl/ *adj* real: *In actual fact he is not as stupid as you think.*

actuality /aktʃʊ'alıtı/ *n* reality.

'actually *adv* **1** really: *She actually saw the accident happen.* **2** in fact: *Actually, I'm doing something else this evening.*

acupuncture /'akjʊpʌŋktʃə(r)/ *n* a method of treating illnesses or pain by sticking needles into the patient's skin at certain points.

acute /ə'kju:t/ *adj* **1** very bad but not lasting very long: *an acute pain.* **2** very great: *There is an acute shortage of teachers.* **3** quick of understanding. **4** less than a right angle: *An angle of 45° is an acute angle.* **a'cutely** *adv.* **a'cuteness** *n.*

ad /ad/ short for **advertisement**.

adapt /ə'dapt/ *v* to change or alter so as to fit a different situation *etc*: *She has adapted the play for television; Children adapt quickly to new surroundings.* **adap'tation** *n.*

a'daptable *adj* willing or able to change to fit in with different circumstances.

a'daptor *n* a kind of electrical plug for connecting a plug of one type to a socket of a different type, or several plugs to one socket.

add /ad/ *v* **1** to put one thing with another: *He added water to his drink.* **2** to find the total of various numbers: *Add 7, 9 and 21 together; Add 124 to 356; He added up the figures.* **3** to say something extra: *He added that he was sorry.*

add on to include as extra: *Did you add the tax on to the total?*

add to to increase: *Don't add to our difficulties by misbehaving.*

add up to add together: *Add up your score.*

add up to to make a total of: *The bill adds up to £55.*

addict /'adıkt/ *n* a person who has become dependent on something, especially drugs.

ad'dicted *adj* dependent on a drug *etc*: *He is addicted to alcohol.* **ad'diction** *n*.

ad'dictive *adj* habit-forming: *Some medicines, like tranquillizers, contain addictive drugs.*

addition /ə'dɪʃən/ *n* **1** the process of adding. **2** something added: *A baby is a welcome addition to a family.*

in addition (to) as well (as): *She is studying chemistry in addition to maths and physics.* **ad'ditional** *adj* extra. **ad'ditionally** *adv*.

additive /'adɪtɪv/ *n* a substance that is added in small amounts, especially to food to improve it or to make it keep fresh longer: *This natural yoghurt is free from additives.*

address /ə'drɛs/ *v* **1** to put a name and address on a letter *etc*: *Address the parcel clearly.* **2** to speak to someone: *to address someone politely.* — *n* **1** the name of the house, street, town *etc* where a person lives: *His address is 30 Main St, Edinburgh.* **2** a speech.

adept /'adɛpt/ *adj* very clever: *He's adept at keeping his balance.*

adequate /'adəkwət/ *adj* **1** sufficient; enough. **2** satisfactory; good enough. **'adequately** *adv*.

> The opposite of **adequate** is **inadequate**.

adhere /əd'hɪə(r)/ *v* to stick: *This stamp won't adhere to the envelope.*

adhesion /əd'hiːʒən/ *n* sticking; adhering.

ad'hesive *adj* able to adhere; sticky: *adhesive tape.* — *n* glue: *Use a strong adhesive to mend the plate.*

adjacent /ə'dʒeɪsənt/ *adj* side by side; next to: *We had adjacent rooms in the hotel*; *Their house is adjacent to ours.*

adjective /'adʒəktɪv/ *n* a word which describes something: *a red flower*; *air which is cool*.

adjoin /ə'dʒɔɪn/ *v* to be next to or joined to something.

ad'joining *adj*: *the adjoining room.*

adjourn /ə'dʒɜːn/ *v* to stop a meeting or conference, intending to continue it at another time or place: *The meeting was adjourned until Tuesday.* **ad'journment** *n*.

adjudicate /ə'dʒuːdɪkeɪt/ *v* to be a judge in a competition or argument.

ad'judicator *n* a competition judge.

adjust /ə'dʒʌst/ *v* **1** to get used to: *He soon adjusted to his new way of life.* **2** to correct or alter a piece of machinery *etc*: *He adjusted the hands of the clock.*

ad'justable *adj* able to be adjusted. **ad'justment** *n*.

ad-lib /ad'lɪb/ *v* to say something not prepared in advance: *She had to ad-lib when she forgot her lines in the play.*

ad lib *adv*: *She had no notes, but spoke ad lib for thirty minutes.*

administer /əd'mɪnɪstə(r)/ *v* **1** to govern or manage. **2** to carry out a law *etc*. **3** to give medicine, help *etc*.

admini'stration *n* **1** management: *the administration of the hospital.* **2** the government of a country *etc.* **ad'ministrative** *adj*. **ad'ministrator** *n*.

admirable /'admərəbəl/ *adj* extremely good. **'admirably** *adv*.

admiral /'admɪrəl/ *n* the commander of a navy.

admire /əd'maɪə(r)/ *v* **1** to look at something with great pleasure; to say that you like something very much: *They were all admiring his new car.* **2** to have a very high opinion of something or someone: *I admire John's courage*; *I admire him for being so brave.*

admi'ration *n*: *They were filled with admiration at the team's performance.*

ad'mirer *n* a person who admires someone or something.

ad'miring *adj*: *an admiring look.* **ad'miringly** *adv*.

admission /əd'mɪʃən/ *n* **1** being allowed to go in: *We paid £2.50 for admission to the football ground.* **2** agreeing that something is true; owning up: *an admission of guilt.*

> **admission** and **admittance** both mean permission to enter, but you pay for **admission** to a public place such as a cinema, and you gain **admittance** to a private place such as a house.

admit /əd'mɪt/ *v* **1** to allow to enter. *This ticket admits one person.* **2** to agree that something is true; to own up: *He admitted that he had told a lie.*

ad'mittedly *adv* it must be admitted: *Admittedly, we don't know all the facts yet.*

> **admitting, admitted** and **admittedly** are spelt with two **t**s.

ad'mittance *n* permission to enter: *The notice said 'No admittance'.*

> See **admission**.

adolescent /adə'lɛsənt/ *adj* in the part of your life between childhood and adulthood. — *n* a person at this stage of life. **ado'lescence** *n*.

adopt /ə'dɒpt/ *v* **1** to take a child of other

parents as your own: *They decided to adopt a baby girl.* **2** to take and use something as your own: *He adopted his friend's ideas.* **a'doption** *n.*

adore /ə'dɔː(r)/ *v* **1** to love or like very much: *He adores his children.* **2** to worship.

a'dorable *adj*: *an adorable little baby.*

ado'ration *n* worship or great love.

adorn /ə'dɔːn/ *v* to make beautiful, with decorations or with jewellery: *The statue was adorned with gold rings and bracelets.* **a'dornment** *n.*

adrenalin /ə'drɛnəlɪn/ *n* a substance that is made inside your body, and that makes your heart beat faster and gives you more energy: *Your body produces adrenalin when you are frightened or excited.*

adrift /ə'drɪft/ *adj*, *adv* drifting; floating: *He untied the rope and set the boat adrift.*

adult /'adʌlt/ or /ə'dʌlt/ *adj* **1** fully grown: *an adult gorilla.* **2** sensible; grown-up: *adult behaviour.* — *n* a fully grown human being: *That film is suitable only for adults.*

adultery /ə'dʌltərɪ/ *n* being unfaithful to your wife or husband.

advance /əd'vɑːns/ *v* **1** to move forward; to progress: *The army advanced towards the town*; *Our plans are advancing well.* **2** to supply someone with money that they need, which they will be able to pay back later: *The bank will advance you £500.* — *n* **1** movement forward; progress. **2** a payment made before the normal time. — *adj* **1** made *etc* before the usual time: *an advance payment.* **2** made beforehand: *an advance booking for two theatre seats.*

ad'vanced *adj* having made a lot of progress; at a high level: *She teaches the advanced students*; *an advanced computer course.*

in advance beforehand; earlier: *Can you pay me in advance?*

advantage /əd'vɑːntɪdʒ/ *n* a gain or benefit: *What are the advantages of air travel?*

advantageous /advən'teɪdʒəs/ *adj* giving an advantage; good; useful.

have an advantage over: *As she could already speak French, she had an advantage over the others in the French class.*

take advantage of 1 to make the best use of something, such as a chance or opportunity. **2** to use unfairly.

advent /'advɛnt/ *n* the invention or first appearance of something: *Life has changed greatly since the advent of electric light.*

adventure /əd'vɛntʃə(r)/ *n* something exciting that you do or that happens to you; a great experience: *He wrote a book about his adventures in the Antarctic.*

ad'venturer *n* a person who is always looking for adventures.

ad'venturous *adj* liking adventures.

adverb /'advɜːb/ *n* a word used to describe a verb or an adjective: *He looked carefully in the box, and found a very small key.* **ad'verbial** *adj.*

adversary /'advəsərɪ/ *n* an opponent: *They summoned up the courage to face their adversaries*; *He'll be playing against his old adversary in the next round of the competition.*

adverse /'advɜːs/ *adj* bad: *Smoking by parents could have an adverse effect on their children's health.* **ad'versely** *adv.*

ad'versity *n* trouble; bad luck; something that causes difficulty: *He always remains cheerful in spite of adversity*; *The athlete injured her ankle while training for the race and had various other adversities to overcome.*

advert /'advɜːt/ short for **advertisement**.

advertise /'advətaɪz/ *v* to make something known to a lot of people: *The time and place for the meeting will be advertised in the newspaper.*

advertisement /əd'vɜːtɪsmənt/ *n* a short film, newspaper announcement, poster *etc* making something known, especially in order to persuade people to buy it: *an advertisement for toothpaste on television*; *She replied to my advertisement for a secretary.*

'advertising *n* making advertisements.

> **advertise** /'advətaɪz/ and **advertising** /'advətaɪzɪŋ/ but **advertisement** /əd'vɜːtɪsmənt/ not /'advətaɪzmənt/.

advice /əd'vaɪs/ *n* helpful suggestions to a person about what he should do: *Let me give you a piece of advice.*

advise /əd'vaɪz/ *v* **1** to give advice to someone: *My teacher advises me to work harder.* **2** to inform; to tell.

ad'visable *adj* wise; sensible: *It is not advisable to swim after a meal.*

ad'viser or **ad'visor** *n* a person who advises.

ad'visory *adj* giving advice.

> **advice** is a noun and never used in the plural: *a piece of advice*; *some advice.*
> **advise** is a verb: *He advises us not to go.*

advocate *v* /'advəkeɪt/ to speak in favour of something; to recommend: *He advocated* the provision of more sports centres. — n /'ædvəkət/ **1** someone who supports a plan, an idea *etc*: *She has always been an advocate of changes to English spelling, to make it easier to learn.* **2** a lawyer who speaks in defence of a person who is being tried in court.

aerial /'ɛərɪəl/ *n* a construction of metal rods that can send or receive radio waves *etc*: *a television aerial.* — *adj* in or from the air: *aerial photographs.*

aerobatics /ɛərə'bætɪks/ *n plural* difficult and dangerous movements made in an aeroplane, such as flying upside down.

aerobics /ɛə'roʊbɪks/ *n* exercises that you do usually to music, to make yourself fit: *Mrs Smith does aerobics in a gymnasium twice a week*; *an aerobics class.*

aerodrome /'ɛərədroʊm/ *n* an airport, especially one for private aircraft.

aerodynamics /ɛərədaɪ'næmɪks/ *n* the study of how objects move through the air. **aerody'namic** *adj.*

aeronautics /ɛərə'nɔːtɪks/ *n* the study of the design and flight of aircraft.

aeroplane /'ɛərəpleɪn/ *n* a machine for flying which is heavier than air and has wings.

> See **in.**

aerosol /'ɛərəsɒl/ *n* a metal container in which a liquid, such as a perfume, is kept under pressure and released as a fine spray: *An aerosol can explode if it gets too hot.*

aerospace /'ɛərəspeɪs/ *n* the earth's atmosphere and outer space beyond it.

aesthetic /iːs'θɛtɪk/ *adj* having to do with enjoying art and beauty.

aes'thetically *adv*: *aesthetically pleasing.*

afar /ə'fɑː(r)/ *adv* from, at or to a distance away: *They travelled from afar*; *the thunderous roar could be heard from afar.*

affair /ə'fɛə(r)/ *n* **1** happenings which are connected with a particular person or thing: *the affair of the missing schoolboy*; *a sad affair.* **2** business; concern: *financial affairs*; *What I spend my money on is my own affair.* **3** a love relationship between two people who are not husband and wife.

affect /ə'fɛkt/ *v* **1** to have an influence on something, or change it in some way: *What you eat affects your health.* **2** to make you feel very sad or angry *etc*: *She was deeply affected by the sight of the starving children.*

> **affect**, *verb*: *How will this drug affect me?*
> **effect**, *noun*: *What effect will this drug have on me?*

affection /ə'fɛkʃən/ *n* liking; fondness: *I have great affection for her.*

af'fectionate *adj* having or showing affection: *an affectionate daughter.* **af'fectionately** *adv.*

affirm /ə'fɜːm/ *v* to state that something is true. **affir'mation** *n.*

af'firmative *adj* expressing agreement. — *n.*

affix /ə'fɪks/ *v* to attach one thing to another: *Affix the stamp to the envelope.*

afflict /ə'flɪkt/ *v* to cause someone a lot of pain or suffering: *She is often afflicted with headaches*; *afflicted by grief.*

af'fliction *n* suffering; something that causes suffering: *Is blindness a worse affliction than deafness?*

affluent /'æfluənt/ *adj* rich; wealthy: *He comes from an affluent family and does not have to work.* **'affluence** *n.*

afford /ə'fɔːd/ *v* **1** to be able to spend money, time *etc* on or for something: *We can't afford to take a holiday.* **2** to be able to do something without trouble, difficulty *etc*: *Shopkeepers can't afford to be unfriendly to customers.*

af'fordable *adj*: *an affordable car.*

affront /ə'frʌnt/ *n* an insult. – *v* to hurt or insult someone: *She was affronted by their comments.*

afloat /ə'floʊt/ *adj* floating.

afraid /ə'freɪd/ *adj* **1** frightened of a person, thing *etc*: *The child is not afraid of the dark*; *She was afraid to go*; *He was afraid of making a mistake.* **2** worried: *She began to run because she was afraid that she would be late*; *He was afraid of upsetting his mother.* **3** sorry: *I'm afraid I don't agree with you.*

> Before a noun, use **frightened** instead of **afraid**: *a frightened child* (not *an afraid child*). After a noun, you can use **frightened** or **afraid**: *The child was frightened or afraid.*

afresh /ə'frɛʃ/ *adj* again and usually in a different way: *I need to make so many changes it would be better to start afresh.*

Afro- /'æfroʊ/ *prefix* African: *Afro-American.*

after /'ɑːftə(r)/ *prep* **1** later in time or place than something else: *She arrived after me.* **2** following something: *one thing after another*; *night after night.* **3** behind: *Shut the* *door after you!* **4** in pursuit of something: *He ran after the bus.* **5** considering: *After all I've done you'd think he'd thank me.* **6** looking for something or someone: *What are you after?*; *The police are after him.* — *adv* later in time or place: *They arrived soon after.* — *conjunction* later than some happening: *After she left we moved house.*

after all 1 considering everything: *I won't invite him. After all, I don't really know him.* **2** in spite of everything that has happened or been said before: *It turned out he went by plane after all.*

'after-effects *n* the usually bad or harmful effects of some action or event: *The after-effects of the war could last for several years.*

afternoon /ɑːftəˈnuːn/ *n* the time between midday and evening: *Come this afternoon*; *tomorrow afternoon.*

aftershave /ˈɑːftəʃeɪv/ *n* liquid that men put on their faces after shaving.

aftertaste /ˈɑːftəteɪst/ *n* a taste remaining in your mouth after eating and drinking.

afterthought /ˈɑːftəθɔːt/ *n* a later thought.

afterwards /ˈɑːftəwədz/ *adv* later: *He told me afterwards that he had not enjoyed the film.*

again /əˈgɛn/ or /əˈgeɪn/ *adv* once more: *He never saw her again*; *Don't do that again!*

against /əˈgɛnst/ or /əˈgeɪnst/ *prep* **1** opposed to something: *They fought against the enemy*; *Dropping litter is against the law.* **2** touching something: *He stood with his back against the wall*; *The rain beat against the window.* **3** to protect from something: *vaccination against tuberculosis.*

age /eɪdʒ/ *n* **1** the number of years you have lived: *He went to school at the age of six*; *What age is she?* **2** the state of being old: *The pages were yellow with age.* **3** a particular period of time: *the last Ice Age.* **4** a very long time: *We've been waiting for ages for a bus.* — *v* to grow old or look old: *He has aged a lot since I last saw him.*

aged *adj* **1** /ˈeɪdʒɪd/ old: *an aged man.* **2** /eɪdʒd/ of a certain age: *a child aged five.*

the aged /ˈeɪdʒɪd/ old people.

under age not legally old enough.

agency /ˈeɪdʒənsɪ/ *n* the office or business of an agent: *an advertising agency.*

agenda /əˈdʒɛndə/ *n* a list of things that have to be done or discussed, especially at a meeting: *the first item on the agenda*; *What's on the agenda today?*

agent /ˈeɪdʒənt/ *n* **1** a thing that can do something: *detergents and other cleaning agents.* **2** a person who acts for someone in business *etc.* **3** a spy: *a secret agent.*

aggravate /ˈagrəveɪt/ *v* **1** to make something worse: *His rudeness aggravated the situation.* **2** to make someone angry: *She was aggravated by his stupid questions.* **aggraˈvation** *n.*

aggressive /əˈgrɛsɪv/ *adj* always wanting to attack or quarrel with someone.

agˈgressively *adv.*

agˈgression *n* actions that start a quarrel, fight or war: *Attacking someone without a reason is an act of aggression.*

agˈgressor *n* a person or country that attacks first.

aggrieved /əˈgriːvd/ *adj* angry or upset.

aghast /əˈgɑːst/ *adj* shocked; horrified.

agile /ˈadʒaɪl/ *adj* able to move quickly and easily: *The antelope is very agile.* **agility** /əˈdʒɪlɪtɪ/ *n.*

agitate /ˈadʒɪteɪt/ *v* **1** to make someone excited and anxious: *The little girl was so agitated that she couldn't answer the headmaster's question.* **2** to try to stir up people's feelings for or against something: *Many people are agitating for a ban on the ivory trade.*

'agitated *adj*: *His face wore an agitated expression.*

agiˈtation *n.*

ago /əˈgoʊ/ *adv* in the past: *two years ago*; *How long ago did he leave?*

> See **since.**

agonize /ˈagənaɪz/ *v* to worry about something for a long time.

'agonizing *adj* causing great suffering: *an agonizing decision.*

agony /ˈagənɪ/ *n* great pain: *The dying man was in agony.*

agree /əˈgriː/ *v* **1** to think or say the same as someone: *I agreed with them that we should try again.* **2** to say that you will do or allow something: *He agreed to go*; *He agreed to our request.* **3** to be good for your health: *Cheese does not agree with me.*

> You **agree with** a person, but **agree to** a thing: *I agree with Jenny*; *I agreed to the plan.*

aˈgreeable *adj* pleasant: *She is a most agreeable person.* **aˈgreeably** *adv.*

aˈgreement *n* **1** thinking or saying the same: *We are all in agreement.* **2** an arrangement or promise between people in business *etc*: *You have broken our agreement.*

agriculture /ˈagrɪkʌltʃə(r)/ *n* growing crops

and rearing farm animals; farming. **agri-'cultural** *adj*.

aground /ə'graʊnd/ *adv* stuck on the bottom of the sea *etc* in shallow water: *The ship ran aground on a sandbank.*

ahead /ə'hɛd/ *adv* in front: *He went on ahead of me; We are well ahead of the others.*

aid /eɪd/ *n* help: *Rich countries give aid to developing countries; He came to my aid when my car broke down.* — *v* to help: *The blind man was aided by his dog.*

in aid of as a help to a charity *etc*: *Money was collected in aid of the blind.*

AIDS /eɪdz/ *n* short for **acquired immune deficiency syndrome**, an illness which destroys the body's natural ability to fight disease.

ailing /'eɪlɪŋ/ *adj* ill or weak: *He had to visit his ailing mother; an ailing economy.*

ailment /'eɪlmənt/ *n* an illness, usually not serious or dangerous.

aim /eɪm/ *v* **1** to point or direct at something: *He aimed his gun at the thief.* **2** to intend to do something: *He aims at finishing his painting tomorrow; We aim to please our customers.* — *n* what a person intends to do: *My aim is to become prime minister.*

'aimless *adj* without aim or purpose. **'aimlessly** *adv*.

air /eə(r)/ *n* **1** the mixture of gases we breathe: *He went outside to get some fresh air.* **2** the space above the ground; the sky: *Birds fly through the air.* **3** an appearance: *The house had an air of neglect.* — *v* **1** to bring something out into the air to dry or freshen *etc*: *to air sheets.* **2** to tell everyone: *He loved to air his opinions.*

'airborne *adj* in the air or flying.

air-con'ditioned *adj* having air-conditioning: *an air-conditioned building.*

air-con'ditioning *n* a method of controlling the temperature of the air in a room or building.

'aircraft *n* a machine for flying in the air.

aircraft carrier a ship which carries aircraft and which aircraft can use for landing and taking off.

'airfield *n* an area of ground where military and private aircraft are kept and where they take off and land: *An airfield is smaller than an airport.*

air force the part of the armed services which uses aircraft.

air hostess a woman who looks after passengers in an aircraft.

'airless *adj* without fresh air: *an airless room.*

air letter a letter sent by airmail.

'airline *n* a company that owns a regular air transport service: *Which airline are you travelling by?*

'airliner *n* a large passenger aircraft.

'airmail *n* a system of sending mail by air: *Send this parcel by airmail.* — *adj*: *an airmail letter.*

'airplane *n* an aeroplane.

'airport *n* a place where passenger aircraft arrive and depart.

'air-raid *n* a bombing attack on a town *etc*.

'airship *n* a large balloon which can be steered or driven.

'airstrip *n* a cleared area where aircraft can take off and land: *The small aeroplane landed on an airstrip in the jungle.*

'airtight *adj* made so that air cannot get in or out: *Food keeps fresh in an airtight container.*

air-traffic controller *n* a person who gives information and instructions to aeroplane pilots.

'airy *adj* **1** with plenty of fresh air: *an airy room.* **2** light-hearted; not serious.

on the air broadcasting on radio or television.

aisle /aɪl/ *n* a passage between seats *etc* in a church, cinema *etc*: *The bride walked up the aisle.*

ajar /ə'dʒɑː(r)/ *adj* partly open: *He left the door ajar.*

alarm /ə'lɑːm/ *n* **1** sudden fear. **2** something that gives warning of danger, attracts attention *etc*: *Sound the alarm!; a fire-alarm.* — *v* to make someone afraid: *Every little sound alarms the old lady.*

a'larming *adj* causing fear or worry: *alarming news.* **a'larmingly** *adv*.

alarm clock a clock that can be set to sound an alarm at a chosen time, especially to wake you up.

alas! /ə'læs/ a cry of sorrow.

album /'albəm/ *n* **1** a book for holding photographs, stamps *etc*. **2** a long-playing record: *I've got the group's latest album.*

alcohol /'alkəhɒl/ *n* a liquid which makes you drunk if you drink too much of it.

alco'holic *adj* **1** containing alcohol. **2** having to do with alcohol. — *n* a person who has become much too dependent on alcoholic drinks.

'alcoholism *n* dependence on alcoholic drinks.

alcove /ˈalkoʊv/ *n* a small part of a room where the wall is set back; a recess: *His bed was in an alcove on one side of the room.*

ale /eɪl/ *n* the name for certain kinds of beer.

alert /əˈlɜːt/ *adj* **1** quick-thinking: *She's old but still very alert.* **2** watchful and aware: *You must be alert to danger.* — *n* a signal to be ready for action. — *v* to make someone alert; to warn: *The alarm alerted us to the fire.* **aˈlertly** *adv.* **aˈlertness** *n.*

on the alert watchful: *He was on the alert for any strange sound.*

algae /ˈaldʒiː/ *n* a group of simple plants which includes seaweed.

algebra /ˈaldʒəbrə/ *n* a method of calculating using letters and signs for numbers.

alias /ˈeɪlɪəs/ *n* a false name. — *adv* otherwise known as: *John Smith, alias Peter Jones.*

alibi /ˈalɪbaɪ/ *n* a fact that proves that a person who is suspected of a crime was somewhere else when the crime was committed: *He has an alibi for the night of the robbery — he was at his aunt's house all evening.*

alien /ˈeɪlɪən/ *adj* **1** foreign: *alien customs.* **2** strange and unfamiliar. — *n* **1** a foreigner: *Aliens are not welcome there.* **2** a creature from another planet.

ˈalienate *v* to make someone dislike you: *She alienated her friends and family by her rude and selfish behaviour towards them.* **alieˈnation** *n.*

alight[1] /əˈlaɪt/ *v* **1** to get down from or out of a vehicle: *to alight from a bus.* **2** to settle or land: *The bird alighted on a branch.*

See **disembark**.

alight[2] /əˈlaɪt/ *adj* burning; on fire: *The bonfire was still alight; He set the house alight.*

align /əˈlaɪn/ *v* to put in a straight line: *Make sure the chairs are carefully aligned.* **aˈligned** *adj.* **aˈlignment** *n.*

be aligned with to form an alliance with another party or country.

alike /əˈlaɪk/ *adj* like one another; similar: *Twins are often very alike.* — *adv* in the same way: *He treated all his children alike.*

alimony /ˈalɪmənɪ/ *n* the money that a court of law orders a husband to pay regularly to his wife, or a wife to pay regularly to her husband, when they are separated or divorced.

alive /əˈlaɪv/ *adj* **1** living: *Do you think any of them will come back alive?* **2** full of activity: *The streets were alive with tourists.*

alive to aware of something: *alive to danger.*

alkali /ˈalkəlaɪ/ *n* a substance able to neutralize acid. **ˈalkaline** *adj.*

all /ɔːl/ *adj, pron* **1** the whole: *He ate all the cake; Did you eat all of it?* **2** every one: *They were all present; All men are equal.* **3** everything; the only thing: *She told me all she knew; All I want is a bit of peace.* — *adv* **1** completely: *all alone; dressed all in white.* **2** much; even: *I feel all the better for a shower.* **3** for each side: *The score is five all.*

all-ˈclear *n* a signal that some danger *etc* is over: *They sounded the all-clear after the attack.*

all along the whole time: *I knew the answer all along.*

all at once 1 all at the same time: *Don't eat those cakes all at once!* **2** suddenly: *All at once the light went out.*

all over 1 over the whole of a person, thing *etc*: *My car is dirty all over.* **2** finished: *It's all over now.* **3** everywhere: *We've been looking all over for you!*

all right 1 fine or well: *You look ill. Are you all right?* **2** used to say yes: *'Will you come?' 'Oh, all right'.*

all right is more formal than **alright**.

at all in any way: *I didn't like the film at all; Is there anything at all I can do to help?*

in all when everything is added up: *It took me five hours in all.*

allege /əˈlɛdʒ/ *v* to say something without proof: *The lady alleged that he had stolen her handbag.* **allegation** /aləˈgeɪʃən/ *n.*

allegiance /əˈliːdʒəns/ *n* loyalty to a person, group, idea *etc*: *The knights swore allegiance to their king.*

allergy /ˈalədʒɪ/ *n* something in your body or skin that makes certain foods or materials disagree with you: *She has an allergy to fish.* **alˈlergic** *adj* affected in a bad way by certain things: *He is allergic to milk.*

alley /ˈalɪ/ *n* a narrow street.

alliance /əˈlaɪəns/ *n* an agreement that joins two countries *etc* together as allies.

allied /ˈalaɪd/ or /əˈlaɪd/ *adj* joined by a special agreement: *The allied forces entered the country.*

alligator /ˈalɪgeɪtə(r)/ *n* a large reptile similar to a crocodile.

allocate /ˈaləkeɪt/ *v* to give each person a share: *He allocated a room to each student.* **alloˈcation** *n.*

allot /əˈlɒt/ *v* to give to each person a share of something; to distribute: *They allotted the money to the winners.*

al'lotment *n* one of the sections into which a large piece of public land is divided, that a person rents to grow vegetables *etc* on.

all-out /ɔːlˈaʊt/ *adj* using the greatest effort possible: *an all-out attempt*.

allow /əˈlaʊ/ *v* **1** to let someone do something: *He allowed me to enter*; *Playing football in the street is not allowed*. **2** to take into consideration in sums, plans *etc*: *These figures allow for price rises*. **3** to give, especially regularly: *His father allows him £5 a week*.

al'lowance *n* **1** the amount that you are allowed: *Your baggage allowance for all flights is 20kg*. **2** a fixed sum or amount given regularly.

make allowances to take someone's special circumstances into consideration.

alloy /ˈalɔɪ/ *n* a mixture of two or more metals.

allude /əˈluːd/ or /əˈljuːd/ *v* to refer to or mention: *He alluded to his personal problems but didn't go into details*. **allusion** /əˈluːʒən/ or /əˈljuːʒən/ *n*.

ally *v* /əˈlaɪ/ or /ˈalaɪ/ to join countries or people together as partners in war, for business *etc*. — *n* /ˈalaɪ/ a state, person *etc* allied with another.

almighty /ɔːlˈmaɪtɪ/ *adj* **1** having complete power: *almighty God*. **2** very great: *an almighty crash*.

almond /ˈɑːmənd/ *n* a long narrow nut with a hard shell.

almost /ˈɔːlmoʊst/ *adv* very nearly: *She is almost five years old*.

alms /ɑːmz/ *n* money *etc* given to the poor.

aloft /əˈlɒft/ *adv* in the air; high up: *He held the flag aloft*.

alone /əˈloʊn/ *adv* **1** with no-one else: *He lived alone*. **2** only: *He alone can remember*.

See **lonely**.

along /əˈlɒŋ/ *prep* **1** from one end to the other: *He walked along the street*. **2** on the length of: *There's a post-box somewhere along this street*. — *adv* **1** onwards: *He ran along beside me*; *Come along, please!* **2** to a place mentioned: *I'll come along in five minutes*. **3** together: *I took a friend along with me*.

alongside /əlɒŋˈsaɪd/ *prep, adv* beside.

aloud /əˈlaʊd/ *adv* so that you can hear it: *He read the letter aloud*.

alphabet /ˈalfəbɛt/ *n* the letters of a language arranged in order.

to learn the letters of the **alphabet** (not **alphabets**).

alpha'betical *adj*. **alpha'betically** *adv*.

alpine /ˈalpaɪn/ *adj* having to do with, or belonging to, the high parts of mountains: *alpine skiing*; *alpine flowers*.

already /ɔːlˈrɛdɪ/ or /ɒlˈrɛdɪ/ *adv* **1** before a particular time: *I had already gone when Tom arrived*; *I don't want that book — I've read it already*. **2** before the expected time: *Are you leaving already?*

also /ˈɔːlsoʊ/ *adv* in addition; too: *He speaks English fluently and he also speaks some Italian*; *Her other son is also a doctor*.

Use **as well** or **too** at the end of a sentence, but not **also**: *We eat meat and we like fish as well*. but: *We eat meat and we also like fish*.

See **either**.

altar /ˈɔːltə(r)/ *n* a table in a church or temple for offerings to God.

alter /ˈɔːltə(r)/ *v* to change: *Will you alter this dress to fit me?*; *The town has altered a lot in the last two years*. **alte'ration** *n*.

altercation /ɔːltəˈkeɪʃən/ *n* an argument: *a noisy altercation in the street*.

alternate *adj* /ɔːlˈtɜːnət/ coming, happening *etc* in turns; first one and then the other: *alternate stripes of red and green*. — *v* /ˈɔːltəneɪt/ to come or happen in turns: *Rain and sun alternated throughout the day*. **al'ternately** *adv*.

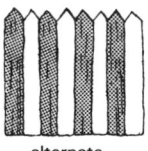

alternate   alternative

alternative /ɔːlˈtɜːnətɪv/ *adj* giving another choice or a second possibility: *An alternative day can be found if you can't come on Tuesday*. — *n* a choice between two possibilities: *I don't like fish. Is there an alternative on the menu?* **al'ternatively** *adv*.

alternative medicine the treatment of disease using acupuncture, homeopathy *etc* rather than drugs and surgery.

although /ɔːlˈðoʊ/ *conjunction* in spite of the fact that: *Although he hurried, the shop was closed when he got there*.

although should not be followed by **but**: *Although he is poor, he is honest* (not *Although he is poor but he is honest*).

altitude /ˈaltɪtjuːd/ or /ˈɔːltɪtjuːd/ *n* height above sea-level.

alto /ˈaltoʊ/ *n* the deepest singing voice for a woman.

altogether /ɔːltəˈɡɛðə(r)/ *adv* **1** completely: *I'm not altogether satisfied.* **2** considering everything: *I'm tired and I'm cold. Altogether I'm not feeling very cheerful.*

aluminium /aljəˈmɪnɪəm/ *n* a light silver-coloured metal.

always /ˈɔːlweɪz/ *adv* **1** at all times: *I always work hard; I'll always remember her.* **2** continually: *He is always making mistakes.*

am /am/ *see* **be**.

amalgamate /əˈmalɡəmeɪt/ *v* to join together with another organization: *The small firm amalgamated with a big company.* **amalgaˈmation** *n*.

amass /əˈmas/ *v* to collect a large quantity.

amateur /ˈamətə(r)/ or /aməˈtɜː(r)/ *n* **1** a person who takes part in a sport *etc* without being paid for it. **2** someone who does something for the love of it and not for money: *For an amateur, he was quite a good photographer.* — *adj*: *an amateur golfer*.

amaze /əˈmeɪz/ *v* to surprise greatly: *I was amazed at his stupidity.*

aˈmazement *n* great surprise: *To my amazement he suddenly stood on his head.*

aˈmazing *adj*: *an amazing sight*.

ambassador /amˈbasədə(r)/ *n* the minister appointed to act for his government in another country: *the British Ambassador to Italy*.

amber /ˈambə(r)/ *n* a hard yellow substance used in jewellery *etc*.

ambiguous /amˈbɪɡjʊəs/ *adj* having more than one possible meaning; not clear in meaning. **amˈbiguously** *adv*. **ambiguity** /ambɪˈɡjuːɪtɪ/ *n*.

ambition /amˈbɪʃən/ *n* the desire for success, fame, power *etc*; the desire to do something special: *His ambition is to be Prime Minister.* **amˈbitious** *adj* wanting fame or success.

amble /ˈambəl/ *v* to walk without hurrying; to stroll: *The boys were ambling home talking about football.*

ambulance /ˈambjʊləns/ *n* a vehicle for carrying the sick and injured to hospital *etc*.

> **ambulance** ends in **-ance** (not **-ence**).

ambush /ˈambʊʃ/ *v* to wait in hiding for someone and make a surprise attack on them: *The soldiers were ambushed in the woods.* — *n* an attack made in this way.

amend /əˈmɛnd/ *v* to correct or improve. **aˈmendment** *n*.

make amends to make up for having done something wrong: *You must make amends to Jenny for breaking her doll.*

amenity /əˈmiːnɪtɪ/ or /əˈmɛnɪtɪ/ *n* something that makes life more pleasant or convenient: *This part of town has a swimming pool, a library, a shopping centre and many other amenities.*

amiable /ˈeɪmɪəbəl/ *adj* likeable; friendly. **ˈamiably** *adv*.

amicable /ˈamɪkəbəl/ *adj* friendly. **ˈamicably** *adv*.

> **amiable** is used about people, but **amicable** is not: *an amiable man; an amicable agreement.*

amid /əˈmɪd/ or **amidst** /əˈmɪdst/ *prep* in the middle of; among: *amid all the confusion; amidst the shadows.*

amiss /əˈmɪs/ *adj, adv* wrong.

ammonia /əˈmoʊnɪə/ *n* a strong-smelling gas.

ammunition /amjʊˈnɪʃən/ *n* bullets, gunpowder or shells used in the firing of a gun *etc*.

amnesia /amˈniːzɪə/ or /amˈniːʒə/ *n* loss of memory.

amnesty /ˈamnəstɪ/ *n* a pardon given by the state to people who have done wrong especially against the government: *All political prisoners were released under the amnesty declared by the new president.*

amok /əˈmɒk/ or /əˈmʌk/ or **amuck** /əˈmʌk/: **run amok** or **run amuck** to rush about madly, attacking everybody and everything: *The gunman ran amok in the crowded supermarket.*

among /əˈmʌŋ/, **amongst** /əˈmʌŋst/ *prep* **1** in the middle of: *a house among the trees.* **2** one of: *Cancer is now amongst the commonest causes of death.* **3** in shares to each person: *Divide the chocolate amongst you.*

> **among** is used for more than two: *She divided the work among the pupils.*
> **between** is used for two: *The twins divided the chocolate between them.*
> See **between**.

among yourselves with each other: *They were just chatting amongst themselves.*

amount /əˈmaʊnt/ *v* to add up to: *The bill amounted to £15.* — *n* a quantity; a sum: *a large amount of money.*

amphibian /amˈfɪbɪən/ *n* **1** any animal that lives both on land and in water: *Frogs are* amphibians. **2** a vehicle for use on land or in the water. **am'phibious** *adj*.

ample /'ampəl/ *adj* enough; plenty: *There is ample space for four people.* **'amply** *adv*.

amplify /'amplɪfaɪ/ *v* **1** to make large. **2** to make the sound from a radio, record-player *etc* louder. **amplifi'cation** *n*.

'amplifier *n* a piece of electrical equipment for increasing the sound of a record-player *etc*.

amputate /'ampjʊteɪt/ *v* to cut off an arm or leg *etc*. **ampu'tation** *n*.

amuse /ə'mjuːz/ *v* **1** to make someone laugh: *I was amused at the clowns.* **2** to keep someone happy or interested: *They amused themselves playing cards.*

a'musement *n* **1** being amused: *a smile of amusement.* **2** an entertainment; an activity: *surfing and other holiday amusements.*

amusement arcade a public building containing machines for gambling and video games.

a'musing *adj* rather funny: *an amusing story.*

an *see* **a**.

anaemia /ə'niːmɪə/ *n* a kind of illness that makes you feel tired and look very pale because your blood cannot carry enough oxygen around your body: *Anaemia is often caused by a lack of iron in your body.* **a'naemic** *adj*.

anaesthetic /anəs'θɛtɪk/ *n* a substance, used by doctors *etc* that causes lack of feeling in a part of the body, or unconsciousness.

anagram /'anəgram/ *n* a word or phrase containing letters which can be rearranged to form another word or phrase: *'Pale' is an anagram of 'leap'.*

analyse /'anəlaɪz/ *v* to examine something carefully: *The doctor analysed the blood sample.*

analyse is spelt **-lyse** (not **-lyze**).

analysis /ə'nalɪsɪs/, *plural* **analyses** /ə'naləsiːz/ *n* a detailed examination of something: *The chemist is making an analysis of the poison.*

analyst /'anəlɪst/ *n* **1** a person who analyses. **ana'lytical** *adj*.

anarchist /'anəkɪst/ *n* **1** a person who believes that it is unnecessary to have any sort of government in a country. **2** a person who tries to destroy the government.

'anarchy *n* **1** a situation where there is no government and people do not obey any laws: *There was total anarchy after the defeat of the government.* **2** disorder: *Anarchy reigned in the classroom after the teacher went out.* **an'archic** *adj*.

anatomy /ə'natəmɪ/ *n* the study of the parts of the body. **ana'tomical** *adj*.

ancestor /'ansɛstə(r)/ *n* a person who was a member of your family a long time ago and from whom you are descended. **an'cestral** *adj*.

'ancestry *n* a person's ancestors.

anchor /'aŋkə(r)/ *n* a heavy piece of metal with points which dig into the sea-bed, for holding a boat in one position. — *v* **1** to hold a boat *etc* steady with an anchor. **2** to fix firmly.

'anchorage *n* a place for anchoring boats.
at anchor anchored: *The ship is at anchor in the bay.*

ancient /'eɪnʃənt/ *adj* **1** of times long ago: *ancient history.* **2** very old: *an ancient shirt.*

The opposite of **ancient** is **modern**.

and /ənd/ or /and/ *conjunction* **1** a word used to join two things, statements *etc*: *I opened the door and went inside; a mother and child.* **2** added to: *2 and 2 makes 4.*

anemone /ə'nɛmənɪ/ *n* a plant that has white, red or purple flowers with black centres.

anesthetic another spelling of **anaesthetic**.

angel /'eɪndʒəl/ *n* **1** a messenger of God: *The angels announced the birth of Christ.* **2** a very good person: *She was an angel to help us.* **an'gelic** *adj*.

anger /'aŋgə(r)/ *n* a violent feeling against someone or something: *He was filled with anger at the way he had been treated.* — *v* to make someone angry: *His rudeness angered her.*

angle[1] /'aŋgəl/ *n* **1** the space between two lines that meet: *an angle of 90°.* **2** a point of view: *from a journalist's angle.* **3** a corner.
at an angle not straight: *He wore his hat at an angle.*

angle[2] /'aŋgəl/ *v* to use a rod and line to try to catch fish: *angling for trout.*
'angler *n* a person who goes angling.
'angling *n*.

Anglo /'aŋgloʊ/ *prefix* English: *Anglo-American.*

angry /'aŋgrɪ/ *adj* full of anger: *He was angry about the broken window; angry words; Are you angry with me?* **'angrily** *adv*.

angry at something: *We were angry at the delay.*
angry with someone: *He is angry with his sister.*

anguish /ˈaŋgwɪʃ/ *n* very great pain or sorrow.

angular /ˈaŋgjʊlə(r)/ *adj* with sharp angles: *angular handwriting.*

animal /ˈanɪməl/ *n* a living being which can feel things and move freely. — *adj*: *animal behaviour.*

animate /ˈanɪmeɪt/ *v* to make lively.
'animated *adj* **1** lively: *an animated discussion.* **2** made to move in a life-like way: *animated cartoons.*
ani'mation *n*.

ankle /ˈaŋkəl/ *n* the joint connecting the foot and leg.

annex or **annexe** /ˈanɛks/ *n* a building that is added to a main building to make it larger: *The new annexe contains extra classrooms and a gymnasium.*

annihilate /əˈnaɪəleɪt/ *v* to destroy completely: *The terrible disease almost annihilated the population of the town.* **annihi'lation** *n*.

anniversary /anɪˈvɜːsərɪ/ *n* a particular day in each year when some event is remembered: *We celebrated our fifth wedding anniversary.*

annotate /ˈanəteɪt/ *v* to add notes and explanations to a book, etc: *Many students annotate their copies of novels they are studying.* **anno'tation** *n*.

announce /əˈnaʊns/ *v* **1** to make something known publicly: *Mary and John have announced their engagement.* **2** to introduce someone to an audience *etc*: *He announced the next singer in the show.* **an'nouncement** *n*.

an'nouncer *n* a person who introduces programmes or reads the news on radio or television.

annoy /əˈnɔɪ/ *v* to make someone rather angry: *His laziness annoyed his teacher.*
an'noyance *n* **1** something which annoys you. **2** a feeling of being annoyed.
an'noyed *adj* made angry: *My mother is annoyed with me*; *He was annoyed at her untidiness.*

annoyed at something: *I was annoyed at the delay.*
annoyed with someone: *The teacher was annoyed with me for being late.*

an'noying *adj*: *annoying habits.*

annual /ˈanjʊəl/ *adj* **1** happening every year: *an annual event.* **2** of one year: *What is his annual salary?* — *n* **1** a book of which a new edition is published every year. **2** a plant that lives for only one year. **'annually** *adv*.

anonymity /anəˈnɪmɪtɪ/ *n* not giving the name of the author, giver *etc*.

anonymous /əˈnɒnɪməs/ *adj* not named: *The writer of this letter wishes to remain anonymous*; *an anonymous gift.* **a'nonymously** *adv*.

anorak /ˈanərak/ *n* a warm, waterproof jacket usually with a hood: *In cool parts of the world most children wear anoraks in the winter.*

anorexia /anəˈrɛksɪə/ *n* an illness in which the sufferer refuses to eat and loses so much weight their life may be in danger.

another /əˈnʌðə(r)/ *pron* **1** a different one: *I don't like this book — can you lend me another?* **2** one more: *I'll have another of those nice biscuits.* — *adj* **1** different: *They're moving to another house.* **2** one more: *Have another piece of cake.*

answer /ˈɑːnsə(r)/ *n* **1** something said, written or done in reply to a question *etc*: *She refused to give an answer to his questions.* **2** The way of solving a problem; a solution: *The answers to the puzzles will be found on page 98.* — *v* **1** to give an answer to a question, problem *etc*: *Answer my questions, please*; *Why don't you answer the letter?* **2** to open the door when there is a knock or ring, or lift up the telephone when it rings: *He answered the telephone as soon as it rang*; *Could you answer the door, please?*

answering machine or **'answerphone** a machine which records telephone messages when no one is able to answer the telephone: *There were three messages on my answering machine when I got back from lunch.*

answer back to reply rudely.

answer for to be punished for something: *He's old enough to answer for his own actions.*

ant /ant/ *n* a type of small insect, thought of as hard-working.

Ants build **nests**.

antagonism /anˈtagənɪzm/ *n* feelings of anger or dislike between people: *There was a lot of antagonism between the two brothers.*
an'tagonist *n* someone who fights with you; an opponent: *His antagonist was too strong for him.*
antago'nistic *adj*: *antagonistic feelings.*
an'tagonize *v* to make someone dislike you:

She antagonized her neighbours by playing loud music at night.

Antarctic /an'tɑːktɪk/ *n* the area round the South Pole. — *adj* belonging to that area.

ant-eater /'antiːtə(r)/ *n* any of several toothless animals with long snouts, that eat ants.

antelope /'antəloʊp/ *n* a kind of quick-moving, graceful animal similar to a deer.

antenna /an'tɛnə/ *n* **1** (*plural* **antennae** /an'tɛniː/) a feeler of an insect. **2** (*plural* **an'tennas**) an aerial for a radio *etc*.

anthem /'anθəm/ *n* a song of praise: *a national anthem.*

ant-hill /'anthɪl/ *n* a heap of earth, leaves *etc* that ants form when they build their nest.

anthology /an'θɒlədʒɪ/ *n* a collection of poems, stories *etc* by various writers: *an anthology of 20th-century poetry.*

anthropology /anθrə'pɒlədʒɪ/ *n* the study of different races of people and of their origins, customs, beliefs *etc*. **anthropo'logical** *adj*. **anthro'pologist** *n*.

anti- /'antɪ/ **1** against, as in **anti-aircraft**. **2** the opposite of, as in **anti-clockwise**.

anti-aircraft /antɪ'ɛəkrɑːft/ *adj* used against enemy aircraft.

antibiotic /antɪbaɪ'ɒtɪk/ *n* a medicine which is used to kill the germs that cause disease.

anticipate /an'tɪsɪpeɪt/ *v* **1** to expect something: *I'm not anticipating any trouble.* **2** to realise beforehand; to be prepared for something: *to anticipate someone's needs.* **antici'pation** *n*.

anticlimax /antɪ'klaɪmaks/ *n* a dull or disappointing ending.

anticlockwise /antɪ'klɒkwaɪz/ *adv*, *adj* moving in the opposite direction to the hands of a clock.

antics /'antɪks/ *n* odd or amusing behaviour: *The children laughed at the monkey's antics.*

antidote /'antɪdoʊt/ *n* **1** a kind of medicine that is given to cure the effects of poison or stop it working: *The doctor gave the man an antidote after he was bitten by a cobra.* **2** anything that prevents something bad or difficult: *Laughter is a good antidote to embarrassment.*

antique /an'tiːk/ *adj* old and valuable: *an antique chair.* — *n* something made long ago which is valuable or interesting: *He collects antiques.*

antiseptic /antɪ'sɛptɪk/ *n* a substance that destroys germs. — *adj*: *antiseptic ointment.*

antler /'antlə(r)/ *n* a deer's horn.

antlers

antonym /'antənɪm/ *n* a word opposite in meaning to another word: *Big and small are antonyms.*

anvil /'anvɪl/ *n* a metal block on which metal objects are hammered into shape: *the blacksmith's anvil.*

anxiety /aŋg'zaɪətɪ/ *n* the feeling of being anxious: *Her son's illness caused her great anxiety.*

anxious /'aŋkʃəs/ *adj* **1** worried: *She is anxious about her father's health.* **2** eager; wanting very much: *He's very anxious to help.* **'anxiously** *adv*.

any /'ɛnɪ/ *pron* **1** it doesn't matter which: *'Which dress shall I wear?' 'Any will do'.* **2** one, some: *John ate all the sweets, so I didn't get any.* — *adj* **1** it doesn't matter which: *Take any book you want.* **2** some: *Have you been to any interesting places?*; *We have hardly any coffee left.* **3** every: *Any schoolboy could tell you the answer.* — *adv* at all; by a small amount: *Is this book any better than the last one?*; *His writing hasn't improved any.*

See **some**.

'anybody or **'anyone** *pron* **1** some person: *Is anybody there?* **2** any person, no matter which: *Get someone to help — anyone will do.* **3** everyone: *Anyone could tell you the answer to that.*

'anyhow *adv* **1** anyway: *Anyhow, even if I run, I will miss the train.* **2** in a careless way: *books piled anyhow on shelves.*

'anything *pron* **1** some thing: *Can you see anything?*; *I can't see anything.* **2** a thing of any kind: *You can buy anything you like.*

'anyway *adv* nevertheless; in spite of what has been said, done *etc*: *My mother says I mustn't go, but I'm going anyway*; *Anyway, she can't stop you.*

'anywhere *adv* in, at or to (any place): *Have you seen my gloves anywhere?*

at any rate at least: *It will be fine tomorrow — at any rate, that's what the weather forecast says.*

in any case nevertheless: *I don't believe the story but I'll check it in any case.*

apart /əˈpɑːt/ *adv* separated by a certain distance: *trees planted three metres apart*; *Stand with feet apart*; *She sat apart from the other people.*

apart from except for: *I can't think of anything I need, apart from a car.*

come apart to break into pieces: *The book came apart in my hands.*

take apart to separate something into the pieces from which it is made: *He took the engine apart.*

apartheid /əˈpɑːtheɪt/ or /əˈpɑːthaɪt/ *n* the system of making people of different races live apart by law, used for many years in South Africa.

apartment /əˈpɑːtmənt/ *n* **1** a room. **2** a flat; a set of rooms for living in.

apathy /ˈapəθɪ/ *n* a lack of interest and enthusiasm: *a worrying apathy towards politics amongst younger people.* **apaˈthetic** *adj*.

ape /eɪp/ *n* a large monkey with little or no tail. — *v* to copy: *He aped everything his older brother did.*

An ape **gibbers**.

aperture /ˈapətʃə(r)/ *n* a small hole or opening.

apex /ˈeɪpɛks/, *plural* **'apexes** or **apices** /ˈeɪpəsiːz/ *n* the highest point: *the apex of his political career.*

apiary /ˈeɪpɪərɪ/ *n* a place where bees are kept, usually in several beehives.

apiece /əˈpiːs/ *adv* each: *The children were given 6 francs apiece.*

apologetic /əpɒləˈdʒɛtɪk/ *adj* sorry for having done something wrong or silly. **apoloˈgetically** *adv*.

apologize /əˈpɒlədʒaɪz/ *v* to say that you are sorry for having done something wrong *etc*: *I must apologize to her for my rudeness.*

apology /əˈpɒlədʒɪ/ *n*: *He made an apology for being late.*

apostle /əˈpɒsəl/ *n* a man sent out to preach the gospel, especially one of the twelve disciples of Christ: *Matthew and Mark were apostles.*

apostrophe /əˈpɒstrəfɪ/ *n* a mark (') to show that letters have been missed out: *can't* (cannot), *don't* (do not); or to show possession: *the boy's coat*; *the boys' coats.*

appal /əˈpɔːl/ *v* to horrify or shock: *We were appalled by the dirtiness of the house.* **apˈpalling** *adj*.

apparatus /apəˈreɪtəs/ or /apəˈrɑːtəs/ *n* machinery, tools or equipment: *chemical apparatus*; *gymnastic apparatus.*

apparent /əˈparənt/ *adj* **1** easy to see; evident: *The mistake was quite apparent to all of us.* **2** seeming but perhaps not real: *his apparent unwillingness.*

apˈparently *adv* it seems that; I hear that: *Apparently he is not feeling well.*

appeal /əˈpiːl/ *v* **1** to ask earnestly for something: *She appealed to him for help.* **2** to take a case you have lost to a higher court to ask a judge for a new decision: *He appealed against a three-year prison sentence.* **3** to be pleasing: *This place appeals to me.* — *n* **1** a request for help *etc*: *a last appeal for help.* **2** a formal request to change a decision: *The judge rejected his appeal.* **3** attraction: *Pop music has no appeal for me.*

apˈpealing *adj* pleasing: *an appealing smile.* **apˈpealingly** *adv*.

appear /əˈpɪə(r)/ *v* **1** to come into view: *A man suddenly appeared round the corner.* **2** to begin to exist; to be invented: *Nylon stockings appeared just after World War 2.* **3** to arrive: *He appeared in time for dinner.* **4** to be seen by the public: *He is appearing on television today.* **5** to seem: *It appears that he is wrong*; *He appears to be wrong.*

apˈpearance *n* **1** what can be seen of a person, thing *etc*: *From his appearance he seemed very wealthy.* **2** when something begins to exist or becomes available: *It's now five years since the appearance of her first novel.* **3** the act of coming into view: *The thieves ran off at the appearance of two policemen.* **4** being seen by the public: *his first appearance on the stage.*

appendicitis /əpɛndɪˈsaɪtɪs/ *n* a painful infection of the appendix in the body.

appendix /əˈpɛndɪks/ *n* **1** (*plural* sometimes **appendices** /əˈpɛndɪsiːz/) a section added at the end of a book *etc*. **2** a small worm-shaped part of the bowels.

appetite /ˈapətaɪt/ *n* a desire for food: *Exercise gives you a good appetite.*

'appetizing *adj* increasing the appetite: *an appetizing smell.*

applaud /əˈplɔːd/ *v* to show approval by clapping the hands *etc*: *to applaud a speech.*

applause /əˈplɔːz/ *n* approval expressed by clapping: *The singer received great applause.*

apple /ˈapəl/ *n* a round fruit, usually with a green or red skin.

apply /əˈplaɪ/ *v* **1** to put or spread something on something: *to apply ointment to a cut.* **2** to use something: *He applied his brains to planning their escape.* **3** to ask for a job: *He applied to the headmaster for the post of art-*

teacher. **4** to ask for money *etc*: *You can apply to the government for a grant to repair your house.* **5** to affect; to concern: *This rule does not apply to him.*

appliance /əˈplaɪəns/ *n* an instrument or tool: *washing-machines and other electrical appliances.*

applicable /əˈplɪkəbəl/ or /ˈaplɪkəbəl/ *adj* able to be applied in a particular case; relevant: *This rule is not applicable to him as he is not a club member; a lesson that is just as applicable now as it was 200 years ago.*

applicant /ˈaplɪkənt/ *n* a person who applies for a job *etc*.

application /aplɪˈkeɪʃən/ *n* **1** applying. **2** a formal request for a job or grant *etc*. **3** hard work; great effort.

ap'plied *adj* put to practical use rather than theoretical: *She is studying applied science at university.*

appoint /əˈpɔɪnt/ *v* to give a person a job: *They appointed him manager.*

ap'pointment *n* **1** an arrangement to meet someone: *I made an appointment to see him.* **2** a job: *a teaching appointment.* **3** choosing a person for a job: *There have been several new appointments recently.*

appreciate /əˈpriːʃieɪt/ or /əˈpriːsieɪt/ *v* **1** to be grateful for something: *I appreciate the help you have given me.* **2** to realise how important or precious someone or something is: *Mothers sometimes complain that their children don't appreciate them enough.* **3** to understand: *I appreciate your difficulties but I cannot help.* **appreciˈation** *n*.

apˈpreciative *adj*. **apˈpreciatively** *adv*.

> **I'd appreciate it** (not **I'd appreciate**) if you could help me.

apprehension /aprɪˈhɛnʃən/ *n* fear; anxiety: *She was filled with apprehension for her child's safety.*

appreˈhensive *adj* anxious; worried: *The students were rather apprehensive about their final exams; She had an apprehensive expression on her face.* **appreˈhensively** *adv*.

apprentice /əˈprɛntɪs/ *n* a person who is being trained to do a job.

apˈprenticeship *n* the time during which a person is an apprentice: *He is serving his apprenticeship as a mechanic.*

approach /əˈproʊtʃ/ *v* to come near: *She approached me and asked what the time was; Christmas is approaching.* — *n* coming near: *The boys ran off at the approach of a policeman.*

apˈproachable *adj* **1** friendly **2** able to be reached: *The village is not approachable by road.*

appropriate /əˈproʊprɪət/ *adj* suitable; right: *Wear appropriate clothes for the picnic.*

apˈpropriately *adv* suitably: *appropriately dressed for the occasion.*

> The opposite of **appropriate** is **inappropriate**.

approval /əˈpruːvəl/ *n* agreeing to something; being pleased with a person, thing *etc*. *Their plan met with her approval; She was full of approval for his new apartment; Their initial wariness was replaced by warm approval.*

on approval able to be given back to a shop *etc* if not satisfactory: *She bought some shoes on approval.*

approve /əˈpruːv/ *v* **1** to be pleased with a person, thing *etc*: *I approve of your decision; I don't approve of my son's girlfriend.* **2** to agree to something: *The committee approved the plan.*

> The opposite of **approve**[1] is **disapprove**.

apˈproving *adj* showing approval.

approximate /əˈprɒksɪmət/ *adj* not exactly right, but nearly correct: *What is the approximate price of a good freezer?*

apˈproximately *adv* nearly; about: *approximately 550.*

apricot /ˈeɪprɪkɒt/ *n* an orange-coloured fruit like a small peach.

April /ˈeɪprəl/ *n* the fourth month of the year.

apron /ˈeɪprən/ *n* a garment worn to protect the front of the clothes: *She tied on her apron before preparing the dinner.*

apt /apt/ *adj* **1** likely: *He is apt to get angry if you ask a lot of questions.* **2** suitable: *an apt remark.* **3** clever; quick to learn: *an apt student.* **ˈaptly** *adv*. **ˈaptness** *n*.

aptitude /ˈaptɪtjuːd/ *n* a talent or ability: *an aptitude for mathematics.*

aquarium /əˈkwɛərɪəm/ *n* a glass tank, for keeping fish and other water animals.

aquatic /əˈkwatɪk/ *adj* living, growing, or taking place in water: *aquatic plants; aquatic sports.*

aqueduct /ˈakwɪdʌkt/ *n* a bridge with many

arches that is used to carry water across a valley or river.

aqueduct

gateway — porch — archway

Arabic /'arəbɪk/: *Arabic numerals* 1, 2, 3, 4 *etc*.

arable /'arəbəl/ *adj* being used, or suitable, for growing crops: *arable land*; *This land is too sandy to be arable*.

arbitrary /'ɑ:bɪtrərɪ/ or /'ɑ:bɪtrɪ/ *adj* not decided by rules or laws but by a person's own opinion: *an arbitrary dismissal*. **arbi-'trarily** *adv*.

arbitrate /'ɑ:bɪtreɪt/ *v* to be a judge or referee in a disagreement. **arbi'tration** *n*.

arc /ɑ:k/ *n* a part of the line which forms a circle or other curve.

arcade /ɑ:'keɪd/ *n* a covered passage or area with shops, stalls *etc*: *a shopping arcade*.

arch /ɑ:tʃ/ *n* a doorway or other opening with a curved top: *He steered the boat through one of the arches of the bridge*. — *v* to bend into the shape of an arch: *The cat arched its back*; *an arched doorway*.

arch- *prefix* most important or chief: *his arch-rival for the job of President*.

archaeology /ɑ:kɪ'ɒlədʒɪ/ *n* the studying of people of ancient times by examining the remains of their buildings, tools, pottery *etc*. **archaeo'logical** *adj*. **archae'ologist** *n*.

archangel /'ɑ:keɪndʒəl/ *n* a chief angel.

archbishop /ɑ:tʃ'bɪʃəp/ *n* a chief bishop.

archer /'ɑ:tʃə(r)/ *n* a person who shoots with a bow and arrows.

'archery *n* the sport of shooting with a bow.

archipelago /ɑ:kɪ'pɛləgoʊ/ *n* a group of islands.

architect /'ɑ:kɪtɛkt/ *n* a person who designs buildings *etc*.

'architecture *n* the art of designing buildings. **archi'tectural** *adj*.

archives /'ɑ:kaɪvz/ *n* a store of documents about the history of a place or organization, *etc*.

archway /'ɑ:tʃweɪ/ *n* an arched passageway or entrance.

Arctic /'ɑ:ktɪk/ *n* the area round the North Pole. — *adj* belonging to this area.

'arctic *adj* very cold.

ardent /'ɑ:dənt/ *adj* enthusiastic; passionate: *an ardent football supporter*. **'ardently** *adv*.

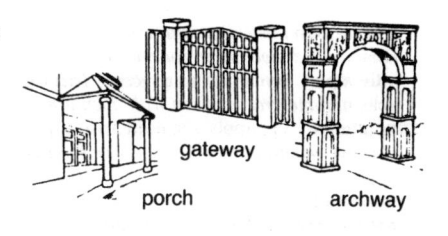

arduous /'ɑ:djʊəs/ *adj* very difficult or tiring: *an arduous task*.

are *see* **be**.

area /'ɛərɪə/ *n* **1** the extent of a flat surface: *This garden is twelve square metres in area*. **2** a place; part of a town *etc*: *Do you live in this area?* **3** a space used for a particular purpose: *a kitchen with dining area*.

arena /ə'ri:nə/ *n* any place for a public show, contest *etc*: *a sports arena*.

aren't short for **are not** and **am not**.

arguable /'ɑ:gjʊəbəl/ *adj* **1** probably true. **2** not certain.

'arguably *adv* probably: *She's arguably our greatest living writer*.

argue /'ɑ:gju:/ *v* to quarrel with a person: *Will you children stop arguing with each other about whose toy that is!* **2** to give reasons for or for not doing something: *I argued against accepting the plan*. **3** to discuss: *She argued very cleverly*.

argument /'ɑ:gjʊmənt/ *n* **1** a quarrel: *They are having an argument about whose turn it is to wash the dishes*. **2** reasoning for or against something: *Let us presume for the purposes of argument that he did this*.

argu'mentative *adj* fond of arguing.

arid /'arɪd/ *adj* dry; having very little water: *The land is so arid that only cactuses can grow on it*. **a'ridity** *n*.

arise /ə'raɪz/ *v* **1** to come into being: *Another difficulty has arisen*. **2** to get up.

> **arise**; **arose** /ə'roʊz/; **arisen** /ə'rɪzən/: *A storm arose*; *A problem has arisen*.

aristocracy /arɪ'stɒkrəsɪ/ *n* the nobility and others of the highest social class.

'aristocrat *n* a member of the aristocracy. **aristo'cratic** *adj*.

arithmetic /ə'rɪθmətɪk/ *n* a way of counting using numbers. **arithmetical** /arɪθ'mɛtɪkəl/ *adj*.

arm[1] /ɑ:m/ *n* **1** the part of the body between the shoulder and the hand. **2** anything similar to this: *the arm of a chair*.

arm-in-'arm *adv* with arms linked together: *They walked along arm-in-arm.*

with open arms with a very friendly welcome: *He greeted them with open arms.*

arm² /ɑːm/ *v* **1** to supply someone with a gun or other weapons: *to arm the police force.* **2** to prepare for battle, war *etc*: *They armed for battle.*

arms *n* **1** weapons: *Does the police force carry arms?* **2** a design *etc* which is used as the symbol of the town, family *etc*.

take up arms to begin fighting: *The peasants took up arms against the dictator.*

armadillo /ɑːməˈdɪloʊ/, *plural* **arma'dillos**, *n* a South American animal with a covering of strong bony scales over its body, that lives in a burrow and eats insects.

armaments /ˈɑːməmənts/ *n* equipment for war.

armchair /ˈɑːmtʃeə(r)/ *n* a chair with arms at each side.

armed /ɑːmd/ *adj* carrying a gun or other weapons: *An armed man robbed the bank; armed forces.*

armful /ˈɑːmfʊl/ *n* as much as a person can hold in one or both arms: *an armful of clothes.*

armhole /ˈɑːmhoʊl/ *n* an opening in a piece of clothing through which you put your arm.

armistice /ˈɑːmɪstɪs/ *n* an agreement to stop fighting in a war, battle *etc*: *An armistice was declared at 11 o'clock on the 11th of November.*

armour /ˈɑːmə(r)/ *n* a protective suit of metal worn by knights.

'armoured *adj* protected by a specially strong metal covering: *armoured vehicles.*

'armoury *n* the place where weapons are kept.

armpit /ˈɑːmpɪt/ *n* the hollow under the arm.

army /ˈɑːmɪ/ *n* **1** a large number of men armed and organized for war: *The army advanced into enemy territory; He served for two years in the army.* **2** a large number of people, insects *etc*: *an army of ants.*

aroma /əˈroʊmə/ *n* a pleasant smell: *the aroma of coffee.*

aromatic /arəˈmatɪk/ *adj*: *aromatic herbs.*

arose *see* **arise**.

around /əˈraʊnd/ *prep* **1** on all sides of something or in a circle about something: *Flowers grew around the tree; They danced around the fire.* **2** here and there in a place: *Clothes had been left lying around the house.* — *adv* **1** near to a time, place *etc*: *around three o'clock.* **2** in the opposite direction: *Turn around!* **3** nearby: *If you need me, I'll be somewhere around.* **4** on all sides: *He looked around for a way of escape.* **5** here and there: *to wander around.*

arouse /əˈraʊz/ *v* to cause or start a feeling *etc*: *His strange behaviour aroused my suspicions.*

arrange /əˈreɪndʒ/ *v* **1** to put in order: *Arrange these books in alphabetical order; She arranged the flowers in a vase.* **2** to plan or fix: *We have arranged a meeting for next week; I have arranged to meet him tomorrow.*

ar'rangement *n* **1** the result of arranging: *flower-arrangements.* **2** an agreement: *They've finally come to an arrangement about sharing the money.* **3** a plan or preparation: *Have you made any arrangements for a meeting with him?*

array /əˈreɪ/ *n* a large collection of things, laid out in front of you: *There was a fine array of cakes and buns in the shop window.*

arrears /əˈrɪəz/: **in arrears** late in paying money that you owe: *He is in arrears with his rent.*

arrest /əˈrest/ *v* **1** to capture or take hold of a person because he or she has broken the law: *The police arrested the thief.* **2** to stop. — *n* the arresting of someone; being arrested: *The police made several arrests; He was questioned after his arrest.*

under arrest having been arrested: *The thief is under arrest.*

arrive /əˈraɪv/ *v* **1** to reach a place, the end of a journey *etc*: *They arrived home last night; The parcel arrived yesterday.* **2** to happen: *The day of the exam had arrived.*

> You **arrive at** the station, bus stop, beach *etc*, but you **arrive in** countries and cities: *to arrive at the airport; to arrive in London, Sweden, the USA.* See also **reach**.

ar'rival *n* **1** the act of arriving: *I was greeted by my sister on my arrival.* **2** a person, thing *etc* that has arrived.

arrive at to reach: *Finally, they arrived at a decision.*

arrogant /ˈarəgənt/ *adj* extremely proud; thinking that you are much more important than other people: *an arrogant person; arrogant behaviour.* **'arrogance** *n.* **'arrogantly** *adv.*

arrow /ˈaroʊ/ *n* **1** a thin, straight stick with a point, which is shot from a bow. **2** a sign shaped like an arrow showing direction: *You can't get lost — just follow the arrows.*

arsenal /'ɑːsənəl/ *n* a factory or store for weapons, ammunition *etc*.

arsenic /'ɑːsənɪk/ *n* a strong poison.

arson /'ɑːsən/ *n* the crime of setting fire to a building *etc* on purpose.

art /ɑːt/ *n* **1** painting, drawing and sculpture: *I'm studying art at school.* **2** a skill: *the art of embroidery.*

arts *n* languages, literature, history, rather than scientific subjects.

the arts *n* the creation and showing of painting, literature, music, dancing and drama *etc*: *The government will spend more on the arts next year.*

artery /'ɑːtərɪ/ *n* a tube that carries blood from the heart through the body. **2** a main route of travel and transport. **arterial** /ɑːˈtɪərɪəl/ *adj*.

arthritis /ɑːˈθraɪtɪs/ *n* a kind of disease that causes pain and stiffness in a joint: *He suffers from arthritis in his hands.*

article /'ɑːtɪkəl/ *n* **1** a thing; an object: *This shop sells articles of all kinds.* **2** a piece of writing in a newspaper or magazine: *He has written an article on the new sports centre for a local magazine.* **3** the name of the words 'the', 'a', 'an'.

articulate *adj* /ɑːˈtɪkjʊlət/ able to express your thoughts clearly: *I enjoy listening to her speaking — she is so articulate.* — *v* /ɑːˈtɪkjʊleɪt/ to speak or pronounce something very clearly: *The teacher articulated the difficult words very carefully.*

articulated /ɑːˈtɪkjʊleɪtɪd/ *adj* made of separate sections which are connected: *an articulated lorry.*

artificial /ɑːtɪˈfɪʃəl/ *adj* made by man; not natural: *artificial flowers.* **artiˈficially** *adv*.

artificial intelligence the study of how to build computers which can learn, understand and make judgements like human beings.

artificial respiration forcing air into and out of the lungs of a person who has stopped breathing.

artillery /ɑːˈtɪlərɪ/ *n* **1** large guns. **2** the part of an army which uses large guns.

artist /'ɑːtɪst/ *n* **1** a person who draws or paints pictures or is a sculptor. **2** a singer, dancer, actor *etc*.

arˈtistic *adj* **1** good at painting, music *etc*: *She draws and paints — she's very artistic.* **2** beautifully done: *an artistic flower arrangement.* **arˈtistically** *adv*.

'artistry *n* skill.

artiste /ɑːˈtiːst/ *n* a person who performs in a theatre, circus *etc*: *a troupe of circus artistes.*

as /az/ or /əs/ **1** when; while: *I met John as I was coming home; We'll be able to talk as we go.* **2** because: *As I am leaving tomorrow, I've bought you a present.* **3** in the same way that: *Always do as I do.* **4** used in comparisons: *The bread was as hard as a brick.* **5** like: *He was dressed as a woman.* **6** doing a particular job: *He works as a librarian.*

as for with regard to; concerning: *The girls are well-behaved, but as for John — he's the naughtiest boy I know.*

as if or **as though**: *You look as if you had seen a ghost!; Behave as though nothing was wrong.*

as of or **as from** starting on a particular date: *As from today, the doors will be locked at 5 o'clock.*

asbestos /asˈbɛstəs/ *n* a grey, poisonous substance that will not burn and that is used to make clothing, mats *etc* which give protection against fire: *an asbestos suit.*

ascend /əˈsɛnd/ *v* to climb or go up: *The smoke ascended into the air.*

> The opposite of **ascend** is **descend**.

ascent /əˈsɛnt/ *n* **1** the act of climbing or going up: *the ascent of Mount Everest.* **2** a slope upwards: *a steep ascent.*

ascend the throne to be crowned king or queen.

ascertain /asəˈteɪn/ *v* to find out; to make sure.

ash /aʃ/ *n* the dust *etc* that remains after anything is burnt: *cigarette ash; the ashes of the bonfire.*

'ashes *n* the remains of a human body after cremation.

ashamed /əˈʃeɪmd/ *adj* feeling shame: *He was ashamed of his bad work; ashamed to admit his mistake; Aren't you ashamed of yourself for telling a lie?*

ashen /'aʃən/ *adj* very pale with shock *etc*: *Her face was ashen.*

ashore /əˈʃɔː(r)/ *adv* on or on to the shore: *The sailor went ashore.*

ashtray /'aʃtreɪ/ *n* a dish for cigarette ash.

aside /əˈsaɪd/ *adv* on or to one side: *They stood aside to let her pass; I've put aside two tickets for you to collect.*

ask /ɑːsk/ *v* **1** to question someone: *He asked me what the time was; Ask her where to go; If you don't know the way, ask a policeman; Have you asked the teacher about the dancing class?* **2** to say to someone that you want

asleep

them to do something or give you something; to request: *I'm going to ask my father for more pocket-money*; *I asked her to help me*. **3** to invite: *He asked her to his house for lunch.*

See **call**.

ask after to ask how someone is: *He always asks after my mother when I see him.*

ask for to express a wish to see or speak to someone: *When he telephoned he asked for you.*

asleep /əˈsliːp/ *adj* **1** sleeping: *The baby is asleep*; *He fell asleep as soon as his head touched the pillow.* **2** numb: *My foot's asleep.*

aspect /ˈaspɛkt/ *n* a part of something to be thought about: *We must consider every aspect of the problem.*

asphalt /ˈasfalt/ *n* a black substance that contains tar and is used to make roads, pavements *etc*: *The workmen are laying asphalt.* — *adj*: *an asphalt courtyard.*

aspire /əˈspaɪə(r)/ *v* to try very hard to reach something difficult, ambitious *etc*: *to aspire to greatness.*

aspiration /aspɪˈreɪʃən/ *n* an ambition.

aspirin /ˈasprɪn/ *n* a pain-killing drug.

ass /as/ *n* **1** a donkey. **2** a stupid person.

An ass **brays**.
A male ass is a **jackass**.

assassinate /əˈsasɪneɪt/ *v* to murder someone very important: *The president was assassinated by terrorists.* **assassi'nation** *n*.

as'sassin *n* a person who assassinates someone.

assault /əˈsɔːlt/ *v* to attack suddenly. — *n* a sudden attack.

assemble /əˈsɛmbəl/ *v* **1** to come together; to meet: *The crowd assembled in the hall.* **2** to bring together: *He assembled his family and told them of his plan.* **3** to put together a machine *etc*: *Before you assemble the model aeroplane, read the instructions.*

assembly /əˈsɛmblɪ/ *n* **1** a gathering of people for a particular purpose: *The school meets for morning assembly at 8.30.* **2** putting together; constructing.

assembly line in a factory, a line of workers or machines that a product is passed along until it is finished: *the latest model of sports car to come off the assembly line.*

assent /əˈsɛnt/ *n* agreement. — *v* to agree: *They assented to the proposal.*

assert /əˈsɜːt/ *v* **1** to say definitely: *He asserted that a modern artist should be in tune with his times.* **2** to insist on: *A teacher has to assert her authority over the class.* **as'sertion** *n*.

as'sertive *adj* speaking and acting in a confident and forceful way: *He needs to be more assertive if he wants to do well as a politician.* **as'sertively** *adv*. **as'sertiveness** *n*.

assess /əˈsɛs/ *v* to judge the quantity or quality of something; to estimate the value or cost of something: *The damage done by the fire was assessed at half a million pounds.* **as'sessment** *n*.

asset /ˈasɛt/ *n* anything useful or valuable; an advantage: *Good pupils are a great asset to the school.*

'assets *n* the total property, money *etc* of a person, company *etc*.

assign /əˈsaɪn/ *v* **1** to give to someone as his share or duty: *They assigned the task to us.* **2** to appoint: *He assigned three men to the job.*

as'signment *n* a task given to someone: *You must complete this assignment by tomorrow.*

assimilate /əˈsɪmɪleɪt/ *v* **1** to learn and understand: *We need people who can assimilate new techniques quickly.* **2** to become part of a community. **as'similation** *n*.

assist /əˈsɪst/ *v* to help: *The junior doctor assisted the surgeon at the operation.*

as'sistance *n* help: *Do you need assistance?*
as'sistant *n* **1** a person who assists: *a laboratory assistant.* **2** a person who serves in a shop. — *adj* helping; deputy: *an assistant headmaster.*

associate *v* /əˈsəʊʃɪeɪt/ or /əˈsəʊsɪeɪt/ **1** to connect something with something else in your mind: *He always associated the smell of tobacco with his father.* **2** to join with someone in friendship *etc*: *After school the pupils have time to associate with each other.* — *adj* /əˈsəʊʃɪət/ or /əˈsəʊsɪət/ joined or connected: *associate organizations.* — *n* /əˈsəʊʃɪət/ or /əˈsəʊsɪət/ a colleague or partner.

associ'ation *n* **1** a club, society *etc*: *She joined the Drama Association.* **2** a friendship or partnership: *a long-lasting association.* **3** a connection in the mind.

in association with together with: *We are organizing a competition in association with the Sports Council.*

assorted /əˈsɔːtɪd/ *adj* mixed; of various kinds: *assorted colours*; *assorted sweets.*

as'sortment *n* a mixture or variety: *an assortment of chocolates*.

assume /əˈsjuːm/ or /əˈsuːm/ *v* **1** to believe that something must be true; to presume: *I assume that you can all spell your names correctly*. **2** to take upon yourself: *He assumed the duties of leader*. **3** to put on a particular appearance *etc*: *He assumed a look of horror*.

> to **assume** is to suppose that something is true for the sake of making plans *etc*: *Let's assume* (or *assuming*) *that we can hold the meeting on 8 May — what shall we discuss at it?*
> to **presume** is to believe that something is true though you have no proof: *Your coat was not on your peg, so I presumed you had left*.

assumption /əˈsʌmʃən/ or /əˈsʌmpʃən/ *n* something assumed.

assure /əˈʃʊə(r)/ or /əˈʃɔː(r)/ *v* **1** to tell someone something positively: *I assured him that the house was empty*. **2** to make someone sure: *He assured her of his faith in her*.

as'surance *n* **1** confidence. **2** a promise. **3** insurance: *life assurance*.
as'sured *adj* confident.

asterisk /ˈastərɪsk/ *n* a star-shaped mark (*).

asteroid /ˈastərɔɪd/ *n* any one of the thousands of very small rocky planets that move around the sun, most of them between Mars and Jupiter.

asthma /ˈasmə/ *n* an illness which causes difficulty in breathing out.
asth'matic *n* a person who suffers from asthma. — *adj*: *an asthmatic child*.

astonish /əˈstɒnɪʃ/ *v* to surprise greatly: *I was astonished at her rudeness*.
a'stonishing *adj*. **a'stonishment** *n*.

astound /əˈstaʊnd/ *v* to surprise very much: *He was astounded by the news*. **a'stounding** *adj*.

astray /əˈstreɪ/ *adv* away from the right direction; missing, lost: *The letter has gone astray*; *We were led astray by the old, out-of-date map*.

astride /əˈstraɪd/ *prep* with legs on each side of something: *She sat astride the horse*. — *adv* apart: *He stood with legs astride*.

astrology /əˈstrɒlədʒɪ/ *n* the study of the stars and their influence on people's lives. **a'strologer** *n*.

astronaut /ˈastrənɔːt/ *n* a person who travels in space.

astronomy /əˈstrɒnəmɪ/ *n* the study of the stars and their movements. **a'stronomer** *n*.

> See **astrologer**.

astro'nomical *adj* **1** of astronomy: *the local astronomical society*. **2** very large: *These prices are really astronomical*.

astrologer   astronomer

astute /əˈstjuːt/ *adj* quick and clever. **a'stutely** *adv*.

asylum /əˈsaɪləm/ *n* a place of safety; protection: *He was granted political asylum*.

at /ət/ or /at/ *prep* showing **1** position: *They are not at home*; *She lives at 9 Forest Road*. **2** direction: *He looked at her*; *She shouted at the boys*. **3** time: *He arrived at ten o'clock*. **4** occupation: *She is at work*. **5** speed: *He drove at 120 kilometres per hour*. **6** cost: *bread at 80p a loaf*.

> You use **in** when speaking of the area within which someone or something is: *I live in Scotland*; *I work in Hamburg*; *My house is in Rose Street*.
> You use **at** when describing an exact position: *I live at 32 Rose Street*; *I work at Brown's Book Shop*.

ate see **eat**.

atheist /ˈeɪθiːɪst/ *n* a person who does not believe in God.

athlete /ˈaθliːt/ *n* a person who is good at sport, *esp* running, jumping *etc*.
ath'letic *adj* **1** of athletics: *He is taking part in the athletic events*. **2** good at athletics; strong and able to move easily and quickly: *He looks very athletic*.
ath'letics *n* the sports of running, jumping *etc*: *Athletics was my favourite activity at school*.

atlas /ˈatləs/ *n* a book of maps.

atmosphere /ˈatməsfɪə(r)/ *n* **1** the air surrounding the earth. **2** any surrounding feeling: *There was a friendly atmosphere in the village*. **'atmospheric** *adj*.

atom /ˈatəm/ *n* the smallest part of an element. **a'tomic** *adj*.

atomic bomb a bomb using atomic energy.
atomic energy very great energy obtained by breaking up the atoms of some substances.

atrocious /əˈtroʊʃəs/ *adj* **1** very bad: *Your behaviour was atrocious.* **2** extremely cruel: *an atrocious punishment.*

atrocity /əˈtrɒsɪtɪ/ *n* an extremely cruel and wicked act: *The invading army committed many atrocities.*

attach /əˈtatʃ/ *v* to fasten or join something to something else: *I attached a label to my bag.*

at'tached *adj* fond of: *I'm very attached to my brother.*

at'tachment *n* **1** something attached: *My camera has a flash and several other attachments.* **2** liking or affection: *There was a strong attachment between the two cousins.*

attack /əˈtak/ *v* **1** to make a sudden, violent attempt to hurt or damage: *The village was attacked from the air.* **2** to speak or write against someone *etc*: *The minister's decision was attacked in the newspapers.* **3** to attempt to score a goal in football *etc*. — *n* **1** an act of attacking: *They made an air attack on the town.* **2** a sudden occurrence of illness: *a heart attack; an attack of 'flu.*

attain /əˈteɪn/ *v* to gain; to achieve.

at'tainable *adj* that can be achieved.

at'tainment *n*.

attempt /əˈtɛmpt/ *v* to try: *He attempted to climb up the cliff but he did not succeed; He did not attempt the last question in the exam.* — *n* **1** a try: *She made no attempt to run away.* **2** an attack: *There has been an attempt on the President's life.*

attend /əˈtɛnd/ *v* **1** to go to; to be present at: *He attended the meeting; He will attend school till he is sixteen.* **2** to give attention to something; to listen: *Attend carefully to what the teacher is saying!* **3** to deal with something: *I'll attend to that problem tomorrow.* **4** to look after someone: *Two doctors attended her.*

at'tendance *n* being present: *His attendance at school was poor because he was often ill; There was a doctor in attendance at the road accident.*

attendance ends in **-ance** (not **-ence**).

at'tendant *n* a person whose job is to look after something: *a car-park attendant.*

in attendance: *There was a doctor in attendance at the road accident.*

attention /əˈtɛnʃən/ *n* **1** notice: *He tried to attract my attention; Pay attention to your teacher!* **2** care: *That broken leg needs urgent attention.* **3** concentration: *His attention wanders.* **4** a position in which you stand very straight with hands by the sides and feet together: *He stood to attention.*

attentive /əˈtɛntɪv/ *adj* giving attention: *The children were very attentive when the teacher was speaking.* **at'tentively** *adv*.

attic /ˈatɪk/ *n* a room at the top of the house under the roof.

attire /əˈtaɪə(r)/ *n* clothing. — *v* to dress.

attitude /ˈatətjuːd/ *n* a way of thinking or acting *etc*: *What is your attitude to politics?*

attorney /əˈtɜːnɪ/ *n* a person who has the legal power to act for another person.

attract /əˈtrakt/ *v* **1** to cause something to come towards something or someone else: *A magnet attracts iron; I tried to attract her attention.* **2** to arouse someone's liking or interest: *I was attracted by her nice smile.*

at'traction *n* **1** the power of attracting. **2** something pleasant, that attracts people: *The attractions of the hotel include a swimming-pool.*

at'tractive *adj* pleasant; good-looking: *an attractive house; an attractive girl.* **at'tractively** *adv*. **at'tractiveness** *n*.

attribute /əˈtrɪbjuːt/ *v* to think that something has been done or caused by something else: *He attributed his illness to the cold weather.*

auction /ˈɔːkʃən/ *n* a public sale in which each thing is sold to the person who offers the highest price.

auctio'neer *n* a person who sells things at an auction.

audible /ˈɔːdɪbəl/ *adj* able to be heard. **'audibly** *adv*. **audi'bility** *n*.

The opposite of **audible** is **inaudible**.

audience /ˈɔːdɪəns/ *n* a group of people watching or listening to a performance *etc*: *the audience at the concert.*

audience ends in **-ence** (not **-ance**).
An **audience** attends a play, show, performance, concert *etc*, and both listens and watches: *There was a large audience at the concert.*
spectators attend a match, game, sports event *etc*, and watch only: *There weren't many spectators at the match.*

audio- /ˈɔːdɪoʊ/ having to do with sound or hearing.

audio-visual /ɔːdɪoʊ ˈvɪʒʊəl/: **audio-visual aids** films, recordings *etc* used in teaching.

audition /ɔːˈdɪʃən/ *n* a test for an actor, singer, musician *etc* to see if they are good enough to take part in a show *etc*.

auditorium /ˌɔːdɪˈtɔːrɪəm/ *n* the part of a theatre *etc* where the audience sits.

August /ˈɔːgəst/ *n* the eighth month of the year.

aunt /ɑːnt/ *n* the sister of your father or mother or the wife of your uncle.

auntie or **aunty** /ˈɑːntɪ/ *n* a name that children use for an aunt.

austere /ɔːˈstɪə(r)/ *adj* very simple and plain; without luxuries. **auˈsterity** *n*.

authentic /ɔːˈθɛntɪk/ *adj* true, real or genuine. **authenticity** /ˌɔːθɛnˈtɪsɪtɪ/ *n*.

author /ˈɔːθə(r)/ *n* the writer of a book, article, play *etc*.

authority /ɔːˈθɒrətɪ/ *n* **1** the power or right to do something: *He gave me authority to collect his money.* **2** a person who is an expert on a particular subject: *He is an authority on twentieth-century art.* **3** the person or people who have power in a city *etc*: *the Polish authorities; the local planning authority; the broadcasting authorities.*

auˈthoritative *adj* said or written by an expert.

authorize /ˈɔːθəraɪz/ *v* to give the power or right to do something: *I authorized him to sign the documents.* **authoriˈzation** *n*.

auto /ˈɔːtəʊ/ short for **automobile** or **automatic**.

autobiography /ˌɔːtəbaɪˈɒgrəfɪ/ *n* the story of a person's life written by himself. **autobioˈgraphical** *adj*.

autograph /ˈɔːtəgrɑːf/ *n* a person's signature, especially one that is collected as a souvenir. – *v* to write your signature on something.

automatic /ˌɔːtəˈmætɪk/ *adj* **1** working by itself: *an automatic washing-machine.* **2** done without thinking: *an automatic action.*

ˈautomated *adj* working by automation.

autoˈmatically *adv*: *This machine works automatically.*

automation /ˌɔːtəˈmeɪʃən/ *n* the use of machines, especially ones that work other machines.

automobile /ˈɔːtəməbiːl/ *n* a motor-car.

autonomy /ɔːˈtɒnəmɪ/ *n* the power or right of a country etc to govern itself.

auˈtonomous *adj* self-governing.

autumn /ˈɔːtəm/ *n* the season of the year in cool parts of the world when leaves change colour and fall, and fruits ripen.

auxiliary /ɔːgˈzɪlɪərɪ/ *adj* helping; additional: *auxiliary forces; an auxiliary nurse.*

avail /əˈveɪl/: **of no avail** or **to no avail** of no use or effect: *His efforts were of no avail.*

available /əˈveɪləbəl/ *adj* able or ready to be obtained, used or bought: *The hall is available on Saturday night; All the available money has been used; Tickets are now available at the box office.* **availaˈbility** *n*.

avalanche /ˈavəlɑːnʃ/ *n* a fall of large masses of snow and ice down a mountain: *Six houses were buried by the avalanche.*

avarice /ˈavərɪs/ *n* a great desire for money: *He is well known for his avarice.*

avenge /əˈvɛndʒ/ *v* to take revenge for something wrong that someone has done to one of your friends or relations: *to avenge a murder.*

> You **avenge** a wrong done to someone else: *He avenged his father's murder.*
> You **revenge yourself**, or **take revenge** for a wrong done to you: *He revenged himself on his enemies for the harm they had done him.*

avenue /ˈavənjuː/ *n* a road, often with trees along either side.

average /ˈavərɪdʒ/ *n* the result of adding several amounts together and dividing the total by the number of amounts: *The average of 3, 1, 4 and 8 is 4.* — *adj* **1** obtained by finding the average of amounts *etc*: *the average temperature for the week.* **2** ordinary; not exceptional: *The average person is not wealthy; His work is average.* — *v* to form an average: *The money he spent over the week averaged £25 a day.*

averse /əˈvɜːs/: **averse to** disliking or objecting to something.

aversion /əˈvɜːʃən/ *n* a feeling of dislike.

avert /əˈvɜːt/ *v* **1** to turn away, especially your eyes: *She averted her eyes from the sun.* **2** to prevent: *to avert trouble.*

aviary /ˈeɪvɪərɪ/ *n* a place in which birds are kept.

aviation /ˌeɪvɪˈeɪʃən/ *n* the art of flying aeroplanes.

aviator /ˈeɪvɪeɪtə(r)/ *n* an old word for the pilot of a plane.

avid /ˈavɪd/ *adj* eager.

avocado /ˌavəˈkɑːdəʊ/ *n* a green, pear-shaped fruit.

avoid /əˈvɔɪd/ *v* **1** to keep away from a place, person or thing: *He drove carefully to avoid the holes in the road; Avoid the subject of money.* **2** to prevent: *Speak loudly and clearly to avoid any confusion.* **3** to find

ways of not doing something: *He frequently managed to avoid doing the washing-up.*
a'voidable *adj* that can be prevented. **a'voidance** *n*.

await /ə'weɪt/ *v* to wait for: *to await someone's arrival.*

awake /ə'weɪk/ *v* to wake from sleep: *He was awoken by a noise; I awoke suddenly.* — *adj* not asleep: *Is he awake?*

> **awake; awoke** /ə'woʊk/; **awoken** /ə'woʊkən/: *The noise awoke me; I was awoken by the birds.*

a'waken *v* to wake or arouse someone or something.

award /ə'wɔːd/ *v* to give someone something that he has won or deserved: *They awarded her first prize.* — *n* a prize *etc* awarded.

> You win an **award** for merit: *He won an award for his design.*
> You get a **reward** for a service you have done: *The owner gave a reward to the boy who found her dog.*

aware /ə'wɛə(r)/ *adj* knowing something: *Is he aware of the problem?; Are they aware that I'm coming?* **a'wareness** *n*.

> The opposite of **aware** is **unaware**.

away /ə'weɪ/ *adv* **1** to or at a distance from someone or somewhere: *He lives three miles away from the town; Go away!; Take it away!* **2** in the opposite direction: *She turned away so that he would not see her crying.* **3** gradually into nothing: *The noise died away.* **4** continuously: *They worked away until dark.* **4** in the future: *The exams were only ten days away.*

awe /ɔː/ *n* wonder and fear: *The child looked in awe at the king.* — *v* to fill with awe: *He was awed by his new school.*
'awe-inspiring *adj* filling you with wonder and respect.
'awesome *adj* impressive.

awful /'ɔːfʊl/ *adj* **1** very great: *an awful rush.* **2** very bad: *This book is awful; an awful headache.*
'awfully *adv* very: *awfully silly.*
'awfulness *n*.

awhile /ə'waɪl/ *adv* for a short time: *Wait awhile.*

awkward /'ɔːkwəd/ *adj* **1** not graceful or elegant: *an awkward movement.* **2** difficult or causing difficulty *etc*: *an awkward question.*
'awkwardly *adv*. **'awkwardness** *n*.

awoke, awoken *see* **awake**.

awry /ə'raɪ/ *adv* wrong; not as planned. – *adj* untidy; not straight.

axe /aks/ *n* a tool with a handle and a metal blade for cutting down trees and cutting wood into pieces. — *v* **1** to reduce the money spent on something. **2** to cancel: *The whole plan has been axed.*

axis /'aksɪs/, *plural* **axes** /'aksiːz/ *n* **1** the imaginary line from North Pole to South Pole, around which the earth turns. **2** a line with measurements on a graph: *Draw the horizontal and vertical axes first.*

axle /'aksəl/ *n* the rod on which the wheels of a car *etc* turn.

azure /'aʒə(r)/ or /'eɪʒʊə(r)/ *adj* having a bright blue colour: *the azure sky.*

B

B or **b** /biː/, *plural* **Bs** or **b's**, *n* the second-highest grade that can be given for an essay or exam: *I got a B for maths.*

babble /'babəl/ *v* to chatter: *The baby was babbling away to himself.* — *n* a chattering noise.

babe /beɪb/ *n* a baby: *a babe in arms.*

baboon /bə'buːn/ *n* a kind of large monkey with a dog-like face.

baby /'beɪbɪ/ *n* a very young child or animal. — *adj*: *a baby boy*; *a baby bird.*

babyish /'beɪbɪʃ/ *adj* like or suitable for a baby: *The toys were too babyish for a six-year-old girl.*

babysit /'beɪbɪsɪt/ *v* to remain in a house to look after a child while its parents are out: *She babysits for the neighbours every Saturday.* **'babysitter**, **'babysitting** *ns*.

bachelor /'batʃələ(r)/ *n* an unmarried man.

back /bak/ *n* **1** the part of a human's or animal's body from the neck to the lower end of the spine: *She lay on her back*; *She put the saddle on the horse's back.* **2** the part of something that is opposite to or furthest from the front: *the back of the house*; *She sat at the back of the hall.* **3** the part of a chair that you lean against. **4** in football *etc* a player who plays behind the forwards. — *adj* of or at the back: *the back door.* — *adv* **1** to the same place or person again: *I went back to the shop*; *He gave the car back to its owner.* **2** away from something; not near something: *Move back — let the ambulance through!* **3** towards the back of something, or on to your back: *Sit back in your chair*; *He lay back on the bed.* **4** in return: *When the teacher is scolding you, don't answer back.* **5** in the past: *It happened back in 1980.* — *v* **1** to move backwards: *He backed his car out of the garage*; *He backed away from the fierce dog.* **2** to help: *Will you back me against the others?* **3** to bet on a horse *etc*: *I backed your horse to win.*

'backache *n* a pain in the back.

'backbone *n* **1** the spine: *the backbone of a fish.* **2** the main strength of something: *The foot-soldiers were the backbone of the army.*

'backbreaking *adj* very difficult or requiring very hard work: *Digging the garden is a backbreaking job.*

back'date *v* to put back to an earlier date.

'backer *n* people who provide money or support for a project *etc*: *She thanked her backers for their support in setting up the business.*

back'fire *v* to have the opposite effect from the one you intended: *The plan backfired and the thieves were all caught red-handed.*

'background *n* **1** the space behind the most a important figures or objects in a picture *etc*: *There are trees in the background of the picture.*

See **foreground**.

2 happenings that go before an event *etc* and help to explain it: *the background to a situation.* **3** a person's family, home and education: *The manager asked about her background.* **4** where you can be seen or heard, but not as the centre of attention: *background music.*

'backhand *n* in tennis *etc*, a stroke or shot with the back of your hand turned towards the ball.

'backing *n* help or support, often in the form of money: *financial backing.*

'backlash *n* a sudden strong feeling or reaction against something: *There has been a backlash against the big industries that use up the world's resources.*

'backlog *n* a pile of uncompleted work *etc* which has collected.

'backpack *n* a rucksack.

'backside *n* your bottom: *He sits on his backside all day long.*

back'stage *adv* behind the stage in a theatre: *We waited backstage to meet the actors.*

'backstroke *n* a stroke used when swimming on your back.

'backup *n* a spare copy of computer files on disc or tape: *She makes a backup of her files every evening before going home.*

back away to move away from a place, person or situation: *He backed away from the argument.*

back down to give way to the other person in an argument *etc*.

back out 1 to move out backwards: *He opened the garage door and backed his car out.* **2** to take back a promise *etc*: *You* *promised to help — you mustn't back out now!*

back to front with the back at the front: *He's got his hat on back to front.*

back and forth backwards and forwards.

back up 1 to help or encourage or agree with: *my sister backed me up in my quarrel with my brother.* **2** to make a spare copy of computer files on a disc or tape: *If you back up your work regularly you won't lose it if the computer breaks down.*

backward /'bakwəd/ *adj* **1** aimed backwards: *A backward glance.* **2** slow in growing up or learning: *Backward children sometimes need extra teaching.* **'backwardness** *n*.

'backwards *adv* **1** towards the back: *He glanced backwards.* **2** with your back facing the direction you are going in: *The boy walked backwards into a lamp-post.* **3** in the opposite way to that which is usual: *Can you count from 1 to 10 backwards?* (starting at 10 and counting back to 1).

backwards and forwards in one direction and then in the opposite direction: *The dog ran backwards and forwards across the grass.*

backyard /bak'jɑ:d/ *n* a garden or yard at the back of a house *etc*.

bacon /'beɪkən/ *n* the meat of the back and sides of a pig, salted and dried.

bacteria /bak'tɪərɪə/ *n* very tiny creatures, too small to be seen, that live in air, in soil and in living bodies. Some are the germs of disease.

bad /bad/ *adj* **1** not good: *He is a bad driver; His eyesight is bad; I am bad at arithmetic.* **2** wicked; naughty: *You're a bad boy; He has done some bad things.* **3** sad; upsetting: *bad news.* **4** rotten: *This meat is bad.* **5** causing harm: *Smoking is bad for your health.* **6** painful or weak: *She has a bad heart; I have a bad leg.* **7** ill: *I feel bad today.* **8** sad or sorry: *I feel bad about losing your book.* **9** serious: *a bad accident; a bad mistake.* **10** wrong or unsuitable: *Is this a bad moment to call?*

> **bad; worse; worst:** *My eyesight is bad, but my mother's is worse, and my father's is worst of all.*

See also **weak**.

not bad quite good: *'Is she a good swimmer?' 'She's not bad'.*

too bad unfortunate: *It's too bad that she lost her purse.*

bade *see* **bid**.

badge /badʒ/ *n* a brooch or a special design worn to show that you are a member of a team, club, school, *etc*: *a school badge on a blazer.*

badger /'badʒə(r)/ *n* a burrowing animal with a black-and-white-striped head.

badly /'badlɪ/ *adv* **1** not well: *He plays tennis very badly.* **2** seriously: *He is badly hurt.* **3** very much: *I badly need some help.*

> **badly; worse; worst:** *She behaved badly, but you behaved worse, and John behaved worst of all.*

badly off not having much money.

badminton /'badmɪntən/ *n* a game played on a court with a shuttlecock and rackets.

bad-tempered /bad'tɛmpəd/ *adj* rude and angry in the way you speak and act.

baffle /'bafəl/ *v* to puzzle: *I was baffled by the teacher's question.*
'baffling *adj* mysterious; puzzling: *a baffling crime.*

bag /bag/ *n* **1** something made of paper, plastic, cloth, leather *etc*, for carrying things in. **2** a closed packet made of paper or plastic: *a bag of crisps.*

handbag briefcase suitcase

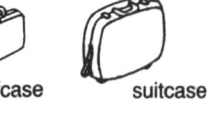

haversack knapsack carrier bag

baggage /'bagɪdʒ/ *n* bags and cases; luggage: *Our baggage was unloaded from the cart.*

> **baggage** is not used in the plural: *How many pieces of baggage have you brought?*

baggy /'bagɪ/ *adj* large and loose: *baggy trousers.*

bagpipes /'bagpaɪps/ *n* a musical instrument made of a bag fitted with pipes, played in Scotland.

bail[1] /beɪl/ *n* a sum of money which is paid to get a prisoner out of prison until his trial.
bail out to set someone free by giving this money to a court of law.

bail[2] /beɪl/ *n* one of the cross-pieces laid on the top of the wicket in cricket.

bait /beɪt/ *n* **1** food that you use to catch

animals, fish *etc* with, such as a worm attached to a fishhook. **2** something that is used to tempt or persuade you: *Free holidays were offered as bait to new customers.* — *v* to put bait on or in a hook, trap *etc*: *He baited the mousetrap with cheese.*

bake /beɪk/ *v* **1** to cook in an oven: *I baked some bread today.* **2** to dry or harden by heat: *The clay pots were put in the sun to bake.*

'**baker** *n* a person who bakes or sells bread and cakes: *My mother is a good baker*; *Get me a loaf at the baker's shop.*

'**bakery** *n* a place where bread and cakes are made or sold.

'**baking** *n* the art of cooking bread, cakes *etc*.

baking powder a powder used in cakes to make them rise.

balance /'baləns/ *n* **1** a machine for weighing. **2** steadiness: *The boy was walking along the wall when he lost his balance and fell.* **3** the state where various things are in a satisfactory relationship with one another: *We try to achieve a balance between work and play.* **4** the amount of money left out of a particular quantity after certain sums have been taken away and certain sums have been added. — *v* **1** to make or keep steady: *She balanced the jug of water on her head*; *The girl balanced on her toes.* **2** to make something equal on both sides.

'**balanced** *adj* **1** fair to all sides of an argument: *Read this article for a balanced view of the problem.* **2** having different parts in the right proportions: *a balanced diet.*

in the balance uncertain: *The company's future is in the balance.*

off balance not steady: *He hit me while I was off balance.*

on balance taking everything into consideration: *On balance, the meeting went well.*

balcony /'balkənɪ/ *n* **1** a platform built out from the wall of a building: *He climbed onto the balcony of the neighbouring building.* **2** the highest floor of seats in a cinema or theatre.

See **veranda**.

bald /bɔːld/ *adj* having no hair, or not very much hair: *a bald man*; *a bald head*; *He is going bald*; *a bald patch on the dog's back.*
'**baldness** *n*.
'**balding** *adj* becoming bald.

bale[1] /beɪl/ *n* a large bundle of cloth, hay *etc* tied together: *a bale of cotton.*

bale[2] /beɪl/ *v* to clear water out of a boat with buckets *etc*.

bale out to jump from a plane with a parachute in an emergency.

ball[1] /bɔːl/ *n* **1** a round object used for games. **2** something else that has a round shape: *a ball of wool.*

on the ball alert and ready to act quickly: *You have to be on the ball to succeed in business these days.*

ball[2] /bɔːl/ *n* a dance: *A ball was held at the palace.*

ballad /'baləd/ *n* **1** a long, simple poem or song that tells a story. **2** a slow, romantic, popular song.

ball-bearings /bɔːl'bɛərɪŋs/ *n* in machinery *etc*, small steel balls that help one part to move over another.

ballerina /balə'riːnə/ *n* a female ballet-dancer.

ballet /'baleɪ/ *n* **1** a performance of dancing, often telling a story. **2** the art of dancing in this way: *She is taking lessons in ballet.* — *adj*: *a ballet class.*
'**ballet-dancer** *n*.

balloon /bə'luːn/ *n* **1** a brightly-coloured object like a very light ball, made of thin rubber or plastic, and filled with air. **2** a much larger object filled with gas *etc* for carrying passengers through the air.

balloon is spelt with **-ll-** and **-oo-**.

ballot /'balət/ *n* a method of voting in secret by marking a paper and putting it into a box: *The government is elected by ballot.*

ballpoint /'bɔːlpɔɪnt/ *n* a pen that has a tiny ball as the writing point.

ballroom /'bɔːlruːm/ *n* a large room in which dances can be held.

ballroom dancing formal dances in which couples use fixed steps and movements.

bamboo /bam'buː/ *n* a kind of plant with a hollow stem that is hard and strong like wood.

ban /ban/ *n* an order that a certain thing may not be done: *a ban on smoking.* — *v* to forbid: *He has been banned from driving for a year.*

banana /bə'nɑːnə/ *n* the long, curved, yellow-skinned fruit, of a very large tropical tree: *What does this bunch of bananas cost?*

band[1] /band/ *n* **1** a strip of material to put round something: *a rubber band.* **2** a stripe of a colour *etc*: *a skirt with a band of* *red round it.* **3** in radio *etc*, a group of wavelengths.

band² /band/ *n* **1** a group: *a band of robbers.* **2** a group of musicians: *a brass band*; *a dance band.* — *v* to join together for a purpose: *A small group of people banded together determined to save the building.*

bandage /'bandɪdʒ/ *n* a piece of cloth *etc* for tying round an injured part of the body or covering up a wound. — *v* to cover with a bandage: *The doctor bandaged the boy's foot.*

bandit /'bandɪt/ *n* a robber, especially a member of a gang: *They were attacked by bandits in the mountains.*

bandwagon /'bandwagən/: **jump on the bandwagon** to do something only because it is fashionable or because it seems to be successful: *He jumped on the bandwagon and joined the Green Party.*

bang /baŋ/ *n* **1** a sudden loud noise: *The door shut with a bang.* **2** a blow or knock: *He got a bang on the head when he fell off his bicycle.* — *v* **1** to close with a sudden loud noise: *He banged the door*; *The door banged.* **2** to hit, often making a loud noise: *The child banged his drum.* **3** to make a sudden loud noise: *We could hear the fireworks banging in the distance.*

go with a bang to be very successful: *The party went with a bang.*

bangle /'baŋgəl/ *n* a bracelet worn on the arm or leg.

banish /'banɪʃ/ *v* to send away as a punishment: *He was banished from the country for betraying secrets.* **'banishment** *n*.

banisters /'banɪstərs/ *n plural* the rail that is supported by posts and fixed to the side of a staircase: *The little boy loves sliding down the banisters.*

banjo /'bandʒoʊ/, *plural* **'banjos**, *n* a stringed musical instrument similar to the guitar.

bank¹ /baŋk/ *n* **1** a mound or ridge: *The ship got struck on a sandbank.* **2** the ground at the edge of a river, lake *etc*: *The river overflowed its banks.*

bank² /baŋk/ *n* **1** a place where money is lent or exchanged, or put for safety: *He has a savings account with the bank.* **2** a place where something is stored for use at a later date: *a blood bank*; *a data bank.* — *v* to put money into a bank.

bank account the arrangement by which a bank looks after your money for you: *open a bank account.*

There are different kinds of **bank account**: you use cheques to take money out of a **current account**, you can save money in a **current** or **deposit account.**

'banker *n* a person who owns or manages a bank.

bank book a book showing you how much money you have put into and taken out of the bank.

'banking *n* the business done by banks: *a career in banking.*

'banknote *n* a piece of paper worth a certain amount of money, printed by a bank.

bank on to depend on: *Don't bank on getting any extra pocket-money from me!*

bankrupt /'baŋkrʌpt/ *adj* having lost all your money; unable to pay your debts. — *n* someone who is unable to pay their debts. **'bankruptcy** *n*.

banner /'banə(r)/ *n* **1** a military flag. **2** a large strip of cloth carried in a procession *etc*, on which something is written: *Many of the demonstrators were carrying banners.*

banquet /'baŋkwɪt/ *n* a dinner for many people, held to celebrate something special.

baptize /bap'taɪz/ *v* to sprinkle someone with water to show that they have been received into the Christian church, usually giving them a name at the same time: *She was baptized Mary.*

baptism /'baptɪzm/ *n* baptizing: *the baptism of the baby.*

bar /bɑː(r)/ *n* **1** a rod: *There were iron bars across the window*; *They fastened the door by pushing a bar across it.* **2** an oblong piece: *a bar of chocolate*; *a bar of soap.* **3** a counter at which articles of a particular kind are sold: *a snack bar.* **4** a public house serving alcoholic drinks. **5** a measured division in music: *Sing the first ten bars.* — *v* **1** to fasten with a bar: *Bar the door.* **2** to prevent from entering: *a policeman put out his arm to bar the way.* **3** to forbid someone officially to do, use or enter something: *She's been barred from the club*; *He was barred from playing international matches for a year.*

behind bars in prison.

barb /bɑːb/ *n* a backward-facing point on a fishing-hook *etc.*

barbarian /bɑː'bɛərɪən/ *n* an uncivilized person.

barbaric /bɑː'barɪk/ *adj* cruel and brutal: *a barbaric form of punishment.* **barbarically** *adv*.

barbarism /'bɑːbərɪzm/ *n* cruel and brutal

behaviour: *acts of barbarism committed in war*.

barbarous /'bɑːbərəs/ *adj* **1** barbaric. **2** rough, rude and uncivilized.

barbecue /'bɑːbɪkjuː/ *n* **1** a frame with bars across it for grilling meat *etc* over a charcoal fire: *We cooked the steak on a barbecue.* **2** a party in the open air, at which food is barbecued. — *v* to cook on a barbecue: *to barbecue a chicken.*

> **barbecue** ends in **-cue** (not **-que**).

barbed wire /bɑːbd 'waɪə(r)/ *n* wire with sharp points, used for fences *etc*.

barber /'bɑːbə(r)/ *n* a person who cuts men's hair, shaves their beards *etc*.

barber   hairdresser

bar code /'bɑːkəʊd/ *n* a group of thin and thick black lines printed on a product giving its price, etc, which can be read by a computer.

bare /beə(r)/ *adj* **1** naked: *bare skin*; *bare bodies*. **2** uncovered: *bare floors*. **3** empty: *bare shelves*. **4** basic, without anything extra: *He only had enough money to buy the bare necessities of life.* — *v* to uncover: *The dog bared its teeth in anger.* '**bareness** *n*.

'**bareback** *adv* without a saddle: *The girl often rides her pony bareback.*

'**barefoot** *adj*, *adv* not wearing shoes or socks *etc*: *The children go barefoot on the beach.*

'**barely** *adv* scarcely or only just: *We have barely enough food.*

bargain /'bɑːgɪn/ *n* **1** something bought cheaply and giving good value for money: *This carpet was a real bargain.* **2** an agreement made between people: *I'll make a bargain with you.* — *v* to argue about or discuss a price *etc*: *I bargained with him over the price.*

'**bargaining** *n* discussion about a price or the kind of agreement that you want.

bargain for to be prepared for something: *They had not bargained for bad weather.*

barge /bɑːdʒ/ *n* **1** a flat-bottomed boat for carrying goods *etc*. **2** a large power-driven boat. — *v* **1** to move clumsily: *He barged about the room.* **2** to bump into someone: *He barged into me.*

barge in to push your way rudely: *She barged in without knocking.*

baritone /'barɪtəʊn/ *n* a man's singing voice, quite deep, but not as deep as a bass.

bark[1] /bɑːk/ *n* the short, sharp cry of a dog. — *v* to make this sound: *The dog barked at the stranger.*

bark[2] /bɑːk/ *n* the covering of the trunk and branches of a tree: *He stripped the bark off the branch.*

barley /'bɑːlɪ/ *n* a type of grain used for food and for making beer and whisky.

barn /bɑːn/ *n* a building in which grain, hay *etc* are stored.

barnacle /'bɑːnəkəl/ *n* a kind of small shellfish that sticks to rocks and the bottoms of ships.

barometer /bə'rɒmɪtə(r)/ *n* an instrument which indicates changes of weather.

barracks /'barəks/ *n* a building in which soldiers live.

barrage /'bɑːrɑːʒ/ *n* **1** heavy gunfire that keeps back an enemy. **2** a very large number: *After his adventure, he had to answer a barrage of questions from his friends.*

barrel /'barəl/ *n* **1** a container made of curved pieces of wood or of metal: *The barrels contain beer.* **2** a long, tube-shaped part of a gun.

barren /'barən/ *adj* not fertile; not able to produce crops, fruit, babies *etc*. '**barrenness** *n*.

barricade /'barɪkeɪd/ *n* a barrier put up to block a street *etc*. — *v* to block a street *etc* with a barricade.

barrier /'barɪə(r)/ *n* **1** something put up as a protection: *He drove through a crash barrier*; *The barrier at the frontier was lifted to let them through.* **2** something that causes difficulty: *Deafness can be a barrier to learning.*

barring /'bɑːrɪŋ/ *prep* **1** except for: *Barring one small problem, the equipment works perfectly.* **2** if a particular thing does not happen: *The journey takes two hours, barring unexpected delays.*

barrister /'barɪstə(r)/ *n* a lawyer who speaks in defence of a person who is being tried in court.

barrow /'barəʊ/ *n* **1** a wheelbarrow. **2** a small cart.

barter /'bɑːtə(r)/ *v* to trade by giving one thing in exchange for another: *The bandits* *bartered gold for guns.* — *n* exchange of goods.

base /beɪs/ *n* **1** the foundation, support, or lowest part of something, or the surface on which something is standing: *the base of the statue.* **2** the main ingredient of a mixture: *This paint has oil as a base.* **3** headquarters: *an army base.* — *v* **1** to have headquarters in a particular place: *Our group was based in Paris.* **2** to make something rest or depend on something: *An opinion should be based on facts, not guesses.*

> **based** (not **basing**) on the facts collected.

baseball /'beɪsbɔːl/ *n* an American game played with bat and ball.
basement /'beɪsmənt/ *n* the lowest floor of a building, usually below ground level: *a basement car park; the students' canteen is in the basement.*

> Use **on** the ground floor, **on** the first floor *etc*, but **in** the basement.

bash /baʃ/ *v* to beat or smash: *The soldiers bashed the door down.* — *n* a heavy blow: *a bash on the head.*
bashful /'baʃfʊl/ *adj* shy. '**bashfully** *adv*. '**bashfulness** *n*.
basic /'beɪsɪk/ *adj* **1** forming a basis; being the main thing on which something depends: *Your basic theory is wrong.* **2** elementary; only as much as necessary: *a basic knowledge of French.*
'**basically** *adv*: *She is basically a very kind person; Basically, I want a job with a higher salary.*
basics /'beɪsɪks/ *n* the simple and most important things about something: *a chance to learn the basics of sailing.*
basin /'beɪsən/ *n* **1** a bowl for washing yourself: *a wash-hand basin.* **2** a wide dish for making food in: *Use three-quarters of the pastry to line the basin.* **3** the low, flat area beside a river: *the basin of the Nile.*
basis /'beɪsɪs/, *plural* **bases** /'beɪsiːz/, *n* **1** something on which a thing rests or depends: *This idea is the basis of my argument.* **2** the way something is organized: *We'll pay you on an hourly basis.*
bask /bɑːsk/ *v* to lie in warmth or sunshine: *The seals basked in the warm sun.*
basket /'bɑːskɪt/ *n* an object for holding and carrying things, made of strips of wood, rushes *etc* woven together.
'**basketball** *n* a game in which goals are scored by throwing a ball into a net on a high post.
'**basketry** *n* basketwork.
'**basketwork** *n* articles made of plaited rushes *etc*: *The stall sold only basketwork.* — *adj*: *a basketwork chair.*
bass /beɪs/ *n* **1** the low notes of a piano *etc*. **2** the lowest male voice. – *adj*: *a bass guitar.*
bassoon /bə'suːn/ *n* a wind instrument which gives a very low sound.
bastard /'bæstəd/ or /'bɑːstəd/ *n* a child born of parents not married to each other.
bat[1] /bæt/ *n* a piece of wood *etc* specially shaped for striking the ball in cricket, baseball, table tennis *etc*. — *v* to strike the ball with a bat: *He batted the ball; It's your turn to bat.*
off your own bat without anyone telling you to.
bat[2] /bæt/ *n* a mouse-like animal which flies, usually at night.
batch /bætʃ/ *n* a number of things made or sent all at one time: *She baked a fresh batch of bread; The letters were sent out in batches.*
bath /bɑːθ/, plural **baths** /bɑːðz/, *n* **1** a long deep container for water in which to wash the whole body. **2** getting washed in a bath: *I had a bath last night.* — *v* to wash in a bath: *She bathed the baby.*

> **bath** means to wash the whole body in a bath: *I'll bath the baby; I bath every morning.*
> **bathe** means to wash a part of the body, especially if it is hurt *etc*: *Go and bathe your cut finger.*
> **bathe** also means to go swimming: *I bathe in the sea every day.*

baths *n* a swimming-pool.
bathe /beɪð/ *v* **1** to clean with water: *I'll bathe that cut on your head.* **2** to go swimming: *She bathes in the sea every day.* — *n* a swim: *We went for a bathe in the river.* '**bather**, '**bathing** *ns*.
'**bathed** *adj* covered in; surrounded by: *bathed in light.*

> See **bath**.

bathing costume *n* a swimsuit.
bathroom /'bɑːθruːm/ *n* **1** a room which contains a bath. **2** a lavatory.
bathtub /'bɑːθtʌb/ *n* a bath.
batik /bə'tiːk/ *n* a method of dyeing patterns on cloth by waxing certain areas so that they remain uncoloured.
baton /'bætɒn/ *n* **1** a short, heavy stick, carried

by a policeman as a weapon. **2** a light stick used by the conductor of an orchestra or choir.

battalion /bəˈtalɪən/ *n* a large group of soldiers that forms part of a brigade.

batter /ˈbatə(r)/ *v* to hit something very hard, many times: *They battered the door down.* — *n* a mixture of flour, eggs, milk and salt that is used to make pancakes or to coat food before frying it.

'battered *adj* old and damaged: *a battered hat.*

battery /ˈbatərɪ/ *n* **1** an object that is fitted inside a clock, watch, radio, flashlight *etc* to supply it with electricity. **2** a set of cages in which hens are kept to lay eggs.

battle /ˈbatəl/ *n* **1** a fight between armies: *Which side won the battle?*; *Where was the battle fought?* **2** a struggle: *a long battle against illness*; *a battle for power.* — *v* to fight.

> A **battle** is a fight between armies, lasting a short time.
> A **war** is a period of armed fighting between nations, that can last several years.

battlefield /ˈbatəlfiːld/ *n* the place where a battle is fought.

battleship /ˈbatəlʃɪp/ *n* a very large ship fitted with guns.

bawl /bɔːl/ *v* to shout or cry very loudly.

bay[1] /beɪ/ *n* a wide inward bend in the coast: *Ships were anchored in the bay.*

bay[2] /beɪ/ *n* an area which has a particular purpose in a building: *a factory loading bay*; *a parking bay.*

bayonet /ˈbeɪənɪt/ *n* a knife-like instrument of steel fixed to the end of a rifle barrel.

> See **gun**.

bazaar /bəˈzɑː(r)/ *n* **1** a market place. **2** a sale of home-made or second-hand goods.

be /biː/ *v* **1** used in describing and giving information about people, things *etc*: *I am tall*; *It is a beautiful day*; *Are you a teacher?* *Tom wants to be a doctor.* **2** to exist: *Is there life on Mars?*; *There is oxygen in the air.* **3** to have a particular job: *She wants to be a doctor*; *What do you want to be when you grow up?* **4** used to help other verbs to form tenses: *Bob is leaving*; *They were beaten.*

I am or **I'm** /aɪm/;
you are /ɑː(r)/ or **you're** /jɔː(r)/;
he is /ɪz/ or **he's** /hiːz/;
she is or **she's** /ʃiːz/;
it is or **it's** /ɪts/;
we are or **we're** /wɪə(r)/;
they are or **they're** /ðɛə(r)/;
are not or **aren't** /ɑːnt/;
is not or **isn't** /ˈɪzənt/:
I am Peter Brown; *I'm clever, aren't I?*; *I am not a fool, am I?*; *Are you going to tell me or aren't you?*; *Bill's a doctor, isn't he?*; *It's time to go, isn't it?*; *You aren't getting tired, are you?*; *We're to leave at 10.00 a.m., aren't we?*; *They're leaving tomorrow, aren't they?*

I was /wɒs/; **you were** /wɜː(r)/;
he was; **she was**; **it was**;
we were; **they were**;
was not or **wasn't** /ˈwɒzənt/;
were not or **weren't** /wɜːnt/:
I was the fastest, wasn't I?; *You were taught English at school, weren't you?*; *It was fun, wasn't it?*; *Was he guilty or wasn't he?*; *We were just going to have tea*; *You were not telling the truth, were you?*

been /biːn/ or /bɪn/: *I have been rather stupid*; *She has been going to school since August*; *Have you been told the news?*; *We have been to the zoo today.*

being /ˈbiːɪŋ/: *You are being very brave*; *She is being trained as a dancer*; *We were being given a history lesson.*

beach /biːtʃ/ *n* the sandy or stony shore of a sea or lake: *Children love playing on the beach.* — *v* to pull a boat up on to a beach.

beacon /ˈbiːkən/ *n* a bonfire or a light that acts as a signal or warning.

bead /biːd/ *n* a little ball of glass *etc* strung with others in a necklace *etc*: *She wore a string of beads.*

'beady *adj* small, round and bright: *the beady eyes of the blackbird.*

beagle /ˈbiːɡəl/ *n* a small hunting-dog with short, smooth, brown and white fur, short legs and long ears.

beak /biːk/ *n* the hard, pointed part of a bird's mouth: *The bird had a worm in its beak.*

beaker /ˈbiːkə(r)/ *n* a drinking-glass or tall cup, without a handle.

beam /biːm/ *n* **1** a long straight piece of wood,

bean

used in ceilings. **2** a ray or shaft of light *etc*: *a beam of sunlight.* — *v* **1** to smile: *She beamed with delight.* **2** to send out rays of light, radio waves *etc*: *This transmitter beams radio waves all over the country.*

bean /biːn/ *n* **1** any of several kinds of vegetable that grow in pods: *mung beans.* **2** the bean-like seed of other plants: *coffee beans.*

bear¹ /beə(r)/ *v* **1** to put up with something; to stand something: *She can't bear that television programme*; *I couldn't bear to touch the snake*; *She bore the pain bravely.* **2** to be able to support: *Will the chair bear my weight?* **3** to have a baby: *to bear a child*; *I was born on 7 July.* **4** to produce fruit: *This tree hasn't borne any fruit this year.* **5** to carry: *He bore the banner proudly in the procession.*

> **bear**; **bore** /bɔː(r)/; **born** or **borne** /bɔːn/: *He bore his disappointment well*; *I was born on 21 December*; *She has borne three children.*

'bearable *adj* able to be endured: *The pain was severe, but bearable.*

> The opposite of **bearable** is **unbearable**.

bear out support; confirm: *I need a witness to bear my story out.*

bear with to be patient with someone: *Bear with him, even if he is a nuisance.*

bear² /beə(r)/ *n* a large heavy animal with thick fur and hooked claws.

> A bear **growls**.
> A baby bear is a **cub**.

beard /bɪəd/ *n* the hair that grows on the chin: *a man's beard*; *a goat's beard.*

'bearded *adj* having a beard: *a bearded man.*

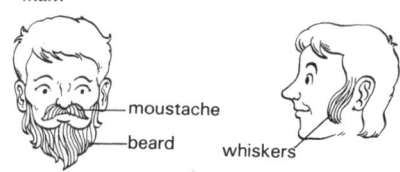

moustache
beard
whiskers

bearer /'beərə(r)/ *n* a person who carries something.

bearing /'beərɪŋ/ *n* a person's way of standing or walking.

get your bearings to find your way; to find where you are.

lose your bearings to lose your way; not to know where you are.

beast /biːst/ *n* **1** an animal: *beasts of the jungle.* **2** a cruel person. **3** a nasty person: *Arthur is a beast for refusing to come!*

'beastly *adj* **1** like a beast. **2** nasty: *What a beastly thing to do!* **'beastliness** *n*.

beat /biːt/ *v* **1** to hit: *Beat the drum.* **2** to win against: *She beat me in the competition.* **3** to stir very strongly and quickly: *to beat an egg.* **4** to make a regular sound or movement: *My heart is beating faster than usual.* **5** to mark time in music: *A conductor beats time for an orchestra.* — *n* a regular stroke or its sound: *heart-beats.*

> **beat**; **beat**; **'beaten**; *I was top in English, but he beat me in geography*; *Our team was badly beaten.*
> See also **win**.

'beater *n* a machine for beating eggs *etc*.

'beating *n* **1** punishment by hitting with a stick *etc*: *The headmaster gave the boys a beating.* **2** a defeat: *Our team took a bad beating.*

beat about the bush to avoid making up your mind.

beat down 1 to force a person selling something to accept less money for it: *I beat him down from five pounds to three.* **2** to be very hot and shining brightly: *The sun beat down on them.* **3** to fall very heavily: *The rain had been beating down all day.*

beat off to succeed in overcoming or preventing: *He beat the attack off easily.*

beat up to punch, kick or hit a person: *He was beaten up by a crowd of boys.*

beauty /'bjuːtɪ/ *n* **1** loveliness in appearance: *the beauty of the mountains*; *the young woman's beauty.* **2** a woman who is lovely: *His daughter is a great beauty.* **3** something very fine: *His new car is a beauty!*

beautician /bjuː'tɪʃən/ *n* a person who works in a beauty salon where women go to have their skin cared for, their nails cut and polished *etc*.

beautiful /'bjuːtɪfʊl/ *adj* full of beauty: *a beautiful woman*; *What a beautiful dress!*; *The flowers are beautiful.* **'beautifully** *adv*.

beautify /'bjuːtɪfaɪ/ *v* to make something more beautiful.

beauty queen a woman who wins a competition to find out which woman is the most beautiful.

beauty spot a place of natural beauty: *We visited several beauty spots.*

beaver /'biːvə(r)/ *n* a brown furry animal with

strong front teeth and a broad flat tail that helps it to swim.

became *see* **become**.

because /bɪˈkɒz/ or /bɪˈkəz/ *conjunction* for the reason that: *I can't go because I am ill.*
because of on account of: *I can't walk because of my broken leg.*

beckon /ˈbɛkən/ *v* to make a sign to someone to come: *He beckoned the waiter over to his table.*

become /bɪˈkʌm/ *v* **1** to grow to be: *She has become very tall.* **2** to train for or take up a particular job: *a farmer's daughter who became a farmer's wife; the actress he helped become a star; I was able to become a mature student in the 1950s.* **3** to happen to someone or something: *What became of her son?*

> **become; became** /bɪˈkeɪm/; **beˈcome**: *She became a dancer; You have become very thin.*

bed /bɛd/ *n* **1** a flat, oblong object on which to sleep: *It's time to go to bed; I put the baby to bed; She got ready for bed; You must make your bed neatly in the mornings.* **2** the bottom of a river, lake or sea. **3** a space specially dug for flowers *etc* in a garden: *a bed of flowers.*

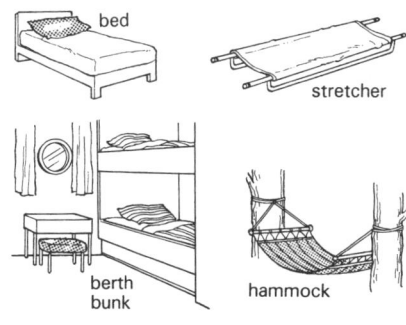

ˈbedclothes *n plural* sheets, blankets *etc*: *He pulled the bedclothes up over his head.*
ˈbedcover *n* a top cover for a bed.
ˈbedding *n* mattress, bedclothes *etc*.

bedraggled /bɪˈdrægəld/ *adj* wet and untidy: *a group of bedraggled and exhausted refugees.*

bedridden /ˈbɛdrɪdən/ *adj* in bed for a long period because of age or sickness: *She has been bedridden since the car accident.*

bedroom /ˈbɛdruːm/ *n* a room for sleeping in.

bedside /ˈbɛdsaɪd/ *n* the place or position next to a person's bed: *He was at her bedside when she woke up.* — *adj*: *a bedside lamp.*

bedspread /ˈbɛdsprɛd/ *n* a top cover for a bed.

bedtime /ˈbɛdtaɪm/ *n* the time when you usually go to bed: *Seven o'clock is the children's bedtime.* — *adj*: *I'll read you a bedtime story.*

bee /biː/ *n* a four-winged insect that makes honey: *A swarm of bees had settled on the branch.*

> Bees live in a **hive**.
> Bees **buzz** or **hum**.

beech /biːtʃ/ *n* a tree with smooth silvery bark.

beef /biːf/ *n* the meat of a bull, cow or ox: *roast beef.*
beefburger /ˈbiːfbɜːgə(r)/ *n* a round, flat piece of minced beef that is fried and then put in a bread roll with slices of onion *etc*: *I had a beefburger for lunch.*
ˈbeefeater *n* one of the guards at the Tower of London, who wear a uniform in the style of the 16th century.
ˈbeefy *adj* big, strong and fat: *a beefy man.*

beehive /ˈbiːhaɪv/ *n* a container in which bees are kept.

been *see* **be**.

> **been** can be used as the past participle of **go** when a return journey has been completed:
> *He's been away.* (and now he's back).
> *He's gone away.* (and he hasn't come back yet).

beep /biːp/ *v* to make a short high noise, for example on the horn of a car: *The car behind beeped us when the traffic lights changed.* – *n*.

beer /ˈbɪə(r)/ *n* a type of alcoholic drink made from barley.

beetle /ˈbiːtəl/ *n* an insect with four wings.

befall /bɪˈfɔːl/ *v* to happen to someone: *She's very late — perhaps some accident has befallen her.*

> **befall; befell** /bɪˈfɛl/; **beˈfallen**: *An accident befell him; What has befallen them?*

before /bɪˈfɔː(r)/ *prep* **1** earlier than: *Food was cheaper before the war.* **2** in front of: *She was before me in the queue.* — *adv* earlier: *I've seen you before.* — *conjunction* earlier than some action or event: *Before I go, I must phone my parents.*
beˈforehand *adv* before the time when something else is done: *If you're coming, let me know beforehand.*
before long soon: *He'll be here before long.*

befriend

befriend /bɪˈfrɛnd/ v to be a friend to someone and treat them kindly: *The lonely girl was befriended by a kind old lady.*

beg /bɛg/ v **1** to ask someone for money, food etc: *The old man was so poor that he had to beg in the street*; *He begged me for money.* **2** to ask very eagerly or desperately: *She begged him not to leave her.*

began *see* **begin**.

beggar /ˈbɛgə(r)/ n a person who lives by begging: *The beggar asked for money to buy food.*

begin /bɪˈgɪn/ v to start: *He began to talk*; *The lesson begins at 10.30.*

> **begin**; **began** /bɪˈgan/; **begun** /bɪˈgʌn/: *She began to sing*; *Have you begun your essay?*

beˈginner n someone who is just learning how to do something: *an English class for beginners.*

beˈginning n the start of something: *at the beginning of term.*

to begin with 1 at first: *I didn't like him to begin with, but now he's my best friend.* **2** first: *There are many reasons why I don't like her — to begin with, she tells lies.*

begrudge /bɪˈgrʌdʒ/ v to be jealous of someone because of something: *I don't begrudge him his success.*

begun *see* **begin**.

behalf /bɪˈhɑːf/: **on behalf of someone** for someone: *On behalf of all the pupils, Jane thanked the teacher for taking them to the movie.*

behave /bɪˈheɪv/ v **1** to act properly; to be good: *If you come, you must behave yourself*; *He always behaves when he's at his grandmother's.* **2** to act in a particular way: *You are behaving stupidly*; *Metals behave in different ways when heated.*

badly-beˈhaved *adj* not well-behaved.

well-beˈhaved *adj* having good manners; behaving well; polite: *Well-behaved children.*

behaviour /bɪˈheɪvjə(r)/ n way of behaving: *The headmistress praised the good behaviour of the pupils.*

behead /bɪˈhɛd/ v to cut off someone's head: *King Henry VIII of England had two of his wives beheaded.*

behind /bɪˈhaɪnd/ prep **1** at the back of something: *He hid behind the door.* **2** remaining after: *Visitors to the park are asked not to leave any litter behind them.* **3** helping; supporting: *It's good to have friends behind you when you're in trouble.* — *adv* **1** at the back: *A car has two wheels in front and two behind.* **2** not keeping up: *You are behind with your reading — try to catch up with the other children.* **3** remaining after someone has gone: *He left his book behind*; *We stayed behind after the party.* — n the bottom: *a spank on the behind.*

behind someone's back without someone's knowledge or permission: *He sometimes bullies his sister behind his mother's back.*

beige /beɪʒ/ n a pale brown colour. — *adj*: *a beige hat.*

being /ˈbiːɪŋ/ n **1** any living person or thing: *a human being*; *strange beings from outer space.* **2** existence: *The company came into being in 1987.*

> See also **be**.

belated /bɪˈleɪtɪd/ *adj* coming late: *belated birthday greetings.* **beˈlatedly** *adv*.

belch /bɛltʃ/ v **1** to make an explosive noise in your throat, especially after eating. **2** to send out a large amount of smoke: *The chimney was belching black smoke.* – n: *He gave a loud belch.*

belief /bɪˈliːf/ n **1** faith or trust: *I have no belief in his ability to save us*; *belief in God.*

> The opposite of **belief**¹ is **disbelief** (not **unbelief**).

2 something you believe: *It's my belief that she will win*; *Christian beliefs.*

believe /bɪˈliːv/ v **1** to feel that something is true; to feel that someone is telling the truth: *I believe his explanation*; *He told me she was ill and I believed him.* **2** to think: *I believe he's ill.* **beˈlievable** *adj*.

> The opposite of **believable** is **unbelievable**.

beˈliever n a person who believes in something.

believe in 1 to accept the existence of something: *Do you believe in ghosts?* **2** to think that something is right: *I don't believe in spanking children when they are naughty.*

belittle /bɪˈlɪtəl/ v to talk about something in a way that makes it seem small or unimportant.

bell /bɛl/ n **1** a hollow metal object that gives a ringing sound when it is shaken or swung: *church bells.* **2** any other device for giving a ringing sound: *He rang the doorbell.* **3** a flower shaped like a hollow bell.

bellow /ˈbɛloʊ/ v to roar like a bull; to shout loudly. — n a roar.

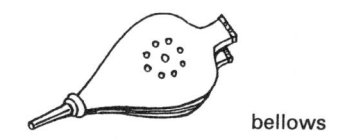

bellows /'bɛloʊz/ *n* an instrument for making a current of air.

belly /'bɛli/ *n* the part of the body between the chest and the legs: *a swollen belly*.

belong /bɪ'lɒŋ/ *v* **1** to be owned by someone: *This book belongs to me*. **2** to be a member *etc* of: *Which swimming club do you belong to?* **3** to go together with something else: *Does this shoe belong with that shoe?* **4** to stay somewhere, or have somewhere as your home: *That clock belongs on the mantelpiece*; *I've don't feel as if I belong here..*

be'longings *n* possessions: *She can't have gone away — all her belongings are still here*.

beloved /bɪ'lʌvɪd/ *adj* much loved: *my beloved country*.

below /bɪ'loʊ/ *prep* lower than something: *Your foot is below your knee*; *The plane flew below the clouds*; *A captain is below a major in the army*. — *adv* in a lower place: *We climbed up the tower and looked at the houses down below*; *Read the questions below before listening to the tape*.

> See **under**.

belt /bɛlt/ *n* **1** a long piece of leather, cloth, plastic *etc* worn round the waist: *a trouser-belt*; *He tightened his belt*. **2** a long narrow strip: *a belt of trees*. **3** a rubber ring used in a machine *etc*.

below the belt unkind and unfair.

bemused /bɪ'mjuːzd/ *adj* puzzled or confused.

bench /bɛntʃ/ *n* **1** a long seat: *They sat on a bench in the park*. **2** a table for a carpenter *etc* to work at: *He laid out his tools on the workbench*.

bend /bɛnd/ *v* **1** to curve: *Bend your arm*; *The road bends to the right*; *He can bend an iron bar*. **2** to crouch: *She bent down to pick up the coin*. — *n* a curve or angle: *a bend in the road*.

> **bend**; **bent** /bɛnt/; **bent**: *He bent down*; *He has bent the spoon*.

'bended: **on bended knee** kneeling: *He begged her forgiveness on bended knee*.

beneath /bɪ'niːθ/ *prep* **1** lower than something; under; below: *The cat crouched beneath the chair*. **2** not worthy of someone: *It is beneath him to cheat*. — *adv* below or underneath: *Who lives in the apartment beneath?*

benefactor /'bɛnɪfæktə(r)/ *n* a person who gives friendly help, usually money.

beneficial /bɛnɪ'fɪʃəl/ *adj* having good effects: *Swimming is beneficial to your health*.

benefit /'bɛnɪfɪt/ *n* something good to receive, an advantage: *the benefits of taking exercise*. — *v* **1** to gain advantage: *He benefited from her advice*. **2** to do good to: *The long rest benefited her*.

> **benefited** and **benefiting** have one **t**.

give someone the benefit of the doubt to believe someone when you don't know for certain that they are telling the truth.

benevolence /bə'nɛvələns/ *n* generosity; kindness.

be'nevolent *adj* kind: *a benevolent father*.
be'nevolently *adv*.

benign /bɪ'naɪn/ *adj* **1** kind and gentle: *a benign smile*. **2** not likely to cause death: *The tumour on her lung is benign*.

bent /bɛnt/ *adj* crooked: *a bent stick*.

> *See also* **bend**.

bent on determined to do something: *He's bent on winning*.

bequeath /bɪ'kwiːð/ *v* to leave money or property to someone when you die: *The old lady bequeathed £200 000 to her niece*.

bequest /bɪ'kwɛst/ *n* something you give away when you die.

bereaved /bɪ'riːvd/ *adj* having lost, through death, someone dear: *a bereaved mother*.
be'reavement *n*.

bereft /bɪ'rɛft/ *adj* not having something any longer; without: *He was bereft of hope*; *The shock left her quite bereft of speech*.

beret /'bɛreɪ/ *n* a round flat hat that has no brim and is made of soft material.

berry /'bɛrɪ/ *n* a kind of small fruit: *ripe strawberries*; *Those berries are poisonous*.

berserk /bəˈzɜːk/ *adj* crazy and violent in a dangerous way: *A man went berserk and shot a lot of people in the street.*

berth /bɜːð/ *n* **1** a sleeping-place in a ship *etc*. **2** a place in a harbour where a ship can be anchored. — *v* to anchor in a harbour: *The ship berthed last night.*

> See **bed**.

beside /bɪˈsaɪd/ *prep* **1** by the side of or near: *The lamp is beside the bed; She sat beside her sister.* **2** compared with: *She looks small beside her brother.*

  be'sides *prep* in addition to; as well as: *I want to talk about something besides kids and illness!* — *adv* also: *The swirl of the tide looked dangerous, and besides, I didn't want to swim.*

  beside the point not important; off the point: *All this discussion is beside the point.*

  beside yourself very worried, angry, amused *etc*: *He was beside himself with worry.*

besiege /bɪˈsiːdʒ/ *v* **1** to surround a town with an army and wait for the people in it to surrender. **2** to pursue and overwhelm: *The reporters besieged me with questions about the plane crash.*

> **besiege** is spelt with **-ie-**.

best /bɛst/ *adj* better than all the others: *Which is the best team?; She is my best friend.* — *pron* something that is better than everything else: *Whose essay was the best?; I want to look my best for the party.* — *adv* better than all the others: *Who can sing best?; Who did best in the English exam?*

  best man the bridegroom's attendant at a wedding.

  do your best to try as hard as possible: *I'll do my best to pass the exam.*

  look your best to look as smart or attractive as possible.

  make the best of to use well: *You don't make the best of all your talents; They made the best of the rain by catching up on their reading indoors.*

bestow /bɪˈstoʊ/ *v* to give an honour to someone: *The President bestowed an award on her for bravery.* **be'stowal** *n*.

bestseller /bɛstˈsɛlə(r)/ *n* a book which sells very well.

bet /bɛt/ *v* **1** to gamble money on a racehorse *etc*: *She bet all the money she had on that horse.* **2** to be very certain: *I bet I can run faster than you.* — *n* **1** an act of betting: *I won the bet I made with my father that it would rain today; I'll take a bet that he wins.* **2** a sum of money betted.

> **bet**; **bet** or **'betted**; **bet** or **'betted**: *She bet all her money on one horse; Have you betted on a horse before?*

  you bet of course: *'Do you want to see the movie?' 'You bet!'.*

betray /bɪˈtreɪ/ *v* **1** to be a traitor to your friend or your country *etc*; to give away: *He betrayed his own brother to the enemy.* **2** to show signs of some feeling: *Her pale face betrayed her fear.* **be'trayal** *n*. **be'trayer** *n*.

betrothed /bɪˈtroʊðd/ *adj* engaged to be married to someone. **be'trothal** *n*.

better /ˈbɛtə(r)/ *adj* **1** superior: *Our new car is better than our old one; She's better at running than I am.* **2** improved in health; recovered from an illness: *I feel better today; She had a headache but it's better now.* **3** preferable: *It would be better to do it now than later.* — *adv* **1** in a superior way: *You will learn to speak English better as you grow older.* **2** preferably: *You had better write to her.* — *pron* someone or something which is superior to another: *This book is the better of the two.*

> *He is better today* (not *He is more better*). *He is much better* is correct.
>
> *You had better come* or *You'd better come* (not *You better come*).

  better off richer; happier in some way: *When I'm better off I'll buy a car; You'd be better off if you cycled to work instead of driving.*

  get the better of to be defeated or conquered by: *He got the better of me in the discussion; Her curiosity got the better of her.*

between /bɪˈtwiːn/ *prep* **1** in the space dividing two things: *between the car and the pavement; between 2 o'clock and 2.30; between meals.* **2** concerning two things or people: *There was a disagreement between them; the difference between right and wrong.* **3** working together: *They managed it between them.* **4** giving some to one person and some to the other: *Divide the chocolate between you.*

> **between** fifty **and** (not **to**) sixty people; the difference between reptiles **and** (not **as well as**) mammals.
> You always say between **you and me** (not **you and I**).
> See also **among**.

in between in the space or time between two things, times or people: *two armchairs with a low table in between.*

beverage /'bevərɪdʒ/ *n* a drink such as tea or coffee.

beware /bɪ'weə(r)/ a cry meaning 'look out!', 'be careful!': *Beware of the dog!*

bewilder /bɪ'wɪldə(r)/ *v* to puzzle: *She was bewildered by the difficult instructions.*
be'wildering confusing or puzzling. **be'wilderment** *n*.

bewitch /bɪ'wɪtʃ/ *v* to cast a spell on; to charm: *She bewitched us with her smile.*

beyond /bɪ'jɒnd/ *prep* **1** on the farther side of something: *My house is beyond those trees.* **2** unable to be affected by: *The doctor saw that she was beyond his help.* **3** more than: *He succeeded beyond all his hopes.* — *adv*: *I could see as far as the fence but not beyond.*
beyond you impossible to understand: *How she did it was beyond him.*
beyond your means 1 too expensive: *A video recorder is beyond my means.* **2** spending too much money: *He lives beyond his means.*

bias /'baɪəs/ *n* an unfair feeling for or against something: *The teacher liked the girls but seemed to have a bias against the boys.*
'biased *adj*: *The old lady was biased against teenagers; a biased opinion.*

bib /bɪb/ *n* a piece of cloth or plastic tied under a baby's chin to catch spilt food *etc.*

Bible /'baɪbəl/ *n* the book containing the holy writings of the Christian Church.
biblical /'bɪblɪkəl/ *adj*.

bibliography /bɪblɪ'ɒɡrəfɪ/ *n* a list of books on a particular subject, by a particular author, or used by you for your own piece of work: *He forgot to put his bibliography at the end of his essay.*

bicentenary /baɪsɛn'tiːnərɪ/ *n* a day or year when you celebrate an event which happened exactly two hundred years earlier: *a concert to celebrate the bicentenary of the composer's birth.*

bicentennial /baɪsɛn'tɛnɪəl/ *n* a bicentenary. — *adj* held to celebrate a bicentenary: *bicentennial celebrations.*

bicker /'bɪkə(r)/ *v* to quarrel, usually about something that is not important: *The children bickered over whose turn it was to ride the bicycle.*

bicycle /'baɪsɪkəl/ *n* a pedal-driven vehicle with two wheels and a seat. — *v* to ride a bicycle: *He bicycled slowly up the hill.*

bicycle

bid /bɪd/ *v* **1** to offer an amount of money for something at an auction: *John bid £1000 for the painting.* **2** to offer to do work for a particular price: *My firm is bidding for the contract for the new road.* **3** to tell someone to do something: *Bid him come in.* **4** to greet someone: *to bid someone good morning.* — *n* **1** an offer: *He made a bid of £20.* **2** an attempt to obtain something: *The prisoner made a bid for freedom.* **'bidder** *n*. **'bidding** *n*.

> **bid; bid** or **bade** /bad/ or /beɪd/; **bidden** /'bɪdən/: *He bid £1000 for the picture; She bade him goodbye; Do as you are bidden.*

bide /baɪd/: **bide your time** to wait for a good opportunity: *I'm just biding my time until he makes a mistake.*

biennial /baɪ'ɛnɪəl/ *adj* **1** for two years. **2** happening every two years: *a biennial tournament.*

big /bɪɡ/ *adj* **1** large in size: *a big car.* **2** important: *a big event.*

bigamy /'bɪɡəmɪ/ *n* marriage to two wives or two husbands at the same time.

bigoted /'bɪɡətɪd/ *adj* not prepared to tolerate or understand the opinions and beliefs of other people: *a bigoted religious fanatic.*

bike /baɪk/ *n* short for **bicycle**: *He got a new bike for his birthday.*

bikini /bɪ'kiːnɪ/ *n* a two-piece swimming costume for women.

bilingual /baɪ'lɪŋɡwəl/ *adj* **1** written or spoken in two languages: *a bilingual dictionary.* **2** speaking two languages equally well: *bilingual children.*

bill[1] /bɪl/ *n* a bird's beak.

bill[2] /bɪl/ *n* **1** a note showing how much money is owed for goods *etc*: *an electricity bill.* **2** a

billiards

banknote: *a five-dollar bill*. **3** a poster used for advertising. — *v* to send a bill to someone: *You will be billed next month*.

billiards /'bɪlɪədz/ *n* a game played on a table with long thin sticks called cues, and balls.

billion /'bɪljən/ *n* and *adj* **1** especially in Britain, one million millions (1 000 000 000 000). **2** especially in America, one thousand millions (1 000 000 000).

billow /'bɪloʊ/ *n* a large wave. — *v* to move like a wave: *The clothes billowed on the washing-line; Smoke was billowing from the burning factory*. **'billowy** *adj*.

bin /bɪn/ *n* a holder for rubbish or for storing something in: *a waste-paper bin; a flour-bin*.

binary /'baɪnərɪ/ *adj* consisting of two: *The binary system uses only the digits 0 and 1*.

bind /baɪnd/ *v* **1** to tie or wrap: *The doctor bound up the patient's injured leg with a bandage; The robbers bound the bank manager with a rope*. **2** to force: *You are bound by law to reply*. **3** to fasten together the pages of a book and put the cover on it: *He is learning how to bind books*.

> **bind; bound** /baʊnd/; **bound**: *She bound up the parcel; This book has been nicely bound.*

'binder *n* a hard cover for keeping loose sheets of paper together.

'binding *n* the covering in which the pages of a book are fixed: *a leather binding*. — *adj* that must be done or obeyed: *This agreement is binding*.

bingo /'bɪŋgoʊ/ *n* a gambling game in which each player has a card with numbers printed on it, and covers the numbers as they are called out; the winner is the first to cover all his or her numbers: *The old lady goes to play bingo every night; a bingo-hall*.

binoculars /bɪ'nɒkjələz/ *n* an instrument that you hold up to your eyes to make distant objects look nearer: *He looked at the ship through his binoculars*.

biodegradable /baɪoʊdɪ'greɪdəbəl/ *adj* able to be decomposed by bacteria or other living organisms: *Most types of plastic are not biodegradable*.

biography /baɪ'ɒgrəfɪ/ *n* the story of someone's life. **bio'graphical** *adj*.

biology /baɪ'ɒlədʒɪ/ *n* the science of living things. **bio'logical** *adj*. **bio'logically** *adv*. **bi'ologist** *n*.

biological warfare the use of germs as a weapon.

bionic /baɪ'ɒnɪk/ *adj* having extraordinary powers, such as being very, very strong or being able to fly: *a bionic man*.

bird /bɜːd/ *n* a feathered creature, with a beak, two legs and two wings, that is usually able to fly: *A flock of birds flew across the sky*.

> Birds live in **nests**.
> Small birds **chirp**.

bird's-eye view a view from above: *a bird's-eye view of the town from an aeroplane*.

birth /bɜːθ/ *n* **1** coming into the world, being born: *the birth of her son*. **2** the beginning: *the birth of civilization*.

birth control the limiting of the number of children that are born.

'birthday *n* the anniversary of the day on which you were born: *Today is his birthday*. — *adj*: *a birthday party*.

'birthmark *n* a mark on the skin that has been there since birth.

'birthplace *n* the place where you were born.

'birthrate *n* the number of children born in a particular place during a particular time.

give birth to to produce a baby: *She has given birth to twins*.

biscuit /'bɪskɪt/ *n* a crisp, thin, flat cake; a cracker or a cookie.

bisect /baɪ'sɛkt/ *v* to cut a line *etc* into two equal parts.

bishop /'bɪʃəp/ *n* **1** a Christian clergyman in charge of all the churches in a city *etc*. **2** one of the pieces in chess.

bison /'baɪsən/ *n* a wild ox.

bit[1] /bɪt/ *n* **1** a small piece: *a bit of bread; a bit of advice*. **2** a short time: *Wait a bit longer*.

a bit rather; slightly: *The brain is a bit like a computer; We've got a bit of a problem here*.

bit by bit gradually: *Move the pile of rocks bit by bit*.

do your bit to share in the work: *We must all do our bit to help*.

not a bit not at all: *He doesn't look a bit like a millionaire*.

in bits, to bits in or into small pieces: *The broken mirror lay in bits on the floor; He tore the letter to bits*.

bits and pieces small things of various kinds: *a few interesting bits and pieces that she had collected*.

bit[2] *see* **bite**.

bitch /bɪtʃ/ *n* the female of the dog, wolf or fox.

bite /baɪt/ *v* to cut through or injure something with the teeth or jaws: *I bit the apple; She sank her teeth in, biting as hard as she could;*

The dog bit my leg; He was bitten by a mosquito. — *n* biting, or the piece or place bitten: *The dog gave him a bite; I took a bite of the cake; He has a mosquito bite on his arm.*

> **bite; bit** /bɪt/; **bitten** /ˈbɪtən/: *That animal bit me; I have been bitten by a flea.*

'biting *adj* **1** very cold: *a biting wind.* **2** unkind: *a biting remark.*

bitter /ˈbɪtə(r)/ *adj* **1** having a sharp taste like lemons: *This juice tastes bitter.* **2** very unpleasant and hard to bear: *bitter disappointment.* **3** full of hatred: *bitter enemies.* **4** very cold: *a bitter wind.* **'bitterness** *n*.
'bitterly *adv*: *bitterly disappointed.*

bitumen /ˈbɪtʃʊmɪn/ *n* a black sticky substance obtained from petroleum.

bizarre /bɪˈzɑː(r)/ *adj* very strange: *a bizarre happening.*

black /blak/ *adj* **1** the colour in which these words are printed: *The photographs are not coloured — they're black and white.* **2** dark: *as black as night.* **3** dark-skinned or black-skinned: *the black peoples of Africa.* **4** dirty: *Your hands are black!* **5** without milk: *black coffee.* **6** funny in a bitter, unpleasant way: *black comedy.* **7** depressed or depressing: *a black mood; The future looks black.* — *n* **1** the colour of the print in this book: *Black and white are opposites.* **2** a dark-skinned or black-skinned person: *The blacks were unfairly blamed for the violence.* **'blackness** *n*.

'blackberry *n* a small, soft, black fruit that grows on a bush.

'blackbird *n* a dark-coloured bird that sings sweetly.

'blackboard *n* a dark-coloured board used in schools *etc*, for writing on in chalk.

'blacken *v* **1** to become black: *The sky blackened before the storm.* **2** to criticize something unfairly: *She blackened his character.*

black eye an eye with bad bruising around it from being hit *etc*: *George gave me a black eye.*

'blackhead *n* a small black spot on the skin.
black magic evil magic.

'blackmail *v* to get money wrongly from someone by threatening to tell people about some bad secret event in their past unless they pay a large sum of money *etc* for keeping the secret: *It is a crime to blackmail someone.* — *n* getting money in this way: *He was imprisoned for blackmail.* **'blackmailer** *n*.

black market dishonest trading in goods that are either against the law, or cannot be obtained by the general public: *He sold the diamonds on the black market.*

in black and white in writing.

'blackout *n* **1** a period of darkness produced by putting out all lights: *Accidents increase during a blackout.* **2** a stopping of news broadcasting: *There is a complete blackout of news about the fall of the government.*

black sheep someone who brings shame on his family because of his wicked behaviour *etc*: *My brother is the black sheep of the family.*

'blacksmith *n* a person who makes things out of iron by hand: *The blacksmith made a new shoe for the horse.*

black and blue badly bruised: *After the fight the boy was black and blue all over.*

black out to become unconscious for a moment; to faint: *He blacked out for almost a minute.*

bladder /ˈbladə(r)/ *n* the bag-like part of the body in which the urine collects.

blade /bleɪd/ *n* **1** the cutting part of a knife *etc*: *His penknife has several different blades.* **2** a long flat leaf or piece of grass: *a blade of grass.*

blame /bleɪm/ *v* **1** to consider that someone is the cause of something bad: *I blame the cyclist for the accident; I didn't break the window — you can't blame it on me!* **2** to think someone is wrong to do something: *I don't blame you for getting angry.* — *n* saying that something is someone's fault: *He always takes the blame when things go wrong.*

'blameless *adj* innocent: *a blameless life.*

to blame being the cause of something bad: *You are not to blame for the accident.*

bland /bland/ *adj* **1** almost without taste: *This fish is very bland.* **2** dull and boring: *a very bland piece of music.* **3** mild and gentle in manner: *a bland person who does not show his emotions.* **'blandly** *adv*.

blank /blaŋk/ *adj* **1** without writing or marks: *a blank sheet of paper.* **2** puzzled; not understanding: *She gave me a blank look when I asked her the question.* **3** bored; uninterested: *blank faces.* **4** having no door, window *etc*: *a blank wall.* — *n* **1** a space left to be filled up with words, on a printed sheet of paper *etc*: *Fill in all the blanks.* **2** a cartridge

blanket 42

without a bullet: *The soldier fired a blank.* **'blankly** *adv.* **'blankness** *n.*

blank cheque a signed cheque where the amount to be paid has been left blank.

draw a blank to get no results or to fail: *All her attempts to find the stolen jewellery have drawn a blank.*

go blank to become empty: *My mind went blank when the teacher questioned me.*

blanket /'blaŋkɪt/ *n* **1** a warm covering made of wool *etc*: *a blanket on the bed.* **2** something which covers like a blanket: *a blanket of mist.* — *v* to cover something as if with a blanket: *The hills were blanketed in mist.*

blare /blɛə(r)/ *v* to make a harsh sound: *The radio blared out music.* — *n*: *the blare of trumpets.*

blaspheme /blas'fi:m/ *v* **1** to speak about God or religion without respect. **2** to swear, using the name of God.

blasphemous /'blasfəməs/ *adj* showing disrespect for God.

blasphemy /'blasfəmɪ/ *n* the saying or writing of something that shows disrespect for God.

blast /blɑːst/ *n* **1** a strong, sudden stream of air *etc*: *a blast of cold air.* **2** a loud sound: *He heard a blast from a car's horn as he stepped into the road.* **3** an explosion: *the blast from a bomb.* — *v* **1** to tear by an explosion: *The door was blasted off its hinges*; *They had to blast the rock to make way for the new road.* **2** to make a loud noise: *Music was blasting out of the radio.*

blast off to take off and start to rise: *The spacecraft will blast off at 11 a.m.* **'blast-off** *n.*

blatant /'bleɪtənt/ *adj* done openly and without shame or disguise: *a blatant lie.* **'blatantly** *adv.*

blaze /bleɪz/ *n* **1** a bright light or fire: *A neighbour rescued her from the blaze.* **2** a violent fit of anger *etc*: *a blaze of fury.* **3** a bright display: *The flowerbeds were a blaze of colour.* — *v* to burn or shine brightly: *A fire was blazing in the hearth*; *The sun blazed down.*

blazer /'bleɪzə(r)/ *n* a type of jacket worn as part of a school uniform *etc*.

bleach /bliːtʃ/ *n* liquid *etc* used for whitening clothes *etc*. — *v* to fade; to become lighter or paler in colour: *The sun has bleached his red shirt*; *His hair bleached in the sun.*

bleak /bliːk/ *adj* **1** cold and bare, with very few trees: *a bleak landscape.* **2** not hopeful: *The future looks bleak.* **'bleakly** *adv.* **'bleakness** *n.*

bleary /'blɪərɪ/ *adj* red and watery; not seeing clearly: *Her eyes were bleary and she had a headache.*

'blearily *adv*: *He looked blearily out of the window.*

bleary-eyed *adj*: *He was bleary-eyed the morning after the party.*

bleat /bliːt/ *v* to make the noise of a sheep, lamb or goat: *The lamb bleated for its mother.* – *n* this sound.

bleed /bliːd/ *v* to pour out blood: *Her nose was bleeding.*

> **bleed**; **bled** /blɛd/; **bled**: *Her finger bled*; *How long has it bled?*

'bleeding *n* blood coming from a cut *etc*: *try to stop the bleeding.*

bleep /bliːp/ *n* a short, high sound made, for instance, by an electronic machine. — *v* to make a short, high sound: *Satellites bleep as they circle the earth.*

'bleeper *n* a small radio receiver used by doctors *etc*, that you can carry in your pocket and which bleeps when you are needed.

blemish /'blɛmɪʃ/ *n* a mark that spoils something: *a blemish on an apple.*

blend /blɛnd/ *v* to mix together: *Blend the eggs and milk together*; *These two colours blend well.* — *n* a mixture: *a blend of eggs and cheese.*

'blender *n* a machine for mixing things together, especially in cooking.

bless /blɛs/ *v* to ask God to look after something: *The priest blessed the children.*

'blessed *adj* holy: *the Blessed Virgin Mary.* **'blessedness** *n.*

blessing /'blɛsɪŋ/ *n* **1** a prayer for happiness or success: *The priest gave them his blessing.* **2** any cause of happiness: *Her son was a great blessing to her.*

a blessing in disguise something that seems bad but turns out to be lucky after all.

blew *see* **blow**².

blind /blaɪnd/ *adj* **1** not able to see: *a blind man.* **2** not wanting to realise something: *She is blind to his faults.* **3** unreasonable: *blind hatred.* **4** not able to be seen properly; not giving a clear view of the road *etc*: *Take care as you approach a blind corner.* — *n* a screen to prevent light coming through a window *etc*: *The sunlight is too bright — pull down the blinds!* — *v* to make blind:

He was blinded in the war. **'blindly** *adv.* **'blindness** *n.*

blindfold /'blaɪndfoʊld/ *n* a piece of cloth *etc* that is tied round your head and over your eyes to prevent you from seeing. — *v* to put a blindfold on someone: *They blindfolded her with a scarf.* — *adj* with the eyes covered by a cloth *etc*: *The prisoner was kept blindfold in a locked room.*

'blinding *adj* very bright, making you unable to see for a moment: *a blinding flash of light.*

to turn a blind eye to pretend not to notice.

blink /blɪŋk/ *v* to shut and open your eyes very quickly: *It is impossible to stare for a long time without blinking.* — *n* a quick shutting and opening of the eyes.

bliss /blɪs/ *n* very great happiness: *the bliss of a young married couple.* **'blissful** *adj.* **'blissfully** *adv.*

blister /'blɪstə(r)/ *n* 1 a thin bubble on the skin, containing liquid: *My feet are covered with blisters after walking so far.* 2 a similar bubble on any surface: *blisters on the paintwork.* — *v* to cause or get blisters: *The sun has blistered the paint on the door*; *Her skin blistered when she got burnt.*

'blistering *adj* 1 very hot. 2 full of anger: *blistering criticism.*

blitz /blɪts/ *n* a sudden bombing attack by a large number of enemy aeroplanes. — *v* to attack a city *etc* with bombs: *London was blitzed during the Second World War.*

blizzard /'blɪzəd/ *n* a very bad snow-storm.

bloated /'bloʊtɪd/ *adj* swollen and puffed up: *He felt bloated after eating so much.*

blob /blɒb/ *n* a small shapeless mass of liquid *etc*: *a blob of paint*; *a blob of wax.*

block /blɒk/ *n* 1 a square or oblong piece of wood or stone *etc*: *blocks of stone.* 2 a piece of wood used for certain purposes: *a chopping-block.* 3 a connected group of houses, offices *etc*: *a block of flats*; *an office block.* 4 a barrier: *a road block.* — *v* to close up; to make progress difficult or impossible: *The crashed cars blocked the road*; *He had a bad cold, so his nose was blocked.*

block'ade *n* the surrounding of a place with ships, troops *etc*, so that nothing can get in or out.

'blockage *n* something that blocks an opening *etc*: *a blockage in the pipe.*

block capital, block letter a printed capital letter: *NAME is written in block capitals.*

blond or **blonde** /blɒnd/ *adj* having yellow or fair hair: *a blond child.*

blonde *n* a woman with fair hair.

blood /blʌd/ *n* 1 the red liquid pumped through the body by the heart: *Blood poured from the wound in his leg.* 2 family or ancestors: *He is of royal blood.*

bloodcurdling /'blʌdkɜːdlɪŋ/ *adj* frightening: *a bloodcurdling scream.*

blood donor a person who gives blood to be put into the body of a person who hasn't enough blood.

blood group one of the four types of human blood.

'bloodhound *n* a large dog with loose wrinkled skin on its head, that has a very good sense of smell and that is used for finding things by smelling them out.

'bloodless *adj* very pale: *bloodless lips.*

'bloodshed *n* death and wounding: *There was much bloodshed in the battle.*

'bloodshot *adj* very red and sore-looking: *bloodshot eyes.*

'bloodstained *adj* covered with blood: *a bloodstained bandage.*

'bloodstream *n* the blood flowing through the body: *The poison entered her bloodstream.*

'bloodthirsty *adj* 1 eager to kill people: *a bloodthirsty warrior.* 2 full of killing: *a bloodthirsty story.*

'blood-vessel *n* the veins and arteries in the body, through which the blood flows.

'bloody *adj* 1 bleeding, or covered with blood: *a bloody wound*; *a bloody shirt.* 2 causing a lot of wounds or deaths: *a bloody battle.*

in cold blood deliberately and cruelly and without emotion: *He was killed in cold blood.*

bloom /bluːm/ *n* 1 a flower: *These blooms are withering now.* 2 the time when a plant produces flowers: *The roses are in full bloom just now.* — *v* to grow or flower: *Daffodils bloomed along the river's edge.*

blossom /'blɒsəm/ *n* flowers, especially those of a fruit tree: *cherry blossom.* — *v* 1 to develop flowers: *The apple tree has blossomed.* 2 to grow up: *She blossomed into a beautiful woman.*

blot /blɒt/ *n* 1 a spot of spilt ink on a written page *etc*: *an ink-blot.* 2 something ugly: *That building is a blot on the landscape.* — *v* 1 to spill a drop of ink *etc* on something. 2 to soak up: *She tried to blot the coffee-stain with a tissue.*

'blotting-paper *n* soft paper used for soaking up ink.

blot out to hide: *The rain blotted out the view.*

blotch /blɒtʃ/ *n* a round mark especially on the skin: *The insect-bite left a red blotch on her leg.*

'blotchy *adj* covered in blotches.

blouse /blaʊz/ *n* a woman's loose garment for the upper half of the body: *She wore a skirt and blouse.*

blow¹ /bloʊ/ *n* 1 a hit or knock: *a blow on the head.* 2 a sudden misfortune: *Her husband's death was a terrible blow to her.*

come to blows start fighting.

blow² /bloʊ/ *v* 1 to move along as the wind does: *The wind blew more strongly.* 2 to make something move, as the wind does: *The wind blew his hat off; The explosion blew off the lid.* 3 to be moved by the wind etc: *The door must have blown shut; The washing blew about on the line.* 4 to breathe hard: *Please blow into this tube.* 5 to make a sound on a wind instrument: *She blew the trumpet.* – *n.*

> **blow; blew** /bluː/; **blown** /bloʊn/: *My hat blew off; The washing has blown away.*

'blowpipe *n* a tube from which a poisonous dart is blown.

blow out to blow on a flame to stop it burning: *blow the candles out.*

blow over to pass or come to an end without having a bad effect: *The storm blew over; She hopes her problems at work will soon blow over.*

blow up 1 to explode; to destroy by an explosion: *The bomb blew up; The bridge was blown up.* 2 to fill with air or gas: *to blow a balloon up.* 3 to begin: *a storm had blown up in the night; an argument suddenly blew up.*

blow your nose to clear your nose by breathing out hard through it.

blue /bluː/ *adj* 1 of the colour of a cloudless sky: *blue paint; Her eyes are blue.* 2 sad: *I'm feeling blue today.* — *n* 1 the colour of a cloudless sky: *a beautiful shade of blue.* 2 the sky: *The balloon floated off into the blue.*

'bluecollar *adj* working in a factory rather than at a desk: *bluecollar workers.*

'blueprint *n* a photographic plan of something that is to be made: *the blueprints for a new aircraft.*

once in a blue moon hardly ever: *He takes a holiday once in a blue moon.*

out of the blue without warning: *He arrived out of the blue, without phoning first.*

the blues 1 a feeling of sadness: *He's got the blues today.* 2 a type of slow, sad jazz music: *a blues singer.*

bluff /blʌf/ *v* 1 to deceive; to trick: *He bluffed them into lending him the money.* 2 to lie or pretend: *He bluffed his way into the palace by pretending to be a policeman.* — *n* a trick; a pretence.

blunder /'blʌndə(r)/ *v* to make a mistake: *There's a mistake on the school time-table — someone has blundered.* — *n* a mistake: *He made a bad blunder in his exam.*

blunt /blʌnt/ *adj* 1 having a point or edge that is no longer sharp: *a blunt knife.* 2 a bit too honest, or rather rude, in the way you speak to people: *She was very blunt, and said that she did not like him.* — *v* to make less sharp: *The knife has been blunted by years of use.*

'bluntly *adv.* **'bluntness** *n.*

blur /blɜː(r)/ *n* a shape that is not clear; a fuzzy image: *Everything becomes a blur when I take my glasses off.* — *v* to make or become unclear: *The rain blurred the view out of the window.*

blurt /blɜːt/: **blurt out** to pour out words suddenly: *He blurted out the whole story.*

blush /blʌʃ/ *n* a red colour on the skin caused by shame, shyness *etc.* — *v* to show shame, shyness *etc* by growing red in the face: *That girl blushes easily.*

bluster /'blʌstə(r)/ *v* to speak loudly and angrily without being able to do anything: *He is only blustering — he can't really carry out his threats.*

boa /'boʊə/ *n* (usually **boa constrictor** /'boʊə kənstrɪktə(r)/) a very large snake that kills animals and birds by winding itself round them.

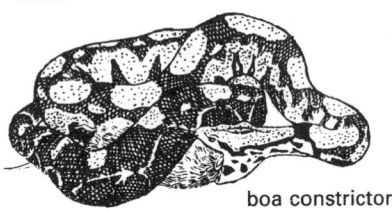

boa constrictor

boar /bɔː(r)/ *n* a male pig.

board /bɔːd/ *n* 1 a flat piece of wood: *The floorboards of the old house were rotten.* 2 a flat piece of wood *etc* for a special purpose: *a notice-board; a chessboard.* 3 meals: *The inn provided board and lodging.* 4 a group of people who direct an organization *etc*:

the board of directors. — *v* **1** to get on to a vehicle, ship, plane *etc*: *This is where we board the bus.* **2** to stay, and have your meals, in someone else's house: *He boards at Mrs Smith's during the week.* **'boarder** *n*.

See **disembark**.

above board open, honest and legal: *The elections were open and above board.*

on board on a ship or aeroplane: *Take your baggage on board with you.*

'board-game *n* a game you play by moving objects on a board, such as chess.

'boarding-house *n* a private house where people stay and have meals as paying guests.

'boarding-school *n* a school at which you sleep and eat as well as have lessons: *He was sent to boarding-school in England.*

'boardroom *n* a room in which the directors of a company meet.

board up to close a hole or entrance *etc* with boards: *The broken window was boarded up.*

boast /bəʊst/ *v* **1** to talk too proudly: *He was always boasting about how clever his son was.* **2** to own proudly: *The school boasts a fine swimming-pool.* — *n* a claim: *His boast is that he has never yet lost a match.* **'boastful** *adj*. **'boastfully** *adv*. **'boastfulness**, **'boasting** *ns*.

boat /bəʊt/ *n* **1** a small vessel for travelling over water: *We'll cross the stream by boat.* **2** a larger vessel; a ship: *to cross the Atlantic in a passenger boat.* — *v* to sail about in a small boat: *They are boating on the river.*

See **in**.

'boatman *n* a man in charge of a boat carrying passengers.

in the same boat suffering in the same way: *Don't be so sorry for yourself — we're all in the same boat!*

boatswain /'bəʊsən/ *n* an officer who looks after a ship's boats, ropes, sails *etc*.

bob /bɒb/ *v* to move up and down: *The cork was bobbing about in the water.*

bodily /'bɒdɪlɪ/ *adj* of your body: *You must eat enough food for your bodily needs.* — *adv* by the whole body: *They lifted him bodily and carried him off.*

body /'bɒdɪ/ *n* **1** the whole of a person or animal: *Athletes have to look after their bodies.* **2** a dead person: *The battlefield was covered with bodies.* **3** the main or central part of something: *a car-body.* **4** a group of people acting together: *They went in a body to complain to the head-teacher.*

'body-building *n* physical exercise which makes your muscles bigger and stronger. **'body-builder** *n*.

'bodyguard *n* a guard or guards to protect an important person: *the president's bodyguard.*

bog /bɒɡ/ *n* very wet ground; marsh.

'boggy *adj*: *boggy ground.*

bogged down prevented from making progress.

bogus /'bəʊɡəs/ *adj* false: *She was fooled by his bogus police uniform.*

boil[1] /bɔɪl/ *n* a red, painful swelling on the skin: *His neck is covered with boils.*

boil[2] /bɔɪl/ *v* **1** to bubble and turn from liquid to vapour when heated; to heat a liquid till it does this: *The water's boiling*; *Boil the water.* **2** to cook by boiling in water *etc*: *I've boiled the potatoes.*

'boiler *n* a container in which water is heated.

'boiling-point *n* the temperature at which something boils.

boil over to boil and overflow: *The pan of milk boiled over and spilt on the floor.*

boisterous /'bɔɪstərəs/ *adj* lively and noisy: *a boisterous little boy.* **'boisterously** *adv*.

bold /bəʊld/ *adj* **1** daring: *a bold plan of attack.* **2** bright and clear: *a bold design.* **3** heavy, black printing: *Use bold type for titles.* **'boldly** *adv*. **'boldness** *n*.

bold as brass very cheeky: *She walked in late as bold as brass.*

bollard /'bɒlɑːd/ *n* **1** one of a number of short, thick posts that are placed round part of a road to keep traffic away from it. **2** a short, strong post in a harbour *etc* that is used for fastening boats to.

bolster /'bəʊlstə(r)/ *n* a long pillow for a double bed.

bolt /bəʊlt/ *n* **1** a small metal bar that slides across to fasten a door *etc*: *We have a bolt as well as a lock on the door.* **2** a type of screw: *nuts and bolts.* **3** a flash of lightning. — *v* **1** to fasten with a bolt: *He bolted the door.* **2** to go away very fast: *The horse bolted in terror.*

a bolt from the blue a sudden, unexpected happening: *His departure was a bolt from the blue.*

bolt upright straight and stiff: *He sat bolt upright.*

bomb /bɒm/ *n* a hollow case containing explosives *etc*: *The enemy dropped a bomb on the factory and blew it up.* — *v* to drop

bombard

bombs on: *London was bombed several times.*

bombard /bɒmˈbɑːd/ *v* **1** to attack with big guns: *They bombarded the town.* **2** to shoot questions *etc* at: *The reporters bombarded the film star with questions.* **bomˈbardment** *n*.

bomber /ˈbɒmə(r)/ *n* an aeroplane built for bombing.

bombshell /ˈbɒmʃɛl/ *n* a piece of amazing news: *What a bombshell the President's announcement was!*

bond /bɒnd/ *n* **1** something used for tying someone up: *They released the prisoner from his bonds.* **2** something that unites or joins people together: *a bond of friendship.*

bondage /ˈbɒndɪdʒ/ *n* slavery.

bone /bəʊn/ *n* **1** the hard substance that forms the skeleton: *Bone lasts longer than flesh.* **2** a part of the skeleton: *She broke two bones in her foot.* — *v* to take the bones out of a fish *etc*, to cook it: *She boned the fish.*

bone-ˈdry *adj* completely dry.

have a bone to pick with someone to have something that you want to complain about to a particular person: *I've got a bone to pick with you — why did you take my umbrella?*

bonfire /ˈbɒnfaɪə(r)/ *n* a large fire in the open air, often built to celebrate something.

bonnet /ˈbɒnɪt/ *n* **1** a hat, especially one for a baby, fastened under the chin. **2** the cover of a motor-car engine.

bonsai /ˈbɒnsaɪ/ *n* a small tree grown in a pot.

bonus /ˈbəʊnəs/ *n* something extra given in addition to the usual amount: *At Christmas the employees received a bonus of £50 in addition to their wages; We were given two extra days' holiday as a bonus.*

bony /ˈbəʊnɪ/ *adj* **1** full of bones: *This fish is very bony.* **2** thin: *bony fingers.*

boo /buː/ *n* a word shouted rudely by a disappointed audience, football crowd *etc*: *the boos of the crowd.* — *v* to shout 'boo' at a person *etc*: *The crowd booed him.*

booby /ˈbuːbɪ/ *n* a stupid person.

booby prize a prize for the lowest score *etc*: *John came last and got the booby prize.*

booby trap a hidden bomb. – *v*: *The room had been booby-trapped.*

book /bʊk/ *n* **1** a number of printed or blank sheets of paper bound together: *an exercise book.* **2** a long piece of writing, printed and made into a book: *She has written a book about dancing.* — *v* to reserve or pay for in advance: *I've booked four seats for Friday's concert; Please book a table at the restaurant for this evening.*

bookbinding /ˈbʊkbaɪndɪŋ/ *n* putting the covers on books. **ˈbookbinder** *n*.

ˈbookcase *n* a set of shelves for books.

ˈbooking *n* the reserving of a travel ticket, theatre seat *etc.*

ˈbooking-office *n* an office where travel tickets *etc* are sold: *There was a queue at the station booking-office.*

ˈbooklet *n* a small, thin book: *a booklet about the history of the town.*

ˈbook-maker *n* a person whose job is to take people's money when they want to bet, and pay them if they win the bet.

ˈbookmark *n* something put in a book to mark a particular page.

books *n* the records of the money a company *etc* has earned and spent: *An accountant will check the books.*

ˈbookshelf *n* a shelf on which books are kept.

ˈbookstall a small shop where books and newspapers *etc* are sold.

bookworm /ˈbʊkwɔːm/ *n* a person who reads a lot.

booked up full: *The course has been booked up for weeks.*

book in to sign your name on the list of guests at an hotel *etc*: *We have booked in at the Royal Hotel.*

boom[1] /buːm/ *n* a sudden increase in a business *etc*: *a boom in the sales of TV sets.* — *v* to increase suddenly: *Business is booming this week.*

boom[2] /buːm/ *v* to make a hollow sound, like a large drum or gun: *His voice boomed out over the loudspeaker.* — *n* a sound like this: *the boom of the guns.*

boomerang /ˈbuːməraŋ/ *n* a curved piece of wood used by Australian aborigines which, when thrown, returns to the thrower.

boost /buːst/ *v* to improve. — *n* help; encouragement.

ˈbooster *n* something that helps to increase or improve something else, for instance, a television mast for improving television reception.

boot /buːt/ *n* **1** a covering for the foot and lower part of the leg, made of leather *etc*: *a pair of suede boots.* **2** a place for luggage in a motor-car *etc.* — *v* to kick: *He booted the ball out of the goal.*

booth /buːð/ *n* **1** a stall selling goods *etc*, especially at a fair. **2** a small compartment for a special purpose: *a telephone booth.*

booty /'bu:tɪ/ *n* property taken from an enemy by force during a war: *The soldiers shared the booty among themselves.*

border /'bɔ:də(r)/ *n* **1** something that forms an edge: *the border of a picture.* **2** the boundary of a country: *They'll ask for your passport at the border.* **3** a flowerbed round the edge of a lawn *etc*: *a flower border.* — *v* to lie next to: *Germany borders on France.*
'**borderline** *n* the border or division between two things: *His exam marks were just on the borderline between passing and failing.*

bore[1] *see* **bear**[1].

bore[2] /bɔ:(r)/ *v* to make a hole through something: *They bored a tunnel under the sea.* — *n* the size of the barrel of a gun.

bore[3] *v* to make someone feel tired and uninterested, by being dull *etc*: *He bores everyone with stories about his travels.* — *n* a dull person or thing: *He's a bore.*
bored *adj*: *You get bored when you have nothing to do.*
'**boredom** *n* being bored: *the boredom of waiting.*
'**boring** *adj*: *a boring book.*

born, borne *see* **bear**[1].

borrow /'bɒrəʊ/ *v* to take something away for a while, intending to return it: *He borrowed a book from the library.* '**borrower,** '**borrowing** *ns*.

> **borrow from:** *I borrow money from a friend.*
> **lend to:** *My friend lends money to me; My friend lends me money.*

bosom /'bʊzəm/ *n* the breast; the chest: *She held him close to her bosom.* — *adj* close: *a bosom friend.*

boss /bɒs/ *n* the person in charge: *the boss of the factory.* — *v* to order: *Stop bossing everyone about!*
'**bossy** *adj* liking to order others about.
'**bossiness** *n*.

botany /'bɒtənɪ/ *n* the scientific study of plants. **bo'tanical** *adj*.
'**botanist** *n* a person who studies botany.
botanical gardens a public park for the growing of plants.

both /bəʊθ/ *adj, pron* the two; the one and the other: *We both went*; *Both men are dead*; *Both the men are dead*; *The men are both dead*; *Both are dead.*

> He is both rich **and** (not **as well as**) handsome.
> See also **neither**.

bother /'bɒðə(r)/ *v* **1** to annoy or worry or disturb: *Don't bother me now — I'm busy.* **2** to make an effort: *Don't bother to write — it isn't necessary.* — *n* **1** trouble: *I don't want to cause any bother.* **2** something that causes trouble; a nuisance: *These flies are such a bother.*

bottle /'bɒtəl/ *n* a hollow narrow-necked container for holding liquids *etc*: *a lemonade bottle.* — *v* to put into bottles.
'**bottled** *adj* sold in bottles: *bottled water.*
'**bottleneck** *n* a part of a road where traffic is held up.
bottle up to keep your feelings hidden inside yourself: *She always bottles up her anger.*

bottom /'bɒtəm/ *n* **1** the lowest part of anything: *the bottom of the sea.* **2** the end of something: *the bottom of the garden*; *the bottom of the bed.* **3** the part of your body on which you sit.
'**bottom** *adj*: *the bottom step*; *He bit his bottom lip.*
'**bottomless** *adj* very deep: *a bottomless pit.*
'**bottoms** *n* the trousers of a set of clothes: *a pair of tracksuit bottoms.*
at the bottom of something the real cause or explanation.
get to the bottom of something to find out the reason or explanation for something.

bougainvillaea /bu:gən'vɪlɪə/ *n* a vine with small flowers and purple or red leaves.

bough /baʊ/ *n* a branch of a tree: *The bough of the apple tree was weighed down with fruit.*

> See **branch**.

bought *see* **buy**.

boulder /'bəʊldə(r)/ *n* a large rock or stone.

bounce /baʊns/ *v* to spring back from the ground, or make something do this: *The ball bounced*; *I can bounce a ball.* — *n* **1** this action: *With one bounce the ball went over the net.* **2** energy: *She has a lot of bounce.*
'**bouncing** *adj* strong and lively: *a bouncing baby.*
bounce back to recover after a period of bad health or bad luck.

bound[1] *see* **bind**.

bound[2] /baʊnd/: **-bound** going in a particular direction: *westbound traffic.*
bound for on the way to: *The ship is bound for Taiwan.*
bound to certain to: *He's bound to notice your mistake.*
bound up closely connected with something.

bound[3] /baʊnd/ *n* a limit: *His story is beyond*

bound

the bounds of probability. — v to enclose: The country is bounded on the west by a range of hills.
out of bounds outside the allowed area or limits: The cinema was out of bounds for the schoolchildren.
bound[4] /baʊnd/ n a big jump: He reached me in one bound. — v to jump, leap: The dog bounded over to me.
boundary /ˈbaʊndərɪ/ n a division or borderline between two things: the boundary between two towns.
boundless /ˈbaʊndləs/ adj having no limit: boundless generosity.
bouquet /buːˈkeɪ/ n a bunch of flowers: The bride carried a bouquet of roses.
bout /baʊt/ n 1 a fit: a bout of coughing. 2 a contest: The boxing-match will consist of a bout of fifteen five-minute rounds.
boutique /buːˈtiːk/ n a small shop, especially one selling clothes.
bow[1] /boʊ/ n 1 a curved rod bent by a string, with which arrows are shot. 2 a rod with horsehair stretched along it, with which to play a violin. 3 a looped knot tied with ribbon, or in shoe-laces etc: Have you learnt how to tie a bow yet?
bow[2] /baʊ/ v to bend your head and the upper part of your body forwards in greeting a person: He bowed to the ladies; They bowed their heads in prayer. — n a bowing movement: He made a bow to the ladies.
bow[3] /baʊ/ or **bows** n the front of a ship or boat: The waves broke over the bows.
bowel /baʊəl/ or **bowels** n a very long twisted and folded tube in the lower part of your body, through which food goes; the intestines.
bowl[1] /boʊl/ n a round, deep dish for holding or mixing food etc: a soup bowl; a baking-bowl.
bowl[2] /boʊl/ n a wooden ball rolled along the ground in playing bowls. — v to deliver or send a ball towards the batsman in cricket.
ˈ**bowler** n a person who bowls the ball in cricket.
ˈ**bowler** or **bowler** ˈ**hat** a man's hard, round, usually black hat.
ˈ**bowling** n the game of bowls.
bowls n a game played on a square patch of smooth grass.
ˈ**bowling-alley** n a room containing long narrow wooden boards along which you roll bowls at skittles.
bowtie /boʊˈtaɪ/ n a tie with a double loop, worn by men on formal occasions.

box[1] /bɒks/ n 1 a case for holding something: a wooden box; a matchbox. 2 a space marked out by straight lines on a piece of paper etc: Write your name in the box at the top of the page. 3 in a theatre etc, a group of seats separated from the rest of the audience.
box office a ticket office in a theatre, concert-hall etc.
box[2] /bɒks/ v to fight someone with your fists: Years ago, fighters used to box without wearing padded gloves. — n a blow; a hit: She gave him a box on the ear. ˈ**boxer** n. ˈ**boxing** n.
ˈ**boxing-glove** n a boxer's padded glove.
ˈ**boxing-match** n.
boy /bɔɪ/ n 1 a male child: She has three girls and one boy. 2 a man or boy who does a certain job: a cowboy; a newspaper-boy.
ˈ**boyfriend** n a girl's favourite male friend.
ˈ**boyhood** n the time of being a boy: He had a happy boyhood.
boycott /ˈbɔɪkɒt/ v to refuse to have anything to do with something. — n a refusal of this sort.
bra /brɑː/ short for **brassière**.
brace /breɪs/ n something that holds something firmly in the right position: He wears a brace to straighten his teeth. — v to make yourself firm or steady: He braced himself for the fight.
ˈ**braces** n straps over the shoulders for holding up the trousers.
bracelet /ˈbreɪslət/ n an ornament worn round the wrist or arm: a gold bracelet.
bracket /ˈbrakɪt/ n 1 a sign written in pairs like this: ( ) or like this: [ ] or a single sign like this: {, used for grouping together one or more words etc. 2 an L-shaped piece of metal etc used to attach shelves to walls. — v to enclose words etc in brackets: He bracketed the last part of the sentence.
brag /brag/ v to boast.
braid /breɪd/ n thick, heavy ornamental ribbon that is used as decoration on uniforms etc: gold braid on the admiral's uniform.
braille /breɪl/ n a system of printing books for blind people, using raised dots.
brain /breɪn/ n 1 the part of you that is inside your head and makes you think and move. 2 cleverness: She has a good brain; He has plenty of brains.
ˈ**brainchild** n the idea etc of a particular person: This project is my wife's brainchild.
ˈ**brainless** adj very silly.
ˈ**brainwash** v to make someone believe

something by continually telling them it is true.

brainwave *n* a sudden good idea: *Your suggestion was a brainwave!*

'brainy *adj* clever; intelligent: *She's very brainy — she always does well in her exams.*

on the brain in your head: *I've had that song on the brain all day.*

pick someone's brains to ask someone who knows more about a subject than you do for help or information: *I'll come and pick your brains if I have any problems.*

brake /breɪk/ *n* the instrument with which you slow down or stop a car, bicycle *etc*: *He put on his brakes.* — *v* to slow down or stop: *He braked suddenly.*

bramble /'bræmbəl/ *n* a wild, prickly blackberry bush: *The boy was badly scratched when he fell into the brambles.*

bran /bræn/ *n* the brown outer parts of wheat grains.

branch /brɑːntʃ/ *n* **1** an arm-like part of a tree: *He cut some branches off the tree.* **2** one of the stores or businesses that are all run by one big firm *etc*: *This store has many branches in different towns.* — *v*.

branch off to separate into different parts like branches: *The road to the coast branches off here.*

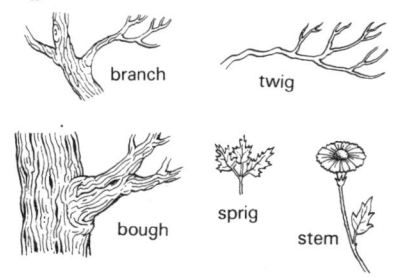

branch / twig / bough / sprig / stem

branch out to develop different interests: *She has left teaching and branched out into giving concert performances.*

brand /brænd/ *n* a name given by a manufacturer to a particular kind of goods that he makes: *This is a new brand of coffee.* — *v* to make a special mark on cattle *etc* with a hot iron.

brand-'new *adj* completely new: *a brand-new dress.*

brandish /'brændɪʃ/ *v* to wave something about: *He brandished the sword above his head.*

brandy /'brændɪ/ *n* a type of very strong alcoholic drink, drunk after a meal.

brass /brɑːs/ *n* **1** a mixture of copper and zinc: *This door-handle is made of brass.* **2** wind musical instruments which are made of brass. — *adj* made of brass: *a brass doorknocker.*

brandish

brass band a band of players of brass wind instruments.

brassière /'bræzɪə(r)/ *n* a woman's undergarment supporting the breasts.

brave /breɪv/ *adj* able to face danger without fear, or to suffer pain without complaining: *a brave soldier; Be brave — don't cry!; It was brave of him to go into the burning house; a brave action.* — *v* to face boldly: *They braved the cold weather.* **'bravely** *adv.* **'bravery** *n.*

bravo /brɑː'voʊ/ a shout from an audience *etc* meaning 'well done!'

brawl /brɔːl/ *n* a noisy quarrel or fight: *The police were called out to deal with a brawl in the street.* — *v* to fight noisily.

brawn /brɔːn/ *n* strong muscles; physical strength: *He is all brawn and no brain.*

'brawny *adj* with big strong muscles: *brawny arms.*

bray /breɪ/ *n* the cry of a donkey. — *v* to make this cry.

brazen /'breɪzən/ *adj* bold in a rude way: *She was brazen enough to tell the teacher that she hadn't done the work because she didn't want to.* **'brazenly** *adv.*

brazier /'breɪzɪə(r)/ *n* a metal container in which coal can be burnt, used for keeping people warm outside in cold weather: *The builders warmed themselves at the brazier.*

breach /briːtʃ/ *n* **1** the breaking of a promise: *a breach of our agreement.* **2** a gap, break or hole: *a breach in the castle wall.* **3** a quarrel causing unfriendliness between two people. — *v* to break or make a hole in a wall *etc*.

bread

bread /brɛd/ n **1** a food made mainly of flour, baked in the oven: *I'll bake another batch of bread today.* **2** enough money to live on: *You must work to earn your daily bread.*

'breadcrumbs n very tiny pieces of bread: *The table was covered with breadcrumbs.*

bread and butter a way of earning enough money to live on: *Writing books is my bread and butter.*

breadth /brɛdθ/ n width; size from side to side: *the breadth of a table.*

breadwinner /'brɛdwɪnə(r)/ n a person who earns money to keep a family: *When her husband died she had to become the breadwinner.*

break /breɪk/ v **1** to divide into two or more pieces, especially with force: *He broke the pencil in two; She broke a piece off the chocolate bar; The mirror dropped and broke.* **2** to damage something or be damaged; not to work any more: *I've broken my hairdryer; The fridge has broken.* **3** to disobey: *You have broken the law.* **4** to fail to keep: *He broke his appointment at the dentist's.* **5** to do better than a previous record: *He broke the record for the high jump.* **6** to end or interrupt: *She broke the silence.* **7** to tell bad news: *She had to break the news of his death to his wife.* **8** to get lower: *The boy's voice broke when he was 13.* **9** to burst out: *The storm broke before they reached shelter.* — n **1** a pause: *Let's stop work and have a break for coffee.* **2** a change: *a break in the weather.* **3** an opening: *a break in the clouds.*

> **break; broke** /brouk/; **broken** /'broukən/: *He broke my watch; The mirror is broken.*

'breakable adj likely to break: *breakable toys.*

'breakage n the breaking of something: *Be careful with the dishes — we have had too many breakages.*

'breaker n a large wave which breaks on the shore.

'break-in n a burglary: *The Smiths have had two break-ins recently.*

'break-up the end of something: *the break-up of his marriage; the break-up of peace talks.*

break away to escape from control: *The dog broke away from its owner.*

break down 1 to stop working properly: *My car has broken down.* **2** to become very upset: *She broke down and wept.* **'breakdown** n.

break in or **break into 1** to force a way into a house *etc*: *Thieves broke in and stole the computer.* **2** to interrupt: *You shouldn't break in on a private conversation.*

break loose to escape from control: *The dog has broken loose.*

break off 1 to remove a part of something by force; to fall from the main part of something: *The light has broken off my bicycle.* **2** to stop; to end: *John and Mary have broken off their engagement.* **3** to stop speaking suddenly: *She broke off in the middle of a sentence.*

break out 1 to happen suddenly: *War has broken out.* **2** to escape from prison *etc*: *A prisoner has broken out.* **'breakout** n.

break the ice to start becoming friendly.

break up 1 to finish or end: *School will break up on 20 December.* **2** to separate into pieces: *He broke the box up with an axe.* **3** to end a relationship: *He has broken up with his girlfriend.*

breakfast /'brɛkfəst/ n the first meal of the day: *I had coffee and toast for breakfast.* — v to have breakfast: *They breakfasted on the train.*

breakthrough /'breɪkθruː/ n an important development or discovery: *There has been a breakthrough in the search for a cure for this disease.*

breakwater /'breɪkwɔːtə(r)/ n a very large wall that is built out into the sea to protect a shore or harbour from strong waves.

breast /brɛst/ n **1** one of a woman's two milk-producing organs on the front of her chest. **2** the front of your body between your neck and waist: *He held the child against his breast.*

'breastfeed v to feed a baby with milk from the breasts. **'breastfed** adj.

'breaststroke n a style of swimming in which the arms are pushed out in front and then swept backwards.

breath /brɛθ/ n **1** the air drawn into, and then sent out from, the lungs: *Your breath smells of peppermint.* **2** the action of breathing: *Take a deep breath.*

breathalyze /'brɛθəlaɪz/ v to ask the driver of a car to breathe into a special kind of plastic bag, called a **'breathalyzer**, that is used by the police to see if the driver has drunk too much alcohol.

breathtaking /'brɛθteɪkɪŋ/ adj very exciting

or beautiful: *The view from the top of the mountain was breathtaking.*

get your breath back to start breathing normally again after exercise.

hold your breath to stop breathing for a moment: *He held his breath as he watched the acrobat flying through the air.*

out of breath breathless from running *etc*: *I'm out of breath after climbing all these stairs.*

take your breath away to surprise or shock: *The news took my breath away.*

under your breath very quietly: *He swore under his breath.*

> **breath** is a noun: *He held his breath.*
> **breathe** is a verb: *He found it difficult to breathe.*

breathe /briːð/ *v* to take air into the lungs and let it out: *He couldn't breathe because of the smoke.*

breathe in to take air into your lungs.

breathe out to send air out of your lungs.

breathless /ˈbrɛθləs/ *adj* unable to breathe easily; short of breath: *He was breathless after climbing the hill.* **'breathlessly** *adv*. **'breathlessness** *n*.

bred *see* **breed**.

breed /briːd/ *v* **1** to produce babies: *Rabbits breed often.* **2** to keep and sell animals: *I breed dogs and sell them as pets.* — *n* a type of animal: *There are many breeds of dogs.*

> **breed; bred** /brɛd/; **bred**: *Who bred this racehorse?; She has bred horses for many years.*

'breeding *n* education and upbringing; good manners: *a man of good breeding.*

breeze /briːz/ *n* a gentle wind: *There's a lovely cool breeze today.*

> See **wind**.

'breezy *adj* **1** windy: *a breezy day.* **2** cheerful, lively: *She had a breezy manner of speaking.*

brevity /ˈbrɛvɪtɪ/ *n* shortness: *Aim at clearness and brevity when you speak or write.*

brew /bruː/ *v* **1** to make beer *etc*. **2** to make tea *etc*: *She brewed another pot of tea.* **3** to be coming; to be on the way: *There's a storm brewing.* **'brewer** *n*.

'brewery *n* a place where beer is brewed.

briar or **brier** /ˈbraɪə(r)/ *n* a wild rose bush or some other kind of prickly bush.

bribe /braɪb/ *n* a gift offered to someone to persuade them to do something for you: *Policemen are not allowed to accept bribes.* — *v* to give someone a bribe: *He bribed the guards to let him out of prison.* **'bribery** *n*.

brick /brɪk/ *n* a block of baked clay used for building: *a pile of bricks.* — *adj* made out of bricks: *a brick wall.*

bricklayer /ˈbrɪkleɪə(r)/ *n* a person who builds houses *etc* with bricks.

'brickwork *n* the part of a building that is made of bricks.

bride /braɪd/ *n* a woman who is getting married: *The bride wore a white dress.* **'bridal** *adj*.

'bridegroom *n* a man who is getting married.

bridesmaid *n* an unmarried girl who looks after the bride at a wedding.

bridge /brɪdʒ/ *n* **1** a construction that takes a road or railway over a river *etc*: *The bridge collapsed in the storm.* **2** the narrow raised platform on a ship, from which the captain directs the ship. **3** the bony part of the nose. — *v* to build a bridge over a river *etc*: *They bridged the stream.*

bridle /ˈbraɪdəl/ *n* the harness on a horse's head to which the reins are attached.

brief /briːf/ *adj* short: *a brief visit; a brief letter.* — *v* to give instructions to someone about a task they have to do: *The astronauts were briefed before the space mission.*

'briefcase *n* a light flat case for papers used by businessmen *etc*.

'briefing *n* instructions and information: *The policemen were given a briefing before they left.*

'briefly *adv*: *He told me briefly what he knew.*

briefs *n* women's or men's pants: *a pair of briefs.*

brier *see* **briar**.

brigade /brɪˈɡeɪd/ *n* **1** a body of troops. **2** a group of people with a special job: *the fire brigade.*

brigadier /brɪɡəˈdɪə(r)/ *n* the commander of a brigade in the army.

brigand /ˈbrɪɡənd/ *n* an old word for a robber, especially one of a gang moving round the countryside: *They were attacked by brigands in the mountains.*

bright /braɪt/ *adj* **1** shining with light: *bright sunshine.* **2** strong and clear: *bright red; bright blue.* **3** cheerful: *a bright smile.* **4** clever: *bright children.* **'brightly** *adv*. **'brightness** *n*.

'brighten *v* to make or become brighter: *The new yellow paint brightens up the room.*

brilliant /ˈbrɪljənt/ *adj* **1** bright and colourful:

the bird's brilliant feathers. **2** very clever: *a brilliant scholar.* **'brilliance** *n.* **'brilliantly** *adv.*

brim /brɪm/ *n* **1** the top edge of a cup, glass *etc*: *The jug was filled to the brim.* **2** the edge of a hat: *She pulled the brim of her hat down over her eyes.* — *v* to be full to the brim: *Her eyes were brimming with tears.*

brim over to overflow.

bring /brɪŋ/ *v* **1** to carry something, or make someone come with you: *I'll bring plenty of food with me; Bring him to me!; You may borrow my umbrella, but please bring it back!* **2** to cause, give or provide: *The news brought him happiness.* **3** to force yourself: *I couldn't bring myself to tell her the news.*

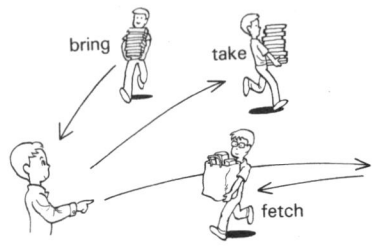

> **bring; brought** /brɔːt/; **brought**: *She brought him his tea; Have you brought my book back?*

> **bring** towards me: *Mary, bring me some coffee.*
> **take** away from me: *Take these cups away.*
> **fetch** from somewhere else and bring to me: *Fetch me my book from the bedroom.*

bring about to cause: *His carelessness brought about his failure in the exam.*

bring back to cause something to return: *Hearing that song again brought back a lot of memories; Parliament may vote to bring hanging back.*

bring down to cause someone to lose their power or important position: *The scandal brought the government down; It brought down the president.*

bring forward to move something to an earlier time: *The match has been brought forward to tomorrow.*

> *The opposite of* **bring forward** *is* **postpone.**

bring in to introduce: *This government has brought in a new tax system.*

bring off to do something successfully: *They brought off their plan.*

bring on to cause: *Her headache was brought on by reading in bad light.*

bring out to produce: *This model was brought out ten years ago.*

bring round 1 to bring back from unconsciousness: *Fresh air brought him round.* **2** to persuade someone to agree with you: *They disagreed at first but we managed to bring them round.*

bring up 1 to train and teach children: *Her parents brought her up to be polite.* **2** to introduce a subject: *Bring the matter up when you see the headmaster.* **3** to vomit.

brink /brɪŋk/ *n* the edge of a river *etc*: *He stood on the brink of the river.*

on the brink to be about to do something: *scientists on the brink of new discoveries.*

brisk /brɪsk/ *adj* fast and lively: *a brisk walk; Business was brisk today.* **'briskly** *adv.* **'briskness** *n.*

bristle /'brɪsəl/ *n* a short, stiff hair on an animal or brush: *This brush has plastic bristles.* — *v* to show that you are angry: *He was bristling with anger.* **'bristly** *adj.*

brittle /'brɪtəl/ *adj* easily broken: *Eggshells are brittle.* **'brittleness** *n.*

broad /brɔːd/ *adj* **1** wide: *a broad street.* **2** from side to side: *two metres broad.* **3** general; without the details: *It should have broad appeal; It was grouped into rather broad categories.* **4** not stern and strict: *He has broad views on bringing up children.* **'broadly** *adv.*

broad daylight the daytime: *The thieves broke into the house in broad daylight.*

'broaden *v* to make broader; to widen.

broad-'minded *adj* allowing people to think and act freely; not strict: *a broad-minded headmaster.*

broadcast /'brɔːdkɑːst/ *v* to send out radio and TV programmes *etc*: *Have they broadcast the interview with the headmistress yet?* — *n* a television or radio programme: *I heard his broadcast last night.* **'broadcaster** *n.* **'broadcasting** *n.*

> **broadcast; broadcast; broadcast**: *They broadcast the programme last night; Has the president's speech been broadcast yet?*

broccoli /'brɒkəlɪ/ *n* a vegetable with green or purple flower-like buds growing on thick green stalks.

brochure /'brəʊʃə(r)/ *n* a booklet giving information about something, for example, holidays: *travel brochures*.

broil /brɔɪl/ *v* to grill food: *She broiled the chicken*.

broke /brəʊk/ *adj* having no money: *I can't afford new jeans — I'm broke!* See also **break**.

broken /'brəʊkən/ *adj* **1** damaged; not working any more: *a broken window*; *My watch is broken*. **2** not continuous: *a broken line*. **3** not kept: *a broken promise*. See also **break**.

'**broken-down** *adj* in bad condition: *a broken-down old car*.

broken-hearted /brəʊkən 'hɑːtɪd/ *adj* very unhappy: *She was broken-hearted when she heard the sad news*.

broker /'brəʊkə(r)/ *n* a person who is employed to buy and sell goods, shares, foreign money *etc* for other people: *He is an insurance broker*.

bronchitis /brɒŋ'kaɪtɪs/ *n* an illness that affects your lungs, making you cough a lot and making it difficult to breathe.

bronze /brɒnz/ *n* a mixture of copper and tin: *The medal is made of bronze*. — *adj* made of bronze, or golden-brown in colour like bronze: *a bronze statue*; *bronze skin*.

bronze medal a medal given as third prize.

brooch /brəʊtʃ/ *n* an ornament like a badge, especially for a woman, fastened by a pin: *She wore a brooch on her dress*.

brood /bruːd/ *v* to worry over something: *It's silly to go on brooding about what happened*. — *n* a number of baby birds all hatched at one time.

'**broody** *adj* thinking deeply and worrying.

brook /brʊk/ *n* a small stream.

broom /bruːm/ *n* a long-handled brush for sweeping the floor.

'**broomstick** *n* the long handle of a broom.

broth /brɒθ/ *n* a kind of soup containing vegetables and barley or rice.

brother /'brʌðə(r)/ *n* **1** a male person who has the same parents as you do: *I have a sister and two brothers*. **2** a member of a monastery *etc*; a monk: *The brothers prayed together*. '**brotherhood** *n*.

'**brother-in-law**, *plural* '**brothers-in-law**, *n* **1** the brother of your husband or wife. **2** the husband of your sister.

'**brotherly** *adj* like a brother: *brotherly love*.

brought *see* **bring**.

brow /braʊ/ *n* **1** an eyebrow: *thick black brows*. **2** your forehead: *The doctor felt her brow*. **3** the top of a slope: *the brow of a hill*.

brown /braʊn/ *n* a dark colour between black, red and yellow. — *adj* **1** having this colour: *Her eyes are brown*; *Soil is brown*. **2** suntanned: *She was very brown after her holiday*. – *v* to make or become brown: *Brown the breadcrumbs in a frying-pan*.

Brownie /'braʊnɪ/ *n* a junior Girl Guide.

browse /braʊz/ *v* **1** to look through a book without reading it: *to browse through a book*. **2** to look casually at things in a shop. – *n*: a browse around the shops.

bruise /bruːz/ *n* an injury caused by a hit, turning the skin a dark colour: *bruises all over his legs*; *apples covered in bruises*. — *v* to cause a bruise on the skin: *When she walked into the lamp-post she bruised her forehead*.

brunette /bruː'net/ *n* a woman or girl with dark brown hair.

brunt /brʌnt/: **bear the brunt** to receive the main force of something: *She bore the brunt of his anger*.

brush /brʌʃ/ *n* **1** an object with bristles, for cleaning scrubbing *etc*: *a toothbrush*; *a hairbrush*; *a sweeping brush*. **2** a brushing: *Give your hair a brush*. **3** the bushy tail of a fox. — *v* **1** to use a brush on something: *He brushed his teeth*; *Brush the floor, please*; *Brush your hair before you come in to a meal*. **2** to touch lightly: *The leaves brushed her face*.

brush aside to take no notice of: *She brushed aside my questions*.

brush away to wipe off: *She brushed away her tears*.

brush up to improve: *You'd better brush up your English if you want to pass that exam*.

Brussels sprout /brʌsəls 'spraʊt/ *n* a green vegetable that looks like a tiny cabbage: *In Britain most people eat Brussels sprouts with their Christmas turkey*.

brute /bruːt/ *n* **1** an animal other than man: *What a big brute their dog is!* **2** a cruel person: *Stop hurting me, you brute!*

'**brutal** *adj* very cruel and violent: *He gave the boy a brutal beating*. '**brutally** *adv*. **bru't-ality** *n*.

bubble /'bʌbəl/ *n* a floating ball containing air or gas: *bubbles in lemonade*; *soap bubbles*. — *v* to be full of bubbles: *The water will bubble when it boils*. '**bubbly** *adj*.

bubble over to be very cheerful and noisy: *The children were bubbling over with excitement*.

buck /bʌk/ *n* the male of the deer, hare, rabbit *etc*: *a buck and a doe*. — *v* to kick and jump

bucket

back: *The horse bucked when it came to the fence.*
buck up to hurry: *You'd better buck up if you want to catch the bus.*
bucket /'bʌkɪt/ *n* a container for holding water *etc*: *We carried water in buckets.*
buckle /'bʌkəl/ *n* a fastening for a strap, belt *etc*: *a belt with a silver buckle.* — *v* **1** to fasten with a buckle: *He buckled his sword on.* **2** to bend because of heat or weakness: *The railings had buckled in the sun.*
bud /bʌd/ *n* a shoot of a tree or plant, from which leaves or flowers will burst out: *Are there buds on the trees yet?*; *a rosebud.* — *v* to begin to grow: *The trees are budding.*
Buddhism /'bʊdɪzm/ *n* the religion founded by Gautama or Buddha.
'Buddhist *n* a believer in Buddhism.
budding /'bʌdɪŋ/ *adj* just beginning to develop: *I want you to write a poem for your homework — I'm sure we shall find some budding poets in the class.*
budge /bʌdʒ/ *v* to move slightly: *I can't budge this heavy chest*; *It won't budge!*
budgerigar /'bʌdʒərɪgɑː(r)/ *n* a small brightly-coloured bird, kept as a pet.
budget /'bʌdʒɪt/ *n* a plan showing how money is to be spent: *Here is my budget for the month.* — *v* to plan carefully how to spend your money: *We must try to budget or we shall be in debt.*

> **budgeted** and **budgeting** have one **t**.

budgie /'bʌdʒɪ/ short for **budgerigar**.
buffalo /'bʌfəloʊ/, *plural* **'buffalos** or **'buffaloes**, *n* a large kind of ox.
buffer /'bʌfə(r)/ *n* a device at a railway station for lessening the force with which a train meets the wall at the end of the track.
buffet /'bʊfeɪ/ *n* **1** a refreshment bar, for example in a railway station or on a train *etc*: *We'll get some coffee at the buffet.* **2** a cold meal set out on tables from which people help themselves: *a table laden with an unappetizing buffet.*

> **buffet** is pronounced 'bʊfeɪ; the **t** is silent.

bug /bʌg/ *n* **1** an insect that lives in dirty houses and beds: *a bedbug.* **2** an insect: *There's a bug crawling up your arm.* **3** a small, hidden microphone. — *v* **1** to hide tiny microphones in a room *etc* in order to be able to listen to what people are saying: *The spy's bedroom was bugged.* **2** to annoy; to worry: *He's always bugging me*; *What's bugging you?*
bugle /'bjuːgəl/ *n* a musical instrument that is played by blowing, and is used especially to give signals in the army. **'bugler** *n*.
build /bɪld/ *v* to form or construct something: *They have built a new school, house, bridge, railway.* — *n* shape and size of body: *a man of broad, heavy build.* **'builder** *n*.

> **build**; **built** /bɪlt/; **built**: *He built a wall*; *The new house is built at last.*

'building *n* **1** the construction of houses *etc*: *building and civil engineering.* **2** anything built: *The new supermarket is a very ugly building.*
build in to fix onto a wall: *He's having some cupboards built in in the kitchen.*
build on to use something as a basis from which to develop further: *We must build on this success.*
build up to increase the size or extent of something: *His father built up that grocery business from nothing.*
'build-up *n* **1** a gradual increase: *a build-up of traffic.* **2** increasing excitement before an event: *during the build-up to the World Cup.*
built-in /bɪlt'ɪn/ *adj* forming a permanent part of the building *etc*: *Built-in cupboards save space.*
built-up /bɪlt'ʌp/ *adj* covered with buildings: *a heavily built-up area.*
bulb /bʌlb/ *n* **1** the ball-shaped part of the stem of certain plants, for example onions, from which their roots grow. **2** a pear-shaped glass globe surrounding the element of an electric light.
bulbous /'bʌlbəs/ *adj* round; swollen.
bulge /bʌldʒ/ *n* a swelling: *The apple made a bulge in his pocket.* — *v* to swell out: *His muscles bulged.* **'bulging** *adj*.
bulk /bʌlk/ *n* **1** most: *The bulk of his money was spent on food.* **2** a large shape: *We saw the dark bulk of the ship in front of us.*
'bulky *adj* large in size and difficult to carry *etc*: *This parcel is too bulky to send by post.*
in bulk in large quantities: *They like to buy household goods in bulk from the supermarket.*
bull /bʊl/ *n* the male of the ox family and of the whale, walrus, elephant *etc*.

> A baby bull is a **calf**.
> Bulls and cows are **cattle**.

bulldozer /'bʊldoʊzə(r)/ *n* a large heavy vehicle for clearing ground for building *etc*.

bullet /'bolɪt/ *n* a piece of metal *etc* fired from a gun: *He was wounded by machine-gun bullets.*
   'bullet-proof *adj* strong enough to stop bullets passing through it: *bullet-proof glass.*

bulletin /'bolətɪn/ *n* **1** an official announcement giving news: *A bulletin about the Queen's illness was broadcast on the radio.* **2** a printed information-sheet: *a monthly bulletin of school news.*

bullfight /'bolfaɪt/ *n* a fight between a bull and men on horseback and on foot. **'bullfighter** *n*.

bullion /'boljən/ *n* gold or silver in lumps or bars *etc*, not made into coins.

bullock /'bolək/ *n* a young bull.

bull's-eye /'bolzaɪ/ *n* the centre of a target used for shooting, or for darts *etc*.

bully /'bolɪ/ *n* a person who hurts or frightens other, weaker people: *Bullies are often cowards.* — *v* to behave like a bully; to hurt and frighten someone: *He bullies his younger brother.*

bump /bʌmp/ *v* to knock something: *She bumped into me; I bumped my head against the ceiling.* — *n* **1** a blow or knock: *We heard a loud bump.* **2** a swelling or bruise; an uneven part: *a bump on the head; This road is full of bumps.* **'bumpy** *adj*.
   'bumper *n* a bar on a motor vehicle to lessen damage when it collides with anything.
   bump into to meet someone by chance: *I bumped into him in the street.*

bumpkin /'bʌmpkɪn/ *n* a clumsy or stupid person.

bun /bʌn/ *n* a kind of sweet cake: *a currant bun.*

bunch /bʌntʃ/ *n* a number of things fastened or growing together: *a bunch of bananas.* — *v* to form into a group: *The children bunched up together in the corner.*

bundle /'bʌndəl/ *n* a number of things tied together: *a bundle of letters.* — *v* **1** to make into bundles: *Bundle up all these old magazines.* **2** to push roughly: *They bundled Harry into the back of the van.*

bungalow /'bʌŋgəloʊ/ *n* a small house of one storey.

bunged-up /'bʌndʌp/ *adj* blocked: *a bunged-up nose.*

bungle /'bʌŋgəl/ *v* to do something badly; to make a mistake.

bunk /bʌŋk/ *n* **1** a bed fixed to the wall, on board a ship; a sleeping-berth. **2** one of a pair of beds fixed one over the other.

See **bed**.

bunker /'bʌŋkə(r)/ *n* **1** an underground shelter built with strong walls to protect people against bombs and heavy gunfire. **2** a large container for storing coal.

bunny /'bʌnɪ/ *n* a child's name for a rabbit.

bunting /'bʌntɪŋ/ *n* flags for use in celebrations.

buoy /bɔɪ/ *n* a large floating ball anchored in the sea as a guide or warning to ships.
   buoyant /'bɔɪənt/ *adj* able to float: *Corks are buoyant.*

burden /'bɜːdən/ *n* **1** something heavy that has to be carried: *The donkey carried its burden up the hill.* **2** something difficult: *Buying school-books is an extra burden for parents.* — *v* to give someone a load to carry: *He was burdened with luggage.*

bureau /'bjʊəroʊ/, *plural* **bureaux** /'bjʊəroʊ/ or **bureaus** /'bjʊəroʊz/, *n* **1** a writing-desk with drawers. **2** an office supplying information *etc*: *a travel bureau.*

bureaucracy /bjʊə'rɒkrəsɪ/ *n* **1** a system of government by officials who are not elected. **2** all the rules and formal stages followed by office and administrative staff, resulting in delays and a loss of money. **bureau'cratic** *adj*: *a long, bureaucratic procedure.*

bureaucrat /'bjʊərəkrat/ *n* **1** an official in a bureaucracy. **2** an official who follows the rules rigidly, causing delays and a loss of money.

burger /'bɜːgə(r)/ *n* **1** a round, flat piece of minced beef that is fried and then put into a bread roll. **2** any item of food made in the same shape but from different ingredients, and eaten in a bread roll: *a nutburger.*

burglar /'bɜːglə(r)/ *n* a person who breaks into a house *etc* to steal: *The burglar stole her jewellery.*
   burglar alarm an alarm that rings if someone tries to enter a building illegally.
   burglary /'bɜːglərɪ/ *n*: *He's in prison for burglary; We had two burglaries in one week.*
   'burgle *v*: *Our house has been burgled.*

burial /'berɪəl/ *n* the burying of someone: *My grandfather's burial was on Tuesday.*

burly /'bɜːlɪ/ *adj* big, strong and heavy: *a big, burly farmer.*

burn /bɜːn/ *v* **1** to destroy, damage or injure, or be destroyed, damaged or injured, by fire, heat, acid *etc*: *The factory has burnt down; Take care not to burn the meat!; I've burnt my finger on the iron; The acid burned*

burp

a hole in my dress. **2** to catch fire: *Paper burns easily.* **3** to feel very hot: *My face is burning.* **4** to feel a very strong emotion: *I was burning with anger.* — *n* an injury or mark caused by fire *etc*: *His burns will take a long time to heal*; *a burn in the carpet.*

> **burn; burnt** /bɜːnt/ or **burned; burnt** or **burned**: *He burnt the meat*; *She has burnt her dress.*

'**burner** *n* the part of a gas cooker *etc* from which the flame rises.

'**burning** *adj* **1** on fire: *The house is burning.* **2** very hot: *the burning sun.* **3** very strong or intense: *a burning desire.* **4** very important or urgent: *a burning issue.*

'**burnt-out** *adj* badly damaged or destroyed by fire: *a burnt-out shell of a car.*

burn out to stop burning because there is nothing left to burn: *The fire has burnt itself out.*

burn up to destroy completely by fire or heat: *The spacecraft burnt up as it entered the earth's atmosphere.*

burp /bɜːp/ *v* to make an explosive noise in your throat, usually after eating or drinking; to belch. – *n*: *a loud burp.*

burrow /'bʌroʊ/ *n* a hole dug for shelter: *a rabbit burrow.* — *v* **1** to make holes underground: *Rabbits are burrowing under our garden.*

burst /bɜːst/ *v* **1** to break suddenly, especially with a bang: *The balloon burst.* **2** to come violently: *He burst into the room without knocking.* **3** to overflow: *The river has burst its banks.* — *n* **1** a break: *a burst in the pipes.* **2** a sudden fit or outbreak: *a burst of clapping*; *The horse put on a burst of speed.*

> **burst; burst; burst**: *She burst the balloon*; *The pipe has burst.*
> See also **explode**.

'**bursting** *adj* **1** very eager: *I'm bursting to tell you my news!* **2** very full of: *His mother is bursting with pride now he has qualified as a doctor.*

burst into flames to start burning suddenly.
burst into tears to start crying.
burst out to start doing something suddenly: *to burst out laughing.*

bury /'beri/ *v* **1** to put a dead body in a grave: *My grandfather was buried in the cemetery.* **2** to hide something underground *etc*: *They buried the treasure.* **3** to cover or hide: *She buried her face in her hands.* **4** to be fully occupied with something: *He was buried in his book.*

bus /bʌs/ *n* a large vehicle for carrying passengers by road: *He goes to school by bus.*

> See **in**.

bus stop a place where buses stop to let passengers on or off.

bush /bʊʃ/ *n* a small, low tree: *a rose bush.*
'**bushy** *adj* thick: *bushy eyebrows.*

business /'bɪznɪs/ *n* **1** trade; buying and selling: *Business was good at the shop today.* **2** a job, occupation: *Book-selling is my business.* **3** a shop; a firm: *He runs a hairdressing business.* **4** concern; interest: *How I spend my money is my business, not yours.* **5** work: *Let's get down to business.* **6** any situation or series of events: *That accident was a terrible business*; *Let's forget the whole business now.*

'**businesslike** *adj* practical and efficient.
'**businessman** or '**businesswoman** *n* a person who makes a living from trade, not a doctor, teacher *etc*.

go out of business to stop operating as a company.

have no business to have no right to do something: *He had no business to read my diary.*

bust /bʌst/ *n* **1** a woman's chest. **2** a sculpture of a person's head and shoulders: *a bust of the president.*

bustle /'bʌsəl/ *v* to rush, hurry or be very busy: *She bustled round the kitchen.* — *n* hurry; rush: *the frenetic bustle of the city.*

busy /'bɪzɪ/ *adj* **1** having a lot of work to do: *The headmaster is too busy to see you just now.* **2** full of traffic, people *etc*: *The roads are busy*; *a busy shop.* '**busily** *adv*.

busy yourself become occupied with: *She busied herself with her knitting.*

'**busybody** *n* a nosey person.

but /bʌt/ *conjunction* a word used to join two statements *etc*, and show that there is a difference between them: *John was there but Peter was not.* — *prep* except: *There was no-one there but Jane*; *I live in the next street but one.*

butcher /'bʊtʃə(r)/ *n* a person who sells meat: *Get me four steaks at the butcher's shop.*

butler /'bʌtlə(r)/ *n* the head male servant in a house.

butt /bʌt/ *v* to hit someone with your head: *He fell over when the goat butted him.* — *n* **1** the thick, heavy end of a rifle or pistol. **2** the end of a finished cigarette or cigar:

cigarette butts. **3** someone whom others criticize or tell jokes about: *He's the butt of all their jokes.*

butt in to interrupt someone speaking.

butter /'bʌtə(r)/ *n* a substance made from cream for spreading on bread *etc* — *v* to spread with butter: *She buttered the bread.*
'**butterfingers** *n* a person who keeps dropping things by mistake.

butterfly /'bʌtəflaɪ/, *plural* '**butterflies**, *n* an insect with large coloured wings.

butterfly

moth

buttocks /'bʌtəks/ *n* the part of the body on which you sit.

button /'bʌtən/ *n* **1** a small, usually round, object, used as a fastening: *I lost a button off my coat.* **2** a small knob that you press to switch something on *etc*: *This button turns the radio on.* — *v* to fasten with buttons: *Button up your jacket.*
'**buttonhole** *n* the hole through which you put a button to fasten it.

buttress /'bʌtrəs/ *n* a support built on to the outside of the wall of a church, castle *etc.* — *v* to support: *These planks of wood buttress the collapsing wall.*

buy /baɪ/ *v* to get something by paying for it with money: *He has bought a car.* – *n*: *a good buy.*

> **buy; bought** /bɔːt/; **bought**: *She bought a book; I've bought a dress.*

buzz /bʌz/ *v* to make the noise that some insects make: *Bees, wasps and flies buzz.* — *n* a sound that reminds you of bees buzzing, for example the sound of a lot of people talking: *a buzz of conversation.*
'**buzzer** *n* an electrical device which makes a buzzing sound, such as an alarm or bell: *The doctor pressed the buzzer when she was ready for the next patient.*

by /baɪ/ *prep* **1** next to; near: *He sat by his sister.* **2** along: *We came by the main road.* **3** used to show who or what does or causes something: *He was hit by a stone*; *This story was written by me*; *I met her by chance.* **4** using something: *He'll let us know the news by telephone*; *The letter came by post*; *We travelled by train.* **5** not later than: *Be home by 6 o'clock.* **6** used to show a difference: *She is taller than he is by ten centimetres.* **7** used to give measurements: *The table is 4 metres by 2 metres.* **8** in particular quantities: *Fruit is sold by the kilo.* **9** during: *by day and by night.* **10** according to: *It's five past three by my watch.* — *adv* **1** near: *They stood by and watched.* **2** past: *A dog ran by.* **3** aside; away: *I have put by some money for an emergency.*

> **by** is used for forms of transport: *by train; by aeroplane; by land; by sea.*
> See also **until**.

by and by after a short time: *By and by, everyone went home.*

by yourself 1 alone: *He was standing by himself at the bus stop.* **2** without anyone else's help: *She did the job all by herself.*

by the way words used in mentioning another subject: *By the way, have you posted that letter?*

bye /baɪ/ or **bye-'bye** an expression you use when leaving someone, instead of 'goodbye'.

by-election /'baɪɪlekʃən/ *n* a special election that is held to elect a new member of parliament for a particular place when the previous member has resigned or died.

bypass /'baɪpɑːs/ *n* a road which avoids a busy area: *Take the bypass round the city.* — *v*: *This road bypasses the town.*

by-product /'baɪprɒdʌkt/ *n* something that is formed during the making of something else: *When lead is manufactured, silver is sometimes obtained as a by-product.*

bystander /'baɪstændə(r)/ *n* someone who watches something happening but does not take part: *There were several bystanders present when the accident happened.*

byte /baɪt/ *n* a group of eight binary digits used as a unit for measuring computer memory.

C

C, c /siː/, *plural* **Cs** or **c's**, *n* **1** the third-highest grade that can be given for an essay or exam: *He only got a C for his essay.* **2** an abbreviation for a century: *a famous 17th c. writer.* **3** Centigrade or Celsius: *temperatures below 8°C.*

cab /kab/ *n* **1** a taxi: *Could you call a cab for me?* **2** the driver's compartment in a lorry or train.

cabaret /ˈkabəreɪ/ *n* an entertainment such as singing or dancing that is given in a restaurant or nightclub: *She is a singer in a cabaret.*

cabbage /ˈkabɪdʒ/ *n* a vegetable with thick green leaves.

cabin /ˈkabɪn/ *n* **1** a small house or hut: *They built a log cabin.* **2** a small room in a ship for sleeping in. **3** the part of an aeroplane where people sit.

cabinet /ˈkabɪnət/ *n* **1** a piece of furniture with shelves and doors or drawers. **2** the group of senior ministers who govern a country: *The Prime Minister has chosen a new Cabinet.*

cable /ˈkeɪbəl/ *n* **1** a thick, strong rope: *The truck towed the car with a cable.* **2** a set of wires for carrying electric current or signals: *They are laying a new cable.* **3** a telegram sent by cable. — *v* to telegraph by cable: *I cabled the news to my aunt.*

cable television a service by which television programmes are transmitted along wires rather than by radio waves.

cacao /kəˈkaʊ/ *n* the tropical tree from whose seeds cocoa and chocolate are made.

cackle /ˈkakəl/ *n* **1** the sound made by a hen or goose. **2** a laugh which sounds like this: *an evil cackle.* — *v* to make this sound.

cactus /ˈkaktəs/ *n* a prickly plant which grows in dry climates.

cadaverous /kəˈdavərəs/ *adj* like a dead person, especially in being very thin and pale: *pale, cadaverous cheeks.*

caddie or **caddy** /ˈkadi/ *n* a person who carries golf-clubs for a golfer.

caddy /ˈkadi/ *n* a small box for keeping tea leaves in: *a tea-caddy.*

cadet /kəˈdɛt/ *n* **1** a student in a military or police school. **2** a schoolboy taking military training.

café /ˈkafeɪ/ or /ˈkafi/ *n* a small restaurant where coffee, tea, snacks *etc* are served.

cafeteria /kafəˈtɪərɪə/ *n* a self-service restaurant: *This school has a cafeteria.*

caffeine /ˈkafiːn/ *n* a substance which keeps you awake, found in tea and coffee: *The doctor told her to cut down on caffeine by drinking less coffee.*

cage /keɪdʒ/ *n* a box of wood, wire *etc* for holding birds or animals: *The lion has escaped from its cage; a bird-cage.* — *v* to put in a cage: *a caged animal.*

cake /keɪk/ *n* **1** a food made by baking a mixture of flour, fat, eggs, sugar *etc*: *Have a piece of cake; She made another batch of creamcakes.* **2** something pressed into a flat, regular shape: *fishcakes; a cake of soap.* — *v* to cover in a dried mass: *His shoes were caked with mud.*

calamity /kəˈlamɪti/ *n* a great misfortune or disaster.

calcium /ˈkalsɪəm/ *n* a substance that is in teeth, bones and chalk.

calculate /ˈkalkjʊleɪt/ *v* to count: *Calculate the number of days in a century.*
'calculated *adj* intended or considered in advance: *a calculated risk.*
'calculating *adj* planning carefully to get what is good for yourself.
calcuˈlation *n*: *We shall have £55 to spend, according to my calculations.*
'calculator *n* a machine for calculating: *She used a calculator to add up the numbers.*

calendar /ˈkalɪndə(r)/ *n* a table showing the months and days of the year: *Have you a calendar for 1988?*

> **calendar** ends in **-ar** (not **-er**).

calf[1] /kɑːf/, *plural* **calves** /kɑːvz/, *n* **1** the baby of a cow, elephant *etc.* **2** leather made from the skin of a calf.

calf[2] /kɑːf/, *plural* **calves** /kɑːvz/, *n* the back part of the leg below the knee.

calibre /ˈkalɪbə(r)/ *n* a person's usually high quality or ability: *The company needs employees of your calibre.*

call /kɔːl/ *v* **1** to give a name to someone or something: *My name is Alexander but I'm called Sandy by my friends; 'What do you call a baby cat?' 'A kitten.'* **2** to shout to someone to get them to come to you: *Call* *everyone over here.* **3** to telephone someone; to ask someone to come, by telephone: *I'll call you this evening; He called me up from the airport; He called a doctor.* **4** to visit: *He called on his friend; I shall call at your house this evening.* **5** to arrange for something to happen: *to call a meeting; to call an election.* — *n* **1** a shout or cry: *a call for help.* **2** a short visit: *The teacher made a call at the boy's home.* **3** calling on the telephone: *I've just had a call from the police; I'll give you a call tomorrow.* **4** a demand: *There have been calls for the president to resign.* **5** a need: *There was no call for you to be so rude.* **6** the song of a bird *etc*: *the call of a blackbird.*

> to **ask** (not **call**) a friend to go out with you.
> to **ask** (not **call**) someone to be quiet.
> **call on** a person: *I'll go and call on Mrs Jones.*
> **call at** a place: *I'll call at the post office on my way home.*

call back 1 to visit again: *He called back a week later.* **2** to telephone again: *Can I call you back in an hour?*
'call-box *n* a telephone box.
'caller *n* **1** a visitor. **2** a person making a telephone call.
call for 1 to need: *This calls for quick action.* **2** to collect: *I'll call for you at eight o'clock.*
call in 1 to visit a place briefly: *She called in at Susan's on the way home.* **2** to ask someone to come and help: *They had to call in the police.*
call off to cancel: *The party's been called off.*
call on or **call upon 1** to visit someone: *I'll try and call on him tomorrow.* **2** to appeal to someone: *They called on me for help.*
call out 1 to shout: *She called out that she was upstairs.* **2** to ask for help from an organization: *He called out the fire brigade when a fire started in his house.*
on call ready to come out to an emergency: *Which of the doctors is on call tonight?*
calligraphy /kə'lɪɡrəfɪ/ *n* the art of beautiful handwriting.
callous /'kaləs/ *adj* showing no concern for other people, cruel and insensitive: *a callous act*; *a callous remark*.
calm /kɑːm/ *adj* **1** still; quiet: *a calm sea; The weather was calm.* **2** not anxious or excited: *a calm person; Please keep calm!* — *n* a time when everything is peaceful and quiet: *He enjoyed the calm of the library.* — *v* to make someone calm: *He tried to calm his mother down; Please calm yourself!* **'calmly** *adv.* **'calmness** *n.*
calorie /'kalərɪ/ *n* a unit of energy given by food: *My diet allows me 1200 calories per day.*
calves *see* **calf**[1] and **calf**[2].
camcorder /'kamkɔːdə(r)/ *n* a small video recorder that can be held in one hand: *She used her camcorder to film the children playing.*
came *see* **come**.
camel /'kaməl/ *n* a desert animal with one or two large humps on its back, that carries goods and people.

camel

cameo /'kamɪoʊ/ *n* **1** a piece of stone with a raised design of a different colour on one side. **2** a small part in a play or film performed by a well-known actor.
camera /'kamərə/ *n* a device for taking still or moving photographs: *He bought a new film for his camera.*
'cameraman *n* a person who operates a film or television camera.
camouflage /'kaməflɑːʒ/ *n* something that makes an animal, person, building *etc* difficult for enemies to see against the background: *The soldiers put leaves round their helmets as camouflage.* — *v* to hide by camouflage: *They camouflaged their tent.*
camp /kamp/ *n* a group of tents, huts *etc* in which people stay for a short time: *a holiday camp; The soldiers left their camp.* — *v* to put up, and live in, a tent: *We camped on the beach; We go camping every year.* **'camper** *n.* **'camping** *n.*
campaign /kam'peɪn/ *n* **1** organized actions in support of a cause: *a campaign against smoking.* **2** military operations with one purpose: *Napoleon's Russian campaign.* — *v* to take part in a campaign: *He has campaigned against smoking for years.* **cam'paigner** *n.*
camp-fire /'kampfaɪə(r)/ *n* the fire on which campers cook, and round which they sit in the evening.

campsite /'kampsaɪt/ n a piece of land on which holidaymakers may put up a tent *etc*.

campus /'kampəs/ n the grounds of a university or college: *Most students live on the campus.*

can[1] /kan/ or /kən/ v **1** to be able to do something: *You can do it if you try hard.* **2** to know how to do something: *She can drive a car, can't she?*; *He can't swim*; *I cannot ride a bicycle.* **3** to have permission to do something: *You can go if you behave yourself.*

> **can; 'cannot** or **can't** /kɑːnt/: *She can speak English, can't she?*; *You cannot swim yet, can you?*
> See also **could** and **may**.
> **Can** is used in the present tense: *He can already read very well.*
> **Could** is the simple past tense of **can**: *He could read before he started school.*
> For other past and future tenses use **be able to**: *She has been able to sing beautifully since she was a little girl*; *The baby will be able to walk soon.*

can[2] /kan/ n a metal container for liquids *etc*: *oilcans*; *beer-cans*; *six cans of beer.* — v to put food *etc* into cans: *a factory for canning raspberries.*

canal /kə'nal/ n a channel cut through land for ships or boats, or to carry water to fields: *the Panama Canal.*

canary /kə'neərɪ/ n a small, yellow, singing bird, kept as a pet.

cancel /'kansəl/ v **1** to decide that something already arranged will not happen: *He cancelled his appointment.* **2** to mark stamps with a postmark. **cancel'lation** n.

> **cancelled** and **cancelling** have two ls.

cancel out to undo the effect of something: *Our profits will be cancelled out by extra expenses.*

cancer /'kansə(r)/ n a disease in which cells in a part of the body grow out of control: *Smoking can cause lung cancer.* **'cancerous** *adj.*

candid /'kandɪd/ *adj* open and honest: *Give me your candid opinion.* **'candidly** *adv.*

candidate /'kandɪdeɪt/ n a person who takes part in a competition or examination for a job, prize *etc*: *a candidate for the job of manager.*

candle /'kandəl/ n a stick of wax with a thread in the centre, that you burn to give light: *We had to use candles when the electric lights went out.*

'candlelight n the light that a candle produces: *read by candlelight.*

'candlestick n a holder for a candle.

candour /'kandə(r)/ n open and honest behaviour: *'I've never liked him, you know,' he said in a moment of candour.*

candy /'kandɪ/ n a sweet; sweets: *That child eats too much candy*; *Have a candy!*

candy floss Sweet that looks like cotton wool and is held on a stick.

cane /keɪn/ n **1** the stem of certain types of plant: *Sugar is made from sugar-cane.* **2** a stick used to help you walk, or to beat schoolchildren with, as a punishment: *The teacher kept a cane in his cupboard.* — v to beat with a cane: *The schoolmaster caned the boy.*

canine /'keɪnaɪn/ *adj* like a dog; having to do with dogs: *canine characteristics.*

canine tooth one of the four pointed teeth near the front of your mouth.

canister /'kanɪstə(r)/ n a small cylindrical container, usually made of metal.

cannabis /'kanəbɪs/ n a drug made from Indian hemp that some people smoke to make them feel relaxed: *Cannabis is illegal in many countries.*

canned /'kand/ *adj* put in cans: *canned peas.*

cannery /'kanərɪ/ n a factory where goods are canned.

cannibal /'kanɪbəl/ n a person who eats human flesh. **'cannibalism** n.

cannon /'kanən/ n a large heavy gun on wheels, used in earlier times.

'cannonball n a ball of iron, shot from a cannon.

cannot /'kanɒt/ or /'kanɒt/ see **can**[1].

canoe /kə'nuː/ n a light narrow boat moved by a paddle or paddles. — v to travel by canoe: *He canoed on the river.* **ca'noeist** n.

canopy /'kanəpɪ/ n a covering that is hung over a throne, bed *etc* as a decoration; a covering that is placed on poles as a shelter: *A canopy was put up to protect the president and his party from the strong sun.*

can't short for **cannot**.

canteen /kan'tiːn/ n a place in a factory, office *etc* where meals can be bought and eaten.

canter /'kantə(r)/ v to gallop at an easy pace: *The horse cantered across the meadow.*

canvas /'kanvəs/ n a strong, coarse cloth used for sails, tents *etc*, and for painting on: *a bag made of heavy canvas.* — *adj*: *canvas sails.*

canvass /ˈkanvəs/ v to go round asking people for votes or opinions *etc*: *The committee chairman had canvassed opinion before announcing the changes.* **'canvasser** n.

canyon /ˈkanjən/ n a deep, steep-sided valley, usually containing a river: *the Grand Canyon.*

cap /kap/ n **1** a flat hat with a piece at the front to shade the eyes: *a chauffeur's cap.* **2** a covering for the head: *a swimming cap; a nurse's cap.* **3** a cover or top of a bottle, pen *etc*: *Replace the cap after you've finished with the pen.* – v **1** to cover the top of something: *mountains capped with snow.* **2** to do something better or more impressive: *She was able to cap every story that was told.*

capable /ˈkeɪpəbəl/ adj **1** clever and sensible: *She'll manage somehow — she's so capable!* **2** able to do something: *He is capable of doing better.* **'capably** adv. **capa'bility** n.

The opposite of **capable** is **incapable**.

capacity /kəˈpasɪti/ n **1** ability to hold, contain *etc*: *This tank has a capacity of 300 gallons.* **2** ability: *He did not doubt their capacity for hard work.* **3** a person's official position: *He was acting in his capacity as chairman.*

cape[1] /keɪp/ n a loose garment without sleeves hanging from the shoulders: *a cycling cape.*

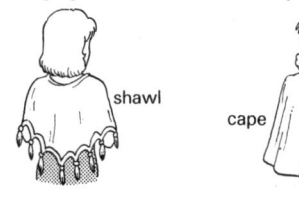

shawl

cape

cape[2] /keɪp/ n a high point of land sticking out into the sea: *The fishing-boat sailed round the cape.*

capital /ˈkapɪtəl/ n **1** the chief city of a country: *London is the capital of Great Britain.* **2** a large letter found at the beginning of sentences, names *etc*: *THESE ARE CAPITALS.* **3** money saved for a particular purpose *etc*: *You need capital to start a new business.* — adj **1** leading to punishment by death: *a capital crime.* **2** excellent: *a capital idea.*

capital city a capital: *Paris is a capital city.*
capital letter a capital: *Write your name in capital letters.*
capital punishment punishment of a crime by death: *Britain no longer has capital punishment.*

capitalism /ˈkapɪtəlɪzm/ n a system of government under which business and industry are controlled by individual people, and not by the state.
'capitalist adj having to do with capitalism: *a capitalist society.* — n a person who believes in capitalism.

capitulate /kəˈpɪtʃʊleɪt/ v to surrender usually on agreed conditions: *We capitulated to the enemy.* **capitu'lation** n.

capsize /kapˈsaɪz/ v to overturn: *The boat capsized and we all fell into the water.*

capsule /ˈkapsjuːl/ or /ˈkapsəl/ n **1** a small edible container holding a quantity of medicine, which you swallow. **2** a closed metal container: *a space capsule.*

captain /ˈkaptɪn/ n **1** the person who commands a ship, an aircraft, or a group of soldiers. **2** the leader of a team or club. — v to be captain of something: *John captained the football team last year.*

caption /ˈkapʃən/ n the words that are written underneath a picture to explain it: *In the newspaper there was a photograph of the girl, with the caption 'Susan Brown, the girl who saved her brother'.*

captivate /ˈkaptɪveɪt/ v to hold all your attention: *She has captivated audiences all over the world.*
'captivating adj interesting, attractive or charming: *a captivating story; a captivating personality.*

captive /ˈkaptɪv/ n a prisoner: *Two of the captives escaped.* — adj kept as a prisoner: *The soldiers were taken captive.*
cap'tivity n being a prisoner or kept in a cage: *Is it right to keep animals in captivity in a zoo?*
'captor n a person who captures someone: *He managed to escape from his captors.*

capture /ˈkaptʃə(r)/ v **1** to take by force: *The soldiers captured the castle; Several animals were captured with a large net.* **2** to represent something perfectly in words, pictures or music *etc*: *The artist has captured her expression exactly.* — n **1** capturing: *the capture of the criminal.* **2** something caught: *A kangaroo was his most recent capture.*

car /kɑː(r)/ n **1** a motor vehicle on wheels for carrying people: *What kind of car do you have?; Did you go by car?; A fleet of cars accompanied the president's vehicle.* **2** a railway carriage for goods or people: *a freight-car; a dining-car.*

See **in**.

car park a piece of land or a building where cars may be parked.

carat /'karət/ *n* **1** a unit for measuring how much pure gold there is in a gold object: *an 18-carat gold ring.* **2** a measure of weight for diamonds and other precious stones that is equal to 0.2 grams.

caravan /'karəvan/ *n* **1** a vehicle on wheels for living in, pulled by a car: *a holiday caravan.* **2** a group of people travelling together for safety especially across a desert on camels.

carbohydrate /kɑːbou'haɪdreɪt/ *n* substances found in food, especially sugar and starch: *Rice is full of carbohydrate.*

carbon /'kɑːbən/ *n* a substance that is found in coal *etc*.

carbon dioxide /kɑːbən daɪ'ɒksaɪd/ a gas present in the air, breathed out by man and animals.

carbon paper a paper coated with carbon, which is placed between two sheets of paper for making copies.

carcase or **carcass** /'kɑːkəs/ *n* the body of a dead animal.

card /kɑːd/ *n* **1** thick paper or thin cardboard: *shapes cut out from card.* **2** a small piece of thick paper with designs, used in playing certain games: *a pack of cards.* **3** a piece of thick paper, plastic *etc* used for sending greetings, storing information *etc*: *a birthday card; a bank card.*

cards *n* the games played with a pack of cards: *Do you like playing cards?*

'cardboard *n* a stiff kind of paper often made up of several layers. — *adj*: *a cardboard box.*

cardigan /'kɑːdɪgən/ *n* a knitted jacket that fastens up the front.

cardigan

jumper / pullover / sweater / jersey

cardinal /'kɑːdɪnəl/ *n* in the Catholic Church, one of the men next in rank to the Pope.

cardinal number a number that is used for counting: *'One', 'two' and 'three' are all cardinal numbers.*

care /kɛə(r)/ *n* **1** attention; concentration: *Carry these cups with care.* **2** protection: *Your belongings will be safe in my care.* **3** worry: *His mind was full of cares; It's nice to be free from care.* — *v* **1** to be anxious or concerned: *Don't you care if you fail your exam?; She really cares about her children.* **2** to want to do something: *Would you care to have tea with me?*

'care for 1 to look after someone: *The nurse will care for you.* **2** to like or love: *Do you really care for him enough to marry him?*

take care to be careful or thorough *etc*: *Take care or you will fall!*

take care of to look after someone or something: *Their aunt took care of them while their parents were abroad.*

career[1] /kə'rɪə(r)/ *n* a way of making a living: *the teaching career; I would like to make nursing my career.*

career[2] /kə'rɪə(r)/ *v* to move fast in an uncontrolled way: *The car came careering around the corner and hit a lamp-post.*

carefree /'kɛəfriː/ *adj* having no worries: *the carefree life of a gypsy.*

careful /'kɛəfʊl/ *adj* **1** taking care: *Be careful when you cross the street; a careful driver.* **2** thorough: *a careful search.* **'carefully** *adv*. **'carefulness** *n*.

careless /'kɛələs/ *adj* not careful: *This work is careless; a careless student.* **'carelessly** *adv*. **'carelessness** *n*.

caress /kə'rɛs/ *v* to touch gently and lovingly: *She caressed the horse's neck.* — *n* a loving, gentle touch: *a loving caress.*

caretaker /'kɛəteɪkə(r)/ *n* a person who looks after a building *etc*.

cargo /'kɑːgoʊ/, *plural* **'cargoes**, *n* a load of goods carried by a ship *etc*: *a cargo of cotton.*

caricature /'karɪkətjʊə(r)/ *n* an unkind drawing of someone which is very easy to recognize: *Caricatures of politicians appear in the newspapers every day.*

'caring *adj* kind, helpful and sympathetic: *a caring person.*

carnival /'kɑːnɪvəl/ *n* a public entertainment, often with processions of people in fancy dress *etc*.

carnivore /'kɑːnɪvɔː(r)/ *n* a flesh-eating

animal: *The lion is a carnivore.* **car'nivorous** *adj.*

carol /'karəl/ *n* a song of joy, especially for Christmas.

carousel /karə'sɛl/ *n* a moving platform which carries luggage for passengers to collect at an airport.

carp /kɑːp/, *plural* **carp**, *n* a freshwater fish found in ponds and rivers.

carpenter /'kɑːpɪntə(r)/ *n* a workman who makes and repairs wooden objects. **carpentry** /'kɑːpɪntrɪ/ *n.*

carpet /'kɑːpɪt/ *n* a thick piece of material for covering the floor or stairs *etc.* — *v* to cover with a carpet: *They haven't carpeted the floor yet.*

carriage /'karɪdʒ/ *n* **1** a vehicle for carrying railway passengers: *the carriage nearest the engine.* **2** a passenger vehicle drawn by horses. **3** the sending or delivery of goods: *She had to pay 10 pounds for the carriage of the books.*

'carriageway *n* the part of a road used by cars *etc*: *The overturned truck blocked the whole carriageway.*

carrier /'karɪə(r)/ *n* **1** a container or frame used for carrying things: *He had a luggage carrier fixed to his bicycle.* **2** (also **carrier bag**) a bag made of plastic or paper for carrying shopping *etc* in. **3** a person who is infected with a disease and can pass it on to other people.

carrot /'karət/ *n* **1** a long orange-coloured root vegetable. **2** an attractive offer that is used to persuade someone to do something: *New customers were offered free theatre tickets as a carrot.*

carry /'karɪ/ *v* **1** to take from one place to another: *She carried the baby into the house*; *Flies carry disease.* **2** to go from one place to another: *Sound carries better over water.* **3** to support: *These stone pillars carry the weight of the whole building.*

get carried away to lose control of your feelings: *She got carried away with excitement.*

carry off to manage to do something successfully: *She had decided to impress them and she carried it off beautifully.*

carry on 1 to continue: *You must carry on working*; *Carry on with your work.* **2** to manage: *He carries on a business as a grocer.*

carry out to finish something successfully: *He carried out the plan.*

carrycot /'karɪkɒt/ *n* a light cot with handles for carrying a small baby.

cart /kɑːt/ *n* a two-wheeled vehicle pulled by a horse, used for carrying loads: *a farm cart.* — *v* **1** to carry in a cart: *He carted the potatoes home.* **2** to carry: *I don't want to cart this luggage around all day.*

cartilage /'kɑːtɪlɪdʒ/ *n* a strong rubbery substance that forms your ears, the tip of your nose and the front part of your ribs.

carton /'kɑːtən/ *n* a cardboard or plastic container: *Orange juice is sold in cartons.*

cartoon /kɑː'tuːn/ *n* **1** a drawing making fun of someone or something: *a cartoon of the Prime Minister in the newspaper.* **2** a film consisting of a series of drawings in which the people and animals give the impression of movement: *a Walt Disney cartoon.*

car'toonist *n* a person who draws cartoons.

cartridge /'kɑːtrɪdʒ/ *n* **1** a case containing gunpowder, and a bullet, for a gun. **2** a tube containing ink for loading a pen.

cartwheel /'kɑːtwiːl/ *n* **1** a wheel of a cart. **2** an acrobatic movement in which you turn your body sideways in the air with the action of a wheel, putting your weight on each hand and each foot in turn: *The gymnast turned a cartwheel.* — *v*: *She cartwheeled across the gymnasium.*

carve /kɑːv/ *v* **1** to cut designs, shapes *etc* out of a piece of wood, stone *etc*: *The statue was carved out of wood.* **2** to cut up meat into slices: *Father carved the joint.*

'carving *n* a design, figure *etc* carved from wood, stone *etc.*

cascade /ka'skeɪd/ *n* **1** a big waterfall: *The water flowing over the edge is transformed into a miniature cascade.* **2** something that seems to flow like a waterfall: *Roses formed a cascade of colour on the wall.* — *v* **1** to pour very fast: *The water cascaded over the rocks.* **2** to pour or hang down like a waterfall: *Her hair cascaded down her back.*

case[1] /keɪs/ *n* **1** an example of something: *A grant will be awarded only in the most exceptional cases*; *This is a bad case of measles.* **2** a particular situation: *It's different in my case.* **3** a crime that is being investigated: *a murder case.* **4** a legal trial: *The magistrate dismissed the case against him.* **5** a fact; the truth: *I don't think that's really the case.* **6** the facts and reasons used to support a proposal: *the case for raising taxes.*

in any case 1 whatever happens: *We don't know who will win the election but in any case we'll have a new president tomorrow.* **2**

anyway: *She didn't tell me and, in any case, I didn't want to know.*

in case in order to guard against a possibility: *I'll take an umbrella in case it rains.*

in case of if a particular thing happens: *In case of fire, telephone the fire brigade.*

in that case if that is happening: *You're going to the shop? In that case, get me a box of matches.*

case² /keɪs/ *n* **1** a container: *a case of medical instruments; a suitcase.* **2** a crate or box: *six cases of oranges.* **3** a piece of furniture for displaying or containing things: *a glass case full of china; a bookcase.*

cash /kaʃ/ *n* coins or paper money, not cheques *etc*: *Do you wish to pay cash?* — *v* to give or get cash for a cheque: *Can you cash a cheque for me?*

cash register the machine in a shop *etc* into which cash is put.

cashew /ˈkaʃuː/ or /kəˈʃuː/ *n* a small curved nut.

cashier /kaˈʃɪə(r)/ *n* a person who receives and pays out money, for example in a bank.

cashmere /ˈkaʃmɪə(r)/ *n* a very fine, soft wool.

casino /kəˈsiːnoʊ/, *plural* **ca'sinos**, *n* a building in which people gamble.

cask /kɑːsk/ *n* a barrel, usually for wine.

casket /ˈkɑːskɪt/ *n* a small case for holding jewels *etc*.

casserole /ˈkasəroʊl/ *n* **1** a dish with a lid used for cooking food slowly in an oven. **2** the food cooked in such a dish: *a chicken casserole.*

cassette /kəˈsɛt/ *n* a container for photographic film or magnetic tape: *I bought a cassette of jazz music.*

cassette player or **cassette recorder** a machine that plays, or makes, recordings on magnetic tape.

cast /kɑːst/ *v* **1** to throw or direct: *The fisherman cast his line into the river; The moon cast a pale light over the garden.* **2** to drop or shed: *Some snakes cast their skins.* **3** to pour liquid metal *etc* into a container to get a desired shape: *The statue was cast in bronze.* **4** to give a part in a play *etc* to someone: *She was cast as a fairy.* **5** to give a vote: *Who will you cast your vote for?* — *n* **1** a throw. **2** a mould in which something is shaped and hardened: *The hot metal was poured into a cast.* **3** all the actors in a play *etc*.

> **cast; cast; cast**: *He cast a glance at me; Have you cast your vote?*

'castaway *n* a shipwrecked person.

cast aside or **cast away** or **cast off** to throw away.

castanets /kastəˈnɛts/ *n plural* a pair of musical instruments used in Spanish dancing, consisting of two small hollow pieces of wood or plastic that you hold between your fingers and thumb and strike together to make a rhythm.

caste /kɑːst/ *n* a social class especially in India.

caster *see* **castor**.

cast-iron /kɑːstˈaɪən/ *adj* **1** made of a hard type of iron. **2** very strong or reliable: *a cast-iron alibi.* **cast 'iron** *n*.

castle /ˈkɑːsəl/ *n* **1** a large building strengthened against attack: *The castle was built on top of a mountain.* **2** a piece in chess.

cast-off /ˈkɑːstɒf/ *adj* no longer needed: *cast-off clothes.*

castor or **caster** /ˈkɑːstə(r)/ *n* a small wheel fixed under the leg of a chair, table or bed, that makes it easier to move.

casual /ˈkaʒʊəl/ *adj* **1** not careful: *I took a casual glance at the book.* **2** not smart or formal: *casual clothes.* **3** happening by chance: *a casual meeting with a friend.* **'casually** *adv.* **'casualness** *n.*

casualty /ˈkaʒʊəltɪ/ *n* a person who is wounded or killed in a battle, accident *etc*: *Attacks from the air would risk civilian casualties; The casualty list included several children.*

cat /kat/ *n* **1** a small, four-legged, fur-covered animal, often kept as a pet. **2** any wild animal of the cat family, such as a lion or tiger: *the big cats in the zoo.*

> *A cat* **purrs** or **mews**.
> A baby cat is a **kitten**.
> A male cat is a **tom**.

let the cat out of the bag to let a secret become known without meaning to.

catacombs /ˈkatəkuːmz/ *n plural* a series of underground tunnels containing burial places: *When she was in Rome she visited the catacombs.*

catalogue /ˈkatəlɒɡ/ *n* a list of names, goods, books *etc* arranged in a particular order: *a library catalogue.* — *v* to list things in order: *She catalogued the books.*

catalyst /ˈkatəlɪst/ *n* **1** a substance that causes or assists a chemical change in other substances without itself changing. **2** something that causes a change in a situation, or makes something happen.

catalytic converter /katəlɪtɪk kən'vɜːtə(r)/ *n* a device which reduces the amount of poisonous gas given off by a motor car.

catamaran /katəmə'ran/ *n* a sailing-boat that looks like two boats side by side, joined together by a deck.

catapult /'katəpʌlt/ *n* a Y-shaped stick with an elastic string for shooting small stones *etc*. — *v* to throw violently: *His bicycle hit a stone, and he was catapulted over the handlebars.*

catastrophe /kə'tastrəfɪ/ *n* a sudden great disaster: *earthquakes and other catastrophes.*
 catastrophic /katə'strɒfɪk/ *adj*.

catch /katʃ/ *v* **1** to stop and hold something which is moving; to capture: *He caught the ball*; *Did you catch any fish?*; *I tried to catch his attention.* **2** to be in time for, or get on, a train, bus *etc*: *I'll have to catch the train to London.* **3** to surprise someone while they are doing something wrong: *I caught him stealing my vegetables.* **4** to become infected with a disease: *He caught flu.* **5** to get attached or held by accident: *The child caught her fingers in the car door.* **6** to hit: *The punch caught him on the chin.* **7** to manage to hear: *Did you catch what she said?* **8** to start burning: *The dry grass caught fire.* — *n* **1** catching something, especially a ball: *She made a good catch.* **2** a total amount of fish *etc* caught: *The fishermen made a big catch.* **3** a trick: *There's a catch in this question.* **4** a device for holding something closed: *The catch on my necklace is broken.*

> **catch; caught** /kɔːt/; **caught**: *He caught a fish*; *The thief was caught at last.*

'catch-phrase *n* a popular, fashionable saying; something that everyone is repeating.

'catchy *adj* attractive and easily remembered: *a catchy tune.*

catch someone's eye to attract someone's attention: *The advertisement caught my eye.*

catch on 1 to become popular: *The fashion caught on.* **2** to understand: *He's sometimes a bit slow to catch on.*

catch out to trick someone into making a mistake: *The question caught them all out.*

catch up 1 to reach or pass someone or something, after following: *We caught him up at the corner*; *We waited for him to catch up.* **2** to reach the same standard or level as someone else: *If he works hard he should soon catch up with the other children.* **3** to do all the work that you have not yet done: *She had a lot of schoolwork to catch up on after her illness.*

get caught up in become involved in something without intending to: *The government didn't want to get caught up in another country's war.*

category /'katəgərɪ/ *n* a class or type of things or people: *Story-books come under the category of fiction.*

cater /'keɪtə(r)/ *v* **1** to provide food *etc*: *This hotel caters for wedding-parties.* **2** to supply what is needed: *We cater for all educational needs.* **'caterer**, **'catering** *ns*.

caterpillar /'katəpɪlə(r)/ *n* a worm-like creature that is the larva of a butterfly or moth.

catfish /'katfɪʃ/ *n* a fish with long whiskers round its mouth.

cathedral /kə'θiːdrəl/ *n* the principal church of a district under a bishop.

Catholic /'kaθəlɪk/ *adj* of the Roman Catholic Church. — *n* a member of the Roman Catholic Church.

Cat's-eye® /'katsaɪ/ *n* a small thick piece of glass fixed into the road to reflect a car's headlights and so guide the driver.

cattle /'katəl/ *n* grass-eating animals, especially cows, bulls and oxen: *A few hardy-looking cattle wandered about.*

> **cattle** takes a plural verb: *The cattle were in the field.*

caught *see* **catch**.

cauldron /'kɔːldrən/ *n* a large deep pot for boiling things in.

cauliflower /'kɒlɪflaʊə(r)/ *n* a vegetable with a large white head.

cause /kɔːz/ *n* **1** something or someone that produces an effect or result: *Lack of money is the cause of all my misery.* **2** a reason for an action: *You had no cause to treat your dog so badly.* **3** an aim for which one person or a group works: *He has worked hard in the cause of peace.* — *v* to make something happen: *What caused the accident?*; *Her son's illness caused her a lot of worry.*

> See **reason**.

causeway /'kɔːzweɪ/ *n* a raised road *etc* over wet ground or shallow water.

caution /'kɔːʃən/ *n* **1** carefulness because of possible danger *etc*: *You should always cross the street with caution.* **2** a warning: *The policeman gave him a caution for speeding.* — *v* to give a warning to someone: *He was*

bridge

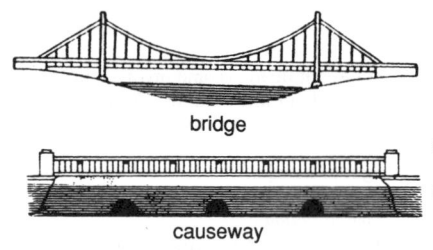

causeway

cautioned for careless driving. **'cautionary** *adj.*

'cautious *adj* careful: *She used to trust everyone but she's more cautious now; a cautious driver.* **'cautiously** *adv.*

cavalier /kavə'lɪə(r)/ *n* in former times, a horseman or knight.

cavalry /'kavəlrɪ/ *n* the part of an army consisting of soldiers who ride on horses.

cave /keɪv/ *n* a large natural hollow in rock or in the earth: *The children explored the cave.*

'caveman *n* a person who lived in a cave thousands of years ago.

cave in to collapse: *The wall caved in.*

cavern /'kavən/ *n* a large cave.

caviar or **caviare** /'kavɪɑː(r)/ *n* the eggs of a large fish called a sturgeon, that are eaten as food: *A small jar of caviar might cost you over ten pounds.*

cavity /'kavɪtɪ/ *n* a hollow place; a hole: *The dentist said she had three cavities in her teeth.*

cease /siːs/ *v* to stop or end: *They were ordered to cease firing; The noise ceased at last.*

'ceasefire *n* an agreement to stop fighting: *Both countries signed the ceasefire which brought the war to an end.*

'ceaseless *adj* continuous: *ceaseless noise.* **'ceaselessly** *adv.*

cedar /'siːdə(r)/ *n* a large tree with needle-like leaves and hard, sweet-smelling wood.

ceiling /'siːlɪŋ/ *n* the inner roof of a room *etc*: *If I stand on a chair I can touch the ceiling.*

celebrate /'sɛləbreɪt/ *v* to have a party *etc* in honour of a happy or important event: *I'm celebrating my birthday today.* **cele'bration** *n.*

'celebrated *adj* famous: *a celebrated actress.* **celebrity** /sə'lɛbrɪtɪ/ *n* a famous person.

celery /'sɛlərɪ/ *n* a vegetable whose long juicy stalks are used in salads.

celestial /sɪ'lɛstɪəl/ *adj* of heaven or the sky: *Stars are celestial bodies.*

cell /sɛl/ *n* **1** a small room especially in a prison. **2** a very small piece of the substance of which all living things are made: *The human body is made up of cells.* **3** a small compartment or division: *the cells of a honeycomb.*

cellar /'sɛlə(r)/ *n* an underground room, usually used for storing coal, wine *etc.*

cello /'tʃɛloʊ/ *n* a musical instrument similar to, but much larger than, a violin. **'cellist** *n.*

The pronunciation of **cello** is /'tʃɛloʊ/.

celsius /'sɛlsɪəs/ *adj* measured on the temperature scale where water freezes at 0° and boils at 100°: *twenty degrees Celsius; 20°C.*

Celsius ends in **-sius** (not **-cius**).

cement /sɪ'mɛnt/ *n* **1** a grey powder which you mix with sand and water and use for sticking bricks *etc* together and for making concrete. **2** a strong glue. — *v* to join firmly with cement.

cemetery /'sɛmətrɪ/ *n* a place where people are buried.

censor /'sɛnsə(r)/ *v* to remove from books, films *etc* anything which might offend people: *Their letters were censored by the authorities.* — *n* a person who censors.

'censorship *n* the censoring of books, films *etc.*

censure /'sɛnʃə(r)/ *v* to criticize or blame: *He was censured for staying away from work.* — *n* criticism or blame.

census /'sɛnsəs/ *n* an official counting especially of a country's inhabitants.

cent /sɛnt/ *n* a coin equal to the hundredth part of a dollar, rupee *etc.*

centenary /sɛn'tiːnərɪ/ or /'sɛntənərɪ/ *n* a hundredth anniversary.

centenarian /sɛntɪ'nɛərɪən/ *n* a person who is a hundred or more years old.

centigrade /'sɛntɪgreɪd/ *adj* another name for Celsius.

centimetre /'sɛntɪmiːtə(r)/ *n* a hundredth part of a metre: *cm is short for centimetre.*

centipede /'sɛntɪpiːd/ *n* a small crawling creature with many legs.

central /'sɛntrəl/ *adj* **1** belonging to, or near, the centre: *His flat is in the central part of the town.* **2** important: *He plays a central part in the story.* **'centrally** *adv.*

'centralize *v* to bring under one control. **centrali'zation** *n.*

centre /'sɛntə(r)/ *n* **1** the middle point or part: *the centre of a circle; the city centre.* **2** a place for an activity of a particular sort: *a* *shopping-centre*; *a sports-centre*. **3** the main point of interest *etc*: *He likes to be the centre of attention.* — *v* **1** to place, or to be, at the centre. **2** to concentrate on: *Her plans always centre on her child.*

century /'sɛntʃərɪ/ *n* a period of a hundred years: *the 19th century*; *for more than a century.*

> See **year**.

ceramic /sɪ'ramɪk/ *adj* made of baked clay: *a ceramic vase.* — *n* something made of baked clay: *She sells ceramics and woodcarvings.*

cereal /'sɪərɪəl/ *n* **1** a grain used as food: *Wheat and barley are cereals.* **2** a breakfast food prepared from grain.

ceremony /'sɛrəmənɪ/ *n* **1** a formal event such as a wedding, funeral *etc*: *a marriage ceremony.* **2** formal behaviour: *The delegates were received with respectful ceremony.*
ceremonial /sɛrə'moʊnɪəl/ *adj* formal or official: *a ceremonial occasion such as the opening of parliament.* **cere'monially** *adv*.

certain /'sɜːtən/ *adj* **1** true or without doubt: *It's certain that the world is round.* **2** sure: *I'm certain he'll come*; *He is certain to forget*; *Being late is a certain way of losing your job.* **3** one; some: *certain areas of Europe*; *in certain circumstances*; *a certain Mrs Smith.* **4** slight; some: *a certain amount.* — *pron* some: *certain of his friends.*

> The opposite of **certain**, meaning without doubt, is **uncertain**.

'certainly *adv* **1** definitely: *I can't come today, but I'll certainly come tomorrow.* **2** of course: *You may certainly have a chocolate.*
'certainty *n* **1** being certain: *We can try, but there is no certainty of success.* **2** something that will definitely happen: *It's an absolute certainty that she'll get the job.*
for certain definitely: *She may come but she can't say for certain.*
make certain to act so that, or check that, something is sure: *Make certain you arrive early*; *I think he's gone home but you'd better make certain.*

certificate /sə'tɪfɪkət/ *n* a written official statement of some fact: *a marriage certificate.*

certify /'sɜːtɪfaɪ/ *v* to put something down in writing as an official promise, statement *etc*: *Here is a document certifying that I was born in France.* **certifi'cation** *n*.

chain /tʃeɪn/ *n* **1** a number of metal rings passing through one another: *The dog was fastened by a chain*; *She wore a silver chain round her neck.* **2** a series: *a chain of events.* — *v* to fasten with chains: *The prisoner was chained to the wall.*
chain store one of a series of shops owned by the same company.

chair /tʃɛə(r)/ *n* a seat for one person, with a back to it: *a table and four chairs.* — *v* to be officially in charge at a meeting *etc*: *a committee chaired by a Labour peer.*
'chairman *n* a person, usually but not always a man, who takes charge of or directs a meeting.

chalet /'ʃaleɪ/ *n* a small wooden house used by holidaymakers *etc*.

chalk /tʃɔːk/ *n* **1** a soft white kind of stone. **2** a piece of a substance like this, used for writing on blackboards. **'chalky** *adj*.
'chalkboard *n* a smooth green board for writing on with chalk.
chalk up to achieve a success: *Our team has chalked up six wins this season.*

challenge /'tʃalɪndʒ/ *v* **1** to ask someone to take part in a contest: *He challenged his brother to a game of golf.* **2** to say that you doubt whether something is true, right *etc*: *She challenged his right to keep the money.* — *n* **1** an invitation to a contest: *a challenge to fight.* **2** a situation, career *etc* which requires a lot of effort and ability: *His new job is a challenge for him.* **'challenger** *n*.
'challenging *adj*.

chamber /'tʃeɪmbə(r)/ *n* **1** a room. **2** the place where an assembly such as Parliament meets: *There were few members left in the chamber.*
'chambermaid *n* a female hotel worker in charge of bedrooms.
chamber music classical music composed for a small group of instruments rather than an orchestra.

chameleon /kə'miːlɪən/ *n* a small lizard which is able to change colour.

champagne /ʃam'peɪn/ *n* a white sparkling wine.

champion /'tʃampɪən/ *n* **1** in games, competitions *etc*, a person who has defeated all others: *this year's golf champion.* **2** a person who strongly supports a cause: *a champion of human rights.* — *adj* being a champion: *a champion boxer.* — *v* to defend or support.

'championship *n* **1** a contest held to decide who is the champion: *a tennis championship.* **2** the title or position of champion: *compete for the championship of the world.*

chance /tʃɑːns/ *n* **1** luck or fortune; something you didn't plan: *She never left things to chance; Card games are games of chance.* **2** an opportunity: *Now you have a chance to do well.* **3** a possibility: *He has no chance of winning.* — *adj* unexpected: *a chance meeting.* — *v* to happen: *I chanced to meet her yesterday.*

by any chance perhaps: *Are you by any chance free tonight?*

by chance by accident; not planned or on purpose: *They met by chance.*

stand a chance to have a possibility of succeeding: *He won last time and stands a good chance of winning again.*

the chances are it is likely that: *The chances are he can't come tomorrow.*

chancellor /'tʃɑːnsələ(r)/ *n* **1** the head of the government in some European countries, such as West Germany. **2** the head of a university.

chandelier /ʃændə'lɪə(r)/ *n* a frame with many holders for lights, which hangs from the ceiling.

change /tʃeɪndʒ/ *v* **1** to make or become different: *They have changed the time of the train; He has changed since I saw him last.* **2** to exchange: *She changed my library books for me.* **3** to remove clothes *etc* and replace them by clean or different ones: *I'm just going to change my shirt; I'll change into an old pair of trousers.* **4** to make into or become something different: *The prince changed into a frog.* **5** to give or receive one kind of money for another: *Could you change this bank-note for coins?* — *n* **1** an alteration: *There is no change in the patient's condition; There will be a change in the programme.* **2** changing one thing for another: *a change of clothes.* **3** coins rather than paper money: *I'll have to give you a note — I have no change.* **4** money left over or given back from the amount given in payment: *He paid with a five pound note and got 50 pence change.* **5** a holiday, rest *etc*: *He has been ill — the change will do him good.*

'changeable *adj* changing often: *In Britain the weather is very changeable.*

change hands to pass from one owner to another: *This car has changed hands three times.*

change of heart a change of opinion or feeling: *She had a sudden change of heart and agreed to the plan.*

change over to replace one system with another: *We have changed over to a new computerized method of payment.* **change-over** *n.*

change your mind to alter your intention or opinion about something: *At first he wanted to go to Los Angeles but he changed his mind.*

for a change to be different; for variety: *I usually go by bus but today I'll walk for a change.*

make a change to be pleasantly different from what usually happens: *It makes a change to see her smiling.*

channel /'tʃænəl/ *n* **1** the hollow in which a river or stream flows. **2** a narrow sea: *the English Channel.* **3** a band of frequencies for radio or television signals: *BBC Television now has two channels.* — *v* **1** to make a channel. **2** to direct into a course: *He channelled all his energies into the project.*

chant /tʃɑːnt/ *v* to repeat something over and over out loud: *The crowd was chanting 'We want more!'* — *n* **1** a song used in religion, in magic spells *etc*. **2** a sentence or phrase that is constantly repeated.

chaos /'keɪɒs/ *n* complete disorder or confusion: *The place was in chaos after the burglary.* **cha'otic** *adj.* **cha'otically** *adv.*

chap /tʃæp/ *n* a man or boy: *He's a nice chap.*

chapel /'tʃæpəl/ *n* **1** a small church. **2** a small apartment for private services *etc*, that is part of a larger church.

chaplain /'tʃæplɪn/ *n* a member of the Christian clergy who works in a hospital, school, prison or the army.

chapped /'tʃæpt/ *adj* cracked and sore: *chapped lips.*

chapter /'tʃæptə(r)/ *n* a division of a book: *The book is divided into 12 chapters; Read Chapter 5.*

char /tʃɑː(r)/ *v* to burn or turn black by fire or heat: *The wood was charred by the heat.*

character /'kærəktə(r)/ *n* **1** the qualities that make someone or something different from others: *He never shows his true character in public.* **2** qualities that are considered admirable in some way: *He showed great character in dealing with the danger.* **3** a person in a play, novel *etc*: *There are six*

characters in the play. **4** a letter, sign *etc* used in writing or printing: *Chinese characters.*
character'istic *adj* typical of a person *etc*: *The ageing population in Britain is characteristic of developed countries.* — *n* a typical quality: *A strong smell is one of the characteristics of oranges.* **characte'ristically** *adv.*

The opposite of **characteristic** is **uncharacteristic**.

'characterize *v* **1** to mark in a special way: *The giraffe is characterized by its long neck.* **2** to describe; to say what the qualities of something are: *He was characterized by his teachers as lazy and dull.* **characteri'zation** *n.*
charades /ʃə'rɑːdz/ *n* a game in which each syllable of a word, and then the whole word, is acted, and the audience has to guess the word.
charcoal /'tʃɑːkoʊl/ *n* the black part of partly burned wood used as fuel and for drawing.
charge /tʃɑːdʒ/ *v* **1** to ask as the price for something: *They charge 50 pence for a pint of milk.* **2** to accuse someone: *He was charged with theft.* **3** to rush forward and attack: *We charged towards the enemy on horseback.* **4** to rush: *The children charged down the hill.* **5** to fill with electricity: *Please charge my car battery.* **6** to load a gun *etc.* — *n* **1** a price: *What is the charge for a telephone call?* **2** something with which a person is accused: *He faces three charges of murder.* **3** an attack: *The soldiers made a charge.* **4** the electricity in something: *a positive or negative charge.* **5** a quantity of gunpowder.
in charge of looking after someone or something: *The teacher is in charge of the pupils.*
take charge to look after or organize: *Who will take charge of the school while the headmaster is away?*
chariot /'tʃærɪət/ *n* a vehicle with two wheels, used in ancient times in fighting and racing.
charisma /kə'rɪzmə/ *n* the power to make people like and respect you, and do what you want: *A good leader must have charisma.* **charis'matic** *adj*: *a charismatic leader.*
charity /'tʃærɪtɪ/ *n* **1** kindness especially in giving money to poor people. **2** an organization set up to collect money for poor people, for medical research *etc*: *Many charities sent money to help the victims of the disaster.*
'charitable *adj* **1** kind and understanding towards other people: *That's not a very charitable description of her.* **2** having to do with charity. **'charitably** *adv.*

The opposite of **charitable** is **uncharitable.**

charm /tʃɑːm/ *n* **1** pleasantness of character: *Her charm won her many friends.* **2** a magic spell: *The witch recited a charm.* **3** something believed to bring good luck: *She wore a lucky charm.* — *v* **1** to delight: *The storyteller charmed all the children.* **2** to influence by magic: *He charmed the snake from its basket.* **'charming** *adj* very attractive: *a charming smile.* **'charmingly** *adv.*
chart /tʃɑːt/ *n* **1** a map, especially of seas or lakes. **2** a diagram giving information: *a weather chart.* — *v* to make a chart of something: *We charted their journey on our map.*
charter /'tʃɑːtə(r)/ *n* a written statement of rights or permission to do something. — *v* to hire an aircraft *etc*: *The travel company had chartered three aircraft for their holiday flights.* — *adj*: *a charter flight.*
chartered /'tʃɑːtəd/ *adj* being fully qualified in certain professions: *a chartered accountant.*
chase /tʃeɪs/ *v* **1** to run after someone or something: *He chased after them but did not catch them*; *We chased them by car.* **2** to cause to run away: *I often have to chase the boys away from my fruit trees.* — *n* **1** the chasing of someone or something: *We caught him after a long chase.* **2** the hunting of animals.
give chase to chase: *The thieves ran off and the policeman gave chase.*
chasm /'kazm/ *n* a deep opening between high rocks *etc.*
chat /tʃat/ *v* to talk in a friendly and easy way: *They chatted about the weather.* — *n* a friendly talk: *We had a chat over coffee.*
chat up to talk to someone in a friendly way, usually because you would like them as your boyfriend or girlfriend: *He has chatted up all the girls in his class.*
chateau /'ʃatoʊ/ or /ʃa'toʊ/, *plural* **chateaux**, *n* a castle or large country house in France.
chatter /'tʃatə(r)/ *v* **1** to talk noisily about unimportant things: *The children chattered among themselves.* **2** to knock together because of cold or fear: *Her teeth were chattering with the cold.* — *n* rapid, noisy talk: *childish chatter.*
'chatterbox *n* a person who chatters a lot.
chatty /'tʃatɪ/ *adj* talkative: *a chatty old lady.*

chauffeur /ˈʃoʊfə(r)/ *n* a person employed as a car-driver for someone important *etc*.

chauvinism /ˈʃoʊvənɪzm/ *n* a silly belief that your own country, party, group *etc* is much better than any other.
  'chauvinist *n* a person who has this kind of belief: *A male chauvinist believes that men are superior to women.* **chauvi'nistic** *adj*.

cheap /tʃiːp/ *adj* **1** low in price; not expensive: *Eggs are cheap just now.* **2** of bad quality or little value: *cheap jewellery.* **'cheaply** *adv*. **'cheapness** *n*.

cheat /tʃiːt/ *v* to act dishonestly to gain an advantage: *He cheated in the exam*; *He was cheated out of the money he had been left by his parents.* — *n* **1** a person who cheats. **2** a dishonest trick.
  'cheating *n*: *He was accused of cheating in the examination.*

check /tʃɛk/ *v* **1** to see if something is correct: *Will you check my addition?* **2** to see if a machine *etc* is in good condition or working properly: *Have you checked the engine?* **3** to stop: *We've checked the flow of water from the burst pipe.* — *n* **1** the checking of something: *Give these sums a check.* **2** the reducing of something: *Keep a check on your spending.* **3** in chess, a position in which the king is attacked. **4** a pattern of squares on material *etc*. **5** a ticket received in return for handing in baggage *etc*. **6** a bill. **7** a cheque.
  checked *adj* having a pattern of check: *She wore a checked skirt.*
  'check-in *n* the place where you show your ticket and leave your luggage before getting on an aeroplane: *the check-in desk.*
  'checkmate *n* in chess, a position from which the king cannot escape.
  'checkout *n* a place in a supermarket where you pay for goods.
  'checkpoint *n* a place where cars, passports *etc* are inspected.
  'check-up *n* an examination by a doctor to make sure you are healthy.
  check in to arrive at a hotel or airport and sign the register or show your tickets: *We checked in last night*; *Passengers are asked to check in half an hour before their flight leaves.*
  check out 1 to leave a hotel *etc* and pay your bill. **2** to find out more information about something: *The offer seemed so good that I decided to check it out.*
  check up to make sure of something: *Please check up on the time of the train.*

cheek /tʃiːk/ *n* **1** the side of your face; the part below your eye: *pink cheeks.* **2** rudeness: *He had the cheek to make fun of his teacher.*
  'cheekbone *n* the bone that is below your eye.
  'cheeky *adj* rude; impolite: *a cheeky remark.*
  'cheekily *adv*. **'cheekiness** *n*.

cheer /tʃɪə(r)/ *n* a shout of joy, encouragement or welcome: *Three cheers for the winner!* — *v* to give a shout of joy *etc*: *The crowd cheered the new champion.*
  'cheerful *adj* full of, or causing, happiness: *a cheerful smile*; *cheerful news.* **'cheerfully** *adv*. **'cheerfulness** *n*.
  cheer on to shout encouragement: *We all jumped about cheering on our horse.*
  cheer up to make or become more cheerful: *He stopped crying and cheered up*; *The flowers will cheer her up.*

cheerio! /tʃɪərɪˈoʊ/ a word for goodbye.

cheers! /tʃɪəz/ **1** a word you say when you drink someone's health *etc*. **2** another word for goodbye or thanks.

cheery /ˈtʃɪərɪ/ *adj* lively and happy. **'cheerily** *adv*.

cheese /tʃiːz/ *n* a solid food made from milk.
  cheesed off bored: *I'm cheesed off with all this rain.*

cheetah /ˈtʃiːtə/ *n* a very swift-running animal of the cat family.

chef /ʃɛf/ *n* a head cook in a hotel *etc*.

chemical /ˈkɛmɪkəl/ *adj* having to do with chemistry: *a chemical reaction.* — *n* a substance which is formed by or used in a chemical process.

chemist /ˈkɛmɪst/ *n* **1** a scientist who studies or works in chemistry. **2** a person who prepares and sells medicines.

chemistry /ˈkɛmɪstrɪ/ *n* the science that deals with the nature of substances and the ways in which they act on, or combine with, each other: *Chemistry was his favourite subject.*

cheque /tʃɛk/ *n* a written order telling a bank to pay money to the person named: *I'll pay for the meal by cheque.*
  'chequebook *n* a book containing cheques.

See **bank**.

chequered /ˈtʃɛkəd/ *adj* partly good and partly bad: *a chequered career*; *a chequered past.*

cherish /ˈtʃɛrɪʃ/ *v* **1** to protect and love a person: *She cherishes that child.* **2** to keep a hope, idea *etc* in the mind: *She cherishes the hope that he will return.*

cherry /ˈtʃɛrɪ/ *n* a small red fruit with a stone.

chess /tʃɛs/ n a game for two played with thirty-two pieces (**'chessmen**) on a board (**'chessboard**) with sixty-four black and white squares.

chest[1] /tʃɛst/ n the part of the body between the neck and waist.

get something off your chest to tell someone about something that has been worrying or annoying you.

chest[2] /tʃɛst/ n **1** a large, strong wooden or metal box. **2** a piece of furniture with drawers, for keeping clothes in *etc*.

chest of drawers a piece of furniture fitted with several drawers.

chestnut /'tʃɛstnʌt/ n **1** a tree with red-brown nuts. **2** the nut of this tree. **3** a red-brown colour. — *adj*: *chestnut hair*.

chew /tʃuː/ v to break food *etc* with the teeth: *You have to chew meat before swallowing it*.

'chewing-gum n a sweet and sticky substance that you chew.

'chewy *adj* needing a lot of chewing: *a chewy piece of meat*.

chic /ʃiːk/ *adj* smart; pretty: *She looks very chic in that hat*.

chick /tʃɪk/ n a baby bird.

chicken /'tʃɪkɪn/ n **1** a young bird, especially a young hen: *She keeps chickens*. **2** its flesh used as food: *a plate of fried chicken*.

'chicken-pox n an infectious disease with fever and red itchy spots.

chicken out to avoid doing something because you are afraid: *He chickened out of swimming in the river*.

chief /tʃiːf/ *adj* most important *etc*: *That was my chief aim*; *Looking after others was her chief source of pleasure*. — n a person who is the head of a tribe or a business *etc*.

'chiefly *adv* mainly: *She became ill chiefly because she did not eat enough*.

'chieftain n the head of a tribe *etc*.

chihuahua /tʃɪ'wɑːwə/ n a tiny dog with short hair that originally comes from Mexico.

child /tʃaɪld/, *plural* **children** /'tʃɪldrən/, n **1** a baby or young person. **2** a son or daughter: *Her youngest child is five years old*.

'childbirth n having a baby.

'childhood n the time during which you are a child: *Did you have a happy childhood?*

'childish *adj* like a child; silly: *a childish remark*. **'childishly** *adv*. **'childishness** n.

'childless *adj* having no children.

'childlike *adj* innocent: *trustful and childlike*.

> **childish** means silly: *a childish joke*.
> **childlike** means innocent; full of trust: *childlike obedience*.

chill /tʃɪl/ n **1** coldness: *There's a chill in the air*. **2** an illness which causes shivering: *I think I've caught a chill*. — *adj* cold: *a chill wind*. — v to make something cool or cold: *Have you chilled the wine?*

'chilly *adj* cold: *a chilly day*.

chilli /'tʃɪlɪ/ n the hot-tasting pod of a type of pepper, often dried and made into a powder.

chilling /'tʃɪlɪŋ/ *adj* frightening: *a chilling story*.

chime /tʃaɪm/ n a ringing sound, usually like a little tune, made by a large clock to tell the time. — v to make this sound: *The church clock chimed 9 o'clock*.

chime in to interrupt a conversation: *'Yes, that's true', Peter chimed in eagerly*.

chimney /'tʃɪmnɪ/ n a structure that contains a passage for the escape of smoke *etc* from a fire: *a factory chimney*.

chimpanzee /tʃɪmpən'ziː/ n a small African ape.

chin /tʃɪn/ n the part of your face below your mouth: *His beard completely covers his chin*.

china /'tʃaɪnə/ n a hard white material used for making cups, plates *etc*; articles made from this: *Wash the china carefully*. — *adj*: *a china vase*.

chink /tʃɪŋk/ n a small, narrow opening: *Light came in through a chink in the wall*.

chip /tʃɪp/ v to knock a small piece off something: *This glass was chipped when I knocked it over*. — n **1** a small piece cut or broken off from glass, stone, wood *etc*. **2** a place from which a small piece is broken: *There's a chip in the cup*. **3** a long thin piece of potato fried in deep fat: *steak and chips*. **4** a small piece of plastic used in place of cash in gambling. **5** a microchip.

have a chip on your shoulder to be angry for a long time because you feel that you have not been as lucky as others.

chip in to interrupt in order to add something to a conversation: *Yvonne chipped in with a suggestion*. **2** to give some money to help pay for something: *They all chipped in and bought me a present*.

chipmunk /'tʃɪpmʌŋk/ n a type of North American squirrel with a bushy tail and black-and-white-striped back.

chiropodist /kɪ'rɒpədɪst/ n a person whose job is to care for people's feet.

chirp /tʃɜːp/ or **chirrup** /'tʃɪrəp/ *ns* the singing sound made by certain birds and insects. — *v* to make this sound.

chisel /'tʃɪzəl/ *n* a tool with a cutting edge at the end. — *v* to cut or shape wood *etc* with a chisel.

chivalry /'ʃɪvəlrɪ/ *n* kindness of men towards women; care for people weaker than yourself. **'chivalrous** *adj*.

chlorine /'klɔːriːn/ *n* a poisonous, strong-smelling gas, often used to keep swimming pool water clean.

chocolate /'tʃɒklɪt/ *n* **1** a substance made from the seeds of the cacao tree. **2** a sweet or drink made from it: *a bar of chocolate*; *a cup of chocolate*. — *adj*: *chocolate ice-cream*; *chocolate biscuits*.

choice /tʃɔɪs/ *n* choosing or the possibility of choosing: *He had to make a difficult choice between the two cars*; *Here is some money to buy a book of your choice*; *You have no choice — you must do it*. — *adj* of especially good quality: *Use only the choicest ingredients for this recipe*.

choir /kwaɪə(r)/ *n* a group of singers: *He used to sing in the church choir*.

choke /tʃəʊk/ *v* **1** to stop or partly stop breathing: *The gas choked him*; *He choked to death*. **2** to block: *This pipe was choked with dirt*.

choke back to try hard not to show a strong emotion: *I could tell he was choking back his tears*.

cholera /'kɒlərə/ *n* a very infectious and serious illness with diarrhoea and vomiting, that can cause death.

cholesterol /kə'lɛstərɒl/ *n* a fatty substance that is found in some foods and in the blood.

choose /tʃuːz/ *v* **1** to take one thing rather than another from a number of things; to select: *There's a huge range of colours to choose from*; *Always choose a book carefully*; *I had to choose between getting married and taking up a career*. **2** to decide: *If he chooses to stay at home, let him do so*.

> **choose; chose** /tʃəʊz/; **chosen** /'tʃəʊzən/: *She chose a new book*; *Have you chosen a partner?*

'choosy *adj* caring very much or too much about choosing carefully; difficult to please: *He's very choosy about his whisky*.

chop /tʃɒp/ *v* to cut something into small pieces: *He chopped up the vegetables*. — *n* a slice of pork *etc* containing a rib.

chop down to cut down a tree *etc* with an axe: *He chopped down the fir tree*.

'chopper *n* **1** a knife *etc* for chopping. **2** a helicopter.

choppy /'tʃɒpɪ/ *adj* rather rough: *The ferry crossing was unpleasant because the sea was so choppy*. **'choppiness** *n*.

chopsticks /'tʃɒpstɪks/ *n* two thin sticks used to eat with.

choral /'kɔːrəl/ *adj* sung by a choir: *choral music*.

chord /kɔːd/ *n* a musical sound made by playing a number of notes together.

chore /tʃɔː(r)/ *n* a piece of housework or any hard or dull job: *everyday chores like shopping and cleaning*.

choreography /kɒrɪ'ɒɡrəfɪ/ *n* the arrangement of movements for dancing, especially ballet.

chorus /'kɔːrəs/ *n* **1** a large group of singers. **2** a group of singers and dancers in a musical show. **3** part of a song repeated after each verse. **4** something said or shouted by a number of people together: *a chorus of cheers*.

chose, chosen *see* **choose**.

Christ /kraɪst/ *n* Jesus.

christen /'krɪsən/ *v* to baptize and give a name to someone: *She was christened Joanna*.
'christening *n* a Christian ceremony in which a baby is christened.

Christian /'krɪstʃən/ *n* a believer in Christ. — *adj*: *the Christian religion*.
Christi'anity *n* the religion based on the teaching of Christ.
Christian name the name you are given in addition to your surname: *Peter is his Christian name*.

Christmas /'krɪsməs/ *n* an annual festival in memory of the birth of Christ, held on December 25, Christmas Day.
Christmas Eve December 24.
Christmas tree an evergreen tree on which decorations and gifts are hung.

chrome /krəʊm/ *n* a hard, silver-coloured, shiny metal: *The bumpers of the car are made of chrome*. — *adj* covered with chrome: *chrome taps*.

chronic /'krɒnɪk/ *adj* never getting better; permanent: *a chronic illness*. **'chronically** *adv*.

chronicle /'krɒnɪkəl/ *n* a record of events, described or listed in the order in which they happened. — *v* to make this kind of record of events: *He chronicled the progress of the war*.

chronological /krɒnə'lɒdʒɪkəl/ *adj* in order

of happening: *a chronological list of events.*
chrono'logically *adv.*
chrysanthemum /krɪ'sanθɪməm/ *n* a garden flower with a large, bushy head.
chubby /'tʃʌbɪ/ *adj* plump: *a baby's chubby face.*
chuck /tʃʌk/ *v* to throw: *Chuck this rubbish away.*
chuckle /'tʃʌkəl/ *v* to laugh quietly: *He sat chuckling over a funny book.* — *n* a quiet laugh: *He gave a chuckle.*
chug /tʃʌg/ *v* to move along with the engine making a gentle noise: *I could hear the boat chugging along the river; The old car chugged up the hill.*
chum /tʃʌm/ *n* a close friend: *a school chum.*
chunk /tʃʌŋk/ *n* a thick piece: *a chunk of bread.* **'chunky** *adj.*
church /tʃɜːtʃ/ *n* a building where Christians meet to pray together.

See **go.**

'churchyard *n* the ground round a church where dead people are buried.
churn /tʃɜːn/ *v* **1** to stir milk hard to produce butter. **2** to move or turn about violently.
churn out to keep on producing ideas, work *etc.*
chute /ʃuːt/ *n* **1** a steep, narrow slope for sending water, rubbish *etc* down. **2** a similar structure in a playground, for children to slide down.
cicada /sɪ'kɑːdə/ *n* an insect that makes a chirping noise.
cider /'saɪdə(r)/ *n* an alcoholic drink made from apples.
cigar /sɪ'gɑː(r)/ *n* a roll of tobacco leaves for smoking.
cigarette /sɪgə'rɛt/ *n* a tube of paper containing finely cut tobacco for smoking.
cigarette lighter a device used for lighting cigarettes and cigars.
cinder /'sɪndə(r)/ *n* a piece of burnt coal, wood *etc.*
cine camera /'sɪniː kamərə/ *n* a camera for taking moving pictures: *She used her new cine camera to film her son taking his first steps.*
cinema /'sɪnɪmə/ *n* **1** a building in which films are shown. **2** films and the film industry: *Are you interested in the cinema?*

See **go.**

cinnamon /'sɪnəmən/ *n* a yellowish-brown spice used in baking and cooking.
cipher /'saɪfə(r)/ *n* secret writing; a code.

circle /'sɜːkəl/ *n* **1** a round shape; a ring: *They stood in a circle.* **2** a group of people: *a circle of close friends.* **3** an upper floor of seats in a theatre *etc*: *We managed to get seats in the lower circle.* — *v* **1** to move in a circle: *The dancers circled round and round.* **2** to draw a circle round a word, number *etc*: *Circle the word you think is wrong.*
circuit /'sɜːkɪt/ *n* **1** a journey round something: *the earth's circuit round the sun; three circuits of the race-track.* **2** a race-track, running-track *etc.* **3** the path of an electric current.
circular /'sɜːkjʊlə(r)/ *adj* **1** having the form of a circle; round: *Plates are usually circular.* **2** leading back to the point from which it started: *a circular road.* — *n* a notice *etc*, especially advertising something, sent to many people: *We often get circulars advertising holidays.* **circu'larity** *n.*
circulate /'sɜːkjʊleɪt/ *v* **1** to go round in a fixed path coming back to a starting-point: *Blood circulates through the body.* **2** to spread around from person to person: *There's a story circulating that the art teacher is getting married.*
circu'lation *n* **1** the action or movement of circulating; the circulation of the blood. **2** the number of people who buy a particular newspaper *etc*: *This paper has a circulation of 1½ million.*
circumference /sə'kʌmfərəns/ *n* the line which marks out a circle; the edge of anything circular in shape; the length of this line: *the circumference of a wheel.*
circumstance /'sɜːkəmstəns/ *n* **1** a fact; a happening: *What were the circumstances that led you to telephone the police?* **2** (**circumstances**) conditions; surroundings: *They live in poor circumstances.*
in or **under no circumstances** never, for any reason at all: *She would not under any circumstances give away her secret.*
in or **under the circumstances** considering a particular situation: *It's not ideal, but it's the best we can do in the circumstances.*
circus /'sɜːkəs/ *n* a travelling show with performances by acrobats, clowns, animals *etc.*
cistern /'sɪstən/ *n* a tank for storing water.
citizen /'sɪtɪzən/ *n* **1** a person who lives in a city or town: *a citizen of London.* **2** a member of a state: *a British citizen; a citizen of the USA.*
'citizenship *n* the rights and duties of a citizen, especially of a particular country.
citrus fruit /'sɪtrəs fruːt/ *n* a type of juicy fruit

with thick skin and a sharp taste, such as the lemon, orange, lime *etc*.

city /'sɪtɪ/ *n* a very large town.

civic /'sɪvɪk/ *adj* having to do with a city or citizen: *The offices of the city council are in the civic centre*; *It is our civic duty to keep the city tidy*.

civil /'sɪvəl/ *adj* **1** polite, courteous. **2** having to do with the state or community: *civil rights*. **3** ordinary; not military or religious: *civil life*.

ci'vilian *n* a person who has a civil job, not in the armed forces.

ci'vility *n* politeness: *Treat strangers with civility*.

'civilly *adv* politely.

civil servant a member of the civil service.

civil service the organization which runs the administration of a state.

civil war a war between citizens of the same state: *the American Civil War*.

civilize /'sɪvəlaɪz/ *v* to change the ways of a primitive people to those found in a more advanced society: *The Romans tried to civilize the ancient Britons*.

civili'zation *n* **1** civilizing or being civilized: *the present state of civilization in the world*. **2** the way of life of a particular people: *the ancient Minoan civilization*.

'civilized *adj* **1** socially and culturally highly developed. **2** polite and reasonable: *Although they were angry, they discussed the problem in a civilized manner*.

clad /klad/ *adj* clothed: *clad in silk*.

claim /kleɪm/ *v* **1** to say that something is a fact: *He claims to be the best runner in the class*. **2** to demand as a right: *You must claim your money back if the goods are damaged*. **3** to say that you own something: *Does anyone claim this book?* — *n* **1** a statement that something is a fact: *His claim was false*. **2** a demand for something which you say you own or have a right to: *a rightful claim to the money*.

'claimant *n* a person who makes a claim.

clam /klam/ *n* a large shellfish with two shells joined together.

clam up to stop talking suddenly and refuse to speak any more: *After giving the police his name, he just clammed up*.

clamber /'klambə(r)/ *v* to climb using hands and feet: *They clambered over the rocks*.

clammy /'klamɪ/ *adj* damp and sticky: *clammy hands*; *clammy weather*.

clamour /'klamə(r)/ *n* a loud, continuous noise, especially of voices. — *v* to make a noise like this: *They're all clamouring to get their money back*.

clamp /klamp/ *n* a device for holding things together tightly. — *v* to hold things together with a clamp.

'clampdown *n* sudden, very strict control: *another government clampdown on pay increases*.

clamp down to bring something under very strict control or stop it altogether: *They are clamping down on illegal parking in the city centre*.

clan /klan/ *n* a tribe or group of related families.

clandestine /klan'dɛstɪn/ *adj* kept hidden or secret: *a clandestine meeting*.

clang /klaŋ/ *v* to make a loud, ringing sound: *The heavy gate clanged shut*. — *n* a ringing sound.

clank /klaŋk/ *v* to produce a sound like that made by metal hitting metal: *The chains clanked*. — *n* a noise like this.

clap /klap/ *v* **1** to strike your hands together: *When the singer appeared, the audience clapped*; *They clapped the song*; *Clap your hands to the music*. **2** to put your hand suddenly over something: *He clapped his hand over his mouth*. — *n* **1** a sudden noise of thunder. **2** the action of clapping: *They gave the performer a clap*.

clarify /'klarɪfaɪ/ *v* to make clear in meaning *etc*: *Please clarify your last statement*. **clarifi'cation** *n*.

clarinet /klarɪ'nɛt/ *n* a musical instrument played by blowing, made of wood: *He plays the clarinet in the school orchestra*. **clari'nettist** *n*.

clarity /'klarɪtɪ/ *n* **1** being easy to see, hear or understand: *She spoke with great clarity*. **2** clearness: *the clarity of the water*.

clash /klaʃ/ *n* **1** a loud noise of metal things striking together: *the clash of swords*. **2** a quarrel or fight: *a clash between the two armies*. — *v* **1** to strike together noisily: *The cymbals clashed*. **2** to disagree, quarrel or fight: *The workers clashed with their employer*. **3** not to go well together: *These two colours clash*. **4** to happen at the same time: *She can't go to the school dance because it clashes with her father's birthday party*.

> the **clash** (not **crash**) of swords.

clasp /klɑːsp/ *n* a hook *etc* used for holding things together: *the clasp of a necklace*. — *v* to grasp, hold tightly: *She clasped the money in her hand*.

class /klɑːs/ *n* **1** a group of people or things that are alike in some way: *The dog won first prize in its class in the dog show.* **2** one of a number of social groups: *the upper class; the middle class; the working class.* **3** a particular grade or level: *work of a very high class.* **4** a number of pupils or students taught together: *John and I are in the same class.* **5** a school lesson or college lecture *etc*: *a French class.* – *v* to put a person or thing in a particular class: *The film has been classed as suitable for adults only.*

'classmate *n* a pupil in the same class as you: *He invited some of his classmates to his party.*

'classroom *n* a room in a school where a class is taught.

classic /'klasɪk/ *n* a book or musical work that is generally considered very good and important: *works by Dickens and other popular classics.* — *adj* **1** known by everyone to be very good, or the best: *This is one of the classic textbooks on English grammar.* **2** simple, neat and smart: *a classic black dress.* **'classical** *adj*: *classical music.*

classify /'klasɪfaɪ/ *v* to put into a particular class or group: *The books are classified according to subject.* **classifi'cation** *n*.

'classified *adj* officially secret: *classified information.*

classified advertisements small advertisements in a newspaper that are put in by people who want to buy or sell something.

classy /'klɑːsɪ/ *adj* expensive and stylish: *They're staying in a classy hotel on the coast.*

clatter /'klatə(r)/ *n* a loud noise like hard objects falling, striking against each other *etc*: *the clatter of pots and pans.* — *v* to make a noise like this: *She clattered the dishes in the sink.*

clause /klɔːz/ *n* **1** a part of a sentence, such as either of the two parts of this sentence: *John has a friend/who is rich.* **2** a part of an official or legal agreement.

claustrophobia /klɒstrə'foʊbɪə/ *n* a feeling of fear and nervousness caused by being in a small, confined space: *He dislikes travelling in cars because he suffers from claustrophobia.* **claustro'phobic** *adj*.

claw /klɔː/ *n* **1** one of the hooked nails of an animal or bird: *The cat sharpened its claws on the tree-trunk.* **2** the foot of an animal or bird with hooked nails. **3** the leg of a crab *etc*. — *v* to scratch or tear at something with claws or nails: *The two cats clawed at each other.*

clay /kleɪ/ *n* a soft, sticky type of earth which is often baked into pottery, china, bricks *etc*.

clean /kliːn/ *adj* **1** free from dirt: *a clean dress.* **2** neat and tidy: *Cats are very clean animals.* **3** not yet used: *a clean sheet of paper.* — *v* to make or become free from dirt *etc*: *Will you clean the windows?* **'cleanly** *adv*. **'cleanness** *n*.

'cleaner *n* **1** a person whose job it is to clean. **2** something which cleans.

cleanliness /'klɛnlɪnəs/ *n* cleanness, especially in personal habits.

clean out to empty something and clean it thoroughly: *I'll clean the wardrobe out and find somewhere to put these new clothes.*

a clean slate a fresh start: *After being in prison he started his new job with a clean slate.*

clean up to clean a place thoroughly: *She cleaned the room up after they went home.*

come clean to tell the truth about something that you have been keeping secret: *She decided to come clean with her parents about her exam results.*

make a clean sweep to get rid of everything unnecessary or unwanted.

cleanse /klɛnz/ *v* to make something clean: *She cleansed her skin with soap and water.* **'cleanser** *n*.

clean-shaven /kliːn'ʃeɪvən/ *adj* without a beard or moustache.

clear /'klɪə(r)/ *adj* **1** easy to see through: *clear glass.* **2** free from cloud: *a clear sky.* **3** easy to see, hear or understand: *a clear explanation; The photograph is very clear.* **4** free from difficulty or dangers: *a clear road.* **5** free from doubt *etc*: *Are you quite clear about what I mean?* – *v* **1** to take something away which is in your way: *She cleared the floor of toys; He cleared the table.* **2** to declare someone innocent: *He was cleared of the murder.* **3** to become bright, free from cloud: *The sky cleared.* **4** to jump over and get past something without touching it: *He's the only athlete ever to have cleared 2.65 metres.* — *adv* away from something; not touching: *The car didn't hit him because he managed to jump clear.* **'clearness** *n*.

'clearance *n* **1** the removal of something: *clearance of trees.* **2** the distance between one object and another passing beside or under it: *The lorry passed under the bridge with a good six inches clearance.* **3** official permission to do something: *The plane did not have clearance to land.*

clear-'cut *adj* clear and definite: *clear-cut plans.*

clear-'headed *adj* able to think clearly.

'clearing *n* a piece of land cleared of trees *etc*: *a clearing in the forest.*

'clearly *adv* **1** in a clear way: *I couldn't see clearly for the mud on my glasses; You'll have to speak clearly – she's a little deaf.* **2** obviously; without doubt: *This has clearly been a great shock to all of you; Clearly we must do something about this at once.*

clear-'sighted *adj* able to understand situations and decide sensibly how to act.

clear away to return things to their proper place after use: *He cleared away the breakfast things; Remember to clear away when you've finished.*

clear off to go away: *He cleared off without saying a word.*

clear out 1 to get rid of something: *He cleared the rubbish out of the attic.* **2** to empty: *He has cleared out the attic.*

clear up 1 to tidy: *Clear up this mess!* **2** to become better *etc*: *If the weather clears up, we'll go for a picnic.* **3** to solve a problem or mystery *etc*: *There seems to be a misunderstanding here that we must clear up.*

clear your throat to cough slightly: *He cleared his throat and we guessed what he was going to say.*

stay clear, **steer clear** to avoid someone: *I always steer clear of her when she's angry.*

cleave /kli:v/ *v* to split. **'cleavage** *n*.

> **cleave**; **cleft** /klɛft/ or **clove** /kloʊv/; **cleft** or **'cloven** /'kloʊvən/: *He cleft (or clove) the rock in two; The rock was cleft (or cloven) in two by the blow.*

clef /klɛf/ *n* a symbol at the beginning of a piece of music, showing the pitch of the notes.

cleft[1] /klɛft/ *n* an opening; a split: *a cleft in the rocks.*

cleft[2] *see* **cleave**.

clemency /'klɛmənsɪ/ *n* mercy: *He appealed for clemency.*

clench /klɛntʃ/ *v* to close tightly together: *He clenched his fist.*

clergy /'klɜːdʒɪ/ *n* the ministers, priests *etc* of the Christian religion.

'clergyman *n* a priest, minister *etc*.

clerical[1] /'klɛrɪkəl/ *adj* having to do with the clergy.

clerical[2] /'klɛrɪkəl/ *adj* having to do with a clerk or with his work: *a clerical error.*

clerk /klɑːk/ *n* a person who deals with letters, accounts *etc* in an office.

clever /'klɛvə(r)/ *adj* **1** quick to learn and understand: *a clever child.* **2** skilful: *a clever carpenter.* **'cleverly** *adv*. **'cleverness** *n*.

> He is **cleverer** (not **more cleverer**) than I am.
> See also **wise**.

cliché /'kli:ʃeɪ/ *n* something that is said which everyone copies, so that it soon becomes boring: *Try not to use clichés when you're writing an essay.*

click /klɪk/ *n* a short, sharp sound: *the click of the camera.* — *v* to make this sound: *The gate clicked.*

client /'klaɪənt/ *n* **1** a person who receives advice from a lawyer, accountant *etc*. **2** a customer.

clientele /kli:ɒn'tɛl/ or /klaɪən'tɛl/ *n* customers or clients: *The shop has an extensive clientele.*

cliff /klɪf/ *n* a high steep rock, especially one facing the sea.

'cliff-hanger *n* an exciting story or situation in which the conclusion is left in doubt until the very end: *The chess match was a real cliff-hanger.*

climate /'klaɪmət/ *n* **1** the weather conditions of a region. **2** a region with certain weather conditions: *They moved to a warmer and drier climate.* **3** people's general opinions and attitudes at a particular time: *the current political climate.* **cli'matic** *adj*.

> **climate** means the general weather conditions, temperature, dryness or dampness *etc* of a country: *a tropical climate.*
> **weather** means the changing conditions from day to day: *windy weather; wet weather; What lovely weather is it today!*

climax /'klaɪmaks/ *n* the event or point of greatest interest or importance.

climb /klaɪm/ *v* to go up or towards the top of a mountain, wall, ladder *etc*: *He climbed up the ladder; The child climbed the tree.* — *n*: *It was a long climb to the top of the hill.* **'climber** *n*.

'climbing *n* the sport of climbing mountains or rocks: *go climbing at the weekend.*

clinch /klɪntʃ/ *v* to settle or come to an agreement about an argument, bargain *etc*: *The two companies clinched a deal which would mean greater profits for them both.*

cling /klɪŋ/ *v* to stick; to grip tightly: *The mud*

was clinging to her shoes; She clung to her husband as he said goodbye.

> **cling; clung** /klʌŋ/; **clung**: *He clung to the rope; They have always clung to the old customs.*

clinic /'klɪnɪk/ *n* a hospital where a particular kind of medical treatment or advice is given: *the skin clinic.* **'clinical** *adj.*

clink /klɪŋk/ *n* a ringing sound: *the clink of coins.* — *v* to make this sound: *They clinked their glasses together.*

clip¹ /klɪp/ *v* to fasten with a clip: *Clip these papers together.* — *n* something for holding things together or in position: *a paper-clip; a hair-clip.*

clip² /klɪp/ *v* **1** to cut with scissors or shears: *The shepherd clipped the sheep; The hedge was clipped.* **2** to hit sharply: *She clipped him over the ear.* — *n* **1** a cutting or clipping. **2** a sharp blow: *a clip on the ear.*
'clippers *n* a tool for clipping: *hedgeclippers; a pair of nail-clippers.*
'clipping *n* something cut out of a newspaper.

clique /kliːk/ *n* a group of people who are friendly with each other but keep others out of the group: *She had a special clique of school friends.*

cloak /kloʊk/ *n* **1** a loose outer garment without sleeves, covering most of the body. **2** something that hides: *They arrived under cloak of darkness.* — *v* to hide: *He used a false name to cloak his activities.*

clock /klɒk/ *n* **1** an instrument for measuring time, but not worn on the wrist like a watch: *an alarm clock.* **2** an instrument in a car that shows how far it has travelled: *This car has 40 000 miles on the clock.*
'clockwise *adv* in the direction of the movement of the hands of a clock.
'clockwork *n* the machinery of a clock or similar machinery.
round the clock all day and all night.
turn or **put the clock back** to return to the old-fashioned ideas or conditions of an earlier period: *The government were accused of wanting to put the clock back.*

clod /klɒd/ *n* a lump of earth.

clog¹ /klɒg/ *n* a shoe with a wooden sole.

clogs

clog² /klɒg/ *v* to block: *The drain is clogged with hair.*

cloister /'klɔɪstə(r)/ *n* a covered passageway round an open courtyard or garden in a monastery, cathedral or college.
'cloistered *adj* quiet and safe; away from the normal busy life of the world: *a cloistered life.*

clone /kloʊn/ *n* an exact copy of a thing or person that is produced artificially. — *v.*

close¹ /kloʊs/ *adv* **1** near in time, place *etc*: *He stood close to his mother; Follow close behind.* **2** tightly; neatly: *a close-fitting dress.* — *adj* **1** near in relationship; very dear: *a close friend.* **2** almost equal: *a close contest; The result was close.* **3** thorough: *Keep a close watch on him.* **4** tight: *a close fit.* **5** without fresh air: *There was a close atmosphere in the room.* **'closely** *adv.* **'closeness** *n.*

> **close**¹ means near: *A sister is a close relation.*
> **closed** means shut: *The door is closed.*

close call or **close shave** *ns* a narrow escape.
'close-up *n* a photograph or film taken near the subject.
close at hand nearby; not far off: *My mother lives close at hand.*
close by not far away: *He put the cup down on a table close by.*
close on almost; nearly: *She's close on sixty.*
close to 1 near in time, place, relationship *etc*: *It's close to 3 o'clock; Our house is close to the hospital; He's very close to his mother.* **2** almost; nearly: *close to fifty years of age.*
close up at or from a very short distance: *You can't see the crack in the vase until you look at it close up.*

close² /kloʊz/ *v* **1** to make or become shut: *The baby closed his eyes; Close the door; The shops close on Sundays.* **2** to finish: *The meeting closed with everyone in agreement.* — *n* the end: *the close of day.*
closed *adj* shut: *a closed door.*

open closed

See **close**¹.

closedown *n* the end of TV or radio programmes at night.

close down to close permanently: *The new supermarket has caused many small shops to close down.*

close in to get gradually nearer to and surround a person or place: *The enemy forces were beginning to close in on the town.*

close up 1 to come or bring closer: *Close up your letters — they're too spread out.* **2** to shut completely: *He closed up the house when he went on holiday.*

closet /ˈklɒzɪt/ *n* a cupboard: *a clothes closet.*

closure /ˈkloʊʒə(r)/ *n* closing: *the closure of a factory.*

clot /klɒt/ *n* soft or fluid matter formed into a solid mass: *a clot of blood.* — *v* to form into clots.

cloth /klɒθ/ *n* woven material from which clothes and many other things are made.

clothe /kloʊð/ *v* **1** to provide with clothes: *The widow did not have enough money to clothe her children.* **2** to dress: *She was clothed in silk.*

clothes *n* things you wear, such as a shirt, trousers, dress *etc*: *Her clothes are always smart and clean.*

> There is no singular form for **clothes**.

clothes line a rope that you hang washing on to dry.

clothes peg a peg for hanging washing up to dry.

ˈclothing *n* clothes: *warm clothing.*

> **clothing** is never used in the plural.

cloud /klaʊd/ *n* **1** a mass of tiny drops of water floating in the sky: *white clouds in a blue sky.* **2** a great number or quantity of anything small moving together: *a cloud of flies.* — *v* to become cloudy: *The sky clouded over and it began to rain.*

ˈcloudless *adj* clear and bright: *a cloudless sky.*

ˈcloudy *adj* **1** full of clouds: *The weather was cloudy today.* **2** not clear: *a cloudy photograph.*

cloud over to become full of clouds: *We abandoned the picnic when it began to cloud over.*

under a cloud not trusted or popular: *He left his job under a cloud when they accused him of unprofessional behaviour.*

clout /klaʊt/ *n* **1** a hit with the hand: *She gave him a clout round the ear.* **2** influence and power: *an organization with a lot of political clout.* — *v* to hit with your hand.

clove[1] /kloʊv/ *n* the flower bud of a tropical tree dried for use as a spice.

clove[2], **cloven** *see* **cleave**.

clown /klaʊn/ *n* a person who works in a circus, performing funny acts.

clown around, **clown about** to behave in a silly way.

club /klʌb/ *n* **1** a heavy stick *etc* used as a weapon. **2** a stick used in certain games, especially golf. **3** a number of people meeting for study, pleasure, games *etc*: *He joined the tennis club.* **4** the place where these people meet: *He goes to the club every Friday.* **5** one of the playing-cards of the suit clubs, which have black shapes on them like this, ♣: *the four of clubs.* — *v* to beat with a stick *etc*: *They clubbed him with a heavy stick.*

club together to share the cost of something: *The boys clubbed together to buy the teacher a bunch of flowers.*

cluck /klʌk/ *n* the sound made by a hen. — *v* to make this sound: *The hen was clucking in the yard.*

clue /kluː/ *n* anything that helps to solve a mystery, problem *etc*: *After she had given me a clue, I knew the answers at once.*

clued-up *adj* well-informed: *He's not at all clued-up about computers.*

not have a clue not to know at all: *'How does that work?' 'I haven't a clue.'*

clump[1] /klʌmp/ *n* a group: *a clump of trees.*

clump[2] /klʌmp/ *v* to walk heavily and noisily.

clumsy /ˈklʌmzɪ/ *adj* awkward in movement *etc*: *He's very clumsy — he's always dropping things.* **ˈclumsily** *adv.* **ˈclumsiness** *n.*

clung *see* **cling**.

cluster /ˈklʌstə(r)/ *n* a group of people or things close together: *a cluster of berries*; *They stood in a cluster.* — *v* to gather in clusters: *The children clustered round the door.*

clutch /klʌtʃ/ *v* **1** to take hold of something: *I clutched at a floating piece of wood to save myself from drowning.* **2** to hold tightly in your hands: *She was clutching a 50-cent piece.* — *n* **1** control or power: *He fell into the clutches of his enemy.* **2** a part of a motor-car engine used in changing the gears.

clutter /ˈklʌtə(r)/ *v* to fill or cover in an untidy way: *He cluttered up his desk*; *The room was cluttered with furniture.* — *n* a lot of useless things that take up too much space and look untidy: *His desk is full of clutter.*

co- /koʊ/ doing something together, as in the words **co-author**, **co-exist**.

coach /koʊtʃ/ n **1** a bus for travelling long distances. **2** a large four-wheeled carriage pulled by horses. **3** a railway carriage for passengers. **4** a person who trains sportsmen: *the tennis coach*. **5** a private teacher who prepares students for examinations. — v to prepare a person for an examination, contest *etc*: *He coached his friend for the Latin exam*.

coal /koʊl/ n a black substance burned as fuel for heating.
  '**coalmine** n a mine from which coal is dug.

coalition /koʊə'lɪʃən/ n a temporary agreement to work together for the same cause, usually between political parties with different opinions: *The government will never be beaten unless the other parties form a coalition*.

coarse /kɔːs/ adj **1** rough; not fine: *This coat is made of coarse material*. **2** rude; impolite: *coarse jokes*. '**coarsely** adv. '**coarseness** n.

coast /koʊst/ n the side or border of land next to the sea: *The coast was very rocky*. — v to travel downhill in a vehicle, on a bicycle *etc* without the use of any power.
  '**coastal** adj near the coast: *a coastal town*.
  '**coaster** n a small mat for putting under a drinking-glass *etc*.
  '**coastguard** n a person or group of people, employed as guards along the coast to help those in danger in boats and to prevent smuggling.
  '**coastline** n a coast as seen on a map or from the sea: *We could just see the coastline of France through the fog*.

coat /koʊt/ n **1** an outdoor garment with sleeves. **2** the hair or wool of an animal: *Some dogs have smooth coats*. **3** a covering of paint *etc*: *This wall will need two coats of paint*. — v to cover: *She coated the biscuits with chocolate*.
  '**coat-hanger** n a curved piece of wood, plastic *etc* with a hook for hanging up your clothes.
  '**coating** n a covering: *chocolate coating*.
  coat of arms a family badge.

coax /koʊks/ v to persuade someone by kindness or flattery: *He coaxed her into going to the dance by saying she was the best dancer he knew*; *He coaxed some money out of his mother*.

cobble[1] /'kɒbəl/ n a rounded stone used for making the surface of a street.
  '**cobbled** adj: *cobbled streets*.

cobble[2] /'kɒbəl/ v to mend shoes.
  '**cobbler** n a person who mends shoes.
  cobble together to make something quickly without enough care: *They just cobbled a report together from old bits of research*.

cobra /'koʊbrə/ n a poisonous snake found in India and Africa.

cobweb /'kɒbwɛb/ n a spider's web.

cocaine /koʊ'keɪn/ n a drug that is used to stop pain, but is also used by drug-addicts.

cock[1] /kɒk/ v **1** to set upright; to lift: *The dog cocked its ears*. **2** to tilt to one side: *He cocked his hat*.

cock[2] /kɒk/ n a male bird, especially of domestic poultry: *a cock and three hens*.

A cock **crows**.

cock-and-'bull story an unbelievable story.

cockatoo /kɒkə'tuː/ n a parrot with a large crest.

cock-crow /'kɒk-kroʊ/ n early morning: *He gets up at cock-crow*.

cockerel /'kɒkərəl/ n a young farmyard cock.

cock-eyed /kɒk'aɪd/ adj ridiculous: *a cock-eyed idea*.

cockle /'kɒkəl/ n a small shellfish that has a round, flat shell divided into two halves.

cockpit /'kɒkpɪt/ n a compartment in which the pilot of an aeroplane or the driver of a racing car *etc* sits.

cockroach /'kɒkroʊtʃ/ n an insect like a beetle that comes out at night in kitchens.

cocktail /'kɒkteɪl/ n **1** a mixed alcoholic drink. **2** a mixed dish: *a fruit cocktail*.

cocky /'kɒkɪ/ adj cheeky; conceited.

cocoa /'koʊkoʊ/ n **1** a powder made from the crushed seeds of the cacao tree, used in making chocolate. **2** a drink made from the powder: *a cup of cocoa*.

coconut /'koʊkənʌt/ n a very large nut containing a white solid lining and a clear liquid.

cocoon /kə'kuːn/ n a silk covering which the larvae of certain insects spin round themselves.

cod /kɒd/, *plural* **cod**, n a large edible fish found in northern seas.

code /koʊd/ n **1** a set of laws or rules: *a code of behaviour*. **2** a set of letters or signs used for writing or signalling: *The message was in a secret code*; *the Morse Code*. — v to put into a code: *Have you coded the material for the computer?*

co-education /koʊɛdjʊ'keɪʃən/ n the education of boys and girls in the same school or college. **co-edu'cational** adj.

coerce /koʊˈɜːs/ v to force a person into doing something: *He was coerced into joining the navy.* **coˈercion** n.

co-exist /koʊɪɡˈzɪst/ v to exist side by side, especially peacefully. **co-exˈistence** n.

coffee /ˈkɒfɪ/ n a drink made from the beans of a plant that grows, for instance, in Brazil. **ˈcoffee-pot** n a jug in which coffee is served. **ˈcoffee shop** n a café serving coffee *etc*. **coffee table** a small low table.

coffin /ˈkɒfɪn/ n a box for a dead body to be buried in.

cog /kɒɡ/ n a point like a tooth at the edge of a gearwheel (a kind of wheel used inside an engine *etc*).

coherent /koʊˈhɪərənt/ adj clear and sensible: *He was able to give a coherent account of what had happened.* **coˈherently** adv. **coˈherence** n.

coil /kɔɪl/ v to twist into rings: *The snake coiled round the tree.* — n a length of something which has been coiled: *a coil of rope; a coil of hair.*

coin /kɔɪn/ n a piece of metal used as money. — v 1 to make metal into money: *When was that sixpence coined?* 2 to invent a word, phrase *etc*: *Scientists often coin new words.*
ˈcoinage n the system of coins used in a country: *decimal coinage.*

coincide /koʊɪnˈsaɪd/ v 1 to happen at the same time: *Her arrival coincided with his departure.* 2 to be like or the same as something: *Their tastes in music coincide.*
coincidence /koʊˈɪnsədəns/ n an unlikely happening that comes about by chance: *By a strange coincidence we were both on the same train.* **coinciˈdental** adj. **coinciˈdentally** adv.

coke /koʊk/ n a fuel made from coal.

colander /ˈkɒləndə(r)/ or /ˈkʌləndə(r)/ n a metal or plastic bowl with a lot of small holes in it for draining water off vegetables *etc*.

cold /koʊld/ adj 1 low in temperature: *cold water; cold meat and salad.* 2 lower in temperature than is comfortable: *I feel cold.* 3 unfriendly: *His manner was cold.* — n 1 cold weather: *She cannot bear the cold in Britain.* 2 being or feeling cold: *He was blue with cold.* 3 an illness with sneezing, coughing *etc*: *She has caught a bad cold; Don't catch cold!* **ˈcoldly** adv. **ˈcoldness** n.
cold-ˈblooded adj 1 having blood like that of a fish, which becomes the same temperature as the surroundings of the body. 2 cruel and deliberate: *cold-blooded murder.*
get cold feet to lose courage: *I was going to apply for the job but I got cold feet.*
give someone the cold shoulder to show that you don't want to be friendly with a person: *All the neighbours gave her the cold shoulder.*

coleslaw /ˈkoʊlslɔː/ n a salad made of chopped raw cabbage, carrots and onions in mayonnaise.

collaborate /kəˈlæbəreɪt/ v 1 to work together with someone on a piece of work: *He and his brother collaborated on a book about aeroplanes.* 2 to give help to enemies who are occupying your country. **collaboˈration** n. **colˈlaborator** n.

collage /kɒˈlɑːʒ/ n a picture made by sticking pieces of paper, cloth *etc* on to a surface.

collapse /kəˈlæps/ v 1 to fall down and break into pieces: *The bridge collapsed under the weight of the traffic.* 2 to fall down because of illness, shock *etc*: *She collapsed with a heart attack.* 3 to break down; to fail: *The talks between the two countries have collapsed.* 4 to fold up: *Do these chairs collapse?* — n: *economic collapse; The storm caused the collapse of several buildings.* **colˈlapsible** adj.

collar /ˈkɒlə(r)/ n 1 the part of a shirt, jacket *etc* which goes round your neck: *This collar is too tight.* 2 a strap *etc* fastened round the neck: *The dog's name was on its collar.*
ˈcollarbone n either one of two long bones joining the shoulder-blade to the base of the neck.

colleague /ˈkɒliːɡ/ n a person who works with you, or who does the same kind of work as you do: *He gets on well with his colleagues.*

collect /kəˈlekt/ v 1 to bring or come together; to gather: *I collect stamps; I'm collecting money for cancer research; He's trying to collect his thoughts; A few people had collected round the man's body.* 2 to fetch: *She collects the children from school each day.*
colˈlection n 1 the collecting of something: *This parcel is waiting for collection.* 2 a set of objects collected: *a stamp collection.* 3 asking for money from a number of people in a church or for a charity *etc*: *a collection for the poor.*
colˈlective adj of a group of people *etc*: *This success was the result of collective effort.* — n a farm or organization run by a group of workers for the good of all of them. **colˈlectively** adv.

col'lector *n* a person who collects: *a ticket-collector; a stamp-collector.*

collect yourself to make an effort to become calm after being angry or upset: *She stopped to collect herself and then continued as if nothing had happened.*

collect your thoughts to prepare yourself mentally: *I tried to collect my thoughts before going into the exam.*

college /ˈkɒlɪdʒ/ *n* a school for higher education: *She went to college after she had finished school.*

collide /kəˈlaɪd/ *v* to strike together with great force: *The cars collided in the fog; The van collided with a lorry.*

> See **knock**.

collision /kəˈlɪʒən/ *n* a crash; a violent striking together: *Ten people were injured in the collision between the bus and the car.*

colloquial /kəˈloʊkwɪəl/ *adj* used in everyday conversation; not formal: *'Cheerio' is a colloquial expression for goodbye.* **col'loquially** *adv*.

colon /ˈkoʊlən/ *n* the punctuation mark (:).

colonel /ˈkɜːnəl/ *n* an army officer in charge of a regiment.

colonial /kəˈloʊnɪəl/ *adj* having to do with a country's colonies abroad: *Britain's former colonial territories.* **co'lonialism** *n*.

colonize /ˈkɒlənaɪz/ *v* to establish a colony in a place: *The settlers colonized the newly-discovered land.* **'colonist** *n*. **coloni'zation** *n*.

colony /ˈkɒlənɪ/ *n* **1** a settlement of people living in a foreign country but governed by their own native country: *a former British colony.* **2** a group of animals, birds *etc*, of the same type, living together: *a colony of gulls.*

colossal /kəˈlɒsəl/ *adj* very big; enormous: *a colossal increase in the price of books.*

colour /ˈkʌlə(r)/ *n* **1** a quality which objects show when light falls on them: *What colour is her dress?*; *Red, blue and yellow are colours.* **2** the shade of a person's skin — white, brown, black *etc*: *People of all colours.* **3** interesting and exciting details: *The article is good, but can you add a little more colour?* — *adj* in colour, not black and white: *a colour film; colour television.* — *v* **1** to put colour on a picture *etc*: *Colour the sea green.* **2** to influence thoughts or opinions *etc*: *Don't allow one bad experience to colour your attitude to everything.*

> I bought a **red** (not **red colour**) jacket.

'coloured *adj* **1** having colour: *The garden is full of brightly coloured flowers.* **2** belonging to a dark-skinned race.

> You say **colour** photographs, a **colour** film, **colour** television, but **coloured** pencils, an orange-**coloured** cat.

'colour-blind *adj* unable to tell the difference between certain colours.

'colourful *adj* **1** full of colour: *a colourful pattern.* **2** full of interesting details: *a colourful description.*

'colouring *n* **1** something used to give colour: *She put pink colouring in the icing.* **2** the colour of a person's skin and hair: *She has fair colouring.*

'colourless *adj* **1** without colour: *a colourless liquid like water.* **2** dull and uninteresting: *He's rather a colourless character.*

off colour unwell: *she's been feeling a bit off colour lately.*

show yourself in your true colours to do something that shows the faults in your character.

with flying colours with great success: *He passed his exam with flying colours.*

colt /koʊlt/ *n* a young horse.

column /ˈkɒləm/ *n* **1** a stone or wooden pillar used to support a building. **2** something similar in shape: *a column of smoke.* **3** a line of numbers, print *etc* stretching from top to bottom of a page: *a column of figures; a newspaper column.* **4** a section in a newspaper, often written regularly by a particular person: *He writes a daily column about sport.* **5** a long line of vehicles *etc*, one behind the other.

'columnist *n* a person who writes a regular article in a newspaper.

coma /ˈkoʊmə/ *n* a long-lasting unconscious state.

comb /koʊm/ *n* **1** an object with a row of teeth for making your hair tidy. **2** a crest that sticks up on the head of some birds. — *v* **1** to tidy your hair with a comb: *Wash your hands and comb your hair before coming to lunch.* **2** to search a place thoroughly: *They combed the hills for the missing climber.*

combat *n* /ˈkɒmbat/ a fight or struggle. — *v* /ˈkɒmbat/ or /kəmˈbat/ to fight or struggle against something: *doing everything possible to combat the government's plans to build a motorway.*

'combatant *n* a person who is fighting.

combination /kɒmbɪˈneɪʃən/ *n* **1** the combining of two or more things: *The colour* *orange is a combination of yellow and red.* **2** a set of numbers used to open certain types of lock: *You need the combination to open the safe.*

combine *v* /kəmˈbaɪn/ to join or mix together: *They combined forces to fight the enemy; You can produce green by combining blue with yellow.* — *n* /ˈkɒmbaɪn/ a group of businesses that have joined together.

combustible /kəmˈbʌstɪbəl/ *adj* capable of catching fire and burning: *combustible materials.*

combustion /kəmˈbʌstʃən/ *n* burning: *the combustion of gases.*

come /kʌm/ *v* **1** to move *etc* towards a place or person: *I'm coming to your house tomorrow; Come here!; John came to see me; Have any letters come for me?* **2** to draw near: *Christmas is coming soon.* **3** to happen or be placed: *The letter 'd' comes between 'c' and 'e' in the alphabet.* **4** to happen: *How did you come to break your leg?* **5** to arrive at a certain state *etc*: *What are things coming to?; We have come to an agreement.* **6** to add up to a certain number: *The total comes to 51.* **7** to be a product of something: *Wool comes from sheep.* **8** to be available: *This dress only comes in sizes 10 – 14.*

> **come; came** /keɪm/; **come:** *He came into the room; A letter has come for you.*

'comeback *n* a return, especially to show business: *The actress made a comeback.*

come about to happen: *How did that come about?*

come across 1 to meet by chance: *He came across some old friends.* **2** to come over: *His speech came across well.*

come along 1 to go with; to accompany: *Come along with me!* **2** to progress: *How are things coming along?*

come at to attack: *He came at me with a knife.*

come back 1 to return: *You must come back again soon.* **2** to be remembered: *The horror of the accident came back to her gradually.* **3** to become popular again: *Trousers with flared bottoms are coming back.*

come by to get: *How did you come by that black eye?*

come down to decrease; to become less: *Tea has come down in price.*

come down with to get an illness: *Jane's come down with flu.*

come forward to offer or present oneself, usually to help in some way: *Several people came forward when he asked for volunteers.*

come from to be born or live in: *She comes from Paris.*

come in for to receive blame *etc*: *The Prime Minister has come in for a lot of criticism recently.*

come off 1 to fall off: *Her shoe came off.* **2** to turn out well; to succeed: *Our plan didn't come off.*

come on 1 to appear on stage or the screen: *They waited for the comedian to come on.* **2** hurry up!: *Come on – we'll be late for the party!* **3** don't be ridiculous!: *Come on, you don't really expect me to believe that!* **4** to make progress: *The new project is coming on fine.*

come out 1 to become known: *The truth finally came out.* **2** to be published: *This newspaper comes out once a week.* **3** to be developed: *This photograph has come out well.* **4** to be removed: *This dirty mark won't come out.* **5** to appear: *The sun has come out.*

come out in to become covered in; to develop: *He has come out in spots.*

come over 1 to affect someone: *I don't know what has come over him.* **2 come over** or **come across** to make a particular impression: *She came across as a very sensible woman.*

come round to change your mind and accept an idea *etc*: *I knew she would eventually come round to our way of thinking.*

come round or **come to** to become conscious again: *He came to several hours after the accident.*

come through to survive or recover from: *He came through the ordeal well; The doctors expect him to come through the operation without any problems.*

come to light to be discovered: *The theft only came to light when the owners returned from holiday.*

come up 1 to be about to happen; to appear: *The schools have a holiday coming up soon.* **2** to happen unexpectedly: *I'm afraid something has come up and I'll be late home.* **3** to be mentioned in a conversation: *The subject of education came up several times.*

come up against to find a problem that you must deal with: *The police are coming up against more violence in the streets these days.*

come upon to find by chance: *She came upon a solution to the problem.*

come up with to think of: *He has come up with a great idea.*

comings and goings movements to and fro: *the comings and goings of people in the street.*

to come in the future: *in the days to come.*

comedian /kə'miːdɪən/ *n* a performer who tells jokes or acts in comedies.

comedy /'kɒmədɪ/ *n* **1** a funny play: *We went to see a comedy last night.* **2** the art of making people laugh: *She has a talent for comedy.*

> The opposite of **comedy** is **tragedy**.

comet /'kɒmɪt/ *n* a sort of star that travels across the sky with a trail of light behind it.

comfort /'kʌmfət/ *v* to calm or console someone: *The mother comforted the weeping child.* — *n* **1** a pleasant condition of being relaxed, happy, warm *etc*: *He enjoys the comfort of home life.* **2** something that makes you happier when you are sad: *The children were a great comfort to her when her husband died.* **3** a luxury: *the comforts of the hotel.*

'comfortable *adj* **1** in comfort: *He looked very comfortable in his chair.* **2** giving comfort: *a comfortable chair.* **'comfortably** *adv*.

> The opposite of **comfort** (sense 1) is **discomfort**.
> The opposite of **comfortable** is **uncomfortable**.

comic /'kɒmɪk/ *adj* **1** having to do with comedy: *a comic actor; a comic opera.* **2** funny: *comic remarks.* — *n* **1** an amusing person, especially a comedian. **2** a children's magazine with funny stories, adventures *etc* in the form of comic strips.

'comical *adj* funny: *It was comical to see the chimpanzee pouring out a cup of tea.*

comic strip a series of small pictures showing stages in an adventure.

comma /'kɒmə/ *n* the punctuation mark (,).

> See the section called **Punctuation** on page 617.

command /kə'mɑːnd/ *v* **1** to order: *I command you to leave the room immediately!* **2** to be in control of something: *He commanded a regiment of soldiers.* — *n* **1** an order: *They obeyed his commands.* **2** control: *He was in command of the operation.* **3** the ability to use your knowledge of something: *She has got a good command of the language.*

comman'dant *n* an officer who has the command of a place or of troops.

commandeer /kɒmən'dɪə(r)/ *v* to take control or possession of something officially or unfairly: *The soldiers commandeered his truck.*

com'mander *n* a person who commands: *He was the commander of the expedition.*

commander-in-'chief *n* the most senior officer in command of an army, or of the entire forces of the state.

com'manding *adj* **1** in a position of power, control or leadership: *a country with a commanding position in world affairs; his commanding officer.* **2** powerful and confident: *She is a strong, commanding woman who isn't afraid of arguing with her opponents.* **3** giving good views all round: *The house is in a commanding position on a hill.*

com'mandment *n* a command given by God, especially one of the ten given to Moses.

commando /kə'mɑːndoʊ/, *plural* **com-'mandos**, *n* a soldier trained for tasks requiring special courage and skill.

commemorate /kə'mɛmərɛɪt/ *v* to remember someone or something by holding a ceremony or putting up a monument: *His death is commemorated every year; This monument commemorates those who died in the war.* **commemo'ration** *n*.

commence /kə'mɛns/ *v* to begin: *When does the school term commence?* **com-'mencement** *n*.

> You commence **working** or **writing** (not **to work** or **to write**).

commend /kə'mɛnd/ *v* to praise: *His ability was commended.*

com'mendable *adj* worthy of praise.

commen'dation *n* praise.

comment /'kɒmɛnt/ *n* a remark: *He made several comments about her untidy appearance.* — *v* to make a remark: *He commented on her appearance.*

'commentary *n* the comments of a reporter at a sports event *etc*, broadcast on radio or television.

'commentate *v* to give a commentary.

'commentator *n* someone whose job is to broadcast a commentary at a sports event *etc*.

no comment a way of refusing to answer a question.

commerce /'kɒmɜːs/ *n* the buying and selling of goods between nations or people; trade.

com'mercial *adj* **1** connected with commerce: *a commercial agreement.* **2** paid for by advertisements: *commercial television.* — *n* a TV or radio advertisement. **com'mercially** *adv.*

commercialized /kəˈmɜːʃəlaɪzd/ *adj* to do with trying to make money: *It's a pity Christmas has become so commercialized.*

commiserate /kəˈmɪzəreɪt/ *v* to express sympathy for a person's sadness or disappointment.
commise'ration *n*: *Congratulations to the winners and commiserations to the losers.*

commission /kəˈmɪʃən/ *n* **1** money earned by a person who sells things for someone else. **2** an order for a work of art: *He was given a commission to paint the president's portrait.* **3** a paper giving authority to an officer in the army *etc.* **4** a group of people appointed to find out about something and make a report: *a commission on education.* — *v* to give a commission or power to someone: *He was commissioned to paint the president's portrait.*

> **commission** is spelt with -mm- and -ss-.

com'missioner *n* a representative of the government in a district *etc.*

commit /kəˈmɪt/ *v* **1** to do something illegal: *He committed the crime when he was drunk.* **2** to make a definite promise or decision: *Think carefully before committing yourself.* **3** to give something or someone to be looked after by someone else: *She was committed to their care.*

> **committing** and **committed** are spelt with two **t**s.

com'mitted *adj* giving a lot of your time and energy to something because you think it is important: *This government is committed to reducing unemployment.*
com'mitment *n* **1** a task that must be done. **2** strong support for something that you believe is right: *We are looking for a teacher with enthusiasm and commitment.*

> **commitment** is spelt with one **t**.

committee /kəˈmɪtɪ/ *n* a number of people selected from a larger group to deal with some special business: *The committee meets today.* — *adj: a committee meeting.*

> **committee** is spelt with -mm-, -tt-, -ee.

commodity /kəˈmɒdɪtɪ/ *n* an article which is bought or sold: *tea, rice and other commodities.*

common /ˈkɒmən/ *adj* **1** seen or happening often; quite normal or usual: *These birds are not common here.* **2** shared by everyone: *We use English as a common language.* **3** of ordinary, not high, social rank: *the common people.*
'commonly *adv: Spinach is commonly believed to give you strength.*
'commonplace *adj* very ordinary and uninteresting: *The comments range from the commonplace to the highly imaginative.*
'common-room *n* a sitting-room for students or teachers in a college *etc.*
common ground something that two or more people agree about: *There seems to be no common ground at all between the two sides.*
common sense practical good sense: *If he has any common sense he'll change jobs.*
in common shared; similar: *He and his girlfriend have a lot of interests in common.*

commonwealth /ˈkɒmənwɛlθ/ *n* an association of states that have joined together for their common good.

commotion /kəˈmoʊʃən/ *n* noise and confusion: *He was woken by a commotion in the streets.*

communal /ˈkɒmjʊnəl/ *adj* shared with others: *a communal kitchen.*

commune /ˈkɒmjuːn/ *n* a group of people living together and sharing everything they own.

communicate /kəˈmjuːnɪkeɪt/ *v* **1** to give someone information *etc*: *She communicated the facts to him.* **2** to speak or write to someone: *We can communicate with each other by telephone.*
com'municating *adj* linking two rooms *etc*: *a communicating door.*
communi'cation *n* **1** sending messages by letter, telephone *etc*: *The telephone is the quickest means of communication.* **2** a means of getting messages and supplies to an army: *Their line of communications was cut off.* **3** a message.
com'municative *adj* enjoying or willing to talk to other people: *The prisoner had not been very communicative so far.*

> The opposite of **communicative** is **uncommunicative**.

communion /kəˈmjuːnjən/ *n* the sharing of thoughts and feelings; fellowship.
communism /ˈkɒmjʊnɪzm/ *n* a system of

government under which there is no private industry and very little private property, most things being owned by the state.

'communist *n* a person who believes in communism.

community /kə'mju:nɪtɪ/ *n* **1** the people who live in a certain area: *It's time this community had a swimming-pool.* **2** the public in general: *He did it for the good of the community.*

commute /kə'mju:t/ *v* to travel regularly between two places, especially between home in the suburbs and work in the city.

com'muter *n* a person who commutes.

compact *adj* /kəm'pakt/ or /'kɒmpakt/ fitted neatly in a small space: *a nice compact kitchen.* — *n* /'kɒmpakt/ a small flat container for women's face powder.

com'pactly *adv*.

compact disc a disc with high-quality sound recorded on it, played on a machine with a laser beam (**a compact-disc player**).

companion /kəm'panjən/ *n* **1** a person *etc* who accompanies another person as a friend: *a travelling companion.* **2** a helpful handbook on a particular subject: *The Gardening Companion.*

com'panionship *n* friendship; being with someone: *She enjoys the companionship of young people.*

company /'kʌmpənɪ/ *n* **1** a number of people joined together for trade *etc*; a business firm: *a glass-manufacturing company.* **2** companionship: *I was grateful for her company; She's always good company.* **3** a group of companions: *He got into bad company.* **4** a large group of soldiers.

keep someone company to go, stay *etc* with someone: *I'll keep you company.*

comparable /'kɒmpərəbəl/ *adj* similar: *These two materials are comparable in thickness.*

comparative /kəm'parətɪv/ *adj* **1** judged by comparing with something else; moderate or reasonable: *the comparative quiet of the suburbs.* **2** 'comparative' is used to describe adjectives and adverbs used in comparisons, like these underlined words: *I'm younger than you; You look better today.* — *n*.

> See the section called **Comparing** on page 614.

com'paratively *adv* moderately; fairly: *This house was comparatively cheap.*

compare /kəm'pɛə(r)/ *v* **1** to put things side by side to see how far they are alike, or which is better: *If you compare his work with hers, you will find hers more accurate; This is a good essay compared with your last one.* **2** to describe as being similar to: *She compared him to a monkey.* **3** to be of the same quality: *His intelligence doesn't compare with that of the other boys.*

> **compare with** is used to bring out similarities and differences between two things of the same type: *He compared his pen with mine and decided mine was better.*
>
> **compare to** is used when pointing out a similarity between two different things: *Stars are often compared to diamonds.*

com'parison *n*: *Living here is cheap in comparison with London.*

compartment /kəm'pɑ:tmənt/ *n* **1** a separate enclosed part: *The drawer was divided into compartments.* **2** a closed-in section of seats in a railway carriage.

compass /'kʌmpəs/ *n* an instrument with a magnetized needle, used to find directions.

'compasses *n* an instrument with two movable legs, for drawing circles *etc*, also called **a pair of compasses**: *My compasses have broken — lend me your pair of compasses.*

compassion /kəm'paʃən/ *n* pity for the sufferings of another person. **com'passionate** *adj*.

compatible /kəm'patɪbəl/ *adj* able to exist or work well together: *I don't know why they got married — they are not compatible at all.* **compati'bility** *n*.

> The opposite of **compatible** is **incompatible**.

compel /kəm'pɛl/ *v* to force: *She compelled me to tell her the truth.*

com'pelling *adj* **1** holding your interest and attention completely: *a compelling story.* **2** convincing: *a compelling argument.*

compensate /'kɒmpənseɪt/ *v* to make up for loss or wrong especially by giving money: *This payment will compensate her for the loss of her job.*

compen'sation *n* money *etc* given for loss or injury.

compère /'kɒmpɛə(r)/ *n* a person who introduces the different acts in an entertainment.

compete /kəm'pi:t/ *v* to try to beat others in a contest *etc*: *We are competing against the South African team in the next round of the competition; The two boys will be competing with each other for the scholarship.*

competent /ˈkɒmpətənt/ *adj* **1** skilled: *a competent pianist*. **2** able; capable: *Is he competent enough to fly solo?*. **'competence** *n*. **'competently** *adv*.

> The opposite of **competent** is **incompetent**.

competition /kɒmpəˈtɪʃən/ *n* **1** competing; rivalry. **2** a contest for a prize: *Have you entered the drawing competition?* **3** the people you are competing against: *We must find out what the competition is planning*.

com'petitive *adj* **1** liking to compete with others: *Most children are competitive*. **2** organized as a competition: *tennis, football and other competitive sports*.

com'petitor *n* a person who takes part in a competition: *All 200 competitors finished the race*.

compile /kəmˈpaɪl/ *v* to make a book, list *etc* from information that you have collected: *He compiled a French dictionary*. **compi'lation** *n*. **com'piler** *n*.

complacent /kəmˈpleɪsənt/ *adj* feeling satisfied with what you have done. **com'placency** *n*. **com'placently** *adv*.

complain /kəmˈpleɪn/ *v* **1** to express your dissatisfaction *etc*: *I'm going to complain to the police about the noise*. **2** to say that you have a pain *etc*: *He's complaining of a pain in his chest*.

com'plaint *n* **1** something you say to show that you are dissatisfied: *The customer made a complaint about the dirt in the food shop*. **2** a sickness *etc*: *A cold is not a serious complaint*.

complement /ˈkɒmplɪmənt/ *n* **1** something that is added to something else to make it complete: *In the sentence 'I am a doctor', 'a doctor' is the complement of 'I am'*. **2** something that goes well with something else: *Yoghurt can be used as a complement to spicy food*. — *v* to go together well with: *His dark good looks complement her blonde beauty*.

> the **complement** (not **compliment**) of a verb.

comple'mentary *adj* combining well to form a complete, single or balanced whole: *two complementary approaches to the same problem*.

complete /kəmˈpliːt/ *adj* **1** whole; with nothing missing: *a complete set of stamps*. **2** thorough; absolute: *a complete surprise*. **3** finished: *My picture will soon be complete*. — *v* to finish: *When will he complete the job?*

com'pletely *adv*: *I am completely satisfied*. **com'pleteness** *n*.

completion /kəmˈpliːʃən/ *n* finishing: *You will be paid on completion of the work*.

complex /ˈkɒmplɛks/ or /kəmˈplɛks/ *adj* **1** composed of many parts: *a complex piece of machinery*. **2** complicated or difficult: *a complex problem*. — *n* **1** something made up of many different pieces: *a sports complex*. **2** emotions that always upset a person in a particular situation or about a particular subject: *She has a complex about her weight and won't accept that she's not fat*.

complexion /kəmˈplɛkʃən/ *n* the colour or appearance of the skin of the face: *She has a pale complexion*.

complexity /kəmˈplɛksɪtɪ/ *n* **1** being complex: *He doesn't understand the complexity of the situation*. **2** one of the many different parts that make something complicated: *I'll explain the complexities of the matter later*.

compliance /kəmˈplaɪəns/ *n* agreement; obedience.

com'pliant *adj* willing to comply.

complicate /ˈkɒmplɪkeɪt/ *v* to make something more difficult: *These extra lessons will complicate the timetable*.

'complicated *adj* difficult to understand: *complicated instructions*.

compli'cation *n* **1** something making a situation more difficult. **2** a development in an illness *etc* which makes it worse.

compliment /ˈkɒmplɪmənt/ *n* something that is said in praise or flattery: *He's always paying her compliments*. — *v* to praise: *He complimented her on her cooking*.

> to pay a **compliment** (not **complement**).

compli'mentary *adj* **1** flattering or praising: *complimentary remarks*. **2** given free: *a complimentary ticket to the circus*.

with compliments with good wishes, used when sending a gift *etc*: *'sent with the compliments of the manager'*.

comply /kəmˈplaɪ/ *v* to obey: *You must comply with the teacher's instructions*.

component /kəmˈpoʊnənt/ *n* one of the pieces that are put together to make a machine *etc*.

compose /kəmˈpoʊz/ *v* **1** to form by putting parts together: *A word is composed of several letters*. **2** to write music, poetry *etc*: *Mozart began to compose when he was six years old*.

com'posed *adj* **1** made up of: *The committee is composed of three women and three men.* **2** calm; in control of your feelings: *She was very nervous, but managed to appear composed.*

com'poser *n* a writer of music.

compo'sition *n* **1** something that has been composed: *a musical composition.* **2** an essay written as a school exercise: *The children had to write a composition about their holiday.* **3** composing: *She studied composition at music college.*

compose yourself to become calm after being angry, upset or nervous: *He gave her a moment to compose herself before telling her the details.*

compost /'kɒmpɒst/ *n* rotting plants and manure that are added to the soil to make it better and richer for growing things: *He uses compost on his garden; a compost heap.*

composure /kəm'poʊʒə(r)/ *n* being calm and in control of your feelings: *He managed to recover his composure.*

compound¹ /'kɒmpaʊnd/ *adj* made up of a number of parts. — *n* a substance, word *etc* formed from two or more parts or words: *The word 'racetrack' is a compound; chemical compounds.*

compound² *n* /'kɒmpaʊnd/ a fenced or walled-in area, for example round a factory, school *etc*. — *v* /kəm'paʊnd/ to add to something and make it worse: *Her sadness was compounded by the knowledge that he had lied to her.*

comprehend /kɒmprɪ'hɛnd/ *v* **1** to understand. **2** to include.

compre'hensible *adj* understandable: *The words were too difficult to be comprehensible to the children.*

> The opposite of **comprehensible** is **incomprehensible**.

compre'hension *n* **1** understanding: *The teacher asked the children questions to test their comprehension of the story she had just read to them.* **2** an exercise that tests how well you understand something: *a listening comprehension.*

compre'hensive *adj* including many things: *This will be one of the most comprehensive reforms yet.*

compress /kəm'prɛs/ *v* to press or squash together very tightly. **com'pression** *n*.

comprise /kəm'praɪz/ *v* to contain: *The team comprises five members.*

> The book **comprises** (not **comprises of**) ten chapters.
> 'The book **consists of** ten chapters' is correct.

compromise /'kɒmprəmaɪz/ *n* an agreement in which each side gives up something it has previously demanded: *We argued for a long time but finally arrived at a compromise.* — *v* **1** to achieve a compromise: *Neither side seems willing to compromise.* **2** to act in a way that leads other people to criticize you: *He refused to compromise himself by taking money from them.*

compulsion /kəm'pʌlʃən/ *n* force that makes you do something: *You are not under any compulsion to go to the disco if you don't want to.*

compulsive /kəm'pʌlsɪv/ *adj* **1** very interesting; fascinating: *a compulsive book.* **2** unable to stop doing something: *She is a compulsive shopper.* **com'pulsively** *adv.*

compulsory /kəm'pʌlsərɪ/ *adj* having to be done; completely necessary: *Is it compulsory for me to attend the class?; a compulsory examination.*

> See **voluntary**.

compute /kəm'pjuːt/ *v* to calculate. **compu'tation** *n.*

com'puter *n* an electronic machine capable of storing and processing large amounts of information and of performing calculations.

com'puterize *v* to organize some process or system so that it is dealt with by computer.

com'puting *n* the skill of using computers: *They study computing at school.*

comrade /'kɒmrɪd/ or /'kɒmreɪd/ *n* a close companion: *his comrades at school.*

'comradeship *n* friendship.

con /kɒn/ *v* to trick: *He conned her into giving him money.* — *n* a dishonest trick.

concave /kɒŋ'keɪv/ *adj* curved inwards: *Spoons are concave.*

> See **convex**.

conceal /kən'siːl/ *v* to hide: *He concealed the letter under his pillow.* **con'cealment** *n.*

concede /kən'siːd/ *v* **1** to admit: *He conceded that he had been wrong.* **2** to allow someone to have something: *to concede a privilege to someone.*

conceit /kən'siːt/ *n* too much pride in yourself.

> **conceit** is spelt with **-ei-**.

con'ceited *adj* having too much pride in yourself: *She's very conceited about her good looks.*

conceive /kən'siːv/ *v* **1** to form an idea *etc* in your mind. **2** to imagine: *I can't conceive why you did that.* **3** to become pregnant. **con'ceivable** *adj* possible to imagine or believe: *We tried every conceivable tool, but the lock wouldn't move.* **con'ceivably** *adv*.

> **conceive** is spelt with **-ei-**.
> The opposite of **conceivable** is **inconceivable**.

concentrate /'kɒnsəntreɪt/ *v* **1** to give all your attention to one thing: *I wish you'd concentrate on what I'm saying.* **2** to make a liquid *etc* thicker or purer. **3** to bring or come together in one place: *He concentrated his troops on the shore.* **concen'tration** *n*.
'concentrated *adj* very strong; not diluted: *concentrated orange juice.*

concentric /kən'sentrɪk/ *adj* used about circles inside each other that all have the same centre.

concept /'kɒnsept/ *n* an idea of something that you have in your mind: *the concept of freedom.*
con'ception *n* **1** conceiving. **2** understanding: *We can have no conception of the size of the universe.*

concern /kən'sɜːn/ *v* **1** to have to do with someone or something: *That new rule doesn't concern us*; *So far as I'm concerned, you can do what you like.* **2** to worry: *Don't concern yourself about my safety*; *You needn't concern yourself with make-up at your age.* — *n* **1** someone's business: *This is not your concern.* **2** worry: *The lack of rain is causing concern.* **3** a business; a firm: *a big textile concern.*
con'cerning *prep* about: *He wrote to me concerning a business arrangement.*

concert /'kɒnsət/ *n* a musical entertainment.

concerted /kən'sɜːtɪd/ *adj* done by a group of people working together: *They made a concerted effort and finished quickly.*

concertina /kɒnsə'tiːnə/ *n* a musical instrument like a small accordion, played by pulling the sides apart and squeezing them together again: *The clown played the concertina.*

concerto /kən'tʃeətoʊ/, *plural* **con'certos**, *n* a piece of music that is written for one or more solo instruments and an orchestra: *a piano concerto.*

concession /kən'seʃən/ *n* **1** something that has been allowed: *As a concession, he was allowed a day off school to go to his sister's wedding.* **2** a reduction in the price of something for certain groups of people: *Concessions are available for students.*

conciliate /kən'sɪlɪeɪt/ *v* to win over someone previously unfriendly or angry. **concili'ation** *n*.

concise /kən'saɪs/ *adj* short and accurate: *a concise statement.* **con'cisely** *adv*.

conclude /kən'kluːd/ *v* **1** to finish; to bring to an end: *to conclude a meeting*; *He concluded by thanking everyone.* **2** to think, as a result of something: *I concluded from the silence that the children were asleep.*

conclusion /kən'kluːʒən/ *n* **1** an end: *the conclusion of his speech.* **2** a judgement: *I came to the conclusion that the house was empty.*
a foregone conclusion something that is or was certain to happen: *His examination success was a foregone conclusion.*
jump to conclusions to make up your mind about something without knowing all the facts.

conclusive /kən'kluːsɪv/ *adj* convincing: *conclusive proof.*
con'clusively *adv*: *This proves conclusively that the thief was a woman.*

> The opposite of **conclusive** is **inconclusive**.

concoct /kən'kɒkt/ *v* **1** to make something by mixing different things together: *He managed to concoct a meal from what was left in the cupboard.* **2** to invent: *He tried to concoct a reasonable excuse, but couldn't think of one.* **con'coction** *n*.

concord /'kɒnkɔːd/ *n* peace and agreement between people.

concrete /'kɒnkriːt/ *n* a mixture of cement with sand *etc* used in building. — *adj* **1** made of concrete: *a concrete path.* **2** real; able to be seen and touched: *Safety is an abstract idea but a safety-pin is a concrete object.* — *v* to cover something with concrete.

concurrent /kən'kʌrənt/ *adj* happening at the same time as something else.
con'currently *adv*: *Their prison sentences ran concurrently.*

concussion /kən'kʌʃən/ *n* harm to the brain caused by a heavy blow on the head, making the person feel sick, or become unconscious: *He banged his head when he fell, and suffered slight concussion.*
con'cussed *adj* suffering from concussion.

condemn /kənˈdɛm/ v **1** to say that something or someone is wrong or evil: *Everyone condemned her for being cruel to her child.* **2** to sentence someone to a punishment: *She was condemned to death.* **3** to say officially that a building is not safe to use. **condemˈnation** n.

condense /kənˈdɛns/ v **1** to shorten: *to condense a book.* **2** to turn to liquid: *Steam condensed on the kitchen windows.* **condenˈsation** n.

condescend /kɒndɪˈsɛnd/ v **1** to behave in a way that shows they think they are better or more important than you. **2** to behave as if you are doing someone a great favour: *Has she condescended to join us?*

condeˈscending adj: *a condescending smile.* **condeˈscendingly** adv.

condeˈscension n: *a manager who treats his workers with condescension.*

condiment /ˈkɒndɪmənt/ n anything added to food to give it flavour, such as salt or pepper.

condition /kənˈdɪʃən/ n **1** the state in which a person or thing is: *The house is in poor condition*; *He is in no condition to leave hospital.* **2** something that has been agreed or that has to happen before something else does: *It was a condition of his going on the trip that he should pay his own fare.* — v **1** to get something into good condition: *a shampoo that cleans and conditions.* **2** to influence the way that someone behaves or develops: *We were conditioned by the world we grew up in.*

conˈditional adj depending on certain things happening: *a conditional offer of a university place.* **conˈditionally** adv.

conˈditioner n something that improves the condition of something: *hair conditioner.*

on condition that only if something is done: *You will be paid tomorrow on condition that the work is finished.*

on no condition not at all; for no reason: *On no condition must you tell anyone this.*

out of condition not fit and healthy: *I'm out of condition because I haven't had any exercise recently.*

condolence /kənˈdoʊləns/ n sympathy: *a letter of condolence.*

condone /kənˈdoʊn/ v to accept or ignore something: *They claim that this government is condoning cruelty to animals.*

conducive /kənˈdjuːsɪv/ adj encouraging something or making it more likely: *The noisy atmosphere was not conducive to a romantic evening.*

conduct v /kənˈdʌkt/ **1** to guide: *We were conducted down a narrow path; a conducted tour.* **2** to direct an orchestra, choir etc. **3** to behave yourself: *He conducted himself well.* **4** to manage, organize or control: *to conduct a meeting.* **5** to transmit heat or electricity. — n /ˈkɒndʌkt/ behaviour: *His conduct at school was disgraceful.*

conˈductor n **1** a director of an orchestra, choir etc. **2** a person who collects fares on a bus etc: *a bus conductor.* **3** a substance that transmits heat or electricity.

conˈductress n a female conductor on a bus.

cone /koʊn/ n **1** a solid shape with a point and a round base. **2** the fruit of the pine, fir etc: *fir-cones.* **3** a pointed wafer holder for ice-cream: *an ice-cream cone.*

confectioner /kanˈfɛktʃənə(r)/ n a person who makes or sells sweets or cakes.

conˈfectionery n sweets, chocolates, ice-cream etc.

confederation /kənfɛdəˈreɪʃən/ n an organization of individuals or small groups that have joined together: *a confederation of southern European states.*

confer /kənˈfɜː(r)/ v **1** to talk together: *The teachers conferred about the new timetable.* **2** to give an honour etc to someone: *The university conferred degrees on two famous scientists.*

ˈconference n a meeting for discussion: *The conference was held in New York.*

confess /kənˈfɛs/ v to say that you are guilty, wrong etc; to admit: *He confessed to the crime*; *He confessed that he had broken the vase.*

conˈfession n **1** admitting that you are guilty, wrong etc: *The boy made a confession to the police officer.* **2** confessing your sins to a priest.

confetti /kənˈfɛti/ n small pieces of coloured paper thrown at weddings etc.

confide /kənˈfaɪd/ v to tell your secrets etc to someone: *He confided in his brother*; *He confided his fears to his brother.*

> You confide **in** someone, but you confide your secrets etc **to** someone.

confidence /ˈkɒnfɪdəns/ n **1** trust or belief in someone: *I have great confidence in you.* **2** belief in your own ability: *She shows a great deal of confidence for her age.*

ˈconfident adj having a great deal of trust,

especially in yourself: *She is confident that she will win*; *a confident boy*. **'confidently** *adv*.

in confidence as a secret: *I'm telling you this in confidence*.

take into your confidence to tell someone a secret or private thing.

confidential /kɒnfɪˈdɛnʃəl/ *adj* not to be told to others: *confidential information*. **confidentiality** /kɒnfɪdɛnʃɪˈælɪtɪ/ *n*.

confiˈdentially *adv* secretly.

confine /kənˈfaɪn/ *v* **1** to keep within limits: *They confined the fire to a small area*. **2** to shut up or keep in one place: *He was confined in a prison cell for two years*; *She was confined to bed with a cold*.

conˈfined *adj* small; narrow: *a confined space*.

conˈfinement *n* being shut up or imprisoned: *solitary confinement*.

'confines *n* boundary: *within the confines of the city*.

confirm /kənˈfɜːm/ *v* **1** to make something certain: *They confirmed their hotel booking by letter*. **2** to admit someone to full membership of a Christian church. **confirˈmation** *n*.

conˈfirmed *adj* settled in a way of life: *a confirmed bachelor*.

confiscate /ˈkɒnfɪskeɪt/ *v* to take something away, as a punishment: *The teacher confiscated the boy's comic*. **confisˈcation** *n*.

conflict *n* /ˈkɒnflɪkt/ **1** disagreement: *Conflict between husband and wife can have a very bad effect on the children*. **2** a fight or battle: *the Gulf conflict*. — *v* /kənˈflɪkt/ to say something different; to disagree: *The two accounts of the accident conflicted with each other*.

conform /kənˈfɔːm/ *v* **1** to behave, dress *etc* in the way that most other people do. **2** to follow or obey: *You must conform to the school rules*.

conˈformist *n* a person who conforms.

conˈformity *n* behaviour which conforms.

confound /kənˈfaʊnd/ *v* **1** to puzzle or surprise: *He was confounded by the decision*. **2** to succeed in doing something other people have tried to stop you from doing: *She confounded all their attempts to have her dismissed from her job*.

confront /kənˈfrʌnt/ *v* **1** to face or meet an enemy, difficulty *etc*. **2** to bring someone face to face with something: *He was confronted with the evidence*. **confronˈtation** *n*.

confuse /kənˈfjuːz/ *v* **1** to put in disorder: *He confused the arrangements by arriving late*. **2** to mix up in your mind: *I always confuse John and his twin brother*. **3** to puzzle: *He confused me by his questions*.

conˈfused *adj* **1** mixed up: *The message was rather confused*. **2** puzzled.

conˈfusing *adj* difficult to understand.

conˈfusion *n*.

congeal /kənˈdʒiːl/ *v* to become or make thicker and more solid: *The blood had congealed round the wound*.

congested /kənˈdʒɛstɪd/ *adj* very crowded; very full. **conˈgestion** *n*.

congratulate /kənˈgrætʃʊleɪt/ *v* to tell someone how glad you are about something good that has happened to them: *She congratulated him on passing his driving test*.

congratuˈlations *n*: *Warmest congratulations on the birth of your baby*.

There is no singular of **congratulations**.

congregate /ˈkɒŋgrɪgeɪt/ *v* to come together: *A large crowd congregated in the street*.

congreˈgation *n* a group gathered together, especially people in a church.

congress /ˈkɒŋgrɛs/ *n* **1** a large meeting of people who have gathered for talks and discussions. **2** the parliament of the United States: *He has been elected to Congress*. **conˈgressional** *adj*.

conical /ˈkɒnɪkəl/ *adj* cone-shaped: *A witch wears a conical hat*.

conifer /ˈkɒnɪfə(r)/ *n* any tree that has cones and evergreen leaves: *Pines, firs and cedars are conifers*.

coˈniferous *adj* having cones.

conjecture /kənˈdʒɛktʃə(r)/ *n* forming opinions or judgements without having all the facts: *What really happened remains a matter for conjecture*.

conjugal /ˈkɒndʒʊgəl/ *adj* relating to marriage and the relationship between a husband and wife: *conjugal happiness*.

conjunction /kənˈdʒʌŋkʃən/ *n* a word that connects sentences or parts of sentences: *John sang and Mary danced*; *I'll do it if you want*.

in conjunction with together with.

conjure /ˈkʌndʒə(r)/ *v* to do tricks that seem magical. **'conjuror** *n*.

conjure up to put a picture into your mind: *The smell of olive oil conjures up the warmth and beauty of Italy*.

con-man /ˈkɒnmæn/ *n* someone who cheats people by tricking them.

connect /kəˈnɛkt/ *v* **1** to join or fasten

together: *How do you connect the printer to the computer?*; *This road connects the two farms*; *This telephone line connects with the President.* **2** to bring together in the mind: *People connect money with happiness.*

con'nection *n* **1** something that connects: *a faulty electrical connection.* **2** being connected; a relationship: *I have no connection with their family.* **3** a train, bus *etc* which you take on the next part of your journey: *As the local train was late, I missed the connection to London.*

in connection with about: *He wrote to me in connection with his son's school report.*

connive /kə'naɪv/ *v* to plan together with someone else to do something that is wrong.

connoisseur /kɒnə'sɜː(r)/ *n* a person who knows a lot about food or art *etc*: *a connoisseur of modern art.*

connotation /kɒnə'teɪʃən/ *n* the impression a word or phrase makes in addition to its straightforward meaning: *'Spinster' means an unmarried woman but it has negative connotations.*

conquer /'kɒŋkə(r)/ *v* to defeat: *The Normans conquered England in the eleventh century*; *You must conquer your fear of the dark.* **'conqueror** *n*.

conquest /'kɒŋkwest/ *n* something that has been won by force or effort; conquering: *the conquest of Mount Everest.*

conscience /'kɒnʃəns/ *n* your sense of right and wrong: *She had a bad conscience because she had lied*; *He had no conscience about telling a lie.*

conscientious /kɒnʃɪ'enʃəs/ *adj* careful and hard-working: *a conscientious pupil.* **consci'entiously** *adv*.

conscious /'kɒnʃəs/ *adj* **1** fully awake; knowing what is happening around you: *The patient was conscious.* **2** realising something: *The children were conscious of their mother's unhappiness.* **'consciously** *adv*.

'consciousness *n*: *The patient soon regained consciousness.*

conscript *n* /'kɒnskrɪpt/ a person ordered to serve in the armed forces. — *v* /kən'skrɪpt/ to make someone join the armed forces. **con'scription** *n*.

consecrate /'kɒnsəkreɪt/ *v* **1** to set aside for religious or holy use: *The church was consecrated in 1966.* **2** to devote or dedicate to some special purpose: *She consecrated her life to God; consecrate your life to helping others.*

consecutive /kən'sekjʊtɪv/ *adj* following one after the other: *He visited us on two consecutive days, Thursday and Friday.* **con'secutively** *adv*.

consensus /kən'sensəs/ *n* the feeling of most people: *The consensus of opinion is that we should do this.*

consent /kən'sent/ *v* to give permission or agree to something: *I consent to that plan.* — *n* agreement; permission: *You have my consent to leave.*

consequence /'kɒnsɪkwəns/ *n* **1** a result: *This decision will have important consequences.* **2** importance: *A small error is of no consequence.*

'consequently *adv* therefore.

conserve /kən'sɜːv/ *v* to keep from being damaged or lost: *This old building should be conserved.*

conser'vation *n* conserving wildlife, the countryside, old buildings *etc*.

con'servatism *n* dislike of change and new ideas.

con'servative *adj* **1** not liking changes: *Older people are often conservative in their opinions.* **2** in politics, wanting to avoid major changes and to keep business and industry in private hands. **3** cautious; not extreme: *a conservative estimate of the cost.* **con'servatively** *adv*: *She always dresses conservatively for work.*

consider /kən'sɪdə(r)/ *v* **1** to have an opinion about someone or something: *I consider him a very clever pupil.* **2** to think about carefully: *I'll consider your suggestion*; *Always consider other people's feelings.*

con'siderable *adj* great: *a considerable amount.*

con'siderably *adv* quite a lot: *Considerably fewer people came than I expected.*

con'siderate *adj* thoughtful about others: *He is always considerate to elderly people.*

The opposite of **considerate** is **inconsiderate**.

consider'ation *n* **1** thinking about something: *She took the job after careful consideration.* **2** something that must be thought about: *The cost of the journey is our main consideration.* **3** thoughtfulness for other people: *He stayed at home out of consideration for his sick mother.*

con'sidering *prep* in spite of: *Considering his deafness he manages to understand very well.*

take into consideration to consider something that will affect your final decision:

We must take the cost of the project into consideration.

consign /kənˈsaɪn/ *v* to send or put something in a particular place.
conˈsignment *n* a load of goods *etc*: *a consignment of books.*

consist /kənˈsɪst/ *v* to be made up of something: *The house consists of six rooms.*

> See **comprise**.

consistent /kənˈsɪstənt/ *adj* **1** in agreement with something: *The second statement is not consistent with the first.* **2** not changing: *He was consistent in his attitude*; *a consistent style of writing.* **conˈsistency** *n.* **conˈsistently** *adv.*

> The opposite of **consistent** is **inconsistent**.

consolation /kɒnsəˈleɪʃən/ *n* **1** the consoling of someone. **2** something that consoles: *Her children were a great consolation to her after her husband died.*

console /kənˈsoʊl/ *v* to comfort; to cheer up: *She could not console the weeping child.*

consolidate /kənˈsɒlɪdeɪt/ *v* to make or become solid; to strengthen: *It revises, consolidates and extends the vocabulary that students will have come across.* **consoliˈdation** *n.*

consonant /ˈkɒnsənənt/ *n* any letter of the alphabet except *a*, *e*, *i*, *o*, *u*.

consort /ˈkɒnsɔːt/ *n* a wife or husband, especially of someone royal.

conspicuous /kənˈspɪkjʊəs/ *adj* very noticeable: *Her blond hair made her conspicuous in the crowd.*

> The opposite of **conspicuous** is **inconspicuous**.

conspire /kənˈspaɪə(r)/ *v* to plan a crime *etc* together in secret: *They conspired to overthrow the government.* **conˈspiracy** *n.*
conˈspirator *n* a person who conspires.

constable /ˈkʌnstəbəl/ *n* a policeman.

constant /ˈkɒnstənt/ *adj* **1** never stopping: *a constant noise.* **2** not changing: *These eggs must be kept at a constant temperature.* **3** faithful: *He remained constant.* **ˈconstantly** *adv.*

constellation /kɒnstɪˈleɪʃən/ *n* a group of stars.

constipate /ˈkɒnstɪpeɪt/ *v* to make someone constipated.
ˈconstipated *adj* finding it difficult to empty your bowels. **constiˈpation** *n.*

constituency /kənˈstɪtjʊənsɪ/ *n* a town or an area that has its own member of parliament: *Our member of parliament spends a lot of time meeting and talking to people in the constituency.*

constitute /ˈkɒnstɪtjuːt/ *v* to form; to be: *Nuclear waste constitutes a serious danger.*
constiˈtution *n* **1** a set of rules, laws *etc* by which a country or group of people is governed: *the constitution of our country.* **2** the health and strength of a person's body: *He has a strong constitution — he's never ill.* **constiˈtutional** *adj.*

constrain /kənˈstreɪn/ *v* to limit; to prevent something from developing or spreading.
conˈstraint *n* a limit or restriction: *There are no constraints on the amount of money you may spend.*

constrict /kənˈstrɪkt/ *v* to squeeze too tightly: *Don't wear shoes that constrict your toes.* **conˈstriction** *n.*

construct /kənˈstrʌkt/ *v* to build: *They are planning to construct a new supermarket.*
conˈstruction *n* **1** the process of building: *A new bridge is under construction.* **2** something built: *That construction won't last long.*
conˈstructive *adj* helpful: *Constructive criticism tells you both what is wrong and also what to do about it.* **conˈstructively** *adv.*

consul /ˈkɒnsəl/ *n* a person who represents his own government in a foreign country and looks after the people from his own country who live there. **consular** /ˈkɒnsjʊlə(r)/ *adj.*
consulate /ˈkɒnsjʊlət/ *n* the place where the consul lives.

consult /kənˈsʌlt/ *v* **1** to ask advice from someone or get information from something: *Consult your doctor about your illness*; *He consulted his watch and found that it was 8.00 a.m.* **2** to give professional advice: *My doctor consults on Mondays and Fridays.* **consulˈtation** *n.*
conˈsultant *n* a person who gives professional advice.
consulting room a room in which a doctor sees patients.

consume /kənˈsjuːm/ *v* **1** to eat or drink: *He consumes a huge amount of food.* **2** to use: *How much electricity do you consume per month?* **3** to destroy: *The entire building was consumed by fire.*
conˈsumer *n* a person who eats, uses, buys things *etc*: *The average consumer spends £10 per year on toothpaste.*
consumer goods goods which can be used

by the consumer, such as clothing, food, TV sets *etc.*

con'sumption *n* **1** the consuming of something. **2** the amount consumed: *The consumption of coffee has increased.*

> consumption is spelt with a **p**.

contact /'kɒntakt/ *n* **1** touch or nearness: *Her hands came into contact with the acid.* **2** communication: *I've lost contact with all my old friends; How can I get in contact with him?* **3** a person you know: *I have some useful contacts in London.* **4** a wire *etc* carrying an electric current: *the contacts on the battery.* **5** a means of communication: *His radio is his only contact with the outside world.* — *v* to get in touch with someone: *I'll contact you by telephone.*

contact lens a small plastic lens which is worn on the surface of the eye to improve its sight.

contagious /kən'teɪdʒəs/ *adj* spreading from one person to another by touch: *Is that skin disease contagious?* **con'tagion** *n.*

contain /kən'teɪn/ *v* **1** to have something inside: *This box contains a pair of shoes.* **2** to control: *He could hardly contain his excitement.*

con'tainer *n* **1** something made to contain things: *He brought his lunch in a plastic container.* **2** a very large metal box for carrying goods on a truck, ship *etc.* — *adj*: *a container truck.*

contaminate /kən'tæmɪneɪt/ *v* to dirty something: *The water has been contaminated by chemicals.* **contami'nation** *n.*

contemplate /'kɒntəmpleɪt/ *v* to think about something or look at something for a long time: *She contemplated her future gloomily; He contemplated his face in the mirror.* **contem'plation** *n.* **con'templative** *adj.*

contemporary /kən'tɛmpərərɪ/ *adj* of the present time; modern: *contemporary art.* — *n* a person living at the same time: *She was one of my contemporaries at school.*

contempt /kən'tɛmpt/ *n* very low opinion; scorn: *She spoke with contempt of his bad behaviour.*

con'temptible *adj* very bad; deserving scorn: *a contemptible lie.*

contemptuous /kən'tɛmptʃʊəs/ *adj* scornful: *He was very contemptuous of my drawing.*

contend /kən'tɛnd/ *v* **1** to struggle against something: *He has many problems to contend with.* **2** to say something firmly: *He contended that he was right.*

con'tender *n* a person who has entered a competition.

content[1] /kən'tɛnt/ *adj* satisfied; happy: *He doesn't want more money — he's content with what he has.* — *n* happiness; satisfaction: *When we go on holiday we can swim to our hearts' content.* — *v* to satisfy: *As the TV's broken, you'll have to content yourself with listening to the radio.*

content[2] /'kɒntɛnt/ *n* the amount of something contained: *Oranges have a high vitamin C content.*

contented /kən'tɛntɪd/ *adj* happy; satisfied. **con'tentedly** *adv.*

contention /kən'tɛnʃən/ *n* disagreement or quarrelling.

con'tentious *adj* that people strongly disagree about: *a contentious issue.*

contentment /kən'tɛntmənt/ *n* happiness; satisfaction.

contents /'kɒntɛnts/ *n* **1** the things contained in something: *He drank the contents of the bottle.* **2** a list of the things contained in a book: *Look up the contents at the beginning of the book.*

contest *n* /'kɒntɛst/ a struggle, competition *etc*: *a sporting contest.* — *v* /kən'tɛst/ **1** to argue that something is wrong, unfair or untrue: *They are going to contest the judge's decision.* **2** to take part in and try to win an election or competition *etc*: *a hotly contested championship.*

con'testant *n* a person who takes part in a contest.

context /'kɒntɛkst/ *n* **1** the parts before and after a word or sentence that help to make its meaning clear: *If you hear the sentence 'She drove the kids to school', you know from the context that 'kids' means children, not baby goats.* **2** the background or situation that something happens in: *We must examine these ideas in the context of recent events.*

continent /'kɒntɪnənt/ *n* **1** one of the five great divisions of the earth's land surface — Europe, America, Australia, Asia or Africa. **2** Europe excluding Britain. **conti'nental** *adj.*

continental breakfast a light breakfast of rolls and coffee.

contingency /kən'tɪndʒənsɪ/ *n* something that may happen: *The government is making contingency plans for war.*

con'tingent *n* a group, especially of soldiers.

continual /kən'tɪnjʊəl/ *adj* going on all the

time; happening again and again: *continual interruptions.* **con'tinually** *adv.*

See **continuous**.

continue /kən'tɪnjuː/ *v* **1** to keep on doing something: *She continued to run; They continued running; He will continue in his present job; The noise continued for several hours.* **2** to go on with something: *He continued his talk after the break; This story is continued on p. 53.* **continu'ation** *n.*

continuity /kɒntɪ'njuːɪtɪ/ *n* being without breaks or stops: *These interruptions break the continuity of the lesson.*

con'tinuous *adj* put together, or going on, without breaks or stops: *continuous rain; continuous movement.* **con'tinuously** *adv.*

continual means frequent, again and again: *continual complaints.*
continuous means never stopping, going on all the time: *a continuous noise.*

contort /kən'tɔːt/ *v* to twist or turn violently or into an unnatural shape: *His face contorted with pain.* **con'tortion** *n.*

contour /'kɒntʊə(r)/ *n* **1** (often **contours**) the shape of something seen in outline: *From the deck of the ship the captain could see the familiar contours of the island.* **2** (also **contour line**) a line drawn on a map showing where the land reaches a certain height: *the 500-metre contour.*

contraband /'kɒntrəbænd/ *n* goods which you are not allowed to bring into a country. — *adj*: *contraband goods.*

contraception /kɒntrə'sɛpʃən/ *n* the prevention of pregnancy; birth control: *reliable methods of contraception.*

contra'ceptive *n* a pill or some other device that a woman uses to prevent her becoming pregnant: *Many women use contraceptives; a contraceptive pill.*

contract *v* /kən'trækt/ **1** to make smaller or become smaller: *'I am' is often contracted to 'I'm'; Your muscles contract to make your body move.* **2** to catch a disease: *He contracted malaria.* **3** to make a business agreement: *The builders contracted to finish the house by December.* — *n* /'kɒntrækt/ a written agreement: *He has a four-year contract of employment with us.*

con'traction *n* **1** the contracting of a muscle. **2** a short form: *'He's' is a contraction of 'he is'.*

con'tractor *n* a person or firm that promises to do work or supply goods at a fixed rate: *a building contractor.*

contradict /kɒntrə'dɪkt/ *v* to say the opposite to something; to argue or disagree with someone: *It's foolish to contradict your boss.* **contra'diction** *n.* **contra'dictory** *adj.*

contraption /kən'træpʃən/ *n* a strange machine or apparatus: *What's this new contraption for?*

contrary /'kɒntrərɪ/ *adj* opposite to something: *That decision was contrary to my wishes.* — *n* the opposite.

on the contrary just the opposite: *'Are you busy?' 'No, on the contrary, I'm out of work.'*

to the contrary saying the opposite: *I suppose they are still coming as I haven't heard anything to the contrary.*

contrast *v* /kən'trɑːst/ **1** to be very different from something else: *His words contrast with his actions.* **2** to compare two things: *Contrast fresh and frozen vegetables and you'll find the fresh ones taste better.* — *n* /'kɒntrɑːst/ **1** the difference between things: *There is often a great contrast between a book and the film made from it.* **2** a thing or person that is very different from another: *She's a complete contrast to her sister.*

contravene /kɒntrə'viːn/ *v* to break or disobey: *This advertisement contravenes the regulations on the advertising of tobacco.* **contra'vention** *n.*

contribute /kən'trɪbjuːt/ *v* **1** to give money, help *etc* together with others: *Have you contributed any money to this charity?* **2** to help to cause something: *His laziness contributed to his failure.*

contri'bution *n* **1** contributing. **2** something contributed, especially money.

con'tributor *n.*

con'tributory *adj* helping to cause something: *The bad weather was a contributory factor to the crash.*

contrive /kən'traɪv/ *v* to manage or succeed: *She contrived to live well on a very small income.*

con'trived *adj* false or unnatural: *The play had a complicated plot but a contrived ending.*

control /kən'trəʊl/ *n* **1** power or authority over something or someone: *She has no control over that dog; He lost control of himself and shouted very loudly.* **2** the inspecting or checking of something: *price controls.* **3** a switch *etc* which operates a car, aircraft *etc.* — *v* **1** to have power or authority over something or someone: *The captain controls the whole ship; Control your* *dog!* **2** to check or regulate something: *A policeman controlled the traffic.*

con'troller *n* a person or thing that controls.

con'trol-tower *n* a building at an airport from which take-off and landing instructions are given.

in control in charge: *Don't worry — the headmaster is in control of the situation.*

out of control not under the power of someone: *The brakes failed and the car went out of control.*

under control: *Everything's under control now.*

controversy /ˈkɒntrəvɜːsɪ/ *n* an argument; a dispute: *There is a controversy over the rules of the game.* **contro'versial** *adj.*

convalesce /kɒnvəˈlɛs/ *v* to rest and become well again after an illness or operation: *She has left hospital and is convalescing at home.* **conva'lescence** *n.*

conva'lescent *n* a person who is convalescing: *Convalescents often need a special diet.* — *adj* **1** becoming well again after an illness or operation: *He is convalescent now.* **2** for convalescents: *a convalescent home in the country.*

convene /kənˈviːn/ *v* to bring together; to assemble: *to convene a meeting.*

convenient /kənˈviːnɪənt/ *adj* **1** suitable: *When would it be convenient for me to come?* **2** easy to use or reach; handy: *Keep this in a convenient place.* **con'veniently** *adv.*

con'venience *n* **1** being convenient: *the convenience of living near the office.* **2** a useful thing that makes life easy, or comfortable, for example, a washing machine.

convenience food food in cans or frozen in packets which has been prepared or partly prepared before you buy it so that it can be cooked and eaten immediately or very quickly: *He always buys a lot of convenience food.*

convent /ˈkɒnvənt/ *n* a building in which nuns live.

convent school a school in which the teachers are nuns.

convention /kənˈvɛnʃən/ *n* **1** a way of behaving that has become usual: *Shaking hands when meeting people is a convention in many countries.* **2** a big meeting of a political party *etc.* **3** a treaty or agreement, especially between nations.

con'ventional *adj* normal; not unusual: *Michael is not the conventional public school type.* **con'ventionally** *adv.*

The opposite of **conventional** is **unconventional**.

converge /kənˈvɜːdʒ/ *v* to come together or meet at one point: *The roads converge in the centre of town.* **con'vergence** *n.* **con'vergent** *adj.*

conversation /kɒnvəˈseɪʃən/ *n* talk: *We had a long conversation about our plans.*

conver'sational *adj* **1** informal: *conversational English.* **2** fond of talking.

converse[1] /kənˈvɜːs/ *v* to talk: *They conversed in Spanish.*

converse[2] /ˈkɒnvɜːs/ *n* the opposite: *The converse of 'good' is 'bad'.* **con'versely** *adv.*

conversion /kənˈvɜːʃən/ *n* **1** the converting of someone: *his conversion to Christianity.* **2** alteration: *the conversion of the house into a hotel.*

convert *v* /kənˈvɜːt/ **1** to change from one thing into another: *He has converted his house into four apartments.* **2** to change from one religion *etc* to another: *He was converted to Christianity.* — *n* /ˈkɒnvɜːt/ a person who has been converted to a religion *etc*: *a convert to Buddhism.*

con'vertible *adj* able to be converted: *a convertible sofa.* — *n* a car with a folding roof.

convex /ˈkɒnvɛks/ *adj* curved outwards, like the surface of your eye: *a convex lens.*

See **concave**.

convey /kənˈveɪ/ *v* to carry or transport: *The goods were conveyed by sea to Rotterdam.*

con'veyance *n* **1** the conveying of something. **2** a vehicle of any kind: *A bus is a public conveyance.*

conveyor belt an endless, moving belt transporting things in a factory *etc.*

convict *v* /kənˈvɪkt/ to prove or declare someone guilty: *She was convicted of theft.* — *n* /ˈkɒnvɪkt/ a person who is in prison for a crime: *Two convicts have escaped from prison.*

con'viction *n* **1** a strong belief: *It's my conviction that he's right.* **2** being found guilty of a crime in a court of law: *He has two previous convictions for burglary.*

convince /kənˈvɪns/ *v* to make someone believe that something is true: *Her smile convinced me that she was happy*; *She is convinced of his innocence.*

con'vincing *adj* likely to be believed: *a convincing argument.*

convoy /ˈkɒnvɔɪ/ *n* a group of ships, lorries,

convulsion

cars *etc* travelling together: *an army convoy.*

convulsion /kən'vʌlʃən/ *n* a sudden jerking movement caused by a muscle movement that you cannot control: *He needed drugs to help control the convulsions.*

coo /kuː/ *n* the sound that a pigeon makes. — *v*: *The pigeons cooed softly.*

cook /kʊk/ *v* to prepare food or become ready by heating: *She cooked the chicken; The chicken is cooking in the oven.* — *n* a person who cooks, especially as a job.

'**cooker** *n* an apparatus for cooking food: *She has an electric cooker.*

'**cookery** *n* the art of cooking food: *She was taught cookery at school.*

'**cooking** *n* preparing food for eating: *Cooking is one of my hobbies.*

cook up to make up a false story *etc*: *He cooked up a story about his car having broken down.*

cookie /'kʊkɪ/ *n* a flat, hard, sweet cake; a biscuit.

cool /kuːl/ *adj* **1** slightly cold: *cool weather.* **2** calm: *He kept cool in spite of his danger.* **3** not very friendly: *He was very cool towards me.* — *v* **1** to make or become less warm: *She cooled her hands in the stream.* **2** to become less strong: *Her anger cooled.*
'**coolly** *adv.* '**coolness** *n.*

cool-'headed *adj* able to act calmly.

cool down 1 to make or become less warm: *Let your food cool down a bit!* **2** to make or become less excited: *Stop shouting — cool down!*

coolie /'kuːlɪ/ *n* an Indian or Chinese labourer.

coop /kuːp/ *n* a cage for hens *etc*.

coop up to keep an animal or person in a small place: *I couldn't live cooped up in that little flat like you do.*

co-operate /koʊ'ɒpəreɪt/ *v* **1** to work together: *We must all co-operate to make the school run smoothly.* **2** to do what somebody asks you to: *They threatened to hurt me if I didn't co-operate.* **co-oper'ation** *n.*

co'operative *adj* **1** managed or owned jointly by a number of people: *a co-operative business venture.* **2** willing to do what somebody asks you to: *The bank manager was not very co-operative.*

> The opposite of **co-operative** is **unco-operative**.

co-ordinate *v* /koʊ'ɔːdɪneɪt/ to make one action *etc* fit in smoothly with another: *In swimming, the movement of your arms and legs must be co-ordinated.* — *n* /koʊ'ɔːdɪnət/ one of two sets of numbers or letters, used to find a point on a map.

co-ordi'nation *n* **1** the organization of different people or things so that they work well together: *You will be responsible for the co-ordination of the whole project.* **2** the ability to control the movements of the different parts of your body: *I'm a very poor dancer – I have no co-ordination at all.*

cop /kɒp/ *n* a slang shortening of **copper**².

cope /koʊp/ *v* to manage; to deal with something successfully: *I can't cope with all this work.*

copier /'kɒpɪə(r)/ *n* a machine that makes copies; a photocopier.

copious /'koʊpɪəs/ *adj* in large amounts: *She put copious notes on the desk in front of her.*
'**copiously** *adv.*

copper¹ /'kɒpə(r)/ *n* **1** a metal of a brown-red colour. **2** a coin made of copper. — *adj* **1** made of copper. **2** having the colour of copper.

copper² /'kɒpə(r)/ *n* a British nickname for a policeman.

copra /'kɒprə/ *n* the dried middle part of the coconut, which gives coconut oil.

copy /'kɒpɪ/ *n* **1** an imitation or reproduction: *a copy of a painting*; *He made two copies of the text on the copying machine.* **2** a single book, newspaper *etc*: *May I have six copies of this dictionary, please?* — *v* to imitate or make a reproduction of something: *Copy the way I speak*; *Copy this passage into your notebook*; *His secretary copied his letter.*

'**copyright** *n* the right that only you have to reproduce, record, film or translate a piece of music or book: *She owns the copyright on her father's novels.*

coral /'kɒrəl/ *n* a hard pink substance made up of the skeletons of tiny sea animals: *a necklace made of coral.* — *adj*: *a coral reef.*

cord /kɔːd/ *n* **1** thin rope or thick string. **2** an electric cable or a flex: *the cord of his electric razor.*

cordial /'kɔːdɪəl/ *adj* friendly: *a cordial welcome.* — *n* a refreshing drink: *lime-juice cordial.* '**cordially** *adv.*

cordon /'kɔːdən/ *n* a line or ring of police *etc*, that prevents people from entering an area.

cordon off to put a cordon around an area: *The police have cordoned off the street where the bomb was found.*

core /kɔː(r)/ *n* the inner part of something: *an apple core*; *the core of the earth.* — *v* to take out the core of fruit.

cork /kɔːk/ *n* **1** the outer bark of the cork tree:

Cork floats well. **2** a stopper for a bottle *etc* made of cork: *Put the cork back in the bottle.* — *adj* made of cork: *cork tiles.* — *v* to put a cork into something: *I've corked the bottle.*

'corkscrew *n* a tool for taking out corks.

corn[1] /kɔːn/ *n* **1** wheat, oats or maize. **2** the seeds of these crops.

corn[2] /kɔːn/ *n* a little lump of hard skin, usually on a toe.

cornea /'kɔːnɪə/ *n* the transparent covering of the eyeball.

corned beef /kɔːnd'biːf/ *n* salted beef usually sold in cans.

corner /'kɔːnə(r)/ *n* **1** a point where two lines, walls, roads *etc* meet: *The chair stood in a corner of the room*; *I met him on the street corner.* **2** a small quiet place: *He found a corner where he could read quietly.* **3** in football, a free kick from the corner of the field. **4** a difficult or embarrassing situation: *He found himself in a very tight corner.* — *v* to force a person or animal into a place from which it is difficult to escape: *The thief was cornered in an alley.*

cut corners to spend less time or money on something than you should.

cornflakes /'kɔːnfleɪks/ *n plural* a light, crunchy breakfast food that is made from maize and eaten with milk: *a bowl of cornflakes.*

cornflour /'kɔːnflaʊə(r)/ *n* fine flour made from maize.

corny /'kɔːnɪ/ *adj* ridiculously simple or well-known: *His jokes are all so corny.*

coronary /'kɒrənərɪ/ *n* a heart attack, in which the blood supply to the heart is cut off.

coronation /kɒrə'neɪʃən/ *n* the ceremony of crowning a king or queen.

coroner /'kɒrənə(r)/ *n* a person whose job is to inquire into the causes of accidental or sudden deaths.

coronet /'kɒrənət/ *n* a small crown.

corporal[1] /'kɔːpərəl/ *n* a soldier of the rank below sergeant.

corporal[2] /'kɔːpərəl/ *adj* having to do with the body: *The head-teacher forbids caning or any other kind of corporal punishment.*

corporate /'kɔːpərɪt/ *adj* united: *corporate effort.*

corpo'ration *n* an organization or business: *the British Broadcasting Corporation.*

corps /kɔː(r)/ *n* **1** a division of an army: *The Royal Medical Corps.* **2** a group: *a corps of dancers.*

The pronunciation of **corps** is kɔː(r), rhyming with **more**.

corpse /kɔːps/ *n* a dead body.

corpuscle /'kɔːpəsəl/ *n* a red or white cell in the blood.

correct /kə'rɛkt/ *v* **1** to make something free from faults and errors: *You must correct this sentence.* **2** to mark errors in something: *The teacher corrected our exercises.* — *adj* **1** free from faults or errors: *This sum is correct.* **2** right; not wrong: *You are quite correct.* **cor'rection** *n.* **cor'rectly** *adv.*

cor'rective *adj* putting something right: *corrective treatment.*

correlate /'kɒrəleɪt/ *v* to be linked or related: *Stress levels and heart disease are strongly correlated.* **corre'lation** *n.*

correspond /kɒrɪ'spɒnd/ *v* **1** to be similar: *A bird's wing corresponds to the arm and hand in humans.* **2** to be in agreement with something: *Her opinion corresponds with what I said.* **3** to write letters to someone: *Do they often correspond with each other?*

corre'spondence *n* **1** agreement; similarity. **2** letters.

corre'spondent *n* **1** a person who writes letters. **2** a person who writes reports for a newspaper *etc.*

corre'sponding *adj* similar; matching: *The word 'gobble' means to eat greedily — is there a corresponding word in Spanish?*

corridor /'kɒrɪdɔː(r)/ *n* a passageway.

corroborate /kə'rɒbəreɪt/ *v* to give evidence that supports what someone else has said: *Several witnesses have corroborated what she told us.* **corrobo'ration** *n.*

corrode /kə'rəʊd/ *v* to destroy or eat away as rust, chemicals *etc* do. **cor'rosion** *n.*

cor'rosive *adj* likely to corrode.

corrugated /'kɒrəgeɪtɪd/ *adj* shaped into regular narrow folds or ridges: *Corrugated paper is used for packing breakable objects*; *The hut has a corrugated-iron roof.*

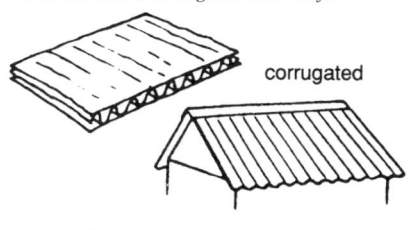

corrugated

corrupt /kə'rʌpt/ *v* **1** to make someone or something evil or bad: *He was corrupted by the bad influence of his companions.* **2** to bribe. — *adj* **1** bad or evil: *The government is corrupt.* **2** willing to accept bribes: *a corrupt police officer.* **cor'ruptible** *adj.* **cor'ruption** *n.*

cortège /kɔː'teɪʒ/ *n* a funeral procession.

cosmetic /kɒz'mɛtɪk/ *n* something that can make your face look more beautiful, such as lipstick, eye-shadow *etc.* — *adj* improving the appearance of something: *cosmetic surgery.*

cosmic /'kɒzmɪk/ *adj* having to do with the universe or outer space: *cosmic rays.*

cosmonaut /'kɒzmənɔːt/ *n* an astronaut.

cosmopolitan /kɒzmə'pɒlɪtən/ *adj* belonging to all parts of the world: *The population of London is very cosmopolitan.*

cosmos /'kɒzmɒs/ *n* the universe.

cost /kɒst/ *v* to have a certain price: *This jacket costs £120.* — *n* **1** the money paid for something: *What was the cost of the meal?* **2** something given in return for something: *The victory was won at the cost of 650 lives.*

> **cost; cost; cost:** *The book cost £5; The repairs have cost more than £5000.*
> to ask the **price** (not **cost**) of a dress.
> to ask what something **costs**.

'costly *adj* expensive: *a costly dress.*

at all costs no matter what the cost may be: *We must prevent disaster at all costs.*

costume /'kɒstjuːm/ *n* **1** an outfit for special use: *a dance costume.* **2** a swimsuit. **3** dress; clothes: *eighteenth-century costume.*

cosy /'kəʊzɪ/ *adj* warm and comfortable: *a cosy scarf; a cosy armchair.* — *n* a covering for keeping a teapot or an egg warm. **'cosily** *adv.* **'cosiness** *n.*

cot /kɒt/ *n* **1** a small bed with high sides for a baby. **2** a folding bed.

cottage /'kɒtɪdʒ/ *n* a small house, especially in the country or in a village.

cotton /'kɒtən/ *n* **1** a soft fluffy substance obtained from the seeds of a plant, which is used for making thread or cloth. **2** a cloth or thread made from cotton: *a reel of cotton; This shirt is made of cotton.* — *adj* made of cotton: *a cotton shirt.*

cotton-'wool *n* loose white fluffy cotton for absorbing liquids, wiping or protecting an injury *etc.*

cotton on to realize or understand: *He still hasn't cottoned on to the fact he is unpopular at school.*

couch /kaʊtʃ/ *n* a sofa for sitting or lying on.

See **bench**.

cough /kɒf/ *v* to make a noise in your throat as you breathe out suddenly: *He's coughing badly because he has a cold.* — *n* **1** an illness causing coughing: *He has a bad cough.* **2** an act of coughing: *She gave a little cough.*

cough up 1 to bring up from the lungs or stomach by coughing: *She's been coughing up blood.* **2** to give especially money or information: *I persuaded her to cough up £20 towards his present; He owes me £20 but he just won't cough up.*

could /kʊd/ or /kəd/ *v* **1** past tense of **can**: *They asked if I could drive a car; I said I couldn't.* **2** used to express a possibility: *I could go but I'm not going to; Could you give me a lift in your car?*

> **could; could not** or **'couldn't** / 'kʊdənt/ or /'kədənt/: *I could help you to pack, couldn't I?; You couldn't lend me a dollar, could you?*

could have used to express a possibility in the past: *We could have gone, but we didn't.*

council /'kaʊnsəl/ *n* a group of people who meet to discuss or give advice: *The town council are discussing the new road.*

'councillor *n* an elected member of a council.

counsel /'kaʊnsəl/ *n* **1** advice: *You must seek counsel from a good lawyer.* **2** a lawyer at a trial: *the counsel for the defence.* — *v* to advise: *The lawyer counselled him to pay the money back.*

'counselling *n* the act of giving specialist advice to people: *The university provides a counselling service for students with problems.*

'counsellor *n* a person who gives advice.

count /kaʊnt/ *v* **1** to say the numbers: *Count up to ten.* **2** to add up: *Count up the number of people in the room.* **3** to be important: *What he says doesn't count.* **4** to have a value; to be added to a score *etc*: *You must write the essay without your parents' help, or your mark won't count.* **5** to consider: *Count yourself lucky to be in the team.* — *n* the counting of something: *They took a count of the people at the meeting.*

'countable *adj* **1** able to be numbered. **2** able to have a plural: *Table is a countable noun, but water is an uncountable noun.*

> The opposite of **countable** is **uncountable**.

'countdown *n* a counting backwards to the exact moment at which to start something, especially a rocket.

count against to be a disadvantage: *Do you think my age will count against me?*

count on to depend on someone or something: *I'm counting on you to help me.*

count out 1 to count notes and coins one by one. **2** not to include someone: *If you're going to her place you can count me out.*

keep count to know how many there are or have been: *I always keep count of how many customers we have each day.*

lose count to forget how many there are or have been: *I've lost count of the number of times he's told that story.*

countenance /ˈkaʊntənəns/ *n* a rather old word for the face: *a gloomy countenance.*

counter- /ˈkaʊntə(r)/ against or opposite: *to move counterclockwise*; *They listened to the arguments and counter-arguments.*

counter /ˈkaʊntə(r)/ *n* **1** a place in a bank or post-office where you are served; a table or surface in a shop where you pay. **2** a small flat disc used in board games. — *v* to react with a return attack: *He countered her criticisms with a long explanation of his methods.*

counter to in the opposite direction: *The results ran counter to expectations.*

counteract /kaʊntərˈakt/ *v* to prevent the effect of something: *How can you counteract this poison?*

counter-attack /ˈkaʊntərətak/ *n* an attack in reply to an attack. — *v*: *Our troops counter-attacked.*

counterfeit /ˈkaʊntəfɪt/ *adj* **1** copied or made in imitation: *counterfeit money.* **2** not real. — *v* to make a copy of something: *to counterfeit banknotes.*

counterfoil /ˈkaʊntəfɔɪl/ *n* part of a cheque, ticket or receipt which you keep as a record: *She always keeps the counterfoil from her theatre ticket as a souvenir.*

countermand /kaʊntəˈmɑːnd/ *v* to cancel an order or command, usually by giving a different one: *The sergeant's order was countermanded by his captain.*

counterpart /ˈkaʊntəpɑːt/ *n* a thing or person that has a similar function or job somewhere else: *Government ministers have been meeting their European counterparts for informal talks.*

countless /ˈkaʊntləs/ *adj* very many: *countless stars.*

country /ˈkʌntrɪ/ *n* **1** any of the nations of the world; the land occupied by a nation: *Canada is a larger country than Spain.* **2** the part of the land which is away from the town: *a quiet holiday in the country.* **3** an area or stretch of land: *hilly country.* **4** the people of a land: *The whole country supported the president.*

'countryside *n* an area away from the town: *They cycled out into the countryside.*

county /ˈkaʊntɪ/ *n* one of several divisions of a country or state with its own local government: *She works for the county council.*

coup /kuː/ *n* **1** a very successful gain. **2** a sudden and violent change in government: *The president was killed during the coup.*

> **coup** is pronounced /kuː/, to rhyme with **too**.

couple /ˈkʌpəl/ *n* **1** two; a few: *May I borrow a couple of chairs?* **2** a man and wife, or boyfriend and girlfriend: *a married couple*; *The young couple have a child.* — *v* to link or connect two or more things or people: *The rain, coupled with the heavy traffic, made the journey difficult.*

couplet /ˈkʌplɪt/ *n* two lines of verse, one following the other, which usually rhyme: *Shakespeare's plays are full of rhyming couplets.*

coupon /ˈkuːpɒn/ *n* a piece of paper *etc* which gives you something, for example a gift or discount price: *This coupon gives 50 cents off your next purchase.*

courage /ˈkʌrɪdʒ/ *n* the ability to do something dangerous in spite of fear; bravery: *He was praised for his courage in saving the children from the fire.*
courageous /kəˈreɪdʒəs/ *adj.* **couˈrageously** *adv.*

courier /ˈkʊərɪə(r)/ *n* **1** a guide who travels with, and looks after, parties of tourists. **2** a messenger.

course /kɔːs/ *n* **1** something planned in stages: *He's doing a course in French*; *She's having a course of treatment for her cough.* **2** a part of a meal: *Now we've had the soup, what's the next course?* **3** the ground over which a race is run or a game is played: *a racecourse*; *a golf-course.* **4** the direction in which something or someone moves: *the course of the River Nile*; *the course of his journey.* **5** a way of dealing with a particular situation: *What's the best course of action here?*

as a matter of course as part of a normal routine or pattern of events.

in due course at the proper time: *In due course, this seed will grow into a tree.*

in the course of during: *In the course of our talk, he told me about the accident.*

in the course of time eventually: *You'll forget all this in the course of time.*

of course naturally; certainly: *Of course, he didn't tell me any secrets; Of course I can swim; Of course I'll help you.*

court /kɔːt/ *n* **1** a place where legal cases are heard: *The accused man is to appear in court on Friday.* **2** a space for certain games: *a tennis-court; a squash court.* **3** the people who look after a king or queen: *the court of King James.* — *v* to try to win the love of a woman: *He courted her for several years.*

courteous /'kɜːtɪəs/ *adj* polite: *He wrote a courteous letter of thanks.* **'courteously** *adv*.

> The opposite of **courteous** is **discourteous**.

courtesy /'kɜːtəsɪ/ *n* politeness.

courtier /'kɔːtɪə(r)/ *n* a member of the court of a king or queen.

courthouse /'kɔːthaʊs/ *n* a building where legal cases are tried.

court-martial /kɔːt'mɑːʃəl/, *plural* **courts-'martial**, *n* a court held by officers of the armed forces to try their members for breaking rules.

courtship /'kɔːtʃɪp/ *n* trying to win the love of someone.

courtyard /'kɔːtjɑːd/ *n* an open area surrounded by walls or buildings.

cousin /'kʌzən/ *n* a son or daughter of your uncle or aunt.

cove /koʊv/ *n* a small bay, especially a sheltered one surrounded by cliffs: *They swam in a quiet cove.*

cover /'kʌvə(r)/ *v* **1** to put or spread something over something: *Have you a cloth to cover the table with?; My shoes are covered in paint.* **2** to be enough to pay for something: *Will 10 dollars cover your expenses?* **3** to travel: *We covered forty miles in one day.* **4** to stretch over a length of time *etc*: *His diary covered three years.* **5** to protect: *Are we covered by your car insurance?* **6** to report on something: *I'm covering the race for the newspaper.* — *n* **1** something which covers, especially a cloth over a table, bed *etc*: *a table-cover; a bed-cover.* **2** something that gives protection: *The soldiers took cover from the enemy gunfire; insurance cover.* **3** something that hides: *He escaped under cover of darkness.* **4** a disguise for a secret or illegal activity: *A journalist seemed to be a good cover for a spy.*

'coverage *n* the extent of news covered by a newspaper *etc*: *The TV coverage of the Olympic Games was extensive.*

'covering *n*: *My car has a covering of dirt.*

'cover-up *n* an attempt to hide something illegal or dishonest.

cover up to hide the truth when someone has done something wrong: *The secretary had been covering up for her boss for years.*

covet /'kʌvɪt/ *v* to want something that belongs to another person: *I coveted her fur coat.* **'covetous** *adj*. **'covetously** *adv*.

cow /kaʊ/ *n* the female of the ox family, kept for its milk.

> Cows **moo** or **low**.
> A baby cow is a **calf**.
> Cows and bulls are **cattle**.

coward /'kaʊəd/ *n* a person who is easily frightened: *I am such a coward — I hate going to the dentist.* **'cowardly** *adj*. **'cowardice** /'kaʊədɪs/ *n*.

cowboy /'kaʊbɔɪ/ *n* a man who looks after cattle, especially in the United States.

cower /'kaʊə(r)/ *v* to move back or downwards because of fear: *The dog cowered away into a corner.*

cowhide /'kaʊhaɪd/ *n* the skin of a cow made into leather.

coy /kɔɪ/ *adj* shy: *a coy smile.* **'coyly** *adv*.

crab /krab/ *n* an edible sea animal with a shell and five pairs of legs, the first pair having claws.

crack /krak/ *v* **1** to break partially, but not into pieces: *The stone hit the window and cracked it.* **2** to make a sudden sharp sound: *The whip cracked.* **3** to make a joke: *He's always cracking jokes.* — *n* **1** a split or break: *There's a crack in this cup.* **2** a sudden sharp sound: *the crack of a whip.* **3** a blow: *a crack on the jaw.*

cracked *adj* damaged by cracks: *a cracked cup.*

'cracker *n* **1** a thin crisp biscuit. **2** a small exploding firework: *fire crackers.* **3** a hollow paper object containing a small gift *etc*, used at parties, that gives a loud bang when pulled apart.

crack down on to take strong action against: *The police are cracking down on speeding.* **'crackdown** *n*.

crack up to become mentally or physically ill, usually because of stress or strain: *She'll*

crack up if she doesn't stop working so hard.
'crack-up *n*.
get cracking to move quickly.
have a crack to try to do something: *He decided to have a crack at fixing the pipe himself.*
the crack of dawn very early in the morning.

crackle /ˈkrakəl/ *v* to make a continuous cracking noise: *The dry branches crackled under my feet.* — *n*.

cradle /ˈkreɪdəl/ *n* a child's bed, especially one in which it can be rocked. — *v* to hold gently: *She cradled the baby in her arms.*

craft /krɑːft/ *n* **1** a skill: *the craft of woodcarving.* **2** (*plural* **craft**) a boat or ship: *a sailing craft.* **3** trickery.
'craftsman *n* a person who is skilled at making things. **'craftsmanship** *n*.
'crafty *adj* cunning and sly. **'craftily** *adv*.

crag /krag/ *n* a rough, steep mountain or rock: *Salisbury Crags.*

cram /kram/ *v* **1** to fill very full: *The drawer was crammed with papers.* **2** to push or force: *He crammed food into his mouth.*

cramp /kramp/ *n* a painful stiffening of the muscles: *The swimmer got cramp in his leg.* — *v* to prevent something from developing or being expressed: *Worry about money cramped our enjoyment of life.*
cramped *adj* unpleasantly small or overcrowded: *The room was cramped and airless with so many people in it.*

crane /kreɪn/ *n* a machine used on building sites *etc* with a long arm and a chain, for raising heavy weights. — *v* to stretch out or twist round: *He craned his neck in order to see round the corner.*

crash /kraʃ/ *n* **1** a noise of something heavy falling and breaking: *There was an awful crash when he dropped all the plates.* **2** a collision; an accident: *an air-crash; He was hurt in a car-crash.* — *v* **1** to fall with a loud noise: *The plate crashed to the floor.* **2** to drive or move with great force against or into something: *He crashed his car; His plane crashed in the mountains.* — *adj* done in a short time to achieve results quickly: *a crash course in German; a crash diet.*

to crash (not **clash**) a car.

'crash-helmet *n* a very strong protective hat worn by motor-cyclists *etc*.
'crash-landing *n* a landing made quickly in an emergency, that causes some damage to the aircraft: *Nobody was seriously injured in the crash-landing.*

crate /kreɪt/ *n* a container for carrying and transporting goods: *a crate of oranges.*

crater /ˈkreɪtə(r)/ *n* **1** the bowl-shaped opening of a volcano. **2** a hollow made in the ground by a bomb *etc*.

crave /kreɪv/ *v* **1** to beg for. **2** to long for; desire extremely.
'craving *n* a longing: *a craving for adventure.*

crawl /krɔːl/ *v* **1** to move on hands and knees or with the front of the body on the ground: *The baby can't walk yet, but she crawls everywhere.* **2** to move slowly: *The traffic was crawling along at ten kilometres per hour.* — *n* **1** a very slow movement or speed: *We drove along at a crawl.* **2** a swimming-stroke used for swimming on your front.

crayfish /ˈkreɪfɪʃ/ *n* a type of edible shellfish.

crayon /ˈkreɪən/ *n* a coloured pencil for drawing with.

craze /kreɪz/ *n* a very popular fashion that lasts only a short time: *There is a craze for wearing black clothes.*

crazy /ˈkreɪzɪ/ *adj* **1** mad: *He must be going crazy; a crazy idea.* **2** liking something very much: *She's crazy about her boyfriend.*

creak /kriːk/ *v* to make a sharp grating sound: *That chair is creaking beneath your weight.* — *n* a sound like this: *The door opened with a creak.* **'creaky** *adj*.

cream /kriːm/ *n* **1** the yellowish-white fatty substance that forms on the top of milk, and from which butter and cheese are made. **2** anything like cream: *ice-cream; face-cream.* **3** a yellowish-white colour. — *v* to make into a cream-like mixture: *Cream the eggs, butter and sugar together.*
'creamy *adj* full of, or like, cream: *creamy milk.*

crease /kriːs/ *n* a mark made by folding or pressing: *There was a smart crease in his trousers; My dress was full of creases after being in my suitcase.* — *v* to make or become creased: *You've creased my newspaper; This fabric creases easily.*

create /kriːˈeɪt/ *v* to cause; to make: *How was the earth created?; The sculptor created a beautiful statue; The circus created great excitement.*
creˈation *n* **1** creating: *the creation of the world.* **2** something designed or made by an artist *etc*: *The dress designer is showing his latest creations.*
creˈative *adj* clever at making things; imaginative. **creˈativity** *n*.

cre'ator *n* a person who creates.
creature /'kri:tʃə(r)/ *n* an animal or human being: *all God's creatures*.
crèche /krɛʃ/ *n* a nursery for babies whose parents are at work *etc*.
credentials /krɪ'dɛnʃəlz/ *n* **1** the qualifications and achievements which are evidence of your ability or authority: *They were impressed with her credentials as an organizer.* **2** the documents or certificates which are proof of these: *She asked the policeman to show her his credentials.*
credible /'krɛdɪbəl/ *adj* likely to be believed: *The story he told was hardly credible.* **'credibly** *adv.* **credi'bility** *n.*

The opposite of **credible** is **incredible**.

credit /'krɛdɪt/ *n* **1** time allowed for payment of goods *etc* after they have been received: *We don't give credit at this shop.* **2** the sum of money which someone has in an account at a bank: *Your credit amounts to 2014 dollars.* **3** praise; approval: *He got all the credit for the work, although I had done most of it.* **4** the list shown at the end of a film or television programme of the names of the people who helped to make it: *Look at the credits for the actor's name.* **5** belief: *The story is gaining credit.* — *v* **1** to think someone has done something: *He was credited with having discovered the island.* **2** to believe: *These reports of official corruption are difficult to credit.* **3** to add some money to a bank account: *They credited my account with $200.*

See **debit**.

'creditable *adj* worthy of praise.
'creditor *n* a person to whom money is owed.
'credit card a card with which you can buy goods *etc* on credit: *I pay by credit card.*
do you credit to cause you to be admired or respected: *Your hard work does you credit.*
give someone credit for something to give someone praise for good work *etc*: *He was given credit for finishing the work so quickly.*
have to your credit to achieve: *By the age of 24 she already had three published novels to her credit.*
on credit payment being made after the date of sale: *Do you sell goods on credit?*
to someone's credit a phrase used to show approval of one thing a person does, after criticizing another: *To her credit, she apologized very quickly.*

credulous /'krɛdjʊləs/ *adj* believing too easily. **cre'dulity** /krə'dju:lɪtɪ/ *n.*
creed /kri:d/ *n* **1** a statement of your religious beliefs. **2** something that you firmly believe in.
creek /kri:k/ *n* **1** a small bay on the sea coast. **2** a small river.
creep /kri:p/ *v* **1** to move slowly, quietly or secretly: *He crept into the bedroom.* **2** to move on hands or knees or with the body close to the ground: *The cat crept towards the bird.* — *n* a nasty word for an unpleasant person: *He's always trying to flatter the teacher — he's a real creep.*

creep; crept; crept /krɛpt/: *He crept forward; The water had crept higher.*

'creep·er *n* a plant growing along the ground or up a wall.
'creepy *adj* causing a feeling of fear: *It was very creepy in the old castle at night; a creepy film about giant spiders.*
'creepy-crawly, plural **'creepy-crawlies**, *n* a small creeping insect: *She hates slugs and snails and all other creepy-crawlies.*
cremate /krɪ'meɪt/ *v* to burn dead bodies. **cre'mation** *n.*
crematorium /krɛmə'tɔ:rɪəm/ *n* a place where cremation is carried out.
crept *see* **creep**.
crescendo /krɪ'ʃɛndoʊ/, plural **cre'scendos**, *n* a gradual increase in loudness, such as in a piece of music: *The noise grew to a crescendo; The last twelve bars form a crescendo.*
crescent /'krɛsənt/ or /'krɛzənt/ *n* **1** the curved shape of the growing moon. **2** a curved street.
crest /krɛst/ *n* **1** the comb or tuft on the head of a cock or other bird. **2** the highest part: *the crest of a wave.*
crestfallen /'krɛstfɔ:lən/ *adj* disappointed.
crevice /'krɛvɪs/ *n* a thin crack in rock.
crew[1] *see* **crow**.
crew[2] /kru:/ *n* **1** the people who work on a ship, aeroplane, bus *etc*. **2** a group of workmen operating machinery *etc*: *a television crew*.
'crewcut *n* a very short hairstyle.
crib /krɪb/ *v* to copy someone else's work: *She cribbed the answers from her friend's exercise book.* — *n* a cradle or cot for a baby: *The baby was asleep in her crib.*
crick /krɪk/ *n* a pain in your neck, caused by moving too suddenly: *I have a crick in my neck.* — *v*: *I've cricked my neck.*

cricket[1] /'krıkıt/ *n* an outdoor game played with bats, a ball and wickets, between two teams of eleven players. **'cricketer** *n*.

cricket[2] /'krıkıt/ *n* an insect similar to a grasshopper; the male cricket can make a chirping sound.

crime /kraım/ *n* **1** an action which is against the law: *Murder is a crime.* **2** something wrong though not against the law: *What a crime to cut down those trees!*
'criminal *adj* **1** against the law: *Theft is a criminal offence.* **2** very wrong; wicked: *a criminal waste of food.* — *n* a person who is guilty of a crime.

crimson /'krımzən/ *n*, *adj* a deep red colour: *He blushed crimson.*

cringe /krındʒ/ *v* **1** to back away in fear, as a dog does when it is about to be hit. **2** to feel shame or embarrassment: *Thinking about how stupid I must have sounded made me cringe.*

crinkle /'krıŋkəl/ *v* to make or become creased or wrinkled: *The paper crinkled in the heat.*

cripple /'krıpəl/ *v* **1** to make someone lame or disabled: *He was crippled by a fall from a horse.* **2** to make weaker: *The war has crippled the country.* — *n* a lame or disabled person: *He has been a cripple since his car accident.*

crisis /'kraısıs/, *plural* **crises** /'kraısi:z/, *n* **1** a deciding moment or a worst point, especially of an illness: *Although she is still very ill, she has passed the crisis.* **2** a time of great danger or difficulty: *The government is good at dealing with a crisis such as the recent flooding.*

crisp /krısp/ *adj* **1** stiff and dry enough to break easily: *crisp biscuits.* **2** firm and fresh: *a crisp lettuce.* **3** firm and clear in the way you say or write something: *a crisp voice.* — *n* short for **potato crisp**. **'crispness** *n*. **'crispy** *adj*.

criss-cross /'krıskrɒs/ *adj* made of lines which cross each other repeatedly: *a criss-cross pattern.*

criterion /kraı'tıərıən/, *plural* **cri'teria**, *n* a standard used in judging something: *What are your criteria for deciding which words to include in this dictionary?*

critic /'krıtık/ *n* **1** a person who writes or talks about new books, plays, films, paintings *etc* and says if they are good or not. **2** a person who finds fault: *Most people praise the president, but he does have a few critics.*
'critical *adj* **1** fault-finding: *He is too critical of his children.* **2** dangerous; very serious: *a critical shortage of food*; *After the accident, his condition was critical.* **'critically** *adv*.
'criticize /'krıtısaız/ *v* **1** to find fault with someone: *He's always criticizing her.* **2** to give an opinion of a book *etc*. **'criticism** *n*.

croak /krəʊk/ *v* to make a low hoarse sound like the noise a frog makes. — *n* this noise.

crochet /'krəʊʃeı/ *v* to knit using a single small needle with a hooked end, called a **crochet hook**. — *n* work done in this way.

crockery /'krɒkərı/ *n* dishes, such as plates, cups *etc*: *a sink full of dirty crockery.*

crockery   cutlery

crocodile /'krɒkədaıl/ *n* a large tropical reptile found in rivers.
crocodile tears false tears.

crocus /'krəʊkəs/ *n* a spring plant that grows from a bulb and has bright yellow, white or purple flowers.

crook /krʊk/ *n* **1** a shepherd's or bishop's stick, bent at the end. **2** a criminal: *The two crooks stole the old woman's jewels.* **3** the bend in your arm inside your elbow.
crooked /'krʊkıd/ *adj* **1** bent: *The man was crooked with age.* **2** not straight: *That picture is crooked.* **3** not honest: *a crooked car-salesman.* **'crookedness** *n*.

croon /kru:n/ *v* to sing or speak in a soft low voice: *She crooned a lullaby to her baby.*

crop /krɒp/ *n* **1** the produce of plants; a plant which is grown by farmers: *a fine crop of rice*; *We grow a variety of crops, including cabbages, wheat and barley.* **2** a short whip used when horse-riding. — *v* to cut or nibble: *The sheep cropped the grass.*
cropped *adj* cut very short: *cropped hair.*
crop up to happen unexpectedly: *Something important cropped up — that's why I'm late.*

croquet /'krəʊkeı/ *n* a game in which players, using wooden hammers, try to hit wooden balls through hoops in the ground.

cross[1] /krɒs/ *adj* angry. **'crossly** *adv*.

cross[2] /krɒs/ *n* **1** a mark or shape formed by two lines placed across each other, like this: + or ×. **2** a cross like this: †; it is a sign used in the Christian religion. **3** a mixture of two things: *A tangelo is a cross between a tangerine and a pomelo.* — *v* **1** to go from one side to the other: *Let's cross the street*; *This bridge crosses the river.* **2** to place two things across each other: *He sat down and crossed his legs.* **3** to go across each other: *The roads cross in the centre of town.* **4** to pass each other: *Our letters must have crossed in the post.* **5** to put a line across: *Remember to cross your 't's.*

'**crossbar** *n* **1** the horizontal metal bar between the handlebars and the saddle on a boy's or man's bicycle. **2** the horizontal bar across a pair of goalposts.

'**crossbow** *n* a bow fixed to a shaft with a device for pulling back and releasing the string with the arrow.

'**cross-breed** *n* an animal bred from two different breeds. '**cross-bred** *adj*.

cross-'country *adj* across fields *etc*, not on roads: *a cross-country run*.

cross-ex'amine *v* to test the evidence of a witness during a trial *etc* by asking them a lot of questions: *The lawyer cross-examined the witness.* **cross-exami'nation** *n*.

'**crossing** *n* **1** a place where a road *etc* may be crossed: *a pedestrian crossing.* **2** a journey over the sea: *It was a very rough crossing.*

'**cross-fire** *n* the crossing of lines of gunfire from two or more points.

See **zebra crossing**.

cross-'legged *adj* with both legs bent at the knee and with the one ankle crossed over the other: *All the children sat cross-legged on the floor.*

'**crossroads** *n* a place where roads cross or meet: *At the crossroads we'll have to decide which road to take.*

'**crossword** or **crossword puzzle** *n* a word-puzzle where small squares have to be filled with letters.

cross section 1 The flat part you can see when you cut straight through something: *a cross section of an apple.* **2** a sample as representative of the whole: *He interviewed a cross section of the audience to get their opinion of the play.*

cross your fingers to place a finger across the one next to it, for good luck.

cross your mind to think of something: *It never crossed my mind that I might have upset her.*

cross off to draw a line through something on a list: *Cross the things off the list as you buy them.*

cross out to draw a line through: *He crossed out all her mistakes.*

crouch /kraʊtʃ/ *v* to get down low, with your knees well bent; to squat down: *He crouched behind the bush*; *The tiger was crouching ready to spring.*

crow /kroʊ/ *n* **1** a large black bird. **2** the cry of a cock. — *v* **1** to cry like a cock. **2** to make happy sounds: *The baby crowed with happiness.*

> **crow; crew** /kruː/; **crowed**: *The cock crew*; *Has the cock crowed yet?*

as the crow flies in a straight line.

crowbar /'kroʊbɑː(r)/ *n* a large iron rod, used to lift heavy stones *etc*.

crowd /kraʊd/ *n* a large number of people or things gathered together: *A crowd of people gathered in the street.* — *v* **1** to gather in a large group: *They crowded round the pop star.* **2** to fill something too full: *Sightseers crowded the building.*

'**crowded** *adj* having or containing a lot of people or things: *crowded buses*.

crown /kraʊn/ *n* **1** a circular head-dress usually made of gold or silver, with jewels, worn by a king or a queen. **2** the top of a head, hat, hill *etc*: *We reached the crown of the hill.* — *v* **1** to make someone king or queen by placing a crown on their head: *She was crowned queen in 1953.* **2** to form a top to something: *The wedding cake was crowned with a red rose.*

'**crowning** *adj* making something perfect or complete: *Her crowning achievement was winning the World Championship.*

crown prince the heir to the throne.

crown princess 1 the wife of a crown prince. **2** the female heir to the throne.

crucial /'kruːʃəl/ *adj* very important: *The next game is crucial — if we lose it, we lose the match.* '**crucially** *adv*.

crucify /'kruːsɪfaɪ/ *v* to put a person to death by fixing his hands and feet to a cross: *Christ was crucified.* **cruci'fixion** *n*.

crucifix /'kruːsɪfɪks/ *n* a model of Christ on the cross.

crude /kruːd/ *adj* **1** not treated; not refined: *crude oil.* **2** rough: *a crude drawing of a house.* **3** impolite: *His manners are rather crude.* '**crudely** *adv*. '**crudeness** *n*.

cruel /'kruəl/ *adj* **1** wanting to cause pain unnecessarily: *The man was very cruel to his dog — he starved and beat it.* **2** sad; painful: *a cruel disappointment.* '**cruelly** *adv*. '**cruelty** *n*.

cruise /kru:z/ v **1** to sail for pleasure: *We're going cruising in the Mediterranean.* **2** to travel by car, plane *etc* at a steady speed: *cruising at 100 kph.* — *n* a voyage made for pleasure: *They went on a cruise.*
'**cruiser** *n* a high-speed battleship.

crumb /krʌm/ *n* a very small piece of bread, cake *etc*: *She swept the crumbs off the table.*

crumble /'krʌmbəl/ v to break into crumbs or small pieces: *She crumbled the bread; The building had crumbled into ruins.* '**crumbly** *adj*.

crumple /'krʌmpəl/ v to make or become creased: *This material crumples easily; She crumpled up the piece of paper.*

crunch /krʌntʃ/ v to crush noisily, with the teeth, feet *etc*: *She crunched sweets all through the film.* — *n* the noise made by crunching.
'**crunchy** *adj*: *crunchy biscuits.*

crusade /kru:'seɪd/ *n* a struggle or campaign in support of a good cause: *the crusade against cigarette advertising.* — *v* to take part in a crusade: *to crusade for women's rights.* **cru'sader** *n*.

crush /krʌʃ/ v **1** to press or squeeze together: *The car was crushed between the two trucks; We were all crushed into the small room.* **2** to crease: *That material crushes easily.* **3** to defeat: *He crushed all his enemies.* — *n* crowding: *There's always a crush in the supermarket on Saturdays.*
'**crushing** *adj* very great: *a crushing defeat.*

crust /krʌst/ *n* **1** the hard outside surface of a loaf of bread: *Eat up your crusts.* **2** a hard surface: *the Earth's crust.* '**crusty** *adj*.

crustacean /krʌ'steɪʃən/ *n* an animal that is covered by a hard shell and lives in water: *Crabs, lobsters, shrimps and barnacles are crustaceans.*

crutch /krʌtʃ/ *n* a stick with a bar at the top to support a lame person: *He can walk only by using crutches.*

crux /krʌks/ *n* the difficult part of something: *This is the crux of the matter.*

cry /kraɪ/ v **1** to let tears come from your eyes; to weep: *The boy cried because he was very sad.* **2** to shout out: *She cried out for help.* — *n* **1** a shout: *a cry of pain.* **2** a time of weeping: *The baby had a little cry before he went to sleep.* **3** the sound made by some animals: *the cry of a wolf.*

> **cry**; '**cry·ing**; **cried**; **cried**: *What are you crying about?*; *The baby cried for a while.*

a far cry a long way from or very different to: *These gentle hills are a far cry from the mountains around my home.*
cry out for to need or deserve something very much: *The city is crying out for a new transport system.*

crypt /krɪpt/ *n* an underground room, especially one under a church used for burials: *Visitors to the cathedral are not allowed into the crypt.*

cryptic /'krɪptɪk/ *adj* containing a hidden meaning that you do not immediately understand: *a cryptic remark.*

crystal /'krɪstəl/ *n* **1** a small regularly shaped part of a solid substance such as salt or ice. **2** a special kind of very clear glass.
'**crystallize** v **1** to form into crystals: *He crystallized salt from sea water.* **2** to organize properly: *He tried to crystallize his ideas.* **crystalli'zation** *n*.
crystal ball a glass ball used in fortune telling.

cub /kʌb/ *n* **1** the baby of certain animals such as foxes, lions *etc*: *a litter of cubs.* **2** a young boy scout.

cube /kju:b/ *n* **1** a solid object with six equal square sides. **2** the result of multiplying a number by itself twice: *The cube of* $4 = 4 \times 4 \times 4 \times 4^3 = 64.$ — *v* to calculate the cube of a number.
'**cubic** *adj* shaped like a cube.

cubicle /'kju:bɪkəl/ *n* a very small room for changing your clothes in *etc*: *There was a row of cubicles at the side of the swimming-pool for changing in.*

cuckoo /'kʊku:/ *n* a bird, named after its call, which lays eggs in the nests of other birds.

cucumber /'kju:kʌmbə(r)/ *n* a long green vegetable.

cud /kʌd/: **chew the cud** to chew food again after bringing it back up from the stomach into the mouth: *Cows, sheep, goats and deer chew the cud.*

cuddle /'kʌdəl/ v to hold someone lovingly in your arms: *The mother cuddled the child until he fell asleep.* — *n*: *She gave the baby a cuddle.*
'**cuddly** *adj*: *a cuddly teddy-bear.*
cuddle up to sit or lie next to someone and hold them close: *They cuddled up together for warmth.*

cue[1] /kju:/ *n* in a play *etc*, something that tells you when to speak or do something.
on cue at exactly the arranged or expected moment: *The door opened right on cue as I walked towards it.*

cue[2] /kju:/ *n* the stick that you use in billiards for hitting the ball.

cuff[1] /kʌf/ *n* the tight part of a sleeve at the wrist: *I've lost a button off one of my shirt cuffs.*

off the cuff without preparation: *I would say, off the cuff, that it will cost about half a million dollars.*

cuff[2] /kʌf/ *v* to hit with a half-open hand or with a paw: *He cuffed the boy on the side of the head; The mother bear cuffed her cub.*

cuisine /kwɪˈziːn/ *n* a style of cookery: *French cuisine.*

cul-de-sac /ˈkʌldəsak/ *n* a street that is closed at one end.

culinary /ˈkʌlɪnərɪ/ *adj* used in the kitchen or in cookery: *culinary herbs.*

cull /kʌl/ *v* **1** to gather or collect. **2** to kill a number of animals of a certain type when there are thought to be too many of them.

culminate /ˈkʌlmɪneɪt/ *v* to reach the highest or most important point: *The celebrations culminated in a firework display.* **culmi'nation** *n*.

culprit /ˈkʌlprɪt/ *n* a person who has done something wrong: *I don't know yet which of you broke the window, but I shall find the culprit.*

cult /kʌlt/ *n* **1** a religious belief or worship. **2** a person or thing that has become extremely popular or fashionable: *a television programme which has become a cult.*

cultivate /ˈkʌltɪveɪt/ *v* **1** to prepare land for growing crops. **2** to grow: *He cultivates tomatoes in his garden.* **culti'vation** *n*.

'**cultivated** *adj* having good manners; educated: *a cultivated young lady.*

'**cultivator** *n* a machine for breaking up ground and removing weeds.

culture /ˈkʌltʃə(r)/ *n* **1** the civilization and customs of a certain race or nation: *the Chinese culture.* **2** improvement of the mind *etc* by education *etc*. **3** a liking for art, literature, music *etc*. '**cultural** *adj*. '**culturally** *adv*.

'**cultured** *adj* well educated.

'**cumbersome** /ˈkʌmbəsəm/ *adj* heavy and clumsy: *a cumbersome piece of furniture.*

cumulative /ˈkjuːmjʊlətɪv/ *adj* the total number or amount after a steady increase: *a cumulative effect.*

cunning /ˈkʌnɪŋ/ *adj* **1** sly; clever at deceiving: *cunning tricks.* **2** clever; very skilful: *cunning workmanship.* — *n* slyness; cleverness.

cup /kʌp/ *n* **1** a small bowl, often with a handle: *a teacup; a cup of tea.* **2** a gold or silver bowl given as a prize in sports events *etc*: *They won the Football League Cup.* — *v* to put your hands into the shape of a cup: *He cupped his hands.*

'**cupful** *n* the amount a cup will hold: *three cupfuls of water.*

cup of tea the sort of thing you like or prefer: *Pop music is not my cup of tea.*

cupboard /ˈkʌbəd/ *n* a piece of furniture with shelves and doors for storing anything: *Put the food in the cupboard; a shoe cupboard.*

curable /ˈkjʊərəbəl/ *adj* able to be cured: *a curable disease.*

> The opposite of **curable** is **incurable**.

curator /kjʊˈreɪtə(r)/ *n* a person in charge of a museum *etc*.

curb /kɜːb/ *n* **1** something which stops or controls something: *He should try to put a curb on his gambling.* **2** a kerb. — *v* to control: *You must curb your spending.*

curd /kɜːd/ *n* the solid substance formed when milk turns sour, used in making cheese.

curdle /ˈkɜːdəl/ *v* to turn into curd: *This milk has curdled.*

cure /kjʊə(r)/ *v* **1** to make better: *That medicine cured me; That pill cured my headache.* **2** to get rid of a bad habit *etc*: *How can I be cured of biting my nails?* **3** to preserve food with salt. — *n* something which cures: *They're trying to find a cure for cancer.*

curfew /ˈkɜːfjuː/ *n* an order forbidding people to be in the streets after a certain hour.

curiosity /ˌkjʊərɪˈɒsɪtɪ/ *n* **1** eagerness to find out about something: *He couldn't bear the curiosity of the neighbours.* **2** something interesting and unusual: *a shop full of old curiosities.*

curious /ˈkjʊərɪəs/ *adj* **1** strange; odd: *a curious habit.* **2** eager to know something: *I'm curious to find out whether he passed his exams.* **3** having too much interest in other people's affairs: *Our neighbours are very curious.* '**curiously** *adv*.

curl /kɜːl/ *v* **1** to twist hair into small coils or rolls. **2** to move in curves; to bend: *The paper curled up at the edges.* — *n* a coil of hair *etc*: *She combed her blonde curls.* '**curly** *adj*. '**curliness** *n*.

'**curler** *n* an object round which hair is rolled to make it curl.

curl up to roll your body into the shape of a ball: *He curled up and went to sleep.*

curly frizzy wavy

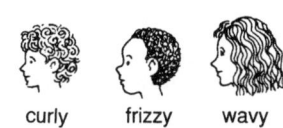

currant /'kʌrənt/ *n* **1** a small, sweet, dried grape used in cakes *etc*. **2** a small red or black juicy fruit.

> a packet of **currants** (not **currents**).

currency /'kʌrənsɪ/ *n* the money of a country: *foreign currencies*.

current /'kʌrənt/ *adj* belonging to the present: *current affairs; the current month*. — *n* **1** a stream of air: *air currents*. **2** the direction a river is flowing in: *Don't swim here — the current is too powerful*. **3** a flow of electricity: *an electric current*.

> **electric current** (not **currant**); **current** (not **currant**) affairs.

'currently *adv* at the present time: *John is currently working as a bus-driver*.

current account a bank account from which money may be withdrawn by cheque.

current affairs important political events happening at the present time: *He always watches the current affairs programmes on the television*.

curriculum /kə'rɪkjʊləm/, *plural* **cur'ricula**, *n* a course of study at school or university.

> **curriculum** is spelt with **-rr-** and **-c-**.

curriculum vitae /'vi:taɪ/ a written account of your personal details, education, qualifications and the jobs you have done, often sent when applying for a new job: *Your curriculum vitae should say what your hobbies are*.

curry /'kʌrɪ/ *n* meat, vegetables *etc* cooked with spices: *chicken curry*. — *v* to cook meat *etc* in this way.

curry powder a mixture of spices ground together and used in making a curry.

curry favour to seek favour by flattery: *She's currying favour with the boss*.

curse /kɜ:s/ *v* **1** to wish evil on something or someone: *The witch cursed him*. **2** to use bad words; to swear: *He cursed when he dropped the hammer on his toe*. — *n* **1** cursing, or the words used: *the witch's curse*. **2** something that is the cause of trouble: *Her shyness is a curse to her*.

cursory /'kɜ:sərɪ/ *adj* done in a hurry and not thoroughly: *The committee only had a cursory look at his report*.

curt /kɜ:t/ *adj* short and sharp: *a curt reply*. **'curtly** *adv*.

curtail /kɜ:'teɪl/ *v* to make less, shorter *etc* than was at first planned: *I've had to curtail my visit*. **cur'tailment** *n*.

curtain /'kɜ:tən/ *n* a piece of material hung up at a window, on a theatre stage *etc*: *In the evening he drew the curtains; The curtain came down at the end of the play*.

curtsy /'kɜ:tsɪ/ *n* a polite movement that women make when meeting a royal person, by bending the knees slightly. — *v*: *The lady curtsied to the queen*.

curtsey

curve /kɜ:v/ *n* a rounded line: *a curve in the road*. — *v* to bend in a curve: *The road curves east*. **curved** *adj*. **'curvy** *adj*.

cushion /'kʊʃən/ *n* **1** a bag filled with feathers *etc*, to make a seat more comfortable. **2** something that gives protection from shock or reduces unpleasant effects: *The hovercraft moves on a cushion of air*. — *v* to lessen the force of a blow *etc*: *The soft sand cushioned his fall*.

custard /'kʌstəd/ *n* a sauce made of milk, sugar and eggs or cornflour for sweet dishes.

custody /'kʌstədɪ/ *n* **1** the duty of caring for children. **2** imprisonment: *The police took the thief into custody; The accused man is in custody*.

custom /'kʌstəm/ *n* something you do from habit, or because it is usual: *It's my custom to go for a walk on Sundays; religious customs*.

'customary *adj* usually done: *It is customary to clap at the end of a concert*.

'customer *n* a person who buys from a shop *etc*: *our regular customers*.

'customize *v* to make or alter to fit a particular client's needs: *The company customizes cars for disabled drivers*.

'customs *n* **1** taxes paid on goods being brought into a country. **2** the place at an airport *etc* where these taxes are collected.

cut /kʌt/ *v* **1** to make an opening in something.

with something sharp, such as a knife or a pair of scissors: *to cut paper.* **2** to divide by cutting: *She cut a slice of bread; The child cut out the pictures.* **3** to shorten by cutting; to trim: *to cut hair; I'll cut the grass.* **4** to reduce: *They cut my wages by ten per cent.* **5** to remove: *They cut several bits out of the film.* **6** to wound or hurt: *I cut my hand on a piece of glass.* **7** to take a short way: *He cut through the park on his way to the office.* **8** to stay away from a class, lecture *etc*: *He cut school and went to the cinema.* **9** to divide a pack of cards into two. — *n* **1** the result of cutting: *a cut on the head; a haircut; a cut in prices.* **2** the shape and style of clothes. **3** a piece of meat cut from an animal.

> **cut; cut; cut**: *He cut his toe; Has she cut herself?*

cut across 1 to go across something to make your journey shorter: *We could get ahead of them if we cut across this field.* **2** to go beyond the divisions of : *The shock of the leader's death has cut across party differences.*
cut back to reduce: *The school cut back its spending on books.* **'cut-back** *n.*
cut down 1 to cause to fall by cutting: *He has cut down the apple tree.* **2** to reduce in quantity *etc*: *I haven't given up smoking but I'm cutting down.*
cut in to interrupt: *She cut in with a remark.*
cut off 1 to remove by cutting: *She cut off a long piece of thread.* **2** to interrupt a telephone conversation. **3** to separate: *The farm was cut off from the village by the snow.*
cut out 1 to stop working: *The engine cut out.* **2** to stop: *I've cut out smoking.* **3** to be suited to something: *She wasn't really cut out for the outdoor life.*
cut short to make something shorter than intended: *He cut short his holiday.*

cut up to divide something into smaller pieces: *Shall I cut up your meat for you?*
cute /kju:t/ *adj* attractive or pleasing: *a cute baby.*
cutlery /'kʌtlərɪ/ *n* knives, forks and spoons.

> See **crockery**.

cutlet /'kʌtlət/ *n* a slice of meat.
cut-price /kʌt'praɪs/ *adj* reduced in price: *The shop sells everything cut-price during the sale.*
cutter /'kʌtə(r)/ *n* **1** a person or thing that cuts: *a woodcutter; a glass-cutter.* **2** a type of small sailing ship.
cut-throat /'kʌtθroʊt/ *n* a murderer. — *adj* fierce: *cut-throat rivalry.*
cutting /'kʌtɪŋ/ *n* **1** a piece cut from a plant to be grown separately. **2** a piece cut out of a newspaper. — *adj* meant to hurt someone's feelings: *cutting remarks.*
cuttlefish /'kʌtəlfɪʃ/ *n* an edible sea-creature like an octopus, that squirts a black liquid.
cyanide /'saɪənaɪd/ *n* a deadly poison.
cycle[1] /'saɪkəl/ *v* to go by bicycle: *He cycles to work every day.* — *n* short for **bicycle**.
cycle[2] /'saɪkəl/ *n* a number of events happening one after the other in a certain order: *the cycle of the seasons.* **'cyclic** *adj.*
cyclist /'saɪklɪst/ *n* a person who rides a bicycle.
cyclone /'saɪkloʊn/ *n* a violent storm of wind.

> See **hurricane**.

cygnet /'sɪgnət/ *n* a young swan.
cylinder /'sɪlɪndə(r)/ *n* **1** an object with a round base and top and straight sides. **2** a piece of machinery of this shape. **cy'lindrical** *adj.*
cymbal /'sɪmbəl/ *n* a brass musical instrument like a plate, two of which are struck together to make a clashing sound.
cynic /'sɪnɪk/ *n* a person who believes the worst about everyone. **'cynical** *adj.*

D

D /diː/: **3-D** abbreviation for three-dimensional: *a 3-D picture.*

dab /dab/ *v* to touch gently: *He dabbed the wound with cotton-wool.* — *n* **1** a small lump of anything soft or moist: *a dab of butter.* **2** a gentle touch.

dabble /'dabəl/ *v* to move about or splash in water: *He dabbled his feet in the river.*

dachshund /'dakshʊnd/ *n* a small dog with a long body and short legs.

dad /dad/, **daddy** /'dadɪ/ *n* children's words for father.

daffodil /'dafədɪl/ *n* a yellow flower which grows from a bulb.

daft /daft/ *adj* stupid or silly: *That's a daft idea.*

dagger /'dagə(r)/ *n* a knife for stabbing.

daily /'deɪlɪ/ *adj* happening every day: *a daily walk; Brushing our teeth is part of our daily lives.* — *adv* every day: *We see each other daily.* — *n* a newspaper published every day.

dainty /'deɪntɪ/ *adj* delicate and pretty: *her dainty figure; dainty frilled curtains and matching bedcover.* **'daintily** *adv.* **'daintiness** *n.*

dairy /'dɛərɪ/ *n* **1** a shop supplying milk, butter, cheese *etc*: *We bought milk at the dairy.* **2** the place on a farm *etc* where milk is kept and butter and cheese are made.

> You buy milk in a **dairy** (not **diary**).

dais /'deɪɪs/ *n* a raised platform in a hall, for people to stand on when speaking to an audience.

daisy /'deɪzɪ/ *n* a small common flower with a yellow centre and white petals.

dam /dam/ *n* **1** a bank or wall of earth, concrete *etc* to keep back water. **2** the water kept back. — *v* to hold back by means of a dam: *The river has been dammed up.*

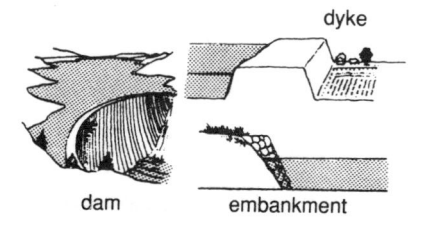

dyke

dam   embankment

damage /'damɪdʒ/ *n* injury or harm, especially to a thing: *The storm caused a lot of damage; She suffered brain-damage as a result of the accident.* — *v* to cause harm to something; to spoil: *The fire damaged several buildings; The book was damaged in the post.*
'damages *n* payment for loss or injury suffered by someone: *The court awarded him £5000 damages.*
'damaging *adj* having a harmful effect.

damn /dam/ *v* to condemn someone or something; to say or show that they are wrong, bad, guilty *etc*: *He said he was innocent of the crime, but the evidence damned him.*
'damning *adj* extremely critical: *a damning remark.*

damp /damp/ *adj* slightly wet: *This towel is still damp.* — *n* slight wetness, especially in the air: *The walls were brown with the damp.*
'dampen *v* **1** to make something damp. **2** to make or become less strong: *The bad news dampened everyone's enthusiasm.*
'dampness *n.*

damp down to make less strong or fierce: *He tried to damp down the flames by hitting them with his hat.*

dance /dɑːns/ *v* **1** to move in time to music: *She began to dance; Can you dance the waltz?* **2** to move with a skipping or jumping step: *The children were dancing up and down with excitement.* — *n* **1** a series of steps made in time to music: *Have you done this dance before?* **2** a party at which people dance: *We're going to a dance next Saturday.* **3** performing dances as a form of art: *She's very interested in modern dance.* — *adj*: *dance music.*
'dancer *n* someone who dances, especially as a job: *She joined a troupe of dancers.*
'dancing *n.*

dandelion /'dandɪlaɪən/ *n* a common wild plant with a yellow flower.

dandruff /'dandrʌf/ *n* dead skin under the hair which falls off in small pieces.

danger /'deɪndʒə(r)/ *n* **1** something that may cause harm or injury: *The cliff is a danger to children.* **2** a situation in which a person or thing may be harmed: *He is in danger; The bridge is in danger of collapsing.*
'dangerous *adj* very unsafe and likely to be a cause of harm: *a dangerous road.* **'dangerously** *adv.*

dangle /ˈdaŋgəl/ v to hang loosely: *Her legs dangled over the wall.*

dank /daŋk/ adj unpleasantly damp and cold: *a dark, dank cellar.*

dappled /ˈdapəld/ adj having patches of a different colour: *a dappled horse.*

dare /dɛə(r)/ v **1** to be brave enough to do something: *I daren't go*; *He wouldn't dare do a thing like that*; *Don't you dare say such a thing again!* **2** to tell a person to do something as proof of courage: *I dare you to jump off the wall.*

> **dare** can be used with or without **to**: *I dare do anything*; *He dares to jump*; *How dare he hit me!*
> **dare not** and **daren't** /dɛənt/ are used without **to**: *I dare not tell* (not *to tell*) *the truth*; *He daren't tell the truth.*

'daredevil n a very bold person.

'daring adj bold; courageous: *a daring pilot*; *She made a daring attempt to rescue the climber.* — n boldness.

I dare say I suppose: *I dare say you're right.*

dark /dɑːk/ adj **1** without light: *a dark room*; *It's getting dark.* **2** not pale; not fair: *a dark red colour*; *Her hair is dark.* **3** evil: *dark deeds.* — n absence of light: *in the dark*; *He never goes out after dark.* **'darkness** n.

'darken v to make or become dark: *The sky darkened.*

'darkroom n a room which gets no natural light, used for developing photographs.

darling /ˈdɑːlɪŋ/ n a dearly loved person: *Is that you, darling?* — adj much loved: *My darling child!*

darn /dɑːn/ v to mend a hole in a sock *etc* with rows of stiches that cross one another.

dart /dɑːt/ n **1** a pointed arrow-like weapon for throwing or shooting. **2** a sudden and quick movement: *the sudden dart of little silvery fish.* — v to move suddenly and quickly: *The mouse darted into a hole.*

darts n a game in which small darts are thrown at a target called a **'dartboard**.

dash /daʃ/ v **1** to move hastily; to rush: *The man dashed into a shop*; *I have to dash off to catch the bus.* **2** to knock, throw *etc* violently: *He dashed the bottle against the wall.* **3** to destroy: *Our hopes were dashed.* — n **1** a sudden rush: *The child made a dash for the door.* **2** a small amount of something: *coffee with a dash of milk.* **3** a short line (—) to show a break in a sentence *etc*.

dash off to write something quickly without thinking.

dashboard /ˈdaʃbɔːd/ n the board with dials, switches *etc* in front of the driver's seat in a car or other vehicle.

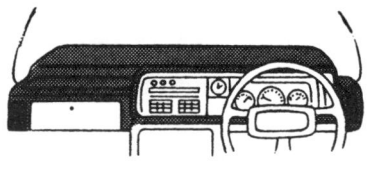

dashboard

dashing /ˈdaʃɪŋ/ adj smart and lively: *He looks very dashing in his new clothes.*

data /ˈdeɪtə/ or /ˈdɑːtə/ n facts or information: *All the data has* (or *have*) *been fed into the computer.*

'data-bank n a large amount of information which is stored in a computer.

'database n a large amount of information stored in a computer in a way which lets you use that information quickly: *The school keeps all the pupils' marks in a database.*

data-'processing n the handling and processing of information by computer.

date¹ /deɪt/ n the brown, sticky fruit of the **date palm**, a tree growing in the tropics.

date² /deɪt/ n **1** the day of the month, month and year: *I can't read the date on this letter.* **2** the time at which something happened or is going to happen: *What is your date of birth?* **3** an appointment, especially to go out with a boyfriend or girlfriend: *He asked her for a date.* — v **1** to put a date on a letter *etc*: *This letter is dated 21 June.* **2** to state or guess when an object was made or produced: *We can date the skeleton to within ten years.*

'dated adj old-fashioned: *The whole film has a very dated feel to it.*

to date until now: *The news to date has not been good.*

out of date 1 old-fashioned: *This coat is out of date.* **2** no longer used; no longer valid: *Your ticket is out of date*; *an out-of-date telephone directory.*

up to date 1 completed up to the present time: *Is the catalogue up to date?* **2** modern; new: *This method is very up-to-date*; *an up-to-date method.*

daughter /ˈdɔːtə(r)/ n a female child.

'daughter-in-law, plural **'daughters-in-law**, n a son's wife.

daunt /dɔːnt/ v to discourage or frighten

slightly: *Children can be daunted if you give them too much information at one time.* **'daunting** *adj*: *a daunting task.*

dawdle /'dɔːdəl/ *v* to waste time by moving slowly: *Hurry up, don't dawdle!*

dawn / dɔːn/*v* to begin to appear: *A new day has dawned.* — *n* **1** the beginning of a day; very early morning: *We must get up at dawn.* **2** the beginning of something: *the dawn of civilization.*

dawn on to become suddenly clear to a person: *It suddenly dawned on me what he meant.*

day /deɪ/ *n* **1** the time from sunrise to sunset: *She worked all day*; *They worked day and night to finish the job.* **2** the time or hours usually spent at work: *How long is your working day?* **3** twenty-four hours from one midnight to the next: *How many days are in the month of September?* **4** a particular time or period: *in my grandfather's day.*

'daybreak *n* dawn: *We left at daybreak.*

'day-dream *n* a dreaming or imagining of pleasant events while awake. — *v*: *She often day-dreams.*

'daylight *n* **1** the light given by the sun: *The sand, as daylight faded, was decorated with pin-points of silvery light.* **2** dawn.

day off a normal working day on which you do not have to go to work: *I've got a day off tomorrow.*

day school a school whose pupils attend only during the day and live at home.

'daytime *n* the time between sunrise and sunset.

day-to-'day *adj* happening every day as part of the usual routine: *She never has enough money for her day-to-day expenses.*

by day during the day.

call it a day to stop working: *I'm so tired that I'll have to call it a day.*

day by day every day: *He's getting better day by day.*

day in, day out happening every day.

from day to day or **from one day to the next** only for or within short periods of time: *The situation has been changing quickly from day to day.*

one day or **some day** at some time in the future: *He hopes to go to America one day*; *I hope to see her again some day.*

the other day not long ago: *I saw Mr Smith the other day.*

these days nowadays.

daze /deɪz/ *v* to confuse someone, for instance because of a blow, a shock *etc*: *She was dazed by the news.* — *n* a state of confusion: *She's been going around in a daze all day.*

dazzle /'dazəl/ *v* **1** to blind for a short time with very bright light: *I was dazzled by the car's headlights.* **2** to impress deeply: *She was dazzled by his charm.*

'dazzling *adj* **1** extremely bright: *a dazzling light.* **2** impressive: *a dazzling display of wit.*

dead /dɛd/ *adj* **1** without life; not living: *a dead body.* **2** without feeling; numb: *My arm's gone dead.* **3** not working: *The engine is dead.* **4** complete: *There was dead silence at his words*; *He came to a dead stop.* **5** without movement or activity: *The phone suddenly went dead.* — *adv* exactly; completely; very: *Keep looking dead ahead*; *You were dead right*; *It's dead easy*; *The train stopped dead.*

'deaden *v* to make less sharp *etc*: *This pill will deaden the pain.*

dead end *n* a road closed off at one end.

dead heat *n* a race in which two or more runners cross the finishing line together.

'deadline *n* a time by which something must be finished: *Monday is the deadline for handing in this essay.*

> to set a **deadline** (not **dateline**) for finishing a job.

'deadlock *n* a situation in which no further progress towards an agreement is possible: *Talks between the two sides ended in deadlock.*

'deadly *adj* **1** causing death: *a deadly poison.* **2** very great: *They are deadly enemies.* — *adv* extremely; very: *I'm deadly serious.*

'deadpan *adj* sounding serious and without laughing or smiling: *a deadpan expression.* — *adv*: *He looked at me deadpan.*

the dead people who have died: *remember the dead.*

the dead of night the darkest and quietest part of the night: *We left the house at the dead of night.*

deaf /dɛf/ *adj* **1** unable to hear: *She has been deaf since birth.* **2** refusing to understand or to listen: *He was deaf to all arguments.* **'deafness** *n*.

'deafen *v* to damage someone's hearing; to make more noise than someone can bear: *I was deafened by the music at the disco.*

'deafening *adj* very loud.

the deaf deaf people: *sign language for the deaf.*

deal /diːl/ *n* **1** a bargain or agreement: *a business deal.* **2** dividing cards among players in a card game. — *v* **1** to do business: *I think he deals in stocks and shares.* **2** to distribute playing cards.

> **deal**; **dealt** /dɛlt/; **dealt**: *She dealt the cards*; *We have dealt with the problem.*

'dealer *n* **1** a person who buys and sells: *a dealer in antiques.* **2** the person who distributes the cards in a card game.

'dealings *n* contact: *I will have no dealings with dishonest people.*

deal with 1 to be concerned with something: *This book deals with methods of teaching English.* **2** to take action about something: *She deals with all the difficult problems.*

a good deal or **a great deal** much; a lot: *They made a good deal of noise*; *She spent a great deal of money on the necklace.*

dear /dɪə(r)/ *adj* **1** high in price: *Cabbages are very dear this week.* **2** very lovable: *He is such a dear little boy.* **3** much loved: *She is very dear to me.* **4** used at the beginning of a letter: *Dear Peter*; *Dear Sir.* — *n* a person who is loved or liked: *Come in, dear.*

'dearly *adv* very much: *She loved him dearly.*

dear, dear! or **oh dear!** or **dear me!** expressions of regret, sorrow *etc*: *Oh dear! I've forgotten my key!*

dearth /dɜːθ/ *n* the state of not having something that is needed, a lack: *There is a dearth of good actresses in this country.*

death /dɛθ/ *n* **1** being dead or dying: *Most people fear death.* **2** something which causes a person to die: *Smoking was the death of him.*

'deathly *adj, adv* as if caused by death: *a deathly silence.*

death penalty capital punishment.

put to death to kill someone, especially a criminal: *The criminal was put to death by hanging.*

debate /dɪˈbeɪt/ *n* a discussion, especially a formal one in front of an audience: *a debate in Parliament.* — *v* to hold a formal discussion about something: *Parliament will debate the question tomorrow.*

de'batable *adj* not certain; that can be argued about: *It's debatable whether animal fats are really bad for you.*

debit /ˈdɛbɪt/ *n* money paid out of a bank account. — *v* to take money out of a bank account: *My bank statement showed that my bank account had been debited with £100.*

> See **credit**.

debrief /diːˈbriːf/ *v* to question a soldier, diplomat or astronaut *etc* after a battle, event or mission to gain information about it: *The spy was debriefed when he returned to his own country.*

dèbris /ˈdɛbriː/ or /ˈdeɪbriː/ *n* **1** the remains of something broken, destroyed *etc*: *The fireman found a dog among the debris of the house.* **2** rubbish: *There was a lot of debris in the house after the builder had left.*

debt /dɛt/ *n* what one person owes to another: *His debts amount to over £3000.*

'debtor *n* a person who owes a debt.

in debt 1 owing money: *He's badly in debt.* **2** grateful for what someone has done for you: *She felt that she would always be in his debt.*

debut /ˈdeɪbjuː/ or /ˈdɛbjuː/ *n* a first public appearance on the stage *etc*: *She made her stage debut at the age of eight.*

decade /ˈdɛkeɪd/ *n* a period of ten years: *the first decade of this century.*

> See **year**.

decadence /ˈdɛkədəns/ *n* a falling from high to low standards, especially moral standards or in art or literature: *societies that have reached a stage of over-prosperous decadence.*

'decadent *adj* having or showing low moral standards: *He was accused of having decadent values.*

decaffeinated /diːˈkafɪneɪtɪd/ *adj* having had the caffeine removed: *She only drinks decaffeinated coffee.*

decapitate /dɪˈkapɪteɪt/ *v* to cut off someone's head: *His body was decapitated after his death.*

decathlon /dɪˈkaθlən/ *n* a contest for men in which each athlete competes in ten different sporting events.

decay /dɪˈkeɪ/ *v* to become rotten or ruined: *Sugar makes your teeth decay.* — *n*: *Sugar causes tooth decay.* **de'cayed** *adj*.

deceased /dɪˈsiːst/ *adj* dead: *His deceased parents had been very wealthy.* — *n*: *Relatives of the deceased brought flowers to the house.*

deceit /dɪˈsiːt/ *n* deceiving: *She was too honest to be capable of deceit.* **de'ceitful** *adj*. **de'ceitfully** *adv*: *You acted deceitfully.* **de'ceitfulness** *n*.

> **deceit** is spelt with **-ei-**.

deceive /dɪˈsiːv/ *v* to make someone believe something that is not true: *She told her father a lie, but he was not deceived by it*;

He was deceived by her innocent appearance.

> **deceive** is spelt with **-ei-**.

December /dɪˈsɛmbə(r)/ *n* the twelfth month of the year.

decency /ˈdiːsənsɪ/ *n* right, proper and respectable behaviour: *In the interests of decency, those using this swimming-pool must not bathe naked; He had the decency to admit that it was his fault.*

decent /ˈdiːsənt/ *adj* **1** respectable; good: *a decent man.* **2** modest; not causing shock or embarrassment: *Keep your language decent!* **ˈdecently** *adv.*

> The opposite of **decent** is **indecent**.

deception /dɪˈsɛpʃən/ *n* an act of deceiving; a trick or lie: *His clever deception fooled the enemy into thinking he was on their side.* **deˈceptive** *adj.*
deˈceptively *adv*: *She made the process look deceptively easy.*

decide /dɪˈsaɪd/ *v* **1** to make up your mind: *I have decided to learn French; What made you decide not to go?* **2** to make the result of something become certain: *The last goal decided the match.*
deˈcided *adj* clear; definite: *There has been a decided improvement in his work.*
deˈcidedly *adv.*

deciduous /dɪˈsɪdjuːəs/ *adj* having leaves that fall off in autumn: *Oaks and chestnuts are deciduous trees.*

> See **evergreen**.

decilitre /ˈdɛsɪliːtə(r)/ *n* one-tenth of a litre.

decimal /ˈdɛsɪməl/ *adj* numbered by tens: *the decimal system.* — *n* a fraction expressed as a decimal number, with amounts less than 1 placed after a point: *In decimal figures,* $\frac{1}{10}$ *is 0.1.*

decipher /dɪˈsaɪfə(r)/ *v* to find the meaning of something which is difficult to read or written in code: *I can't decipher his handwriting; They deciphered the spy's letter.*

decision /dɪˈsɪʒən/ *n* deciding; a judgement: *You will soon have to make a decision whether or not to leave school; I think you made the wrong decision.*

decisive /dɪˈsaɪsɪv/ *adj* **1** final; putting an end to a contest *etc*: *The battle was decisive.* **2** firm: *a decisive person.* **deˈcisively** *adv.* **deˈcisiveness** *n.*

deck /dɛk/ *n* **1** a platform extending from one side of a ship to the other and forming the floor: *The cars are on the lower deck.* **2** a floor in a bus: *Let's go on the top deck.* **3** a pack of playing-cards.
ˈdeck-chair *n* a light chair that can be folded up: *They were sitting in deck-chairs on the beach.*

> See **bench**.

declare /dɪˈklɛə(r)/ *v* **1** to say firmly: *'I don't like him at all,' she declared.* **2** to announce publicly: *They declared war on their enemies.* **3** to tell the people in authority that you have goods on which duty must be paid, income on which tax should be paid *etc*: *Do you have anything to declare?* **declaˈration** *n.*

decline /dɪˈklaɪn/ *v* **1** to say 'no' to an invitation *etc*; to refuse: *We declined his offer of a lift in his car.* **2** to become less strong or less good *etc*: *His health has declined recently.* — *n* becoming less or worse: *There has been a decline in the number of students.*

decode /diːˈkoʊd/ *v* to translate a coded message into ordinary language.

decompose /diːkəmˈpoʊz/ *v* to rot or decay: *The dead leaves decomposed quickly.* **decompoˈsition** *n.*

decor /ˈdɛkɔː(r)/ *n* the style of furniture and decoration in a room: *a flat with decor and furnishings in the 1930's style.*

decorate /ˈdɛkəreɪt/ *v* **1** to add some kind of ornament *etc* to something to make it more beautiful *etc*: *We decorated the Christmas tree with glass balls.* **2** to put paint, paper *etc* on the walls of a room: *He spent a week decorating the living-room.* **3** to give a medal to someone as a mark of honour: *He was decorated for bravery.*
decoˈration *n* something used to decorate: *Christmas decorations.*
ˈdecorative *adj* ornamental or beautiful.
ˈdecorator *n* a person who paints rooms, houses *etc.*

decoy /ˈdiːkɔɪ/ *n* anything intended to lead someone or something into a trap: *The policewoman acted as a decoy when the police were trying to catch the murderer.*

decrease *v* /dɪˈkriːs/ to make or become less: *The number of pupils has decreased.* — *n* /ˈdiːkriːs/ a growing less: *a decrease of fifty per cent; a gradual decrease in unemployment.*

> The opposite of **decrease** is **increase**.

decree /dɪˈkriː/ *n* an order or law: *a decree forbidding the killing of certain wild animals.* — *v* to order: *The court decreed that he should pay a fine of £800.*

decrepit /dɪˈkrɛpɪt/ *adj* worn out with age; broken down: *a decrepit building*; *Grandfather says he's getting old and decrepit.*

dedicate /ˈdɛdɪkeɪt/ *v* **1** to give up or devote your time, life *etc* to something: *He dedicated his life to helping those who had been crippled in the war.* **2** to state that a book *etc* is written in honour of someone: *The author dedicated the book to his father*; *He dedicated that song to her.* **dedication** *n*.

'dedicated *adj* giving a lot of time and effort to something you believe is important: *Only the most dedicated nurses could work in these conditions.*

deduce /dɪˈdjuːs/ *v* to work out something from facts you know or guess: *From the height of the sun I deduced that it was about ten o'clock.* **de'duction**[1] /dɪˈdʌkʃən/ *n*.

deduct /dɪˈdʌkt/ *v* to take away: *They deducted the expenses from his salary.*

de'duction[2] *n* something that has been deducted: *A deduction had been made from his pay.*

deed /diːd/ *n* something done; an act: *a good deed*.

deep /diːp/ *adj* **1** going far down or back: *a deep lake*; *a deep wound*; *deep shelves*. **2** very much occupied in something: *He was deep in a book.* **3** strong; dark: *The sea is a deep blue colour.* **4** low: *His voice is very deep.* **5** sound: *They are in a deep sleep.* — *adv* far down or into something: *They wandered deep into the wood.* **'deepness** *n*.

'deepen *v* to make or become deeper: *He deepened the hole.*

deep-'freeze *n* a kind of refrigerator which freezes food quickly and can keep it for a long time. — *v* to freeze food in this.

deep-'fried *adj* fried in enough fat to be completely covered by it: *He does not like deep-fried chicken.*

'deeply *adv* very: *We are deeply grateful to you.*

deep-'rooted or **deep-'seated** *adj* firmly fixed and not easily changed: *deep-rooted prejudices.*

in deep water in difficulties or trouble: *You will get into deep water if you start borrowing money.*

deer /dɪə(r)/, *plural* **deer**, *n* a large, grass-eating animal, the male of which has antlers.

> A deer **barks** or **bellows**.
> A baby deer is a **fawn** or a **calf**.
> A female deer is a **doe** or a **hind**.
> A male deer is a **buck** or a **stag**.

deface /dɪˈfeɪs/ *v* to spoil the appearance of something: *The statue had been defaced with red paint.* **de'facement** *n*.

default /dɪˈfɔːlt/ *n* the procedure a computer follows when it is given no other instruction. **by default** happening because it was not prevented: *The job became hers by default when no other candidates applied.*

defeat /dɪˈfiːt/ *v* to beat; to win a victory over someone or something: *They defeated our team by three goals*; *We will defeat the enemy eventually.* — *n* the loss of a game, battle *etc*: *We suffered yet another defeat.*

de'featism *n* the attitude of someone who expects to be defeated.

de'featist *n*: *You are all such defeatists!*

defect *n* /ˈdiːfɛkt/ a fault: *She has a few defects in her character*; *a defect in the china.* — *v* /dɪˈfɛkt/ to leave a country, political party *etc* to go and join another: *He defected to the Liberal Party.* **de'fection** *n*.

de'fective *adj* having a fault: *a defective machine.*

defence /dɪˈfɛns/ *n* **1** the defending of something or someone against attack: *the defence of Rome*; *He spoke in defence of the government's plans.* **2** the method or equipment used to guard or protect: *The walls were built as a defence against flooding.* **3** a person's answer to an accusation, especially in a law court: *What is your defence?* **4** the lawyers speaking and acting for the accused person in a court of law: *The defence has (or have) already asked that question.* **de'fenceless** *adj* without protection.

defend /dɪˈfɛnd/ *v* to guard or protect someone or something against attack: *The soldiers defended the castle.* **de'fender** *n*.

de'fendant *n* an accused person in a lawcourt.

de'fensive *adj* protective; resisting attack: *They had to take defensive action against their attackers.*

defer /dɪˈfɜː(r)/ *v* to put off to another time: *They can defer their departure.*

> **deferred** and **deferring** have two **r**s.

deference /ˈdɛfərəns/ *n* respectful, polite behaviour: *In my day, teachers were always treated with deference.*

in deference to because of the respect you feel: *In deference to her parents' wishes, she didn't mention the matter again.*

defiance /dɪˈfaɪəns/ *n* openly refusing to obey; opposition: *He went swimming in defiance of my orders.* **de'fiant** *adj*. **de'fiantly** *adv*.

in defiance of openly refusing to obey a thing or person: *She continued to wear make-up in defiance of the school rules.*

deficient /dɪˈfɪʃənt/ *adj* not having enough of something: *Their food is deficient in vitamins.* **deˈficiency** *n*.

deficit /ˈdɛfəsɪt/ *n* the amount by which a sum of money *etc* is too little: *The total should have been £500, but there was a deficit of £49.*

> The opposite of **deficit** is **surplus**.

defile /dɪˈfaɪl/ *v* to make something dirty; to spoil or destroy the purity of something: *Some video films are so horrible that they must defile the minds of the people who watch them.*

define /dɪˈfaɪn/ *v* to state the exact meaning of a word *etc*: *Words are defined in a dictionary.* **definition** /dɛfɪˈnɪʃən/ *n*.

definite /ˈdɛfɪnət/ *adj* clear; fixed or certain: *I'll give you a definite answer later.*
 ˈdefinitely *adv* clearly; certainly: *She definitely said that she'd arrive at 9.00 a.m*; *Her dress is definitely red.*
 definite article the name of the word **the**.

definitive /dɪˈfɪnɪtɪv/ *adj* the best or most satisfactory that has ever been done: *the definitive performance of a play.* **deˈfinitively** *adv*.

deflate /diːˈfleɪt/ *v* to let air out of a tyre *etc*. **deˈflation** *n*.

> The opposite of **deflate** is **inflate**.

deflect /dɪˈflɛkt/ *v* **1** to make something turn away from the direction it is going in: *He deflected the blow with his arm.* **2** to stop someone doing what they intend: *Don't try to deflect me from my purpose!* **deˈflection** *n*.

deform /dɪˈfɔːm/ *v* to alter the shape of something from what is normal and natural: *The disease can severely deform the fingers.*
 deˈformed *adj* twisted out of the right shape: *His foot was deformed.* **deˈformity** *n*.

defrost /diːˈfrɒst/ *v* **1** to remove frost or ice from a refrigerator *etc*: *I keep forgetting to defrost the freezer.* **2** to thaw: *Make sure you defrost the chicken thoroughly.*

deft /dɛft/ *adj* quick, neat and skilful in movement: *He was very deft with his fingers and was always making things.* **ˈdeftly** *adv*. **ˈdeftness** *n*.

defuse /diːˈfjuːz/ *v* to remove the fuse from a bomb *etc*.

defy /dɪˈfaɪ/ *v* **1** to disobey openly: *He defied the headmaster's authority.* **2** to challenge someone to do something that you believe is impossible: *I defy you to prove me wrong.* **3** to be too difficult to explain or understand: *The beauty of the place defies description.*

degenerate /dɪˈdʒɛnəreɪt/ *v* to become worse in some way, such as in health: *His behaviour has been degenerating ever since he left school.* **degeneˈration** *n*.

degrade /dɪˈɡreɪd/ *v* to take dignity and pride away from someone: *He felt degraded by having to beg for food.* **degraˈdation** *n*.
 deˈgrading *adj*: *Cleaning the public toilets shouldn't be considered a degrading job.*

degree /dɪˈɡriː/ *n* **1** an amount or extent: *Children will need some degree of skill to answer the third question.* **2** a unit of temperature: *twenty degrees* (usually written 20°) *Celsius.* **3** a unit by which angles are measured: *an angle of ninety degrees* (usually written 90°). **4** an award given by a university to a person who has passed their final examinations: *He has a degree in chemistry.*
 by degrees gradually; step by step; little by little: *We are achieving our aim by degrees.*

dehydrate /diːˈhaɪdreɪt/ *v* to remove water from something; to dry: *Vegetables can be dehydrated so that they keep for a long time.* **dehyˈdration** *n*.
 dehyˈdrated *adj* having lost too much water from the body: *Climbers can easily become dehydrated on these exposed slopes.*

deity /ˈdeɪəti/ *n* a god or goddess: *Apollo was one of the Greek deities.*

dejected /dɪˈdʒɛktɪd/ *adj* sad; miserable: *His defeat made him very dejected.* **deˈjectedly** *adv*. **deˈjection** *n*.

delay /dɪˈleɪ/ *v* **1** to put off to a later time: *We delayed our holiday for a week.* **2** to hold up; to make late: *The bus was delayed ten minutes*; *We were delayed by the traffic.* — *n* lateness; a hold-up: *He came without delay.*

delegate *v* /ˈdɛlɪɡeɪt/ to give a piece of work, power *etc* to someone else: *He delegates a great deal of work to his assistant.* — *n* /ˈdɛlɪɡət/ a person chosen to act for or represent others at a conference, meeting *etc*.
 deleˈgation *n* a group of delegates.

delete /dɪˈliːt/ *v* to remove or cross out a word *etc*: *Delete his name from the list.* **deˈletion** *n*.

deliberate *adj* /dɪˈlɪbərət/ **1** intentional; not by accident: *That was a deliberate insult.* **2** slow and careful: *He had a very deliberate* *way of talking.* — *v* /dɪˈlɪbəreɪt/ to think carefully before making a decision: *I'm still deliberating over the job offer.*

deˈliberately *adv* **1** intentionally. **2** slowly and carefully.

delibeˈration *n*: *The committee carried on its deliberations in secret.*

delicacy /ˈdɛlɪkəsɪ/ *n* **1** the quality of being delicate. **2** something delicious and special to eat.

delicate /ˈdɛlɪkət/ *adj* **1** requiring special treatment or careful handling: *delicate china*; *a delicate situation*. **2** fine; done with skill: *The ring had a very delicate design.* **3** able to do fine, accurate work: *a delicate instrument.* **4** not strong or bright: *a delicate shade of blue.* **5** soft; fine: *the delicate skin of a child.* **ˈdelicately** *adv.*

delicatessen /dɛlɪkəˈtɛsən/ *n* a shop selling unusual and foreign foods: *I bought some smoked sausage at the delicatessen.*

delicious /dɪˈlɪʃəs/ *adj* very nice to eat or smell: *a delicious meal; The food smells delicious.* **deˈliciously** *adv.*

delight /dɪˈlaɪt/ *v* **1** to please greatly: *I was delighted by the news.* **2** to enjoy something very much: *He delights in teasing me.* — *n* pleasure.

deˈlightful *adj* causing delight: *a delightful surprise.* **deˈlightfully** *adv.*

delinquent /dɪˈlɪŋkwənt/ *n* someone who breaks the law; someone who commits a crime. **deˈlinquency** *n.*

delirious /dɪˈlɪrɪəs/ *adj* **1** confused and talking nonsense usually because of high fever. **2** very excited or happy.

deˈliriously *adv*: *The couple seemed deliriously happy.*

deliver /dɪˈlɪvə(r)/ *v* **1** to take goods, letters *etc* to the person for whom they are intended: *The postman delivers letters.* **2** to make a speech *etc*: *He delivered a long speech.* **3** to assist a woman at the birth of her child: *The doctor delivered the twins safely.*

deˈlivery *n* **1** delivering goods, letters *etc.* **2** giving birth to a child.

delta /ˈdɛltə/ *n* a triangular area of land formed at the mouth of a river which reaches the sea in two or more branches: *the Nile Delta.*

delude /dɪˈluːd/ *v* to deceive: *He is deluding himself if he thinks she is going to marry him.*

deluge /ˈdɛljuːdʒ/ *n* **1** a great flood of water; very heavy rain. **2** a great number: *a deluge of questions.* — *v* to flood; to overwhelm.

delusion /dɪˈluːʒən/ *n* a false belief.

de luxe /dɪˈlʌks/ *adj* very luxurious or elegant: *a de luxe model of a car.*

delve /dɛlv/ *v* to search deeply for something: *to delve into the past*; *She delved into her shopping bag and brought out the key.*

demand /dɪˈmɑːnd/ *v* **1** to ask firmly for something: *I demanded an explanation.* **2** to require; to need: *This demands careful thought.* — *n* **1** a request made very firmly: *The employees made a demand for higher wages.* **2** a need felt by the public for certain goods *etc*: *There's no demand for books of this kind.*

deˈmanding *adj* requiring a lot of effort, ability *etc*: *a demanding job.*

in demand wanted by a lot of people: *Good teachers will always be in demand.*

on demand whenever you ask for it: *Your money will be available on demand.*

demeanour /dɪˈmiːnə(r)/ *n* a person's way of behaving, especially towards others: *Her demeanour is always polite.*

democracy /dɪˈmɒkrəsɪ/ *n* a form of government in which the people freely elect representatives to govern them.

democrat /ˈdɛməkrat/ *n* a person who believes in democracy. **demoˈcratic** *adj.* **demoˈcratically** *adv.*

demolish /dɪˈmɒlɪʃ/ *v* to pull down; to tear down: *They're demolishing the old buildings in the centre of town.* **demoˈlition** *n.*

demon /ˈdiːmən/ *n* an evil spirit; a devil.

demonstrate /ˈdɛmənstreɪt/ *v* **1** to show clearly: *That silly answer he gave demonstrates how stupid he is.* **2** to show how something works: *He demonstrated the new vacuum cleaner.* **3** to express an opinion by marching, carrying banners *etc* in public: *A crowd collected to demonstrate against the new taxes.*

demonˈstration *n* **1** a showing of how something works *etc*: *The salesman gave me a demonstration of all the things the dishwasher could do.* **2** a public protest or expression of opinion, especially in the form of a big meeting or a procession with banners *etc.* **ˈdemonstrator** *n.*

deˈmonstrative *adj* showing feeling, especially affection, openly and easily.

demoralize /dɪˈmɒrəlaɪz/ *v* to take away a person's confidence and enthusiasm: *His failure to pass his final examination has completely demoralized him.* **deˈmoralization** *n.*

demote /diːˈmoʊt/ v to reduce someone to a lower rank: *He was demoted for misconduct.* **deˈmotion** n.

> The opposite of **demote** is **promote**.

demure /dɪˈmjʊə(r)/ adj quiet and well-behaved: *a very demure young woman.*

den /dɛn/ n **1** the home of a wild animal: *a lion's den.* **2** a private room for working in etc.

denial /dɪˈnaɪəl/ n **1** a statement that something that has been said is not true: *She made a complete denial of the accusation.* **2** a refusal: *Come on — play the piano — we'll take no denial!*

denim /ˈdɛnɪm/ n a cotton cloth, often blue, used for making jeans, overalls *etc*.
ˈdenims n jeans made of denim.

denominator /dɪˈnɒmɪneɪtə(r)/ n the number that stands under the line in a fraction: *The denominator in the fraction ¾ is 4.*

denote /dɪˈnoʊt/ v to mean: *The symbol £ denotes pounds sterling.* **denoˈtation** n.

denounce /dɪˈnaʊns/ v to accuse someone publicly of a crime *etc*: *He was denounced as a murderer.*

dense /dɛns/ adj closely packed together: *a dense forest.* **2** thick: *The fog was so dense that we could not see anything.* **ˈdensely** adv.
ˈdensity n the number of things, people *etc* found in a particular area, compared with other areas: *the density of the population.*

dent /dɛnt/ n a small hollow made by a blow: *My car has a dent where it hit a tree.* — v to make a dent in something: *The car was dented when it hit a wall.*

dental /ˈdɛntəl/ adj having to do with the teeth: *Regular dental care is essential for healthy teeth.*

dentist /ˈdɛntɪst/ n a person who cares for diseases *etc* of the teeth, by filling or removing them *etc*: *I hate going to the dentist.*
ˈdentistry n a dentist's work.

dentures /ˈdɛntʃəz/ n a set of artificial teeth.

deny /dɪˈnaɪ/ v **1** to say that something that has been said is not true: *He denied the charge of murder.* **2** to refuse to give someone something; to say 'no' to a request: *He was denied a chance to put his side of the story.*

deodorant /diˈoʊdərənt/ n a pleasant-smelling substance that people put on their bodies to prevent, or hide the smell of, sweat.

depart /dɪˈpɑːt/ v **1** to go away; to leave: *The train departed from the station at 9 a.m.* **2** to turn away from what you had planned: *We departed from our original plan.*

department /dɪˈpɑːtmənt/ n a part or section of a government, university, office or shop: *the Department of Justice; the sales department.* **departˈmental** adj.
department store a large shop with different departments selling many kinds of goods.

> a **department** (not **departmental**) store.

departure /dɪˈpɑːtʃə(r)/ n departing: *The departure of the train was delayed.*

depend /dɪˈpɛnd/ v **1** to rely on something or someone: *You can't depend on your parents to keep giving you money; You can depend on Jack — he's very reliable; If I were you, I wouldn't depend on getting a day off school.* **2** to be decided by something: *Our success depends on everyone working hard.*
deˈpendable adj able to be trusted: *I know he'll remember to buy the drinks — he's very dependable.*
deˈpendant n a person who is supported by another: *He has five dependants to support — a wife and four children.*
deˈpendent adj relying on someone for support: *A child is dependent on his parents.*
deˈpendence n needing something or someone constantly: *drug dependence.*

> The opposite of **dependent** is **independent**.
> **dependent on** but **independent of**.

it depends it is uncertain until something else is known: *I don't know whether we'll have a picnic — it depends on the weather.*

depict /dɪˈpɪkt/ v **1** to draw or paint someone or something: *The artist depicted the king on horseback.* **2** to describe: *Her book depicts the life of a policewoman.* **deˈpiction** n.

deplete /dɪˈpliːt/ v to reduce the amount of something: *Stocks have been seriously depleted by increased demand.*
deˈpletion n: *the depletion of the ozone layer.*

deplorable /dɪˈplɔːrəbəl/ adj very bad: *deplorable behaviour.* **deˈplorably** adv.

deplore /dɪˈplɔː(r)/ v to say that something is wrong or very bad: *We all deplore the waste of food in rich countries when there is so much hunger in poor countries.*

deploy /dɪˈplɔɪ/ v to put something where it will be most effective.
deˈployment n: *the deployment of troops.*

deport /dɪˈpɔːt/ v to send a person out of the country: *Some immigrants had entered the* *country illegally, and were deported.* **deportation** /diːpɔːˈteɪʃən/ *n.*

depose /dɪˈpoʊz/ *v* to remove someone from a high position, for example, a king from his throne.

deposit /dɪˈpɒzɪt/ *v* **1** to put down: *She deposited her shopping-basket in the kitchen.* **2** to put something somewhere for safe keeping: *He deposited the money in the bank.* — *n* **1** the money you pay as part of the payment for something which you intend to buy: *We decided we could not afford to go on holiday and managed to get back the deposit we had paid.* **2** the money you put into a bank. **3** solid matter that has settled at the bottom of a liquid: *There was a white deposit in the bottle.* **4** a layer of coal, iron *etc* occurring naturally in rock.

deposit account a bank account which pays you interest on money that you save in it: *She used money from her deposit account to pay for her holiday.*

See **bank**.

deˈpositor *n* a person who deposits money in a bank.

depot /ˈdɛpoʊ/ or /ˈdiːpoʊ/ *n* **1** the place where railway engines, buses *etc* are kept and repaired: *a bus depot.* **2** a storehouse.

depreciate /dɪˈpriːʃieɪt/ *v* to lose value. **depreciˈation** *n.*

depress /dɪˈprɛs/ *v* to make someone sad: *It depressed her to think that maybe she would never get a job.*

deˈpressed *adj* sad; unhappy: *The news made me very depressed.*

deˈpressing *adj*: *What depressing news!*

deˈpression *n* sadness and low spirits: *She was treated by the doctor for depression.*

deprive /dɪˈpraɪv/ *v* to take something away from someone: *They deprived him of food and drink.* **depriˈvation** *n.*

deˈprived *adj* not having the advantages in life that most people have: *deprived children.*

depth /dɛpθ/ *n* the distance from the top downwards; deepness: *The submarine travelled at a depth of 200m.*

in depth thoroughly: *I have studied the subject in depth.*

out of your depth 1 in water that is too deep for you to stand up in: *Don't swim out of your depth.* **2** in a situation that is too difficult for you: *I'm out of my depth in mathematical discussions.*

deputation /dɛpjʊˈteɪʃən/ *n* a group of people chosen to speak or act for others: *They sent a deputation to the President.*

ˈdeputize *v* to act as a deputy: *She deputized for her father at the meeting.*

ˈdeputy *n* someone chosen to help a person and take over some of his jobs if necessary: *While the boss was ill, his deputy ran the office.*

derail /diːˈreɪl/ *v* to make a train come off the railway lines.

deˈrailment *n*: *Our train was delayed because of a derailment earlier in the day.*

deranged /dɪˈreɪndʒd/ *adj* gone mad.

derelict /ˈdɛrəlɪkt/ *adj* abandoned and left to fall to pieces: *a derelict building.*

deride /dɪˈraɪd/ *v* to laugh scornfully at someone.

derision /dɪˈrɪʒən/ *n* scornful laughter.

derisive /dɪˈraɪsɪv/ *adj.*

deˈrisively *adv*: *She grinned derisively at the suggestion.*

deˈrisory *adj* so small that it is ridiculous: *a derisory offer.*

derive /dɪˈraɪv/ *v* to come or develop from something: *The word caterpillar derives from an old French word.* **deriˈvation** *n.*

deˈrivative *n* a word that has been formed from another: *'Teaching' and 'teacher' are derivatives of 'teach'.*

derogatory /dɪˈrɒɡətrɪ/ *adj* expressing disapproval or scorn: *He made a derogatory remark about my wife.*

derrick /ˈdɛrɪk/ *n* a device like a crane, for lifting weights: *Derricks were used to unload the ship.*

descend /dɪˈsɛnd/ *v* **1** to go down or climb down from a higher place or position: *He descended the staircase.* **2** to slope downwards: *The hills descend to the sea.* **3** to be passed down from parent to child: *The business descended to his son.*

deˈscendant *n* your child, grandchild *etc*: *This is a photograph of my grandmother with her descendants.*

descended from to belong to a later generation of the same family: *She says that she is descended from Shakespeare.*

deˈscent *n* **1** the action of descending: *The descent of the hill was easy.* **2** a slope: *a steep descent.* **3** family: *She is of royal descent.*

> The noun **descendant** ends in **-ant** (not **-ent**).

describe /dɪˈskraɪb/ *v* to say what happened or what something or someone is like: *He described what had happened; He described* her as tall and dark, with glasses; *Describe your brother to me.*

> to **describe** (not **describe about**) a scene.

description /dɪˈskrɪpʃən/ *n* the describing of something: *I recognized him from your description*; *He gave a description of his holiday.*

desˈcriptive *adj* describing: *She writes descriptive travel articles for the newspaper.*

desert[1] /ˈdɛzət/ *n* a region where almost no plants can grow, because there is very little rain: *the Gobi Desert.*

> the Sahara **desert** (not **dessert**).

desert[2] /dɪˈzɜːt/ *v* **1** to leave or abandon someone: *Why did you desert us?* **2** to run away from the army: *The soldier was shot for trying to desert.*

deˈserted *adj* **1** with no people *etc*: *The streets were completely deserted.* **2** abandoned: *his deserted wife and children.* **deˈserter** *n.* **deˈsertion** *n.*

deserve /dɪˈzɜːv/ *v* to have earned something by what you have done: *She deserves to be called the best pupil in the class*; *He deserves a good mark.*

deˈservedly *adv* rightly; as someone deserves: *She was expelled from the school – deservedly in my opinion.*

deˈserving *adj* that deserves help or rewards: *to give money to a deserving cause.*

desiccated /ˈdɛsɪkeɪtɪd/ *adj* dried: *desiccated coconut.*

design /dɪˈzaɪn/ *v* to invent and prepare a plan of something before it is built or made: *A famous architect designed this building.* — *n* **1** a sketch or plan produced for something that is to be made: *a design for a dress.* **2** style; appearance: *The car is very modern in design*; *I don't like the design of that building.* **3** a pattern *etc*: *The curtains have a flower design on them.* **deˈsigner** *n.*

designate *v* /ˈdɛzɪɡneɪt/ to choose someone or something for a special purpose *etc*: *The forest was designated a conservation area*; *He has been designated as successor to the President.* — *adj* /ˈdɛzɪɡnət/ chosen to do a particular job but not yet having started it: *the ambassador designate.*

desigˈnation *n* a name; a title.

desire /dɪˈzaɪə(r)/ *n* a wish: *I have a sudden desire for a bar of chocolate*; *I have no desire to see him again.* — *v* to want something very much: *After a day's work, all I desire is a hot bath.*

deˈsirable *adj* pleasing or worth having: *a desirable house.* **desiraˈbility** *n.*

desk /dɛsk/ *n* a table for writing, reading *etc*: *He was sitting at his desk.*

ˈdesktop *adj* small enough to be used on a desk or table: *a desktop computer.*

desolate /ˈdɛsələt/ *adj* **1** very lonely: *a desolate landscape.* **2** very sad, lonely and unhappy: *He is desolate because his wife has died.* **desoˈlation** *n.*

despair /dɪˈspɛə(r)/ *v* to give up hope: *He despaired of ever seeing his son again.* — *n* **1** the giving up of hope: *He was filled with despair at the news.* **2** something which causes someone to despair: *He is the despair of his mother.*

desˈpairing *adj*: *She gave me a despairing look.* **desˈpairingly** *adv.*

despatch *see* **dispatch**.

desperate /ˈdɛspərət/ *adj* **1** ready to do anything violent; not caring what you do: *a desperate criminal.* **2** very eager indeed: *She was desperate to get into university.* **3** very bad; almost hopeless: *We are in a desperate situation.* **4** urgent: *He made a desperate appeal for help.* **ˈdesperately** *adv.* **despeˈration** *n.*

despicable /dɪˈspɪkəbəl/ *adj* very bad; wicked; deserving to be despised: *His behaviour was despicable.*

despise /dɪˈspaɪz/ *v* to look upon someone or something with scorn and contempt: *He despised her for being stupid.*

despite /dɪˈspaɪt/ *prep* in spite of something: *He didn't get the job despite all his qualifications.*

> to go **despite** (not **despite of**) the warnings.

despondent /dɪˈspɒndənt/ *adj* feeling miserable, unhappy, *etc*: *She was despondent at her failure.* **desˈpondency** *n.* **desˈpondently** *adv.*

despot /ˈdɛspɒt/ *n* a person with very great or complete power which they use cruelly and unjustly: *The country is being ruled by a despot.*

dessert /dɪˈzɜːt/ *n* the sweet course of a meal; pudding: *We had ice-cream for dessert.*

> to eat a **dessert** (not **desert**).

desˈsertspoon *n* a medium-sized spoon.
destination /dɛstɪˈneɪʃən/ *n* the place to which

destined

you are going: *We've arrived at our destination at last.*

destined /'dɛstɪnd/ *adj* **1** decided in advance by fate: *She was destined for success.* **2** on the way to a place: *a packet of mail destined for the New York office.*

destiny /'dɛstɪnɪ/ *n* the power which is thought to control events; fate.

destitute /'dɛstɪtjuːt/ *adj* having no money or home: *Many people have been made destitute by the war.* **desti'tution** *n*.

destroy /dɪ'strɔɪ/ *v* **1** to knock something to pieces; to make something useless; to ruin: *The building was destroyed by fire.* **2** to kill animals: *The horse broke its leg and had to be destroyed.*

de'stroyer *n* a small fast warship.

destruction /dɪ'strʌkʃən/ *n* the destroying of something: *the destruction of the city.*

de'structive *adj* causing destruction: *Small children can be very destructive.*

detach /dɪ'tatʃ/ *v* to remove: *I detached the lower part of the form and sent it back.*

de'tachable *adj* designed to be removed or separated: *Men's shirts used to have detachable collars.*

de'tached *adj* **1** standing apart or by itself: *a detached house.* **2** not personally involved: *He felt calm and detached.*

de'tachment *n* a group of soldiers *etc*, sent to do a particular job.

detail /'diːteɪl/ *n* a small point in a story *etc*, or something small shown in a picture *etc*: *She paid close attention to the details.* — *v* to list or describe something fully: *Detail your requirements and we will supply them for you.*

'detailed *adj* with nothing left out: *His instructions were very detailed.*

go into detail or **go into details** to explain something thoroughly: *Give me a rough idea of what happened without going into details.*

in detail giving attention to the details: *I'll tell you the story in detail.*

to describe the accident **in detail** (not **in details**).

detain /dɪ'teɪn/ *v* **1** to hold back; to delay: *I won't detain you — I can see you're in a hurry.* **2** to keep under guard: *Three suspects were detained at the police station.*

detect /dɪ'tɛkt/ *v* to notice: *She detected a slight smell of gas as she opened the door.*

de'tection *n* discovery: *Some crimes escape detection for many years.*

de'tective *n* a person who tries to find criminals or watches suspected persons: *She was questioned by detectives.*

de'tector *n* an instrument used to discover the presence of something: *a smoke detector.*

detention /dɪ'tɛnʃən/ *n* imprisonment.

deter /dɪ'tɜː(r)/ *v* to make someone less willing to do something; to frighten someone out of doing something: *She was not deterred by his threats.*

deterred and **deterring** have two **r**s.

detergent /dɪ'tɜːdʒənt/ *n* a substance used for cleaning: *She poured detergent into the washing-machine.*

deteriorate /dɪ'tiːrɪəreɪt/ *v* to become worse: *Her health began to deteriorate after her husband's death.* **deterio'ration** *n*.

determination /dɪtɜːmɪ'neɪʃən/ *n* firmness of character: *She showed her determination by refusing to give way.*

determine /dɪ'tɜːmɪn/ *v* **1** to fix: *Together they determined the rules of the game.* **2** to find out exactly: *He tried to determine what had gone wrong.*

de'termined *adj* having firmly made up your mind: *She is determined to win the prize.*

deterrent /dɪ'tɛrənt/ *n* something that stops people doing something, especially by frightening them: *Imprisonment punishes the criminal and is a deterrent to other people with criminal intentions.*

detest /dɪ'tɛst/ *v* to hate: *I detest cruelty.* **de'testable** *adj*.

detonate /'dɛtəneɪt/ *v* to cause a bomb *etc* to explode: *The bomb was detonated.*

deto'nation *n* an explosion.

detour /'diːtʊə(r)/ *n* part of a journey where you leave the direct route and travel by a longer route: *We made a detour through the mountains in order to look at the beautiful scenery.*

detract /dɪ'trakt/ *v* to make something seem less good or important: *A crack will certainly detract from the value of the plate.*

detriment /'dɛtrɪmənt/ *n* harming or damaging: *He took up sport to the detriment of his academic progress.*

detri'mental *adj* harmful or damaging: *Smoking is detrimental to health.*

deuce /djuːs/ *n* a score of forty points each in tennis.

devastate /'dɛvəsteɪt/ *v* to ruin: *The fire devastated the countryside.*

'devastated *adj* badly shocked or upset: *We*

were completely devastated by the announcement.

'devastating *adj* **1** badly damaging. **2** very shocking. **'devastatingly** *adv.*

devas'tation *n*: *The forest fires caused devastation over a huge area.*

develop /dɪˈvɛləp/ *v* **1** to grow bigger or to a more advanced state: *The plan developed slowly in his mind*; *The village developed into a very large city.* **2** to use chemicals to make a photograph visible: *My brother develops all his own films.* **3** to get; to have or show: *She developed a high fever*; *A rash developed on her face.*

de'velopment *n* **1** developing: *Learning to share is an important stage in the development of a child.* **2** a new process or discovery: *the latest developments in science.*

deviate /ˈdiːvɪeɪt/ *v* to think or do something differently from usual: *He never deviated from his principles.* **devi'ation.**

device /dɪˈvaɪs/ *n* something made for a purpose, such as a tool or instrument: *This is a new device for opening cans.*

> **device**, unlike **advice**, can be used in the plural: *mechanical devices.*
> **devise** is a verb: *to devise a scheme.*

devil /ˈdɛvəl/ *n* **1** the spirit of evil: *The Devil rules in Hell.* **2** any wicked or mischievous being.

devious /ˈdiːvɪəs/ *adj* **1** secretive and not direct: *I don't trust politicians because they can be so devious.* **2** complicated; with many curves and bends: *a devious route through the backstreets.*

devise /dɪˈvaɪz/ *v* to invent; to think out something: *She devised a new method of doing the work faster.*

> See **device**.

devoid /dɪˈvɔɪd/ *adj* completely without: *He's quite devoid of humour.*

devote /dɪˈvoʊt/ *v* to give up your time, money *etc* to something: *She devotes her life to music.*

de'voted *adj* **1** loving and loyal: *a devoted friend*; *I am devoted to him.* **2** very keen: *He is devoted to his work.*

'devotee *n* someone who is very keen on something: *a devotee of football.*

de'votion *n* **1** great love. **2** devoting or being devoted: *a soldier's devotion to duty.*

devour /dɪˈvaʊə(r)/ *v* to eat up greedily: *She devoured the chocolates.*

devout /dɪˈvaʊt/ *adj* very sincere, especially in religion: *a devout Muslim.* **de'voutly** *adv.*

dew /djuː/ *n* tiny drops of water coming from the air as it cools at night: *The grass is wet with dew.*

dexterity /dɛkˈstɛrɪtɪ/ *n* skill at doing things with your hands: *I admired her dexterity with a needle.*

diabetes /daɪəˈbiːtiːz/ *n* a disease in which there is too much sugar in the blood.

diabetic /daɪəˈbɛtɪk/ *adj* to do with diabetes or suitable for people who suffer from it: *diabetic chocolate.* — *n* a person suffering from diabetes.

diabolical /daɪəˈbɒlɪkəl/ *adj* very, very bad; very unpleasant: *His behaviour is diabolical*; *We had diabolical weather yesterday with a lot of wind and rain.* **dia'bolically** *adv.*

diagnose /daɪəgˈnoʊz/ *v* to say what is wrong with a sick person after making an examination: *The doctor diagnosed her illness as flu.*

diagnosis /daɪəgˈnoʊsɪs/, *plural* **diagnoses** /daɪəgˈnoʊsiːz/, *n.*

diagonal /daɪˈagənəl/ *n* a line going from one corner to the opposite corner. — *adj*: *a diagonal line.* **di'agonally** *adv.*

diagram /ˈdaɪəgram/ *n* a drawing that explains something that is difficult to understand: *This book has diagrams showing the parts of a car engine.*

dial /daɪl/ *n* **1** the face of a watch or clock: *My watch has a dial you can see in the dark.* **2** the turning disc over the numbers on a telephone. — *v* to turn a telephone dial to get a number: *She dialled the wrong number.*

dialect /ˈdaɪəlɛkt/ *n* a form of a language spoken in one part of a country.

dialogue /ˈdaɪəlɒg/ *n* talk between two or more people especially in a play, film, *etc.*

diameter /daɪˈamɪtə(r)/ *n* a straight line drawn from side to side of a circle, passing through its centre: *Measure the diameter of this circle.*

diamond /ˈdaɪəmənd/ *n* **1** a very hard, colourless precious stone: *Her brooch had three diamonds in it.* **2** a four-sided figure or shape like this, ♦: *There was a pattern of diamonds on the floor.* **3** one of the playing cards of the suit diamonds, with red shapes like this on them.

diarrhoea /daɪəˈrɪə/ *n* a disease or disorder of the bowels which makes you empty your bowels too often and makes your excretions too liquid.

diary /ˈdaɪərɪ/ *n* a small book in which you write your appointments or what has hap-

dice

pened each day: *The explorer kept a diary of his adventures.*

> You make a note in your **diary** (not **dairy**).

dice /daɪs/, *plural* **dice**, *n* a small cube, with numbered sides, used in certain games: *It is your turn to throw the dice.*

dictate /dɪkˈteɪt/ *v* **1** to say or read out something for someone else to write down: *The boss dictated his letters to his secretary.* **2** to give orders to someone; to command: *I won't be dictated to by you.* **dicˈtation** *n*.

dicˈtator *n* an all-powerful ruler: *The dictator governed the country as he liked.* **dicˈtatorship** *n*.

dictionary /ˈdɪkʃənərɪ/ *n* a book having the words of a language in alphabetical order along with their meanings *etc*: *an English dictionary.*

did *see* **do**.

didn't short for **did not**.

die /daɪ/ *v* **1** to stop living; to become dead: *Those flowers are dying*; *She died of old age*. **2** to want something very much: *I'm dying for a drink*; *I'm dying to see her.*

> **die**; **'dying**; **died**; **died**: *This plant is dying*; *Mine died last week*; *It seems to have died already.*

die away to become gradually quieter, fainter or less: *The storm died away.*

die down to lose strength or power: *I think the wind has died down a bit.*

die hard to change only slowly: *old habits die hard.*

die out to exist no longer anywhere: *All dinosaurs died out when it became too cold for them.*

dying for or **dying to** wanting something or to do something very much: *I'm dying for a cup of tea*; *She was dying to tell them her news.*

diesel oil /ˈdiːzəl ɔɪl/ *n* a heavy oil used as fuel.

diet /ˈdaɪət/ *n* special food, usually for losing weight or as treatment for an illness *etc*: *a diet of fish and vegetables*; *She went on a diet to lose weight.* — *v* to eat only certain kinds of food so as to lose weight: *She has to diet to stay slim.*

differ /ˈdɪfə(r)/ *v* **1** to be not alike: *Our opinions always differed*; *Her house differs from mine.* **2** to disagree: *She differed from me on that question.*

> **differed** and **differing** have one **r**.

difference /ˈdɪfrəns/ *n* **1** the quality of being not the same; a variation: *I can't see any difference between these two pictures.* **2** a disagreement: *We had a difference of opinion.* **3** the amount by which one number is greater than another: *The difference between 7 and 3 is 4.*

make a difference to alter the situation in some way.

make no difference or **not make any difference** to be unimportant: *It makes no difference to us if you stay for one day or one week.*

different /ˈdɪfrənt/ *adj* not the same: *These gloves are not a pair — they're different*; *My ideas are different from his.* **'differently** *adv*.

> **different** is followed by **from** (not **than**).

differentiate /dɪfəˈrenʃɪeɪt/ *v* **1** to see or show the difference between things: *Children must be taught to differentiate between right and wrong.* **2** to make something different from another: *What differentiates him from previous presidents?* **3** to treat people differently: *We never differentiated between the girls and the boys.*

difficult /ˈdɪfɪkʌlt/ *adj* **1** hard to do or understand; not easy: *difficult sums*; *a difficult task*; *It is difficult to know what to do for the best.* **2** hard to deal with: *a difficult child.* **'difficulty** *n* **1** the quality of being difficult: *I have difficulty in understanding him.* **2** anything difficult: *There are so many difficulties in English that you wonder why people want to learn it.* **3** trouble, especially money trouble: *The firm was in difficulties.*

diffident /ˈdɪfɪdənt/ *adj* shy and nervous; lacking in confidence: *He's diffident about his abilities.* **'diffidence** *n*. **'diffidently** *adv*.

diffuse /dɪˈfjuːz/ *v* to spread in all directions: *Sunlight was diffusing through the trellis of oaks and evergreens.* **difˈfusion** *n*.

dig /dɪɡ/ *v* to turn up earth *etc* with a spade *etc*: *to dig the garden*; *We had to dig the car out of the mud*; *They are digging up the road yet again*; *The child dug a tunnel in the sand.* — *n* **1** digging: *The garden needs a good dig*; *He gave me a dig in the ribs.* **2** Something that you say to hurt or embarrass someone.

> **dig**; **dug** /dʌɡ/; **dug**: *The dog dug a hole*; *A hole has been dug in the road.*

dig in or **dig into** to press one thing into

another: *She dug her elbow sharply into my side.*

dig out to find something by searching for it: *We'll get all the details by digging out the old records.*

dig up to find out facts that are not generally known: *The journalists have been trying to dig up some information about his private life.*

digest /'daɪdʒɛst/ *v* to break up food in your stomach and turn it into a form that your body can use: *Your body digests some foods more easily than others.*

di'gestible *adj*: *Raw vegetables are not as digestible as cooked ones.*

> **digestible** ends in **-ible** (not **-able**). The opposite of **digestible** is **indigestible**.

digestion /daɪ'dʒɛstʃən/ *n*.
di'gestive *adj*: *the digestive system.*

digit /'dɪdʒɪt/ *n* **1** any of the figures 0 to 9: *105 is a number with three digits.* **2** a finger or toe.

'digital *adj* using the numbers 0 to 9: *a digital computer.*

digital watch a watch which shows the time in numbers instead of on a dial.

digital watch

dignified /'dɪgnɪfaɪd/ *adj* showing dignity: *She decided that it would not be dignified to run for the bus.*

> The opposite of **dignified** is **undignified**.

dignitary /'dɪgnətrɪ/ *n* a person with an important position or rank: *A bishop is a church dignitary.*

dignity /'dɪgnɪtɪ/ *n* **1** a serious and calm manner: *Holding her head high, she retreated with dignity.* **2** importance and seriousness: *The Queen's coronation was an occasion of great dignity.* **3** your personal pride: *His rude remarks wounded her dignity.*

dike *see* **dyke**.

dilapidated /dɪ'læpɪdeɪtɪd/ *adj* falling to pieces; needing repair: *a dilapidated old house.* **dilapi'dation** *n*.

dilemma /dɪ'lɛmə/ or /daɪ'lɛmə/ *n* a situation in which you have to make a difficult choice between two courses of action: *He was faced with a dilemma: should he leave the party early in order to get a lift home in his friend's car, or stay at the party and have to walk four miles home?*

diligent /'dɪlɪdʒənt/ *adj* hardworking: *a diligent student.* **'diligently** *adv*. **'diligence** *n*.

dilly-dally /'dɪlɪdælɪ/ *v* to waste time: *Hurry up — don't dilly-dally!*

dilute /daɪ'luːt/ *v* to lessen the strength of a liquid by mixing with water: *You should dilute that lime juice with water.* — *adj* reduced in strength; weak: *dilute acid.* **di'lution** *n*.

dim /dɪm/ *adj* not bright; not clear: *a dim light in the distance; a dim memory.* — *v* to make or become dim: *Her eyes were dimmed with tears; The theatre lights dimmed.* **'dimly** *adv*. **'dimness** *n*.

dimension /daɪ'mɛnʃən/ *n* a measurement of height, length, breadth, thickness *etc*: *The dimensions of the box are 20cm by 10cm by 4cm.*

di'mensional *adj*: *a three-dimensional object.*

diminish /dɪ'mɪnɪʃ/ *v* to make or become less: *Our supplies are diminishing rapidly.* **dimi'nution** *n*.

di'minutive *adj* very small.

dimple /'dɪmpəl/ *n* a small hollow, especially on the cheek or chin: *She has a dimple in her cheek when she smiles.*

din /dɪn/ *n* a loud continuous noise: *What a terrible din that machine makes!*

dine /daɪn/ *v* to have dinner: *We shall dine at half past eight; They dined on chicken and rice.*

'diner *n* **1** a restaurant. **2** someone having dinner.

'dining-room *n* a room used for eating in.
'dining-table *n* a table round which people sit to eat.
dine out to have dinner at a restaurant.

dinghy /'dɪŋɪ/ *n* a small sailing boat or rowing boat: *The boy rowed his rubber dinghy across the lake.*

dinghy

dingy /'dɪndʒɪ/ *adj* **1** dull, drab and depressing: *The old man's room is dark and dingy.* **2** dirty; faded: *The beggar wore a dingy grey coat.*

dinner /'dɪnə(r)/ *n* **1** the main meal of the day eaten usually in the evening: *Is it time for* *dinner yet?* **2** a party in the evening, when dinner is eaten: *They asked me to dinner.* — *adj*: *a dinner party*.

dinner jacket a man's smart, usually black, jacket worn at formal events: *You must wear a dinner jacket when you dine with the queen.*

dinosaur /'daɪnəsɔː(r)/ *n* any of several types of large reptile which no longer exist.

dinosaur

dint /dɪnt/ *n* a hollow made by a blow; a dent. **by dint of** by means of: *He succeeded by dint of hard work.*

dip /dɪp/ *v* **1** to put something into any liquid for a moment: *He dipped his bread in the soup.* **2** to go downwards: *The sun dipped below the horizon.* **3** to lower the beam of car headlights: *He dipped his lights as the other car approached.* — *n* **1** a hollow in a road *etc*: *The car was hidden by a dip in the road.* **2** a soft, savoury mixture in which a biscuit *etc* can be dipped: *a cheese dip.* **3** a short swim: *a dip in the sea.*

dip into 1 to read passages from different parts of a book. **2** to spend some, but not all, of a particular amount of money: *We had to dip into our savings to pay for the new car.*

diploma /dɪ'pləʊmə/ *n* a written statement saying that you have passed an examination *etc*: *She has a diploma in teaching.*

diplomacy /dɪ'pləʊməsɪ/ *n* **1** the business of making agreements, treaties *etc* between countries; the business of looking after the affairs of your country in a foreign country. **2** skill in dealing with people, persuading them *etc*: *Use a little diplomacy and she'll soon agree to help.*

diplomat /'dɪpləmæt/ *n* a person who works for his country in diplomacy: *He is a diplomat at the American embassy.*

diplo'matic *adj* having to do with diplomacy: *a diplomatic mission.* **diplo'matically** *adv*.

dire /'daɪə(r)/ *adj* terrible; urgent: *She is in dire need of help.*

direct /daɪ'rɛkt/ or /dɪ'rɛkt/ *adj* **1** straight; shortest: *Is this the most direct route?* **2** honest: *a direct answer.* **3** immediate: *His dismissal was a direct result of his rudeness to* the manager. **4** exact; complete: *Her opinions are the direct opposite of his.* — *adv* **1** straight: *I drove direct to the office.* **2** face to face with someone: *I won't write her a note — I'd rather speak to her direct.* — *v* **1** to point or turn in a particular direction: *He directed my attention towards the notice.* **2** to show the way: *She directed him to the station.* **3** to order: *We shall do as you direct.* **4** to control: *A policeman was directing the traffic.*

The opposite of the adjective **direct** (senses **1**, **2** and **3**) is **indirect**.
direct means straight: *This bus goes direct to the town centre.*

di'rection *n* **1** the place or point to which you move, look *etc*: *What direction did he go in?*; *He looked in my direction.* **2** (usually **di'rections**) instructions, such as how to get somewhere, use something *etc*: *We asked the policeman for directions*; *I have lost the directions for using my washing-machine.*

di'rective *n* an official instruction: *A directive came from the management concerning safety at work.*

di'rectly *adv* immediately; almost at once: *He will be here directly.* **di'rectness** *n*.

directly is used to mean immediately: *Go home directly!*

di'rector *n* **1** a person who directs, especially one of a group of people who manage the affairs of a business. **2** a person who is in charge of the making of a film, play *etc*: *He is on the board of directors of our firm.*

di'rectory *n* a book giving names, addresses, telephone numbers *etc*: *a telephone directory.*

direct speech the words that are actually said by someone: *He said 'I will come'.*

dirt /dɜːt/ *n* any unclean substance, such as mud, dust *etc*: *His shoes are covered in dirt.*

dirt is never used in the plural: *The workmen left a lot of dirt behind.*

'dirty *adj* **1** not clean: *dirty clothes.* **2** nasty; unfair: *a dirty trick.* — *v* to make something dirty: *He dirtied his hands.* **'dirtiness** *n*.

disability /dɪsə'bɪlɪtɪ/ *n* an injury or a physical or mental illness or handicap that affects your way of life or restricts what you can do: *He has a disability which prevents him from walking very far.*

disabled /dɪs'eɪbəld/ *adj* having a disability: *The car has been adapted for disabled drivers.*

disadvantage /dɪsəd'vɑːntɪdʒ/ n something which is not helpful: *There are several disadvantages to this plan.* **disadvan'tageous** *adj.*

disad'vantaged *adj* in a bad position, especially not having the social and educational opportunities that people usually have: *Unemployment is leading to more and more people becoming disadvantaged.*

disagree /dɪsə'griː/ v **1** to have different opinions *etc*: *We disagree about everything; I disagree with you on that point.* **2** to quarrel: *We never meet without disagreeing.* **3** to be bad for someone and cause pain: *Onions disagree with me.*

disa'greeable *adj* unpleasant: *a disagreeable task; a most disagreeable person.* **disa'greeably** *adv.*

disa'greement n **1** disagreeing. **2** a quarrel: *a violent disagreement.*

disallow /dɪsə'laʊ/ v to not permit, accept or approve something: *The goal was disallowed because the whistle had already been blown.*

disappear /dɪsə'pɪə(r)/ v **1** to go out of sight: *The sun disappeared behind the clouds.* **2** to exist no longer: *This custom had disappeared by the end of the century.* **3** to go away so that other people do not know where you are: *A little boy disappeared from his home on Monday.* **disap'pearance** n.

disappoint /dɪsə'pɔɪnt/ v to fail to be what you had hoped or expected: *London disappointed her after all she had heard about it.*

disap'pointed *adj*: *I was disappointed to hear that the party had been cancelled; You shouldn't have told a lie — I'm disappointed in you; The teacher was a bit disappointed with Tom's work.*

disap'pointing *adj*: *disappointing results.* **disap'pointingly** *adv.*

disap'pointment n: *His bad exam results were a great disappointment to his parents.*

disapprove /dɪsə'pruːv/ v to think that something is bad, wrong *etc*: *Her mother disapproved of her behaviour.* **disap'proval** n. **disap'proving** *adj*: *a disapproving look.* **disap'provingly** *adv.*

disarm /dɪs'ɑːm/ v **1** to take away weapons from someone. **2** to get rid of weapons of war: *Not until peace was made did the victors consider it safe to disarm.*

dis'armament n getting rid of war weapons.

disarrange /dɪsə'reɪndʒ/ v to make untidy: *The strong wind had disarranged her hair.* **disar'rangement** n.

disaster /dɪ'zɑːstə(r)/ n a terrible event, especially one that causes great damage, loss *etc*: *The earthquake was the greatest disaster the country had ever experienced.* **di'sastrous** *adj.* **di'sastrously** *adv.*

disband /dɪs'bænd/ v to stop existing as a group: *The pop group disbanded when the lead singer made a solo recording.*

disbelieve /dɪsbɪ'liːv/ v not to believe; to doubt: *He disbelieved her story.*

disbelief /dɪsbɪ'liːf/ n the state of not believing: *She stared at him in disbelief.*

disc /dɪsk/ n **1** a flat, thin, round object: *The full moon looks like a silver disc.* **2** a gramophone record. **3** another spelling for **disk**.

disc jockey a person who introduces and plays recorded pop-music for radio programmes *etc*.

discard /dɪs'kɑːd/ v to throw something away: *They discarded the empty bottles.*

discern /dɪ'sɜːn/ v to see or notice something with difficulty: *I discerned a note of fear in his voice.*

dis'cernible *adj* that can be seen, observed, noticed or realized: *A faint scar was discernible on her left cheek.*

> **discernible** ends in **-ible** (not **-able**).

dis'cerning *adj* good at judging the quality of things or people: *She was a discerning judge of character.*

discharge v /dɪs'tʃɑːdʒ/ **1** to allow someone to leave: *The prisoner was at last discharged; She was discharged from hospital.* **2** to fire a gun: *He discharged his gun at the policeman.* **3** to perform a task *etc*: *He discharges his duties well.* **4** to let something out: *The chimney was discharging clouds of smoke; The drain discharging into the street.* — n /'dɪstʃɑːdʒ/ the discharging of someone or something: *He was given his discharge from the army; the discharge of your duties.*

disciple /dɪ'saɪpl/ n a person who believes in the teaching of another, especially one of the first followers of Christ: *Jesus and his twelve disciples.*

discipline /'dɪsəplɪn/ n **1** training in an orderly way of life: *All children need discipline.* **2** strict self-control. — v to control: *You must discipline youself so that you do not waste time.* **'disciplinary** *adj.*

disclose /dɪs'kloʊz/ v to make known: *He refused to disclose his identity.* **dis'closure** n.

disco /'dɪskoʊ/ n short for **discotheque**.

discolour /dɪs'kʌlə(r)/ v to lose or make some-

thing lose its original colour: *Cigarette-smoking tends to discolour the teeth.*
discomfort /dɪsˈkʌmfət/ *n* **1** lack of comfort; pain: *Her broken leg caused her great discomfort.* **2** something that causes lack of comfort: *the discomforts of living in a tent.*
disconcert /dɪskənˈsɜːt/ *v* to confuse or worry: *She was disconcerted by his long silence.*
  discon'certing *adj*: *The child gave me a disconcerting stare.* **discon'certingly** *adv.*
disconnect /dɪskəˈnɛkt/ *v* to separate; to break the connection between things: *Our phone has been disconnected.* **discon'nection** *n.*
discontent /dɪskənˈtɛnt/ *n* not being contented: *There is a lot of discontent among young people.*
  discon'tented *adj* not satisfied; not happy: *She's discontented with her life.* **discon'tentment** *n.*
discontinue /dɪskənˈtɪnjuː/ *v* to stop or stop producing something: *That particular design has now been discontinued.*
discord /ˈdɪskɔːd/ *n* **1** disagreement or quarrelling. **2** in music, a group of notes played together which give an unpleasant sound. **dis'cordant** *adj.*
discotheque /ˈdɪskətɛk/ *n* a place at which recorded music is played for dancing.
discount *n* /ˈdɪskaʊnt/ a sum taken off the price of something: *The shopkeeper gave me a discount of 20%.* — *v* /dɪsˈkaʊnt/ to ignore something that you consider untrue or unimportant: *We discounted her idea because it would have been too expensive.*
discourage /dɪsˈkʌrɪdʒ/ *v* **1** to take away the confidence, hope *etc* of someone: *His lack of success discouraged him.* **2** to prevent: *The rain discouraged him from going camping.*
  dis'couraged *adj*: *He was feeling depressed and discouraged about his future.*
  dis'couragement *n.*

> The opposite of **discourage** is **encourage**.

discourteous /dɪsˈkɜːtɪəs/ *adj* not polite; rude: *It was very discourteous of him not to thank her for the present*; *a discourteous shop assistant.* **dis'courtesy** *n.*
discover /dɪsˈkʌvə(r)/ *v* **1** to be the first person who finds something: *Columbus discovered America.* **2** to find out: *Try to discover what's going on!*
  dis'covery *n*: *a voyage of discovery*; *She made several important discoveries in medicine.*

> We **discover** something that existed but was not yet known: *He discovered a cave.*
> We **invent** something that was not in existence: *They invented a new machine.*

discredit /dɪsˈkrɛdɪt/ *v* **1** to show that something is wrong or doubtful: *That theory has been totally discredited.* **2** to damage a person's reputation: *an effort to discredit a particular politician.*
discreet /dɪsˈkriːt/ *adj* careful not to say anything which might cause trouble or embarrassment: *He made some discreet enquiries about the company before he started to work there.* **dis'creetly** *adj.*

> The opposite of **discreet** is **indiscreet**.

discrepancy /dɪˈskrɛpənsɪ/ *n* an unexpected difference: *They have discovered some discrepancies in the accounts.*
discretion /dɪsˈkrɛʃən/ *n* **1** being careful not to cause embarrassment: *to behave with discretion.* **2** good sense in making decisions: *I leave the arrangements to your discretion.*
discriminate /dɪsˈkrɪmɪneɪt/ *v* **1** to see a difference: *Some people find it hard to discriminate between good books and bad ones.* **2** to treat a certain person or group of people differently from others: *He was accused of discriminating against female employees.* **discrimi'nation** *n.*
discus /ˈdɪskəs/ *n* a heavy disc of metal *etc* used in a throwing competition.
discuss /dɪsˈkʌs/ *v* to talk about something: *We had a meeting to discuss our plans for the future.*
  dis'cussion *n* talking about something: *I think there has been too much discussion of this subject*; *His parents had a discussion with his teacher about his work.*
  under discussion being discussed: *The company's future is still under discussion.*

> to **discuss** (not **discuss about**) a problem.

disdain /dɪsˈdeɪn/ *n* scorn.
  dis'dainful *adj*: *He was disdainful of his wife's writing activities.* **dis'dainfully** *adv.*
disease /dɪˈziːz/ *n* an illness: *She's suffering from a disease of the heart.*
  di'seased *adj*: *The diseased tree had to be destroyed.*
disembark /dɪsɪmˈbɑːk/ *v* to go from a ship on to land. **disembar'kation** *n.*
disenchanted /dɪsɪnˈtʃɑːntɪd/ *adj* dissatisfied

with something you once liked, enjoyed or approved of: *She was disenchanted with her job.* **disen'chantment** *n*.

disentangle /dɪsɪn'tæŋgəl/ *v* to free something from a tangle: *The bird could not disentangle itself from the net.* **disen'tanglement** *n*.

disfigure /dɪs'fɪgə(r)/ *v* to spoil the appearance of something: *Her face had been badly disfigured in a fire.*

disgrace /dɪs'greɪs/ *n* **1** being out of favour: *He is in disgrace because of his bad behaviour.* **2** shame: *He brought disgrace on his family.* **3** something to be ashamed of: *Your clothes are a disgrace!* — *v* to bring shame upon someone or something: *The pupils who had been caught stealing disgraced the whole school.*

dis'graceful *adj* very bad or shameful: *disgraceful behaviour.* **dis'gracefully** *adv*.

disgruntled /dɪs'grʌntəld/ *adj* disappointed, dissatisfied or angry about something.

disguise /dɪs'gaɪz/ *v* **1** to change someone's appearance so that they won't be recognized: *He disguised himself as a policeman.* **2** to hide your feelings *etc*: *He tried to disguise his real intentions.* — *n* a disguised appearance: *He was in disguise; He was wearing a false beard as a disguise.*

disgust /dɪs'gʌst/ *v* to cause strong feelings of dislike: *The smell of that soup disgusts me; She was disgusted by the mess.* — *n* a strong feeling of dislike: *She left the room in disgust.*

dis'gusted *adj*: *I was disgusted with myself for not trying harder.*

dis'gusting *adj*: *What a disgusting smell!* **dis'gustingly** *adv*.

dish /dɪʃ/ *n* **1** a plate, bowl *etc* in which food is brought to the table. **2** food prepared for the table: *She cooked a dish containing chicken and almonds.*

'dishes *n* all the plates and cutlery *etc* that you use during a meal: *I do the cooking and she washes the dishes.*

'dishwasher *n* a machine for washing dishes.

dish out to serve to people: *He dished out the potatoes.*

dish up to serve food: *Will you dish up the potatoes?*

dishearten /dɪs'hɑːtən/ *v* to take courage or hope away from someone: *The failure of her first attempt disheartened her.* **dis'heartening** *adj*.

dishevelled /dɪ'ʃɛvəld/ *adj* with untidy clothes and hair.

dishonest /dɪs'ɒnɪst/ *adj* not honest; deceitful: *She was dishonest about her age when she applied for the job.* **dis'honestly** *adv*. **dis'honesty** *n*.

dishonour /dɪs'ɒnə(r)/ *n* disgrace; shame. — *v* to cause shame to someone: *You have dishonoured your family by your wicked act.* **dis'honourable** *adj*: *a dishonourable action.*

disillusion /dɪsɪ'luːʒən/ *v* to make you sad or disappointed that something or someone is not as good as you thought they were. **disil'lusioned** *adj*: *She is very disillusioned with her job.* **disil'lusionment** or **disil'lusion** *ns*.

disinfect /dɪsɪn'fɛkt/ *v* to rid a place of germs: *The washbasins should be disinfected regularly.*

disin'fectant *n* a substance that destroys germs.

disintegrate /dɪs'ɪntɪgreɪt/ *v* to fall to pieces: *The paper bag was so wet that the bottom disintegrated and all the groceries fell out.* **disinte'gration** *n*.

disinterested /dɪs'ɪntrəstɪd/ *adj* not influenced by private or selfish feelings; fair: *a disinterested judgement.*

See **uninterested**.

disjointed /dɪs'dʒɔɪntɪd/ *adj* confused; not developing logically: *She could only give a disjointed account of what had happened.* **dis'jointedly** *adv*.

disk /dɪsk/ *n* a circular piece of plastic with a magnetic coating, used in a computer to store information.

disk drive the device that controls the transfer of information to or from a floppy disk.

dislike /dɪs'laɪk/ *v* not to like: *I dislike lazy people.* — *n* a strong feeling against someone or something: *He has a strong dislike of (or for) crowds.*

take a dislike to to start to hate or dislike someone: *She took an immediate dislike to her new music teacher.*

dislocate /'dɪsləkeɪt/ *v* to cause a bone to slip out of its joint: *The old lady dislocated her hip when she fell; You'll dislocate your jaw if you yawn like that!* **dislo'cation** *n*.

dislodge /dɪs'lɒdʒ/ *v* to make something move out of its position: *A few tiles have been dislodged from the roof by the wind.*

disloyal /dɪs'lɔɪəl/ *adj* not loyal: *He was disloyal to his country.* **dis'loyalty** *n*.

dismal /'dɪzməl/ *adj* sad: *dismal news; Don't look so dismal!* **'dismally** *adv*.

dismantle /dɪs'mæntəl/ *v* to take to pieces: *The*

bridge was erected in May and dismantled in September.

dismay /dɪsˈmeɪ/ v to shock or upset: *We were dismayed by the bad news.* — n shock and worry: *a shout of dismay.*

dismiss /dɪsˈmɪs/ v **1** to send away: *The pupils will be dismissed at 12.30 p.m.* **2** to remove someone from their job; to sack: *He was dismissed from his post for being lazy.* **dis-ˈmissal** n.

disˈmissive adj rejecting or refusing to consider something seriously.

disˈmissively adv: *She spoke dismissively of the other competitors.*

dismount /dɪsˈmaʊnt/ v to get off a horse or bicycle.

disobey /dɪsəˈbeɪ/ v to fail to obey: *He disobeyed his mother.* **disobedience** /dɪsəˈbiːdɪəns/ n. **disoˈbedient** adj.

disorder /dɪsˈɔːdə(r)/ n **1** lack of order; confusion: *The strike has thrown the whole country into disorder.* **2** a disease: *a disorder of the lungs.*

disˈorderly adj **1** in confusion: *His clothes lay in a disorderly heap.* **2** causing trouble: *a disorderly group of people.*

disorganized /dɪsˈɔːgənaɪzd/ adj in confusion; not organized: *The meeting was very disorganized.* **disorganiˈzation** n.

disorientated /dɪsˈɔːrɪənteɪtɪd/ adj confused about where you are or what time of day it is: *She woke up feeling very disorientated, not remembering where she was.* **disorienˈtation** n.

disown /dɪsˈoʊn/ v to refuse to admit that something belongs to you: *He's disowned his son.*

dispatch /dɪˈspatʃ/ v to send off: *He dispatched several letters.*

dispel /dɪˈspɛl/ v to remove doubts, worries or fears *etc*: *All doubts were now dispelled.*

dispensable /dɪˈspɛnsəbəl/ adj not necessary: *Some of these items are dispensable extras.*

> The opposite of **dispensable** is **indispensable**.

dispensary /dɪˈspɛnsərɪ/ n a place in a hospital where medicines are given out.

dispense /dɪˈspɛns/ v **1** to give or deal out. **2** to prepare medicines for giving out.

disˈpenser n a machine or container from which you get something: *a cash-dispenser.*

dispense with to get rid of: *We could save money by dispensing with two assistants.*

disperse /dɪˈspɜːs/ v **1** to scatter in all directions: *Some seeds are dispersed by the wind.* **2** to spread news *etc*: *News is dispersed by newspapers.* **disˈpersal** n.

displace /dɪsˈpleɪs/ v **1** to put something out of place. **2** to take the place of someone or something: *There was a revolution and the government was displaced by a group of army officers.* **disˈplacement** n.

display /dɪˈspleɪ/ v **1** to set out for show: *The china was displayed in a special glass cabinet.* **2** to show: *She displayed a talent for painting.* — n **1** the showing of something: *a display of military strength.* **2** a show; an entertainment: *a dancing display.*

on display laid out for people to see: *The children's work is on display in their classrooms.*

displease /dɪsˈpliːz/ v to offend or annoy someone: *The children's behaviour displeased their father.*

disˈpleasure n the feeling of being displeased: *She showed her displeasure by leaving at once.*

dispose /dɪˈspoʊz/ v to get rid of something: *I have disposed of your old coat.* **disˈposal** n.

disˈposable adj intended to be thrown away or destroyed after use: *disposable cups.*

disposition /dɪspəˈzɪʃən/ n a person's nature or character: *He has a calm disposition.*

disproportionate /dɪsprəˈpɔːʃənət/ adj surprisingly or unreasonably large or small. **disproˈportionately** adv: *His ears seemed disproportionately small.*

disprove /dɪsˈpruːv/ v to prove something to be false or wrong: *His theories have been disproved.*

dispute /dɪsˈpjuːt/ v **1** to say that something is not true: *I'm not disputing what you say.* **2** to argue or quarrel about something: *They disputed the ownership of the land.* — n an argument or quarrel: *a dispute over wages.*

disqualify /dɪsˈkwɒlɪfaɪ/ v to put someone out of a competition *etc* for breaking rules *etc*: *She was disqualified because she was too young.* **disqualifiˈcation** n.

disregard /dɪsrɪˈgɑːd/ v to pay no attention to something: *He disregarded my warnings.* — n lack of attention: *He has a complete disregard for his own safety.*

disrepair /dɪsrɪˈpɛə(r)/ n bad condition; in need of repair: *The building has fallen into a state of disrepair.*

disreputable /dɪsˈrɛpjʊtəbəl/ adj not to be trusted; having a bad reputation: *I had heard of his disreputable business activities.*

disrepute /dɪsrɪ'pjuːt/ n having a bad reputation: *The poor examination results brought the school into disrepute.*

disrespect /ˌdɪsrɪ'spɛkt/ n rudeness; lack of respect: *He spoke of his parents with disrespect.*
disre'spectful adj showing disrespect: *Never be disrespectful to older people.* **disre'spectfully** adv.

disrupt /dɪs'rʌpt/ v to break up or put into disorder: *Some noisy people disrupted the meeting; Traffic was disrupted by floods.* **dis'ruption** n.
dis'ruptive adj causing disorder.

dissatisfy /dɪ'sætɪsfaɪ/ v to fail to satisfy: *The teacher was dissatisfied with the pupil's work.* **dissatis'faction** n. **dis'satisfied** adj.

> **dissatisfied** means not pleased: *I'm dissatisfied with this hotel.*
> **unsatisfactory** means not good enough: *This hotel is unsatisfactory.*

dissect /daɪ'sɛkt/ or /dɪ'sɛkt/ v to cut the body of a dead person or animal into parts for examination: *The biology students dissected frogs and tadpoles.* **dis'section** n.

dissent /dɪ'sɛnt/ n disagreement. — v to have a different opinion; to disagree: *I dissent from the general opinion.* **dis'sension** n.

dissident /'dɪsɪdənt/ n a person who expresses disagreement with the policies of a government. **'dissidence** n.

dissimilar /dɪ'sɪmɪlə(r)/ adj different: *Fashions today are not dissimilar to those of the 30's.*

dissolve /dɪ'zɒlv/ v 1 to melt something, especially by putting in a liquid: *He dissolved the pills in water; The pills dissolved easily in water.* 2 to put an end to a parliament, a marriage *etc*.

dissuade /dɪ'sweɪd/ v to persuade someone not to do something: *She tried to dissuade me from going to London.* **dis'suasion** n.

distance /'dɪstəns/ n 1 the space between things, places *etc*: *Some of the children have to walk long distances to school; It is quite a distance to the bus stop; It is difficult to judge distance when driving at night; What's the distance from here to London?* 2 a far-off place or point: *We could see the town in the distance; The picture looks better at a distance.* — v 1 to make you feel less close or involved: *She refused to let her job distance her from her family.* 2 to show that you are not involved in something: *He tried to distance himself from the views of his son.*
'distant adj 1 far away or far apart, in place or time: *the distant past; a distant country; Our house is two kilometres distant from the school.* 2 not close: *He is a distant cousin of mine.* 3 not friendly: *Her manner was rather distant.*

distaste /dɪs'teɪst/ n disapproval, disgust or dislike: *He looked around the room with an expression of distaste.* **dis'tasteful** adj.

distended /dɪs'tɛndɪd/ adj swollen or stretched: *His stomach was distended after a large meal.*

distil /dɪ'stɪl/ v to get a liquid in a pure state by heating it till it becomes steam, then cooling it again.

> **distil** has one **l**.

distinct /dɪ'stɪŋkt/ adj 1 easily seen, heard or noticed: *Her voice is very distinct.* 2 different: *You would never mistake one of those twins for the other — they're quite distinct.* **dis'tinctly** adv. **dis'tinctness** n.
dis'tinction n 1 a difference: *The teacher seemed to make no distinction between the slow pupils and the lazy ones.* 2 a grade awarded to an excellent pupil, student *etc*: *She passed her exams with distinction; It's important to draw a distinction between the old methods and the new ones.*

distinctive /dɪ'stɪŋktɪv/ adj different from others; easy to distinguish and recognize: *The distinctive pink colour of the flamingo makes it easy to recognize.* **dis'tinctively** adv. **dis'tinctiveness** n.

distinguish /dɪ'stɪŋgwɪʃ/ v 1 to make something different from others: *What distinguishes this school from all the others?* 2 to see; to recognize: *He could just distinguish his friend in the crowd.* 3 to recognize a difference: *I can't distinguish between the two types of cheese — they both taste the same to me.* 4 to make yourself noticed through your achievements: *He distinguished himself at school by winning a prize in every subject.* **dis'tinguishable** adj.
dis'tinguished adj famous or excellent: *a distinguished scientist.*

distort /dɪ'stɔːt/ v to twist out of shape: *The heat distorted the metal.* 2 to change a voice *etc*, so that it sounds wrong: *Her voice was distorted by the recording.* **dis'tortion** n.

distract /dɪ'strækt/ v to draw aside someone's attention: *He was constantly being distracted from his work by the noisy conversation of his colleagues.* **dis'traction** n.
dis'tracted adj too anxious or worried to think clearly.

distraught /dɪˈstrɔːt/ *adj* very upset or worried: *She looks very distraught.*

distress /dɪˈstrɛs/ *n* great sorrow, trouble or pain: *She was in great distress over her son's disappearance*; *Is the cut on your leg causing you any distress?*; *The loss of all their money left the family in distress.* — *v* to cause pain or sorrow to someone: *Her husband's lies distressed her.* **dis'tressing** *adj*.

distribute /dɪˈstrɪbjuːt/ or /ˈdɪstrɪbjuːt/ *v* **1** to divide something among several people: *He distributed sweets to all the children in the class.* **2** to spread out widely: *Branches of this shop are distributed throughout the city.* **distri'bution** *n*.

dis'tributor *n* a person or company that supplies goods, especially to shops: *an electrical goods distributor.*

district /ˈdɪstrɪkt/ *n* a part of a country, town etc: *He lives in a poor district of London.*

distrust /dɪsˈtrʌst/ *n* suspicion; lack of trust: *He has always had a distrust of politicians.* — *v* to have no trust in someone or something: *He distrusts even his friends.* **dis'trustful** *adj*.

disturb /dɪˈstɜːb/ *v* **1** to interrupt someone when they are busy *etc*: *I'm sorry, am I disturbing you?* **2** to worry someone or make them anxious: *The news has disturbed me very much.* **3** to stir up or throw into confusion: *A violent storm disturbed the surface of the lake.*

dis'turbance *n* **1** a noisy or disorderly happening: *He was thrown out of the meeting for causing a disturbance.* **2** an interruption: *I want no more disturbances during this lesson!*

dis'turbed *adj* having mental or emotional problems: *We will never know what went on in her disturbed mind.*

dis'turbing *adj* causing concern and worry: *These disturbing developments may lead to war.*

disuse /dɪsˈjuːs/ *n* not being used any more: *Some ancient customs have fallen into disuse.*

disused /dɪsˈjuːzd/ *adj*: *a disused warehouse.*

ditch /dɪtʃ/ *n* a long narrow hollow dug in the ground especially one to drain water from a field, road *etc*.

dither /ˈdɪðə(r)/ *v* to hesitate and be unable to make a decision: *She's still dithering about whether to move house.*

divan /dɪˈvan/ *n* a long, low seat without a back which can be used as a bed.

See **bench**.

dive /daɪv/ *v* **1** to go headfirst into water; to plunge: *He dived off a rock into the sea.* **2** to go under water: *The submarine dived.* **3** to go quickly and suddenly out of sight: *She suddenly dived into a shop.* — *n*: *She did a beautiful dive into the pool.*

'diver *n* a person who dives, especially one who works under water.

'diving-board *n* a platform from which to dive, built beside a swimming-pool.

diverge /daɪˈvɜːdʒ/ *v* to separate and go in different directions: *The roads diverge three kilometres further on.*

diverse /daɪˈvɜːs/ *adj* different from each other; various: *There were diverse activities to choose from at the holiday camp — swimming, cycling, horse-riding and many others.* **di'versely** *adv*.

diversion /daɪˈvɜːʃən/ *n* **1** a change to the usual route of traffic: *There's a diversion at the end of the road.* **2** an amusement; something interesting that makes the time pass quickly.

diversity /daɪˈvɜːsɪtɪ/ *n* the state of being different; variety: *buildings in a great diversity of architectural styles.*

divert /daɪˈvɜːt/ *v* to make traffic *etc* turn aside or change direction: *Traffic had to be diverted because of the accident.*

divide /dɪˈvaɪd/ *v* **1** to separate into parts or groups: *The wall divided the garden in two*; *The children are divided into 12 classes according to age and ability.* **2** to share: *We divided the sweets between us.* **3** to find out how many times one number contains another: *6 divided by 2 equals 3.*

> You divide a cake **in two** or **in half**, but you divide it **into three parts, five parts, eight parts** *etc*.

divine /dɪˈvaɪn/ *adj* belonging to God: *divine mercy.*

di'vinity *n* **1** the study of religion: *She is doing divinity at university.* **2** the state of being a god: *Muslims believe in the divinity of Allah.* **3** a god: *Vishnu is one of many Hindu divinities.*

divisible /dɪˈvɪzəbəl/ *adj* able to be divided: *100 is divisible by 4.*

division /dɪˈvɪʒən/ *n* **1** the dividing of something. **2** something that separates; a dividing line: *A ditch formed the division between their two fields.* **3** a part or section of an army *etc*: *He belongs to B division of the local police force.* **4** the finding of how many times one number is contained in another.

divisive /dɪˈvaɪsɪv/ *adj* causing disagreement

or arguments between people: *a divisive policy*.

divorce /dɪˈvɔːs/ *n* the legal ending of a marriage. — *v*: *The girl was very sad when her parents got divorced.*

diˈvorced *adj*: *I'm not married – I'm divorced.*

divorˈcee *n* a divorced person.

divulge /daɪˈvʌldʒ/ *v* to make known: *Doctors shouldn't divulge information about their patients.*

dizzy /ˈdɪzɪ/ *adj* **1** confused; giddy: *If you spin round and round like that, you'll make yourself dizzy.* **2** causing a dizzy feeling: *dizzy heights.* **ˈdizzily** *adv*. **ˈdizziness** *n*.

do /duː/ *v* **1** to carry out something: *What shall I do?*; *That was a terrible thing to do*; *She does the cooking and I do the washing-up.* **2** to act or behave: *Do as you please.* **3** to get on: *He is doing well.* **4** to be enough: *One onion will do.* **5** to study or work at something: *He is at university doing mathematics*; *She is doing sums.* **6** to put something in order: *Have you done your hair?* **7** to cause: *The storm did a lot of damage.* **8** used with a more important verb in questions, in sentences with *not* or to emphasize something: *Do you speak English?*; *'Do you have the time, please?' 'No, I don't have a watch'*; *You don't speak German, do you?*; *I do not smoke*; *He doesn't try hard enough*; *I do think you should apologize to the teacher*; *I thought she wouldn't come, but she did.* — *n* an affair or a party: *The school is having a do for Christmas.*

> **do**; he, she, it **does** /dʌz/ ; **did** /dɪd/; **done** /dʌn/; *Do your homework!*; *Does he swim every day?*; *He did his sums*; *I've done the dishes.*
>
> **do not** or **don't** /dount/;
> **does not** or **ˈdoesn't** /ˈdʌzənt/;
> **did not** or **ˈdidn't** /ˈdɪdənt/:
> *I don't care*; *It doesn't take long*; *You saw her, didn't you?*

do-it-yourˈself *n* doing your own decorating, repairs *etc*: *I've just bought a book on do-it-yourself so I can try to tile the bathroom.* — *adj*: *a do-it-yourself book*.

I could do with used to express a wish or need: *I could do with a cup of coffee*.

do away with to get rid of something: *They did away with uniforms at that school years ago*.

do out of to prevent someone from having something in an unfair way: *We've been done out of £1000!*

do up 1 to fasten a piece of clothing: *He put on his hat and did up his coat.* **2** to repair and decorate a building: *She did the house up and sold it for a huge profit*.

do without to manage without something: *We'll just have to do without a phone*; *If you're too lazy to fetch the ice-cream you can just do without*.

to do with connected with something; about something: *Is this decision anything to do with what I said yesterday?*; *This letter is to do with Bill's plans for the summer*.

docile /ˈdousaɪl/ *adj* quiet and easy to manage or control: *He found her a particularly docile horse to ride*.

dock /dɒk/ *n* **1** a deepened part of a harbour *etc* where ships go for loading, unloading, repair *etc*: *The ship was in dock for three weeks.* **2** the area surrounding this: *He works down at the docks.* **3** the place in a law court where the accused person sits or stands. — *v* to enter a dock and tie up alongside a quay: *The ship docked in Southampton this morning*.

ˈdocker *n* a person who works in the docks.

ˈdockyard *n* a harbour with docks, stores *etc*.

doctor /ˈdɒktə(r)/ (written **Dr** before names) *n* **1** a person who is trained to treat ill people: *You should call the doctor if you are ill*; *I'll have to go to Dr Smith.* **2** a person who has gained the highest university degree in any subject. — *v* **1** to change something dishonestly to deceive others: *He had doctored the statistics to fit his theory.* **2** to put poison or a drug in food or drink.

doctrine /ˈdɒktrɪn/ *n* a belief which is taught: *religious doctrines*.

document /ˈdɒkjəmənt/ *n* a written statement giving information, proof, evidence *etc*: *She signed several documents concerned with the sale of her house*.

docuˈmentary *n* a film, programme *etc* giving information on a certain subject.

dodge /dɒdʒ/ *v* to avoid something by a sudden or clever movement: *She dodged the blow*; *He dodged round the corner out of sight.* — *n* **1** a quick movement to avoid something. **2** a clever way of avoiding something: *He knows all the tax dodges*.

doe /dou/ *n* the female of certain animals, such as the deer, the rabbit and the hare.

does *see* **do**.

doesn't short for **does not**.

dog /dɒg/ *n* a meat-eating animal often kept as a pet.

> A dog **barks** or **growls**.
> A baby dog is a **puppy**.
> A female dog is a **bitch**.
> A dog lives in a **kennel**.

'dog-eared *adj* having the pages turned down at the corner: *a dog-eared book; Several pages were dog-eared.*

dogged /'dɒgɪd/ *adj* keeping on doing something in a determined way: *By dogged perseverance she managed to learn the work well enough to pass her exam.* **'doggedness** *n*. **'doggedly** *adv*: *He doggedly went on with his work despite the loud noise.*

dogmatic /dɒg'matɪk/ *adj* arrogantly forcing one's opinions on others: *You should try to be less dogmatic.*

dole /doʊl/ *v* to give out small shares of something: *She doled out the food.*

doleful /'doʊlfəl/ *adj* sad; unhappy: *a doleful expression.* **'dolefully** *adv*. **'dolefulness** *n*.

doll /dɒl/ *n* a toy in the shape of a small human being: *Little girls like to play with dolls.*

dollar /'dɒlə(r)/ *n* the main unit of money in the USA, Canada, Australia, Singapore and other countries, often written $: *It costs ten dollars* (or *$10*).

dolphin /'dɒlfɪn/ *n* a sea-animal about three metres long, closely related to the porpoise.

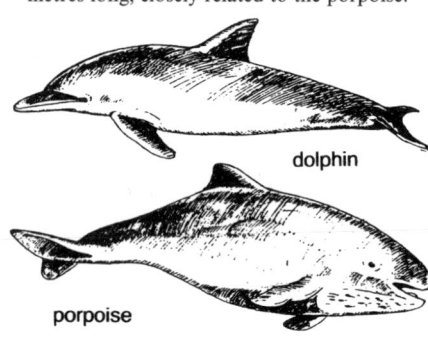

dolphin

porpoise

domain /də'meɪn/ *n* land that someone owns or controls: *The travellers were now entering the domain of King Zog of the West.*

dome /doʊm/ *n* a roof shaped like half a ball: *the dome of the cathedral.*

domestic /də'mɛstɪk/ *adj* **1** used in the house or home: *washing-machines and other domestic equipment.* **2** concerning your private life or family: *domestic problems.* **3** tame and living with or used by people: *domestic animals.* **4** to do with inside a particular country; not international: *a domestic airline.*

dominate /'dɒmɪneɪt/ *v* **1** to have command over someone: *The stronger man dominates the weaker.* **2** to be most important or most noticeable *etc*: *steep cliffs that dominate the northern beaches of France.* **'dominant** *adj*. **domi'nation** *n*.

domineering /dɒmɪ'nɪərɪŋ/ *adj* arrogantly trying to control what other people do: *Her elder brother is a domineering bully.*

dominion /də'mɪnjən/ *n* **1** control or power: *The general seized power in the country and nobody dared to challenge his dominion.* **2** a country or territory ruled over by someone, especially a foreign power: *Britain used to have many overseas dominions.*

domino /'dɒmɪnoʊ/, *plural* **'dominoes**, *n* a small piece of wood *etc* marked with spots with which the game of **'dominoes** is played.

donate /doʊ'neɪt/ *v* to give money to a charity *etc*: *He donated £100 to the fund.* **do'nation** *n* a gift of money or goods: *All donations are welcome.*

done /dʌn/ *adj* **1** finished or complete: *That job is done at last.* **2** completely cooked and ready to eat: *I don't think the meat is quite done yet.* **3** a word used to agree to a bargain or bet with someone: *'I'll give you £250 for it' 'Done!'.* See also **do**.

over and done with completely finished; in the past: *That part of my life is over and done with.*

donkey /'dɒŋkɪ/ *n* **1** an animal with long ears related to the horse but smaller. **2** a stupid person: *Don't be such a donkey!*

> A donkey **brays**.

donor /'doʊnə(r)/ *n* **1** a person who gives something, especially a gift to a charity. **2** someone who gives a part of their body to replace the same part in the body of an ill person: *a kidney-donor; a blood-donor.*

don't short for **do not**.

doodle /'du:dəl/ *v* to scribble, or make meaningless drawings. — *n*.

doom /du:m/ *n* a person's fate; something terrible and final which you can't stop happening to you: *He could not escape his doom.* — *v* to condemn; to make something certain to fail *etc*: *The plan was doomed to failure; He was doomed from the moment he first took drugs.*

door /dɔː(r)/ *n* a large flat piece of wood that closes the entrance of a room, house *etc*.

'**doorbell** *n* a bell on the outside of the front door of a house.

'**doorknob** *n* a round handle for opening and closing a door.

'**doormat** *n* a mat kept in front of the door for people to wipe their feet on.

'**doorstep** *n* a raised step just outside the door of a house.

door-to-'door *adj* calling at each house in turn: *a door-to-door salesman*.

'**doorway** *n* the space usually filled by a door: *He was standing in the doorway*.

dope /doʊp/ *v* to drug: *The race-horse had been doped*.

dormant /'dɔːmənt/ *adj* quiet or inactive: *a dormant volcano*.

dormitory /'dɔːmətrɪ/ *n* a room used for sleeping in, with many beds, in a boarding-school *etc*.

dose /doʊs/ *n* **1** the quantity of medicine *etc* to be taken at one time: *It's time you had a dose of your medicine*. **2** an amount of something unpleasant: *He has had a bad dose of flu*. — *v* to give someone medicine: *She dosed herself with aspirin and went to bed*.

dot /dɒt/ *n* a small, round mark.

'**dotted** *adj* **1** made of dots: *a dotted line*. **2** having dots: *dotted material*.

on the dot exactly on time: *The meeting started at ten o'clock on the dot*.

dote /doʊt/ *v* to love someone so much that you cannot see their faults: *She dotes on her only nephew*.

'**doting** *adj*: *My doting grandparents paid for me to go to a private school*.

double /'dʌbəl/ *adj* **1** twice the weight, size *etc*: *We shall need a double quantity of milk today*. **2** two of a sort together or occurring in pairs: *double doors*. **3** consisting of two parts or layers: *a double thickness of paper*. **4** for two people: *a double bed*. — *adv* **1** twice: *I gave her double the usual quantity*. **2** in two: *The coat had been folded double*. — *n* **1** a double quantity: *Whatever the women earn, the men earn double*. **2** someone who is exactly like another: *My uncle is my father's double*. — *v* **1** to make or become twice as much: *He doubled his income in three years*; *Road accidents have doubled since 1960*. **2** to fold in two: *She doubled the blanket*. **3** to have a second job, use or function: *The kitchen table doubles as a desk*.

double bass *n* the largest instrument in the violin family, that you play standing up.

double-'breasted *adj* having wide front parts that fasten over each other with two rows of buttons: *a double-breasted jacket*.

double-'check *v* to check again; to check with great care: *The examination results are double-checked before being sent to the candidates*.

double-'cross *v* to cheat the person you are supposed to be helping: *I paid him to lose the fight but he double-crossed me and tried to win*.

double-'decker *n* a bus with two floors for passengers. — *adj*: *a double-decker bus*.

double figures the numbers between 10 and 99.

'**doubles** *n* a tennis match *etc* in which there are two players on each side.

double standard a rule applied more strictly to some people than to others, especially yourself: *It's clear you have a double standard if you let your daughter stay out until midnight but expect her twin brother to return home two hours earlier*.

'**doubly** *adv* **1** especially; extra: *When you are away I am doubly careful about locking the doors*. **2** in two ways: *He was doubly responsible for the accident*.

double up to bend completely over: *He doubled up with the pain*.

doubt /daʊt/ *v* **1** to be unsure about something: *I doubt if he'll come now*; *He might have an iron, but I doubt it*. **2** not to trust something: *She doubted his sincerity*. — *n* a feeling of not being sure and sometimes of being suspicious: *There is some doubt as to what happened*; *I have my doubts about his explanation*.

See **suspect**.

'**doubtful** *adj* **1** feeling doubt: *The headmaster is doubtful about the future of the school*. **2** not clear: *The meaning is doubtful*; *a doubtful result*. **3** unlikely: *It is doubtful whether this will work*. **4** suspicious: *He's rather a doubtful character*. '**doubtfully** *adv*. '**doubtfulness** *n*.

'**doubtless** *adv* probably: *John has doubtless told you about me*.

beyond doubt certainly: *Beyond doubt, they will arrive tomorrow*.

cast doubt to suggest that something is not true or reliable: *These new facts cast doubt on the old theory*.

in doubt uncertain: *The result of the election is still in doubt.*

no doubt surely; probably: *No doubt you would like to see your bedroom; He will come back again tomorrow, no doubt.*

without doubt or **without a doubt** definitely: *He is without doubt the most selfish person I know.*

dough /doʊ/ *n* a mixture of flour and water *etc* used for making bread, cakes *etc*.

'doughnut *n* a small, round cake fried and covered with sugar.

dour /dʊə(r)/ *adj* rather stern and unfriendly. **'dourly** *adv*.

dove /dʌv/ *n* a kind of pigeon.

dowdy /'daʊdɪ/ *adj* dull and unfashionable: *Do I look dowdy in this hat?*

down[1] /daʊn/ *n* small, soft feathers: *a quilt filled with down.* **'downy** *adj*.

down[2] /daʊn/ *adv* **1** towards or in a lower place or position: *He climbed down to the bottom of the ladder.* **2** to the ground: *The little boy fell down and cut his knee.* **3** from a greater to a smaller size, amount *etc*: *Prices have been going down steadily.* **4** on paper: *I can prove it — it's all down here in black and white.* — *prep* **1** in a lower position in or on something: *Their house is halfway down the hill.* **2** to a lower position in or on something: *Water poured down the wall.* **3** along: *The teacher looked down the line of children.* — *adj* **1** miserable or depressed: *I'm feeling down today.* **2** not working: *Our computer's down so we can't do any more just now.*

'downcast *adj* sad; depressed: *a downcast expression.*

'downfall *n* a final failure or ruin: *It was his own foolishness that caused his downfall.*

down'grade *v* to reduce to a lower grade: *His job was downgraded.*

down'hearted *adj* depressed and in low spirits: *Don't be downhearted! — we may win after all.*

down'hill *adv* **1** down a slope: *The road goes downhill all the way from our house to yours.* **2** towards a worse state: *His work has been going downhill since he became ill.*

'downpour *n* a very heavy fall of rain.

See **rain**.

'downstairs *adj*, **down'stairs** *adv* on or towards a lower floor: *He walked downstairs; I left my book downstairs; a downstairs flat.*

down'stream *adv* towards the mouth of a river: *The boat floated away downstream.*

down-to-'earth practical and sensible.

'downward *adj* leading, moving *etc* down: *a downward curve.*

'downwards *adv* towards a lower position: *The path led downwards towards the sea.*

down and out having no money and no home.

down with a cry meaning get rid of someone or something: *Down with the dictator!*

get down to to begin working seriously on something: *I must get down to some letters!*

go down with to be or become ill with something: *He's gone down with flu.*

dowry /'daʊrɪ/ *n* money and property brought by a woman to her husband when they marry.

doze /doʊz/ *v* to sleep lightly: *The old lady dozed in her chair.* — *n* a short, light sleep.

doze off to fall asleep without meaning to.

dozen /'dʌzən/ *n* a group of twelve: *There are two dozen (24) children in the class; Half-a-dozen (6) of them speak Italian.*

dozens very many: *I've been there dozens of times.*

several **dozen** (not **dozens**): *two dozen red roses.*

drab /drab/ *adj* dull, especially in colour: *drab factory buildings.*

draft /drɑːft/ *n* **1** a rough outline of something such as a speech. **2** an order to someone to serve in the army *etc*. — *v* **1** to make a rough outline of a speech *etc*: *Could you draft a report on this meeting?* **2** to order someone to serve in the army *etc*: *He was drafted into the Navy.*

draftsman another spelling of **draughtsman**.

drag /drag/ *v* **1** to pull, especially by force, or roughly: *She was dragged to safety from the burning car.* **2** to pull something slowly: *He dragged the heavy table across the floor.* **3** to move along the ground: *His coat was so long it dragged on the ground.* **4** to be boring; to seem to last a long time: *The second half of the concert dragged terribly.* — *n* **1** something that slows you down: *His lack of education was a drag on his career.* **2** someone or something that is dull and boring: *He's such a drag — he won't come to the football match with me; It's a drag to have to do the washing-up every day.* **3** women's clothes when worn by a man: *a male dancer in drag.* **4** an act of drawing in smoke from a cigarette *etc*: *He took a long drag on his cigar.*

drag on to continue longer than necessary and leave you feeling bored and tired: *The meeting dragged on for hours.*

drag out to make something last as long as possible: *She dragged out her lunch to avoid doing her work.*

dragon /'dragən/ *n* a creature you find in stories and pictures; it usually breathes fire, its body is covered with scales, and it has wings, claws and a long tail.

dragonfly /'dragənflaɪ/ *n* an insect with a long body and double wings.

drain /dreɪn/ *v* **1** to flow away: *The water drained away into the ditch.* **2** to remove liquid from something: *Would you drain the vegetables?*; *He drained the petrol tank.* **3** to empty your cup *etc* by finishing your drink: *He drained his glass.* **4** to use up completely: *The effort drained all his energy.* — *n* **1** a ditch, trench, waterpipe *etc* that carries away water: *The heavy rain has caused several drains to overflow.* **2** something that uses up strength and resources: *The fees for the special school were a drain on their savings.* **'drainage** *n.*

'drainpipe *n* a pipe which carries water from the roof of a building to the ground.

down the drain wasted: *All our hard work has just gone down the drain.*

drake /dreɪk/ *n* a male duck.

drama /'drɑːmə/ *n* **1** a play for acting on the stage. **2** the art of acting in plays: *He studied drama at college.* **3** exciting events: *the drama and excitement of the auction.*

dra'matic *adj* **1** having to do with plays or acting; put into the form of a play: *a dramatic entertainment.* **2** sudden or exciting: *a dramatic improvement.*

dra'matically *adv.*

'dramatist *n* a writer of plays.

'dramatize *v* **1** to turn a story into a play: *She dramatized the novel for television.* **2** to make something seem more serious or more exciting than it really is: *The story was dramatized so much by the papers that I became a hero!* **dramati'zation** *n.*

drank *see* **drink**.

drape /dreɪp/ *v* to hang or arrange cloth, especially in loose folds: *She draped sheets over the furniture to protect it from dust.*

drastic /'drastɪk/ *adj* very great or severe: *There has been a drastic reduction in the number of teachers at this school.* **'drastically** *adv.*

draught /drɑːft/ *n* a movement of air: *He closed the window, because he didn't like sitting in the draught.*

draughts /drɑːfts/ *n* a game for two people, played with small discs on a board.

draughts

draughtsman or **draftsman** /'drɑːftsmən/ *n* a person who is employed in making drawings: *This firm of engineers employs three draughtsmen.*

draughty /'drɑːftɪ/ *adj* full of draughts: *a draughty room.*

draw /drɔː/ *v* **1** to make a picture with a pencil, crayons *etc*: *She watched him sketch, then stop and change what he had drawn.* **2** to pull something out or along: *He drew a gun and fired*; *All water had to be drawn from a well*; *The cart was drawn by a pony.* **3** to move; to come: *The car drew away from the kerb*; *Christmas is drawing closer.* **4** to play a game in which neither side wins: *The match was drawn*; *The two sides drew at 1–1.* **5** to get money from a bank *etc*: *to draw a pension.* **6** to open or close curtains. **7** to attract: *She was trying to draw my attention to something.* — *n* **1** a drawn game: *The match ended in a draw.* **2** the selecting of winning tickets in a lottery *etc*: *a prize draw.*

> **draw**; **drew** /druː/; **drawn** /drɔːn/: *He drew a picture*; *The curtains were drawn.*

draw a blank to fail to find what you wanted.

draw a conclusion to come to a conclusion after thinking about what you have learned: *Don't draw the wrong conclusion from what I've said!*

draw in to come to a halt at the side of the road: *A car drew in beside me.*

draw lots to decide who is going to do something by drawing names out of a box *etc*: *Five of us drew lots for the two pop-concert tickets.*

draw out 1 to move your car *etc* out into the road from the side. **2** to take money from a bank: *I drew out £40 yesterday.*

draw up 1 to stop your car: *We drew up outside their house.* **2** to prepare and write out a document or list *etc*: *We're drawing up a new timetable.*

drawback /'drɔːbak/ *n* a disadvantage: *There are several drawbacks to his plan.*

drawbridge /'drɔːbrɪdʒ/ *n* a bridge that goes across the moat of a castle to its entrance, which can be lifted up to stop enemies getting into the castle: *They raised the drawbridge when they saw the strange horsemen approaching.*

drawer /drɔː(r)/ *n* a sliding box without a lid which fits into a chest, table *etc*: *The letter is in the bottom drawer of my desk*; *She put the pullover away in the chest of drawers.*

drawing /'drɔːɪŋ/ *n* **1** making pictures with a pencil *etc*: *Are you good at drawing?* **2** a picture made with a pencil *etc*: *She made a drawing of a house.*

drawing-pin /'drɔːɪŋ pɪn/ *n* a pin with a broad, flat head used for fastening paper to a board *etc*.

drawing-room /'drɔːɪŋ ruːm/ *n* a sitting-room.

drawl /drɔːl/ *v* to speak in a slow, lazy manner. — *n*.

drawn /drɔːn/ *adj* **1** looking tired, ill or worried. **2** pulled across: *We sat in the dark with the curtains drawn.* See also **draw**.

dread /drɛd/ *n* great fear: *The thief lived in dread of being found out.* — *v* to fear greatly: *We were dreading having to see the headmaster.*

  'dreaded *adj* terrible; causing fear: *I'm off to see the dreaded dentist.*

  'dreadful *adj* **1** terrible: *a dreadful accident.* **2** very bad: *What dreadful weather!*

  'dreadfulness *n*. **'dreadfully** *adv*.

dream /driːm/ *n* **1** thoughts and pictures in the mind that come mostly during sleep: *I had a terrible dream last night.* **2** the state of being occupied with your own thoughts: *Don't sit there in a dream!* **3** an ambition or hope: *It's my dream to win a Nobel Prize.* — *v* to see pictures in your mind, especially when asleep: *She often dreams of being a great artist*; *I dreamt last night that the house had burnt down.*

> **dream**; **dreamt** /drɛmt/ or **dreamed**; **dreamt** or **dreamed**: *She dreamt about her grandmother*; *I would never have dreamt that this could happen.*

  'dreamer *n* an unrealistic person who makes impossible plans.

  'dreamy *adj* having or showing thoughts that are far away from the real world: *a dreamy expression.* **'dreamily** *adv*.

  dream up to invent: *However did you dream up such a strange idea?*

  would not dream of would definitely not do something: *I wouldn't dream of telling your mother.*

dreary /'drɪərɪ/ *adj* making you miserable; dull: *What dreary weather!*; *I've got lots of dreary sums to do.* **'drearily** *adv*. **'dreariness** *n*.

dredge /drɛdʒ/ *v* to clear mud from the bottom of a river or harbour *etc*.

  dredge up to mention again something unpleasant that people have forgotten: *The papers had dredged up some embarrassing details from his past.*

drench /drɛntʃ/ *v* to soak completely: *They went out in the rain and were drenched to the skin.*

dress /drɛs/ *v* **1** to put clothes on: *We dressed in a hurry and my wife dressed the children*; *Get dressed!*; *She was dressed in white.* **2** to treat and bandage wounds: *He was sent home from hospital after his burns had been dressed.* — *n* **1** what you are wearing: *His dress was always rather strange.* **2** a piece of women's clothing with the top and skirt in one piece: *Shall I wear a dress or a blouse and skirt?*

  'dressing *n* **1** a sauce added especially to salads: *oil and vinegar dressing.* **2** a bandage *etc* used to dress a wound: *He changed the patient's dressing.*

  'dressing-gown *n* a loose garment worn over pyjamas *etc*.

  'dressing-table *n* a table in a bedroom with a mirror and drawers.

  'dressmaker *n* a person who makes clothes for women.

  dress rehearsal a full performance of a play *etc* done for practice but with costumes *etc*.

  dress up to put on special clothes: *He dressed up as a clown for the party.*

drew see **draw**.

dribble /'drɪbəl/ *v* **1** to fall in small drops: *Water dribbled out of the tap.* **2** to let liquid trickle from your mouth: *His mouth was so full of ice-cream it was dribbling out of the corners.* **3** in football, hockey *etc* to kick or hit the ball along little by little: *He dribbled the ball up the field.*

dried /draɪd/ *see* **dry**.

drier another spelling of **dryer**.

drift /drɪft/ *n* **1** snow that has been driven into a heap by the wind: *His car stuck in a snowdrift.* **2** a slow movement towards or away from something: *the drift away from traditional values.* **3** the general meaning of something: *I couldn't understand every word he said but I got his general drift.* — *v* **1** to float or be blown along: *Sand drifted across the road; The boat drifted down the river.* **2** to move slowly or with no particular purpose: *The guests began to drift towards the food.*

'driftwood *n* wood that is floating on the sea, or down a river; wood that has been cast up from the water on to the shore: *The children made a fire with dry driftwood that they found on the beach.*

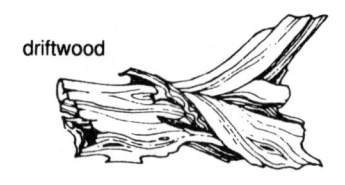

driftwood

drill /drɪl/ *v* **1** to make a hole with a drill: *He drilled holes in the wood; to drill for oil.* **2** to exercise or be exercised: *The soldiers drilled every morning.* — *n* **1** a tool for making holes: *an electric drill.* **2** exercise or practice, especially in the army: *The soldiers have an hour of drill after breakfast.*

drink /drɪŋk/ *v* **1** to swallow a liquid: *Drink plenty of water; She drank a glass of lemonade.* **2** to take alcohol: *I never drink.* — *n* **1** a liquid for drinking: *He had a drink of water; Lemonade is a refreshing drink.* **2** alcoholic liquor: *He had a drink with his friends.*

drink; drank /draŋk/; **drunk** /drʌŋk/: *The cat drank the milk; He has drunk his tea.*

'drinking *n* drinking alcohol: *the dangers of drinking and driving.*

drink to someone or **drink someone's health** to offer good wishes to someone while drinking; to drink a toast to someone.

drip /drɪp/ *v* to fall in single drops: *Rain dripped off the roof.* — *n* a small quantity of liquid falling in drops: *A drip of water ran down her arm.*

drive /draɪv/ *v* **1** to control or guide a car *etc*: *Can you drive a car?; Do you want to drive, or shall I?* **2** to bring or take someone in a car: *My mother is driving me to the airport.* **3** to force along: *Two men and a dog were driving a herd of cattle across the road.* **4** to hit hard: *He drove a nail into the door.* **5** to force someone into a particular state or to do a particular thing: *That noise is driving me crazy; What drove him to do such a thing?* — *n* **1** a journey in a car, especially for pleasure: *We decided to go for a drive.* **2** a private road leading from a gate to a house *etc*: *There were trees growing along the drive.* **3** a name used for other roads: *They live in Cherrytree Drive.* **4** the energy, enthusiasm and determination necessary to get things done. **5** a slot in a computer into which you put disks or the mechanism that turns them on: *Put a 3.5-inch disk in Drive A.*

drive; drove /droʊv/; **driven** /'drɪvən/: *He drove a truck; He had driven for many miles.*

'drive-in *n* a cinema, restaurant *etc* for people who stay in their cars while watching a film, eating *etc.* — *adj*: *a drive-in café.*
'driver *n* a person who drives a car *etc*: *a bus-driver.*
'driving *n* controlling a car *etc*: *He was arrested for dangerous driving.* — *adj* very strong: *driving rain; Who's the driving force behind this plan?*
be driving at to mean: *What are you driving at?*
drive mad to annoy and upset: *The noise is driving me mad.*
drive off to keep something away: *He used his handkerchief to drive off the flies.*
drive on to push forward: *His eagerness to win drove him on.*
driving licence a card or certificate showing that you are qualified to drive.

drizzle /'drɪzəl/ *v* to rain in small drops: *It drizzled all morning.* — *n* fine, light rain.

See **rain.**

drone /droʊn/ *n* a deep, humming sound: *the distant drone of traffic.* — *v* to make a low, humming sound: *An aeroplane droned overhead.*
drone on to go on speaking for a long time in a boring manner: *The teacher droned on and on.*

drool /druːl/ *v* **1** to allow liquid to drip from your mouth. **2** to admire something in a silly way: *They were all drooling over the new baby.*

droop /druːp/ *v* to hang down: *The willows drooped over the pond.*
'drooping *adj*: *a drooping moustache.*

drop /drɒp/ *n* **1** a small round or pear-shaped

drought

blob of liquid: *a drop of rain*. **2** a small quantity of liquid: *If you want more wine, there's a drop left*. **3** a fall: *a drop in temperature*; *From the top of the mountain there was a drop of a thousand feet*. — *v* **1** to let something fall, usually by accident: *She dropped a box of pins all over the floor*. **2** to fall: *The coin dropped through the hole*; *The cat dropped on to its paws*. **3** to give up something: *I think she's dropped the idea of going to London*. **4** to let someone get out of a car *etc*: *The bus dropped me at the end of the road*. **5** to say or write in a casual manner: *I'll drop her a note*.

'drop-out *n* a person who leaves school or university without completing their studies.

drop back or **drop behind** to move into a position behind others because you are moving more slowly.

drop by or **drop in** to visit someone casually: *Do drop in if you happen to be passing!*; *I'll drop by at your house on my way home*.

drop off 1 to get separated; to fall off: *The door-handle dropped off*; *This button dropped off your coat*. **2** to fall asleep: *I must have dropped off for a few minutes*.

drop out to leave or stop doing something before you have finished: *to drop out of a competition*.

drought /draʊt/ *n* a long period without rain: *The reservoir dried up completely during the drought*.

> The opposite of a **drought** is a **flood**.

drove *see* **drive**.

drown /draʊn/ *v* **1** to sink in water and so die; to cause someone to do this: *He drowned in the river*; *He fell off the ship and was drowned*. **2** to cause a sound not to be heard by making a louder sound: *His voice was drowned by the roar of the traffic*.

drowsy /'draʊzɪ/ *adj* sleepy: *drowsy children*. **'drowsily** *adv*. **'drowsiness** *n*.

drug /drʌg/ *n* **1** any substance used in medicine: *She has been prescribed a new drug for her stomach-pains*. **2** a substance taken by some people to get a certain effect, such as happiness or excitement: *It is very dangerous to take drugs*. — *v* to make someone become unconscious by giving them a drug: *She drugged him and tied him up*.

drug addict *n* a person who has become dependent on drugs.

drum /drʌm/ *n* **1** a musical instrument made of skin stretched on a round frame, played by beating: *He plays the drums*. **2** something shaped like a drum, especially a container: *an oil-drum*. — *v* **1** to beat a drum. **2** to tap continuously, especially with your fingers: *Stop drumming on the table!* **3** to make a sound like someone beating a drum: *The rain drummed on the metal roof*.

drums

'drummer *n* a person who plays the drums.
'drumstick *n* **1** a stick used for beating a drum. **2** the lower part of the leg of a cooked chicken *etc*.

drum into to repeat something to someone until they learn it: *We had our multiplication tables drummed into us at school*.

drum up to persuade a number of people to give help or support *etc*: *We expect to drum up a good audience for the concert*.

drunk /drʌŋk/ *adj* not able to think, talk or walk properly, after drinking too much alcohol: *A drunk man fell into the river*. — *n* someone who is drunk. See also **drink**.

'drunkard *n* a person who is often drunk: *I'm afraid he's turning into a drunkard*.
'drunken *adj* drunk: *drunken soldiers*. **'drunkenness** *n*. **'drunkenly** *adv*.

dry /draɪ/ *adj* **1** not moist or wet: *The ground is very dry*; *The leaves are dry and withered*. **2** uninteresting: *a very dry book*. **3** not sweet: *dry wine*. **4** funny, while seeming serious: *a dry sense of humour*. — *v* to make or become dry: *I prefer drying dishes to washing them*; *The clothes dried quickly in the sun*. **'dryness** *n*.

> **dry; 'drying; dried; dried**: *I'm drying my hair*; *She dried the dishes*; *dried peas*.

dry-'clean *v* to clean clothes *etc* with chemicals, not with water.
'dryer or **'drier** *n* a machine *etc* that dries: *a spin-drier*; *a hair-dryer*.

dry out to become completely dry: *Allow the paper to dry out before writing on it*.

dry up 1 to become or make completely

dry: *All the rivers dried up in the heat; The sun dried up the puddles in the road.* **2** to forget what you were going to say next.

dual /'dju:əl/ *adj* double: *The driving instructor's car has dual controls.*

> a car with **dual** (not **duel**) controls.

dub /dʌb/ *v* **1** to put new voices into a film, especially in a different language. **2** to add sound effects or music to a film *etc*. **'dubbing** *n*.

dubious /'dju:bɪəs/ *adj* doubtful: *Both men were dubious about how long someone could endure the winter weather.* **'dubiously** *adv.* **'dubiousness** *n*.

duchess /'dʌtʃɪs/ *n* **1** the wife of a duke. **2** a woman of the same rank as a duke.

duck[1] /dʌk/ *v* **1** to push someone under water for a moment: *They splashed about, ducking each other.* **2** to lower your head suddenly to avoid a blow *etc*: *He ducked as the ball came at him.*

duck[2] /dʌk/ *n* a water-bird with short legs and a broad flat beak.
'duckling *n* a baby duck.

> A duck **quacks**.
> A baby duck is a **duckling**.
> A male duck is a **drake**.

duct /dʌkt/ *n* a tube or pipe that carries a liquid or gas: *a ventilation duct; Your tear ducts drain water from your eyes.*

due /dju:/ *adj* **1** owed: *200 francs are still due to us for the parcel of books we sent you.* **2** expected to be ready, to arrive *etc*: *The bus is due in three minutes.* — *adv* exactly: *We decided to travel due west.*
due to caused by something: *His success was due to hard work.*

> The accident **was due to** (not **happened due to**) his carelessness.
> See also **owing to**.

duel /'dju:əl/ *n* a fight with swords or pistols between two people.

> to fight a **duel** (not **dual**).

duet /dju:'ɛt/ *n* a piece of music for two singers or two players: *The two sisters played a piano duet.*

dug *see* **dig**.

duke /dju:k/ *n* a nobleman of the highest rank.

> The wife of a **duke**, or a woman of the same rank, is a **duchess**.

dull /dʌl/ *adj* **1** slow to learn or to understand: *The clever children help the dull ones.* **2** not bright, shining or clear: *a dull day.* **3** not exciting or interesting: *a very dull book.* **'dullness** *n.* **'dully** *adv.*

duly /'dju:lɪ/ *adv* properly; as expected: *He was duly punished.*

dumb /dʌm/ *adj* not able to speak: *She was born deaf and dumb; He was struck dumb with fear.* **'dumbness** *n.* **'dumbly** *adv.*

dumbfounded /dʌm'faʊndɪd/ *adj* too surprised to say anything.

dummy /'dʌmɪ/ *n* **1** something which looks real but is not: *The boxes of chocolates in the shop window were dummies.* **2** an object that you put in a baby's mouth to comfort it. — *adj*: *We'll only be using dummy bullets in the exercise.*

dump /dʌmp/ *v* **1** to put down heavily: *She dumped the heavy shopping-bag on the table.* **2** to get rid of rubbish *etc*: *Some people just dump their rubbish in the countryside.* — *n* a place for leaving unwanted things: *a rubbish dump.*

dumpling /'dʌmplɪŋ/ *n* **1** a steamed pudding. **2** a ball of dough served with meat.

dumpy /'dʌmpɪ/ *adj* small and fat. **'dumpiness** *n*.

dunce /dʌns/ *n* a person who is slow at learning or stupid: *I was a dunce at school.*

dune /dju:n/ *n* a low hill or bank of sand: *There were lots of sand dunes between the beach and the road.*

dung /dʌŋ/ *n* the excretion of horses and cattle, used as a soil fertilizer.

dungarees /dʌŋgə'ri:z/ *n plural* trousers with a top part that covers your chest and has straps going over your shoulders: *He bought two pairs of dungarees; Your dungarees are lying on the chair.*

dungeon /'dʌndʒən/ *n* a dark underground prison.

dupe /dju:p/ *v* to trick: *He duped me into paying twice for the ticket.*

duplicate *adj* /'dju:plɪkət/ exactly the same: *He had a duplicate key made.* — *n* **1** another thing of exactly the same kind: *This ring is almost the duplicate of the one I lost.* **2** a copy: *She gave her boss a duplicate of her report.* — *v* /'dju:plɪkeɪt/ to make a copy of something: *He duplicated the letter.* **dupli'cation** *n*.

durable /'djʊərəbəl/ *adj* lasting well: *durable cloth.* **dura'bility** *n*.

duration /djʊ'reɪʃən/ *n* the length of time something continues: *Everybody stayed indoors for the duration of the hurricane; a* *training course of three months' duration.*

during /'djʊərɪŋ/ *prep* **1** all through the time that something lasts: *We couldn't get enough food during the war.* **2** at a particular time while something is happening: *He died during the war.*

dusk /dʌsk/ *n* the time of evening when the light is disappearing, after the sun sets. **'dusky** *adj* dark-coloured. **'duskiness** *n*.

dust /dʌst/ *n* **1** powdery dirt: *The furniture was covered in dust.* **2** any fine powder: *golddust; sawdust.* — *v* to wipe the dust off furniture: *She dusts the house once a week.* **'dusty** *adj.* **'dustiness** *n*.

> **dust** is never used in the plural.

'dustbin *n* a container for rubbish.
'duster *n* a cloth for removing dust.
'dustman *n* a person who collects the rubbish from houses.
'dustpan *n* a flat container for sweeping dust into.
throw dust in someone's eyes to try to deceive someone.

dutiful /'dju:tɪfəl/ *adj* careful to do what you should: *a dutiful daughter.*

duty /'dju:tɪ/ *n* **1** something you ought to do: *It is your duty to share in the housework.* **2** a task that you do as part of your job *etc*: *What are your duties as a school prefect?* **3** a tax on goods: *You must pay duty when you bring wine into the country.*
off duty not working: *The doctor is off duty this weekend.*
on duty working: *Which nurses are on duty this evening?*

dwarf /dwɔ:f/, *plural* **dwarfs** or **dwarves**, *n* in fairy tales *etc*, a creature like a tiny man, with magic powers: *Snow White and the seven dwarfs.* — *v* to make a smaller thing look very small indeed: *The little man was completely dwarfed by his two tall sons.*

> The opposite of a **dwarf** is a **giant**.

dwell /dwɛl/ *v* to live in a place.

> **dwell; dwelt** /dwɛlt/; **dwelt**: *The witch dwelt in a dark wood; She had dwelt there for a hundred years.*

'dwelling *n* a house, flat *etc*.
dwell on to think or worry for too long about something: *Don't dwell on your troubles.*

dwindle /'dwɪndəl/ *v* to grow less: *His money dwindled away.*

dye /daɪ/ *v* to give a permanent colour to clothes, cloth or hair: *I've just dyed my coat green; I'm sure she dyes her hair.* — *n* a powder or liquid for colouring: *a bottle of green dye.*

> **dye; dyeing; dyed; dyed**: *I'm dyeing this blouse; She dyed her hair green.*

dying /'daɪɪŋ/ *see* **die**.

dyke or **dike** /daɪk/ *n* a thick wall that is built to prevent water flooding on to land from the sea or a river.

dynamic /daɪ'næmɪk/ *adj* full of energy; having a lot of new ideas: *A dynamic teacher can make even the most uninterested pupils enthusiastic.* **dy'namically** *adv.* **'dynamism** *n*.

dynamite /'daɪnəmaɪt/ *n* a powerful explosive.

dynamo /'daɪnəmoʊ/, *plural* **'dynamos**, *n* a device that produces electricity, for example from the movement of wheels: *A small dynamo on a bicycle produces power for its lights.*

dynasty /'dɪnəstɪ/ *n* a series of rulers of the same family: *the Ming dynasty.* **dy'nastic** *adj.*

E

each /iːtʃ/ *adj* every person or thing: *Each house in this street has a garden*; *The boys each have 50 pence*; *I gave them each an apple.* — *pron* every one: *She called at each of the houses.* — *adv* to every one: *I gave them a pound each.*

> Each girl **has** a book.
> They each **have** a book.
> Each of the boys **has** a book in his hand.
> See also **every**.

each other used as the object when an action takes place between two or more people *etc*: *People welcomed each other*; *Two tired men holding on to each other.*

> You can use **each other** of two people: *The twins used to fight each other.*
> You can use **one another** of several people: *The children helped one another.*

eager /ˈiːgə(r)/ *adj* keen; wanting something very much: *They are eager for success*; *He is eager to win*; *He tried not to look too eager.* **'eagerly** *adv.* **'eagerness** *n.*

eagle /ˈiːgəl/ *n* a large bird that attacks smaller creatures and has very good eyesight.

ear /ɪə(r)/ *n* **1** the part of you that you hear with: *You must have sharp ears to hear a bat squeaking.* **2** the top part of a plant that contains the seeds: *an ear of corn.*

be all ears to listen keenly: *The children were all ears when the headmaster told them about the competition.*

go in one ear and out the other not to be heard: *I keep telling the children to be quiet, but my words go in one ear and out the other.*

play by ear to play a tune without the help of printed music.

play it by ear to decide what to do according to how a situation develops, instead of planning in advance.

up to your ears very busy with something: *I'm up to my ears in work.*

earache /ˈɪəreɪk/ *n* pain inside your ear.

eardrum /ˈɪədrʌm/ *n* the thin piece of skin that vibrates inside your ear.

earlobe /ˈɪəloʊb/ *n* the soft lower part of your ear: *You have to have your earlobes pierced in order to be able to wear earrings.*

early /ˈɜːlɪ/ *adv* **1** near the beginning: *I started writing poems early in my life*; *The accident happened early in the afternoon.* **2** before other people; sooner than usual; sooner than expected: *He arrived early*; *She came an hour early.* — *adj* **1** near the beginning of something: *in the early morning*; *in the early part of the century.* **2** belonging to the first, or primitive, stages: *early musical instruments.* **3** before the usual time: *He died an early death*; *It's too early to get up yet.* **'earliness** *n.*

at the earliest not before a particular time: *She can't see you until 3 o'clock at the earliest.*

early on soon after the beginning: *We had some problems early on in the project, but solved them quickly.*

earmark /ˈɪəmɑːk/ *v* to set something aside for a particular purpose: *This money has been earmarked for our holiday in New Zealand.*

earn /ɜːn/ *v* **1** to get money for work: *He earns £500 a week*; *He earns his living by cleaning shoes.* **2** to deserve: *I've earned a rest.* **'earnings** *n* money etc earned: *His earnings are not sufficient to support his family.*

earnest /ˈɜːnɪst/ *adj* **1** serious: *an earnest student.* **2** determined; sincere: *He made an earnest attempt to improve his work.* **'earnestness** *n.* **'earnestly** *adv.*

in earnest 1 not joking: *I am in earnest when I say this.* **2** determination: *He set to work in earnest.*

earphones /ˈɪəfoʊnz/ *n plural* a pair of receivers connected to a radio, cassette recorder *etc*, that you wear over your ears in order to listen to music *etc* without other people hearing it.

earring /ˈɪərɪŋ/ *n* a piece of jewellery that you attach to your ear.

> **an** (not **a**) earring.

earshot /ˈɪəʃɒt/ *n* the distance at which you can hear a sound: *He was out of earshot, so he couldn't hear what she was saying.*

earth /ɜːθ/ *n* **1** the planet on which we live: *Is Earth nearer the Sun than Mars is?*; *the geography of the earth.* **2** the world: *heaven and earth.* **3** soil: *Fill the plant-pot with earth.* **4** dry land; the ground: *the earth, sea and sky.* **5** the wire that is connected to the

earthenware

ground to make an electrical system safe: *Which of these wires is the earth?* **6** the hole of a fox.

cost the earth to be very expensive.

on earth used for emphasis: *What on earth are you doing?*; *the stupidest man on earth*.

globe

earth

earthenware /'ɜːθənweə(r)/ *n* pots, bowls *etc* made of baked clay; pottery: *She collects earthenware.* — *adj*: *an earthenware dish*.

earthly /'ɜːθlɪ/ *adj* belonging to this world, not to heaven: *We cannot take our earthly possessions with us when we die*.

earthquake /'ɜːθkweɪk/ *n* a shaking of the earth's surface: *The village was destroyed by an earthquake*.

earthworm /'ɜːθwɜːm/ *n* a worm.

ease /iːz/ *n* **1** freedom from pain or from worry or hard work: *He led a life of ease.* **2** freedom from difficulty: *He passed his exam with ease.* — *v* **1** to make or become better: *The pill eased his headache*; *The pain has eased a bit now*. **2** to move something heavy or awkward gently or gradually: *They eased the wardrobe carefully up the narrow staircase*.

at ease not shy or anxious: *He is completely at ease among strangers*.

ease off to become less severe: *I think the rain's eased off a little*.

stand at ease to stand with legs apart and hands clasped behind the back.

take your ease to make yourself comfortable; to relax: *There he was — taking his ease in his father's chair!*

easel /'iːzəl/ *n* a stand for supporting a blackboard or an artist's picture.

easily /'iːzɪlɪ/ *adv* **1** without difficulty: *She won the race easily.* **2** by far: *This is easily the best book I've read*; *He is easily the cleverest pupil in the class*.

east /iːst/ *n* **1** the direction from which the sun rises, or any part of the earth lying in that direction: *The wind is blowing from the east*; *The oil field lies to the east of Shetland*; *in the east of England*. **2** (often written **E**) one of the four main points of the compass. — *adj* **1** in the east: *the east coast*. **2** from the direction of the east: *an east wind.* — *adv* towards the east: *The house faces east*.

east and west is always said in this order.

the East 1 the countries east of Europe: *the Middle East*; *the Far East*. **2** the countries of eastern Asia, and the countries of eastern Europe that have or used to have Communist governments.

Easter /'iːstə(r)/ *n* a Christian festival held in the spring, to celebrate Christ's coming back to life after the Crucifixion.

Easter egg a decorated egg, usually made of chocolate, eaten at Easter.

easterly /'iːstəlɪ/ *adj* **1** coming from the east: *an easterly wind*. **2** towards the east: *We are travelling in an easterly direction*.

eastern /'iːstən/ *adj* belonging to the east: *an eastern custom*.

eastward /'iːstwəd/ *adj, adv* towards the east: *in an eastward direction*; *moving eastward*.

eastwards /'iːstwədz/ *adv* towards the east: *They are travelling eastwards*.

easy /'iːzɪ/ *adj* **1** not difficult: *This is an easy job to do*. **2** free from pain, trouble, anxiety *etc*: *He had an easy day at the office*. **3** friendly; relaxed: *an easy manner*; *an easy smile*. '**easiness** *n*.

easy chair a chair that is soft and comfortable, for example, an armchair.

easy-'going *adj* not inclined to worry.

easier said than done more difficult than it at first seems: *Getting tickets for the match is easier said than done*.

go easy on to be careful with: *Go easy on the sandwiches — there won't be enough for the rest of the guests*.

take it easy not to work hard: *The doctor told him to take it easy*.

eat /iːt/ *v* to chew and swallow; to take food: *They are forbidden to eat meat*; *They ate up all the cakes*; *We must eat to live*.

eat; ate /eɪt/; '**eaten**: *She ate up all her pudding*; *You haven't eaten your dinner yet*.

'**eatable** *adj* able to be eaten: *The meal was scarcely eatable*.

eat out to have a meal at a restaurant.

eat into to destroy or waste gradually: *Acid eats into metal*.

eat your words to admit that you were mistaken in saying something.

eaves /iːvz/ *n* the edges of a roof that stick

out beyond the walls: *The nest was under the eaves.*

eavesdrop /ˈiːvzdrɒp/ *v* to listen secretly to a private conversation: *He eavesdropped on my discussion with his parents.*

ebb /ɛb/ *v* **1** the word used to describe the tide going out from the land: *The tide began to ebb.* **2** to become less: *His strength was ebbing fast.*

ebb and flow frequent changes, often between good and bad or between positive and negative: *Governments must be aware of the ebb and flow of public opinion.*

ebony /ˈɛbənɪ/ *n* a type of very hard, almost black wood. — *adj.*

eccentric /ɪkˈsɛntrɪk/ *adj* odd; unusual: *He had an eccentric habit of writing notes on his shirt-sleeve; The old man is growing more eccentric every day.* — *n* an eccentric person: *She has always been an eccentric.* **ec'centrically** *adv.* **eccen'tricity** *n.*

echo /ˈɛkoʊ/, plural **'echoes**, *n* the repeating of a sound caused by its striking a surface and coming back: *The children shouted loudly in the cave so that they could hear the echoes.* — *v* to send back an echo: *The hills echoed his shout.* **2** to repeat; to copy: *She echoed her sister's words.*

éclair /ɪˈklɛə(r)/ *n* a long, narrow cake made of very light pastry, that is usually filled with cream and has chocolate icing.

eclipse /ɪˈklɪps/ *n* the disappearance of the whole or part of the sun when the moon comes between it and the earth, or of the moon when the earth's shadow falls across it.

ecology /ɪˈkɒlədʒɪ/ *n* **1** the relationships between living things and their surroundings: *He is very interested in the ecology of the desert; a chain of events disastrous to the ecology of two continents.* **2** the study of these relationships. **e'cologist** *n.*

eco'logical *adj* **1** relating to the relationships between living things and their surroundings: *She is studying the ecological problems of the area.* **2** interested in preserving animals and plants and the environment in which they live: *He belongs to an ecological group which is fighting to stop pollution.*

economic /iːkəˈnɒmɪk/ or /ɛkəˈnɒmɪk/ *adj* **1** having to do with economy. **2** economical.

economical /iːkəˈnɒmɪkəl/ or /ɛkəˈnɒmɪkəl/ *adj* good at saving; not using up a lot of money *etc*: *an economical housewife; This car is very economical to run.* **eco'nomically** *adv.*

economics /iːkəˈnɒmɪks/ or /ɛkəˈnɒmɪks/ *n* the study of the management of money and goods.

economist /ɪˈkɒnəmɪst/ *n* a person who is an expert in economics.

economize /iːˈkɒnəmaɪz/ or /ɪˈkɒnəmaɪz/ *v* to spend money or use goods carefully: *We must economize on fuel.*

economy /ɪˈkɒnəmɪ/ *n* **1** the careful management of money and materials to avoid waste: *Please use the water with economy.* **2** a saving: *We must make economies in household spending.* **3** organization of money earned and spent: *the country's economy; household economy.*

ecstasy /ˈɛkstəsɪ/ *n* very great joy. **ec'static** *adj.* **ec'statically** *adv.*

edge /ɛdʒ/ *n* **1** the part farthest from the middle of something; a border: *Don't put that cup so near the edge of the table — it will fall off; the edge of the lake; He stood at the water's edge.* **2** the cutting side of something sharp, for example a knife or weapon: *the edge of the sword.* — *v* to move little by little: *She edged her way through the crowd.*

edged *adj* having a border: *a handkerchief edged with lace.*

'edging *n* a border: *a jacket with gold edging.*

'edgy *adj* nervous and a bit bad-tempered. **'edgily** *adv.* **'edginess** *n.*

on edge nervous: *She was on edge when she was waiting for her exam results.*

edible /ˈɛdɪbəl/ *adj* able to be eaten: *Are these berries edible?* **edi'bility** *n.*

The opposite of **edible** is **inedible**.

edifice /ˈɛdɪfɪs/ *n* a large, important-looking building: *The new bank is a magnificent edifice.*

edit /ˈɛdɪt/ *v* to prepare a book, film *etc* for publication or for showing to the public, by correcting, altering, shortening *etc.*

edition /ɪˈdɪʃən/ *n* **1** a number of copies of a book, magazine or newspaper printed at one time: *There is going to be a new edition of this dictionary.* **2** one copy of a particular edition: *a paperback edition of the novel.* **3** a television or radio programme that is part of a series: *Don't forget to watch next week's edition.*

'editor *n* **1** a person who edits books *etc.* **2** a person who is in charge of a newspaper, journal *etc* or a part of it: *the editor of The*

edi'torial *adj*: *She does editorial work for a publisher.* — *n* an article in a newspaper that gives the opinion of the editor or the publishers: *The editorial criticized the education minister's decision.*

educate /'ɛdjʊkeɪt/ *v* to teach, especially at a school or college: *He was educated at an American school.*
'educated *adj* having a lot of knowledge in various subjects: *a highly educated person.*
edu'cation *n* the teaching of children and young people in schools, universities *etc*: *He received a good education.* **edu'cational** *adj.*

eel /i:l/ *n* a kind of fish like a big long worm.

eel

eerie /'ɪərɪ/ *adj* very strange and a bit frightening: *There was an eerie silence in the dark woods.* **'eerily** *adv.* **'eeriness** *n.*

effect /ɪ'fɛkt/ *n* **1** a result: *Getting too fat is one of the effects of eating too much.* **2** an impression made by something: *The television programme had a strong effect on her.* — *v* to make something happen: *The new headmistress effected several changes at the school.*

to have a bad **effect** (not **affect**).
See also **affect**.

ef'fective *adj* **1** producing the result that is wanted: *These new teaching methods have proved very effective.* **2** pleasing: *an effective display of flowers.* **3** in use: *The new law becomes effective next week.* **ef'fectively** *adv.* **ef'fectiveness** *n.*
ef'fects *n* **1** in drama *etc*, devices for producing suitable sounds, lighting *etc* to accompany a play *etc*: *sound effects.* **2** your personal possessions.
come into effect to come into use: *The law came into effect last month.*
in effect 1 in use: *That rule is no longer in effect.* **2** a phrase used to explain the reality of a situation: *It sounds as if I'm getting a pay rise, but in effect I'm losing money.*
put into effect to carry out a plan *etc*: *I'll put my plan into effect tomorrow.*
take effect to begin to work: *When will the drug take effect?*
to this effect or **to that effect** with this or that general meaning: *He told me to go away, or words to that effect.*

effeminate /ɪ'fɛmɪnət/ *adj* not manly; like a woman or girl: *He behaves in a very effeminate way.*
effervesce /ɛfə'vɛs/ *v* to give off bubbles; to fizz: *The drink effervesced in the glass.* **effer'vescence** *n.* **effer'vescent** *adj.*
efficient /ɪ'fɪʃənt/ *adj* **1** capable; skilful: *a very efficient secretary.* **2** producing satisfactory results: *The new bread knife is much more efficient than the old one.* **ef'ficiently** *adv.* **ef'ficiency** *n.*

The opposite of **efficient** is **inefficient**.

effort /'ɛfət/ *n* **1** hard work; energy: *Learning a foreign language requires effort*; *The effort of climbing the hill made the old man very tired.* **2** an attempt; a struggle: *He made a big effort to improve his work.* **3** a try: *Your drawing was a good effort.*
'effortless *adj* done very easily: *The dancer's movements looked effortless.* **'effortlessly** *adv.*
egg¹ /ɛg/: **egg on** to encourage someone: *He egged his friend on to steal the radio.*
egg² /ɛg/ *n* **1** an object covered with shell, laid by a bird, snake *etc*, from which a young one is hatched: *The female bird is sitting on the eggs in the nest.* **2** one of these laid by a hen and used as food: *Would you like boiled, fried or scrambled eggs?* **3** in a female animal, the cell from which the baby is formed.
'egg-cup *n* a small cup-shaped container for holding a boiled egg while it is being eaten.
'egg-plant *n* a dark purple fruit used as a vegetable.

egg-plant

'eggshell *n* the shell of an egg.
ego /'i:goʊ/, *plural* **egos**, *n* your opinion of how important you are, personal pride: *He has an enormous ego* (he thinks he is very important indeed).
'egotism *n* selfish behaviour that shows that you think you are more important than anyone else.
'egotist *n* a person who behaves selfishly. **ego'tistical** *adj.*
eight /eɪt/ *n* **1** the number 8: *Four and four are eight.* **2** the age of 8: *children of eight and over.* — *adj* **1** 8 in number: *eight people*; *He is eight years old.* **2** aged 8: *He is eight today.*

eighth *n* one of eight equal parts: *They each received an eighth of the money.* — *n, adj* the next after the seventh in order: *His horse was eighth in the race; Is it the eighth of November today?; When the eighth wicket went down, England was still nine behind.*

eighteen /eɪˈtiːn/ *n* **1** the number 18. **2** the age of 18: *a girl of eighteen.* — *adj* **1** 18 in number: *eighteen horses.* **2** aged 18: *He is eighteen now.*

eighty /ˈeɪtɪ/ *n* **1** the number 80; **2** the age of 80. — *adj* **1** 80 in number. **2** aged 80.

either /ˈaɪðə(r)/ or /ˈiːðə(r)/ *pron* the one or the other of two: *You may borrow either of these books; I offered him coffee or tea, but he didn't want either.* — *adj* **1** the one or the other: *He can write with either hand.* **2** the one and the other; both: *at either side of the garden.* — *adv* also: *If you don't go, I won't either.*

> I have not been to Denmark **either** (not **also**).

either...or used to introduce two things you must choose between: *Either go and make a noise outside, or stay here and keep quiet.*

> Either John or Mary **is** telling a lie.
> Either Michael or his parents **are** going to see the headmaster.

ejaculate /ɪˈdʒakjʊleɪt/ *v* **1** to discharge semen from the penis. **2** a rather old word for exclaim: *'Goodness!' she ejaculated.* **ejacuˈlation** *n*.

eject /ɪˈdʒɛkt/ *v* **1** to force someone to leave a house: *They were ejected from their house for not paying the rent.* **2** to leave an aircraft in an emergency, causing your seat to be ejected: *The pilot had to eject when his plane caught fire.* **eˈjection** *n*.

eke /iːk/: **eke out** to make something last as long as possible: *We must eke out our supplies until we can get to a shop.*

eke out a living to survive on very little money.

elaborate *adj* /ɪˈlabərət/ very detailed or complicated: *The brooch had an elaborate design.* — *v* /ɪˈlabəreɪt/ to give more details about something: *The minister refused to elaborate on his statement.*

eˈlaborately *adv*: *an elaborately embroidered blouse.*

elapse /ɪˈlaps/ *v* to pass: *Many years have elapsed since we met.*

elastic /ɪˈlastɪk/ *adj* able to return to its proper shape or size after being pulled or pressed out of shape: *Rubber is an elastic substance.* — *n* a type of cord containing strands of rubber: *Her hat was held on with a piece of elastic.* **elasˈticity** *n*.

elastic band a small thin ring of rubber for holding things together: *He put an elastic band round the papers.*

elated /ɪˈleɪtɪd/ *adj* very cheerful: *She felt elated after winning.* **eˈlation** *n*.

elbow /ˈɛlboʊ/ *n* the joint where your arm bends: *He leant on his elbows.* — *v* to push with your elbow: *He elbowed his way through the crowd.*

ˈelbow-room *n* space enough for doing something: *Get out of my way and give me some elbow-room!*

at your elbow close to you: *When you are reading, always keep a dictionary at your elbow.*

elder /ˈɛldə(r)/ *adj* older: *He has three elder sisters; He is the elder of the two.* — *n* a person who is older: *Take the advice of your elders.*

ˈelderly *adj* rather old: *an elderly lady.*

ˈeldest *adj* oldest: *She is the eldest of the three children.*

> **elder** and **eldest** can be used instead of **older** and **oldest** when you are talking about members of a family: *my elder sisters; my eldest sister;* **but** *My sister is older than me.*

elect /ɪˈlɛkt/ *v* **1** to choose by vote: *He was elected chairman.* **2** to decide: *She elected to stay at home.*

eˈlection *n* the choosing of someone by vote: *When does the election take place?; He is standing for election as president again.*

eˈlector *n* a person who has the right to vote at an election.

eˈlectoral *adj* to do with elections: *the electoral process.*

electric /ɪˈlɛktrɪk/ *adj* **1** produced by or worked by electricity: *electric light.* **2** very tense or exciting: *The atmosphere in the room was electric.*

eˈlectrical *adj* having to do with electricity: *electrical goods; an electrical fault.* **eˈlectrically** *adv*.

elecˈtrician *n* a person whose job is to make, fit and repair electrical equipment: *The electrician mended the electric fan.*

elecˈtricity *n* a form of energy used to give heat, light, power *etc*: *This machine is worked by electricity; Don't waste electricity.*

electrify /ɪˈlɛktrɪfaɪ/ *v* to equip something,

such as railway lines, with electric power.

electrocute /ɪˈlɛktrəkjuːt/ v to kill accidentally by electricity. **electroˈcution** n.

electrode /ɪˈlɛktroʊd/ n a small metal connector where an electric current enters or leaves a battery etc.

electron /ɪˈlɛktrɒn/ n a very small particle within an atom.

electronic /ɪlɛkˈtrɒnɪk/ adj 1 worked by, or produced by, the action of electrons: *an electronic calculator*. 2 having to do with electronics: *an electronic engineer*. **elecˈtronically** adv.

elecˈtronics n the science that deals with the study of electrons and their use in machines etc.

electronic mail sending information using a computer.

elegant /ˈɛlɪɡənt/ adj smart; stylish: *elegant clothes*. **ˈelegance** n. **ˈelegantly** adv.

elegy /ˈɛlədʒɪ/ n a sad poem or song, often on the subject of death or a dead person: *an elegy for their dead king*.

element /ˈɛləmənt/ n 1 a substance that cannot be split by chemical means into simpler substances: *Hydrogen, chlorine, iron and uranium are elements*. 2 surroundings necessary for life: *Water is a fish's natural element*. 3 a slight amount: *an element of doubt*. 4 the heating part in an electric kettle etc.

eleˈmentary adj very simple: *elementary mathematics*.

ˈelements n the first things to be learned in any subject: *the elements of musical theory*.

in your element in the situation that you find most natural and enjoyable: *He's in his element in a roomful of people*.

elephant /ˈɛləfənt/ n a very large animal with thick skin, a trunk and two tusks.

An elephant **trumpets**.

elevate /ˈɛləveɪt/ v to raise: *The mechanics had to elevate the car so that they could look underneath it*. **eleˈvation** n.

ˈelevator n a lift for taking people, goods etc to a higher or lower floor.

eleven /ɪˈlɛvən/ n 1 the number 11. 2 the age of 11. 3 in football etc, a team of eleven players: *He plays for the school's first eleven*. adj 1 11 in number. 2 aged 11.

eˈleventh n one of eleven equal parts. — n, adj the next after the tenth.

at the eleventh hour just in time: *She sent in her entry for the competition at the eleventh hour*.

elf /ɛlf/, plural **elves** /ɛlvz/, n a tiny mischievous fairy.

eligible /ˈɛlɪdʒəbəl/ adj 1 suitable to be chosen: *the most eligible candidate*. 2 being the right age etc for something: *Is he eligible to join the Scouts?* **eligiˈbility** n.

eliminate /ɪˈlɪmɪneɪt/ v 1 to put someone out of a competition etc; to exclude: *He was eliminated from the tennis tournament in the first round*. 2 to get rid of something. **elimiˈnation** n.

elite /ɪˈliːt/ or /eɪˈliːt/ n the best, most important or powerful people in a society or group: *He is a member of the scientific elite*. — adj of or belonging to these people: *an elite school*.

ellipse /ɪˈlɪps/ n an oval.

elˈliptical adj: *an elliptical shape*.

elocution /ɛləˈkjuːʃən/ n the art of speaking clearly and effectively: *Actors must study elocution as part of their training*.

elongated /ˈiːlɒŋɡeɪtɪd/ adj long and narrow; stretched out: *elongated leaves*; *An ellipse looks like an elongated circle*. **elonˈgation** n.

elope /ɪˈloʊp/ v to run away secretly with another person to marry them: *Her parents would never agree to her marriage so she decided to elope with her fiancé*.

eloquence /ˈɛləkwəns/ n the ability to speak so well that you deeply affect people's feelings: *a speaker of great eloquence*. **ˈeloquent** adj. **ˈeloquently** adv.

else /ɛls/ adj, adv besides; other than yourself; other than the thing or person already named: *I know it's wrong to tell a lie, but if I have to keep the secret what else can I do?*; *Can we go anywhere else?*; *He took someone else's pencil*.

elseˈwhere adv in, or to, another place; somewhere or anywhere else: *You must try elsewhere if you want a less tiring job*.

or else otherwise: *He must have missed the train — or else he's ill*.

elude /ɪˈluːd/ v to escape or avoid by quickness or cleverness: *He eluded his pursuers*.

eˈlusive adj escaping or vanishing, often or cleverly: *an elusive criminal*.

elves plural of **elf**.

emaciated /ɪˈmeɪsɪeɪtɪd/ adj very thin and weak, usually because of illness or starvation: *She looked pale and emaciated when she left hospital*.

e-mail /ˈiːmeɪl/ n electronic mail.

emancipate /ɪˈmansɪpeɪt/ v to set someone free from slavery etc. **emanciˈpation** n.

embankment /ɪmˈbaŋkmənt/ n a bank made

to keep back water or to carry a railway over low-lying places *etc*.

embargo /ɪmˈbɑːgoʊ/, *plural* **emˈbargoes**, *n* an official order by a government stopping trade with another country: *The government ordered an embargo on the sale of weapons.*

embark /ɪmˈbɑːk/ *v* to go on board ship: *Passengers should embark early; Two hours was enough to embark the men in Cherbourg harbour.* **emˈbarkation** *n*.
embark on to start: *She embarked on a new career.*

> See **disembark**.

embarrass /ɪmˈbarəs/ *v* to make someone feel shy and uneasy: *She was embarrassed by his praise.*
emˈbarrassment *n*.

> **embarrass** is spelt with two **r**s and two **ss**.

emˈbarrassing *adj*: *an embarrassing question.*

embassy /ˈɛmbəsɪ/, *plural* **ˈembassies**, *n* an ambassador and his staff or the house where he lives: *the American embassy in London.*

embedded /ɪmˈbɛdɪd/ *adj* deeply fixed: *The bullet was embedded in the wall.*

embellish /ɪmˈbɛlɪʃ/ *v* **1** to increase the interest of a story *etc* by adding details, especially untrue ones: *He thought about how he could embellish the presentation without substituting fiction for reality.* **2** to decorate *etc*: *a uniform embellished with gold braid.*
emˈbellishment *n*.

embers /ˈɛmbəz/ *n* the sparking or glowing remains of a fire.

embezzle /ɪmˈbɛzəl/ *v* to steal money that has been given to you to look after, especially money belonging to a firm *etc*. **emˈbezzlement** *n*. **emˈbezzler** *n*.

emblem /ˈɛmbləm/ *n* an object chosen to represent something such as an idea, a quality, a country *etc*: *The dove is the emblem of peace.*

embody /ɪmˈbɒdɪ/ *v* to be a perfect example of something: *He embodied every woman's dream of the ideal husband.*

embrace /ɪmˈbreɪs/ *v* to hug: *She embraced her brother warmly.* — *n* a hug: *a loving embrace.*

embroider /ɪmˈbrɔɪdə(r)/ *v* to decorate with designs in needlework: *She embroidered her name on her handkerchief.* **emˈbroidery** *n*.

embryo /ˈɛmbrɪoʊ/, *plural* **ˈembryos**, *n* a young animal or plant in its earliest stages in seed, egg or womb: *An egg contains the embryo of a chicken.* **embryˈonic** *adj*.

emerald /ˈɛmərəld/ *n* **1** a precious green stone. **2** its colour. — *adj*: *She wore an emerald dress.*

emerge /ɪˈmɜːdʒ/ *v* to come out; to come into view: *The swimmer emerged from the water.* **eˈmergence** *n*.

emergency /ɪˈmɜːdʒənsɪ/ *n* an unexpected happening, especially a dangerous one: *Call the doctor — it's an emergency; You must save some money for emergencies.* — *adj*: *an emergency exit.*

emigrate /ˈɛmɪgreɪt/ *v* to leave your country and settle in another: *Many doctors emigrate to America.* **emiˈgration** *n*.

> The opposite of **emigrate** is **immigrate**.

ˈemigrant *n* someone who emigrates.

eminent /ˈɛmɪnənt/ *adj* famous and clever: *an eminent lawyer.* **ˈeminence** *n*. **ˈeminently** *adv*.

emit /ɪˈmɪt/ *v* to give out light, heat, a sound, a smell *etc*. **eˈmission** *n*.

emotion /ɪˈmoʊʃən/ *n* a strong feeling of any kind: *Fear, joy, anger, love, jealousy are all emotions.* **eˈmotional** *adj*. **eˈmotionally** *adv*.

emperor /ˈɛmpərə(r)/ *n* the head of an empire: *the Emperor Napoleon.*

emphasis /ˈɛmfəsɪs/ *n* **1** stress put on certain words in speaking *etc*; greater force of voice used in words or parts of words to make them more noticeable: *In writing we sometimes underline words to show emphasis.* **2** importance given to something: *At this school the emphasis is on hard work.*
ˈemphasize *v* to put emphasis on something: *You emphasize the word 'too' in the sentence 'Are you going too?'*

> *to* **emphasize** (not **emphasize on**) a point.

emphatic /ɪmˈfatɪk/ *adj* firm and definite: *an emphatic refusal.* **emˈphatically** *adv*.

empire /ˈɛmpaɪə(r)/ *n* **1** a group of states *etc* under a single ruler or ruling power: *the Roman empire.* **2** a large group of companies controlled by a single person or organization: *Their publishing empire is continuing to expand.*

employ /ɛmˈplɔɪ/ *v* **1** to pay someone to do some work: *He employs three typists; She is employed as a teacher.* **2** to keep someone busy; to occupy someone: *She was employed in writing letters.* **3** to use: *You should employ your time better.*

em'ployed *adj* having a job.
em'ployee *n* a person employed by a firm *etc*: *That firm has fifty employees.*
em'ployer *n* the person who employs you: *His employer dismissed him.*
em'ployment *n* being employed: *They came to the town to search for employment.*

See **unemployed** and **unemployment**.

emporium /ɪmˈpɔːrɪəm/ *n* a large, usually rather grand shop that sells many kinds of goods.
empress /ˈɛmprɪs/ *n* **1** a female head of an empire. **2** the wife of an emperor.
empty /ˈɛmptɪ/ *adj* having nothing or no-one inside: *an empty box; an empty cup; an empty room; That house is empty now.* — *v* **1** to make or become empty: *He emptied the jug; The classroom emptied quickly at lunch-time; He emptied out his pockets.* **2** to tip, pour, or fall out of a container *etc*: *She emptied the milk into a pan; The rubbish emptied out on to the ground.* **'emptiness** *n*.
empty-'handed *adj* without the thing you wanted, or should have: *I went to buy my sister a present but returned empty-handed.*
emu /ˈiːmjuː/ *n* an Australian bird that cannot fly.
emulate /ˈɛmjʊleɪt/ *v* to copy someone you admire.
enable /ɪˈneɪbəl/ *v* to make someone able to do something: *The money I inherited enabled me to go on a world cruise.*
enamel /ɪˈnaməl/ *n* **1** a kind of hard covering for metal dishes and pans *etc*, made of glass. **2** the hard covering of the teeth. **3** a glossy paint.
e'namelled *adj* covered with enamel.
encamp /ɪnˈkamp/ *v* to set up a camp: *The soldiers encamped in a field.*
en'campment *n* a place where troops *etc* have made their camp.
enchant /ɪnˈtʃɑːnt/ *v* **1** to delight: *I was enchanted by the children's concert.* **2** to put a magic spell on someone: *A wizard had enchanted her.* **en'chantment** *n*.
en'chanter *n* a person who enchants.
en'chantress *n* a female who enchants.
encircle /ɪnˈsɜːkəl/ *v* to surround: *The town was encircled by hills.*
enclose /ɪnˈkloʊz/ *v* **1** to put something inside a letter or its envelope: *I enclose a cheque for £4.00.* **2** to shut in: *The garden was enclosed by a high wall.*
enclosure /ɪnˈkloʊʒə(r)/ *n* a piece of land surrounded by a fence or wall: *He keeps a donkey in that enclosure.*
encore /ˈɒŋkɔː(r)/ *n* a call from an audience for a performer to sing or play something more: *The number of encores varies according to how well the concert has gone.*
encounter /ɪnˈkaʊntə(r)/ *v* to meet someone or something, especially unexpectedly: *She encountered the headmistress in the street; We've encountered a problem in our computer programme.* — *n* **1** a meeting with someone that happens by chance: *a brief encounter with a friend.* **2** a fight: *a fierce encounter between two armies.*
encourage /ɪnˈkʌrɪdʒ/ *v* **1** to make someone feel confident and hopeful: *The general tried to encourage the troops.* **2** to urge someone to do something: *You must encourage him to try again.* **en'couraging** *adj*. **en'couragingly** *adv*. **en'couragement** *n*.

The opposite of **encourage** is **discourage**.

encroach /ɪnˈkroʊtʃ/ *v* to take up more and more of something you have no right to: *His work is beginning to encroach on his weekends.*
encyclopaedia /ɪnˌsaɪkləˈpiːdɪə/ *n* a large book, or a book in several volumes, containing information on all subjects, or a lot of information on one particular subject.
end /ɛnd/ *n* **1** the last or furthest part: *the house at the end of the road; both ends of the room.* **2** the finish: *the end of the week; The talks have come to an end; The war is at an end; He is at the end of his strength.* **3** death: *How did he meet his end?* **4** a small piece left over: *cigarette ends.* — *adj* at the end of a street *etc*: *We live at the end house.* — *v* to bring or come to an end: *How does the play end?; The plan ended in failure; How should I end this letter?*
end up to reach or come to an end, usually unpleasant: *I knew that he would end up in prison.*
in the end finally: *He had to work very hard but he passed his exam in the end.*
make ends meet not to get into debt: *The widow and her four children found it difficult to make ends meet.*
no end a lot: *These changes have confused me no end; No end of people have complained about it.*
on end continuously: *She hadn't left the house for days on end.*
put an end to to stop: *The doctor put an*

end to her fears about her son's health.

endanger /ɪnˈdeɪndʒə(r)/ v to put something in danger: *Drunk drivers endanger the lives of others.*

endangered species types of animal *etc* that are in danger of becoming extinct: *The whale is no longer considered an endangered species.*

endear /ɪnˈdɪə(r)/ v to make someone like you: *She endeared herself to everyone by her kindness.*

enˈdearing *adj*: *She has a very endearing way of speaking.* **enˈdearingly** *adv*.

endeavour /ɪnˈdɛvə(r)/ v to try to do something: *He endeavoured to teach the children some grammar.* — *n* an attempt: *He succeeded in his endeavour to climb Everest.*

ending /ˈɛndɪŋ/ *n* the end, especially of a story, poem *etc*: *Fairy stories have happy endings.*

endless /ˈɛndləs/ *adj* **1** going on for ever: *endless arguments.* **2** continuous: *an endless chain.* **ˈendlessly** *adv*.

endure /ɪnˈdjʊə(r)/ v **1** to bear: *She endures her troubles bravely; I can endure her rudeness no longer.* **2** to last: *The actress died many years ago, but the memory of her great acting has endured.* **enˈdurable** *adj*. **enˈdurance** *n*.

enemy /ˈɛnəmɪ/ *n* **1** a person who hates you and wants to harm you: *She is so good and kind that she has no enemies.* **2** a member of a country that is fighting your country: *The Germans were the enemies of the British in the two world wars; The French and British were enemies in the Napoleonic wars.* — *adj*: *enemy troops.*

the enemy your enemies in war: *The enemy marched on the city and captured it.*

energetic /ɛnəˈdʒɛtɪk/ *adj* **1** strong and active: *an energetic child.* **2** requiring energy: *an energetic walk.* **enerˈgetically** *adv*.

energy /ˈɛnədʒɪ/ *n* **1** strength and vigour: *The old man has amazing energy for his age.* **2** the power, of electricity *etc*, of doing work: *electrical energy; nuclear energy.*

enforce /ɪnˈfɔːs/ v to make sure that a law or command is carried out: *It is the job of the police to enforce the law.* **enˈforcement** *n*.

engage /ɪnˈɡeɪdʒ/ v **1** to appoint someone to work for you: *She engaged a woman to clean the house.* **2** to catch and hold someone's attention: *The toy engaged the baby's attention for a moment.* **3** to fit into one another: *The gears failed to engage.* **4** to start using a particular gear: *Engage second gear.*

enˈgaged *adj* **1** having given a promise to marry someone: *She became engaged to John.* **2** occupied: *She is engaged in writing children's books.* **3** busy; not free: *Please come if you are not already engaged for that evening.* **4** being used by someone else: *The telephone line is engaged.*

enˈgagement *n* **1** a promise to get married: *When shall we announce our engagement?* **2** an appointment: *Have you any engagements tomorrow?* **3** a battle: *a naval engagement.*

engine /ˈɛndʒɪn/ *n* **1** a machine in which heat *etc* is used to produce motion: *The car has a new engine.* **2** a railway engine: *He likes to sit in a seat facing the engine.*

ˈengine-driver *n* a person who drives a railway engine.

engiˈneer *n* **1** a person who designs, makes, or works with machinery: *an electrical engineer.* **2** a person who designs and constructs roads, railways, bridges *etc*. — *v* to cause something to happen after careful and usually secret planning: *The strike had been engineered by one of the directors.*

engiˈneering *n* the job of an engineer: *He is studying engineering at university.*

English /ˈɪŋɡlɪʃ/ *adj* belonging to England. — *n* the main language of England and the rest of Britain, North America, a great part of the British Commonwealth and some other countries.

ˈEnglishman, ˈEnglishwoman *n* a man or woman born in England.

engrave /ɪŋˈɡreɪv/ v to cut letters or designs on stone, wood, metal *etc*: *His initials were engraved on the silver cup.*

engrossed /ɪŋˈɡrəʊst/ *adj* giving all your attention to something: *He is completely engrossed in his book.*

engulf /ɪŋˈɡʌlf/ v to close around; to cover completely: *The house was already engulfed in flames when the fire brigade arrived; The enormous waves seemed to engulf the little boat.*

enhance /ɪnˈhɑːns/ v to increase or improve something: *Working harder will enhance his chances of passing the examination.*

enigma /ɪˈnɪɡmə/ *n* a person, thing or event that is mysterious or difficult to understand: *Her death remains an enigma.*

enigmatic /ɛnɪɡˈmatɪk/ *adj*: *an enigmatic smile.*

enjoy /ɪnˈdʒɔɪ/ v to get pleasure from something: *Did you enjoy your meal?; I enjoy walking, running and swimming.* **enˈjoyable** *adj*. **enˈjoyment** *n*.

enjoy needs an object: *to enjoy a book*; *to enjoy yourself* (not *to enjoy very much*).

enjoy yourself to have a good time; to feel happy: *She enjoyed herself at the party.*

enlarge /ɪn'lɑːdʒ/ *v* to make something larger: *They enlarged their house*; *She had the photograph enlarged.* **en'largement** *n*.

enlarge on to give more details about something: *He was asked to enlarge on his plans.*

enlighten /ɪn'laɪtən/ *v* to give more information about something: *If you need to know anything about gardening, this book will enlighten you.*

enlist /ɪn'lɪst/ *v* **1** to join an army *etc*: *He enlisted in the British army.* **2** to get help from someone: *They enlisted the support of five hundred people for their campaign.*

enliven /ɪn'laɪvən/ *v* to make more lively or cheerful: *The funny games enlivened the party.*

enmity /'ɛnmɪtɪ/ *n* a strong feeling of dislike between people; hatred: *There is still too much enmity between the nations of the world*; *The two men never overcame their enmity towards each other.*

enormity /ɪ'nɔːmɪtɪ/ *n* **1** wickedness or great crime or sin: *The programme discussed the enormities committed during the war.* **2** great size or importance: *The enormity of the task worried her.*

enormous /ɪ'nɔːməs/ *adj* very large: *The new building is enormous*; *We had an enormous lunch.* **e'normously** *adv*.

enough /ɪ'nʌf/ *adj* **1** as much as you need: *Have you enough money to pay for the books?*; *There is enough food for everyone.* **2** as much as you can bear: *That's enough cheek from you!* — *pron* **1** as much as you need: *He has had enough to eat.* **2** as much as you can bear: *I've had enough of her rudeness.* — *adv* as much *etc* as necessary: *Is it hot enough?*; *He swam well enough to pass the test.*

enquire, **en'quiry** a different way of spelling **inquire** and **inquiry**. See **inquire**.

enrage /ɪn'reɪdʒ/ *v* to make someone very angry: *His son's rudeness enraged him.*

enrich /ɪn'rɪtʃ/ *v* to improve something: *Fertilizers enrich the soil*; *Reading enriches your mind.*

enrol /ɪn'rəʊl/ *v* to make someone a member of, or become a member of, a school, class, club *etc*: *We enrolled for the gym class*; *You must enrol your child before the start of the school term.* **en'rolment** *n*.

enrolment is spelt with one **l**.

ensemble /ɒn'sɒmbəl/ *n* **1** all the clothes that someone is wearing: *She was wearing a matching pink ensemble.* **2** a small group of musicians who regularly perform together.

enslave /ɪn'sleɪv/ *v* to make someone a slave: *The land was conquered and the people were enslaved.* **en'slavement** *n*.

ensue /ɪn'sjuː/ *v* to come after, especially as a result: *The meeting broke up in confusion and fighting ensued.*

en'suing *adj* coming after; happening as a result: *She was hurt in the ensuing riots*; *He met her on holiday and wrote to her often during the ensuing months.*

ensure /ɪn'ʃʊə(r)/ *v* to make sure: *Ensure that your television set is switched off at night.*

entail /ɪn'teɪl/ *v* to cause; to require: *These alterations will entail great expense.*

entangle /ɪn'taŋɡəl/ *v* to tangle something with something else: *Her long scarf entangled itself in the bicycle wheel.* **en'tanglement** *n*.

enter /'ɛntə(r)/ *v* **1** to go or come into a place: *Enter by this door*; *He entered the room.* **2** to give your own or someone else's name for a competition *etc*: *He entered for the race*; *I entered my pupils for the examination.* **3** to write something in a particular place: *Please enter your choice in the space below.* **4** to start in a particular place: *She entered the school last term.*

enter into 1 to start to be involved in something: *I have no intention of entering into a discussion about it.* **2** to affect or have an influence on a situation: *I hired her because she's good; our friendship never entered into it.*

to **enter** (not **enter into**) a room.

enterprise /'ɛntəpraɪz/ *n* **1** a scheme or plan; a business: *We wish him success in his enterprise.* **2** willingness to try out something new: *We need someone with enterprise for this job.*

'enterprising *adj* keen to try new things, and willing to take risks.

entertain /ɛntə'teɪn/ *v* **1** to give a meal *etc* to guests: *They entertained us to dinner.* **2** to amuse: *His stories entertained us for hours.*

enter'tainer *n* someone who gives amusing performances as a job.

enter'taining *adj* amusing: *entertaining stories.*

enter'tainment *n* **1** a theatrical show *etc*:

The school is staging a Christmas entertainment. **2** amusement; interest: *There is always plenty of entertainment in a big city.*

enthral /ɪnˈθrɔːl/ *v* to delight or thrill someone: *His stories enthralled the children.* **enˈthralling** *adj.*

enthrone /ɪnˈθroʊn/ *v* to place someone on a throne; to crown someone as a king, queen *etc*: *The queen was enthroned with great ceremony.* **enˈthronement** *n.*

enthusiasm /ɪnˈθjuːzɪazm/ *n* great liking and interest; keenness: *He has a great enthusiasm for travelling.*

enˈthusiast *n* a person who is very keen on something: *a computer enthusiast.* **enthusiˈastic** *adj.* **enthusiˈastically** *adv.*

entice /ɪnˈtaɪs/ *v* to tempt or persuade someone by showing or promising something nice: *She was enticed into the shop by the lovely window display.*

enˈticing *adj* very tempting and attractive: *That meal looks very enticing.*

entire /ɪnˈtaɪə(r)/ *adj* whole: *I spent the entire day on the beach.*

enˈtirely *adv* completely: *The house is entirely hidden by trees; This arrangement is not entirely satisfactory; The twins look entirely different.*

entirety /ɪnˈtaɪərətɪ/ *n* completeness.

entitle /ɪnˈtaɪtl/ *v* **1** to give someone a right to, or to do, something: *You are not entitled to free school lunches; He was not entitled to borrow money from the cash box.* **2** to give a title to a book *etc*: *a story entitled 'The White Horse'.* **enˈtitlement** *n.*

entity /ˈɛntɪtɪ/ *n* something that exists separately from something else: *The shops share the same building but they are each separate entities.*

entrance¹ /ˈɛntrəns/ *n* **1** a place where you enter, for example, an opening, a door *etc*: *the entrance to the tunnel; The church has a very fine entrance.* **2** the action of entering, for instance on to a stage: *Cinderella at last made her entrance.* **3** the right to enter: *He has applied for entrance to university.* — *adj*: *an entrance exam.*

> The opposite of **entrance¹** is **exit**.

entrance² /ɪnˈtrɑːns/ *v* to delight someone very much: *The audience were entranced by her singing.*

entrant /ˈɛntrənt/ *n* someone who enters a competition *etc*: *There were sixty entrants for the musical competition.*

entreat /ɪnˈtriːt/ *v* to ask someone earnestly; to beg or implore: *He entreated her to help him.*

enˈtreaty *n*: *She refused to listen to his entreaties.*

entrenched /ɪnˈtrɛntʃt/ *adj* firmly fixed and not easy to change: *His conservative views are well entrenched.*

entrust /ɪnˈtrʌst/ *v* to trust somebody with something: *I entrusted this secret to her; I entrusted her with the duty of locking up.*

entry /ˈɛntrɪ/ *n* **1** coming in or going in: *They were silenced by the entry of the headmaster.* **2** the right to enter: *We can't go in — the sign says 'No Entry'.* **3** a passage or small entrance hall: *Don't bring your bike in here — leave it in the entry.* **4** a person or thing entered for a competition: *There are forty-five entries for the painting competition.* **5** a single item that is written in a diary, computer or dictionary *etc*: *She read again the entry for 25 November.*

entwine /ɪnˈtwaɪn/ *v* to wind something round and round.

envelop /ɪnˈvɛləp/ *v* to cover by wrapping; to surround completely: *She enveloped herself in a long cloak.*

> **envelop**, without an -e, is a verb.
> **envelope**, with an -e, is a noun.

envelope /ˈɛnvəloʊp/ *n* a paper cover for a letter: *Don't forget to put a stamp on the envelope.*

envious /ˈɛnvɪəs/ *adj* feeling or showing envy: *He is envious of my new car.*

environment /ɪnˈvaɪərənmənt/ *n* surroundings or conditions in which a person or animal lives: *An unhappy home environment may drive a teenager to crime; We should protect the environment.* **environˈmental** *adj.*

environˈmentalist *n* a person who wants to protect the natural environment from the bad effects of pollution and industry *etc*: *Environmentalists are very worried about the dangers of nuclear energy.*

envisage /ɪnˈvɪzɪdʒ/ *v* to imagine or think that something is likely to happen: *We don't envisage being able to borrow more money.*

envoy /ˈɛnvɔɪ/ *n* a messenger: *He was sent to France as the king's envoy.*

envy /ˈɛnvɪ/ *v* to look greedily at someone and wish that you had what they have: *He envied me; She envied him his money; I've always envied that house of yours.* — *n* the feeling you have when you envy someone: *She was filled with envy at his wealth.*

epic /ˈɛpɪk/ *n* a long story, film *etc* about great

events and deeds in history *etc*. — *adj*.

epidemic /ɛpɪˈdɛmɪk/ *n* an outbreak of a disease that affects very many people: *an epidemic of influenza*.

epilepsy /ˈɛpɪlɛpsɪ/ *n* a medical condition which causes a person to become unconscious and suffer convulsions: *He has suffered from epilepsy ever since his accident*.
epiˈleptic *adj* of, for or suffering from epilepsy: *an epileptic fit*. — *n* a person suffering from epilepsy: *He has been diagnosed as an epileptic*.

epilogue /ˈɛpɪlɒg/ *n* a short passage or scene at the end of a book, play or film.

> See **prologue**.

episode /ˈɛpɪsoʊd/ *n* **1** an event that is part of a longer story *etc*: *The episode concerning the donkeys is in Chapter 3*. **2** a part of a radio or television serial: *This is the last episode of the serial*.

epistle /ɪˈpɪsəl/ *n* a letter, especially in the Bible from an apostle: *The Epistles of St Paul*.

epitaph /ˈɛpɪtɑːf/ *n* something written on a gravestone in memory of the dead person.

epitome /ɪˈpɪtəmɪ/ *n* a perfect example of something: *His mother was the epitome of kindness*.
eˈpitomize *v* to be a perfect example of: *She epitomizes the modern businesswoman*.

epoch /ˈiːpɒk/ *n* a particular period in the history or development of the world: *With the collapse of communism, we are entering a new epoch*.

equal /ˈiːkwəl/ *adj* the same in size, amount, value *etc*: *four equal slices*; *coins of equal value*; *Are these pieces equal in size?*; *Women want equal wages with men*. — *n* someone of the same age, rank, ability *etc*: *I am not his equal at running*. — *v* to be the same in amount, value, size *etc*: *I cannot hope to equal him*; *She equalled his score of twenty points*; *Five and five equals ten*. **ˈequally** *adv*.
equality /ɪˈkwɒlɪtɪ/ *n* being equal: *Women want equality of opportunity with men*.
ˈequalize *v* to make or become equal: *Our team were winning by one goal — but the other side soon equalized*.
equal to fit or ready for something: *I didn't feel equal to telling him the truth*.

> The opposite of **equal** is **unequal**.
> The opposite of **equality** is **inequality**.

equation /ɪˈkweɪʒən/ *n* a statement, especially in mathematics, that two things are equal or the same: *2+3=5 is an equation*.

equator /ɪˈkweɪtə(r)/ *n* the imagined line that circles the earth, lying at an equal distance from the North and South Poles: *The country is almost on the equator*. **equaˈtorial** *adj*.

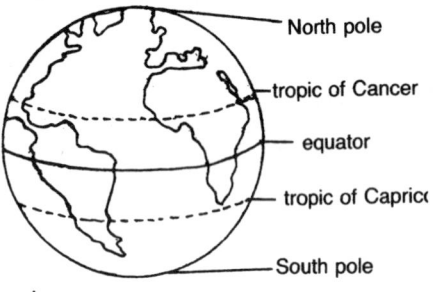

the equator

equilateral /iːkwɪˈlætərəl/ *adj* having all sides equal: *an equilateral triangle*.

equip /ɪˈkwɪp/ *v* to provide someone or something with everything needed: *He was fully equipped for the journey*; *The school is equipped with four computers*.
eˈquipment *n* the clothes, machines, tools *etc* necessary for a particular kind of work, activity *etc*: *Without the right equipment the mechanic could not repair the car*.

> **equipment** is never used in the plural.

equivalent /ɪˈkwɪvələnt/ *adj* **1** equal: *A metre is not quite equivalent to a yard*. **2** the same in meaning: *Would you say that 'brave' and 'courageous' are exactly equivalent?* — *n* something or someone that is equivalent to something or someone else: *This word has no equivalent in Arabic*.

era /ˈɪərə/ *n* a particular period in history or in the development of man: *This is the era of the motor car*.

eradicate /ɪˈrædɪkeɪt/ *v* to get rid of something completely: *Smallpox is a disease that has almost been eradicated*. **eradiˈcation** *n*.

erase /ɪˈreɪz/ *v* to rub out pencil marks *etc*: *The pupil tried to erase the mistake*.
eˈraser *n* a piece of rubber *etc* for rubbing out pencil marks.

erect /ɪˈrɛkt/ *adj* upright: *He held his head erect*. — *v* **1** to put up or to build something: *They erected a statue in the hero's memory*; *They plan to erect an office block there*. **2** to set upright: *to erect a mast*. **eˈrection** *n*.

erode /ɪ'rood/ v to wear away or destroy gradually: *Acids erode certain metals.* **e'rosion** n.

erotic /ɪ'rɒtɪk/ adj arousing feelings of sexual desire or pleasure: *an erotic dance.*

err /ɜː(r)/ v to make a mistake.

errand /'ɛrənd/ n a short journey to get or do something for someone else: *He sent the child on an errand; The boy will run errands for you.*

erratic /ɪ'ratɪk/ adj not regular; not dependable: *His work is erratic.* **er'ratically** adv.

erroneous /ɪ'roʊnɪəs/ adj wrong: *an erroneous statement.*

error /'ɛrə(r)/ n a mistake: *His composition is full of errors.*

in error by mistake; as a result of a mistake: *The letter was sent to you in error.*

erudite /'ɛrʊdaɪt/ adj showing or having a lot of knowledge: *an erudite professor.*

erupt /ɪ'rʌpt/ v **1** used to describe the action of a volcano — to burst and throw out lava etc: *When did this volcano last erupt?* **2** to burst out: *The demonstration started quietly but suddenly violence erupted.* **e'ruption** n.

See **explode**.

escalate /'ɛskəleɪt/ v to increase more and more quickly: *The argument escalated into a fight; Prices are escalating.* **esca'lation** n.

escalator /'ɛskəleɪtə(r)/ n a moving staircase in a big shop, underground railway etc.

escape /ɪ'skeɪp/ v **1** to get away free or safe: *He escaped from prison; She escaped the infection.* **2** to slip from the memory etc: *His name escapes me.* **3** to leak; to find a way out: *Gas was escaping from a hole in the pipe.* — n an act of escaping: *Make your escape while the guard is away; There have been several escapes from that prison.*

escort n /'ɛskɔːt/ **1** one or more people accompanying others to protect or guide them: *He offered to be my escort round the city.* **2** one or more cars, ships etc accompanying a ship, vehicle etc for protection or courtesy: *The truck carrying the dangerous chemical was under police escort.* — v /ɪ'skɔːt/ to accompany someone as escort: *He offered to escort her to the dance.*

especially /ɪ'spɛʃəlɪ/ adv particularly: *These insects are quite common, especially in hot countries.*

See **specially**.

espionage /'ɛspɪənɑːʒ/ n **1** the use of spies to get secret information about an enemy or rival: *Spying on rival firms is called industrial espionage.* **2** the activity of spying: *He was arrested for espionage.*

esplanade /'ɛsplənerd/ n a level space for walking or driving, especially at the seaside.

essay /'ɛseɪ/ n a written composition: *Write an essay on your holiday.*

essence /'ɛsəns/ n **1** the most important part or quality: *This is the essence of what he said.* **2** a substance obtained from a plant etc: *vanilla essence.*

essential /ɪ'sɛnʃəl/ adj absolutely necessary: *It is essential that you arrive punctually.* — n a thing that is essential: *Is a television set an essential?* **es'sentially** adv.

establish /ɪ'stablɪʃ/ v **1** to settle someone firmly in a job, business etc: *He established himself as a jeweller in the city.* **2** to set up a university, a business etc: *How long has the firm been established?* **3** to show that something is true: *The police have established that he was guilty.*

es'tablishment n **1** the establishing of something. **2** a firm, shop, hotel etc: *I want to speak to the manager of this establishment.*

estate /ɪ'steɪt/ n **1** a large piece of land, especially in the country, owned by someone. **2** a piece of land for building etc: *a housing estate.*

esteem /ɪ'stiːm/ v to respect greatly. — n respect: *His foolish behaviour lowered him in my esteem.*

estimate v /'ɛstɪmeɪt/ to judge size, amount, value etc, especially without measuring or calculating exactly: *He estimated that the journey would take two hours.* — n /'ɛstɪmət/ an approximate calculation: *He gave us an estimate of the cost of repairing the car; a rough estimate.*

esti'mation n opinion: *In my estimation, he is the better pupil of the two.*

estuary /'ɛstjʊərɪ/ n the wide part of a river that flows into the sea.

et cetera /ɛt'sɛtərə/ and so on, usually shortened to **etc**.

etch /ɛtʃ/ v **1** to make designs on metal, glass etc by using an acid to cut out the lines: *The artist made a drawing and then etched it on to copper.* **2** to fix something firmly in your memory as if by printing it there: *The scene he saw in that room remained etched on his mind.*

'etching n a picture printed from etched metal, glass etc.

eternal /ɪ'tɜːnəl/ adj **1** without end; lasting for

ethics

ever: *God is eternal*; *eternal life*. **2** never stopping: *I am tired of your eternal complaints*. **e'ternally** *adv*.

e'ternity *n* **1** time without end. **2** the state or time after death.

ethics /'ɛθɪks/ *n* a set of moral principles and beliefs about right and wrong: *The law may be effective but there are several questions about its ethics*. **'ethical** *adj*.

ethnic /'ɛθnɪk/ *adj* having to do with nations or races or their customs, dress, food *etc*: *ethnic groups*; *ethnic dances*.

etiquette /'ɛtɪkɛt/ *n* rules for correct or polite behaviour between people.

eucalyptus /juːkə'lɪptəs/ *n* a large Australian evergreen tree, giving timber, gum and an oil that is used for treating colds.

euphemism /'juːfəmɪzm/ *n* a pleasant name for something that is unpleasant: *'Pass on' is a euphemism for 'die'*. **euphe'mistic** *adj*.

euphoria /juː'fɔːrɪə/ *n* a feeling of wild excitement or happiness. **eu'phoric** *adj*.

euthanasia /juːθə'neɪzɪə/ *n* the painless killing of someone who is suffering from a painful illness that cannot be cured: *Doctors are not allowed to practise euthanasia*.

evacuate /ɪ'vakjʊeɪt/ *v* to leave a place, or make someone leave a place, especially because of danger: *Children were evacuated from the city to the country during the war*. **evacu'ation** *n*.

evade /ɪ'veɪd/ *v* **1** to avoid something: *He tried to evade paying his taxes*. **2** to avoid answering: *She evaded his question by talking about the weather*.

evaluate /ɪ'valjʊeɪt/ *v* to find out the value of someone or something: *It is difficult to evaluate his work*. **evalu'ation** *n*.

evangelist /ɪ'vandʒɪlɪst/ *n* someone who tries to convert other people, especially to Christianity, usually by preaching at large public meetings: *Billy Graham is a well-known American evangelist*.

evaporate /ɪ'vapəreɪt/ *v* to change into vapour and disappear: *The small pool of water evaporated in the sunshine*. **evapo'ration** *n*.

e'vaporated *adj* having had some liquid removed by evaporation: *evaporated milk*.

evasive /ɪ'veɪsɪv/ *adj* not open and honest: *Her answer was evasive*.

e'vasion *n* avoiding something: *tax evasion*.

take evasive action to act to avoid trouble or problems, especially a collision: *The driver had to take evasive action to avoid crashing*.

eve /iːv/ *n* **1** the day or evening before a festival: *Christmas Eve*; *New Year's Eve*. **2** the time just before an event: *on the eve of the battle*.

even¹ /'iːvən/ *adj* **1** the same in height, amount *etc*: *Are the table-legs even?*; *an even temperature*. **2** smooth: *Make the path more even*. **3** regular: *He has a strong, even pulse*. **4** able to be divided by 2: *2, 4, 6, 8, 10 etc are even numbers*. **5** equal in number, amount *etc*: *The teams have scored one goal each and so they are even now*. **6** calm: *She has a very even temper*. — *v* to make even or equal: *to even the score*. **'evenly** *adv*. **'evenness** *n*.

get even with to harm someone who has harmed you: *He tricked me, but I'll get even with him*.

even out to become or make even: *The road rose steeply and then evened out*; *He raked the soil to even it out*.

even² /'iːvən/ *adv* **1** used to point out something unexpected in what you are saying: *'Have you finished yet?' 'No, I haven't even started.'*; *Even the winner got no prize*. **2** yet; still: *My boots were dirty, but his were even dirtier*.

even if no matter whether: *Even if I leave now, I'll be too late*.

even so in spite of that: *It rained, but even so we enjoyed the day*.

even though in spite of the fact that: *I like the job even though it's badly paid*.

evening /'iːvnɪŋ/ *n* the part of the day between the afternoon and the night: *in the evening*; *summer evenings*; *tomorrow evening*; *on Tuesday evening*; *In the course of the evening, we sampled a wide variety of wines*.

evening dress clothes worn for formal occasions in the evening.

event /ɪ'vɛnt/ *n* **1** something, especially something important, that happens: *That night a terrible event occurred*. **2** an individual race or contest in a sporting competition: *The high jump is the next event*.

e'ventful *adj* full of events; exciting: *We had an eventful day*.

> The opposite of **eventful** is **uneventful**.

at all events or **in any event** in any case: *At all events, we can't make things worse than they already are*.

in the event of if something happens: *In the event of rain, the match will have to be cancelled*.

eventual /ɪ'vɛntʃʊəl/ *adj* happening in the end: *Her eventual return caused great joy*.

e'ventually *adv* finally; in the end: *We thought he wasn't going to come but eventually he arrived.*

ever /'ɛvə(r)/ *adv* **1** at any time: *Nobody ever visits us; She hardly ever writes to her mother; Have you ever ridden on an elephant?; Her dancing is better than ever; the brightest star they had ever seen.* **2** always; continually: *They lived happily ever after; He said he would love her for ever; I've known her ever since she was a baby.*

'evergreen *adj* having green leaves all the year round: *Holly is evergreen.* — *n* an evergreen tree: *Firs and pines are evergreens.*

ever'lasting *adj* **1** not changing; not dying: *everlasting flowers; everlasting life.* **2** endless; continual: *I'm tired of your everlasting grumbles.*

ever'more *adv* for ever.

for ever *adv* for all time: *I'll love you for ever (and ever).*

every /'ɛvrɪ/ *adj* each one; all: *Every room is painted white; Not every family has a car; The ladder on my shoulder was getting heavier with every step.*

> **each** can be used rather than **every** when you are talking about members of a group: *Every house needs a roof; Each pupil in the class has a copy of the book.*

'everybody or **'everyone** *prons* every person: *Everybody got down very quickly as another shell exploded; Everyone thinks I'm mad.*

> **everybody** and **everyone** are singular: *Everybody is* (not *are*) *tired*; *Is everyone leaving already?*

'everyday *adj* **1** happening or done every day: *her everyday duties.* **2** common; usual: *an everyday event.*

'everything *pron* **1** all things: *Everything is repeated down to the smallest detail; Have you everything you want?* **2** the most important thing: *Money isn't everything.*

'everywhere *adv* in or to every place: *The flies are everywhere; Everywhere I go, he follows me.*

every now and then or **every so often** occasionally: *We get a letter from him every now and then.*

every other day *etc*, **every second day** *etc*: on the first, third, fifth day *etc*; on alternate days: *I visit my mother every other day; We go to the supermarket every second week.*

every time 1 always: *We use this method every time.* **2** whenever: *Every time he comes, we quarrel.*

evict /ɪ'vɪkt/ *v* to force someone by law to move out of a house or leave a piece of land, for instance because they haven't paid the rent: *The man was evicted from his flat as he hadn't paid his rent for six months.* **e'viction** *n*.

evidence /'ɛvɪdɛns/ *n* **1** proof used in a law case *etc*: *Have you enough evidence of his guilt to arrest him?*; *We have several new pieces of evidence to consider.* **2** a sign: *Her bag on the table was the only evidence of her presence.*

> **evidence** is never used in the plural.

evident /'ɛvɪdənt/ *adj* clearly to be seen or understood: *his evident satisfaction; It is evident that you have been telling lies.* **'evidently** *adv*.

evil /'iːvəl/ *adj* very bad; wicked: *an evil man; He looks evil; evil deeds.* — *n* **1** harm or wickedness: *He tries to ignore all the evil in the world.* **2** anything evil, such as crime, misfortune *etc*: *The evils of war.* **3** harmful words: *Never speak evil of anyone.* **'evilly** *adv*. **'evilness** *n*.

evoke /ɪ'vouk/ *v* **1** to cause or produce a response, reaction *etc*: *His letter in the newspaper evoked a storm of protest.* **2** to cause to be remembered or recalled: *The photographs evoked her memories of the past.*

evolution /iːvə'ljuːʃən/ *n* **1** gradual development: *the evolution of our form of government.* **2** the development of the higher kinds of animals, plants *etc*, from the lower kinds. **evo'lutionary** *adj*.

evolve /ɪ'vɒlv/ *v* to develop: *Man evolved from the apes.*

ewe /juː/ *n* a female sheep: *The ewe had two lambs.*

exact /ɪg'zakt/ *adj* accurate or correct in every detail: *What are the exact measurements of the room?*; *an exact copy*; *What is the exact time?*

ex'acting *adj* needing a lot of hard work, care and attention: *an exacting job.*

ex'actly *adv* **1** just; quite: *He's exactly the right man for the job.* **2** in accurate detail: *Work out the prices exactly*; *What exactly did you say?* **3** used as a reply meaning 'I quite agree'. **ex'actness** *n*.

not exactly 1 not quite, but almost true: *She's not exactly an expert, but she is very good.* **2** not really; not at all: *The meeting* *wasn't exactly long – it only lasted five minutes!*

exaggerate /ɪgˈzadʒəreɪt/ *v* to make something seem larger, greater *etc* than it really is: *You are exaggerating his faults*; *That dress exaggerates her thinness*; *You can't trust her — she always exaggerates.* **exagge'ration** *n*.

exalted /ɪgˈzɔːltɪd/ *adj* **1** high in rank, position *etc*; very important: *He hoped one day to reach the exalted position of prime minister.* **2** very happy and triumphant: *She felt exalted when she reached the summit of the mountain.*

examination /ɪgzamɪˈneɪʃən/ *n* **1** a test of knowledge or ability (shortened to **ex'am**): *school examinations*; *He passed the English exam*. **2** looking at something closely; inspection: *The doctor gave him a thorough examination.* **3** the questioning of a witness *etc* in a law court.

examine /ɪgˈzamɪn/ *v* **1** to look at something closely: *They examined the animal tracks and decided that they were those of a fox.* **2** to inspect someone thoroughly to check for disease *etc*: *The doctor examined the child and said she was healthy.* **3** to test the knowledge or ability of students *etc*: *She examines pupils in mathematics.* **4** to question: *The lawyer examined the witness in the court case.*
ex'aminer *n* a person who examines.

example /ɪgˈzɑːmpəl/ *n* **1** something that shows what other things of the same kind are like: *This poem is a good example of the poet's work.* **2** something that shows clearly a fact *etc*: *Can you give me an example of how this word is used?* **3** a person or thing that is a pattern to be copied: *She was an example to the rest of the class.* **4** a warning: *Let this be an example to you, and never do it again!*
for example as an example; such as.
set an example to act in such a way that other people will copy your behaviour: *Teachers must set a good example to their pupils.*

exasperate /ɪgˈzɑːspəreɪt/ *v* to make someone very angry: *He was exasperated by their stupid questions.*
ex'asperating *adj*: *an exasperating series of delays.*
exaspe'ration *n*.

excavate /ˈɛkskəveɪt/ *v* to dig up a piece of ground *etc*; to uncover by digging: *The archaeologist excavated an ancient fortress.*
exca'vation *n*.
'excavator *n* a machine or person that excavates.

exceed /ɪkˈsiːd/ *v* **1** to be greater than something: *His expenditure exceeds his income.* **2** to go beyond something: *He exceeded the speed limit on the motorway.*
ex'ceedingly *adv* very: *exceedingly nervous.*

excel /ɪkˈsɛl/ *v* **1** to do very well: *He excelled in mathematics*; *His friend excelled at football.* **2** to be better than others: *She excels them all at swimming.* **'excellence** *n*.
'excellent *adj* unusually or extremely good: *She is an excellent pupil.* **'excellently** *adv*.

except /ɪkˈsɛpt/ *prep* leaving out; not including: *They're all here except him*; *Your essay was good except that it was too long.* — *v* to leave out; to exclude.

> to work every day **except** (not **accept**) Sunday (not **Sunday only**).

ex'ception *n* **1** something or someone not included: *With the exception of Jim we all went home early.* **2** something unusual: *We normally eat very little at lunchtime, but Sunday is an exception.*
ex'ceptional *adj* unusual; remarkable: *His ability is exceptional.* **ex'ceptionally** *adv*.
except for except: *Except for John, they all arrived punctually.*
take exception to to object to something: *The old lady took exception to the bad behaviour of the children.*
without exception happening in all cases: *Everyone without exception must fill in a form.*

excerpt /ˈɛksɜːpt/ *n* a short piece of writing, music or film taken from the whole work.

excess *n* /ɪkˈsɛs/ or /ˈɛksɛs/ **1** going beyond what is usual or proper: *He ate well, but not to excess*; *a proposal that there should be some form of excess profits tax.* **2** an amount by which something is greater than something else: *He found he had paid an excess of £5 over what was actually on the bill.* — *adj* /ˈɛksɛs/ extra; additional: *He had to pay extra for his excess baggage.*
ex'cessive *adj* too much, too great *etc*.
ex'cessively *adv*.
in excess of greater than: *The debts are in excess of £3 million.*

exchange /ɪksˈtʃeɪndʒ/ *v* **1** to give in return for something else: *Can you exchange a pound note for two 50-pence pieces?* **2** to give and receive in return: *They exchanged a few remarks.* — *n* **1** the giving and taking of one thing for another: *He gave me a pencil in exchange for the marble*; *An exchange of opinions is helpful.* **2** the exchanging of the money of one country for that of another. **3** a place where business shares are bought and sold. **4** a central telephone system where lines are connected.

excite /ɪkˈsaɪt/ v to cause strong feelings of expectation, happiness etc in someone: *The children were excited about the party.* **exˈcitement** n.
exˈcitable adj easily made excited or nervous.
exˈcited adj: *She was so excited she couldn't think about anything else.* **exˈcitedly** adv.
exˈciting adj: *an exciting adventure.*

exclaim /ɪkˈskleɪm/ v to call out, or say, suddenly and loudly: *'Good!' he exclaimed.* **exclaˈmation** n.
exclaˈmation mark the mark (!) used after an exclamation.

exclude /ɪkˈskluːd/ v **1** to prevent someone from sharing or taking part in something: *They excluded her from the meeting.* **2** to shut out; to keep out: *Fill the bottle to the top so as to exclude all air.* **3** to leave out of consideration: *We cannot exclude the possibility that he was lying.* **exˈclusion** n.

> The opposite of **exclude** is **include**.

exˈcluding prep not counting: *The bill came to £20, excluding the wine.*

exclusive /ɪkˈskluːsɪv/ adj **1** given to only one person or group etc: *The story is exclusive to this newspaper.* **2** fashionable and expensive: *exclusive shops.* **exˈclusively** adv. **exˈclusiveness** n.
exˈclusion n not including someone or something.
exclusive of not including.

excrete /ɪkˈskriːt/ v to get rid of the waste from your bowels. **exˈcretion** n.

excruciating /ɪkˈskruːʃieɪtɪŋ/ adj causing extreme pain.

excursion /ɪkˈskɜːʃən/ n a trip; an outing: *an excursion to the seaside.*

excuse v /ɪkˈskjuːz/ **1** to forgive: *Excuse me — can you tell me the time?*; *I'll excuse your being late this time.* **2** to free someone from a task, duty etc: *May I be excused from writing this essay?* — n /ɪkˈskjuːs/ a reason for being excused, or a reason for excusing: *He has no excuse for being so late.* **exˈcusable** adj pardonable.

> The opposite of **excusable** is **inexcusable**.

execute /ˈɛksəkjuːt/ v **1** to put someone to death by order of the law: *when Henry VIII was executing his wives down the road at the Tower.* **2** to carry out instructions etc: *He executed an order.*
exeˈcution n **1** killing by law: *The judge ordered the execution of the murderer.* **2** the carrying out of orders etc.

executive /ɪɡˈzɛkjʊtɪv/ n **1** the branch of the government that puts the laws into effect. **2** a person in an organization etc who has power to direct or manage: *He is an executive in an insurance company.* — adj.

exempt /ɪɡˈzɛmpt/ v to free a person from a duty, task, tax etc: *He was exempted from military service.* — adj free from a duty, tax etc: *If your income is below £14 000, you are exempt from this tax.* **exˈemption** n.

exercise /ˈɛksəsaɪz/ n **1** training through action or effort: *Swimming is one of the healthiest forms of exercise*; *Take more exercise.* **2** an activity intended as training: *ballet exercises*; *spelling exercises.* — v to train; to give exercise to: *Dogs should be exercised frequently*; *I exercise every morning*; *You should exercise every part of your body.*

exert /ɪɡˈzɜːt/ v **1** to bring into use or action: *He likes to exert his authority.* **2** to make yourself make an effort: *It's time you exerted yourselves a bit.* **exˈertion** n.

exhale /ɛksˈheɪl/ v to breathe out.

> The opposite of **exhale** is **inhale**.

exhaust /ɪɡˈzɔːst/ v **1** to make someone very tired: *She was exhausted by her long walk.* **2** to use all of something: *We have exhausted our supplies.* **3** to say all that can be said about a subject etc: *We've exhausted that subject.* — n the set of metal pipes that takes away the fumes etc from the engine of a car, motorcycle etc.
exˈhausting adj causing extreme tiredness: *Looking after young children can be exhausting.*
exˈhaustion n extreme tiredness.
exˈhaustive adj extremely thorough; including everything: *an exhaustive investigation.*

exhibit /ɪɡˈzɪbɪt/ v **1** to show in public: *My picture is to be exhibited in the art gallery.* **2** to show a quality etc: *He exhibited a complete lack of concern for others.* — n an object displayed in a museum etc: *One of the exhibits is missing.*
exhiˈbition n a public display of works of art, industrial goods etc: *an exhibition of children's books*; *The sculpture exhibition's to be taken down today.*

exhilarate /ɪgˈzɪləreɪt/ v to fill with a lively cheerfulness or excitement: *She was exhilarated by the news.*
exˈhilarating adj: *an exhilarating ride on horseback.* **exhilaˈration** n.

exile /ˈɛksaɪl/ or /ˈɛgzaɪl/ n **1** a long stay in a foreign land, usually as a punishment: *He was sent into exile.* **2** a person who lives outside his own country, either by choice or because he is forced to do so. — v to send a person away from his own country.

exist /ɪgˈzɪst/ v **1** to be real: *Do ghosts really exist?* **2** to stay alive; to live: *It is possible to exist on bread and water.* **exˈistence** n. **exˈistent** adj.

exit /ˈɛksɪt/ or /ˈɛgzɪt/ n **1** a way out of a building *etc*: *the emergency exit.* **2** going out; departure: *She made a noisy exit.* — v.

The opposite of **exit** is **entrance**.

exorcize /ˈɛksɔːsaɪz/ v to get rid of an evil spirit by means of prayers and ceremonies: *They asked a priest to exorcize the evil spirits from the house*; *The priest exorcized the haunted house.* **ˈexorcism** n.
ˈexorcist n a person who exorcizes.

exotic /ɪgˈzɒtɪk/ adj **1** coming from a foreign country, especially from the tropics: *exotic plants.* **2** unusual or strange: *exotic clothes.*

expand /ɪkˈspænd/ v to make or grow larger; to spread out wider: *Metals expand when heated*; *They expanded their business.* **exˈpansion** n: *the expansion of metals.*
expand on to give more information about something: *You can improve the essay by expanding on your first point.*

expanse /ɪkˈspæns/ n a wide area: *an expanse of water.*

expect /ɪkˈspɛkt/ v **1** to think that something or someone is likely to happen or come: *I'm expecting a letter today*; *We expect her on tomorrow's train.* **2** to think or suppose: *I expect that he will go*; *'Will she go too?' 'I expect so'*; *I expect you're tired.* **3** to require: *You are expected to tidy your own room.* **4** to believe or hope that you will do something: *He expects to be home tomorrow.*
exˈpectant adj **1** full of hope or expectation: *the expectant faces of the audience.* **2** expecting a baby: *an expectant mother.*
exˈpectancy n. **exˈpectantly** adv.
expecˈtation n the state of expecting: *In expectation of a wage increase, he bought a washing-machine*; *In spite of the teacher's expectations, the boy failed the exam.*

expedition /ɛkspəˈdɪʃən/ n **1** a journey with a purpose: *an expedition to the South Pole.* **2** a group making an expedition: *He was a member of the expedition that climbed Mount Everest.*

expel /ɪkˈspɛl/ v **1** to send someone away for ever, from a school *etc*, because they have done something wrong: *The child was expelled from school for stealing.* **2** to get rid of something: *an electric fan for expelling kitchen smells.*

expend /ɪkˈspɛnd/ v to use or spend supplies, money *etc*.
exˈpendable adj not considered absolutely necessary to keep: *No-one likes to think that they are expendable.*

expenditure /ɪkˈspɛndɪtʃə(r)/ n spending: *His expenditure amounted to £500.*

exˈpense n **1** the spending of money *etc*; cost: *I've gone to a lot of expense to educate you well.* **2** a cause of spending: *What an expense clothes are!*
exˈpenses n money spent in carrying out a job *etc*: *His firm paid his travelling expenses.*
exˈpensive adj costing much money: *expensive clothes.*
exˈpensively adv: *She was expensively dressed.*

The opposite of **expensive** is **cheap** or **inexpensive**.

experience /ɪkˈspɪərɪəns/ n **1** knowledge or skill gained through the doing of something: *Learn by experience — don't make the same mistake again*; *Has she had experience in teaching?* **2** an event that affects or involves you: *The big fire was a terrible experience.* — v to have experience of something; to feel: *I have never before experienced such pain.*
exˈperienced adj having gained knowledge from experience; skilled: *an experienced teacher.*

The opposite of **experienced** is **inexperienced**.

experiment /ɪkˈspɛrɪmənt/ n a test done in order to find out something: *He performs chemical experiments*; *We shall find out by experiment.* — v to try to find out something by making tests: *The doctor experimented with various medicines*; *Some people think it's wrong to experiment on animals.* **experiˈmental** adj. **experiˈmentally** adv.

expert /ˈɛkspɜːt/ adj skilled through training or practice: *I'm expert at map-reading*; *Get expert advice on repainting your car.* — n a person who is an expert: *He is an expert on*

computers. **'expertly** *adv.* **'expertness** *n.*
expertise /ɛkspɜːˈtiːz/ *n* special skill or knowledge: *a lawyer's expertise.*
expire /ɪkˈspaɪə(r)/ *v* **1** to come to an end: *His membership expires at the end of the year*; *Your ticket expired last month.* **2** to die. **ex'piry** *n.*
explain /ɪkˈspleɪn/ *v* **1** to make something clear or easy to understand: *Can you explain to me how this machine works?*; *Did she explain why she was late?* **2** to give, or be, a reason for something: *I cannot explain his failure*; *That explains his silence.* **explanation** /ɛkspləˈneɪʃən/ *n.* **explanatory** /ɪkˈsplanətərɪ/ *adj.*
explicable /ɛkˈsplɪkəbəl/ *adj* able to be explained.

The opposite of **explicable** is **inexplicable**.

explicit /ɪkˈsplɪsɪt/ *adj* stated, or stating, fully and clearly: *explicit instructions*; *Can you be more explicit?* **ex'plicitly** *adv.*
explode /ɪkˈspləʊd/ *v* **1** to blow up with a loud noise: *The bomb exploded.* **2** to show strong feelings suddenly: *The teacher exploded with anger*; *The children exploded into laughter.*

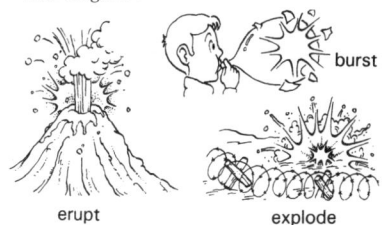

erupt   burst   explode

exploit *n* /ˈɛksplɔɪt/ a brave deed or action: *stories of his military exploits.* — *v* /ɪkˈsplɔɪt/ **1** to make good use of something: *to exploit the country's natural resources.* **2** to use a person unfairly for your own advantage. **exploi'tation** *n.*
explore /ɪkˈsplɔː(r)/ *v* **1** to search or travel through a place for the purpose of discovery: *The oceans have not yet been fully explored*; *Let's go exploring in the caves.* **2** to investigate carefully: *I'll explore the possibilities of getting a job here.* **explo'ration** *n.*
ex'plorer *n* a person who explores unknown regions: *explorers in space.*
explosion /ɪkˈspləʊʒən/ *n* **1** the blowing up of something; the noise caused by this: *a gas explosion*; *The explosion could be heard a long way off.* **2** the exploding of something: *the explosion of the atom bomb.* **3** a sudden great increase: *an explosion in food prices.*
ex'plosive *adj* likely to explode: *a dangerously explosive gas.* — *n* a material that is likely to explode.
export *v* /ɪkˈspɔːt/ to send goods to another country for sale: *Jamaica exports bananas to Britain.* — *n* /ˈɛkspɔːt/ **1** exporting: *the export of rubber.* **2** something that is exported: *Rubber is an important Malaysian export.* **expor'tation** *n.* **ex'porter** *n.*
expose /ɪkˈspəʊz/ *v* **1** to uncover; to leave unprotected from the sun, wind, cold, danger *etc*: *Paintings should not be exposed to direct sunlight*; *Don't expose children to danger.* **2** to discover and make known a hidden evil, crime *etc*: *His secret life was at last exposed.* **3** to allow light to fall on a photographic film as you take a photograph. **exposure** /ɪkˈspəʊʒə(r)/ *n.*
exposition /ɛkspəˈzɪʃən/ *n* an exhibition.
expound /ɪkˈspaʊnd/ *v* to explain something in detail.
express /ɪkˈsprɛs/ *v* **1** to put into words: *He expressed his ideas very clearly.* **2** to put your own thoughts into words: *You haven't expressed yourself clearly.* **3** to show by looks, actions *etc*: *She nodded to express her agreement.* — *adj* **1** travelling, carrying goods *etc*, especially fast: *an express train*; *express delivery.* **2** clearly stated: *You have disobeyed my express wishes.* — *adv* by express train or fast delivery service: *Send your letter express.* — *n* an express train: *the London to Cardiff express.*
ex'pression *n* **1** a look on your face which shows your feelings: *He always has a bored expression.* **2** a word or phrase: *'Dough' is a slang expression for 'money'.* **3** a showing of thoughts or feelings by words, actions *etc*: *A smile is an expression of happiness.*
expressive /ɪkˈsprɛsɪv/ *adj* lively; showing or expressing feelings well: *She has an expressive face*; *an expressive voice.*
expressly /ɪkˈsprɛslɪ/ *adv* **1** clearly: *She had expressly asked him not to mention it.* **2** for a special purpose: *We chose that holiday expressly so that Mother could join us.*
expressway /ɪkˈsprɛsweɪ/ *n* a motorway.
expulsion /ɪkˈspʌlʃən/ *n* the expelling of someone; getting rid of something: *Expulsion is the usual punishment for anyone caught stealing at this school.*

exquisite /ɪkˈskwɪzɪt/ *adj* very beautiful or skilful: *exquisite jewellery*.

extend /ɪkˈstɛnd/ *v* **1** to make something longer or larger: *He extended his vegetable garden*. **2** to reach or stretch: *The school grounds extend as far as this fence*. **3** to hold out or stretch out a limb *etc*: *He extended his hand to her*. **4** to offer: *May I extend a welcome to you all?*

exˈtension *n* **1** the extending of something. **2** an added part: *He built an extension to his house*. **3** a telephone line from a central switchboard to a room or office: *Could I have extension 281, please*.

exˈtensive *adj* large in area or amount: *extensive plantations*; *He suffered extensive injuries in the accident*.

exˈtensively *adv*: *The buildings were extensively damaged in the fire*.

exˈtent *n* **1** the area or length to which something extends: *The garden is nearly a kilometre in extent*. **2** amount: *What is the extent of the damage?*; *To what extent can we trust him?*

to a certain extent or **to some extent** partly but not completely.

exterior /ɪkˈstɪərɪə(r)/ *adj* on or from the outside; outer: *an exterior wall of a house*. — *n* the outside of something: *the grey stone exterior of the hospital*.

See **interior**.

exterminate /ɪkˈstɜːmɪneɪt/ *v* to destroy completely: *Rats must be exterminated from a building or they will cause disease*. **extermiˈnation** *n*.

external /ɪkˈstɜːnəl/ *adj* **1** outside or on the outside. **2** on your skin: *The liquid in that medicine bottle is for external use only*. **exˈternally** *adv*.

extinct /ɪkˈstɪŋkt/ *adj* **1** no longer in existence: *Dinosaurs became extinct in prehistoric times*. **2** no longer active: *That volcano was thought to be extinct until it suddenly erupted ten years ago*. **exˈtinction** *n*.

extinguish /ɪkˈstɪŋgwɪʃ/ *v* to put out a fire *etc*: *Please extinguish your cigarettes*.

exˈtinguisher *n* a spraying device containing chemicals for putting out fire.

extort /ɪkˈstɔːt/ *v* to obtain something from someone by threats or violence: *He extorted money from the old lady*. **exˈtortion** *n*.

exˈtortionate *adj* unfairly high or great: *The prices in that shop are extortionate*.

extra /ˈɛkstrə/ *adj* additional; more than is usual or necessary: *They demanded an extra £10 a week*; *We need extra men for this job*. — *adv* unusually: *an extra-large box of chocolates*. — *n* **1** something extra: *His parents bought him a bicycle, but he had to buy the lamp and pump and other extras himself*. **2** a person employed to be one of a crowd in a film.

extract *v* /ɪkˈstrakt/ **1** to pull out: *I had to have a tooth extracted*. **2** to obtain a substance from something by crushing *etc*: *Oil is extracted from sunflower seeds*. — *n* /ˈɛkstrakt/ **1** a passage selected from a book *etc*: *a short extract from his play*. **2** a substance extracted from something: *beef extract*; *extract of malt*. **exˈtraction** *n*.

extraordinary /ɪkˈstrɔːdənərɪ/ *adj* surprising; unusual: *What an extraordinary thing to say!*; *She wears extraordinary clothes*. **exˈtraordinarily** *adv*.

extravagant /ɪkˈstravəgənt/ *adj* using or spending too much; wasteful: *He's extravagant with money*. **exˈtravagance** *n*. **exˈtravagantly** *adv*.

extreme /ɪkˈstriːm/ *adj* **1** very great; much more than usual: *extreme pleasure*; *He is in extreme pain*. **2** very far from the centre: *the extreme south-western tip of England*. **3** very strong; not ordinary; not usual: *He holds extreme views on education*. — *n* something as far, or as different, as possible from something else: *the extremes of sadness and joy*.

exˈtremely *adv* very: *extremely kind*.

exˈtremities *n* hands and feet.

in the extreme very: *dangerous in the extreme*.

extrovert /ˈɛkstrəvɜːt/ *n* a friendly and sociable person: *He is getting to be more of an extrovert*.

See **introvert**.

exuberant /ɪgˈzjuːbərənt/ *adj* cheerful and excited; full of energy: *She was exuberant about passing her exams*; *He was in an exuberant mood*. **exˈuberance** *n*.

eye /aɪ/ *n* **1** the part of the body with which you see: *She has blue eyes*. **2** anything like or suggesting an eye, such as the hole in a needle. **3** a talent for noticing and judging: *She has an eye for a good horse*. — *v* to look at someone or something: *The dog eyed the bone*; *The thief eyed the policeman nervously*.

ˈeyeball *n* the whole rounded part of the eye.

'eyebrow *n* the curved line of hair above each eye.

'eye-catching *adj* noticeable, especially if attractive: *an eye-catching advertisement*.

'eyelash *n* one of the hairs that grow on the edge of the eyelids.

'eyelid *n* the piece of skin that covers or uncovers the eye when you shut or open it.

'eyesight *n* the ability to see: *I have good eyesight*.

'eyesore *n* something, especially a building, that is ugly to look at.

'eye-witness *n* a person who sees something happen: *Eye-witnesses were questioned by the police after the accident*.

be up to the eyes to be very busy: *She's up to the eyes in work*.

close your eyes to to take no notice of something wrong: *She closed her eyes to the children's misbehaviour*.

keep an eye on 1 to watch someone or something closely: *Keep an eye on the patient's temperature*. **2** to look after: *Keep an eye on the baby while I am out!*

keep an eye out for or **keep an eye open for** to watch or look for someone or something: *I'll keep an eye out for a suitable present when I'm shopping*.

see eye to eye to agree: *I don't see eye to eye with my wife on this matter*.

F

F an abbreviation for Fahrenheit.

fable /'feɪbəl/ *n* a story, usually about animals, that teaches a lesson about human behaviour.

fabric /'fabrɪk/ *n* cloth or material: *Nylon is a man-made fabric.*

fabricate /'fabrɪkeɪt/ *v* to make up something that is not true: *to fabricate an excuse.*
fabri'cation *n* a lie.

fabulous /'fabjʊləs/ *adj* **1** wonderful: *This is a fabulous idea!* **2** existing only in old stories *etc*: *A dragon is a fabulous beast.*

facade /fə'sɑ:d/ *n* **1** the front of a building: *The bank's facade needs painting.* **2** a false appearance that hides the truth: *There is a very bad-tempered person behind that smiling facade.*

face /feɪs/ *n* **1** the front part of the head, where your eyes, nose *etc* are: *a beautiful face.* **2** a front surface: *the face of a clock; a rock face.* — *v* **1** to be opposite to something: *My house faces the park.* **2** to look, turn *etc* in the direction of someone: *She faced him across the desk.* **3** to bear bravely: *She faced many difficulties.*

'facecloth *n* a small square cloth for washing yourself with.

'face-powder *n* make-up in the form of fine powder for putting on your face.

face the music to bear your punishment bravely.

face to face in person; in the actual presence of one another: *I'd like to meet him face to face some day — I've heard so much about him.*

face up to meet and bear bravely: *He faced up to his difficult situation.*

in the face of in spite of something: *He succeeded in the face of great difficulties.*

lose face to suffer shame: *You will really lose face if you are defeated.*

make a face, pull a face to twist your face into a strange expression: *He pulled faces at the baby to make it laugh.*

save your face to avoid shame; to avoid seeming silly or wrong. **'face-saving** *n, adj.*

to someone's face openly and directly: *I told him to his face that he was wrong.*

facet /'fasɪt/ *n* **1** a side of a many-sided object: *the facets of a diamond.* **2** an aspect of a subject: *There are several facets to this problem.*

facetious /fə'si:ʃəs/ *adj* funny, not serious; intended to be humorous: *a facetious remark; Don't be facetious about serious matters.* **fa'cetiously** *adv.* **fa'cetiousness** *n.*

facial /'feɪʃəl/ *adj* having to do with your face: *A smile is a facial expression.*

facilitate /fə'sɪlɪteɪt/ *v* to make something possible or easier: *The new doors will facilitate the entry of wheelchairs.*

facility /fə'sɪlɪtɪ/ *n* **1** ease: *She speaks English with great facility.* **2** a talent: *He has a facility for solving problems.*

fa'cilities *n* the means to do something: *There are facilities for cooking meals in the hostel.*

facing /'feɪsɪŋ/ *prep* opposite: *The hotel is facing the church.*

fact /fakt/ *n* **1** something known to be true: *It is a fact that smoking is a danger to health.* **2** reality: *He sometimes can't distinguish fact from fiction.*

> The opposite of **fact** is **fiction**.

as a matter of fact or **in fact** actually; really: *She doesn't like him much — in fact, I think she hates him!*

factor /'faktə(r)/ *n* **1** a fact, circumstance *etc* that has to be remembered or considered: *There are various factors to be considered before you decide where to go for your holiday.* **2** a number which exactly divides into another: *3 is a factor of 6.*

factory /'faktərɪ/ *n* a workshop where goods are made in large numbers: *a car factory.* — *adj*: *a factory worker.*

factual /'faktjʊəl/ *adj* containing facts: *a factual account.*

faculty /'fakəltɪ/ *n* **1** a power of the mind: *the faculty of reason.* **2** a natural power of the body: *the faculty of hearing.* **3** an ability or skill: *He has a faculty for saying the right thing.* **4** a department of a university: *the Faculty of Mathematics.*

fad /fad/ *n* **1** a strong liking for something; something that people are keen on for a short time: *He's no longer keen on roller-skating — it was only a passing fad.* **2** a dislike, especially for some kind of food: *It's difficult to cook for someone who has a lot of fads.*

fade /feɪd/ v to lose strength, colour, loudness etc: *The noise gradually faded away*; *The colours faded in the sun.*

faeces or **feces** /ˈfiːsiːz/ n plural solid waste matter from the bowels of people and animals: *Animal faeces on city streets are a danger to health as well as a nuisance.*

Fahrenheit /ˈfarənhaɪt/ adj measured on a Fahrenheit thermometer, which shows the temperature at which water freezes as 32°, and that at which it boils as 212°: *fifty degrees Fahrenheit (50°F).*

fail /feɪl/ v **1** to be unsuccessful; not to manage to do something: *They failed in their attempt*; *I failed my exam*; *I failed to post the letter.* **2** to break down or stop working: *The brakes failed.* **3** to be not enough: *His courage failed him.* **4** to reject a candidate: *The examiner failed half the class.* **5** to disappoint: *She promised to send him a present, and she did not fail him.* — n a failure in an examination: *six passes and two fails.*

> The opposite of **to fail** is **to succeed** or **to pass**: *She tried to smile but did not succeed*; *He passed all his examinations with top marks.*

ˈfailing n a fault; a weakness: *You should try to forgive people's failings.*

failing that if something is not possible: *Wear a suit, or failing that, your school uniform.*

failure /ˈfeɪljə(r)/ n **1** failing: *She was upset by her failure in the exam*; *There was a failure in the electricity supply.* **2** an unsuccessful person or thing: *He felt he was a failure.* **3** not being able or willing to do something: *I was surprised by his failure to reply.*

> The opposite of **failure** is **success**.

without fail definitely; certainly: *I shall do it tomorrow without fail.*

faint /feɪnt/ adj **1** dim; not clear: *The sound grew faint*; *a faint light.* **2** weak and about to lose consciousness: *Suddenly she felt faint.* — v to lose consciousness: *She fainted on hearing the bad news.* — n loss of consciousness: *She fell down in a faint.* **ˈfaintly** adv.

fair¹ /fɛə(r)/ adj **1** light-coloured; with light-coloured hair and skin: *fair hair*; *Many Scandinavian people are fair.* **2** just; not favouring one side: *a fair test.* **3** fine; without rain: *fair weather.* **4** quite good; neither bad nor good: *His work is only fair.* **5** quite big, long etc: *a fair size.* — adv fairly: *to play fair in a game.* **ˈfairness** n.

fair enough a phrase used to express agreement or understanding: *'I'll let you know tomorrow.' — 'Fair enough.'*

ˈfairly adv **1** justly; honestly: *The competition was fairly judged.* **2** quite; rather: *The work was fairly hard.*

fair play honest and equal treatment.

fair² /fɛə(r)/ n **1** a collection of movable stalls and entertainments that travels from town to town: *She won a doll at the fair.* **2** a large market held at fixed times. **3** an exhibition of goods from different countries, firms etc: *a trade fair.*

ˈfairground n a piece of land where fairs are held.

fairy /ˈfɛərɪ/ n a small creature in a story etc that looks like a human being and has magical powers: *Many children believe in fairies.*

fairy story 1 an old story of fairies, magic etc: *a book of fairy stories.* **2** a lie: *I don't want to hear any fairy stories!*

fairy tale a fairy story.

faith /feɪθ/ n **1** trust: *He had faith in his ability.* **2** religious belief: *She has a strong faith in God.* **3** loyalty to someone or to a promise: *We kept faith with our friends.*

ˈfaithful adj **1** loyal and true; not changing: *a faithful friend*; *He was faithful to his promise.* **2** true; exact: *Give me a faithful account of what happened.* **ˈfaithfully** adv. **ˈfaithfulness** n. **ˈfaithless** adj. **ˈfaithlessness** n.

> **faithfully** has two **l**s; **faithfulness** has one **l**.

yours faithfully a phrase used to end letters which begin 'Dear Sir' or 'Dear Madam'.

> See **sincerely**.

fake /feɪk/ n **1** a worthless imitation, especially one which is intended to deceive: *That picture is a fake.* **2** a person who pretends to be something they are not: *He pretended to be a doctor, but he was a fake.* — adj **1** made in imitation of something more valuable: *fake diamonds.* **2** pretending to be something you are not: *a fake policeman.* — v to pretend or imitate in order to deceive: *He tried to fake his father's signature.*

falcon /ˈfɔːlkən/ n a bird of prey sometimes used for hunting.

fall /fɔːl/ v **1** to drop down: *The apple fell from*

fallacious

the tree; *The leaves of many trees fall in autumn*; *She fell over.* **2** to become lower or less: *The temperature is falling.* **3** to enter a certain state or condition: *He had fallen asleep by the time I came back*; *They fell in love.* — *n* **1** a tumble; a drop: *He had a fall on the icy path and hurt his leg*; *a fall in the price of oil.* **2** something that has fallen: *a fall of snow.* **3** capture or defeat: *the fall of Rome.* **4** autumn: *Leaves change colour in the fall.*

> **fall; fell** /fɛl/; **fallen** /ˈfɔːlən/: *She fell off her chair*; *He has just fallen downstairs.*

fall apart to break into pieces: *This book fell apart when I opened it.*

fall away 1 to become less in number: *The crowd began to fall away.* **2** to slope downwards: *The ground fell away steeply.*

fall back on to use in an emergency: *Whatever happens, you have your father's money to fall back on.*

fall behind 1 to be slower than someone else: *Hurry up! You're falling behind the others*; *He is falling behind in his schoolwork.* **2** to become late in regular payment, letter-writing *etc*: *Don't fall behind with the rent!*

fall for 1 to fall in love with: *She fell for him immediately.* **2** to be deceived by a trick or lie: *You didn't fall for that old story, did you?*

fall in with to agree with a plan, idea *etc*: *They fell in with our suggestion.*

fall off to become smaller in number or amount: *The number of guests at the hotel falls off in the winter.*

fall on, fall upon to attack: *He fell on me and started to hit me.*

fall out to quarrel: *I have fallen out with my brother.*

fall short to be not enough or not good enough *etc*: *The money we have falls short of what we need.*

fall through to fail: *Our plans fell through.*

fallacious /fəˈleɪʃəs/ *adj* wrong because of being based on wrong information: *a fallacious argument.*

fallacy /ˈfaləsɪ/ *n* a wrong idea, usually one that many people believe to be true: *The belief that girls are less intelligent than boys is a fallacy.*

fallible /ˈfalɪbəl/ *adj* able or likely to make mistakes: *We are all fallible.*

> The opposite of **fallible** is **infallible**.

fallout /ˈfɔːlaʊt/ *n* radioactive dust from a nuclear explosion *etc*.

fallow /ˈfaloʊ/ *adj* left to lie after being ploughed, without being planted with seeds, so that the soil can improve: *The farmer let several fields lie fallow for a year.*

falls /fɔːlz/ *n* a waterfall: *the Niagara Falls.*

false /fɔːls/ *adj* **1** not true; not correct: *He made a false statement to the police.* **2** intended to deceive: *He has a false passport.* **3** not natural; artificial: *false teeth.* **4** not loyal: *false friends.*

ˈfalsehood *n* a lie.

falsify /ˈfɔːlsɪfaɪ/ *v* to change dishonestly: *He falsified the firm's accounts.* **falsifiˈcation** *n*.

false alarm a warning of something which in fact does not happen.

falter /ˈfɔːltə(r)/ *v* to stumble or hesitate: *The blind girl walked across the room without faltering*; *His voice faltered.* **ˈfaltering** *adj*.

fame /feɪm/ *n* being known to many people: *His novels brought him fame.*

familiar /fəˈmɪlɪə(r)/ *adj* **1** already well known: *The house was familiar to him*; *His face looks familiar to me.* **2** knowing about something: *I am not familiar with that custom.* **familiˈarity** *n*.

faˈmiliarize *v* to make something well known to someone: *You must familiarize yourself with the rules.*

family /ˈfamɪlɪ/ *n* **1** parents and their children. **2** a group of people related to each other, including cousins, grandchildren *etc*: *He comes from a wealthy family.* **3** a group of plants, animals, languages *etc* that are connected in some way: *The lion is a member of the cat family.*

> **family** can be used with a singular or plural verb: *Are your family all well?*; *My family has owned this house for a long time.*

family name a surname; the name you share with the rest of your family.

family tree a plan showing a person's ancestors and relations.

famine /ˈfamɪn/ *n* a great lack or shortage especially of food: *Some parts of the world suffer frequently from famine.*

famished /ˈfamɪʃt/ *adj* very hungry.

famous /ˈfeɪməs/ *adj* known to many people for a good or worthy reason: *She is a famous actress*; *Scotland is famous for its whisky.*

> See **notorious**.

fan[1] /fan/ *n* **1** a thin flat object that you wave

in front of your face to keep cool in hot weather. **2** a mechanical instrument causing a current of air: *an electric fan.* — *v* **1** to cool yourself with a fan *etc*: *She fanned herself with her newspaper.* **2** to make a fire burn more strongly by waving a flat object in front of it: *to fan the flames.*

fan out to move forwards and outwards from a central point: *The six planes flew in a straight line and then fanned out.*

fan[2] /fan/ *n* an admirer of an actor, singer, football team *etc*: *I'm going to see him in his new play — I'm a great fan of his; football fans.*

fanatic /fəˈnatɪk/ *n* a person who is too enthusiastic about something: *a religious fanatic.* **faˈnatical** *adj.* **faˈnatically** *adv.* **faˈnaticism** *n.*

fanciful /ˈfansɪfəl/ *adj* **1** inclined to have strange ideas: *She's a very fanciful girl.* **2** unlikely; unrealistic: *That idea is rather fanciful.* **ˈfancifully** *adv.*

fancy /ˈfansɪ/ *n* **1** a liking or desire: *I used to have quite a fancy for pickled onions.* **2** something imagined: *I was sure I saw her in the crowd, but it was just my fancy.* — *adj* decorated; not plain: *fancy cakes.* — *v* **1** to like the idea of having or doing something: *I fancy a cup of tea; Do you fancy going for a swim?* **2** to think or imagine: *I fancied you were angry.*

fancy dress unusual clothes for disguising yourself, often representing a famous character: *He went to the party in fancy dress.* — *adj*: *a fancy-dress party.*

take a fancy to to become fond of someone or something: *He bought that house because his wife took a fancy to it.*

take someone's fancy to attract someone; to appeal to someone: *None of these pictures takes my fancy.*

fanfare /ˈfanfɛə(r)/ *n* a short tune played loudly on trumpets *etc*: *The king's entry was signalled by a fanfare.*

fang /faŋ/ *n* **1** a long, sharp tooth of a fierce animal: *The wolf bared its fangs.* **2** the poison-tooth of a snake.

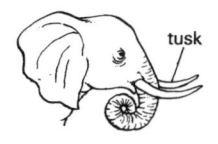

fantasize /ˈfantəsaɪz/ *v* to dream about doing something impossible or very unlikely: *She fantasizes about becoming a famous model.*

fantastic /fanˈtastɪk/ *adj* **1** strange or like a fantasy: *She told me some fantastic story about her father being a prince.* **2** wonderful; very good: *You look fantastic!* **fanˈtastically** *adv*: *He's fantastically rich!*

fantasy /ˈfantəsɪ/ *n* something imagined; an impossible dream: *She was always having fantasies about becoming rich and famous.*

far /fɑː(r)/ *adv* **1** a long way away: *He went far away.* **2** very much: *He was a far better swimmer than his friend.* — *adj* **1** distant; a long way away: *a far country.* **2** more distant, usually of two things: *He lives on the far side of the lake.*

> **far**; **'further** or **'farther**; **'furthest** or **'farthest**: *adv*: *I live far from school. Jane lives further away but the teacher lives the furthest away.*
> *adj*: *The earth is far from the sun, Mars is further and Jupiter is the furthest of the three.*
> The forms **farther** and **farthest** are used only for distance. See **farther** and **further**.

ˈfaraway *adj* distant: *faraway places.*

as far as 1 to a particular place: *We walked as far as the lake.* **2** as great a distance as: *He did not walk as far as his friends did.* **3** according to what: *As far as I know, he is well.*

by far by a large amount: *They have by far the largest house in the village.*

far from instead of; different from: *Far from being pleased, she seemed annoyed; I'm not angry. Far from it!*; *Her bedroom was far from tidy.*

go too far to behave in an unsuitably extreme way: *He's often rude, but this time he's gone too far.*

so far until now: *So far, nothing had gone right for him.*

farce /fɑːs/ *n* **1** a comic play in which the characters and the events are ridiculous and unlikely. **2** a funny or stupid situation: *The meeting was a farce — only five people were present.* **ˈfarcical** *adj.*

fare /fɛə(r)/ *n* the price of a journey on a train, bus, ship *etc*: *He hadn't enough money to pay the bus fare.* — *v* to do; to get on: *How did you fare in the examination?*; *The team from the other school fared badly against our team.*

farewell /fɛəˈwɛl/ an expression meaning goodbye.

far-fetched /fɑːˈfɛtʃt/ *adj* very unlikely: *a far-fetched story.*

farm /fɑːm/ *n* **1** a piece of land, used for growing crops, and keeping cows, sheep, pigs *etc*: *Much of England is good agricultural land and there are many farms.* **2** the farmer's house and the buildings near it: *She lives at the farm.* — *v* to work on the land in order to grow crops, and keep animals *etc*: *He farms 5000 acres.*

'farmer *n* a person who owns or looks after a farm and works on the land *etc*. **'farming** *n*.

'farmhouse *n* the house in which a farmer lives.

'farmyard *n* the open area surrounded by the farm buildings.

far-'reaching *adj* having a great influence: *far-reaching changes.*

far-'sighted *adj* able to guess what will happen in the future and make sensible plans: *Politicians need to be far-sighted to plan properly for the country's future.*

farther /ˈfɑːðə(r)/ *adv*, *adj* can be used instead of **further** when you talk about distance: *I can't walk any farther.*

'farthest *adv*, *adj* can be used instead of **furthest** when you talk about distance: *40 kilometres is the farthest I've ever walked.*

fascinate /ˈfæsɪneɪt/ *v* to attract or interest someone very strongly: *The children were fascinated by the monkeys in the zoo.* **fasci'nation** *n*.

'fascinating *adj* very attractive or interesting: *a fascinating story.*

fashion /ˈfæʃən/ *n* **1** the style and design of clothes: *Are you interested in fashion?* **2** the way of behaving, dressing *etc* that is popular at a certain time: *Fashions in music and art are always changing.* **3** a way of doing something: *She spoke in a very strange fashion.*

'fashionable *adj* following the newest style of dress, newest ideas and likings: *a fashionable woman; a fashionable café.*

'fashionably *adv*.

> The opposite of **fashionable** is **unfashionable** or **old-fashioned**.

in fashion fashionable: *Long skirts are in fashion.*

out of fashion not fashionable.

fast[1] /fɑːst/ *adj* **1** quick-moving: *a fast car.* **2** quick: *a fast worker.* **3** showing a time later than the correct time: *My watch is five minutes fast.* — *adv* quickly: *She speaks so fast I can't understand her.*

fast food food that can be quickly prepared, such as hamburgers.

fast[2] /fɑːst/ *v* to go without food, especially for religious or medical reasons: *Muslims fast during Ramadan.* — *n* a time of fasting.

fast[3] /fɑːst/ *adj* **1** firm, fixed: *He made his end of the rope fast to a tree.* **2** that will not come out of a fabric when it is washed: *fast colours.*

fast asleep deeply asleep: *The baby fell fast asleep in my arms.*

fasten /ˈfɑːsən/ *v* **1** to fix; to attach: *She fastened a flower to her dress.* **2** to close firmly: *It was difficult to fasten the buttons; Please fasten the gate.*

'fastener *n* something that fastens things: *a zip-fastener.*

fastidious /fæˈstɪdɪəs/ *adj* fussy about details and about being tidy and clean: *She is very fastidious about her clothes.*

fat /fæt/ *n* an oily substance found in the bodies of animals and some plants: *This meat has got a lot of fat on it.* — *adj* **1** containing fat: *fat meat.* **2** large, heavy and round in shape: *He was a very fat child.* **'fatness** *n*.

fatal /ˈfeɪtəl/ *adj* causing death or disaster: *a fatal accident; She made a fatal mistake.* **'fatally** *adv*.

fa'tality *n* death: *There are far too many fatalities on the roads.*

fate /feɪt/ *n* **1** a power that seems to control events: *She blamed fate for everything that went wrong.* **2** a final result, death, or an end: *A terrible fate awaited her.*

'fateful *adj* having an important, especially bad, effect on the future: *a fateful decision.*

father /ˈfɑːðə(r)/ *n* **1** a male parent: *The eldest child looked like his father.* **2** the title of a priest: *I met Father Sullivan this morning.* **3** a person who invents or first makes something: *Thomas Edison was the father of electric light.*

'father-in-law, *plural* **fathers-in-law**, *n* the father of your wife or husband.

'fatherly *adj* like a father; kind: *He showed a fatherly interest in his friend's child.*

fathom /ˈfæðəm/ *v* to understand something after thinking about it; to work something out: *I cannot fathom why he should have left home without telling anyone.* — *n* a measure of depth of water, equal to 6 feet or 1.8 metres: *The water is 3 fathoms deep.*

fatigue /fəˈtiːɡ/ *n* **1** great tiredness: *He was*

suffering from fatigue after walking 40 kilometres. **2** weakness caused by continual use: *metal fatigue.*
fa'tigued *adj* tired: *They were fatigued by the journey.*

fatten /'fatən/ *v* to give a bird or animal a lot of food so that it becomes very fat, especially to make it ready for eating.
'fattening *adj* making people fat: *Is bread fattening?*
'fatty *adj* containing a lot of fat: *This pork is very fatty.*

fault /fɔːlt/ *n* **1** a mistake; something for which you are to blame: *The accident was your fault.* **2** something wrong: *There is a fault in this machine.* **3** a crack in the rock surface of the earth. — *v* to find a fault or mistake in something: *I couldn't fault her English.*
'faultless *adj* without fault; perfect: *a faultless performance.* **'faultlessly** *adv.*
'faulty *adj* not made correctly; not working correctly: *a faulty machine.*
at fault wrong; deserving blame: *Which side is at fault in this dispute?*
find fault with to complain about someone or something: *She is always finding fault with the way he eats.*

fauna /'fɔːnə/ *n* the animals of a district or country as a whole.

favour /'feɪvə(r)/ *n* **1** a kind action: *Will you do me a favour and lend me your bicycle?* **2** kindness; approval: *Any teacher looks with favour on a pupil who tries hard.* **3** unfair preference: *The teacher was inclined to show favour to the girls.* — *v* to support or show preference for someone or something: *Which side do you favour?*
favourable *adj* **1** showing approval: *Was his answer favourable or unfavourable?* **2** helpful: *a favourable wind.* **'favourably** *adv.*
'favourite *adj* best-liked; preferred: *his favourite city.* — *n* a person or thing that you like best: *Of all his paintings that is my favourite.*

favour, favourable and **favourite** are spelt with **-our-**.

'favouritism *n* the fault of unfairly preferring one person or group to the others: *Why did you give Jill more sweets than me? That's favouritism!*
in favour generally approved of: *Grammar-teaching is in favour again.*
in favour of in support of something: *I am in favour of higher pay for nurses.*
in someone's favour giving an advantage to someone: *The wind was in our favour.*
out of favour no longer popular or approved of: *Her views are out of favour with the present government.*

fawn /fɔːn/ *n* **1** a baby deer. **2** its colour, a light yellowish brown.

fax /faks/ *n* **1** (also **fax machine**) a machine that sends a copy of a document along a telephone line: *We need a new fax for the office.* **2** a copy of a document sent in this way: *Send me a fax of the agreement.* — *v* to send someone a copy of a document using a fax machine: *She faxed me a copy of the picture; Fax the letter to me.*

fear /fɪə(r)/ *n* a feeling of great worry or anxiety; being afraid: *The soldier tried not to show his fear; He can't learn to swim because of his fear of water; The people lived in fear of another earthquake.* — *v* **1** to feel fear because of something: *She feared her father when he was angry; I fear for my father's safety.* **2** to regret: *I fear that the doctor is too busy to see you today.*
'fearful *adj* **1** afraid: *a fearful look.* **2** terrible: *The lion gave a fearful roar.* **3** very bad: *a fearful mistake.* **'fearfully** *adv.*
'fearless *adj* without fear; brave. **'fearlessly** *adv.*

feasible /'fiːzəbəl/ *adj* able to be done or achieved, possible: *There is only one feasible solution to the problem.* **feasi'bility** *n.*

feast /fiːst/ *n* **1** a large and rich meal: *The king invited them to a feast in the palace.* **2** an annual religious celebration: *Easter and Christmas are important feasts.* — *v* to eat rich food, especially at a feast: *We feasted all day.*

feat /fiːt/ *n* something that is a difficult thing to do: *She could perform some extraordinary feats of gymnastics; It was quite a feat to built a viaduct across the deep valley.*

feather /'fɛðə(r)/ *n* one of the objects that grow from a bird's skin and form a soft covering over its body: *We found a seagull's feather; They cleaned the oil off the bird's feathers.* **'feathered** *adj.* **'feathery** *adj.*

feature /'fiːtʃə(r)/ *n* **1** one of the parts of your face, such as your eyes, nose *etc.* **2** a special quality: *Sport is a strong feature of life at this school.* **3** a piece of writing in a newspaper. **4** the main film in a cinema programme. — *v* **1** to have as an important part: *This exhibition features the work of two young artists.* **2** to have a part in something: *He features in some of my stories, but certainly not all of them.*

February

February /'fɛbruərɪ/ *n* the second month of the year.

feces *see* **faeces**.

fed *see* **feed**.

federal /'fɛdərəl/ *adj* having to do with a form of government or a country where there is one central and several regional governments: *the Federal Republic of Germany*; *the federal government of the United States*.

fede'ration *n* a group of states or organizations which act together: *The banks formed a federation*.

fee /fiː/ *n* the price paid for work done by a doctor, lawyer *etc* or for some special service or right: *an entrance fee*; *university fees*.

feeble /'fiːbəl/ *adj* weak: *The old lady has been rather feeble since her illness*. **'feebleness** *n*. **'feebly** *adv*.

feed /fiːd/ *v* **1** to give food to animals, babies *etc*: *He fed the child with a spoon*. **2** to eat: *Cows feed on grass*. — *n* food for a baby or animals: *Have you given the baby his feed?*; *cattle feed*.

> **feed; fed** /fɛd/; **fed**: *She fed the baby*; *Have you fed the cat today?*

'feedback *n* comments that you collect from people about something you are involved in, that are useful in organizing or improving it: *We are waiting for feedback from the students' parents on the new scheme for buying school-books*.

fed up bored and annoyed: *I'm fed up with all this work!*

feel /fiːl/ *v* **1** to become aware of something through touch: *She felt his hand on her shoulder*. **2** to find out the shape, size *etc* of something by touching it with your hands: *The blind man felt the object carefully*. **3** to experience an emotion, sensation *etc*: *She felt horribly jealous*; *He felt very unhappy*; *She feels sick*. **4** to think: *She feels that the firm treated her badly*. **5** to have a particular physical quality: *The parcel felt quite light*; *His forehead felt hot*. — *n* the impression something gives when it is touched: *I like the feel of this material*.

> **feel; felt** /fɛlt/; **felt**: *She felt happy*; *He had never felt so ill before*.

'feeler *n* one of the two long thin parts on the heads of certain creatures such as insects or snails, that are used to feel things; an antenna.

'feeling *n* **1** ability to feel: *I have no feeling in my little finger*. **2** something that you feel: *a painful feeling*; *a feeling of happiness*; *It was the greatest feeling I had ever had*. **3** a belief: *I have a feeling that this plan won't work*. **4** emotion; passion: *He spoke with great feeling*.

'feelings *n* your own pride and dignity: *His rudeness hurt my feelings*.

feel for 1 to feel sympathy for: *I really feel for her now she has lost her job*. **2** to try to find by feeling: *She felt for her key in the dark*.

feel like 1 to have the feelings that you would have if you were someone else: *I feel like a princess in this beautiful dress*. **2** to feel that you would like to have, do *etc* something: *I feel like a drink*; *Do you feel like going to the cinema?*

feel your way to find your way by feeling: *I had to feel my way to the door in the dark*.

feet plural of **foot**.

feign /feɪn/ *v* to pretend: *His feigned illness*.

feline /'fiːlaɪn/ *adj* of or like a cat: *a vet specializing in feline problems*.

fell[1] *see* **fall**.

fell[2] /fɛl/ *v* to cut down or knock down: *They are felling all the trees in this area*.

> **fell; felled; felled**: *He felled the tree*; *Many trees have been felled*. See also **fall**.

fellow /'fɛloʊ/ *n* **1** a man or boy: *He's quite a nice fellow*. **2** a companion. — *adj* belonging to the same group, country *etc*: *a fellow student*; *a fellow countryman*.

'fellowship *n* **1** an association, club or society. **2** friendliness between people who work or live together *etc*.

felt[1] /fɛlt/ *see* **feel**.

felt[2] /fɛlt/ *n* a cloth made of wool that has been pressed together, not woven. — *adj*: *a felt hat*.

felt pen /fɛlt 'pɛn/ or **felt tip** or **felt-tip pen** *n* a pen with a point made of felt.

female /'fiːmeɪl/ *n* **1** the sex that gives birth to children, produces eggs *etc*. **2** a person or animal of this sex. — *adj*: *a female blackbird*.

> The opposite of **female** is **male**.

feminine /'fɛmɪnɪn/ *adj* **1** having to do with women; typical of women: *feminine beauty*. **2** belonging to the female class of nouns in some languages: *Is this noun masculine or feminine?* **femi'ninity** *n*.

fib

> The opposite of **feminine** is **masculine**.

fence[1] /fɛns/ *n* a line of wooden or metal posts joined by wood, wire *etc* to stop people, animals *etc* moving on to or off a piece of land: *The garden was surrounded by a wooden fence.* — *v* to put a fence round an area of land.

fence in to put a fence around something: *The dogs are safely fenced in and can't escape.*

fence off to separate one area from another with a fence: *Part of the park has been fenced off as a play area.*

sit on the fence to avoid supporting either side in an argument.

fence[2] /fɛns/ *v* to fight with swords as a sport. **'fencing** *n* the sport of fighting with swords.

fend /fɛnd/: **fend for yourself** to look after yourself: *He is old enough to fend for himself.*
fend off to defend yourself against something: *He put up his hands to fend off the birds.*

ferment /fə'mɛnt/ *v* **1** to change chemically, as dough does when yeast is added to it: *Grape juice ferments to become wine.* **2** to encourage bad feeling between people, so that they quarrel or rebel: *He tried to ferment discontent among his fellow-workers.*

fern /fɜːn/ *n* a plant with feather-like leaves.

ferocious /fə'rouʃəs/ *adj* fierce or savage: *a ferocious animal.* **fe'rociously** *adv.* **ferocity** *n*.

ferry /'fɛrɪ/ *n* a boat that carries people, cars *etc* from one place to another: *We went by ferry from Dover to Calais.* — *v* to carry people *etc* in a boat: *They were ferried across the river in a motor-boat.*

fertile /'fɜːtaɪl/ *adj* **1** producing a lot: *fertile fields.* **2** able to produce fruit, children, young animals *etc.* **fer'tility** *n*.

> The opposite of **fertile** is **infertile**.

fertilize /'fɜːtɪlaɪz/ *v* to make fertile: *He fertilized his fields with manure; An egg must be fertilized before it can develop.* **ferti-li'zation** *n*.

'fertilizer *n* a substance used to make land more fertile.

fervent[1] /'fɜːvənt/ *adj* keen and very sincere: *fervent hope.* **'fervently** *adv* **'fervour** *n*.

festival /'fɛstɪvəl/ *n* **1** a celebration, especially a public one: *Christmas is a Christian festival.* **2** a season of musical or theatrical performances: *a music festival; a drama festival.*

festive /'fɛstɪv/ *adj* having to do with celebrations; joyful: *Christmas is a festive occasion; a festive atmosphere.*
fes'tivity *n* a celebration.

festoon /fɛ'stuːn/ *v* to decorate something with ribbons, strings of flowers *etc*: *The streets were festooned with flags.*

fetch /fɛtʃ/ *v* **1** to go and get something or someone and bring it: *Fetch me some bread.* **2** to be sold for a certain price: *The picture fetched £100.*

> See **bring**.

fête /feɪt/ *n* an event held outdoors, with stalls, games and amusements, usually to raise money for charity: *The school holds a fête each summer.*

fetters /'fɛtəz/ *n* chains that hold the feet of a prisoner, animal *etc.*

fetus another spelling of **foetus**.

feud /fjuːd/ *n* a long-lasting quarrel or war between families, tribes *etc.* — *v*.

feudal /'fjuːdəl/ *adj* having to do with the old system by which people served a more powerful man in return for land and protection. **'feudalism** *n*.

fever /'fiːvə(r)/ *n* **1** a high body temperature and quick heart-beat, usually caused by illness: *She is in bed with a fever.* **2** an illness causing fever.
'feverish *adj* **1** having a slight fever: *She seems a bit feverish tonight.* **2** very excited: *feverish activity.* **'feverishly** *adv*.

few /fjuː/ *adj* not many: *Few people visit me nowadays*; *He asked me questions every few minutes.* — *pron*: *Few of you are old enough to remember the disaster.*

a few a small number: *There are a few books in this library about geography*; *We have only a few left.*

a good few or **quite a few** quite a lot: *There have been quite a few letters to the newspapers about this.*

few and far between very few: *Interesting jobs are few and far between.*

> **few** means 'not many'.
> **a few** means 'some'.
> See also **less** and **little**.

fiancé /fɪɑːn'seɪ/ or /fɪ'ɒnseɪ/ *n* the man to whom a woman is engaged to be married.
fi'ancée *n* the woman to whom a man is engaged to be married.

fiasco /fɪ'æskoʊ/, *plural* **fi'ascos**, *n* a complete failure.

fib /fɪb/ *n* a harmless lie: *to tell fibs.* — *v* to

tell a fib: *She fibbed about her age.*

fibre /ˈfaɪbə(r)/ *n* **1** a fine thread or something like a thread: *a nerve fibre.* **2** a material made up of fibres: *coconut fibre.* **ˈfibrous** *adj.*

ˈfibreglass *n* a material made of very fine threadlike pieces of glass, used for many purposes, for instance building boats.

fickle /ˈfɪkəl/ *adj* always changing your mind: *You can't rely on him — he's so fickle.* **ˈfickleness** *n.*

fiction /ˈfɪkʃən/ *n* stories which tell of imagined, not real, characters and events. **ˈfictional** *adj.*

> The opposite of **fiction** is **fact**.

fictitious /fɪkˈtɪʃəs/ *adj* **1** not true: *a fictitious account.* **2** not real: *All the characters in the book are fictitious.*

fiddle /ˈfɪdəl/ *n* a violin: *He played the fiddle.* — *v* **1** to play a violin: *He fiddled a little tune.* **2** to play with something or interfere with something: *Stop fiddling with your pencil!*; *Who's been fiddling with the television?* **ˈfiddler** *n.*

ˈfiddly *adj* difficult to do because needing careful or delicate handling: *Building model ships out of matchsticks is very fiddly.*

fidelity /fɪˈdɛlɪtɪ/ *n* **1** loyalty: *his fidelity to his wife; fidelity to a promise.* **2** exactness in recording or reproducing something: *high fidelity.*

fidget /ˈfɪdʒɪt/ *v* to move your hands, feet *etc* restlessly: *Stop fidgeting while I'm talking to you!* **ˈfidgety** *adj.*

field /fiːld/ *n* **1** a piece of land used for growing crops, keeping animals *etc*: *Our house is surrounded by fields.* **2** a wide area for games, sports *etc*: *a football field.* **3** a piece of land where minerals *etc* are found: *an oilfield; a coalfield.* **4** an area of knowledge, interest, study *etc*: *There has been a great deal of progress this century in the field of medicine.* — *v* in some games, such as cricket, to catch or fetch the ball and return it. **ˈfielder** *n.*

ˈfield-glasses *n* a small double telescope.

fiend /fiːnd/ *n* **1** a devil. **2** a very evil or cruel person. **ˈfiendish** *adj.*

ˈfiendishly *adv* very; extremely: *a fiendishly clever plan.*

fierce /fɪəs/ *adj* **1** very angry and likely to attack: *a fierce dog; a fierce expression.* **2** intense or strong: *fierce heat.* **ˈfiercely** *adv.*

fiery /ˈfaɪərɪ/ *adj* **1** like fire: *a fiery light.* **2** easily made angry: *a fiery temper.*

fiesta /fɪˈɛstə/ *n* a holiday to celebrate a religious festival, especially in Spain and South America.

fifteen /fɪfˈtiːn/ *n* the number 15. — *adj* **1** 15 in number. **2** aged 15: *Are you fifteen yet?*

fifth /fɪfθ/ *n* one of five equal parts. — *n, adj* the next one after the fourth.

fifty /ˈfɪftɪ/ *n* the number 50. — *adj* **1** 50 in number. **2** aged 50.

fifty-ˈfifty *adv* in half: *We'll divide the money fifty-fifty.* — *adj* equal: *a fifty-fifty chance.*

fig /fɪg/ *n* a soft pear-shaped fruit that can be dried and kept.

fight /faɪt/ *v* **1** to struggle against someone with your hands or weapons: *The two boys are fighting over some money they found.* **2** to take strong action against something or for something: *to fight a fire; We must fight for our freedom.* **3** to quarrel: *His parents were always fighting.* **4** to make your way with difficulty: *He fought his way through the crowd.* — *n* **1** a struggle or battle: *There was a fight going on in the street.* **2** strong action for or against something: *the fight for freedom of speech; the fight against disease.*

> **fight; fought** /fɔːt/; **fought**: *He fought with his brother; She had fought for freedom all her life.*

ˈfighter *n* **1** a person who fights. **2** a fast aircraft designed to shoot down other aircraft.

fight back to defend yourself against an attack.

fight it out to fight or argue till one person wins: *Fight it out between yourselves.*

fight off to drive away by fighting: *He managed to fight off his attacker.*

figurative /ˈfɪgərətɪv/ *adj* not used with its exact meaning, but in an imaginative way: *'Her eyes were glued to the television screen'* is a figurative use of the word 'glued'. **ˈfiguratively** *adv.*

figure /ˈfɪgə(r)/ *n* **1** a symbol for a number: *'240' has three figures.* **2** an amount; a sum: *a figure of £1000 was paid.* **3** the form or shape of a person: *That girl has a good figure.* **4** a shape: *Triangles, squares and circles are geometrical figures.* **5** a drawing to explain something: *The parts of a flower are shown in figure 3.* **6** a picture, model or small statue: *There was a wooden figure of Buddha on the table.* — *v* to think; to guess: *I figured that you would arrive before half past eight.*

'figurehead *n* a person who is officially leader but has little power.

figure on to have something in your plans: *I figure on finishing the book by the end of the year.*

figure out to understand: *I can't figure out why he said that.*

good at figures good at arithmetic: *Are you good at figures?*

filament /'fɪləmənt/ *n* the very thin, fine wire in an electric light bulb, or some other very fine thread-like object.

file[1] /faɪl/ *n* a line of people walking one behind the other. — *v* to walk in a file: *The children filed into the school hall.*

in single file one behind the other: *They went along the passage in single file.*

file[2] /faɪl/ *n* **1** something for keeping papers together and in order. **2** a collection of papers on a particular subject. **3** in computing, a collection of data. — *v* to put papers *etc* in a file: *He filed the letter under P.*

on file or **on the files** kept in a file for reference: *We've kept all your letters on file.*

file[3] /faɪl/ *n* a steel tool with a rough surface for smoothing or rubbing away wood, metal *etc*. — *v* to shape or make something smooth with a file: *She filed her nails.*

filial /'fɪlɪəl/ *adj* suitable for a son or daughter: *filial obedience.*

filing cabinet /'faɪlɪŋ kabɪnət/ a piece of office furniture with drawers which can be locked, for storing documents *etc*: *She keeps all the letters she receives in a filing cabinet.*

filings /'faɪlɪŋz/ *n* pieces of wood, metal *etc* rubbed off with a file: *iron filings.*

fill /fɪl/ *v* **1** to make or become full: *to fill a cupboard with books*; *Her eyes filled with tears.* **2** to put something in a hole to stop it up: *They've filled up that hole in the road*; *The dentist filled two of my teeth yesterday.* **3** to find someone for a job; to occupy a job: *They couldn't find anybody to fill the job.* — *n* as much as fills or satisfies you: *He ate his fill.*

'filling *n* anything used to fill something: *The filling has come out of my tooth*; *She put an orange filling in the cake.*

filling station *n* a place where petrol is sold.

fill in 1 to add or put in whatever is needed to make something complete: *to fill in the details*; *Have you filled in your tax form yet?* **2** to do another person's job while they are away: *I'm filling in for his secretary.*

fill out 1 to write the information asked for in the blank spaces on a form: *She filled out her application for a bank loan.* **2** to become fatter: *He used to be very thin but he has filled out a bit recently.*

fill up to make or become completely full: *Fill up the petrol tank, please.*

fillet /'fɪlɪt/ *n* a piece of meat or fish without bones: *fillet of veal*; *cod fillet.*

> The pronunciation of **fillet** is 'fɪlɪt.

filly /'fɪlɪ/ *n* a young female horse.

film /fɪlm/ *n* **1** a thin strip of material on which photographs are taken: *photographic film.* **2** a story, play *etc* shown as a motion picture in a cinema, on television *etc*: *to make a film.* **3** a thin skin or covering: *a film of oil.* — *v* to make a motion picture: *They are going to film the race.*

'filmstar *n* a famous actor or actress in films.

filter /'fɪltə(r)/ *n* a device through which liquid, gas, smoke *etc* can pass, but not solid material: *A filter is used to make sure that the oil is clean.* — *v* **1** to make or become clean by passing through a filter: *The rainwater filtered into a tank.* **2** to come bit by bit or gradually: *The news filtered out.*

filth /fɪlθ/ *n* anything very dirty: *Look at that filth on your boots!*

'filthy *adj* very dirty: *The whole house is absolutely filthy.*

fin /fɪn/ *n* a thin movable part on a fish's body by which it balances and swims.

final /'faɪnəl/ *adj* **1** the very last: *the final chapter of the book.* **2** decided and not to be changed: *The judge's decision is final.* — *n* (often **finals**) the last part of a competition: *the tennis finals.*

finale /fɪ'nɑːlɪ/ *n* a grand final scene or ending to a performance.

> **final** is an adjective meaning last, or a noun meaning the last round of a competition.
> **finale** is a grand final scene.

'finalist *n* a person who reaches the final stage in a competition.

'finalize *v* to make a final decision about plans, arrangements *etc*: *We must finalize the arrangements by Friday.*

'finally *adv* **1** last: *The soldiers rode past, then came the Royal visitors, and finally the Queen.* **2** at last, after a long time: *The train finally arrived.*

'finals *n* the last examinations for a university degree *etc*: *I am taking my finals in June.*

finance /faɪˈnans/ or /ˈfaɪnans/ *n* money affairs: *He is an expert in finance*; *The government is worried about the state of the country's finances.* — *v* to give money for a plan, business *etc*: *Will the company finance your trip abroad?*

fiˈnancial *adj* concerning money: *financial affairs*. **fiˈnancially** *adv*.

finch /fɪntʃ/ *n* a kind of small bird: *a greenfinch*.

find /faɪnd/ *v* **1** to come upon or meet with accidentally, or after searching: *Look what I've found!* **2** to discover: *I found that I couldn't unlock the door.* **3** to form an idea or opinion of something: *I find the British weather very cold.* — *n* something found, especially something of value or interest: *That old book is quite a find!*

> **find; found** /faʊnd/; **found**: *She found some beautiful shells*; *He has just found the missing piece.*
> See also **search**.

ˈfindings *n* the information or conclusions that you have after a period of study or inquiry: *He presents his findings in a report.*
find out 1 to discover: *I found out what was worrying her.* **2** to discover the truth about someone, usually that they have done wrong: *He had been stealing for years, but eventually they found him out.*

fine[1] /faɪn/ *adj* **1** very good; excellent: *fine paintings*; *a fine performance*. **2** bright; not raining: *a fine day*. **3** well; healthy: *I was ill yesterday but I am feeling fine today.* **4** thin or delicate: *a fine material*; *fine hair*. **5** enjoyable: *We had a fine time.* **6** made of small pieces, grains *etc*: *fine sand*; *fine rain*. **7** good: *There's nothing wrong with your work — it's fine.* — *adv* well: *This table will do fine.* **ˈfinely** *adv*.

fine[2] /faɪn/ *n* money that must be paid as a punishment: *I had to pay a £20 fine.* — *v* to make someone pay a fine: *He was fined £10.*

finery /ˈfaɪnərɪ/ *n* beautiful clothes, jewellery *etc*: *She arrived in all her finery.*

finger /ˈfɪŋgə(r)/ *n* **1** one of the five end parts of the hand: *She pointed her finger at the thief.* **2** anything shaped *etc* like a finger: *a fish finger.* — *v* to touch or feel with your fingers: *She fingered the material.*

ˈfingernail *n* the nail at the tip of the finger.
ˈfingermark *n* a dirty mark left on a surface by a finger: *The window was covered with fingermarks.*
ˈfingerprint *n* the mark made by the tip of the finger: *The thief wiped his fingerprints off the safe.*
ˈfingertip *n* the very end of a finger: *She burnt her fingertips on the stove.*
have something at your fingertips: *You must have all the facts at your fingertips.*
keep your fingers crossed to hope that something will happen, come true or go well.
put your finger on to point out or describe exactly: *He put his finger on the cause of our problem.*

finish /ˈfɪnɪʃ/ *v* **1** to bring or come to an end: *She has finished her work*; *The music finished.* **2** to use, eat, drink *etc* the last of something: *Have you finished your tea?* — *n* **1** the last touch of paint, polish *etc* that makes the work perfect: *It gives a waterproof satin finish.* **2** the last part of a race *etc*: *It was a close finish.*

ˈfinished *adj* **1** done; completed: *Is the job finished?*; *a finished product.* **2** having been completely used, eaten *etc*: *The food is finished.* **3** ruined: *He's finished!*
finish off 1 to complete: *She finished off the painting yesterday.* **2** to eat, drink or use the last part of: *Who would like to finish off the cake?* **3** to kill a person who is usually already ill or injured: *He'd been ill for years and the pneumonia finally finished him off.*
finish up 1 to use, eat *etc* the last of something: *Finish up your meal as quickly as possible.* **2** to end: *It was no surprise to me when he finished up in jail.*

finite /ˈfaɪnaɪt/ *adj* having an end or limit: *We only have a finite amount of time to do this job.*

> The opposite of **finite** is **infinite**.

fiord or **fjord** /ˈfiːɔːd/ or /fjɔːd/ *n* a long narrow stretch of sea between high cliffs or mountains: *Norway is famous for its fiords.*

fir /fɜː(r)/ *n* an evergreen tree that bears cones.

fire /ˈfaɪə(r)/ *n* **1** a pile of wood, coal *etc* that is burning to give heat: *to sit by a warm fire.* **2** something that is burning by accident: *Several houses were destroyed in the fire.* **3** a device for heating: *an electric fire.* **4** attack by guns: *The soldiers were under fire.* — *v* **1** to heat pottery *etc* in an oven in order to harden and strengthen it: *The pots must be fired.* **2** to make someone enthusiastic: *The story fired his imagination.* **3** to use a gun *etc*; to shoot: *He fired his revolver three times*; *He fired three bullets at the target*; *They suddenly fired at us.* **4** to dismiss someone from a job: *He was fired for being late.*

fire alarm a bell *etc* that gives warning of a fire.

'firearm *n* any type of gun.

fire brigade a company of firemen.

fire engine a vehicle carrying firemen and their equipment.

fire escape a means of escape, especially an outside metal staircase that people can use to leave a burning building.

'fire-extinguisher *n* a device containing chemicals for putting out fires.

'firelight the light that is produced by a fire: *I could see her smile in the firelight.*

'fireman *n* a man whose job is to put out fires.

'fireplace *n* a space in a wall of a room with a chimney above, for a fire.

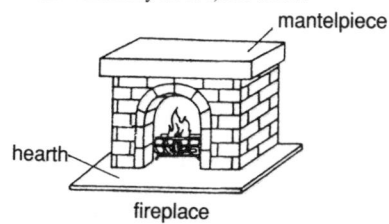

mantelpiece
hearth
fireplace

fire station a building for firemen and their equipment.

'firewood wood for burning as fuel.

'firework *n* a small exploding device giving off a colourful display of lights. — *adj*: *a firework display.*

catch fire to begin to burn: *Dry wood catches fire easily.*

on fire burning: *The building is on fire!*

open fire to begin shooting at someone: *The enemy opened fire on us.*

set fire to something or **set something on fire** to cause something to begin burning: *They set fire to the school*; *He has set the house on fire.*

firing squad /ˈfaɪərɪŋ skwɒd/ a group of soldiers ordered to shoot a person sentenced to death: *He was executed by firing squad.*

firm[1] /fɜːm/ *adj* **1** strong and steady: *The castle was built on firm ground*; *a firm handshake.* **2** not changing your mind: *a firm decision.*

'firmly *adv*. **'firmness** *n*.

firm[2] /fɜːm/ *n* a business company: *an engineering firm.*

first /fɜːst/ *adj* before all others: *the first person to arrive*; *The first snowflakes fluttered down between the trees.* — *adv* **1** before all others: *The boy spoke first*; *Who came first in the race?.* **2** before doing anything else: *'Shall we eat now?' 'Wash your hands first!'* — *n* the person, animal *etc* that does something before any other person, animal *etc*: *the first to arrive.*

first aid treatment of a wounded or sick person before the doctor's arrival.

first-'class *adj* **1** being of the best quality: *a first-class hotel.* **2** very good: *This food is first-class!* **3** for travelling in the best and most expensive part of the train, plane, ship *etc*: *a first-class passenger ticket.* — *adv*: *He always travels first-class.*

first floor 1 in British English, the floor of a building above the ground floor. **2** in American English, the ground floor of a building.

first'hand *adj* learnt through personal involvement, not from other people: *He had had firsthand experience of jungle warfare.* — *adv*: *She had seen it done firsthand and would never forget it.*

'firstly *adv* in the first place: *I have two reasons for not going — firstly, it's cold, and secondly, I'm tired!*

first name the name you are given in addition to your surname: *Susan is her first name.*

first-'rate *adj* very good: *He is a first-rate doctor.*

at first at the beginning: *At first I didn't like him.*

first of all to begin with; the most important thing is: *First of all, let's clear up the mess*; *First of all, the plan is impossible — secondly, we can't afford it.*

fish /fɪʃ/ *n* **1** a creature that lives in water and breathes through gills: *There are plenty of fish around the coast.* **2** its flesh eaten as food: *Do you prefer meat or fish?* — *v* **1** to catch fish: *He likes fishing.* **2** to search for something: *She fished around in her desk for a pencil.*

> The plural **fish** is never wrong, but sometimes **fishes** is used in talking about different kinds of: *How many fish did you catch?*; *the fishes of the Indian Ocean.* **fish** as a food is usually singular: *Fish is good for you*; but: *The fish were jumping about in the net.*

'fishball or **'fishcake** *n* mashed fish shaped into a ball and fried.

'fisherman *n* a man who fishes as a job or as a hobby.

'fishing *n* the sport or business of catching fish.

'fishing-line *n* a fine strong thread made of nylon, used with a rod *etc* for catching fish.

'fishing-rod *n* a long thin rod used with a fishing-line and hooks *etc* for catching fish.

'fishmonger *n* **1** a person who sells fish. **2** a shop that sells fish.

'fishy *adj* **1** like a fish: *a fishy smell*. **2** suspicious: *There's something fishy about that man*.

fist /fɪst/ *n* a tightly closed hand: *He shook his fist at me in anger*.

fit[1] /fɪt/ *adj* **1** in good health: *I am feeling very fit*. **2** suitable: *a dinner fit for a king*. — *n* the right size or shape for a particular person, purpose *etc*: *Your dress is a very good fit*. — *v* **1** to be the right size or shape for someone or something: *The coat fits very well*; *This dress won't fit me any more*. **2** to be suitable for a particular purpose: *His speech fitted the occasion*. **3** to fix something: *You must fit a new lock on the door*. **4** to equip with something: *He fitted the cupboard with shelves*.

> The opposite of the adjective **fit** is **unfit**.

'fitness *n* being healthy, especially as a result of exercise: *fitness classes*.

'fitted *adj* made or cut to fit a particular space and fixed there: *fitted cupboards*; *a fitted carpet*; *a fitted kitchen*.

'fitting *adj* right; suitable: *It seemed fitting to make a short speech*. — *n* something fixed in a building or on a piece of furniture.

fit in to be able to live peacefully with others: *She doesn't fit in with the other children*.

fit out to provide someone with everything necessary: *The shop fitted them out with everything they needed for their journey*.

fit[2] /fɪt/ *n* a sudden occurrence; a sudden attack: *a fit of laughter*; *a fit of coughing*; *He hit her in a fit of anger*.

in fits and starts often stopping and starting again: *We progressed in fits and starts*.

five /faɪv/ *n* the number 5. — *adj* **1** 5 in number. **2** aged 5: *He is five today*.

fix /fɪks/ *v* **1** to make or keep something firm or steady: *He fixed the post firmly in the ground*. **2** to attach: *He fixed the shelf to the wall*. **3** to mend; to repair: *He has fixed my watch*. **4** to direct attention, a look *etc* at someone or something: *She fixed all her attention on me*; *He fixed his eyes on the door*. **5** to arrange: *to fix a price*; *We fixed up a meeting*. **6** to prepare something; to get something ready: *I'll fix dinner tonight*. — *n* trouble; a difficulty: *I'm in a terrible fix!*

fixed *adj* not changing; not movable; steady.

fixture /'fɪkstʃə(r)/ *n* a fixed piece of furniture *etc*: *We can't move the cupboard — it's a fixture*.

fix on to decide on something, choose: *Have you fixed on a date for the wedding?*

fix someone up with something to provide someone with something: *Can you fix me up with a car for tomorrow?*

fizz /fɪz/ *v* to give off many small bubbles: *I like the way lemonade fizzes*. — *n* the sound or feeling of something fizzing. **'fizzy** *adj*.

fizzle out to end in a weak and disappointing way: *The party fizzled out well before midnight*.

fjord see **fiord**.

flabbergasted /'flabəgɑːstɪd/ *adj* very surprised.

flabby /'flabɪ/ *adj* fat, but not firm and healthy: *flabby cheeks*.

flag[1] /flag/ *n* a piece of cloth with a particular design representing a country *etc*, or used for signalling messages: *The ship was flying a British flag*.

'flag-pole *n* the pole on which a flag is hung.

'flagship *n* **1** the ship that flies the flag of the commander of the fleet: *Nelson's flagship was the 'Victory'*. **2** the most important ship in a fleet: *The QE2 is the flagship of the Cunard shipping line*. **3** a company's most important product: *That particular car is the maker's flagship*.

flag[2] /flag/ *v* to become tired or weak: *Halfway through the race he began to flag*.

flagrant /'fleɪɡrənt/ *adj* wrong and shocking, but not concealed: *She told a flagrant lie*.

flair /fleə(r)/ *n* a natural ability for doing something: *She has a flair for drawing*.

flake /fleɪk/ *n* a small piece: *a snowflake*. — *v* to come off in flakes off the walls *etc*: *The paint is flaking*. **'flaky** *adj*.

flamboyant /flam'bɔɪənt/ *adj* **1** very confident, lively and excited: *a very flamboyant actor*. **2** bright, colourful and attracting attention or notice: *flamboyant clothes*. **flam'boyantly** *adv*.

flame /fleɪm/ *n* the bright light of something burning: *A small flame burned in the lamp.* — *v* to burn with flames: *The fire flamed up.* **'flaming** *adj.*

flamingo /fləˈmɪŋgoʊ/, *plural* **fla'mingos**, *n* a large bird with pink and red feathers and long legs.

flammable /ˈflaməbəl/ *adj* able or likely to burn: *flammable material.*

See **inflammable**.

flank /flaŋk/ *n* **1** the side of an animal's body, especially a horse's. **2** the side of an army arranged for battle: *They marched around the enemy's flank.* — *v* to be at the side of someone or something: *The prisoner appeared, flanked by two policemen.*

flannel /ˈflanəl/ *n* loosely woven woollen cloth.

flap /flap/ *v* to wave about; to flutter: *The curtains were flapping in the breeze; The bird flapped its wings.* — *n* **1** this movement: *a flap of wings.* **2** anything broad or wide that hangs loosely: *a flap of canvas.*

flare /fleə(r)/ *v* to burn with a bright unsteady light: *The firelight flared.* — *n* **1** a sudden bright light or flame. **2** a device for producing a bright light, used as a signal.

flared *adj* widening; spreading out: *a flared skirt.*

flare up 1 to burn strongly suddenly: *The fire flared up.* **2** to become very angry suddenly: *He flared up at me because I told him to leave.*

flash /flaʃ/ *n* **1** a sudden bright light: *a flash of lightning.* **2** a moment; a very short time: *He was with her in a flash.* — *v* **1** to shine quickly: *A blue light flashed across the window; He flashed a torch.* **2** to pass quickly: *The days flashed by; The cars flashed past.*

'flashback *n* a scene from the past in a film, play *etc*: *As the hero is sleeping, there is a flashback to his childhood.*

'flashing *adj*: *flashing lights.*

'flashlight *n* **1** a torch. **2** a device that flashes, to give a bright light for taking photographs.

'flashy *adj* smart, new and too obviously expensive: *flashy clothes; a flashy car.*

flask /flɑːsk/ *n* **1** a bottle. **2** a special container for keeping drinks *etc* hot: *a flask of tea.*

flat /flat/ *adj* **1** level: *a flat surface; flat shoes.* **2** having lost most of its air: *His car had a flat tyre.* **3** used up; having no power left: *a flat battery.* — *adv* stretched out: *She was lying flat on her back.* — *n* **1** an apartment on one floor, with kitchen and bathroom, in a larger building: *Do you live in a house or a flat?* **2** a sign (♭) in music, that makes a note lower by another half note. **3** a level, even part: *the flat of her hand.*

'flatly *adv* **1** without interest. **2** definitely; absolutely: *She flatly refused to help.*

'flatten *v* to make or become flat: *He flattened himself against the wall.*

fall flat to fail to achieve the effect that you wanted: *My joke fell completely flat.*

flat out as fast as possible, with as much effort as possible: *He was running flat out.*

flatter /ˈflatə(r)/ *v* **1** to praise someone too much, or not sincerely: *She flattered him by complimenting him on his singing.* **2** to make someone seem better than they really are: *The photograph flatters him.* **'flatterer** *n.*

'flattering *adj* making you look attractive or seem important: *a flattering photo.*

'flattery *n* praise that is not sincere.

flaunt /flɔːnt/ *v* to show something off: *He liked to flaunt his wealth.*

flavour /ˈfleɪvə(r)/ *n* **1** taste: *The tea has a wonderful flavour.* **2** atmosphere; quality: *The story has a flavour of mystery.* — *v* to give a flavour to something: *She flavoured the cake with lemon.*

'flavouring *n* anything used to give a particular taste: *lemon flavouring.*

flaw /flɔː/ *n* a fault; something that spoils a thing slightly: *There is a flaw in this material.*

flawed *adj* containing a flaw: *a flawed argument.*

'flawless *adj* perfect.

flea /fliː/ *n* a small insect that jumps instead of flying and lives on the blood of animals or people.

fleck /flɛk/ *n* a spot: *a fleck of dust.*

fled *see* **flee**.

fledgling /ˈflɛdʒlɪŋ/ *n* a young bird ready to fly.

flee /fliː/ *v* to run away from danger: *He fled from the burning house.*

flee; fled /flɛd/; **fled**: *She fled when she saw us coming; He had fled by the time his enemies arrived.*

fleece /fliːs/ *n* a sheep's wool. **'fleecy** *adj.*

fleet /fliːt/ *n* **1** a number of ships or boats under one command or sailing together: *a fleet of fishing boats.* **2** the entire navy of a country: *the British fleet.*

'fleeting *adj* passing quickly: *She caught a fleeting glimpse of the deer through the trees.*

flesh /flɛʃ/ *n* **1** the muscles and fat that cover

the bones of animals. **2** the soft part of fruit: *the flesh of a peach.*
'fleshy *adj* fat: *a fleshy face.*

flew *see* **fly**².

flex /flɛks/ *n* a covered wire for carrying electricity attached to an electrical device: *Don't trip over the flex!* — *v* to bend; to contract: *She slowly flexed her arm to find out if it was still painful*; *He flexed his muscles to show how strong he was.*

flexible /'flɛksəbəl/ *adj* **1** able to be bent easily: *Wire is flexible.* **2** able to be altered: *My holiday plans are very flexible.* **flexi'bility** *n.*

flick /flɪk/ *n* a quick, sharp movement: *a flick of the wrist.* — *v* to make this kind of movement: *He flicked some dust from his jacket.*

flick through to look quickly through: *He flicked through the magazine.*

flicker /'flɪkə(r)/ *v* **1** to burn unsteadily: *the candle flickered.* **2** to move quickly: *A smile flickered across her face.* — *n* an unsteady light or flame.

flight¹ /flaɪt/ *n* **1** the action of flying: *the flight of a bird*; *Have you seen geese in flight?* **2** a journey in a plane: *How long is the flight to New York?* **3** a set of steps or stairs: *a flight of steps.*

flight² /flaɪt/ *n* the act of running away from an enemy or from danger; fleeing.

put to flight to make someone flee or run away: *The army put the rebels to flight.*

flimsy /'flɪmzɪ/ *adj* **1** made of thin material: *You'll be cold in that flimsy dress.* **2** badly made; likely to break: *His boat is far too flimsy to take out to sea.* **3** not very convincing: *The teacher will never believe that flimsy excuse.*

flinch /flɪntʃ/ *v* to make a sudden movement in fear, pain *etc*: *She flinched when he shook his fist at her.*

fling /flɪŋ/ *v* to throw with great force: *He flung his golf clubs down on the bank, exasperated.*

> **fling; flung** /flʌŋ/; **flung**: *She flung herself into a chair*; *Clothes had been flung all over the floor.*

flint /flɪnt/ *n* a very hard kind of stone.

flip /flɪp/ *v* **1** to toss something lightly so that it turns in the air: *They flipped a coin to see which side it landed on.* **2** to turn over quickly: *She flipped over the pages of the book.* — *n* the action of flipping.

flippant /'flɪpənt/ *adj* not serious enough about important matters: *Some students had a rather flippant attitude to their work.*

flipper /'flɪpə(r)/ *n* **1** one of the two short arm-like limbs of a seal, walrus *etc*, that it uses for swimming. **2** a large flat rubber shoe that helps you swim underwater.

flirt /flɜːt/ *v* to behave as though you were in love but without being serious: *She flirts with every man she meets.* **flir'tation** *n.*

flit /flɪt/ *v* to move quickly and lightly from place to place: *Butterflies flitted around in the garden.*

float /fləʊt/ *v* to stay on the surface of a liquid: *A piece of wood was floating in the stream.* — *n* a floating ball on a fishing-line: *If the float moves, there is probably a fish on the hook.*

flock /flɒk/ *n* a group of animals or birds: *a flock of sheep*; *a flock of geese.* — *v* to go somewhere in a crowd: *People flocked to the cinema.*

flog /flɒg/ *v* to beat; to whip: *You will be flogged for stealing the money.*
'flogging *n*: *I gave the boy a good flogging.*

flood /flʌd/ *n* **1** a great quantity of water lying on the land, after very heavy rain *etc*: *If it goes on raining like this we shall have floods.* **2** any great quantity: *There is always a flood of letters at Christmas.* — *v* to overflow over land *etc*; to cause an overflow of water: *The river burst its banks and flooded the fields*; *She left the tap running and flooded the bathroom.*

> The opposite of a **flood** is a **drought**.

'floodlight *n* a very strong light used to light up the outside of buildings *etc*: *There were floodlights in the sports stadium.* **'floodlighting** *n.* **'floodlit** *adj.*

floor /flɔː(r)/ *n* **1** the surface in a room *etc* on which you stand and walk. **2** all the rooms on the same level in a building: *My office is on the third floor.* — *v* **1** to make a floor for a room: *We've floored the kitchen with tiles.* **2** to knock down: *He floored him with one blow.* **3** to surprise or confuse with a question: *Her query floored me.*

flop /flɒp/ *v* **1** to fall heavily: *She flopped into an armchair*; *Her hair flopped over her face.* **2** to be unsuccessful with the public. — *n* a failure: *Most of his plays were flops.*
'floppy *adj*: *a floppy hat.*

floppy disk a flexible magnetic disc used to store information from a computer: *She keeps copies of all her computer files on floppy disks.*

flora /'flɔːrə/ *n* the plants of a district or country as a whole.

floral /ˈflɔːrəl/ *adj* having to do with flowers; made of flowers: *floral decorations.*

See **flowery**.

florist /ˈflɒrɪst/ *n* a person who grows or sells flowers.

flour /ˈflaʊə(r)/ *n* wheat, or other cereal, ground into powder and used for baking *etc.*

flour is never used in the plural.

flourish /ˈflʌrɪʃ/ *v* **1** to be healthy; to grow well: *My plants are flourishing.* **2** to be successful: *His business is flourishing.* **3** to wave something as a show, threat *etc*: *He flourished his sword.* — *n* a grand gesture with an arm or a hand: *He removed his hat with a flourish.*

flout /flaʊt/ *v* to disobey an order deliberately: *Too many drivers flout the law on speeding.*

flow /fləʊ/ *v* to move along in the way that water does: *The river flowed into the sea.* — *n* the action of flowing; something that flows: *a flow of blood; the flow of traffic.*

flower /ˈflaʊə(r)/ *n* **1** a bloom or blossom on a plant. **2** a plant that has blooms: *We grow roses, carnations and other flowers.* — *v* to produce flowers: *This plant flowers in early May.*

flowery   floral

'flowery *adj* full of flowers or decorated with flowers: *a flowery hat.*

'flowerbed *n* a piece of land prepared and used for the growing of flowers.

'flowerpot *n* a container for growing plants in.

in flower having flowers in bloom: *These trees are in flower in May.*

flown see **fly**².

flu /fluː/ short for **influenza**.

fluctuate /ˈflʌktjʊeɪt/ *v* to change often: *The price of petrol continually fluctuates*; *He fluctuates between loving school and hating it.* **fluctu'ation** *n.*

fluent /ˈfluːənt/ *adj* able to speak or write quickly, easily and well, especially in a foreign language: *She is fluent in English.* **'fluency** *n.* **'fluently** *adv.*

fluff /flʌf/ *n* small pieces of soft, wool-like material from blankets *etc.*

'fluffy *adj* soft and furry, or woolly: *a fluffy kitten; fluffy chickens.*

fluid /ˈfluːɪd/ *n* any liquid substance: *cleaning fluid.* — *adj* **1** liquid; able to flow like a liquid: *Blood is a fluid substance.* **2** able to be changed easily: *My plans are fluid.*

fluke /fluːk/ *n* a success that has happened by chance.

flung see **fling**.

fluorescent /flʊəˈresənt/ *adj* **1** giving out radiation in the form of light: *Many sea creatures are fluorescent at night.* **2** very bright: *She marked the spelling mistakes using a fluorescent yellow pen.*

fluorescent lamp or **light** a type of electric lamp or light using tubes filled with gas: *Fluorescent lights are often used in bathrooms.*

flurry /ˈflʌrɪ/ *n* **1** a sudden rush of wind *etc.* **2** a confused rush: *a flurry of activity.*

flush /flʌʃ/ *n* redness of the face; a blush. — *v* **1** to become red in the face: *She flushed with excitement.* **2** to clean by a rush of water: *to flush a toilet.*

flushed *adj* covered with a red flush: *Your face gets flushed when you run hard.*

fluster /ˈflʌstə(r)/ *v* to make someone confused or nervous: *Don't fluster me!*

flute /fluːt/ *n* a musical wind instrument in the form of a metal pipe with holes.

flutter /ˈflʌtə(r)/ *v* **1** to move the wings quickly: *The bird fluttered in its cage.* **2** to move in a quick or irregular way: *A leaf fluttered to the ground; The flags fluttered in the wind.* — *n*: *They could hear the flutter of bats' wings in the dark.*

fly¹ /flaɪ/ *n* **1** a small insect with wings. **2** a fish hook made to look like a fly. **3** a piece of material with buttons or a zip, especially at the front of trousers.

fly² /flaɪ/ *v* **1** to go through the air on wings *etc* or in an aeroplane; to pilot an aeroplane: *The pilot flew over the sea; to fly a plane.* **2** to move or pass quickly: *She flew along the road to catch the bus; The days flew past.* **3** to run away; to flee: *Fly, before it's too late!*

fly; flew /fluː/; **flown** /fləʊn/: *The bird flew away; Has he ever flown a helicopter?*

flying visit a very short visit.

fly sheet the outer covering of a tent.

'flyover *n* a road *etc* that is built on pillars so as to cross over another.

fly into to get into a sudden rage, temper

foal

etc: *He flew into a rage when she spoke rudely to him.*
fly off the handle to lose your temper; to get angry.
let fly to attack angrily with words or actions: *The boy suddenly let fly at me with his fists.*
send flying to knock someone or something over, with great force: *She hit him and sent him flying.*

foal /fəʊl/ *n* a baby horse.

foam /fəʊm/ *n* a mass of small bubbles on the surface of liquids *etc*. — *v* to produce foam.
foam rubber a form of rubber which looks like a sponge and is used for stuffing chairs *etc*.

focus /ˈfəʊkəs/ *n* **1** the point at which rays of light meet after passing through a lens. **2** a point to which light, a look, attention *etc* is directed: *She was the focus of everyone's attention.* — *v* **1** to adjust a camera *etc* in order to get a clear picture. **2** to direct attention *etc* to one point: *The children's attention was focused on the stage.*
in focus, **out of focus** giving, or not giving, a clear picture: *This photograph is out of focus.*

fodder /ˈfɒdə(r)/ *n* food for farm animals.

foe /fəʊ/ *n* an enemy.

foetus or **fetus** /ˈfiːtəs/ *n* the fully developed embryo of a human being or animal before it is born. **ˈfoetal** or **ˈfetal** *adj*.

fog /fɒg/ *n* a thick cloud of moisture in the air that makes it difficult to see. — *v* to cover with fog: *Her glasses were fogged up with steam.*
ˈfoggy *adj*: *foggy weather.*
ˈfog-horn *n* a device that makes a loud booming or whining noise, used as a warning to, or by, ships in fog.

foil¹ /fɔɪl/ *v* to defeat; to disappoint: *They were foiled in their attempt to overthrow the President.*

foil² /fɔɪl/ *n* very thin sheets of metal that resemble paper: *silver foil.*

foist /fɔɪst/ *v* to force someone to receive something: *They tried to foist their ideas on us throughout our education.*

fold¹ /fəʊld/ *v* **1** to double over material, paper *etc*: *She folded the paper in half.* **2** to tuck one arm or hand under the other: *She folded her arms.* — *n* **1** a folded part in material *etc*: *Her dress hung in folds.* **2** a mark made especially on paper by folding: *There was a fold in the page.*

ˈfolder *n* a cover for keeping loose papers together.
ˈfolding *adj* able to be folded: *a folding chair.*

fold² /fəʊld/ *n* a place surrounded by a fence or wall, in which sheep are kept.

foliage /ˈfəʊliːɪdʒ/ *n* leaves: *This plant has dark foliage.*

folk /fəʊk/ *n* people: *The folk in this town are very friendly.* — *adj* belonging to the people of a country: *a folk dance; folk music.*

> **folk** takes a plural verb.

ˈfolklore *n* the customs, beliefs and stories of a particular people.
folks *n* family: *I spent my holiday with my folks.*

follow /ˈfɒləʊ/ *v* **1** to go or come after someone: *I will follow you.* **2** to go along a road, river *etc*: *Follow this road.* **3** to understand: *Do you follow me?* **4** to act according to something: *I followed his advice.* **5** to take an interest in the way something develops or continues: *Have you been following the murder trial?*

> I'll **go with** or **come with** you; I'll **go** or **come shopping with** you (not I'll **follow** you).

as follows a phrase used to introduce a list *etc*: *Saturday's team is as follows ...*
ˈfollower *n* a person who follows, especially someone who supports the ideas *etc* of another person: *the followers of Jesus.*
ˈfollowing *adj* **1** coming after: *the following day.* **2** about to be mentioned: *You will need the following things: paper, pencil and scissors.* — *n* a group of supporters or admirers: *She has a keen following among rock fans.* — *prep* after; as a result of: *There was a silence following his announcement.*
follow up to investigate further; to find out more about something: *The police are following up a clue.*

folly /ˈfɒlɪ/ *n* foolishness; stupidity.

fond /fɒnd/ *adj* **1** loving; affectionate: *a fond mother; She gave him a fond look.* **2** liking something or someone: *She is very fond of her children; I'm fond of swimming.* **ˈfondly** *adv*. **ˈfondness** *n*.

> **fond** is followed by **of**.

fondle /ˈfɒndəl/ *v* to touch or stroke affectionately.

food /fuːd/ *n* what living things eat: *Horses and cows eat different food from dogs.*

food poisoning an illness caused by eating food that is bad.

food-processor an electric machine for chopping or mixing food.

'foodstuff *n* food: *frozen foodstuffs.*

fool /fu:l/ *n* a stupid, silly person — *v* **1** to deceive: *She completely fooled me with her story.* **2** to act like a fool: *Stop fooling about!*

'foolish *adj* stupid; silly. **'foolishly** *adv.* **'foolishness** *n.*

'foolhardy *adj* taking foolish risks.

'foolproof *adj* unable to go wrong: *His new plan seems completely foolproof.*

fool about or **fool around** to behave in a silly way: *Stop fooling around with that knife or someone will get hurt.*

make a fool of someone to make someone appear stupid.

foot /fʊt/, *plural* **feet** /fi:t/, *n* **1** the part of your leg on which you stand or walk. **2** the lower part of anything: *at the foot of the hill.* **3** a measure of length equal to 30.48 cm: *She is five feet* (or *five foot*) *tall.*

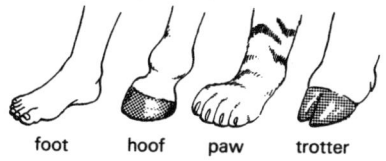

foot · hoof · paw · trotter

'football *n* **1** a game played by kicking a large ball. **2** the ball used in this game.

'foothill *n* a small hill at the foot of a range of mountains: *the foothills of the Alps.*

See **mountain**.

'foothold *n* a place to put your foot when climbing: *He lost his foothold and fell onto the ledge below.*

'footing *n* **1** balance: *It was difficult to keep his footing on the slippery path.* **2** foundation: *The business is now on a firm footing.*

'footmark *n* a footprint.

'footnote *n* a note at the bottom of a page.

'footpath *n* a path or way for walking, not for cars, bicycles *etc.*

'footprint *n* the mark of a foot: *She followed his footprints through the snow.*

'footstep *n* the sound made by walking: *She heard his footsteps on the stairs.*

'footwear *n* boots, shoes, slippers *etc.*

follow in someone's footsteps to do the same as someone has done before you.

on foot walking: *She came on foot.*

put your foot down to be firm about something: *I put my foot down and refused.*

put your foot in it to say something embarrassing that upsets someone.

stand on your own two feet to look after yourself without help.

for /fɔː(r)/ *prep* **1** intended to be given or sent to someone: *This letter is for you.* **2** towards; in the direction of somewhere: *We set off for London.* **3** through a certain time or distance: *He worked hard for three hours; They drove on for three miles.* **4** as payment of something: *He paid £2 for his ticket.* **5** having a particular purpose: *He gave her money for her bus fare; I'm saving up for a bicycle.* **6** in order to help; on behalf of: *Please do this for me; He works for a building firm.* **7** supporting; in favour of: *Are you for or against this plan?* **8** because of: *for this reason.* **9** considering that it is: *It's very cold for August.* **10** used in several other ways: *He asked his father for money; I'll go for a walk; Are you coming for a swim?* — *conjunction* because: *I stopped to rest, for I was very tired.*

> I've lived here **for** a year (a period of time).
> I've lived here **since** last year (a point in time).

forbid /fə'bɪd/ *v* to tell someone not to do something: *She forbade him to go.*

> **forbid; forbade** /fə'beɪd/; **forbidden** /fə'bɪdən/: *Her mother forbade her to shout; His father had forbidden him to smoke, but he did it nevertheless.*

for'bidden *adj* not allowed.

for'bidding *adj* rather frightening: *a forbidding face.*

force /fɔːs/ *n* **1** strength; power: *the force of the wind; There are many forces we do not control.* **2** violence: *They used force to make him do what they wanted.* **3** a group of people organized for police or military duties: *the police force; the Royal Air Force.* — *v* **1** to make someone do something against their will, by using violence or threats: *He forced me to give him money.* **2** to push with violence; to break: *They forced the door open.*

'forceful *adj* powerful: *a forceful argument.*

'Forces *n* the army, navy and air force of a country.

in force in large numbers: *The police were out in force when the president visited the city.*

forcible

into force or **in force** in or into operation: *The new law is now in force.*

forcible /'fɔːsəbəl/ *adj* using physical force. **'forcibly** *adv*: *The demonstrators were forcibly removed from the town square.*

ford /fɔːd/ *n* a shallow place in a river, where you can cross.

forearm /'fɔːrɑːm/ *n* the lower part of your arm, between your wrist and elbow.

foreboding /fɔː'boʊdɪŋ/ *n* a feeling of approaching trouble or disaster: *She tossed and turned in her bed that night, full of forboding.*

forecast /'fɔːkɑːst/ *v* to tell about something before it happens: *He forecast good weather for the next three days.* — *n* a statement about what is going to happen: *the weather forecast.*

> **forecast; forecast; forecast**: *She forecast trouble*; *A week of rain had been forecast.*

forecourt /'fɔːkɔːt/ *n* an open area in front of a building such as a petrol station.

forefathers /'fɔːfɑːðəz/ *n* ancestors.

forefinger /'fɔːfɪŋgə(r)/ *n* the finger next to the thumb.

foregone /'fɔːgɒn/: **a foregone conclusion** an obvious or certain result: *It was a foregone conclusion who would win.*

foreground /'fɔːgraʊnd/ *n* the part of a view or picture nearest to the person looking at it: *He painted a picture of hills and fields, with two horses in the foreground.*

> See **background**.

forehand /'fɔːhænd/ *n* a stroke in tennis that is made with the palm of your hand facing forward.

forehead /'fɔːhɛd/ *n* the part of the face above the eyebrows: *Her hair covers her forehead.*

foreign /'fɒrɪn/ *adj* belonging to a country other than your own: *a foreign passport.* **'foreigner** *n* a person from another country.

foreleg /'fɔːlɛg/ *n* an animal's front leg.

foreman /'fɔːmən/, *plural* **'foremen**, *n* the leader of a group, especially of workmen.

foremost /'fɔːmoʊst/ *adj* first in time or place; most famous or important: *the foremost modern artist.*

forensic /fə'rɛnsɪk/ *adj* having to do with the science and medicine of criminal investigations: *The objects found in the vehicle have been sent for forensic analysis.*

foresee /fɔː'siː/ *v* to see or know about something before it happens: *He could foresee the difficulties.* **fore'seeable** *adj*.

> **foresee; foresaw** /fɔː'sɔː/; **foreseen** /fɔː'siːn/: *He foresaw what would happen*; *She had foreseen the delay.*

foresight /'fɔːsaɪt/ *n* the ability to see in advance what may happen and to plan for it.

forest /'fɒrɪst/ *n* a large piece of land covered with trees. **forestry** /'fɒrɪstrɪ/ *n* the science of growing and looking after forests.

foretaste /'fɔːteɪst/ *n* a small sample or experience of something before it happens: *This cold weather is just a foretaste of winter.*

foretell /fɔː'tɛl/ *v* to tell about something before it happens: *to foretell the future from the stars.*

> **foretell; foretold** /fɔː'toʊld/; **foretold**: *The prophet foretold Christ's birth*; *The birth of Christ had been foretold.*

forethought /'fɔːθɔːt/ *n* careful planning and preparation: *A little forethought can save you a lot of money.*

forever /fə'rɛvə(r)/ *adj* **1** for ever: *I'll love you forever.* **2** always: *You're forever asking silly questions.*

foreword /'fɔːwɜːd/ *n* an introduction at the beginning of a book.

forfeit /'fɔːfɪt/ *n* something you must give up because you have done something wrong, especially in a game: *to pay a forfeit.* — *v* to lose: *He forfeited our respect by telling lies.*

forgave *see* **forgive**.

forge[1] /fɔːdʒ/ *n* a place where metal is heated and hammered into shape. — *v* to shape metal by heating and hammering: *He forged a horseshoe out of an iron bar.*

forge[2] /fɔːdʒ/ *v* **1** to copy a letter, a signature *etc*, for a dishonest purpose: *He forged my signature on the cheque.* **2** to paint a picture *etc* and say it is by another more important artist, in order to make money dishonestly. **'forgery** *n*.

forge[3] /fɔːdʒ/ *v* to move steadily: *They forged ahead with their plans.*

forget /fə'gɛt/ *v* **1** to fail to remember: *He has forgotten my name.* **2** to leave something behind accidentally: *She has forgotten her handbag.*

forget; forgot /fəˈgɒt/; **forgotten** /fəˈgɒtən/: *He forgot her telephone number*; *She had forgotten to ring him.*

forˈgetful *adj* often forgetting things: *She is a very forgetful person.* **forˈgetfully** *adv.*

forgivable /fəˈgɪvəbəl/ *adj* that can be forgiven: *I thought that her anger was forgivable in the circumstances.*

The opposite of **forgivable** is **unforgivable**.

forgive /fəˈgɪv/ *v* to stop being angry with someone who has done something wrong: *He forgave her for breaking his watch.*

forgive; forgave /fəˈgeɪv/; **forgiven** /fəˈgɪvən/: *She forgave him for telling lies*; *She has forgiven his bad behaviour.*

forˈgiveness *n* the forgiving of something: *He asked God for forgiveness for all the bad things he had done.*

forˈgiving *adj* willing to forgive: *She's a very forgiving wife.*

forgot, forgotten see **forget**.

fork /fɔːk/ *n* **1** an eating tool or a farming tool with several points for piercing and lifting things: *We eat with a knife, fork and spoon.* **2** the point at which a road etc divides into two or more branches: *They came to a fork in the road.* **3** one of the branches into which a road divides: *Take the left fork.* — *v* **1** to divide into branches: *The main road forks here.* **2** to lift or move with a fork: *The farmer forked the hay into the truck.*

fork-lift truck a small vehicle with two steel prongs on the front that can lift and carry heavy loads.

forlorn /fəˈlɔːn/ *adj* lonely and unhappy.

form¹ /fɔːm/ *n* **1** a shape; an appearance: *He thought he saw the form of a man in the darkness.* **2** a kind; a type: *There are many different forms of religion.* **3** a paper containing certain questions, the answers to which must be written on it: *If you would like to apply for the job, please fill in this application form.* **4** a school class: *He is in the sixth form.* — *v* **1** to make a shape etc: *The children formed a circle and held hands*; *Form yourselves into three groups.* **2** to grow: *An idea slowly formed in his mind.* **3** to organize: *They formed a drama club.* **4** to be: *These exercises form part of the lesson.*

form² /fɔːm/ *n* a long seat without a back; a bench.

formal /ˈfɔːməl/ *adj* **1** done according to certain rules, especially the rules of politeness: *a formal letter.* **2** suitable for important occasions and ceremonies: *You must wear formal dress for weddings and funerals.* **3** polite but not very friendly: *formal behaviour.* **ˈformally** *adv.* **forˈmality** *n.*

The opposite of **formal** is **informal**.

format /ˈfɔːmat/ *n* something's size, shape or style: *Her novel was published in a paperback format.* — *v* to arrange something in a particular format for a computer.

formation /fɔːˈmeɪʃən/ *n* **1** the forming of something. **2** a shape made by a group *etc*: *The planes flew in an arrow-shaped formation.*

former /ˈfɔːmə(r)/ *adj* belonging to an earlier time: *In former times people did not travel so much.*

ˈformerly *adv* in earlier times: *Formerly, this large town was a small village.*

the former the first of two things mentioned: *We visited America and Australia, staying longer in the former than in the latter.*

formidable /ˈfɔːmɪdəbəl/ *adj* **1** rather frightening: *He looked formidable in his black uniform.* **2** very difficult to deal with: *They were faced with formidable problems.* **ˈformidably** *adv.*

formula /ˈfɔːmjʊlə/, *plural* **formulas** or **formulae** /ˈfɔːmjʊliː/, *n* **1** a set of signs or letters used in chemistry, arithmetic *etc* to express an idea briefly: *The formula for water is H_2O.* **2** a special way of making something, and the special substances used to make it: *The shampoo was made to a new formula.*

formulate /ˈfɔːmjʊleɪt/ *v* **1** to express or explain something in words. **2** to invent and develop a plan in detail: *to formulate a new policy.*

forsake /fɔːˈseɪk/ *v* to leave someone or something for ever: *He was forsaken by his friends.*

forsake; forsook /fɔːˈsʊk/; **forsaken** /fɔːˈseɪkən/: *She forsook her children*; *She was forsaken by her husband.*

fort /fɔːt/ *n* a place of defence against an enemy.

forth /fɔːθ/ *adv* forward; onward: *They went forth into the desert.*

back and forth first in one direction and then in the other: *We had to go back and forth many times before we moved all our furniture to the new house.*

forthcoming /fɔːθˈkʌmɪŋ/ *adj* happening soon: *forthcoming events*.

forthright /ˈfɔːθraɪt/ *adj* openly saying what you think, frank: *She was forthright in her criticism of the plan*.

fortify /ˈfɔːtɪfaɪ/ *v* to strengthen: *The king fortified his castle against attack*; *Some hot soup will fortify you for the walk*. **fortifiˈcation** *n*.

fortnight /ˈfɔːtnaɪt/ *n* two weeks: *It's a fortnight since I last saw her*.
ˈ**fortnightly** *adj* every fortnight: *a fortnightly visit* — *adv*: *He is paid fortnightly*.

fortress /ˈfɔːtrəs/ *n* a fort; a castle; a fortified town.

fortunate /ˈfɔːtʃənət/ *adj* lucky: *It was fortunate that nobody was hurt in the accident*.
ˈ**fortunately** *adv*.

fortune /ˈfɔːtʃən/ *n* **1** good or bad luck: *We have to go on, whatever fortune may bring*. **2** a large amount of money: *That ring must be worth a fortune!*
ˈ**fortune-teller** *n* someone who tells fortunes.
tell someone's fortune to foretell what will happen to someone in the future: *The gypsy told my fortune*.

forty /ˈfɔːtɪ/ *n* the number 40. — *adj* **1** 40 in number. **2** aged 40: *Her father is forty*.

> forty (not **fourty**).

forum /ˈfɔːrəm/ *n* a place for public discussion and argument.

forward /ˈfɔːwəd/ *adj* **1** advancing: *a forward movement*. **2** at or near the front: *The forward part of a ship is called the 'bows'*. — *adv* in a forward direction: *They pushed the car forward*. — *v* to send letters *etc* on to another address: *I have asked the post office to forward my mail*.
ˈ**forwards** *adv* forward: *The rope swung backwards and forwards*.
forwarding address a new address to which post should be sent.

fossil /ˈfɒsəl/ *n* the hardened remains of an animal or vegetable, found in rock.
ˈ**fossilize** *v* to change into a fossil.

foster /ˈfɒstə(r)/ *v* **1** to bring up a child that is not your own. **2** to encourage ideas *etc*: *She fostered the child's talents*.
ˈ**foster-child** *n* a child fostered by a family.
ˈ**foster-father**, **foster-mother** *ns* a man or woman who looks after a child who is not his or her own child.

fought *see* **fight**.

foul /faʊl/ *adj* **1** smelling or tasting very bad: *This food is foul*. **2** very dirty: *a foul place*. **3** very unpleasant: *foul weather*. — *n* an action *etc* which breaks the rules of a game: *The other team committed a foul*.

found[1] *see* **find**.

found[2] /faʊnd/ *v* **1** to start or set up something: *The school was founded by the President*. **2** to base on something: *The story was founded upon fact*.

foundation /faʊnˈdeɪʃən/ *n* **1** the founding of something: *the foundation of a new university*. **2** the base on which something is built: *First they laid the foundations, then they built the walls*.
ˈ**founder** *n* a person who founds a school, college, organization *etc*.

fountain /ˈfaʊntɪn/ *n* a device that produces a spring of water that rises into the air: *In the middle of the garden was a carved fountain in the shape of a fish*.
ˈ**fountain pen** a pen with a supply of ink inside.

four /fɔː(r)/ *n* the number 4. — *adj* **1** 4 in number. **2** aged 4: *My sister is four*.
fourth *n* one of four equal parts. — *n*, *adj* the next one after the third.
on all fours on hands and knees: *He climbed the steep path on all fours*.

fourteen /fɔːˈtiːn/ *n* the number 14. — *adj* **1** 14 in number. **2** aged 14: *Her brother is fourteen*.

fowl /faʊl/ *n* a bird, especially a hen, duck, goose *etc*: *He keeps fowls and a few pigs*.

fox /fɒks/ *n* a wild animal like a small dog, with red fur and a long bushy tail.

> A fox **barks**.
> A baby fox is a **cub**.
> A female fox is a **vixen**.
> A fox lives in an **earth**.

foyer /ˈfɔɪeɪ/ or /ˈfɔɪə(r)/ *n* a large entrance hall to a theatre, hotel *etc*.

> See **lobby**.

fraction /ˈfrakʃən/ *n* a part; an amount that is not a whole number, for example $\frac{1}{2}$, $\frac{1}{3}$, $\frac{1}{4}$, *etc*. ˈ**fractional** *adj*.
ˈ**fractionally** *adv* slightly: *This brand is fractionally better*.

fracture /ˈfraktʃə(r)/ *n* a break in a hard substance, especially a bone. — *v* to break: *He fractured his leg in the accident*.

fragile /ˈfradʒaɪl/ *adj* easily broken: *a fragile glass vase*. **fraˈgility** *n*.

fragment /ˈfragmənt/ *n* **1** a broken piece; a bit: *The floor was covered with fragments of glass*. **2** something that is not complete: *a* *fragment of poetry.* **'fragmentary** *adj.*

fragrant /'freɪgrənt/ *adj* having a sweet smell: *fragrant flowers.* **'fragrance** *n.*

frail /freɪl/ *adj* weak, especially in health: *a frail old lady.* **'frailty** *n.*

frame /freɪm/ *n* **1** a hard main structure round which something is built or made: *the steel frame of the aircraft.* **2** something that forms a border or edge: *a picture-frame; a windowframe.* **3** the body: *He has a small frame.* — *v* **1** to put a frame around something: *to frame a picture.* **2** to act as a frame for something: *Her hair framed her face.* **3** to arrange things dishonestly so that an innocent person appears to be guilty of a crime: *He said that he had been framed by his enemies.*

'framework *n* the basic supporting structure of anything: *The building will be made of concrete on a steel framework.*

frame of mind a state of mind; a mood: *He is in a strange frame of mind.*

frank /fraŋk/ *adj* saying or showing openly what is in your mind; honest: *a frank person; a frank reply.* — *v* to mark a letter by machine to show that postage has been paid. **'frankly** *adv.* **'frankness** *n.*

frantic /'frantɪk/ *adj* very upset or excited, because of worry, pain *etc*: *His mother became frantic when he did not return home.* **'frantically** *adv.*

fraternity /frə'tɜːnɪtɪ/ *n* **1** brotherhood; a community or society of men, for example monks. **2** people with the same job *etc*: *the medical fraternity.*

'fraternize *v* to meet together as friends: *The townspeople did not fraternize with the soldiers living on the nearby army base.*

fraud /frɔːd/ *n* **1** dishonest behaviour, especially in business: *He was sent to prison for fraud.* **2** a person who pretends to be something that they are not: *He said he was a famous doctor, but he was just a fraud.* **'fraudulent** *adj.* **'fraudulence** *n.*

fray /freɪ/ *v* to become worn at the ends or edges, so that the threads or strands come loose: *If you don't sew a hem on this cloth, it will fray; The rope frayed and broke where it had been rubbing against the rock; When you get angry and lose your temper, people say that your temper is fraying.*

frayed *adj*: *He was wearing a pair of frayed old jeans.*

freak /friːk/ *n* a very unusual event, person or thing: *A storm as bad as that one is a freak of nature.*

freckle /'frɛkəl/ *n* a small brown spot on the skin: *In summer her face was always covered with freckles.* **'freckled** *adj.*

free /friː/ *adj* **1** allowed to move where you want; not shut in, tied, fastened *etc*: *The prison door opened, and out he went — a free man at last; One end of the string was tied to the handle — the other end was left free.* **2** not forced or persuaded to act, speak *etc* in a particular way: *You are free to do what you like.* **3** generous: *He is always free with his money.* **4** frank, open, saying what you really think: *a frank and free discussion; free speech.* **5** costing nothing: *a free gift.* **6** not working; not busy: *I shall be free at five o'clock.* **7** not occupied; not engaged: *Is this seat free?* **8** without: *She is free from pain now.* — *adv* without payment: *We were allowed into the circus free; We shall mend the tyre free of charge.* — *v* to set someone free: *He freed all the prisoners.*

'freedom *n* not being under control; being able to do whatever you want: *The prisoner was given his freedom; She had hoped for a new freedom, but had found a trap.*

'freehand *adj* done by hand without the help of an instrument such as a ruler: *a freehand drawing.* — *adv.*

'freelance *adj* working on your own; not employed by a firm *etc*: *He is a freelance journalist.*

'freely *adv* **1** generously: *Give freely to charity.* **2** openly, frankly: *You can speak freely to a friend.* **3** willingly: *I freely admit I was wrong.*

free-'range *adj* produced by hens and animals that are allowed to move about freely: *free-range eggs.*

free and easy informal and casual: *Their attitude to discipline was very free and easy.*

free kick a kick in football allowed to a player of one team after a member of the other team has broken a rule.

free speech the right to express an opinion freely: *All citizens should have a right to free speech.*

free will the ability to choose and act freely: *He did it of his own free will.*

-free /friː/ *suffix* free from, not having or troubled by: *You can buy duty-free goods at the airport; tax-free.*

freeze /friːz/ *v* **1** to become ice: *It's so cold that the river has frozen over.* **2** to be at or below freezing-point: *If it freezes again tonight, all my plants will die.* **3** to make food very cold in order to preserve it: *You*

freight

can freeze the rest of that food and eat it later. **4** to make or become stiff or unable to move with cold, fear *etc*: *She froze when she heard the strange noise.* **5** to fix prices, wages *etc* at a certain level. — *n* a period of very cold weather when temperatures are below freezing-point: *How long do you think the freeze will last?*

> **freeze; froze** /froʊz/; **frozen** /ˈfroʊzən/: *The water froze in the tank; The lake has frozen over.*

'freezer *n* a cabinet for freezing food or keeping it frozen.

'freezing *adj* very cold: *This room's freezing.*

'freezing-point *n* the temperature at which water *etc* becomes ice.

freight /freɪt/ *n* the transport of goods: *air-freight.*

'freighter *n* a ship that carries goods rather than passengers.

French /frɛntʃ/ *adj* belonging to France. — *n* the language of France.

frenzy /ˈfrɛnzɪ/ *n* great excitement or anxiety. **'frenzied** *adj.*

frequency /ˈfriːkwənsɪ/ *n* **1** the occurrence of something often: *The teacher was surprised at the frequency of this mistake in the children's work.* **2** the rate at which something happens or is repeated. **3** in radio *etc*, the number of waves *etc* occurring per second. **4** the number of radio waves per second at which a radio station broadcasts.

frequent *adj* /ˈfriːkwənt/ happening often: *He makes frequent journeys to Britain.* — *v* /frɪˈkwɛnt/ to visit a place often: *This jungle used to be frequented by tigers.*

'frequently *adv* often: *He frequently arrived late.*

> The opposite of the adjective **frequent** *adj* is **infrequent**.

fresh /frɛʃ/ *adj* **1** newly made, gathered *etc*: *fresh bread; fresh fruit; fresh flowers.* **2** not tired: *You are looking very fresh this morning.* **3** new; not already used, worn, heard *etc*: *a fresh piece of paper; fresh news.* **4** cool; refreshing: *a fresh breeze; fresh air.* **5** without salt: *The swimming-pool has fresh water in it, not sea water.*

'freshen *v* **1** to make or become fresh: *A cool drink will freshen you up.* **2** to become strong: *The wind began to freshen.*

'freshly *adv* newly; recently: *freshly gathered grapes.* **'freshness** *n.*

'freshwater *adj* belonging to inland rivers or lakes, not to the sea: *freshwater fish.*

fret /frɛt/ *v* to worry or be unhappy: *The dog frets whenever its master goes away.* **'fretful** *adj.*

friction /ˈfrɪkʃən/ *n* **1** the rubbing together of two things: *The friction between the head of the match and the matchbox causes a spark.* **2** quarrelling; disagreement: *There seems to be some friction between the workmen and their manager.*

Friday /ˈfraɪdɪ/ *n* the sixth day of the week; the day following Thursday.

fridge /frɪdʒ/ *n* short for **refrigerator**.

friend /frɛnd/ *n* someone you know well and like: *He is my best friend.* **'friendship** *n.*

'friendless *adj* without friends.

'friendly *adj* kind: *She is very friendly to everybody.*

make friends with to become the friend of someone: *She tried to make friends with the new neighbours.*

frieze /friːz/ *n* a narrow strip with a decorative pattern, that is put round the wall of a room or building, usually near the top.

fright /fraɪt/ *n* a sudden feeling of fear: *The noise gave me a terrible fright.*

'frighten *v* to make someone afraid: *The large dog frightened the boy.* **'frightened** *adj.* **'frightening** *adj.*

> See **afraid**.

'frightful *adj* terrible; frightening: *a frightful experience.* **'frightfully** *adv.*

take fright to become frightened: *She took fright when she saw the lion, and ran away.*

frill /frɪl/ *n* a narrow strip of cloth that has been pulled up into folds along one side and sewn on a dress, skirt *etc* as a decoration. **'frilly** *adj* decorated with frills: *The little girl was wearing a frilly pink dress.*

fringe /frɪndʒ/ *n* **1** a border of loose threads on a carpet, shawl *etc*. **2** hair cut to hang over the forehead: *You should have your fringe cut before it covers your eyes.* **3** the outer area; the edge: *on the fringe of the city.* — *v* to make or be a border around something: *Trees fringed the pond.*

> See **plait**.

frisk /frɪsk/ *v* **1** to jump about playfully: *The lambs are frisking in the fields.* **2** to search somebody's body to check that they are not hiding a weapon *etc*: *We were frisked at the airport.* **'frisky** *adj.*

fritter /ˈfrɪtə(r)/: **fritter away** *v* to waste something gradually: *He frittered away his money* on computer games; *She frittered away her time watching television.*

frivolous /ˈfrɪvələs/ *adj* not sensible; silly: *Why don't you spend your money on serious things like books, instead of frivolous things like toys?* **friˈvolity** *n*.

frizzy /ˈfrɪzɪ/ *adj* in very small curls: *frizzy hair.*

frock /frɒk/ *n* a woman's or girl's dress: *a cotton frock.*

frog /frɒg/ *n* a small jumping animal, without a tail, that lives on land and in water.

> A frog **croaks**.
> A baby frog is a **tadpole**.

ˈfrogman *n* an underwater swimmer who uses breathing apparatus and flippers.

frolic /ˈfrɒlɪk/ *v* to play happily: *The puppies frolicked in the garden.*

from /frɒm/ or /frəm/ *prep* **1** used in giving a starting-point: *to travel from Europe to Asia; The office is open from Monday to Friday; a letter from her father.* **2** used to show separation: *Take it from him; She took a book from the shelf.* **3** used to show a cause or reason: *He is suffering from a cold.* **4** used to show the material with which something is made: *Paper is made from trees.*

front /frʌnt/ *n* **1** the part of anything that you see first, or is most important: *the front of the house.* **2** the part of a vehicle *etc* that faces the direction in which it moves: *the front of the ship.* **3** in a war *etc*, the place where the fighting is: *They are sending more soldiers to the front.* — *adj* at the front: *the front page of a book; the front seat of a bus.* **ˈfrontal** *adj* from the front: *a frontal attack.*

at the front of in the front part of something: *They stood at the front of the crowd.*

in front further forward than others; ahead of others: *He stayed in front throughout the race.*

in front of 1 outside something on its front or forward-facing side: *There is a garden in front of the house.* **2** in the presence of: *Please don't say that in front of my parents.*

frontier /ˈfrʌntɪə(r)/ *n* a boundary between countries: *We crossed the frontier between Germany and France.* — *adj*: *a frontier town.*

frost /frɒst/ *n* **1** a thin, white layer of frozen dew, vapour *etc*: *The ground was covered with frost this morning.* **2** the coldness of weather needed to form ice: *There'll be frost tomorrow.* — *v* to become covered with frost: *The windscreen of my car frosted up last night.* **ˈfrosty** *adj*.

ˈfrostbite *n* injury caused to the body by freezing: *He was suffering from frostbite in his feet.* **ˈfrostbitten** *adj*.

froth /frɒθ/ *n* a mass of small bubbles on the top of a liquid *etc*: *Some types of beer have more froth than others.* — *v* to produce froth: *The sea frothed and foamed over the rocks.* **ˈfrothy** *adj*.

frown /fraʊn/ *v* to draw your eyebrows together and wrinkle your forehead, because of worry, anger, being puzzled *etc*: *He frowned at her bad behaviour.* — *n* a frowning expression: *a frown of anger.*

frown on or **frown upon** to disapprove of: *Smoking is frowned upon in the staffroom.*

froze *see* **freeze**.

frozen /ˈfrəʊzən/ *adj* **1** below freezing point; turned to ice; covered with ice: *frozen foods; a frozen river.* **2** very cold: *Your hands are frozen.* See also the verb **freeze**.

frugal /ˈfruːgəl/ *adj* **1** preferring to save money rather than spend it: *Her parents taught her to be frugal with her money.* **2** not costing very much: *We had a frugal meal of bread and cheese.* **fruˈgality** *n*. **ˈfrugally** *adv*.

fruit /fruːt/ *n* the part of a plant that contains seeds, and can sometimes be eaten: *Is the fruit of this tree safe to eat?; Apples, bananas and strawberries are my favourite fruits.*

> **fruit** is singular: *Fruit is good for you; The tree bears fruit* (not *fruits*).
> The plural **fruits** is used in talking about different types of fruit: *oranges, mangoes and other fruits.*

ˈfruitful *adj* producing good results: *a fruitful discussion.*

ˈfruitless *adj* useless; not successful: *a fruitless attempt.*

ˈfruity *adj* like fruit: *a fruity taste.*

frustrate /frʌˈstreɪt/ *v* to make someone or something fail: *His efforts were frustrated; We were frustrated in our attempt to swim across the river.* **fruˈstration** *n*.

fruˈstrated *adj* disappointed; not satisfied: *She is unhappy and frustrated in her job.*

fruˈstrating *adj* making you angry and dissatisfied.

fry /fraɪ/ *v* to cook in hot oil or fat: *Shall I fry the eggs or boil them?*

> **fry; ˈfrying; fried** /fraɪd/; **fried**: *I'm frying an egg; He fried the fish; a plate of fried potatoes.*

ˈfrying-pan *n* a shallow pan, with a long handle, for frying food in.

fuel /ˈfjuːəl/ *n* any substance, such as petrol, oil, coal, by which a fire burns, or an engine *etc* is made to work: *The machine ran out of fuel.* — *v* to provide fuel for something.

fugitive /ˈfjuːdʒɪtɪv/ *n* a person who is running away from danger, from an enemy, from the police *etc*.

fulfil /fʊlˈfɪl/ *v* to carry out or perform a task, promise *etc*: *He fulfilled his promises.* **fulˈfilment** *n*.

fulˈfilled *adj* satisfied and happy: *With her career and family she's a very fulfilled person.*

fulˈfilling *adj* making you happy and satisfied: *Most people want a fulfilling job.*

> fulfil begins with ful- (not full-) and ends with -fil (not -fill); but note **fulfilled** and **fulfilling**.

full /fʊl/ *adj* **1** holding or containing as much as possible: *My basket is full.* **2** complete: *a full year; a full account of what happened.* **3** having had enough to eat or drink: *I am full.* **4** rounded or plump: *a full face.* **5** containing a large amount of material: *a full skirt.* — *adv* **1** completely: *Fill the petrol tank full.* **2** exactly; directly: *She hit him full in the face.*

ˈfull-length *adj* **1** showing your whole body: *a full-length mirror; a full-length portrait.* **2** not shorter than normal: *a full-length film.*

full moon the moon when it appears at its most complete: *There is a full moon tonight.*

ˈfull-scale *adj* **1** the same size as the subject: *a full-scale model.* **2** using every means available: *a full-scale police investigation.*

full stop a point (.) marking the end of a sentence.

ˈfull-time *adj* occupying someone's working time completely: *a full-time job.* — *adv*: *She works full-time now.*

ˈfully *adv* **1** completely: *He was fully aware of what was happening; a fully-grown dog.* **2** at least: *It will take fully three days to finish the work.*

full of containing or holding a lot: *The bus was full of people.*

full of yourself talking a lot about yourself and your own importance.

in full completely: *Write your name in full; He paid his bill in full.*

to the full as much as possible: *to enjoy life to the full.*

fumble /ˈfʌmbəl/ *v* **1** to feel about clumsily with your hands: *She fumbled about in her bag for her key.* **2** to use your hands clumsily: *He fumbled with the key.*

fume /fjuːm/ *v* to be very angry: *He was fuming with rage.*

fumes *n* smoke; vapour: *He smelt the petrol fumes.*

fun /fʌn/ *n* enjoyment; a good time: *They had a lot of fun at the party; Isn't this fun!*

ˈfunfair *n* a collection of amusements, stalls and roundabouts *etc*: *They took their children to the funfair.*

for fun or **in fun** as a joke; for amusement: *The children threw stones for fun; I said it in fun.*

make fun of to laugh at someone, usually unkindly: *They made fun of her strange clothes; They made fun of him for working so hard at school.*

function /ˈfʌŋkʃən/ *n* **1** a special job of a machine, part of the body *etc*: *The function of the brake is to stop the car.* **2** an important social event: *The prince attends many different functions every month.* — *v* to work: *This typewriter isn't functioning very well.* **ˈfunctional** *adj*.

fund /fʌnd/ *n* **1** a sum of money for a special purpose: *Have you given money to the repair fund for the school?* **2** a supply: *He has a fund of funny stories.* — *v*.

fundamental /fʌndəˈmentəl/ *adj* very important; basic: *Being interested in the subject is fundamental to learning it well.* — *n* a basic part of anything: *Learning to read is one of the fundamentals of education.* **fundaˈmentally** *adv*.

funeral /ˈfjuːnərəl/ *n* the ceremony before the burying of a dead body: *A large number of people attended the funeral.*

fungus /ˈfʌŋgəs/, plural **fungi** /ˈfʌŋgaɪ/ or /ˈfʌndʒaɪ/, *n* the class of plants to which mushrooms belong: *edible fungi; That tree has a fungus growing on it.*

funnel /ˈfʌnəl/ *n* a tube with a wide opening through which liquid can be poured into a narrow bottle *etc*.

funny /ˈfʌnɪ/ *adj* **1** amusing; making you laugh: *a funny story.* **2** strange: *I heard a funny noise.* **ˈfunnily** *adv*.

fur /fɜː(r)/ *n* **1** the short, fine hair of certain animals. **2** the skin of these animals, often used to make clothes *etc* for people: *a hat made of fur.* **3** a coat, cape *etc* made of fur: *She was wearing her fur.* — *adj*: *a fur jacket.*

furious /ˈfjʊərɪəs/ *adj* **1** very angry: *She was furious with him.* **2** violent: *a furious argument.* **ˈfuriously** *adv*.

furl /fɜːl/ *v* to roll up a flag, sail or umbrella.

furnace /ˈfɜːnɪs/ *n* a very hot oven or closed

chimney

funnel

chimney

fireplace for melting metals, making steam for heating *etc*.

furnish /'fɜːnɪʃ/ *v* to provide a house *etc* with furniture: *We spent a lot of money on furnishing our house.*
'furnished *adj* supplied with furniture.
'furnishings *n* furniture, equipment *etc*: *The office had very expensive furnishings.*
furniture /'fɜːnɪtʃə(r)/ *n* things in a house *etc* such as tables, chairs, beds *etc*: *modern furniture.*

furniture is never used in the plural.

furrow /'fʌroʊ/ *n* **1** a line cut into the earth by a plough. **2** a line in the skin of the face; a wrinkle: *The furrows in her forehead made her look older.* — *v* to make furrows in something: *Her face was furrowed with worry.*
furry /'fɜːrɪ/ *adj* **1** covered with fur: *a furry animal.* **2** like fur: *furry material.*
further /'fɜːðə(r)/ *adv* **1** at or to a greater distance; more: *I cannot go any further.* **2** more; in addition: *I cannot explain further.* — *adj* more: *There is no further news.* — *v* to help something to go forward quickly: *He furthered our plans.*

See **far**

further'more *adv* in addition.
'furthest *adv* at or to the greatest distance or extent: *Who lives furthest away?*
furtive /'fɜːtɪv/ *adj* done secretly; avoiding attention: *a furtive action*; *a furtive look.*
'furtively *adv.*
fury /'fjʊərɪ/ *n* a very great anger; rage: *She was in a terrible fury.*
fuse[1] /fjuːz/ *v* **1** to melt together as a result of a great heat: *Copper and tin fuse together to make bronze.* **2** to stop working because of the melting of a fuse: *Suddenly all the lights fused.* — *n* a piece of easily-melted wire included in an electric circuit for safety.
fuse[2] /fjuːz/ *n* a device that makes a bomb *etc* explode at a particular time.
fuselage /'fjuːzəlɑːʒ/ *n* the main body of an aircraft: *The fuselage broke in two when the aircraft crashed.*
fusion /'fjuːʒən/ *n* the uniting of different things into one: *fusion of metals.*
fuss /fʌs/ *n* unnecessary excitement, worry or activity, often about something unimportant: *Don't make such a fuss.* — *v* to worry too much: *She fusses over the children.*
'fussy *adj* too concerned with details; difficult to satisfy: *He'll make you do it all over again if you make a mistake — he's very fussy*; *She is very fussy about her food.*
kick up a fuss or **make a fuss** to complain: *She kicked up a fuss when the airline lost her luggage during a flight.*
make a fuss of to pay a lot of attention to someone or something: *He always makes a fuss of his grandchildren.*
futile /'fjuːtaɪl/ *adj* useless; having no effect: *a futile attempt.* **fu'tility** *n.*
future /'fjuːtʃə(r)/ *n* **1** the time to come: *He was afraid of what the future might bring.* **2** the future tense: *'I shall go' is the future of 'I go'.* — *adj* happening *etc* at a later time; belonging to a later time: *his future wife.*
in future *adv* from now on: *Don't do that again in future.*
fuzz /fʌz/ *n* a mass of soft, light material such as fine light hair *etc*.
'fuzzy *adj* **1** covered with fuzz. **2** not clear: *The television picture was fuzzy.*

G

gabble /ˈgabəl/ v to talk very quickly and not very clearly. — n fast talk.

gad about to go from place to place looking for fun or entertainment: *He spends his weekends gadding about.*

gadget /ˈgadʒɪt/ n a small tool, machine *etc*.

gag /gag/ v to prevent someone from talking or making a noise by putting something in or over their mouth: *The guards tied up and gagged the prisoners.* — n something that is used to gag a person.

gaiety /ˈgeɪəti/ n the feeling of being gay and cheerful; merriment: *The New Year is a time of gaiety.*

gaily /ˈgeɪli/ adv in a gay, cheerful manner: *She walked gaily along; gaily decorated streets.*

gain /geɪn/ v 1 to get something good by doing something: *What have I to gain by staying here?* 2 to have an increase in something: *He gained strength after his illness.* 3 to go too fast: *This clock gains four minutes a day.* — n 1 an increase in weight *etc*: *a gain of one kilo.* 2 advantage, wealth *etc*: *His loss was my gain; He'd do anything for gain.*

> The opposite of **to gain** is **to lose**.
> The opposite of **a gain** is **a loss**.

gain ground to make progress.

gain on to get or come closer to someone that you are pursuing: *Drive faster — the police car is gaining on us.*

gala /ˈgɑːlə/ n 1 an occasion of entertainment and enjoyment out of doors: *a children's gala.* 2 a meeting for certain sports: *a swimming gala.*

galaxy /ˈgaləksɪ/ n a very large group of stars.

gale /geɪl/ n a strong wind: *Many trees were blown down in the gale.*

> See **wind**.

gallant /ˈgalənt/ adj brave: *a gallant soldier.* **ˈgallantly** adv. **ˈgallantry** n.

gallery /ˈgalərɪ/ n 1 a large room or building in which paintings, statues *etc* are on show: *an art gallery.* 2 the top floor of seats in a theatre.

gallon /ˈgalən/ n a measure for liquids; eight pints (in Britain, 4·5 litres; in the US, 3·8 litres).

gallop /ˈgaləp/ n the fastest pace of a horse: *The horse went off at a gallop.* — v 1 to move at a gallop: *The horse galloped round the field.* 2 to do something very quickly: *He galloped through the work.*

gallows /ˈgaloʊz/ n a wooden frame from which criminals were once hanged.

galore /gəˈlɔː(r)/ adv in plenty: *food galore.*

gamble /ˈgambəl/ v 1 to play games of chance for money: *He made a living by gambling.* 2 to risk money on the result of a game, race *etc*: *I like to gamble on a horse race occasionally.* — n something which involves a risk: *The plan was a bit of a gamble.* **ˈgambler** n. **ˈgambling** n.

take a gamble to do something risky in the hope that it will succeed.

game /geɪm/ n 1 an enjoyable activity, *esp* one for children: *a game of pretending.* 2 a competitive form of activity, with rules: *Football, tennis and chess are games.* 3 a match or part of a match: *a game of tennis; He won by three games to one.* 4 certain birds and animals that are hunted for sport. — adj willing; ready: *Those little kids are game for anything.*

ˈgamekeeper n a person who looks after wild birds and animals for the owner of the land on which they are kept for shooting or hunting: *The gamekeeper caught the poacher who had been shooting the young pheasants.*

game reserve an area of land set aside for the protection of animals.

games n an athletic competition: *the Olympic Games.*

give the game away to tell a person something that should have been kept secret: *He said he hadn't been out, but his muddy shoes gave the game away.*

the game is up the plan or trick has failed or has been found out.

gander /ˈgandə(r)/ n a male goose.

gang /gaŋ/ n 1 a number of workmen *etc* working together. 2 a group of people, usually formed for a bad purpose: *a gang of jewel thieves.*

gang up on someone to join with others against someone: *He complained that the other children were always ganging up on him.*

gangling /ˈgaŋglɪŋ/ adj very tall and thin.

gangplank /ˈgaŋplaŋk/ n a gangway for getting on to or off a ship.

gangrene /ˈgaŋgriːn/ n the decay of tissue on

part of the body caused by the blood not flowing to it: *If frostbite isn't treated it can lead to gangrene.* **'gangrenous** *adj.*

gangster /'gaŋstə(r)/ *n* a member of a gang of criminals.

gangway /'gaŋweɪ/ *n* **1** a passage between rows of seats. **2** a movable bridge by which to get on or off a ship.

gaol /dʒeɪl/, **gaoler** /'dʒeɪlə(r)/ different spellings of **jail**, **jailer**.

> to put a criminal in **gaol** (not **goal**).

gap /gap/ *n* an open space: *a gap between his teeth.*

gape /geɪp/ *v* to stare at something with your mouth open in wonder *etc*: *The children gaped at the monkeys.*
'gaping *adj* wide open: *a gaping hole.*

garage /'garɑːʒ/ or /'garɪdʒ/ *n* **1** a building in which a car *etc* is kept: *a house with a garage.* **2** a building where cars are repaired, and petrol, oil *etc* is sold: *He has taken his car to the garage to be repaired.*

garbage /'gɑːbɪdʒ/ *n* rubbish.
garbage can a dustbin.

garbled /'gɑːbəld/ *adj* confused; unclear: *a garbled message.*

garden /'gɑːdən/ *n* a piece of ground on which flowers, vegetables *etc* are grown: *a garden at the front of the house.* — *v* to work in a garden, usually as a hobby: *The old lady does not garden much nowadays.*
'gardener *n* a person who works in, and looks after, a garden.
'gardening *n* the work of looking after a garden: *Gardening is his favourite hobby.*
'gardens *n* a park: *We went for a walk in the public gardens.*
garden party a large party held in the garden of a house *etc*.

gargle /'gɑːgəl/ *v* to wash your throat with a soothing liquid without swallowing it, when you have a sore throat *etc*.

garish /'geərɪʃ/ *adj* unpleasantly bright: *garish colours.*

garland /'gɑːlənd/ *n* flowers or leaves tied together so that they form a ring: *She made a garland to go round his neck.*

garlic /'gɑːlɪk/ *n* a plant with a bulb shaped like an onion, that has a strong taste and smell and is used in cooking.

garment /'gɑːmənt/ *n* any article of clothing: *pullovers, trousers and other garments.*

garnish /'gɑːnɪʃ/ *v* to decorate food: *The cook garnished the fried fish with lemon slices and parsley.* — *n* something that is used to decorate food: *She used tomato slices as a garnish for the chicken dish.*

garrison /'garɪsən/ *n* a number of soldiers guarding a fortress, town *etc*.

gas /gas/ *n* **1** a substance like air: *Oxygen is a gas.* **2** a substance of this sort used as a fuel for heating, cooking *etc* or as a weapon: *Do you cook by electricity or gas?*; *The police used tear gas to chase away the angry crowds.* **3** petrol. — *v* to poison or kill someone with gas.

gas mask a device that covers your mouth and nose and prevents you breathing poisonous gas.

gas meter a device that measures the amount of gas that has been used as fuel.

gash /gaʃ/ *n* a long deep cut: *The sword had made a gash in his leg.* — *v*: *His upper arm was badly gashed.*

gasoline /'gasəliːn/ *n* petrol.

gasp /gɑːsp/ *n* the sound made by suddenly breathing in, because of surprise, sudden pain *etc*: *a gasp of fear.* — *v* to take a sudden sharp breath: *He gasped with pain*; *He was gasping for breath after running so hard*; *The news left them gasping with astonishment.*

gastric /'gastrɪk/ *adj* having to do with the stomach.

gasworks /'gaswɜːks/ *n* a place where gas is made.

gate /geɪt/ *n* a device like a door for closing the opening in a wall, fence *etc* that people *etc* go through: *Close the gate after you, so that the cattle do not escape on to the road*; *The park gates were locked.*
'gate-crash *v* to go to a party *etc* without being invited. **'gate-crasher** *n*.
'gate-post *n* a post to which a gate is fixed.
'gateway *n* an opening that contains a gate; an entrance.

> See **archway**.

gather /'gaðə(r)/ *v* **1** to bring or come together in one place: *A crowd of people gathered near the accident*; *Gather round and hear the news!*; *Gather your books together now, please.* **2** to learn from what you have seen, heard *etc*: *I gather you are leaving tomorrow.* **3** to collect; to pick: *She gathered flowers.*
'gathering *n* a meeting of people: *a family gathering.*

gaudy /'gɔːdɪ/ *adj* very bright; too bright: *gaudy colours.*

gauge /geɪdʒ/ *v* **1** to measure something accurately: *They gauged the hours of sunshine.* **2**

gaunt

to estimate, judge: *It is difficult to gauge how much wine we shall need.* — *n* an instrument for measuring amount, size, speed *etc*: *a petrol gauge.*

gaunt /gɔːnt/ *adj* thin and bony in appearance: *a gaunt old woman*; *He grew more and more gaunt as his illness got worse.* **'gauntness** *n.*

gauze /gɔːz/ *n* a thin cloth, often used to cover wounds.

gave *see* **give**.

gay /geɪ/ *adj* **1** happy: *The children were gay and cheerful*; *gay music*. **2** bright: *gay colours*. **3** sexually attracted to people of the same sex as yourself; homosexual: *He is gay.* — *n* a person, especially a man, who is homosexual.

> The noun from **gay** is **gaiety**; the adverb is **gaily**.

gaze /geɪz/ *v* to look steadily for some time: *She gazed at the strange animal in amazement.* — *n* a long steady look.

gazelle /gəˈzɛl/ *n* a nimble animal of the goat family.

gear /gɪə(r)/ *n* **1** a set of toothed wheels that make the connection between the engine and the wheels of a car *etc*: *The car is in first gear.* **2** the things needed for a particular job, sport *etc*: *sports gear.*

geese the plural of **goose**.

gel /dʒɛl/ *n* a jelly-like substance that is between a liquid and a solid: *a jar of hair gel.*

gelatine /ˈdʒɛlətiːn/ *n* a clear, tasteless substance that is made by boiling animal bones and skins and is used to make liquids become firm: *The jelly wouldn't set as she hadn't used enough gelatine.*

gem /dʒɛm/ *n* **1** a precious stone, especially one that is cut into a particular shape, for a ring, necklace *etc*. **2** anything or anyone that is especially good: *This picture is the gem of my collection.*

gender /ˈdʒɛndə(r)/ *n* either of the classes masculine or feminine.

gene /dʒiːn/ *n* a tiny part of a cell in a person, animal or plant that is responsible for the way they look, their growth or development, and is passed on from parents to their children.

genealogy /dʒiːnɪˈalədʒɪ/ *n* **1** the study of the history of families: *This book is an introduction to the subject of genealogy.* **2** the history of a particular family, usually shown by a diagram: *She has been trying to trace her family's genealogy for years.* **geneˈalogist** *n.*

general /ˈdʒɛnərəl/ *adj* **1** having to do with, or affecting all or most people *etc*: *There was a general expectation among the pupils that Marion would win first prize.* **2** covering a large number of cases: *Children start school at the age of five, as a general rule.* **3** without details; rough: *I'll just give you a general idea of the plan.* — *n* an army officer of a very high rank.

'generally *adv* usually: *He generally wins at chess.*

general election an election in which the voters in all parts of the country elect members of parliament.

general knowledge knowledge about very many different subjects.

in general usually; in most cases: *In general we found the people of Britain helpful and friendly when we went on holiday there.*

'generalize *v* to talk in general terms and without details: *It's time we stopped generalizing and discussed each case separately.*

generaliˈzation *n* a statement or rule that is true in most cases: *This book is full of generalizations and very little detail.*

generate /ˈdʒɛnəreɪt/ *v* to produce: *This machine generates electricity*; *His silly remarks generated a lot of trouble.*

geneˈration *n* **1** the generating of something: *the generation of electricity.* **2** one stage in the descent of a family: *All three generations — children, parents and grandparents — lived together quite happily.* **3** people who are about the same age: *People of my generation all think the same way about this.*

'generator *n* a machine that produces electricity, gas *etc*.

generous /ˈdʒɛnərəs/ *adj* **1** giving willingly; kind: *It is very generous of you to pay for our holiday*; *He was given a bicycle by a generous uncle.* **2** large; larger than necessary: *a generous sum of money*; *a generous piece of cake.* **'generously** *adv.* **geneˈrosity** *n.*

genetic /dʒəˈnɛtɪk/ *adj* having to do with genes.

geˈnetically *adv*: *Some diseases can be passed on genetically from parents to children.*

genial /ˈdʒiːnɪəl/ *adj* friendly; good-natured: *a genial person.*

genitals /ˈdʒɛnɪtəlz/ *n plural* the external

organs of the body concerned with the production of babies.

genius /'dʒiːnɪəs/ *n* a person who is very clever.

gents /dʒɛnts/ *n* short for **gentlemen**, a public toilet for men.

gentle /'dʒɛntəl/ *adj* **1** behaving, talking *etc* in a kind, pleasant way: *a gentle old lady*; *The doctor was very gentle*. **2** not strong or rough: *a gentle breeze*. **3** rising gradually: *a gentle slope*. **'gentleness** *n*. **'gently** *adv*.

gentleman /'dʒɛntəlmən/, *plural* **'gentlemen**, *n* **1** a polite word for a man: *Two gentlemen arrived this morning*. **2** a polite, well-mannered man: *He's a real gentleman*. **'gentlemanly** *adj*.

genuine /'dʒɛnjʊɪn/ *adj* **1** real; not fake: *a genuine pearl*. **2** honest; sincere: *She has a genuine concern for other people's happiness*. **'genuinely** *adv*.

geography /dʒɪ'ɒgrəfɪ/ *n* the science that describes the surface of the Earth and its inhabitants. **ge'ographer** *n*. **geo'graphical** *adj*.

geology /dʒɪ'ɒlədʒɪ/ *n* the study of the earth's structure and how it developed to what it is today: *She is very interested in geology*. **geo'logical** *adj*. **ge'ologist** *n*.

geometry /dʒɪ'ɒmətrɪ/ *n* a branch of mathematics dealing with the study of lines, angles *etc*.
geo'metric or **geo'metrical** *adj* made up of lines, circles *etc*; having a regular shape: *geometrical designs*.

geriatric /dʒɛrɪ'atrɪk/ *adj* to do with old people and their illnesses: *a geriatric hospital*.

germ /dʒɜːm/ *n* an extremely tiny live thing that causes diseases: *You should stay at home when you have a cold, so that you don't pass your germs on to other people*.

germinate /'dʒɜːmɪneɪt/ *v* to make seeds grow; to begin to grow. **germi'nation** *n*.

gesture /'dʒɛstʃə(r)/ *n* **1** a movement of your head, hand *etc* to express an idea, *etc*: *The speaker emphasized his words with violent gestures*. **2** something you do to show your feelings: *He sent her a Christmas card as a gesture of friendship*. — *v*: *She gestured to me that I should not say any more*; *I gestured him to sit down*.

get /gɛt/ *v* **1** to receive; to obtain: *I got a letter this morning*. **2** to bring; to buy: *Please get me some food*. **3** to move, go, take, put *etc*: *He couldn't get across the river*; *I got the book down from the shelf*. **4** to bring someone or something into a particular state: *I got the work finished*; *You'll get me into trouble*. **5** to become: *You're getting old*; *She got very wet in the rain*. **6** to persuade or ask someone: *I'll try and get my aunt to lend us the money*; *Get an electrician to mend that lamp*. **7** to arrive: *When did they get home?* **8** to catch a disease *etc*: *She got measles last week*. **9** to catch someone: *The police will soon get the thief*. **10** to understand: *I didn't get the joke*. **11** used with the verb **have** to mean the same as **have**: *I've got blue eyes*.

> **get; got** /gɒt/; **got**: *She got a new dress*; *He has got what he always wanted*.

get about or **get around 1** to become well known: *The story got about that she was leaving*. **2** to be able to move or travel about: *The old lady doesn't get about much nowadays*.

get across to make something understood: *The teacher is good at getting the subject across to the pupils*.

get ahead to be successful: *If you want to get ahead, you must work hard*.

get along to be friendly with someone: *I get along very well with him*.

get around *see* **get about**.

get at 1 to reach a place, thing *etc*: *The farm is very difficult to get at*. **2** to mean: *What are you getting at?* **3** to point out a person's faults: *He's always getting at me*.

get away to escape: *The thieves got away in the stolen car*. **'getaway** *n*.

get away with something to do something bad without being punished for it.

get back 1 to move away: *The policeman told the crowd to get back*. **2** to receive again: *She eventually got back the book she had lent him*.

get back to to return to a previous job or state *etc*: *She got back to work after lunch*.

get by to manage: *I can't get by on such a small salary*.

get down to something to concentrate on something: *I must get down to work tonight*.

get in 1 to arrive: *What time does the train from Glasgow get in?* **2** to be elected: *Which party do you think will get in at the next election?* **3** to bring in, collect or harvest: *She got the washing in when it started to rain*. **4** to manage to say or do: *They were arguing so loudly I couldn't get a word in*.

get into 1 to put on clothes or shoes: *Get into your pyjamas*. **2** to begin to be in a particular state or behave in a particular way: *He got into a temper; What's got into her?*

get nowhere to make no progress: *You'll get nowhere if you don't try hard.*

get off 1 to take off clothes or shoes: *I can't get my boots off.* **2** to remove stains *etc*: *I'll never get this mark off my dress.* **3** to step out of a vehicle: *He got off the train at George Town.* **4** to receive little or no punishment for doing something wrong: *He got off lightly with an official warning.*

get on 1 to progress; to be successful: *How are you getting on in your new job?* **2** to work, live *etc* in a friendly way: *We get on very well together; I get on well with him.* **3** to grow old: *Our doctor is getting on a bit now.* **4** to put clothes *etc* on: *Go and get your coat on.* **5** to continue doing something: *I must get on with my work.* **6** to climb onto a bus, train, bicycle or horse: *Several people got on our bus at the next stop; He fell off the bike almost immediately after getting on.*

get out 1 to escape: *No-one knows how the lion got out.* **2** to become known: *News got out that she was leaving.*

get out of 1 to avoid doing something: *You can't get out of washing the dishes.* **2** to take off clothes: *He got out of his school uniform and into his jeans.* **3** to leave a vehicle and continue on foot: *He got out of the car and ran into the shop.*

get over to recover from an illness, disappointment, surprise *etc*: *I've got over my cold now; He's very disappointed, but he'll get over it.*

get over with to do something immediately rather than go on worrying about it: *I was glad to get my visit to the dentist over with.*

get round or **get around 1** to persuade someone to agree with you: *My father said I couldn't come out this evening but I managed to get round him.* **2** to find a way of avoiding or dealing successfully with a problem.

get round to to manage to do something: *I don't know when I'll get round to painting the door.*

get there to succeed: *There have been a lot of problems but we're getting there.*

get through 1 to finish work *etc*: *We got through a lot of jobs today.* **2** to pass a test *etc*: *He got through his exam easily.* **3** to contact someone: *I just can't get through to her on the telephone.* **4** to make someone understand or realize something: *I can't seem to get through to them how important this is.*

get together to meet: *We get together once a week.*

'get-together *n* a meeting.

get up 1 to get out of bed: *I got up at seven o'clock.* **2** to stand up: *He got up off the floor.*

get up to something to do something bad: *He's always getting up to mischief.*

geyser /'giːzə(r)/ *n* **1** an underground spring that produces hot water and steam. **2** a small gas or electric water heater in a bathroom, kitchen *etc*.

ghastly /'gɑːstlɪ/ *adj* **1** very bad: *a ghastly mistake.* **2** horrible; terrible: *a ghastly murder.* **ghastliness** *n*.

ghetto /'gɛtoʊ/, *plural* **'ghetto(e)s**, *n* a poor part of a city where a lot of people of a particular nationality or religion have come to live: *A lot of big cities have ghettoes.*

ghost /goʊst/ *n* the spirit of a dead person: *Do you believe in ghosts?*

'ghostly *adj* like a ghost: *a ghostly figure.*

GI /dʒiː 'aɪ/ *n* a soldier in the US army: *This bar is popular with GIs.*

giant /'dʒaɪənt/ *n* **1** a huge, frightening person in fairy tales *etc*. **2** a person or thing that is unusually large. — *adj* unusually large: *He caught a giant fish.*

'giantess *n* a female giant.

The opposite of a **giant** is a **dwarf**.

gibber /'dʒɪbə(r)/ *v* to make chattering noises: *Monkeys and apes gibber.*

'gibberish *n* fast talk or chatter which does not make sense: *His speech sounded like gibberish to me.*

gibbon /'gɪbən/ *n* an ape with long arms.

gibe /dʒaɪb/ another spelling of **jibe**.

giblets /'dʒɪbləts/ *n* the eatable parts from inside a chicken *etc* such as the heart and liver.

giddy /'gɪdɪ/ *adj* dizzy: *I was dancing round so fast that I felt giddy; a giddy feeling.* **'giddiness** *n*.

gift /gɪft/ *n* **1** something given; a present: *a birthday gift.* **2** a natural ability: *She has a gift for music.*

'gifted *adj* having great ability: *a gifted musician.*

gigantic /dʒaɪ'gæntɪk/ *adj* very large: *a gigantic wave.*

giggle /'gɪɡəl/ *n* to laugh in a silly way: *They couldn't stop giggling at the joke.* — *n* a laugh of this kind.

gill /gɪl/ *n* one of the openings on the side of a fish's head through which it breathes.

gilt /gɪlt/ *n* a thin layer of gold used to decorate something: *The book's title was marked in gilt on the cover.* — *adj* decorated with gilt: *a mirror with a gilt frame.*

gimmick /'gɪmɪk/ *n* something used to attract people's attention: *The tyre manufacturers were using an airship as an advertising gimmick.* **'gimmicky** *adj.*

gin /dʒɪn/ *n* an alcoholic drink made from grain.

ginger /'dʒɪndʒə(r)/ *n* a hot-tasting root that is used as a spice. — *adj* **1** flavoured with ginger: *a ginger biscuit.* **2** reddish-brown in colour: *a ginger cat.*

ginger ale, **ginger beer** a non-alcoholic drink flavoured with ginger.

'gingerbread *n* a cake flavoured with ginger.

gingerly /'dʒɪndʒəlɪ/ *adv* very gently and carefully: *He gingerly stood on his injured foot.*

ginseng /'dʒɪnseŋ/ *n* the root of a plant from North America, China and Korea which is used in medicine in some countries: *She takes ginseng in tablet form.*

gipsy /'dʒɪpsɪ/ another spelling of **gypsy**.

giraffe /dʒɪ'rɑːf/ *n* an African animal with a very long neck, long legs and spots.

> **giraffe** is spelt with one **r** and two **fs**.

girder /'gɜːdə(r)/ *n* a large beam of steel *etc*, used in the construction of buildings, bridges *etc*.

girdle /'gɜːdəl/ *n* **1** a narrow belt or cord for tying round the waist. **2** an elastic, tight-fitting undergarment for women, worn round the waist, hips and bottom, to make them look slimmer.

girl /gɜːl/ *n* **1** a female child. **2** a young woman.

'girlfriend *n* a female friend, especially a close female friend of a man or boy: *I don't like my son's girlfriend.*

'girlish *adj* like a girl.

Girl Guide a member of the Girl Guide Association, an organization for girls.

gist /dʒɪst/ *n* the main points of a story *etc*: *Just give me the gist of what he said.*

give /gɪv/ *v* **1** to hand over; to present as a gift; to present freely; to offer: *My aunt gave me a book for my birthday; They have given a lot of time and money to this project; Give me your opinion on this question.* **2** to produce something: *Cows give milk but horses do not.* **3** to do something for others to enjoy *etc*: *He gave a talk on his travels; Won't you give us a performance on the piano?* **4** to pay: *I gave £200 for this bicycle.* **5** to bend; to break: *We pushed hard against the door, and at last the lock gave.* **6** to organize some event *etc*: *We're giving a party next week.* **7** to perform some action; to make some noise: *She gave him a push; He gave a shout.*

> **give**; **gave** /geɪv/; **given** /'gɪvən/: *She gave him the key; Has he given her back the key?*

give-and-'take *n* a willingness to listen to and accept the views of other people: *We can easily settle this argument with a little give-and-take.*

'given *adj* **1** definitely stated: *to do a job in a given time.* **2** inclined to do something: *He's given to making silly remarks.* **3** taking something as a fact: *Given that x equals three, x plus two equals five.*

give away 1 to give something to others free: *I'm going to give some of my books away.* **2** to tell a secret: *He gave away our hiding-place.*

give back to return something: *She gave me back the book that she borrowed last week.*

give in 1 to stop fighting; to surrender: *The soldiers gave in to the enemy.* **2** to hand something to a person in charge: *Do we have to give in our books at the end of the lesson?*

give off to produce: *That fire is giving off a lot of smoke.*

give out 1 to give to several people; to distribute: *The teacher gave out the exam papers; The headmaster's wife is going to give out the prizes.* **2** to come to an end: *They were planning to camp for another week, but their supplies of food gave out.*

give rise to to cause: *This new situation gives rise to a large number of problems.*

give up 1 to stop: *I must give up smoking; They gave up the search.* **2** to stop using or having something: *You'll have to give up cigarettes.* **3** to hand over something to someone else: *The police made him give up his gun.*

give way 1 to allow other people, drivers *etc* to go before you do: *Give way to traffic coming from the right.* **2** to break, collapse *etc*: *The bridge will give way soon.* **3** to agree against your will: *She had to give way to the children's wishes.*

give yourself up surrender yourself as a

prisoner: *He gave himself up to the police.*
glacier /ˈglasɪə(r)/ or /ˈgleɪsɪə(r)/ *n* a slowly moving mass of ice that is formed from the snow on mountains.
glad /glad/ *adj* pleased; happy: *I'm very glad that you are here.* **'gladly** *adv.* **'gladness** *n.*
'gladden *v* to make someone glad: *The news gladdened her.*
gladiator /ˈgladɪeɪtə(r)/ *n* in ancient Rome, a man trained to fight with other men or with animals for the amusement of spectators.
glamour /ˈglamə(r)/ *n* **1** beauty, especially if it is rather false. **2** excitement that comes from being rich, famous *etc*: *the glamour of a career in films.* **'glamorous** *adj.*

> **glamour**, noun, ends in **-our**.
> **glamorous**, adjective, is spelt with **-or**.

glance /glɑːns/ *v* to look very quickly: *He glanced at the book; Glancing down, her toes seemed miles away.* — *n* a quick look: *He gave her a friendly glance.* — *v* to hit and bounce off: *The ball glanced off the edge of his bat.*
at a glance at once: *I could tell at a glance that something was wrong.*
glance off to hit something at an angle and move off in another direction: *The ball glanced off the goalpost and into the net.*
gland /gland/ *n* a kind of cell or organ in the body that stores substances for the body to use, or to get rid of.
glare /gleə(r)/ *v* **1** to look angrily: *She glared at the cheeky boy.* **2** to shine with an unpleasantly bright light: *The sun glared down on them as they crossed the desert.* — *n* **1** an angry look. **2** unpleasantly bright light: *the glare of the sun.* **'glaring** *adj.*
glass /glɑːs/ *n* **1** a hard transparent substance: *This bottle is made of glass.* **2** a hollow object made of glass, used for drinking: *There are six glasses on the tray; sherry glasses.* **3** the contents of a glass: *She drank two glasses of water.* **4** a mirror. **'glassy** *adj.*
'glasses *n* spectacles.

> **glasses**, meaning spectacles, is plural: *His reading glasses are broken*; but **a pair of glasses** takes a singular verb: *A pair of glasses has been found.*

'glassful *n* the amount that a drinking glass will hold: *two glassfuls of water.*
glaze /gleɪz/ *v* **1** to fit glass into a window: *The house has been built, but the windows are not glazed yet.* **2** to cover with a glaze: *The potter glazed the vase; She glazed the cake with icing.* — *n* a shiny coating.
glazier /ˈgleɪzɪə(r)/ *n* a person who puts glass in window frames *etc*: *The glazier fitted a new pane in the shop window.*
glaze over to lose any expression of interest: *His eyes glazed over as she talked on and on.*
gleam /gliːm/ *v* to shine faintly: *a light gleaming in the distance.* — *n* **1** a glow; a sparkle: *There was a gleam in her eyes.* **2** a slight amount: *a gleam of hope.*
glean /gliːn/ *v* to collect or pick up news, facts *etc.*
glee /gliː/ *n* great joy: *The children shouted with glee when they saw their presents.* **'gleeful** *adj.* **'gleefully** *adv.*
glib /glɪb/ *adj* speaking or spoken quickly and easily, but not sincerely: *a glib talker; glib promises.* **'glibly** *adv.*
glide /glaɪd/ *v* **1** to move smoothly and easily: *The dancers glided across the floor.* **2** to fly a glider. — *n* a gliding movement.
'glider *n* a small, light aeroplane that has no engine. **'gliding** *n.*
glimmer /ˈglɪmə(r)/ *v* to shine faintly: *A single candle glimmered in the darkness.* — *n* **1** a faint light. **2** a slight amount: *a glimmer of hope.*
glimpse /glɪmps/ *n* a very brief look: *I caught only a glimpse of the Queen.* — *v* to see very briefly: *He glimpsed her in the crowd.*
glint /glɪnt/ *v* to gleam or sparkle: *The windows glinted in the sunlight.* — *n* a gleam or sparkle: *the glint of steel.*
glisten /ˈglɪsən/ *v* to shine; to sparkle: *Her eyes glistened with tears.*
glitter /ˈglɪtə(r)/ *v* to sparkle: *Her diamonds glittered in the light.* — *n*: *the glitter of her diamonds.* **'glittering** *adj.*
gloat /gloʊt/ *v* to feel very pleased about your own success or about other people's failure: *She is gloating because she passed the exam and you didn't.*
globe /gloʊb/ *n* **1** the Earth: *I've travelled to all parts of the globe.* **2** a ball with a map of the Earth on it. **3** a ball-shaped object.

> See **earth**.

'global *adj* affecting the whole world: *a global problem.* **'globally** *adv.*
gloom /gluːm/ *n* **1** a state of not quite complete darkness: *I could not tell the colour of the car in the gloom.* **2** sadness: *The king's death cast a gloom over the whole country.*
'gloomy *adj* sad: *Don't look so gloomy;*

gloomy news. **2** dark: *gloomy rooms.* **'gloominess** *n.*

glory /'glɔːrɪ/ *n* **1** fame; honour: *He took part in the competition for the glory of the school.* **2** beauty; splendour: *The sun rose in all its glory.*

glorify /'glɔːrɪfaɪ/ *v* **1** to make something seem better or more beautiful than it really is: *This book glorifies school life.* **2** to praise or worship: *to glorify God.* **glorifi'cation** *n.* **'glorious** *adj* **1** splendid; deserving great praise: *a glorious victory.* **2** very pleasant; delightful: *glorious weather.*

glory in to feel or show great pleasure or pride in something: *He gloried in his unexpected success.*

gloss /glɒs/ *n* brightness on a surface: *Her hair has a lovely gloss.*

glossary /'glɒsərɪ/ *n* a list of special words with their meanings: *There is a glossary of technical terms at the back of the book.*

glossy /'glɒsɪ/ *adj* smooth and shining: *The dog has a glossy coat.* **'glossiness** *n.*

glove /glʌv/ *n* a covering for the hand: *a pair of gloves.*

glow /gloʊ/ *v* **1** to give out heat or light without any flame: *The coal was glowing in the fire.* **2** to be rosy; to blush: *Her cheeks were glowing after her brisk walk.* — *n* a gleam; a brightness: *The glow of the sunset.* **'glowing** *adj* full of praise and admiration: *a glowing report.*

glower /'glaʊə(r)/ *v* to stare angrily: *He glowered at me.*

glucose /'gluːkoʊs/ *n* a kind of sugar found in the juice of fruit.

glue /gluː/ *n* a substance used for sticking things together: *That glue will stick plastic to wood.* — *v* to join things with glue: *She glued the pieces together.*

glum /glʌm/ *adj* gloomy; sad.

glut /glʌt/ *n* too great a supply: *There has been a glut of apples this year.*

glutinous /'gluːtɪnəs/ *adj* sticky: *glutinous rice.*

glutton /'glʌtən/ *n* a person who eats too much: *You mustn't eat all the cake at once — don't be such as glutton!* **'gluttony** *n* greediness.

gnarled /nɑːld/ *adj* **1** full of lumps and knots; twisted: *The tree was gnarled with age.* **2** bony and twisted: *The old man had gnarled hands.*

gnash /naʃ/ *v* to grind your top teeth and bottom teeth together, in anger *etc*: *The dog growled and gnashed its teeth.*

gnat /nat/ *n* a small fly that can bite you.

gnaw /nɔː/ *v* to bite or chew with a scraping action: *The dog was gnawing a bone.*

gnome /noʊm/ *n* a small man who lives underground, sometimes guarding treasure: *Fairy stories are full of gnomes.*

go /goʊ/ *v* **1** to walk, travel, move *etc*: *He is going across the field*; *Go straight ahead.* **2** to lead somewhere: *Where does this road go?* **3** to visit; to attend: *He goes to school every day*; *I decided not to go to the movie.* **4** to be removed, destroyed *etc*: *He's completely useless — he'll have to go.* **5** to be done, carried out *etc*: *The meeting went very well.* **6** to leave: *I think it is time we were going.* **7** to disappear: *My purse has gone!*; *All the green fields had gone.* **8** to do some action or activity: *I'm going for a walk*; *I'm going sailing next week-end.* **9** to be working *etc*: *I don't think that clock is going.* **10** to become: *These apples have gone bad.* **11** to be: *Many people in the world go hungry.* **12** to be put; to belong: *Spoons go in that drawer.* **13** to pass: *Time goes quickly when you are enjoying yourself.* **14** to be spent; to be used: *All her pocket-money goes on sweets.* **15** to be given, sold *etc*: *The prize goes to the best pupil*; *The painting went for £1000.* **16** to make a particular noise: *Dogs go woof, not miaow.* **17** to have a particular tune *etc*: *How does that song go?* — *n* **1** (*plural* **goes**) an attempt: *I'm not sure how to do it, but I'll have a go.* **2** energy: *She's full of go.*

> **go, goes; went** /went/; **gone** /gɒn/: *He goes to St Michael's School*; *She went home*; *He hasn't gone yet.*

> to go **to the cinema** (not **for a show**).
> to go **to the pictures** (not **to see pictures**).
> to **go to school** means to be a student; to **go to the school** means to visit the school.
> to **go to church** means to attend a service or go and pray; to **go to the church** means to visit the church.
> See also **been**.

from the word go from the very beginning.
get going to get started: *If you want to finish that job you'd better get going.*
go about to work at something: *I don't know the best way to go about this job.*
go after 1 to follow: *Go after him and give him his book back.* **2** to try to get or win: *to go after a job*; *to go after a prize.*

go against to oppose; to disagree with someone or something: *I don't like to go against my parent's wishes.*

go ahead to start or continue: *We went ahead with the project after we were given permission.*

'go-ahead *n* permission: *We can't begin the building work until we get the go-ahead from the bank.* — *adj* ambitious; successful: *This is a very go-ahead firm.*

go along to progress: *Check your work as you go along.*

go along with to agree something or support someone: *I'm happy to go along with whatever you suggest.*

go around to be passed from one person to another: *There's a rumour going around that you are leaving.*

go around with to be friendly with someone: *I don't like the people you're going around with.*

go at to attack: *The little boys went at each other with their fists.*

go back to return: *Let's go back to what we were talking about yesterday.*

go back on to break a promise *etc*: *I never go back on a promise.*

go by 1 to believe; to depend on: *You can't go by what Jeremy says — he doesn't really know.* **2** to pass: *Four years went by before I saw her again.*

go down 1 to be received: *The teacher suggested a walk, and the idea went down well with the children.* **2** to become lower: *The price has gone down.* **3** to set: *The sun is going down.* **4** to catch an illness: *At the start of their holiday they all went down with flu.*

go far to be successful: *Try hard, and you'll go far.*

go for 1 to go to fetch: *He has just gone for a doctor.* **2** to attack: *The two dogs went for each other.*

go in for 1 to enter a competition. **2** enjoy something that you do regularly: *He doesn't go in for outdoor sports much.*

going to intending to, or about to do something: *I'm going to have a shower; It's going to rain soon.*

go into 1 to examine carefully: *We must go into this plan in detail.* **2** to start working in a certain type of job: *She left school and went into the police force.*

go off 1 to explode: *The firework went off.* **2** to ring: *When the alarm went off the thieves ran away.* **3** to begin to dislike: *I've gone off chocolates.* **4** to become rotten: *That meat has gone off.* **5** to happen or take place in a certain way: *The party went off really well.*

go on 1 to continue: *Go on reading — I won't disturb you.* **2** to talk too much: *She goes on and on about her troubles.* **3** to keep complaining to someone about something: *She's always going on at me to stop smoking.* **4** to happen: *What is going on here?*

go out 1 to stop burning *etc*: *The light suddenly went out.* **2** to meet and go about regularly with a particular girlfriend or boyfriend: *He has been going out with her for a year.*

go over 1 to read carefully; to examine: *I want to go over your work.* **2** to repeat; to list: *Do you want me to go over the instructions again?* **'going-over** *n*.

go round to be enough for everyone: *Is there enough food to go round?*

go through 1 to search: *I've gone through all my pockets but I still can't find my key.* **2** to suffer: *I went through a difficult time.* **3** to use up: *We went through a lot of money on holiday.*

go through with it to do something though it is difficult or unpleasant: *We may not enjoy it but we must go through with it.*

go together to match; to look nice together: *Those two colours don't go together.*

go towards to help to buy *etc*: *The money we collect will go towards new computers for the school.*

go up 1 to increase: *The price had gone up.* **2** to be built: *There are office blocks going up all over town.*

go up in flames to be destroyed by fire.

go with to match; to look right with something: *This tie goes with the shirt nicely.*

go without not to have: *I can't go without breakfast.*

have a go to try to do something: *I can't play the piano very well but I'll have a go.*

on the go very busy: *He's always on the go, from morning to night.*

goad /goʊd/ *v* to nag, annoy or tease someone till they react: *She goaded me into hitting her.*

goal /goʊl/ *n* **1** in football, hockey *etc*, the posts between which the ball is to be kicked, hit *etc*. **2** the point gained by doing this: *He scored six goals.* **3** an aim or purpose: *My goal in life is to write a book.*

to score a **goal** (not **gaol**).

'goalkeeper *n* the player whose job is to

defend the goal and keep the ball out of it.
'goalpost *n* one of the two upright posts which form the goal in football, rugby *etc*.
goat /gəʊt/ *n* an animal of the sheep family, with horns and a long-haired coat.

> A goat **bleats**.
> A baby goat is a **kid**.
> A female goat is a **nanny-goat**.

gobble /'gɒbl/ *v* to swallow food *etc* quickly: *It's bad for you to gobble your food.*

go-between /'gəʊbɪtwiːn/ *n* a person who takes messages between two people or groups who do not or cannot meet: *They used the boy as their go-between.*

goblet /'gɒblət/ *n* a glass or metal cup with a long stem but no handles: *She was given six silver goblets as a present.*

goblin /'gɒblɪn/ *n* a small, ugly and evil creature that exists only in fairy tales *etc*.

god /gɒd/ *n* **1** (with a capital letter) the creator and ruler of the world: *He prayed to God for help.* **2** a being who is worshipped: *the gods of Greece and Rome; a river god.*
'goddess *n* a female god.
'godfather, 'godmother, 'godparent *ns* a person who, at a child's christening, promises to make sure that the child is brought up according to the beliefs of the Christian church; the child is called a **'godchild, 'goddaughter** or **'godson**.

goggles /'gɒɡlz/ *n* spectacles used to protect the eyes from dust, water *etc*: *Many swimmers wear goggles in the water.*

going /'gəʊɪŋ/ *n* **1** progress: *That was good going to walk all that way in an hour!* **2** the situation or conditions that affect your progress: *When it started to rain, the going began to get tough.*
the going rate the usual cost: *They paid well below the going rate.*

go-kart /'gəʊkɑːt/ *n* a frame with four wheels and an engine, used as a very simple kind of racing vehicle.

gold /gəʊld/ *n* a precious yellow metal used for making jewellery *etc*: *This watch is made of gold.* — *adj* made of gold: *a gold coin.*
'golden *adj* **1** like gold; of the colour of gold: *golden hair.* **2** fiftieth: *a golden wedding anniversary.* **3** very good: *a golden opportunity.*

> **golden** usually means 'like gold': *golden sunlight*
> **gold** means 'made of gold': *gold coins.*

'goldfish, *plural* **'goldfish,** *n* a small golden-yellow fish that can be kept as a pet.
gold medal in competitions, the medal awarded as first prize.
'gold-mine *n* a place where gold is mined.
'goldsmith *n* a person who makes jewellery, ornaments *etc* of gold.

as good as gold very well-behaved: *The baby was as good as gold during his christening.*

golden opportunity a very good opportunity.

golf /gɒlf/ *n* a game in which a small white ball is hit across open ground and into small holes with golf-clubs.
'golf-club *n* a long thin stick with a wooden or metal head, used to hit the ball in golf.
'golfer *n* a person who plays golf.

gondola /'gɒndələ/ *n* **1** a long, narrow boat that is used especially on the canals of Venice. **2** a cabin that hangs under an airship or balloon; a cabin that hangs from a cable across a valley *etc*.

gone /gɒn/ *adj* **1** no longer existing or present; used up: *When I looked again he was gone; I can offer you more to drink but the food is all gone.* **2** see **go**.

gong /gɒŋ/ *n* a metal disc hanging from a frame, which, when struck, gives a ringing sound: *a dinner gong.*

good /gʊd/ *adj* **1** well-behaved; not causing trouble *etc*: *Be good!; She's a good baby.* **2** correct: *good manners; good English.* **3** of high quality: *a good radio; good food.* **4** skilful; able to do something well: *a good doctor; She's good at tennis.* **5** kind: *You've been very good to him; a good father.* **6** helpful; giving benefit: *Vegetables are good for you.* **7** pleased, happy *etc*: *She is in a good mood today.* **8** pleasant; enjoyable: *a good book; Ice-cream is good to eat.* **9** large: *a good salary; She talked a good deal of nonsense.* **10** suitable: *a good man for the job.* **11** sound; fit: *good health; good eyesight.* **12** showing approval: *We've had very good reports about you.* — *n* **1** advantage or benefit: *He worked for the good of the poor; The teacher told Peter she was punishing him for his own good; I'll take your advice, but what good will it do?; It won't do any good.* **2** goodness: *I always try to see the good in people.* — an expression of gladness: *Good! I'm glad you've come!* **'goodness** *n*.

> **good; 'better** /'betə(r)/; **best** /best/: *I am a good swimmer, my father is a better one, but my sister is the best.*
> See also **well**.

goose

to be **good at** (not **in**) English.
See also **strong**.

good'bye an expression you use when leaving someone.

good-for-'nothing *n* a person who is useless or lazy.

Good Friday the Friday before Easter Day: *Christ was crucified on Good Friday.*

good humour kindliness and cheerfulness.

good-'humoured *adj* cheerful: *She is always good-humoured.*

'goodies *n* delicious food: *There were cakes, jellies, ice-cream and other goodies at the party.*

good-'looking *adj* handsome; pretty: *a good-looking girl; He is very good-looking.*

good morning, good afternoon, good-'day, good evening, good night words you use when meeting or leaving someone: *Good morning, Mrs Brown; Good night, everyone — I'm going to bed.*

good-'natured *adj* kindly; not easily made angry: *He is very good-natured — he never loses his temper; a good-natured fellow.*

goods *n* **1** objects *etc* for sale; products: *leather goods.* **2** articles sent by rail: *This station is for passengers and goods.* — *adj*: *a goods train.*

good'will *n* kind thoughts; friendliness: *He has always shown a lot of goodwill towards us.*

as good as almost: *The job is as good as done.*

do someone good to bring benefit to someone: *Drink this soup — it will do you good.*

for good for ever: *He's not going to France for a holiday — he's going for good.*

good for you!, good for her! *etc* an expression of pleasure or approval at someone's success *etc*: *You did well in the race — good for you!*

goodness gracious, goodness me, my goodness expressions of surprise.

no good useless: *It's no good crying for help — no-one will hear you; This penknife is no good — the blade is blunt.*

thank goodness an expression you use when you are glad or relieved about something: *Thank goodness it isn't raining!*

up to no good doing mischief: *Those children are a bit too quiet — I'm sure they're up to no good.*

goose /guːs/, *plural* **geese** /giːs/, *n* a bird like a duck, but larger.

A goose **cackles** or **hisses**.
A baby goose is a **gosling**.
A male goose is a **gander**.

'goose-flesh or **'goosepimples** *n* small bumps on the skin caused by cold or fear.

gooseberry /'gʊzbərɪ/ *n* a round, edible green berry with a hairy skin, that grows on a prickly bush.

gore /gɔː(r)/ *n* blood. — *v* to pierce with horns, tusks *etc*: *The bull gored the farmer.*

gorge /gɔːdʒ/ *n* a deep narrow valley. — *v* to eat greedily until you are full: *He gorged himself at the party.*

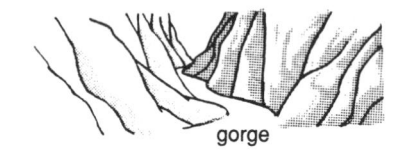

gorgeous /'gɔːdʒəs/ *adj* beautiful; splendid: *a gorgeous dress; These colours are gorgeous.*

gorilla /gə'rɪlə/ *n* the largest kind of ape.

gory /'gɔːrɪ/ *adj* bloody; violent: *a gory tale.*

gosh /gɒʃ/ an expression of surprise.

gosling /'gɒzlɪŋ/ *n* a baby goose.

go-slow /gəʊ'sləʊ/ *n* a form of protest by workers in a factory *etc* in which they work more slowly than usual.

gospel /'gɒspəl/ *n* the life and teaching of Christ; one of the four books in the Bible that describes these: *the Gospel according to St Luke.*

gossip /'gɒsɪp/ *n* **1** talk or chatter that is about

other people, and is sometimes unkind or untrue: *I never pay any attention to gossip.* **2** a person who listens to and passes on gossip: *She's a dreadful gossip.* — *v*: *Try never to gossip about other people.*

got *see* **get**.

gouge /gaʊdʒ/ *v* to dig out, especially with a tool: *He gouged a hole in the wood.*

   gouge out to take something out by force, usually with a sharp tool or your fingers: *We tried to gouge the nail out of the wood.*

gourd /gʊəd/ *n* a fruit whose dried shells can be used as bottles, bowls *etc*.

gourmet /ˈgʊəmeɪ/ *n* a person who knows a lot about, and enjoys, good food and wine: *This restaurant is popular with local gourmets.*

govern /ˈgʌvən/ *v* **1** to rule: *The emperor governed the country wisely and well.* **2** to guide; to influence: *Be governed by your head and not by your heart!*

government /ˈgʌvəmənt/ *n* **1** the people who rule a country or state: *the British Government.* **2** the way in which a country or state is ruled: *Democracy is one form of government.* **3** the job of governing. **'governmental** *adj*.

governor /ˈgʌvənə(r)/ *n* **1** a person who governs a province or state: *After the independence ceremony, the former governor left the colony.* **2** a person who is in charge of a particular organization: *She wants to be a prison governor.*

gown /gaʊn/ *n* **1** a woman's dress, especially one for dances, parties *etc*. **2** a loose robe worn by lawyers, teachers *etc*.

GP /ˌdʒiː ˈpiː/ *n* a doctor who works in a particular town or area and who treats all types of illness: *She went to see her GP when she thought she might be getting flu.*

grab /grab/ *v* to seize or grasp suddenly: *He grabbed a biscuit.* — *n* a sudden attempt to grasp or seize: *He made a grab at the bag of money.*

grace /greɪs/ *n* **1** beauty in appearance or in movement: *A dancer needs grace.* **2** politeness: *He at least had the grace to thank her for her present.* **3** a short prayer of thanks for a meal. **4** favour; mercy: *the grace of God.*

   'graceful *adj* having a lovely shape, or moving beautifully: *a graceful dancer.* **'gracefully** *adv*.

   'gracious *adj* kind; polite: *a gracious smile.* **'graciously** *adv*.

grade /greɪd/ *n* **1** one level in a scale of qualities, sizes *etc*: *There are several grades of paper.* **2** a class or year at school: *We're in the fifth grade now.* **3** a mark for an examination *etc*: *He always got good grades at school.* — *v* to sort into grades: *to grade eggs.*

   make the grade to do well.

gradient /ˈgreɪdɪənt/ *n* the steepness of a slope: *The hill has a gradient of 1 in 4 (25%).*

gradual /ˈgradʒʊəl/ *adj* happening slowly: *a gradual rise in temperature.* **'gradually** *adv*.

graduate *v* /ˈgradʒʊeɪt/ to receive a university degree, diploma *etc*: *He graduated in German and French.* — *n* /ˈgradʒʊət/ a person who has got a university degree or diploma: *a graduate in mathematics.* **gradu'ation** *n*.

graffiti /grəˈfiːtɪ/ *n plural* words or drawings that are scratched or painted on walls *etc*: *The bus shelter was covered with graffiti; Graffiti are difficult to remove.*

graft /grɑːft/ *v* to move skin, bone *etc* from one part of the body to a damaged part, to help it to heal. — *n* the piece of skin or bone that is moved.

grain /greɪn/ *n* **1** the seed of wheat, oats, maize *etc*: *Grain is ground into flour.* **2** a very small, hard piece: *a grain of sand.* **3** the natural pattern of lines in wood or stone *etc*: *Saw the wood across the grain.*

   go against the grain to be against your principles or natural character: *It went against the grain to say I was sorry but I did it anyway.*

gram /gram/ another spelling of **gramme**.

grammar /ˈgramə(r)/ *n* the rules for forming words and for combining words to form correct sentences. — *adj*: *a grammar book.*

> **grammar** ends in **-ar** (not **-er**).

   gram'matical *adj* **1** having to do with grammar. **2** correct according to the rules of grammar: *a grammatical sentence.* **gram'matically** *adv*.

gramme or **gram** /gram/ *n* the basic unit of weight in the metric system: *1 kilogramme = 1000 grammes.*

gramophone /ˈgraməfoʊn/ *n* the old name for a record-player.

gran /gran/ short for **granny**.

granary /ˈgranərɪ/ *n* a storehouse for grain.

grand /grand/ *adj* **1** splendid; magnificent: *a grand procession; It would be nice to live in a grand house.* **2** very pleasant: *a grand day at the seaside.* **3** liked and respected: *a grand old man.* **'grandly** *adv*.

grandchild /ˈgræntʃaɪld/ *n* the child of your son or daughter.

granddad /ˈgrændæd/ *n* a grandfather.

grand-daughter /ˈgrændɔːtə(r)/ *n* the daughter of your son or daughter.

grandeur /ˈgrændʒə(r)/ *n* greatness; magnificence: *the grandeur of the mountains.*

grandfather /ˈgrænfɑːðə(r)/ *n* the father of your father or mother.

grandfather clock a tall clock which stands on the floor.

grandma /ˈgrænmɑː/ *n* a grandmother.

grandmother /ˈgrænmʌðə(r)/ *n* the mother of your father or mother.

grandpa /ˈgrænpɑː/ *n* a grandfather.

grandparent /ˈgrænpɛərənt/ *n* a grandfather or grandmother.

grandson /ˈgrænsʌn/ *n* the son of your son or daughter.

grandstand /ˈgrænstænd/ *n* the rows of seats at a sports ground *etc.*

granite /ˈgrænɪt/ *n* a very hard, usually pale grey rock that is used for building: *houses built of granite.*

granny or **grannie** /ˈgrænɪ/ *n* a grandmother.

grant /grɑːnt/ *v* **1** to give: *Would you grant me one favour?*; *The teacher granted the boy permission to leave.* **2** to admit: *I grant that I behaved wrongly.* — *n* money given for a particular purpose: *He was awarded a grant for studying abroad.*

take something for granted 1 to believe something without checking: *I took it for granted that you had heard the story.* **2** not to worry about something: *People take electricity for granted until their supply is cut off.*

granulated /ˈgrænjʊleɪtɪd/ *adj* coarsely ground: *granulated sugar.*

granule /ˈgrænjuːl/ *n* a small, hard piece or grain of something: *coffee granules.*

grape /greɪp/ *n* a green or black eatable berry from which wine is made: *She bought two bunches of grapes at the supermarket.*

'grapevine *n* the vine on which grapes grow.

sour grapes saying that something is not worth having, when you cannot get it.

grapefruit /ˈgreɪpfruːt/ *n* a large yellow fruit similar to an orange.

graph /grɑːf/ *n* a diagram in which there is a line or lines drawn to show changes in some quantity: *a graph of temperature changes.*

'graphic *adj* **1** very clear; told with many details: *She gave the police a graphic description of the robbery.* **2** having to do with drawing and designing, especially in a mathematical way: *a graphic artist.* **'graphically** *adv.*

'graphics 1 *n* the art of designing or drawing, especially in a mathematical way: *He's studying computer graphics.* **2** *n* plural designs and drawings: *The graphics in this book are good.*

graph paper paper ruled in little squares, for making graphs on.

grapple /ˈgræpəl/ *v* to struggle: *to grapple with a problem.*

grasp /grɑːsp/ *v* **1** to take hold of something very firmly: *He grasped the rope*; *He grasped her by the arm.* **2** to understand: *I can't grasp the meaning of what you said.* — *n* **1** a grip with your hand *etc*: *Have you got a good grasp of that rope?* **2** the ability to understand: *His ideas are quite beyond my grasp.*

'grasping *adj* greedy, especially for money.

grass /grɑːs/ *n* the green plant that covers fields, garden lawns *etc.* **'grassy** *adj.*

'grasshopper *n* an insect that jumps and makes a noise by rubbing its wings.

grate /greɪt/ *v* **1** to rub cheese, vegetables *etc* into small pieces with a grater. **2** to make an unpleasant grinding sound when two surfaces rub together: *the sound of knives grating on dinner plates.* **3** to irritate or annoy: *Her voice grates on me.* — *n* a framework of iron bars for holding coal or wood in a fireplace.

grateful /ˈgreɪtfʊl/ *adj* feeling thankful: *I am grateful to you for your help.* **'gratefully** *adv.*

The opposite of **grateful** is **ungrateful**.

grater /ˈgreɪtə(r)/ *n* a kitchen device with a rough surface for grating food.

grating /ˈgreɪtɪŋ/ *n* a framework of bars: *a grating in the road.*

gratitude /ˈgrætɪtjuːd/ *n* the feeling of being grateful to someone for something: *She kissed her father to show her gratitude for his present.*

The opposite of **gratitude** is **ingratitude**.

grave¹ /greɪv/ *n* a hole in the ground, in which a dead person is buried.

grave² /greɪv/ *adj* **1** serious, sad: *a grave expression.* **2** dangerous: *a grave situation.* **3** important: *grave decisions.* **'gravely** *adv.*

gravel /ˈgrævəl/ *n* very small stones.

gravestone /ˈgreɪvstoʊn/ *n* a stone placed at

a grave on which the dead person's name *etc* is written.

graveyard /'greɪvjɑːd/ *n* a place where dead people are buried.

gravity¹ /'grævɪtɪ/ *n* the quality of being grave; sadness; seriousness; importance.

gravity² /'grævɪtɪ/ *n* the force which attracts things towards the earth and causes them to fall to the ground.

gravy /'greɪvɪ/ *n* a sauce made from the juices of meat that is cooking.

gray /greɪ/ another spelling of **grey**.

graze¹ /greɪz/ *v* to eat grass that is growing: *Cows and sheep were grazing in the fields.*

graze² /greɪz/ *v* to scrape skin from a part of your body: *I've grazed my hand on that stone wall.* — *n* the mark left by this: *I've got a graze on my knee.*

grease /griːs/ *n* **1** soft, thick, animal fat. **2** any thick, oily substance. — *v* to put grease on or in something.

'greasy *adj*: *His long greasy hair hung down on his shoulders.*

great /greɪt/ *adj* **1** very important; remarkable: *a great writer; Napoleon was a great man.* **2** very large: *a great crowd of people.* **3** a lot of: *Take great care of that book.* **4** very good; very pleasant: *We had a great time at the party.* **'greatly** *adv.* **'greatness** *n*.

great- /greɪt/ *prefix* used before nouns to show another generation in family relationships: *my great-grandparents; your great-aunt; our great-grandson.*

greed /griːd/ *n* too great a desire for food, money *etc*: *Eating five cakes one after the other is nothing but greed.* **'greedy** *adj*. **'greedily** *adv*. **'greediness** *n*.

green /griːn/ *adj* **1** having the colour of growing grass. **2** not ripe: *green bananas.* **3** without experience: *Only someone as green as you would believe a story like that.* **4** pale; sick-looking. — *n* the colour of grass. **5** to do with protecting the environment and the natural world: *green politics; green products.*

'greenery *n* leaves: *Add some greenery to that vase of flowers.*

'greengrocer *n* a person who sells fruit and vegetables: *Fetch me a melon from the greengrocer's shop.*

'greenhouse *n* a building, usually made of glass, in which plants are grown: *In Holland tomatoes are grown in huge greenhouses.*

greens *n* green vegetables.

green with envy very jealous.

greet /griːt/ *v* to welcome: *She greeted me when I arrived.*

'greeting *n* words of welcome; a kind message: *a friendly greeting; Christmas greetings.*

gremlin /'gremlɪn/ *n* an imaginary creature responsible for faults in machinery: *The computer failure was blamed on gremlins.*

grenade /grə'neɪd/ *n* a small bomb, especially one thrown by hand.

grew see **grow**.

grey or **gray** /greɪ/ *n* a colour between black and white. — *adj* **1** having this colour: *a grey donkey.* **2** having hair that is becoming white; grey-haired: *He's going grey.*

greyhound /'greɪhaʊnd/ *n* a breed of dog that can run very fast and is used for racing.

grid /grɪd/ *n* **1** a pattern of straight lines forming squares on a map, which help you find places on that map: *She found the correct map reference using the grid.* **2** a system of wires and cables which carry electricity over a large area: *the National Grid.*

grief /griːf/ *n* great sorrow or unhappiness: *She was filled with grief at the news of her sister's death.*

grievance /'griːvəns/ *n* a cause for complaining.

grieve /griːv/ *v* **1** to be very sad: *She was grieving for her dead husband.* **2** to upset someone: *Your bad behaviour grieves me.*

grievous /'griːvəs/ *adj* very bad; causing a lot of suffering: *a grievous illness.*

'grievously *adv*: *He was grievously injured.*

grill /grɪl/ *v* **1** to cook directly under heat: *to grill steaks.* **2** to question someone repeatedly and for a long time: *The detective grilled him about what he had done the previous evening.* — *n* **1** the part of a cooker used for grilling. **2** a frame of metal bars for grilling food on. **3** a dish of grilled food: *a mixed grill.*

'grilling *n* repeated or continuous questioning: *Her parents gave her a grilling when she got home.*

grim /grɪm/ *adj* **1** horrible: *a grim accident.* **2** angry; stern: *The boss looks a bit grim this morning.* **'grimly** *adv*. **'grimness** *n*.

grimace /'grɪməs/ or /grɪ'meɪs/ *n* a twisted expression on the face, sometimes made from pain or disgust, sometimes as a joke: *He made a rude grimace behind the teacher's back.* — *v* to make a grimace: *He grimaced with pain as the doctor touched his wound.*

grime /graɪm/ *n* dirt that is difficult to remove. **'grimy** *adj*.

grin /grɪn/ v to smile very cheerfully. — n a wide smile.

grind /graɪnd/ v **1** to crush something into powder or small pieces: *This machine grinds coffee.* **2** to rub two surfaces together: *stop grinding your teeth!* — n boring hard work: *Learning vocabulary is a bit of a grind.*

> **grind; ground** /graʊnd/; **ground**: *She ground the coffee*; *He has ground the spices.*

'grinder n.

'grindstone n a wheel-shaped stone against which knives are sharpened as it turns.

grip /grɪp/ v to take a firm hold of something or someone: *Grip my hand*; *He gripped his stick*; *The speaker gripped the attention of his audience.* — n **1** a firm hold: *He had a firm grip on the rope*; *He has a very strong grip*; *The land was in the grip of a terrible storm.* **2** a bag used by travellers. **3** understanding: *He has a good grip of the subject.*
get to grips with something to begin to deal successfully with something: *We are still trying to get to grips with our new computer system.*
'gripping adj exciting: *a gripping story.*
lose your grip to lose control.

grisly /ˈgrɪzlɪ/ adj horrible; very nasty: *a grisly sight.*

gristle /ˈgrɪsəl/ n a tough, rubbery substance found in meat: *There's too much gristle in this steak.*

grit /grɪt/ n **1** very small pieces of stone. **2** courage: *He's got a lot of grit.* — v to keep your teeth tightly closed together: *He gritted his teeth to stop himself crying out in pain.*

grizzly /ˈgrɪzlɪ/ n or **grizzly bear** a large bear of North America.

groan /groʊn/ v to make a deep sound in your throat from pain, unhappiness etc: *to groan with pain.* — n: *a groan of despair.*
groaning with loaded with something: *The table was groaning with food.*

grocer /ˈgroʊsə(r)/ n a person who sells food and household supplies.
'groceries n food etc sold in a grocer's shop.

groggy /ˈgrɒgɪ/ adj weak and unable to think clearly because of illness etc.

groin /grɔɪn/ n the part of the lower body where the abdomen and legs are joined: *He pulled a muscle in his groin playing football.*

groom /gruːm/ n **1** a person who looks after horses. **2** a bridegroom. — v to clean and brush a horse's coat.

groove /gruːv/ n a long, narrow cut made in a surface: *the groove in a record.* **grooved** adj.

grope /groʊp/ v to search by feeling with your hands: *He groped for the door.*

gross /groʊs/ adj **1** very bad: *gross errors*; *gross behaviour.* **2** very fat indeed: *He has become quite gross.* **3** total: *gross weight.* — n the total made by several things added together. **'grossly** adv.

grotesque /groʊˈtɛsk/ adj unnatural and strange-looking: *a grotesque carving.*

grouch /graʊtʃ/ v to complain. — n a complaint. **'grouchy** adj.

ground[1] /graʊnd/ *see* **grind**.

ground[2] /graʊnd/ n **1** the solid surface of the earth: *lying on the ground*; *high ground.* **2** a piece of land used for some purpose: *a football ground.* **3** an area of discussion or study: *The lesson covered a lot of new ground.* — v **1** to let a ship run against sand, rocks *etc*, and become stuck: *The ship was grounded on rocks.* **2** to prevent an aeroplane or pilot from flying: *All planes have been grounded because of the fog.*
'grounding n the teaching of the basic facts of a subject: *a grounding in mathematics.*
'groundless adj without reason: *Your fears are groundless.*
ground floor the rooms of a building that are at street level.
'groundnut *see* **peanut**.
grounds n **1** the land round a large house *etc*: *the castle grounds.* **2** good reasons: *Have you any grounds for calling him a liar?*
'groundsheet n a waterproof sheet that is spread on the ground in a tent *etc*.
break new ground to achieve something new or unusual: *Scientists have been breaking new ground in cancer research.*
get off the ground to make a successful start: *The youth club has only been open a week and hasn't really got off the ground yet.*

group /gruːp/ n **1** a number of people or things together: *a group of boys.* **2** a group of people who play or sing together: *a pop group*; *a folk group.* — v to form into a group or groups: *The children grouped round the teacher.*

grouse /graʊs/ v to complain: *He's always grousing about something or other.*

grove /groʊv/ n a group of trees.

grovel /ˈgrɒvəl/ v to crawl; to go down on the floor, especially in fear or humbleness.

grow /groʊ/ v **1** to make a plant develop from a seed *etc*; to develop in this way: *He grows* *roses*; *Carrots grow well in this soil.* **2** to increase: *Their friendship grew as time went on.* **3** to let hair get longer; to get longer: *Your hair has grown a lot*; *Are you growing a beard?* **4** to get bigger; to develop: *You've grown since I last saw you*; *She has grown into a lovely young woman.* **5** to become: *It's growing dark*; *He has grown old.*

> **grow**; **grew** /gruː/; **grown** /groʊn/: *She grew flowers in her garden*; *He has grown tall.*

grow into to become big enough to fit clothes *etc*: *The jacket is too big for him just now, but he'll soon grow into it.*

grow on to become more pleasing: *I used to hate that song but now I've found that it's grown on me.*

grow out of to become too big or too old for something: *I used to wear my big brother's clothes when he had grown out of them.*

grow up to become an adult: *My children are growing up fast*; *I want to be a doctor when I grow up.*

growl /graʊl/ *v* to make a deep, rough sound in the throat: *The dog growled angrily.* — *n*: *a growl of anger.*

grown /groʊn/ *adj* adult: *My son is a grown man now*; *a fully grown dog.*

'**grown-up** *n* an adult: *The grown-ups go to bed late.* — *adj* adult: *I'm pleased with you for behaving in such a grown-up way.*

growth /groʊθ/ *n* **1** the process of growing: *The growth of a plant.* **2** the amount grown: *Can we measure the growth of a tree during the year?* **3** a patch of cancer in the body.

grub /grʌb/ *n* **1** the form of an insect after it hatches from its egg: *A caterpillar is a grub.* **2** a slang term for food: *Have we enough grub to eat?*

grubby /'grʌbɪ/ *adj* dirty: *a grubby little boy.*

grudge /grʌdʒ/ *v* **1** to be unwilling to do, give *etc*; to do, give *etc* unwillingly: *I grudge wasting time on this silly job*; *We shouldn't grudge help to those that need it.* **2** to be jealous of something: *He grudges her the success she has had.* — *n* a feeling of anger *etc*: *He has a grudge against me.*

'**grudging** *adj* unwilling. '**grudgingly** *adv*.

gruelling /'gruːəlɪŋ/ *adj* difficult and tiring: *a gruelling journey.*

gruesome /'gruːsəm/ *adj* horrible.

gruff /grʌf/ *adj* deep and rough; sounding a bit unfriendly: *a gruff voice*; *He's a bit gruff, but really very kind.* '**gruffly** *adv*. '**gruffness** *n*.

grumble /'grʌmbəl/ *v* **1** to complain in a bad-tempered way: *He grumbled at the way he had been treated.* **2** to make a low deep sound: *Thunder grumbled in the distance.* — *n* **1** a complaint: *I'm tired of your grumbles.* **2** a low, deep sound.

grumpy /'grʌmpɪ/ *adj* bad-tempered. '**grumpily** *adv*. '**grumpiness** *n*.

grunt /grʌnt/ *v* to make a low, rough sound: *The pigs grunted when the farmer brought their food.* — *n* this sound: *a grunt of pleasure.*

guarantee /gærən'tiː/ *n* a statement by the maker of something that it will work well and a promise to repair it if it goes wrong within a certain period of time: *This guarantee is valid for one year.* — *v* **1** to give a guarantee: *This watch is guaranteed for six months.* **2** to state that something is true, definite *etc*: *I can't guarantee that what he told me is correct.*

guard /gɑːd/ *v* **1** to protect someone or something from danger or attack: *The soldiers were guarding the palace.* **2** to prevent a person from escaping: *The soldiers guarded their prisoners.* **3** to prevent something from happening: *to guard against mistakes.* — *n* **1** someone, or a group, that protects: *There was always a guard round the king.* **2** something that protects: *She put a guard in front of the fire.* **3** someone whose job is to prevent a person from escaping: *There was a guard with the prisoner every hour of the day.* **4** a person in charge of a train. **5** the duty of guarding.

'**guarded** *adj* cautious: *a guarded reply.*

keep guard: *The soldiers kept guard over the prisoner.*

off guard unprepared: *He hit me while I was off guard*; *to catch someone off guard.*

on guard prepared: *Be on your guard against his tricks.*

stand guard: *The policeman stood guard at the gates.*

guardian /'gɑːdɪən/ *n* **1** a person who takes care of a child, usually an orphan. **2** a person who looks after something: *the guardian of the castle.*

'**guardianship** *n* the duty of being a guardian.

guava /'gwɑːvə/ *n* a yellow fruit, shaped like a pear, that is grown in the tropics.

guerrilla or **guerilla** /gə'rɪlə/ *n* a member of an armed group of fighters: *The guerrillas made an attack on the army base*; *guerrilla warfare.*

guess /gɛs/ v **1** to say what you think is likely or probable: *I'm trying to guess the height of this building*; *If you don't know the answer, just guess.* **2** to think: *I guess I'll have to leave now.* — n an answer that is guessed: *I didn't know her age, but I made a guess that she was 26.*

'guesswork n guessing: *I got the answer by guesswork.*

guest /gɛst/ n a visitor received in a house, in a hotel *etc*: *We are having guests for dinner.*

'guesthouse n a small hotel.

guffaw /gʌˈfɔː/ v to laugh loudly: *He guffawed loudly through the whole film.* — n a loud laugh: *He let out a guffaw at the joke.*

guidance /ˈgaɪdəns/ n **1** leadership, instruction: *work done under the guidance of the teacher.* **2** advice.

guide /gaɪd/ v to lead, direct or show someone the way: *I don't know how to get to your house — I'll need someone to guide me*; *Should children always be guided by their parents?* — n **1** a person who shows the way to go, points out interesting things *etc*: *A guide will show you round the castle.* **2** a book that contains information for tourists: *a guide to London.* **3** a Girl Guide. **4** something you use to guide you: *I've drawn a diagram, which you can use as a guide.*

'guidebook n a book of information for tourists.

guide dog a dog which has been trained to lead blind people safely.

'guidelines n advice about how something should be done.

guilt /gɪlt/ n **1** a feeling of shame for having done wrong: *Do you feel no guilt after telling such a lie?* **2** being guilty of a crime or other wrong act: *The fingerprints on the gun proved the man's guilt.*

'guilty adj **1** having committed a crime or done some other wrong: *The judge said the man was guilty of murder.* **2** feeling guilt: *I've got a guilty conscience.* **'guiltily** adv.

The opposite of **guilty** is **innocent**.

guinea-pig /ˈgɪnɪpɪg/ n **1** a small animal like a rabbit but with short ears, that can be kept as a pet. **2** a person who is used in an experiment.

guitar /gɪˈtɑː(r)/ n a musical instrument with strings. **guiˈtarist** n.

gulf /gʌlf/ n a large bay: *the Gulf of Mexico.*

gull /gʌl/ n a large sea bird with grey and white, or black and white, feathers; a seagull.

gullet /ˈgʌlɪt/ n the tube by which food passes from the mouth to the stomach.

gullible /ˈgʌləbəl/ adj easily tricked or fooled: *He persuaded some gullible people to lend him money and then he left the country.*

gully /ˈgʌlɪ/ n a channel worn by running water, often on the side of a mountain: *They looked down into the deep, snow-filled gully.*

gulp /gʌlp/ v to swallow eagerly or in large mouthfuls: *He gulped down the water.* — n the action of swallowing: *He drank the glass of water in one gulp*; *He took a large gulp of coffee.*

gum[1] /gʌm/ n the firm flesh in which your teeth grow.

gum[2] /gʌm/ n **1** a sticky juice got from some trees and plants. **2** glue. **3** a kind of sweet: *a fruit gum.* **4** chewing-gum. — v to glue; to stick: *Gum the two bits of paper together.*

gun /gʌn/ n a weapon that fires bullets, shells *etc*: *He fired a gun at the burglar.*

'gunboat n a small warship with large guns.

'gunfire n the firing of guns: *I could hear the sound of gunfire.*

'gunman n a criminal who uses a gun.

'gunpowder n an explosive powder.

'gunshot n the sound of a gun firing: *I heard a gunshot.*

at gunpoint being threatened with a gun: *Over twenty customers were held at gunpoint while the robbers took the money.*

gun down to shoot and kill or seriously injure someone.

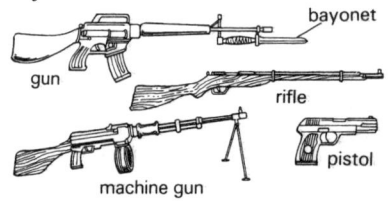

guppy /ˈgʌpɪ/ n a small brightly-coloured freshwater fish.

gurgle /ˈgɜːgəl/ v **1** to make a bubbling sound while flowing: *They could hear a stream gurgling nearby.* **2** to make a bubbling sound in your throat: *The baby gurgled with pleasure.* — n a gurgling sound: *The baby gave a gurgle of delight.*

gush /gʌʃ/ v to flow out suddenly and strongly: *Blood gushed from his wound.* — n: *a gush of water.*

'gushing adj: *a gushing stream.*

gust /gʌst/ *n* a sudden blast of wind.

gusto /'gʌstoʊ/ *n* enjoyment: *He told the story with gusto.*

gut /gʌt/ *n* **1** a very long coiled tube in the lower part of your body, through which food passes. **2** a strong thread made from the gut of an animal, used for violin strings *etc.* — *v* **1** to take the guts out of fish *etc.* **2** to destroy the inside of a building: *The fire gutted the house.*

    guts *n* **1** the gut, liver, kidneys *etc.* **2** courage: *He's got a lot of guts.*

gutter /'gʌtə(r)/ *n* a channel for carrying away water, especially at the edge of a road.

guy /gaɪ/ *n* a man: *I don't know the guy you're talking about.*

gym /dʒɪm/ short for **gymnasium** and **gymnastics**.

gymnasium /dʒɪm'neɪzɪəm/ *n* a building or room with equipment for physical exercise.

gymnast /'dʒɪmnast/ *n* a person who does gymnastics.

    gym'nastic *adj* having to do with gymnastics: *gymnastic exercises.*

    gym'nastics *n* exercises to strengthen and train your body.

gypsy or **gipsy** /'dʒɪpsɪ/ *n* a member of a race of wandering people.

H

ha! /hɑː/ an expression of surprise, triumph etc: *Ha! I've found it!*

habit /'habɪt/ *n* something that a person does usually or regularly: *He has the habit of going for a run before breakfast; She could not get out of the habit of smoking; I switched on the light from habit, forgetting it was broken.*

habitable /'habɪtəbəl/ *adj* fit to be lived in: *This old house is no longer habitable.*

habitat /'habɪtat/ *n* the natural home of an animal or plant.

habitual /həˈbɪtʃʊəl/ *adj* **1** always doing something; constant: *He's a habitual criminal.* **2** regular: *He took his habitual walk before bed.* **ha'bitually** *adv*.

hack /hak/ *v* **1** to cut or chop up roughly: *The butcher hacked the beef into large pieces.* **2** to use your own computer to get information from another computer's files without permission.

hackneyed /'haknɪd/ *adj* used too much and no longer meaning anything: *a hackneyed expression of regret.*

hacksaw /'haksɔː/ *n* a saw for cutting metal.

had /had/ *see* **have**.

hadn't short for **had not**.

haemorrhage /'hɛmərɪdʒ/ *n* very serious bleeding, either inside the body or from a wound: *He suffered a haemorrhage during the operation.*

hag /hag/ *n* an ugly old woman.

haggard /'hagəd/ *adj* looking very tired and thin-faced: *She was haggard after a sleepless night.*

haggis /'hagɪs/ *n* a Scottish dish made from the internal organs of sheep and calves mixed with finely ground oats.

haggle /'hagəl/ *v* to argue about the price of something.

hail¹ /heɪl/ *n* small balls of ice falling from the clouds: *There was some hail during the rainstorm last night.* — *v*: *It is hailing.*

'hailstone *n* a ball of hail.

hail² /heɪl/ *v* **1** to call or shout to someone: *He hailed me from across the street; We hailed a taxi.* **2** to greet; to welcome: *The Queen was hailed by the crowd.*

hair /hɛə(r)/ *n* **1** one of the thread-like things that grow from your skin: *He brushed the dog's hairs off his jacket.* **2** the mass of these on your head: *He still has plenty of hair, but it's going grey.*

a piece of hair is a **lock** of hair.

'hairbrush *n* a brush that you use on your hair.

'haircut *n* the cutting of a person's hair, or the style in which it is cut: *I like your new haircut; Go and get a haircut.*

'hair-do *n* a hairstyle: *I like her new hair-do.*

'hairdresser *n* a person who washes, cuts, curls *etc* people's hair. **'hairdressing** *n*.

'hair-drier *n* an electrical device that dries your hair by blowing hot air over it.

-haired: *a fair-haired girl.*

'hairless *adj* without hair.

'hairpin *n* a U-shaped pin that is used for holding hair in place.

'hair-raising *adj* causing great fear: *a hair-raising adventure.*

'hair's-breadth *n* a very small distance: *The bullet missed him by a hair's-breadth.*

'hairstyle *n* the style or shape in which you have your hair cut and arranged: *a simple hairstyle.*

'hairy *adj* **1** covered in hair: *a hairy chest.* **2** dangerous or frightening: *The ice and snow made the journey north a bit hairy.*

let your hair down to relax and enjoy yourself: *After the exams we let our hair down at a party.*

make someone's hair stand on end to terrify someone.

split hairs to worry about unimportant details.

half /hɑːf/, *plural* **halves** /hɑːvz/, *n* one of two equal parts of anything: *He cut the apple into two halves and gave one half to me; half a kilo of sugar; a kilo and a half of sugar; one and a half kilos of sugar.* — *adj* being half the usual size or amount: *The children were given half portions at the restaurant; a half-bottle of wine.* — *adv* **1** to the extent of one half: *This cup is only half full; It's half empty; They met a strange creature that was half man and half horse.* **2** almost; partly: *I'm half hoping he won't come; They were half dead from hunger.*

'half-brother, **'half-sister** *n* a brother or sister who is the child of only one of your parents: *My father has been married twice, and I have two half-brothers.*

half-'hearted *adj* not eager; unwilling: *a half-hearted attempt.* **half-'heartedly** *adv.*

half-'price *adv* half the usual price: *We bought the furniture half-price in a sale.* — *adj.*

half-'time *n* a short rest between two halves of a game of football *etc.*

'half-way *adj, adv* of or at a point equally far from the beginning and the end: *We are half-way through the work now; the half-way point.*

at half mast flying at a position half-way up a mast *etc* to show that someone of importance has died: *The flags are at half mast.*

half past thirty minutes past the hour: *He's arriving at half past two.*

in half in two equal parts: *He cut the cake in half; The pencil broke in half.*

hall /hɔːl/ *n* **1** a room or passage at the entrance to a house: *We left our coats in the hall.* **2** a large public room, used for concerts, meetings *etc.* **3** a building with offices where the running of a town *etc* is carried out: *a town hall.*

'hallmark *n* **1** a mark on a silver or gold article which guarantees its quality: *Don't buy a piece of gold jewellery unless it has a hallmark.* **2** a typical feature or quality: *Neatness is a hallmark of her work.*

hallo!, hello!, hullo! /həˈloʊ/ a word used as a greeting, or to attract attention: *Hallo! How are you?; Say hallo to your aunt.*

hallucination /həluːsɪˈneɪʃən/ *n* the seeing of something that is not really there: *He had a very high fever which gave him hallucinations.*

halt /hɔːlt/ *v* to come or bring to a stop: *The driver halted the train; The train halted at the signals.* — *n* a stop: *The train came to a halt.*

halve /hɑːv/ *v* **1** to divide something in two equal parts: *He halved the apple.* **2** to reduce something a lot: *This new device will halve your housework.*

halves the plural of **half**.

ham /ham/ *n* the top of the back leg of a pig, salted and dried, used as meat.

hamburger /ˈhambɜːgə(r)/ *n* a round, flat piece of minced beef, that is fried and then put into a bread roll with slices of onion *etc.*

hammer /ˈhamə(r)/ *n* **1** a tool with a heavy metal head, used for driving nails into wood *etc.* **2** a device inside a piano *etc* that hits against some other part, so making a noise. — *v* to hit something with a hammer: *He hammered the nail into the wall.*

hammock /ˈhamək/ *n* a long piece of material hung up by the corners and used as a bed.

See **bed**.

hamper[1] /ˈhampə(r)/ *v* to make it difficult for someone to do something: *I tried to run but I was hampered by my long dress.*

hamper[2] /ˈhampə(r)/ *n* a large basket, especially for picnics.

hamster /ˈhamstə(r)/ *n* a small, light brown animal, rather like a big mouse with a tiny tail, that can be kept as a pet.

hand /hand/ *n* **1** the part of your body at the end of your arm. **2** a pointer on a clock, watch *etc*: *Clocks usually have an hour hand and a minute hand.* **3** a person employed as a helper, crew member *etc*: *a farm hand; All hands on deck!* **4** help; assistance: *Can I lend a hand?; Give me a hand with this box, please.* **5** handwriting: *a letter written in a neat hand.* — *v* to give; to pass: *I handed him the book; He handed it back to me; I'll go up the ladder, and you can hand the tools up to me; That is the end of the news — I'll now hand you back to Jack Frost for the weather report.*

'handbag *n* a small bag carried by women, for personal belongings.

'handbook *n* a small book giving information about something: *a handbook of European birds; a bicycle-repair handbook.*

'handbrake *n* a brake operated by the driver's hand.

'handcuff *v* to put handcuffs on someone: *The police handcuffed the criminal.*

'handcuffs *n* steel rings, joined by a short chain, put round the wrists of prisoners: *a pair of handcuffs.*

'handful *n* **1** as much as you can hold in your hand: *a handful of sweets.* **2** a small number: *Only a handful of people came to the meeting.*

at hand 1 near: *The bus station is close at hand.* **2** available: *Help is at hand.*

by hand 1 with your hands, or with tools that you hold in your hands, rather than with machinery: *furniture made by hand.* **2** not by post but by a messenger *etc*: *This parcel was delivered by hand.*

get your hands on 1 to catch: *If I ever get my hands on him, I'll make him sorry for what he did!* **2** to obtain: *I'd love to get my hands on a car like that.*

give someone a hand to help someone: *Give me a hand with these dishes.*

hand down to pass something on to your children: *These stories have been handed down from parents to children for many generations.*

hand in to give something to a person who is in charge: *The teacher told the children to hand in their exercise-books.*

hand in hand with one person holding the hand of another: *The boy and girl were walking along hand in hand.*

hand on to give something you have received to someone else: *When you have read the book, please hand it on to the other students.*

hand out to give something to several people; to distribute: *The teacher handed out books to all the pupils.* **'handout** *n*.

hand over to give up something to someone: *We know you have the jewels, so hand them over*; *They handed the thief over to the police.*

hands off! do not touch!

hands up! raise your hands above your head: *'Hands up!' shouted the gunman.*

have a hand in something to be one of the people who have taken part in some project *etc*: *Did you have a hand in writing this dictionary?*

have, get or **gain the upper hand** to win; to be in a position in which you can win.

have your hands full to be very busy, especially with a number of different jobs.

in good hands receiving care and attention: *The patient is in good hands.*

in hand 1 not yet used: *We still have £50 in hand*; *We finished the job with three days in hand.* **2** being dealt with; under control: *Don't worry — everything is in hand.*

lend a hand to help: *Lend a hand with this luggage, please!*

off your hands no longer your responsibility: *I was glad to have the problem off my hands.*

on hand near; present; ready for use *etc*: *We always keep some candles on hand in case there's an electricity cut.*

on the one hand ... on the other hand used to show two opposite sides of an argument: *We could, on the one hand, wait for the rain to stop*; *on the other hand, it might be better to cancel the expedition.*

on your hands being your responsibility: *We seem to have a problem on our hands.*

out of hand unable to be controlled: *The angry crowd was getting out of hand.*

shake hands with someone or **shake someone's hand** to grasp and shake a person's hand as a form of greeting or as a sign of agreement. **'handshake** *n*.

to hand near; easy to reach: *I don't have your letter to hand at the moment.*

handicap /'hændɪkæp/ *n* **1** something that makes doing something more difficult: *The loss of a finger would be a handicap for a pianist.* **2** a disadvantage of some sort, for instance, having to run a greater distance, given to the best competitors in a race, competition *etc*, so that others have a better chance of winning. — *v* to make something more difficult for someone: *He wanted to be a pianist, but was handicapped by his deafness.*

'handicapped *adj* disabled: *He is physically handicapped and cannot walk*; *Some severely handicapped children die at an early age.*

handicraft /'hændɪkrɑːft/ *n* skilled work done by hand, such as knitting, pottery *etc*.

handiwork /'hændɪwɜːk/ *n* things made by hand: *Examples of the pupils' handiwork were on show for their parents to see.*

> **handiwork** is never used in the plural.

handkerchief /'hæŋkətʃɪf/ *n* a small square piece of cloth or paper tissue used for wiping your nose.

handle /'hændəl/ *n* the part of an object that you hold: *I've broken the handle off this cup*; *You've got to turn the handle in order to open the door.* — *v* **1** to touch or hold in your hand: *Please wash your hands before handling food.* **2** to manage or deal with someone; to treat someone or something in a particular way: *He'll never make a good teacher — he doesn't know how to handle children*; *Never handle animals roughly.*

'handlebars *n* the curved bar at the front of a bicycle *etc*, that the rider holds, and uses for steering.

handmade /hænd'meɪd/ *adj* made by hand, not machine: *handmade furniture.*

hand-picked /hænd'pɪkt/ *adj* carefully chosen: *A hand-picked group of students stood ready to talk to the Queen.*

handrail /'hændreɪl/ *n* a narrow bar fitted beside steps or a path *etc* for people to hold on to for safety.

handset /'hændsɛt/ *n* the part of a telephone that you hold in your hand.

handsome /'hænsəm/ *adj* **1** good-looking: *a handsome man.* **2** generous: *He gave a handsome sum of money to charity.* **'handsomely** *adv*.

handstand /'hændstænd/ *n* the acrobatic act

of balancing your body upside down on your hands: *We all had to do a handstand in our gymnastics lesson.*

handwriting /'hændraɪtɪŋ/ *n* the way you write: *I can't read your handwriting.*

handwritten /hænd'rɪtən/ *adj* written by hand, not typed or printed.

handy /'hændɪ/ *adj* **1** easy to reach; in a convenient place: *I like to keep my tools handy; This house is handy for the shops.* **2** easy to use; useful: *a handy tool.* **'handiness** *n*.

'handyman *n* a man who does jobs, for himself or other people, especially around the house.

come in handy to be useful: *I'll keep these bottles — they might come in handy.*

hang /hæŋ/ *v* **1** to fix or be fixed above the ground by a hook, cord, chain *etc*: *We'll hang the picture on that wall; The picture is hanging on the wall.* **2** to be drooping or falling downwards: *The dog's tongue was hanging out; Her hair was hanging down.* **3** to bend; to lower: *He hung his head in shame.* **4** to kill someone by putting a rope round their neck and letting them drop: *Murderers used to be hanged in Britain.*

> **hang; hung** /hʌŋ/; **hung**: *She hung up her coat; I've hung the laundry in the garden.* But: *He **hanged** himself; The murderer was **hanged**.*

get the hang of something to learn how to use or do something: *After a few lessons, I began to get the hang of the new equipment.*

hang about, **hang around** or **hang round** to stay in a place not doing anything, often because you are waiting for someone or have nothing else to do: *He hung round in the park with his friends.*

hang on **1** to wait: *Hang on a minute — I'm not quite ready.* **2** to hold: *Hang on to that rope.* **3** to keep: *He likes to hang on to his money.*

hang out to put wet clothes *etc* outside on a line to dry.

hang up to put the receiver back on the telephone: *I tried to talk to her, but she hung up.*

hangar /'hæŋə(r)/ *n* a shed for aeroplanes.

hanger /'hæŋə(r)/ *n* a shaped wooden, plastic or metal object with a hook, for hanging jackets *etc* on.

hang-glider /'hæŋglaɪdə(r)/ *n* an aircraft with no engine that looks like a large kite, to which you can attach yourself, and fly from the top of a mountain *etc*.

'hang-gliding *n* the activity of flying in a hang-glider: *They went up into the mountains to do some hang-gliding.*

hanging /'hæŋɪŋ/ *n* the killing of a criminal by hanging.

hangings /'hæŋɪŋz/ *n* **1** curtains. **2** woven decorations hung on the wall.

hangman /'hæŋmən/ *n* a man whose job is to hang criminals.

hangover /'hæŋoʊvə(r)/ *n* the unpleasant effects of having had too much alcohol, such as a headache and feeling sick: *On the morning after the party he woke up with a dreadful hangover.*

hang-up /'hæŋʌp/ *n* something that always makes you feel anxious and nervous: *I've got a hang-up about money matters.*

hanker /'hæŋkə(r)/ *v* to want something very much: *He was hankering after fame.*

hankie, **hanky** /'hæŋkɪ/ short for **handkerchief**.

haphazard /hæp'hæzəd/ *adj* not planned or organized; left to chance: *Their plans for the holiday are rather haphazard; He put the books on the shelf in a haphazard way.* **hap-'hazardly** *adv*.

happen /'hæpən/ *v* **1** to occur: *What happened next?* **2** to befall; to affect someone or something: *She's late — something must have happened to her; Something funny has happened to the television.* **3** to do or be by chance: *I happened to find him; He happens to be my friend; As it happens, I have the key in my pocket.*

'happening *n* an occurrence; an event: *strange happenings.*

happy /'hæpɪ/ *adj* **1** having or showing a feeling of pleasure: *a happy smile; I feel happy today.* **2** willing: *I'd be happy to help you.* **3** lucky: *By a happy chance I have the key with me.* **'happiness** *n*. **'happily** *adv*.

happy-go-'lucky *adj* not worrying about what might go wrong.

harass /'hærəs/ *v* **1** to annoy or trouble someone constantly: *The children have been harassing me all morning.* **2** to make frequent sudden attacks on an enemy. **'harassment** *n*.

'harassed *adj* worried and anxious because you have too much to do: *She was hurrying along with two bags of shopping, looking harassed.*

harbour /'hɑːbə(r)/ *n* a place of shelter for ships: *All the ships stayed in the harbour during the storm.* — *v* to give shelter or a

hiding-place to someone: *It is against the law to harbour criminals.*
'harbour-master *n* the official in charge of a harbour.

hard /hɑːd/ *adj* **1** firm; solid; not easy to break, scratch *etc*: *The ground is too hard to dig.* **2** not easy to do, learn, solve *etc*: *Is English a hard language to learn?*; *He is a hard man to please*; *a chronic illness that made it hard to do even basic things.* **3** not feeling or showing kindness: *a hard master.* **4** severe: *a hard winter.* **5** having or causing suffering: *a hard life*; *hard times.* — *adv* **1** with great effort: *He works very hard*; *Think hard.* **2** with great force; heavily: *Don't hit him too hard*; *It was raining hard.* **3** with great attention: *He stared hard at the man.* **'hardness** *n*.
'hardback *n* a book with a hard cover: *That book is available both in hardback and in paperback.* — *adj*: *the hardback edition.*
hard-'boiled *adj* boiled until solid: *a hard-boiled egg.*
hard disk the metal disc in a computer where information, files and software are stored.
'harden *v* to make or become hard: *Wait for the cement to harden.*
'hard-earned *adj* earned by hard work: *I deserve every cent of my hard-earned wages.*
hard facts information that is true, not simply someone's opinion.
hard-'headed *adj* not influenced by feelings: *a hard-headed businessman.*
hard-'hearted *adj* having no pity or kindness: *a hard-hearted employer.*
hard 'line a firm or strict attitude or policy: *The government is taking a hard line on tax evasion.*
hard-'hitting *adj* openly and usually strongly critical: *a hard-hitting report about the growing poverty in the country.*
hard lines or **hard luck** bad luck: *It's hard luck that he broke his leg just before his holiday.*
hard of hearing rather deaf: *He is a bit hard of hearing nowadays.*
hard up not having much money: *I'm a bit hard up at the moment.*

hardly /'hɑːdlɪ/ *adv* **1** almost no, none, never *etc*: *There is hardly any rice left*; *I hardly ever go out.* **2** only just; almost not: *My feet are so sore, I can hardly walk*; *I had hardly got on my bicycle when I got a puncture.*

See **rarely** and **scarcely**.

hardship /'hɑːdʃɪp/ *n* **1** pain, suffering *etc*: *a life full of hardship.* **2** something that causes suffering: *Hardships came one after another.*

hardware /'hɑːdweə(r)/ *n* **1** metal goods such as pans, tools *etc*: *This shop sells hardware.* **2** the electronic machinery used in computing.

See **software**.

hardwearing /hɑːd'weərɪŋ/ *adj* lasting a long time: *a hardwearing material.*

hardy /'hɑːdɪ/ *adj* tough; strong; able to bear cold, tiredness *etc*: *He's very hardy — he takes a cold shower every morning.* **'hardiness** *n*.

hare /heə(r)/ *n* an animal with long ears, like a rabbit but slightly larger.
harebrained /'heəbreɪnd/ *adj* silly, foolish: *His boss thought his ideas were harebrained.*

harem /'hɑːriːm/ *n* **1** the part of a Muslim house occupied by the women. **2** the women who live in a harem.

hark! /hɑːk/ listen!

harm /hɑːm/ *n* damage; injury: *I'll make sure you come to no harm*; *He meant no harm*; *It'll do you no harm to have some exercise.* — *v* to cause someone harm: *There's no need to be frightened — he won't harm you.*
'harmful *adj* doing harm: *A medicine can be harmful if you take too much of it.*
'harmless *adj* not dangerous: *Don't be frightened of that snake — it's harmless.*
'harmlessly *adv*. **'harmlessness** *n*.

harmonic /hɑː'mɒnɪk/ *adj* having to do with harmony.

harmonica /hɑː'mɒnɪkə/ *n* a small musical instrument that you play with your mouth.

harmonious /hɑː'məʊnɪəs/ *adj* **1** pleasant-sounding: *a harmonious melody.* **2** pleasant to look at: *harmonious colours.* **3** without quarrels; peaceful: *a harmonious relationship.* **har'moniously** *adv*.

harmonize /'hɑːmənaɪz/ *v* **1** to go well with each other: *The colours in this room harmonize nicely.* **2** to sing or play musical instruments in harmony. **harmoni'zation** *n*.

harmony /'hɑːmənɪ/ *n* **1** a pleasant combination of musical notes: *The singers sang in harmony.* **2** peace between people: *Few married couples live in perfect harmony.*

harness /'hɑːnɪs/ *n* the leather straps *etc* by which a horse is attached to a cart *etc* which it is pulling. — *v* to put the harness on a horse.

harp /hɑːp/ *n* a large musical instrument that is held upright, and that has many strings that you pluck with your fingers. **'harpist** *n*.

harp

harp on *v* to keep on talking about something: *He's forever harping on about his football team.*

harpoon /hɑːˈpuːn/ *n* a spear fastened to a rope, used especially for killing whales.

harrow /ˈharoʊ/ *n* a farm tool with a row of spikes fixed to a frame, that is used to break up big lumps of soil.

harrowing /ˈharoʊɪŋ/ *adj* terrible: *a harrowing experience.*

harsh /hɑːʃ/ *adj* **1** very strict; cruel: *a harsh punishment.* **2** rough and unpleasant to hear, see *etc*: *a harsh voice; harsh colours.* **'harshly** *adv*. **'harshness** *n*.

harvest /ˈhɑːvɪst/ *n* the gathering in of ripe crops: *the rice harvest.* — *v* to gather in crops *etc*: *We harvested the apples yesterday.* **'harvester** *n* a person or machine that harvests corn.

has /haz/ or /həs/ *see* **have**.

has-been /ˈhazbiːn/ *n* someone who was once successful but is no longer thought to be important.

hash /haʃ/ or **make a hash of** to do something badly: *He couldn't perform the simplest task without making a hash of it.*

hasn't short for **has not**.

hassle /ˈhasəl/ *n* trouble; bother: *It's such a hassle getting all this homework done.* — *v*.

haste /heɪst/ *n* hurry; speed: *He did his homework in great haste.*

hasten /ˈheɪsən/ *v* to hurry: *He hastened towards me; We must hasten the preparations.*

hasty /ˈheɪsti/ *adj* **1** done *etc* in a hurry: *a hasty snack.* **2** done without thinking carefully: *a hasty decision.* **3** easily made angry: *a hasty temper.* **'hastily** *adv*. **'hastiness** *n*.

hat /hat/ *n* a garment for the head.

take your hat off to someone to admire someone.

talk through your hat to talk nonsense.

hatch[1] /hatʃ/ *n* **1** an opening in a wall, floor, ship's deck *etc*. **2** the door or cover for this opening.

hatch[2] /hatʃ/ *v* **1** to produce baby birds from eggs: *My hens have hatched ten chicks.* **2** to break out of an egg: *These chicks hatched this morning.* **3** to plan something in secret: *to hatch a plot.*

hatchback /ˈhatʃbak/ *n* a car with a door at the back that opens upwards.

hatchet /ˈhatʃɪt/ *n* a small axe held in one hand.

hate /heɪt/ *v* to dislike very much: *I hate them for their cruelty; I hate getting up in the morning.* — *n* great dislike: *a look of hate.*
'hateful *adj* very bad; nasty: *That was a cruel and hateful thing to say to her.*
'hatred *n* great dislike: *I have a hatred of liars.*

haughty /ˈhɔːti/ *adj* very proud: *a haughty look.* **'haughtily** *adv*. **'haughtiness** *n*.

haul /hɔːl/ *v* to pull something: *Horses are used to haul barges along canals.* — *n* **1** a strong pull: *He gave the rope a haul.* **2** the amount of anything, especially fish, that is got at one time: *The fishermen had a good haul.*
'haulage *n* the business of transporting goods, especially by road.

haunt /hɔːnt/ *v* **1** to visit a place as a ghost: *A ghost is said to haunt this house.* **2** to keep coming back into your mind: *The terrible memory still haunts me.* — *n* a place you often visit: *This wood is one of my favourite haunts.*
'haunted *adj* lived in by ghosts: *a haunted castle.*
'haunting *adj* having a strange quality that stays in your mind: *a haunting tune.*

have /hav/ *v* **1** used with other verbs to show that an action is in the past, and has been completed: *I have just heard the news; I've read that book; He has gone home, hasn't he?* **2** to possess; to be keeping: *We have two cars; The teacher has your pencil; Do you have a cat?; Has she a video?* **3** to possess something as a part of you: *She has blue eyes.* **4** to feel something; to suffer something: *I have a headache; I've no doubt you'll win the prize.* **5** to get; to receive: *I had some news from my brother yesterday; Thank you for lending me the book — you can have it back tomorrow.* **6** to produce a baby: *She's had a baby girl.* **7** to enjoy; to pass: *We had a lovely holiday; They had a terrible time in the war.* **8** to get something done: *I'm having a tooth taken out.* **9** to think of something: *I've had a good idea.* **10** to eat or drink something; to give yourself something: *Have* *a rest*; *Have you had a long enough look?*; *I've had supper*; *Will you have a drink?* **11** to allow: *I won't have you wearing such awful clothes!* **12** to ask someone to your house as a guest, or to do a job: *She had a friend round to play with her*; *We're having the painters in next week.* **13** often used with **got** in meanings **2**, **3** and **4**: *The teacher has got your pencil*; *Have you got a cat?*; *She's got blue eyes, hasn't she?*; *I've got a pain.*

I have or **I've** /aɪv/; **you have** or **you've** /juːv/; **he has** or **he's** /hiːz/; **she has** or **she's** /ʃiːz/; **it has** or **it's** /ɪts/; **we have** or **we've** /wiːv/; **they have** or **they've** /ðeɪv/.

have not or **haven't** /ˈhavənt/; **has not** or **hasn't** /ˈhazənt/: *They've finished, haven't they?*; *She has long hair, hasn't she?*; *John's gone already, hasn't he?*

I had or **I'd** /aɪd/; **you had** or **you'd** /juːd/; **he had** or **he'd** /hiːd/; **she had** or **she'd** /ʃiːd/; **it had** or **it'd** /ˈɪtəd/; **we had** or **we'd** /wiːd/; **they had** or **they'd** /ðeɪd/;

had not or **hadn't** /ˈhadənt/: *I'd better tell the teacher, hadn't I?*; *They hadn't finished, had they?*

had: *We've had enough English for today.*

I have (not **I'm having**) *a bad cold.*

have had it to be completely ruined, broken or dead; to be worn out: *He knew he'd had it if the police found out*; *I had had it by the time we reached the top of the hill.*

have it in for someone to want to cause trouble for someone: *He's had it in for me ever since I got the job he applied for.*

have on 1 to be wearing something: *What a nice dress you have on today!* **2** to have made an arrangement to do something: *I thought we could go to the concert if you've got nothing else on?*

have someone on to fool or tease someone: *You're having me on — that's not really true, is it?*

have to or **have got to** not to be able to avoid doing something: *I don't want to punish you, but I have to*; *Do you have to go away so soon?*; *I've got to finish this homework.*

have to do with 1 to be about something; to concern something: *The meeting had something to do with teachers' salaries*; *What has your remark to do with the present subject?* **2** to concern someone; to be someone's business: *This is a private letter to me — it has nothing to do with you.* **3** to have some responsibility for something: *Had she anything to do with this murder?* **4** to have a connection with someone or something: *Have nothing to do with liars!*

I have it! I know!

haven /ˈheɪvən/ *n* a harbour; a place of safety.

haven't short for **have not**.

haversack /ˈhavəsak/ *n* a bag carried over one shoulder by a walker, for holding food *etc*.

havoc /ˈhavək/ *n* great destruction or damage: *The storm created havoc along the coast.*

play havoc with to confuse or upset something: *These computer breakdowns are playing havoc with our schedule.*

hawk¹ /hɔːk/ *n* a bird of prey that hunts small animals *etc*.

hawk² /hɔːk/ *v* to sell goods in the street or by carrying them around and showing them to people: *The old man lives by hawking herbs and spices.*

'hawker *n* a person who sells goods in the street.

hay /heɪ/ *n* grass, cut and dried, used as food for cattle *etc*.

'hay-fever *n* an illness like a bad cold, caused by the pollen of flowers *etc*.

'hay-stack *n* hay built up into a large pile.

'haywire *adj*, *adv* wrong; crazy: *Our computer has gone haywire.*

hazard /ˈhazəd/ *n* a risk; a danger: *the hazards of mountain-climbing.* — *v* **1** to risk something: *His mother hazarded her life to rescue him from the fire.* **2** to make a guess that you know could be wrong: *I don't know how much a car like that costs but I could hazard a guess.*

'hazardous *adj* dangerous.

haze /heɪz/ *n* a thin mist.

'hazy *adj* **1** misty: *a hazy view of the mountains.* **2** not clear: *a hazy idea.* **'haziness** *n*.

hazel /ˈheɪzəl/ *n* a small tree on which nuts grow. — *adj* light-brown in colour: *hazel eyes.*

'hazelnut *n* the edible round nut of the hazel.

he /hiː/ or /hɪ/ *pron* (used as the subject of a verb) a male person or animal: *When I spoke to John, he told me he had seen you.* — *n* a male person or animal: *Is a cow a he or a she?*

head /hɛd/ *n* **1** the top part of the human body, containing the eyes, mouth, brain *etc*; the same part of an animal's body. **2** your mind: *An idea came into my head last night.* **3** the chief or most important person of an organization, country *etc*: *Kings and presidents are heads of state.* **4** anything that is like a head in shape or position: *the head of a pin*; *The boy knocked the heads off the flowers.* **5** the top or front part of anything: *He walked at the head of the procession*; *His name was at the head of the list.* **6** the most important end: *Father sat at the head of the table.* **7** a headmaster or headmistress: *You'd better ask the Head.* **8** one person: *This dinner costs £25 a head.* — *v* **1** to go at the front of something, or at the top of something: *The procession was headed by the band*; *Whose name headed the list?* **2** to be the leader of a group *etc*: *He heads a team of scientists.* **3** to move in a certain direction: *The explorers headed south*; *The boys headed for home.* **4** to hit a ball with your head: *He headed the ball into the goal.*

'**headache** *n* a pain in your head: *Loud noise gives me a headache.*

'**headband** *n* a strip of material worn round your head to keep your hair back.

'**head-dress** *n* something worn on your head, especially something decorative: *The bridesmaids wore head-dresses of pink flowers.*

-'**headed**: *a two-headed monster*; *a bald-headed man.*

head'first *adv* with your head leading: *He fell headfirst into the swimming-pool.*

'**headgear** *n* anything that you wear on your head: *Hats, caps and helmets are types of headgear.*

'**heading** *n* the title written at the beginning of a chapter, article, page *etc*.

'**headlamp** *n* a headlight.

'**headland** *n* a point of land that sticks out into the sea.

headland

'**headlight** *n* a powerful light at the front of a vehicle: *As it was getting dark, the driver switched on his headlights.*

'**headline** *n* the words written in large letters at the top of newspaper articles.

'**headlines** *n* a brief statement of the most important items of news, on television or radio: *The news headlines come first.*

'**headlong** *adj, adv* **1** moving forwards or downwards, with your head in front: *He fell headlong into the pit.* **2** without stopping to think properly: *He rushed headlong into disaster.*

head'master *n* a man who is in charge of a school.

head'mistress *n* a woman who is in charge of a school.

head-'on *adv* with the front of one car *etc* hitting the front of another: *The two cars crashed head on.* — *adj*: *a head-on collision.*

'**headphones** *n* a pair of receivers connected to a radio *etc*, that you wear over your ears.

head'quarters *n* the place from which the leaders of an organization direct and control its activities.

heads *n*, *adv* the side of a coin with the head of a king, president *etc* on it: *He tossed the penny and it came down heads.*

head start an advantage that you have from the beginning of a race or competition.

'**headstone** *n* a stone placed at the end of a grave with the dead person's name on it.

'**headstrong** *adj* wanting to do things your own way; difficult to control: *a headstrong, disobedient child.*

'**headway** *n* progress: *We've made headway today.*

go to your head to make you conceited or too pleased with yourself: *Don't keep telling him how clever he is or it will go to his head.*

head over heels 1 completely: *He fell head over heels in love.* **2** turning over completely: *He fell head over heels into a pond.*

heads or tails? used when tossing a coin to decide which of two people does, gets *etc* something: *Heads or tails? Heads you do the dishes, tails I do them.*

keep your head to remain calm and sensible.

laugh, scream or **shout your head off** to laugh, scream or shout very loudly in an uncontrolled way: *I didn't think it was funny but the others laughed their heads off.*

lose your head to become excited or confused.

make head or tail of something to understand: *I can't make head or tail of these instructions.*

off the top of your head without preparing or referring to something or someone else: *I can't tell you off the top of my head exactly* *how much money we have in the bank.*

heal /hi:l/ *v* to make or become healthy: *That scratch will heal up in a couple of days*; *This ointment will soon heal your cuts.* **'healer** *n.*

health /helθ/ *n* the state of being well or ill: *He is in good health*; *The man was in poor health because he didn't have enough to eat.*
   'healthy *adj* **1** having good health: *I'm rarely ill — I'm a very healthy person.* **2** helping to produce good health: *a healthy climate.*
   drink someone's health to drink a toast to someone, wishing them good health.

heap /hi:p/ *n* a large pile: *a heap of sand.* — *v* **1** to pile things into a heap: *I'll heap these stones in a corner of the garden.* **2** to cover something with a heap: *He heaped his plate with food.*
   heaped *adj* very full: *A heaped spoonful of sugar.*

hear /hɪə(r)/ *v* **1** to receive sounds by ear: *I don't hear very well; Speak louder — I can't hear you; I didn't hear you come in.* **2** to receive information, news *etc*, not only by ear: *I hear that you're leaving*; *'Have you heard from your sister?' 'Yes, I got a letter from her today'*; *I've never heard of him — who is he?*

> **hear; heard** /hɜ:d/; **heard**: *He heard a strange noise; She has heard the news.*

> to **hear** is to receive sounds with your ears; to **listen** is to pay attention to what you hear: *I heard him speaking, but I didn't listen to what he was saying.*

hear! hear! an expression used to show that you agree with what has just been said.
   'hearing *n* **1** the ability to hear: *My hearing is not very good.* **2** the distance within which something can be heard by someone: *You mustn't use that word in the children's hearing; I think we're out of hearing now.* **3** a court case: *The hearing is tomorrow.*
   'hearing-aid *n* a small electronic device that helps deaf people to hear better by making sounds louder.
   'hearsay *n* what other people have told you, which may or may not be true: *Is it true that he's seriously ill or is it only hearsay?*
   not hear of something not to allow: *He would not hear of her going home alone in the dark.*

hearse /hɜ:s/ *n* a car used for carrying a dead body in a coffin to a cemetery *etc*.

heart /hɑ:t/ *n* **1** the organ that pumps blood through your body: *How fast does a person's heart beat?* **2** the central part: *I live in the heart of the city; in the heart of the forest.* **3** your conscience; your feelings toward other people: *She has a kind heart; You know in your heart that you shouldn't have told a lie; You're very cruel — you have no heart.* **4** courage; enthusiasm: *The soldiers were beginning to lose heart.* **5** a shape supposed to represent the heart, like this, ♥: *a white dress with little pink hearts on it; heart-shaped.* **6** one of the playing cards of the suit hearts, which have red symbols of this shape on them.

'heartache *n* great sadness.

heart attack a sudden failure of the heart to work properly, sometimes causing death.

'heartbeat *n* the regular sound of the heart.

'heartbreak *n* great sorrow.

'heartbreaking *adj* very sad.

'heartbroken *adj* very unhappy: *a heartbroken widow.*

-'hearted: *kind-hearted; hard-hearted.*

'hearten *v* to encourage: *We were heartened by the good news.*

heart failure a condition in which the heart gradually stops working, often causing death: *The doctor told her she is suffering from heart failure.*

'heartfelt *adj* sincere: *heartfelt thanks.*

a change of heart a change in your opinion: *She's had a change of heart and has decided not to marry him.*

at heart really: *He seems rather stern but he is at heart a very kind man.*

break someone's heart to cause someone great sorrow: *It'll break her heart if you leave her.*

by heart from memory: *Actors must learn their speeches by heart.*

have a heart! show some pity!

have at heart to have a concern for or interest in: *He has the interest of his workers at heart.*

heart and soul with all your attention and energy: *She devoted herself heart and soul to caring for her husband.*

lose heart to lose courage or interest: *When he realized how much work there was to do, he lost heart.*

not have the heart to to be unwilling to do something that will hurt someone: *I hadn't the heart to tell him the bad news.*

take something to heart to be greatly affected by something: *He took her advice to heart and did as she had suggested.*

with all my heart very sincerely: *I hope with*

all my heart that you will be happy.

hearth /hɑːθ/ *n* the floor of a fireplace: *an armchair by the hearth.*

heartless /'hɑːtləs/ *adj* cruel: *a heartless remark.* **'heartlessly** *adv.* **'heartlessness** *n.*

heartrending /'hɑːtrɛndɪŋ/ *adj* filling you with sadness and pity: *The child's father made a heartrending appeal to the public for help.*

hearty /'hɑːtɪ/ *adj* **1** friendly; sincere: *a hearty welcome*; *a hearty cheer.* **2** large: *He ate a hearty breakfast*; *She has a hearty appetite.* **'heartily** *adv.* **'heartiness** *n.*

heat /hiːt/ *n* **1** how hot something is: *Test the heat of the water before you bath the baby.* **2** the warmth from something that is hot: *The heat from the fire will dry your coat*; *the heat of the sun.* **3** anger or excitement: *He didn't mean to be rude — he just said that in the heat of the moment.* **4** a division or round in a competition: *He won his heat, so he will run in the final.* — *v* to make or become hot or warm: *I'll heat the soup*; *The day heats up quickly once the sun has risen.* **'heated** *adj* **1** having been made hot or warm: *a heated swimming-pool.* **2** angry; excited: *a heated argument.* **'heatedly** *adv.*

'heater *n* an apparatus that warms a room *etc,* or heats water.

'heating *n* the system of heaters *etc* that heat a room, building *etc.*

'heatstroke *n* a serious condition caused by too much sun, causing a feeling of faintness and fever: *She got heatstroke from lying on the beach all day.*

'heatwave *n* a period of very hot weather.

heave /hiːv/ *v* **1** to lift or pull, with great effort: *They heaved the wardrobe up into the truck.* **2** to throw something heavy: *He heaved a big stone into the river.* **3** to shift; to move violently: *The earthquake made the ground heave.* **4** to let out: *He heaved a sigh of relief.* — *n* the action of heaving: *He gave one heave and the rock moved.*

heaven /'hɛvən/ *n* **1** the place where God lives and where good people are believed to go when they die. **2** (often **heavens**) the sky: *He raised his eyes to the heavens.*

'heavenly *adj* **1** very pleasant: *What a heavenly colour!* **2** having to do with heaven.

heavenly body the sun, moon, a star or planet.

'heavens! or **good heavens!** expressions of surprise, dismay *etc*: *Heavens! I forgot to buy your birthday present.*

heaven-'sent *adj* very lucky: *a heaven-sent opportunity.*

for heaven's sake! an expression used to show anger, surprise *etc*: *For heaven's sake, stop making that noise!*

thank heavens! an expression used to show that you are glad something has or has not happened: *Thank heavens you found the car key!*; *Thank heavens for that!*

heavy /'hɛvɪ/ *adj* **1** having great weight: *a heavy parcel.* **2** having a particular weight: *I wonder how heavy our little baby is.* **3** great in amount, force *etc*: *heavy rain*; *He gave the burglar a heavy blow on the neck.* **4** doing something a lot: *He's a heavy smoker.* **5** sad: *He said goodbye to his son with a heavy heart.* **'heavily** *adv.* **'heaviness** *n.*

heavy-'duty *adj* made to stand up to very hard use: *heavy-duty tyres.*

heavy industry industries such as coal-mining, ship-building *etc.*

heavy metal a type of loud fast rock music played on electric instruments.

'heavyweight *n* a boxer who is in the heaviest class, weighing more than 175 pounds (79 kg): *a heavyweight boxer*; *the world heavyweight boxing champion.*

heckle /'hɛkəl/ *v* to interrupt a public speaker or performer with loud, rude or critical comments or questions: *She was used to being heckled by her opponents.* **'heckler** *n.* **'heckling** *n*: *There was a lot of heckling from the back of the hall.*

hectare /'hɛktɛə(r)/ *n* 10 000 square metres.

hectic /'hɛktɪk/ *adj* very busy; rushed: *Life is hectic these days.* **'hectically** *adv.*

he'd short for **he had** or **he would**.

hedge /hɛdʒ/ *n* a line of bushes *etc* planted closely together forming a boundary for a garden, field *etc.* — *v* to avoid directly answering a question or giving your opinion: *Get a definite yes or no from her — don't let her hedge.*

'hedgehog *n* a small animal with prickles all over its back.

heed /hiːd/ *v* to pay attention to something: *He refused to heed my warning.*

'heedless *adj* careless; paying no attention: *Heedless of the danger, he ran into the burning building to rescue the girl.* **'heedlessly** *adv.*

heel /hiːl/ *n* **1** the back part of your foot: *I have a blister on my heel.* **2** the part of a sock *etc* that covers this part of the foot: *I have a hole in the heel of my sock.* **3** the part of a shoe, boot *etc* under the heel of the foot: *The heel has come off this shoe.* — *v* to put a heel on a shoe *etc.*

hefty

-**heeled**: *high-heeled shoes.*

at or **on someone's heels** close behind: *The thief ran off with the policeman close on his heels.*

kick your heels to have to wait, with nothing to do.

take to your heels to run away: *The thief took to his heels.*

hefty /'hɛftɪ/ *adj* **1** big and strong: *Her husband is pretty hefty.* **2** powerful: *a hefty kick.*

height /haɪt/ *n* **1** the distance from the bottom to the top of something: *What is the height of this building?*; *He is 1·75 metres in height.* **2** the highest, greatest, strongest *etc* point: *He is at the height of his career*; *The storm was at its height.* **3** the extreme: *Your behaviour was the height of foolishness.* **4** (often **heights**) a high place: *We looked down from the heights at the valley beneath us.*

'**heighten** *v* **1** to make higher: *to heighten the garden wall.* **2** to increase.

heir /ɛə(r)/ *n* a person who by law receives wealth, property *etc* when the owner dies: *A king's eldest son is the heir to the throne.*

> The **h** in **heir** is not sounded.
> **an** (not **a**) **heir** to the throne.

'**heiress** *n* a female heir.

'**heirloom** *n* something valuable that has been handed down in a family from parents to children.

held *see* **hold**.

helicopter /'hɛlɪkɒptə(r)/ *n* a flying-machine kept in the air by large propellers fixed on top of it which go round very fast.

hell /hɛl/ *n* the place where the Devil is believed to live and where evil people are believed to be punished after death.

he'll /hiːl/ short for **he will**.

hello /hə'ləʊ/ another spelling of **hallo**.

helm /hɛlm/ *n* the wheel or handle by which a ship is steered: *to take the helm.*

'**helmsman** *n* the person who steers a ship.

helmet /'hɛlmɪt/ *n* a metal, plastic *etc* covering to protect the head, worn by soldiers, firemen, motorbike riders *etc*.

help /hɛlp/ *v* **1** to do something necessary or useful for someone: *Will you help me with my work?*; *My sister helped me to write the letter*; *Can I help?*; *He fell down and I helped him up.* **2** to improve: *Good exam results will help his chances of a job.* **3** to make less bad: *An aspirin will help your headache.* **4** to avoid or prevent something: *He looked so funny that I couldn't help laughing*; *Can I help it if it rains?* — *n* **1** the act of helping: *Can you give me some help?*; *Your digging the garden was a big help.* **2** someone or something that is useful: *You're a great help to me.* '**helper** *n*.

'**helpful** *adj* useful; giving help: *You have been most helpful to me*; *She gave me some helpful advice.* '**helpfully** *adv*. '**helpfulness** *n*.

'**helping** *n* a share of food served at a meal: *a large helping of pudding.*

'**helpless** *adj* unable to do anything for yourself: *A baby is almost completely helpless.* '**helplessly** *adv*. '**helplessness** *n*.

help yourself to serve yourself with food *etc*: *Help yourself to another cake*; '*Can I have a pencil?' 'Certainly — help yourself'.*

help out to help occasionally, when your help is needed: *I help out in the shop from time to time*; *Could you help me out by looking after the baby?*

helter-skelter /hɛltə'skɛltə(r)/ *adv* in great hurry and confusion.

hem /hɛm/ *n* the edge of a piece of clothing, folded over and sewn. — *v* to make a hem on a piece of clothing.

hem in to prevent someone from escaping by surrounding them: *They found themselves hemmed in by the crowd.*

hemisphere /'hɛmɪsfɪə(r)/ *n* **1** one half of the Earth: *Europe and the British Isles are in the northern hemisphere.* **2** one half of a sphere.

hemp /hɛmp/ *n* a plant from which is obtained a coarse fibre used to make rope *etc*.

hen /hɛn/ *n* **1** the female farmyard bird: *Hens lay eggs.* **2** the female of any bird.

> A hen **clucks** or **cackles**.
> The male of the hen is a **cock**.
> A baby hen or cock is a **chicken** or **chick**.
> A hen lives in a **hen-coop** or **henhouse**.

hence /hɛns/ *adv* **1** for this reason: *Hence, I shall have to stay.* **2** from this time: *a year hence.* **3** away from this place.

hence'forth *adv* from now on: *Henceforth I shall refuse to work with him.*

henpecked /'hɛnpɛkt/ *adj* ruled over too much by your wife: *a henpecked husband.*

her /hɜː(r)/ or /hə(r)/ *pron* (used as the object of a verb or preposition) a female person or animal: *I'll ask my mother when I see her*; *He came with her.* — *adj* belonging to a female person or animal: *My mother has her own car*; *a cat and her kittens.*

herald /'hɛrəld/ *v* to be a sign of something

that is about to happen: *The return of the swallows heralds the beginning of summer.*

herb /hɜ:b/ *n* a plant used to flavour food or to make medicines: *herbs and spices.*
   'herbal *adj*: *herbal medicine.*

herd /hɜ:d/ *n* a group of animals of one kind that stay, or are kept, together: *a herd of cattle; a herd of elephants.* — *v* to gather together in a group: *The dogs herded the sheep together; The tourists were herded into a tiny room.*

> **herd** is used for a group of **sheep** or **cattle**; it is used for groups of other animals too, for instance **goats**, **deer**, **elephants**, **buffalos**, **antelopes**.

-herd a person who looks after a herd of certain kinds of animals: *a goatherd.*

here /hɪə(r)/ *adv* **1** at, in or to this place: *He's here; Come here; He lives not far from here; Here they come; Here's your lost book.* **2** at this point: *Here she paused in her story to wipe away her tears.* — **1** a shout of surprise, disapproval *etc*: *Here! What do you think you're doing?* **2** a shout used to show that you are present: *Shout 'Here!' when I call your name.*

   here and there in, or to, various places: *Books were scattered here and there.*

   here's to words used when you wish someone success, or drink their health: *Here's to the success of the new company.*

   here, there and everywhere everywhere: *People were running around here, there and everywhere.*

   here you are here is what you want *etc*: *'Can you lend me a pen?' 'Yes, here you are.'*

   neither here nor there not important: *Do what you want to do — what he thinks is neither here nor there.*

hereditary /həˈrɛdɪtərɪ/ *adj* able to be passed on from parents to children: *Eye colour is hereditary.*

heredity /həˈrɛdɪtɪ/ *n* the passing on of qualities such as appearance and intelligence from parents to children.

heresy /ˈhɛrəsɪ/ *n* a belief which is contrary to the principles and beliefs of a particular religion: *Many Christians believe that it is a heresy to ordain women.*
   'heretic *n* a person who holds a belief thought by many to be a heresy: *He is thought by many Muslims to be a heretic.*
   he'retical *adj* of heretics or heresy.

heritage /ˈhɛrɪtɪdʒ/ *n* things which are passed on from one generation to another: *We must all take care to preserve our national heritage.*

hermit /ˈhɜ:mɪt/ *n* a person who lives alone, especially for religious reasons.

hero /ˈhɪərou/, *plural* **'heroes**, *n* **1** a person who is admired by many people for brave deeds: *The boy was regarded as a hero for saving his friend's life.* **2** the chief person in a story, play *etc*: *The hero is a boy called Peter Pan.*
   he'roic *adj* **1** very brave: *heroic deeds.* **2** having to do with heroes or heroines: *heroic tales.* **heroically** /hɪˈrouɪklɪ/ *adv.*

heroin /ˈhɛrouɪn/ *n* a drug obtained from opium.

> to take **heroin** (not **heroine**).

heroine /ˈhɛrouɪn/ *n* a female hero.

> the **heroine** (not **heroin**) of a story.

heroism /ˈhɛrouɪzm/ *n* great bravery: *He was awarded a medal for his heroism.*

heron /ˈhɛrən/ *n* a large water-bird, with long legs and a long neck.

herring /ˈhɛrɪŋ/ *n* a small, edible sea fish.

hers /hɜ:z/ *pron* something that belongs to a female: *It's not my book — is it hers?; No, hers is on the shelf; Are you a friend of hers?*

herself /hɜ:ˈsɛlf/ or /həˈsɛlf/ *pron* **1** used as the object of a verb or preposition when a female person or animal is both the subject and object: *The cat licked herself; She looked at herself in the mirror.* **2** used to emphasize **she**, **her** or a name: *She herself stayed behind; Mary answered the letter herself.* **3** without help: *Did she do it all herself?* **4** in her normal, healthy state: *She hasn't been herself recently.*

he's short for **he is** or **he has**.

hesitate /ˈhɛzɪteɪt/ *v* to pause briefly because of uncertainty: *He hesitated before answering; Some may hesitate to do what is right.*
   hesi'tation *n.*
   'hesitant *adj* hesitating a lot, usually because you are not sure of what you are doing: *He gave a hesitant speech.* **2** a bit unwilling to do something: *He was rather hesitant about giving her advice.* **'hesitantly** *adv.*

heterosexual /hɛtərouˈsɛkʃuəl/ *adj* sexually attracted to people of the opposite sex: *Most people are heterosexual.*

het /hɛt/: **het up** *adj* worried or upset: *He was getting all het up over having to make a speech.*

hew /hjuː/ v to cut: *He hewed a path through the forest.*

> **hew; hewed; hewn** /hjuːn/: *He hewed down the tree; Several trees had been hewn down.*

hexagon /ˈhɛksəgən/ n a six-sided figure. **hexˈagonal** adj.

hey! /heɪ/ a shout used to attract attention: *Hey! What are you doing there?*

heyday /ˈheɪdeɪ/ n the time when a thing or person is at their most famous, successful, powerful *etc*: *In her heyday she was the most popular star on Broadway.*

hi! /haɪ/ a word of greeting: *Hi! How are you?*

hibernate /ˈhaɪbəneɪt/ v to pass the winter in a kind of sleep: *Hedgehogs hibernate.* **hiberˈnation** n.

hibiscus /hɪˈbɪskəs/ n a tropical plant with brightly-coloured flowers.

hiccup or **hiccough** /ˈhɪkʌp/ n a sudden and repeated jumping feeling in your throat, that makes you make a sharp noise: *I got hiccups after drinking the lemonade so fast.* — v: *He hiccuped loudly.*

hidden /ˈhɪdən/ adj difficult to see or find: *a hidden door; a hidden meaning.*

hide[1] /haɪd/ v to put or keep something or someone in a place where they cannot be seen or easily found; to go or be somewhere where you cannot be found: *I'll hide the children's presents; You hide, and I'll come and look for you; She was hiding in the cupboard; He tries to hide his feelings.*

> **hide; hid** /hɪd/; **ˈhidden**: *She hid from her friends; He has hidden my book.*

hide[2] /haɪd/ n the skin of an animal: *The bag was made of cow-hide.*

hide-and-seek /haɪdənˈsiːk/ n a children's game in which one person searches for others who have hidden.

hideous /ˈhɪdɪəs/ adj extremely ugly: *a hideous face.* **ˈhideously** adv. **ˈhideousness** n.

hide-out /ˈhaɪdaʊt/ n a hiding-place: *The gang used a cellar as a hide-out.*

hiding[1] /ˈhaɪdɪŋ/ n the state of being hidden: *He went into hiding because his enemies were looking for him.*

hiding[2] /ˈhaɪdɪŋ/ n a beating: *He got a good hiding for breaking the window.*

hieroglyphics /haɪərəˈglɪfɪks/ n plural a form of writing in which little pictures are used instead of words: *Hieroglyphics were used in ancient Egypt.*

hi-fi /ˈhaɪfaɪ/ n 1 short for **high fidelity**. 2 a very good stereo record-player *etc*.

high /haɪ/ adj 1 rising a long way above the ground: *a high mountain; a high diving-board.* 2 having a particular height: *This building is about 20 metres high.* 3 great; large: *The car was travelling at high speed; He has a high opinion of her work; They charge high prices; The child has a high temperature.* 4 good: *The teacher sets high standards.* 5 very important: *a high official.* 6 strong: *The wind is high tonight.* 7 not deep in sound; shrill: *the high voices of children.* 8 near the top of the range of musical notes: *What is the highest note you can sing?* — adv far above: *The plane was flying high in the sky.* — n a maximum level: *Sales reached an all-time high last year.*

> See **tall**.

high-ˈclass adj very good: *This is a high-class hotel.*

higher education education at a university, college *etc*.

high-fiˈdelity adj being of very good quality in the reproduction of sound (often shortened to **hi-fi**): *a high-fidelity tape recorder.*

high jump a sports contest in which people jump over a bar that is raised until no-one can jump over it.

ˈhighlands n a mountainous part of a country. **ˈhighland** adj.

ˈhighlight n the best part of something: *The highlight of my holiday was the trip in the helicopter.* — v to give special attention to something: *The minister highlighted the need for immediate action to be taken.*

ˈhighly adv 1 very; very much: *She was highly delighted; I value the book highly.* 2 with approval: *He speaks very highly of you.*

highly-ˈstrung adj rather nervous and easily upset or excited: *a highly-strung, sensitive child; She's always been very highly strung.*

ˈhighness n a title of a prince, princess *etc*: *Your Highness; Her Highness.*

high-ˈpitched adj high, sharp: *a high-pitched voice.*

ˈhigh-powered adj very powerful: *a high-powered motorbike.*

ˈhigh-rise adj with many storeys: *She does not like living in a high-rise block.*

high school a secondary school.

high-ˈspirited adj lively: *a high-spirited horse.*

high street the main shopping street in a town.

high tea in Britain, a large meal, often with tea to drink, in the late afternoon: *We have high tea at five o'clock and our parents have dinner at eight.*

high-tech or **hi-tech** *adj* high technology; using advanced, especially electronic equipment and methods.

high tide the time when the sea is at its highest level.

'highway *n* a main road.

Highway Code a set of official rules for road-users.

high wire a high tightrope for an acrobat to walk along.

high and low everywhere: *I've searched high and low for that book.*

high and mighty behaving as if you think you are very important: *Don't be so high and mighty — you're no-one special.*

it is high time (used with the past tense of the verb) it is time something was done: *It's high time somebody spanked that child!*

the high seas the open sea, far from land.

hijack /'haɪdʒæk/ *v* **1** to take control of an aeroplane while it is moving and force the pilot to fly to a particular place. **2** to stop and rob a vehicle: *Thieves hijacked a lorry carrying £20 000 worth of whisky.* — *n* the hijacking of a plane or vehicle: *a daring hijack.* **'hijacker** *n*.

hike /haɪk/ *n* a long walk, especially in the country. — *v* to go for a long walk in the country. **'hiker** *n*.

hilarious /hɪ'lɛərɪəs/ *adj* very funny: *a hilarious play.* **hi'lariously** *adv*.

hilarity /hɪ'lærɪtɪ/ *n* amusement; laughter.

hill /hɪl/ *n* **1** a piece of high land, smaller than a mountain: *We went for a walk in the hills yesterday.* **2** a slope on a road: *This car has difficulty going up steep hills.*

See **mountain**.

'hilly *adj* having many hills: *hilly country.*

'hillside *n* the side or slope of a hill: *The hillside was covered with new houses.*

'hilltop *n* the top of a hill. — *adj*: *a hilltop bungalow.*

hilt /hɪlt/ *n* the handle of a sword, dagger *etc*.

to the hilt completely; very much: *He supported me to the hilt throughout the argument.*

him /hɪm/ *pron* (used as the object of a verb or preposition) a male person or animal: *I saw him yesterday*; *I gave him a book*; *I came with him.*

him'self *pron* **1** used as the object of a verb or preposition when a male person or animal is both the subject and the object: *He hurt himself*; *He looked at himself in the mirror.* **2** used to emphasize **he**, **him** or a name: *Henry himself never had anything interesting to do.* **3** without help: *He did it himself.* **4** in his normal healthy state: *He didn't seem himself yesterday.*

hind[1] /haɪnd/ *n* a female deer.

hind[2] /haɪnd/ *adj* back: *The cat has hurt one of its hind legs.*

hinder /'hɪndə(r)/ *v* to delay someone or something: *All these interruptions are hindering my work*; *The noise hinders me from working.*

hindrance /'hɪndrəns/ *n* a person, thing *etc* that hinders: *I know you are trying to help but you're just being a hindrance.*

hindsight /'haɪndsaɪt/ *n* wisdom or knowledge about an event after it has happened: *I thought I was doing the right thing, but with hindsight I can see that I made a mistake.*

Hindu /'hɪnduː/ or /hɪn'duː/ *n* a person who believes in the religion of **'Hinduism**. — *adj*: *the Hindu religion.*

hinge /hɪndʒ/ *n* the moving joint by which a door is fastened to the side of a doorway, or a lid is fastened to a box *etc*: *I must oil the hinges of this door.*

hinge on to depend on: *The result of the whole competition hinges on this match.*

hint /hɪnt/ *n* **1** something that is said in a roundabout way, not stated clearly: *He didn't actually say he wanted more money, but he dropped a hint.* **2** a helpful suggestion: *some useful gardening hints.* **3** a small amount that can only just be noticed: *There was a hint of fear in his voice.* — *v* to try to tell someone something in a roundabout way, without stating it clearly or directly: *He hinted that he would like more money.*

hip /hɪp/ *n* **1** the top part of either leg: *She fell and broke her left hip.* **2** (**hips**) the part of your body around your bottom and the top of your legs: *What do you measure round the hips?*; *This exercise is good for the hips.*

hippopotamus /hɪpə'pɒtəməs/ *n* a large African animal with very thick skin that lives near rivers.

hippopotamus

hire /'haɪə(r)/ *v* **1** to get the use of something by paying money: *He's hiring a car from Dicksons for the week.* **2** to employ someone: *They have hired a team of labourers to dig the road.* — *n* money paid for hiring: *How much is the hire of the hall?* **'hirer** *n*.

See **let**².

hire-'purchase *n* a way of buying goods by paying the price in several weekly or monthly parts: *He bought a video recorder on hire-purchase.*
for hire able to be hired: *Is this car for hire?*
hire out to allow someone to use something for a short time in exchange for money: *They hire out rowing boats in the summer.*
on hire being borrowed for money: *This crane is on hire from a building firm.*

his /hɪz/ *adj, pron* belonging to a male person: *John says it's his book*; *He says the book is his*; *No, his is on the table*; *I'm a friend of his*; *His fantasy had become reality.*

hiss /hɪs/ *v* to make a sound like that of the letter *s*, especially to show anger or dislike: *The children hissed the witch when she came on stage*; *The geese hissed at the dog.* — *n* a sound like this: *The speaker ignored the hisses of the audience.*

history /'hɪstərɪ/ *n* **1** the study of events *etc* that happened in the past: *She is studying British history.* **2** a description of events connected with something: *I'm writing a history of the American Civil War.* — *adj*: *a history lesson.*

historian /hɪ'stɔːrɪən/ *n* a person who studies and writes about history.

historic /hɪ'stɒrɪk/ *adj* famous or important in history: *a historic battle*; *This is the historic spot where the explorer first landed.*

historical /hɪ'stɒrɪkəl/ *adj* having to do with history; having to do with people or events from history: *historical research*; *historical novels.* **hi'storically** *adv.*

hit /hɪt/ *v* **1** to give someone or something a blow; to knock, or knock into something: *The ball hit him on the head*; *He hit his head against a low branch*; *The car hit a lamppost*; *Stop hitting me on the head!*; *He was hit by a bullet*; *That boxer certainly hits hard!* **2** to give something a blow that makes it move: *The golfer hit the ball over the wall.* **3** to reach: *His second arrow hit the bull's-eye.* **4** to happen to someone or something: *The city was hit by an earthquake.* — *n* **1** the hitting of something, such as a target: *That was a good hit!* **2** something that is popular or successful: *The record is a hit.* — *adj*: *a hit song.*

hit; hit; hit: *He hit the dog*; *The dog was hit by a car.*

hit-and-'run *adj* causing injury to a person and driving away without stopping.

hit-or-'miss *adj* without planning; careless: *hit-or-miss methods.*

hit back to hit someone who has hit you: *He hit me, so I hit him back.*

hit it off to become friendly: *I hit it off with Paul as soon as I met him.*

hit on to find an answer *etc*: *We've hit on the solution at last.*

hit out at 1 to criticize strongly: *She hit out at the government.* **2** to fight against: *He hit out at his attackers.*

hitch /hɪtʃ/ *v* **1** to fasten something to something: *He hitched his horse to the post.* **2** to hitch-hike: *I can't afford the train-fare — I'll have to hitch.* — *n* **1** a problem that holds you up: *The workmen have met a hitch.* **2** a kind of knot.

'hitch-hike *v* to travel by means of free rides in other people's cars: *He has hitch-hiked all over Britain.* **'hitch-hiker** *n*.

hitherto /hɪðə'tuː/ *adv* up to this or that time: *She'd always been a happy child hitherto.*

HIV /eɪtʃaɪ'viː/ *n* the virus that causes AIDS: *The test showed he was HIV-positive but hadn't yet developed AIDS.*

hive /haɪv/ *n* **1** a box in which bees live and store up honey: *He's building a hive so that he can keep bees.* **2** the bees that live in such a place: *The whole hive flew after the queen bee.*

hoard /hɔːd/ *n* a store of treasure, food *etc*: *She was on a diet but she kept a secret hoard of potato crisps in a cupboard.* — *v* to store up large quantities of something: *His mother told him to stop hoarding old comics.* **'hoarder** *n*.

hoarding /'hɔːdɪŋ/ *n* a large board in the street on which advertisements are displayed.

hoarse /hɔːs/ *adj* **1** rough; harsh: *a hoarse cry.* **2** having a hoarse voice, because of a sore throat, or shouting too much: *You sound hoarse — have you a cold?*; *The spectators shouted themselves hoarse.* **'hoarsely** *adv.* **'hoarseness** *n*.

hoax /hoʊks/ *n* a trick; a joke: *They were told there was a bomb in the school, but it was just a hoax.* — *v* to trick: *They found that they had been hoaxed.*

hob /hɒb/ *n* the flat cooking surface on top of a cooker.

hobble /'hɒbəl/ *v* to walk with difficulty; to limp: *The old lady hobbled along with a stick.*

hobby /'hɒbɪ/ *n* something you enjoy doing in your spare time: *Stamp-collecting is a popular hobby.*

hockey /'hɒkɪ/ *n* a game for two teams of eleven players, played with sticks that are curved at one end, and a ball, or, in **ice hockey**, a round flat disc called a **puck**.

hoe /hoʊ/ *n* a long-handled tool for removing weeds *etc*. — *v* to remove weeds with a hoe.

hog /hɒg/ *n* a pig. — *v* to take or use more than your fair share of something: *She hogs the bathroom for at least an hour every morning, so that the rest of us can't use it.*

hoist /hɔɪst/ *v* **1** to lift something heavy: *He hoisted the sack on to his back; He hoisted the child up on to his shoulders.* **2** to lift with a rope *etc*: *The cargo was hoisted on to the ship; They hoisted the flag.*

hold¹ /hoʊld/ *v* **1** to have in your hand: *He was holding a knife; Hold that dish with both hands; He held the little boy by the hand; Hold my hand.* **2** to grip with something: *He held the pencil in his teeth.* **3** to support something or keep it firmly in one position: *The shelf was being held up by a pile of bricks; Hold your hands above your head; Hold his arms so that he can't struggle.* **4** to remain fixed: *Will the anchor hold in a storm?* **5** to keep someone in your power: *He was held by the police for questioning.* **6** to contain: *This jug holds two pints.* **7** to make something take place; to organize: *The meeting will be held next week; We'll hold the Christmas party in the hall.* **8** to have a festival *etc*: *The festival is held on 30 August.* **9** to have a job *etc*: *He held the position of manager for five years.* **10** to believe in something: *He holds some very strange opinions.* **11** to defend: *They held the castle against the enemy.* **12** to keep a person's attention: *A good teacher should always be able to hold the children's attention.* **13** to remain; to last: *Our offer holds till 31 June; I hope the weather holds until after the school sports.* **14** to wait on the telephone: *Mr Brown is busy at the moment — will you hold or would you like him to call you back?* — *n* **1** the holding of something; a grip: *He got hold of her arm; Take hold of this rope; She caught hold of his coat; Keep hold of that rope.* **2** a way of holding your opponent in wrestling *etc*. **3** an influence or control: *He seemed to have some mysterious hold over her.*

> **hold; held** /hɛld/; **held**: *He held her hand; Has the meeting been held yet?*

'**holder** *n* a container: *a pencil-holder.*

get hold of 1 to manage to speak to: *I've been trying to get hold of you by phone all morning.* **2** to find: *I've been trying to get hold of a copy of that book for years.*

hold back 1 to refuse to tell something, or show your feelings *etc*: *Tell me everything — don't hold anything back; She managed to hold back her tears.* **2** to hesitate; to be unwilling or reluctant to do something: *They were asking for help but for some reason she held back.* **3** to prevent someone from making progress or moving forward: *Her parents had held her back by stopping her from going to college; The police tried to hold the crowd back.*

hold good to be true; to remain firm: *Does that rule hold good in every case?*

hold it to wait: *Hold it! Don't start till I tell you to.*

hold on 1 to keep holding: *She held on to me to stop herself slipping.* **2** to wait: *The telephonist asked the caller to hold on while she connected him.*

hold out 1 to extend something towards someone: *He held out his hand to me and I took it; She held out her money to pay.* **2** to last in a difficult situation: *Can you hold out until the ambulance comes?* **3** to continue to ask for something until you get it: *The women held out for equal pay with the male workers.*

hold up 1 to delay: *I'm sorry I'm late — I got held up at the office.* **2** to stop and rob: *The bandits held up the travellers.* '**hold-up** *n*.

hold² /hoʊld/ *n* the place where luggage or cargo is carried in a ship or aircraft.

hole /hoʊl/ *n* **1** an opening or gap in something: *a hole in the fence; There are big holes in my socks.* **2** a hollow: *a hole in my tooth; Many animals live in holes in the ground.*

holiday /'hɒlɪdeɪ/ *n* **1** a day when you do not have to work: *Next Monday is a holiday.* **2** (often **holidays**) a period of time when you do not have to work: *The summer holidays will soon be here; We're going to Tuscany for our holidays; I'm taking two weeks' holiday in June.*

'**holidaymaker** *n* a person who is having a

holiday away from home: *The beach was crowded with holidaymakers.*
on holiday not working; having a holiday: *Mrs Smith has gone on holiday*; *She is on holiday in France.*
holiness /'hoʊliːnəs/ *n* **1** the state of being holy. **2** a title of the Pope: *His Holiness.*
hollow /'hɒloʊ/ *adj* having an empty space inside: *a hollow tree*; *Bottles, pipes and tubes are hollow.* — *n* a hollow part; a dip: *You can't see the farm from here because it's in a hollow.* **'hollowness** *n.*
hollow out to remove the inside of something solid: *Their canoes are hollowed-out tree-trunks.*
holly /'hɒli/ *n* a type of evergreen tree with prickly leaves and red berries.
holocaust /'hɒləkɔːst/ *n* great destruction and loss of life, especially by fire or in war: *When the hotel burned down, a lot of people died in the holocaust.*
hologram /'hɒləgram/ *n* a kind of photograph created with a laser beam which shows objects in three dimensions: *Holograms are sometimes used on credit cards.*
holster /'hoʊlstə(r)/ *n* the leather case for a pistol, worn on a belt.
holy /'hoʊli/ *adj* **1** belonging to or connected with God, Jesus, a saint *etc*; sacred: *the Holy Bible*; *holy ground.* **2** good; pure; following the rules of religion: *a holy life.*
homage /'hɒmɪdʒ/ *n* great respect shown to someone in authority or to someone you admire: *All her children paid homage to the work she did during her life.*
home /hoʊm/ *n* **1** the house, town, country *etc* where you live: *I work in the city, but my home is in the country*; *Barcelona is my home*; *He invited me round to his home*; *Africa is the home of the lion*; *Her husband came home on Friday night.* **2** the place from which a person, thing *etc* comes originally: *America is the home of jazz.* **3** a place where people who need to be looked after live: *an old people's home.* — *adj* **1** to do with your home and your life there: *home cooking*; *a happy home life.* **2** to do with your own country, not with a foreign country: *home affairs*; *goods for the home market.* **3** played on a team's own ground: *a home game.* — *adv* to your home: *I'm going home now.*

> Your **home** is the place where you live or belong: *The fox trotted back to its home in the woods.*
> A **house** is a building: *How many windows does your house have?*

'homecoming *n* a return home: *We had a party to celebrate his homecoming from America.*
'home-grown *adj* grown in your own garden: *These tomatoes are home-grown.*
'homeland *n* your native land.
'homeless *adj* without a place to live in: *This charity was set up to help homeless people to find somewhere to live.* — *n* people with nowhere to live: *help for the homeless.* **'homelessness** *n.*
'homely *adj* pleasantly simple and ordinary: *The furnishings were homely and comfortable rather than smart.*
home-'made *adj* made by a person at home: *home-made jam.*
'homesick *adj* missing your home and family: *When the boy first went to boarding school he was very homesick.* **'homesickness** *n.*
'homeward *adj* going towards home: *the homeward journey.* **'homewards** *adv.*
'homework *n* work done at home, by a school pupil: *Finish your homework!*
at home 1 in your house: *I'm afraid he's not at home.* **2** playing on your own ground: *The team is at home today.* **3** relaxed and at ease; accustomed to your surroundings or situation: *He's quite at home with cows — he used to live on a farm.*
bring something home to someone to make someone realize something: *The talk by the doctor brought home to them the dangers of taking drugs.*
leave home 1 to leave your house: *I usually leave home at 7.30am.* **2** to leave your home to go and live somewhere else: *He left home at the age of fifteen to get a job in Australia.*
make yourself at home to make yourself as comfortable and relaxed as you would be at home.
homeopathy or **homoeopathy** /hoʊmɪ'ɒpəθɪ/ *n* the treating of diseases with medicines which give you a very mild form of the disease they are supposed to cure: *Many doctors now study homeopathy as part of their medical degree.*
'homeopath or **'homoeopath** *n* a person who treats diseases using homeopathy: *She went to a homeopath about her skin problems.* **homeo'pathic** or **homoeo'pathic** *adj*: *homeopathic remedies.*
homicide /'hɒmɪsaɪd/ *n* murder. **homi'cidal** *adj.*
homonym /'hɒmənɪm/ *n* a word having the same sound as another word, but a different

meaning: *The words 'there' and 'their' are homonyms.*

homosexual /hɒməˈsɛkʃʊəl/ *adj* sexually attracted to people of the same sex as yourself: *He is homosexual.* — *n* a homosexual person: *a meeting-place for homosexuals.* **homosexu'ality** *n*

honest /ˈɒnɪst/ *adj* truthful; not cheating, stealing *etc*: *The servants are absolutely honest; Give me an honest opinion.* **'honesty** *n*.

an (not **a**) **honest** person.

The opposite of **honest** is **dishonest**.

'honestly *adv* **1** in an honest way: *He made his money honestly.* **2** used to stress the truth of what you are saying: *I honestly don't think it's possible.*

honey /ˈhʌnɪ/ *n* a sweet, thick liquid made by bees from the nectar of flowers.

honeycomb /ˈhʌnɪkoʊm/ *n* the mass formed by rows of wax cells in which bees store their honey.

'honeymoon *n* a holiday spent immediately after your marriage: *We went to London for our honeymoon.*

honk /hɒŋk/ *v* to sound the horn of a car.

honorary /ˈɒnərərɪ/ *adj* **1** not paid: *the honorary secretary of the club.* **2** given as an honour: *He has an honorary degree.*

honorary is spelt with **-or-** (not **-our-**).

honour /ˈɒnə(r)/ *n* **1** truthfulness; honesty; the ability to be trusted: *He is a man of honour.* **2** pride; good reputation: *We must fight for the honour of our country.* **3** fame; glory: *He won honour as a scholar.* **4** respect; memory: *This ceremony is being held in honour of those who died in the war.* **5** something to be proud of: *It is a great honour to be asked to give the prizes.* — *v* **1** to show great respect to a person, thing *etc*: *We should honour the President.* **2** to make someone pleased and proud by doing something for them: *Will you honour us by being the chairman of our meeting?* **3** to keep a promise *etc*: *We'll honour our agreement.* **'honourable** *adv*.

honour and **honourable** are spelt with **-our-**.

You use **an** (not **a**) before **honorary**, **honour** and **honourable**.

'honours *n* **1** a degree awarded by universities, colleges *etc* to students who achieve good results. **2** a ceremony performed as a mark of respect: *The dead soldiers were buried with full military honours.* — *adj*: *He got an honours degree in English.*

hood /hʊd/ *n* **1** a loose covering for the whole head, usually attached to a coat, cloak *etc*. **2** a folding cover on a car, pram *etc*: *Put the hood of the pram up — the baby is getting wet.* **3** the cover over the engine of a car: *He raised the hood to look at the engine.*

'hooded *adj* with a hood.

hoodwink /ˈhʊdwɪŋk/ *v* to trick: *He was hoodwinked into giving his money to a thief.*

hoof /huːf/, *plural* **hooves** /huːvz/ or **hoofs**, *n* the hard part of the feet of horses, cows *etc*.

See **foot**.

hook /hʊk/ *n* **1** a small piece of metal shaped like a J, fixed at the end of a fishing-line to catch fish: *a fish-hook.* **2** a bent piece of metal *etc* used for hanging coats, cups *etc* on, or a smaller one sewn on to a garment, for fastening it: *Hang your jacket on that hook behind the door; hooks and eyes.* — *v* **1** to catch a fish with a hook: *He hooked a large salmon.* **2** to fasten by a hook: *He hooked the ladder on to the branch.*

hooked *adj* **1** curved like a hook: *a hooked nose.* **2** very keen on something; addicted to something: *He's hooked on jazz.*

by hook or by crook by one means or another; in any way possible: *I'll get her to marry me, by hook or by crook.*

hook up to connect or link: *Each caravan can hook up to the local electricity supply while it is here.*

off the hook 1 used when a telephone receiver is not in its normal resting position and calls cannot be received: *I've been trying to get in touch with her all day but her phone has been off the hook.* **2** out of a difficult situation: *You're off the hook because they have found who really stole the money.*

hooligan /ˈhuːlɪɡən/ *n* a person who behaves violently or very badly.

'hooliganism *n*: *football hooliganism.*

hoop /huːp/ *n* a ring of metal, wood *etc*: *At the circus we saw a dog jumping through a hoop.*

hoorah, hooray other spellings of **hurrah**.

hoot /huːt/ *v* **1** to sound the horn of a car *etc*: *The driver hooted at the old lady.* **2** to cry like an owl: *An owl hooted in the wood.* **3** to laugh or shout loudly: *The audience hooted with laughter.* — *n* **1** the sound of a car horn *etc*. **2** the call of an owl.

> See **horn**.

'hooter *n* an instrument that makes a hooting sound: *The hooter goes off to mark the end of one shift and the beginning of the next.*

Hoover /'hu:və(r)/ *n* (trademark) a type of vacuum cleaner.

'hoover *v* to clean a floor, carpet *etc* with a vacuum cleaner: *She hoovers the sitting-room twice a week; He hoovered up the crumbs.*

hooves plural of **hoof**.

hop /hɒp/ *v* **1** to jump on one leg: *The children had a competition to see who could hop the furthest; He hopped about shouting with pain when the hammer fell on his foot.* **2** to jump on both legs or all legs: *The sparrow hopped across the lawn; The frog hopped on to the stone.* **3** to jump: *He hopped out of bed; Hop into the car and I'll drive you home.* — *n* **1** a jump on one leg. **2** a jump made by a bird or animal: *With a hop, the frog landed beside her.*

hope /hoʊp/ *v* to want something to happen and believe that it may happen; to expect: *He's very late, but we are still hoping he will come; I hope to be in London next month; All we can hope to do is get ourselves organized; 'Do you think it will be fine today?' 'I hope so'; 'Is it going to rain today?' 'I hope not'.* — *n* **1** the feeling that what you want may happen; expectation: *He has lost all hope of winning the scholarship; He came to see me in the hope that I would help him; The rescuers said there was no hope of finding anyone else alive in the mine.* **2** someone or something that you depend on for help: *He's my last hope — there is no-one else I can ask.*

'hopeful *adj* full of hope: *The police are hopeful that they will soon find the thief; The dog looked at the sausages with a hopeful expression; The future looks quite hopeful.* **'hopefulness** *n*. **'hopefully** *adv*.

'hopeless *adj* **1** without hope; not likely to succeed: *It's hopeless to try to persuade him to help us.* **2** very bad: *I'm a hopeless dancer; He's hopeless at arithmetic.* **'hopelessly** *adv*. **'hopelessness** *n*.

hope for the best to hope that something will succeed or that nothing bad will happen.

hopscotch /'hɒpskɒtʃ/ *n* a game in which a stone is thrown on to a set of squares marked out on the ground, and you have to hop or jump from square to square to get it back: *Some children were playing hopscotch in the playground.*

horde /hɔːd/ *n* a moving crowd: *Hordes of tourists crowded the temple.*

horizon /hə'raɪzən/ *n* the line at which the earth and the sky seem to meet: *The sun went down below the horizon; A ship could be seen on the horizon.*

horizontal /hɒrɪ'zɒntəl/ *adj* lying level or flat; not upright: *The floor is horizontal and the walls are vertical.* **hori'zontally** *adv*.

hormone /'hɔːmoʊn/ *n* any of a number of chemicals produced in your body to perform a particular task: *Adrenalin is a hormone that makes your heart beat faster when you are frightened or excited.* **hor-'monal** *adj*.

horn /hɔːn/ *n* **1** a hard pointed object that grows on the head of a cow, sheep *etc*: *A ram has horns.* **2** an animal's horn used as a material to make things from: *These spoons are made of horn.* **3** the device in a car *etc* which gives a warning sound: *The driver sounded his horn.* **4** an instrument, made of brass, that is played by blowing: *a hunting-horn.* — *adj* made of an animal's horn: *a horn spoon.*

> **horn** is not used as a verb; say **sound**, **hoot**, **toot** or **blow** your horn.

horned *adj* having horns: *a horned animal; a four-horned sheep.*

hornet /'hɔːnɪt/ *n* a kind of large wasp.

horoscope /'hɒrəskoʊp/ *n* the telling of a person's future from the position of the stars and planets at the time of their birth.

horrendous /hə'rendəs/ *adj* very unpleasant and shocking: *a horrendous accident.* **hor'rendously** *adv*: *horrendously expensive.*

horrible /'hɒrɪbəl/ *adj* **1** causing horror; dreadful: *a horrible sight.* **2** unpleasant: *What a horrible smell!* **'horribleness** *n*. **'horribly** *adv*.

horrid /'hɒrɪd/ *adj* **1** unpleasant: *That was a horrid thing to say.* **2** dreadful: *a horrid shriek.*

horrific /hə'rɪfɪk/ *adj* terrible; terrifying: *a horrific accident.* **hor'rifically** *adv*.

horrify /'hɒrɪfaɪ/ *v* to shock greatly: *Mrs Smith was horrified to find that her son had grown a beard.* **'hor'rifying** *adj*.

horror /'hɒrə(r)/ *n* **1** great fear: *She has a horror of spiders.* **2** shock and dismay: *She* *looked at me in horror when I told her the bad news.* **3** something horrific: *the horrors of war.*

hors d'œuvre /ɔː'dɜːv/, *plural* **hors d'œuvres** /ɔː'dɜːvz/, *n* a dish of food served before the main meal to give you an appetite: *She served several different types of hors d'œuvre.*

horse /hɔːs/ *n* **1** a large four-footed animal which is used to pull carts *etc* or to carry people: *The carriage was pulled by a team of horses.* **2** an object used for jumping, vaulting *etc* in a gymnasium.

> A horse **neighs** or **whinnies**.
> A baby horse is a **foal**.
> A male horse is a **stallion**.
> A female horse is a **mare**.
> A horse lives in a **stable**.

'horseman, 'horsewoman *n* someone who rides a horse: *She's a good horsewoman.* **'horsemanship** *n*.

'horsepower *n* a unit for measuring the power of car-engines (shortened to **h.p.**).

'horseshoe *n* a U-shaped piece of iron that is nailed to the bottom of a horse's hoof, and is regarded as a symbol of luck.

on horseback riding on a horse: *The soldiers rode through the town on horseback.*

horticulture /'hɔːtɪkʌltʃə(r)/ *n* the science and art of gardening. **horti'cultural** *adj*.

hose /həʊz/ *n* a rubber or plastic tube which bends and which is used to spray water *etc*: *a garden hose; a fireman's hose.* — *v* to wash with a hose: *I'll go and hose the car.*

'hosepipe *n* a hose.

hosiery /'həʊzɪərɪ/ *n* socks, tights and stockings: *The shop has a big hosiery department.*

hospitable /hɒ'spɪtəbəl/ *adj* kind in inviting people to your house: *It was very hospitable of you to invite us to your party.* **ho'spitably** *adv*.

hospital /'hɒspɪtəl/ *n* a building where people who are ill or injured are given treatment: *After the train crash, the injured people were taken to hospital.*

> If you are ill, you are **in hospital**; you go **to hospital** or are taken **to hospital** (not **the hospital**); if you are visiting or working there, you go **to the hospital** or you work **at the hospital**.

hospitality /hɒspɪ'talɪtɪ/ *n* a friendly welcome in your home for guests or strangers.

host /həʊst/ *n* someone who invites guests to his house: *The host must always make sure that the guests have enough food and drink.*

hostage /'hɒstɪdʒ/ *n* a person who is taken prisoner by people who will not let him go till they get what they want: *The terrorists were holding three people hostage.*

hostel /'hɒstəl/ *n* **1** a building where people can stay the night when they are on a walking or cycling trip *etc*: *a youth hostel*. **2** a building where students *etc* live: *a nurses' hostel.*

hostess /'həʊstəs/ *n* a female host.

hostile /'hɒstaɪl/ *adj* **1** not friendly; behaving like an enemy: *hostile tribes; a hostile army.* **2** showing dislike: *She gave him a hostile look.* **hostility** /hɒ'stɪlɪtɪ/ *n*.

hot /hɒt/ *adj* **1** full of heat; very warm: *a hot oven; That water is hot; a hot day; Running makes me feel hot.* **2** having a sharp, burning taste: *a hot curry.* **3** easily made angry: *He has a hot temper.*

'hotbed *n* a place which allows something, especially something bad, to grow quickly: *The universities are a hotbed of revolution.*

hot dog a sandwich containing a hot sausage.

hot'headed *adj* easily made angry; acting too quickly, without thinking first.

'hotly *adv* **1** eagerly; quickly: *The thieves were hotly pursued by the police.* **2** angrily: *He hotly denied the accusation that he had told a lie.*

'hot-plate *n* a flat, usually circular, metal surface on a cooker on which food is heated for cooking.

hot up to become more exciting: *The election campaign began slowly but hotted up after a few days.*

like hot cakes very quickly: *These toys are selling like hot cakes.*

hotel /həʊ'tɛl/ *n* a large building where people can stay and have meals in return for payment: *The new hotel has over 500 bedrooms.*

ho'telier *n* a person who owns or manages a hotel.

hotline /'hɒtlaɪn/ *n* a direct telephone line.

hound /haʊnd/ *n* a dog, especially one used for hunting foxes. — *v* to chase someone: *The film star was hounded by newspaper reporters.*

hour /'aʊə(r)/ *n* (sometimes shortened to **hr**) **1** a period of sixty minutes: *There are 24 hours in a day; He spent an hour at the swimming-pool this morning; She'll be home in half an hour; a five-hour delay.* **2** the time at which a particular thing happens: *The dog stayed beside him until the hour of his*

house

death; *This firm's business hours are from 9.00 to 16.00 hrs.*

an (not **a**) **hour**.

'hour-glass *n* a device that measures hours, in which sand passes from one glass container through a narrow tube into a lower container.

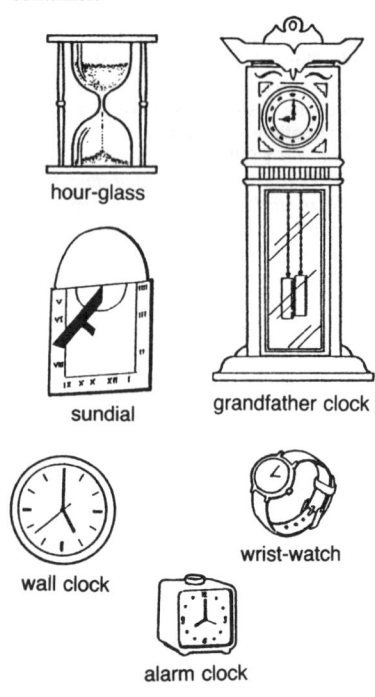

hour-glass

sundial

grandfather clock

wall clock

wrist-watch

alarm clock

hour hand the smaller of the two hands of a watch or clock, which shows the time in hours.

'hourly *adj, adv* every hour: *Take his temperature hourly*; *hourly reports*.

at all hours at any time of the day or night, especially the night.

for hours for a very long time: *We waited for hours for the train*.

on the hour exactly at one, two, three, *etc* o'clock: *Trains for Manchester leave on the hour*.

the early hours or **the small hours** very early in the morning; the period after midnight: *Don't stay awake worrying until the small hours*.

house /haʊs/, *plural* **houses** /'haʊzɪz/, *n* **1** a building in which people, especially a single family, live. **2** a place or building used for a particular purpose: *a hen-house*; *a cowhouse*. **3** a theatre; an audience: *There was a full house for the first night of the play*. **4** a family, usually important or noble, including its ancestors: *Jesus came from the house of David*. — *v* /haʊz/ **1** to provide people *etc* with somewhere to live: *All these homeless people will have to be housed*; *The animals are housed in the barn*. **2** to keep somewhere: *The gardening equipment is housed in the garage*.

See **home**.

'houseboat *n* a boat where someone lives which actually stays in one place on a river or canal *etc*.

'housebound *adj* unable to leave your house because you are too old or too ill.

'housebreaker *n* a burglar. **'housebreaking** *n*.

'house-fly *n* the common fly, found throughout the world.

'household *n* the people who live together in a house: *How many people are there in this household?*

'housekeeper *n* a person, especially a woman, who is paid to look after a house.

'housekeeping *n* **1** managing a household and doing the cooking, cleaning and shopping. **2** the money that you need to manage a household.

house-to-'house *adj* going to each house in an area: *The police are making a house-to-house search*.

'house-warming *n* a party that you give after moving into a new house.

'housewife, *plural* **'housewives**, *n* a woman who spends most of her time looking after her house, her husband and her family.

'housework *n* the work of keeping a house clean and tidy: *My mother has a woman to help her with the housework*.

housing /'haʊzɪŋ/ *n* **1** houses: *The government will provide housing for the immigrants*. **2** the hard cover round a machine.

housing estate an area where a large number of houses or blocks of flats are planned and built at the same time.

hovel /'hɒvəl/ *n* a small, dirty house.

hover /'hɒvə(r)/ *v* **1** to remain in the air without moving in any direction: *The bird hovered over the rock*. **2** to stay near a place in an uncertain way, as though waiting for something: *She looked up to see a small child hovering in the doorway*.

'hovercraft *n* a vehicle which is able to move over land or water, supported by a layer of air.

how /haʊ/ *adv, conjunction* **1** in what way: *How do you make bread?*; *I know how to do this sum.* **2** to what extent: *How do you like my new dress?*; *How often do we see scenes like this on television?*; *How far is Paris from London?* **3** by what means: *I've no idea how he got out of the locked room.* **4** in what state: *How are you today?*; *How do I look?* **5** why; for what reason: *How can you be so rude to your parents?*

how about used for suggesting something, or asking what someone else thinks: *'Where shall we go tonight?' 'How about the cinema?'*; *We're going to the cinema tonight. How about you?*

See **what about**.

how come why; for what reason: *How come I didn't get any cake?*

how do you do? words that you say when you meet someone for the first time: *'How do you do? My name is William,' he said, shaking her hand.*

however /haʊ'evə(r)/ *adv* **1** but: *She earns very little money — however, she manages with what she has.* **2** how: *However did you get over such a high wall?* **3** no matter how: *However hard I try, I still can't swim.*

howl /haʊl/ *v* to make a long, loud noise: *The wolves howled*; *He howled with pain*; *The wind howled through the trees.* — *n* a sound like this: *a howl of pain.*

HQ /eɪtʃ'kjuː/ *n* headquarters: *The general returned to his HQ.*

hub /hʌb/ *n* **1** the centre of a wheel. **2** a centre of activity or business.

hubbub /'hʌbʌb/ *n* a confused noise containing many different sounds: *He could hardly hear what she was saying above the hubbub of voices.*

huddle /'hʌdəl/ *v* **1** to crowd closely together: *The cows huddled together in the corner of the field.* **2** to curl up in a sitting position: *The old man was huddled near the fire to keep warm.* — *n* a small, dense group: *People were standing about in huddles, discussing the news.*

hue[1] /hjuː/ *n* colour: *flowers of many hues.*

hue[2] /hjuː/: **hue and cry** a loud protest: *There will be a hue and cry over this unfair decision.*

huff /hʌf/ *n* a period of being angry and not speaking to anyone: *He is in a huff because he wasn't invited to the disco.*

hug /hʌɡ/ *v* to put your arms round someone and hold them tight: *The mother hugged her child.* — *n* a tight grasp with the arms: *As they said good-bye she gave him a hug.*

huge /hjuːdʒ/ *adj* very large: *a huge dog*; *a huge sum of money*; *Their new house is huge.* **'hugeness** *n*. **'hugely** *adv*.

hulk /hʌlk/ *n* **1** the body of an old ship from which everything has been taken away: *The hulk was towed away for scrap.* **2** a ship which is or looks difficult to steer: *You won't get very far in that old hulk.* **3** a large, awkward person or thing: *The darkness made the castle ruins look like a hulk.*

hull /hʌl/ *n* the frame or body of a ship: *The hull of the ship was painted black.*

hullo /hə'loʊ/ another spelling of **hallo**.

hullabaloo /ˌhʌləbə'luː/ *n* **1** a noise: *The teacher told the pupils to stop making such a hullabaloo.* **2** a loud public protest.

hum /hʌm/ *v* **1** to make a musical sound with closed lips: *He was humming a tune to himself.* **2** to make a sound like this: *The bees were humming round the hive.* — *n* a humming sound: *I could hear the hum of conversation in the room next door.*

human /'hjuːmən/ *adj* of, natural to, concerning, or belonging to, mankind: *human nature*; *The dog was so clever that he seemed almost human.* — *n* a person: *Humans are not as different from animals as we think.*

human being a human.

human nature feelings and behaviour that all human beings normally have.

human rights the rights that every person has to justice and freedom.

the human race mankind; all people.

humane /hjʊ'meɪn/ *adj* kind; not cruel. **hu'manely** *adv*.

The opposite of **humane** is **inhumane**.

humanity /hjʊ'mænɪtɪ/ *n* **1** kindness: *Prisoners must be treated with humanity.* **2** people: *all humanity.*

humanitarian /hjʊˌmænɪ'teərɪən/ *n* a person who tries to make life better for everyone and tries to stop the suffering in the world. — *adj*: *humanitarian actions.*

humble /'hʌmbəl/ *adj* **1** having a low opinion of yourself; not proud: *You have plenty of ability, but you are too humble.* **2** not great and important: *I do quite a humble job at the hospital.* **'humbly** *adv*. **'humbleness** *n*.

humbug /'hʌmbʌɡ/ *n* **1** a person who pretends to be better than he or she is: *Someone who drops litter and then complains about other* *people's dirtiness is a real humbug.* **2** talk or words that try to deceive you; nonsense: *People talk a lot of humbug about today's children being lazy and selfish.* **3** in Britain, a hard sweet, usually flavoured with peppermint.

humdrum /'hʌmdrʌm/ *adj* dull or ordinary: *He'd climbed so many mountains that it had become humdrum.*

humid /'hju:mɪd/ *adj* damp: *a humid climate.* **humidity** /hju:'mɪdɪtɪ/ *n.*

humiliate /hjʊ'mɪlɪeɪt/ *v* to make someone feel ashamed: *He was humiliated to find that his girlfriend could run faster than he could.* **hu'miliating** *adj.* **humili'ation** *n.*

humility /hjʊ'mɪlɪtɪ/ *n* modesty; humbleness: *In spite of his important job, he was a man of great humility.*

humming-bird /'hʌmɪŋbɜ:d/ *n* a small brightly-coloured bird that makes a humming sound with its wings.

humorous /'hju:mərəs/ *adj* funny; amusing: *a humorous remark.* **'humorously** *adv.*

humour /'hju:mə(r)/ *n* the ability to amuse people; quickness to see a joke: *He has a great sense of humour.* — *v* to please someone by agreeing with them or doing as they wish, so as to avoid trouble: *Don't tell him he is wrong — just humour him instead.*

> **humour** ends in **-our**.
> **humorous** is spelt with **-or-**.

-humoured having, or showing, feelings or a personality of a particular sort: *a good-humoured person; an ill-humoured remark.*

humourless /'hju:mələs/ *adj* very serious; not able to see when things are funny: *His writing style was dry and humourless.*

hump /hʌmp/ *n* **1** a lump on the back of an animal, person *etc*: *a camel's hump.* **2** part of a road *etc* which rises in the shape of a hump.

humus /'hju:məs/ *n* a dark brown mass of rotten plants that you dig into the soil to improve it.

hunch[1] /hʌntʃ/ *n* a feeling: *I have a hunch that something is wrong.*

hunch[2] /hʌntʃ/ *v* to bring your shoulders upwards and forwards: *He hunched his shoulders*; *She hunched herself up in front of the fire to keep warm.*

'hunchback *n* a person with a hump on his back.

hundred /'hʌndrəd/, *plural* **'hundred**, *n* the number 100: *Ten times ten is a hundred*; *more than one hundred*; *Three hundred of the children already speak some English.* — *adj* **1** 100 in number: *six hundred people*; *a few hundred pounds.* **2** aged 100: *He is a hundred today.*

> You use **hundred** (not **hundreds**) after a number: *nine hundred boxes.*

'hundred-: *a hundred-dollar bill.*

'hundredth *n* one of a hundred equal parts. — *n, adj* the last of a hundred people, things *etc*.

hundreds of 1 several hundred: *He has hundreds of pounds in the bank.* **2** very many: *I've got hundreds of things to do.*

hung *see* **hang**.

hunger /'hʌŋgə(r)/ *n* **1** the desire for food: *A cheese roll won't satisfy my hunger.* **2** not having enough food: *Poor people in many parts of the world are dying of hunger.* **3** eagerness: *a hunger for success.* — *v* to want very much: *The children hungered for love.*

hungry /'hʌŋgrɪ/ *adj* wanting food *etc*: *a hungry baby; I'm hungry — I haven't eaten all day; He's hungry for adventure.* **'hungrily** *adv.*

go hungry to have too little to eat: *If the harvest is not good, the population will go hungry.*

hunger strike a refusal to eat: *The prisoners went on hunger strike.*

hunk /hʌŋk/ *n* a large piece: *a hunk of cheese.*

hunt /hʌnt/ *v* **1** to chase and catch animals *etc* for food or for sport: *He spent the whole day hunting deer.* **2** to search: *She hunted for the lost book.* — *n* **1** the act of hunting animals *etc*: *a tiger hunt.* **2** a search: *I'll have a hunt for that lost necklace.*

'hunter *n* a person who hunts animals. **'hunting** *n.*

hunt high and low to search everywhere.

hurdle /'hɜ:dəl/ *n* **1** a frame to be jumped in a race. **2** a difficulty; a difficult test: *We still have several hurdles to get over.* **'hurdler** *n.* **'hurdling** *n.*

hurl /hɜ:l/ *v* to throw violently: *He hurled himself to the ground*; *They hurled rocks at their attackers.*

hurrah, **hoorah** /hʊ'rɑ:/, **hooray**, **hurray** /hʊ'reɪ/ a shout of joy *etc*: *Hurrah! We're getting an extra day's holiday!*; *Hip, hip, hooray!*

hurricane /'hʌrɪkən/ *n* a violent storm with winds blowing at over 120 kilometres per hour.

> A **hurricane** is a violent, destructive tropical wind, or a wind blowing at over 120 kilometres per hour.
> A **cyclone** is a violent storm with winds blowing in a circle round a calm central area.
> A **tornado** is a violent storm with winds that whirl round in a circle.
> A **typhoon** is a violent tropical storm, especially in the seas east of China.
> A **whirlwind** is a wind with a violent circular motion, moving across the land or sea.

hurry /'hʌrɪ/ v **1** to be quick: *You'd better hurry if you want to catch that bus.* **2** to make someone be quick: *If you hurry me, I'll make mistakes.* **3** to take quickly: *After the accident, the injured man was hurried to the hospital.* — n quickness in doing something; a rush; haste: *In his hurry to leave, he fell over the dog.*
'**hurried** *adj* done too quickly: *a hurried job.* '**hurriedly** *adv.*
hurry up to be quick, or make someone be quick: *Do hurry up!*; *Please hurry the children up — we're late!*
in a hurry 1 quickly; in a rush: *I did this in a hurry.* **2** wanting to be quick: *Don't stop me now — I'm in a hurry*; *She was in a hurry to get home and cook the meal.*
in no hurry 1 having plenty of time: *Take it easy and slow down – we're in no hurry.* **2** unwilling: *I'm in no hurry to repeat that experience.*

hurt /hɜːt/ v **1** to injure: *I hurt my hand when I fell over.*; *Were you badly hurt?* **2** to be painful: *My tooth hurts.* **3** to upset someone: *She was hurt by her friend's cruel words.*

> **hurt**; **hurt**; **hurt**: *He hurt his foot*; *I've hurt my toe.*

'**hurtful** *adj* cruel: *a hurtful remark.*
hurtle /'hɜːtəl/ v to move very quickly: *The car hurtled downhill.*
husband /'hʌzbənd/ n a man to whom a woman is married: *Some husbands do the housework, while their wives go out to work.*
hush /hʌʃ/ a warning to be quiet: *Hush! Don't wake the baby.* — n silence: *A hush came over the room.*
hushed *adj* silent: *a hushed crowd.*
hush up to keep something secret: *The government want to hush the matter up.*
husky[1] /'hʌskɪ/ *adj* low and rough in sound: *He had a husky voice.* '**huskiness** *n.* '**huskily** *adv.*
husky[2] /'hʌskɪ/ n a dog used for pulling sledges.
hustle /'hʌsəl/ v to push quickly and roughly: *The man was hustled out of the office and into the car.* — n hurry; rush.
hut /hʌt/ n a small house or shelter, made of wood *etc.*
hutch /hʌtʃ/ n a box with a wire front in which rabbits are kept.
hyacinth /'haɪəsɪnθ/ n a plant of the lily family with a sweet-smelling flower, that grows from a bulb.
hybrid /'haɪbrɪd/ n an animal or plant that has been bred from two different kinds of animal or plant: *A mule is a hybrid between a horse and a donkey*; *a hybrid rose.*
hydrant /'haɪdrənt/ n a pipe connected to the main water supply in a street.
hydraulic /haɪ'drɔːlɪk/ *adj* worked by water or some other fluid which is kept under pressure: *a hydraulic drill.*
hydroelectricity /ˌhaɪdrouɪlɛk'trɪsɪtɪ/ n electricity produced by means of water-power.
hydroe'lectric *adj*: *hydroelectric power stations.*
hydrofoil /'haɪdrəfɔɪl/ n a fast, light boat that rests on special supports and travels above the surface of the water.
hydrogen /'haɪdrədʒən/ n the lightest gas, which burns easily and which, when combined with oxygen, produces water.
hyena /haɪ'iːnə/ n a dog-like animal with a howl which sounds like human laughter.

> A hyena **laughs** or **screams**.

hygiene /'haɪdʒiːn/ n healthiness and cleanliness in the way we live and in our surroundings. **hy'gienic** *adj.* **hy'gienically** *adv.*
hymn /hɪm/ n a religious song of praise.
hyperactive /ˌhaɪpər'aktɪv/ *adj* more active than is normal: *She is worried that her young son is hyperactive.*
hypermarket /'haɪpəmɑːkɪt/ n a very large supermarket: *A new hypermarket has just opened on the outskirts of the town.*
hyphen /'haɪfən/ n a short stroke (-) which is used to join parts of a word *etc*, as in: *a sleeping-bag*; *a well-thought-out plan.*
hypnosis /hɪp'noʊsɪs/ n a sleep-like state into which you are put by the words of another person who can then make you obey his commands. **hyp'notic** *adj.*
hypnotism /'hɪpnətɪzm/ n the practice or the skill of putting people under hypnosis.

'hypnotist *n* a person who practices hypnotism.

'hypnotize *v* to use hypnosis on someone.

hypochondriac /haɪpəˈkɒndrɪak/ *n* a person who worries a lot about their health even when there is nothing wrong with them: *Hypochondriacs waste a lot of their time visiting the doctor.*

hypocrisy /hɪˈpɒkrɪsɪ/ *n* pretending to be better than you are.

hypocrite /ˈhɪpəkrɪt/ *n* someone who pretends they are better than they are. **hypoˈcritical** *adj.* **hypoˈcritically** *adv.*

hypodermic /haɪpəˈdɜːmɪk/ *n* a medical instrument with a thin hollow needle that is used for injecting a drug under the skin. — *adj*: *a hypodermic syringe.*

hypothesis /haɪˈpɒθəsɪs/, *plural* **hypotheses** /haɪˈpɒθəsiːz/, *n* an idea or suggestion that you put forward, for instance about how something happened: *The most likely hypothesis was that the murderer had been hiding behind the door when his victim entered.* **hypoˈthetical** *adj.* **hypoˈthetically** *adv.*

hysteria /hɪˈstɪərɪə/ *n* **1** a bad nervous upset that makes you behave strangely, for instance crying or screaming or laughing a lot. **2** a great deal of excitement and screaming among a crowd of people: *There was mass hysteria at the football match.*

hysˈterical *adj*: *He became hysterical after the shock of the accident.* **hyˈsterically** *adv.*

hyˈsterics *n* an uncontrollable emotional or excited state: *Please don't tell my mother – she'll have hysterics.*

in hysterics laughing uncontrollably: *She had the audience in hysterics.*

I

I /aɪ/ pron (used as the subject of a verb) the word you use when you are talking about yourself: *I can't find my book*; *John and I have always been friends.*

ice /aɪs/ n **1** frozen water: *The pond is covered with ice*; *Would you like ice in your orange juice?* **2** an ice cream: *Three ices, please.* — v to cover a cake *etc* with icing: *She iced the birthday cake.*

'iceberg n a huge mass of ice floating in the sea.

ice cream a sweet, creamy, frozen food: *a bowl of ice cream*; *two strawberry ice creams.*

ice cube a small cube of ice used for cooling drinks *etc*.

ice lolly a frozen block of ice cream or fruit juice on a stick.

ice rink a large room or building with a floor of ice for skating.

ice skates boots with thick metal blades on the soles for sliding over ice.

ice tray a metal or plastic tray for making ice-cubes in a refrigerator.

ice up or **ice over** to become covered with ice because the weather is very cold: *The roads had iced over during the night.*

the tip of the iceberg a small part of a much larger problem.

icicle /'aɪsɪkəl/ n a long hanging spike of ice formed by water freezing as it drops: *Icicles had formed on the edges of the roof.*

icing /'aɪsɪŋ/ n a mixture of sugar, water *etc*, used for covering and decorating cakes.

icon /'aɪkɒn/ n **1** a picture of Jesus Christ or a saint painted on wood: *He had an icon hanging above his bed.* **2** a symbol on a computer screen which represents a particular function: *If you choose that icon, the computer will print the work you have done.*

icy /'aɪsɪ/ adj **1** very cold: *icy winds.* **2** covered with ice: *icy roads.* **3** unfriendly: *She spoke in an icy voice.*

ID /aɪ'diː/ n identification; an official document that proves who you are: *an ID card*; *Do you have any ID with you?*

I'd short for **I had**, **I should** or **I would**.

idea /aɪ'dɪə/ n **1** opinion; belief: *I've an idea that he isn't telling the truth.* **2** a plan: *I've an idea for solving this problem.* **3** a picture in your mind: *This will give you an idea of what I mean.* **4** the aim or purpose of something: *The idea of the game is to win as many cards as possible.*

get the idea 1 to get a feeling or impression: *I got the idea that the work was not going well.* **2** to understand something or how to do something: *I got the idea of the game really quickly.*

ideal /aɪ'dɪəl/ adj perfect: *This tool is ideal for the job I have in mind.* — n **1** a person, thing *etc* that you believe is perfect: *She was clever and beautiful — in fact she was his ideal of what a wife should be.* **2** a person's standard of behaviour *etc*: *a man of high ideals.*

> an **ideal** (not **quite** or **most ideal**) place for a holiday.

i'dealism n the belief that the world can be made perfect: *She was full of youthful idealism.* **idea'list** n. **idea'listic** adj.

i'dealize v to think of as perfect or better than it really is: *She has a very idealized opinion of marriage.*

i'deally adv **1** perfectly: *He is ideally suited to this job.* **2** in an ideal situation: *Ideally, we should check this again, but we haven't enough time.*

identical /aɪ'dɛntɪkəl/ adj exactly the same: *His new car is identical to his old one*; *The twins wore identical dresses.* **i'dentically** adv.

identify /aɪ'dɛntɪfaɪ/ v to recognize: *Would you be able to identify the man who robbed you?*; *He identified the coat as his brother's.*

identifi'cation n.

identikit /aɪ'dɛntɪkɪt/ n a drawing of the face of a person whom the police want to find, made from a description of the face: *An identikit picture of the bank robber was shown on television.*

identity /aɪ'dɛntɪtɪ/ n who a person is: *The police still do not know the dead man's identity.*

i'dentity card a card that proves who you are.

ideology /aɪdɪ'ɒlədʒɪ/ n a set of beliefs and principles on which a faith, political ideas *etc* are based: *He is very interested in Marxist ideology.* **ideo'logical** adj.

idiocy /'ɪdɪəsɪ/ n stupidity; silliness.

idiom /'ɪdɪəm/ n **1** an expression used in speaking; a special way of saying something:

The idiom 'drop in' means to visit someone. **idio'matic** *adj.* **idio'matically** *adv.*

idiot /'ɪdɪət/ *n* a silly person; a fool: *She was an idiot to give up such a good job.* **idi'otic** *adj*: *idiotic actions.*

idle /'aɪdəl/ *adj* **1** lazy: *He has work to do, but he's idle and just sits around.* **2** not being used: *Ships were lying idle in the harbour.* **3** not really meant: *idle threats.* **4** unnecessary: *idle fears.* — *v* to be idle or lazy: *He just idles from morning till night.* **'idleness** *n.* **'idly** *adv.*

idle away to spend time doing nothing: *They idled the hours away on the beach.*

idol /'aɪdəl/ *n* **1** an image of a god that is worshipped: *The tribesmen bowed down before their idol.* **2** someone who is greatly admired: *The singer was the idol of thousands of teenagers.*

'idolize *v* to love or admire too much: *Many young people idolize pop stars.*

idyllic /ɪ'dɪlɪk/ *adj* very pleasant, peaceful and happy: *It was idyllic sitting in the sun by the river.*

if /ɪf/ *conjunction* **1** used when you are talking about possibilities: *He will have to go into hospital if his illness gets any worse; I'll only stay if you can stay too; If the head-teacher walked in now, and saw what we were doing, we would be in trouble; I wondered if I had misheard.* **2** whenever: *If I sneeze, my nose bleeds.* **3** whether: *I don't know if I can come or not.*

if only I wish: *If only I were rich!*

igloo /'ɪgluː/ *n* an Eskimo hut, built of blocks of snow.

igloo

ignite /ɪg'naɪt/ *v* to catch fire; to make something catch fire: *Petrol is easily ignited; Petrol ignites easily.*

ignition /ɪg'nɪʃən/ *n* **1** the device in a car *etc* which ignites the petrol in the engine: *He switched on the car's ignition.* **2** the igniting of something.

ignorant /'ɪgnərənt/ *adj* **1** knowing very little: *He's very ignorant — he ought to read more; I'm ignorant about money matters.* **2** not realizing something: *He continued on his way, ignorant of the dangers that lay ahead.* **'ignorantly** *adv.* **'ignorance** *n.*

ignore /ɪg'nɔː(r)/ *v* to take no notice of something or someone: *He ignored all my warnings.*

iguana /ɪ'gwɑːnə/ *n* a tropical American lizard that lives in trees.

ill /ɪl/ *adj* **1** not well; having a disease: *Jane is ill in bed — she has flu.* **2** bad: *ill health; These pills have no ill effects.* — *n* **1** bad luck: *I would never wish anyone ill.* **2** a trouble: *all the ills of this world.*

> **ill** means not well: *He is very ill with a fever.*
> **sick** means vomiting or feeling that you want to vomit: *He was sick twice in the car; I feel sick; I want to be sick.*

ill- badly: *ill-equipped.*

be taken ill to become ill: *He was taken ill at the party and was rushed to hospital.*

I'll short for **I will** or **I shall**.

illegal /ɪ'liːgəl/ *adj* not allowed by the law; not legal: *It is illegal to park a car here.* **il'legally** *adv.* **ille'gality** *n.*

illegible /ɪ'ledʒɪbəl/ *adj* very difficult or impossible to read: *His writing is illegible.* **il'legibly** *adv.* **illegi'bility** *n.*

illegitimate /ɪlə'dʒɪtɪmət/ *adj* **1** born of parents not married to each other. **2** not allowed by the law; against the rules: *It is our view that the contracts are illegitimate.* **ille'gitimately** *adv.* **ille'gitimacy** *n.*

ill-feeling /ɪl'fiːlɪŋ/ *n* an unkind feeling towards another person: *The two men parted without any ill-feelings.*

illicit /ɪ'lɪsɪt/ *adj* not allowed by law or by the social customs of a country: *an illicit trade in drugs.*

illiterate /ɪ'lɪtərət/ *adj* **1** unable to read and write. **2** having little education. **il'literacy** *n.*

ill-mannered /ɪl'manəd/ *adj* rude; having bad manners: *He's an ill-mannered young man.*

ill-natured /ɪl'neɪtʃəd/ *adj* bad-tempered: *Just because you're tired, there's no need to be so ill-natured.*

illness /'ɪlnɪs/ *n* bad health; a disease: *There is a lot of illness amongst the pupils just now; the illnesses of childhood.*

illogical /ɪ'lɒdʒɪkəl/ *adj* not sensible or reasonable; not logical: *It seems illogical to ask me when you already know the answer.*

ill-treat /ɪl'triːt/ *v* to treat badly: *She often ill-treated her children.* **ill-'treatment** *n.*

illuminate /ɪ'luːmɪneɪt/ *v* **1** to light up: *The gardens were illuminated by rows of lamps.* **2** to explain something or make it easier to understand. **il'luminating** adj. **illumi'nation** n.

illumi'nations n coloured lights that are put up to decorate a street etc.

illusion /ɪˈluːʒən/ n **1** a false idea, belief or impression that you have: *The old man was under the illusion that he still looked young and handsome.* **2** a sight or appearance that cheats your eyes, so that you see something that isn't really there: *The men in the desert thought they saw a lake in the distance, but it was only an optical illusion.*

illustrate /ˈɪləstreɪt/ v **1** to put pictures into a book etc: *The book is illustrated with drawings and photographs.* **2** to make what you are saying clearer by giving an example etc: *Let me illustrate my point; This diagram will illustrate what I mean.*

'illustrated adj having pictures etc: *an illustrated catalogue.*

illu'stration n **1** a picture: *coloured illustrations.* **2** an example.

'illustrator n.

I'm short for **I am**.

image /ˈɪmɪdʒ/ n **1** a copy or model of a person etc made of wood, stone etc: *a carved image of Jesus.* **2** something that is like a copy of something else: *She's the image of her sister.* **3** a reflection: *She looked at her image in the mirror.* **4** a picture in your mind: *I have an image of his face in my mind.*

imaginary /ɪˈmadʒɪnərɪ/ adj existing only in your mind; not real: *A dragon is an imaginary beast, not a real one.*

imagination /ɪmadʒɪˈneɪʃən/ n **1** the part of your mind in which you see pictures: *I could see the house in my imagination.* **2** the ability to think of ideas by yourself, and to describe things in your own words: *This composition shows a lot of imagination.* **3** the seeing etc of things which do not exist: *There was no-one there — it was just your imagination.*

imaginative /ɪˈmadʒɪnətɪv/ adj full of imagination: *an imaginative writer; This composition is interesting and imaginative.*

imaginable /ɪˈmadʒɪnəbəl/ adj that can be imagined: *the most wonderful food imaginable; They have every imaginable luxury in their home.*

imagine /ɪˈmadʒɪn/ v **1** to realize or understand: *I can imagine how you felt.* **2** to believe that you can see or hear something which is not really there: *Children often imagine that there are frightening animals under their beds; You're just imagining things!* **3** to think: *I imagine that he will be late.*

imbalance /ɪmˈbaləns/ n a difference in fairness or equality: *There is an imbalance between the many opportunities open to men and the few open to women.*

imbecile /ˈɪmbəsiːl/ n an unkind word for someone who is stupid; an idiot: *Don't be such an imbecile!*

imitate /ˈɪmɪteɪt/ v to do as someone else etc does; to copy: *Children imitate their friends rather than their parents; He could imitate the song of many different birds.*

imi'tation n imitating: *Children learn how to speak by imitation; He did a good imitation of the teacher's way of speaking.* — adj made to look like something else: *imitation pearls.* **'imitative** adj. **'imitativeness** n.

'imitator n a person who imitates.

immaculate /ɪˈmakjʊlət/ adj **1** very clean, neat and tidy: *immaculate white shirts; Her house is always immaculate.* **2** perfectly correct; with no mistakes: *an immaculate performance.*

immaterial /ɪməˈtɪərɪəl/ adj not important; not relevant: *It's immaterial whether you agree or not; He collects old books of all kinds — their condition is immaterial to him.*

immature /ɪməˈtjʊə(r)/ adj childish; behaving as if you are younger than you are.

imma'turity n.

immediate /ɪˈmiːdɪət/ adj **1** happening at once, without any delay: *I want an immediate reply to my question.* **2** without anything coming between: *in the immediate future.*

im'mediately adv **1** at once: *He answered immediately.* **2** directly; very closely: *He wasn't immediately involved in the crime.* **3** nearest in time or position: *I couldn't see because there was a tall man sitting immediately in front of me; I always check that I have got my keys immediately before leaving the house.* — conjunction as soon as: *I knew she had bad news immediately I saw her face.*

immense /ɪˈmɛns/ adj very large: *an immense forest.* **im'mensely** adv. **im'mensity** n.

immerse /ɪˈmɜːs/ v **1** to put something into a liquid: *She immersed the vegetables in boiling water.* **2** to involve yourself deeply in something; to give something your whole attention: *She's immersed herself in her work at the moment.* **im'mersion** n.

immigrant /ˈɪmɪɡrənt/ n a person who has come into a foreign country to live. — adj: *immigrant workers.*

'immigrate v to enter a country in order to live there.

The opposite of **immigrate** is **emigrate**.

immi'gration n entering a country in order to live there.

imminent /'ɪmɪnənt/ adj expected very soon: *A storm is imminent*. **'imminence** n.

immobile /ɪ'moʊbaɪl/ adj not able to move or be moved; not moving: *His leg was put in plaster and he was immobile for several weeks*; *She sat immobile*. **immo'bility** n.
im'mobilize v to prevent something from working or moving: *The bomber attacks completely immobilized the enemy's tanks*.

immoral /ɪ'mɒrəl/ adj wrong; wicked: *immoral behaviour*. **im'morally** adv. **immo'rality** n.

immortal /ɪ'mɔːtəl/ adj living for ever; never dying: *A person's soul is said to be immortal*. **immor'tality** n.
im'mortalize v to make famous forever or for a very long time: *Her beauty was immortalized in the films she made*.

immovable /ɪ'muːvəbəl/ adj impossible to move: *The rock was immovable*.

immune /ɪ'mjuːn/ adj protected against something: *immune to measles*; *immune to danger*. **im'munity** n.
'immunize v to prevent someone from getting a disease by giving them an injection, especially one that contains the germs of a weak form of the disease. **immuni'zation** n.

imp /ɪmp/ n a mischievous little being, especially a child: *Her son is a little imp*.

impact /ɪm'pækt/ n **1** the force of one object *etc* hitting another: *The bomb exploded on impact*. **2** an effect: *The film made quite an impact on the children*.

impair /ɪm'pɛə(r)/ v to damage, weaken or make less good: *He was told that smoking would impair his health*. **im'pairment** n.

impart /ɪm'pɑːt/ v to give information *etc*: *She said she had information to impart*.

impartial /ɪm'pɑːʃəl/ adj not favouring one person *etc* more than another: *an impartial judge*. **im'partially** adv. **imparti'ality** n.

impassive /ɪm'pæsɪv/ adj showing no emotion or feeling: *Her face remained totally impassive throughout the interview*. **im'passively** adv.

impatient /ɪm'peɪʃənt/ adj not willing to wait; not patient: *Don't be so impatient — it will soon be your turn on the swing*. **im'patience** n. **im'patiently** adv.

impeccable /ɪm'pɛkəbəl/ adj without a fault, flaw or mistake: *His clothes are always impeccable*. **im'peccably** adv.

impede /ɪm'piːd/ v to make it difficult for someone or something to move or make progress: *Recent developments have been impeded by a shortage of money*.

impediment /ɪm'pɛdɪmənt/ n **1** a person or thing that makes development or progress difficult: *Are there any impediments to their marriage?* **2** a slight fault or problem when speaking: *A stammer is a common speech impediment*.

impending /ɪm'pɛndɪŋ/ adj about to happen: *There was a feeling of impending disaster at the meeting*.

imperative /ɪm'pɛrətɪv/ adj very important; very urgent: *It is imperative that you bring written permission from your parents for the school trip*. — n a verb used in the form of a command; a word that tells you to do something: *Come here!*; *Listen!*; *Stop it!*

imperceptible /ɪmpə'sɛptəbəl/ adj too small or quiet to be noticed: *an almost imperceptible change of expression*.

imperfect /ɪm'pɜːfɪkt/ adj having a fault: *This coat is being sold cheap because it is imperfect*. **im'perfectly** adv. **imper'fection** n.

imperial /ɪm'pɪərɪəl/ adj belonging to an empire or an emperor: *the imperial crown*.
im'perialism n the policy of trying to control other countries. **im'perialist** n, adj.

impersonal /ɪm'pɜːsənəl/ adj not friendly: *Her voice was cold and impersonal*.

impersonate /ɪm'pɜːsəneɪt/ v to copy the behaviour *etc* of someone else or pretend to be another person: *An actor impersonated the prime minister*. **imperso'nation** n.

impertinent /ɪm'pɜːtɪnənt/ adj rude; not showing respect: *The headmaster punished the boy for being impertinent to his teacher*. **im'pertinently** adv. **im'pertinence** n.

impervious /ɪm'pɜːvɪəs/ adj **1** not affected or influenced by something: *You never quite become impervious to criticism*. **2** not allowing water to pass through: *The outer surface of the jacket is completely impervious to rain*.

impetuous /ɪm'pɛtjʊəs/ adj acting or done very quickly and without thought: *She is a very impetuous person*.

impetus /'ɪmpɪtəs/ n a force or energy which causes something to happen or progress: *The discovery of a vaccine gave new impetus to the fight against the disease*.

impinge /ɪm'pɪndʒ/ v to affect or interfere

with something in some way: *I'm not going to let my job impinge on my private life.*

implant /ɪmˈplɑːnt/ *v* **1** to put ideas *etc* into a person's mind. **2** to put a replacement for a damaged part of someone's body permanently into their body. **implan'tation** *n*.

implausible /ɪmˈplɔːzəbəl/ *adj* difficult to believe: *a ridiculously implausible excuse.*

implement *n* /ˈɪmpləmənt/ a tool, device or instrument: *garden implements; Chopsticks are eating implements.* — *v* /ˈɪmpləment/ to start using a plan or system *etc*: *The new parking system will be implemented next month.* **implemen'tation** *n*.

implicate /ˈɪmplɪkeɪt/ *v* to show or suggest that someone is involved in a crime *etc*: *The discovery of his footprints at the scene of the crime certainly implicated him.*
impli'cation *n* something that is suggested or implied by an event or situation: *What are the implications of the President's speech?*

implicit /ɪmˈplɪsɪt/ *adj* suggested; not directly stated: *It was implicit in her criticism that she thought he could have done it better.*
im'plicitly *adv* completely: *He trusts all his workers implicitly.*

implore /ɪmˈplɔː(r)/ *v* to ask earnestly: *She implored her husband to give up smoking; She implored his forgiveness.* **im'ploring** *adj*.

imply /ɪmˈplaɪ/ *v* to suggest; to mean: *Are you implying that I am not telling the truth?*

impolite /ɪmpəˈlaɪt/ *adj* not polite; rude: *You must not be impolite to the teacher.* **impo'litely** *adv*. **impo'liteness** *n*.

import *v* /ɪmˈpɔːt/ to bring in goods from abroad to sell in your own country: *Britain imports wine from France.* — *n* /ˈɪmpɔːt/ **1** something which is imported from abroad: *Our imports are greater than our exports.* **2** the bringing of goods into your country from abroad: *the import of wine.* **impor'tation** *n*. **im'porter** *n*.

important /ɪmˈpɔːtənt/ *adj* **1** mattering a lot: *Your eighteenth birthday is an important occasion; It is important that you should all know the rules.* **2** powerful: *He is an important man; She has an important job.* **im'portantly** *adv*.
im'portance *n*: *matters of great importance.*

impose /ɪmˈpəʊz/ *v* **1** to charge a tax, fine *etc*: *The government have imposed a new tax on cigarettes.* **2** to give someone a task: *You mustn't impose any extra tasks on him.* **impo'sition** *n*.

imposing /ɪmˈpəʊzɪŋ/ *adj* having a very impressive appearance: *an imposing building; Her father was a tall, imposing man with clear blue eyes.*

impossible /ɪmˈpɒsɪbəl/ *adj* not able to be done; too difficult to do: *It is impossible to sing and drink at the same time; an impossible task.* **im'possibly** *adv*. **impossi'bility** *n*.

impostor /ɪmˈpɒstə(r)/ *n* a person who pretends to be someone else in order to deceive another person: *He called at her house saying he was a policeman — but he was just an impostor.*

impostor is spelt **-or**.

impractical /ɪmˈpræktɪkəl/ *adj* not practical, reasonable or sensible: *an impractical suggestion.*

imprecise /ɪmprɪˈsaɪs/ *adj* not precise, accurate or clear: *imprecise instructions; I've only got a very imprecise idea of what happened.*

impress /ɪmˈpres/ *v* **1** to cause feelings of admiration *etc* in someone: *I was impressed by his good behaviour; The children's concert greatly impressed her.* **2** to fix something in someone's mind: *I must impress on you the need for hard work; Impress this date on your memory.* **3** to make a hollow mark by pressing: *A footprint was impressed on the sand.*

im'pression *n* **1** the effect produced in someone's mind by a person, experience *etc*: *The film made a great impression on me.* **2** an idea or opinion that you form about something: *I have the impression that he's not pleased.* **3** a hollow mark made by pressing: *an impression of a dog's paw in the cement.* **4** an attempt to look and talk like another person, usually someone famous, as a way of amusing or entertaining others: *My brother does a good impression of the headmaster.*

im'pressionable *adj* easily impressed or influenced by others: *Teenagers can be very impressionable.*

im'pressive *adj* making a great impression on your mind and feelings: *an impressive ceremony.* **im'pressively** *adv*. **im'pressiveness** *n*.

imprint *n* /ˈɪmprɪnt/ a mark made by pressing: *the imprint of a foot in the sand.* — *v* /ɪmˈprɪnt/: *The scene was imprinted on her memory.*

imprison /ɪmˈprɪzən/ *v* to put someone in prison; to take or keep someone prisoner: *He was imprisoned for twenty years for his crimes.* **im'prisonment** *n*.

improbable /ɪmˈprɒbəbəl/ *adj* **1** not likely to

impromptu

happen; not probable: *It is improbable that men will ever fly like birds.* **2** hard to believe: *He told us an improbable story.* **im'probably** *adv.* **improba'bility** *n.*

impromptu /ɪmˈprɒmptjuː/ *adj, adv* without preparation: *an impromptu speech; He spoke impromptu.*

improper /ɪmˈprɒpə(r)/ *adj* wrong: *Reading comics in school is an improper use of your time.* **im'properly** *adv.* **impro'priety** *n.*

improper fraction a fraction which is larger than 1: $\frac{5}{4}$ *is an improper fraction.*

improve /ɪmˈpruːv/ *v* to make or become better: *His work has improved; They have recently improved the engine of that car.*

im'provement *n* **1** the improving of something: *There has been a great improvement in her work.* **2** something that makes a thing better than it was: *I've made several improvements to the house.*

improve on to make something better than it is: *Your performance was good, but I think you can still improve on it.*

improvise /ˈɪmprəvaɪz/ *v* **1** to make something quickly, from whatever you can find: *They improvised a shelter from branches and blankets.* **2** to make up music as you play it: *He improvised a tune on the piano.* **improvi'sation** *n.*

impudent /ˈɪmpjʊdənt/ *adj* rude: *an impudent remark.* **'impudently** *adv.* **'impudence** *n.*

impulse /ˈɪmpʌls/ *n* **1** a sudden force: *an electrical impulse.* **2** a sudden desire: *I felt an impulse to hit him.*

im'pulsive *adj* inclined to act suddenly, without careful thought: *She has an impulsive nature.* **im'pulsively** *adv.* **im'pulsiveness** *n.*

impure /ɪmˈpjʊə(r)/ *adj* dirty; mixed with other substances; not pure: *impure air; The water is impure.* **im'purity** *n.*

in /ɪn/ *prep* **1** inside; within: *My mother is in the house; The house is in London; I am in bed; He came in his car.* **2** into: *He put his hand in his pocket.* **3** during a particular period: *I'll come in the morning.* **4** at the end of a particular period: *I'll be back in a week.* **5** used in many other kinds of expression: *She was dressed in a brown coat; They were walking in the rain; I'm in a hurry; The book is written in English; He is in the army; The letters were tied up in bundles; His daughter is in her teens; Pink shoes are in fashion.* — *adv* **1** at home; in your office etc: *Is your mother in?; The boss won't be in today.* **2** arrived: *Is the train in yet?* **3** in fashion: *Short skirts are in.*

> You travel **in** or **on** a **bus, train, boat, ship** or **(aero)plane**; you travel **in** a **car**. See also **at**.

day in, day out day after day without a break: *I do the same boring job day in, day out.*

in for going to have: *We're in for some bad weather; You're in for trouble if you broke that window!*

> **in spite of** see **spite**.

in that because: *This is not a good plant for your garden in that its seeds are poisonous.*

inability /ɪnəˈbɪlɪtɪ/ *n* a lack of ability: *my inability to remember people's names.*

inaccessible /ɪnəkˈsɛsəbəl/ *adj* difficult or impossible to approach, reach or obtain: *That beach is inaccessible by car.* **inaccessi'bility** *n.*

inaccurate /ɪnˈakjʊrət/ *adj* not correct; not accurate: *an inaccurate translation.* **in'accuracy** *n.*

inactive /ɪnˈaktɪv/ *adj* **1** not taking much exercise: *You're fat because you're so inactive.* **2** not active; no longer active: *an inactive volcano.*

in'action, inac'tivity *ns.*

inadequate /ɪnˈadɪkwət/ *adj* not enough or suitable: *This house is inadequate for such a big family.* **in'adequately** *adv.* **in'adequacy** *n.*

inadvertent /ɪnədˈvɜːtənt/ *adj* done by accident, without thinking.

inad'vertently *adv: I had inadvertently stood on someone's foot.*

inadvisable /ɪnədˈvaɪzəbəl/ *adj: It would be inadvisable for you to go alone.*

inane /ɪˈneɪn/ *adj* silly or stupid: *We have learnt not to listen to her inane remarks.*

inappropriate /ɪnəˈprəʊprɪət/ *adj* not suitable or appropriate: *The tools I had with me were completely inappropriate for the job.*

inattentive /ɪnəˈtɛntɪv/ *adj* not paying attention; not attentive: *inattentive pupils.* **inat'tention, inat'tentiveness** *ns.*

inaudible /ɪnˈɔːdɪbəl/ *adj* not loud or clear enough to be heard: *Her voice was inaudible because of the noise.* **in'audibly** *adv.* **inaudi'bility** *n.*

inaugural /ɪˈnɔːɡərəl/ *adj* officially marking the beginning of something: *The new chairman will make her inaugural speech on Thursday.*

inaugurate /ɪˈnɔːgjʊreɪt/ v **1** to install a new president or other leader at an official ceremony. **2** to start, introduce or open something new.
inauguˈration n: *We had an invitation to attend the inauguration ceremony.*

inborn /ɪnˈbɔːn/ adj natural: *an inborn ability to paint.*

incalculable /ɪnˈkælkjʊləbəl/ adj too great to judge or calculate: *This had done incalculable harm to the peace process.*

incapable /ɪnˈkeɪpəbəl/ adj not able: *He seems to be incapable of learning anything.* **incapaˈbility** n.

See **unable**.

incarnate /ɪnˈkɑːnɪt/ adj in human form: *The dictator was so evil that the people called him the devil incarnate.* **incarˈnation** n.

incendiary /ɪnˈsendɪərɪ/ adj designed to cause a fire: *an incendiary bomb.*

incense n /ˈɪnsens/ a substance which is burned in religious services *etc*, and which smells pleasant. — v /ɪnˈsens/ to make someone very angry: *The boy's rudeness incensed the teacher.*

incentive /ɪnˈsentɪv/ n something that encourages you: *The teacher always praised the children if they had done well, as an incentive to hard work.*

incessant /ɪnˈsesənt/ adj going on and on without stopping; continual: *The neighbours complained to the police about the incessant noise.*
inˈcessantly adv: *She talked incessantly so that no-one else could say anything.*

inch /ɪntʃ/ n **1** a measure of length, equal to 2·54 centimetres. **2** a small amount: *There is not an inch of room to spare.* — v to move slowly and carefully: *He inched along the narrow ledge.*

incidence /ˈɪnsɪdəns/ n how often something happens or occurs: *There is a higher incidence of left-handedness among boys than girls.*

incident /ˈɪnsɪdənt/ n an event or happening: *There was a strange incident in the supermarket today.*

inciˈdental adj occurring *etc* by chance in connection with something else: *an incidental remark.*

inciˈdentally adv by the way: *Incidentally, where were you last night?*

incinerate /ɪnˈsɪnəreɪt/ v to destroy something completely by burning.

inˈcinerator n a container in which rubbish is burnt.

incision /ɪnˈsɪʒən/ n a cut, especially one made by a surgeon: *The incision will not leave a very big scar.*

incite /ɪnˈsaɪt/ v to encourage someone to do something, especially something bad: *He incited the people to rebel against the king.*
inˈcitement n.

inclination /ɪnklɪˈneɪʃən/ n a slight desire or preference: *I felt an inclination to hit him; Have you any inclinations towards teaching?*

incline v /ɪnˈklaɪn/ to bow your head *etc*: *He inclined his head in agreement.* — n /ˈɪnklaɪn/ a slope.

inclined /ɪnˈklaɪnd/ adj **1** likely to behave in a particular way: *He is inclined to be a bit lazy.* **2** having a slight wish or desire: *I am inclined to accept their invitation.*

include /ɪnˈkluːd/ v to add someone or something into a group *etc*: *Am I included in the team?; Your duties include making the tea.*

The opposite of **include** is **exclude**.

inˈcluding prep: *The whole family has been ill, including the baby.*

inclusion /ɪnˈkluːʒən/ n: *The inclusion of all that violence in the film was unnecessary.*

inˈclusive adj including everything: *The price of the holiday is fully inclusive; The meal cost £25, inclusive of drinks; May 4 to May 6 inclusive is a period of three days.*

incognito /ɪnkɒgˈniːtəʊ/ adv, adj without letting people know who you are, for example by using a false name: *He travelled incognito to Paris.*

incoherent /ɪnkəʊˈhɪərənt/ adj difficult to understand or not clear: *He made a rambling, incoherent speech.* **incoˈherently** adv. **incoˈherence** n.

income /ˈɪnkʌm/ n money received by a person as wages *etc*: *He cannot support his family on his income.*

income tax a tax paid on income that is more than a certain amount.

incoming /ˈɪnkʌmɪŋ/ adj coming in: *the incoming tide; incoming telephone calls.*

incomparable /ɪnˈkɒmpərəbəl/ adj extraordinary; exceptional: *incomparable skill.*

incompatible /ɪnkəmˈpætɪbəl/ adj not able to work or live together: *The two computer systems are incompatible.* **incompatiˈbility** n.

incompetent /ɪnˈkɒmpɪtənt/ adj not very good at doing a job *etc*: *a very incompetent teacher.* **inˈcompetence** n. **inˈcompetently** adv.

incomplete /ɪnkəmˈpliːt/ *adj* not finished; with some part missing: *His book was still incomplete when he died*; *an incomplete pack of cards.*

incomprehensible /ɪnkɒmprɪˈhɛnsəbəl/ *adj* impossible to understand: *an incomprehensible explanation.*

inconceivable /ɪnkənˈsiːvəbəl/ *adj* impossible or very difficult to believe or imagine: *It was inconceivable that her mother wanted to hurt her.*

inconclusive /ɪnkənˈkluːsɪv/ *adj* not leading to a definite conclusion, result or decision: *an inconclusive discussion*; *The medical tests were inconclusive and will have to be repeated.* **inconˈclusively** *adv.*

incongruous /ɪnˈkɒŋɡruəs/ *adj* not suited to a particular situation; strange: *He was an incongruous figure in the coffee shop, wearing his dinner jacket.* **inˈcongruously** *adv.* **inconˈgruity** *n.*

inconsiderate /ɪnkənˈsɪdərət/ *adj* not caring about the feelings or comfort of other people: *It was inconsiderate of you to borrow the car without asking first.* **inconˈsiderately** *adv.* **inconˈsiderateness** *n.*

inconsistent /ɪnkənˈsɪstənt/ *adj* **1** not in agreement: *What you're saying today is quite inconsistent with the statement you made yesterday.* **2** changeable; sometimes good and sometimes bad *etc*: *His work is inconsistent.* **inconˈsistency** *n.* **inconˈsistently** *adv.*

inconspicuous /ɪnkənˈspɪkjuəs/ *adj* not easily noticed: *Our store detectives make themselves as inconspicuous as possible.*

inconvenience /ɪnkənˈviːnɪəns/ *n* something that causes difficulty; trouble: *He apologized for the inconvenience caused by his late arrival.* — *v* to cause inconvenience to someone: *I hope I haven't inconvenienced you.*

inconvenient /ɪnkənˈviːnɪənt/ *adj* causing trouble or difficulty: *He has come at a very inconvenient time.*

incorporate /ɪnˈkɔːpəreɪt/ *v* **1** to include something so that it forms part of the whole: *Most of the children's ideas were incorporated into the new school play.* **2** to contain something as part of the whole: *The shopping centre also incorporates a restaurant and a bank.*

incorrect /ɪnkəˈrɛkt/ *adj* not accurate; not correct; wrong: *an incorrect translation of a word.* **incorˈrectly** *adv.* **incorˈrectness** *n.*

incorrigible /ɪnˈkɒrɪdʒəbəl/ *adj* too bad to be improved.

increase *v* /ɪnˈkriːs/ **1** to grow in size, number *etc*: *The number of children in this school has increased greatly in recent years.* **2** to make something more or bigger: *My father has increased my pocket money.* — *n* /ˈɪnkriːs/ growth: *The increase in the population of the city over the last ten years was 20 000.*

> The opposite of **increase** is **decrease**.

inˈcreasingly *adv* more and more: *They found it increasingly difficult to pay for their children's school-books.*

incredible /ɪnˈkrɛdɪbəl/ *adj* hard to believe: *She has an incredible memory*; *What an incredible story!* **inˈcredibly** *adv.* **incrediˈbility** *n.*

incredulous /ɪnˈkrɛdjʊləs/ *adj* hardly believing; amazed. **increˈdulity** *n.* **inˈcredulously** *adv.*

> **incredible** means hard to believe: *What incredible luck!*
> **incredulous** means hardly believing: *He was incredulous when he heard about his luck.*

increment /ˈɪnkrəmənt/ *n* an increase in salary *etc.*

incubate /ˈɪnkjʊbeɪt/ *v* **1** to hatch eggs by keeping them warm, especially by sitting on them. **2** to develop in a person who has caught it: *How long does chickenpox take to incubate?* **incuˈbation** *n.*

ˈincubator *n* a heated container for hatching eggs; a special container in which babies who are born too early are kept and fed till they are strong and well.

incur /ɪnˈkɜː(r)/ *v* **1** to bring something unpleasant on yourself: *to incur someone's displeasure.* **2** to cause yourself expense: *to incur bills.*

> **incurred** and **incurring** are spelt with two **r**s.

incurable /ɪnˈkjʊərəbəl/ *adj* not able to be cured: *an incurable disease*; *an incurable habit.*

indebted /ɪnˈdɛtɪd/ *adj* grateful: *I am indebted to you for your help.* **inˈdebtedness** *n.*

indecent /ɪnˈdiːsənt/ *adj* not decent; disgusting: *indecent behaviour*; *indecent clothing.* **inˈdecency** *n.* **inˈdecently** *adv.*

indecision /ɪndɪˈsɪʒən/ *n* not being able to decide; hesitation.

indecisive /ɪndɪˈsaɪsɪv/ *adj* **1** not having a definite result: *an indecisive battle*. **2** unable to make firm decisions: *an indecisive person*.

indeed /ɪnˈdiːd/ *adv* **1** certainly; of course: *'He's very clever, isn't he?' 'He is indeed'*; *'Do you remember your grandmother?' 'Indeed I do!'* **2** used for emphasis: *Thank you very much indeed*; *This is very good indeed*; *By two o'clock he was very drunk indeed*. **3** used to express surprise, disbelief, interest or anger at what someone has just said: *'They were talking about you last night' — 'Were they indeed!'*

indefinite /ɪnˈdɛfɪnət/ *adj* not fixed; not definite: *The road will be out of use for an indefinite length of time*; *His plans are indefinite at the moment*. **inˈdefinitely** *adv*.

indefinite article the name given to the words **a** and **an**.

indelible /ɪnˈdɛləbəl/ *adj* making a mark that cannot be removed: *indelible ink*; *an indelible memory*.

independent /ɪndɪˈpɛndənt/ *adj* **1** not under the control of another country: *Latvia is an independent republic*; *When did it become independent of Britain?* **2** not willing to accept help: *an independent old lady*. **3** having enough money to support yourself: *She is completely independent and receives no money from her family*. **4** seeing for yourself, making up your own mind *etc*: *an independent observer*; *Would you like to hear my own independent opinion?* **indeˈpendence** *n*. **indeˈpendently** *adv*.

> The opposite of **independent** is **dependent**.

indescribable /ɪndɪsˈkraɪbəbəl/ *adj* too good or bad to be described accurately: *The pain she felt was indescribable*.

indesˈcribably *adv*: *The lecture was indescribably boring*.

indestructible /ɪndɪˈstrʌktəbəl/ *adj* so strong or tough that it cannot be broken or destroyed: *The new tanks were supposed to be indestructible*.

index /ˈɪndɛks/ *n* **1** an alphabetical list of names, subjects *etc* at the end of a book, telling you the page on which you will find them in the book. **2** (*plural* **indices** /ˈɪndɪsiːz/) in mathematics, the figure which indicates the number of times a number must be multiplied by itself *etc*: *In 6^3 and 7^5, the figures 3 and 5 are the indices*. — *v* to create an index of all the items in a book or collection *etc*: *She spent the afternoon indexing her record collection*.

index finger the finger next to the thumb: *She pointed at the map with her index finger*.

indicate /ˈɪndɪkeɪt/ *v* to show: *We can paint an arrow here to indicate the right path*.

indiˈcation *n* a sign: *There are indications that the weather is going to improve*; *He had given no indication that he was intending to leave the country*.

ˈindicator *n* a pointer, sign *etc* that indicates something: *The right indicator was flashing on the car in front*.

indices plural of **index**.

indifferent /ɪnˈdɪfərənt/ *adj* **1** not caring about something: *She is indifferent to other people's suffering*. **2** not very good: *He is an indifferent tennis-player*. **inˈdifference** *n*.

indigenous /ɪnˈdɪdʒənəs/ *adj* existing, living or growing in a place from the beginning, not brought from other places: *indigenous people*; *The domestic cat is not indigenous to Europe*.

indigestible /ɪndɪˈdʒɛstəbəl/ *adj* difficult to digest: *indigestible food*. **indigestiˈbility** *n*.

indigestion /ɪndɪˈdʒɛstʃən/ *n* pain that is caused by difficulty in digesting food: *She suffers from indigestion after eating fatty food*.

indignant /ɪnˈdɪgnənt/ *adj* angry, usually because of some wrong that has been done to you or someone else: *The indignant customer complained to the manager*. **inˈdignantly** *adv*. **indigˈnation** *n*.

indigo /ˈɪndɪgoʊ/ *n* a dark colour between blue and purple. — *adj*: *an indigo skirt*.

indirect /ɪndɪˈrɛkt/ *adj* not leading straight to a place; not direct: *We arrived late because we took an indirect route*.

indiˈrectly *adv*: *She feels indirectly responsible for what happened*.

indirect speech the form of speech you use when you are telling what someone has said: *He said that he would come is indirect speech for He said 'I will come'*.

indiscipline /ɪnˈdɪsəplɪn/ *n* bad behaviour; unwillingness to obey orders.

indiscreet /ɪndɪˈskriːt/ *adj* not careful or polite in what you say or do. **indiˈscreetly** *adv*.

indiscretion /ɪndɪˈskrɛʃən/ *n* **1** the quality of being indiscreet: *Her main fault is indiscretion*. **2** behaviour that is indiscreet: *a minor indiscretion*.

indiscriminate /ɪndɪˈskrɪmɪnət/ *adj* not carefully done or chosen with careful thought:

Indiscriminate terrorist attacks on civilians are still occurring.

indi'scriminately *adv*: *They fired their guns indiscriminately into the crowd.*

indispensable /ˌɪndɪˈspɛnsəbəl/ *adj* necessary: *A dictionary is an indispensable possession.*

indisputable /ˌɪndɪˈspjuːtəbəl/ *adj* definitely true; that cannot be proved wrong.

indistinct /ˌɪndɪˈstɪŋkt/ *adj* not clear, confused: *They could just see the indistinct outline of a ship through the haze.* **indi'stinctly** *adv.* **indi'stinctness** *n.*

individual /ˌɪndɪˈvɪdjʊəl/ *adj* **1** single; separate: *Put price labels on each individual item.* **2** for one person only: *All the children have their own individual pegs to hang their coats on.* — *n* a single person: *Every individual has a right to justice.* **individu'ality** *n.*
indi'vidually *adv* each separately: *I'll deal with each question individually.*

indivisible /ˌɪndɪˈvɪzəbəl/ *adj* not able to be divided or separated. **indivisi'bility** *n.*

indoctrinate /ɪnˈdɒktrɪneɪt/ *v* to fill people's minds with particular ideas or opinions until they accept them as the truth and think other ideas and opinions are wrong: *The dictator tried to indoctrinate the people with his false ideals.* **indoctri'nation** *n.*

indoor /ˈɪndɔː(r)/ *adj* inside a building: *indoor games; an indoor swimming-pool.*

> The opposite of **indoor** is **outdoor**.

in'doors *adv* in or into a building: *Stay indoors till you've finished your homework; He went indoors when the rain started.*

induce /ɪnˈdjuːs/ *v* **1** to persuade someone to do something: *He induced her to tell him her secret by promising to buy her an ice-cream.* **2** to cause something: *The doctor gave him some medicine that induced sleep.* **in'ducement** *n.*

indulge /ɪnˈdʌldʒ/ *v* to let someone have what they want or do what they want: *His mother indulges him too much; Life would be dull if you didn't indulge yourself sometimes.* **in'dulgence** *n.*
in'dulgent *adj* very kind, especially too kind: *an indulgent grandmother.*

industrial /ɪnˈdʌstrɪəl/ *adj* concerned with industry: *an industrial town.*
industrial estate an area set aside for factories.
in'dustrialist *n* a person who owns or controls an industry.
in'dustrialize *v* to develop a country or an area so that lots of industries grow up in it: *the industrialized countries of the world.* **industriali'zation** *n.*

industrious /ɪnˈdʌstrɪəs/ *adj* hardworking: *industrious pupils.*

industry /ˈɪndəstrɪ/ *n* **1** the manufacture of goods *etc*: *the ship-building industry; the rubber industry.* **2** hard work: *He owed his success to both ability and industry.*

inedible /ɪnˈɛdɪbəl/ *adj* not fit to be eaten: *The meal was inedible.*

ineffective /ˌɪnɪˈfɛktɪv/ *adj* useless: *ineffective methods.*

inefficient /ˌɪnɪˈfɪʃənt/ *adj* not working in the best way and so wasting time *etc*: *an inefficient workman; old-fashioned, inefficient machinery.* **inef'ficiently** *adv.* **inef'ficiency** *n.*

inequality /ˌɪnɪˈkwɒlɪtɪ/ *n* the difference in size, value *etc* between two or more things: *There is bound to be inequality between a manager's salary and a workman's wages.*

inert /ɪˈnɜːt/ *adj* **1** not having the power to move: *A stone is inert.* **2** not wanting to move, act or think: *He sits inert in his armchair watching television all day.*

inevitable /ɪnˈɛvɪtəbəl/ *adj* certain to happen *etc*: *The Prime Minister said that war was inevitable.* **inevita'bility** *n.* **in'evitably** *adv.*

inexcusable /ˌɪnɪkˈskjuːzəbəl/ *adj* too bad *etc* to be excused: *inexcusable rudeness.* **inex'cusably** *adv.*

inexhaustible /ˌɪnɪɡˈzɔːstəbəl/ *adj* that can never be used up: *Our energy supplies are not inexhaustible.*

inexpensive /ˌɪnɪkˈspɛnsɪv/ *adj* not expensive; cheap: *inexpensive clothes.* **inex'pensively** *adv.*

inexperience /ˌɪnɪkˈspɪərɪəns/ *n* lack of experience or knowledge: *He failed to get the job because of inexperience.*
inex'perienced *adj* lacking knowledge and experience: *You are still too young and inexperienced to leave home.*

inexplicable /ˌɪnɪkˈsplɪkəbəl/ *adj* impossible to explain or understand: *the inexplicable disappearance of the schoolgirl.* **inex'plicably** *adv.*

infallible /ɪnˈfaləbəl/ *adj* **1** never wrong; never making a mistake. **infalli'bility** *n.* **in'fallibly** *adv.*

infamous /ˈɪnfəməs/ *adj* famous because of being very bad: *an infamous criminal.* **'infamy** *n.*

> See **notorious**.

infant /ˈɪnfənt/ *n* a baby; a very young child.

'infancy *n* the time of being a baby: *He was very ill during infancy.*

infantile /'ɪnfəntaɪl/ *adj* very silly and childish: *grown men making infantile jokes.*

infantry /'ɪnfəntrɪ/ *n* soldiers who are on foot, not on horses: *The infantry marched behind the cavalry.*

infatuated /ɪn'fatjʊeɪtɪd/ *adj* having a strong, foolish and unreasonable love: *She is infatuated with him.* **infatu'ation** *n*.

infect /ɪn'fɛkt/ *v* to fill with germs that cause disease; to give a disease to someone: *You must wash that cut on your knee in case it becomes infected*; *She had a bad cold last week and has infected the rest of the class.*

in'fection *n* **1** infecting or being infected: *You should wash your hands after handling raw meat to avoid infection.* **2** a disease: *a throat infection.*

in'fectious *adj* likely to spread to others: *Measles is an infectious disease.*

infer /ɪn'fɜː(r)/ *v* to judge from facts: *I inferred from your silence that you were angry.* **'inference** *n*.

inferior /ɪn'fɪərɪə(r)/ *adj* **1** less good than something else: *This carpet is inferior to that one.* **2** bad: *This is very inferior work, Paul.* **3** lower in rank: *Is a colonel inferior to a brigadier?* **inferi'ority** *n*.

The opposite of **inferior** is **superior**.

This carpet is **inferior to** (not **than**) that one.

inferno /ɪn'fɜːnoʊ/, *plural* **in'fernos**, *n* a place of fire, horror and destruction: *The explosion turned the petrol station into a blazing inferno.*

infertile /ɪn'fɜːtaɪl/ *adj* **1** not fertile; not producing good crops: *The land was stony and infertile.* **2** unable to have babies. **infer'tility** *n*.

infest /ɪn'fɛst/ *v* to cover with insects or other pests: *The dog was infested with fleas*; *The house was infested with mice.* **infe'station** *n*.

infiltrate /'ɪnfɪltreɪt/ *v* **1** to get through enemy lines a few at a time: *to infiltrate enemy territory.* **2** to enter an organization in small numbers so as to be able to influence decisions *etc*.

infinite /'ɪnfɪnət/ *adj* **1** without end or limits: *We believe that space is infinite.* **2** very great: *Infinite damage could be caused by such a mistake.* **'infinitely** *adv*.

infinitive /ɪn'fɪnɪtɪv/ *n* the basic form of a verb: *'Have', 'be' and 'do' are infinitive forms.*

infinity /ɪn'fɪnɪtɪ/ *n* space, time or quantity that is without limit: *The night sky seemed to stretch away into infinity.*

infirm /ɪn'fɜːm/ *adj* weak or ill: *elderly and infirm people.* **in'firmity** *n*.

inflame /ɪn'fleɪm/ *v* to make feelings become violent: *to inflame someone's anger.*

in'flamed *adj* hot, red and sore, usually because of infection: *Her throat was very inflamed.*

inflammable /ɪn'flaməbəl/ *adj* easily set on fire: *Paper is highly inflammable.*

inflammable means the same as **flammable**: *a highly inflammable gas.*

inflammation /ɪnflə'meɪʃən/ *n* pain, redness and swelling in a part of the body: *inflammation of the throat.*

inflate /ɪn'fleɪt/ *v* to fill something with air; to blow something up: *He used a bicycle pump to inflate the ball.*

The opposite of **inflate** is **deflate**.

in'flatable *adj*: *an inflatable beach ball.*

in'flation *n* **1** a general increase in prices caused by an increase in the amount of money people are spending: *Inflation was brought down to below 5 per cent.* **2** the act of blowing something up.

inflict /ɪn'flɪkt/ *v* to give something unpleasant to someone: *Was it necessary to inflict such a punishment on him?* **in'fliction** *n*.

influence /'ɪnfluəns/ *n* **1** the power to affect people, actions or events: *He used his influence as a friend of the headmaster to get his daughter into a higher class*; *Never drive a car while under the influence of alcohol.* **2** a person or thing that has this power: *She is a bad influence on him.* — *v* to have an effect on someone or something: *The weather seems to influence her moods.*

influ'ential *adj* powerful; important: *He is in quite an influential job.*

influenza /ɪnflʊ'ɛnzə/ *n* an infectious illness with a headache, fever *etc*.

influx /'ɪnflʌks/ *n* a sudden arrival of people or things in large numbers: *We are expecting to see the usual influx of tourists to the island.*

inform /ɪn'fɔːm/ *v* **1** to tell: *Please inform your teacher if you wish to go on the outing to the zoo*; *I was informed that you were absent from the office.* **2** to tell the police about a criminal *etc*: *He informed against his fellow thieves.*

informal /ɪnˈfɔːməl/ *adj* not formal; friendly and relaxed: *The two prime ministers will meet for informal discussions today*; *Will the party be formal or informal?*; *friendly, informal manners*. **inforˈmality** *n*. **inˈformally** *adv*.

informant /ɪnˈfɔːmənt/ *n* someone who informs: *He passed on the news to us, but would not say who his informant had been.*

information /ɪnfəˈmeɪʃən/ *n* facts told to you or knowledge gained or given: *Can you give me any information about planes to Zurich?*; *He is full of interesting bits of information.*

> **information** is not used in the plural: *some information*; *any information*.

informative /ɪnˈfɔːmətɪv/ *adj* giving useful information: *an informative book.*

informed /ɪnˈfɔːmd/ *adj* having knowledge or information about something: *The police had no news but they promised to keep us informed.*

informer /ɪnˈfɔːmə(r)/ *n* a person who informs against a criminal.

infrequent /ɪnˈfriːkwənt/ *adj* happening only rarely or occasionally: *His visits to the hospital became increasingly more infrequent.* **inˈfrequently** *adv*.

infringe /ɪnˈfrɪndʒ/ *v* to break a law *etc* or interfere with a person's freedom. **inˈfringement** *n*.

infuriate /ɪnˈfjʊərieɪt/ *v* to make someone very angry: *I was infuriated by his rudeness.*
inˈfuriating *adj*: *I find his silly jokes infuriating.* **inˈfuriatingly** *adv*.

ingenious /ɪnˈdʒiːnɪəs/ *adj* clever: *He was ingenious at making up new games for the children*; *an ingenious plan.* **inˈgeniously** *adv*. **inˈgeniousness**, **ingenuity** /ɪndʒəˈnjuːɪtɪ/ *ns*.

ingot /ˈɪŋgət/ *n* a mass of metal, gold or silver cast in a mould.

ingrained /ɪnˈgreɪnd/ *adj* fixed firmly; difficult to change or remove: *The dirt was deeply ingrained in the carpet*; *ingrained stains*; *Selfishness was ingrained in his character.*

ingratitude /ɪnˈgrætɪtjuːd/ *n* the state of not being grateful: *After all the help I'd given him I expected something more than his ingratitude.*

ingredient /ɪnˈgriːdɪənt/ *n* one of the things that go into a mixture: *Could you give me a list of the ingredients of the cake?*

inhabit /ɪnˈhæbɪt/ *v* to live in a place: *Polar bears inhabit the Arctic region*; *That house is inhabited by an English family.*

inˈhabitant *n* a person or animal that lives permanently in a place: *the inhabitants of the village*; *tigers, leopards and other inhabitants of the jungle.*

inhale /ɪnˈheɪl/ *v* to breathe in: *It is very unpleasant to have to inhale the smoke from other people's cigarettes.*

> The opposite of **inhale** is **exhale**.

inherent /ɪnˈhɪərənt/ *adj* belonging naturally to someone or something: *The desire to win is inherent in us all.*
inˈherently *adv*: *She is inherently kind — she would never hurt anyone.*

inherit /ɪnˈherɪt/ *v* **1** to receive property or money that belonged to someone who has died: *He inherited the house from his father*; *She inherited £4000 from her father.* **2** to have qualities the same as your parents *etc*: *She inherits her quick temper from her mother.* **inˈheritance** *n*.

inhibit /ɪnˈhɪbɪt/ *v* to stop or hinder someone from doing something.
inˈhibited *adj* unable to relax and express your feelings: *She was a bit inhibited about speaking in front of the class.*
inhiˈbition *n*: *Actors have few inhibitions.*

inhospitable /ɪnhɒˈspɪtəbəl/ *adj* not friendly and welcoming.

inhuman /ɪnˈhjuːmən/ *adj* not seeming to be human: *inhuman cruelty*; *inhuman strength.* **inhuˈmanity** *n*.

inhumane /ɪnhjʊˈmeɪn/ *adj* unkind; cruel. **inhuˈmanely** *adv*.

> **inhuman** and **inhumane** both mean cruel, but **inhuman** also means 'more than human': *He made an inhuman effort.*

initial /ɪˈnɪʃəl/ *n* the letter that begins a word, especially a name: *The picture was signed with the initials J J B, standing for John James Brown.* — *adj* first; early; at the beginning: *In the initial stage of the disease, the patient developed bright red spots on his face.* — *v* to write your initials on something.
iˈnitially *adv* at first; in the beginning: *Initially the situation seemed far more serious than it really was.*

initiate *v* /ɪˈnɪʃɪeɪt/ **1** to start: *He initiated a scheme for helping old people with their shopping.* **2** to accept someone into a society *etc*, especially with secret ceremonies. — *n* /ɪˈnɪʃɪət/ a person who has been initiated.

initiative /ɪˈnɪʃətɪv/ *n* **1** a first step or move

that leads the way: *He took the initiative in making friends with the new neighbours.* **2** the ability to lead the way; the ability to make decisions for yourself: *He is quite good at his job, but lacks initiative.*

inject /ɪnˈdʒɛkt/ *v* to force a liquid into the body of a person using a needle and syringe: *The doctor injected the drug into her arm.* **inˈjection** *n.*

injure /ˈɪndʒə(r)/ *v* to harm or damage: *He injured his arm when he fell; They were badly injured when the car crashed.*

See **wound**.

'injured *adj* hurt in body or feelings: *The injured people were taken to hospital after the accident; 'There's no need to be so rude,' he said in an injured voice.*

injurious /ɪnˈdʒʊərɪəs/ *adj* harmful: *Smoking is injurious to your health.*

'injury *n* harm or damage; a wound *etc*: *Badly-made chairs can cause injury to your back; The motorcyclist received severe injuries in the crash.*

injury time playing time added to the end of a football or rugby match to make up for time taken to treat injured players during the match.

injustice /ɪnˈdʒʌstɪs/ *n* unfairness; lack of justice: *He complained of injustice in the way he had been dismissed from his job.*

ink /ɪŋk/ *n* a black or coloured liquid used for writing, printing *etc*: *Please sign your name in ink rather than pencil.*

inkling /ˈɪŋklɪŋ/ *n* a slight idea: *I had no inkling of what was going on.*

inland *adj* /ˈɪnlənd/ not beside the sea: *inland areas.* — *adv* /ɪnˈlænd/ in, or towards, the parts of the land away from the sea: *These flowers grow best inland; He travelled inland for many miles.*

in-laws /ˈɪnlɔːz/ *n* your husband or wife's parents: *We're going to visit my in-laws at the weekend.*

-in-'law related to you by marriage: *The man my sister is married to is my brother-in-law; My mother is his mother-in-law.*

inlet /ˈɪnlɛt/ *n* a small bay.

inmate /ˈɪnmeɪt/ *n* a person who lives in an institution, for instance a prison.

inmost /ˈɪnməʊst/ *adj* most secret: *her inmost desires.*

inn /ɪn/ *n* a small hotel or public house, especially in the countryside; a house providing food and lodging for travellers.

'innkeeper *n* a person who runs an inn.

innate /ɪˈneɪt/ *adj* being a natural quality of someone: *an innate ability.*

inner /ˈɪnə(r)/ *adj* further inside: *The inner tube of his tyre was punctured; It's difficult to guess someone's inner thoughts.*

The opposite of **inner** is **outer**.

'innermost *adj* **1** furthest from the edge or outside: *the innermost parts of the castle.* **2** most secret or hidden: *his innermost feelings.*

innings /ˈɪnɪŋz/ *n* a team's or player's turn at batting in a cricket match: *Pakistan need to score two hundred runs in their second innings if they are to win.*

innocent /ˈɪnəsənt/ *adj* **1** not guilty of a crime; not guilty of doing any wrong: *He is innocent of the crime; They hanged an innocent man.* **2** harmless: *an innocent remark.* **3** free from evil *etc*: *an innocent child.* **'innocently** *adv.* **'innocence** *n.*

The opposite of **innocent** is **guilty**.

innocuous /ɪˈnɒkjʊəs/ *adj* harmless: *This drug is innocuous unless taken together with anotherone.*

innovation /ɪnəˈveɪʃən/ *n* a change or a new arrangement *etc*: *The headmistress made some innovations.* **'innovator** *n.*

innumerable /ɪˈnjuːmərəbəl/ *adj* too many to be counted: *innumerable difficulties.*

inoculate /ɪˈnɒkjʊleɪt/ *v* to protect someone against a serious disease with an injection: *Has she been inoculated against measles?*

inoffensive /ɪnəˈfɛnsɪv/ *adj* harmless: *an inoffensive remark.*

inoperable /ɪnˈɒpərəbəl/ *adj* not able to be removed by an operation: *inoperable cancer.*

inorganic /ɪnɔːˈgænɪk/ *adj* things such as stone or metal, that do not consist of, or contain, living matter.

in-patient /ˈɪnpeɪʃənt/ *n* a person who lives in a hospital while receiving treatment there.

input /ˈɪnpʊt/ *n* **1** an amount of energy, labour *etc* that is put into something. **2** information put into a computer for processing.

The opposite of **input** is **output**.

inquest /ˈɪnkwɛst/ *n* a legal inquiry into a case of sudden and unexpected death.

inquire or **enquire** /ɪnˈkwaɪə(r)/ *v* **1** to ask: *He inquired the way to the art gallery; She inquired what time the bus left.* **2** to ask for information about something: *They inquired about trains to London.* **3** to ask about a person's health: *He inquired after her mother.* **4** to try to discover the truth about something: *The police are inquiring into the matter.*

> to **inquire** means to ask for information: *to inquire about lessons in German.*
> to **query** means to express doubt about something: *to query a bill.*

in'quiring *adj* eager to discover or learn new things: *Children usually have inquiring minds.*

in'quiry or **en'quiry** *n* **1** a question; a request for information: *Your inquiry is being dealt with.* **2** an investigation: *An inquiry is being held into the disaster.*

> an **inquiry** can be a request for information or an investigation: *a police inquiry.*
> a **query** is a question: *to answer a query.*

make inquiries to ask for information.

inquisitive /ɪnˈkwɪzɪtɪv/ *adj* eager to find out about other people's affairs: *The neighbours are very inquisitive about us.*

inroads /ˈɪnrəʊdz/: **make inroads on 1** to use up large amounts of: *He has made inroads on his savings.* **2** to attack and begin to destroy: *She hasn't finished the job but she has made inroads on it.*

insane /ɪnˈseɪn/ *adj* **1** mad. **2** extremely foolish: *It was insane to think he would give you the money.* **in'sanity** *n*.

inscribe /ɪnˈskraɪb/ *v* to carve or write: *Several names were inscribed on the gravestone.*

inscription /ɪnˈskrɪpʃən/ *n* something written, for instance on a gravestone or on a coin.

inscription

insect /ˈɪnsɛkt/ *n* any small creature with six legs, wings and a body divided into sections: *We were bothered by swarms of flies, wasps and other insects.*

insecticide /ɪnˈsɛktɪsaɪd/ *n* a substance for killing insects.

insecure /ɪnsɪˈkjʊə(r)/ *adj* **1** afraid; not confident: *Whenever he was in a crowd of people he felt anxious and insecure.* **2** not safe; not firm: *This chair-leg is insecure; an insecure lock.* **inse'curity** *n*.

> She feels **insecure** (not **insecured**).

insensible /ɪnˈsɛnsəbəl/ *adj* unconscious.

insensitive /ɪnˈsɛnsətɪv/ *adj* not feeling or not reacting to touch, light, the feelings of other people *etc*: *The dentist's injection made the tooth insensitive to the drill*; *He was insensitive to her sorrow.* **insensi'tivity** *n*.

inseparable /ɪnˈsɛpərəbəl/ *adj* **1** always together: *inseparable friends.* **2** closely linked; always considered together: *These two issues are inseparable — we cannot deal with one without dealing with the other.*

insert /ɪnˈsɜːt/ *v* to put something into something else: *He inserted the money in the parking meter*; *An extra chapter has been inserted into the book.* **in'sertion** *n*.

inset /ˈɪnsɛt/ *n* a small map, picture *etc* that has been put in the corner of a larger one.

inside *n* /ɪnˈsaɪd/ or /ˈɪnsaɪd/ the inner side, or the part or space within: *The inside of this apple is rotten.* — *adv* /ɪnˈsaɪd/ **1** to, in, or on, the inside: *The door was open and he went inside*; *She shut the door but left her key inside by mistake.* **2** in a house or building: *You should stay inside in such bad weather.* — *adj* /ˈɪnsaɪd/ on or in the inside: *The inside pages of the newspaper.* — *prep* **1** within; to or on the inside of something: *She is inside the house*; *He went inside the shop.*

in'sides *n* your internal organs, especially your stomach.

inside out 1 with the inner side out: *Haven't you got your shirt on inside out?* **2** very thoroughly: *He knows the book inside out.*

insight /ˈɪnsaɪt/ *n* an understanding of something: *He shows a lot of insight into children's problems.*

insignia /ɪnˈsɪɡnɪə/ *n* things worn or carried as a mark of high office: *The crown and sceptre are the insignia of a king.*

insignificant /ɪnsɪɡˈnɪfɪkənt/ *adj* having little value or importance: *They paid me an insignificant sum of money*; *an insignificant person.* **insig'nificance** *n*.

insincere /ɪnsɪnˈsɪə(r)/ *adj* not sincere: *His praise was insincere*; *insincere promises.* **insin'cerity** *n*.

insinuate /ɪnˈsɪnjʊeɪt/ *v* to suggest something unpleasant in an indirect way: *Newspaper reports insinuated that she had lied in court.* **insinu'ation** *n*.

insipid /ɪnˈsɪpɪd/ *adj* **1** dull and boring: *Many people find the president insipid.* **2** without taste or flavour: *A lot of the food he cooks is insipid.*

insist /ɪnˈsɪst/ *v* **1** to hold firmly to an opinion, plan *etc*: *He insists that I was to blame for the accident*; *I insisted on driving him home.* **2** to demand; to urge: *The teacher insists on good behaviour*; *She insisted on coming with me*; *He insisted that I should go.*

See **persist**.

in'sistence *n*: *She went to see the doctor at her husband's insistence.* in'sistent *adj.*

insolent /'ɪnsələnt/ *adj* rude; insulting: *an insolent remark.* 'insolently *adv.* 'insolence *n.*

insoluble /ɪn'sɒljʊbəl/ *adj* **1** too difficult to solve: *an insoluble problem.* **2** impossible to dissolve in a liquid: *a mineral which is insoluble in water.*

insomnia /ɪn'sɒmnɪə/ *n* the state of not being able to sleep: *He suffers from insomnia, so he takes sleeping-pills to help him to sleep.*

inspect /ɪn'spɛkt/ *v* **1** to examine carefully: *He inspected the bloodstains.* **2** to visit a restaurant or school officially, to make sure that it is properly run. **in'spection** *n.*

in'spector *n* **1** a person appointed to make an inspection: *a school inspector.* **2** a police officer of senior rank.

inspire /ɪn'spaɪə(r)/ *v* to encourage someone by filling them with confidence, enthusiasm *etc*: *The players were inspired by the loyalty of their supporters.* **inspi'ration** *n.*

in'spired *adj* showing more talent or skill than expected: *She gave an inspired performance*

in'spiring *adj* very exciting or interesting: *We didn't find the speech very inspiring.*

instability /ɪnstə'bɪlɪtɪ/ *n* the condition of not being steady or stable: *a period of economic instability.*

install /ɪn'stɔːl/ *v* **1** to put equipment *etc* in place ready for use: *The engineer installed the telephone yesterday.* **2** to put a person in a place or position: *He was installed as president yesterday*; *They soon installed themselves in the new house.*

instal'lation *n* **1** the process of installing something. **2** a piece of equipment that has been installed: *the cooker, fridge and other electrical installations.*

instalment /ɪn'stɔːlmənt/ *n* **1** a small sum of money that you pay regularly instead of paying a large bill all at once: *The new car is being paid for by monthly instalments.* **2** a part of a story that is printed one part at a time in a weekly magazine *etc*, or read in parts on the radio *etc*: *Did you hear the final instalment last week?*

instalment has one **l**.

instance /'ɪnstəns/ *n* an example; a particular case: *As a social worker, he saw many instances of extreme poverty.*

for instance for example: *Some birds, penguins for instance, cannot fly at all.*

instant /'ɪnstənt/ *adj* **1** immediate: *His latest play was an instant success.* **2** able to be prepared *etc* almost immediately: *instant coffee.* — *n* **1** a point in time: *He climbed into bed and at that instant the telephone rang.* **2** a moment or very short time: *It all happened in an instant*; *In an instant he had vaulted over the side of their car.*

instantaneous /ɪnstən'teɪnɪəs/ *adj* happening at once, or very quickly: *The effect of the injection was instantaneous.*

instan'taneously *adv*: *When you press the button, the television comes on almost instantaneously.*

'instantly *adv* immediately: *He went to bed and instantly fell asleep.*

instead /ɪn'stɛd/ *adv* in place of something or someone: *I don't like coffee. Could I please have tea instead?*; *Please take me instead of him*; *You should have been working instead of watching television.*

instep /'ɪnstɛp/ *n* **1** the middle, arched part of your foot. **2** the part of a sock, shoe *etc* that covers this.

instigate /'ɪnstɪɡeɪt/ *v* to suggest and encourage a wrong or criminal action. **insti'gation** *n.*

instil /ɪn'stɪl/ *v* to put ideas *etc* into someone's mind by teaching or training: *The importance of working hard was instilled into me by my father.*

instil has one **l**.

instinct /'ɪnstɪŋkt/ *n* a natural habit of behaving in a particular way, without thinking and without having been taught: *As winter approaches, swallows fly south from Britain by instinct*; *He has an instinct for saying the right thing.* **in'stinctive** *adj.* **in'stinctively** *adv.*

institute /'ɪnstɪtjuːt/ *n* a society or organization, or the building it uses. — *v* to start or establish: *When was the Red Cross instituted?*

insti'tution *n* an organization, a society or a building that has a particular purpose, especially the care of people, or education: *schools, hospitals, prisons and other institutions.* **insti'tutional** *adj.*

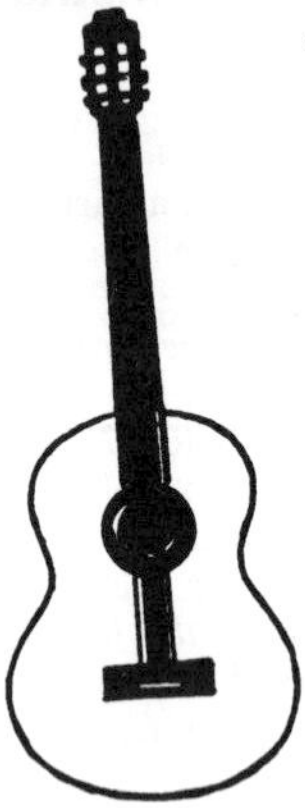

guitar

saxophone

oboe

clarinet

flute

trombone

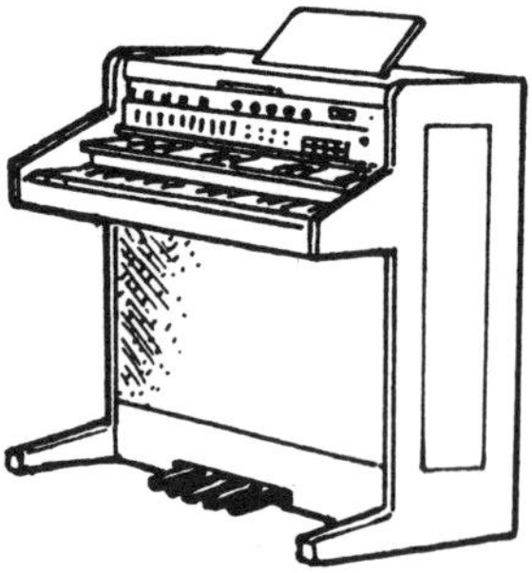

organ

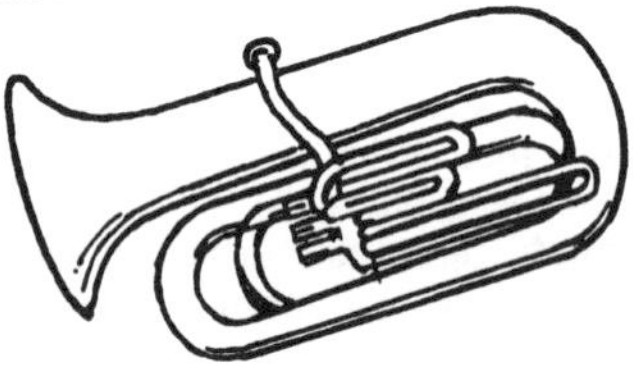

tuba

french horn

grand piano

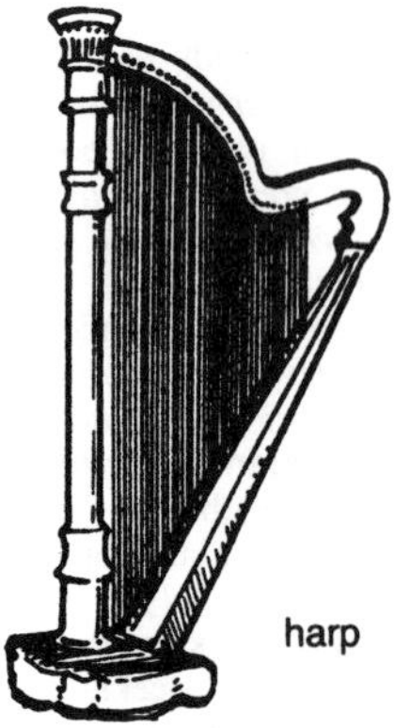

harp

instruct /ɪn'strʌkt/ v **1** to teach or train a person in a subject or skill: *Girls as well as boys should be instructed in woodwork.* **2** to order or direct a person to do something: *He was instructed to come here at nine o'clock.*

in'struction n **1** teaching: *She sometimes gives instruction in gymnastics.* **2** an order or direction: *You must learn to obey instructions.*

in'structions n information on how to do or use something: *Please read the instructions carefully before attempting to use this machine.*

in'structive adj giving useful information: *an instructive film.*

in'structor n a person who gives instruction in a skill *etc*: *a ski-instructor.*

instrument /'ɪnstrəmənt/ n **1** a tool, especially if used for delicate scientific or medical work: *medical instruments.* **2** an object whose purpose is to produce musical sounds: *He can play the piano, violin and several other instruments.*

instru'mental adj **1** performed on musical instruments, not by voices: *instrumental music.* **2** helpful: *She was instrumental in finding them a new home.*

insufferable /ɪn'sʌfərəbəl/ adj extremely annoying: *He's insufferable because he thinks he knows everything.*

insufficient /ɪnsə'fɪʃənt/ adj not enough: *There is insufficient food to last the week.* **insuf-'ficiently** adv. **insuf'ficiency** n.

insular /'ɪnsjʊlə(r)/ adj not interested in meeting new people or listening to new ideas or opinions.

insulin /'ɪnsjʊlɪn/ n a hormone which controls the amount of sugar in the blood: *If your body does not produce enough insulin, you may develop diabetes.*

insulate /'ɪnsjʊleɪt/ v to cover something with a material that does not let electrical currents or heat *etc* pass through it: *Rubber and plastic are used for insulating electric wires and cables.* **insu'lation** n.

insult v /ɪn'sʌlt/ to treat someone rudely: *He insulted her by telling her she was not only ugly but stupid too.* — n /'ɪnsʌlt/ a remark or action that insults someone: *Why do so many people use the word 'old' as an insult?* **in'sulting** adj: *insulting words.*

insurance /ɪn'ʃʊərəns/ n **1** an agreement made with a company, that if you pay them a regular sum, they will give you money if something of yours is lost, stolen, damaged *etc*. **2** the payment made to or by an insurance company: *Have you paid the insurance on your camera?*; *He received £100 insurance.*

insure /ɪn'ʃʊə(r)/ v to arrange insurance for something: *Is your camera insured?*; *Employers have to insure employees against accident.*

intact /ɪn'takt/ adj whole; not damaged: *The box was washed up on the beach with its contents still intact.*

intake /'ɪnteɪk/ n the thing or quantity taken in: *This year's intake of students is smaller than last year's.*

intangible /ɪn'tandʒɪbəl/ adj difficult to describe, understand or explain; not tangible: *She has an intangible quality which attracts people to her.*

integral /'ɪntɪɡrəl/ adj absolutely necessary; essential: *Learning how to keep fit and healthy should be an integral part of our education.*

integrate /'ɪntɪɡreɪt/ v **1** to fit parts together to form a whole. **2** to mix with other groups in society *etc*: *The immigrants are not finding it easy to integrate into the life of our city.* **inte'gration** n.

integrity /ɪn'tɛɡrɪti/ n honesty: *He is a man of absolute integrity.*

intellect /'ɪntəlɛkt/ n the thinking power of your mind: *He was a person of great intellect.*

intellectual /ɪntə'lɛktʃʊəl/ adj having to do with your intellect: *He does not play football — his interests are mainly intellectual.* — n a person who is interested in ideas, literature, art, *etc*: *He found himself in a room full of intellectuals discussing philosophy and politics.*

intelligence /ɪn'tɛlɪdʒəns/ n **1** the power of understanding: *His job doesn't require much intelligence.* **2** secret information about other countries *etc*: *the intelligence services.* **in'telligent** adj **1** clever and quick at understanding: *an intelligent child.* **2** showing intelligence: *an intelligent question.* **in'telligently** adv.

intelligible /ɪn'tɛlɪdʒəbəl/ adj able to be understood: *His answer was barely intelligible because he was speaking through a mouthful of food.* **intelligi'bility** n. **in'telligibly** adv.

intend /ɪn'tɛnd/ v **1** to mean to do something; to plan that something should happen: *Do you still intend to go?*; *Do you intend them to go?*; *I didn't intend that this should happen!*; *Did you intend this to happen?* **2** to mean something to be understood in a particular way: *His remarks were intended to be a com-*

pliment. **3** to direct something towards someone: *That letter was intended for me.*

intense /ɪn'tɛns/ *adj* very great: *intense heat.* **in'tensity** *n.*

in'tensely *adv* very much: *I dislike that sort of behaviour intensely.*

in'tensify *v* to increase; to make or become greater: *The police are intensifying their efforts to find the murderer; She called a doctor when the pain intensified.* **intensifi'cation** *n.*

in'tensive *adj* very thorough: *The police began an intensive search for the murderer; The hospital has just opened a new intensive care unit.* **in'tensively** *adv.*

intent /ɪn'tɛnt/ *adj* **1** meaning, planning or wanting to do something: *He's intent on going.* **2** concentrating hard on something: *He was intent on the job he was doing.* — *n* purpose; what a person means to do: *He broke into the house with intent to steal.*

in'tently *adv* with great attention: *He watched her intently.*

intention /ɪn'tɛnʃən/ *n* what a person plans or intends to do: *He has no intention of leaving; If I have offended you, it was quite without intention; good intentions.*

in'tentional *adj* done, said *etc* on purpose and not by accident: *I'm sorry I offended you — it wasn't intentional; intentional cruelty.* **in'tentionally** *adv.*

interact /ɪntər'akt/ *v* to have some effect on one another. **inter'action** *n.*

inter'active *adj* involving two-way communication between, for example, a machine and the person using or operating it: *interactive video games.*

intercept /ɪntə'sɛpt/ *v* to stop someone or something before they arrive at a particular place: *The police intercepted the bank robbers on their way to the airport; Jenny tried to pass a note to me but the teacher intercepted it.* **inter'ception** *n.*

interchange /'ɪntətʃeɪndʒ/ *n* **1** a place where two or more main roads or motorways at different levels are connected by means of several small roads, so allowing vehicles to move from one road to another. **2** an exchange: *an interchange of ideas.*

inter'changeable *adj* able to be put in the place of one another: *a saw with interchangeable blades.*

intercom /'ɪntəkɒm/ *n* a system of communication within an aeroplane, factory *etc* by means of microphones and loudspeakers: *The pilot spoke to the passengers over the intercom.*

intercontinental /ɪntə'kɒntɪ'nɛntəl/ *adj* travelling between or connecting different continents: *intercontinental air flights.*

intercourse /'ɪntəkɔːs/ *see* **sexual intercourse**.

interest /'ɪntərəst/ or /'ɪntərɛst/ *n* **1** curiosity; attention: *That newspaper story is bound to arouse interest; He used to be very active in politics, but he has lost interest now.* **2** a matter, activity *etc* that is of special concern to you: *Gardening is one of my main interests.* **3** money paid in return for borrowing a sum of money: *You will have to pay interest on this loan.* **4** a share in the ownership of a business firm *etc*. — *v* to hold the attention of someone; to be important to someone: *Sport doesn't interest him at all; The story interested her.*

'interested *adj* **1** eager to know about something; curious: *He's not interested in politics; Don't tell me any more — I'm not interested; I'll be interested to see what happens next week.* **2** keen to do something: *Are you interested in buying a car?*

'interesting *adj*: *an interesting book.*

'interestingly *adv* used to introduce something you think another person will find interesting: *Interestingly, I was told that by someone else only yesterday.*

in the interests of in order to protect or obtain something: *In the interests of safety, please do not smoke.*

lose interest to stop being interested: *He has lost interest in his work.*

take an interest to be interested: *I take a great interest in everything they do.*

interfere /ɪntə'fɪə(r)/ *v* **1** to try to organize or change something that is not your business; to meddle: *I wish you would stop interfering with my plans; Don't interfere in other people's business!* **2** to prevent or hinder something: *He doesn't let anything interfere with his game of golf on Saturday mornings.*

inter'ference *n*: *She was furious at his mother's interference in their holiday arrangements.* **inter'fering** *adj.*

> **interfered** and **interfering** are spelt with one **r**.

interior /ɪn'tɪərɪə(r)/ *adj* belonging to, or on the inside of something: *the interior walls of a building.* — *n* **1** the inside of a building *etc*: *The interior of the house was very attractive.* **2** the part of a country away from the coast: *The explorers landed on the coast, and then travelled into the interior.*

See **exterior**.

interjection /ɪntə'dʒɛkʃən/ *n* a word or words, or some noise, used to express surprise, pain or other feelings: *Oh dear! I've lost my key; Ouch! That hurts!*

interlock /ɪntə'lɒk/ *v* to fit or fasten together: *The pieces of a jigsaw puzzle interlock.*

interlude /'ɪntəluːd/ *n* a short period or gap, for instance between the acts of a play.

intermarry /ɪntə'marɪ/ *v* to marry one another: *Some of the soldiers stationed in the area intermarried with the local population.* **inter'marriage** *n*.

intermediary /ɪntə'miːdɪərɪ/ *n* a person who takes messages from one person or group to another during negotiations: *She acted as intermediary between the two families in their dispute over the garden.*

intermediate /ɪntə'miːdɪət/ *adj* in the middle; placed between two things, stages *etc*: *an intermediate English course.*

interminable /ɪn'tɜːmɪnəbəl/ *adj* having or appearing to have no end: *The meeting was interminable.* **in'terminably** *adv*.

intermission /ɪntə'mɪʃən/ *n* a pause or an interval during a film, concert *etc*.

intermittent /ɪntə'mɪtənt/ *adj* stopping for a while and then starting again: *Intermittent rain has been forecast for this morning; She was suffering from intermittent pain in her leg.*

inter'mittently *adv*: *It rained intermittently.*

intern /'ɪntɜːn/ *n* a junior doctor who works and sleeps at a hospital.

internal /ɪn'tɜːnəl/ *adj* on the inside of something, for instance a person's body: *The man suffered internal injuries in the accident.* **in'ternally** *adv*.

international /ɪntə'naʃənəl/ *adj* happening between nations: *international trade; an international football match.* — *n* a football match *etc* played between teams from two countries. **inter'nationally** *adv*.

interpret /ɪn'tɜːprɪt/ *v* **1** to translate a speaker's words, while he is speaking, into the language of his hearers: *He spoke to the audience in French and she interpreted.* **2** to show or explain the meaning of something: *How do you interpret these lines of the poem?* **interpre'tation** *n*. **in'terpreter** *n*.

interrelated /ɪntərɪ'leɪtɪd/ *adj* connected with each other: *He found that the two problems were interrelated.*

interrogate /ɪn'tɛrəgeɪt/ *v* to question a person thoroughly: *The police spent five hours interrogating the prisoner.* **interro'gation** *n*. **in'terrogator** *n*.

interrupt /ɪntə'rʌpt/ *v* **1** to stop someone while they are saying or doing something: *He interrupted her while she was speaking; He interrupted her speech; Listen to me and don't interrupt!* **2** to stop or make a break in an activity *etc*: *He interrupted his work to eat his lunch.*

inter'ruption *n*: *How can I work properly with so many interruptions?*

intersect /ɪntə'sɛkt/ *v* to cross; to meet each other: *Where do the two roads intersect?*

inter'section *n* a place where roads or lines intersect: *The accident happened at the intersection.*

interspersed /ɪntə'spɜːst/ *adj* placed at various points: *His speech was interspersed with jokes.*

interval /'ɪntəvəl/ *n* **1** a passing of time: *He returned home after an interval of two hours.* **2** a short break in a play, concert *etc*: *We had ice-cream in the interval.*

at intervals here and there; now and then: *Trees grew at intervals along the road.*

intervene /ɪntə'viːn/ *v* to try to stop a quarrel: *He intervened in the dispute.*

intervening /ɪntə'viːnɪŋ/ *adj* coming between two events: *It was a long time since my last visit and the place had changed a lot in the intervening years.*

inter'vention *n*: *This government is opposed to military intervention in another country's civil war.*

interview /'ɪntəvjuː/ *n* **1** a meeting and discussion with someone applying for a job *etc*. **2** a discussion in which a television or radio reporter asks a person questions that he thinks listeners would like to hear the answer to. — *v* to question a person in an interview: *They interviewed seven people for the job; He was interviewed by reporters about his policies.* **'interviewer** *n*.

intestines /ɪn'tɛstɪnz/ *n* the lower parts of the food passage in man and animals. **intestinal** /ɪn'tɛstɪnəl/ *adj*.

intimate /'ɪntɪmət/ *adj* **1** close and affectionate: *intimate friends.* **2** private; personal: *the intimate details of his correspondence.* **3** deep and thorough: *an intimate knowledge of English grammar.* — *n* a close friend. **'intimacy** *n*. **'intimately** *adv*.

intimidate /ɪn'tɪmɪdeɪt/ *v* to frighten,

into

especially by threatening violence. **intimi-'dation** n.

in'timidating adj frightening: *She can be a very intimidating woman.*

into /'ɪntuː/ prep **1** to the inside of something: *The eggs were put into the box*; *They went into the house.* **2** against: *The car ran into the wall.* **3** to a different state *etc*: *A tadpole turns into a frog*; *She translated the book into Spanish.* **4** expressing the idea of division: *Two into four goes twice.*

be into to be interested in or enthusiastic about something: *She's into classical music and all that.*

intolerable /ɪn'tɒlərəbəl/ adj not able to be endured: *intolerable pain*; *This delay is intolerable.* **in'tolerably** adv.

in'tolerant adj unwilling to accept people whose ideas *etc* are different from your own; not able to bear other people's weaknesses *etc*: *an intolerant attitude*; *He is intolerant of others' faults.* **in'tolerance** n.

intonation /ɪntə'neɪʃən/ n the rise and fall of your voice when you speak: *Radio newsreaders should have clear intonation.*

intoxicate /ɪn'tɒksɪkeɪt/ v **1** to make someone drunk: *Two glasses of wine were enough to intoxicate her.* **2** to make someone very excited: *He was intoxicated by his success.* **in'toxicating** adj. **intoxi'cation** n.

intransigent /ɪn'trænsɪdʒənt/ adj unwilling to change your behaviour or opinions, stubborn: *His intransigent attitude is a great problem.*

intravenous /ɪntrə'viːnəs/ adj in or into a vein: *an intravenous drip.*

intrepid /ɪn'trepɪd/ adj bold; brave; not easily frightened: *The intrepid mountaineers climbed the steepest side of the mountain*; *an intrepid explorer.*

intricate /'ɪntrɪkət/ adj complicated: *an intricate knitting pattern.* **'intricacy** n.

intrigue n /'ɪntriːg/ or /ɪn'triːg/ a secret plan; a plot. — v /ɪn'triːg/ **1** to make someone interested or curious: *The book intrigued me.* **2** to make secret plots. **in'triguing** adj.

intrinsic /ɪn'trɪnsɪk/ adj belonging to a thing as a basic and important part of it: *The painting has no intrinsic value.* **in'trinsically** adv.

introduce /ɪntrə'djuːs/ v **1** to make people known by name to each other: *He introduced the guests to each other*; *Let me introduce you to my mother*; *May I introduce myself? I'm John Brown.* **2** to bring in something new: *Grey squirrels were introduced into Britain from Canada.* **3** to start instruct-

ing someone in a particular subject *etc*: *Children are introduced to algebra at about the age of eleven.*

intro'duction n **1** the introducing of something: *the introduction of new methods.* **2** the introducing of one person to another: *The hostess made the introductions and everyone shook hands.* **3** something written at the beginning of a book explaining the contents. **intro'ductory** adj.

introvert /'ɪntrəvɜːt/ n a person who prefers to spend time on their own and does not enjoy social events: *As an introvert, she really dislikes having to go to parties.*

> See **extrovert**.

'introverted adj quiet or shy: *It seems odd that his wife is so introverted.*

intrude /ɪn'truːd/ v to come in when you are not wanted or invited; to take up someone's time: *I'm sorry to intrude on your time.*

in'truder n a person who intrudes, for example a burglar.

in'trusion n an act of intruding: *She was angry at his intrusion into the meeting.*

in'trusive adj disturbing your peace or privacy: *I thought the attention we received from journalists was often intrusive.*

intuition /ɪntjʊ'ɪʃən/ n the power of understanding or realizing something without thinking it out: *She knew by intuition that he was telling her the truth.*

inundate /'ɪnʌndeɪt/ v **1** to cover a place with water; to flood: *The river burst its banks and inundated the fields.* **2** to heap or pile a great quantity of something on someone: *The students were inundated with work for their exams.* **inun'dation** n.

invade /ɪn'veɪd/ v to enter a country *etc* with an army: *Britain was twice invaded by the Romans.* **in'vader** n.

invalid[1] /ɪn'vælɪd/ adj not able to be used legally; not valid: *Your passport is out of date and therefore invalid.*

invalid[2] /'ɪnvəlɪd/ n a person who is ill or disabled: *During the last few years of his life, he was a permanent invalid.*

invaluable /ɪn'væljʊəbəl/ adj very precious; very useful: *Thank you for your invaluable help.*

> **invaluable** means very valuable; it is not the opposite of **valuable**.

invariable /ɪn'veərɪəbəl/ adj not changing: *an invariable habit.*

in'variably adv always.

invasion /ɪnˈveɪʒən/ *n* the invading of a country *etc*.

invent /ɪnˈvɛnt/ *v* **1** to be the first person to make a machine, use a method *etc*: *Who invented the microscope?*; *When was printing invented?* **2** to make up a story *etc*: *I'll have to invent some excuse for not going with him.*

See also **discover**.

in'vention *n* something invented: *What a marvellous invention the sewing-machine was!*

in'ventive *adj* good at thinking of new and original ways of doing things.

in'ventor *n* a person who invents something.

inverse /ˈɪnvɜːs/ *n* the opposite: *If 5 = 5/1, then its inverse is 1/5.*

invert /ɪnˈvɜːt/ *v* to turn something upside down. **in'version** *n*.

inverted commas commas, the first being turned upside down, used in writing to show where direct speech begins and ends; quotation marks: *'It is a lovely day,' she said.*

invertebrate /ɪnˈvɜːtɪbrət/ *n* a creature that has no backbone, such as a worm, insect or shark.

invest /ɪnˈvɛst/ *v* to put money into a business in order to make a profit: *He invested in a building firm.*

investigate /ɪnˈvɛstɪgeɪt/ *v* to examine carefully: *The police are investigating the mystery.* **investi'gation** *n*. **in'vestigator** *n*.

in'vestigative *adj* trying to find out all the facts about something: *investigative journalism.*

investment /ɪnˈvɛstmənt/ *n* the investing of money in a business *etc*, or the money invested. **in'vestor** *n*.

invigilate /ɪnˈvɪdʒəleɪt/ *v* to sit with students and be in charge of them while they are doing an examination. **invigi'lation** *n*. **in'vigilator** *n*.

invigorate /ɪnˈvɪgəreɪt/ *v* to make someone feel stronger or fresher; to strengthen and refresh: *Her walk in the cool air invigorated her.*

in'vigorating *adj*: *an invigorating shower.*

invincible /ɪnˈvɪnsɪbəl/ *adj* not able to be defeated: *an invincible army.*

invisible /ɪnˈvɪzəbəl/ *adj* not able to be seen: *Only in stories can people make themselves invisible.* **invisi'bility** *n*.

invitation /ɪnvɪˈteɪʃən/ *n* a request made to someone to go somewhere *etc*: *Have you received an invitation to their party?*

invite /ɪnˈvaɪt/ *v* **1** to ask a person politely to come to your house, to a party *etc*: *They have invited us to dinner tomorrow.* **2** to ask a person politely to do something: *He was invited to speak at the meeting.* **3** to ask for suggestions *etc*: *He invited suggestions for a project from the pupils.*

in'viting *adj* attractive: *There was an inviting smell coming from the kitchen.*

invoice /ˈɪnvɔɪs/ *n* a list sent with goods giving details of price and quantity.

involuntary /ɪnˈvɒləntərɪ/ *adj* not intentional; not done on purpose; happening too quickly to be controlled: *She gave an involuntary cry when he stepped on her toe.* **in'voluntarily** *adv*.

involve /ɪnˈvɒlv/ *v* **1** to require: *His job involves a lot of travelling.* **2** to interest or concern someone: *He has always been involved in the theatre; Don't ask my advice — I don't want to get involved.* **in'volvement** *n*.

in'volved *adj* very complicated: *The plot of the film was so involved that I didn't really understand the ending.*

inward /ˈɪnwəd/ *adj* being inside or moving towards the inside: *an inward curve; inward happiness.*

The opposite of **inward** is **outward**.

'inward or **'inwards** *adv* towards the inside or the centre: *When one of your eyes turns inwards, we call the effect a squint.*

'inwardly *adv* secretly: *She was laughing inwardly.*

iodine /ˈaɪədiːn/ or /ˈaɪədaɪn/ *n* a black substance in the form of crystals or a liquid, used in medicine.

irate /aɪˈreɪt/ *adj* angry.

iris /ˈaɪrɪs/ *n* **1** the coloured part of your eye. **2** a brightly-coloured flower similar to a lily.

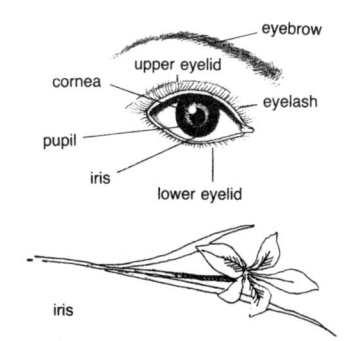

iron /'aɪən/ *n* **1** the most common metal, which is very hard, and is used for making tools *etc*: *Steel is made from iron*; *The ground is as hard as iron*; *She sat on a rickety iron seat halfway down the garden*. **2** a flat-bottomed instrument that is heated up and used for smoothing clothes *etc*: *I've burnt a hole in my dress with the iron*. — *adj* made of iron: *iron tools*. — *v* to smooth clothes *etc* with an iron: *This dress needs to be ironed*.

'ironing *n* clothes waiting to be ironed, or just ironed: *What a huge pile of ironing!*

'ironing-board *n* a padded board on which to iron clothes.

strike while the iron is hot to act while the situation is favourable.

ironic /aɪ'rɒnɪk/ or **ironical** /aɪ'rɒnɪkəl/ *adj* **1** meaning the opposite of what you are saying; not serious: *If you say 'What a brilliant remark' to someone who has just said something stupid, you are being ironic*. **2** funny; strange: *It's really ironic that now she's got a bicycle she prefers to walk*. **i'ronically** *adv*.

irony /'aɪrənɪ/ *n* **1** a way of speaking that shows other people that you really mean the opposite of what you are saying: *'That was clever', she said with irony, when he sat on her glasses*. **2** a funny or strange side of a situation: *He cheated in the test by copying the answers from the teacher's answer-book, but the irony was that he copied the answers to the wrong test*.

irrational /ɪ'raʃənəl/ *adj* not the result of clear, logical thought: *His decision was irrational*.

irregular /ɪ'rɛgjʊlə(r)/ *adj* **1** not regular: *The bus-service is irregular*. **2** not even: *His pulse was irregular*. **ir'regularly** *adv*.

irregu'larity *n*.

irrelevant /ɪ'rɛləvənt/ *adj* not connected with the subject that is being discussed *etc*: *irrelevant remarks*. **ir'relevance, ir'relevancy** *ns*. **ir'relevantly** *adv*.

irreplaceable /ɪrɪ'pleɪsəbəl/ *adj* so valuable or rare that it cannot be replaced.

irrepressible /ɪrɪ'prɛsɪbəl/ *adj* always lively, cheerful and enthusiastic.

irresistible /ɪrɪ'zɪstəbəl/ *adj* too strong to be resisted: *He had an irresistible desire to hit her*.

irrespective /ɪrɪ'spɛktɪv/: **irrespective of** without considering something: *The pupils are taught together, irrespective of age or ability*.

irresponsible /ɪrɪ'spɒnsɪbəl/ *adj* not sensible: *It was very irresponsible to leave the child alone outside the shop*; *irresponsible behaviour*. **irresponsi'bility** *n*. **irre'sponsibly** *adv*.

irreverent /ɪ'rɛvərənt/ *adj* not showing proper respect: *The programme takes an irreverent look at the medical profession*. **ir'reverence** *n*.

irreversible /ɪrɪ'vɜːsəbəl/ *adj* impossible to stop, change or turn back: *It seems that the decision is irreversible*.

irrigate /'ɪrɪgeɪt/ *v* to supply water to land by canals or other means. **irri'gation** *n*.

irritate /'ɪrɪteɪt/ *v* **1** to annoy someone; to make someone angry: *The children's chatter irritated him*. **2** to make a part of the body sore, red, itchy *etc*: *Soap can irritate a baby's skin*. **irri'tation** *n*.

'irritable *adj* easily annoyed; grumpy: *He was in an irritable mood*. **'irritably** *adv*. **irrita'bility** *n*.

is see **be**.

-ish /ɪʃ/ *suffix* slightly, fairly: *reddish hair*.

Islam /'ɪzlɑːm/ *n* the Muslim religion. **Is'lamic** *adj*.

island /'aɪlənd/ *n* **1** a piece of land surrounded by water: *The island lay a mile off the coast*. **2** a small section of pavement built in the middle of a street, for pedestrians to stand on.

'islander *n* someone living on an island.

See **isthmus**.

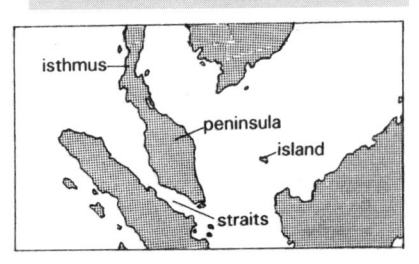

isle /aɪl/ *n* an island, used especially in names of islands: *the Isle of Wight*.

isn't short for **is not**.

isolate /'aɪsəlɛɪt/ *v* to separate, cut off or keep apart from others: *Several houses have been isolated by the flood water*; *A child with an infectious disease should be isolated*. **iso'lation** *n*.

issue /'ɪʃuː/ *v* **1** a problem or subject for discussion: *I hope to raise the issue at tomorrow's meeting*; *Your own personal views are not really the issue*. **2** to come out from something: *A strange noise issued from the room*. **3** to give out officially: *The police* *issued a description of the criminal*; *Rifles were issued to the troops.* — *n* **1** the giving out of something: *Stamp collectors like to buy new stamps on the day of issue.* **2** one number in the series of a newspaper, magazine *etc*: *Have you seen the latest issue of that magazine?*

make an issue of to treat something as very important and something to be argued about: *We disagree on this, but let's not make an issue of it.*

isthmus /'ɪsməs/ *n* a narrow strip of land joining two larger pieces: *the Isthmus of Panama.*

it /ɪt/ *pron* **1** (used as the subject of a verb or object of a verb or preposition) a thing, a fact *etc*, also an animal or a baby: *If you find my pencil, please give it to me*; *The dog is in the garden, isn't it?*; *I picked up the baby because it was crying*; *He said he could drive, but it wasn't true.* **2** used as a subject in certain kinds of sentences, for example, when you are talking about the weather, distance or time: *Is it raining very hard?*; *It's cold*; *It is five o'clock*; *Is it the fifth of March?*; *It's two miles to the village*; *Is it your turn to make the tea?*; *It is impossible for him to finish the work*; *It was nice of you to come.* **3** used with the verb **be** to emphasize a certain word: *It was you that I wanted to see, not Mary.*

italics /ɪ'talɪks/ *n* letters or writing which slopes to the right: *Examples are printed in italics in this dictionary.*

itch /ɪtʃ/ *n* a feeling in your skin that makes you want to scratch: *He had an itch in the middle of his back and could not scratch it easily.* — *v* to be itchy: *Wool can make your skin itch.*

'itchy *adj* itching: *an itchy rash*; *I feel itchy all over.* **'itchiness** *n*.

it'd short for **it had** or **it would**.

item /'aɪtəm/ *n* **1** an object or article that is one of several, for instance, in a list: *He ticked the items as he read through the list.* **2** a piece of news in a newspaper *etc*: *Did you see the item about dogs in the newspaper?* **'itemize** *v* to list or mention things separately: *an itemized bill.*

itinerary /aɪ'tɪnərərɪ/ *n* a route for a journey.

it'll short for **it will**.

its /ɪts/ *adj, pron* belonging to it: *The bird has hurt its wing.*

> **its** is an adjective or pronoun expressing possession: *a cat and its kittens.*
> **it's** is short for **it is** or **it has**: *It's raining heavily.*

it's short for **it is** or **it has**.

itself /ɪt'sɛlf/ *pron* **1** used as the object of a verb or preposition when a thing, animal *etc* is both the subject and the object: *The cat looked at itself in the mirror*; *The cat stretched itself by the fire.* **2** used to emphasize **it** or the name of an object, animal *etc*: *The house itself is quite small, but the garden is big*; *I've met several French people — one day I'd like to visit France itself.* **3** without help: *'How did the dog get in?' 'Oh, it can open the gate itself.'*

I've /aɪv/ short for **I have**.

ivory /'aɪvərɪ/ *n* the hard white substance of which the tusks of an elephant *etc* are formed: *Ivory was once used to make piano keys.* — *adj*: *ivory chessmen.*

ivy /'aɪvɪ/ *n* a type of climbing evergreen plant with shiny leaves that grows up trees and walls.

J

jab /dʒab/ *v* to poke; to prod: *He jabbed me in the ribs with his elbow.* — *n* **1** a sudden hard poke or prod: *He gave me a jab with his finger.* **2** a medical injection: *You should have a typhoid jab before you go on holiday there.*

jabber /'dʒabə(r)/ *v* to talk very quickly and not clearly: *I can't understand you when you jabber like that.*

jack /dʒak/ *n* **1** a device for raising part of a motor car *etc* off the ground. **2** the playing-card between the ten and queen: *The jack, queen and king are the three face cards.*

jack up to raise a motor car *etc* with a jack: *They had to jack up the car to change the wheel.*

jackal /'dʒakəl/ *n* a wild animal similar to a dog or wolf.

jackass /'dʒakas/ *n* **1** a male ass. **2** a stupid person: *the silly jackass!*

jacket /'dʒakɪt/ *n* **1** a short coat: *He wore brown trousers and a blue jacket.* **2** a loose paper cover for a book: *I like the design on this book-jacket.*

jack-in-the-box /'dʒakɪnðəbɒks/ *n* a doll fixed to a spring inside a box, that jumps out when the lid is opened.

jack-knife /'dʒaknaɪf/ *n* a large folding knife. — *v* to bend in the middle and therefore go out of control: *The lorry jack-knifed after it slowed down too quickly on the wet road.*

jackpot /'dʒakpɒt/ *n* in card-games *etc* that are played for money, a large amount of prize-money that keeps increasing till it is won.

hit the jackpot to win, or suddenly earn, a large amount of money.

jade /dʒeɪd/ *n* a type of hard stone, usually green in colour. — *adj*: *jade ornaments.*

jaded /'dʒeɪdɪd/ *adj* tired and bored: *jaded employees*; *You look a bit jaded — can't you take a short holiday?*

jagged /'dʒagɪd/ *adj* having rough or sharp and uneven edges: *jagged rocks.*

jaguar /'dʒagjʊə(r)/ *n* a South American animal of the cat family, similar to a leopard in appearance, with a spotted coat.

jail or **gaol** /dʒeɪl/ *n* prison: *You ought to be sent to jail for doing that.* — *v* to put someone in prison: *He was jailed for two years.*

to put a criminal in jail or **gaol** (not **goal**).

'jailer or **'gaoler** *n* a person who is in charge of a jail or of prisoners: *The jailer was knocked unconscious in the riot.*

'jailbird or **'gaolbird** *n* a person who is in jail, or has often been in jail.

jam[1] /dʒam/ *n* a thick sticky substance made of fruit *etc* boiled with sugar: *raspberry jam.*

jam[2] /dʒam/ *v* **1** to crowd: *The gateway jammed with angry people.* **2** to get stuck; to make something get stuck: *This drawer has jammed*; *My door-key got jammed in the lock.* — *n* **1** a crowding together of vehicles *etc* so that nothing can move: *a traffic jam.* **2** a difficult situation: *I'm in a jam — I haven't got enough money to pay for this meal — can you lend me some?*

jam on to put on suddenly and with force: *When the dog ran in front of his car he jammed on his brakes.*

jamboree /dʒambə'riː/ *n* a large gathering of people, especially Boy Scouts, Girl Guides *etc.*

jangle /'dʒaŋgəl/ *v* to make or cause to make a sound like metal objects hitting each other: *Her earrings jangled as she ran.*

janitor /'dʒanɪtə(r)/ *n* **1** a caretaker. **2** a man on duty at the door of a hotel *etc.*

'janitress *n* a female janitor.

January /'dʒanjʊərɪ/ *n* the first month of the year, the month following December.

jar[1] /dʒɑː(r)/ *n* a container made of glass or pottery with a wide neck: *a jar of honey*; *jam-jars.*

jar[2] /dʒɑː(r)/ *v* **1** to have an unpleasant effect on someone: *Her sharp voice jarred on my ears*; *The car accident had jarred her nerves.* **2** to hurt or damage something as a result of a jerk or bump: *He fell back and jarred his back.*

jargon /'dʒɑːgən/ *n* special words used by a particular group of people when they talk to each other, that are difficult for other people to understand: *criminals' jargon*; *doctors' jargon.*

jarring /'dʒɑːrɪŋ/ *adj* startling; harsh: *The orange curtains with the purple carpet had a jarring effect.*

jaundice /'dʒɔːndɪs/ *n* an illness in which your

skin and whites of your eyes become yellow.

jaunt /dʒɔːnt/ *n* a journey made for pleasure; a trip: *Did you enjoy your jaunt to Cornwall?*

jaunty /'dʒɔːntɪ/ *adj* cheerful; bright; lively: *He walked along with a jaunty step.* **'jauntily** *adv.* **'jauntiness** *n.*

javelin /'dʒævəlɪn/ *n* a light spear for throwing, especially in an athletic competition.

jaw /dʒɔː/ *n* either of the two bones of your mouth that hold your teeth: *the upper jaw; the lower jaw; His jaw was broken in the fight.*

jaws *n* an animal's mouth: *The crocodile opened its jaws wide.*

jaywalker /'dʒeɪwɔːkə(r)/ *n* a person who walks carelessly among traffic. **'jaywalking** *n.*

jazz /dʒæz/ *n* popular music that was first played and sung by black Americans.

jazz up to make something seem brighter or livelier: *I suppose we could jazz the walls up with some posters.*

jealous /'dʒeləs/ *adj* **1** feeling envy; envious: *She is jealous of her sister's beauty.* **2** having feelings of dislike for any possible rivals: *a jealous husband.* **'jealously** *adv.* **'jealousy** *n.*

jeans /dʒiːnz/ *n* trousers made of denim.

jeep /dʒiːp/ *n* a small motor vehicle used, especially by the armed forces.

jeer /dʒɪə(r)/ *v* **1** to shout scornfully at someone: *He was jeered as he tried to speak to the crowd.* **2** to make fun of someone rudely: *He's always jeering at her stupidity.* — *n* a rude shout: *the jeers of the audience.*

'jeering *adj* mocking: *a jeering tone.*

jelly /'dʒelɪ/ *n* **1** the juice of fruit boiled with sugar until it is firm, used like jam, or served with meat. **2** a sweet, transparent food, usually with a flavour of fruit: *I've made raspberry jelly for the party.* **3** any jelly-like substance: *Frogs' eggs are enclosed in a kind of jelly.*

jellyfish /'dʒelɪfɪʃ/, *plural* **'jellyfish** or **'jelly-fishes**, *n* a kind of sea animal with a jelly-like body.

jeopardize /'dʒepədaɪz/ *v* to risk damaging or destroying: *Don't jeopardize your chances of promotion by arguing with your boss.*

jeopardy /'dʒepədɪ/ *n* danger.

jerk /dʒɜːk/ *n* a short, sudden movement: *We felt a jerk as the train started.* — *v* to move with a jerk: *The car jerked to a halt.* **'jerky** *adj.* **'jerkily** *adv.*

jersey /'dʒɜːzɪ/ *n* a knitted garment for the top part of your body; a sweater: *She put on a jersey over her blouse when it got colder.*

jest /dʒest/ *n* a joke; something done or said to make people laugh. — *v* to joke.

'jester *n* in earlier times, a man employed in the courts of kings *etc* to amuse them with jokes *etc.*

in jest jokingly: *speaking in jest.*

jet /dʒet/ *n* **1** a strong stream of liquid, gas, flame or steam, forced through a narrow opening: *The firemen directed jets of water at the burning house.* **2** a narrow opening through which a jet of water, gas *etc* comes: *This gas jet is blocked.* **3** an aeroplane driven by **jet engines** that work by sucking gas in and forcing it out behind: *We flew by jet to America; Low-flying military jets blasted down the glen.*

'jetlag *n* tiredness caused by travelling quickly from one time zone to another: *Jetlag can be a serious problem for international businessmen.* **'jetlagged** *adj.*

jettison /'dʒetɪsən/ *v* to throw cargo *etc* overboard to lighten a ship, aircraft *etc* in times of danger.

jetty /'dʒetɪ/ *n* a small pier for use as a landing-place.

See **quay**.

jewel /'dʒuəl/ *n* a precious stone: *rubies, emeralds and other jewels.*

'jewelled *adj* covered with jewels: *a jewelled crown.*

'jeweller *n* a person who makes, or sells, jewellery *etc*, made of precious stones and metals.

jewellery /'dʒuəlrɪ/ *n* articles that you wear to decorate your body, such as bracelets, necklaces, brooches, rings *etc.*

jibe or **gibe** /dʒaɪb/ *n* a cruel remark: *cruel jibes.* — *v*: *He kept jibing at his wife.*

jiggle /'dʒɪgəl/ *v* to move jerkily: *The television picture kept jiggling up and down.*

jigsaw /'dʒɪgsɔː/ *n* a puzzle made up of many pieces of various shapes that fit together to form a picture.

jihad /dʒɪ'hɑːd/ *n* a holy war fought by Muslims.

jilt /dʒɪlt/ *v* to reject someone with whom you have been in love.

jingle /'dʒɪŋgəl/ *n* **1** a ringing sound made by coins, small bells *etc*: *the jingle of coins.* **2** a little rhyme: *nursery rhymes and other jingles; advertising jingles.* — *v* to make a ringing sound: *He jingled the coins in his pocket.*

jinx /dʒɪŋks/ *n* an evil spell or bad luck: *She believes there is a jinx on my car which makes it keep breaking down.*
    jinxed *adj*: *The project was jinxed from the start — everything went wrong that could go wrong.*

jittery /'dʒɪtərɪ/ *adj* nervous and anxious: *She's feeling jittery about her exam tomorrow.*

job /dʒɒb/ *n* **1** a person's daily work: *She has a job as a bank-clerk.* **2** a piece of work; a task: *I have several jobs to do before going to bed.* **3** a function or responsibility: *Your job is to turn the light on when I tell you to.*
    make a good job of to do something well: *You've made a good job or ironing my shirts.*
    'jobless *adj* wanting, but not having, paid work. — *n*: *The jobless are all the people who don't have jobs.*

jockey /'dʒɒkɪ/ *n* a person employed to ride horses in races.

jodhpurs /'dʒɒdpəz/ *n* special trousers that you wear for riding a horse.

jog /dʒɒg/ *v* **1** to push, shake or knock gently: *He jogged my arm and I spilt my coffee; I have forgotten what I was going to say, but something may jog my memory later on.* **2** to travel slowly and jerkily: *The cart jogged along the rough track.* **3** to take exercise by running at a gentle pace: *She goes jogging round the park for half an hour every morning.* — *n*: *He goes for a jog around the park every evening; The photo gave my memory a jog.*
    'jogger *n* a person who goes jogging for exercise.

join /dʒɔɪn/ *v* **1** to put together; to connect: *The electrician joined the wires up wrongly; You must join this piece on to that piece; He joined the two pieces together; The island is joined to the mainland at low tide.* **2** to connect two points by a line: *Join point A to point B.* **3** to become a member of a group: *Join our club!* **4** to meet: *This lane joins the main road; Do you know where the two rivers join?; I'll join you later in the café.* — *n* a place where two things are joined: *You can hardly see the join in the material.*
    join hands to hold one another's hands for dancing *etc*: *Join hands with your partner; They joined hands in a ring.*
    join in to take part: *We're playing a game — do join in!*; *He would not join in the game.*
    join up 1 to connect or attach: *I think you've joined the front and the back up wrongly.* **2** to become a member of the army, navy or air force: *She joined up in 1940 and was immediately posted abroad.*

joint /dʒɔɪnt/ *n* **1** the place where two or more things join: *The plumber tightened up all the joints in the pipes.* **2** a part of your body where two bones meet and are able to move like a hinge: *Your shoulders, elbows, wrists, hips, knees and ankles are joints.* **3** a piece of meat for cooking containing a bone: *A leg of mutton is a large joint.* — *adj* **1** united; done together: *the joint efforts of the whole team.* **2** shared: *She and her husband have a joint bank account*; *a joint responsibility.*
    'jointed *adj* having movable joints: *a jointed doll.*
    'jointly *adv* together: *They worked jointly on this book.*

joist /dʒɔɪst/ *n* any of the beams supporting a floor or ceiling.

joke /dʒəʊk/ *n* **1** anything said or done to make people laugh: *He told the old joke about the elephant in the refrigerator*; *He dressed up as a ghost for a joke*; *He played a joke on us — he pretended he was a ghost.* **2** something that makes people laugh: *The children thought it a great joke when the cat stole the fish.* — *v* **1** to make a joke: *They joked about my mistake.* **2** to tease; to say something as a joke: *I hope you weren't upset when I said you looked like a monkey — I was only joking.*
    'joker *n* **1** in a pack of playing-cards, an extra card with a picture of a figure like a clown, used in some games. **2** a person who enjoys telling jokes, playing tricks *etc*.
    'jokingly *adv*: *He looked out at the rain and jokingly suggested a walk.*
    it's no joke it is a serious matter: *It's no joke when water gets into the petrol tank.*
    see the joke to understand what is funny about a joke or situation.
    take a joke to accept a trick or joke about you without getting angry.
    you must be joking an expression used when you are very surprised.

jolly /'dʒɒlɪ/ *adj* merry; cheerful: *He's in quite a jolly mood today.* — *adv* very: *Taste this — it's jolly good!* **'jolliness**, **'jollity** *ns*.

jolt /dʒəʊlt/ *v* to move jerkily; to jerk: *The bus jolted along the road*; *The train jolted and began to move.* — *n* a sudden movement or shake: *The car gave a jolt and started.*

joss stick /'dʒɒs stɪk/ a stick of incense used to give a sweet smell to a room.

jostle /'dʒɒsəl/ *v* to push roughly: *We were*

jostled by the crowd; *I felt people jostling against me in the dark.*

jot /dʒɒt/ *n* a small amount: *I haven't a jot of patience left.* — *v* to write something quickly: *He jotted down the telephone number in his notebook.*

'**jotter** *n* a notebook.

journal /'dʒɜ:nəl/ *n* **1** a magazine, especially one that deals with a particular subject, and comes out regularly: *the British Medical Journal.* **2** a diary giving an account of each day's activities.

'**journalism** *n* the business of running, or writing for, newspapers or magazines.

'**journalist** *n* a writer for a newspaper, magazine *etc.*

journey /'dʒɜ:ni/ *n* a person's travels from one place to another, or the distance travelled, especially over land: *By train, it is a two-hour journey from here to the coast*; *I'm going on a long journey.* — *v* to travel: *They journeyed to Kathmandu.*

jovial /'dʒəʊvɪəl/ *adj* cheerful. **jovi'ality** *n*. '**jovially** *adv.*

joy /dʒɔɪ/ *n* **1** great happiness: *The children jumped for joy when they saw their new toys.* **2** something that makes you happy: *all the joys and sorrows of life.*

'**joyful** *adj* filled with, showing or causing joy: *a joyful mood*; *joyful faces*; *joyful news.* '**joyfully** *adv.* '**joyfulness** *n.*

'**joyless** *adj* unhappy: *a joyless marriage.* '**joyous** *adj* joyful. '**joyously** *adv.*

'**joystick** /'dʒɔɪstɪk/ *n* a lever used for controlling movement of an aircraft or on a computer screen *etc*: *Push the joystick in the direction required.*

jubilant /'dʒu:bɪlənt/ *adj* triumphant: *The team were jubilant after their victory.* '**jubilantly** *adv.*

jubi'lation *n* rejoicing: *There was great jubilation over the victory*; *The jubilations went on till midnight.*

jubilee /'dʒu:bɪli:/ *n* a celebration of a special anniversary of some event, for example, the beginning of the reign of a king or queen: *The king celebrated his golden jubilee* (50th anniversary of his coming to the throne) *last year.*

judge /dʒʌdʒ/ *v* **1** to hear and try cases in a court of law: *Who will be judging this murder case?* **2** to decide which is the best in a competition *etc*: *She was asked to judge the singing in the music competition*; *to judge the entries for a painting competition*; *Who is judging at the horse show?* **3** to form an idea of something; to estimate: *You can't judge a man by his appearance*; *Watch how a cat judges the distance before it jumps.* **4** to blame someone for doing wrong: *We have no right to judge him — we might have done the same thing ourselves.* — *n* **1** a person who hears and decides cases in a law-court: *The judge asked if the jury had reached a verdict.* **2** a person who decides which is the best in a competition *etc*: *He was asked to be one of the judges at the beauty contest.* **3** a person who is skilful at deciding how good something is: *He's a good judge of horses.*

'**judgement** *n* **1** the decision of a judge in a court of law. **2** the judging or estimating of something: *Faulty judgement in overtaking is a common cause of traffic accidents.* **3** the ability to make right and sensible decisions: *You showed good judgement in buying this book for me.* **4** opinion: *In my judgement, he is a very good actor.*

judicial /dʒu'dɪʃəl/ *adj* having to do with judgement in a court of law: *judicial procedures.*

judicious /dʒu'dɪʃəs/ *adj* sensible or wise: *The portrait shows a judicious use of colour.* **ju'diciously** *adv.*

judo /'dʒu:dəʊ/ *n* a Japanese form of wrestling: *He learns judo at the sports centre.*

jug /dʒʌg/ *n* a deep container for liquids, usually with a handle and a shaped part for pouring: *a milk-jug.*

juggle /'dʒʌgəl/ *v* to keep throwing a number of balls or other objects in the air and catching them: *He entertained the audience by juggling with four balls and four plates at once.* '**juggler** *n.*

juice /dʒu:s/ *n* **1** the liquid part of fruit or vegetables: *She squeezed the juice out of the orange*; *tomato juice.* **2** the fluid contained in meat, that flows out when you cook it: *the turkey's juices.* **3** fluid contained in the organs of your body, for instance to help you digest your food: *digestive juices.* '**juicy** *adj.* '**juiciness** *n.*

July /dʒʊ'laɪ/ *n* the seventh month of the year, the month following June.

jumble /'dʒʌmbəl/ *v* to mix up; to throw things together untidily: *In this puzzle, the letters of all the words have been jumbled up*; *His shoes and clothes were all jumbled together in the cupboard.* — *n* **1** a confused mixture: *He found an untidy jumble of things in the drawer.* **2** unwanted possessions suitable for a jumble sale: *Have you any jumble to spare?*

jumble sale a sale of unwanted clothes and other things, usually to raise money for a charity *etc*.

jumbo /'dʒʌmboʊ/, *plural* **'jumbos**, or **'jumbo jet** *n* a very large jet aeroplane: *He flew by jumbo to London.*

jump /dʒʌmp/ *v* **1** to spring off the ground; to leap: *He jumped off the wall, across the puddle, over the fallen tree and into the swimming-pool.* **2** to rise; to move quickly: *She jumped to her feet; He jumped into the car.* **3** to make a startled movement: *The noise made me jump.* **4** to get over something by leaping: *He jumped the stream easily.* **5** to make a horse jump: *Don't jump the horse over that high fence!* — *n* **1** a leap; a spring: *She crossed the stream in one jump.* **2** a fence *etc* to be jumped over: *Her horse fell at the third jump.* **3** a jumping competition: *He won the high jump.* **4** a startled movement: *She gave a jump when the door suddenly banged shut.*

jump at to grasp a chance *etc* eagerly: *He jumped at the chance to go to Helsinki for a fortnight.*

jump for joy to be very happy.

jump on to make a sudden attack on someone: *He was waiting round the corner and jumped on me in the dark.*

jump the queue to move ahead of others in a queue without waiting for your turn.

jumper /'dʒʌmpə(r)/ *n* a sweater or jersey.

jumpy /'dʒʌmpɪ/ *adj* nervous; anxious.

junction /'dʒʌŋkʃən/ *n* a place at which things meet or join, for example roads, railway lines *etc*: *a railway junction.*

juncture /'dʒʌŋktʃə(r)/: **at this juncture** at this moment: *At this juncture the doorbell rang.*

June /dʒuːn/ *n* the sixth month of the year, the month following May.

jungle /'dʒʌŋɡəl/ *n* a thick growth of trees and plants in tropical areas: *Tigers are found in the jungles of Asia.* — *adj*: *soldiers trained for jungle warfare.*

junior /'dʒuːnɪə(r)/ *adj* **1** younger in years or lower in rank: *junior pupils; the junior school; She is junior to me at school.* **2** used for the son of someone who has the same name (often written **Jnr**, **Jr** or **Jun.**): *John Jones Junior.* — *n* someone who is younger, or lower in rank: *The school sent two juniors and two seniors to take part in the competition.*

> You say **younger than**, but **junior to**.

> The opposite of **junior** is **senior**.

junk¹ /dʒʌŋk/ *n* unwanted things; rubbish: *That cupboard is full of junk.*

junk food food which is not very good for your health but is quick to prepare and eat: *Children shouldn't eat too much junk food.*

junk² /dʒʌŋk/ *n* a Chinese flat-bottomed sailing ship.

Chinese junk

jury /'dʒʊərɪ/ *n* **1** a group of people from the ordinary public, who are chosen to sit in a law-court while a case is going on, listen to what the judge says, and then together decide what the verdict should be, for example, whether a prisoner is guilty or not guilty. **2** a group of judges for a competition *etc*.

'juror or **'juryman** *ns* a member of a jury in a law-court.

just¹ /dʒʌst/ *adj* **1** fair; not favouring one more than another: *The head-teacher's decision to punish both the boys was a just one.* **2** reasonable: *He certainly has a just claim to the money.* **3** deserved: *He got his just reward for all his hard work when he won first prize.*
'justly *adv*.

> The opposite of **just** is **unjust**.

just² /dʒʌst/ *adv* **1** exactly: *This penknife is just what I needed; He was behaving just as if nothing had happened.* **2** entirely; quite: *This dress is just as nice as that one.* **3** very recently: *He has just gone out of the house.* **4** on the point of; at this very moment: *She is just coming through the door.* **5** at a particular moment: *The telephone rang just as I was leaving.* **6** barely: *We have only just enough milk to last till Friday; I just managed to escape; You came just in time.* **7** only; merely: *They waited for six hours just to catch a glimpse of the Queen; Could you wait just a minute?* **8** used for emphasis: *Just look* at that mess!; That just isn't true!; I just don't know what to do; It just won't do! **9** absolutely: *The weather is just marvellous.*

just about more or less: *Is your watch just about right?*

just now 1 at this particular moment: *I can't do it just now.* **2** a short while ago: *She fell and banged her head just now, but she feels better again.*

just then 1 at that particular time: *I was feeling rather angry just then.* **2** in the next minute: *She opened the letter and read it. Just then the door bell rang.*

justice /'dʒʌstɪs/ *n* **1** fairness between people: *Everyone has a right to justice.* **2** the law: *a court of justice.* **3** a judge.

bring to justice to arrest, try and sentence a criminal: *The murderer escaped but was finally brought to justice.*

do yourself justice to do as well as you are capable of doing in a test or competition *etc.*

justify /'dʒʌstɪfaɪ/ *v* **1** to prove or show that something is just or right: *How can the government justify the spending of millions of pounds on weapons when there is so much poverty in the country?* **2** to be a good excuse for something: *Watching television during breakfast does not justify your being late for school.* **justi'fiable** *adj.*

justifi'cation *n* a good reason for something you do; an excuse.

jut /dʒʌt/ *v* to stick out: *His top teeth jut out.*

juvenile /'dʒuːvənaɪl/ *adj* **1** young: *juvenile offenders.* **2** childish: *juvenile behaviour.* — *n* a young person: *She is still a juvenile, so she will not go to prison for her crime.*

K

K /keɪ/ *n* **1** one thousand: *She earns £20K a year.* **2** a kilobyte, used for measuring computer memory space: *This computer has 40K of hard-disk space.*

kaleidoscope /kəˈlaɪdəskoʊp/ *n* a tube in which you can see changing patterns formed by coloured bits of glass *etc* reflected in two mirrors.

kaleido'scopic *adj* full of colour, change and variety.

kangaroo /kaŋɡəˈruː/ *n* a type of large Australian animal with very long hind legs and great power of leaping, the female of which carries her baby in a pouch on the front of her body.

karaoke /karɪˈoʊkɪ/ *n* a form of entertainment in which people take it in turns to sing pop songs to recorded music played by a **karaoke machine**.

karate /kəˈrɑːtɪ/ *n* a Japanese form of unarmed fighting, using blows and kicks.

kayak /ˈkaɪak/ *n* a canoe made of skins stretched over a frame.

kebab /kɪˈbab/ *n* small pieces of meat *etc*, cooked on a metal spike.

keel /kiːl/ *n* the long piece of a ship's frame that lies along the bottom from bow to stern: *The boat's keel stuck in the mud near the shore.*

keel over to fall over, faint or collapse: *Several soldiers keeled over in the heat.*

keen /kiːn/ *adj* **1** eager: *He is a keen collector of stamps*; *I'm keen to succeed.* **2** sharp: *The teacher may be a lot older than you are, but her eyesight is as keen as ever.* **'keenly** *adv.* **'keenness** *n.*

keen on liking something or someone very much: *She's keen on sailing*; *She has been keen on that boy for years.*

keep /kiːp/ *v* **1** to have for ever, or for a very long time: *He gave me the picture to keep.* **2** not to give away or throw away: *I threw away some of my books, but I kept the most interesting ones*; *Can you keep a secret?* **3** to remain in a certain state or make sure that something or someone else does: *How do you keep cool in this heat?*; *Will you keep me informed of what happens?*; *I keep this gun loaded.* **4** to go on doing something: *He kept walking.* **5** to have in store: *I always keep a tin of beans for emergencies.* **6** to have a particular place for something: *Where can I keep my books?* **7** to look after something: *She keeps the garden beautifully.* **8** to have animals, a pet *etc*: *Our neighbours keep hens.* **9** to remain in good condition: *That meat won't keep in this heat unless you put it in the fridge.* **10** to make entries in a diary *etc*: *She keeps a diary to remind her of her appointments.* **11** to delay: *Sorry to keep you.* **12** to provide food, clothes, housing for someone: *He has a wife and child to keep.* **13** not to break a promise *etc*: *She kept her promise.* — *n* food and a place to live: *She gives her mother money every week for her keep.*

> **keep; kept** /kɛpt/; **kept**: *She kept the letter in her pocket*; *Have you kept your promise?*

'keeper *n* a person who looks after something, for example animals in a zoo: *The lion attacked its keeper.*

keep-'fit *n* exercises that are intended to make you fit and strong. — *adj*: *keep-fit exercises.*

keep at something to continue to work hard at something: *She didn't find maths easy but she kept at it and began to make progress.*

keep away to remain at a distance: *Keep away — it's dangerous!*

keep back 1 not to move forward: *Everybody keep back from the door!* **2** not to tell something: *I think he's keeping back the truth.*

keep your distance to stay quite far away: *The deer did not trust us and kept their distance.*

keep someone from doing something to stop someone from doing something: *She held onto the rail to keep herself from falling.*

keep going to go on doing something in spite of difficulties.

keep in to stay close to the side of a road *etc*: *Keep in! There's a truck coming.*

keep in mind to remember something: *Always keep this in mind.*

keep it up to go on doing something as well as you are already doing it: *Your work is good — keep it up!*

keep off to stay away: *There are notices round the bomb warning people to keep off*;

The rain kept off and we had sunshine for the wedding.

keep on 1 to continue: *He kept on writing in spite of the noise*; *Keep on until you come to a petrol station.* **2** to continue talking or complaining about something: *I wish you wouldn't keep on at me about my driving*; *He keeps on at her to give up her job.*

keep out not to enter: *The notice at the building site said 'Keep out!'*

keep out of: *Do try to keep out of trouble!*

keep time to show the time accurately: *Does this watch keep good time?*

keep to not to go away from: *We kept to the roads we knew.*

keep something to yourself not to tell anyone something: *He kept the bad news to himself.*

keep up 1 to move fast enough not to be left behind: *Don't run — I can't keep up with you.* **2** to continue: *How can the baby keep up that crying for such a long time?* **3** to know about what is happening: *I try to keep up with the latest developments if I can.*

keep watch to have the job of staying awake and watching for danger.

keeping /ˈkiːpɪŋ/: **in keeping** fitting in; suitable: *You need furniture which is in keeping with the style of the house.*

out of keeping not fitting in; unsuitable: *Don't wear your jeans tomorrow — they would be out of keeping with the seriousness of the occasion.*

keg /kɛg/ *n* a small barrel: *a keg of beer.*

kennel /ˈkɛnəl/ *n* **1** a type of small hut for a dog. **2** a place where dogs can be looked after.

kept *see* **keep**.

kerb /kɜːb/ *n* the row of stones that form the edge of a pavement.

kernel /ˈkɜːnəl/ *n* the softer substance inside the shell of a nut, or inside the stone of a fruit such as a plum, peach *etc.*

kerosene /ˈkɛrəsiːn/ *n* paraffin oil, obtained from petroleum or from coal.

ketchup /ˈkɛtʃəp/ *n* a sauce made from tomatoes or mushrooms *etc.*

kettle /ˈkɛtəl/ *n* a metal pot for heating water, with a spout for pouring and a lid.

'kettledrum *n* a large drum that consists of a metal bowl covered with a stretched skin and usually stands on three legs.

key /kiː/ *n* **1** an instrument for opening a lock *etc*: *Have you the key for this door?* **2** in musical instruments, one of the small parts you press to sound the notes: *piano keys.* **3** on a typewriter, calculator *etc*, one of the parts you press to print or display a letter *etc.* **4** something that explains a mystery or gives an answer to a mystery, a code *etc*: *the key to the whole problem.* **5** in a map *etc*, a table explaining the signs that are used in it. **6** a series of musical notes related to one another: *a song in the key of C.* — *adj* most important: *the country's key industries.* — *v* to type on a computer.

'keyboard *n* the keys of a piano, typewriter *etc*: *The pianist sat down at the keyboard and began to play*; *A computer keyboard looks like that of a typewriter.*

'keyhole *n* the hole in which the key of a door *etc* is placed: *Never look through keyholes.*

'keynote *n* the most important part or point of something: *The keynote of the president's speech was 'working together'.*

'keyring *n* a ring for keeping keys on.

keyed up excited; anxious.

khaki /ˈkɑːkɪ/ *n, adj* a colour between pale brown and green, used for soldiers' uniforms.

kick /kɪk/ *v* to hit with your foot: *The child kicked his brother*; *He kicked the ball into the next garden*; *He kicked at the locked door*; *He kicked the gate open.* — *n* a blow with the foot: *The horse gave her a kick on the leg.*

kick around to treat someone badly; to bully: *The bigger boys are always kicking him around.*

kick off to start a football game by kicking the ball: *We kick off at 2.30.* **'kick-off** *n*.

kick out to make someone leave, usually using force: *He was kicked out of the club for fighting.*

kick up to make: *She kicked up a fuss when he refused to help her tidy the house.*

kid[1] /kɪd/ *n* **1** a word for a child or teenager: *They've got three kids now, two boys and a girl*; *More than a hundred kids went to the disco last night.* **2** a young goat. **3** the leather made from a goat's skin. — *adj* younger: *my kid brother and sister.*

kid[2] /kɪd/ *v* to trick, deceive or tease someone, especially harmlessly: *He kidded his sister into thinking he'd forgotten her birthday*; *Don't cry — I'm only kidding!*

kidnap /ˈkɪdnap/ *v* to take someone away by force, usually demanding money in exchange for their safe return: *The children were kidnapped by a gang and taken to a secret place in the country.* **'kidnapper** *n*.

kidney /ˈkɪdnɪ/ *n* a part of your body that removes waste material from your blood and produces urine.

kill /kɪl/ *v* to cause the death of a person, animal or plant: *He killed the rats with poison*; *Cancer kills many people every day*. **ˈkiller** *n* someone or something that kills; a murderer: *He searched for his father's killer*. **killer whale** a large black and white whale. **ˈkilling** *n* a murder: *There have been several brutal killings in the area recently*.
kill off to destroy completely: *The acid in the river has killed off all the fish*.
kill time to find something to do to use up spare time: *He went for a walk to kill time till dinner*.

kiln /kɪln/ *n* a large oven for baking pottery or bricks.

kilogramme /ˈkɪləgram/, or **kilo** /ˈkiːloʊ/, *plural* **ˈkilos**, *n* a unit of weight equal to 1000 grammes.

kilometre /ˈkɪləmiːtə(r)/ or /kɪˈlɒmɪtə(r)/ *n* a unit of length equal to 1000 metres.

kilt /kɪlt/ *n* a garment like a short pleated skirt, made of checked material, part of a Scottish man's national costume.

kimono /kɪˈmoʊnoʊ/, *plural* **kiˈmonos**, *n* a loose Japanese robe, fastened with a sash.

kin /kɪn/ *n* your own relations: *my own kin*. — *adj* related.
next of kin your nearest relation.

kind¹ /kaɪnd/ *n* a sort; a type: *What kind of car is it?*; *He is not the kind of boy who would steal*.
a kind of used for giving a rough description or idea: *The curtains are a kind of pinkish-orange*; *I had a kind of feeling that something was wrong*.
kind of rather; a little: *I was feeling kind of sad*; *I kind of hoped he'd dance with me*.
of a kind not very good; of poor quality: *I've worked out a timetable of a kind*.

kind² /kaɪnd/ *adj* generous and good to other people; helpful and friendly: *It was kind of you to look after the children yesterday*; *a kind father*; *The teacher was very kind to him when he felt ill in school*. **ˈkindness** *n*.

kindergarten /ˈkɪndəɡɑːtən/ *n* a school for very young children.

kind-hearted /kaɪndˈhɑːtɪd/ *adj* kind: *She is too kindhearted to hurt an animal*.

kindle /ˈkɪndəl/ *v* to catch fire; to set fire to something: *I kindled a fire using twigs and grass*; *The fire kindled easily*; *His speech kindled the anger of the crowd*.

kindly /ˈkaɪndlɪ/ *adv* **1** in a kind manner: *She kindly lent me a handkerchief*; *He talked kindly to them*. **2** please: *Would you kindly stop talking!* — *adj* gentle and friendly: *a kindly smile*; *a kindly old lady*. **ˈkindliness** *n*.

kindred /ˈkɪndrəd/ *n* your relations. — *adj* of the same sort: *climbing and kindred sports*.

kinetic /kɪˈnɛtɪk/ *adj* having to do with movement: *Kinetic energy is produced when something moves*.

king /kɪŋ/ *n* **1** a male ruler of a nation, who inherits his position by right of birth: *He became king when his father died*; *King Charles III*. **2** the playing-card with the picture of a king: *the king of diamonds*. **3** the most important piece in chess.
ˈkingdom *n* **1** a state that has a king or queen as its head: *The United Kingdom of Great Britain and Northern Ireland*; *He rules over a large kingdom*. **2** any of the three great divisions of natural objects: *the animal, vegetable and mineral kingdoms*.

kingfisher /ˈkɪŋfɪʃə(r)/ *n* a type of bird with bright blue feathers, that feeds on fish.

kingfisher

kingly /ˈkɪŋlɪ/ *adj* royal; fit for a king: *kingly robes*; *a kingly feast*. **ˈkingliness** *n*.

king-size /ˈkɪŋsaɪz/ *adj* of a large size; larger than normal: *king-size cigars*.

kink /kɪŋk/ *n* a bend or twist in something that should be straight: *The hosepipe had a kink in it which stopped the water getting through*. **ˈkinky** *adj*.

kiosk /ˈkiːɒsk/ *n* **1** a small roofed stall for the sale of newspapers, sweets *etc*: *I bought a magazine at the kiosk at the station*. **2** a public telephone box: *She phoned from the telephone-kiosk outside the post-office*.

kiss /kɪs/ *v* to touch someone's face or lips with your lips as a sign of your love for them: *She kissed him when he arrived home*; *The child kissed his parents good-night*. — *n*: *He gave her a kiss*.

kit /kɪt/ *n* **1** a set of tools, clothes *etc* for a particular purpose: *He carried his tennis kit in a bag*; *She had a repair kit for mending* *punctures in bicycle tyres.* **2** a collection of the materials *etc* required to make something: *He bought a model-aeroplane kit.*

kit out to provide the clothes and equipment needed for a particular occupation or job: *We kitted her out for her trip to Africa*; *It took a week to get the boys kitted out for their school trip.*

kitchen /'kɪtʃən/ *n* a room where food is cooked: *A smell of burning was coming from the kitchen.*

kitchenette /kɪtʃə'nɛt/ *n* a small kitchen.

kite /kaɪt/ *n* a light frame covered with paper or another material, with string attached, for flying in the air: *The children were flying their kites in the park.*

kith and kin friends and relations: *She invited all her kith and kin to her wedding.*

kitten /'kɪtən/ *n* a young cat: *The cat had five kittens last week*; *There were five kittens in the litter.*

kitty /'kɪtɪ/ *n* a sum of money kept for a particular purpose, to which members of a group jointly contribute: *The three friends shared a flat and kept a kitty for buying food.*

kiwi /'ki:wi:/ *n* a type of bird that cannot fly, found in New Zealand.

kiwi fruit an oval fruit with furry brown skin, green juicy flesh and black seeds inside.

knack /nak/ *n* the ability to do something easily and skilfully: *Once you get the knack of putting in your contact lenses, you'll do it very quickly.*

knapsack /'napsak/ *n* a small bag for food, clothes *etc* carried on your back.

knead /ni:d/ *v* to squeeze dough *etc* with your fingers.

knee /ni:/ *n* the part of your leg that bends: *He fell and cut his knee*; *The child sat on her father's knee*; *He fell on his knees and begged for mercy.*

'kneecap *n* a flat, round bone on the front of the knee joint.

knee-'deep *adj, adv* deep enough to reach the knees: *She was standing knee-deep in water*; *The mud by the river was knee-deep.*

kneel /ni:l/ *v* to drop down on to your knees; to rest your weight on your knees: *She knelt down to fasten the child's shoes*; *She was kneeling on the floor.*

---

kneel; **knelt** /nɛlt/; **knelt**: *He knelt down*; *Have you ever knelt on a drawing-pin?*

---

knell /nɛl/ *n* the ringing of a bell for a death or funeral.

knelt *see* **kneel**.

knew *see* **know**.

knickers /'nɪkəz/ *n* women's and girls' pants.

knife /naɪf/, *plural* **knives** /naɪvz/, *n* **1** a tool with a blade for cutting: *He carved the meat with a large knife.* **2** a sharp knife used as a weapon: *She stabbed him with a knife.* — *v* to stab with a knife: *He knifed her in the back.*

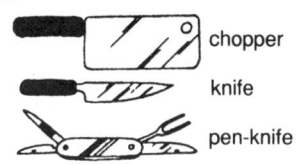

chopper

knife

pen-knife

knight /naɪt/ *n* **1** in earlier times, a man of noble birth who was trained to fight, especially on horseback: *King Arthur and his knights.* **2** a man who has been given the title 'Sir' as a special honour. **3** a piece used in chess, shaped like a horse's head. — *v* to make a person a knight as a reward for important work *etc*: *He was knighted for his medical work.*

'knighthood *n* the rank of a knight: *He was given a knighthood last year.*

knit /nɪt/ *v* to make pullovers *etc* from woollen thread *etc*, using knitting-needles or a machine: *She knitted him a sweater for Christmas.*

'knitting *n*: *This long piece of knitting is going to be a scarf.*

'knitting-needle *n* a thin rod of steel or plastic *etc*, used in knitting.

'knitwear *n* knitted clothes.

knives *see* **knife**.

knob /nɒb/ *n* **1** a hard rounded object, attached to something else: *There were brass knobs on the end of the bed.* **2** a rounded handle on a door or drawer: *wooden doorknobs.*

knock /nɒk/ *v* **1** to make a sharp noise by tapping on a door *etc*: *Someone knocked at the door.* **2** to hit something or someone, making them fall: *She knocked the vase over when she was dusting*; *I knocked him down with one punch*; *He was knocked down in the street by a car.* **3** to bump into: *She knocked against the table and spilt my coffee*; *I knocked my head on the car door.* — *n* the sound or action of knocking: *They heard a loud knock at the door*; *The jug fell off the* *shelf and gave him a knock on the head.*

> The bus **collided with** (not **knocked against**) the truck.

'knocker *n* an object made of metal *etc*, fixed to a door and used for knocking.

knock about or **knock around 1** to hit repeatedly: *He was knocked around by a gang who stole his money.* **2** to be in a place: *Have you seen yesterday's paper knocking about anywhere?*

knock back to drink quickly: *She knocked her drink back and left without a word.*

knock down 1 to injure or kill a person by hitting them when driving a vehicle: *She was knocked down by a bus.* **2** to remove or destroy a building completely: *A row of houses had to be knocked down to make way for the new road.*

knock out 1 to hit someone so that they become unconscious: *The boxer knocked his opponent out in the third round.* **2** to make someone sleepy or unconscious with a drug: *The doctor gave her an injection which knocked her out for a few hours.* **3** to beat a team or person in a competition so that they cannot compete in it anymore: *We were knocked out in the third round of the tennis tournament.* — **'knockout** *n*.

knot /nɒt/ *n* **1** a join made in string, rope *etc* by tying and pulling tight: *She tied a knot in her shoe-laces.* **2** a lump in wood at the join between a branch and the trunk. — *v* to tie something in a knot: *He knotted the rope around the post.*

know /noʊ/ *v* **1** to be aware of something; to have information about something: *He knows everything; I know he is at home because his car is in the drive; He knows all about it; Hunt knew he had the faster car; He knew he couldn't have been dozing very long.* **2** to have learned and remembered something: *He knows a lot of poetry.* **3** to be able to recognize someone; to be friendly with someone: *I know Mrs Smith — she lives near me; You would hardly know my son now — he has grown up so much recently.* **4** to call someone or something by a particular name: *His real name is Michael, but his friends know him as Mick; He's known as Mick to his friends.*

> **know; knew** /njuː/; **known** /noʊn/: *She knew the answer; Have you known him long?*

'know-all *n* a person who thinks they know everything.

'know-how *n* the knowledge and skill needed to deal with something: *She has acquired a lot of know-how about cars.*

'knowing *adj* showing secret understanding: *She gave him a knowing look.*

'knowingly *adv* **1** on purpose: *I would never knowingly upset you.* **2** in a knowing way: *He smiled knowingly.*

in the know having information that other people have not: *People in the know say that the minister is going to resign.*

know how to to have learned the way to do something: *She already knew how to read before she went to school.*

let someone know to tell or inform someone about something: *Let me know if you're going to be late.*

knowledge /'nɒlɪdʒ/ *n* **1** knowing: *The knowledge that her husband was safe made her very happy.* **2** information; understanding: *For this job you need a good knowledge of computers; He had a vast amount of knowledge about boats.*

> **knowledge** is never used in the plural.

'knowledgeable *adj* knowing a lot: *He is very knowledgeable about the history of the city.*

general knowledge knowledge about a lot of different subjects: *The teacher sometimes tests our general knowledge.*

known *see* **know**.

knuckle /'nʌkəl/ *n* a joint of a finger: *She hit her hand against the wall and hurt her knuckles.*

koala /koʊ'ɑːlə/ *n* a type of Australian tree-climbing animal like a small bear, the female of which carries her baby in a pouch (also called a **koala bear**).

kookaburra /'kʊkəbʌrə/ *n* a large Australian bird with bright feathers and a cackling cry.

Koran /kɔː'rɑːn/ *n* the holy book of the Muslims.

kung fu /kʌŋ 'fuː/ *n* a Chinese type of fighting using only your hands and feet.

L

lab /lab/ *n* short for **laboratory**.

label /'leɪbəl/ *n* a small written note fixed on something to say what it is or whose it is *etc*: *luggage labels; The label on the blouse said 'Do not iron'.* — *v* to put a label on something: *She labelled all the boxes of books carefully.*

laboratory /lə'bɒrətərɪ/ *n* a place where scientific experiments are done or drugs *etc* are prepared: *a chemical laboratory; a hospital laboratory.*

laborious /lə'bɔːrɪəs/ *adj* difficult; requiring hard work: *Moving house is always a laborious process.* **la'boriously** *adv*.

labour /'leɪbə(r)/ *n* **1** hard work: *The building of the cathedral took much labour.* **2** workmen on a job: *The firm is having difficulty getting labour.* **3** the pains that a woman feels when her baby is being born. — *v* **1** to work as a labourer: *to labour on a building site.* **2** to work very hard: *They laboured to get the work finished in time.* **3** to move with difficulty: *They laboured through the dense jungle.*

'laboured *adj* done slowly or with difficulty: *laboured breathing.*

'labourer *n* a workman: *He employed four labourers to build the wall.*

'labour-saving *adj* reducing the amount of work needed to do something: *A washing-machine is a labour-saving device.*

labyrinth /'labərɪnθ/ *n* a place full of long, winding passages; a maze.

lace /leɪs/ *n* **1** a string for fastening shoes *etc*: *I need a new pair of laces for my tennis shoes.* **2** delicate, patterned net-like material made with fine thread: *Her dress was trimmed with lace.* — *adj*: *a lace collar.* — *v* to fasten with a lace which is threaded through holes: *Lace up your boots firmly.*

'lace-ups *n* shoes with laces: *All of his shoes are lace-ups.*

lack /lak/ *v* to have too little of something or none at all: *He lacked the courage to join the army.* — *n* the state of not having enough of something: *They were prevented from going on holiday by their lack of money.*

'lacking *adj* **1** not having enough of something: *He's lacking in brains.* **2** not enough: *Money is lacking for the repairs to the hospital.*

lackadaisical /lakə'deɪzɪkəl/ *adj* having or showing no enthusiasm or energy: *Her work is very lackadaisical.*

lacklustre /'laklʌstə(r)/ *adj* having no brightness or energy, dull: *a lacklustre performance of the play.*

lacquer /'lakə(r)/ *n* a type of paint: *He painted the table with black lacquer.*

lacy /'leɪsɪ/ *adj* made with, decorated with or looking like lace: *lacy table mats; a lacy jumper.*

lad /lad/ *n* a boy.

ladder /'ladə(r)/ *n* **1** a set of steps between two long supporting pieces of wood, metal *etc*, for climbing up or down: *She was standing on a ladder painting the ceiling; the ladder of success.* **2** a long hole in a stocking: *I've got a ladder in my tights.*

platform ladder
straight ladder
extension ladder
step stool
fruit-picking ladder
hook ladder
rope ladder
step ladder

laden /'leɪdən/ *adj* carrying a lot; heavily loaded: *People left the shops laden with their* *shopping*; *The laden truck went slowly up the hill.*

ladle /'leɪdəl/ *n* a bowl-like spoon with a long handle for lifting out liquid from a container: *a soup ladle.*

lady /'leɪdɪ/ *n* **1** a woman: *Stand up and let that lady sit down*; *This shop sells ladies' shoes.* **2** a woman who has good manners: *Be quiet! — Ladies do not shout in public.* **3** a special title for certain women: *Sir James and Lady Brown.*

'ladybird *n* a little round beetle, usually red with black spots.

'ladylike *adj* behaving in a polite and dignified way: *That's not a very ladylike thing to say!*

lag /lag/ *v* to move too slowly and get left behind: *We waited for the smaller children to catch up, as they were lagging behind the rest.* — *n* the amount by which one thing is later than another: *There is sometimes a time-lag of several seconds between seeing lightning and hearing thunder.*

lager /'lɑːgə(r)/ *n* a light beer: *He never drinks lager.*

lagoon /lə'guːn/ *n* an area of shallow water that is separated from the sea by a long bank of sand: *We went for a swim in the lagoon.*

laid /leɪd/ *see* **lay**[1].

lain /leɪn/ *see* **lie**[2].

lair /lɛə(r)/ *n* the home of a wild beast: *The bear had its lair among the rocks.*

lake /leɪk/ *n* a large area of water surrounded by land: *They go sailing on the lake.*

lamb /lam/ *n* **1** a young sheep: *The ewe has had three lambs.* **2** its flesh eaten as food: *a roast leg of lamb.*

A lamb **bleats**.

lame /leɪm/ *adj* **1** unable to walk properly: *He was lame for several weeks after his fall.* **2** not good enough: *a lame excuse.* **'lamely** *adv.* **'lameness** *n.*

lament /lə'mɛnt/ *v* to feel or express sadness about something: *We all lament his death.* — *n* an expression of sorrow: *This song is a lament for those killed in battle.* **'lamentable** *adj.* **lamen'tation** *n.*

lamp /lamp/ *n* a light, usually with a cover: *a table lamp*; *a street-lamp.*

lamp post the post supporting a streetlamp.

'lampshade *n* a cover for a light-bulb.

lance /lɑːns/ *n* a weapon of earlier times with a long handle and a sharp point.

land /land/ *n* **1** the dry, solid parts of the surface of the earth: *We had been at sea a week before we saw land.* **2** a country: *foreign lands.* **3** the ground or soil: *The land was poor and stony.* **4** a piece of countryside belonging to someone: *This is private land.* — *v* **1** to come down to the ground: *She jumped across the stream and landed safely on the other side.* **2** to come down to earth in a plane *etc*: *The plane landed in a field*; *They managed to land the helicopter safely.* **3** to bring a ship *etc* from the sea to land: *After being at sea for three months, they landed at Plymouth.* **4** to get into trouble *etc*: *Don't drive so fast — you'll land up in hospital*; *You're going to land yourself in trouble!*

'landing *n* **1** bringing a plane down to the ground: *The pilot had to make an emergency landing.* **2** the level part of a staircase between flights of steps: *Her room was on the first floor, across the landing from mine.*

landing stage a platform where passengers either get on to or leave a boat.

'landlady *n* a female landlord.

'landlord *n* **1** a person who rents rooms, flats or houses to people: *My landlord has just put up my rent.* **2** a person who keeps a hotel or bar where people drink.

'landmark *n* **1** a building *etc* that can be easily seen and recognized: *The church tower is a landmark for sailors because it stands on the top of a cliff.* **2** an important event in the development of something: *landmarks in the history of science, such as the invention of the telescope.*

'land-mine *n* a mine laid near the surface of the ground, that is set off by something passing over it.

'landowner *n* a person who owns a lot of land.

landscape /'landskeɪp/ *n* **1** the scenery or countryside that you see laid out in front of you: *He stood on the hill admiring the landscape.* **2** a picture of a countryside scene: *There were watercolour landscapes on every wall.*

'landslide *n* a piece of land that falls down from the side of a hill *etc*: *His car was buried in the landslide.*

land with to give someone an unpleasant job: *She was landed with the job of telling him the bad news.*

lane /leɪn/ *n* **1** a narrow road or street: *a winding lane.* **2** used in the names of certain roads or streets: *His address is 12 Penny Lane.* **3** a division of a road for one line of traffic: *The new motorway has three lanes in each direction.* **4** a division of an athletics track or swimming pool for the use of an individual competitor in a race: *The winner was in lane two.*

language /ˈlæŋgwɪdʒ/ *n* **1** human speech: *How did humans develop language?* **2** the speech of a particular nation: *She is very good at learning languages; Russian is a difficult language.* **3** the special words used by a particular group of people *etc*: *medical language.*

bad language swearing.

language laboratory a room that has equipment such as tape recorders to help students learn foreign languages.

languish /ˈlæŋgwɪʃ/ *v* to grow weak.

lank /læŋk/ *adj* straight and greasy: *lank hair.*

lanky /ˈlæŋkɪ/ *adj* too tall and thin: *a lanky fellow.* ˈ**lankiness** *n*.

lantern /ˈlæntən/ *n* a case for holding or carrying a light.

lap[1] /læp/ *v* **1** to drink by licking with the tongue: *The cat lapped up the milk from a saucer.* **2** to make a soft sound as water splashes gently against something: *The sea lapped against the side of the boat.*

lap up to enjoy hearing praise, gossip or information: *She stood at the front of the stage, lapping it up as the audience clapped and cheered.*

lap[2] /læp/ *n* the part of you from your waist to your knees, when you are sitting; your thighs: *The baby was lying in its mother's lap.*

ˈ**laptop** *n* a small computer that can be carried in a briefcase and used on your lap: *She uses her laptop on long train journeys.*

lap[3] /læp/ *n* one round of a race-course *etc*: *The runners have completed five laps, with three still to run.* — *v* to overtake another competitor who is one lap behind you in a race.

lapel /ləˈpɛl/ *n* one of the two parts of a coat or jacket that are joined to the collar and folded back across your chest: *He had a small badge fixed to the left lapel of his jacket.*

lapis lazuli /ˌlæpɪs ˈlæzjʊlɪ/ *n* a bright blue stone used as a gem: *earrings made of silver and lapis lazuli.*

lapse /læps/ *v* to get worse or lower: *I'm afraid our standards of tidiness have lapsed.* — *n* **1** a fault; a failure: *I had a lapse of memory and forgot his name.* **2** a length of time that has passed: *I saw him again after a lapse of five years.*

lard /lɑːd/ *n* the melted fat of the pig, used in cooking.

larder /ˈlɑːdə(r)/ *n* a room or cupboard where food is stored.

large /lɑːdʒ/ *adj* great in size, amount *etc*; not small: *a large number of people; a large house; a large family; This house is too large for two people.* ˈ**largeness** *n*.

ˈ**largely** *adv* mainly: *Training is very largely to do with improving technical skills.*

ˈ**large-scale** *adj* affecting a lot of people or a wide area: *A large-scale search for survivors is continuing.*

at large 1 generally; as a whole: *I know that the public at large aren't interested in this issue.* **2** free; not in captivity: *They were warned that an escaped prisoner was at large in the area.*

by and large mostly; in general: *By and large it was a successful holiday.*

lark /lɑːk/ *n* a name for several types of singing-bird, especially the skylark, which flies high into the air as it sings.

laryngitis /ˌlærɪnˈdʒaɪtɪs/ *n* an infection affecting your larynx and making it difficult to speak.

larynx /ˈlærɪŋks/ *n* a hollow organ in the throat which contains the vocal cords: *Singers must be careful not to strain the larynx.*

larva /ˈlɑːvə/, *plural* **larvae** /ˈlɑːviː/, *n* a developing insect in its first stage after coming out of the egg; a grub or caterpillar. ˈ**larval** *adj*.

laser /ˈleɪzə(r)/ *n* an instrument that produces a narrow and very strong beam of light: *The men were cutting the sheets of metal with a laser.* — *adj*: *a laser beam.*

laser printer a fast computer printer which produces very good quality work: *She is hoping to buy a laser printer to use at home.*

lash /læʃ/ *n* **1** an eyelash: *She looked at him through her thick lashes.* **2** a whip. **3** a stroke with a whip *etc*: *The sailor was given twenty lashes as a punishment.* — *v* **1** to strike with a lash: *He lashed the horse.* **2** to fasten something with rope: *All the equipment had to be lashed to the deck of the ship.* **3** to make a movement like a whip: *The tiger crouched in the tall grass, its tail lashing from side to side.* **4** to come down very heavily: *The rain was lashing down.*

lash out to attack violently: *He lashed out at us with his fists.*

lass /læs/ *n* a girl.

lasso /lə'suː/, *plural* **las'soes**, *n* a long rope with a loop that tightens when the rope is pulled, used for catching wild horses *etc*. — *v* to catch with a lasso: *The cowboy lassoed the horse.*

last[1] /lɑːst/ *adj* **1** at the end; final: *the last day of November; He was last in the race; He caught the last bus home; She was the last guest to arrive.* **2** previous: *Our last house was much smaller than this; last year; last month; last week; The last time I went to Britain, it rained all the time.* **3** only remaining: *This is my last ten pounds.* — *pron*: *I've spent the last of my money.* — *adv* after all the others: *He took his turn last.*

See **past**.

'lastly *adv* finally: *Lastly, I would like to thank you all for listening so patiently to what I have been saying.*

last-'minute *adj* done or made at the latest possible time: *It is too late to make any last-minute changes.*

at last or **at long last** in the end, especially after a long delay: *Oh, there he is at last!; They succeeded at long last.*

last but one, two, three *etc* one, two or three *etc* places before the final one of a series.

last but not least at the end of a list but just as important as all the others.

the last word 1 the final remark in an argument *etc*: *She always must have the last word!* **2** the final decision: *The last word rests with the chairman.*

to the last until the very end: *He kept his courage to the last.*

last[2] /lɑːst/ *v* **1** to continue: *I hope this fine weather lasts.* **2** to remain in good condition or supply: *This carpet has lasted well; The bread won't last another two days — we'll need more; This coat will last me a long time.*
'lasting *adj*: *A good education is a lasting benefit.*

last out to be enough; to keep going: *I hope the petrol lasts out until we reach a petrol station; I hope we can last out till help arrives.*

latch /latʃ/ *n* a catch of wood or metal used to fasten a door *etc*: *She lifted the latch and walked in.*

See **bolt**.

'latchkey *n* a small front-door key.
latch on to to understand or realize what something means: *It took her a moment to latch on to what they were arguing about.*

late /leɪt/ *adj* **1** after the expected or usual time: *The train is late tonight; I try to be punctual, but I'm always late.* **2** far on in the day or night: *late in the day; late at night; It was very late when I got to bed.* **3** dead, especially recently: *the late king.* **4** the last to hold a job before the present person: *our late chairman, Mr Brown.* — *adv* **1** after the expected or usual time: *He arrived late for his interview.* **2** far on in the day or night: *They always go to bed late.* **'lateness** *n*.

later see **latter**.

'latecomer *n* a person who arrives late for an event after it has begun.
'lately *adv* recently; not long ago: *Have you seen her lately?*
later on at a later time: *He hasn't come yet but I expect he'll arrive later on.*
of late lately: *She has been less friendly of late.*

latent /'leɪtənt/ *adj* hidden; not yet developed: *a latent talent for music.*

lateral /'latərəl/ *adj* having to do with the side; sideways: *lateral movement.* **'laterally** *adv*.

latest /'leɪtɪst/ *adj* most recent: *Her latest book is about her travels in Egypt; What's the latest news?* — *n*: *They have the very latest in new machinery; Have you heard the latest?*
at the latest not later than: *I have to return these books to the library by Friday at the latest.*

latex /'leɪtɛks/ *n* the milky juice of some plants, especially rubber trees.

lathe /leɪð/ *n* a machine for shaping wood *etc*.

lather /'lɑːðə(r)/ *n* foam made of soap bubbles: *This soap gives plenty of lather.*

Latin /'latɪn/ *n* the language spoken in ancient Rome.

latitude /'latɪtjuːd/ *n* the distance, measured in degrees on the map, between a particular place and the Equator, whether north or south: *The latitude of Singapore is 10° south.*

See **longitude**.

latrine /lə'triːn/ *n* a lavatory used by soldiers *etc*.

latter /'latə(r)/ *adj* towards the end: *the latter part of our holiday.*
the latter the second of two things *etc* mentioned: *John and Mary arrived, the latter wearing a green dress.*

to choose the second or **latter** (not **later**) of two suggestions.

'latterly *adv* lately; recently: *She hasn't been feeling well latterly.*

lattice /'latɪs/ *n* a framework made of crossed strips of wood, metal *etc*: *The gardener built a lattice for the roses to climb up.*

laudable /'lɔːdəbəl/ *adj* worthy of being praised: *a laudable effort.* **'laudably** *adv.*

laugh /lɑːf/ *v* to make a sound that shows you are happy or amused: *We laughed at the funny film; Children were laughing in the garden as they played.* — *n* an act or sound of laughing: *He gave a laugh; a loud laugh.*

'laughable *adj* so bad that it should be laughed at: *He made a laughable attempt at ordering breakfast in French.*

'laughing *adj* showing or involving laughter: *laughing faces; This is no laughing matter.*

'laughter *n* the act or sound of laughing: *We could hear laughter in the classroom next-door.*

for a laugh for fun; as a joke: *She hid his shoes for a laugh.*

launch[1] /lɔːntʃ/ *v* **1** to make a boat or ship slide into the water, or make a rocket leave the ground: *As soon as the alarm was given, the lifeboat was launched; The Russians have launched a rocket.* **2** to start something new or show something for the first time: *to launch a new product onto the market; The enemy launched an attack at midnight.* — *n*: *The launch of the shuttle has been delayed by 24 hours.*

'launching-pad *n* a platform from which a rocket is launched.

launch[2] /lɔːntʃ/ *n* a large, power-driven boat, used for short trips or for pleasure: *We cruised round the bay in a motor-launch.*

launder /'lɔːndə(r)/ *v* to wash and iron: *to launder clothes.*

launderette /lɔːndə'rɛt/ *n* a shop where customers can wash clothes in washing machines.

'laundress *n* a woman employed to launder.

'laundry *n* **1** a place where clothes *etc* are washed, especially in return for payment: *She took the sheets to the laundry.* **2** clothes *etc* that are waiting to be washed, or have been washed: *a bundle of laundry.*

laurel /'lɒrəl/ *n* a type of tree, once used for making wreaths to crown winners of races or competitions *etc.*

lava /'lɑːvə/ *n* liquid, melted rock *etc* thrown out from a volcano and becoming solid as it cools.

lavatory /'lavətrɪ/ *n* **1** a receptacle for waste matter from the body. **2** a room in which there is a lavatory.

lavender /'lavəndə(r)/ *n* **1** a plant with lots of tiny, sweet-smelling, bluish-purple flowers on long stalks. **2** a pale, bluish-purple colour.

lavish /'lavɪʃ/ *adj* very generous; too generous: *lavish gifts.* — *v* to spend a lot; to give generously: *She lavishes presents on her nephew.* **'lavishly** *adv.* **'lavishness** *n.*

law /lɔː/ *n* **1** the rules according to which people live or a country *etc* is governed: *Stealing is against the law; The police have to keep law and order.* **2** one of these rules: *A new law has been passed by Parliament.* **3** a rule in science that says that under certain conditions certain things always happen: *the law of gravity.*

law-abiding /'lɔːəbaɪdɪŋ/ *adj* obeying the law: *a law-abiding citizen.*

law court or **court of law** a place where people accused of crimes are tried and legal disagreements between people are judged.

'lawful *adj* **1** allowed by law: *He was going about his lawful business as usual.* **2** rightful: *She is the lawful owner of the property.* **'lawfully** *adv.*

'lawless *adj* breaking the law, especially violently.

'lawlessness *n*: *a growth in lawlessness.*

law and order a situation in which the law is obeyed and respected: *There has been a breakdown in law and order in some cities.*

lawn /lɔːn/ *n* an area of smooth, short grass in a garden: *He is mowing the lawn.*

'lawnmower *n* a machine for cutting grass: *an electric lawnmower.*

lawsuit /'lɔːsuːt/ *n* a quarrel that is taken to a court of law for an agreement: *He brought a lawsuit against his neighbour over the constant loud noise from her radio.*

lawyer /'lɔːjə(r)/ *n* a person whose job is to know about the law and give advice and help people in matters that concern the law: *When he was arrested, he sent for his lawyer.*

lax /laks/ *adj* careless; not strict enough: *Pupils have been rather lax about some of the school rules recently.* **'laxity** *n.*

lay[1] /leɪ/ *v* **1** to put; to put down: *She laid the clothes in a drawer; Lay your hat on this chair; He laid down his pencil.* **2** to place in a lying position; to flatten: *She laid the baby on his back; The dog laid back its ears.* **3** to put in order; to arrange: *She went to lay the table for dinner; I need time to lay my plans for revenge; They laid a trap for him.* **4** to produce eggs: *The hen laid four eggs*; *My hens are laying well.* **5** to bet: *I'll lay five pounds that you don't succeed.*

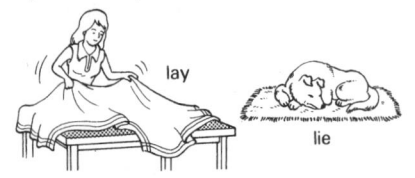

lay

lie

lay¹; **laid** /leɪd/; **laid**: *Watch how she lays the table*; *He laid the baby in its cot*; *The hens have laid twelve eggs.*

lay¹ means to **put** something: *to lay a carpet*; *to lay a book on the table.*

lie² means to **rest** in a flat position: *to lie on the carpet*; the past tense is **lay**²: *He lay on the bed.*

lay aside to put something away so that it can be used or dealt with at a later time: *She laid the books aside for later use.*

lay down 1 to give up: *They laid down their arms*; *The soldiers laid down their lives in the cause of peace.* **2** to order; to instruct: *The rule book lays down what should be done in such a case.*

lay your hands on something 1 to find something; to be able to obtain something: *I wish I could lay my hands on that book!* **2** to catch: *The police have been trying to lay hands on the criminal for months.*

lay off 1 to dismiss employees for a time: *Because of a shortage of orders, the firm has laid off a quarter of its workers.* **2** to stop annoying someone: *Can't you lay off your little sister for a while?*

lay on to provide: *The teachers laid on a tea party for the pupils.*

lay out 1 to arrange; to plan: *He was the architect who laid out the public gardens.* **2** to spread something out so that it can be easily seen: *She laid out her jewellery on her dressing-table.* **3** to knock someone unconscious.

lay² the past tense of **lie**².

lay³ /leɪ/ *adj* **1** not a priest; not a clergyman: *lay preachers.* **2** not an expert in a particular subject: *Doctors use words that lay people don't understand.*

layabout /'leɪəbaʊt/ *n* a lazy person.

layer /'leɪə(r)/ *n* **1** a thickness; a covering: *The ground was covered with a layer of snow.* **2** a hen that lays eggs: *This hen is a good layer.*

layman /'leɪmən/ *n* **1** a person who is not a clergyman. **2** a person who is not one of the experts in a particular subject.

layout /'leɪaʊt/ *n* the way something is arranged: *They spent a lot of time planning the layout of the garden.*

laze /leɪz/ *v* to relax and not do anything: *She lazed on the beach all day.*

lazy /'leɪzɪ/ *adj* not wanting to work hard; not wanting to take exercise: *Henry is lazy at his school-work*; *I take the bus to work as I'm too lazy to walk*; *Lazy people tend to become fat.* **'lazily** *adv.* **'laziness** *n.*

'lazy-bones *n* a name for a lazy person.

lead¹ /lɛd/ *n* **1** heavy, grey metal: *Are these pipes made of lead or copper?* **2** the part of a pencil that makes a mark: *The lead of my pencil has broken.* — *adj*: *The old lead water-pipes were replaced with copper ones.* **'leaden** *adj.*

lead² /liːd/ *v* **1** to guide or take a person or animal in a certain direction: *Follow my car and I'll lead you to the motorway*; *She took the child by the hand and led him across the road*; *He was leading the horse into the stable*; *The sound of hammering led us to the garage*; *You led us to believe that we would be paid!* **2** to go to a particular place or along a particular course: *A small path leads through the woods.* **3** to cause or bring about a certain situation or state of affairs: *The heavy rain led to serious floods.* **4** to be at the front; to be ahead of others: *An official car led the procession*; *He is still leading in the competition.* **5** to live a certain kind of life: *Cats lead a pleasant life.* — *n* **1** the front place or position: *He has taken over the lead in the race*; *He has a lead of 20 metres over the other runners.* **2** the act of leading: *We all followed his lead.* **3** a leather strap or chain for leading a dog: *All dogs must be kept on a lead.* **4** a bit of information that may help to solve a mystery; a clue: *Have the police any leads yet?* **5** a leading part in a play *etc*: *Who plays the lead in that film?* **6** a piece of wire for carrying electricity to an electrical device: *The lead on the television isn't long enough to plug it in by the door.*

lead; **led** /lɛd/; **led**: *She led him out of the wood*; *He has led a wicked life.*

'leader *n* **1** a person who is in front or goes first: *The leader is well ahead of the other* *cyclists; the leader of a procession.* **2** a person who is in charge of something: *The leader of the expedition is a scientist.*

'**leadership** *n* **1** the position of leader: *He took over the leadership of the Labour party.* **2** the quality of being a leader: *Is he capable of leadership?*

'**leading** *adj* **1** the most important: *He is one of our leading authors.* **2** in front; in first position: *The leading team has not been defeated this season.*

lead on to go first; to show the way: *Lead on to victory!*

lead the way to go first in order to show the way: *She led the way upstairs.*

lead up to 1 to develop in such a way as to cause a particular situation: *the events leading up to the war.* **2** to direct the conversation towards a particular subject: *I wondered what you were leading up to.*

leaf /li:f/, *plural* **leaves** /li:vz/, *n* **1** a part of a plant growing from the side of a stem, usually green, flat and thin, but of various shapes depending on the plant: *Many trees lose their leaves in autumn.* **2** the page of a book: *Several leaves had been torn out of the book.* **3** a part of a table that can be folded down or taken off.

'**leaflet** *n* a small, printed sheet containing information *etc*.

'**leafy** *adj* having many leaves: *a leafy plant.*

leaf through to turn the pages of a book *etc* quickly without looking at them carefully: *She sat in the waiting-room, leafing through a magazine.*

turn over a new leaf to begin a new and better way of behaving, working *etc*.

league /li:g/ *n* **1** a union of people, nations *etc* for the benefit of each other: *the League for the Protection of Shopkeepers.* **2** a sports association: *the Football League.* **3** a class or standard of quality: *She is so much better than the others — they just aren't in her league.*

in league with having a secret arrangement with someone: *She was accused of being in league with the murderer.*

leak /li:k/ *n* **1** a crack or hole through which liquid or gas escapes: *Water was escaping through a leak in the pipe.* **2** the passing of gas, water *etc* through a crack or hole: *a gas leak.* **3** the giving away of secret information: *a leak of Government plans.* — *v* **1** to have a leak: *This bucket leaks.* **2** to pass through a leak: *Gas was leaking from the cracked pipe.* **3** to tell secret news or information to the public: *He leaked the news of the royal divorce to the press.* '**leakage** *n.* '**leaky** *adj.*

leak out to become known to the public: *The government did not want the details to leak out.*

lean[1] /li:n/ *v* **1** to slope over to one side; not to be upright: *The lamp-post was leaning dangerously.* **2** to rest against or on something: *She leant the ladder against the wall; Don't lean your elbows on the table; He leant on the gate.*

> **lean; leant** /lɛnt/ or **leaned; leant** or **leaned**: *She leaned over to talk to me; Someone had leant against the fence and damaged it.*

lean[2] /li:n/ *adj* **1** thin: *a tall, lean man.* **2** not containing much fat: *lean meat.* **3** producing little to eat: *a lean harvest; the lean years after the war.* '**leanness** *n.*

leant *see* **lean**[1].

leap /li:p/ *v* **1** to jump: *He leapt into the boat.* **2** to jump over: *The dog leapt the wall.* — *n* **1** the action of leaping: *He got over the stream in one leap.* **2** a sudden or great change or increase: *a leap in the price of petrol; The development of penicillin was a great leap forward in the field of medicine.*

> **leap; leapt** /lɛpt/ or **leaped; leapt** or **leaped**: *The cat leapt off the roof; The dog had leapt the gate many times before.*

'**leap-frog** *n* a game in which one person leaps over another's bent back, pushing off with his hands.

leap year every fourth year, which has 366 days instead of 365, because of February having 29 days, as in 1992, 1996, 2000, 2004 *etc*.

by leaps and bounds extremely rapidly: *Your work has improved by leaps and bounds.*

leap at to accept something eagerly: *She leapt at the chance to spend her summer working in Australia.*

learn /lɜ:n/ *v* **1** to gain knowledge or skill: *A child is always learning; to learn French; She is learning to swim; It's time you learnt how to make your bed properly.* **2** to get to know: *Where did you learn that news?*

> **learn; learnt** /lɜ:nt/ or **learned; learnt** or **learned**: *He learnt French at school; Have you learnt that poem?* See also **study**.

lease

learned /'lɜːnɪd/ *adj* knowing a lot: *a learned professor*.

'learner *n* a person who is learning: *Be patient — I'm only a learner.* — *adj*: *a learner driver*.

'learning *n* knowledge: *The professor was a man of great learning*.

lease /liːs/ *n* an agreement giving the use of a house *etc* on payment of rent: *We signed the lease yesterday*; *a twenty-year lease*. — *v* to give or get the use of a house *etc* for payment: *He leases the land from the town council*.

leash /liːʃ/ *n* a lead for a dog.

least /liːst/ *adj* the smallest or the smallest possible: *She wanted to know how to do the work with the least amount of effort*. — *pron* the smallest; the smallest thing; the smallest amount: *After being so rude, the least you could do is apologize!* — *adv* to the smallest or lowest extent: *I like her least of all the girls*; *That is the least important of our problems*.

See **little**.

at least 1 at any rate; anyway: *I think she's well — at least, she was when I saw her last.* 2 not less than: *He must weigh at least 300 pounds.* 3 even if other things are wrong: *I know my car's old but at least it goes.*

least of all especially not: *No-one was prepared for the shock — least of all me*; *You musn't worry about a thing — least of all my safety*.

not in the least not at all: *She didn't seem in the least worried*; *It doesn't matter in the least*.

leather /'lɛðə(r)/ *n* the skin of an animal prepared for making clothes, luggage *etc*: *shoes made of leather*. — *adj*: *Is your case leather?*; *a leather jacket*.

leave[1] /liːv/ *v* 1 to go away; to depart from someone or something: *Please don't leave me!*; *He left the room for a moment*; *They left at about six o'clock*; *I have left that job.* 2 to go without taking something: *She left her gloves in the car*; *He left his children behind when he went to France.* 3 to allow something to remain in a particular state or condition: *She left the job half-finished.* 4 to let a person or a thing do something without being helped or attended to: *I'll leave the meat to cook for a while*; *The teacher left them to work out the problem by themselves.* 5 to let something be done by someone else: *Don't play with electricity — leave that job to the experts!* 6 to give someone something in your will: *She left all her property to her son*.

leave; left /lɛft/; **left**: *She left the house*; *He has already left*.

leave alone not to disturb, upset or tease: *Why can't you leave your little brother alone?*

leave behind 1 to go away without taking something with you: *I arrived at the meeting to find I'd left my notes behind*; *We had to leave our pets behind when we moved to the city.* 2 to progress much faster than someone else: *She left the other runners far behind*.

leave off 1 not to include: *She left three names off the list.* 2 to stop doing: *He left off working to watch the television*.

leave out not to include: *You've left out the 't' in 'Christmas'*.

left over not used; extra: *When everyone took a partner there was one person left over*; *We divided out the left-over food*.

See also **leftovers**.

leave[2] /liːv/ *n* 1 permission to do something: *The teacher gave him leave to go home early.* 2 a holiday: *Some of the soldiers are home on leave at the moment*.

leaves plural of **leaf**.

lectern /'lɛktən/ *n* a stand for holding a book *etc* to be read from, for a lecture or in a church.

lecture /'lɛktʃə(r)/ *n* 1 a formal talk given to students *etc*: *a history lecture.* 2 a scolding: *The teacher gave the children a lecture for running in the passage.* — *v* 1 to give a lecture: *He lectures on modern history.* 2 to scold: *His parents lectured him about getting home late*.

'lecturer *n* a person who lectures to students *etc*.

led see **lead**[2].

ledge /lɛdʒ/ *n* a shelf or an object that sticks out like a shelf: *He keeps plant-pots on the window-ledge*; *a rock-ledge*.

ledger /'lɛdʒə(r)/ *n* the book of accounts of an office or shop.

lee /liː/ *n* the sheltered side, away from the wind: *We sat in the lee of the rock*.

leech /liːtʃ/ *n* a kind of blood-sucking worm.

leek /liːk/ *n* a type of vegetable related to the onion with green leaves and a white base.

leeway /'liːweɪ/ *n* scope or possibility for freedom of movement or action: *A tight schedule won't leave you much leeway*.

left¹ *see* **leave¹**.

left² /lɛft/ *adj* on the side of the body that in most people has the less skilful hand: *They drive on the left side of the road in Britain.* — *adv* to or towards this side: *He turned left at the end of the road.* — *n* the left side, part *etc*: *You ought to know your right from your left*; *He sat on her left*; *She turned to her left*; *Take the first road on the left*; *Keep to the left!*

> The opposite of **left** is **right**.

'left-hand *adj* at the left; to the left: *It's in the bottom left-hand drawer of the desk.*
left-'handed *adj* having the left hand more skilful than the right. **left-'handedness** *n*.
left wing the members of a political party that want more social change than the others in their party.
left-'wing *adj*: *left-wing politicians*; *They're both very left-wing*.

> See also **right-wing**.

'leftovers *n* food that has not been eaten at a meal.

leg /lɛg/ *n* **1** one of the limbs by which animals and humans walk: *The horse injured a front leg*; *She stood on one leg*. **2** the part of an article of clothing that covers a leg: *He has torn the leg of his trousers*. **3** a long, narrow support of a table, chair *etc*: *One of the legs of the chair was broken.*
-legged /'lɛgɪd/ *adj*: *a long-legged girl*; *a four-legged animal*.
pull someone's leg to tease someone by trying to make them believe something that is not true.

legacy /'lɛgəsɪ/ *n* something left to you by someone who has died: *He was left a legacy by his great-aunt.*

legal /'liːgəl/ *adj* **1** allowed by the law: *Is it legal to teach your children at home instead of sending them to school?*; *a legal contract*. **2** concerned with the law: *He belongs to the legal profession*. **'legally** *adv*. **le'gality** *n*.

> The opposite of **legal** is **illegal**.

'legalize *v* to allow something by law.
legend /'lɛdʒənd/ *n* a myth; a story about heroes *etc* of long ago: *the legend of Monkey and his friends*. **'legendary** *adj*.
legible /'lɛdʒɪbəl/ *adj* clear enough to be read: *The writing was faded but still legible.*
'legibly *adv*. **legi'bility** *n*.

> The opposite of **legible** is **illegible**.

legislate /'lɛdʒɪsleɪt/ *v* to make laws: *The government plans to legislate against the importing of foreign cars.*
legi'slation *n* **1** making laws. **2** a law; a set of laws.
'legislator *n* a person who makes laws.
legitimate /lɪ'dʒɪtɪmət/ *adj* lawful; allowed by law. **le'gitimately** *adv*. **le'gitimacy** *n*.

> The opposite of **legitimate** is **illegitimate**.

leisure /'lɛʒə(r)/ *n* time that you can spend as you like, when you have no work to do: *I seldom have the leisure to watch television.*
'leisurely *adj* taking plenty of time: *She had a leisurely bath.*
at leisure or **at your leisure** at a convenient time and without hurrying: *I don't want the book back so you can finish reading it at your leisure.*

lemon /'lɛmən/ *n* a type of juicy fruit with thick, yellow skin and very sour juice: *She added the juice of a lemon to the pudding.*
lemonade /lɛmə'neɪd/ *n* a drink, usually fizzy, flavoured with lemons.

lend /lɛnd/ *v* **1** to give someone the use of something for a time: *She had forgotten her umbrella so I lent her mine to go home with.* **2** to give: *Desperation lent him strength.*

> **lend**; **lent** /lɛnt/; **lent**: *He lent me a pound*; *You shouldn't have lent him money.*
> **lend to**: *I lent my pencil to John.*
> See also **borrow**.

length /lɛŋθ/ *n* **1** the distance from one end to the other of an object, period of time *etc*: *What is the length of your car?*; *Please note down the length of time it takes you to do this.* **2** a piece of something, especially cloth: *I bought a 3-metre length of silk.*
'lengthen *v* to make or become longer: *I'll have to lengthen this skirt*; *The days are lengthening now that the spring has come.*
'lengthways *adv* in the direction along the length of something: *fold the sheets lengthways.*
'lengthy *adj* very long: *This essay is interesting but lengthy.*
at length 1 in detail: *She told us at length about her accident.* **2** at last: *At length the walkers arrived home.*
go to great lengths to take a lot of trouble to achieve something.
the length and breadth of to or in all parts

lenient

of a place: *They travelled throughout the length and breadth of India.*

lenient /'li:nɪənt/ *adj* merciful; not punishing severely: *You are much too lenient with those naughty children.* **'leniently** *adv.* **'lenience**, **'leniency** *ns.*

lens /lɛnz/ *n* **1** a curved piece of glass *etc* used in spectacles, microscopes, cameras *etc*: *I need new lenses in my spectacles; She lost one of her contact lenses.* **2** a similar curved, transparent part of your eye.

> **lens** is singular; the plural is **lenses**.

lent *see* **lend**.

lentil /'lɛntɪl/ *n* a small round vegetable like a bean, that can be dried and then used in cooking: *lentil soup.*

leopard /'lɛpəd/ *n* a large spotted animal of the cat family.

leotard /'lɪətɑːd/ *n* a tight-fitting garment worn for dancing, gymnastics *etc*.

leper /'lɛpə(r)/ *n* a person who has leprosy.

leprosy /'lɛprəsɪ/ *n* a skin disease, causing serious damage to the body.

lesbian /'lɛzbɪən/ *n* a woman who is sexually attracted to other women. — *adj*.

lesion /'liːʒən/ *n* an injury or wound: *a serious lesion on the abdomen.*

less /lɛs/ *adj* not as much as: *Think of a number less than forty; He drank his tea and wished he had put less sugar in it; The salary for that job will be not less than £20 000.* — *adv* not as much; to a smaller extent: *You should smoke less if you want to remain healthy.* — *pron* a smaller part or amount: *He earns less than I do; Use less of the red paint and more of the yellow when you're painting flesh.* — *prep* minus: *He earns £180 a week, less £60 income tax.*

> **less** is used in speaking about quantity or amount: *People should eat less fat; I've less than £100 in the bank.*
> **fewer** is used in speaking about numbers of things or people: *I've fewer books than he has; There were fewer than 50 people at the meeting.*
> See also **little**.

lessen /'lɛsən/ *v* to make or become less: *The noise lessened gradually.*

'lesser *adj* smaller; not as important: *the lesser of the two towns.*

less and less becoming smaller and smaller in amount or degree: *He visited his parents less and less; I find I have less and less time for reading these days.*

the less...: *The less I see of him, the better!; The less I practise, the worse I become.*

lesson /'lɛsən/ *n* **1** a period of teaching: *during the French lesson.* **2** something that is learnt by experience: *He burnt his fingers when he touched the kettle — that taught him a lesson!* **3** a piece from the Bible, read in church.

lest /lɛst/ *conjunction* in case: *He was scared lest he should fail his exam.*

let[1] /lɛt/ *v* **1** to allow; to permit: *She refused to let her children go out in the rain; Let me see your drawing.* **2** used for giving orders or making suggestions: *If they will not work, let them starve; Let us pray.*

> **let; let; let**: *He let me in; Have you let the cat out?*

> **let's** is short for **let us**: *Let's go for a walk!*

let alone and certainly not: *There's no room for her, let alone her children and animals.*

let someone or **something alone**, **let someone** or **something be** to leave alone; not to disturb or worry: *Why don't you let him be when he's not feeling well!; Do let your father alone.*

let down 1 to lower: *She let down the blind.* **2** to disappoint: *You must get him a present — you can't let him down on his birthday.*

let go to stop holding something: *Will you let go of my coat!; When he was nearly at the top of the rope he suddenly let go and fell.*

let in or **let out** to allow someone or something to come in or go out: *Let me in!; I let the dog out.*

let me see or **let's see** used when you are thinking or trying to remember something: *Now let me see — where did I put my car keys?*

let someone know to tell someone: *I'll let you know what the price of the book is.*

let off 1 to fire a gun *etc*: *He let the gun off accidentally.* **2** to allow someone to go without punishment *etc*: *The policeman let him off with a warning.*

let[2] /lɛt/ *v* to give the use of a house *etc* in return for payment: *He lets his house to visitors in the summer.*

to let for letting: *The notice said 'House to let'.*

> **let, rent, hire**: You **let** or **rent** a place to live, but you **hire** equipment.
> **let to**: *to let your flat to visitors.*
> **rent to, rent out to**: *He rents his flat out to university students.*
> **rent from**: *I rent my flat from a landlord who lives abroad.*
> **hire from**: *I hired a bicycle from the shop.*
> **hire out**: *This shop hires out cycles.*

lethal /ˈliːθəl/ *adj* causing death: *The poison is lethal to rats; a lethal blow to the head.*

lethargic /ləˈθɑːdʒɪk/ *adj* having no interest, energy or enthusiasm: *He has been very lethargic since he was ill.* **ˈlethargy** *n*.

letter /ˈlɛtə(r)/ *n* **1** a mark that means a sound: *the letters of the alphabet.* **2** a written message, especially one sent by post in an envelope: *Did you post my letter?*

> See **alphabet**.

ˈlettering *n* letters painted or written carefully, for display *etc*.

ˈletterbox *n* **1** an oblong hole in a door, sometimes with a box behind it, through which mail is put: *He put the postcard through the letterbox.* **2** a postbox.

lettuce /ˈlɛtɪs/ *n* a type of green plant with large leaves, used in salads.

leukaemia or **leukemia** /luːˈkiːmɪə/ *n* a very serious blood disease.

level /ˈlɛvəl/ *n* **1** height: *The level of the river rose.* **2** a standard: *There is a high level of intelligence amongst the pupils.* **3** a floor: *the third level of the multi-storey car park.* **4** a kind of instrument for showing whether a surface is level. **5** a flat area, not sloping up or down: *It was difficult running uphill but he could run fast on the level.* — *adj* **1** flat; horizontal: *a level surface; a level spoonful.* **2** of the same height, standard, amount *etc*: *When he stood up, his eyes were level with the window-sill; The scores of the two teams are level.* **3** steady: *a calm, level voice.* — *v* **1** to make something flat or smooth: *He levelled the soil.* **2** to make things equal: *His goal levelled the scores of the two teams.* **3** to aim a gun *etc*: *He levelled his pistol at the target.* **ˈlevelness** *n*.

level crossing a place where a road crosses a railway on the same level.

level-ˈheaded *adj* calm and sensible.

do your level best to do your very best.

level off or **level out** to become flat or horizontal after rising or falling; to remain steady after increasing or decreasing: *The road climbed steeply and then levelled out; Unemployment figures are at last levelling off.*

on a level with level with: *His eyes were on a level with the shop counter.*

lever /ˈliːvə(r)/ *n* **1** a tool *etc* used to move things that are heavy or to loosen things that are firmly fixed: *You can use a coin as a lever to get a lid off a tin.* **2** a bar or handle for working a machine *etc*: *This is the lever that switches on the power.* — *v* to move something with a lever: *He levered the lid off with a coin.*

ˈleverage *n* the force or power gained by using a lever.

levitate /ˈlɛvɪteɪt/ *v* to float or cause to float in the air: *He claimed to be able to levitate.* **ˈlevitation** *n*.

levy /ˈlɛvɪ/ *v* to collect a tax: *A tax was levied on tobacco.* — *n* **1** money collected by order: *a levy on imports.* **2** the collecting of soldiers for an army.

liable /ˈlaɪəbl/ *adj* **1** likely to be affected by something: *This road is liable to flooding; He is liable to pneumonia.* **2** likely to do something: *Watch the milk — it's liable to boil over; He's liable to make careless mistakes.* **3** responsible in law for something: *Is a wife liable for her husband's debts?* **liaˈbility** *n*.

liaison /lɪˈeɪzən/ *n* contact; communication: *liaison between parents and teachers.* — *adj*: *a liaison officer.*

liˈaise *v* to communicate as an official duty.

liar /ˈlaɪə(r)/ *n* a person who tells lies; an untruthful person: *If he told you that, he's a liar.*

libel /ˈlaɪbəl/ *n* something written that is harmful to a person's reputation. — *v* to damage the reputation of someone by libel.

liberal /ˈlɪbərəl/ *adj* **1** generous: *She gave me a liberal helping of apple pie; She is very liberal with her money.* **2** not severe or strict; allowing people to do what they want, as much as possible: *a liberal headmaster.* — *n* a person who thinks in a liberal way. **ˈliberally** *adv*.

liberate /ˈlɪbəreɪt/ *v* to set someone free: *The prisoners were liberated by the new government.*

libeˈration *n*: *the women's liberation movement.*

ˈliberated *adj* not sharing traditional opinions or ways of behaving.

liberty /ˈlɪbətɪ/ *n* **1** freedom from captivity or

from slavery: *The new president ordered that all prisoners should be given their liberty.* **2** freedom to do as you want: *Children have a lot more liberty now than they used to.* **3** a lack of politeness in speech or action: *I think you were taking a liberty to ask her how old she was!*

at liberty free; allowed to do something: *You are at liberty to leave when you wish; I am not at liberty to tell you where I got this information.*

library /'laɪbrərɪ/ *n* **1** a building or a room containing a large collection of books, especially for people to borrow: *He works in the public library.* **2** a collection of other things, for example gramophone records, for borrowing.

librarian /laɪ'brɛərɪən/ *n* a person who is employed in a library.

lice plural of **louse**.

licence /'laɪsəns/ *n* a printed form giving you permission to do something, for example, drive a car, sell alcoholic drinks *etc*: *a driving licence.*

'license *v* to give a licence to someone; to permit someone to do something: *He is licensed to sell alcohol.*

> **licence** is a noun: a **licence** (not **license**) to sell alcohol.
> **license** is a verb: **licensed** (not **licenced**) to drive a goods vehicle.

licen'see *n* a person to whom a licence to keep a licensed hotel *etc* has been given.

lichee another spelling of **lychee**.

lichen /'laɪkən/ *n* a tiny, primitive kind of plant that grows in patches on tree-trunks, rocks, walls *etc*.

lick /lɪk/ *v* to pass your tongue over something: *The dog licked her hand; She licked the stamp.* — *n*: *The child gave the ice-cream a lick.*

lap   lick   suck

lid /lɪd/ *n* **1** a cover for a pot, box *etc*: *He lifted the lid of the box and looked inside.* **2** an eyelid.

lie¹ /laɪ/ *n* a false statement made in order to deceive someone: *He said he had stayed away from school because he was ill, but he was telling a lie — he had been at a football match.* — *v* to tell a lie: *Some people are inclined to lie about their age.*

> **lie**¹; **'lying**; **lied**; **lied**: *I knew she was lying*; *He lied about the money.*

lie² /laɪ/ *v* **1** to be in, or get into, a flat position: *She went into the bedroom and lay on the bed; Lie back in the chair; He lay down on the floor; The book was lying in the hall.* **2** to be in a particular place, condition *etc*; to be found, or belong, somewhere: *The farm lay three miles from the sea; The shop is lying empty now; The secret of good golf lies in the wrist action; The responsibility for the mistake lies with you.*

> **lie**²; **'lying**; **lay**; **lain**: *Lie down!*; *She's lying on the couch*; *He lay on the beach*; *The factory had lain empty for years.* See also **lay**¹.

lie about or **lie around** to spend your time relaxing and not working: *I like to spend my weekends just lying about.*

lie ahead to be going to happen in the future: *I just don't know what lies ahead for the company.*

lie down to get into a flat or horizontal position, especially to sleep or have a rest.
'lie-down *n*: *He had a lie-down on the bed.*
lie in to stay in bed longer than usual.
'lie-in *n*: *She has a lie-in on her day off.*
lie low to stay quiet or hidden: *The criminal lay low until the police stopped looking for him.*
lie with to be the responsibility of: *The fault lies with you.*

lieutenant /lɛf'tɛnənt/ or /lu:'tɛnənt/ *n* (often written **Lt**, **Lieut**) a junior officer in the army or navy.

life /laɪf/, *plural* **lives** /laɪvz/, *n* **1** the quality that plants and animals have that makes them different from stones and rocks *etc*; the thing that goes out of you when you die: *Doctors are fighting to save the child's life.* **2** the time between birth and death: *He had a long and happy life.* **3** liveliness: *She was full of life and energy.* **4** a manner of living: *She lived a life of ease and idleness.* **5** a particular part of life: *School life has changed in the last 20 years.* **6** living things: *It is now believed that there is no life on Mars*; *animal life.* **7** the story of a life: *He has written a life of Sir Stamford Raffles.*

life-and-'death *adj* deciding between life and death: *a life-and-death struggle.*

'lifebelt *n* a ring which floats and can support a person who has fallen into water.

'lifeboat *n* a boat for saving shipwrecked people.

life cycle the various stages through which a living thing passes: *the life cycle of the snail.*

life expectancy the length of time a person can expect to live.

'lifeguard *n* a person employed to protect and rescue swimmers at a swimming pool, beach *etc.*

life insurance *n* an agreement made with an insurance company, that if you pay them a regular sum, they will give you money when you reach a certain age; an agreement that a certain amount of money will be given to the wife, husband, or children when the person who paid the insurance dies.

life jacket a jacket filled with material that will float, for keeping a person afloat.

'lifeless *adj* **1** dead: *a lifeless body.* **2** not lively: *The actress gave a lifeless performance.*

'lifelike *adj* like a living person, animal *etc*: *The statue was very lifelike.*

'lifeline *n* a rope used for support in dangerous jobs, or thrown to rescue a drowning person.

'lifelong *adj* lasting the whole length of a life: *a lifelong friendship.*

'life-saving *n* the skill of rescuing people from drowning.

'life-size or **'life-sized** *adj* as large as the original: *a lifesize statue.*

'lifespan *n* the length of time that a thing or person lives.

'lifestyle *n* a person's or group's way of living: *He has a very expensive lifestyle.*

life-support machine a machine which keeps a person alive when they are very ill or in a dangerous environment: *Astronauts depend on their life-support machines when they are in space.*

'lifetime *n* the period of a person's life: *There have been many changes in his lifetime.*

bring to life to make a subject interesting: *His lectures brought the subject to life.*

for life until death: *They became friends for life.*

take someone's life to kill someone.

take your own life to kill yourself; to commit suicide.

lift /lɪft/ *v* **1** to raise up: *The box was so heavy that I couldn't lift it*; *She lifted the child on to her back.* **2** to rise: *The helicopter lifted into the air.* **3** to disappear: *The plane can't take off till the fog lifts.* **4** to cancel a rule or law *etc*: *The emergency speed limit has been lifted.* — *n* **1** a small compartment that moves up and down between floors carrying goods or people; an elevator: *As she was too tired to climb the stairs, she went up in the lift.* **2** a ride in someone's car: *Can I give you a lift into town?* **3** a feeling of happiness: *Winning the competition gave me quite a lift.*

lift off to leave the ground: *The rocket will lift off at 14.00 hours.* **'lift-off** *n.*

ligament /'lɪgəmənt/ *n* a band of tough tissue that joins bones and muscles together: *He strained the ligaments in his knee playing football.*

light¹ /laɪt/ *n* **1** the brightness given by the sun, or by a flame, or a lamp, that makes things able to be seen: *It was nearly dawn and the light was getting stronger*; *Sunlight streamed into the room.* **2** an electric lamp *etc* in a street or building: *Suddenly all the lights went out.* **3** something that can be used to set fire to something else; a flame; a match. — *adj* **1** having plenty of light; not dark: *The studio was a large, light room.* **2** pale in colour; closer to white than black: *light green.* — *v* **1** to give light to a place: *The room was lit only by candles.* **2** to make something catch fire; to catch fire: *She lit the gas*; *I think this match is damp, because it won't light.* **'lightness**¹ *n.*

> **light**; **lit** /lɪt/; **lit**: *She lit the candles*; *The fire had been lit.*

light bulb a bulb for producing electric light.

come to light to be found or known: *New evidence came to light during the court case.*

in the light of considering; because of: *We shall have to make our decision in the light of everything we have heard today.*

light up 1 to make, be or become bright or full of light: *A flash of lightning lit up the whole sky.* **2** to make or become happy: *Her face lit up when she saw him*; *A sudden smile lit up her face.*

light² /laɪt/ *adj* **1** easy to lift or carry; weighing little: *Aluminium is a light metal*; *I bought a light suitcase for plane journeys.* **2** easy; not hard; not severe: *Next time the punishment will not be so light*; *He was given light work after his illness.* **3** consisting of only a small amount of food: *a light meal.* **4** lively; nimble: *She was very light on her feet.* **5** cheerful; not serious: *light music.* **6** little in quantity: *light rain.* **'lightly** *adv.* **'lightness**² *n.*

get off lightly to escape or be allowed to go without severe punishment *etc*.

travel light to travel with little luggage.

lighten¹ /'laɪtən/ *v* to make or become brighter: *The sky was lightening as dawn approached.*

lighten² /'laɪtən/ *v* to make or become less heavy: *Let me carry one of your bags — that will lighten your load a bit.*

lighter /'laɪtə(r)/ *n* a device for lighting a gas oven, cigarette *etc*.

light-headed /'laɪthedɪd/ *adj* dizzy.

light-hearted /'laɪthɑ:tɪd/ *adj* happy; not anxious; not sad or serious: *I'm in a light-hearted mood today.*

lighthouse /'laɪthaʊs/ *n* a tall building built on a coastline *etc*, with a light, especially one that flashes, to guide or warn ships.

lighting /'laɪtɪŋ/ *n* the lights provided in a room *etc*: *The lighting was so bad in the café that we could hardly see.*

lightning /'laɪtnɪŋ/ *n* a flash of electricity during a storm, usually followed by thunder: *The house was struck by lightning.*

> a flash of **lightning** (not **lightening**).
> **lightning** is never used in the plural.

lightweight /'laɪtweɪt/ *adj* light in weight: *a lightweight raincoat.*

light-year /'laɪtjɪə(r)/ *n* the distance light travels in a year, 9.5 million million kilometres.

like¹ /laɪk/ *prep* **1** the same as or similar to; in the same or a similar way to: *He climbs like a cat; She is like her mother.* **2** typical of a particular person: *It isn't like her to be late.* **3** used in asking someone to describe someone or something: *What is she like?; What is it like?* **4** such as; for example: *outdoor sports like running and climbing; They keep hugging and kissing like they do in films.*

feel like to want: *I don't feel like going out; I expect he feels like a cup of tea.*

look like 1 to appear similar to someone or something: *She looks very like her mother.* **2** to show signs of something: *It looks like rain.*

like² /laɪk/ *v* **1** to be pleased with something; to find someone or something pleasant: *I like him very much; I like the way you've decorated this room.* **2** to enjoy: *I like gardening.* **'likeable** *adj.*

> The opposite of **like**² is **dislike**.

if you like used for agreeing to a suggestion: *'Shall we go out tonight?' 'If you like.'*

should like or **would like** want: *I should like to say thank you; Would you like a cup of tea?*

likelihood /'laɪklɪhʊd/ *n* probability.

likely /'laɪklɪ/ *adj* **1** probable; expected: *What is the likely result?; It's likely that she'll succeed; She's likely to win.* **2** suitable: *a likely spot for a picnic; She's the most likely person for the job.*

not likely! certainly not!: *'Would you put your head in a lion's mouth?' 'Me? Not likely!'*

like-minded /laɪk'maɪndɪd/ *adj* agreeing in opinion or purpose: *like-minded people.*

liken /'laɪkən/ *v* to compare: *He likened the earth to an apple.*

likeness /'laɪknəs/ *n* **1** a similarity: *The likeness between them is amazing.* **2** a picture of a person *etc* in a photograph or portrait *etc*: *That photo of Mary is a good likeness.*

likes /laɪks/: **likes and dislikes** the things that you do and do not like.

likewise /'laɪkwaɪz/ *adv* the same: *Mary gave some of her pocket money to the Red Cross, and you should do likewise.*

liking /'laɪkɪŋ/ *n* **1** a fondness: *He has too great a liking for chocolate.* **2** satisfaction: *Is this meal to your liking?*

take a liking to to begin to like: *I've taken a liking to him.*

lilac /'laɪlək/ *n* **1** a small tree with bunches of tiny, sweet-smelling, pale purple or white flowers. **2** a pale purple colour. — *adj*: *a lilac blouse.*

lily /'lɪlɪ/ *n* a type of tall plant grown from a bulb, with white or coloured flowers.

limb /lɪm/ *n* **1** an arm or leg. **2** a branch.

out on a limb on your own, without support from other people.

limber /'lɪmbə(r)/: **limber up** to do some exercises before you start training properly.

lime¹ /laɪm/ *n* the white substance left after heating limestone, used in making cement.

lime² /laɪm/ *n* **1** a small, sour, green fruit related to the lemon. **2** the colour of this fruit. — *adj*: *lime walls.*

lime³ /laɪm/ *n* a tree with rough bark and small heart-shaped leaves.

limelight /'laɪmlaɪt/: **in the limelight** attracting the public's attention.

limerick /'lɪmərɪk/ *n* a funny poem with five lines, the third and fourth lines being shorter than the others.

limestone /'laɪmstoʊn/ *n* a kind of rock.

limit /'lɪmɪt/ *n* **1** the farthest point; the boundary: *the outer limits of the city*. **2** a control: *We must put a limit on our spending*. — *v* to control; to say where the finishing-point must be: *The teacher limited the time for the composition to one hour*.

limi'tation *n* **1** controlling something or making something smaller; a condition that controls or limits what you can do: *arms limitation talks*; *There are certain limitations on what the committee can do*. **2** the extent of a thing or person's ability: *know your limitations*; *Acupuncture is good for some medical conditions but it has its limitations*.

'limited *adj* **1** not very large: *We have a limited amount of money to spend on this project*. **2** (usually written **Ltd**.) a word used in the titles of some business companies: *W. and R. Chambers Ltd*.

'limitless *adj* very large: *The possibilities are limitless*.

within limits to a certain extent; as long as it is not too much, great *etc*: *You can spend as much as you like within limits!*

limousine /ˌlɪməˈziːn/ *n* a large type of motor car.

limp[1] /lɪmp/ *adj* lacking stiffness or strength; drooping: *a limp lettuce*; *limp flowers*.

limp[2] /lɪmp/ *v* to walk unevenly, usually because you have hurt your foot or leg: *He twisted his ankle and came limping home*. — *n*: *He walks with a limp*.

line[1] /laɪn/ *n* **1** a thread, cord, rope *etc*: *She hung the washing on the line*; *a fishing-rod and line*. **2** a long, narrow mark: *She drew straight lines across the page*; *a dotted line*; *a wavy line*. **3** a mark or wrinkle on your face: *Don't frown — you'll get lines on your forehead*. **4** a row of objects or people arranged side by side or one behind the other: *The children stood in a line*; *a line of trees*. **5** a short letter: *I'll drop him a line*. **6** a series of people that come one after the other, especially in the same family: *a line of kings*. **7** the railway; a single track of the railway: *Passengers must cross the line by the bridge only*. **8** a system of pipes or electrical cables or telephone cables connecting one place with another: *All telephone lines to Bangkok are engaged*. **9** a row of written or printed words: *a poem with sixteen lines*. **10** the words that an actor has to learn: *I hope I don't forget my lines*. **11** a direction or course of thought or action; an attitude or policy towards something: *a line of argument*; *If this policy doesn't work, we'll have to take a different line*. **12** a route along which vehicles travel regularly: *lines of communication*; *As the city grew, more lines were opened on the underground system*. — *v* to form lines along a road *etc*: *Crowds lined the pavement to see the Queen*.

drop a line to write a short note or letter to someone: *Drop me a line sometime*.

in line for likely to get something: *She's next in line for promotion*.

in line with similar to something and fitting in with it: *This policy is in line with the school's traditions*.

line up to form a line; to group things or people into a line: *The children lined up ready to leave the classroom*; *She lined up the chairs*.

on line connected to a computer system.

line[2] /laɪn/ *v* to cover something on the inside: *She lined the drawer with newspaper*; *She lined the dress with silk*.

lined[1] *adj*: *a lined skirt*.

lined[2] /laɪnd/ *adj* **1** ruled with lines: *lined paper*. **2** covered with wrinkles: *a lined face*.

linen /'lɪnɪn/ *n* a kind of cloth that is heavier than cotton, sometimes used to make sheets, dish-towels *etc*: *This handkerchief is made of linen*. — *adj* made of linen: *linen sheets*.

liner[1] /'laɪnə(r)/ *n* a large ship or aircraft: *They went aboard the liner*.

liner[2] /'laɪnə(r)/ *n* a plastic bag *etc* used for lining a container *etc*: *a dustbin-liner*.

linesman /'laɪnzmən/ *n* a person who watches the boundary line of a football field, tennis court *etc* during a match, and gives a sign when the ball goes over the line.

linger /'lɪŋɡə(r)/ *v* to remain; to stay; to move very slowly: *The smell of the bad fish lingered for days*; *We lingered in the hall looking at the pictures*.

lingerie /'lænʒərɪ/ *n* women's underwear and nightclothes: *The lingerie department is on the second floor of the department store*.

linguist /'lɪŋɡwɪst/ *n* a person who studies language or is good at languages. **lin'guistic** *adj*.

linguistics /lɪŋˈɡwɪstɪks/ *n* the science of languages.

lining /'laɪnɪŋ/ *n* a covering on the inside: *The lining of my jacket is torn*.

link /lɪŋk/ *n* **1** one of the rings that are joined together to form a chain. **2** something that joins or connects one thing with another: *a link in an argument*; *These old photographs are a link with the past*. — *v* to connect; to join: *The children stood in a circle and linked* hands; *The new train service links the suburbs with the heart of the city*; *An electrician is coming to link up our house to the electricity supply.*

linoleum /lɪˈnoʊliəm/ *n* a smooth, hard covering for floors (often shortened to **lino** /ˈlaɪnoʊ/): *We have grey lino on our kitchen floor.*

lint /lɪnt/ *n* linen in the form of soft fluffy material for putting over wounds.

lion /ˈlaɪən/ *n* a large, flesh-eating animal of the cat family, the male of which has a thick mane: *A group of lions is called a pride of lions.*

ˈlioness *n* a female lion.

> A lion **roars**.
> A baby lion is a **cub**.
> A lion lives in a **den** or **lair**.

the lion's share the largest share.

lip /lɪp/ *n* **1** either of the pieces of flesh that form the edge of your mouth: *She bit her lip.* **2** the edge of something: *the lip of a cup.*

-lipped: *a thin-lipped mouth.*

ˈlip-read *v* to understand what someone is saying by watching the movement of their lips: *Many deaf people learn to lip-read.*

ˈlipstick *n* make-up for colouring the lips usually in the form of a short stick: *She was wearing bright red lipstick.*

liquid /ˈlɪkwɪd/ *n* a substance that flows, like water: *Water is a clear liquid.* — *adj* able to flow; not solid: *The ice-cream has become liquid.*

ˈliquidize *v* to make solid food into a liquid or smooth cream: *He liquidized the vegetables to make soup.*

ˈliquidizer *n* a machine for liquidizing food.

liquor /ˈlɪkə(r)/ *n* strong alcoholic drink.

lisp /lɪsp/ *v* to pronounce *s* and *z* as *th.* — *n*: *He speaks with a lisp.*

list /lɪst/ *n* a series of names, numbers, prices *etc* written down or said one after the other: *a shopping-list*; *We have a long list of people who are willing to help.* — *v* to put something on a list: *He listed the things he had to do.*

> to **list** (not **list down** or **list out**) the things you need.

listen /ˈlɪsən/ *v* **1** to pay attention to what someone is saying, or to some other sound, so as to hear it properly: *I told her three times how to do it, but she wasn't listening*; *Do listen to the music!* **2** to follow someone's advice: *If she'd listened to her mother, she wouldn't have got into trouble.*

> See **hear**.

ˈlistener *n* someone who listens.

listen for or **listen out for** to wait to hear something: *She sat listening for the sound of his key in the lock*; *Listen out for the baby crying, won't you?*

listen in to listen secretly to a private conversation: *I became aware that someone was listening in on the telephone downstairs.*

listless /ˈlɪstləs/ *adj* having no energy or interest: *The heat made us listless.* **ˈlistlessly** *adv*.

lit *see* **light**¹.

literacy /ˈlɪtərəsɪ/ *n* the ability to read and write.

literal /ˈlɪtərəl/ *adj* **1** exact: *the literal truth.* **2** giving the exact meaning of each word: *a literal translation.* **ˈliterally** *adv*.

literary /ˈlɪtərərɪ/ *adj* having to do with literature, or the writing of books.

literate /ˈlɪtərət/ *adj* able to read and write.

literature /ˈlɪtərətʃə(r)/ *n* books; writings; poems, novels, plays *etc*, especially good ones.

lithe /laɪð/ *adj* able to bend easily, supple: *Gymnasts need to be as lithe as possible.*

litre /ˈliːtə(r)/ *n* a measure of liquid: *a litre of wine.*

litter /ˈlɪtə(r)/ *n* **1** an untidy mess of paper, rubbish *etc*: *Put your litter in a rubbish bin.* **2** a number of animals born to the same mother at the same time: *a litter of kittens.* — *v* to cover the ground *etc* with scattered objects: *Papers littered the table.*

litter bin a container to put litter in.

little /ˈlɪtəl/ *adj* **1** small: *a little book.* **2** very young: *He is only a little boy*; *When I was little, I was afraid of the dark.* **3** not much: *topics that have very little to do with the art of display*; *The storm did little harm.* **4** not important: *I did not expect her to make a fuss about such a little thing.* — *n* not much: *There's little we can do to help him.* — *adv* **1** not much: *She goes out very little nowadays.* **2** not at all: *He little knew how close he was to danger.*

> **little; less; least:** *We have little reason to be pleased, but you have less, and they have least of all.*
> See also **few**.

little-ˈknown *adj* not famous: *a little-known author.*

a little 1 a short time or distance: *Move a*

little to the right! **2** a small quantity of something: *He has a little money to spare; 'Is there any soup left?' 'Yes, a little'.* **3** slightly: *She was a little frightened.*

> **little** means 'not much': *You have little reason to boast.*
> **a little** means 'some', 'a small quantity': *There's a little milk left.*

little by little gradually: *Little by little we began to get to know him.*

live¹ /lɪv/ *v* **1** to be alive: *This poison is dangerous to everything that lives.* **2** to stay alive; to survive: *The doctors say he is very ill, but they think he will live.* **3** to have your home in a particular place: *She lives next to the church; They went to live in Brisbane.* **4** to pass your life: *He lived a life of luxury; She lives in fear of being attacked.* **5** to get enough money, food *etc* to keep alive: *She lives by writing books; He lived by fishing.*

live down to make people forget something bad or embarrassing that you did or that happened to you: *We lost 10 – 0 and we'll never live it down!*

live on 1 to keep yourself alive by eating particular foods: *He lives on fish and potatoes.* **2** to buy enough food *etc* to keep alive, using the money that you get or earn: *You can't live on £30 a week.*

live up to to be as good as expected: *She couldn't live up to her parents' expectations.*

live² /laɪv/ *adj* **1** having life; not dead: *They found a live mouse in the tin of biscuits.* **2** heard or seen on the radio or television while it is actually happening; not recorded: *I watched a live broadcast of the football match on television.* **3** not exploded; still active: *a live bomb.* **4** burning: *a live coal.* **5** an electric current: *a live wire.* — *adv* as the event takes place: *The competition will be broadcast live.*

livelihood /'laɪvlɪhʊd/ *n* enough pay or wages for you to live on, feed yourself *etc*: *He earns a livelihood as a newspaper reporter.*

lively /'laɪvlɪ/ *adj* active; full of life or movement: *lively music; She did a lively dance; a lively discussion.* **'liveliness** *n.*

liven /'laɪvən/: **liven up** to become or make something livelier, more interesting or more exciting: *Some pictures on the walls should liven this place up a bit; When the band began to play, the party livened up.*

liver /'lɪvə(r)/ *n* **1** a large organ in your body that purifies your blood. **2** this organ, taken from certain animals, used as food.

lives plural of **life**.

livestock /'laɪvstɒk/ *n* animals kept on a farm *etc* such as horses, cattle, sheep, pigs.

livid /'lɪvɪd/ *adj* **1** very angry: *He was absolutely livid when he was sacked.* **2** black and blue: *livid bruises.*

living /'lɪvɪŋ/ *adj* **1** having life; alive: *living creatures; Is there anything living on Mars?* **2** alive at present: *He is the greatest living artist.* — *n* the money that you earn and live on: *He earns his living as a taxi-driver; She makes a living by painting portraits.*
'living-room *n* a sitting-room.

lizard /'lɪzəd/ *n* a small, four-footed reptile.

llama /'lɑːmə/ *n* a South American animal with soft, thick hair, that is like a small camel without a hump: *Llamas are kept for carrying loads and for their wool, meat and skin.*

lo and behold /ˌloʊ ənd bɪˈhoʊld/ an expression of surprise *etc* at seeing or finding something.

load /loʊd/ *n* **1** something that is being carried: *The truck had to stop because its load had fallen off; She was carrying a load of groceries.* **2** as much as can be carried at one time: *two truck-loads of earth.* **3** a large amount: *We ate loads of ice-cream.* — *v* **1** to put a load on to a vehicle *etc*: *They loaded the luggage into the car.* **2** to put bullets *etc* into a gun: *He loaded the revolver and fired.* **3** to put a film into a camera: *Is this camera loaded?* **4** to put a program or disk into a computer so that it may be used: *Load the disk immediately after switching the machine on.*

'loaded *adj* **1** carrying a load: *a bus loaded with children.* **2** giving an advantage: *The system is loaded in our favour.*

loaf¹ /loʊf/, *plural* **loaves** /loʊvz/, *n* a shaped mass of bread: *a sliced loaf.*

loaf² /loʊf/ *v* to walk about idly, or waste time doing nothing: *They were loafing about the street.*
'loafer *n*: *an idle loafer.*

loan /loʊn/ *n* **1** anything lent, especially money: *I shall ask the bank for a loan.* **2** the lending of something: *I gave him the loan of my bicycle.* — *v*: *My mother loaned me the money I needed.*
on loan borrowed: *This picture is on loan from the museum.*

loathe /loʊð/ *v* to hate very much: *I loathe arithmetic.*
'loathing *n*: *I remember my maths teacher with loathing.*

loaves plural of **loaf**[1].

lob /lɒb/ *n* a slow, high throw or hit of a ball *etc*. — *v* to throw or strike a ball *etc* so that it moves high and slowly: *He lobbed the ball over the net.*

lobby /ˈlɒbɪ/ *n* a small entrance-hall or passage.

> A **lobby** is a small entrance-hall or passage.
> A **foyer** is a large entrance-hall in a theatre, cinema or hotel.

lobe /loʊb/ *n* the soft lower part of your ear.

lobster /ˈlɒbstə(r)/ *n* a shellfish with large claws.

local /ˈloʊkəl/ *adj* belonging to a certain place or district: *The local shops are very good*; *He likes to read the local newspaper.* — *n* a person who lives in a particular area: *One of the locals agreed to be my guide.* **ˈlocally** *adv*.

locality /loʊˈkalɪtɪ/ *n* an area; a neighbourhood: *There is only one school in this locality.*

locate /loʊˈkeɪt/ *v* to find the place or position of something: *He located the street he was looking for on the map*; *The kitchen is located in the basement.*

loˈcation *n* position or situation.

on location made in a suitable place outside a studio: *The film was shot entirely on location in Brazil.*

lock[1] /lɒk/ *n* a device for fastening doors *etc*: *He put the key in the lock.* — *v* **1** to fasten or become fastened with a lock: *She locked the drawer*; *This door doesn't lock.* **2** to stop someone getting through a door by locking it: *Don't forget to take your key with you — you mustn't lock yourself out of the house!*; *She found she was locked in, and had to climb out through a window.*

> See **bolt**.

lock in or **lock out** to lock a door so that a person cannot get in or out: *She found that she was locked out of the house.*

lock up 1 to lock someone into a room *etc*; to lock something into a drawer *etc*: *to lock up a prisoner*; *She locked up her jewellery.* **2** to lock the door and whatever else should be locked: *He locked up and left the shop.*

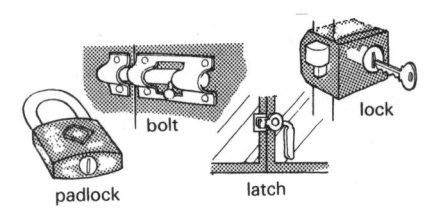

lock[2] /lɒk/ *n* a piece of hair: *She cut off a lock of his hair.*

locker /ˈlɒkə(r)/ *n* a small cupboard, for holding sports equipment *etc*.

locket /ˈlɒkɪt/ *n* a small case for holding tiny photographs, worn on a chain as jewellery: *She kept the pictures of her grandchildren in a locket round her neck.*

locksmith /ˈlɒksmɪθ/ *n* a person who makes and repairs locks.

locomotive /ˌloʊkəˈmoʊtɪv/ *n* a railway engine.

locust /ˈloʊkəst/ *n* a large insect of the grasshopper family, found in Africa and Asia, that moves in very large groups and destroys crops by eating them.

lodge /lɒdʒ/ *n* a small house, especially one at the entrance to a large house. — *v* **1** to live in rented rooms: *He lodges with the Smiths.* **2** to become fixed: *The bullet was lodged in his spine.*

> See **dislodge**.

ˈlodger *n* a person who lives in rented rooms: *The old lady likes to have a lodger in her house.*

ˈlodging *n* a place to stay: *He paid the landlady for board and lodging.*

ˈlodgings *n* a room or rooms rented in someone else's house: *She lives in lodgings.*

loft /lɒft/ *n* a room or space under a roof: *They kept a lot of old furniture in the loft.*

ˈlofty *adj* **1** very high: *a lofty building.* **2** proud: *a lofty attitude.*

log /lɒg/ *n* **1** a thick piece of wood: *The trees were sawn into logs.* **2** a book in which the official record of an air or sea journey is written: *The captain of the ship entered the details in the log.* — *v* to write down something in a log.

log in, **log into** or **log on** to begin using a computer system by typing a personal and usually secret password: *You can't use the computer unless you log in.*

log out or **log off** to stop using a computer system by typing a command: *He forgot to* *log off before going home for the night.*

logarithm /'lɒgərɪðəm/ *n* one of a series of numbers arranged in special tables that help you to solve mathematical problems.

loggerheads /'lɒgəhɛdz/: **at loggerheads** quarrelling: *They're always at loggerheads with their neighbours.*

logic /'lɒdʒɪk/ *n* correct reasoning.
 'logical *adj* according to the rules of logic: *She is always logical in her thinking.*
 'logically *adv.*

The opposite of **logical** is **illogical**.

logistics /lə'dʒɪstɪks/ *n* **1** the art of moving and supplying soldiers and military equipment: *The general was in charge of the logistics of the campaign.* **2** the organizing of everything needed for a complicated operation: *Planning the school holiday involved some very difficult logistics.*

logo /'loʊgoʊ/, *plural* **logos**, *n* a small design used as the symbol of an organization: *The company logo is a blue cross in a white circle.*

loin /lɔɪn/ *n* the back of an animal when cut into pieces for food.

loiter /'lɔɪtə(r)/ *v* to move *etc* slowly or to stand doing nothing in particular: *They were loitering outside the shop.*

loll /lɒl/ *v* **1** to sit or lie lazily: *to loll in a chair.* **2** to hang down or out: *The dog lay down with his tongue lolling.*

lollipop /'lɒlɪpɒp/ *n* a large sweet on a stick.

lolly /'lɒlɪ/ *n* a lollipop, or another kind of food on a stick: *an ice-lolly.*

lone /loʊn/ *adj* without companions, by itself *etc*: *a lone figure on the beach.*

lonely /'loʊnlɪ/ *adj* **1** sad because you are alone: *Aren't you lonely, living by yourself?* **2** far away from busy places; having few people: *a lonely island.* **'loneliness** *n.*

loner /'loʊnə(r)/ *n* a person who prefers to be alone.

long[1] /lɒŋ/ *adj* **1** measuring a lot from one end to the other: *a long journey; a long road; long legs.* **2** taking a lot of time: *The book took a long time to read; a long conversation; a long delay.* **3** measuring a certain amount in distance or time: *The wire is two centimetres long; The television programme was just over an hour long; How long was the film?* — *adv*: *This happened long before you were born; Have you been waiting long?; She had no idea how long it had taken her to cross the river; I'm going shopping — I won't be long.* — *n*: *It won't take long to get there.*

long-'distance *adj* travelling *etc* a long way: *a long-distance lorry-driver.*

long jump a sports contest in which people jump as far as possible.

as long as or **so long as 1** if: *So long as you're happy, it doesn't matter what you do.* **2** during the time that: *As long as he's here I'll have more work to do.*

before long soon: *Come in and wait — he'll be here before long!*

in the long run in the end: *We thought we would save money, but in the long run our spending was about the same as usual.*

no longer not now; not any more: *This cinema is no longer used.*

so long! goodbye!

long[2] /lɒŋ/ *v* to wish very much: *He longed to go home; I am longing for a drink.*

longhand /'lɒŋhand/ *n* ordinary writing, not shorthand.

longing /'lɒŋɪŋ/ *n* a great wish for something: *She looked at the cakes with longing.*
 'longingly *adv*: *She looked longingly at the chocolate.*

longitude /'lɒŋɪtjuːd/ *n* the distance, measured in degrees on the map, that a place is east or west of the north-south line passing through Greenwich in England.

See **latitude**.

long-playing /lɒŋ'pleɪɪŋ/ *adj* playing for a long time: *a long-playing gramophone record.*

long-range /'lɒŋreɪndʒ/ *adj* **1** to do with the distant future: *a long-range prediction; the long-range weather forecast.* **2** able to travel long distance: *long range nuclear missiles.*

long-sighted /lɒŋ'saɪtɪd/ *adj* having difficulty in seeing close objects clearly. **long-'sightedness** *n.*

long-standing /lɒŋ'standɪŋ/ *adj* that has lasted for a long time: *a long-standing disagreement.*

long-suffering /lɒŋ'sʌfərɪŋ/ *adj* bearing trouble and problems patiently.

long-term /lɒŋ'tɜːm/ *adj* of or for a long period of time: *the company's long-term plans; the long-term effects of the drug.*

long-winded /lɒŋ'wɪndɪd/ *adj* taking too long to say something.

look /lʊk/ *v* **1** to turn your eyes in a certain direction so as to see: *He looked out of the window; I've looked everywhere, but I can't find him; He looked at me angrily.* **2** to seem: *It looks as if it's going to rain; She looks sad.* **3** to face: *The house looks west.* — *n* **1**

an act of looking; a chance to see: *Let me have a look!* **2** a glance; an expression: *a look of surprise.* **3** appearance: *The house had a look of neglect.*

looker-'on *n* a person who is watching something happening; an onlooker.

-'looking: *good-looking; strange-looking.*

'lookout *n* **1** a careful watch: *a sharp lookout.* **2** a high place for watching from. **3** a person who has been given the job of watching.

looks *n* appearance: *She lost her good looks as she grew older.*

be on the lookout or **keep a lookout** to watch to make sure that you see something when it appears: *She kept a lookout for the bus; He's on the lookout for a new job.*

by the look of or **from the look of** judging by the appearance: *By the look of the sky I'd say it's going to rain.*

look after to take care of someone or something: *Who is looking after the children?*

look ahead to consider what will happen in the future.

look back to think about something in your past: *She looked back on her life with sadness.*

look down your nose at something to despise something.

look down on to regard as inferior: *The rich often look down on the poor.*

look for to search for someone or something: *I have been looking for you everywhere.*

See **search**.

look forward to to wait with pleasure for something: *We are looking forward to the holidays; I am looking forward to seeing you.*

look here!: *Look here! Isn't that what you wanted?; Look here, Mary, you're being unfair!*

look into to find out about something; to investigate: *The manager will look into your complaint.*

look on 1 to watch: *No, I don't want to play — I'd rather look on.* **2** to consider: *I have lived with my aunt since I was a baby, and I look on her as my mother.*

look out 1 to wait and watch for something: *She was looking out for him from the window.* **2** to find by searching: *I've looked out these books for you.*

look out! be careful!

look over to examine: *We have been looking over the new house.*

look round 1 to look at lots of things before deciding which to buy: *She looked round for a week before deciding on his present.* **2** to visit a place of interest *etc*: *Let's look round the castle this afternoon.*

look through to examine briefly: *I've looked through your notes.*

look to someone to expect someone to provide something or do something for you: *She always looked to her parents for support; They looked to the state to give them a home.*

look up 1 to improve: *Things have been looking up lately.* **2** to pay a visit to: *I looked up several old friends.* **3** to search for something in a book of reference: *You should look the word up in a dictionary.*

look up to to respect someone: *He has always looked up to his father.*

loom[1] /luːm/ *n* a machine in which thread is woven into a fabric.

loom[2] /luːm/ *v* to appear as a large, vague shape, sometimes with frightening suddenness: *Suddenly a huge ship loomed out of the fog; Tall skyscrapers loomed over the city.*

loop /luːp/ *n* **1** a doubled-over part of a piece of rope, chain *etc*: *She made a loop in the string.* **2** a U-shaped bend in a river *etc.* — *v* to fasten with, or form into, a loop or loops: *He looped the rope round a post.*

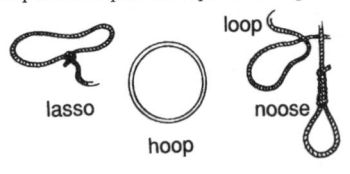

lasso   hoop   loop   noose

'loophole *n* a small mistake or something left out in a law that lets people do things that are really not allowed: *He found a loophole in the new tax law and took advantage of it.*

loose /luːs/ *adj* **1** not tight: *a loose coat; This belt is loose.* **2** not firmly fixed: *This button is loose.* **3** not tied; free: *The horses are loose in the field.* **4** not in a packet: *loose biscuits.*
'loosely *adv.* **'looseness** *n.*

a **loose** (not **lose**) screw.

loose-'leaf *adj* with pages that can be removed or added: *a loose-leaf folder.*

'loosen *v* to make or become loose: *She loosened the string; The screw had loosened and fallen out.*

at a loose end with nothing to do and feeling bored.

break loose to escape: *The prisoner broke loose.*

loosen up to become less tense or stiff: *Do some exercises to loosen up your muscles before the race begins*; *A gentle swim helped her loosen up after a long day.*

loot /luːt/ *n* something which is stolen: *The thieves got away with a lot of loot.* — *v* to rob or steal from a place: *The soldiers looted the shops of the captured town.*

lop /lɒp/ *v* to cut off: *to lop branches off a tree.*

lopsided /lɒpˈsaɪdɪd/ *adj* bigger or heavier on one side than on the other; not evenly balanced; crooked: *an old lopsided hut*; *The load on the back of the lorry looked very lopsided.*

lord /lɔːd/ *n* **1** a master; a man or animal that has power over others or over an area: *The lion is lord of the jungle.* **2** a nobleman or man of rank.

the Lord God; Christ.

lorry /ˈlɒrɪ/ *n* a motor vehicle for carrying heavy loads; a truck: *a coal-lorry.*

lose /luːz/ *v* **1** not to be able to find something: *I've lost my watch.* **2** to have something taken away from you by death, accident *etc*: *She lost her father last year*; *The ship was lost in the storm.* **3** to put something where it cannot be found: *My secretary has lost your letter.* **4** not to win: *I always lose at cards.* **5** to confuse someone so that they cannot understand you: *I'm afraid you've lost me — could you repeat that please?*

> **lose; lost** /lɒst/; **lost**: *He lost his ticket*; *She has lost her job.*
> to **lose** (not **loose**) a match.

'loser *n* a person who loses: *The losers congratulated the winners.*

lose your memory to stop being able to remember things.

loss /lɒs/ *n* **1** losing: *suffering from loss of memory*; *the loss of our friend.* **2** something which is lost. **3** an amount of money *etc* that is lost: *a loss of £500.*

at a loss not knowing what to do, say *etc*: *He was at a loss for words.*

lost /lɒst/ *adj* **1** missing; no longer to be found: *a lost ticket.* **2** not won: *The game is lost.* **3** wasted; not used properly: *a lost opportunity.* **4** no longer knowing where you are, or in which direction to go: *I don't know whether to turn left or right — I'm lost.*

> **loss** is a noun: *She is suffering from loss of memory.*
> **lost** is an adjective: *a lost cat.*
> See also **lose**.

a lost cause an aim or ideal that will never be achieved.

lot /lɒt/ *n* **1** a person's fortune or fate: *It seemed to be her lot to be always unlucky.* **2** a separate group: *She gave one lot of clothes to a jumble sale and threw another lot away.*

lots *n* a large quantity or number: *lots of people*; *She had lots and lots of food left over from the party.*

a lot 1 a large quantity or number: *He's written a lot of stuff down on paper*; *What a lot of letters!* **2** very often: *Although the children are grown up, we still see them a lot.*

draw lots to decide who is going to do something *etc* by putting everyone's name on pieces of paper in a hat *etc* and taking one out: *The six girls drew lots to see which of them should use the two concert tickets.*

lotion /ˈləʊʃən/ *n* a liquid for soothing or cleaning your skin: *hand-lotion.*

lottery /ˈlɒtərɪ/ *n* a way of raising money in which many people buy tickets, and a few of the tickets win prizes: *They held a public lottery in aid of charity.*

lotus /ˈləʊtəs/ *n* a type of waterlily.

loud /laʊd/ *adj* **1** making a great sound; not quiet: *a loud voice*; *loud music.* **2** too bright: *loud colours*; *a loud shirt.* — *adv*: *Could you speak a bit louder please?* **'loudly** *adv.* **'loudness** *n.*

loud'speaker *n* an instrument for increasing the loudness of your voice *etc* to make it more widely heard.

out loud so that people can hear: *He read part of the letter out loud.*

lounge /laʊndʒ/ *v* **1** to lie back comfortably: *lounging on a sofa.* **2** to move about lazily: *I spent the day lounging about the house.* — *n* a sittingroom in a hotel *etc*: *They watched television in the hotel lounge.*

louse /laʊs/, *plural* **lice** /laɪs/, *n* a small blood-sucking insect, sometimes found on the bodies of animals and people.

lout /laʊt/ *n* a rough and aggressive man or boy: *A group of louts caused trouble at the party.*

love /lʌv/ *n* **1** a feeling of great fondness for a person or thing: *She has a great love of music*; *her love for her children.* **2** a person or thing of which you are fond: *Ballet is* *the love of her life*; *Goodbye, love!* — *v* **1** to be very fond of someone: *She loves her children dearly.* **2** to take pleasure in something: *They both love dancing.*

'lovable *adj* easy to love or like; attractive: *a lovable child.*

love affair a romantic and sexual relationship, especially one which does not last very long: *He has had a lot of love affairs but none of them have lasted more than a couple of months.*

loved one a member of your family or a very close friend: *She remembers all her loved ones in her prayers.*

'lovely *adj* **1** beautiful; attractive: *She is a lovely girl*; *She looked lovely in that dress.* **2** pleasant: *What a lovely day!* **'loveliness** *n*.

'love-letter *n* a letter expressing love.

'lover *n* a person who enjoys or admires something: *an art-lover*; *He is a lover of sport.*

'loving *adj*. **'lovingly** *adv*.

be in love with to love someone very much: *She was in love with him.*

fall in love with to develop feelings of love for someone: *He fell in love with her straightaway.*

make love to have sexual intercourse.

send your love or **give your love** to send or give a friendly greeting to someone: *Give my love to your sister when you see her next.*

low[1] /loʊ/ *adj* **1** not high: *low hills*; *a low ceiling*; *This chair is too low for the child to reach the table*; *low temperatures.* **2** not loud: *She spoke in a low voice.* **3** small: *a low price.* **4** not strong: *The fire was very low.* **5** near the bottom in grade, rank, class *etc*: *the lower classes of the school.* — *adv* in or to a low position, manner or state: *The ball flew low over the net*; *He turned the music down low.*

> a **short** (not **low**) person.

low tide the time when the sea is at its lowest level.

low[2] /loʊ/ *v* to make the noise of cattle; to moo: *The cows were lowing.*

lower /'loʊə(r)/ *v* to make something less high or less loud; to take down: *Lower your voice, please!*; *She lowered her umbrella.* — *adj* **1** the bottom one of two things: *She bit her lower lip.* **2** the bottom part of something: *lower back pain.*

> The opposite of the verb **lower** is **raise**. The opposite of the adjective **lower** is **upper**.

low-key /loʊ'kiː/ *adj* controlled and quiet: *a low-key wedding with only six guests.*

lowlands /'loʊləndz/ *n* low-lying land; land that is low compared with the rest of a country *etc*.

lowly /'loʊlɪ/ *adj* low in rank; humble.

low-paid /loʊ'peɪd/ *adj* not paying or earning much money: *low-paid workers.*

loyal /'lɔɪəl/ *adj* faithful: *a loyal friend*; *I'm loyal to my country.* **'loyally** *adv*. **'loyalty** *n*.

> The opposite of **loyal** is **disloyal**.

LP /ɛl'piː/ *n* a record which plays for between 20 and 30 minutes on each side: *He has a large collection of LPs.*

L-plate /'ɛlpleɪt/ *n* a small sign with a red letter *L* on it, put on cars that are driven by learners.

lubricate /'luːbrɪkeɪt/ *v* to oil a machine *etc* to make it move more easily and smoothly. **lubri'cation** *n*.

'lubricant *n* something that lubricates.

lucid /'luːsɪd/ *adj* **1** easy to understand; clear: *She has a lucid style of writing.* **2** thinking clearly; not confused: *Although he is 94 he is still very lucid.* **'lucidly** *adv*. **lu'cidity** *n*.

luck /lʌk/ *n* **1** the state of happening by chance: *Whether you win or not is just luck — there's no skill in this game.* **2** something good which happens by chance: *What a bit of luck!*

'luckless *adj* unfortunate: *luckless children.*

'lucky *adj* **1** having good luck: *We were lucky to survive the crash.* **2** bringing good luck: *a lucky number.* **'luckily** *adv*.

lucky dip a form of amusement at a fair *etc* in which prizes are drawn from a container without the taker seeing what he is getting.

bad luck! or **hard luck!** an expression of sympathy for someone who has failed or been unlucky.

good luck! something you say to encourage someone who is about to take part in a competition, sit an exam *etc*: *She wished him good luck.*

in luck lucky: *I was in luck: they had the shoes in my size.*

out of luck unlucky: *If you want more cake, I'm afraid you're out of luck because it's all gone.*

lucrative /'luːkrətɪv/ *adj* bringing you a lot of

money or profit: *This is a very lucrative business.*

ludicrous /'luːdɪkrəs/ *adj* very silly; deserving to be laughed at: *You look ludicrous wearing climbing boots with your pyjamas*; *He's always making ludicrous suggestions.* **'ludicrously** *adv.*

ludo /'luːdoʊ/ *n* a game played with counters on a board.

lug /lʌg/ *v* to pull something with difficulty: *She lugged the heavy trunk across the floor.*

luggage /'lʌgɪdʒ/ *n* the suitcases, trunks *etc* of a traveller: *He carried her luggage to the train.* — *adj*: *a luggage compartment.*

> **luggage** is never used in the plural; you say *two pieces of luggage.*

lukewarm /luːk'wɔːm/ *adj* **1** a little bit warm: *The baby's milk should be heated till it is lukewarm but not hot.* **2** not showing much interest or enthusiasm: *People gave only lukewarm support to his plans.*

lull /lʌl/ *v* to make calm or quiet: *The sound of the waves lulled him to sleep.* — *n* a short period of calm.

lullaby /'lʌləbaɪ/ *n* a song sung to make children go to sleep.

lumber[1] /'lʌmbə(r)/ *n* **1** old unwanted furniture *etc*. **2** timber sawn up.
  'lumberjack *n* a person employed to cut down, saw up and move trees.

lumber[2] /'lʌmbə(r)/ *v* to move about heavily and clumsily.

luminous /'luːmɪnəs/ *adj* shining, or giving out light, especially in the dark: *a luminous light-switch*; *Are the hands of your watch luminous?*

lump /lʌmp/ *n* **1** a small solid mass of no particular shape: *The custard was full of lumps and no-one would eat it.* **2** a swelling: *She had a lump on her head where she had knocked it.* **3** a small cube-shaped mass of sugar.
  'lumpy *adj* containing lumps: *lumpy custard.* **'lumpiness** *n.*
  lump sum an amount of money given all at once, not in parts over a period of time.

lunacy /'luːnəsɪ/ *n* insanity; madness.

lunar /'luːnə(r)/ *adj* of the moon: *a lunar eclipse.*

lunatic /'luːnətɪk/ *n* a mad person. — *adj*: *lunatic behaviour.*

lunch /lʌntʃ/ *n* a meal eaten in the middle of the day. — *v* to eat lunch.
  luncheon /'lʌntʃən/ *n* a polite word for lunch: *The president gave a luncheon for all the ambassadors.*
  'lunchtime *n* the time in the middle of the day when you have lunch.

lung /lʌŋ/ *n* one of two parts of the body which fill and empty with air when you breathe.

lunge /lʌndʒ/ *v* to make a sudden strong forward movement: *Her attacker lunged at her with a knife.* — *n* a movement of this sort: *He made a lunge at her.*

lurch /lɜːtʃ/ *v* to move forward with a sudden jerk, without full control of the movement: *The drunken man lurched towards the bar.* — *n*: *The train gave a lurch and moved off.*
  leave someone in the lurch to leave someone in a difficult situation and without help: *Soon after their child was born he went off and left his wife in the lurch.*

lure /lʊə(r)/ or /ljʊə(r)/ *n* attraction; something very attractive or tempting: *The lure of his mother's good cooking brought him back home.* — *v* to attract: *The bright lights of the city lured him away from home.*

lurid /'lʊərɪd/ *adj* **1** unpleasantly bright: *lurid colours.* **2** shocking or unpleasant because it is violent or disgusting: *The newspaper gave all the lurid details of the killing.*

lurk /lɜːk/ *v* to wait in hiding especially with a dishonest purpose: *She saw someone lurking in the shadows.*

luscious /'lʌʃəs/ *adj* richly sweet and juicy: *a luscious mango.*

lush /lʌʃ/ *adj* green and fertile: *lush meadows.*

lust /lʌst/ *n* a very strong desire: *a lust for power.* **'lustful** *adj.* **'lustfully** *adv.*

lustre /'lʌstə(r)/ *n* brightness; a shine: *Her hair had a brilliant lustre.* **'lustrous** *adj.*

lusty /'lʌstɪ/ *adj* strong and healthy: *a lusty young man.*

luxurious /lʌg'zjʊərɪəs/ *adj* supplied with luxuries: *a luxurious flat.* — **lux'uriously** *adv.*

luxury /'lʌkʃərɪ/ *n* **1** great comfort: *They live in luxury.* **2** a pleasant, often expensive thing which is not necessary and which you cannot often have: *A new car is a luxury we can't afford.* **3** a pleasure that you do not often have: *An evening in by myself is a real luxury.* — *adj*: *fur coats, jewellery and other luxury goods.*

lychee or **lichee** /laɪ'tʃiː/ *n* a small round fruit with white juicy flesh.

lying /'laɪɪŋ/ *see* **lie**[1], **lie**[2].

lyrical /'lɪrɪkəl/ *adj* poetic and song-like: *Her writing is very lyrical.* **'lyrically** *adv.*

lyrics /'lɪrɪks/ *n* the words of a song: *The tune is good, but I don't like the lyrics.*

M

mac /mak/ short for **mackintosh**.

macabre /mə'kɑːbrə/ *adj* strange and horrible, often because dealing with death: *a story so macabre it will give you nightmares.*

macaroni /makə'rouni/ *n* a form of pasta, pressed out to form tubes, and dried.

macaroon /makə'ruːn/ *n* a sweet cake or biscuit flavoured with almonds or coconut.

mace /meɪs/ *n* an ornamental rod used as a mark of authority on ceremonial occasions.

machine /mə'ʃiːn/ *n* a working arrangement of wheels, levers or other parts, driven by human power, electricity *etc*, or operating electronically, producing power or motion for a particular purpose: *a sewing-machine.* — *v* to sew with a sewing-machine: *to machine seams.*

machinery /mə'ʃiːnəri/ *n* machines in general: *Many products are made by machinery rather than by hand.*

> **machinery** is never used in the plural.

ma'chinist *n* a person whose job is to operate a machine, such as a sewing-machine, or an electrical tool: *She's a machinist in a clothes factory.*

machine code a code used for writing instructions in a form a computer can understand.

machine gun an automatic gun that fires very rapidly. — *v*: *He machine-gunned a crowd of villagers.*

> See **gun**.

macho /'matʃoʊ/ *adj* masculine in a very aggressive way: *She doesn't like macho men.*

mackerel /'makərəl/, *plural* **mackerel**, *n* a type of edible sea-fish, blue-green with wavy markings.

mackintosh or **macintosh** /'makɪntɒʃ/ *n* a waterproof raincoat (often shortened to **mac**).

mad /mad/ *adj* **1** insane: *He went mad; to drive someone mad; You must be mad to refuse such a good offer.* **2** very angry: *She was mad at me for losing my keys; Then she got really mad and started screaming at us.* **3** having a great liking or desire for: *He was mad about football; My husband is mad on golf.* **'madly** *adv.* **'madness** *n.*

like mad wildly, desperately, very quickly *etc*: *struggling like mad.*

madam /'madəm/ *n* a polite form of address to a woman.

madden /'madən/ *v* to make someone, or an animal, mad or angry: *The bull was maddened by the pain.*

'maddening *adj*: *The children can be quite maddening at times.*

made *see* **make**.

Madonna /mə'dɒnə/ *n* the Virgin Mary, mother of Christ: *a painting of the Madonna and Child.*

magazine /magə'ziːn/ *n* a paper that is published every week, every month *etc* with articles, stories *etc* by various writers: *women's magazines.*

maggot /'magət/ *n* the worm-like larva of a fly.

magic /'madʒɪk/ *n* **1** any power that produces results that cannot be explained or which are remarkable: *The prince was turned by magic into a frog.* **2** the art of performing tricks that deceive your eyes: *The conjuror's magic delighted the children.* **3** the wonderful or charming quality of something: *I'll never forget the special magic of that evening.* — *adj* **1** used in or using magic: *a magic spell; This bracelet has strange magic powers.* **2** excellent: *That was a magic film!*

'magical *adj* **1** produced by, or as if by, the art of magic: *magical power.* **2** mysterious; very wonderful: *a magical experience.*
'magically *adv.*

magician /mə'dʒɪʃən/ *n* a person skilled in the art of magic: *They hired a magician to entertain the children.*

magistrate /'madʒɪstreɪt/ *n* a person who has power to put the laws into force and deal with cases of minor crime.

magnanimous /mag'nanɪməs/ *adj* generous and forgiving, usually towards someone you have beaten: *The winner was magnanimous towards the other runners in the race, praising their efforts.*

magnate /'magneɪt/ *n* a person of great power or wealth: *He is a rich shipping magnate.*

magnet /'magnɪt/ *n* a piece of iron, steel *etc* which attracts or repels other pieces of iron *etc*.

magnetic /mag'nɛtɪk/ *adj* **1** having the powers of a magnet: *magnetic force.* **2** having charming and very attractive qualities: *She has a lively, magnetic pesonality.*

'magnetism *n* **1** the power that a magnet has to attract iron and other metals. **2** strong personal attraction: *His magnetism made him a powerful political figure.*

magnetic tape narrow plastic tape with a magnetic coating, used for recording sound, television pictures or information from a computer.

magnetic field the area in which the pull of a magnet is felt: *the earth's magnetic field.*

magnificent /mag'nɪfɪsənt/ *adj* great and splendid: *a magnificent costume*; *a magnificent performance.* **mag'nificently** *adv.* **mag'nificence** *n.*

magnify /'magnɪfaɪ/ *v* to make something appear greater: *The image is magnified many times.* **magnifi'cation** *n.*

magnifying glass *n* a piece of glass with curved surfaces that makes an object appear larger: *This print is so small that I need a magnifying glass to read it.*

magnitude /'magnɪtjuːd/ *n* **1** importance: *He'd never had to deal with a problem of such magnitude.* **2** size: *a star of great magnitude.*

magpie /'magpaɪ/ *n* a black-and-white bird of the crow family, known for its habit of collecting shiny objects.

mahogany /mə'hɒgəni/ *n* a hard, reddish-brown wood used to make furniture. — *adj*: *a mahogany table.*

maid /meɪd/ *n* a female servant.

maiden /'meɪdən/ *n* a young unmarried women.

maiden name a woman's surname before her marriage: *Mrs Johnson's maiden name was Scott.*

maiden voyage a ship's first voyage.

mail /meɪl/ *n* letters, parcels *etc* sent by post: *He needs a large staff to handle the colossal amount of mail that arrives with every post.* — *v* to send a letter or parcel by post.

'mailbag *n* a bag for letters *etc.*

'mailbox *n* a postbox.

mail order buying and selling goods by post: *a mail order catalogue.*

maim /meɪm/ *v* to injure someone badly, especially with permanent effects: *He had been maimed for life in an accident with a firework.*

main /meɪn/ *adj* chief; most important: *the main purpose*; *the main reason*; *the main road north*; *the main character in the story.* — *n* the chief pipe or cable bringing gas, water or electricity to a street *etc*: *The water has been turned off at the mains.*

'mainly *adv* mostly; largely: *This skirt is mainly dark grey.*

'mainland *n* a large piece of land near an island: *The islanders had to get their stores from the mainland*; *Britain is not part of the mainland of Europe.*

in the main mostly or generally: *Our customers are, in the main, foreign businessmen*; *In the main, we think the scheme has worked.*

mainstream /'meɪnstriːm/ *n* the way that most people think or behave: *the mainstream of political thought.* — *adj*: *mainstream politics.*

maintain /meɪn'teɪn/ *v* **1** to continue; to keep up: *to maintain a silence*; *to maintain high standards.* **2** to keep something in good condition: *He maintains his car very well.* **3** to support: *How can you maintain a wife and three children on your small salary?* **4** to say definitely: *I maintain that the theory is true.*

maintenance /'meɪntənəns/ *n* keeping something in good condition: *car maintenance.*

maisonette /meɪzə'nɛt/ *n* an apartment on two floors.

maize /meɪz/ *n* a cereal, grown especially in America.

majestic /mə'dʒɛstɪk/ *adj* having great dignity: *He looked truly majestic in his ceremonial robes*; *a magestic and ancient cedar tree.* **ma'jestically** *adv.*

majesty /'madʒəstɪ/ *n* **1** greatness: *the majesty of God.* **2** a title used when speaking to, or about, a king or queen: *Her Majesty the Queen*; *Their Majesties*; *Your Majesty.*

major /'meɪdʒə(r)/ *adj* great, or greater, in size, importance *etc*: *major and minor roads*; *a major discovery.* — *n* an army officer of high rank.

The opposite of **major** is **minor**.

majority /mə'dʒɒrɪtɪ/ *n* the greater number: *The majority of people can read and write.*

make /meɪk/ *v* **1** to create; to produce: *God made the Earth*; *She makes all her own clothes*; *He made it out of paper*; *to make coffee*; *We made an arrangement.* **2** to force or cause someone to do something: *They made her do it*; *He made me laugh.* **3** to cause to be: *I made it clear*; *You've made me very unhappy.* **4** to gain or earn: *He makes £100 a week*; *to make a profit.* **5** to amount to a total: *2 and 2 make 4.* **6** to appoint someone to a post *etc*: *He was made manager.* **7** to perform some action *etc*: *She made a wish*; *They made a long journey.*

8 to reach a place; to arrive in time for something: *We planned to make Kuala Lumpur before nightfall*; *If we hurry we could make the earlier train.* — *n* a brand; a type: *What make is your new car?*

> **make**; **made** /meɪd/; **made**: *She made lunch*; *He has made a mess.*

> **made of** is used in speaking of the material from which an object is constructed *etc*: *This table is made of wood.*
> **made from** is used in speaking of the raw material from which something has been produced by a process of manufacture: *Paper is made from wood.*

make-be'lieve *n* pretending and imagining: *a world of make-believe.*

'maker *n* a person who makes something: *a tool-maker*; *a dressmaker.*

'makeshift *adj* built or made very quickly, usually in an emergency, and intended to last only a short time: *He built a makeshift shelter of old planks of wood.*

'make-up *n* **1** lipstick, powder and other cosmetics that you put on your face: *She never wears any make-up.* **2** a person's character or nature: *A bad temper is part of his make-up.*

-'making: *glass-making*; *road-making.*

make a bed to tidy and straighten the sheets, blankets *etc* on a bed after it has been used: *The children make their own beds every morning.*

make do to use something as a poor substitute for something else: *There's no meat, so we'll have to make do with potatoes.*

make for 1 to move towards a place: *We didn't tell them where we were making for*; *He jumped up suddenly and made for the door.* **2** to help or allow something to happen: *Fine weather made for an enjoyable holiday.*

> to **make friends** (not **make friend**) with someone.

make it to be successful in doing or being something: *Do you think she could make it as a professional singer?*

make it up 1 to become friends again after a quarrel: *It's time you two made it up with each other.* **2** to do something to show you are sorry about some wrong you have done to someone: *I'm sorry I've broken your toy — I'll make it up to you somehow.*

make off to leave, especially in a hurry or secretly: *The thieves made off in a van*; *One of the guests made off with our car.*

make out 1 to see, hear or understand something: *He could make out a ship in the distance*; *I couldn't make out what he was saying.* **2** to claim; to pretend: *He made out that he was earning a huge amount of money.* **3** to write or fill in something: *The doctor made out a prescription.*

make up 1 to invent: *He made up the whole story.* **2** to form: *Eleven players make up one team.* **3** to complete: *We need one more player — will you make up the number?* **4** to put make-up on your face: *She made up her face in the mirror.* **5** to become friends again after a quarrel *etc*: *They've finally made up their disagreement.*

make up for to replace something that is gone or lost; to correct a bad situation: *We'll each have to work harder to make up for having fewer people in our team.*

make up your mind to make a decision: *He finally made up his mind about the job.*

malady /'malədɪ/ *n* an illness; a disease.

malaria /mə'lɛərɪə/ *n* a fever caused by the bite of a certain type of mosquito.

male /meɪl/ *adj* of the same sex as a man: *the male rabbit.* — *n* a male person, animal *etc*.

> The opposite of **male** is **female**.

malevolent /mə'lɛvələnt/ *adj* wanting to do evil and bad things to other people: *Harry's eyes narrowed and he shot a malevolent glance at Jennifer.*

malfunction /mal'fʌŋkʃən/ *n* something that is going wrong in a machine *etc*.

malice /'malɪs/ *n* the wish to harm other people *etc*: *There was no malice intended in what she said.*

malicious /mə'lɪʃəs/ *adj* unkind: *a malicious remark.*

malignant /mə'lɪgnənt/ *adj* **1** likely to cause death: *The tumour on his lung is malignant.* **2** cruel, harmful: *malignant behaviour.*

mallet /'malɪt/ *n* **1** a large wooden hammer: *We hammered the tent pegs into the ground with a mallet.* **2** a wooden hammer with a long handle for playing croquet or polo.

malnutrition /malnjʊ'trɪʃən/ *n* a diseased condition caused by not getting enough food or the right kind of food: *About half of the population of the country were suffering from malnutrition.*

malt /mɔːlt/ *n* barley or other grain prepared for making beer, whisky *etc*.

mamma or **mama** /mə'mɑː/ *n* a name some children use for their mother.

mammal /'mamǝl/ *n* any member of the class of animals in which the females feed the young with their own milk: *Monkeys are mammals.*

mammoth /'mamǝθ/ *n* a large hairy elephant of a kind no longer found living. — *adj* very large: *a mammoth project.*

man /man/, *plural* **men** /mɛn/, *n* **1** an adult male human being: *hundreds of men, women and children.* **2** human beings taken as a whole: *the development of man.* — *v* to supply something with enough men to operate or run it: *We need twelve men to man the ship*; *Man the guns!*

-man a person doing a particular job: *postman*; *fireman*; *chairman etc.*

as one man together: *They rose as one man to applaud his speech.*

the man in the street the ordinary, average person: *The man in the street has little interest in politics.*

manage /'manɪdʒ/ *v* **1** to be in control or charge of something: *The survey found that most people didn't know how to manage their money.* **2** to be manager of something: *James manages the local football team.* **3** to deal with something; to control: *She's good at managing people.* **4** to be able to do something: *Will you manage to repair your bicycle?*; *Can you manage to eat some more meat?*

manageable /'manɪdʒǝbǝl/ *adj* that can be done or dealt with without too much difficulty: *The garden is a nice, manageable size.*

management /'manɪdʒmǝnt/ *n* **1** the managing of something: *Hand over the management of your money to an expert.* **2** the managers of a firm *etc* as a group: *The management have agreed to pay the workers more money.*

'manager *n* a person who is in charge of a business, football team *etc*: *the manager of the new store.*

manageress /manɪdʒǝ'rɛs/ *n* a woman who is a manager.

mandarin /'mandǝrɪn/ *n* **1** a kind of small orange. **2** an official of high rank in the Chinese Empire.

mandolin /mandǝ'lɪn/ *n* a musical instrument similar to a guitar.

mandolin

mandrill /'mandrɪl/ *n* a West African monkey with a short tail, brown hair and a blue and red face.

mane /meɪn/ *n* the long hair on the back of the neck of a horse, lion *etc.*

man-eating /'manːɪtɪŋ/ *adj* likely to eat people: *a man-eating tiger.* **man-eater** /'manːɪtǝ(r)/ *n.*

maneuver another spelling of **manoeuvre**.

manger /'meɪndʒǝ(r)/ *n* a box in which food for horses and cattle is placed.

mangle /'maŋgǝl/ *v* **1** to crush to pieces: *The car was badly mangled in the accident.* **2** to spoil by bad mistakes *etc*: *He mangled the music by his terrible playing.*

mango /'maŋgoʊ/, *plural* **mangoes** or **mangos**, *n* **1** the yellow fruit of an Indian tropical tree. **2** the tree.

mangrove /'maŋgroʊv/ *n* a tropical tree growing in or near water.

manhole /'manhoʊl/ *n* a hole usually in the middle of a road or pavement through which someone may go to inspect sewers *etc.*

manhood /'manhʊd/ *n* the state of being a man, or of being manly: *He died before he reached manhood.*

mania /'meɪnɪǝ/ *n* **1** a very strong liking for something: *She has a mania for writing lists of things to do.* **2** a form of mental illness in which the sufferer is very excited and sometimes behaves violently.

maniac /'meɪnɪak/ *n* a mad and dangerous person: *He drives like a maniac.*

manicure /'manɪkjʊǝ(r)/ *n* special treatment to keep the hands and nails attractive and in good condition: *She had her nails polished as part of her manicure.*

manifesto /manɪ'fɛstoʊ/, *plural* **manifestos** or **manifestoes**, *n* a usually written statement of the policies and beliefs of a politician or political party: *They published a new manifesto before the last election.*

manipulate /mǝ'nɪpjʊleɪt/ *v* **1** to handle something skilfully: *I watched him manipulating the controls of the aircraft.* **2** to influence cleverly but not very honestly: *A clever lawyer can manipulate a jury.* **manipu'lation** *n.* **ma'nipulator** *n.*

mankind /man'kaɪnd/ *n* the human race as a whole: *He worked for the benefit of all mankind.*

manly /'manlɪ/ *adj* having the qualities expected of a man, such as strength, determination, courage *etc*: *He is strong and manly.* **'manliness** *n.*

man-made /manˈmeɪd/ *adj* made by man, not natural: *a man-made lake*; *Plastic is a man-made material*.

manned /mand/ *adj* supplied with men: *a manned spacecraft*.

mannequin /ˈmanɪkɪn/ *n* **1** a person who models clothes: *Some mannequins earn a lot of money*. **2** a life-size model of the human body, put in shop windows to show clothes.

manner /ˈmanə(r)/ *n* **1** a way in which anything is done *etc*: *She greeted me in a friendly manner*. **2** the way in which a person behaves, speaks *etc*: *I don't like her manner*.

'mannerism *n* a particular movement or way of speaking that is typical of a person: *She had one or two odd mannerisms that frightened the children*.

manners /ˈmanəz/ *n* polite behaviour: *Why doesn't she teach her children manners?*

all manner of all kinds of: *The market sells all manner of exotic fruit and vegetables*.

manoeuvre or **maneuver** /məˈnuːvə(r)/ *n* a planned movement of troops, ships, aircraft, vehicles *etc*: *Can you perform all the manoeuvres required by the driving test?* — *v* to perform manoeuvres: *She had difficulty manoeuvring her car into the narrow space*.

manor /ˈmanə(r)/ *n* an old word for a large house with land round it, once built by a nobleman: *the lord of the manor*; *the manor house*.

manpower /ˈmanpaʊə(r)/ *n* the number of people available for employment *etc*: *There's a shortage of manpower in the building industry*.

manservant /ˈmansɜːvənt/, *plural* **'menservants**, *n* a male servant.

mansion /ˈmanʃən/ *n* a large house.

man-sized /ˈmansaɪzd/ *adj* of a size suitable for a man: *a man-sized breakfast*.

manslaughter /ˈmanslɔːtə(r)/ *n* the crime of killing someone from carelessness, for example, rather than intention: *He was found guilty of manslaughter*.

mantelpiece /ˈmantəlpiːs/ *n* the shelf above a fireplace: *We have some china ornaments and a clock on our mantelpiece*.

manual /ˈmanjʊəl/ *adj* **1** having to do with your hands: *manual skills*. **2** working with your hands: *a manual worker*. **3** worked or operated by hand: *a car with manual gears*. — *n* a handbook, especially of information about a machine *etc*: *an instruction manual*.

'manually *adv* by hand: *You have to operate this sewing-machine manually*.

manufacture /manjʊˈfaktʃə(r)/ *v* **1** to make articles *etc* by machinery and in large quantities: *This firm manufactures cars at the rate of two hundred per day*. **2** to invent something false: *He manufactured an excuse for being late*. — *n* the process of manufacturing: *the manufacture of glass*.

manuˈfacturer *n* a person or firm that manufactures goods.

manure /məˈnjʊə(r)/ *n* a mixture containing animal dung, spread on soil to help produce better crops *etc*. — *v* to put manure on soil or fields.

manuscript /ˈmanjʊskrɪpt/ *n* **1** the handwritten or typed material for a book *etc*. **2** a book or document written by hand: *a collection of ancient manuscripts*.

many /ˈmɛnɪ/ *adj* a great number: *Many languages are spoken in Africa*; *There weren't very many people at the meeting*; *You've made a great many mistakes*. — *pron* a great number: *A few people survived, but many died*; *Many of them died*.

> **many; more; most**: *Many people in Britain play rugby, more play football, but most just watch.*

> **many** is used with countable nouns: *How many pupils are there in your class?* **much** is used with uncountable nouns: *He put too much salt into the soup.*

a good many or **a great many** a lot: *The library is used by a great many people*.

many- having a great number: *many-coloured*; *many-sided*.

many a a great number: *I've told him many a time to be more polite*.

map /map/ *n* a drawing or plan of the surface of the earth or part of it, with rivers, seas, towns *etc*: *a map of the world*; *a road map*. — *v* to make a map of an area: *Africa was mapped by many different explorers*.

map out to plan: *to map out a route*.

mar /maː(r)/ *v* to spoil or damage something: *Her beauty was marred by a scar on her cheek*.

marathon /ˈmarəθən/ *n* a race on foot of 42 km (26 miles).

marble /ˈmɑːbəl/ *n* **1** a kind of hard polished stone: *This table is made of marble*. **2** a small solid ball of glass used in children's games.

marbles *n* any of several games played with marbles: *The boys were playing marbles in the playground*.

March /mɑːtʃ/ *n* the third month of the year.

march /mɑːtʃ/ *v* **1** to walk with regular steps: *Soldiers were marching across the street.* **2** to go on steadily: *Time marches on.* — *n* **1** a distance marched by soldiers *etc*: *a long march.* **2** progress: *the march of time.*

mare /meə(r)/ *n* a female horse.

margarine /mɑːdʒəˈriːn/ *n* a butter-like substance made mainly from vegetable fats: *We use margarine instead of butter.*

margin /ˈmɑːdʒɪn/ *n* **1** the blank edge round a page of writing or print: *Please write your comments in the margin.* **2** an extra amount of something, available if you need it: *a safety margin*; *We've allowed ourselves a margin of about an hour in case the train is late.*

'marginal *adj* not important or significant: *a marginal difference.*

'marginally *adv* slightly; to a small degree: *It is marginally wetter than it was this time last year.*

marijuana or **marihuana** /mærɪˈwɑːnə/ *n* a drug made from the dried flowers and leaves of the hemp plant.

marinate /ˈmærɪneɪt/ *v* to soak in oil, lemon juice or vinegar *etc* before cooking: *She marinated the fish in a mixture of lemon juice and spices.*

marine /məˈriːn/ *adj* having to do with the sea; belonging to the sea: *marine animals.* — *n* a soldier serving on board a ship: *He has joined the marines.*

mariner /ˈmærɪnə(r)/ *n* a sailor.

marionette /mærɪəˈnet/ *n* a puppet or doll whose arms and legs can be moved by strings.

marital /ˈmærɪtəl/ *adj* having to do with marriage: *his marital and other personal relationships.*

maritime /ˈmærɪtaɪm/ *adj* **1** having to do with the sea, shipping *etc*: *maritime law.* **2** concerned with the sea; involved in trade by sea; having a navy: *Britain is a maritime nation.*

mark /mɑːk/ *n* **1** a sign or spot: *My dog has a white mark on his nose.* **2** a point given as a reward for good work *etc*: *She got good marks in her exam.* **3** a stain: *That spilt coffee has left a mark on the carpet.* **4** a sign used as a guide to position *etc*: *There's a mark on the map showing where the church is.* **5** something you do as a sign of something: *People bow to the Queen as a mark of respect.* — *v* **1** to put a mark or stain on something, or to become marked or stained: *Every boy's coat must be marked with his name*; *That coffee has marked the tablecloth*; *This white material marks easily.* **2** to give marks for a piece of work: *I have forty exam-papers to mark tonight.* **3** to show: *On the map, X marks the spot where the treasure is buried.* **4** to note: *Mark it down in your notebook.* **5** to stay close to a player in the opposite team in a game like football, so that they cannot get the ball or score.

marked *adj* easily noticeable: *There has been a marked improvement in her work.*

'marker *n* **1** something used for marking: *He put a marker in the book to keep his place.* **2** a type of pen with a thick point.

'markings *n* coloured areas that form a pattern on the surface of something: *The cheetah's markings are more like spots.*

mark out 1 to mark the boundary of a football pitch *etc*: *The pitch was marked out with white lines.* **2** to choose someone for some particular purpose *etc* in the future: *He had been marked out for an army career from early childhood.*

market /ˈmɑːkɪt/ *n* **1** a public place where people meet to buy and sell or the public event at which this happens: *He has a clothes stall in the market*; *He went to market to sell his cow.* **2** a demand for certain things: *The market for British films has expanded steadily.* — *v* to sell: *I produce the goods and my brother markets them all over the world.*

> to **go to market** means to go shopping at a market: *She goes to market twice a week.*
> to **go to the market** means to visit a particular market: *He went to the market to buy a melon.*

'marketing *n* the business techniques involved in selling things: *a marketing manager*; *She's gone to college to study marketing.*

market place, **market square** the open space or square in a town in which a market is held.

on the market on sale and available for you to buy: *Electric cars have been on the market for some years*; *The new drug will come on the market next year.*

marksman /ˈmɑːksmən/ *n* a person who shoots well with a gun: *A police marksman shot the robber in the leg to prevent him escaping.*

marmalade /ˈmɑːməleɪd/ *n* a jam made from oranges, lemons or grapefruit.

maroon[1] /mə'ru:n/ *n* a dark red colour. — *adj*: *a maroon car*.

ma'roon[2] /mə'ru:n/ *v* **1** to leave someone on a lonely island from which they cannot escape. **2** to leave someone in a helpless or uncomfortable position: *I was marooned on a lonely country road when my car broke down*.

marquee /mɑ:'ki:/ *n* a very large tent used for circuses, parties *etc*.

marriage /'marɪdʒ/ *n* **1** the ceremony by which a man and woman become husband and wife: *Their marriage took place last week*. **2** the state of being married; married life: *Their marriage lasted for thirty happy years*. — *adj*: *the marriage ceremony*.

> **marriage** can mean the state of being married, or the ceremony of getting married.
> A **wedding** is the marriage ceremony.

marrow /'maroʊ/ *n* **1** the soft substance in the hollow parts of bones. **2** a large, green thick-skinned vegetable.

marrow

marry /'marɪ/ *v* **1** to take someone as your husband or wife: *John married my sister*; *He is married to a doctor*; *They married in church*. **2** to join as husband and wife: *The priest married them*. **3** to give your son or daughter as a husband or wife to someone: *He married his son to a rich woman*.
'**married** *adj*: *She has two married daughters*.

marsh /mɑ:ʃ/ *n* an area of soft wet land: *The heavy rainfall turned the land into a marsh*. '**marshy** *adj*. '**marshiness** *n*.

marshal /'mɑ:ʃəl/ *n* **1** an official who arranges ceremonies, processions *etc*. **2** an official with certain duties in the lawcourts.

marsupial /mɑ:'su:pɪəl/ *n* any member of the group of animals of which the females carry their babies in a pouch at the front of their bodies: *In Australia there are many kinds of marsupials, for example the kangaroo and the koala*.

martial /'mɑ:ʃəl/ *adj* having to do with war or military life: *martial music*.

   martial arts any of various sports which teach self-defence, such as judo and karate: *He practises martial arts in his spare time*.

   martial law the ruling of a country by the army in time of war or great national emergency.

martyr /'mɑ:tə(r)/ *n* a person who suffers death or hardship for what they believe: *St Stephen was the first Christian martyr*.

marvel /'mɑ:vəl/ *n* something or someone astonishing or wonderful: *the marvels of the circus*; *She's a marvel at producing delicious meals*. — *v* to feel astonishment: *They marvelled at the fantastic sight*.
'**marvellous** *adj* **1** wonderful: *The Great Wall of China is a marvellous sight*. **2** excellent: *a marvellous idea*. '**marvellously** *adv*.

mascara /ma'skɑ:rə/ *n* make-up that is used to make eyelashes look thicker and darker.

mascot /'maskət/ *n* a person, animal or thing supposed to bring good luck.

masculine /'maskjʊlɪn/ *adj* **1** having qualities expected of a man: *masculine strength*. **2** belonging to the male class of nouns, in some languages: *The French word for 'floor' is masculine, not feminine*. **mascu'linity** *n*.

> The opposite of **masculine** is **feminine**.

mash /maʃ/ *v* to crush into small pieces or a soft mass: *to mash potatoes*.

mask /mɑ:sk/ *n* **1** a covering in the form of a face, for putting over your own face, as a disguise *etc*. **2** a covering for the top part of your face, with holes for your eyes: *The thief wore a black mask*. — *v* to hide; to disguise: *He managed to mask his feelings*.

masochist /'masəkɪst/ *n* a person who enjoys suffering: *Only a masochist would enjoy that*. **maso'chistic** *adj*.

mason /'meɪsən/ *n* a skilled worker or builder in stone.
'**masonry** *n* the stone or bricks of which a building is made: *He was killed by falling masonry*.

masquerade /maskə'reɪd/ *n* pretence; disguise: *Her show of friendship was a masquerade*. — *v* to pretend to be someone else: *The criminal was masquerading as a respectable businessman*.

mass /mas/ *n* **1** a large lump or quantity, gathered together: *a mass of concrete*; *a mass of people*. **2** a large quantity: *I've masses of things to do*. **3** the main part; the majority: *The mass of people are in favour of peace*. — *v* to bring or come together in large numbers or quantities: *The troops massed for an attack*. — *adj* consisting of large quantities or numbers: *a mass meeting*.
   the mass media the things from which most

people get news and other information, such as television, radio, newspapers *etc*.

Mass /mas/ *n* a service in the Roman Catholic church that commemorates Christ's last supper with his disciples: *What time do you go to Mass?*

massacre /'masəkə(r)/ *n* the cruel killing of a large number of people. — *v*: *The soldiers massacred the villagers.*

massage /'masɑːʒ/ *v* to treat parts of the body by rubbing *etc* to remove pain or stiffness: *She massaged my sore back.* — *n* treatment by massaging.

massive /'masɪv/ *adj* huge or heavy: *a massive building*; *a massive load*.

mass-produced /maspɹəˈdjuːst/ *adj* all exactly the same and produced in great quantities: *mass-produced plastic toys*. **mass-pro'duce** *v*. **mass-pro'duction** *n*.

mast /mɑːst/ *n* a long upright pole for supporting the sails of a ship, an aerial, flag *etc*: *The sailor climbed the mast.*

master /'mɑːstə(r)/ *n* **1** a person that commands or controls: *I'm master in this house!* **2** an owner of a dog *etc*. **3** a male teacher: *the Maths master*. **4** the commander of a trading ship: *the ship's master*. **5** a person very skilled in an art, science *etc*: *He's a master with a paint brush.* — *adj* fully qualified and experienced: *a master builder*. — *v* **1** to overcome: *She has mastered her fear of heights*. **2** to become skilful in something: *I don't think I'll ever master arithmetic*.

> The feminine form of **master** is **mistress**.

master key a key which opens a number of locks.

'mastermind *n* a very intelligent person, especially one who directs a scheme: *He was the mastermind behind the scheme.* — *v* to plan and direct a scheme: *Who masterminded the robbery?*

'masterpiece *n* an excellent, or the most excellent, piece of work of an artist, craftsman *etc*: *He considers this picture his masterpiece.*

'mastery *n* control or great skill: *We have gained mastery over the enemy.*

mat /mat/ *n* a flat piece of material for wiping shoes on, covering a floor, putting dishes on *etc*: *Wipe your shoes on the doormat*; *a table mat*.

matador /'matədɔː(r)/ *n* the man who kills the bull in a bullfight.

match[1] /matʃ/ *n* a short piece of wood or other material tipped with a substance that catches fire when rubbed against a rough or specially-prepared surface: *He struck a match*.

match[2] /matʃ/ *n* **1** a contest; a game: *a football match*. **2** a thing that is similar to or the same as another in colour, pattern *etc*: *These trousers are not an exact match for my jacket*. **3** a person who is able to equal another: *She has finally met her match at arguing*. **4** a marriage: *She hoped to arrange a match for her daughter.* — *v* **1** to be similar to something: *That dress matches her red hair*. **2** to set two things, people *etc* against each other: *He matched his skill against the champion's.*

matchbox /'matʃbɒks/ *n* a box for holding matches.

matched /matʃt/ *adj* paired or joined together: *a well-matched couple*; *The competitors were evenly matched*.

matchless /'matʃləs/ *adj* having no equal: *a woman of matchless beauty*.

matchmaker /'matʃmeɪkə(r)/ *n* a person who tries to arrange marriages between people.

matchstick /'matʃstɪk/ *n* the stick of wood from a used match: *He builds models out of old matchsticks*.

mate /meɪt/ *v* to come, or bring animals or birds together for breeding: *It is difficult to get pandas to mate in a zoo.* — *n* **1** an animal *etc* with which another is paired for breeding: *Some birds sing in order to attract a mate*. **2** a companion or friend: *We've been mates for years*.

material /məˈtɪərɪəl/ *n* **1** anything out of which something is, or may be, made: *Tables are made of solid material such as wood*. **2** cloth: *I'd like three metres of blue woollen material.* — *adj* **1** consisting of solid substances *etc*: *the material world*. **2** belonging to the world; not spiritual: *He wanted material things like money and possessions*.

ma'terialism *n* a strong interest in material things, such as money, possessions *etc* and little interest in spiritual and intellectual things. **materia'listic** *adj*.

ma'terialize *v* to happen; to appear or become real: *We'll have to wait and see if the promised pay rise ever materializes*.

maternal /məˈtɜːnəl/ *adj* **1** suitable to a mother: *maternal feelings*. **2** related to you on your mother's side of the family: *my maternal grandfather*.

maternity /məˈtɜːnɪtɪ/ *adj* having to do with

mathematics

having a baby: *a maternity hospital*; *maternity clothes*.

mathematics /maθə'matıks/ *n* the science dealing with measurements, numbers and quantities. **mathe'matical** *adj*.

mathematician /maθəmə'tıʃən/ *n* **1** a person who is good at mathematics: *For a young boy he's an excellent mathematician*. **2** someone who works in mathematics: *He is a mathematician with a local engineering firm*.

maths /maθs/ *n* short for **mathematics**.

matinée /'matıneı/ *n* a performance at a theatre, circus, cinema *etc* given in the afternoon or morning: *They do three matinées every week*.

matriarch /'meıtrıɑ:k/ *n* a woman who is head of a family or community: *My grandmother is the matriarch in my family*.

matrimony /'matrımənı/ *n* the state of being married.

matrix /'meıtrıks/, *plural* **matrices** /'meıtrısi:z/, *n* **1** an arrangement of numbers in rows and columns: *Arrange these numbers in a matrix*. **2** the place in which anything develops or is formed: *This disease has developed in a matrix of poverty, bad health and poor food*.

matron /'meıtrən/ *n* a senior nurse in charge of a hospital.

matt or **mat** /mat/ *adj* not shiny: *matt paint*.

matted /'matıd/ *adj* in a thick untidy mess: *matted hair*.

matter /'matə(r)/ *n* **1** solid substances, liquids and gases in any form, from which everything physical is made: *The entire universe is made up of different kinds of matter*. **2** a subject or topic of discussion *etc*: *a private matter*; *money matters*. — *v* to be important: *That car matters a great deal to him*; *It doesn't matter*.

matter-of-'fact *adj* calm, showing no emotion: *She spoke about her husband's death in a matter-of-fact way*.

for that matter as well; in addition: *My wife was very angry and I was too, for that matter*.

no matter who, what, where, etc whoever, whatever, wherever *etc*: *They won't hear you no matter how loud you shout*; *No matter what the problem is, she's always happy to help*.

the matter the thing that is wrong; the trouble, problem or difficulty: *Is anything the matter?*; *What's the matter with you?*; *He would not tell me what the matter was*.

mattress /'matrəs/ *n* a thick, firm layer of padding, covered in cloth *etc* for lying on, usually as part of a bed.

mature /mə'tjʊə(r)/ *adj* fully grown or developed; grown up: *a very mature person*. — *v* to make or become mature: *She matured early*.

to be very **mature** (not **matured**) for your age.

The opposite of **mature** is **immature**.

maul /mɔ:l/ *v* to injure a person or animal by rough treatment: *He was badly mauled by an angry lion*.

mausoleum /mɔ:sə'lıəm/ *n* a tomb in the form of a large building: *The bodies of their dead leaders are placed in a mausoleum*.

mauve /moʊv/ *n* a pale purple colour. — *adj*: *a mauve scarf*.

maxim /'maksım/ *n* a well-known wise saying or piece of advice: *'He who hesitates is lost' is a well-known maxim*.

maximize /'maksımaız/ *v* to make something as great as possible: *The company's first aim is to maximize profits*; *Use the maximize button to see more of your computer text*.

maximum /'maksıməm/ *adj* greatest: *This requires maximum effort*; *We must put the maximum amount of effort into the job*. — *n* the greatest quantity or the highest point: *Two hundred pencils an hour is the maximum we can produce*; *The temperature reaches its maximum at mid-day*.

The opposite of **maximum** is **minimum**.

may /meı/ *v* **1** to have permission to do something: *You may go home now*; *You may not run in the passage*. **2** used to express a possibility in the present or future: *He may be here — I don't know*; *I may not go to Sidney after all*. **3** used to express a wish: *May you live a long and happy life*. **4** used to contrast two facts: *You may think it's silly, but it works*; *She may be the boss, but I still think she's an idiot*.

can means to be able to: *How can I improve my English?*
may means to be allowed to: *May I open the window, please?*
See also **might**[1].

may have used to express a possibility in the past: *He may have been here, but we cannot be sure*.

May /meɪ/ *n* the fifth month of the year.

maybe /'meɪbɪ/ *adv* perhaps: *Maybe he'll come.*

mayn't /'meɪənt/ short for **may not**.

mayonnaise /meɪə'neɪz/ *n* a cold, thick, creamy sauce that is made from egg yolk, oil, salt and pepper, and vinegar or lemon juice: *Egg mayonnaise is a dish of hard-boiled eggs with mayonnaise.*

mayor /mɛə(r)/ *n* the chief public official of a city or town.

mayoress /'mɛərəs/ *n* **1** a mayor's wife. **2** a female mayor.

maze /meɪz/ *n* a deliberately confusing series of paths from which it is difficult to find the way out.

me /miː/ *pron* (used as the object of a verb or preposition and sometimes instead of I) the word you use when you are talking about yourself: *He hit me*; *Give that to me*; *It's me*; *He can go with John and me.*

> He is shorter **than I** (or **than I am** or **than me**).
> between **you and me** (not **you and I**).

meadow /'mɛdoʊ/ *n* a field of grass: *There were cows in the meadow.*

meagre /'miːɡə(r)/ *adj* poor; not enough: *It's a meagre award for all that effort.*

meal /miːl/ *n* the food taken at one time: *We eat three meals a day.*

mean¹ /miːn/ *adj* **1** not generous with money *etc*: *He's very mean with his money.* **2** not kind; nasty: *It is mean to tell lies.* **'meanness** *n*.

mean² /miːn/ *v* **1** to express something, or intend to express something: *'Vacation' means 'holiday'*; *What do you mean by saying that?* **2** to intend: *I'm sorry, I didn't mean to stand on your toe*; *For whom was that letter meant?* **3** to be important to someone: *My family mean a lot to me.* **4** to make something likely; to cause something: *No rain means a poor harvest.*

> **mean; meant** /mɛnt/; **meant**: *He meant to post the letter*; *It was meant to be a joke.*

mean well to have good intentions: *He meant well by what he said.*

meander /mɪ'andə(r)/ *v* to flow slowly along with many bends and curves: *The stream meandered through the meadows.*

meaning /'miːnɪŋ/ *n* what a statement, action, word *etc* means: *What is the meaning of this phrase?*; *What is the meaning of his behaviour?*

'meaningful *adj* **1** intended to express something: *He gave me a meaningful look and we both left the room.* **2** useful or important: *The tests have produced no real meaningful results yet.*

'meaningless *adj* **1** having no purpose or importance: *Life can seem meaningless at times.* **2** without meaning: *I'm afraid his explanation was meaningless to me.*

means¹ /miːnz/ *n* the instrument, method *etc* that is used to get a result: *By what means can we find out?*

by all means yes, of course: *If you want to use the telephone, by all means do.*

a means to an end a way of achieving something: *For me, the computer course is just a means to an end.*

by means of using: *We escaped by means of a secret tunnel.*

by no means 1 definitely not: *'Have you finished yet?' 'By no means!'* **2** not at all: *I'm by no means certain to win.*

means² /miːnz/ *n* money available or necessary for living *etc*: *She's a person of considerable means.*

meant see **mean**.

meantime /'miːntaɪm/ *n* the time between two events: *I'll hear her account of the matter later — in the meantime, I'd like to hear yours.*

meanwhile /'miːnwaɪl/ *adv* during this time; at the same time: *The child had gone home. Meanwhile, his mother was searching for him in the street.*

measles /'miːzəlz/ *n* a children's disease with small red spots on the skin.

> **measles** is always in the plural form but takes a singular verb: *Measles is an infectious disease.*

measure /'mɛʒə(r)/ *n* **1** a device for finding the size, amount *etc* of something: *a glass measure for liquids*; *a tape-measure.* **2** a unit: *The metre is a measure of length.* **3** a plan of action; something done: *We must take certain measures to stop the increase in crime.* — *v* **1** to find the size, amount *etc* of something: *He measured the table.* **2** to show the size, amount *etc* of something: *A thermometer measures temperature.* **3** to be a certain size: *This table measures two metres by one metre.*

'measurement *n* size, amount *etc*, found

meat

out by measuring: *What are the measurements of this room?*

made to measure made to fit the measurements of a particular person: *Was your jacket made to measure?* — *adj*: *a made-to-measure suit.*

measure up to reach the desired or required standard: *Compared with last year's results, how do this year's students measure up?*

meat /miːt/ *n* the flesh of animals or birds used as food: *He doesn't eat meat or fish.*

'meaty *adj* full of meat: *a meaty soup.*

mechanic /mɪˈkanɪk/ *n* a skilled worker who repairs machinery or keeps it in good condition.

meˈchanical *adj* **1** having to do with machines: *mechanical engineering.* **2** worked or done by machinery: *a mechanical saw.* **3** done without thinking, from habit: *a mechanical action.* **meˈchanically** *adv*.

meˈchanics *n* **1** the way in which a process or system works: *I'm not really familiar with the mechanics of the legal system.* **2** the study of the effects of physical forces on objects.

'mechanism /ˈmɛkənɪzm/ *n* a part of a machine *etc* that does a particular job: *The winding mechanism of the old clock has broken.*

mechanize /ˈmɛkənaɪz/ *v* to use machines instead of people to carry out work: *Car production has become increasingly mechanized.*

medal /ˈmɛdəl/ *n* a piece of metal like a large coin, with a design, inscription *etc* stamped on it, given as a reward or made to celebrate a special occasion: *He won a medal for bravery.*

'medallist *n* a person who has won a medal in a competition *etc*.

medallion /məˈdalɪən/ *n* a large, medal-like piece of jewellery, worn on a chain: *Men sometimes wear medallions.*

meddle /ˈmɛdəl/ *v* to concern yourself with things that are not your business; to fiddle with something: *She was always trying to meddle in my affairs*; *Don't meddle with the television.* **'meddler** *n*.

media /ˈmiːdɪə/ plural of **medium**.

mediaeval *see* **medieval**.

mediate /ˈmiːdɪeɪt/ *v* to try to settle a disagreement between people. **mediˈation** *n*. **'mediator** *n*.

medical /ˈmɛdɪkəl/ *adj* having to do with healing, medicine or doctors: *medical care*; *medical insurance.* — *n* a medical examination. **'medically** *adv*.

medicated /ˈmɛdɪkeɪtɪd/ *adj* having a healing or health-giving substance mixed in: *medicated shampoo.*

medication /mɛdɪˈkeɪʃən/ *n* medicine that a doctor gives to a patient: *Are you taking the medication?*

medicine /ˈmɛdsɪn/ *n* **1** a substance that is used to treat disease or illness: *a dose of medicine.* **2** the science of curing people who are ill: *He is studying medicine.*

> The pronunciation of **medicine** is /ˈmɛdsɪn/.

medieval or **mediaeval** /mɛdɪˈiːvəl/ *adj* having to do with the period between about the 11th and the 15th centuries, especially in Europe: *There are still many medieval buildings in the old town centre of Edinburgh.*

mediocre /miːdɪˈoʊkə(r)/ *adj* not very good; ordinary: *a mediocre performance.* **mediocrity** /miːdɪˈɒkrɪtɪ/ *n*.

meditate /ˈmɛdɪteɪt/ *v* to think deeply: *He was meditating on his troubles.* **mediˈtation** *n*.

medium /ˈmiːdɪəm/, *plural* **'media** or **'mediums,** *n* **1** something by which an effect is transmitted: *Air is the medium through which sound is carried.* **2** a means, especially radio, television and newspapers, by which news *etc* is made known: *the news media.* **3** a person through whom spirits of dead people are believed to speak. — *adj* middle or average in size, quality *etc*: *Would you like the small, medium or large packet?*

medley /ˈmɛdlɪ/ *n* **1** a piece of music put together from a number of other pieces: *She sang a medley of old songs.* **2** a mixture.

meek /miːk/ *adj* humble; not likely to complain, argue *etc*: *a meek little man.* **'meekly** *adv*. **'meekness** *n*.

meet /miːt/ *v* **1** to come face to face with someone by chance: *It was on a train that I first met the man who became my husband*; *Michael politely said 'Good morning' when he met the headmaster in the passage.* **2** to come together with a person *etc*, by arrangement: *The committee meets every Monday.* **3** to be introduced to someone for the first time: *Come and meet my wife.* **4** to join: *Where do the two roads meet?* **5** to satisfy requirements *etc*: *Will there be sufficient stocks to meet the public demand?*

> **meet; met** /mɛt/; **met**: *He met her on his way home*; *Have you met her before?*

'meeting *n* a coming together of people for discussion or another purpose: *to attend a committee meeting.*

meet with to experience; to suffer: *We have met with a few problems while writing this dictionary.*

megaphone /'mɛgəfoʊn/ *n* a device for speaking through, that causes sounds to be made louder: *He shouted instructions to the crowd through a megaphone.*

melancholy /'mɛlənkɒli/ *adj* very sad; showing sadness: *The refugees felt melancholy when they thought of their homeland*; *a melancholy film*; *He had a melancholy expression on his face.* — *n* sadness: *a feeling of melancholy.*

mellow /'mɛloʊ/ *adj* **1** mature and sweet: *a mellow wine.* **2** soft, not strong or unpleasant: *The lamplight was soft and mellow.* **3** having become pleasant and agreeable with age: *a mellow old man.* — *v*: *She never smiled much and she hasn't mellowed with age.* **'mellowness** *n*.

melodious /mə'loʊdiəs/ *adj* **1** having a sweet tune: *a melodious tune.* **2** nice to listen to: *a melodious voice.* **me'lodiously** *adv.*

melodrama /'mɛlədrɑːmə/ *n* a play, film *etc* full of adventure and romance, in which people are either very good or very bad.

melodramatic /mɛlədrə'matɪk/ *adj* showing your feelings too strongly, as though you are acting on stage: *I don't like his melodramatic behaviour.*

melody /'mɛlədi/ *n* a tune: *He played Spanish melodies on his guitar.*

melon /'mɛlən/ *n* a large, juicy fruit with many seeds.

melon   water-melon

melt /mɛlt/ *v* to make or become soft or liquid through heat: *She melted the sugar in a pan*; *The ice has melted.*

'melting-point *n* the temperature at which a solid melts: *The melting-point of ice is 0° Celsius.*

member /'mɛmbə(r)/ *n* a person who belongs to a group, club, society *etc*.

'membership *n* **1** being a member: *membership of a political party.* **2** all the members of a club *etc*: *a society with a large membership.*

membrane /'mɛmbreɪn/ *n* a thin skin that covers or connects the organs or cells of your body.

memento /mə'mɛntoʊ/, *plural* **mementos**, *n* something kept or given as a reminder or souvenir: *They gave her a small gift as a memento.*

memo /'mɛmoʊ/, *plural* **memos**, *n* a note from one member of a company or organization to another: *She sent a memo to all her staff.*

memoirs /'mɛmwɑːz/ *n* a book that a person writes about his or her own life: *the recently published memoirs of her political career.*

memorable /'mɛmərəbəl/ *adj* worthy of being remembered: *a memorable event.*

memorial /mə'mɔːriəl/ *n* something, for example a monument, made to remind people of an event or a person: *a memorial to Mao Tse-tung*; *a war memorial.*

memorize /'mɛməraɪz/ *v* to learn something so well that you can remember it without looking: *She memorized the instructions.*

memory /'mɛməri/ *n* **1** the power to remember things: *a good memory for details.* **2** the store of remembered things in your mind: *Her memory is full of interesting stories.* **3** something remembered: *memories of her childhood.* **4** the time as far back as can be remembered: *the greatest fire in memory.* **5** a part of a computer in which information is stored for immediate use.

in memory of done as a way of remembering a person who has died: *A monument was erected in the town square in memory of the people who died in the fire.*

men plural of **man**.

menace /'mɛnəs/ *n* **1** something likely to cause injury, damage *etc*: *Cholera is an ever-present menace to the poor in Africa and South Asia.* **2** a threat: *His voice was full of menace.* — *v* to threaten: *The village was menaced by the volcano.*

'menacing *adj*: *He gave us a menacing look.*

menagerie /mə'nadʒəri/ *n* a collection of wild animals; a zoo.

mend /mɛnd/ *v* **1** to put something broken, torn *etc* into good condition again; to repair: *Can you mend this broken chair?* **2** to heal or recover: *My broken leg is mending very well.* — *n* a repaired place: *This shirt has a mend in the sleeve.*

'mending *n* things needing to be mended, especially clothes: *a pile of mending.*

on the mend to be getting better after an illness or injury: *She was seriously ill but*

menial /ˈmiːnɪəl/ *adj* needing no skill, dull and boring: *If you don't get some qualifications you'll end up doing menial jobs all your life.*

meningitis /mɛnɪnˈdʒaɪtɪs/ *n* a serious disease of the brain.

menstruation /mɛnstrʊˈeɪʃən/ *n* the natural bleeding from the womb of a woman every 28 days. **'menstruate** *v*.

mental /ˈmɛntəl/ *adj* **1** having to do with your mind: *mental illnesses*. **2** done or made by your mind: *mental arithmetic*; *a mental picture*. **3** for those who have an illness that affects their mind: *a mental hospital*. **4** suffering from an illness of the mind: *a mental patient*.

mentality /mɛnˈtalɪtɪ/ *n* a way of thinking: *He has a rather strange mentality.*
'mentally *adv*: *He is mentally ill.*

menthol /ˈmɛnθɒl/ *n* a sharp-smelling substance got from peppermint oil used to help to give relief from colds *etc*.

mention /ˈmɛnʃən/ *v* **1** to speak of something briefly: *He mentioned the plan.* **2** to remark: *She mentioned that she might be leaving.* — *n* a remark: *No mention was made of this matter.*

don't mention it not at all (used as a polite reply to someone who thanks you): *'You are very kind. Thank you very much.' 'Don't mention it.'*

not to mention and also; as well as: *He is one of the most intelligent, not to mention handsome people I know.*

menu /ˈmɛnjuː/ *n* a list of dishes that may be ordered in a restaurant or are served at a meal: *What's on the menu today?*

mercenary /ˈmɜːsənərɪ/ *adj* too strongly influenced by desire for money: *a mercenary attitude.* — *n* a soldier who is hired to fight for a foreign army.

merchandise /ˈmɜːtʃəndaɪz/ *n* goods to be bought and sold: *This store sells merchandise from all over the world.*

merchant /ˈmɜːtʃənt/ *n* a trader, especially in goods of a particular kind: *tea merchants*.

merciful /ˈmɜːsɪfəl/ *adj* willing to forgive or to punish only lightly: *a merciful judge.*
'mercifully *adv* luckily: *We arrived at the station late but, mercifully, the train had been delayed.*

merciless /ˈmɜːsɪləs/ *adj* without mercy; cruel.

mercury /ˈmɜːkjʊrɪ/ *n* a poisonous, silvery, liquid metal used in thermometers *etc*.

mercy /ˈmɜːsɪ/ *n* **1** kindness towards an enemy, wrongdoer *etc*: *He showed his enemies no mercy.* **2** a piece of good luck: *It was a mercy that it didn't rain.*

at the mercy of someone or **something** wholly in the power of someone or something: *A sailor is at the mercy of the sea.*

have mercy on someone to give kindness to an enemy *etc*: *Have mercy on me!*

mere /mɪə(r)/ *adj* no more than: *a mere child.*
'merely *adv* simply; only: *I was merely trying to help.*

the merest even a small amount of something: *The merest mention of the subject makes her angry.*

merge /mɜːdʒ/ *v* **1** to combine or join: *The sea and sky appear to merge at the horizon.* **2** to change gradually into something else: *Summer slowly merged into autumn.*
'merger *n* the joining together of two or more business companies to form a single large company.

meridian /məˈrɪdɪən/ *n* an imaginary line on the earth's surface, running from one pole to the other and cutting through the equator: *Meridians on maps help you find the place you are looking for.*

See also **longitude**.

meringue /məˈraŋ/ *n* a kind of light, crisp, white cake that is made of whites of eggs whipped up with sugar.

merit /ˈmɛrɪt/ *n* **1** that which deserves praise or reward: *He reached his present position through merit.* **2** a good point or quality: *His speech had at least the merit of being short.* — *v* to deserve: *Her work merits a high mark.*

mermaid /ˈmɜːmeɪd/ *n* a woman with a fish's tail instead of legs, who only exists in fairytales *etc*.

merriment /ˈmɛrɪmənt/ *n* fun and laughter: *There was a great deal of merriment at the party.*

merry /ˈmɛrɪ/ *adj* happy and cheerful: *merry children*; *a merry party*. **'merrily** *adv*. **'merriness** *n*.
'merry-go-round *n* a round, moving platform carrying toy horses *etc* on which children ride at the fair.
'merrymaking *n* joyful celebrating.

mesh /mɛʃ/ *n* **1** the openings between the threads of a net: *a net of very fine mesh.* **2** (**'meshes**) a network: *A fly was struggling in the meshes of the spider's web.*

mesmerize /ˈmɛzməraɪz/ *v* to hold all your attention: *Audiences all over the country have been mesmerized by this performance.*

mess /mɛs/ n disorder; confusion; an untidy or unpleasant sight: *This room is in a terrible mess!*; *The spilt food made a mess on the carpet.* — v to put something into disorder or confusion: *Don't mess the room up!* **'messy** adj dirty: *a messy job.* **'messily** adv.
make a mess of 1 to make something dirty or untidy: *The heavy rain has made a real mess of the garden.* **2** to do something badly: *He made a mess of his essay.*
mess about or **mess around 1** to do things with no particular plan: *He didn't know how to repair the car — he was only messing about with it.* **2** to behave in a foolish way: *The children were shouting and messing about.* **3** to treat someone badly or unfairly: *I wish they'd stop messing me about and tell me exactly what to do.*
mess up to make something untidy or dirty; to spoil or damage something: *Don't mess your suit up when you change the wheel*; *This has really messed up our plans.*

message /'mɛsɪdʒ/ n **1** a piece of information passed from one person to another: *I have a message for you from Mr Johnson.* **2** the teaching given by a story, religion, prophet *etc*: *What message is this story trying to give us?*
messenger /'mɛsɪndʒə(r)/ n a person who carries a message.

Messiah /mə'saɪə/ n Jesus Christ.

metabolism /mə'tabəlɪzm/ n the system of chemical processes in the body that produce energy and growth from food: *Her metabolism is more efficient than mine.* **metabolic** /mɛtə'bɒlɪk/ adj.

metal /'mɛtəl/ n any of a group of substances, usually shiny and able to conduct heat: *Gold, silver, copper and iron are all metals.* — adj: *a metal object.*
metallic /mə'talɪk/ adj **1** containing or consisting of metal: *a metallic substance.* **2** like a metal in appearance or sound: *metallic blue*; *a metallic noise.*
'metalwork n **1** the art or craft of making objects from metal: *She learnt metalwork at school.* **2** objects made from metal: *a collection of metalwork.*

metamorphosis /mɛtə'mɔːfəsɪs/, *plural* **metamorphoses** /mɛtə'mɔːfəsiːz/, n a change of form, appearance, character *etc*: *a caterpillar's metamorphosis into a butterfly.*

metaphor /'mɛtəfə(r)/ n a way of describing someone or something in which you call them by the name of a thing that has the same quality as they do: *'She is a tigress when she is really angry'* and *'Their new house is a dream'* are examples of metaphors.
metaphorical /mɛtə'fɒrɪkəl/ adj. **meta'phorically** adv.

meteor /'miːtɪə(r)/ n a small mass or body travelling very quickly through space, which appears very bright after entering the earth's atmosphere.
mete'oric adj very fast or successful: *the singer's meteoric rise to fame.*
meteorite /'miːtɪəraɪt/ n a kind of large rock that has fallen to earth from space.
meteorology /miːtɪə'rɒlədʒɪ/ n the study of changes in the earth's atmosphere and the weather they produce: *You need to study meteorology if you want to forecast the weather.* **meteorological** /miːtɪərə'lɒdʒɪkəl/ adj.

meter[1] /'miːtə(r)/ n an instrument for measuring quantities of electricity, gas, water *etc*: *If you want to know how much electricity you have used you will have to look at the meter.* — v to measure with a meter.

meter[2] another spelling of **metre**.

method /'mɛθəd/ n **1** a way of doing something: *methods of training athletes.* **2** fixed series of actions for doing something: *Follow the method shown in the instruction book.*
methodical /mə'θɒdɪkəl/ adj having or using a careful and well-organized method: *She's very methodical in the kitchen.*
me'thodically adv: *We watched as he worked his way methodically down the list.*

meticulous /mə'tɪkjʊləs/ adj very careful, almost too careful, about small details: *He paid meticulous attention to detail.* **me'ticulously** adv.

metre /'miːtə(r)/ n the chief unit of length in the metric system, about 1.1 yard: *This table is one metre wide*; *One metre is often written as 1 m.*

metric /'mɛtrɪk/ adj having to do with the metre or metric system: *Are these scales metric?*

metricate /'mɛtrɪkeɪt/ v to change from measuring things in non-metric units to measuring them in metric units, such as metres or grammes: *The system of measurement has been metricated.*

the metric system a system of weights and measures based on tens, for example, 1 metre = 10 decimetres = 100 centimetres = 1000 millimetres.

metropolis /mə'trɒpəlɪs/ n a large city, especially a country's capital.

metropolitan /mɛtrə'pɒlɪtən/ *adj*: *We miss the theatres, restaurants and other aspects of metropolitan life.*

mew /mjuː/ *v* to make the cry of a cat: *The kittens mewed.* — *n* this cry.

miaow /mɪ'aʊ/ *v* to make the cry of a cat: *The cat miaowed all night.* — *n* this cry.

mice plural of **mouse**.

micro- /'maɪkrəʊ/ **1** very small: *microprint*; **2** one millionth part: *a microvolt*.

microchip /'maɪkrətʃɪp/ *n* a tiny piece of silicon *etc* designed to act as a complex electronic circuit.

microcomputer /maɪkrəʊkəm'pjuːtə(r)/ *n* a small computer containing microchips.

microfiche /'maɪkrəfiːʃ/ *n* a piece of film the size of a postcard, used for storing miniature copies of text, which can be read using a **microfiche reader** which magnifies the image: *Many libraries now keep their catalogues on microfiche.*

microfilm /'maɪkrəfɪlm/ *n* a piece of photographic film on to which a document or a book is copied, in a size very much smaller than its actual size: *The library has copies of lots of newspapers on microfilm; I borrowed a microfilm of the book at the library.*

microphone /'maɪkrəfəʊn/ *n* an electronic instrument for picking up sound waves to be broadcast, recorded or amplified as in radio, the telephone, a tape-recorder *etc*: *Speak into the microphone.*

microscope /'maɪkrəskəʊp/ *n* an instrument with lenses, that makes very tiny objects look much larger, so that you can study them closely: *Germs are very small, and can only be seen with the aid of a microscope.*

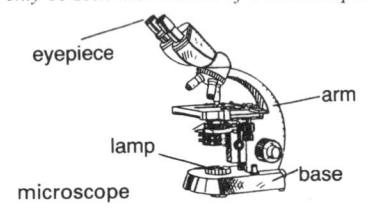

eyepiece
arm
lamp
base
microscope

microscopic /maɪkrə'skɒpɪk/ *adj* **1** able to be seen only through a microscope: *microscopic fungi.* **2** very small: *I can't read his microscopic writing.*

microwave /'maɪkrəweɪv/ *n* (also **microwave oven**) an oven which cooks food very quickly using radiation rather than heat: *You can use a microwave to defrost food from the freezer.*

mid /mɪd/ *adj* at, or in, the middle of something: *a midweek football match; in mid air.*

midday /mɪd'deɪ/ *n* the middle of the day; twelve o'clock: *We'll meet you at midday.* — *adj*: *a midday meal.*

middle /'mɪdəl/ *n* **1** the central point or part: *the middle of a circle.* **2** your waist: *You're getting rather fat round your middle.* — *adj* equally distant from both ends: *the middle seat in a row.*

middle age the years between youth and old age: *She is well into middle age.* **middle-'aged** *adj.*

Middle Ages the period between the 11th and the 15th centuries, especially in Europe: *People were very superstitious during the Middle Ages.*

'middleman *n* a dealer who buys goods from the person who makes or grows them, and sells them to shopkeepers or to the public.

be in the middle of doing something to be busy doing something: *I was in the middle of washing my hair when the telephone rang.*

midget /'mɪdʒɪt/ *n* a person who is fully developed but has not grown to normal height.

midnight /'mɪdnaɪt/ *n* twelve o'clock at night: *I'll go to bed at midnight.*

midst /mɪdst/: **in the midst 1** among; in the centre: *in the midst of a crowd of people.* **2** at the same time as: *in the midst of all these troubles.*

in our midst among us: *We have an enemy in our midst.*

midway /mɪd'weɪ/ *adj* in the middle between two points; half-way: *the midway point.* — *adv*: *Their house is midway between the two villages.*

midweek /mɪd'wiːk/ *adj* happening in the middle of the week: *The midweek match has been cancelled.* — *adv*: *We like to do the shopping midweek.*

midwife /'mɪdwaɪf/, *plural* **midwives** /'mɪdwaɪvz/, *n* a trained nurse who helps at the birth of children. **midwifery** /'mɪdwɪfərɪ/ *n.*

might[1] /maɪt/ *v* **1** past tense of **may**: *I thought I might find you here; He might come if you offered him a meal; I might never have known the truth, if you hadn't told me.* **2** used instead of 'may', for example to make a possibility seem less likely: *He might win if he tries hard.* **3** used to ask permission very politely: *Might I give you some advice?* **4** used to scold someone for not doing something: *You might help me wash the car!*

> **might not** or **mightn't** /'maɪtənt/: *I mightn't be able to come after all.*

might have 1 used to suggest that something would have been possible: *You might have caught the bus if you had run.* **2** used to scold someone for not doing something: *You might have apologized!*

might² /maɪt/ *n* power; strength: *the military might of the NATO alliance.*

mightn't short for **might not**.

mighty /'maɪtɪ/ *adj* having great power: *a mighty nation.* **'mightily** *adv.* **'mightiness** *n.*

migraine /'miːgreɪn/ *n* a very painful headache: *She suffers from frequent attacks of migraine; I have a migraine today.*

migrate /maɪ'greɪt/ *v* **1** to travel from one region to another at certain times of the year: *Many birds migrate in the early winter.* **2** to move from one place to another, especially to another country: *The whole population migrated to the East.* **mi'gration** *n.*

> See also **emigrate**.

migrant /'maɪgrənt/ *n* a person, bird or animal that migrates: *The swallow is a summer migrant to Britain.* — *adj*: *migrant workers.*

mike /maɪk/ *n* a microphone.

mild /maɪld/ *adj* **1** gentle: *He has a mild temper.* **2** not severe: *a mild punishment.* **3** not cold; rather warm: *a mild spring day.* **4** not sharp or hot in taste: *a mild curry.* **'mildly** *adv.* **'mildness** *n.*

mile /maɪl/ *n* a measure of length equal to 1.61 km: *We walked ten miles today; a speed of 70 miles per hour; a ten-mile hike.*

mileage /'maɪlɪdʒ/ *n* the number of miles travelled: *What mileage did you do on your trip?; What's the mileage on that old car?*

miles *n* a lot: *I'm feeling miles better today.*

'milestone *n* a very important event in the history of something: *The invention of the mercury thermometer by Daniel Fahrenheit in 1714 was a milestone in the history of physics.*

militant /'mɪlɪtənt/ *adj* taking strong, sometimes violent action; aggressive: *The militant workers went on strike and prevented the others from working normally.* — *n* a militant person. **'militancy** *n.*

military /'mɪlɪtərɪ/ *adj* having to do with soldiers or armed forces generally: *military power.*

milk /mɪlk/ *n* a white liquid produced by female mammals as food for their young: *The chief source of milk is the cow.* — *v* to obtain milk from a cow *etc*: *The farmer milks his cows each day.*

> **milk** is never used in the plural: *How much milk shall I buy today?*; *They drink a lot of milk.*

'milkmaid *n* a woman employed to milk cows by hand.

'milkman *n* a man who delivers milk.

'milkshake *n* a drink made by whipping milk and a particular flavouring: *I'd like a strawberry milkshake.*

milk teeth the first set of teeth that a baby develops.

'milky *adj* like milk: *A milky substance.*

the Milky Way a huge collection of stars stretching across the sky.

mill /mɪl/ *n* **1** a machine for grinding coffee, pepper *etc* by crushing it between rough, hard surfaces: *a coffee-mill*; *a pepper-mill.* **2** a building where grain is ground: *The farmer took his corn to the mill.* **3** a building where certain things are manufactured: *a woollen-mill*; *a steel-mill.* — *v* to grind or press: *This flour was milled at a local mill.*

mill about or **mill around** to move around a place with no real purpose, often waiting for something to happen.

millennium /mɪ'lenɪəm/, *plural* **millennia** /mɪ'lenɪə/, *n* a period of 1000 years.

> See **year**.

millet /'mɪlɪt/ *n* a grain used as food.

milli- /'mɪlɪ/ a thousandth part of something: *millimetre; milligramme.*

million /'mɪljən/ *n* one thousand thousand; the number 1 000 000: *a million; one million; five million.* — *adj* 1 000 000 in number: *six million people.*

> You use **million** (not **millions**) after a number: *two million dollars.*

millionaire /mɪljə'neə(r)/ *n* a person having a million pounds, dollars *etc* or more.

millio'nairess *n* a woman who is a millionaire.

millipede /'mɪlɪpiːd/ *n* a small many-legged creature with a long body.

mime /maɪm/ *n* **1** in dancing *etc* the art of using movements, especially of the hands, to express what you normally put into words: *She is studying mime.* **2** a play in which no words are spoken and the actions tell the story: *The children performed a mime.* — *v* to act using movements rather than words: *He mimed his love for her by holding his hands over his heart.*

mimic /'mɪmɪk/ *v* to imitate someone or something, especially with the intention of making them appear ridiculous or funny: *The comedian mimicked the Prime Minister's way of speaking.* — *n* a person who mimics: *Some children are good mimics.* '**mimicry** *n*.

mimosa /mɪ'moʊzə/ *n* a plant with small flowers and fern-like leaves that close when touched.

minaret /mɪnə'rɛt/ *n* a tower on a mosque from which the call to prayer is sounded.

See **steeple**.

mince /mɪns/ *v* to cut meat *etc* into very small pieces; to chop finely: *Would you like me to mince the meat for you?* — *n* meat that has been minced and cooked: *mince and potatoes.*
'**mincer** *n* a machine for mincing meat *etc*.

mind /maɪnd/ *n* the power by which you think *etc*; your intelligence or understanding: *The girl was very grown-up — she seemed already to have the mind of an adult.* — *v* **1** to look after someone or something: *Would you mind the baby?* **2** to be upset by something: *Do you mind if I smoke?* **3** to be careful of something: *Mind the step!* — a cry of warning: *Mind! There's a car coming!*
-minded: *narrow-minded*.
'**mindless** *adj* done without a reason: *mindless violence*.
bear in mind or **keep in mind** to remember something; to take something into consideration: *You should keep that in mind when you apply for another job.*
be out of your mind to be mad: *He must be out of his mind!*
have a good mind to do something to feel inclined to do something: *I've a good mind to tell your father what a naughty girl you are!*
mind out to be careful: *Mind out! There's a hole in the road.*
make up your mind to decide: *They've made up their minds to stay in Africa.*
mind your own business not to interfere in other people's affairs: *Go away and mind your own business!*
never mind don't bother; it's all right: *Never mind, I'll do it myself.*

on your mind making you anxious: *I can't think about that now — I've got too much else on my mind.*
speak your mind to say frankly what you mean or think: *You must allow me to speak my mind.*
take your mind off to help you not to worry about something: *He says that having visitors takes his mind off the pain.*

mine[1] /maɪn/ *pron* something that belongs to me: *Are these pencils yours or mine?*; *He is a friend of mine.*

This pencil isn't yours — it's **mine** (not **my one**).

mine[2] /maɪn/ *n* **1** a place, usually underground, from which metals, coal, salt *etc* are dug: *a coalmine*; *My father worked in the mines.* **2** a kind of bomb used underwater or placed just beneath the surface of the ground: *The ship has been blown up by a mine.* — *v* to dig for coal, metals *etc* in a mine: *Coal is mined in this valley.*
'**minefield** *n* an area of land or water in which explosive mines have been hidden.
'**miner** *n* a person who works in a mine.

mineral /'mɪnərəl/ *n* a substance found in the earth and mined: *Metals, coal and salt are minerals.* — *adj*: *mineral oil*.
mineral water a kind of water containing small quantities of health-giving minerals.

mingle /'mɪŋgəl/ *v* to mix: *He mingled with the crowd.* '**mingled** *adj*.

mini /'mɪnɪ/ *n* **1** short for **miniskirt**. **2** (**Mini**®) a type of small car. — *adj* small: *a mini dictionary*; *a minibus*.

miniature /'mɪnɪtʃə(r)/ *adj* smaller than normal, often very small: *a miniature radio.* — *n* **1** a very small painting of a person. **2** a copy or model of something, made on a small scale.

minibus /'mɪnɪbʌs/ *n* a small bus: *The school choir hired a minibus.*

minimal /'mɪnɪməl/ *adj* very small indeed: *The cost of the project will be minimal.*

minimize /'mɪnɪmaɪz/ *v* **1** to reduce something as far as possible: *to minimize the danger.* **2** to make something seem small or not important: *He minimized the mistakes he had made.*

minimum /'mɪnɪməm/ *adj* smallest or lowest: *The minimum temperature last night was −28° Celsius.* — *n* the smallest possible number, quantity *etc* or the lowest level: *Tickets will cost a minimum of £20.*

> The opposite of **minimum** is **maximum**.

miniskirt /'mɪnɪskɜːt/ *n* a very short skirt.

minister /'mɪnɪstə(r)/ *n* **1** a clergyman in certain branches of the Christian Church: *He is a minister in the Presbyterian church.* **2** the head of a department of government: *the Minister for Education.* **ministerial** /mɪnɪ'stɪərɪəl/ *adj.*

ministry /'mɪnɪstrɪ/ *n* **1** the work of a minister of religion: *His ministry lasted for fifteen years.* **2** a department of government or the building where its employees work: *the Transport Ministry.*

mink /mɪŋk/ *n* **1** a small animal like a weasel. **2** its fur: *a hat made of mink.* — *adj*: *a mink coat.*

minor /'maɪnə(r)/ *adj* less, or little, in importance, size *etc*: *Always halt when driving from a minor road to a major road; She has to go into hospital for a minor operation.* — *n* a person who is not yet legally an adult; in Great Britain, a person under 18 years old.

> The opposite of **minor** is **major**.

minority /mɪ'nɒrɪtɪ/ or /maɪ'nɒrɪtɪ/ *n* a small number; less than half: *Only a minority of people live in the countryside; a political minority.*

minstrel /'mɪnstrəl/ *n* in earlier times, a musician who travelled around the country and sang songs or recited poems: *The band of minstrels entertained the king with songs about famous battles.*

mint[1] /mɪnt/ *n* a place where coins are made by the government. — *v* to make coins.

in mint condition in perfect, fresh condition.

mint[2] /mɪnt/ *n* **1** a plant with strong-smelling leaves, used as a flavouring. **2** a sweet with the flavour of these leaves: *a box of mints.* — *adj*: *mint chocolate.*

minus /'maɪnəs/ *prep* used to show subtraction: *Ten minus two equals eight* $(10 - 2 = 8)$. — *adj* negative; less than zero: *Twelve subtracted from ten leaves a minus number.*

minuscule /'mɪnəskjuːl/ *adj* very small: *The risks are minuscule.*

minute[1] /'mɪnɪt/ *n* **1** the sixtieth part of an hour; sixty seconds: *It is twenty minutes to eight.* **2** in measuring an angle, the sixtieth part of a degree. **3** a very short time: *Wait a minute; It will be done in a minute.* **4** a particular point in time: *At that minute, the telephone rang.*

'minutes *n* an official written record of what is said at a formal meeting: *Copies of the minutes will be made available to all members.*

minute hand the larger of the two pointers on a clock or watch.

any minute or **any moment** very soon: *I expect him back any minute now; She was going to spot the mistake at any moment.*

the minute as soon as: *Telephone me the minute he arrives!*

minute[2] /maɪ'njuːt/ *adj* **1** very small: *a minute particle of dust.* **2** paying attention to the smallest details: *minute care.* **mi'nutely** *adv.* **mi'nuteness** *n.*

miracle /'mɪrəkəl/ *n* **1** a wonderful act or event that cannot be explained by the known laws of nature: *Christ's turning of water into wine was a miracle.* **2** an extremely fortunate happening: *It was a miracle that he wasn't killed when he fell down the cliff.*

miraculous /mɪ'rakjʊləs/ *adj* wonderful and amazing: *She has made a miraculous recovery.*

mirage /'mɪrɑːʒ/ *n* something not really there that you imagine you see, especially an area of water in the desert or on a road *etc.*

mirror /'mɪrə(r)/ *n* a surface that reflects light, especially a piece of glass which shows the image of the person looking into it. — *v* to reflect as a mirror does: *The smooth surface of the lake mirrored the surrounding mountains.*

mirth /mɜːθ/ *n* laughter; amusement: *He rolled about the floor with mirth.*

misadventure /mɪsəd'ventʃə(r)/ *n* an unlucky happening.

misbehave /mɪsbɪ'heɪv/ *v* to behave badly: *If you misbehave, I'll send you to bed.* **misbe'haviour** *n.*

miscalculate /mɪs'kalkjʊleɪt/ *v* to make a mistake in calculating: *I miscalculated the bill.* **miscalcu'lation** *n.*

miscarriage /'mɪskarɪdʒ/ *n* **1** the loss of the baby from the womb before it is able to survive. **2** a failure.

mis'carry *v* to have a miscarriage.

miscellaneous /mɪsə'leɪnɪəs/ *adj* composed of several kinds; mixed: *a miscellaneous collection of pictures.*

mischief /'mɪstʃɪf/ *n* **1** behaviour that causes trouble or annoyance to others: *That boy is always up to some mischief.* **2** damage; harm. **'mischievous** *adj*: *a mischievous child.*

make mischief to cause trouble *etc*.

misconduct /mɪsˈkɒndʌkt/ *n* bad behaviour.

miser /ˈmaɪzə(r)/ *n* a mean person who spends very little money, so that he can store up wealth: *That old miser won't give you a cent!* **'miserly** *adv*. **'miserliness** *n*.

miserable /ˈmɪzərəbəl/ *adj* **1** very unhappy: *She's been miserable since her son went away.* **2** very poor in quantity or quality: *The house was in a miserable condition.*

misery /ˈmɪzəri/ *n* great unhappiness: *Forget your miseries and come out with me!*

misfire /mɪsˈfaɪə(r)/ *v* to go wrong; to have a wrong result: *Her little scheme misfired.*

misfit /ˈmɪsfɪt/ *n* a person who behaves differently from other people in a group and is not liked by them: *Everybody was glad when he left the club because he had always been a misfit there.*

misfortune /mɪsˈfɔːtʃən/ *n* bad luck: *I had the misfortune to break my leg.*

misgivings /mɪsˈɡɪvɪŋz/ *n* doubts or worries: *She has a few misgivings about getting married again.*

misguided /mɪsˈɡaɪdɪd/ *adj* acting on or based on beliefs which are wrong: *a misguided view of the situation.*

mishap /ˈmɪshap/ *n* an unlucky accident.

misinform /mɪsɪnˈfɔːm/ *v* to give someone incorrect information: *You have been misinformed — the woman was my sister, not my wife.*

misinterpret /mɪsɪnˈtɜːprɪt/ *v* to understand something wrongly: *He realized that he had misinterpreted her smile.* **misinterpre'tation** *n*.

misjudge /mɪsˈdʒʌdʒ/ *v* to judge something badly or wrongly; to have an unfair opinion of someone: *I had misjudged the distance between the cars in front; He apologized for having misjudged her.* **mis'judgement** *n*.

mislay /mɪsˈleɪ/ *v* to lose something for a while because you have forgotten where you put it: *I seem to have mislaid my pen.*

mis'lay; mislaid /mɪsˈleɪd/; mis'laid.

mislead /mɪsˈliːd/ *v* to deceive: *Her friendly attitude misled me into thinking I could trust her.*

mis'lead; misled /mɪsˈled/; mis'led.

mis'leading *adj*: *a misleading remark.*

misogynist /mɪˈsɒdʒɪnɪst/ *n* a person, usually a man, who hates women: *He has never married because he is a misogynist.*

misplace /mɪsˈpleɪs/ *v* **1** to lose. **2** to give trust, love *etc* to someone who does not deserve it: *Your trust in him was misplaced.*

misprint /ˈmɪsprɪnt/ *n* a mistake in printing.

mispronounce /mɪsprəˈnaʊns/ *v* to pronounce words wrongly. **mispronunci'ation** *n*.

misrepresent /mɪsreprɪˈzent/ *v* to give a false idea or impression of: *He felt that the newspaper article misrepresented him.*

Miss /mɪs/ *n* **1** a polite title given to an unmarried woman or girl: *Miss Wilson will type my letter; Those three sisters are the Misses Brown; Excuse me, miss — what is the time?* **2** a girl: *She's a cheeky little miss!*

miss /mɪs/ *v* **1** to fail to hit, catch *etc*: *The arrow missed the target.* **2** to fail to arrive in time for something: *He missed the 8 o'clock train.* **3** to fail to take advantage of something: *You've missed your opportunity.* **4** to feel sad because of the absence of someone or something: *You'll miss your friends when you go to live abroad.* **5** to notice the absence of something: *I didn't miss my purse till several hours after I'd dropped it.* **6** to fail to hear or see something: *He missed what you said because he wasn't listening.* **7** to fail to go to something: *I'll have to miss my lesson next week, as I'm going to the dentist.* **8** to fail to meet: *We missed you in the crowd.* **9** to avoid: *The thief only just missed being caught by the police.* — *n* a failure to hit, catch *etc*: *two hits and two misses.*

miss out 1 not to include someone or something: *Tell me the whole story and don't miss out a single detail; Have I missed anyone out?* **2** not to have an opportunity that others have: *If you go now you'll miss out on the free food; When I saw what other children had, I felt that I was missing out.*

miss the boat to be left behind, miss an opportunity *etc*: *I meant to send her a birthday card but I missed the boat — her birthday was last week.*

missile /ˈmɪsaɪl/ *n* **1** a weapon that is thrown; something that is fired from a gun *etc*. **2** a rocket-powered weapon carrying an explosive charge: *a ground-to-air missile.*

missing /ˈmɪsɪŋ/ *adj* not able to be found: *The little boy has been missing for three days; I haven't found those missing papers yet.*

mission /ˈmɪʃən/ *n* **1** a purpose for which a person or group of people is sent: *His mission was to seek help.* **2** something that you may feel is the main purpose of your life: *He regards it as his mission to help* the cause of world peace. **3** a place where missionaries live. **4** a group of missionaries: *a Catholic mission.*

'missionary *n* a person who is sent to teach and spread a particular religion.

misspell /mɪsˈspɛl/ *v* to spell a word wrongly.

> **misspell; misspelt** /mɪsˈspɛlt/ or **misspelled** /mɪsˈspɛld/; **misspelt** or **misspelled**.

mist /mɪst/ *n* a cloud of moisture in the air, close to the ground, that makes it difficult to see things clearly: *The hills are covered in thick mist.* **'misty** *adj.* **'mistiness** *n.*

mist up to cover or be covered with mist: *His glasses misted up when he walked into the bathroom.*

mistake /mɪˈsteɪk/ *v* **1** to think that one person or thing is another: *I mistook you for my brother in the dark.* **2** to be wrong about something: *They mistook the date, and arrived two days early.* — *n* something done wrong; an error; a slip: *a spelling mistake; It was a mistake to trust him; I took your umbrella by mistake — it looks like mine.*

> **mi'stake; mistook** /mɪˈstʊk/; **mi'staken**: *He mistook the date; I was mistaken.*

mi'staken *adj* wrong: *You are mistaken if you think the train leaves at 10.30 — it leaves at 10.15.* **mi'stakenly** *adv.*

Mister /ˈmɪstə(r)/ the long way of writing **Mr.**

mistletoe /ˈmɪsəltoʊ/ *n* a small plant with white berries that grows on the branches of trees: *At Christmas she decorated the room with twigs of holly and mistletoe.*

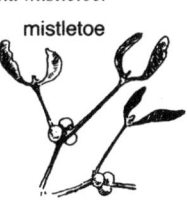

holly   mistletoe

mistreat /mɪsˈtriːt/ *v* to treat cruelly: *You shouldn't mistreat animals.*

mistress /ˈmɪstrəs/ *n* **1** a woman who is the lover of a man to whom she is not married. **2** a female teacher: *the games mistress.* **3** a woman who commands, controls or owns: *a dog and its mistress.*

mistrust /mɪsˈtrʌst/ *v* to be suspicious of something; not to trust someone: *We mistrusted the little information the papers were giving us.* — *n.*

misunderstand /mɪsʌndəˈstand/ *v* not to understand correctly: *You have misunderstood this sentence.*

> **misunderstand; misunderstood** /mɪsʌndəˈstʊd/; **misunder'stood**.

misunder'standing *n* **1** a confusion; a mistake: *a misunderstanding about the date of the meeting.* **2** a slight quarrel.

misuse *n* /mɪsˈjuːs/ a wrong or bad use: *The machine was damaged by misuse.* — *v* /mɪsˈjuːz/ **1** to use wrongly. **2** to treat badly: *They misused the tools.*

mitten /ˈmɪtən/ *n* a kind of glove with two sections, one for the thumb and the other for the fingers: *a pair of mittens.*

mix /mɪks/ *v* **1** to put or blend things together to form one mass: *She mixed the butter and sugar together; He mixed the blue paint with the yellow paint to make green paint.* **2** to go together to form one mass: *Oil and water don't mix.* **3** to go together socially: *People of different races were mixing together happily.* — *n* **1** the result of mixing things or people together: *London has an interesting racial mix.* **2** a collection of ingredients used to make something: *a cake-mix.*

mixed *adj* **1** consisting of different kinds: *I have mixed feelings about leaving home; a mixed population.* **2** for both girls and boys, or both women and men: *a mixed school.*

'mixer *n*: *an electric food-mixer.*

'mixture /ˈmɪkstʃə(r)/ *n* **1** the result of mixing things together: *a mixture of eggs, flour and milk.* **2** a liquid medicine: *The doctor gave the baby some cough mixture.*

'mix-up *n* a muddle: *a mix-up over the concert tickets.*

mix up 1 to blend: *I need to mix up another tin of paint.* **2** to confuse; to muddle: *I'm always mixing the twins up.*

moan /moʊn/ *v* **1** to give a low cry of grief, pain *etc*: *The wounded soldier moaned.* **2** to complain: *She's always moaning about how hard she has to work.* — *n* a sound of grief, pain *etc*: *a moan of pain.*

> **to moan** (not **mourn**) with pain.

moat /moʊt/ *n* a deep ditch, dug round a castle *etc* and filled with water.

mob /mɒb/ *n* a noisy or violent crowd of people: *He was attacked by an angry mob.* — *v* to crowd closely round someone in a noisy, violent way: *The pop singer was mobbed by a huge crowd of his fans.*

mobile /'məʊbaɪl/ *adj* able to move: *The van supplying country districts with library books is called a mobile library; The old lady is no longer mobile — she has to stay in bed all day.* **mo'bility** *n.*

See **immobile**.

mobilize /'məʊbɪlaɪz/ *v* **1** to get ready to fight a war: *The country mobilized its armed forces.* **2** to get a group of people to do something: *She mobilized her neighbours to protest against the noise of the traffic.* **mobili'zation** *n.*

moccasin /'mɒkəsɪn/ *n* a flat shoe that is made of soft leather and has a seam at the front above the toes: *a pair of black moccasins.*

mock /mɒk/ *v* to make fun of someone or something: *They mocked her efforts at cooking.* — *adj* pretended; not real: *a mock battle; He looked at me in mock horror.*

'**mockery** *n* making fun of something: *She could not bear the mockery of the other children.*

'**mocking** *adj*: *a mocking laugh.*

'**mock-up** *n* a detailed model of something: *Tests were carried out on a mock-up of the space shuttle.*

mode /məʊd/ *n* **1** a manner of doing something: *She is a foreigner, and has some unusual modes of expression.* **2** a kind; a type: *modes of transport.*

model /'mɒdəl/ *n* **1** a copy of something on a much smaller scale: *a model of a sports car.* **2** a particular type or design of something that is manufactured in large numbers: *Our car is the latest model.* **3** a person who wears something to show to possible buyers: *He has a job as a fashion model.* **4** someone who poses for an artist, photographer *etc.* **5** a person or thing that is an excellent example: *She is a model of politeness.* — *adj* perfect: *model behaviour.* — *v* **1** to wear something to show to possible buyers: *They model underwear for a living.* **2** to pose as a model for an artist, photographer *etc.* **3** to make a model of a person or thing: *He modelled a figure in clay.* '**modelling** *n.*

modem /'məʊdɛm/ *n* a piece of equipment which allows one computer to send information to another by means of a standard telephone line.

moderate *v* /'mɒdəreɪt/ to make or become less extreme: *He was forced to moderate his opinions.* — *adj* /'mɒdərət/ not extreme: *The prices were moderate; moderate opinions.*

'**moderately** *adv* slightly; quite: *a moderately attractive young woman; It's only moderately more expensive than the other one.*

mode'ration *n* the quality of being moderate: *Alcohol isn't harmful if it's taken in moderation.*

modern /'mɒdən/ *adj* belonging to the present; recent; not old or ancient: *modern music.*

'**modernize** *v* to bring up to date: *We should modernize the school buildings.* **moderni'zation** *n.*

The opposite of **modern** is **ancient**.

modest /'mɒdɪst/ *adj* **1** having a humble or moderate opinion of your merits: *He's very modest about his success.* **2** decent; not shocking: *modest clothing.* '**modestly** *adv.* '**modesty** *n.*

modify /'mɒdɪfaɪ/ *v* to change something: *We had to modify the original design.* **modifi'cation** *n.*

module /'mɒdjuːl/ *n* a unit forming part of a building, spacecraft *etc*: *a lunar module.*

moist /mɔɪst/ *adj* damp, slightly wet: *Alan's eyes were moist with tears.* '**moistly** *adv.* '**moistness** *n.*

moisten /'mɔɪsən/ *v* to wet slightly: *He moistened his lips.*

moisture /'mɔɪstʃə(r)/ *n* dampness: *This soil needs moisture.*

'**moisturize** *v* to add or restore moisture to the skin, air *etc.* '**moisturizer** *n.*

molar /'məʊlə(r)/ *n* a tooth used for grinding food.

mole[1] /məʊl/ *n* a permanent dark spot on the skin.

mole[2] /məʊl/ *n* a small burrowing animal with small eyes and soft fur.

molecule /'mɒlɪkjuːl/ *n* the group of atoms that is the smallest unit into which a substance can be divided without losing its basic nature. **molecular** /mə'lɛkjʊlə(r)/ *adj.*

molehill /'məʊlhɪl/ *n* a heap of earth dug up by a mole while tunnelling.

molest /mə'lɛst/ *v* to annoy or interfere with someone: *The children kept molesting her.*

mollusc /'mɒləsk/ *n* any of a number of animals that have a soft body, no backbone and often a hard shell: *Mussels, clams, octopuses, snails and slugs are molluscs.*

molten /'məʊltən/ *adj* in a liquid state, having been melted: *molten rock.*

moment /ˈmoʊmənt/ *n* **1** a short space of time: *I'll be ready in a moment.* **2** a particular point in time: *At that moment, the telephone rang.*

'momentary *adj* lasting for only a moment: *a momentary feeling of fear.* **'momentarily** *adv.*

momentous /məˈmɛntəs/ *adj* very important: *The invention of the motorcar was a momentous event.*

at the moment at this particular time; now: *She's rather busy at the moment.*

for the moment for now; used to suggest that more will happen, be done or be needed in the future: *Let's leave the subject for the moment and come back to it later*; *We've got enough work for the moment.*

the moment that exactly when: *I want to see him the moment that he arrives.*

momentum /məˈmɛntəm/ *n* the ability of an object to keep moving, or that something has to continue to progress: *Momentum kept the ball bouncing*; *The movement for independence has gained momentum.*

monarch /ˈmɒnək/ *n* a king, queen, emperor, or empress.

'monarchy *n* a country *etc* that has government by a monarch.

monastery /ˈmɒnəstrɪ/ *n* a house in which monks live.

monastic /məˈnæstɪk/ *adj* **1** of or relating to monasteries, monks or nuns: *monastic vows.* **2** simple and without luxuries: *lead a monastic lifestyle.*

Monday /ˈmʌndɪ/ *n* the second day of the week, the day following Sunday.

monetary /ˈmʌnɪtərɪ/ *adj* having to do with money: *monetary problems.*

money /ˈmʌnɪ/ *n* coins or banknotes used in trading: *Have you any money in your purse?*

> **money** is not used in the plural: *All her money is donated to charity.*

'moneylender *n* a person who lends money and charges interest.

lose money, make money to make a loss or a profit: *This film is making a lot of money in America.*

mongrel /ˈmʌŋgrəl/ *n* an animal, especially a dog, bred from different types.

monitor /ˈmɒnɪtə(r)/ *n* **1** a pupil who helps to see that school rules are kept. **2** any of several kinds of instrument *etc* by which something can be constantly checked, especially a small screen in a television studio showing the picture being transmitted at any given time. — *v* to act as, or to use, a monitor; to keep a careful check on something: *These machines monitor the results constantly.*

monk /mʌŋk/ *n* a member of a male religious group, who lives in a monastery.

monkey /ˈmʌŋkɪ/ *n* **1** a small, long-tailed animal of the type most like man: *You children are naughtier than a troop of monkeys.* **2** a mischievous child: *Their son is a little monkey.*

> A monkey **chatters**.

monkey business mischievous or illegal activities.

mono /ˈmɒnoʊ/ *adj* using one sound channel only: *This record is mono, not stereo.*

monologue /ˈmɒnəlɒg/ *n* a long speech given by one actor or person.

monopoly /məˈnɒpəlɪ/ *n* the sole right of making or selling something: *This company has a monopoly on soap-manufacturing.*

monopolize /məˈnɒpəlaɪz/ *v* to have a monopoly of or over something: *They've monopolized the fruit-canning industry.*

monorail /ˈmɒnəreɪl/ *n* a railway with trains which run hanging from, or along the top of, one rail.

monotonous /məˈnɒtənəs/ *adj* lacking in variety; dull: *a monotonous lesson.* **moˈnotonously** *adv.* **monotony** /məˈnɒtənɪ/ *n.*

monsoon /mɒnˈsuːn/ *n* **1** a wind that blows in Southern Asia, from the SW in summer, from the NE in winter. **2** the rainy season caused by the SW monsoon.

monster /ˈmɒnstə(r)/ *n* **1** something of unusual size, form or appearance: *a prehistoric monster.* **2** a horrible creature that only exists in fairytales *etc*. **3** an evil person: *The man must be a monster to treat his children so badly!* — *adj* extremely large: *a monster potato.*

monstrous /ˈmɒnstrəs/ *adj* **1** huge; horrible. **2** shocking: *a monstrous lie.*

monˈstrosity *n* something large and ugly: *We think the monument is a monstrosity that spoils the town square.*

month /mʌnθ/ *n* one of the twelve divisions of the year: *January is the first month of the year.*

'monthly *adj* happening, or produced, once a month: *a monthly magazine.* — *adv* once a month: *Would you like to be paid weekly or monthly?*

monument /ˈmɒnjʊmənt/ *n* **1** something built in memory of a person or event: *They built* *a monument in his honour.* **2** any ancient building or structure that is historically important: *We must carefully preserve our national monuments.*

monu'mental *adj* very large; very important: *a monumental achievment.*

moo /muː/ *v* to make the sound of a cow. — *n* this sound.

mood /muːd/ *n* a person's feelings, temper *etc* at a particular time: *What kind of mood is she in today?*

'moody *adj* often bad-tempered. **'moodily** *adv.* **'moodiness** *n.*

moon /muːn/ *n* the heavenly body that moves round the earth: *The moon was shining brightly.*

moonlight /'muːnlaɪt/ *n* the light reflected by the moon.

moonlit /'muːnlɪt/ *adj* lit by the moon: *a moonlit hillside.*

moor¹ /mɔː(r)/ *n* a large stretch of open, unfarmed land with poor soil.

moor² /mɔː(r)/ *v* to fasten by a rope, cable or anchor: *We moored the yacht in the bay; They moored in the canal for the night.*

moose /muːs/, *plural* **moose**, *n* a type of large deer.

mop /mɒp/ *n* **1** a pad for washing floors, dishes *etc.* **2** a thick mass of hair. **3** an act of mopping: *He gave the floor a quick mop.* — *v* **1** to rub or wipe with a mop: *She mopped the kitchen floor.* **2** to wipe or clean: *He mopped his face.*

mop up to clean away using a mop *etc*: *He mopped up the mess with his handkerchief.*

mope /moʊp/ *v* to behave in a bored and depressed way, not wanting to do anything: *You should stop moping about the house and do something you enjoy.*

moped /'moʊpɛd/ *n* a light motorcycle that you can also pedal like a bicycle.

moral /'mɒrəl/ *adj* having to do with character or behaviour, especially right behaviour: *high moral standards; John is a very moral man.* — *n* **1** the lesson to be learned from something: *The moral of this story is that crime doesn't pay.* **2** (*plural*) beliefs about what is right and wrong: *Parents are responsible for their children's morals.*

'morally *adv*: *It would be morally wrong to accept money for a job I haven't done.*

mo'rality *n* whether something is right or wrong: *We had a discussion about the morality of killing animals for food.*

See **immoral**.

morale /məˈrɑːl/ *n* the level of courage and confidence in an army, team *etc*: *In spite of the defeat, morale was still high.*

morbid /'mɔːbɪd/ *adj* having or showing a strange interest in death or unpleasant things: *She must have a morbid imagination to write books like that.*

more /mɔː(r)/ *adj* **1** a greater number or quantity of something: *I've more pencils than he has.* **2** an additional number or quantity of something: *We need some more milk.* — *adv* **1** used to form the comparative of many adjectives and adverbs: *She can do it more easily than I can.* **2** to a greater extent: *I'm exercising more now than I used to.* **3** again: *Play it once more.* — *pron* **1** a greater number or quantity: *'Are there a lot of people?' 'There are more than we expected.'* **2** an additional number or amount: *We've run out of paint. Would you get some more?; We need more of the red paint.*

more than one is always followed by a singular verb: *More than one of the girls has already gone home.*

See also **many** and **much**.

more'over *adv* also; what is more important: *I don't like the idea, and moreover, I think it's illegal.*

any more any longer: *He doesn't go to church any more.*

more and more increasingly: *It's becoming more and more difficult to see without my spectacles.*

more or less about: *We live more or less ten minutes from town.*

the more ... the more *etc*: *The more I see her, the more I like her; The more I hear about New York, the less I want to go there.*

what's more used to add another fact: *He won the race and what's more, he broke the world record.*

morning /'mɔːnɪŋ/ *n* the part of the day up to noon.

moron /'mɔːrɒn/ *n* an unkind word for a very stupid person: *He doesn't understand anything — he's a real moron.*

morose /məˈroʊs/ *adj* angry and silent.

morphia /'mɔːfɪə/ or **morphine** /'mɔːfiːn/ *ns* a drug used to cause sleep or deaden pain.

Morse /mɔːs/ *n* a code for signalling and telegraphy, consisting of long and short signals.

morsel /'mɔːsəl/ *n* a small piece of something, especially food: *a morsel of fish.*

mortal /'mɔːtəl/ *adj* **1** unable to live for ever: *Man is mortal*. **2** having to do with death; causing death: *a mortal illness*; *mortal enemies*. — *n* a human being.

mor'tality *n* **1** the state of being mortal; the fact that people die: *Going to the funeral reminded him of his own mortality*. **2** the number of people that die in a certain period or place: *Infant mortality was much higher at the beginning of the century*.

'mortally *adv* in such a way as to cause death: *He has been mortally wounded*.

mortar /'mɔːtə(r)/ *n* **1** a mixture of cement, sand and water, used in building, to hold bricks in place. **2** a type of heavy gun: *the sound of mortar fire*.

mortar-board /'mɔːtəbɔːd/ *n* a university cap, with a square flat top.

mortgage /'mɔːgɪdʒ/ *n* a legal agreement by which a sum of money is lent for the purpose of buying buildings, land *etc*. — *v* to give someone the right to own your land, house *etc* in return for money that they are lending you.

mortuary /'mɔːtjʊərɪ/ *n* a building or room where dead bodies are kept before burial or cremation.

mosaic /moʊ'zeɪɪk/ *n* a design formed by fitting together small pieces of coloured marble, glass *etc*.

mosque /mɒsk/ *n* a Muslim place of worship.

mosquito /mɒ'skiːtoʊ/ *n* any of several types of small insect, which suck blood from animals and people.

moss /mɒs/ *n* a small flowerless plant, found in damp places, forming a soft green covering. **'mossy** *adj*.

most /moʊst/ *adj* **1** greatest number or quantity of: *Which of them has read the most books?*; *Who did the most work on this project?* **2** the majority or greater part of: *Most boys like playing football*. — *adv* **1** used to form the superlative of many adjectives and adverbs: *the most delicious cake I've ever tasted*; *Of all his family, John sees his mother most often*. **2** to the greatest degree or extent: *They like sweets and biscuits but they like ice-cream most of all*. **3** very; extremely: *a most annoying child*. — *pron* **1** the greatest number or quantity: *I ate two cakes, but Mary ate more, and John ate the most*. **2** the greatest part; the majority: *He'll be at home for most of the day*; *Most of these students speak English*.

> Most of the **eggs have** been eaten, but most of the **cheese has** been left.

See also **many** and **much**.

'mostly *adv* mainly: *The air we breathe is mostly nitrogen and oxygen*; *Mostly I go to the library rather than buy books*.

at the most taking the greatest estimate: *There were fifty people in the audience at the most*.

motel /moʊ'tɛl/ *n* a hotel with special units for accommodating motorists and their cars.

moth /mɒθ/ *n* any of a large number of insects seen mostly at night and attracted by light.

'mothball *n* a small ball made of a chemical used to protect clothes from moths.

'moth-eaten *adj* old and worn: *Her clothes always look moth-eaten*.

mother /'mʌðə(r)/ *n* a female parent: *John's mother is a widow*. — *adj*: *The mother bird feeds her young*. — *v* to care for someone like their mother would: *The women in the office always mother the boy who collects the post*.

'mother-country or **'motherland** *ns* the country where you were born.

'motherhood *n* being a mother: *Motherhood seemed to suit her*.

'mother-in-law, *plural* **'mothers-in-law**, *n* the mother of your husband or wife.

'motherless *adj* having no mother: *The children were left motherless by the accident*.

'motherly *adj* like a mother: *a motherly woman*; *motherly love*. **'motherliness** *n*.

'mother-tongue *n* your native language: *My mother-tongue is Hindi*.

motif /moʊ'tiːf/ *n* a shape or design that may be repeated to form a pattern.

motion /'moʊʃən/ *n* **1** the act of moving: *the motion of the planets*; *He lost the power of motion*. **2** a single movement or gesture: *He summoned the waiter with a motion of the hand*. **3** a suggestion that is discussed and voted on at a formal meeting. — *v* to make a movement or sign: *He motioned to her to come nearer*.

'motionless *adj* not moving.

motion picture a cinema film.

in motion moving: *Don't jump on the bus while it is in motion*.

motivate /'moʊtɪveɪt/ *v* **1** to cause someone to act in a particular way: *Most of them were motivated by greed*. **2** to make someone feel interested and enthusiastic: *a lively, young teacher who motivates her pupils*. **moti'vation** *n*.

motive /'moʊtɪv/ *n* something that makes a person choose to act in a particular way; a

motor

reason: *What was his motive for murdering the old lady?*

motor /'moʊtə(r)/ *n* a machine, usually a petrol engine or electrical device, that gives motion or power: *A washing-machine has an electric motor.* — *adj: a motor boat.* — *v* to travel by car: *We motored down to my mother's house at the weekend.*

  '**motorbike** or '**motorcycle** *n* a bicycle moved by a motor.

  motor car a four-wheeled vehicle, but not a lorry or van, moved by a motor.

  '**motorcyclist** *n* a person who rides a motorbike.

  '**motorist** *n* someone who drives a motor car.

  '**motorized** *adj* powered or operated by a motor.

  '**motorway** *n* a fast road for motor vehicles.

mottled /'mɒtəld/ *adj* covered with patches of different colours or shades: *mottled leaves*; *His face was red and mottled.*

motto /'mɒtoʊ/, *plural* '**mottoes**, *n* a short sentence or phrase that expresses a pinciple of behaviour *etc*: *'Honesty is the best policy' is my motto.*

mould¹ /moʊld/ *n* **1** soil that is full of rotted leaves *etc*. **2** green patches that form on stale food *etc. This bread is covered with mould because it has been kept too long.*

  '**mouldy** *adj* covered with mould: *mouldy cheese.* '**mouldiness** *n*.

mould² /moʊld/ *n* **1** a shape into which a substance in liquid form is poured so that it may take on that shape when it cools and hardens: *a jelly mould.* **2** something, especially a food, formed in a mould. — *v* **1** to form in a mould: *The gold is moulded into long bars.* **2** to shape something with your hands: *He moulded the clay into a ball.*

moult /moʊlt/ *v* to shed feathers, hair, a skin *etc*: *My budgerigars often moult.*

mound /maʊnd/ *n* **1** a small hill or heap of earth *etc*: *a grassy mound.* **2** a heap or pile of anything: *There's a mound of ironing to do.*

mount /maʊnt/ *v* **1** to climb up on to something: *He mounted the platform*; *She mounted the horse and rode off.* **2** to rise in level: *Prices are mounting quickly.* **3** to put something into a frame, or stick it on to card *etc*: *to mount a photo.* **4** to hang or put up on a stand, support *etc*: *He mounted the tiger's head on the wall.* **5** to organize: *to mount an exhibition*; *to mount an attack.* — *n* an animal that you ride, such as a horse or donkey.

  mount up to increase: *Our savings will soon mount up if we don't spend them.*

Mount /maʊnt/ *n* a name for a mountain: *Mount Everest.*

mountain /'maʊntɪn/ *n* a high hill: *Mount Everest is the highest mountain in the world.* — *adj: a mountain stream.*

  mountaineer /maʊntɪ'nɪə(r)/ *n* a person who climbs mountains as an occupation.

  mountai'neering *n* mountain-climbing.

  '**mountainous** *adj* full of mountains: *The country is very mountainous.*

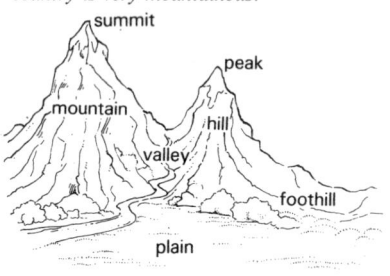

[Diagram of a mountain with labels: summit, peak, mountain, hill, valley, foothill, plain]

mounted /'maʊntɪd/ *adj* on horseback: *mounted policemen.*

mourn /mɔːn/ *v* to feel great sorrow; to grieve: *She mourned for her dead son.*

> to **mourn** (not **moan**) the death of a friend.

  '**mourner** *n*: *The mourners stood round the graveside.*

  '**mournful** *adj* very sad; showing sorrow: *Don't look so mournful*; *Her face had a mournful expression.* '**mournfully** *adv*.

  '**mourning** *n* grief shown for someone's death *etc*: *The family didn't want callers while they were in mourning.*

mouse /maʊs/, *plural* **mice** /maɪs/, *n* **1** a small furry gnawing animal with a long tail, found in houses and in fields. **2** a device attached to a computer, used for entering commands without using the keyboard.

> A mouse (sense **1**) **squeaks** or **squeals**.

  '**mousetrap** *n* a mechanical trap for a mouse.

mousse /muːs/ *n* **1** a cold dish, usually sweet, that is made with whipped cream and eggs: *We had chocolate mousse for dessert.* **2** a kind of foam for putting on your hair to make it easier to style.

moustache /mə'stɑːʃ/ *n* the hair on the upper lip of a man: *He has a moustache.*

> See **beard**.

mousy /'maʊsɪ/ *adj* **1** dull brown in colour: *He had mousy hair.* **2** timid; not interesting: *a mousy person.*

mouth *n* /maʊθ/, *plural* **mouths** /maʊðz/ **1** the opening in the head by which a human or animal eats and speaks or makes noises: *What's in your mouth?* **2** the opening or entrance to something: *the mouth of the harbour.* — *v* /maʊð/ to move your lips to form words, but make no sound.

'mouthful *n* as much as fills your mouth: *I swallowed the last mouthful of chocolate cake.*

'mouthorgan *n* a small musical instrument played by blowing or sucking air through its metal pipes; a harmonica.

'mouthpiece *n* the part of a musical instrument or telephone *etc* that is put into or held near the mouth: *When you are talking on the telephone, speak clearly into the mouthpiece and don't put your hand over it.*

'mouthwash *n* an antiseptic liquid used for cleaning out your mouth.

'mouth-watering *adj* looking or smelling delicious or tempting: *That cake looks mouth-watering.*

move /muːv/ *v* **1** to cause to change position; to go from one place to another: *He moved his arm; Please move your car.* **2** to change houses: *We're moving on Saturday.* **3** to affect the feelings of someone: *I was moved by the film.* — *n* **1** a change of position: *He was watching every move she made.* **2** the moving of a piece in a board-game such as chess: *You can win this game in three moves.* **3** a change to another home: *How did your move go?* **movable** or **moveable** /'muːvəbəl/ *adj.*

'movement *n* **1** a change of position: *The animal turned with a swift movement.* **2** activity: *He stood at the door listening for any movement.* **3** the art of moving gracefully: *She teaches movement and drama.* **4** an organization; an association: *the Scout movement.*

movie /'muːvɪ/ *n* a moving film: *a horror movie.*

> **the movies** means the cinema, or films in general: *We often go to the movies.*

'moving *adj* having an effect on your feelings: *a moving speech.* **'movingly** *adv.*

move along to keep moving: *Move along now!*

move house to change your home: *They're moving house today.*

> to **move** (not **remove**) **house**.

move in to go into and occupy a house *etc*: *We can move in on Saturday.*

move off to begin moving away: *The bus moved off as I got to the bus stop.*

move out to leave a house *etc*: *She has to move out before the new owners arrive.*

move up to move so as to make more space: *Move up and let me sit down.*

on the move 1 moving from place to place: *The circus is always on the move.* **2** advancing; making progress.

mow /moʊ/ *v* to cut with a scythe or mower: *He mowed the lawn.*

> **mow; mowed; mown**: *She mowed the grass; The grass has been mown.*

'mower *n* a machine for cutting grass.

harvest / reap

trim

mow

Mr /'mɪstə(r)/ *n* a title given to a man: *Good morning, Mr Black; Ask Mr White.*

Mrs /'mɪsɪz/ *n* a title given to a married woman: *Come in, Mrs Green; Where is Mrs Brown?*

Ms /mɪz/ *n* a title for a woman whether married or unmarried, used in writing: *The letter is addressed to Ms Scarlet.*

much /mʌtʃ/ *adj* a great amount; a certain amount: *This job won't take much effort; How much sugar is there left?; There's far too much salt in my soup.* — *pron* a large amount: *He didn't say much about it; Did you eat much?; not much; too much; as much as I wanted; You haven't drunk much of the wine; How much does this fish cost?; How much is that fish?* — *adv* **1** a great deal: *She's much prettier than I am; much more easily.* **2** greatly; a lot: *He will be much missed; We don't see her much; I thanked her very much; much too late; I've much too much to do; The accident was as much my*

muck

fault as his; *Much to my dismay, she began to cry.*

> **much; more; most**: *I didn't eat much cake*; *George ate more, and Anne ate most of all.*
> See also **many**.

much the same not very different: *His condition is much the same as it was yesterday.*

nothing much nothing important: *'What are you doing?' 'Nothing much'.*

not much not impressive: *My car isn't much to look at but it's fast.*

think too much of to have too high an opinion of someone: *He thinks too much of himself.*

too much for too difficult for someone: *Is this job too much for you?*

muck /mʌk/ *n* **1** dung, filth, rubbish etc: *farmyard muck*. **2** dirt.

'**mucky** *adj* very dirty: *Your face and hands are mucky.*

muck up to do something badly: *She thinks she's mucked her exam up.*

mucus /'mju:kəs/ *n* the fluid from your nose.

mud /mʌd/ *n* wet soft earth.

'**muddy** *adj* covered with mud, or containing mud: *muddy boots*; *muddy water*. — *v* to make something muddy: *You've muddied the floor!*

> **mud** is never used in the plural.

muddle /'mʌdəl/ or **muddle up** *v* to confuse; to mix up: *Don't talk while I'm counting, or you'll muddle me*; *The books on this shelf have all been muddled up.* — *n* a state of confusion: *These papers keep getting in a muddle.*

'**muddled** *adj*: *muddled thinking.*

'**muddle-headed** *adj* not capable of clear thinking: *John is too muddle-headed to look after the club's money.*

mudguard /'mʌdgɑ:d/ *n* the piece of metal or plastic that covers a wheel to stop mud and water from splashing up.

muezzin /mu:'ɛzɪn/ *n* an official at a mosque who calls people to prayer.

muffin /'mʌfɪn/ *n* a round, flat cake eaten hot with butter.

muffle /'mʌfəl/ *v* to deaden the sound of something: *The snow muffled his footsteps.*

mug[1] /mʌg/ *n* a cup with tall sides: *a mug of coffee.*

'**mugful** *n*: *two mugfuls of coffee.*

mug[2] /mʌg/ *n* a slang word for the face.

mug[3] /mʌg/ *v* to attack and rob someone: *He was mugged on his way home last night.*

'**mugger** *n* a person who attacks others in this way.

'**mugging** *n* an occasion when someone is mugged.

mulberry /'mʌlbərɪ/ *n* **1** a tree on whose leaves silkworms feed. **2** its fruit.

mule /mju:l/ *n* an animal whose parents are a horse and an ass.

mull /mʌl/: **mull over** to think about carefully: *He mulled the plans over in his mind.*

mullet /'mʌlɪt/ *n* an edible fish.

multicoloured /'mʌltɪkʌləd/ *adj* having many colours: *a multicoloured shirt.*

multimillionaire /mʌltɪmɪljə'nɛə(r)/ *n* someone who has wealth valued at several million pounds, dollars *etc.*

multinational /mʌltɪ'naʃənəl/ *n* a company with branches in several different countries: *This oil company is a multinational.*

multiple /'mʌltɪpəl/ *adj* **1** many: *She suffered multiple injuries when she fell out of the window.* **2** involving many things of the same sort: *Fifteen vehicles were involved in the multiple crash on the motorway.* — *n* a number that contains another number an exact number of times: *65 is a multiple of 5.*

multiple-'choice *adj* showing several possible answers from which you must choose: *a multiple-choice test.*

multiply /'mʌltɪplaɪ/ *v* **1** to add a number to itself a given number of times and find the total: $4+4+4$, or 4 multiplied by 3, or $4^3 = 12$. **2** to increase in number: *Rabbits multiply very rapidly.*

multipli'cation *n* the multiplying of numbers.

multiracial /mʌltɪ'reɪʃəl/ *adj* including people of many races: *Britain is a multiracial society.*

multi-storey or **multi-story** /mʌltɪ'stɔ:rɪ/ *adj* having many floors or storeys: *a multi-storey car park.*

multitude /'mʌltɪtju:d/ *n* a very large number of people or things: *a multitude of people*; *I didn't want to see her, for a multitude of reasons.*

mum /mʌm/ *n* a name used by children for their mother: *Goodbye, Mum!*

mumble /'mʌmbəl/ *v* to speak so that the words are difficult to hear: *The old man mumbled a few words to himself.*

mummy[1] /'mʌmɪ/ *n* a name used by small children for their mother: *Where's my mummy?*; *Hallo, Mummy!*

mummy² /'mʌmɪ/ *n* a dead body preserved by being wrapped in bandages and treated with spice, wax *etc.*

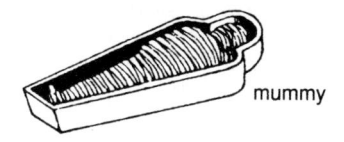

mumps /mʌmps/ *n* an infectious disease causing painful swelling at the sides of your neck and face.

> **mumps** is always in the plural form, but takes a singular verb: *Mumps is a painful illness.*

munch /mʌntʃ/ *v* to chew something with your lips closed: *He was munching his breakfast.*

mundane /mʌn'deɪn/ *adj* ordinary or dull: *a mundane job.*

municipal /mjʊ'nɪsɪpəl/ *adj* of or relating to the local government of a town or region: *There will be municipal elections next month to elect the new town councillors.*

mural /'mjʊərəl/ *n* a painting that is painted directly on to a wall.

murder /'mɜːdə(r)/ *n* **1** the deliberate and illegal killing of someone: *The police are treating his death as murder.* **2** any killing or causing of death that is considered as bad as this: *the murder of innocent people by terrorists.* — *v* to kill someone deliberately and illegally.

'**murderer** *n*: *Murderers are no longer hanged in Britain.*

'**murderess** *n* a woman who is a murderer.

'**murderous** *adj* intending murder: *There was a murderous look in his eye.* '**murderously** *adv.*

murky /'mɜːkɪ/ *adj* dark and gloomy: *deep trenches filled with murky water.*

murmur /'mɜːmə(r)/ *n* a quiet low sound, of voices *etc*: *There was a low murmur among the crowd.* — *v* to make this sound: *The child murmured something in his sleep.* '**murmuring** *adj.*

muscle /'mʌsəl/ *n* any of the bundles of fibres in your body which cause movement: *He has well-developed muscles in his arms.*

'**muscular** *adj* **1** having to do with muscles: *great muscular strength.* **2** having well-developed muscles; strong: *She is tall and muscular.*

museum /mjuː'zɪəm/ *n* a place where collections of things of interest are set out for people to see.

musk /mʌsk/ *n* a substance with a strong, sweet smell, used in making perfume: *She doesn't like perfumes which smell heavily of musk.*

mush /mʌʃ/ *n* something soft and wet: *Babies like to eat mush.* '**mushy** *adj.*

mushroom /'mʌʃrʊm/ *n* an edible fungus. — *v* to grow in size very rapidly: *The town has mushroomed recently.*

music /'mjuːzɪk/ *n* **1** the art of arranging and combining sounds able to be produced by the human voice or instruments: *She is studying music.* **2** the written or printed form of these sounds: *The pianist has forgotten her music.* — *adj*: *a music lesson.*

> **music** is not used in the plural: *This composer has written a lot of choral music.*

musical /'mjuːzɪkəl/ *adj* **1** having to do with music: *a musical instrument.* **2** like music: *a musical voice.* **3** having a talent for music: *Their children are musical.* — *n* a film or play that includes a large amount of singing and dancing. '**musically** *adv.*

musician /mjuː'zɪʃən/ *n* **1** a person who is skilled in music: *The conductor of this orchestra is a fine musician.* **2** someone who plays a musical instrument.

Muslim /'mʊzlɪm/ *n* a person of the religion known as Islam.

mussel /'mʌsəl/ *n* an edible shellfish.

must /mʌst/ *v* **1** used with another verb to express need: *We must go to the shops.* **2** used to suggest a probability: *They must be finding it very difficult to live in such a small house.* **3** used to express duty, an order, rule *etc*: *You must come home before midnight.* — *n* something necessary; something not to be missed: *This new tent is a must for the serious camper.*

> **must not** or **mustn't** /'mʌsənt/: *You mustn't do that again*; *You must hurry, mustn't you?*

mustard /'mʌstəd/ *n* a seasoning made from the seeds of the mustard plant.

muster /'mʌstə(r)/ *v* **1** to gather together for a reason: *The soldiers mustered for duty.* **2** to gather: *He mustered his energy for a final effort.*

mustn't short for **must not**.

musty /'mʌstɪ/ *adj* damp or stale in smell or taste: *musty old books*.

mutate /mju:'teɪt/ *v* to change or develop in a different way: *This flu virus can mutate to become resistant to vaccine*.

mute /mju:t/ *adj* **1** unable to speak; dumb. **2** silent: *She gazed at him in mute horror*.

muted /'mju:tɪd/ *adj* not bright or loud: *muted colours*.

mutilate /'mju:tɪleɪt/ *v* to damage very badly: *the mutilated bodies of the bomb victims*. **muti'lation** *n*.

mutiny /'mju:tɪnɪ/ *n* refusal to obey your senior officers in the navy or other armed services: *There has been a mutiny on HMS Tigress*. — *v* to refuse to obey commands from those in authority: *The sailors mutinied because they did not have enough food*.

mutter /'mʌtə(r)/ *v* to say words in a quiet voice especially when grumbling: *She muttered something under her breath*. — *n* this sound: *He spoke in a mutter*.

mutton /'mʌtən/ *n* the flesh of sheep, used as food.

mutual /'mju:tʃʊəl/ *adj* **1** given by people to one another: *mutual help*. **2** shared by two or more people *etc*: *a mutual friend*.

muzzle /'mʌzəl/ *n* **1** the jaws and nose of an animal such as a dog. **2** an arrangement of straps round the muzzle of an animal to stop it biting. — *v She muzzled the dog*.

my /maɪ/ *adj* belonging to me: *That is my book*. — a cry used to express surprise: *My, how you've grown!*

See also **mine**[1].

myself /maɪ'sɛlf/ *pron* **1** (used as the object of a verb or preposition) the word you use when you yourself are both the subject and the object: *I cut myself while shaving*. **2** used to emphasize **I** or **me**: *I myself can't tell you, but my friend will*; *I don't intend to go myself*. **3** without help: *I did it myself*.

mynah /'maɪnə/ *n* a tropical bird that can mimic human speech.

myriad /'mɪrɪəd/ *n* a large number of people or things: *myriads of stars in the sky*.

mystery /'mɪstərɪ/ *n* **1** something that cannot be, or has not been, explained: *the mystery of how the universe was formed*; *How she passed her exam is a mystery to me*. **2** obscurity; secrecy: *Her death was surrounded by mystery*.

mysterious /mɪ'stɪərɪəs/ *adj* difficult to understand or explain; full of mystery: *mysterious happenings*; *He's being very mysterious about what his work is*. **my'steriously** *adv*.

mysticism /'mɪstɪsɪzm/ *n* a religious practice in which people try to get closer to God through prayer and meditation: *He practises a form of Christian mysticism*.

mystify /'mɪstɪfaɪ/ *v* to make someone very puzzled: *Her sudden disappearance mystified her family*; *The children were completely mystified by the teacher's strange question*.

myth /mɪθ/ *n* an ancient story, especially one dealing with gods, heroes *etc*.

mythical /'mɪθɪkəl/ *adj* existing only in stories; not real: *a mythical prince*.

mythology /mɪ'θɒlədʒɪ/ *n* ancient myths in general: *characters from Greek mythology*.

N

nab /nab/ v to take something; to catch or get hold of someone: *The police nabbed the thief.*

nadir /'neɪdɪə(r)/ n the lowest point: *the nadir of despair.*

nag /nag/ v to complain or criticize continually: *She nags her husband about their lack of money; My parents are always nagging at me to do my homework.*

'nagging adj continuously troublesome: *a nagging pain.*

nail /neɪl/ n **1** a piece of horn-like substance that grows over the ends of your fingers and toes: *I've broken my nail; toe-nails; Don't bite your finger-nails.* **2** a thin pointed piece of metal used to fasten pieces of wood together *etc*: *He hammered a nail into the wall and hung a picture on it.* — v to fasten with nails: *He nailed the picture to the wall.*

'nail-file n a small instrument with a rough surface, used for smoothing or shaping the edges of your fingernails.

naïve or **naive** /naɪ'iːv/ adj **1** simple and straightforward in your way of thinking, speaking *etc*: *a naïve assumption.* **2** ignorant; simple: *a naïve young girl.* **na'ïvely** adv. **na'ïvety** n.

naked /'neɪkɪd/ adj **1** without clothes: *a naked child.* **2** not hidden: *the naked truth.* **3** uncovered or unprotected: *Naked flames are dangerous.* **'nakedly** adv. **'nakedness** n.

the naked eye the eye by itself, without the help of any artificial means such as a telescope, microscope *etc*: *Germs are too small to be seen by the naked eye.*

name /neɪm/ n **1** a word by which a person, place or thing is called: *My name is Rachel.* **2** reputation; fame: *He has a name for honesty.* — v **1** to give a name to someone or something: *They named the child Thomas.* **2** to speak of or list by name: *He could name all the kings of England.* **3** to suggest a date or price: *They haven't named the date for their wedding yet.*

'nameless adj not mentioned by name: *The person who gave me the information must remain nameless.*

'namely adv that is: *Only one student passed the exam, namely John.*

'namesake n a person with the same name as yourself: *She invited John Smith and his namesake, the other John Smith.*

by name using a person's name: *The headmaster knows every pupil by name.*

in the name of for the sake of; for this reason: *They acted in the name of their country.*

make a name for yourself or **make your name** to become famous, get a reputation: *He made a name for himself as a concert pianist; She wanted to make her name in politics.*

name after to give a child or a thing the name of another person: *Peter was named after his father; George Street was named after King George IV.*

nanny /'nanɪ/ n a children's nurse.

nanny-goat /'nanɪgəʊt/ n a female goat.

nap /nap/ n a short sleep. — v.

nape /neɪp/ n the back of your neck: *His hair curled over the nape of his neck.*

napkin /'napkɪn/ n **1** a small piece of cloth or paper for protecting your clothes at mealtimes, and for wiping your lips — also called a **table napkin**. **2** the full form of **nappy**.

nappy /'napɪ/ n a piece of cloth or paper put between a baby's legs to soak up urine *etc*.

narcotic /nɑː'kɒtɪk/ n a drug that stops pain and makes you sleepy: *Morphine and opium are narcotics.*

narrate /nə'reɪt/ v to tell a story: *He narrated the events of the afternoon.* **nar'ration** n.

narrative /'narətɪv/ n a story.

nar'rator n someone who tells a story.

narrow /'narəʊ/ adj **1** not wide; being only a small distance from side to side: *The bridge is too narrow for large trucks to use.* **2** only just managed: *a narrow escape.* **3** not extensive enough: *John has narrow views about teaching.* — v to make or become narrow: *The road suddenly narrowed.*

'narrowly adv closely; only just: *The ball narrowly missed his head.* **'narrowness** n.

narrow-'minded adj unwilling to accept ideas different from your own.

narrow down to reduce or limit a large number of choices or possibilities: *We've narrowed down the list of applicants to the five who will be interviewed.*

nasal /'neɪzəl/ adj **1** having to do with your

nose: *a nasal infection.* **2** sounding through the nose: *a nasal voice.*

nasty /'nɑːstɪ/ *adj* **1** unpleasant: *What nasty weather!*; *a nasty smell.* **2** unfriendly; rude; mean: *The man was nasty to me*; *He has a nasty temper.* **3** serious; bad: *The dog gave her a nasty bite.* **'nastily** *adv.* **'nastiness** *n.*

nation /'neɪʃən/ *n* **1** the people who live in a particular country: *the Swedish nation.* **2** a large number of people who may be scattered in different countries, who share the same history, ancestors, culture *etc*: *the Jewish nation.*

national /'naʃnəl/ or /'naʃənəl/ *adj* having to do with a particular nation: *Many countries have a national health service.* **'nationally** *adv.*

'nationalism *n* **1** great pride in your own nation: *International football matches bring out a strong feeling of nationalism in football supporters.* **2** the desire to bring the people of a nation together under their own government: *Scottish nationalism.*

'nationalist *adj* having to do with the desire to bring the people of a nation together under their own government: *The Nationalist Party won the local election.* — *n* a person who believes in nationalism.

nationa'listic *adj* having to do with great pride in your own nation: *nationalistic feelings.*

nationality /naʃə'nalɪtɪ/ *n* membership of a particular nation: *'What nationality are you?' 'I'm German.'*

'nationalize *v* to make an industry or company the property of the state: *The railways in Britain were nationalized in 1947.* **nationali'zation** *n.*

national anthem a nation's official song or hymn.

national service in some countries, a period in the armed forces that all young men must serve.

nation'wide *adj, adv* throughout the whole nation: *a nationwide broadcast*; *They travelled nationwide.*

native /'neɪtɪv/ *adj* **1** where you were born: *my native land.* **2** belonging to that place: *my native language.* **3** belonging by race to a country: *a native Englishman.* — *n* **1** someone born in a certain place: *a native of Scotland*; *a native of London.* **2** one of the first inhabitants of a country: *Columbus thought the natives of America were Indians.*

natural /'natʃrəl/ or /'natʃərəl/ *adj* **1** made by nature; not made by men: *Coal and oil are natural resources*; *Wild animals are happier in their natural state than in a zoo.* **2** born in someone; not artificial or learned: *natural beauty*; *He had a natural ability for music.* **3** simple; without pretence: *a nice, natural smile.* **4** normal; as you would expect: *It's quite natural to dislike going to the dentist.* — *n* **1** a person who is naturally good at something. **2** in music, a note that is neither sharp nor flat.

natural gas gas suitable for burning, found underground or under the sea.

natural history the study of plants and animals.

naturalist /'natʃrəlɪst/ *n* a person who studies plants and animals.

naturalize /'natʃrəlaɪz/ *v* to make someone a citizen of a country that he or she was not born in: *Mr Singh is a naturalized Australian.*

'naturally *adv* **1** of course: *Naturally, I didn't want to miss the train.* **2** by nature: *She is naturally kind.* **3** normally; in a relaxed way: *Although he was nervous, he behaved quite naturally.*

natural resources sources of energy, wealth *etc* which are not made by man: *Coal and oil are natural resources.*

nature /'neɪtʃə(r)/ *n* **1** the world untouched by man; the power which made it: *the beauty of nature*; *the forces of nature*; *the study of nature.* **2** personality: *She has a generous nature.* **3** quality; what something is or consists of: *What is the nature of your work?*

-'natured having a certain type of personality: *good-natured*; *ill-natured.*

naught /nɔːt/ *n* nothing.

naughty /'nɔːtɪ/ *adj* badly-behaved: *a naughty boy.* **'naughtily** *adv.* **'naughtiness** *n.*

nausea /'nɔːzɪə/ *n* a feeling of sickness.

nauseating /'nɔːzɪeɪtɪŋ/ *adj* **1** sickening: *a nauseating smell.* **2** disgusting; offensive: *nauseating behaviour.*

nautical /'nɔːtɪkəl/ *adj* having to do with ships or sailors: *a nautical expression*; *a nautical cap.*

naval /'neɪvəl/ *adj* of the navy: *a naval officer.*

nave /neɪv/ *n* the main part of a church, where people sit.

navel /'neɪvəl/ *n* the small hollow in the belly, just below the middle of your waist.

navigate /'navɪgeɪt/ *v* **1** to direct, guide or move something in a particular direction: *He navigated the ship past the dangerous rocks.* **2** to find or follow your route when in a vehicle: *If I drive, will you navigate?*

navi'gation *n* the art of navigating.

'navigator *n* someone who navigates.

navy /'neɪvɪ/ *n* **1** a country's warships and the people who work in and with them: *He wanted to join the navy when he left school.* **2** a dark blue colour. — *adj* of this colour: *a navy jersey.*

near /nɪə(r)/ *adj* **1** close in place or time: *The station is quite near; The exams are too near for comfort.* **2** close in relationship: *He is a near relation.* — *adv* **1** at a short distance from somewhere: *He lives quite near.* **2** close to: *Don't sit too near to the window.* — *prep* at a very small distance from: *She lives near the church; It was near midnight when they arrived.* — *v* to come near to: *The roads became busier as they neared the town.* **'nearness** *n*.

nearby /nɪə'baɪ/ *adv* close: *He lives nearby; a cottage with a stream running nearby.* — *adj*: *We stopped at a nearby village for lunch.*

nearly /'nɪəlɪ/ *adv* not far from; almost: *nearly one o'clock.*

near miss something not quite achieved or only just avoided: *She's had two accidents in her car and three near misses.*

near-sighted /nɪə'saɪtɪd/ *adj* short-sighted.

not nearly far from: *I tried on a size 8 but it wasn't nearly big enough.*

neat /niːt/ *adj* **1** tidy: *She is very neat and tidy.* **2** skilfully done: *He has made a neat job of the repair.* **'neatness** *n*.

'neatly *adv* tidily; skilfully: *Write neatly!*

nebulous /'nɛbjʊləs/ *adj* vague or hazy: *These plans are only nebulous.*

necessary /'nɛsəsərɪ/ *adj* needed; essential: *Is it necessary to sign your name?* **necessarily** /nɛsə'sərɪlɪ/ or /nɛsə'sɛrɪlɪ/ *adv*.

necessitate /nɪ'sɛsɪteɪt/ *v* to make necessary: *This development necessitates immediate action.*

necessity /nɪ'sɛsɪtɪ/ *n* something needed; something essential: *Food is one of the necessities of life; There is no necessity for such haste.*

neck /nɛk/ *n* **1** the part of your body between your head and chest: *She wore a scarf round her neck.* **2** the part of a garment that covers that part of the body: *The neck of that shirt is dirty.* **3** anything like a neck in shape or position: *the neck of a bottle.*

necklace /'nɛkləs/ *n* a string of jewels, beads *etc* worn round the neck: *a diamond necklace.*

'necktie *n* a man's tie.

neck and neck exactly equal: *The horses were neck and neck at the finish.*

up to your neck deeply involved: *I can't see you today because I'm up to my neck in paperwork.*

nectar /'nɛktə(r)/ *n* **1** the sweet liquid collected by bees to make honey. **2** a delicious drink.

need /niːd/ *v* **1** to require: *This page needs to be checked; This page needs checking.* **2** to have to: *You need to work if you want to succeed; They don't need to come until six o'clock.* — *n* **1** something necessary; something you must have: *Food is one of our basic needs.* **2** a reason: *There is no need for panic.*

> **need not** or **needn't** /'niːdənt/: *You needn't do exercises 4 and 5 if you're short of time.*

needle /'niːdəl/ *n* **1** a small, sharp piece of steel with a hole for thread: *a sewing needle.* **2** any of various instruments of a long narrow pointed shape: *a knitting-needle; a hypodermic needle.* **3** a moving pointer: *the needle of a compass.*

needless /'niːdləs/ *adj* unnecessary: *a needless fuss.* **'needlessly** *adv*.

needless to say of course: *Needless to say, the little girl couldn't move the wardrobe on her own.*

needlework /'niːdəlwɜːk/ *n* work done with a needle; sewing, embroidery *etc*.

needn't short for **need not**.

needy /'niːdɪ/ *adj* poor: *We must help needy people.*

negative /'nɛɡətɪv/ *adj* **1** meaning or saying 'no'; denying something: *a negative answer.* **2** without enthusiasm; only considering the bad qualities of something: *He seems to have a very negative attitude towards his work at the moment.* **3** less than zero: *−4 is a negative or minus number.* — *n* **1** a word by which something is denied: *'No' and 'never' are negatives.* **2** the photographic film from which prints are made: *I gave away the print, but I still have the negative.* **'negatively** *adv*.

> The opposite of **negative** is **positive**.

neglect /nɪ'ɡlɛkt/ *v* **1** to treat someone or something carelessly; to give too little attention to something: *He neglected his work.* **2** to fail to do something: *He neglected to answer the letter.* — *n* lack of care and attention: *The garden is suffering from neglect.*

negligence /ˈnɛglɪdʒəns/ *n* not giving the proper amount of care and attention: *She was accused of professional negligence.* **'negligent** *adj*.

negligible /ˈnɛglɪdʒəbəl/ *adj* too small or not important enough to be considered: *The amount of rainfall in the desert is negligible.*

negotiate /nɪˈgoʊʃieɪt/ *v* to bargain or discuss a subject in order to agree: *He negotiated a good price with the supplier.* **neˈgotiator** *n*.
negotiˈation *n*: *The disagreement was settled by negotiation.*

Negro /ˈniːgroʊ/ *n* (*offensive*) a person belonging to, or descended from, the black-skinned races of Africa.
Negress /ˈniːgrɪs/ *n* a woman of this race.

neigh /neɪ/ *v* to make the cry of a horse: *The horse neighed in fright.* — *n*: *The horse gave a neigh.*

neighbour /ˈneɪbə(r)/ *n* someone who lives near you: *my next-door neighbour.*
'neighbourhood *n* **1** a district, especially in a town or city: *a poor neighbourhood.* **2** an area surrounding a particular place: *He lives somewhere in the neighbourhood of the station.*
'neighbouring *adj* near together; next to each other: *France and Belgium are neighbouring countries.*
'neighbourly *adj* friendly or willing to give help: *It was very neighbourly of you to offer to help.*

neither /ˈnaɪðə(r)/ or /ˈniːðə(r)/ *adj, pron* not the one nor the other of two: *Neither window faces the sea*; *Neither of the twins is good at mathematics.*
neither...nor used to introduce alternatives that are both negative: *Neither John nor David could come*; *He can neither read nor write.*

> She knows **neither of us** (not She doesn't know **both of us**); She knows **both of us** is correct.
>
> As with **either ... or**, the verb usually follows the noun or pronoun that comes closest to it: *Neither she nor her children speak English*; *Neither the twins nor Jeremy was at home.*

neolithic /niːəˈlɪθɪk/ *adj* of or belonging to the period when people started to make and use stone tools: *There are neolithic paintings on the walls of some caves.*

neon /ˈniːɒn/ *n* a colourless gas used in certain forms of electric lighting, such as advertising signs.

nephew /ˈnɛfjuː/ *n* the son of your brother or sister.

> The son of your brother or sister is your **nephew**.
>
> The daughter of your brother or sister is your **niece**.

nerve /nɜːv/ *n* **1** one of the cords that carry messages between all parts of your body and your brain. **2** courage: *He must have needed a lot of nerve to do that*; *He lost his nerve.*
nerve-racking /ˈnɜːvrækɪŋ/ *adj* making you very anxious or worried: *The first five minutes in the air were pretty nerve-racking.*
nerves *n* a nervous or anxious state: *He thought a brandy might calm his nerves.*
nervous /ˈnɜːvəs/ *adj* **1** having to do with your nerves: *the nervous system.* **2** rather afraid: *a nervous old lady.* **'nervously** *adv*. **'nervousness** *n*.
nervous system the brain and nerves of a person or animal.
get on someone's nerves to irritate someone: *John really gets on my nerves.*

nest /nɛst/ *n* the home that birds and some animals and insects build, in which to hatch or give birth to and look after their babies: *a wasp's nest*; *The swallows are building a nest under the roof of our house.* — *v* to build a nest and live in it: *A pair of robins are nesting in that bush.*
'nest-egg *n* a sum of money saved up for the future.

nestle /ˈnɛsəl/ *v* **1** to lie close together as if in a nest: *They nestled together for warmth.* **2** to settle comfortably: *She nestled down amongst the cushions.*

net¹ /nɛt/ *n* a loose open material made of knotted string, thread, wire *etc*; an object made of this: *a fishing-net*; *a hair-net*; *a tennis-net.* — *adj*: *a net curtain.* — *v* to catch in a net: *They netted several tons of fish.*

net² or **nett** /nɛt/ *adj* **1** remaining after all expenses have been paid: *The net profit from the sale was £200.* **2** not including the packaging or container: *The sugar has a net weight of 1 kilo*; *The sugar weighs one kilo net.*

netball /ˈnɛtbɔːl/ *n* a team-game in which you try to throw the ball into a net hanging high up on a pole.

nett another spelling of **net**².

netting /ˈnɛtɪŋ/ *n* material made in the form of a net: *wire netting.*

nettle /'nɛtəl/ n a plant covered with hairs that sting when touched: *There are a lot of nettles growing wild in that field.*

network /'nɛtwɜːk/ n a system with lots of branches and connections: *A network of roads covered the countryside*; *a radio network*; *The information will be transferred to each computer on the network.*

neurology /njʊ'rɒlədʒɪ/ n the study of the structure and diseases of the nervous system. **neu'rologist** n.

neurotic /'njʊ'rɒtɪk/ adj more worried than it is sensible or reasonable to be: *I know you are worried about your children but it won't help to get neurotic.*

neutral /'njuːtrəl/ adj 1 taking no part in a quarrel or war: *A neutral observer settled the argument.* 2 not strong or definite in colour: *Grey is a neutral colour.* — n The position that the gears of a car, *etc* are in when no power is connected to the wheels: *Put the car in neutral and turn the key in the ignition.*

neutralize /'njuːtrəlaɪz/ v to stop something having an effect; to make something useless: *The doctor gave him an injection that neutralized the snake poison.*

never /'nɛvə(r)/ adv not ever; at no time: *I shall never go there again.*

never-'ending adj lasting a very long time: *The war seemed to be never-ending.*

nevertheless /nɛvəðə'lɛs/ adv in spite of that: *I am feeling ill, but I shall come with you nevertheless.*

new /'njuː/ adj 1 only just built, made, bought etc: *She is wearing a new dress*; *We are building a new house.* 2 not done before: *Flying in an aeroplane was a new experience for her.* 3 changed: *He is a new man.* 4 just arrived *etc*: *The schoolchildren teased the new boy*; *Is your teacher new?* — adv freshly: *new-laid eggs.* **'newness** n.

newcomer /'njuːkʌmə(r)/ n a person who has just arrived: *He is a newcomer to this district.*

'newly adv recently: *She is newly married*; *Her hair is newly cut.*

new to having no previous experience of something: *He's new to this kind of work.*

news /njuːz/ n 1 a report about recent events: *You can hear the news at 9 o'clock.* 2 information: *Is there any news of your friend?* — adj: *a news broadcast.*

news is singular: *The news is good.*

'newsagent n someone who has a shop selling newspapers and other goods.

'newscaster n a person who presents a news broadcast.

'newsflash n a brief announcement of important news during a television or radio programme: *We interrupt this programme to bring you a newsflash.*

'newsletter n a sheet containing news about a group, organization *etc*.

newspaper /'njuːspeɪpə(r)/ n a paper, printed daily or weekly, containing news.

'newsroom n 1 an office where news reports are prepared for printing in a newspaper: *The reporters write their articles in the newsroom.* 2 a radio or television studio used for broadcasting news: *The president was interviewed in the newsroom.*

'newsvendor n a person who sells newspapers.

'newsworthy adj interesting or important enough to be reported as news: *The accident was not thought to be newsworthy.*

newt /njuːt/ n a small animal which lives on land and in water.

newt

next /nɛkst/ adj nearest; immediately following: *When you have called at that house, go on to the next one*; *The next person to arrive late will be sent away.* — adv immediately after, in place or time: *John arrived first and Jane came next.* — pron the person or thing nearest in place, time *etc*: *Finish one question before you begin to answer the next.*

next door adv in the next house: *I live next door to Mrs Smith.*

next but one not the next one, but the one after: *His name is next but one on the waiting list.*

next to 1 beside: *She sat next to me.* 2 closest to: *In height, George comes next to me.*

next to nothing almost nothing: *I know next to nothing about art.*

nib /nɪb/ n the part of a pen from which the ink flows.

-nibbed: *a fine-nibbed pen.*

nibble /'nɪbəl/ v to take very small bites of something: *She nibbled a biscuit.* — n: *I was only having a nibble.*

nice /naɪs/ adj 1 pleasant: *nice weather*; *a nice*

person. **2** used jokingly: *We're in a nice mess now.* **3** exact: *a nice sense of timing.* **'nicely** *adv.*

niche /niːʃ/ *n* a hollow in a wall for a statue, ornament *etc*.

nick /nɪk/ *n* a small cut: *He cut a few small nicks in the canvas.* — *v* to make a small cut in something: *He nicked his chin while he was shaving.*

in the nick of time just in time: *He arrived in the nick of time.*

nickel /ˈnɪkəl/ *n* **1** a greyish-white metal, often mixed with other metals. **2** a coin worth five cents in America or Canada.

nickname /ˈnɪkneɪm/ *n* a special, usually joking, name for someone or something: *Napoleon Bonaparte's nickname was 'Boney'.* — *v* to give a nickname to someone or something: *We nicknamed him 'Four-eyes' because he wore spectacles.*

nicotine /ˈnɪkətiːn/ *n* a substance contained in tobacco.

niece /niːs/ *n* the daughter of your brother or sister: *My brother's two daughters are my nieces.*

See **nephew**.

niggle /ˈnɪɡəl/ *v* to bother or worry slightly: *There are still some doubts niggling me.* — *n* a slight worry: *I just have a couple of niggles left to discuss with you.*

'niggling *adj*: *a niggling doubt at the back of your mind.*

nigh /naɪ/ *adv* an old word for **near**.

well-nigh /ˈwɛlnaɪ/ *adv* nearly; almost: *The puzzle was well-nigh impossible.*

night /naɪt/ *n* **1** the time from sunset to sunrise: *We sleep at night.* **2** the time of darkness: *In the Arctic in winter, night lasts for twenty-four hours out of twenty-four.* — *adj* happening, taking place *etc* at night: *He does night work.*

She arrived **last night** (not **yesterday night**).

'night-club *n* a club open at night for drinking, dancing and entertainment.

'nightdress or **'nightgown** *n* a garment for wearing in bed.

'nightfall *n* the beginning of night; dusk.

nightingale /ˈnaɪtɪŋɡeɪl/ *n* a small bird with a beautiful song.

nightlife /ˈnaɪtlaɪf/ *n* entertainment found in the city late at night: *Paris is famous for its nightlife.*

nightly /ˈnaɪtlɪ/ *adj*, *adv* every night: *a nightly news programme*; *He goes there nightly.*

nightmare /ˈnaɪtmɛə(r)/ *n* **1** a frightening dream: *I often have nightmares.* **2** a very unpleasant or frightening experience: *Driving in the rush-hour traffic is a nightmare.* **'nightmarish** *adj.*

night school /ˈnaɪtskuːl/ educational classes in the evening for adults: *He's studying computing at night school.*

night-time /ˈnaɪt-taɪm/ *n* the time when it is night: *Owls are usually seen at night-time.*

nil /nɪl/ *n* nothing; zero: *Our team won two-nil*; *We lost by two goals to nil.*

nimble /ˈnɪmbəl/ *adj* quick and light in movement: *a nimble jump.* **'nimbly** *adv.*

nincompoop /ˈnɪŋkəmpuːp/ *n* a fool or idiot: *You great nincompoop!*

nine /naɪn/ *n* **1** the number 9. **2** the age of 9. — *adj* **1** 9 in number. **2** aged 9.

ninth /naɪnθ/ *n* one of nine equal parts. — *n*, *adj* the next after the eighth.

nineteen /naɪnˈtiːn/ *n* **1** the number 19. **2** the age of 19. — *adj* **1** 19 in number. **2** aged 19.

ninety /ˈnaɪntɪ/ *n* **1** the number 90. **2** the age of 90. — *adj* **1** 90 in number. **2** aged 90.

nip /nɪp/ *v* **1** to press something between your thumb and a finger, or between claws or teeth, causing pain; to pinch or bite: *A crab nipped her toe*; *The dog nipped her ankle.* **2** to cut with this action: *He nipped off the heads of the flowers.* **3** to go quickly: *Nip along to the shop and get me some rice.* — *n*: *The dog gave her a nip on the ankle.*

nipple /ˈnɪpəl/ *n* **1** the darker, pointed part of a woman's breast from which a baby sucks milk; the same part of a male breast. **2** the rubber mouth-piece of a baby's feeding-bottle; a teat.

nit /nɪt/ *n* **1** the little white egg of a louse, which sticks to people's hair. **2** an unkind word for a stupid person: *Stop shouting, you nit!*

nit-picking /ˈnɪtpɪkɪŋ/ *n* the activity of worrying or arguing about small and unimportant details or looking for tiny faults in things.

nitrate /ˈnaɪtreɪt/ *n* a chemical compound that includes nitrogen and oxygen: *Nitrate is used in fertilizers.*

nitrogen /ˈnaɪtrədʒən/ *n* a type of gas making up nearly four-fifths of the air we breathe.

nitty-gritty /ˈnɪtɪˈɡrɪtɪ/ *n* the basic or most important part of a situation, activity *etc*: *get down to the nitty-gritty of the problem.*

no[1] /noʊ/, *plural* **nos**, a shortening of **number**.

no[2] /noʊ/ *adj* **1** not any: *We have no food*; *No other person could have done it.* **2** not allowed: *No smoking.* **3** not a: *He is no friend of mine*; *This will be no easy task.* — *adv* not any: *He is no better at golf than at swimming*; *He went as far as the shop and no further.* — a word used for denying, disagreeing, refusing *etc*: *'Do you like travelling?' 'No, I don't.'*; *No, I don't agree*; *'Will you help me?' 'No, I won't.'* — *n* a refusal: *She answered with a definite no.*

nobility /noʊˈbɪlɪtɪ/ *n* **1** the state of being noble. **2** people who are of high birth.

noble /ˈnoʊbəl/ *adj* **1** honourable; unselfish: *a noble deed.* **2** of high birth or rank: *a noble family*; *of noble birth.* — *n* a person of high birth: *The nobles planned to murder the king.* **'nobleman** *n* a noble.

nobody /ˈnoʊbədɪ/ *pron* no-one: *Nobody likes him.* — *n* a very unimportant person: *She's just a nobody.*

nocturnal /nɒkˈtɜːnəl/ *adj* **1** active at night: *The owl is a nocturnal bird.* **2** happening at night: *a nocturnal adventure.*

nod /nɒd/ *v* **1** to make a quick forward and downward movement of your head to show agreement, or as a greeting: *You nod your head to say 'yes'*; *I asked him if he agreed and he nodded*; *He nodded to the man as he passed him in the street.* **2** to let your head fall forward and downward when you're sleepy: *Grandmother sat nodding by the fire.* — *n*: *He answered with a nod.*

nod off to fall asleep: *He nodded off while she was speaking to him.*

Noel, Nowell or **Noël** /noʊˈɛl/ *n* an old word for Christmas.

noise /nɔɪz/ *n* **1** a sound: *I heard a strange noise outside.* **2** an unpleasantly loud sound: *I hate noise.*
'noiseless *adj* without any sound: *a noiseless burglar.* **'noiselessly** *adv.*
'noisy *adj* making a loud noise: *noisy children.* **'noisily** *adv.* **'noisiness** *n.*

nomad /ˈnoʊmad/ *n* one of a group of people with no permanent home who travel about with their herds. **no'madic** *adj.* **no'madically** *adv.*

nominal /ˈnɒmɪnəl/ *adj* **1** in name only; not in reality: *He is only the nominal head of the company.* **2** small: *He had to pay only a nominal fine.*

nominate /ˈnɒmɪneɪt/ *v* to name someone for possible election to a particular job *etc*: *They nominated her as president.* **nomiˈnation** *n.*

non- /nɒn/ used with many words to change their meanings to the opposite; not: *non-alcoholic drinks*; *Three of the horses in yesterday's race were non-starters.*

nonchalant /ˈnɒnʃələnt/ *adj* calm and not worried: *She managed to appear nonchalant even though she was very upset.* **'nonchalance** *n.* **'nonchalantly** *adv.*

non-committal /nɒnkəˈmɪtəl/ *adj* not expressing any definite opinion: *The minister gave a typically non-commital reply.*

non-conductor /nɒnkənˈdʌktə(r)/ *n* a substance that does not conduct heat or electricity.

nonconformist /nɒnkənˈfɔːmɪst/ *n* a person who does not behave as other people do or believe what they believe. — *adj*: *She has a rather nonconformist approach to education.* **nonconˈformity** *n.*

nondescript /ˈnɒndɪskrɪpt/ *adj* with no particular or distinctive features: *a nondescript face in the crowd.*

none /nʌn/ *pron* not one; not any: *'How many tickets have you got?' 'None'*; *He asked me for some food but there was none in the house*; *None of us have* (or *has*) *seen today's newspaper*; *None of your cheek!* — *adv* not at all: *He is none the worse for his accident.*

> **none** can be followed by a singular or plural verb: *None of the children like* (or *likes*) *the new teacher.*

nonetheless or **none the less** /nʌnðəˈlɛs/ nevertheless; in spite of this: *Jim had a headache, but he wanted to come with us nonetheless.*

non-existent /nɒnɪgˈzɪstənt/ *adj* not existing; not real: *Jean worries about non-existent difficulties.* **non-exˈistence** *n.*

non-fiction /nɒnˈfɪkʃən/ *n* books about real events or things which exist, as opposed to stories: *The library has a large non-fiction section.*

non-flammable /nɒnˈflaməbəl/ *adj* non-inflammable.

non-inflammable /nɒnɪnˈflaməbəl/ *adj* not able to burn or be set alight: *Asbestos is non-inflammable.*

nonplussed /nɒnˈplʌst/ *adj* puzzled; not knowing what to do or say next.

nonsense /ˈnɒnsəns/ *n* foolishness; foolish words or actions *etc*; something that is ridiculous: *He's talking nonsense*; *What nonsense!* **nonsensical** /nɒnˈsɛnsɪkəl/ *adj.*

non-stop /nɒn'stɒp/ *adj* continuing without a stop: *non-stop entertainment*; *Is this train non-stop?* — *adv*: *It has rained non-stop for three days.*

noodle /'nuːdəl/ *n* a strip of pasta made with water, flour and egg: *fried noodles.*

nook /nʊk/ *n* a quiet, dark corner or place.
  every nook and cranny every part of a room: *He dusted in every nook and cranny.*

noon /nuːn/ *n* twelve o'clock midday: *They arrived at noon.*

> to arrive at **noon** (not **twelve noon**).

no-one /'noʊwʌn/ *pron* no person; nobody: *No-one is to blame*; *I spoke to no-one.*

> **no-one** takes a singular verb.

noose /nuːs/ *n* **1** a loop in rope, wire *etc* that becomes tighter when pulled. **2** a loop like this in a rope used for hanging a person.

nor /nɔː(r)/ *conjunction* and not: *He did not know then, nor did he ever find out*; *Emma was neither young nor old*; *I'm not going, nor is John.*

norm /nɔːm/ *n* what people normally do: *social norms*; *It has become the norm for wives to work.*

normal /'nɔːməl/ *adj* usual; without any special characteristics or circumstances: *She left at the normal time*; *normal people*; *His behaviour is not normal.* — *n*: *Her temperature was slightly above normal*; *The situation soon returned to normal.*
  'normally *adv* **1** in a usual, ordinary way: *He was behaving quite normally yesterday.* **2** usually; most often: *I normally eat toast for breakfast.*

north /nɔːθ/ *n* **1** the direction to your left when you face the rising sun; any part of the earth lying in that direction: *The wind is blowing from the north*; *I used to live in the north of England.* **2** (often written **N**) one of the four main points of the compass. — *adj* **1** in the north: *on the north bank of the river.* **2** from the direction of the north: *a north wind.* — *adv* towards the north: *The stream flows north.*
  northbound /'nɔːθbaʊnd/ *adj* travelling or leading towards the north: *northbound traffic*; *the northbound carriageway of a motorway.*
  northeast /nɔːθ'iːst/, **northwest** /nɔːθ'wɛst/ *ns* the direction midway between north and east, or north and west: *a village in the northeast of the country.* — *adjs*: *a northwest wind.* — *advs*: *to travel northeast.*
  north'easterly *adj* **1** coming from the northeast. **2** towards the northeast.
  north'eastern, **north'western** *adjs* of the northeast or northwest.
  northerly /'nɔːðəlɪ/ *adj* **1** coming from the north: *a northerly breeze.* **2** towards the north: *in a northerly direction.*
  northern /'nɔːðən/ *adj* of the north or the North.
  'northerner *n* a person who lives in, or comes from, the north of a country.
  northward /'nɔːθwəd/ *adj*, *adv* towards the north: *in a northward direction.*
  northwards /'nɔːθwədz/ *adv* towards the north: *They were travelling northwards.*
  the North Pole the northern end of the earth's axis of rotation.

> **north and south** is always used in this order.

nose /noʊz/ *n* **1** the part of your face you use for breathing and smelling: *She held the flower to her nose.* **2** the sense of smell: *Police dogs have good noses and can sniff out explosives.* **3** the part of anything which is like a nose in shape or position: *the nose of an aeroplane.* — *v* **1** to make a way by pushing carefully forward: *The ship nosed its way through the ice.* **2** to look or search as if by smelling: *He nosed about in the cupboard.*
  -nosed: *a long-nosed dog.*
  'nosedive *n* a dive or fall by an aeroplane with its head or nose pointing down. — *v* to make a dive like this: *Suddenly the plane nosedived.*
  nose about or **nose around** to look around a private place, trying to find something interesting: *A couple of journalists were nosing around outside.*
  pay through the nose to pay too much.
  turn your nose up to refuse something because you don't think it is good enough: *You can't turn your nose up at an opportunity like this!*
  under someone's nose right in front of someone: *He stole the money from under my nose.*

nosey another spelling of **nosy**.

nostalgia /nɒ'stældʒə/ *n* a longing or fondness for the past: *She felt a great nostalgia for her childhood.* **no'stalgic** *adj*. **nostalgically** /nɒ'stældʒɪklɪ/ *adv*.

nostril /'nɒstrɪl/ *n* one of two openings in your nose.

nosy or **nosey** /'noʊzɪ/ *adj* too interested in

other people's affairs: *a nosy neighbour.*

not /nɒt/ *adv* **1** a word used for denying, forbidding, refusing, or expressing the opposite of something (often shortened to **n't** /ənt/): *I did not see him; I didn't see him; He isn't here, is he?; Isn't he coming?; They told me not to go; Not a single person came to the party; We're going to London, not Paris; That's not true!* **2** used with certain verbs such as **hope**, **seem**, **believe**, **expect** and also with **afraid**: *'Have you got much money?' 'I'm afraid not'; Is she going to fail her exam?; 'I hope not'.*

not at all it does not matter; it is not important *etc*: *'Thank you for helping me.' 'Not at all.'*

notable /'nəʊtəbəl/ *adj* worth taking notice of; important: *a notable scholar.* **nota'bility** *n.* **'notably** *adv.*

notch /nɒtʃ/ *n* a small V-shaped cut: *He cut a notch in his stick.* — *v* to make a notch in something.

note /nəʊt/ *n* **1** a piece of writing to call attention to something: *He left me a note about the meeting.* **2** (usually **notes**) ideas for a speech, details from a lecture *etc* written down in short form: *The students took notes.* **3** a written or mental record: *Have you kept a note of her name?* **4** a short explanation: *There is a note at the bottom of the page about that difficult word.* **5** a short letter: *She wrote a note to her friend.* **6** a piece of paper used as money; a banknote: *a five-pound note.* **7** a musical sound; a symbol used to represent this. **8** an impression, a feeling or a mood: *There was a note of panic in her voice; The film ends on a happy note.* — *v* **1** to write down: *He noted down her telephone number in his diary.* **2** to notice; to be aware of: *He noted a change in her behaviour.*

'noted *adj* well-known: *a noted author; This town is noted for its cathedral.*

'notebook *n* a small book in which to write notes.

'notepaper *n* paper for writing letters.

'noteworthy *adj* worthy of notice; remarkable. **'noteworthiness** *n.*

take note of to notice and remember: *He took note of the change in her appearance.*

nothing /'nʌθɪŋ/ *pron* no thing; not anything: *I have nothing new to say.* — *n* the number 0; nought: *a telephone number with three nothings in it.* — *adv* not at all: *He's nothing like his father.*

for nothing 1 free; without payment: *I'll do that job for you for nothing.* **2** without result; in vain: *I've been working on this book for six years, and all for nothing!*

nothing but only: *There's nothing but rubbish on the television.*

nothing for it but no other possible action: *There was nothing for it but to wait for the phone to ring.*

(there's) nothing to it (it's) very easy: *I thought it would be difficult but there was actually nothing to it.*

notice /'nəʊtɪs/ *n* **1** a written or printed statement to announce something publicly: *He stuck a notice on the door, saying that the gymnasium was closed for repairs; They put a notice in the paper announcing the birth of their daughter.* **2** attention: *His skill attracted their notice; I'll bring the problem to his notice as soon as possible.* **3** a warning that something is going to happen: *We were prepared to leave at a moment's notice; How much notice must you give before you move out?* — *v* to see; to observe: *I noticed a book on the table; He noticed her leave the room; Did he say that? I didn't notice.*

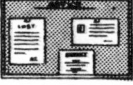

notice   advertisement   poster

'noticeable *adj* likely to be easily noticed: *There's a slight stain on this dress but it's not really noticeable.*

'noticeably *adv*: *He was noticeably more relaxed after she had gone.*

'notice-board *n* a board, for instance in a hall, school *etc* on which notices are put.

take notice to pay attention: *Don't take any notice of my mother — she always complains like that; They're just trying to scare you — take no notice.*

notify /'nəʊtɪfaɪ/ *v* to inform or warn someone about something: *If there has been an accident you must notify the police.* **notifi'cation** *n.*

notion /'nəʊʃən/ *n* **1** understanding: *I've no notion what he's talking about.* **2** an idea: *He has some very odd notions.* **3** a desire for something or to do something: *He had a sudden notion to visit his aunt.*

notorious /nəʊ'tɔːrɪəs/ *adj* well-known for badness or wickedness: *a notorious murderer.* **no'toriously** *adv.*

a **notorious** or **infamous** criminal, but a **famous** musician.

notoriety /noʊtəˈraɪətɪ/ n the quality of being notorious: *They had gained notoriety for being the most violent gang in Chicago.*

notwithstanding /nɒtwɪðˈstandɪŋ/ prep in spite of: *Notwithstanding his extreme youth, he has done some brilliant work.*

nougat /ˈnuːɡɑː/ n a hard, usually white sweet that contains nuts.

nought /nɔːt/ n **1** nothing. **2** the figure 0: *The number contained five noughts.*

noun /naʊn/ n a word used as the name of something: *The words 'boy', 'James' and 'happiness' are all nouns.*

nourish /ˈnʌrɪʃ/ v to give a person, animal or plant the food needed for health and growth: *These children have not been properly nourished for months.*
'**nourishing** adj: *nourishing food.*
'**nourishment** n something that nourishes; food: *Plants draw nourishment from the earth.*

novel[1] /ˈnɒvəl/ n a book telling a long story: *the novels of Charles Dickens.*
'**novelist** n the writer of a novel.

novel[2] /ˈnɒvəl/ adj new and strange: *a novel idea.*
'**novelty** n **1** newness and strangeness: *The pupils were excited by the novelty of life in the senior school.* **2** something new and strange: *Snow is a novelty to people from hot countries.* **3** a small, cheap thing that is sold as a toy or souvenir: *a stall selling novelties.*

November /noʊˈvɛmbə(r)/ n the eleventh month of the year, the month following October.

novice /ˈnɒvɪs/ n **1** a beginner at something: *David was a novice at swimming.* **2** a monk or nun who has not yet taken all their vows.

now /naʊ/ adv **1** at present: *I am now living in England.* **2** immediately: *I can't do it now — you'll have to wait.* **3** at this moment: *He'll be at home now.* **4** then; at that time: *We were now very close to the city.* **5** because of what has happened: *Paul now knew he could not trust Richard.* **6** a word that is used in explanations, warnings, commands *etc*: *Now, this is what happened*; *Stop that, now!*; *Do be careful, now.* — conjunction because or since something has happened: *Now you have left school, you will have to find a job*; *Now that he's 18, he can vote.*

nowadays /ˈnaʊədeɪz/ adv at the present time: *Food is very expensive nowadays.*

for now: *That will be enough for now — we'll continue our conversation tomorrow.*

just now a moment ago: *I saw him just now in the street.*

every now and then or **now and again** sometimes: *We go to the theatre every now and then*; *It happens now and again.*

nowhere /ˈnoʊwɛə(r)/ adv not anywhere: *The book was nowhere to be found.*

noxious /ˈnɒkʃəs/ adj harmful or poisonous: *noxious gases.*

nozzle /ˈnɒzəl/ n a narrow end-piece fitted to a pipe, tube *etc*: *The fireman pointed the nozzle of the hose-pipe at the fire.*

n't /ənt/ *see* **not**.

nuance /ˈnjuːɑːns/ n a slight or delicate difference in colour, tone, meaning *etc*: *The actress could use her voice to achieve nuances of meaning.*

nuclear /ˈnjuːklɪə(r)/ adj **1** using atomic energy: *a nuclear power station.* **2** belonging to a nucleus.
nuclear energy atomic energy.
nuclear-'free adj where nuclear weapons and nuclear energy are not allowed.
nuclear reactor a large machine for producing nuclear energy.

nucleus /ˈnjuːklɪəs/, *plural* **nuclei** /ˈnjuːklɪaɪ/, n **1** the central part of an atom. **2** the part of a plant or animal cell that controls its growth.

nude /njuːd/ adj without clothes; naked: *a nude model.* — n a photograph, picture *etc* of an unclothed human figure.
nudity /ˈnjuːdɪtɪ/ n nakedness.
in the nude without clothes.

nudge /nʌdʒ/ n a gentle push: *He gave her a nudge.* — v to hit gently: *She nudged him in the ribs.*

nugget /ˈnʌɡɪt/ n a small lump, especially of gold: *a gold nugget.*

nuisance /ˈnjuːsəns/ n someone or something that is annoying or troublesome: *That child is a terrible nuisance.*

numb /nʌm/ adj not able to feel or move: *She was numb with cold.* — v to make numb: *The cold numbed her fingers.* '**numbly** adv. '**numbness** n.

number /ˈnʌmbə(r)/ n **1** a word or figure expressing quantity, or the position of something in a series *etc*: *Seven was often considered a magic number*; *Answer nos 1—10 of Exercise 2.* **2** a quantity or group of people or things: *He has a number of* *records*; *There were a large number of people in the room.* **3** a copy of a magazine: *Back numbers can be ordered from the publisher.* — *v* **1** to put a number on: *He numbered the pages in the top corner.* **2** to include: *He numbered her among his closest friends.* **3** to come to in total: *The group numbered ten altogether.*

> **a number of**, meaning 'several', is plural: *A number of boys are absent today.*
> **the number of**, meaning 'the total quantity of something', is singular: *The number of girls in the class is small.*

any number of a large quantity of: *There are any number of ways to answer this question.*
'number-plate *n* one of the metal plates carried on the front and back of a motor vehicle showing the registration number.
numeral /'nju:mərəl/ *n* a figure used to express a number: *1, 10, 50 are Arabic numerals*; *I, X, L are Roman numerals.*
numerate /'nju:mərət/ *adj* knowing how to use numbers and do calculations.
numerator /'nju:məreɪtə(r)/ *n* the number that stands above the line in a fraction: *The numerator in the fraction is 3.*
numerical /nju:'mɛrɪkəl/ *adj* using numbers; consisting of numbers: *He punched in the numerical code.* **nu'merically** *adv*.
numerous /'nju:mərəs/ *adj* very many: *His faults are too numerous to mention.*
nun /nʌn/ *n* a member of a female religious community.
nunnery /'nʌnərɪ/ *n* a house in which a group of nuns live; a convent.
nurse /nɜ:s/ *n* a person who looks after sick or injured people in hospital: *She wants to be a nurse.* — *v* **1** to look after sick or injured people, especially in a hospital: *He was nursed back to health.* **2** to give a baby milk from the breast. **3** to hold with care: *She was nursing a kitten.*
nursery /'nɜ:sərɪ/ *n* **1** a room *etc* for young children. **2** a place where young plants are grown.
nursery rhyme a short poem for children.

nursery school a school for very young children.
nursery slope a lower, gentle snow-covered slope for people who are learning to ski.
nursing /'nɜ:sɪŋ/ *n* the job of a nurse who cares for the sick.
nursing home a small private hospital, especially one for very old people.
nurture /'nɜ:tʃə(r)/ *v* to feed and look after a young child, animal, plant *etc*: *a constant supply of water and minerals nurtures the young plantlets.*
nut /nʌt/ *n* **1** a fruit consisting of a single seed in a hard shell: *a hazelnut.* **2** a small round piece of metal with a hole through it, for screwing on the end of a bolt to hold pieces of wood, metal *etc* together: *a nut and bolt.*
'nutcracker *n* an instrument for cracking nuts open: *a pair of nutcrackers.*

hazelnut **peanut** **walnut**

nutmeg /'nʌtmɛg/ *n* a hard seed ground into a powder and used as a spice in food.
nutrient /'nju:trɪənt/ *n* a substance in food that helps growth and health.
nutrition /nju:'trɪʃən/ *n* nourishment, or the scientific study of this. **nu'tritional** *adj*.
nutritious /nju:'trɪʃəs/ *adj* valuable as food; nourishing: *Sweets are not very nutritious.*
nutshell /'nʌtʃɛl/ *n* the hard covering of a nut.
in a nutshell using few words: *What, in a nutshell, is the problem here?*
nutty /'nʌtɪ/ *adj* **1** containing, or tasting of, nuts: *a nutty flavour.* **2** a slang word for mad: *He's quite nutty.*
nuzzle /'nʌzəl/ *v* to press, rub or caress with the nose: *The horse nuzzled against her cheek.*
nylon /'naɪlɒn/ *n* a type of material made from chemicals and used for clothes, ropes, brushes *etc.* — *adj*: *a nylon shirt.*
nymph /nɪmf/ *n* a goddess or spirit of the rivers, trees *etc*.

O

oaf /oʊf/ n a stupid or clumsy person: *That stupid oaf is always knocking things over.* **'oafish** adj.

oak /oʊk/ n a type of large tree with hard wood. — adj: *oak furniture.*

oar /ɔː(r)/ n a long piece of wood with a flat end for rowing a boat.

oasis /oʊˈeɪsɪs/, plural **oases** /oʊˈeɪsiːz/, n an area in a desert where water is found: *The travellers stopped at an oasis.*

oath /oʊθ/, plural **oaths** /oʊθs/ or /oʊðz/, n **1** a solemn promise: *He swore an oath to support the king.* **2** a word or phrase used when you are swearing: *curses and oaths.*

on oath or **under oath** having made a promise to tell the truth: *The lawyer told the witness to remember that he was under oath to tell the truth.*

oats /oʊts/ n a type of cereal plant or its grain: *Horses eat oats.*

obedience /əˈbiːdɪəns/ n **1** the obeying of someone or something: *obedience to an order.* **2** willingness to obey: *Most teachers would like more obedience from their pupils.* **obedient** /əˈbiːdɪənt/ adj: *an obedient child.* **oˈbediently** adv.

> The opposite of **obedient** is **disobedient**.

obese /oʊˈbiːs/ adj very fat.

oˈbesity n: *Obesity is a danger to health.*

obey /əˈbeɪ/ or /oʊˈbeɪ/ v to do what you are told to do: *I obeyed the order.*

> The opposite of **obey** is **disobey**.

obituary /əˈbɪtjʊərɪ/ n a notice in a newspaper *etc* that announces a person's death, often with a short account of their life.

object¹ /ˈɒbdʒɛkt/ n **1** something that can be seen or felt: *There were various objects on the table.* **2** an aim; an intention: *His main object in life was to become rich.* **3** the word or words in a sentence *etc*, that stand for the person or thing affected by the verb: *He hit me; You can eat what you like.*

no object not a problem; not important: *I will buy you anything you like — money is no object.*

object² /əbˈdʒɛkt/ v to dislike something; to disapprove of something: *I object to her rudeness; Chris objected to going to bed so early.*

obˈjection n **1** an expression of disapproval: *He raised no objection to the idea.* **2** a reason for disapproving: *My objection is that he is too young.*

obˈjectionable adj very unpleasant; offensive: *He is a most objectionable person; Everybody thinks that drug-dealing is objectionable.*

objective /əbˈdʒɛktɪv/ n a goal you try to reach: *Our objective is freedom.* — adj not influenced by personal opinions: *He took an objective view of the problem.* **obˈjectively** adv. **objecˈtivity** n.

oblige /əˈblaɪdʒ/ v **1** to do something to help someone: *Could you oblige me by carrying this, please?*

obligation /ɒblɪˈɡeɪʃən/ n a promise or duty: *You are under no obligation to buy this.*

obligatory /əˈblɪɡətərɪ/ adj that must be done: *It is obligatory to pay tax.*

oˈbliged adj **1** having to do something: *I was obliged to invite him to my party, although I didn't want to.* **2** grateful: *I am obliged to you for all your help.*

oˈbliging adj willing to help other people: *He'll help you — he's very obliging.* **oˈbligingly** adv.

obliterate /əˈblɪtəreɪt/ v to destroy completely: *A nuclear attack could obliterate whole towns and cities.*

oblique /əˈbliːk/ adj sloping: *He drew an oblique line from one corner of the paper to the other.*

oblivion /əˈblɪvɪən/ n **1** the state of not being aware of what is going on around you: *She was staring at the sky in complete oblivion.* **2** the state of being forgotten: *The poet's name has sunk into oblivion over the centuries.*

oˈblivious adj not aware of what is happening: *A toddler makes endless demands on his mother, oblivious to her exhaustion.*

oblong /ˈɒblɒŋ/ n a rectangular shape that has one pair of opposite sides longer than the other pair. — adj shaped like an oblong: *an oblong table.*

obnoxious /əbˈnɒkʃəs/ adj very unpleasant: *Some adults think that all children are obnoxious.*

oboe /'oʊboʊ/ n a woodwind musical instrument. **'oboist** n.

obscene /əb'siːn/ adj disgusting, especially sexually: *obscene photographs*. **ob'scenely** adv.

  obscenity /əb'sɛnɪtɪ/ n **1** the state of being obscene. **2** a word or act that is obscene.

obscure /əb'skjʊə(r)/ adj **1** not clear; difficult to see: *an obscure shape; an obscure outline*. **2** difficult to find; hidden: *an obscure corner of the library*. — v to hide something; to make something difficult to understand: *Our view was obscured by a high wall*. **ob'scurity** n.

observance /əb'zɜːvəns/ n obeying or following a law or custom: *observance of the rules; religious observances*.

observant /əb'zɜːvənt/ adj quick to notice: *An observant boy remembered the car's number.*

observation /ɒbzə'veɪʃən/ n **1** the noticing or watching of someone or something: *She is in hospital for observation*. **2** the ability to notice things and remember them accurately: *a game of observation*. **3** a remark: *He made a couple of observations about the weather before beginning the interview.*

observatory /əb'zɜːvətərɪ/ n a place with large telescopes for observing and studying the moon, stars *etc*.

observe /əb'zɜːv/ v **1** to notice: *I observed her unhappy face; I observed that she was crying*. **2** to watch carefully: *She observed his actions with interest*. **3** to obey: *We must observe the rules*. **4** to make a remark: *'It's a lovely day,' he observed.*

  ob'server n someone who observes.

obsess /əb'sɛs/ v to occupy someone's mind too much: *He is obsessed by death*.

  obsession /əb'sɛʃən/ n: *an obsession about motorbikes*.

  ob'sessive adj continually thinking or behaving in a particular way and unable to stop: *obsessive tidiness*.

obsolete /'ɒbsəliːt/ or /ɒbsə'liːt/ adj no longer used; out of date: *Now that we have diesel and electric trains, the steam locomotive has become obsolete*.

obstacle /'ɒbstəkəl/ n something which prevents progress: *His inability to learn foreign languages was an obstacle to his career*.

obstetrician /ɒbstə'trɪʃən/ n a doctor specializing in the health of pregnant women, the growth of the baby in the womb and birth: *All pregnant women should see an obstetrician regularly*.

obstinate /'ɒbstɪnət/ adj refusing to give in to someone or something; not wanting to obey someone: *She won't change her mind — she's very obstinate*. **obstinacy** /'ɒbstɪnəsɪ/ n. **'obstinately** adv.

obstruct /əb'strʌkt/ v **1** to block: *The road was obstructed by a fallen tree*. **2** to stop something moving past or making progress: *The crashed lorry obstructed the traffic*.

  ob'struction n something that obstructs: *an obstruction in the pipe*.

  ob'structive adj deliberately trying to stop something from happening.

obtain /əb'teɪn/ v to get: *He obtained a large sum of money by selling houses; Antiseptic ointment can be obtained from the chemist*. **ob'tainable** adj.

obtuse /əb'tjuːs/ adj greater than a right-angle: *an obtuse angle*.

obvious /'ɒbvɪəs/ adj easily seen or understood: *It was obvious that she was ill; an obvious improvement; an obvious reason*.

  'obviously adv: *Obviously, I'll need some help.*

occasion /ə'keɪʒən/ n **1** a particular time: *I've heard him speak on several occasions*. **2** a special event: *The wedding was a great occasion*.

  oc'casional adj happening now and then: *I take an occasional trip to London*.

  oc'casionally adv now and then: *I occasionally go to the theatre*.

  on occasion occasionally.

occidental /ɒksɪ'dɛntəl/ adj of or from the West: *occidental cultures*.

occult /ə'kʌlt/ or /'ɒkʌlt/ n the knowledge and study of what is supernatural or magical: *She finds the occult frightening*.

occupant /'ɒkjʊpənt/ n someone who occupies a house *etc*: *the occupants of the flat*.

occupation /ɒkjʊ'peɪʃən/ n **1** your job or work. **2** something that you do in your free time: *Reading is his favourite occupation*. **3** the occupying of a house, town *etc*: *The new houses are now ready for occupation*. **4** the time during which a town, country *etc* is occupied by the army of another country: *During the occupation, there was a shortage of food*.

  occu'pational adj connected with a person's work or profession.

occupier /'ɒkjʊpaɪə(r)/ n the person who lives in a particular house, *etc*.

occupy /'ɒkjʊpaɪ/ v **1** to fill up space: *A table occupied the centre of the room*. **2** to fill up time: *He occupied his time until lunch by reading a book*. **3** to live in: *The family* *occupied a small flat.* **4** to capture: *The soldiers occupied the town.*

occur /əˈkɜː(r)/ *v* **1** to happen: *The accident occurred yesterday morning.* **2** to come into your mind: *An idea occurred to him.* **3** to be found: *Giants occur in fairy tales.*

occurrence /əˈkʌrəns/ *n* something that happens or exists: *a strange occurrence.*

> **occurrence, occurred** and **occurring** have two **r**s.

> **occur** means to happen by chance: *The accident occurred at 8.00 p.m.*
> **take place** should be used when you mean to happen according to plan: *The prize-giving ceremony will take place on 30 June.*

ocean /ˈoʊʃən/ *n* **1** the salt water that covers most of the earth's surface. **2** a name given to each of its five main divisions: *the Atlantic Ocean.*

o'clock /əˈklɒk/ *adv* used, in saying the time, for a particular hour: *It's five o'clock.* — *adj*: *the three o'clock train.*

octagon /ˈɒktəgən/ *n* a flat shape with eight sides.

octagonal /ɒkˈtagənəl/ *adj* having eight sides: *an octagonal coin.*

October /ɒkˈtoʊbə(r)/ *n* the tenth month of the year, the month following September.

octopus /ˈɒktəpəs/ *n* a sea-creature with eight tentacles.

odd /ɒd/ *adj* **1** unusual; strange: *He's wearing very odd clothes*; *an odd young man.* **2** not able to be divided exactly by 2: *5 and 7 are odd numbers.* **3** not one of a pair, set *etc*: *an odd shoe.* **4** unused; left over: *Have you got any odd bits of wood I could use?* **5** not regular or fixed: *odd moments*; *She makes the odd mistake when she speaks English.* **'oddness** *n*.

'oddity *n* a strange or unusual person or thing: *He's always been a bit of an oddity.*

'oddly *adv* strangely: *He is behaving oddly.*

'oddment *n* a piece left over from something larger: *She made the jacket from oddments of material that she found in the house.*

odds /ɒdz/ *n* **1** chances: *The odds are that he will win.* **2** a difference in strength, in favour of one side: *They are fighting against heavy odds.*

odd jobs small jobs of various kinds, often done for other people: *He hasn't got a regular job, but earns some money by doing odd jobs for old people.*

odd man out or **odd one out** one in a group that is noticeably different from the rest: *Look at these pictures and decide which is the odd one out.*

odds and ends small objects of different kinds: *There were various odds and ends lying about on the table.*

ode /oʊd/ *n* a poem written in praise of a person or thing: *Keats' 'Ode to a Nightingale'.*

odious /ˈoʊdɪəs/ *adj* hateful, unpleasant or offensive: *an odious person.*

odour /ˈoʊdə(r)/ *n* a smell: *the unpleasant odour of burning fat.* **'odourless** *adj*.

o'er /ˈoʊə(r)/ *adv, prep*, short for **over**: *o'er the sea.*

of /ɒv/ or /əv/ *prep* **1** belonging to: *Where is the lid of this box?*; *a friend of mine.* **2** away from: *I live within five miles of London.* **3** written by: *the plays of Shakespeare.* **4** belonging to a group: *He is one of my friends.* **5** showing: *a picture of my father.* **6** made from; consisting of: *a dress of silk*; *a collection of pictures.* **7** used to show an amount or measurement of something: *a gallon of petrol*; *five bags of coal.* **8** about: *the story of his adventures.* **9** containing: *a box of chocolates.* **10** used to show a cause: *She died of hunger.* **11** used to show a loss or removal: *She was robbed of her jewels.* **12** used to show the connection between an action and its object: *the smoking of a cigarette.* **13** used to show character, qualities *etc*: *a man of courage.*

off /ɒf/ *adv* **1** away from a place, time *etc*: *He walked off*; *She cut her hair off*; *The holidays are only a week off*; *She took off her coat.* **2** not working; not giving power *etc*: *The water's off*; *Switch off the light*; *Put the light off*; *Have you turned off the machine?* **3** not at work: *He's taking tomorrow off*; *He's off today.* **4** completely: *Finish off your meal.* **5** not as good as usual, or as it should be: *His work has gone off recently.* **6** bad: *This milk has gone off — we can't drink it.* **7** out of a vehicle, train *etc*: *The bus stopped and we got off.* **8** cancelled: *The wedding is off.* — *adj* **1** not as good as usual: *an off day.* **2** rotten: *This fish is definitely off.* — *prep* **1** away from; down from: *It fell off the table*; *a mile off the coast*; *He cut about five centimetres off my hair.* **2** out of a vehicle: *We got off the bus.*

off day a day when things go badly for you or you can do nothing right.

be off with you! go away!

off and on or **on and off** happening occasionally; sometimes.

the off season the period, at a hotel, holiday area *etc*, when there are few visitors: *It's very quiet here in the off season.* — *adj*: *off-season rates*.

offal /'ɒfəl/ *n* the internal organs of an animal that are used as food.

off-chance /'ɒftʃɑːns/ *n* a slight possibility.

on the off-chance hoping to succeed, but thinking that it is unlikely: *I called in on the off-chance and was delighted to see her there.*

offence /ə'fɛns/ *n* **1** disgust, anger, displeasure, hurt feelings *etc*: *His rudeness caused offence.* **2** a cause of these feelings: *That rubbish dump is an offence to the eye.* **3** a crime: *The police charged him with several offences.*

take offence at to be offended by something: *He took offence at her nasty remark.*

offend /ə'fɛnd/ *v* **1** to make someone feel upset or angry: *If you don't go to her party she will be offended.* **2** to disgust: *Cigarette smoke offends me.* **3** to break a law *etc*: *to offend against the law.*

of'fender *n* a person who offends against the law.

of'fensive *adj* **1** insulting: *offensive remarks*. **2** disgusting: *an offensive smell*. **3** used for or to do with attacking: *offensive weapons.* — *n* an attack. **of'fensively** *adv*.

offer /'ɒfə(r)/ *v* **1** to put forward a gift, suggestion *etc* for acceptance or refusal: *He offered her £20 for the picture.* **2** to say that you are willing: *He offered to help her.* — *n* **1** an act of offering: *an offer of help*. **2** something offered; an amount of money offered: *They made an offer of £50 000 for the house.*

'offering *n* **1** a gift: *a birthday offering*. **2** money given during a religious service: *a church offering*.

on offer for sale, often cheaply: *That shop has chairs on offer at £20 each*.

off'hand *adj* rude and impolite: *She often behaves in an offhand way.* — *adv* without having or taking time to think carefully: *Can you tell me offhand how much it might cost?*

office /'ɒfɪs/ *n* **1** the room or building in which the business of a company is done: *The firm's head offices are in New York.* **2** the room in which a particular person works: *the bank manager's office*. **3** a room or building used for a particular purpose: *You buy train tickets at the ticket-office.* **4** a position of responsibility or authority: *The president will hold office for four years.* — *adj*: *office furniture*; *office stationery*.

'officer *n* **1** someone holding a commission in the army, navy or air force: *a naval officer*. **2** someone who carries out a public duty: *a police-officer*.

official /ə'fɪʃəl/ *adj* **1** having to do with authority: *official powers*; *The policeman was wearing his official uniform*. **2** done, said, announced *etc* by people in authority: *the official result of the race*. **3** announced publicly: *Have they made their engagement official yet?* — *n* a person who holds a position of authority: *a government official*.

officialdom /ə'fɪʃəldəm/ *n* the work of officials as a group

of'ficially *adv* **1** as an official: *He attended the ceremony officially*. **2** formally; by someone in authority: *The new library was officially opened yesterday*.

officious /ə'fɪʃəs/ *adj* too ready to give other people orders: *An officious little man told us to move away from the gates*.

offing /'ɒfɪŋ/: **in the offing** likely to come happen soon: *There seems to be some trouble in the offing*.

offload /ɒf'ləʊd/ *v* to get rid of something you do not want by giving it to someone else: *He managed to offload his old books onto one of his pupils*.

off-peak /ɒf'piːk/ *adj* when there is lowest demand for something: *The train fare is less if you travel during off-peak periods*.

off-putting /'ɒfpʊtɪŋ/ *adj* unpleasant or unattractive: *His description of the hotel was a bit off-putting*.

offset /'ɒfsɛt/ *v* to balance the effect of something: *The price rises will be offset by cuts in taxes*.

offshore /'ɒfʃɔː(r)/ *adj* **1** in or on the sea, not far from the coast: *an offshore oil-rig*. **2** blowing away from the coast, out to sea: *offshore breezes*.

offside /ɒf'saɪd/ *adv* in a position not allowed by the rules of football *etc*: *The player was offside so the goal was disallowed.* — *adj*.

offspring /'ɒfsprɪŋ/, *plural* **offspring**, *n* a child; a baby animal: *How many offspring does a cat usually have at one time?*

off-white /ɒf'waɪt/ *adj* not pure white.

often /'ɒfən/ or /'ɒftən/ *adv* many times: *I often go to the theatre*; *I should see him more often*.

every so often occasionally: *We get a letter from him every so often*.

more often than not on most occasions: *More often than not, students get financial help from their parents.*

ogre /'oʊgə(r)/ *n* a frightening cruel giant in fairy tales.

oh /oʊ/ a cry of surprise, admiration *etc*: *Oh, what a lovely present!*

oil /ɔɪl/ *n* a greasy liquid that will not mix with water: *olive oil; whale oil; vegetable oil; cooking oil; He put some oil on the hinges of the door.* — *v* to put oil on or into something: *The machine will work better if it's oiled.*

'oilfield *n* a place where mineral oil is found: *There are oilfields in the North Sea.*

oil painting a picture painted with paints made with oil.

oil palm a palm tree whose fruit and seeds give oil.

'oil-rig *n* a structure used to drill wells from which oil is obtained: *The ship sailed past an enormous oil-rig.*

'oil-tanker *n* a ship used for carrying oil: *An oil-tanker sank near here.*

oil well a hole that is drilled into the ground or seabed in order to obtain oil.

'oily *adj* like, or covered with, oil: *an oily liquid; an oily rag.*

ointment /'ɔɪntmənt/ *n* any greasy substance that you rub on your skin to heal injuries *etc.*

OK or **okay** /oʊ'keɪ/ all right: *'Will you do it?' 'O.K., I will'; Is my dress O.K.?; That's O.K. with me.* — *n* approval: *He gave the plan his O.K.*

old /oʊld/ *adj* **1** having lived a long time: *an old man.* **2** having a certain age: *He is thirty years old.* **3** having existed for a long time: *an old building; Those trees are very old.* **4** no longer useful: *She threw away the old shoes.* **5** belonging to times long ago: *the good old days.*

> **older** *see* **elder** and **senior**.

old age the later part of your life: *He wrote most of his poems in his old age.*

old boy, **old girl** a former pupil of a school: *The new prime minister is an old girl of our school.*

old-fashioned /oʊld'fæʃənd/ *adj* in a style common some time ago: *old-fashioned clothes.*

old hand someone who is good at something because they have done it often before.

old maid an unmarried woman who is past the usual age of marriage.

the old old people: *hospitals for the old.*

olive /'ɒlɪv/ *n* **1** an edible fruit that gives oil for cooking, and is also used as a decoration on food. **2** the tree on which it grows: *a grove of olives.*

olive oil the oil from olives.

Olympic /ə'lɪmpɪk/: **the Olympic Games** or **the Olympics** a sports competition held once every four years for amateur sportsmen and sportswomen from all parts of the world.

omelette or **omelet** /'ɒmlət/ *n* a food made of eggs beaten and fried, sometimes with vegetables, meat *etc*: *a mushroom omelette.*

omen /'oʊmən/ *n* a sign of a future event: *Long ago, storms were regarded as bad omens.*

ominous /'ɒmɪnəs/ *adj* giving a suggestion or warning about something bad that is going to happen: *an ominous cloud.* **'ominously** *adv.*

omission /ə'mɪʃən/ or /oʊ'mɪʃən/ *n* the leaving out of something; something that has been left out: *I have made several omissions in the list of names.*

omit /ə'mɪt/ or /oʊ'mɪt/ *v* **1** to leave out: *You can omit the last chapter of the book.* **2** not to do something: *I omitted to tell him about the meeting.*

> **omitted** and **omitting** have two **t**s.

omnipotent /ɒm'nɪpətənt/ *adj* having very great or complete power: *Only God is omnipotent.*

on /ɒn/ *prep* **1** touching, fixed to, covering *etc* the upper or outer side of something: *The book was lying on the table; She wore a hat on her head.* **2** in or into a vehicle: *There were 14 people on the bus; I got on the wrong bus.* **3** during a certain day: *on Monday.* **4** just after: *On his arrival, he went straight to bed.* **5** about: *a book on the theatre.* **6** having; in the middle of: *He's on holiday.* **7** supported by: *She was standing on one leg.* **8** receiving; taking: *He's on drugs; She's on a diet.* **9** taking part in: *He is on the committee.* **10** towards: *They marched on the town.* **11** near or beside: *a shop on the main road.* **12** by means of: *I spoke to him on the telephone.* **13** being carried by: *The thief had the stolen jewels on him.* **14** as a result of something done; after: *On investigation, there proved to be no need to panic.* **15** followed by: *disaster on disaster.* — *adv* **1** so as to be touching, fixed to, covering *etc* the upper or outer side of something: *She put her hat on.* **2** used to show a continuing state *etc*; onwards: *She kept on asking questions; They moved on.* **3** working; giving power: *Switch on the light; Put the television on; Have you turned the engine on?* **4** being shown: *There's a good film on at the cinema.* **5** into a vehicle: *The bus stopped and we got on.* — *adj* **1** in progress: *The fight was on.* **2** not cancelled: *Is the party on tonight?*

See **in**.

not on not acceptable: *I know you like the idea, but it's just not on.*

on and on used with certain verbs to emphasize the length of an activity: *She kept on and on asking questions.*

on time at the right time.

on time means at the right time: *Jane arrived on time.*
in time means early enough to do something: *Susan arrived in time for tea.*

on to to a position on: *He lifted the box on to the table.*

once /wʌns/ *adv* **1** a single time: *He did it once.* **2** at a time in the past: *I once wanted to be a dancer.* — *conjunction* when; as soon as: *Once it had been unlocked, the door opened easily.*

all at once suddenly: *I was walking along when all at once there was a loud bang.*

at once 1 immediately: *Go away at once!* **2** at the same time: *I can't do three things at once!*

just for once or **just this once** on this occasion only: *I'll tell you the answer just this once.*

once again or **once more** again: *Try to do that once again.*

once and for all once and finally: *Once and for all, I refuse!*

once in a while occasionally: *I see him once in a while.*

oncoming /'ɒnkʌmɪŋ/ *adj* moving towards you: *oncoming traffic.*

one /wʌn/ *n* **1** the number 1: *One and one is two; 1+1=2.* **2** the age of 1: *Babies start to walk and talk at one.* — *pron* **1** a single person or thing: *She's the one I like the best; I like both these scarves but I think I'll buy the red one.* **2** anyone; you: *One can see the city from here.* — *adj* **1** 1 in number: *one person; He took one book.* **2** aged 1: *The baby will be one tomorrow.* **3** of the same opinion *etc*: *We are one in our love of freedom.*

one- having one of something: *a one-legged man.*

one-'off *n* made or happening on one occasion only: *That car was a one-off.* — *adj*: *a one-off opportunity.*

one'self *pron* **1** used as the object of a verb or preposition, when the subject is **one**: *One should wash oneself every morning.* **2** used in emphasis: *One always has to do these things oneself.*

One ought to keep **oneself** (not **himself** or **herself**) fit and healthy.

one-sided /wʌn'saɪdɪd/ *adj* **1** with one person or side having a great advantage over the other: *a one-sided contest.* **2** showing only one view of a subject: *a one-sided discussion.*

one-to-'one *adj* between only two people: *one-to-one teaching.*

one-'way *adj* in which traffic can move in one direction only: *a one-way street.*

one another used as the object of a verb when an action takes place between people *etc*: *People must love one another.*

See **each**.

one by one one after the other: *He examined the vases one by one.*

one or two a few: *I don't want a lot of nuts — I'll just take one or two.*

one of is followed by a plural noun or pronoun, but takes a singular verb: *One of the girls works as a hairdresser.*

ongoing /'ɒngoʊɪŋ/ *adj* continuing: *the ongoing fight against cancer.*

onion /'ʌnjən/ *n* a vegetable with an edible bulb that has a strong taste and smell: *Put plenty of onions in the stew.*

on-line /'ɒnlaɪn/ *adj* directly connected to or controlled by a computer: *on-line information in the library.*

onlooker /'ɒnlʊkə(r)/ *n* someone who watches something happening: *A crowd of onlookers had gathered round them.*

only /'oʊnlɪ/ *adj* without any others of the same type: *He has no brothers or sisters — he's an only child; the only book of its kind.* — *adv* **1** not more than: *We have only two cups left; He lives only a mile away.* **2** alone: *Only you can do it.* **3** merely; just: *I only scolded the child — I did not smack him.* **4** not longer ago than: *I saw him only* *yesterday*. **5** showing the one probable result of an action: *If you do that you'll only make him angry*. — *conjunction* except that; but: *I'd like to go, only I have to work*.

> **only** should be put directly before the word *etc* that it refers to: **Only** *Chris saw the book* means nobody else saw it; *Chris* **only** *saw the book* means he didn't read it; *Chris saw* **only** *the book* means he didn't see anything else.

See also **except**.

not only used to introduce the first of two statements where the second is more surprising: *He not only bought me a present, but also took me out to lunch*.

only child a child with no brothers or sisters.

only just almost not: *We can only just hear you — could you speak up please?*

only too very: *I'll be only too pleased to come*.

onset /ˈɒnsɛt/ *n* a beginning: *the onset of a cold*.

onslaught /ˈɒnslɔːt/ *n* a fierce attack: *The rain stopped and I hurried home before the next onslaught of rough weather could begin*.

onto *see* **on to**.

onward /ˈɒnwəd/ or **onwards** /ˈɒnwədz/ *adv* forward; on: *He led them onward through the night*.

ooze /uːz/ *v* to flow slowly; to have a liquid flowing slowly out: *The glue oozed out of the tube*; *His finger was oozing blood*; *She felt her courage oozing away*.

opal /ˈoʊpəl/ *n* a precious stone that is milky in colour, with slight traces or streaks of other colours.

opaque /oʊˈpeɪk/ *adj* not transparent: *an opaque liquid*. **oˈpaqueness**, **opacity** /oʊˈpasɪtɪ/ *ns*.

open /ˈoʊpən/ *adj* **1** not shut: *an open box*; *The gate is wide open*. **2** allowing the inside to be seen: *an open book*. **3** ready for business, use *etc*: *The shop is open on Sunday afternoons*; *The gardens are open to the public*. **4** obvious; not secret: *He watched her dancing with open admiration*. **5** frank: *He was very open with me about his work*. **6** empty, with no trees, buildings *etc*: *I like to be out in the open country*; *an open space*. **7** still being considered; not yet decided: *The matter is still open for discussion*. — *v* **1** to make or become open: *He opened the door*; *The door opened*; *The new shop opened last week*. **2** to begin: *He opened the meeting with a speech of welcome*.

> The door is **open** (not **opened**);
> Someone has **opened** it.
> See also **closed**.

ˈopen-air *adj* outside: *an open-air meeting*.

open day a day when the public is allowed to enter a school, *etc*.

ˈopener *n* something that opens something: *a tin-opener*.

ˈopening *n* **1** a hole; a space: *an opening in the fence*. **2** a beginning: *the opening of the film*. **3** becoming open or making open: *the opening of a flower*; *the opening of the new theatre*. — *adj* said, done *etc* at the beginning: *the teacher's opening words*.

ˈopenly *adv* frankly: *She talked openly about her illness*.

open-minded /oʊpənˈmaɪndɪd/ *adj* willing to consider new ideas: *an open-minded attitude to education*.

ˈopenness *n* honesty; frankness: *His openness about his past was quite surprising*.

open-ˈplan *adj* with the space kept as one large room and not divided up into smaller individual rooms: *Her sitting-room, dining-room and kitchen are all open-plan*; *an open-plan office*.

in the open outside; in the open air: *It's healthy for children to play in the open*.

in the open air not in a building: *If it doesn't rain, we'll have the party in the open air*.

open out to become wider: *At that point the road opened out and we passed the car in front*.

open up 1 to open a shop *etc*: *I open up the shop at nine o'clock every morning*. **2** to open the door of a building *etc*: *'Open up!' shouted the policeman*.

with open arms in a very friendly way: *They received their visitors with open arms*.

opera /ˈɒpərə/ *n* a musical play in which the words are sung: *an opera by Verdi*. **operˈatic** *adj*.

opera house a theatre especially built for the performance of operas.

operate /ˈɒpəreɪt/ *v* **1** to work: *The sewing-machine isn't operating properly*; *Can you operate this machine?* **2** to perform a surgical operation: *The surgeon operated on her for appendicitis*.

operating theatre a room where surgical operations are done.

operation /ɒpəˈreɪʃən/ *n* **1** a carefully

planned action: *a rescue operation.* **2** the process of working: *Our plan is now in operation.* **3** the cutting of a part of the body, usually by a surgeon, in order to cure disease: *an operation for appendicitis.*

ope'rational *adj* in good working order.

'operative *adj* working; having an effect. — *n* a worker.

'operator *n* **1** someone who works a machine: *a lift operator.* **2** someone who connects telephone calls: *Ask the operator to connect you to that number.*

opinion /ə'pɪnjən/ *n* **1** what you think or believe: *My opinions about education have changed.* **2** a professional judgement, usually of a doctor, lawyer *etc*: *He wanted a second opinion on his illness.* **3** what you think of the worth or value of someone or something: *I have a very high opinion of his work.*

a matter of opinion a subject on which people do not agree.

in my opinion according to what I think: *In my opinion, he's right.*

be of the opinion that to think or believe something: *We are of the opinion that you have done the right thing.*

opium /'oʊpɪəm/ *n* a drug made from the dried juice of a poppy.

opponent /ə'poʊnənt/ *n* someone who opposes you: *He beat his opponent by four points.*

opportunity /ɒpə'tjuːnɪtɪ/ *n* a chance to do something: *I'd like to have an opportunity to go to Rome.*

oppose /ə'poʊz/ *v* **1** to fight against someone or something by force or argument: *We opposed the government on this question.* **2** to compete against: *Who is opposing him in the election?*

as opposed to in contrast with: *We are interested in your professional, as opposed to your personal opinion.*

op'posed to disagreeing with; against: *We are opposed to physical violence.*

opposite /'ɒpəzɪt/ *adj* **1** on the other side of something: *on the opposite side of town.* **2** completely different: *The two men walked off in opposite directions.* — *prep, adv* facing: *He lives in the house opposite mine*; *Who lives in the house opposite?*; *Angela's house is opposite to ours.* — *n* something that is completely different: *Good is the opposite of bad.*

opposite number the person who has the same job or position in another company or team *etc*: *The Foreign Secretary is going to America for talks with his opposite number there.*

opposition /ɒpə'zɪʃən/ *n* **1** resisting or fighting against someone or something by force, or argument: *The teacher found a lot of opposition to her new ideas amongst the parents.* **2** your competitors; the people you are fighting: *a strong opposition.* **3** the politicians who oppose the party in government.

oppress /ə'prɛs/ *v* **1** to govern cruelly: *The king oppressed his people.* **2** to worry; to depress: *The heat oppressed Jim.*

oppression /ə'prɛʃən/ *n*: *After five years of oppression, the peasants revolted.*

op'pressive *adj* **1** cruel and unjust: *oppressive government.* **2** causing worry: *an oppressive situation.* **3** unpleasantly hot: *the oppressive heat of the desert.*

op'pressor *n* a ruler who oppresses his people; a tyrant.

opt /ɒpt/ *v* to choose to do one thing instead of something else: *He opted to stay on another year at school and take his exams again.*

opt for to choose one thing rather than any other.

opt out to decide not to do something: *John opted out of the exam.*

optical /'ɒptɪkəl/ *adj* having to do with sight or what you see: *optical instruments.*

optical illusion a picture or thing which has an appearance which deceives the eye: *He thought he could see water in the distance, but it was in fact an optical illusion caused by the light.*

optician /ɒp'tɪʃən/ *n* someone who makes and sells spectacles: *The optician mended my spectacles.*

optimism /'ɒptɪmɪzm/ *n* a state of mind in which you hope or expect something good to happen: *Even though it was obvious that he would not win, he was full of optimism.* **'optimist** *n*.

> The opposite of **optimism** is **pessimism**.

optimistic /ɒptɪ'mɪstɪk/ *adj* hoping or believing something good will happen: *an optimistic person.* **opti'mistically** *adv*.

option /'ɒpʃən/ *n* **1** choice: *You have no option.* **2** a thing that you choose or that may be chosen: *There were several options open to him and he chose the most difficult one.*

'optional *adj* a matter of choice: *Music is optional at our school.*

opulent /'ɒpjələnt/ *adj* very rich; showing wealth: *There are a lot of opulent people in America*; *She lived in opulent surroundings.* **'opulence** *n.*

or /ɔː(r)/ *conjunction* **1** used to show an alternative: *Is that your book or is it mine?* **2** because if not: *Hurry or you'll be late.* **3** used to correct or explain something that you have just said: *She's in her room, or she was a minute ago.*

See **either**.

or so about; approximately: *I bought a dozen or so books.*

oral /'ɔːrəl/ *adj* **1** spoken; not written: *an oral examination.* **2** with the mouth: *oral hygiene.* — *n* a spoken examination: *He passed the written exam, but failed his oral.* **'orally** *adv* by mouth: *medicine to be taken orally.*

orange /'ɒrɪndʒ/ *n* **1** a juicy citrus fruit with a thick skin of a colour between red and yellow. **2** the colour of this fruit. — *adj*: *She was wearing an orange dress*; *orange juice*; *an orange drink.*

orang-utan /ɔːraŋuːˈtan/ *n* a large, man-like ape.

orang-utan

oration /əˈreɪʃən/ *n* a formal speech, especially in fine language: *a funeral oration.*
orator /'ɒrətə(r)/ *n* someone who makes public speeches.

orbit /'ɔːbɪt/ *n* the path along which something moves around a planet, star *etc*: *The spaceship is in orbit round the moon.* — *v* to go round in space: *The spacecraft orbits the Earth every 24 hours.*

orchard /'ɔːtʃəd/ *n* an area where fruit trees are grown: *a cherry orchard.*

orchestra /'ɔːkɪstrə/ *n* a group of musicians playing together. **orchestral** /ɔːˈkɛstrəl/ *adj.*

orchid /'ɔːkɪd/ *n* a plant with brightly-coloured or unusually-shaped flowers.

ordain /ɔːˈdeɪn/ *v* to make a member of the Christian clergy: *Some Christian churches have decided to ordain women.*

ordeal /ɔːˈdiːl/ *n* a difficult, painful experience: *The exam was a great ordeal.*

order /'ɔːdə(r)/ *n* **1** a command: *He gave me my orders.* **2** an instruction to supply something: *We have received several orders for this dictionary.* **3** an arrangement of people, things *etc*: *Put the names in alphabetical order*; *I'll deal with the questions in order of importance.* **4** an organized state when things are in their proper places: *It was time to bring some order into my life.* **5** a peaceful condition: *law and order.* — *v* **1** to tell someone to do something: *He ordered me to stand up.* **2** to give an instruction to supply something: *He called the waiter and ordered a steak.*

'order-form *n* a form on which a customer's order is written.

'orderly *adj* well-behaved; quiet: *an orderly queue of people.*

in order 1 correct according to what is regularly done: *It is quite in order to end the meeting now.* **2** in a good efficient state: *Everything is in order for the party.*

in order that so that: *Sarah read the page again in order that she might understand it better.*

in order to for the purpose of: *I went home in order to change my clothes.*

in working order ready for use and working properly.

made to order made when and how a customer wishes: *curtains made to order.*

order about or **order around** to keep telling someone what to do and how to do it.

out of order not working properly: *The machine is out of order.*

ordinal /'ɔːdɪnəl/: **ordinal numbers** the numbers that show order in a series — first, second, third *etc*.

ordinary /'ɔːdɪnrɪ/ *adj* **1** usual; normal: *She was behaving in a perfectly ordinary way.* **2** not especially good *etc*: *Stripped of his power to inflict harm, he seemed quite ordinary.*

The opposite of **ordinary** is **extraordinary**.

ordinarily /'ɔːdənərəlɪ/ *adv* usually.
out of the ordinary unusual; different;

strange: *I'm looking for a gift that is a little out of the ordinary.*

ore /ɔː(r)/ *n* any mineral, rock *etc* from which a metal is obtained: *iron ore.*

organ[1] /ˈɔːɡən/ *n* a part of your body or of a plant which has a special purpose: *the organs of reproduction.*

organ[2] /ˈɔːɡən/ *n* a large musical instrument like a piano, with or without pipes.

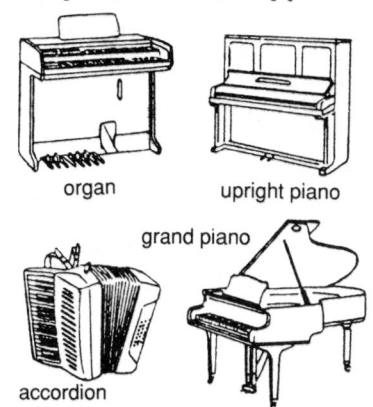

organ upright piano grand piano accordion

ˈorganist *n* someone who plays the organ.

organic /ɔːˈɡænɪk/ *adj* **1** of or produced by living things: *organic fertilizers.* **2** produced without the use of chemical fertilizers: *He will only buy organic vegetables.*

organism /ˈɔːɡənɪzm/ *n* a tiny living animal or plant: *organisms resistent to pencillin.*

organization /ˌɔːɡənaɪˈzeɪʃən/ *n* **1** a group of people working together for a purpose: *a business organization.* **2** the organizing of something: *The success of the project depends on good organization.* **organiˈzational** *adj.*

organize /ˈɔːɡənaɪz/ *v* **1** to arrange; to prepare for something: *to organize a conference.* **2** to arrange things into a system or logical order: *She organized his papers so that he could find what he wanted easily.* **ˈorganizer** *n.*

ˈorganized *adj* well-arranged; efficient; methodical: *Always work in an organized way.*

orgasm /ˈɔːɡazm/ *n* during sexual intercourse, the strongest point of sexual excitement.

Orient /ˈɔːrɪənt/: **the Orient** the east: *the mysteries of the Orient.*

oriˈental *adj* in or from the east: *oriental art.* — *n* someone who comes from the east.

orientate /ˈɔːrɪənteɪt/ *v* **1** to get yourself used to unfamiliar surroundings, conditions *etc*: *It will take him at least a week to orientate himself.* **2** to find out your position in relation to something else: *The hikers tried to orientate themselves before continuing their walk.* **orienˈtation** *n.*

orienteering /ˌɔːrɪənˈtɪərɪŋ/ *n* a sport in which you run across country, finding your way with a map and compass.

origami /ˌɒrɪˈɡɑːmɪ/ *n* the art of paper-folding that comes originally from Japan.

origin /ˈɒrɪdʒɪn/ *n* the place or point from which anything first comes; the cause: *the origins of the English language*; *What was the origin of his fear of flying?.*

original /əˈrɪdʒɪnəl/ *adj* **1** existing at the beginning; first: *This part of the house is new but the rest is original.* **2** new; fresh; able to produce ideas which have not been thought of before: *original ideas*; *He has a very original mind.* **3** done by the artist himself: *The original painting is in the museum, but there are hundreds of copies.* — *n* the earliest version: *This is the original — all the others are copies.*

origiˈnality *n* the quality of being new and different: *His writing lacks originality.*

oˈriginally *adv* **1** in or from the beginning: *He lives in Wales but his family originally came from Scotland.* **2** in a new and different way: *She dresses very originally.*

originate /əˈrɪdʒɪneɪt/ *v* to bring or come into being: *This style of painting on silk originated in China.*

ˈorigins *n* a person's place of birth, family, background *etc*: *He tried to hide his origins.*

ornament /ˈɔːnəmənt/ *n* a decorative object intended to make a room *etc* more beautiful: *There were some china ornaments in the shape of little animals on the mantelpiece.* — *v* to decorate: *The ceiling of the church was richly ornamented.* **ornamenˈtation** *n.*

ornaˈmental *adj* for decoration: *an ornamental pond.*

ornate /ɔːˈneɪt/ *adj* with a complicated and beautiful design: *an ornate doorway.* **orˈnately** *adv.* **orˈnateness** *n.*

ornithology /ˌɔːnɪˈθɒlədʒɪ/ *n* the study of birds. **orniˈthologist** *n.*

orphan /ˈɔːfən/ *n* a child whose parents have both died: *She became an orphan at the age of ten.* — *adj*: *an orphan child.* — *v* to cause a child to become an orphan: *He was orphaned at the age of three.*

orphanage /'ɔːfənɪdʒ/ *n* a home for orphans.

orthodox /'ɔːθədɒks/ *adj* **1** accepted, or thought correct, by most people: *The teacher sometimes allowed the children to walk about the classroom and chatter, instead of sitting quietly at desks in the orthodox way.* **2** in religion, keeping the old, traditional beliefs, opinions and practices: *He is an orthodox Jew.* **'orthodoxy** *n*.

oscillate /'ɒsɪleɪt/ *v* **1** to move or swing backwards and forwards like the pendulum of a clock: *Radio waves oscillate.* **2** to keep changing from one thing to the other; to waver: *He oscillated between eating meat and being a vegetarian.* **oscil'lation** *n*.

ostentatious /ɒstɛn'teɪʃəs/ *adj* designed or intended to attract admiration and attention: *ostentatious jewellery.* **osten'tatiously** *adv*.

ostracize /'ɒstrəsaɪz/ *v* to deliberately exclude a person from a group: *He was ostracized by his workmates for refusing to join the strike.*

ostrich /'ɒstrɪtʃ/ *n* a large bird that cannot fly.

other /'ʌðə(r)/ *adj, pron* **1** the second of two things: *I have lost my other glove; Here is one, but where is the other?* **2** the rest: *Some of the boys have arrived — where are the others?; The baby is here and the other children are at school.* **3** extra; more; different: *If you don't want these books, there are others in the cupboard; We can try out other methods if this doesn't work.* — *adj* recently past: *I saw him just the other day.*

   otherwise /'ʌðəwaɪz/ *adv* in every other way except this: *Jim has a bad temper but otherwise he's very nice.* — *conjunction* or else; if not: *Take a taxi — otherwise you'll be late.*

   other than except: *There was no-one there other than an old woman.*

   somehow or other in some way or by some means: *I'll finish this job on time, somehow or other.*

otter /'ɒtə(r)/ *n* a small furry river animal that eats fish.

ouch /aʊtʃ/ a word used to express pain: *Ouch! That hurt.*

ought /ɔːt/ *v* **1** used to show duty; should: *You ought to help them; She ought not to work so hard.* **2** used to show that you would expect something to happen; should: *He ought to have been able to do it — I don't know why he couldn't manage it.*

oughtn't /'ɔːtənt/ the short form of **ought not**: *You ought to thank her, oughtn't you?*

ounce /aʊns/ *n* a unit of weight, 28·35 grammes, usually written **oz**.

our /'aʊə(r)/ *adj* belonging to us: *This is our house.*

   ours *pron* the one, or ones, belonging to us: *The house is ours; These books are ours.*

   ourselves /aʊə'sɛlvz/ *pron* **1** (used as the object of a verb or preposition) the word you use when you and other people are both the subject and the object of the sentence *etc*: *We saw ourselves in the mirror.* **2** used to emphasize **we** or **us**: *We ourselves played no part in this.* **3** without help *etc*: *We'll just have to finish the job ourselves.*

oust /aʊst/ *v* to force to leave a job, position or place: *The President has been ousted by his political opponents.*

out /aʊt/ *adv* **1** not in a building *etc*; from inside a building *etc*; in or into the open air: *The children are out in the garden; They went out for a walk.* **2** from inside something: *He opened the desk and took out a pencil.* **3** away from home, or from the office *etc*: *We had an evening out; The manager is out.* **4** far away: *He went out to India.* **5** loudly and clearly: *He shouted out the answer.* **6** completely: *She was tired out.* **7** known to everyone: *The secret is out.* **8** with the water at or going to its lowest level: *The tide is going out; The tide is out.*

   out of 1 from inside: *He took it out of the bag.* **2** not in: *Mr Smith is out of the office; out of danger; out of sight.* **3** from among: *Four out of five people like this song.* **4** having none left: *She is quite out of breath.* **5** because of: *He opened the box out of curiosity.* **6** from: *He drank the lemonade out of the bottle.*

   out of doors outside: *We like to eat out of doors in summer.*

out-and-out /aʊtən'aʊt/ *adj* complete or thorough: *an out-and-out liar.*

outback /'aʊtbak/ *n* the part of a country, especially Australia, that is a long way from where people live: *a cattle station in the outback.*

outboard /'aʊtbɔːd/ or **outboard motor** *n* an engine that can be fixed to the back of a small boat.

outbreak /'aʊtbreɪk/ *n* a sudden beginning, usually of something unpleasant: *the outbreak of war.*

outburst /'aʊtbɜːst/ *n* an explosion, especially of angry feelings: *a sudden outburst of rage.*

outcast /'aʊtkɑːst/ *n* someone who has been driven away from friends *etc*: *an outcast from society*.

outcome /'aʊtkʌm/ *n* the result: *What was the outcome of your discussion?*

outcry /'aʊtkraɪ/ *n* a strong reaction or protest by a large number of people: *The decision produced a public outcry*.

outdated /aʊt'deɪtɪd/ *adj* out of fashion and no longer used: *outdated ideas*.

outdo /aʊt'duː/ *v* to do better than someone or something: *He worked very hard as he did not want to be outdone by anyone*.

> **out'do**; **outdid** /aʊt'dɪd/; **outdone** /aʊt'dʌn/.

outdoor /'aʊtdɔː(r)/ *adj* outside; for use outside: *outdoor shoes*; *outdoor activities*.

> The opposite of **outdoor** is **indoor**.

outdoors /aʊt'dɔːz/ *adv* outside; not inside a building: *She sat outdoors in the sun*; *Don't go outdoors if it's raining*.

outer /'aʊtə(r)/ *adj* far from the centre of something: *outer space*; *outer layers*.
  'outermost *adj* nearest the edge, outside *etc*: *the outermost ring on the target*.

outfit /'aʊtfɪt/ *n* a set of clothes, especially for a particular occasion: *a wedding outfit*.

outgoing /aʊt'gəʊɪŋ/ *adj* 1 friendly and enjoying social events: *a lively, outgoing young woman*. 2 leaving: *the outgoing president*.
  outgoings *n* the amounts of money that you spend: *Our outgoings have been increasing*.

outgrow /aʊt'grəʊ/ *v* to grow too big or too old for something: *He has outgrown all his clothes*.

> **out'grow**; **outgrew** /aʊt'gruː/; **outgrown** /aʊt'grəʊn/.

outing /'aʊtɪŋ/ *n* a short trip, made for pleasure: *an outing to the seaside*.

outlandish /aʊt'lændɪʃ/ *adj* very strange or unusual: *outlandish clothes*; *outlandish ideas*.

outlast /aʊt'lɑːst/ *v* to last or live longer than someone or something.

outlaw /'aʊtlɔː/ *n* someone who is given no protection by the law in his country because he is a criminal. — *v* to make something illegal: *The sale of alcohol was outlawed*.

outlay /'aʊtleɪ/ *n* money that is spent, especially in order to start a business or project.

outlet /'aʊtlɛt/ *n* a way out; a way of letting something out: *That pipe is an outlet from the main tank*; *Football is an outlet for his energy*.

outline /'aʊtlaɪn/ *n* 1 the line forming, or showing, the outer edge of something: *He drew the outline of the face first, then added the features*. 2 a short description of the main details of a plan *etc*: *Don't tell me the whole story — just give me an outline*. — *v* to draw or give the outline of something.

outlive /aʊt'lɪv/ *v* to live longer than someone: *He outlived his older brother by fifteen years*.

outlook /'aʊtlʊk/ *n* 1 a view: *Their house has a wonderful outlook*. 2 your view of life *etc*: *He has a strange outlook on life*. 3 what is likely to happen in the future: *The weather outlook is bad*.

outlying /'aʊtlaɪɪŋ/ *adj* distant; away from a city or central area: *He comes from a small outlying village*.

outmoded /aʊt'məʊdɪd/ *adj* out of date; no longer in fashion.

outnumber /aʊt'nʌmbə(r)/ *v* to be more in number than: *The boys in the class outnumber the girls*.

out-of-date /aʊtəv'deɪt/ *adj* 1 old-fashioned: *an out-of-date dress*. 2 old; no longer usable: *an out-of-date telephone directory*.

out-of-the-way /aʊtəvðə'weɪ/ *adj* difficult to reach: *out-of-the-way places*.

outpatient /'aʊtpeɪʃənt/ *n* someone who comes to hospital for treatment but does not stay there for the night: *She went to the out-patient department of the hospital to have the cut on her hand stitched*.

output /'aʊtpʊt/ *n* 1 a quantity of goods that is produced, or an amount of work that is done: *The output of this factory increased last year*. 2 the information produced by a computer.

> The opposite of **output** is **input**.

outrage /'aʊtreɪdʒ/ *n* a wicked action: *The decision to close the hospital is an outrage*. — *v* to hurt, shock or insult: *She was outraged by his behaviour*.

outrageous /aʊt'reɪdʒəs/ *adj* terrible: *outrageous behaviour*. **out'rageously** *adv*. **out'rageousness** *n*.

outright *adv* /aʊt'raɪt/ 1 honestly: *I told him outright what I thought*. 2 immediately: *He was killed outright*. — *adj* /'aʊtraɪt/ without any doubt: *He is the outright winner*.

outset /'aʊtsɛt/ *n* the beginning of something: *At the outset of his career he earned very little money*; *She enjoyed going to school from the outset*.

outshine /aʊtˈʃaɪn/ v to be brighter or better than others: *She outshone all the other students.*

out'shine; outshone /aʊtˈʃɒn/; out-'shone.

outside /aʊtˈsaɪd/ n **1** the outer surface: *The outside of the house was painted white.* **2** the area surrounding something: *I'd like to look at the house from the outside.* — adj **1** of, on, or near the outer part of anything: *the outside surface.* **2** not from within your own group, firm *etc*: *We shall need outside help to finish this work.* — adv **1** out of, not in a building *etc*: *He went outside; He stayed outside.* **2** on the outside: *The house is beautiful both inside and outside.* — prep on the outer part or side of; not inside: *He stood outside the house.*

out'sider n **1** anyone who is not a member: *The members of the secret society had to promise not to tell any outsiders about their meetings.* **2** someone who is in some way different from other people in a group and is not liked by them or does not feel liked by them: *The new boy in the class felt like an outsider.*

at the outside at the most: *A new part would cost £20 at the outside.*

outskirts /ˈaʊtskɜːts/ n the outer parts or area, especially of a town: *I live on the outskirts of London.*

outspoken /aʊtˈspoʊkən/ adj saying exactly what you mean, even if it upsets people: *She sometimes makes enemies because she is very outspoken; an outspoken remark.*

outstanding /aʊtˈstændɪŋ/ adj **1** excellent: *an outstanding student.* **2** not yet paid, done *etc*: *You must pay all outstanding bills.*

out'standingly adv very: *outstandingly good.*

outstretched /aʊtˈstretʃt/ adj spread out as far as possible: *She ran into his outstretched arms.*

outward /ˈaʊtwəd/ adj **1** on or towards the outside; able to be seen: *Judging by his outward appearance, he's not very rich; She showed no outward sign of unhappiness.* **2** away from a place: *The outward journey will be by sea, but they will return home by air.*

'**outwardly** adv in appearance: *Outwardly he is cheerful, but he is really an unhappy person.*

'**outwards** adv towards the outside edge or surface; away from the centre: *Moving outwards from the centre of the painting, we see that the figures become smaller.*

outweigh /aʊtˈweɪ/ v to be of greater value or importance: *The advantages of the scheme far outweigh the disadvantages.*

outwit /aʊtˈwɪt/ v to defeat someone by being cleverer than they are: *She managed to outwit the police and escape.*

oval /ˈoʊvəl/ adj shaped like an egg: *an oval table.* — n an oval shape: *He drew an oval.*

ovary /ˈoʊvərɪ/ n one of the two organs in a woman's body which produce the eggs from which babies grow.

ovation /əˈveɪʃən/ n cheering or applause to express approval, welcome *etc*: *They gave the president an ovation after his speech.*

oven /ˈʌvən/ n a closed box-like container that is heated for cooking food: *She put the cake into the oven.*

'**ovenproof** adj that will not crack when hot: *ovenproof dishes and plates.*

over /ˈoʊvə(r)/ prep **1** higher than; above in position, number, authority *etc*: *Hang that picture over the fireplace; He's over 90 years old.* **2** from one side to another, on or above the top of; on the other side of: *He jumped over the gate; She fell over the cat; My friend lives over the street.* **3** covering: *He put his handkerchief over his face.* **4** across: *You find people like him all over the world.* **5** about: *a quarrel over money.* **6** by means of: *He spoke to her over the telephone.* **7** during: *Over the years, she grew to hate her husband.* **8** while having *etc*: *He fell asleep over his dinner.* — adv **1** moving above you, from one side to another: *The plane flew over about an hour ago.* **2** used to show a turning movement: *He rolled over on his back; He turned over the page.* **3** across: *He went over and spoke to them.* **4** down: *He fell over.* **5** more, in number, age *etc*: *jobs for people aged twenty and over.* **6** remaining: *There are two cakes for each of us, and two over.* **7** through from beginning to end: *Read it over.* — adj finished: *The affair is over now.*

over again once more: *Play the tune over again; Do the whole thing over again.*

> to speak **over twenty** (not **twenty over**) languages.
> to put your hand **over** (not **above**) a cup; the opposite of **over** is **under**.
> to hang a picture **over** or **above** a fireplace; the opposite of **above** is **below**.

overall n /ˈoʊvərɔːl/ a garment worn over ordinary clothes to protect them: *She wears* an overall when cleaning the house. — adj including everything: *the overall cost*. — adv /ˈoʊvərˈɔːl/ **1** including everything: *What is the length overall?* **2** as a whole; in general: *Overall, your son's schoolwork has not been bad.*

overalls /ˈoʊvərɔːlz/ *n* trousers or a suit made of hardwearing materials worn by workmen to protect their ordinary clothes: *The painter put on his overalls before starting work.*

overawe /oʊvərˈɔː/ *v* to impress someone and make them feel a little afraid: *He was overawed by the magnificent mountains.*

overbalance /oʊvəˈbæləns/ *v* to fall over, or nearly fall over because you are not standing in a steady position.

overboard /ˈoʊvəbɔːd/ *adv* over the side of a ship or boat into the water: *He jumped overboard.*

go overboard to become too enthusiastic about something.

overcast /oʊvəˈkɑːst/ *adj* dark with clouds: *In the afternoon it became overcast but it didn't rain.*

overcharge /oʊvəˈtʃɑːdʒ/ *v* to charge too much: *I have been overcharged for these goods.*

overcoat /ˈoʊvəkoʊt/ *n* a heavy coat worn over all other clothes.

overcome /oʊvəˈkʌm/ *adj* helpless; very upset in your feelings: *overcome with grief.* — *v* to defeat; to conquer: *She overcame her fear of the dark.*

> **over'come; overcame** /oʊvəˈkeɪm/; **over'come**.

overcrowded /oʊvəˈkraʊdɪd/ *adj* containing too many people *etc*: *overcrowded buses.*
over'crowding *n*: *There is often overcrowding in cities.*

overdo /oʊvəˈduː/ *v* **1** to do something too much; to go too far: *It's good to work hard, but don't overdo it.* **2** to cook for too long: *The meat was rather overdone.*

> **over'do; overdid** /oʊvəˈdɪd/; **overdone** /oʊvəˈdʌn/.

overdose /ˈoʊvədoʊs/ *n* more of a drug or medicine than is safe: *Don't take more than one tablet — an overdose could be dangerous.*

overdue /oʊvəˈdjuː/ *adj* **1** late: *The train is overdue.* **2** not yet paid, done, delivered *etc*, although the date for doing this has passed: *overdue library books.*

overestimate /oʊvərˈɛstɪmeɪt/ *v* to think that something is bigger or more important *etc* than it really is: *We overestimated the amount of food we would need — there was a lot left over.*

overflow /oʊvəˈfloʊ/ *v* to flow over the edge or limits of something: *The river overflowed its banks*; *The crowd overflowed into the next room.*

overgrown /oʊvəˈgroʊn/ *adj* **1** full of plants that have grown too large or thick: *Our garden is overgrown with weeds.* **2** grown very large: *He behaves like an overgrown schoolboy.*

overhang /oʊvəˈhæŋ/ *v* to stick out or hang over: *The stream was overhung by the branches of a tree.*

overhaul *v* /oʊvəˈhɔːl/ to examine something carefully and repair any faults: *He had his car overhauled at the garage before he took it away on holiday.* — *n* /ˈoʊvəhɔːl/: *The mechanic gave the car a complete overhaul.*

overhead /oʊvəˈhɛd/ or /ˈoʊvəhɛd/ *adv, adj* above; over your head: *The plane flew overhead*; *an overhead bridge.*

> See **zebra crossing**.

overheads /ˈoʊvəhɛdz/ *n plural* the money that a business has to spend regularly on rent, electricity *etc*: *This firm has very high overheads, which make its products more expensive.*

overhear /oʊvəˈhɪə(r)/ *v* to hear what you shouldn't hear: *I overheard them talking about me*; *Your plan was overheard!*

> **over'hear; overheard** /oʊvəˈhɜːd/; **over'heard**.

overjoyed /oʊvəˈdʒɔɪd/ *adj* very glad: *She was overjoyed to hear that he was safe.*

overland /ˈoʊvəlænd/ *adv, adj* across land, rather than by sea or air: *an overland safari*; *They are travelling overland across America.*

overlap *v* /oʊvəˈlæp/ **1** to cover a part of something; to lie partly over each other: *Each roof-tile overlaps the one below it*; *The curtains should be wide enough to overlap.* **2** to happen partly at the same time; to be partly the same: *I couldn't watch the whole film because it overlapped with the news on the fourth channel, which my dad always watches*; *Although history and geography are separate subjects, they quite often overlap.* — *n* /ˈoʊvəlæp/: *There is an overlap of half an hour between the two programmes.*

overleaf /oʊvəˈliːf/ *adv* on the other side of the page: *See the tables overleaf.*

overload /oʊvə'loʊd/ v **1** to put too many things or people in or onto something: *an overloaded bus; I can't take any more work for a week — I'm already overloaded.* **2** to put too much electricity through something: *The circuit will become overloaded if all the machines are switched on together.*

overlook /oʊvə'lʊk/ v **1** to look down on: *The house overlooked the river.* **2** to take no notice of something; to forgive: *We shall overlook your lateness this time.* **3** to fail to see or notice something: *Small details are easily overlooked, but they can be very important.*

overnight /'oʊvənaɪt/ or /oʊvə'naɪt/ adj, adv **1** for the night: *an overnight bag; We stayed in Paris overnight.* **2** sudden; suddenly: *He became a hero overnight; She was an overnight success.*

overpower /oʊvə'paʊə(r)/ v to be stronger and therefore to win: *The man tried to run away but he was overpowered by two policemen.*

over'powering adj very strong: *an overpowering feeling of sadness; An overpowering smell of sulphur filled the air.*

overrate /oʊvə'reɪt/ v to think that something is better than it really is: *I think his books are overrated.*

overriding /oʊvə'raɪdɪŋ/ adj most important: *the overriding consideration.*

overrule /oʊvə'ruːl/ v to decide that another person's decision is wrong: *The chairman has the power to overrule the committee's decision; The judge overruled the lawyer's objection.*

overrun /oʊvə'rʌn/ v **1** to spread quickly all over a place; to occupy a place quickly: *The cellar was overrun with mice; The country was overrun by the enemy troops.* **2** to continue longer than intended: *The live television show overran by ten minutes.*

overseas /oʊvə'siːz/ or /'oʊvəsiːz/ adv, adj across the sea; abroad: *He went overseas; an overseas job.*

> **overseas** (not **oversea**) trade.

oversee /oʊvə'siː/ v to supervise: *He oversees production at the factory.*

> **over'see**; **oversaw** /oʊvə'sɔː/; **overseen**.

overseer n: *The overseer reported her for being late.*

oversight /'oʊvəsaɪt/ n a mistake, especially one that you make because you have not noticed something: *It was a serious oversight on his part.*

oversleep /oʊvə'sliːp/ v to sleep longer than you intended: *He overslept and missed the train.*

> **over'sleep**; **overslept** /oʊvə'slɛpt/; **over'slept**.

overspend /oʊvə'spɛnd/ v to spend too much money: *He overspent on his new house.*

> **over'spend**; **overspent** /'oʊvəspɛnt/; **over'spent**.

overtake /oʊvə'teɪk/ v to pass a car etc while driving etc: *He overtook a police car.*

> **over'take**; **overtook** /oʊvə'tʊk/; **overtaken** /oʊvə'teɪkən/.

overthrow v /oʊvə'θroʊ/ to defeat and force out of power: *The government has been overthrown.* — n /'oʊvəθroʊ/.

> **over'throw**; **overthrew** /oʊvə'θruː/; **overthrown** /oʊvə'θroʊn/.

overtime /'oʊvətaɪm/ n time spent in working more than your set number of hours etc: *He did five hours' overtime this week.*

overture /'oʊvətjʊə(r)/ n **1** a piece of music written as the introduction to an opera or ballet etc. **2** a friendly approach or proposal: *She seemed to be making friendly overtures but I wasn't completely sure that I trusted her.*

overturn /oʊvə'tɜːn/ v to turn over: *They overturned the boat; The car overturned.*

overview /'oʊvəvjuː/ n a brief, general description: *He presented an overview of the results so far.*

overweight /oʊvə'weɪt/ adj too heavy; too fat: *If I eat too much I soon get overweight.*

overwhelm /oʊvə'wɛlm/ v **1** to have a very strong and sudden effect on someone: *When she won the prize she was overwhelmed with joy and didn't know what to say.* **2** to win a complete victory over someone; to defeat completely: *Our soldiers were overwhelmed by the enemy.*

over'whelming adj very great or strong: *an overwhelming feeling of relief; an overwhelming victory.* **over'whelmingly** adv.

overwork /oʊvə'wɜːk/ n the act of working too hard: *Overwork made him ill.*

over'worked adj made to work too hard: *His staff are overworked.*

owe /oʊ/ v to be in debt to someone: *I owe him £10.*

'**owing** *adj* still to be paid: *There is some money still owing.*

owing to because of: *Owing to the rain, the football has been cancelled.*

> **owing to** is used to mean 'because of': *The shop is closed owing to* (not *due to*) *the manager's illness.*
> **due to** is used to mean 'caused by': *The accident was believed to be due to his negligence.*

owl /aʊl/ *n* a bird that flies at night and feeds on small birds and animals.

> An owl **hoots**.

owl

own /oʊn/ *v* **1** to have as a possession: *I own a car*; *These buildings are owned by the University.* **2** to admit that something is true: *I own that I made a mistake.* — *adj*, *pron* belonging to you: *The house is my own*; *I saw it with my own eyes.*

> **I did it by myself** (not **I did it my ownself**).

'**owner** *n* a person who owns something: *Are you the owner of that car?* '**ownership** *n*.

hold your own to not be defeated: *She's perfectly capable of holding her own in an argument.*

on your own 1 by yourself; without help: *Did he do it all on his own?* **2** by yourself; alone: *Don't leave me on my own in this horrible place.*

own up to admit that you have done something: *None of the children owned up to breaking the window.*

ox /ɒks/, *plural* **oxen** /'ɒksən/, *n* **1** a bull used to pull carts, ploughs *etc*: *an ox-drawn cart*. **2** any bull or cow.

oxygen /'ɒksɪdʒən/ *n* a gas without taste, colour or smell, forming part of the air: *He died from lack of oxygen.*

oyster /'ɔɪstə(r)/ *n* an edible shellfish from which we get pearls.

ozone /'oʊzoʊn/ *n* a type of oxygen with a strong smell.

ozone layer the layer of ozone that is part of the earth's atmosphere and that protects the planet from the radiation of the sun: *Scientists are worried that the ozone layer may be getting thinner.*

P

pace /peɪs/ n **1** a step: *He took a pace forward.* **2** speed of movement: *a fast pace.* — v to walk: *The tiger paced to and fro in its cage.*

'pacemaker n **1** an electronic device for making a heart beat regularly: *He was suffering from heart disease and had to have a pacemaker fitted next to his heart.* **2** a person who runs at the front in a race and sets the speed.

keep pace to go as fast or as slowly as another person: *I managed to keep pace with him throughout the race.*

set the pace to do something at the speed others must follow: *The Russian athlete set the pace for the first two laps of the race.*

pacifist /'pasɪfɪst/ n a person who believes that all war is wrong.

pacify /'pasɪfaɪ/ v to make calm or peaceful: *She soothed and pacified the screaming child.*

pack /pak/ n **1** things tied up together or put in a bag, especially for carrying on your back: *He carried his luggage in a pack on his back.* **2** a set of playing-cards: *a pack of cards.* **3** a number or group of certain animals: *a pack of wolves.* **4** a packet: *a pack of cigarettes.* — v **1** to put clothes *etc* into a bag, suitcase or trunk for a journey: *I've packed all I need and I'm ready to go.* **2** to come together in large numbers and fill a small space: *They packed into the hall to hear his speech*; *The hall was packed with people.*

pack in to succeed in doing a lot in a short time: *You seem to have packed a lot into your weekend*; *They saw as much as they could pack in.*

pack out to fill with people: *The theatre was packed out for the first performance.*

pack up 1 to put things into containers in order to take them somewhere else: *She packed up the contents of her house.* **2** to tidy your working area and put everything away: *It will soon be time to pack up and go home.*

package /'pakɪdʒ/ n **1** things wrapped up and tied for posting *etc*: *to deliver a package.* **2** a number of things that must be bought or accepted together: *a word-processing package*; *If you buy this car, free insurance is part of the package.* — v to wrap things up into a package: *He packaged up the clothes.*

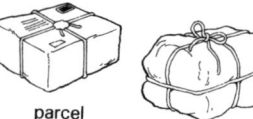

parcel

package

packet

packaging /'pakɪdʒɪŋ/ n all the material that is used to wrap and pack something before it is sold or sent somewhere: *Remove all the packaging carefully.*

package holiday or **package tour** a holiday or tour, arranged by a travel agent, which includes travel and accommodation in the price.

packed lunch /'pakt lʌntʃ/ food that you take with you to work or school.

packet /'pakɪt/ n a small, flat, usually paper or cardboard, container: *a packet of biscuits.*

See **package**.

packing /'pakɪŋ/ n **1** the putting of things in bags, cases *etc*: *He has done his packing already.* **2** the materials used to wrap things for posting: *He unwrapped the vase and threw away the packing*; *There will be a small extra charge for postage and packing.*

packing case a wooden box in which things are transported or stored.

pact /pakt/ n a formal agreement between two or more people, groups or countries: *The three countries have signed a non-aggression pact.*

pad¹ /pad/ v to walk softly: *The dog padded along the road.*

pad² /pad/ n **1** a soft, cushion-like object made of or filled with a soft material: *She knelt on a rubber pad to clean the floor.* **2** sheets of paper fixed together: *a writing-pad.* **3** a platform from which rockets are sent off: *a launching-pad.* — v to put a pad in or on something: *The shoes were too big so she padded them with cottonwool.*

'padding n material used to make a pad: *He used old blankets as padding.*

pad out to make an essay, book, *etc* longer by adding things which are not really necessary: *Her letter seemed too short so* *she padded it out with descriptions of the weather.*

paddle[1] /'padəl/ *v* to walk about in shallow water: *The children went paddling in the sea.*

paddle[2] /'padəl/ *n* a short, light oar, often with a blade at each end used in canoes *etc*. — *v* to move with a paddle: *He paddled the canoe along the river.*

> to **paddle** (not **pedal**) a canoe.

paddock /'padək/ *n* a small enclosed field, usually near a house or stable, where horses are kept.

paddy /'padɪ/ *n* (also **paddy field**) a field where rice is grown.

padlock /'padlɒk/ *n* a movable lock with a U-shaped bar that can be passed through a ring, chain *etc*: *He has put a padlock on the gate.* — *v* to fasten with a padlock: *She padlocked her bike.*

> See **bolt**.

paediatrician /pi:dɪə'trɪʃən/ *n* a doctor specializing in children's health and diseases: *a paediatrician working at the local children's hospital.*

page[1] /peɪdʒ/ *n* one side of a sheet of paper in a book, magazine *etc*: *page ninety-four; a three-page letter.*

page[2] /peɪdʒ/ *n* **1** a boy in a hotel *etc* who takes messages, carries luggage *etc*. **2** a boy servant, also called a **'page-boy**. — *v* to try to find someone in a public place by calling out their name, usually through a loudspeaker: *I could not see my friend in the hotel, so I had him paged.*

pageant /'padʒənt/ *n* **1** a colourful parade or show made up of different scenes, usually taken from history: *The children were dressed in beautiful costumes for the pageant.* **2** any great and splendid show or display: *the colourful pageant of Scotland's history.*

'pageantry *n* the impressive and colourful display of a ceremony or show: *The pageantry of a coronation.*

pagoda /pə'ɡoʊdə/ *n* a Chinese temple, built in the shape of a tall tower, each storey of which has its own strip of over-hanging roof.

paid *see* **pay**.

pail /peɪl/ *n* a bucket: *Fetch a pail of water.*

pain /peɪn/ *n* suffering, in your body or mind: *a pain in the chest.* — *v* to upset: *It pained her to have to scold him.*

> The bruise was **very sore** or **very painful** (not **very pain**).
> I **have a pain** in my chest, or my chest **is hurting** (not **is paining**).

pained *adj* showing that you are upset or offended: *a pained expression.*

'painful *adj* causing pain: *a painful injury.* **'painfully** *adv.*

'painless *adj* without pain. **'painlessly** *adv.*

'painkiller *n* a drug *etc* that takes away pain.

'painstaking *adj* **1** very careful; paying attention to every detail: *She is a very painstaking student.* **2** needing a lot of care and attention to detail: *Building a model aeroplane is painstaking work.* **'painstakingly** *adv.*

be at pains or **take pains** to take great care and trouble to do something well: *He was at pains to sound relaxed; She took great pains to make the party a success.*

paint /peɪnt/ *n* a colouring substance in the form of liquid or paste: *The artist's clothes were covered with paint.* — *adj*: *a paint pot.* — *v* **1** to put paint on walls *etc*: *He is painting the kitchen.* **2** to make a picture of something or someone using paint: *She painted her mother and father.*

'paint-box *n* a box containing different paints for making pictures.

'paint-brush *n* a brush used for putting on paint.

'painter *n* **1** a person whose job is to put paint on walls, doors *etc*: *We employed a painter to paint the outside of the house.* **2** an artist who makes pictures in paint: *Who was the painter of this portrait?*

'painting *n* **1** the activity of painting pictures or walls *etc*: *Painting is very relaxing.* **2** a painted picture: *There were four paintings on the wall.*

pair /peə(r)/ *n* **1** two things of the same kind that are used *etc* together: *a pair of shoes.* **2** a single thing made up of two parts: *a pair of scissors; a pair of pants.* **3** two people, animals *etc* who are thought of together for some reason: *a pair of giant pandas; John and James are the guilty pair.*

> **pair** is singular: *That pair of trousers needs mending; There is a pair of gloves on the table.*

in pairs in groups of two: *Do the exercise alone and then discuss your answers in pairs; Those vases are only sold in pairs.*

pair off to form a pair or pairs: *She had paired me off with her brother before he even arrived*; *We'll all meet together first and then pair off.*

pair up to join together with another person or group: *Please pair up with your neighbour and share the books between you.*

pajamas another spelling of **pyjamas**.

pal /pal/ *n* a friend: *My son brought a pal home for tea.*

palace /'palɪs/ *n* a large and magnificent house, especially one lived in by a king or queen: *Buckingham Palace.*

palate /'palət/ *n* **1** the top part of the inside of your mouth. **2** a person's particular taste or liking: *In London you can get food to suit every palate.*

palatial /pə'leɪʃəl/ *adj* like a palace: *a palatial house*; *palatial rooms.*

pale /peɪl/ *adj* **1** having less colour than normal: *a pale face*; *You look pale — are you ill?*; *She went pale with fear.* **2** light in colour; not bright: *pale green.* — *v* to become pale: *She paled at the bad news.* **'paleness** *n*.

palette /'palət/ *n* a small flat piece of wood *etc* on which artists mix their colours.

pall /pɔːl/ *v* to begin to bore: *He thought the film began to pall after two hours.*

pallid /'palɪd/ *adj* unnaturally pale; without colour: *He looked tired and pallid*; *She had a pallid face.*

pally /'palɪ/ *adj* a slang word for friendly: *My son is a bit too pally with that girl.*

palm[1] /pɑːm/ *n* the inner surface of your hand between your wrist and fingers: *She held the mouse in the palm of her hand.*

palm off 1 to get rid of something that you don't want by giving it to someone else: *They palmed the cracked plate off on the next customer.* **2** to try dishonestly to persuade someone to accept something: *I won't let him palm me off with any more excuses.*

palm[2] /pɑːm/ *n* a tall tree, with broad, spreading leaves, which grows in hot countries: *a coconut palm.*

pamper /'pampə(r)/ *v* to spoil a child *etc* by giving too much attention to it: *He has been pampered by his parents, and now expects to get everything he wants.*

pamphlet /'pamflɪt/ *n* a small book usually giving information, expressing an opinion *etc*: *a political pamphlet.*

pan /pan/ *n* a metal pot used for cooking food: *a frying-pan*; *a sauce-pan.*

'pancake *n* a thin cake made of milk, flour and eggs, fried in a pan *etc*.

pancreas /'paŋkrɪəs/ *n* in the body, the organ which produces insulin: *If cells in the pancreas fail to produce insulin, you may develop diabetes.*

panda /'pandə/ *n* a large black and white bear-like animal that lives in the mountains of China.

pandemonium /pandɪ'moʊnɪəm/ *n* a state of great noise and wild confusion: *Pandemonium broke out as soon as the teacher left the classroom.*

pane /peɪn/ *n* a flat piece of glass: *a window-pane.*

panel /'panəl/ *n* **1** a flat, straight-sided piece of wood *etc* used in a door, wall *etc*: *a door-panel.* **2** a group of people chosen for a particular purpose, for example to judge a contest, take part in a quiz or other game: *members of the judging panel.*

'panellist *n* a member of a panel (sense **2**).

pang /paŋ/ *n* a sudden sharp feeling: *a pang of grief.*

panic /'panɪk/ *n* a sudden great fear, especially the kind that spreads through a crowd *etc*: *The fire caused a panic in the city.* — *v* to become so frightened that you lose the power to think clearly: *He panicked at the sight of the audience when he walked on stage.*

> There is a **k** in **'panicking** and **'panicked**.

panic-stricken /'panɪk-strɪkən/ *adj* filled with extreme fear or anxiety: *He helped to calm the panic-stricken horses.*

panorama /panə'rɑːmə/ *n* a wide view, of a landscape *etc*, in all directions: *There is a wonderful panorama from the top of that hill.*

pano'ramic *adj*: *a panoramic view of the city.*

pant /pant/ *v* **1** to gasp for breath: *He was panting heavily as he ran.* **2** to say while gasping for breath: *'Wait for me!' she panted.*

panther /'panθə(r)/ *n* **1** a leopard, especially a black one. **2** in America, a puma.

panties /'pantɪz/ *n* pants (sense **1**).

pantomime /'pantəmaɪm/ *n* a play performed at Christmas time, based on a popular fairy tale, with music, dancing, comedy *etc*.

pantry /'pantrɪ/ *n* a small room for storing food.

pants /pants/ *n* **1** in British English, a short

undergarment covering your bottom: *a pair of pants*. **2** in American English, trousers.

> **pants** takes a plural verb, but **a pair of pants** is singular: *Where are my pants?*; *Here is a clean pair of pants*.

papa /pə'pɑː/ *n* a name sometimes used for father: *You must ask your papa*.

papaya /pə'paɪə/ *n* a kind of tropical tree, or its fruit.

paper /'peɪpə(r)/ *n* **1** a material made from wood, rags *etc* and used for writing, printing, wrapping parcels *etc*: *I need paper and a pen to write a letter*. **2** a single piece of this: *There were papers all over his desk*. **3** a newspaper: *Have you read the paper?* — *adj: paper handkerchiefs*; *a paper bag*; *paper hats*.

'**paperback** *n* a book with a paper cover. — *adj: paperback novels*.

'**paper clip** a small clip for holding papers together.

'**paper knife** a knife used for opening envelopes *etc*.

'**paperwork** *n* written work which needs to be done regularly: *She does all her paperwork on Mondays*.

on paper 1 in writing: *Let's get these ideas down on paper*; *I haven't received my results on paper yet*. **2** in theory: *The scheme looks good on paper, but would it work in practice?*

papier mâché /papɪeɪ'mɒʃeɪ/ *n* a substance consisting of paper mixed together with glue, which can be made into models, bowls, boxes *etc*. — *adj: a papier mâché puppet*.

par /pɑː(r)/ *n* the number of strokes considered necessary for a golfer to complete a hole or course.

below par or **not up to par** not as good or as well as usual: *Your work has not been up to par recently*; *I'm feeling a little below par today*.

on a par with equivalent to; of equal quality or importance: *As a footballer, he's on a par with many first division players*.

parable /'parəbəl/ *n* a story, especially in the Bible, that is intended to teach a lesson: *Jesus told parables*.

parachute /'parəʃuːt/ *n* an umbrella-shaped piece of light material with ropes attached, with which a person can come slowly down to the ground from an aeroplane. — *v* to come down to the ground using a parachute.

'**parachutist** *n* a person who uses a parachute.

parade /pə'reɪd/ *n* **1** a line of people, vehicles *etc* moving forward in order, often as a celebration of some event: *a circus parade*. **2** an arrangement of soldiers in a particular order: *The troops are on parade*. — *v* **1** to march in line moving forward in order: *They paraded through the town*. **2** to arrange soldiers in order.

paradise /'parədaɪs/ *n* **1** a place or state of great happiness: *It's paradise to be by a warm fire on a cold night*. **2** heaven.

paradox /'parədɒks/ *n* a strange statement *etc* that sounds impossible, but has some truth in it: *When he told them that he was twelve years old but had had only three birthdays, they were puzzled by the paradox — till he explained that he was born on February 29*. **para'doxical** *adj*.

paraffin /'parəfɪn/ *n* a kind of oil that is used as a fuel: *This heater burns paraffin*. — *adj*: *a paraffin lamp*.

paragraph /'parəgrɑːf/ *n* a part of a piece of writing, marked by beginning the first sentence on a new line: *Start a new paragraph*.

parallel /'parəlɛl/ *adj* going in the same direction and always staying the same distance apart: *The road is parallel to the river*; *Draw two parallel lines*. — *adv* in the same direction but always about the same distance away: *We sailed parallel to the coast*. — *n* **1** a parallel line. **2** a thing or situation that is similar to another one: *His success is without parallel in his field*. **3** a comparison: *She drew a parallel between her problem and mine*.

> **parallel** has **ll** in the middle and **l** at the end.

parallelogram /parə'lɛləgram/ *n* a four-sided figure with opposite sides equal and parallel.

paralyse /'parəlaɪz/ *v* to make unable to move: *Her legs are paralysed*; *He was paralysed with fear*.

paralysis /pə'ralǝsɪs/ *n* a loss of the ability to move: *The paralysis affects his legs*.

paramedic /parə'mɛdɪk/ *n* a person who is not a doctor, but who can give emergency medical treatment.

paramount /'parəmaʊnt/ *adj* more important than anything else: *The safety of the population should be paramount*.

paranoid /'parənɔɪd/ *adj* very suspicious and afraid of others: *He has a paranoid distrust of people in uniform*.

parapet /ˈparəpɪt/ *n* a low wall along the edge of a bridge, balcony *etc*: *She leant over the parapet and looked down at the river.*

paraphernalia /parəfəˈneɪlɪə/ *n* a large number of different objects that you need for a particular purpose: *The television crew packed up all their paraphernalia and left.*

paraphrase /ˈparəfreɪz/ *n* a repeating of something written or spoken using different words: *He gave a paraphrase of his speech.* — *v*.

parasite /ˈparəsaɪt/ *n* an animal or plant that lives on another animal or plant without giving anything in return: *Fleas are parasites*; *He is a parasite on society.* **parasitic** /parəˈsɪtɪk/ *adj*.

paratroops /ˈparətruːps/ *n plural* soldiers who are trained to drop by parachute into enemy country.

parcel /ˈpɑːsəl/ *n* something wrapped and tied, usually to be sent by post: *I got a parcel in the post today.*

parcel up to wrap something up in a parcel: *He parcelled up the books and sent them to his friend.*

See **package**.

parch /pɑːtʃ/ *v* to make hot and very dry: *The sun parched the earth.*

parched *adj* **1** dried by the sun: *parched soil.* **2** thirsty: *I'm parched — I'd like a drink!*

pardon /ˈpɑːdən/ *v* **1** to forgive: *Pardon my asking, but can you help me?* **2** to free someone from prison, punishment *etc*: *The king pardoned the prisoners.* — *n* the forgiving of something. — a word used to indicate that you have not heard properly what was said: *Pardon? Could you repeat that last sentence?*

ˈpardonable *adj* that can be excused or forgiven: *a pardonable error.*

I beg your pardon I'm sorry: *I beg your pardon — what did you say?*

pardon me I am sorry: *Pardon me for interrupting you.*

parent /ˈpɛərənt/ *n* a mother or father: *His parents are very kind.* **ˈparenthood** *n*.

pariah /pəˈraɪə/ *n* a person driven out of a group or community; an outcast.

parish /ˈparɪʃ/ *n* a district with a particular church and a priest or minister: *Our house is in the parish of St Mary.*

parity /ˈparətɪ/ *n* equality: *They want parity of pay for all the workers in the factory.*

park /pɑːk/ *n* **1** a public piece of ground with grass and trees: *The children go to the park every morning to play.* **2** the land surrounding a large country house. — *v* to stop and leave a motor car *etc* for a time: *He parked in front of our house*; *Don't park your car on the pavement.*

parking meter a coin-operated meter that shows how long a car may be left parked.

parliament /ˈpɑːləmənt/ *n* the highest law-making council of a nation: *an Act of Parliament.* **parliaˈmentary** *adj*.

parlour /ˈpɑːlə(r)/ *n* **1** an old word for a sitting-room: *She asked the guests into the parlour.* **2** a room for customers: *She is a beautician and has her own beauty parlour*; *an ice-cream parlour.*

parody /ˈparədɪ/ *n* an amusing copying of a work, or of the style of an author or composer *etc*: *The film presents a parody of life in a hospital.* — *v*.

parole /pəˈroʊl/ *n* the setting free of someone from prison before the end of their full time there, on condition that they will behave well: *He was released from prison on parole.*

parquet /ˈpɑːkeɪ/ *n* a floor-covering made of pieces of wood arranged in a design. — *adj*: *a parquet floor.*

parrot /ˈparət/ *n* a bird found in warm countries with a hooked beak and usually brightly-coloured feathers, that can be taught to imitate human speech.

A parrot **talks** or **screeches**.

parrot fashion without understanding the meaning: *She had learnt the poem parrot fashion in French.*

parsley /ˈpɑːslɪ/ *n* a herb with very curly green leaves, used in cookery.

parsley

parson /ˈpɑːsən/ *n* the priest, minister *etc* of a parish.

part /pɑːt/ *n* **1** something which, together with other things, makes a whole; a piece: *We spent part of the time at home and part at the seaside.* **2** an equal division: *He divided the cake into three parts.* **3** a character in a play *etc*: *She played the part of the queen.* **4** the words, actions *etc* of a character in a play *etc*: *He learned his part quickly.* — *v* to separate; to divide: *They parted from each other at the gate.*

for my part as far as it concerns me: *I, for my part, cannot agree with that.*

for the most part usually: *For the most part, our students take five subjects.*

in part to some extent; not completely: *The delay was in part due to the heavy rain.*

on the part of or **on someone's part** done or felt by a particular person: *It was a mistake on her part to leave at that moment; There is concern on the part of the workers that the company will close.*

part of speech nouns, verbs, adjectives *etc*: *What part of speech is 'must'?*

part with to give away: *He doesn't like parting with his money.*

> **part from** someone: *I hate parting from my family.*
> **part with** something: *You'll have to part with that old car one day.*

play a part be involved in or have an influence on something: *Our grandparents played an important part in our childhood.*

take part in to be one of a group of people doing something: *He never took part in the other children's games.*

the best or **better part** most: *He was away for the best part of the year.*

partial /ˈpɑːʃəl/ *adj* **1** not complete; in part only: *a partial success; partial payment.* **2** having a liking for a person or thing: *He is very partial to sweets.*

See **impartial**.

parti'ality *n* preferring one particular side in a competition or trial: *The referee was accused of partiality towards the visiting team.*

partially /ˈpɑːʃəlɪ/ *adv* not completely; partly: *The story was partially true.*

participate /pɑːˈtɪsɪpeɪt/ *v* to be one of a group of people doing something: *Did you participate in the discussion?* **partici'pation** *n*.

par'ticipant *n* a person who participates.

particle /ˈpɑːtɪkəl/ *n* a very small piece: *a particle of dust.*

particular /pəˈtɪkjʊlə(r)/ *adj* meaning one definite person or thing considered separately from others: *this particular man.*

par'ticularly *adv* more than usually; especially: *He was particularly pleased to see his brother because he had a favour to ask him.*

par'ticulars *n* facts; details: *He gave the police all the particulars about the accident.*

in particular especially: *I'm not doing anything in particular this afternoon.*

parting /ˈpɑːtɪŋ/ *n* **1** the act of leaving someone, saying goodbye *etc*: *Their final parting was at the station.* **2** a line dividing hair brushed in opposite directions on the head.

partisan /pɑːtɪˈzan/ *n* **1** a keen supporter of a party, person or cause: *He is a partisan of the government.* **2** a person who fights against an enemy that has invaded their country: *She joined the partisans.*

partition /pɑːˈtɪʃən/ *n* **1** something that divides, for example a wall between rooms: *The office was divided in two by a wooden partition.* **2** the dividing of something: *the partition of India.* — *v* to divide: *They partitioned the room with a curtain.*

partly /ˈpɑːtlɪ/ *adv* **1** to a certain extent: *She was tired, partly because of the journey and partly because of the heat.* **2** not completely: *The work is partly finished.*

partner /ˈpɑːtnə(r)/ *n* **1** a person who shares the ownership of a business *etc* with one or more others: *She was made a partner in the firm.* **2** one of two people who dance, play in a game *etc* together: *a tennis partner.* — *v* to be a partner to someone: *He partnered his wife in the last dance.*

'partnership *n* the relationship in which people work as partners: *They decided to go into partnership together; Marriage is a partnership.*

part-time /pɑːtˈtaɪm/ *adj* not taking up your whole time; for only a few hours or days a week: *a part-time job.* — *adv*: *She works part-time in a restaurant.*

party /ˈpɑːtɪ/ *n* **1** a meeting of guests for entertainment, celebration *etc*: *a birthday party; She's giving a party tonight.* **2** a group of people travelling *etc* together: *a party of tourists.* **3** an organized group of people who share the same political beliefs: *Which party are you going to vote for in the next election?* **4** a person or group involved in a legal case or contract, *etc*: *All three parties must sign the agreement.*

pass /pɑːs/ *v* **1** to move towards and then beyond something, by going past, through, by, over *etc*: *I pass the shops on my way to work.* **2** to move along; to go: *The procession passed along the street.* **3** to give from one person to another: *They passed the photographs round; The tradition has been passed on from father to son; Pass your plates up to the end of the table.* **4** to overtake: *The* *sports car passed me at a dangerous bend in the road.* **5** to spend time: *They passed several weeks in the country.* **6** to end or go away: *His sickness soon passed.* **7** to be successful in an examination *etc*: *I passed my driving test.* — *n* **1** a narrow gap through which a road *etc* goes, between mountains: *a mountain pass.* **2** a ticket or card allowing a person to do something, for example to travel free or to get into a building. **3** a throw, kick, hit *etc* of the ball from one player to another: *He made a pass towards the goal.* **4** a successful result in an examination: *She got good passes in her written papers.*

> Use **passed** only as part of the verb **pass**: *We passed the food round; Have we passed the zoo yet?*
> Otherwise use **past**: *The time for discussion is past.*

pass away to die: *Her grandmother passed away last night.*

> We played a game to **pass** (not **pass away**) the time.

pass down to give to following generations: *Sewing skills that are passed down from mother to daughter.*

pass off to go away: *By the evening, his sickness had passed off and he felt better.*

pass on 1 to give to someone else: *I passed on his message.* **2** to die: *His mother passed on yesterday.*

pass out 1 to faint: *I feel as though I'm going to pass out.* **2** to give to several people: *The teacher passed out books to her class.*

pass up not to accept a chance, opportunity *etc*: *He passed up the offer of a good job.*

> You **hand in** (not **pass up**) your books to the teacher.

passable /ˈpɑːsəbəl/ *adj* **1** quite good but not very good: *Your work has been passable.* **2** clear enough for travelling along; not completely blocked: *The roads are now passable after the flood.*

passage /ˈpæsɪdʒ/ *n* **1** a long narrow way or a corridor: *There was a dark passage leading down to the river between tall buildings.* **2** a tube from an opening in the body: *Her air passage was blocked.* **3** a part of a piece of writing or music: *That is my favourite passage from the Bible.* **4** passing: *the passage of time.*

passenger /ˈpæsɪndʒə(r)/ *n* a person who travels in any vehicle, boat, aeroplane *etc*; not the driver or anyone working there: *a passenger on a train.* — *adj*: *a passenger train.*

passer-by /pɑːsəˈbaɪ/, *plural* **passers-by**, *n* a person who is going past a place when something happens: *He asked the passers-by if they had seen the accident.*

passing /ˈpɑːsɪŋ/ *adj* **1** going past: *a passing car.* **2** lasting only a short time: *a passing interest.*

in passing done or said while you are doing or talking about something else: *She mentioned his name in passing but I can't remember it now.*

passion /ˈpæʃən/ *n* very strong feeling, especially anger or love: *He argued with great passion; He has a passion for chocolate.*
ˈ**passionate** *adj* with or showing strong emotions: *a passionate plea for help.*
ˈ**passionately** *adv*.

passive /ˈpæsɪv/ *adj* **1** not reacting; not showing any feeling or action: *The child lay passive while the doctor examined her.* **2** used to describe the form of a verb when its subject is affected by the action: *The boy was bitten by the dog.* — *n*: *The verb is in the passive.* ˈ**passively** *adv*.

> the opposite of **passive** is **active**.

passport /ˈpɑːspɔːt/ *n* a card or booklet that gives the name and description of a person, and is needed to travel in another country: *a British passport.*

password /ˈpɑːswɜːd/ *n* a secret word that you must give in order to be allowed to go past a particular point, or enter a place: *The guard on duty at the gate asked him for the password; When you want to use a big computer, you must first type your password.*

past /pɑːst/ *adj* **1** just finished: *the past year.* **2** over or ended: *The time for discussion is past.* **3** showing that the action is in the past: *In 'He did it', the verb is in the past tense.* — *prep* **1** up to and beyond; by: *He ran past me.* **2** after: *It's past six o'clock.* — *adv* up to and beyond a place, person *etc*: *The soldiers marched past.* — *n* **1** a person's earlier life or career: *He never spoke about his past.* **2** the past tense: *The verb is in the past.*

the past the time that was, before the present: *In the past, people used candles to light their homes.*

> **In the past** (not **last time**) I used to walk to school.
> See also **passed**.

pasta /'pæstə/ *n* a dried mixture of flour and water prepared in various shapes, such as spaghetti, macaroni *etc*.

paste /peɪst/ *n* **1** a soft, moist mixture: *toothpaste*. **2** a thin kind of glue for sticking paper on walls *etc*. **3** any of several types of food made into a soft mass: *almond paste*; *tomato paste*. — *v* to stick with paste: *He pasted pictures into his scrapbook.*

pastel /'pæstəl/ *adj* pale, containing a lot of white: *a pastel green*. — *n* a coloured pencil, made with chalk, which makes a pale colour.

pasteurize /'pɑːstʃəraɪz/ *v* to heat milk for a time to kill germs in it. **pasteuri'zation** *n*.

pastime /'pɑːstaɪm/ *n* a hobby: *Playing chess is his favourite pastime.*

> **pastime** is spelt with one **t**.

pastor /'pɑːstə(r)/ *n* a minister of religion.

pastry /'peɪstrɪ/ *n* **1** a mixture of flour, fat, water *etc* used in making pies, tarts *etc*. **2** a pie, tart *etc* made with this: *Danish pastries*.

pasture /'pɑːstʃə(r)/ *n* a field covered with grass for cattle *etc* to eat: *The horses were out in the pasture.*

pasty /'pæstɪ/ *n* a small pie made by folding meat, vegetables *etc* in pastry: *Cornish pasties contain beef, potatoes and onions.*

pat /pæt/ *n* **1** a light, gentle blow or touch, usually with the hand and showing affection: *She gave the child a pat on the head.* **2** a small piece: *a pat of butter.* — *v* to strike gently with your hand, as a sign of affection: *He patted the horse's neck.*

a pat on the back congratulations for something good that you have done.

patch /pætʃ/ *n* **1** a piece of material sewn on to a garment *etc* to cover a hole: *She sewed a patch on the knee of her jeans*. **2** a small piece of ground: *a vegetable patch*. **3** a small piece of material that is used to cover and protect an injured eye: *an eye patch*. **4** a small area of something that is different in some way from its surroundings: *a patch of sunlight*; *fog patches*; *a wet patch on the floor*. — *v* to mend clothes *etc* by sewing on pieces of material: *to patch clothes*.

'patchwork *n* cloth made by sewing small pieces of material together.

'patchy *adj* **1** occurring in small quantities; not spread evenly: *The paint on the door was patchy*. **2** not complete; good or correct only in parts: *I only have some patchy information on the subject.*

patch up 1 to mend, especially hastily: *He patched up the roof with bits of wood.* **2** to settle a quarrel: *They soon patched up their disagreement.*

patent /'peɪtənt/ *n* a licence from the government that gives one person or company the right to make and sell a particular product and to prevent others from copying it: *He took out a patent on the electric car he had designed.* — *v* to get a patent for something: *She patented her new invention.* — *adj* **1** obvious; easy to see: *The omission of relevant evidence is most patent in surveys with a political bias.* **2** made by one manufacturer only: *a patent medicine.*

patent leather very shiny hard leather: *His dancing shoes were made of black patent leather.*

paternal /pə'tɜːnəl/ *adj* **1** like a father: *paternal feelings.* **2** on your father's side of the family: *my paternal grandmother.*

path /pɑːθ/, *plural* **paths** /pɑːðz/, *n* **1** a way made across ground by the passing of people or animals: *There is a path through the fields*; *a mountain path*. **2** the line along which someone or something is moving: *She stood right in the path of the bus.*

'pathway *n* a path.

pathetic /pə'θetɪk/ *adj* **1** making you feel pity: *The lost dog looked so pathetic that we took him home with us.* **2** very bad and annoying; useless: *His singing is pathetic!*; *What a pathetic performance!* **pa'thetically** *adv*.

pathologist /pəˈθɒlədʒɪst/ *n* a doctor specializing in the study of diseases, usually by examining dead bodies to find out the cause of death: *The pathologist tried to find out what had killed the man.*

path'ology *n* the study of the diseases of the body.

patience /'peɪʃəns/ *n* **1** the ability or willingness to be patient: *She has a lot of patience with children.* **2** a card game played by one person: *She often plays patience.*

patient /'peɪʃənt/ *adj* suffering delay, pain *etc* quietly and without complaining: *It will be your turn soon — you must just be patient!* — *n* a person who is being treated by a doctor, dentist *etc*: *The hospital had too many patients.* **'patiently** *adv*.

> The opposite of the adjective **patient** is **impatient**.

patriarch /ˈpeɪtrɪɑːk/ n the male head of a family or tribe.

patriot /ˈpatrɪət/ or /ˈpeɪtrɪət/ n a person who loves and serves their country.
  patriotic /patrɪˈɒtɪk/ or /peɪtrɪˈɒtɪk/ adj showing love for your own country; very loyal: *a patriotic song.* **patri'otically** adv.
  patriotism /ˈpatrɪətɪzm/ or /ˈpeɪtrɪətɪzm/ n great love for your own country.

patrol /pəˈtroʊl/ v to watch or protect an area by moving continually around or through it: *Soldiers patrolled the streets.* — n **1** a group of people *etc* who patrol an area. **2** watching or guarding by patrolling: *The soldiers went out on patrol.* — adj: *patrol duty.*

> a police **patrol** (not **petrol**); to **patrol** (not **petrol**) the streets.

patron /ˈpeɪtrən/ n **1** a person who supports an artist, musician, writer, form of art *etc*: *He's a patron of the arts.* **2** a regular customer of a shop *etc*.
  patronage /ˈpatrənɪdʒ/ n the support given by a patron.
  patronize /ˈpatrənaɪz/ v **1** to treat someone as if you were more important, clever *etc* than they are. **2** to be a patron to someone or something. **'patronizing** adj. **'patronizingly** adv.

patter /ˈpatə(r)/ v to make a quick, tapping sound: *She heard the mice pattering behind the walls.* — n the sound made in this way: *the patter of rain on the roof.*

pattern /ˈpatən/ n **1** a model or guide for making something: *a dress-pattern.* **2** a repeated design on material *etc*: *The dress is nice but I don't like the pattern.* **3** the way in which something happens, develops or is organized: *behaviour patterns; Discuss the pattern of events that led up to the war.*
  'patterned adj having a design.

paunch /pɔːntʃ/ n a large, round belly.

pauper /ˈpɔːpə(r)/ n a very poor person.

pause /pɔːz/ n a short stop: *There was a pause in the conversation.* — v to stop talking, working *etc* for a short time: *They paused for a cup of tea.*

pave /peɪv/ v to cover a street, path *etc* with stones or concrete to make a flat surface for walking on *etc*: *He wants to pave the garden.*
  'pavement n a paved footpath along the sides of a road.
  paving stone a flat stone that is part of a path or pavement.

pavilion /pəˈvɪlɪən/ n a building on a sports ground in which players change their clothes, store equipment *etc*.

paw /pɔː/ n the foot of an animal with claws or nails: *The dog had a thorn in its paw.* — v to touch, hit *etc* with a paw: *The cat was pawing the mouse.*

> See **foot**.

pawn /pɔːn/ v to give a valuable article to a shopkeeper called a **'pawnbroker** in exchange for money which may be repaid at a later time to get the article back: *I had to pawn my watch to pay the bill.* — n a piece of the lowest value in the game of chess.

pay /peɪ/ v **1** to give money to someone in exchange for goods, or for doing something for you: *He paid £5 for the book.* **2** to return money that you owe: *It's time you paid your debts.* **3** to suffer punishment: *You'll pay for that remark!* **4** to be useful or profitable: *Crime doesn't pay.* **5** to give: *Pay attention!* — n money given or received for work *etc*; wages: *How much pay do you get?*

> **pay**; **paid** /peɪd/; **paid**: *She paid £10; Have you paid your debts?*

  'payable adj that can or must be paid: *Make the cheque payable to me.*
  pay'ee n a person to whom money is paid.
  'payload n the number of passengers, or amount of cargo, that an aircraft can carry: *The space shuttle can carry a heavy payload.*
  'payment n: *The radio can be paid for in ten weekly payments; He gave me a book in payment for my kindness.*
  'payphone n a public telephone operated by coins or a credit card: *You'll find a payphone at the station.*
  pay back 1 to give back: *I'll pay you back as soon as I can.* **2** to punish: *I'll pay you back for that!*
  pay up to give money that you owe: *You have three days to pay up.*

> to **pay** (not **pay up**) for goods at the cash-desk.

PC /piːˈsiː/ n a personal computer: *She has bought herself a new PC.*

pea /piː/ n **1** the round green seed of a climbing plant, eaten as a vegetable: *We had roast beef, potatoes and peas for dinner.* **2** the plant that produces these seeds.

peace /piːs/ n **1** freedom from war: *These two countries have always been at peace; to make* *peace.* **2** quietness: *I need some peace and quiet.* — *adj: The two countries have signed a peace treaty.*

'**peaceful** *adj* quiet; calm: *It's very peaceful in the country.* '**peacefully** *adv.* '**peacefulness** *n.*

'**peacemaker** *n* a person who tries to make peace between enemies, people who are quarrelling *etc.*

'**peacetime** *n* any period that is free from war: *The army continues to train soldiers in peacetime.*

in peace 1 without disturbance: *Why can't you leave me in peace?* **2** not wanting to fight: *They said they came in peace.*

peach /piːʃ/ *n* **1** a juicy, soft-skinned fruit with a stone-like seed. **2** the orange-pink colour of the fruit: *She wore peach satin underwear.*

peacock /ˈpiːkɒk/ *n* a large bird noted for its magnificent tail-feathers.

peahen /ˈpiːhɛn/ *n* the female of the peacock.

peak /piːk/ *n* **1** the pointed top of a mountain or hill: *snow-covered peaks.* **2** the highest, greatest, busiest *etc* point, time *etc*: *He was at the peak of his career.* **3** the front part of a cap, which shades the eyes: *The boy wore a cap with a peak.* — *v* to reach the highest, greatest, busiest *etc* point, time *etc*: *Prices peaked in July and then began to fall.*

See **mountain**.

peal /piːl/ *n* **1** the ringing of bells. **2** a set of church bells. **3** a loud noise: *peals of laughter; peals of thunder.* — *v*: *Thunder pealed through the valley; The bells pealed.*

peanut /ˈpiːnʌt/ *n* a kind of nut that looks rather like a pea (also called a '**groundnut**).

pear /pɛə(r)/ *n* a fruit of the apple family, round at the bottom and narrowing towards the stem or top.

pearl /pɜːl/ *n* a valuable, hard, round object formed by oysters and several other shellfish: *The necklace consists of three strings of pearls.* — *adj: a pearl necklace.*

'**pearl-diver** or '**pearl-fisher** *n* a person who dives or fishes for pearls.

'**pearly** *adj* like pearls: *pearly teeth.*

peasant /ˈpɛzənt/ *n* a person who lives and works on the land, especially in a poor area.

'**peasantry** *n* the peasants of a country.

pebble /ˈpɛbəl/ *n* a small, smooth stone: *small pebbles on the beach.* '**pebbly** *adj.*

peck /pɛk/ *v* **1** to strike or pick up with the beak: *The birds pecked at the corn.* **2** to eat very little: *She just pecks at her food.* — *n* a tap or bite with the beak.

peckish /ˈpɛkɪʃ/ *adj* a little hungry: *I'm feeling peckish — when's lunch?*

peculiar /pɪˈkjuːlɪə(r)/ *adj* **1** strange; odd: *peculiar behaviour.* **2** belonging to one person, place or thing in particular and to no other: *customs peculiar to France.* **peculi'arity** /pɪˌkjuːlɪˈarɪtɪ/ *n.* **pe'culiarly** *adv.*

pedal /ˈpɛdəl/ *n* a lever worked by the foot, as on a bicycle, piano, organ *etc*: *the brake pedal in a car.* — *v* to operate the pedals on something; to ride a bicycle *etc*: *He pedalled down the road.*

to **pedal** (not **paddle**) a bicycle.

pedantic /pɪˈdantɪk/ *adj* too concerned with correctness of details or rules.

peddle /ˈpɛdəl/ *v* to go from place to place or house to house selling small objects.

pedestal /ˈpɛdɪstəl/ *n* the base of a statue *etc.*

pedestrian /pəˈdɛstrɪən/ *n* a person who is walking along a street *etc*: *A pedestrian was knocked down by a car.* — *adj: a pedestrian walkway.*

pedigree /ˈpɛdɪɡriː/ *n* **1** a list of the parents, grandparents *etc* of a dog, cat or other animal: *This poodle has a good pedigree.* **2** a person's background. — *adj* coming from parents, grandparents *etc* all of the same breed: *pedigree dogs; a herd of pedigree cows.*

pedlar /ˈpɛdlə(r)/ *n* a person who peddles: *I bought this comb from a pedlar.*

peek /piːk/ *v* to look, especially quickly and in secret: *Cover your eyes and don't peek.* — *n* a quick look.

peek and **peep** both mean to look quickly, especially secretly: *She opened the box and peeked inside; He peeped round the corner to see if anyone was there.*
peer means to look hard at something that is difficult to see: *She peered at the ship through the thick fog.*

peel /piːl/ *v* **1** to take off the skin or outer covering of a fruit or vegetable: *She peeled the potatoes.* **2** to take off or come off in small pieces: *The paint is beginning to peel off.* — *n* the skin of certain fruits and vegetables *etc*: *orange peel.*

'**peeler** *n* a tool that peels: *a potato-peeler.*

'**peelings** *n*: *He threw the potato-peelings away.*

peep[1] /piːp/ *v* **1** to look through a narrow

opening or from behind something: *She peeped through the letter-box*. **2** to look quickly and in secret: *He peeped at the answers at the back of the book*. — *n* a quick look: *She took a peep at the visitor*.

See **peek**.

peep² /piːp/ *v* to sound the horn of a car: *She peeped the horn*.

peer /pɪː(r)/ *v* to look with difficulty: *He peered at the small writing*.

See **peek**.

peg /pɛg/ *n* **1** a short piece of wood, metal *etc* used to fasten or mark something: *There were four pegs stuck in the ground*. **2** a hook for hanging clothes *etc* on: *Hang your clothes on the pegs in the cupboard*. **3** a wooden or plastic clip for holding clothes *etc* to a rope while drying. — *v* to fasten with a peg: *She pegged the clothes on the washing-line*.

pejorative /pɪˈdʒɒrətɪv/ *adj* expressing or showing disapproval or criticism: *He did not like the pejorative comments made about him in the newspaper*.

pelican /ˈpɛlɪkən/ *n* a large water-bird with a large beak with a pouch for carrying fish.

pellet /ˈpɛlɪt/ *n* a little ball or similarly-shaped object: *He bought a box of lead pellets for his gun*.

pelt /pɛlt/ *v* **1** to throw things at someone or something: *The children pelted each other with snowballs*. **2** to run very fast: *He pelted down the road*.

pelvis /ˈpɛlvɪs/ *n* the bones that form a hollow framework in your body below the waist. **'pelvic** *adj*.

pen¹ /pɛn/ *n* a small enclosure for sheep, cattle *etc*.

pen² /pɛn/ *n* a tool for writing in ink: *a felt-tip pen; a fountain pen*.

penalize /ˈpiːnəlaɪz/ *v* to punish someone for doing something that is against the rules: *He was penalized for cheating in the examination*.

penalty /ˈpɛnəltɪ/ *n* **1** a punishment for doing wrong: *They did wrong and they will have to pay the penalty; The death penalty has been abolished in that country*. **2** in sport *etc*, a disadvantage given to a player or team for breaking a rule of a game: *The referee gave the team a penalty*.

penance /ˈpɛnəns/ *n* punishment that a person suffers willingly to make up for doing something wrong: *He did penance for his sins*.

pence /pɛns/ the plural of **penny**.

pencil /ˈpɛnsəl/ *n* a tool for writing or drawing: *This pencil needs sharpening; He wrote in pencil, not ink*. — *v* to write or draw with a pencil: *He pencilled an outline of the house*.

pendant /ˈpɛndənt/ *n* an ornament hung from a necklace.

pending /ˈpɛndɪŋ/ *adj* waiting to be decided or dealt with: *The court's decision is still pending*. — *prep* until: *He was held in prison pending trial*.

pendulum /ˈpɛndjʊləm/ *n* a swinging weight that operates the mechanism of a clock.

penetrate /ˈpɛnɪtreɪt/ *v* **1** to manage to get into or through something: *The rain penetrated through the roof; The bullet penetrated his left shoulder*. **2** to understand or be understood: *They could not penetrate the mystery; They told me I had won, but the news took a long time to penetrate*. **pene'tration** *n*.
'penetrating *adj* **1** loud and unpleasant: *Her voice is harsh and penetrating*. **2** hard; full of concentration: *She gave him a penetrating look*. **3** quick at understanding: *He has a penetrating mind*.

pen-friend /ˈpɛnfrɛnd/ *n* a person living abroad with whom you exchange letters: *My daughter has pen-friends in India and Spain*.

penguin /ˈpɛŋgwɪn/ *n* a large sea-bird of Antarctic regions that cannot fly.

penicillin /pɛnɪˈsɪlɪn/ *n* a medicine used to treat illnesses and infections caused by bacteria.

peninsula /pəˈnɪnsjʊlə/ *n* a piece of land that is almost surrounded by water: *the Malay peninsula*. **pe'ninsular** *adj*.

The adjective **peninsular** is spelt with an **r**.
See also **isthmus**.

penis /ˈpiːnɪs/ *n* the male sexual organ in humans and many animals.

penitent /ˈpɛnɪtənt/ *adj* sorry for something wrong you have done: *He felt penitent after shouting at his son*.

pen-knife /ˈpɛn-naɪf/ *n* a small pocket-knife with blades that fold into the handle.

pen-name /ˈpɛn-neɪm/ *n* a name used by writers instead of their own name: *Samuel Clemens used the pen-name Mark Twain*.

pennant /ˈpɛnənt/ *n* a small flag, in the shape of a long narrow triangle.

pen-nib /ˈpɛn-nɪb/ *n* the nib of a pen.

penny /'pɛnɪ/, *plural* **pence** or **pennies**, *n* **1** in British currency, the hundredth part of £1: *It costs seventy-five pence; Please give me five pennies for this five-penny piece.* **2** in certain countries, a coin of low value.
'**penniless** *adj* very poor; with little or no money: *a penniless old man.*

pen-pal /'pɛnpal/ *n* a pen-friend.

pension /'pɛnʃən/ *n* a sum of money paid regularly to a widow, a person who has retired from work, a soldier who has been seriously injured in war *etc*: *He lives on his pension; a retirement pension.*
'**pensioner** *n* a person who receives a pension, especially one who receives a retirement pension.

pensive /'pɛnsɪv/ *adj* thoughtful: *She looked pensive.*

pentagon /'pɛntəgən/ *n* a flat, 5-sided shape. **pen'tagonal** *adj.*

pentathlon /pɛn'taθlən/ *n* a sports contest with five separate events: *Pupils competed in a pentathlon consisting of a running race, a swimming race, a bicycle race, a high jump and a long jump.*

penthouse /'pɛnthaʊs/ *n* a luxurious flat at the top of a building.

pent-up /pɛnt'ʌp/ *adj* not released or expressed: *pent-up anger; pent-up energy.*

penultimate /pɛn'ʌltɪmət/ *adj* the one before the last one in a series: *The marathon is the penultimate race in the Olympics.*

people /'pi:pəl/ *n* **1** persons: *There were three people in the room.* **2** men and women in general: *People often say such things.* **3** a nation or race: *all the peoples of this world.* **4** the public; the population of a country: *A government should serve the people.*

> **people** is usually plural: *The people waiting at the airport were impatient.*
> **people** is singular, and has the plural **peoples**, when it means a nation: *a defeated people; the peoples of Europe.*

pep /pɛp/ *n* energy: *full of pep.*

pepper /'pɛpə(r)/ *n* **1** the dried, hot-tasting berries of the pepper plant, which are ground and used for seasoning food: *black pepper; This soup has too much pepper in it.* **2** any of several red, yellow, or green hollow fruits used as a vegetable: *red peppers stuffed with rice.*
'**peppermint** *n* **1** a strong flavouring obtained from a plant, used in sweets, toothpaste *etc*. **2** a sweet flavoured with peppermint: *a bag of peppermints.*

per /pɜ:(r)/ *prep* **1** for each: *The dinner will cost £15 per person.* **2** in each: *six times per week.*

perceive /pə'si:v/ *v* to notice: *At last he perceived her in the crowd; She perceived that something was wrong with him.*

per cent /pə'sɛnt/ out of every hundred; often written % with figures: *25% of people go to church on Sundays.*

> **per cent** is written as two words.

percentage /pə'sɛntɪdʒ/ *n* **1** an amount or rate per hundred: *Write these fractions as percentages.* **2** a part of something: *A large percentage of the population can't read or write.*

perceptible /pə'sɛptəbəl/ *adj* that can be noticed: *The change was hardly perceptible.*

> The opposite of **perceptible** is **imperceptible**.

perception /pə'sɛpʃən/ *n* **1** the ability to see, hear or understand: *increase your powers of perception.* **2** a particular way of looking at or understanding something: *They have a different perception of how a business should operate.*

perceptive /pə'sɛptɪv/ *adj* good at noticing or realizing things: *A doctor has to be perceptive to find out what is wrong with a patient; She wrote a perceptive essay about life in a big city.* **per'ceptively** *adv.*

perch /pɜ:tʃ/ *n* **1** a branch *etc* on which a bird sits or stands: *The pigeon would not fly down from its perch.* **2** any high seat or position: *He looked down from his perch on the roof.* — *v* **1** to sit or stand on a perch: *The bird perched on the highest branch of the tree.* **2** to sit on something narrow: *They perched on the fence.*

percolator /'pɜ:kəleɪtə(r)/ *n* a kind of pot in which coffee is made by pouring boiling water through ground coffee beans in a small container at the top of the pot.

percussion /pə'kʌʃən/ *n* musical instruments that you play by striking them, for example drums, cymbals *etc*.

perennial /pə'rɛnɪəl/ *adj* that happens often or lasts for a long time: *a perennial problem.*

perfect *adj* /'pɜ:fɪkt/ **1** without fault; excellent: *a perfect day for a holiday; a perfect rose.* **2** exact: *a perfect copy.* **3** complete: *a perfect stranger.* — *v* /pə'fɛkt/ to make perfect: *He went to France to perfect his French.* **perfection** /pə'fɛkʃən/ *n*. '**perfectly** *adv.*

perforate /'pɜ:fəreɪt/ *v* to make a hole or holes

perform

in something, especially a line of small holes in paper, so that it may be torn easily. **'perforated** adj: a perforated line.

perfo'ration n: Tear along the perforations.

perform /pə'fɔːm/ v **1** to do; to carry out: The doctor performed the operation. **2** to act a play or provide any kind of entertainment for an audience: The company will perform a Greek play; She performed on the violin.

per'formance n **1** the doing of something: He is very careful in the performance of his duties. **2** the way in which something or someone performs: His performance in the exams was not very good. **3** something done on stage etc: The company gave a performance of 'Macbeth'.

per'former n a person who performs, especially in the theatre, or on a musical instrument.

perfume n /'pɜːfjuːm/ **1** a sweet smell: the perfume of roses. **2** a liquid for putting on your skin, that has a sweet smell. — v /'pɜːfjuːm/ or /pə'fjuːm/ **1** to put perfume on or in something: She perfumed herself after her shower. **2** to give a sweet smell to the air: Flowers perfumed the room.

perhaps /pə'haps/ adv possibly: Perhaps it will rain.

peril /'pɛrəl/ n great danger: The perils of rock-climbing; You are in great peril.

perilous /'pɛrələs/ adj very dangerous.

perimeter /pə'rɪmɪtə(r)/ n the outside edge of any area: the perimeter of the city; the perimeter of a circle.

period /'pɪərɪəd/ n **1** any length of time: a period of three days. **2** a stage in the Earth's development or in history: the modern period. **3** a full stop (.), put at the end of a sentence. **4** the natural bleeding from the womb of a woman every 28 days; menstruation: She always feels unwell at the start of her period.

peri'odic or **peri'odical** adj at regular intervals or every now and then: He made periodic visits to check on our progress. **periodically** /pɪərɪ'ɒdɪklɪ/ adv.

peri'odical n a magazine that is issued every week, month etc.

periscope /'pɛrɪskoʊp/ n an instrument that, by a special arrangement of mirrors, makes it possible for you to see things that you can't see from the position you are in, used especially in submarines to show you what is on the surface of the water.

perish /'pɛrɪʃ/ v to die, especially in war, accidents etc: Many people perished in the earthquake.

'perishable adj likely to go bad quickly: Fresh fruit is perishable.

perjury /'pɜːdʒərɪ/ n the crime of lying after swearing an oath to tell the truth in a court of law: The lawyer accused him of perjury.

perk[1] /pɜːk/: **perk up** to become more lively or cheerful: I gave her a cup of tea and she soon perked up.

perk[2] /pɜːk/ n a benefit or advantage that you get from your job in addition to your pay: One of the perks of the job is having a company car.

perm /pɜːm/ n short for **permanent wave**, a long-lasting, usually curly, hair-style given to your hair by a special process. — v: She's had her hair permed.

permanent /'pɜːmənənt/ adj lasting for ever, or for a long time; not temporary: After many years of travelling, they made a permanent home in England. **'permanently** adv. **'permanence** n.

permissible /pə'mɪsəbəl/ adj that is allowed: I understood that it was permissible to ask a question.

permission /pə'mɪʃən/ n the permitting of something: She gave me permission to leave.

permissive /pə'mɪsɪv/ adj allowing people a lot of freedom to do whatever they want, even things that are usually disapproved of: The girl's parents are too permissive — they allow her to stay out all night. **per'missiveness** n.

permit v /pə'mɪt/ to allow or let someone do something: Permit me to answer your question; Smoking is not permitted. — n /'pɜːmɪt/ a written order allowing a person to do something: We have a permit to export our products.

perpendicular /pɜːpən'dɪkjʊlə(r)/ adj standing straight upwards; vertical: a perpendicular cliff.

perpetual /pə'pɛtʃʊəl/ adj continuous; lasting for ever; never stopping: The criminal lived in perpetual fear of being discovered by the police; I can't stand the perpetual noise the children make. **per'petually** adv.

perpetuate /pə'pɛtʃʊeɪt/ v to cause to continue: The bad feeling between the families was perpetuated by each generation.

perplex /pə'plɛks/ v to puzzle: She was perplexed by his strange question and didn't know how to answer it. **per'plexed** adj. **per'plexity** n.

persecute /'pɜːsɪkjuːt/ v to make someone

suffer, especially because of their opinions or beliefs: *They were persecuted for their religion.* **perse'cution** *n.* **'persecutor** *n.*

persevere /pɜːsɪ'vɪə(r)/ *v* to continue to do something in spite of difficulties: *He persevered in his task.* **perse'verance** *n.*

persist /pə'sɪst/ *v* to keep on doing something in spite of opposition or difficulty: *It will not be easy but you will succeed if you persist.* **per'sistence** *n.* **per'sistent** *adj.* **per'sistently** *adv.*

> **persist in** means to go on doing something: *He persisted in asking her annoying questions.*
>
> **insist on** means to be very firm in doing or saying what you want to: *He insisted on carrying her case for her.*

person /'pɜːsən/ *n* **1** a human being: *There's a person outside who wants to speak to you.* **2** your body: *Never carry a lot of money on your person.*

'personal *adj* **1** own: *This is his personal opinion.* **2** private: *This is a personal matter between him and me.* **3** appearing yourself: *The Prime Minister will make a personal appearance on television.*

personal computer a small computer which can be used on a desk at home or at work: *He uses his personal computer when he needs to work at home at the weekends.*

perso'nality *n* **1** your character; your qualities: *What a pleasant personality she has!* **2** strong and usually attractive qualities: *She is not beautiful but she has a lot of personality.* **3** a well-known person: *a television personality.*

'personally *adv* **1** used when giving your own opinion: *Personally, I'm very disappointed with this result.* **2** done yourself without anyone else acting for you: *The manager serves important customers personally.* **3** concerning a particular individual as a person: *I admire firemen, although I've never met one personally.*

personify /pə'sɒnɪfaɪ/ *v* **1** to be an example in human form of a particular quality: *She is patience personified.* **2** to describe something as if it were a person, for example in a poem, *etc.*

in person being present personally; face to face: *He decided to deliver it in person*; *She broke the news in person, rather than on the telephone.*

personnel /pɜːsə'nɛl/ *n* the people employed in a firm, factory, shop *etc*; the staff: *Our personnel are very highly trained.*

perspective /pə'spɛktɪv/ *n* the way of drawing solid objects, natural scenes *etc* on a flat surface, so that they appear to have the correct shape and distance from each other *etc*: *Try and draw the house so that the door and windows are properly in perspective*; *That chair is out of perspective.*

perspire /pə'spaɪə(r)/ *v* to lose moisture through your skin when you are hot; to sweat: *He was perspiring in the heat.*
perspi'ration *n*: *The perspiration was running down his face.*

persuade /pə'sweɪd/ *v* to make someone do something, or not do something, by arguing with them and advising them: *We persuaded him to help us*; *How can we persuade people not to drive after drinking?*

persuasion /pə'sweɪʒən/ *n* the act of persuading: *He gave in to our persuasion and did what we wanted him to do.*

persuasive /pə'sweɪzɪv/ *adj* able to persuade you to do or believe something: *a persuasive argument.* **per'suasively** *adv.* **per'suasiveness** *n.*

pertinent /'pɜːtɪnənt/ *adj* relevant; directly related: *a pertinent question.*

perturbed /pə'tɜːbd/ *adj* worried: *She was not a bit perturbed by all the problems.*

pervade /pə'veɪd/ *v* to spread to every part of a place: *The smell of smoke pervaded the whole house.* **pervasive** /pə'veɪsɪv/ *adj.*

perverse /pə'vɜːs/ *adj* doing things that you know are wrong or silly, usually because someone wants you to do the opposite: *His mother told him not to go outside in the rain, but he went out just to be perverse.* **per'versely** *adv.* **per'versity** *n.*

pervert *v* /pə'vɜːt/ to change something from the way it should be; to change something for the worse; to spoil: *People think that violent and disgusting films can pervert the minds of children who watch them.* — *n* /'pɜːvɜːt/ a person who does things, especially of a sexual kind, that are unnatural and disgusting. **per'version** *n.* **per'verted** *adj.*

peso /'peɪsoʊ/, *plural* **pesos**, *n* the standard unit of currency in many South and Central American countries and in the Philippines.

pessimism /'pɛsɪmɪzm/ *n* the state of mind of a person who always expects bad things to happen.

> The opposite of **pessimism** is **optimism**.

'pessimist *n* a person who expects bad

things to happen: *He is such a pessimist that he always expects the worst.* **pessi'mistic** *adj.* **pessimistically** /pɛsɪˈmɪstɪklɪ/ *adv.*

pest /pɛst/ *n* **1** a creature, such as a rat, a mosquito *etc*, that is harmful or that destroys things. **2** a person or thing that causes trouble: *He is always annoying me — he is an absolute pest!*

pesticide /ˈpɛstɪsaɪd/ *n* a substance that kills animal and insect pests.

pester /ˈpɛstə(r)/ *v* to annoy someone continually: *He pestered me with stupid questions.*

pestle /ˈpɛsəl/ or /ˈpɛstəl/ *n* a tool for grinding substances into a powder.

pet /pɛt/ *n* **1** a tame animal that you keep in your home: *She keeps a rabbit as a pet.* **2** a favourite child: *the teacher's pet.* — *adj*: *We have a pet rabbit.* — *v* to stroke in a loving way: *She petted her dog.*

pet name a particular name used to express affection: *His pet name for his daughter was 'Kitten'.*

petal /ˈpɛtəl/ *n* one of the parts of the head of a flower: *This rose has yellow petals edged with pink.*

peter /ˈpiːtə(r)/: **peter out** to finish or come to an end gradually: *The path peters out when it reaches the wood.*

petite /pəˈtiːt/ *adj* small and neat: *Women from Eastern countries are generally more petite than European women.*

petition /pəˈtɪʃən/ *n* a request, especially one signed by many people and sent to a government or authority. — *v* to make a petition: *They petitioned the government for the release of the prisoners.* **pe'titioner** *n.*

petrify /ˈpɛtrəfaɪ/ *v* to make someone very frightened: *The sight of the snake petrified her.* **'petrified** *adj.*

petro- /ˈpɛtroʊ/ having to do with petrol, as in the word **petrochemical**.

petrochemical /pɛtroʊˈkɛmɪkəl/ *n* any chemical obtained from petroleum or natural gas. — *adj*: *the petrochemical industry.*

petrol /ˈpɛtrəl/ *n* a liquid got from petroleum, used as fuel for motor cars *etc*: *I'll stop at the next garage and buy more petrol.*

See also **patrol**.

petroleum /pəˈtroʊlɪəm/ *n* oil in the raw state in which it is found in natural wells below the earth's surface and from which petrol is obtained.

petrol pump an apparatus at a petrol station which pumps petrol into cars *etc*.

petrol station a garage where petrol is sold.

petticoat /ˈpɛtɪkoʊt/ *n* an undergarment worn by girls and women.

petty /ˈpɛtɪ/ *adj* having very little importance: *petty details.* **'pettily** *adv.* **'pettiness** *n.*

pew /pjuː/ *n* a seat or bench in a church.

See **bench**.

pewter /ˈpjuːtə(r)/ *n* a metal made by mixing tin and lead. — *adj*: *a pewter mug.*

phantom /ˈfantəm/ *n* a ghost.

pharmaceutical /fɑːməˈsjuːtɪkəl/ *adj* connected with the production of medicines: *the pharmaceutical industry.*

pharmacy /ˈfɑːməsɪ/ *n* **1** the preparation of medicines: *He is studying pharmacy.* **2** a shop *etc* where medicines are sold or given out: *the hospital pharmacy.*

'pharmacist *n* a person who prepares and sells medicines; a chemist.

phase /feɪz/ *n* **1** a stage in the development of something: *We are entering a new phase in the war.* **2** one in a series of regular changes in the shape or appearance of something: *the phases of the moon.*

phase in to introduce something slowly or gradually over a period of time: *The tax changes will be phased in over the next two years.*

phase out to remove something slowly or gradually over a period of time: *The old equipment is being phased out and replaced by new machines.*

pheasant /ˈfɛzənt/ *n* a bird with a long tail, the male of which has brightly-coloured feathers.

phenomenal /fəˈnɒmɪnəl/ *adj* unusually great or good; extraordinary: *Her memory is phenomenal; He has phenomenal strength; He earns a phenomenal amount of money.* **phe'nomenally** *adv.*

phenomenon /fəˈnɒmɪnən/, *plural* **phenomena** /fəˈnɒmɪnə/, *n* something that can be seen or experienced; a natural happening that is interesting or unusual: *Lightning is an interesting phenomenon; An eclipse of the sun is a phenomenon that you don't see very often.*

phew /fjuː/ a word used to express tiredness, relief *etc*: *Phew! It's hot today!*

philanthropy /fɪˈlanθrəpɪ/ *n* love for mankind, shown by money given to, or work done for other people. **phi'lanthropist** *n.*

philately /fɪˈlatəlɪ/ *n* the study and collecting of postage-stamps. **phi'latelist** *n.*

philosophy /fɪˈlɒsəfɪ/ *n* the search for know-

ledge and truth, especially about the nature of humans and their behaviour and beliefs.

phi'losopher *n* a person who studies philosophy.

philo'sophical *adj* **1** having to do with philosophy: *a philosophical discussion.* **2** calm; not easily upset: *She has a philosophical attitude to life; He's had a lot of bad luck, but he's philosophical about it.* **philosophically** /fɪləˈsɒfɪklɪ/ *adv*.

phlegm /flɛm/ *n* thick, slimy liquid brought up from the throat by coughing.

phobia /ˈfoʊbɪə/ *n* an intense fear or hatred of something: *She has a phobia about birds.*

phoenix /ˈfiːnɪks/ *n* a bird that is found only in stories, that burns itself and is born again from its own ashes.

phone /foʊn/ *n* a telephone: *We were talking on the phone.* — *v* to telephone: *I'll phone you this evening; Phone him up and ask him to help.*

'phone-in *n* a radio or television programme during which you may ask questions or give opinions by telephone.

on the phone or **telephone 1** using the telephone: *Would you mind waiting outside while I'm on the phone, please?* **2** having a telephone in your house: *You can't ring them because they're not on the phone.*

phonetic /fəˈnɛtɪk/ *adj* having to do with the sounds of language. **phonetically** /fəˈnɛtɪklɪ/ *adv*.

pho'netics *n* **1** the study of sounds of language. **2** a system of symbols used to show the pronunciation of words.

phoney /ˈfoʊnɪ/ *adj* fake; false: *He spoke in a phoney accent.* — *n*: *This passport is a phoney.*

photo /ˈfoʊtoʊ/, *plural* **photos**, *n* short for **photograph**.

photocopier /ˈfoʊtoʊkɒpɪə(r)/ *n* a machine that makes photocopies.

photocopy /ˈfoʊtoʊkɒpɪ/ *n* a copy of a document *etc* made by a machine which photographs it: *I'll get some photocopies made of this letter.* — *v* to make a copy in this way: *Will you photocopy this letter for me?*

> **photocopy** is a general word for a copy made by photographing; **Photostat** and **Xerox** are trademarks; all three words can be used as verbs.

photograph /ˈfoʊtoʊɡrɑːf/ *n* a picture taken by a camera: *I took a lot of photographs during my holiday.* — *v* to take a photograph or photographs of a person, thing *etc*: *He photographed the mountain from many different points.*

photographer /fəˈtɒɡrəfə(r)/ *n*: *He is a professional photographer.*

photo'graphic *adj* connected with photographs or photography.

pho'tography *n* the art of taking photographs: *He's very keen on photography.*

Photostat /ˈfoʊtəstat/ *n* the tradename of a kind of photocopying machine; a copy made by it. — *v*: *to Photostat a document.*

> See **photocopy**.

phrasal /ˈfreɪzəl/ *adj* having to do with phrases; in the form of a phrase, as in **phrasal verb**, a phrase consisting of a verb and adverb or preposition, which together behave like a verb: *'Leave out', 'go without', 'go away', are phrasal verbs.*

phrase /freɪz/ *n* a small group of words that forms part of a sentence: *He arrived after dinner.* — *v* to express something in words: *I phrased my explanations in simple language.*

phrase book a book that gives common words and phrases in a foreign language.

physical /ˈfɪzɪkəl/ *adj* **1** having to do with your body: *Playing football is one form of physical exercise.* **2** having to do with things that can be seen or felt: *the physical world.* **3** having to do with the laws of nature: *It's a physical impossibility for a man to fly like a bird.* **4** relating to the natural features of the surface of the Earth: *physical geography.* **5** relating to physics: *physical chemistry.* **physically** /ˈfɪzɪklɪ/ *adv*.

physician /fɪˈzɪʃən/ *n* a doctor who specializes in medical rather than surgical treatment of patients: *My doctor sent me to a physician at the hospital.*

physics /ˈfɪzɪks/ *n* the study of things that occur naturally, such as heat, light, sound, electricity, magnetism *etc*: *the laws of physics.* **physicist** /ˈfɪzɪsɪst/ *n*.

physiotherapy /fɪzɪoʊˈθɛrəpɪ/ *n* the treatment of injury by physical exercise and massage: *He had physiotherapy on the injured leg.* **physio'therapist** *n*.

physique /fɪˈziːk/ *n* the structure of a person's body: *He has a powerful physique.*

piano /pɪˈanoʊ/, *plural* **pianos**, *n* a large musical instrument played by pressing keys: *He's learning to play the piano.*

pianist /ˈpɪənɪst/ *n* a person who plays the piano.

piccolo /ˈpɪkəloʊ/ *n* a small, high-sounding flute.

pick /pɪk/ v **1** to choose; to select: *Pick the one you like best.* **2** to take flowers from a plant, fruit from a tree *etc*: *Pick some wild flowers for me*; *It's time this fruit was picked.* **3** to lift: *He picked up the child.* **4** to unlock a lock with a tool other than a key: *She picked the lock with a bit of wire.* — n **1** whatever you want: *Take your pick of these prizes.* **2** the best: *These grapes are the pick of the bunch.*

pick a fight to start an argument or fight deliberately: *She had been trying to pick a fight for days.*

pick and choose to choose carefully: *When I'm buying apples, I like to pick and choose.*

pick at to eat very little of something: *He was not very hungry, and just picked at the food on his plate.*

pick on 1 to choose someone to do a difficult or unpleasant job: *Why do they always pick on me to do the washing-up?* **2** to be nasty to a particular person: *Stop picking on me!*

pick out 1 to choose: *She picked out one dress that she particularly liked.* **2** to see or recognize a person, thing *etc*: *I couldn't pick him out in the crowd.*

pick someone's pocket to steal something from a person's pocket.

pick up 1 to learn gradually: *I never studied French — I just picked it up when I was in France.* **2** to let someone into a car *etc* in order to take them somewhere: *I picked him up at the station and drove him home.* **3** to get something by chance: *I picked up a bargain at the shops today*; *I picked up an interesting piece of information the other day.* **4** to stand up: *He fell over and picked himself up again.* **5** to collect something from somewhere: *I ordered some meat from the butcher — I'll pick it up on my way home tonight.* **6** to increase: *The car picked up speed as it ran down the hill.*

'pickaxe or **pick** n a tool with a point at one end of its head and a blade for chopping at the other: *He used a pickaxe to break up the rocks.*

picket /'pɪkɪt/ v to stand outside a factory or other place of work in order to protest about something and to persuade other workers not to go to work there, or not to deliver goods there: *The workers picketed the factory for three weeks.* — n a person or a group of people who are picketing a factory *etc*: *The pickets tried to stop lorries getting through the factory gates.*

pickle /'pɪkəl/ n a vegetable, or vegetables, preserved in vinegar, salt water *etc*: *a jar of pickles*; *Have some pickle.* — v to preserve in vinegar, salt water *etc*: *to pickle cucumbers.*

pickpocket /'pɪkpɒkɪt/ n a thief who steals things out of people's pockets *etc*.

pick-up /'pɪkʌp/ n a small truck or van.

picky /'pɪkɪ/ adj difficult to please; fussy: *She won't eat that — she's very picky.*

picnic /'pɪknɪk/ n a meal eaten in the open air, usually on a trip: *We'll go to the seaside and take a picnic*; *Let's go for a picnic!* — v to have a picnic: *We picnicked on the beach.*

> **picnicking** and **picnicked** are spelt with a **k**.

pictorial /pɪk'tɔːrɪəl/ adj **1** having many pictures: *a pictorial magazine.* **2** consisting of a picture or pictures: *a pictorial map.* **pic-'torially** adv.

picture /'pɪktʃə(r)/ n **1** a painting or drawing: *This is a picture of my mother.* **2** a photograph: *I took a lot of pictures when I was on holiday.* **3** a cinema film: *There's a good picture on at the cinema tonight.* **4** an image or view: *He had a clear picture in his mind of the man who had attacked him*; *The plan provided a good picture of how the finished building would look.* **5** what you see on a television screen: *We don't get a very good picture up here in the hills.* **6** a perfect example of something: *She looked the picture of health.* **7** a beautiful sight: *She looked a picture in her new dress.* **8** a clear description: *He gave me a good picture of what was happening.* — v **1** to imagine: *I can picture the scene.* **2** to show or represent something in a picture: *They are pictured in front of the Taj Mahal.*

picturesque /pɪktʃə'rɛsk/ adj pretty and interesting: *The little old village was very picturesque.*

the pictures the cinema: *We went to the pictures last night, but it wasn't a good film.*

> See **go**.

pidgin /'pɪdʒɪn/ n any of a number of languages which consist of a mixture of a European language and a local one, used in Asia and Africa for trade, business *etc*: *pidgin English.*

pie /paɪ/ n food baked in a covering of pastry: *a steak pie*; *an apple pie.*

piece /piːs/ n **1** a part of anything: *a piece of cake.* **2** an example of something; a bit: *a piece of paper*; *a piece of news.* **3** something written or composed: *He has written a piece* *about drugs in this week's newspaper*; *She had played the piece many times before.* **4** a coin of a particular value: *a five-penny piece.* **5** One of the objects you move on a board in a board-game: *a chess-piece.*

piece'meal *adv* a little bit at a time: *He did the work piecemeal.*

go to pieces to get so anxious or upset that you lose your ability to deal with things like you usually do: *She gradually went to pieces as one disaster followed another.*

in pieces 1 with its various parts not joined together: *The bed was delivered in pieces and he had to put it together himself.* **2** broken: *The vase was lying in pieces on the floor.*

piece together 1 to put together: *They tried to piece together the fragments of the broken vase.* **2** to collect information and understand how it fits together to make a story or the truth *etc*: *They pieced together what happened on the day before she died.*

to pieces into separate small pieces: *The material was so old that it fell to pieces when I touched it.*

pier /pɪə(r)/ *n* a platform of stone, wood *etc* stretching from the shore into the sea or a lake, used as a landing-place for boats: *The passengers stepped down on to the pier.*

See **quay**.

pierce /pɪəs/ *v* **1** to go into or through something: *The arrow pierced his arm.* **2** to make a hole in or through something with a pointed object: *Pierce the lid before removing it from the jar*; *She had her ears pierced so that she could wear earrings.*

'piercing *adj* **1** loud; shrill: *a piercing scream.* **2** sharp; intense: *a piercing wind*; *piercing cold.*

piety /'paɪətɪ/ *n* goodness, especially of the religious kind.

pig /pɪg/ *n* **1** a farm animal whose flesh is eaten as pork, ham and bacon: *He keeps pigs.* **2** a greedy or dirty person: *You pig!*

A pig **grunts** or **squeals**.
A baby pig is a **piglet**.
A male pig is a **boar**.
A female pig is a **sow**.
A pig lives in a **sty**.

pigeon /'pɪdʒɪn/ *n* a bird of the dove family.

A pigeon **coos**.

'pigeon-hole *n* a small compartment for letters, papers *etc* in a desk *etc*.

piggy /'pɪgɪ/ *n* a child's word for a pig.

'piggyback *n* a ride on someone's back: *Please give me a piggyback, Daddy.*

'piggybank *n* a small container that children use for saving money in.

pigheaded /pɪg'hɛdɪd/ *adj* refusing to take advice; obstinate. **pig'headedness** *n*.

piglet /'pɪglət/ *n* a baby pig.

pigment /'pɪgmənt/ *n* **1** any substance used for colouring, making paint *etc*. **2** a substance in plants or animals that gives colour to the skin, leaves *etc*: *Some people have darker pigment in their skin than others.*

pigmen'tation *n* colouring of skin *etc*.

pigmy another spelling of **pygmy**.

pigskin /'pɪgskɪn/ *n* leather made of a pig's skin. — *adj*: *a pigskin purse.*

pigsty /'pɪgstaɪ/ *n* **1** a pen for pigs. **2** a very dirty untidy place: *This room is a pigsty!*

pigswill /'pɪgswɪl/ *n* soft food given to pigs.

pigtail /'pɪgteɪl/ *n* a plait of hair.

See **plait**.

pike /paɪk/, *plural* **pike**, *n* a large fresh-water fish.

pile[1] /paɪl/ *n* **1** a number of things lying one on top of another; a heap: *There was a neat pile of books in the corner of the room*; *There was a pile of rubbish at the bottom of the garden.* **2** a large quantity: *He must have piles of money to own a car like that.* — *v* to make a pile of something: *He piled the boxes on the table.*

'pile-up *n* an accident involving several vehicles.

pile into, **pile out of** to come or go in a disorganized way: *As soon as the doors opened, the people piled into the cinema.*

pile up to make or become a pile: *He piled up the earth at the end of the garden*; *The rubbish piled up in the kitchen.*

pile[2] /paɪl/ *n* a large pillar or stake driven into the ground as a foundation for a building, bridge *etc*: *Venice is built on piles.*

pilfer /'pɪlfə(r)/ *v* to steal small things.

pilgrim /'pɪlgrɪm/ *n* a person who travels to a holy place.

'pilgrimage *n* a journey to a holy place.

pill /pɪl/ *n* a small tablet containing a medicine.

pillar /'pɪlə(r)/ *n* **1** an upright post used in building as a support or decoration: *an elegant courtyard with fountains and pillars.* **2** an active supporter or an important member: *He is a pillar of the golf club.*

pillion /'pɪljən/ *n* a passenger seat on a motorcycle. — *adj*: *a pillion passenger.*

pillow /ˈpɪloʊ/ *n* a cushion for your head, especially on a bed.
  'pillowcase or **'pillowslip** *n* a cover for a pillow.
pilot /ˈpaɪlət/ *n* **1** a person who flies an aeroplane. **2** a person who directs a ship in and out of a harbour, river *etc*. — *adj* experimental: *a pilot scheme*. — *v* to guide as a pilot: *He piloted the ship*.
pimple /ˈpɪmpəl/ *n* a small round red swelling on the skin; a spot: *He had a pimple on his nose*. **'pimply** *adj*.
pin /pɪn/ *n* a short, thin, pointed piece of metal used to hold pieces of fabric, paper *etc* together: *The papers are fastened together by a pin*. — *v* **1** to fasten with a pin: *She pinned the material together*; *She pinned the notice on the board*. **2** to hold something down, or against something: *The fallen tree pinned him to the ground*.
  pins and needles sharp little pains that you get in a part of your body after it has been in one position for too long: *I've got pins and needles in my legs after kneeling for so long*.
pinafore /ˈpɪnəfɔː(r)/ *n* **1** a kind of apron for covering your clothes: *The children wore pinafores at nursery school*. **2** a dress with no sleeves, worn over a blouse, sweater *etc*.
pincers /ˈpɪnsəz/ *n* **1** a tool for gripping things tightly: *Where are my pincers?*; *Whose is this pair of pincers?* **2** the claws of lobsters, crabs *etc*.

> **pincers** takes a plural verb, but **a pair of pincers** is singular.

pinch /pɪntʃ/ *v* **1** to squeeze someone's flesh tightly between your thumb and forefinger: *He pinched her arm*. **2** to hurt by being too small or tight: *My new shoes are pinching*. **3** to steal: *Who pinched my bicycle?* — *n* **1** a squeeze: *He gave her cheek a pinch*. **2** a small amount; what can be held between your thumb and forefinger: *a pinch of salt*.
  pinched *adj* thin and pale because of cold or illness *etc*: *the pinched faces of homeless children*.
  at a pinch if absolutely necessary: *We should be able to feed two extra people at a pinch*.
pincushion /ˈpɪnkʊʃən/ *n* a small cushion into which pins are pushed for keeping.
pine[1] /paɪn/ *n* **1** an evergreen tree with cones (**'pine-cones**) and needlelike leaves (**'pine-needles**). **2** its wood: *The table is made of pine*. — *adj*: *a pine table*.

pine[2] /paɪn/ *v* **1** to become weak with pain, grief *etc*: *He pined away after his wife's death*. **2** to want something very much: *He knew that his wife was pining for home*.
pineapple /ˈpaɪnæpəl/ *n* a large tropical fruit shaped like a large pine-cone, the flesh of which is sweet and juicy.
ping /pɪŋ/ *n* a sharp, ringing sound: *His knife struck the wine-glass with a loud ping*. — *v*: *The glass pinged*; *He pinged the wire*.
ping-pong /ˈpɪŋpɒŋ/ *n* the game of table tennis: *Do you play ping-pong?*
pinhole /ˈpɪnhoʊl/ *n* a hole made by a pin.
pink /pɪŋk/ *n* a colour between red and white. — *adj*: *a dress of pink satin*. **'pinkness** *n*.
  'pinkish *adj* slightly pink in colour: *a pinkish blue*.
pinnacle /ˈpɪnəkəl/ *n* **1** a tall thin spire built on the roof of a church, castle *etc*. **2** a high pointed rock or mountain: *It was a dangerous pinnacle to climb*. **3** the highest point of something: *She was at the pinnacle of her success*.
pinpoint /ˈpɪnpɔɪnt/ *v* **1** to place or show very exactly: *He pinpointed the position on the map*. **2** to discover or explain exactly: *They are trying to pinpoint the cause of the pain*.
pint /paɪnt/ *n* a unit for measuring liquids; in Britain, 0.57 litre; in the US, 0.47 litre: *a pint of beer*.
pioneer /paɪəˈnɪə(r)/ *n* **1** a person who goes to a new country to live and work there: *the American pioneers*. **2** a person who is the first to study some new subject, or develop a new skill, method *etc*: *a pioneer of progressive teaching methods*. — *v* to be the first to do or make something: *Edward Jenner pioneered the use of vaccine against smallpox*.
pious /ˈpaɪəs/ *adj* very good; always doing or thinking what is right, especially in a religious way. **'piously** *adv*.
pip /pɪp/ *n* a seed of a fruit: *an orange pip*.

> The small seeds inside apples, melons, pears, oranges *etc* are **pips**.
> The stone of a plum, cherry, peach, apricot *etc* is a **pit**.

  pip at the post to overtake or defeat someone at the last moment.
pipe /paɪp/ *n* **1** a tube, made of metal, plastic *etc*, through which water, gas *etc* can flow: *a water pipe*; *a drainpipe*. **2** a small tube

with a bowl at one end, in which tobacco is smoked: *He smokes a pipe.* **3** a musical instrument consisting of a hollow wooden or metal tube through which the player blows to make a sound: *He played a tune on a bamboo pipe.* — *v* **1** to carry gas, water *etc* by a pipe: *Water is piped to the town from the reservoir.* **2** to play the pipes.

piped music music played through loudspeakers in public places: *There is often piped music in the shopping centre.*

pipe dream an ambition or hope which will never happen: *She wastes too much time on pipe dreams.*

'pipeline *n* a long line of pipes used for conveying oil, gas, water *etc*: *an oil pipeline.*

'piper *n* a person who plays a pipe, or the pipes.

pipes *n* bagpipes or some similar instrument: *He plays the pipes.*

'piping *n* **1** the art of playing a pipe or the pipes. **2** a length of pipe for water, gas *etc* or number of pipes: *lead piping.* — *adj* highsounding: *a piping voice.*

piping hot very hot: *piping-hot soup.*

in the pipeline being planned or prepared: *There are some major changes in the pipeline that will soon be announced.*

piranha /pɪˈrɑːnə/ *n* a small, fierce fish with very sharp teeth that lives in South American rivers: *Piranhas attack and eat other, larger fish.*

piranha

pirate /ˈpaɪrət/ *n* **1** a person who attacks and robs ships at sea: *Their ship was attacked by pirates.* **2** a person who illegally copies and sells things such as video tapes and computer programs: *a software pirate.* — *adj*: *a pirate ship*; *a pirate video.* — *v* to publish, broadcast *etc* without the legal right to do so: *The dictionary was pirated and sold abroad.* **'piracy** *n*.

pistol /ˈpɪstəl/ *n* a small gun held in one hand.

See **gun**.

piston /ˈpɪstən/ *n* a round piece of metal that fits inside a cylinder and moves up and down or backwards and forwards inside it.

pit[1] /pɪt/ *n* **1** a large hole in the ground: *The campers dug a pit for their rubbish.* **2** a place from which minerals are dug, especially a coal mine: *He works down the pit.* — *v* **1** to mark with shallow holes: *The surface of the moon is pitted with craters.* **2** to set one person against another in a fight, competition *etc*: *He was pitted against a much stronger man.*

the pits the areas beside a motor-racing track where vehicles can stop for fuel, new tyres *etc* during a race.

pit[2] /pɪt/ *n* the hard stone of a peach, cherry *etc.* — *v* to remove the stone from a peach *etc.*

See **pip**.

pitch[1] /pɪtʃ/ *v* **1** to set up a tent or camp: *They pitched their tent in the field.* **2** to throw: *He pitched the stone into the river.* **3** to fall heavily: *He pitched forward.* **3** to set something at a particular level: *She pitched her voice low so that no-one else could hear her*; *His lecture was pitched at a level that everyone could understand.* — *n* **1** the ground for certain games: *a football pitch.* **2** the degree of highness or lowness of a musical note, voice *etc.* **3** an extreme point: *His anger reached such a pitch that he hit her.*

-pitched having a certain pitch: *a high-pitched noise*; *low-pitched voice.*

pitched battle a battle between armies that have been prepared and arranged for fighting beforehand: *They fought a pitched battle.*

pitch in to join in or make a contribution to something: *If everyone pitches in, we'll soon be finished.*

pitch[2] /pɪtʃ/ *n* a thick black substance obtained from tar: *as black as pitch.*

pitch-'black or **pitch-'dark** *adj* as black, or dark, as pitch; completely black or dark.

pitcher[1] /ˈpɪtʃə(r)/ *n* a large jug: *a pitcher of water.*

pitcher[2] /ˈpɪtʃə(r)/ *n* the player who throws the ball in baseball.

piteous /ˈpɪtiəs/ *adj* making you feel great pity or sadness: *the piteous cries of the lost children.* **'piteously** *adv.*

pitfall /ˈpɪtfɔːl/ *n* a possible danger; something that it is easy to make a mistake about: *English grammar is full of pitfalls.*

pith /pɪθ/ *n* **1** the white substance between the peel of an orange, lemon *etc* and the fruit itself. **2** the soft substance in the centre of the stems of plants. **3** the most important part of anything: *the pith of the argument.*

pithy /ˈpɪθɪ/ *adj* expressed clearly and cleverly

without using too many words: *a pithy comment*.

pitiful /'pɪtɪfʊl/ *adj* **1** very sad; causing pity: *a pitiful sight*. **2** very poor, bad, insufficient *etc*: *a pitiful attempt*; *a pitiful amount of money*. **'pitifully** *adv*.

pitiless /'pɪtɪləs/ *adj* having or showing no pity.

pitter-patter /'pɪtəpatə(r)/ *n* a light, tapping sound: *the pitter-patter of rain on a window*. — *v* to make this sound. — *adv*: *The mouse ran pitter-patter across the floor*.

pity /'pɪtɪ/ *n* **1** a feeling of sorrow for the troubles of others: *He reluctantly agreed, more out of pity than anything else*. **2** a cause of sorrow or regret: *What a pity that she can't come*. — *v* to feel pity for someone: *She pitied him*.

have pity on to feel pity for someone: *Have pity on the old man*.

take pity on to act kindly, or relent towards someone, from a feeling of pity: *He took pity on the hungry children and gave them food*.

'pitying *adj* showing pity: *a pitying look*.

pivot /'pɪvət/ *n* the pin or centre on which anything balances and turns. — *v* to turn: *The door pivoted on its hinge*.

pixy or **pixie** /'pɪksɪ/ *n* a kind of fairy.

pizza /'pi:tsə/ *n* a flat piece of dough spread with tomato, cheese *etc* and baked.

placard /'plakɑːd/ *n* a notice printed on wood or cardboard and carried, hung *etc*, in a public place: *The protesters were carrying placards attacking the government's policy*.

placate /plə'keɪt/ *v* to stop an angry person feeling angry: *The relaxation of an oppressive regime, far from placating its opponents, encourages further opposition*.

place /pleɪs/ *n* **1** a particular spot or area: *a quiet place in the country*; *I spent my holiday in various different places*. **2** an empty space: *There's a place for your books here*. **3** an area or building with a particular purpose: *a market-place*. **4** a seat: *He went to his place and sat down*. **5** a position in an order, series, queue *etc*: *She is in first place in the competition*; *I lost my place in the queue*. **6** a point in the text of a book *etc*: *I kept losing my place in the book*. **7** a job or position in a team, organization *etc*: *He's got a place in the team*. **8** house; home: *Come over to my place*. **9** a number or one of a series of numbers following a decimal point: *Make the answer correct to four decimal places*. — *v* **1** to put: *He placed it on the table*. *I was placed in a difficult position*. **2** to recognize someone and remember where you met them and what their name is: *I knew we had met before but I couldn't place her*.

to make **room** (not **place**) *for something*.
Is there enough **room** *or* **space** (not **place**) *in here*?

'place-name *n* the name of a place.

change places or **swap places** to take someone's seat or position and give them yours: *If we change places you'll be able to see better*.

fall into place to become clear in your mind: *The details are beginning to fall into place after the discoveries we made this morning*.

in place in the proper position; tidy: *He left everything in place*.

in my, your *etc* **place** used when considering a situation from another person's point of view: *What would you do if you were in my place?*

in place of instead of: *Jim went to the party in place of John*.

in the first, second *etc* **place** expressions used to show steps in an argument, explanation *etc*: *He decided not to buy the house, because in the first place it was too expensive, and in the second place it was too far from his office*.

out of place 1 not in the correct position: *All of these books are out of place*. **2** not appropriate or suitable: *He is out of place here*.

put someone in their place to remind someone, often in a rude or angry way, of their lack of importance.

take place to happen, especially according to plan: *The meeting took place on 17 March*; *What took place after that?*

See **occur**.

take the place of to be used instead of something: *I don't think television will ever take the place of books*.

placid /'plasɪd/ *adj* calm; not easily upset: *a placid child*. **'placidly** *adv*.

plagiarize /'pleɪdʒəraɪz/ *v* to steal or copy someone else's ideas and pretend that they are yours: *She was accused of plagiarizing the work of other authors*.

plague /pleɪg/ *n* **1** an extremely infectious and deadly disease. **2** a large and annoying quantity: *a plague of flies*. — *v* to annoy continually: *The child was plaguing her with questions.*

a **plague** (not a **plaque**) of frogs.

plaice /pleɪs/, *plural* **plaice**, *n* a flat fish.

plain /pleɪn/ *adj* **1** all one colour; without decoration or a pattern: *a plain carpet*; *a plain brown envelope*. **2** simple; ordinary: *plain living*. **3** easy to understand; clear: *His words were quite plain.* **4** absolutely honest: *plain speaking*; *I'll be quite plain with you.* **5** obvious: *It's plain you haven't been practising your music.* **6** not pretty: *a plain child.* — *n* a large flat level piece of land: *the plains of central Canada.* **'plainly** *adv.* **'plainness** *n.*

See **mountain**.

plain chocolate chocolate not containing milk.

plain clothes ordinary clothes, not a uniform: *Detectives usually wear plain clothes.* — *adj*: *a plain-clothes policeman.*

plain sailing progress without difficulty.

plaintiff /'pleɪntɪf/ *n* a person who starts a legal case against someone in a court of law.

plaintive /'pleɪntɪv/ *adj* full of sadness or suffering: *His tone was plaintive rather than angry.* **'plaintively** *adv.*

plait /plat/ or /pleɪt/ *n* **1** a length of hair arranged by dividing it into sections and passing these over one another in turn: *She wore her hair in a long plait.* **2** a similar arrangement of any material: *a plait of straw.* — *v* to arrange hair *etc* in this way: *She plaited her hair.*

fringe

plait   ponytail   pigtail

plan /plan/ *n* **1** an idea of how to do something; a method of doing something: *If everyone follows this plan, we will succeed*; *I have worked out a plan for making a lot of money.* **2** an intention; an arrangement: *What are your plans for tomorrow?* **3** a drawing showing a building, town *etc* as if seen from above: *a street-plan*; *These are the plans for our new house.* — *v* **1** to intend to do something: *We are planning on going to Italy this year*; *We were planning to go last year but we hadn't enough money*; *They are planning a trip to Italy.* **2** to decide how something is to be done; to arrange something: *We are planning a party.* **3** to design something: *They employed an architect to plan the building.*

plane[1] /pleɪn/ *n* an aeroplane.

See **in**.

plane[2] /pleɪn/ *n* **1** a level; a standard. **2** in geometry, a flat surface.

plane[3] /pleɪn/ *n* a carpenter's tool for making a level or smooth surface. — *v* to make a surface level, smooth or lower by using a plane.

planet /'planɪt/ *n* any of the bodies which move round the Sun or round another star: *Mars and Jupiter are planets, but the Moon is not.* **'planetary** *adj.*

planetarium /planə'tɛərɪəm/ *n* a building that contains an apparatus for showing the positions and movements of the planets and stars.

plank /plaŋk/ *n* a long, flat piece of wood: *The floor was made of planks.*

planner /'planə(r)/ *n* **1** someone whose job is to plan buildings, streets, shopping centres *etc*. **2** a large calendar on which to mark your plans for the year.

planning /'planɪŋ/ *n* making plans or arrangements for something: *town-planning*; *This project will need careful planning.*

plant /plɑːnt/ *n* **1** anything that grows from the ground and has a stem, roots and leaves: *Trees are plants.* **2** industrial machinery: *engineering plant.* **3** a factory. — *v* **1** to put something into the ground so that it will grow: *We have planted vegetables in the garden*; *The garden was planted with shrubs*; *We're going to plant an orchard.* **2** to put something firmly in a certain position: *He planted himself in the front row and refused to move*; *She planted a kiss right in the middle of his forehead.* **3** to deliberately put something in another person's belongings so that when it is found, they will be accused of a crime: *He didn't know how to prove that the evidence had been planted on him.*

plan'tation *n* **1** a place that has been planted with trees. **2** a piece of land for growing certain crops, especially cotton, sugar, rubber, tea and tobacco: *He owned a rubber plantation in Malaysia.*

'planter *n* the owner of a plantation: *a tea planter.*

plaque

plaque[1] /'plɑːk/ *n* a metal plate bearing a name etc: *His name was inscribed on a brass plaque.*

> to put a **plaque** (not **plague**) on your front door.

plaque[2] /'plɑːk/ *n* a substance that forms on teeth and encourages the growth of harmful bacteria.

plasma /'plæzmə/ *n* the clear, liquid part of blood: *She was given plasma during her operation as there was no blood available for a transfusion.*

plaster /'plɑːstə(r)/ *n* **1** a substance put on walls, ceilings *etc* that dries to form a hard smooth surface: *He mixed up some plaster to repair the wall.* **2** a similar quick-drying substance used for supporting broken limbs, making models *etc* (also called **plaster of Paris**): *She's got her arm in plaster.* **3** sticky tape used to cover a wound *etc* (also called **'sticking-plaster**): *You should put a plaster on that cut.* — *adj* made of plaster: *a plaster ceiling; a plaster model.* — *v* **1** to put plaster on something: *They plastered the walls.* **2** to cover something thickly: *The car was plastered with mud from the field.*

plastic /'plæstɪk/ *n* any of many chemically manufactured substances that can be moulded when still soft: *This cup is made of plastic.* — *adj* **1** made of plastic: *a plastic cup.* **2** easily made into different shapes.

plastic surgery surgery to repair damage to the skin, such as burns, or to improve your appearance: *She had plastic surgery to make her nose smaller.*

plate /pleɪt/ *n* **1** a shallow dish for holding food *etc*: *china plates.* **2** a sheet of metal *etc*: *The ship was built of steel plates.* **3** a flat piece of metal with letters or information printed on it: *Her name was on the plate beside the doorbell.* **4** a large picture or photograph in a book: *See plate 3 on page 20.* **5** articles made of, or plated with, gold or silver: *a collection of gold plate.*

plateau /'platoʊ/, *plural* **plateaus** or **plateaux** /'platoʊz/, *n* **1** an area of high flat land; a mountain with a wide flat top. **2** a state where there is little development or change.

plated /'pleɪtɪd/ *adj* covered with a thin layer of a different metal: *gold-plated dishes.*

plateful /'pleɪtfʊl/ *n* the contents of a plate: *a plateful of potatoes.*

platform /'platfɔːm/ *n* **1** a raised part of a floor for speakers, entertainers *etc*: *The orchestra arranged themselves on the platform.* **2** the raised area between or beside the lines in a railway station: *The London train will leave from platform 6.*

plating /'pleɪtɪŋ/ *n* a thin covering of metal: *silver plating.*

platinum /'platɪnəm/ *n* a heavy, valuable grey metal, often used in making jewellery. — *adj*: *a platinum ring.*

platoon /plə'tuːn/ *n* a small group of soldiers that is commanded by a lieutenant.

platter /'platə(r)/ *n* a large, flat plate: *a wooden platter.*

plausible /'plɔːzɪbəl/ *adj* reasonable or likely: *His explanation certainly sounds plausible.*

> the opposite of **plausible** is **implausible**.

play /pleɪ/ *v* **1** to amuse yourself: *He is playing with his toys.* **2** to take part in games *etc*: *He plays football; Brazil played Germany in the final.* **3** to act in a play *etc*; to act a character: *She's playing Lady Macbeth; The company is playing in London this week.* **4** to perform on a musical instrument: *She plays the piano.* **5** to listen to a recording of something: *They sat around playing records in the holidays.* **6** to carry out a trick: *He played a trick on me.* — *n* **1** recreation; amusement: *You must have time for both work and play.* **2** an acted story; a drama: *Shakespeare wrote many plays.*

'playboy *n* a rich man who spends his time and money on pleasure.

'player *n* **1** a person who plays: *How many players are there in a football team?; We need four players for this card-game.* **2** an actor.

'playful *adj* **1** happy; full of the desire to play: *a playful kitten.* **2** joking; not serious: *a playful remark.* **'playfully** *adv*. **'playfulness** *n*.

'playground *n* an area where children can play.

playing card one of a pack of cards used in card games.

playing field an area of ground where games are played.

'playmate *n* a childhood friend.

'playschool *n* a nursery school.

'plaything *n* a toy.

'playtime *n* a time for children to play: *The children go outside at playtime.*

playwright /'pleɪraɪt/ *n* a person who writes plays: *He is a famous playwright.*

at play playing: *The children were at play.*

child's play something that is very easy: *Of course you can do it — it's child's play.*

play at 1 to pretend to be *etc*: *The children were playing at cowboys and Indians.* **2** used when asking angrily what someone is doing: *What does he think he's playing at?*

play back to play music *etc* on a record or tape after it has been recorded: *Press the red button to play back your phone messages.* **'play-back** *n*.

play down to present as being less important than it really is: *He played down the seriousness of his injury.*

play fair to act honestly and fairly.

play a part in, **play no part in** to be one of the people, or not be one of the people, taking part in something: *He played no part in the robbery.*

play safe to take no risks.

play up 1 to behave badly or not in the way you want: *Her children are always playing up*; *His car is playing up.* **2** to cause you pain or discomfort: *Is your back still playing up?* **3** to make something seem more important: *He played up the fact that he could speak French.*

plea /pliː/ *n* **1** a prisoner's answer to a charge: *He made a plea of guilty.* **2** an urgent request: *The hospital sent out a plea for blood-donors.*

plead /pliːd/ *v* **1** to answer a charge, saying whether you are guilty or not: *'How does the prisoner plead?' 'He pleads guilty.'* **2** to make an urgent request: *He pleaded to be allowed to go.*

pleasant /'plɛzənt/ *adj* giving pleasure; agreeable: *a pleasant day*; *a pleasant person.* **'pleasantly** *adv*. **'pleasantness** *n*.

please /pliːz/ *v* **1** to do what is wanted by someone; to give pleasure or satisfaction to someone: *You can't please everyone all the time*; *It pleases me to read poetry.* **2** to want; to like: *He does as he pleases.* — *adv* a word added to an order or request in order to be polite: *Please open the window*; *Close the door, please*; *Will you please come with me?*
pleased *adj* happy; satisfied: *She was pleased with her new dress.*
'pleasing *adj* giving pleasure; attractive: *a pleasing view.* **'pleasingly** *adv*.
if you please please: *Come this way, if you please.*

pleasurable /'plɛʒərəbəl/ *adj* giving pleasure; agreeable: *a pleasurable pastime.* **'pleasurably** *adv*.

pleasure /'plɛʒə(r)/ *n* something that gives you enjoyment; joy or delight: *I get a lot of pleasure from listening to music*; *It's a pleasure to meet you.*
'pleasure-boat, **'pleasure-craft** *ns* a boat used for pleasure.
take pleasure in to get enjoyment from doing something: *He takes great pleasure in annoying me.*
with pleasure gladly; willingly; of course: *I joined them for dinner with pleasure*; *'Would you accept this gift?' 'With pleasure.'*

pleat /pliːt/ *n* a fold sewn or pressed into cloth *etc*: *a skirt with pleats.* — *v* to make pleats in something.
'pleated *adj*: *a pleated skirt.*

pledge /plɛdʒ/ *n* **1** a promise: *He gave me his pledge.* **2** something that you give to someone when you borrow money *etc* from them, to keep until you return the money *etc*: *He borrowed £20 and left his watch as a pledge.* **3** a sign or token: *They exchanged rings as a pledge of their love.* — *v* **1** to promise: *He pledged his help.* **2** to give something to someone when you borrow money *etc*: *to pledge your watch.*

plentiful /'plɛntɪfʊl/ *adj* existing in large amounts: *a plentiful supply of food.*

plenty /'plɛntɪ/ *pron* **1** enough: *I don't need any more books — I've got plenty*; *We've got plenty of time to get there.* **2** a large amount: *He's got plenty of money.* — *adj*: *That's plenty, thank you!*

pliable /'plaɪəbəl/ *adj* easy to bend: *Wire is pliable.* **plia'bility** *n*.

pliers /'plaɪəz/ *n* a tool used for gripping, bending or cutting wire *etc*: *He used a pair of pliers to pull the nail out*; *Where are my pliers?*

> **pliers** always takes a plural verb, but **a pair of pliers** is singular.

plight /plaɪt/ *n* a bad situation: *She was in a terrible plight, as she had lost all her money, and was far from home.*

plimsoll /'plɪmsəl/ *n* a light canvas shoe worn for games: *The children put their plimsolls on for their games lesson.*

plod /plɒd/ *v* **1** to walk heavily and slowly: *The elderly man plodded down the street.* **2** to work slowly but thoroughly: *They plodded on with the work.*

plonk /plɒŋk/ *v* to put down noisily and clumsily: *He plonked his books on the table*; *She plonked herself down in front of the fire.* — *n* the sound made by something dropping heavily: *There was a loud plonk as the vase fell over.*

plop /plɒp/ *n* the sound of a small object falling into water *etc*: *The raindrop fell into her teacup with a plop.* — *v*: *A stone plopped into the pool.*

plot /plɒt/ *n* **1** a plan, especially for doing something evil: *a plot to assassinate the President.* **2** the story of a play, novel *etc*: *The play has a very complicated plot.* **3** a small piece of land for use as a gardening area or for building a house on *etc*. — *v* **1** to plan to bring about something evil: *They were plotting the death of the king.* **2** to mark something on a map, diagram or graph: *to plot results on a graph*; *He was plotting the route they were taking on his own map.*

plough /plaʊ/ *n* a farm tool pulled through the top layer of the soil to break it up. — *v* **1** to break up earth with this tool: *The farmer was ploughing a field.* **2** to crash: *The lorry ploughed into the back of a bus.*

ploy /plɔɪ/ *n* a carefully thought-out plan or method of achieving something: *The boys had thought of a ploy to get an afternoon off school.*

pluck /plʌk/ *v* **1** to pull: *She plucked a grey hair from her head*; *He plucked at my sleeve.* **2** to pull the feathers off a bird before cooking it. **3** to pick flowers *etc*. — *n* courage: *He showed a lot of pluck.*

'**plucky** *adj* brave: *a plucky young fellow*. '**pluckily** *adv*. '**pluckiness** *n*.

pluck up courage, energy *etc* to gather up your courage *etc* to do something: *She plucked up the courage to ask the headmaster a question.*

plug /plʌg/ *n* **1** an object that you fit into a socket in the wall, in order to allow an electric current to reach an electrical apparatus that you want to use: *She changed the plug on the electric kettle.* **2** an object shaped for fitting into the hole in a bath or sink to prevent the water from running away, or a piece of material for blocking any hole. — *v* to block a hole by putting a plug in it: *He plugged the hole in the window with a piece of newspaper.*

'**plughole** *n* the hole through which the water flows out from a sink or bath.

plug in to connect up an electrical apparatus by inserting its plug into a socket: *Could you plug in the electric kettle?*

plum /plʌm/ *n* a soft, usually red fruit with a stone in the centre.

plum cake or **plum pudding** a cake or pudding containing raisins, currants *etc*.

plumage /ˈpluːmɪdʒ/ *n* the feathers of a bird: *The peacock has brilliant plumage.*

plumber /ˈplʌmə(r)/ *n* someone who fits and mends water, gas and sewage pipes in your home: *Send for a plumber — we have a leaking pipe.*

The pronunciation of **plumber** is /ˈplʌmə(r)/, to rhyme with **summer**.

plumbing /ˈplʌmɪŋ/ *n* the system of water and gas pipes in a building: *The house needs new plumbing.*

plume /pluːm/ *n* a large decorative feather: *She wore a plume in her hat.*

plump[1] /plʌmp/ *adj* pleasantly fat: *plump cheeks.* **plumply** *adv*. '**plumpness** *n*.

plump up to shake and squeeze something until it has a full, rounded shape: *We plumped up all the cushions on the chairs.*

plump[2] /plʌmp/: **plump for** to choose from a selection, especially after hesitating or careful thought: *In the end, I plumped for the single diamond in a gold setting.*

plunder /ˈplʌndə(r)/ *v* to rob; to steal from a place: *The soldiers plundered the city.* — *n* the things stolen: *They ran off with their plunder.* '**plunderer** *n*.

plunge /plʌndʒ/ *v* **1** to throw yourself down into deep water *etc*; to dive: *He plunged into the river.* **2** to push something violently or suddenly into something: *He plunged a knife into the meat.* — *n* a dive: *He took a plunge into the pool.*

take the plunge to decide to do something that is difficult, especially after hesitating for a while: *When are you two going to take the plunge and get married?*

plural /ˈplʊərəl/ *n* the form of a word which expresses more than one: *'Mice' is the plural of 'mouse'*; *Is the verb in the singular or the plural?* — *adj*: *a plural verb.*

plus /plʌs/ *prep* used to show addition: *Two plus three equals five*; *2+3=5.* — *n* **1** a sign (+) used to show addition or positive quality (also called a **plus sign**). **2** an advantage or benefit: *My company car is an important plus in this job.* — *adj* **1** positive; more than zero: *a plus quantity*; *The temperature was plus fifteen degrees.* **2** rather above the amount, number or grade stated: *He earned a thousand plus for that job*; *She got a C plus* (written *C+*) *for her essay.*

See **minus**.

plush /plʌʃ/ *adj* smart, elegant and usually expensive: *very plush surroundings.*

plutonium /pluːˈtoʊnɪəm/ *n* a radioactive

ply[1] /plaɪ/ v **1** an old word for to work at: *He plies his trade as weaver.* **2** to travel regularly on a particular route: *ships that ply the oceans of the world.*

ply with to keep offering or giving someone food or drink or to keep asking them questions: *As an honoured guest, he was plied with the best food and wine; The boy plied his father with questions about his trip.*

ply[2] /plaɪ/ n a thickness, layer or strand, as in *three-ply wool.*

'**plywood** n a material made up of thin layers of wood glued together. — adj: *a plywood box.*

pneumonia /njuː'moʊnɪə/ n a serious illness of the lungs which makes breathing difficult.

poach[1] /poʊtʃ/ v to cook something in boiling liquid, especially water or milk: *Will I fry or poach the eggs?*

poached adj: *a poached egg.*

poach[2] /poʊtʃ/ v to hunt illegally on someone else's land. '**poacher** n.

pocket /'pɒkɪt/ n **1** a small bag sewn into or on to clothes, for carrying things in: *He stood with his hands in his pockets; a coat-pocket.* **2** a container for small or thin articles fitted to the inside of a suitcase, car door etc: *The safety instructions are in the pocket of the seat in front of you.* **3** your income or amount of money available for spending: *a range of prices to suit every pocket.* — adj: *a pocket handkerchief.* — v to put something in a pocket: *He pocketed his wallet.*

'**pocketful** n the amount contained by a pocket: *a pocketful of coins.*

pocket knife a pen-knife.

'**pocket-money** n money for personal use, especially a child's regular allowance: *He gets £2 a week pocket-money.*

'**pocket-size** adj small enough to carry in your pocket: *a pocket-size dictionary.*

pockmark /'pɒkmɑːk/ n a scar or small dent in the skin caused by smallpox etc. '**pockmarked** adj.

pod /pɒd/ n the long seed-case of the pea, bean etc.

podgy /'pɒdʒɪ/ adj a rather unkind word meaning plump or fat: *He is a small, podgy boy; She has podgy fingers.*

podium /'poʊdɪəm/ n a platform on which a lecturer, conductor of an orchestra etc stands.

poem /'poʊɪm/ n a piece of writing arranged in lines that usually have a regular rhythm and often rhyme: *the poems and songs of Robert Burns.*

poet n someone who writes poems.

'**poetess** n a female poet.

poetic /poʊ'ɛtɪk/ adj like poetry: *a poetic expression.* **po'etically** adv.

poetry /'poʊətrɪ/ n poems: *He writes poetry.*

poignant /'pɔɪnjənt/ adj sad and moving: *a poignant scene in a film.* '**poignancy** n. '**poignantly** adv.

point /pɔɪnt/ n **1** the sharp end of anything: *the point of a pin; a sword point; at gunpoint.* **2** a piece of land that reaches out into the sea etc: *The ship came round Lizard Point.* **3** a small round dot or mark (·): *a decimal point; five point three six (5·36); In punctuation, a point is another name for a full stop.* **4** an exact spot: *When we reached this point in the journey we stopped to rest.* **5** an exact moment: *Her husband walked in at that point.* **6** a place on a scale, especially a temperature scale: *the boiling-point of water.* **7** a mark in scoring a competition, game, test etc: *He has won by five points to two.* **8** a personal characteristic or quality: *We all have our good points and our bad ones.* **9** a fact, idea or opinion that is a part of an argument or discussion etc: *Could I make a point here?; I see your point.* **10** a detail that needs to be considered or dealt with: *I think we need to check a few small points; They went through the agreement point by point.* **11** the most important part of what is being said; the main piece of information: *That's not the point; She always takes ages to get to the point;* **12** the purpose of an activity: *What's the point of doing this?; There's no point in trying to start a car with no petrol in it.* — v **1** to aim in a particular direction: *He pointed the gun at her.* **2** to call attention to something by stretching your forefinger in its direction: *He pointed at the door; He pointed to a sign; It's rude to point your finger at people.* **3** to show that something is likely to be true, to exist or to happen: *All the evidence points to murder.* **4** to fill worn places in a stone or brick wall etc with mortar.

beside the point irrelevant; not connected with the subject being discussed.

make a point of to make a special effort to do something; to be especially careful to do something: *The writer makes a point of explaining all the new words.*

on the point of about to do something: *I*

was on the point of going out when the telephone rang.

point of view your particular opinion or attitude to something: *Try to see it from my point of view.*

point out to indicate; to draw attention to something: *He pointed out his house to her; I pointed out that we needed more money.*

take someone's point to understand and accept what someone is saying: *I take your point and I now understand the problem better.*

to the point relevant; connected with what is being discussed: *The speech was short and to the point; Please try to keep to the point or we'll never finish the discussion.*

up to a point partly: *I agree with you up to a point; The story was true up to a point.*

point-blank /pɔɪnt'blaŋk/ *adj, adv* **1** very close: *He fired at her at point-blank range.* **2** abruptly; without warning or explanation: *He asked her point-blank how old she was.*

pointed /'pɔɪntɪd/ *adj* having a sharp end: *pointed shoes.*

pointer /'pɔɪntə(r)/ *n* **1** a long stick used to point to places on a large map *etc.* **2** a needle on a dial: *The pointer is at zero.*

pointless /'pɔɪntlɪs/ *adj* having no purpose or meaning: *It is pointless trying to change his mind.* **'pointlessly** *adv.* **'pointlessness** *n.*

poise /pɔɪz/ *v* to balance: *She poised herself on the back of his scooter.* — *n* **1** balance and control in bodily movement: *Good poise is important for a dancer.* **2** dignity and self-confidence: *He lost his poise for a moment.*

poised *adj* **1** staying balanced and still: *The car was poised on the edge of the cliff.* **2** having the body in a state of tension and readiness to act: *The animal was poised ready to leap.*

> to **poise** (not **pose**) yourself ready to somersault on a tightrope.

poison /'pɔɪzən/ *n* anything that causes death or illness when taken into your body: *She killed herself by taking poison.* — *adj: poison gas.* — *v* **1** to kill or harm with poison: *He poisoned his wife.* **2** to put poison into food *etc*: *He poisoned her coffee.* **'poisoner** *n.*

'poisoned *adj*: containing poison: *a poisoned drink.*

'poisonous *adj* **1** causing illness or death when taken into your body: *That fruit is poisonous.* **2** producing poison: *a poisonous snake.* **'poisonously** *adv.*

poke /pəʊk/ *v* **1** to push something sharp into something; to prod: *He poked a stick into the hole; He poked her in the ribs.* **2** to make a hole by doing this: *She poked a hole in the sand with her finger.* **3** to stick; to push: *She poked her head in at the window; His foot was poking out of the blankets.* — *n*: *He gave me a poke in the arm.*

poke about or **poke around** to look; to search.

poke fun at to laugh at someone unkindly: *The children often poked fun at him because he was so small.*

poker /'pəʊkə(r)/ *n* **1** a heavy metal rod used for moving wood or coal in a fire. **2** a card game played for money.

polar /'pəʊlə(r)/ *adj* having to do with the earth's North or South Pole or the region around it: *the polar ice-cap; the polar regions.*

polar bear a bear found near the North Pole.

pole[1] /pəʊl/ *n* **1** the north and south end of the Earth's axis: *the North Pole; the South Pole.* **2** the points in the sky opposite the Earth's North and South Poles, around which stars seem to turn. **3** either of the opposite ends of a magnet: *The opposite poles of magnets attract each other.*

pole[2] /pəʊl/ *n* a long, thin, rounded piece of wood, metal *etc*: *a telegraph pole; a tent pole.*

'pole-vault *n* a jump made with the help of a pole.

police /pə'liːs/ *n* the men and women whose job is to prevent crime, keep order, see that laws are obeyed *etc*: *Call the police!; The police are investigating the crime.* — *adj: a police officer.* — *v* to supply a place with police: *We cannot police the whole area.*

police constable a police officer of the lowest rank.

police dog a dog trained to work with the police.

police force all the police officers in a country or area.

po'liceman, po'licewoman *n* a male or female police officer.

police officer a member of a police force.

police station the office or headquarters of a police force: *He was taken to the tiny village police station.*

> **police**, *noun*, is plural: *The police are coming.*
> **police force** is singular: *The police force is large.*

policy /'pɒlɪsɪ/ n **1** a planned course of action: *the government's policies on education.* **2** a document which contains the terms of a contract with an insurance company: *an insurance policy.*

polio /'pəʊlɪəʊ/ n a disease that can afffect the brain and nerves and cause paralysis.

polish /'pɒlɪʃ/ v **1** to make something smooth and shiny by rubbing: *She polished her shoes.* **2** to improve: *Polish up your English!* — n **1** an act of polishing: *I'll give the table a quick polish.* **2** liquid, or other substance used to make something shiny: *furniture polish; shoe polish*
 'polished adj **1** shiny from polishing: *polished wood.* **2** of a high standard: *a polished performance.*

polite /pə'laɪt/ adj having good manners; courteous: *a polite child; a polite apology.* **po'litely** adv. **po'liteness** n.

the opposite of **polite** is **impolite**.

politics /'pɒlɪtɪks/ n the science or business of government: *young people's interest and involvement in politics.*
 po'litical adj having to do with politics: *for political reasons.* **po'litically** adv.
 politician /pɒlɪ'tɪʃən/ n someone whose job is politics; a member of parliament.

poll /pəʊl/ n **1** an election: *They organized a poll to elect a president.* **2** a way of finding out political opinion by asking a lot of people their views on something. — v.
 'polling-booth n a small compartment where you can mark your voting-paper.
 'polling-station n a place where you go to vote.

pollen /'pɒlən/ n the powder inside a flower that fertilizes other flowers: *Bees carry pollen from flower to flower.*
 pollinate /'pɒlɪneɪt/ v to make a plant fertile by carrying pollen to it from another flower: *Insects pollinate flowers.* **polli'nation** n.

pollute /pə'luːt/ v to make dirty: *Chemicals are polluting the air.* **po'lution** n.
 pol'lutant n a substance that pollutes.

polo /'pəʊləʊ/ n a game like hockey, played on horseback.
 polo-neck n a garment with a high, close-fitting neck: *He was wearing a polo-neck.* — adj: *a polo-neck sweater.*

poltergeist /'pɒltəɡaɪst/ n a kind of ghost that can move furniture, throw objects through the air and do other strange things in a house: *He had never seen the poltergeist that was supposed to haunt the house.*

polyester /'pɒlɪɛstə(r)/ n a type of man-made material used for clothes and sheets *etc*: *He bought a shirt made from a mixture of polyester and cotton.*

polygon /'pɒlɪɡɒn/ n a flat shape with three or more sides: *A hexagon is a polygon.*
 polygonal /pə'lɪɡənəl/ adj.

polystyrene /pɒlɪ'staɪriːn/ n a very light kind of plastic: *All the breakable ornaments were packed in polystyrene chips.*

polytechnic /pɒlɪ'tɛknɪk/ n a college where you can go after leaving school to study various subjects, especially technical ones: *She is taking a course in photography at the polytechnic.*

polythene /'pɒlɪθiːn/ n any of several types of plastic that can be moulded when hot. — adj: *a polythene bag.*

pomegranate /'pɒmɪɡranɪt/ n a fruit with a thick skin and many seeds.

pomelo /'pɒmɛləʊ/, plural **pomelos**, n a large tropical citrus fruit similar to a grapefruit.

pomp /pɒmp/ n solemn stateliness and magnificence: *all the pomp and ceremony of the coronation.*

pompous /'pɒmpəs/ adj using words that are rather long and grand, instead of simple ones, and behaving as though you were more important than you are: *People laugh at him for being so pompous*; *'Toiletries' is a rather pompous word for soap and toothpaste.* **'pompously** adv.

poncho /'pɒntʃəʊ/, plural **ponchos**, n a garment like a blanket, with a hole for your head.

pond /pɒnd/ n a small lake or pool: *the village pond.*

ponder /'pɒndə(r)/ v to consider carefully: *He pondered the suggestion.*

ponderous /'pɒndərəs/ adj **1** slow-moving, heavy and clumsy: *The hippopotamus approached with ponderous steps.* **2** dull, too solemn: *He gave a boring, ponderous speech.*

pong /pɒŋ/ n a bad or unpleasant smell: *There's a nasty pong coming from the kitchen.* — v to smell badly: *Your socks pong!*

pontiff /'pɒntɪf/ n a bishop, especially the Pope.

pontoon /pɒn'tuːn/ n a temporary bridge across a river, made from boats and barges tied together: *The soldiers built a pontoon across the river.*

pony /'pəʊnɪ/ n a small horse: *The child was riding a brown pony.*

'ponytail *n* hair tied in a bunch at the back of the head: *She wore her hair in a ponytail.*

See also **plait**.

poodle /'puːdəl/ *n* a breed of dog whose curly hair is often clipped in a decorative way.

pool¹ /puːl/ *n* **1** a small area of still water; a puddle: *The rain left pools in the road.* **2** an area of liquid: *a pool of blood; a pool of oil.* **3** a deep part of a stream or river: *He was fishing in a pool near the river-bank.* **4** a swimming-pool: *They spent the day at the pool.*

pool² /puːl/ *n* a stock or supply: *We put our money into a general pool.* — *v* to put together for general use: *We pooled our money and bought a car.*

poor /pʊə(r)/ *adj* **1** having little money or property: *the poor nations of the world.* **2** not good; of bad quality: *His work is very poor.* **3** deserving pity: *Poor fellow!*
 'poorly *adv* not well; badly: *a poorly written essay.* — *adj* ill: *He is very poorly.*
 the poor poor people.

See **rich**.
See also **weak**.

pop¹ /pɒp/ *n* a sharp, quick, explosive noise, like that made by a cork as it comes out of a bottle: *The paper bag burst with a loud pop.* — *v* **1** to make a pop; to make something pop: *The balloon popped; He popped the balloon.* **2** to spring upwards or outwards: *His eyes nearly popped out of his head in amazement.* **3** to go quickly and briefly somewhere: *He popped out to buy a newspaper.* **4** to put quickly: *He popped the letter into his pocket.*
 pop up to appear: *I never know where he'll pop up next.*

pop² /pɒp/ *adj* (short for **popular**) **1** written, played *etc* in a modern style: *pop music.* **2** performing or playing pop music: *a pop group; a pop singer; pop records.*

popcorn /'pɒpkɔːn/ *n* maize that bursts open when heated.

pope /poʊp/ *n* (often written with a capital letter) the bishop of Rome, head of the Roman Catholic church: *A new Pope has been elected.*

pop-gun /'pɒpɡʌn/ *n* a toy gun.

popper /'pɒpə(r)/ *n* a small metal or plastic device for fastening clothes, one piece being sewn on either side of the garment: *The dress had poppers down the back.*

poppy /'pɒpɪ/ *n* a plant with large, usually red flowers.

popular /'pɒpjʊlə(r)/ *adj* **1** liked by most people: *a popular holiday resort.* **2** believed by most people: *a popular theory.*
 'popularly *adv* amongst, or by, most people: *He was popularly believed to have magical powers.*
 popu'larity *n* the state of being well liked.
 'popularize *n* to make something known to a lot of people; to make popular: *Television is important in popularizing new scientific ideas; She has done a lot to popularize the monarchy.*

populate /'pɒpjʊleɪt/ *v* to fill a land with people: *The country was populated during the last century.*
 popu'lation *n* the people living in a particular country, area *etc*: *the population of London is 8 million.*

population is singular: *The population of the city increases in the summer.*

populous /'pɒpjʊləs/ *adj* full of people: *London is the most populous area in Britain.*

porcelain /'pɔːslɪn/ *n* a kind of fine china: — *adj*: *a porcelain figure.*

porch /pɔːtʃ/ *n* **1** a covered entrance to a building: *They waited in the porch until it stopped raining.* **2** a veranda.

See **archway**.

porcupine /'pɔːkjʊpaɪn/ *n* a gnawing animal covered with long prickles.

pore¹ /pɔː(r)/ *n* a tiny hole, especially in the skin.

pore² /pɔː(r)/: **pore over** *v* to study with great attention: *He pored over his books.*

pork /pɔːk/ *n* the flesh of a pig used as food.

pornography /pɔːˈnɒɡrəfɪ/ *n* magazines, books, films *etc* that are intended to excite people sexually by showing naked people and sexual acts.
 porno'graphic *adj*: *a pornographic film.*

porous /'pɔːrəs/ *adj* having lots of tiny holes that water, air *etc* can pass through: *Many types of rock are porous.*

porpoise /'pɔːpəs/ *n* a sea animal of the dolphin family.

porridge /'pɒrɪdʒ/ *n* a food made from oatmeal boiled in water or milk.

port¹ /pɔːt/ *n* **1** a harbour: *The ship came into port.* **2** a town with a harbour: *the port of Haiphong.*

port² /pɔːt/ *n* the left side of a ship or aircraft:

The helmsman steered the ship to port. — *adj*: *the port wing.*

See **starboard**.

portable /ˈpɔːtəbəl/ *adj* easy to carry from place to place: *a portable radio.*

porter /ˈpɔːtə(r)/ *n* **1** someone whose job is to carry luggage in a railway station *etc*: *The old lady could not find a porter to carry her suitcase.* **2** someone whose job is to carry things where there is no other form of transport: *He set off into the jungle with three porters.*

portfolio /pɔːtˈfoʊlioʊ/, *plural* **portfolios**, *n* **1** a flat, thin case for carrying documents, photographs, drawings *etc*: *The artist kept all her work in a portfolio.* **2** a government minister's particular department: *He was given the education portfolio.* **3** a document showing how you have invested your money and what shares you own: *The bank put together a portfolio of possible investments for her.*

porthole /ˈpɔːthoʊl/ *n* a small round window in a ship.

portion /ˈpɔːʃən/ *n* **1** a part: *I read a portion of the newspaper.* **2** a share: *Her portion of the money was £200.* **3** an amount of food for one person: *a portion of salad.*

to eat a **portion** (not **potion**) of cake.

portion out to divide into portions or shares: *The money was portioned out between the three children.*

portly /ˈpɔːtlɪ/ *adj* an old word meaning rather fat: *a portly old gentleman.* **ˈportliness** *n*.

portrait /ˈpɔːtrɪt/ or /ˈpɔːtreɪt/ *n* **1** a drawing, painting, photograph *etc* of someone: *She had her portrait painted*; *She sat for her portrait.* **2** a written description of a person, place *etc*: *a book called 'A portrait of London'.*

portray /pɔːˈtreɪ/ *v* **1** to make a portrait of someone: *In this painting, the king is portrayed sitting on his throne.* **2** to show or represent a thing or person in a particular way: *In his book, he portrays the city as something evil*; *The grandfather in the play was well portrayed by a surprisingly young actor.* — **porˈtrayal** *n*.

pose[1] /poʊz/ *n* a position into which you put your body: *a relaxed pose.* — *v* **1** to position yourself: *She posed in the doorway.* **2** to pretend to be: *He posed as a doctor.*

to **pose** (not **poise**) for a photograph.

pose[2] /poʊz/ *v* to set a question or problem for answering or solving: *Children who are clever but lazy pose a problem for the teacher*; *Tigers rarely pose any threat to humans.*

posh /pɒʃ/ *adj* of a superior type or class: *a posh family*; *posh clothes.*

position /pəˈzɪʃən/ *n* **1** a way of standing, sitting *etc*: *He lay in an uncomfortable position.* **2** a place or situation: *The house is in a beautiful position.* **3** a job; a post: *He has a position with a bank.* **4** a point of view: *Let me explain my position on employment.* **5** the situation you are in at a particular time: *our financial position*; *They are not in a position to help.* — *v* to put; to place: *He positioned the lamp in the middle of the table.* **be in** or **out of position** to be in the right place, not in the right place: *Is everything in position for the photograph?*; *This vase is out of position.*

positive /ˈpɒzɪtɪv/ *adj* **1** meaning or saying 'yes': *a positive answer*; *They tested the water for the bacteria and the result was positive.* **2** definite; leaving no doubt: *positive proof.* **3** certain; sure: *I'm positive he's right.* **4** greater than zero: *4 is a positive quantity, but −4 is a negative quantity.* **5** helpful; encouraging: *a positive suggestion.* **6** hopeful; confident: *We are feeling more positive about the situation now.*

The opposite of **positive** is **negative**.

ˈpositively *adv* **1** absolutely; extremely: *She was positively furious.* **2** used to emphasize what you are saying: *This is positively the last time that I'll lend you money.*

possess /pəˈzɛs/ *v* **1** to own; to have: *How much money does he possess?* **2** to control your mind or actions: *What possessed you to behave like that?*

posˈsession *n* **1** the state of having or owning something: *He took possession of the house and everything in it*; *He was found in possession of a gun.* **2** something that is owned by a person, country *etc*: *She lost all her possessions in the fire.*

posˈsessive *adj* **1** showing that someone or something possesses something: *'Yours', 'mine', 'his', 'hers', 'theirs' are possessive pronouns*; *'your', 'my', 'his', 'their' are possessive adjectives.* **2** not willing to share your possessions with other people: *Children can be very possessive with their toys.*

posˈsessor *n*: *He is the proud possessor of a new car.*

possibility /ˌpɒsɪˈbɪlɪtɪ/ *n* something that is

possible; being possible; a likelihood: *There isn't much possibility of that happening*; *There's a possibility of war.*

possible /'pɒsɪbəl/ *adj* **1** able to happen or be done: *It's important that the fishing tackle is as light as possible.* **2** satisfactory; acceptable: *I've thought of a possible solution to the problem.*

> **possible** means 'able to happen': *It's possible that he may arrive today.*
> **probable** means 'likely to happen': *It's probable that he's gone home now.*

possibly /'pɒsɪblɪ/ *adv* **1** perhaps: *'Will you have time to do it?' 'Possibly'.* **2** in any possible way: *I'll come as fast as I possibly can; I can't possibly eat any more.*

post[1] /poʊst/ *n* a long piece of wood, metal *etc*, usually fixed upright in the ground: *The notice was nailed to a post; a gate-post; the winning-post.*

post[2] /poʊst/ *n* **1** a job: *a teaching post; He has a post in the government.* **2** a place of duty: *The soldier remained at his post.* — *v* to send someone to work somewhere: *The diplomat was posted to the embassy in New York.*

post[3] /poʊst/ *n* the system of collecting, transporting and delivering letters, parcels *etc*: *I sent the book by post; Has the post arrived yet?; Is there any post for me?* — *v* to send a letter *etc* by post: *He posted the parcel yesterday.*

'**postage** *n* the money paid for sending a letter *etc* by post: *The postage was £1·20.*

postage stamp a small printed label fixed to a letter, parcel *etc* to show that postage has been paid.

'**postal** *adj* having to do with the system of sending letters *etc*: *the postal service.*

postal order a printed document bought at a post office, that can be exchanged at another post office for the amount of money paid for it.

'**postbox** *n* a box into which letters *etc* are put to be collected and sent to their destination (also called a '**letterbox** or a '**mail box**).

'**postcard** *n* a card on which a message may be sent by post, often with a picture on one side (a **picture postcard**): *Bob sent me a postcard of the Taj Mahal.*

'**postcode** *n* a series of letters or numbers that you add at the end of an address.

poster /'poʊstə(r)/ *n* a large notice or advertisement for sticking on a wall *etc*: *Have you seen the posters advertising the circus?*

posterity /pɒ'stɛrɪtɪ/ *n* people coming after; future generations: *The treasures must be kept for posterity.*

postgraduate /poʊst'grædjuːət/ *n* a student who already has a first degree and is studying for another: *She is a postgraduate working for her doctor's degree.* — *adj* of such a student, or the degree they are studying for: *postgraduate research.*

posthumous /'pɒstjʊməs/ *adj* happening, published, awarded *etc* after death: *He received a posthumous medal.* '**posthumously** *adv*.

postman /'poʊstmən/ *n* a person whose job is to collect and deliver letters *etc*: *Has the postman been this morning?*

postmark /'poʊstmaːk/ *n* a mark put on a letter at a post office, showing the date and place of posting, and cancelling the postage stamp: *The postmark read 'Beirut'.*

post-mortem /poʊst'mɔːtəm/ *n* a medical examination of a dead body made to find out how the person died: *The post-mortem on the man revealed that he had been poisoned.*

post office /'poʊst ɒfɪs/ an office for receiving and sending letters, parcels *etc*: *Where is the nearest post office?*

postpone /poʊst'poʊn/ *v* to cancel something until a future time: *The football match has been postponed till tomorrow.* **post-'ponement** *n*.

postscript /'poʊstskrɪpt/ *n* the words that the writer of a letter sometimes adds below the signature, with the letters **P.S.** (short for **postscript**).

posture /'pɒstʃə(r)/ *n* **1** the way you hold your body when standing, sitting, walking *etc*: *Good posture is important for a dancer.* **2** a position or pose: *He knelt in an uncomfortable posture.*

postwar /poʊst'wɔː(r)/ *adj* of or belonging to the period following a war: *postwar housing.*

posy /'poʊzɪ/ *n* a small bunch of flowers: *a posy of primroses.*

pot /pɒt/ *n* any of many kinds of deep container used in cooking, for holding food, liquids *etc* or for growing plants: *a cooking-pot; a plant-pot; a jam-pot; The waiter brought her a pot of tea.* — *v* to plant in a pot.

take pot luck to take whatever happens to be available, usually when you are an unexpected guest at a meal-time.

potassium /pə'tæsɪəm/ *n* a soft, silver-white

metallic element: *Potassium is used in making soap and fertilizers.*

potato /pəˈteɪtoʊ/, *plural* **potatoes**, *n* a plant with round underground stems called **tubers**, which are used as a vegetable; the tuber of this plant: *She bought 2 kilos of potatoes.*

potato crisp or **potato chip** a thin, crisp, fried slice of potato: *a packet of potato crisps.*

potent /ˈpoʊtənt/ *adj* powerful; having a very strong effect: *one of the most fascinating and potent aspects of his writing; This plant contains a very potent poison.* **'potency** *n.*

potential /pəˈtɛnʃəl/ *adj* possible: *That hole in the road is a potential danger.* — *n* the possibility of successful development: *The land has great farming potential; He shows potential as a teacher.* **po'tentially** *adv.*

pothole /ˈpɒthoʊl/ *n* **1** a hole in the road surface. **2** a cave or deep hole that was created by water wearing away soft rock.

potion /ˈpoʊʃən/ *n* a drink containing medicine or poison, or having a magic effect: *a love potion.*

to drink a magic **potion** (not **portion**).

potted /ˈpɒtɪd/ *adj* pressed into a pot or jar: *potted meat; potted shrimps.*

potter[1] /ˈpɒtə(r)/ *v* to wander about doing small jobs or doing nothing important: *I spent the afternoon pottering about.*

potter[2] /ˈpɒtə(r)/ *n* someone who makes plates, cups, vases *etc* out of clay and fires them in an oven called a **kiln**.

'pottery *n* **1** articles made of baked clay: *He is learning how to make pottery.* **2** a place where these articles are made: *He is working in the pottery.*

potty /ˈpɒtɪ/ *adj* a slang word for mad; crazy: *He must be potty to go running in this heat.*

pouch /paʊtʃ/ *n* **1** a small bag: *a tobacco-pouch.* **2** something bag-like: *This animal stores its food in two pouches under its chin.* **3** a pocket of skin on the belly of the female of animals such as kangaroo, in which the baby is reared.

pouffe or **pouf** /puːf/ *n* a large firm kind of cushion used as a seat.

poultry /ˈpoʊltrɪ/ *n* farmyard birds: *They keep poultry.*

pounce /paʊns/ *v* to jump suddenly, in order to seize or attack: *The cat waited behind the birdcage, ready to pounce.* — *n* the action of pouncing; a sudden attack: *The cat made a pounce at the bird.*

pounce on to leap upon someone or something in order to attack or grab: *The tiger pounced on its victim.*

pound[1] /paʊnd/ *n* **1** the standard unit of British currency, 100 pence (also called **pound sterling**; written **£**): *A pound is equal to about eight French francs; £40.* **2** a measure of weight, equal to 0·454 kilograms (written **lb**, plural **lbs**).

pound[2] /paʊnd/ *n* a pen into which stray animals are put: *a dog-pound.*

pound[3] /paʊnd/ *v* **1** to hit heavily; to thump: *He pounded at the door; The children were pounding on the piano.* **2** to walk or run heavily: *He pounded down the road.* **3** to break up a substance into powder or liquid: *She pounded the dried herbs.*

pour /pɔː(r)/ *v* **1** to empty; to flow in a stream: *She poured the milk into a bowl; Water poured down the wall.* **2** to rain heavily: *It was pouring this morning.*

pout /paʊt/ *v* to push your lips out as a sign of displeasure. — *n* this expression of the face.

poverty /ˈpɒvətɪ/ *n* the condition of being poor: *They lived in extreme poverty.*

poverty-stricken /ˈpɒvətɪ-strɪkən/ *adj* very poor.

powder /ˈpaʊdə(r)/ *n* **1** any substance in the form of fine particles: *soap powder; milk-powder.* **2** a special kind of substance used as make-up *etc*: *face-powder; talcum powder.* — *v.*

'powdered *adj* in the form of fine particles: *powdered chocolate.*

'powdery *adj* like powder: *powdery soil.*

power /ˈpaʊə(r)/ *n* **1** ability: *He no longer has the power to walk; This plant has magic powers.* **2** strength; force; energy: *muscle power; water-power.* **3** authority; control: *All politicians want power; I have him in my power at last.* **4** the result obtained by multiplying a number by itself a number of times: $2 \times 2 \times 2$ or 2^3 *is the third power of 2, or 2 to the power of 3.*

'powered *adj* supplied with mechanical power: *The machine is powered by electricity; an electrically-powered machine.*

'powerful *adj* having great strength, influence *etc*: *a powerful engine; He's powerful in local politics.* **'powerfully** *adv.*

'powerless *adj* having no power: *The king was powerless to prevent the execution.*

power cut or **power failure** a break in the electricity supply: *We had a power cut last night.*

power point a socket on a wall *etc* into which an electric plug can be fitted: *Is there a power point in the attic?*

power station a building where electricity is produced.

power tool a tool worked by electricity.

practical /'præktɪkəl/ *adj* **1** concerned with the doing of something: *practical difficulties; His knowledge is practical rather than theoretical.* **2** useful: *You must try to find a practical answer to the problem.* **3** good at dealing with problems and making sensible decisions: *We need someone practical to lead the team.*

practi'cality *n* **1** the state of being sensible or possible: *I am not sure of the practicality of the scheme.* **2** the practical matters involved in a scheme or situation, rather than the ideas: *Let's discuss the practicalities of the proposed project.*

practically /'præktɪklɪ/ *adv* **1** almost: *The room was practically full.* **2** in a practical way.

practical joke a joke consisting of an action, not words: *He nailed my chair to the floor as a practical joke.*

practice /'præktɪs/ *n* **1** the actual doing of something: *We thought the plan would work all right, but in practice there were a lot of difficulties.* **2** the usual way of doing things; a habit: *It was his usual practice to rise at 6.00 a.m.* **3** the repeated exercise of something in order to learn to do it well: *She has musical talent, but she needs a lot of practice; Have a quick practice before you start.* **4** the work done by doctors or lawyers: *He has been in practice since 1965.* **5** the place where doctors or lawyers work: *a group practice; a country practice.*

> **practice** is a noun: *practice makes perfect.*
> **practise** is a verb: *to practise the guitar.*

out of practice not having had a lot of practice recently: *I haven't played the piano for months — I'm very out of practice.*

practise /'præktɪs/ *v* **1** to do exercises to improve your performance: *She practises the piano every day; You must practise more if you want to enter the competition.* **2** to make something a habit: *to practise self-control.* **3** to work as a doctor or lawyer: *She practises as a doctor in the city centre.*

> See **practice**.

practised /'præktɪst/ *adj* skilful because of having practised a lot: *a practised performer.*

pragmatic /præg'mætɪk/ *adj* practical, sensible and reasonable: *She has a very pragmatic approach to the problem.*

prairie /'prɛərɪ/ *n* in America, an area of flat land, without trees and covered with grass.

praise /preɪz/ *v* **1** to speak highly of someone or something: *He praised her singing; She was often praised for her tidiness.* **2** to worship God by singing hymns *etc*: *Praise the Lord!* — *n* the expressing of approval: *He has received a lot of praise for his courage.*

'**praiseworthy** *adj* deserving praise: *a praiseworthy attempt.*

pram /præm/ *n* a small carriage on wheels for a baby, pushed by someone on foot.

prance /prɑːns/ *v* to dance or jump about.

prank /præŋk/ *n* a trick; a practical joke.

prattle /'prætəl/ *v* to talk in a foolish or childish way. — *n* childish talk; chatter.

prawn /prɔːn/ *n* an edible shellfish like a shrimp.

pray /preɪ/ *v* to speak to God to give thanks, make a request *etc*: *Let us pray; She prayed to God to help her.*

> **pray** is a verb: to **pray** (not **prey**) for peace.

'**prayer** *n* **1** the words that you use when you pray: *a book of prayer; The child said his prayers.* **2** the act of praying: *They were kneeling in prayer.*

preach /priːtʃ/ *v* to give a talk, usually during a religious service, about religious or moral matters: *The vicar preached about pride.*

precarious /prɪ'kɛərɪəs/ *adj* risky; dangerous.
pre'cariously *adv*.

precaution /prɪ'kɔːʃən/ *n* care taken to avoid accidents, disease *etc*: *They took every precaution to ensure that their journey would be safe and enjoyable.*

pre'cautionary *adj*: *take precautionary measures.*

precede /prɪ'siːd/ *v* to go before: *She preceded him into the room.*

precedence /'presɪdəns/ *n* the right of coming first in order of importance *etc*: *This matter is urgent and should be given precedence over others at the moment.*

precedent /'presɪdənt/ *n* something that can be used as an example or rule for present or future action: *There is no precedent for making such a decision.*

precinct /'priːsɪŋkt/ *n* **1** an area of shops in the centre of a town or city where no cars, motorcycles *etc* are allowed: *a pedestrian precinct; a shopping precinct.* **2** (also **precincts**) an area of ground with walls *etc* around it: *Ball games are not allowed within the cathedral precincts.* **3** in America, a district in a city.

precious /'prɛʃəs/ *adj* very valuable: *precious jewels.*

precious metal a valuable metal such as gold, silver or platinum.

precious stone a jewel; a gem: *diamonds, emeralds and other precious stones.*

precipice /'prɛsɪpɪs/ *n* a steep cliff.

precise /prɪ'saɪs/ *adj* **1** exact: *Give me his precise words; precise instructions.* **2** careful to be accurate and exact in manner, speech *etc*: *He is always very precise.* **pre'ciseness** *n.*

pre'cisely *adv: at midday precisely; He spoke very precisely.*

precision /prɪ'sɪʒən/ *n* the quality of being clear and exact: *His work shows great precision.*

precocious /prɪ'koʊʃəs/ *adj* more advanced in speech, learning *etc* than is usual: *precocious reading ability; Their little boy is very precocious.*

preconception /priːkən'sɛpʃən/ *n* an idea or opinion that you form before you have enough knowledge or experience of that person or thing.

preconceived /priːkən'siːvd/ *adj: When they had children themselves, they changed a lot of their preconceived ideas about family life.*

predator /'prɛdətə(r)/ *n* a bird or animal that attacks and kills others for food: *A lion is a predator.* **'predatory** *adj.*

predecessor /'priːdəsɛsə(r)/ *n* **1** a person who has had a particular job or position before the present person: *He was my predecessor as manager.* **2** an ancestor: *My predecessors came from Scotland.*

predicament /prɪ'dɪkəmənt/ *n* a difficulty: *It is not your fault that you are in such a predicament.*

predict /prɪ'dɪkt/ *v* to say in advance: *He predicted a change in the weather.*

pre'dictable *adj* **1** that could be expected: *The ending of the film was totally predictable.* **2** dull and boring because it always happens: *He's very predictable — I knew what he would say and I was right.* **pre'dictably** *adv.*

pre'diction *n* something predicted: *I'd rather not make any predictions about the result of the race in case I'm wrong.*

predominant /prɪ'dɒmɪnənt/ *adj* most common, most important or most noticeable: *The English language has always been predominant in America; Blue and white are the predominant colours in our bathroom.* **pre'dominance** *n.*

pre'dominantly *adv* mostly: *The population of this part of Switzerland is predominantly French-speaking.*

pre'dominate *v* **1** to be greater or greatest in number: *In this school girls predominate over boys.* **2** to be most important or most noticeable: *His good qualities predominate over his bad ones.*

pre-empt /priː'ɛmpt/ *v* to do something which makes what another person planned to do pointless: *If she has already told you my news, then she has pre-empted me.*

pre-emptive /priː'ɛmptɪv/ *adj* **1** having the effect of making someone else's plan pointless: *He took pre-emptive action to prevent the strike.* **2** military action taken to destroy the enemy's weapons before they can be used against you: *They destroyed several enemy aircraft in a pre-emptive attack.*

preen /priːn/ *v* **1** to arrange feathers: *The seagulls were preening themselves.* **2** to improve your appearance, put on your make-up *etc.*

prefabricated /priː'fabrɪkeɪtɪd/ *adj* made of parts manufactured in advance and ready to be put together: *prefabricated houses.*

preface /'prɛfɪs/ *n* an introduction to a book *etc*: *The preface explained how to use the dictionary.*

prefect /'priːfɛkt/ *n* one of a number of senior pupils having special powers in a school *etc.*

prefer /prɪ'fɜː(r)/ *v* to like better: *Which do you prefer — tea or coffee?; I prefer reading to watching television; She would prefer to come with you rather than stay here.*

> **preferred** and **preferring** are spelt with **-rr-**.

> I **prefer** apples **to** (not **than**) oranges.

preferable /'prɛfrəbəl/ *adj* better: *Is it preferable to write or make a telephone call?* **'preferably** *adv.*

preference /'prɛfərəns/ *n* **1** a liking for one thing rather than another: *He likes most music but he has a preference for classical music.* **2** special treatment that you give to one person or group rather than another: *Workers who have been here longer than two years will get preference.*

preferable, adjective, is spelt with -r-.
preference, noun, is spelt with -r-.

preferential /prɛfəˈrɛnʃəl/ *adj* giving preference: *Why is he getting preferential treatment?*

prefix /ˈpriːfɪks/ *n* a syllable added to the beginning of a word to change its meaning: <u>dis</u>*like;* <u>un</u>*employed;* <u>re</u>*make.*

pregnant /ˈprɛgnənt/ *adj* carrying an unborn baby in the womb. **'pregnancy** *n.*

prehistoric /priːhɪˈstɒrɪk/ *adj* belonging to the time before history was written down: *prehistoric tools; prehistoric animals.*

prejudice /ˈprɛdʒʊdɪs/ *n* an opinion that you form, especially against something, before you have proper knowledge or experience: *The jury must listen to the witness's statement without prejudice; We must work to prevent racial prejudice.* — *v* **1** to influence someone to have a bad opinion of a thing or person: *The story she told me prejudiced me against him from the start.* **2** to harm something or put it in danger: *Bad handwriting prejudices your chances of passing the exam.*

'prejudiced *adj* having or showing prejudice: *I'm not prejudiced against foreigners.*

preliminary /prɪˈlɪmɪnərɪ/ *adj* said or done in preparation for something: *The judge in the contest made a few preliminary remarks before presenting the prizes to the winners.* — *n.*

prelude /ˈprɛljuːd/ *n* **1** an event that happens before something, or leads the way to it: *The meeting of the two presidents was the prelude to a new friendship between the two countries.* **2** a piece of music played as an introduction to the main piece.

premature /ˈprɛmətʃʊə(r)/ *adj* happening before the right or expected time: *a premature birth; The baby was three weeks premature. Our decision was premature — we should have waited until we knew all the results.* **premaˈturely** *adv.*

premeditated /priːˈmɛdɪteɪtɪd/ *adj* planned before it is done: *premeditated murder.*

premier /ˈprɛmɪə(r)/ *adj* first; leading: *Italy's premier industrialist.* — *n* a prime minister: *the French premier.*

premiere /ˈprɛmɪɛə(r)/ *n* the first public performance of a play or film *etc: a world premiere.*

premises /ˈprɛmɪsɪz/ *n* a building and the area of ground belonging to it: *The firemen made sure that everyone was off the premises.*

premium /ˈpriːmɪəm/ *n* **1** an extra amount of money that someone pays for something: *The factory owner paid the workers a high premium for working overtime.* **2** a regular payment to an insurance company for insuring something.

premonition /prɛməˈnɪʃən/ *n* a strange feeling that something will happen before it actually does: *She had a premonition about her uncle's death about a month before he died.*

preoccupation /priːɒkjʊˈpeɪʃən/ *n* something that you think about all or most of the time: *Buying clothes is one of his main preoccupations.*

preoccupied /prɪˈɒkjʊpaɪd/ *adj* thinking about something all the time and not paying attention to other things: *He tried to talk to her, but she seemed preoccupied; He neglects his family because he is always so preoccupied with his work.*

preˈoccupy *v* to fill a person's thoughts; to take all someone's attention.

preparation /prɛpəˈreɪʃən/ *n* **1** the work of preparing: *You can't pass an exam without preparation.* **2** something done to prepare: *She was making hasty preparations for her departure.*

prepare /prɪˈpɛə(r)/ *v* to make or get ready: *My mother prepared a meal; He prepared to go out; Prepare yourself for a shock.*

preˈpared *adj* **1** ready: *We must be prepared to help when we are asked to; You should be prepared for a disappointment.* **2** willing: *I'm not prepared to lend him more money.*

preposition /prɛpəˈzɪʃən/ *n* a word put before a noun or pronoun to show how it is related to another word: <u>through</u> *the window;* <u>in</u> *the garden; written* <u>by</u> *me.* **prepoˈsitional** *adj.*

preposterous /prɪˈpɒstərəs/ *adj* ridiculous or foolish: *a preposterous suggestion.*

prerogative /prɪˈrɒgətɪv/ *n* a special right, privelege or power that someone has: *It is the bride's prerogative to fix the day for her wedding; Skiing holidays are the prerogative of the rich.*

prescribe /prɪˈskraɪb/ *v* to advise the use of something: *My doctor prescribed some pills for my cold; Here is a list of books prescribed by the examiners for the exam.*

prescription /prɪˈskrɪpʃən/ *n* a doctor's written instructions for the preparing and taking of a medicine: *He gave me a prescription to give to the chemist.*

presence /ˈprɛzəns/ *n* the state of being present: *The committee requests your presence at Thursday's meeting.*

in the presence of someone while someone is present: *This document must be signed in the presence of a witness*; *Don't talk about such shocking things in my mother's presence.*

present[1] /'prɛzənt/ *n* a gift: *a wedding present*; *birthday presents.*

present[2] /'prɛzənt/ *adj* **1** being here, or at a particular place, occasion *etc*: *Who else was present at the wedding?*; *Now that the whole class is present, we can begin the lesson.* **2** belonging to the time in which we are now living: *the present moment*; *the present prime minister.* **3** showing action now: *In the sentence 'She wants a chocolate', the verb is in the present tense.*

the present the time now: *Forget the past — think more of the present and the future!*

at present at the present time: *He's away from home at present.*

for the present as far as the present time is concerned: *You've done enough work for the present.*

present[3] /prɪ'zɛnt/ *v* **1** to give: *The child presented a bunch of flowers to the Queen*; *He was presented with a gold watch when he retired.* **2** to introduce: *May I present my wife?* **3** to show; to express; to produce: *She presents her ideas very clearly*; *This new situation presents a problem.* **4** to introduce various parts of a television or radio programme: *Each episode will be presented by a different actor.*

pre'sentable *adj* suitable to be seen in public: *You don't look very presentable in those dirty old clothes.*

presen'tation *n* the presenting of something: *the presentation of the prizes.*

pre'senter *n* the person who introduces a television or radio programme.

presently /'prɛzəntlɪ/ *adv* soon: *Take a seat in the waiting-room — the dentist will see you presently.*

preserve /prɪ'zɜːv/ *v* **1** to keep safe from harm: *Heaven preserve us from danger!* **2** to keep in existence, or in good condition: *They have managed to preserve many old documents.* **3** to treat food so that it will not go bad: *If you preserve the meat by salting it it will last for many months.* — *n* jam: *blackberry jam and other preserves.* **preser'vation** *n*.

pre'servative *n* something that preserves, especially that prevents food *etc* from going bad: *a chemical preservative.*

preside /prɪ'zaɪd/ *v* to be chairman of a meeting *etc*: *The prime minister presided at the meeting.*

presidency /'prɛzɪdənsɪ/ *n* **1** the rank or office of a president: *His ambition is the presidency.* **2** the period of time for which somebody is president: *during the presidency of Dwight D. Eisenhower.*

president /'prɛzɪdənt/ *n* **1** the leading member of a club, association *etc*: *She was elected president of the Music Society.* **2** the leader of a republic: *The President of the United States.* **presi'dential** *adj.*

press /prɛs/ *v* **1** to push: *Press the bell twice!*; *I don't like being in a crowd with people pressing against me*; *He pressed her hand to comfort her.* **2** to squeeze: *The grapes are pressed to extract the juice.* **3** to iron: *Your trousers need to be pressed.* **4** to try to get someone to agree to do something: *They pressed him to accept the offer*; *You must press them for an answer.* — *n* **1** the action of pressing: *He gave her hand a press*; *You had better give your shirt a press.* **2** a printing machine. **3** the newspapers: *It was reported in the press.* — *adj*: *a press photographer.*

press conference a meeting in which information is given to journalists.

'press-cutting *n* an article cut out of a newspaper or magazine.

'pressing *adj* that must be done immediately: *a pressing engagement.*

press stud a popper.

'press-up *n* an exercise where you lie face downwards and push your body up with your arms.

pressed for not having enough: *I'm pressed for time just now — can we meet again later?*

press on to continue to go or do something in a determined way, without delay: *We decided to press on with our journey as soon as the engine was repaired.*

pressure /'prɛʃə(r)/ *n* **1** the action of pressing: *to apply pressure to a cut to stop the bleeding.* **2** the force with which something presses against a surface *etc*: *air pressure*; *blood pressure.* **3** stress or worry: *the pressures of family life.* — *v* to pressurize.

pressurize /'prɛʃəraɪz/ *v* to make someone do something: *He was pressurized into giving up his job.*

'pressurized *adj* having a pressure inside that is different from the pressure outside: *The cabin of an aeroplane is pressurized so that it has the same pressure as that on the ground.*

pressure cooker a pan in which food is cooked quickly by steam kept under great pressure.

prestige /prɛˈstiːʒ/ *n* reputation or influence due to success, high rank *etc*: *His fame brought great prestige to the family.*

prestigious /prɛˈstɪdʒəs/ *adj* generally admired and respected: *He graduated from the most prestigious university in the country.*

presume /prɪˈzjuːm/ *v* to believe that something is true without proof: *When I found the room empty, I presumed that you had gone home*; '*Has he gone?*' '*I presume so*'.

> See **assume**.

presumably /prɪˈzjuːməblɪ/ *adv* I presume: *Presumably you didn't mean to hit the headmistress when you threw the ball.*

presumption /prɪˈzʌmpʃən/ *n* something that you think is the case, but have no proof of.

presumptuous /prɪˈzʌmptjʊəs/ *adj* bold in a rude way: *It was a bit presumptuous of you to tell the teacher she was wrong.* **preˈsumptuousness** *n*.

pretence /prɪˈtɛns/ *n* pretending something: *Under the pretence of friendship, he persuaded her to give him £1000.*

pretend /prɪˈtɛnd/ *v* **1** to make believe that something is true, in play: *Let's pretend we're having a real tea party*; *Pretend to be a lion!* **2** to put on a false show: *She was only pretending to be asleep*; *He pretended not to mind.*

pretentious /prɪˈtɛnʃəs/ *adj* trying to appear more important than they really are: *Only pretentious people drive such big, showy cars.*

pretext /ˈpriːtɛkst/ *n* a false reason given for doing something: *Her claim that she arrived late because the train broke down is just a pretext to cover the fact she got up late.*

pretty /ˈprɪtɪ/ *adj* pleasing; attractive: *a pretty girl*; *a pretty dress.* — *adv* rather: *That's pretty good*; *He's pretty old now.*
ˈprettily *adv.* **ˈprettiness** *n.*
pretty well nearly: *I've pretty well finished.*

prevail /prɪˈveɪl/ *v* to win; to succeed: *Truth must prevail in the end.*
preˈvailing *adj* most frequent or usual: *the prevailing fashion*; *The prevailing winds are from the west.*
prevalent /ˈprɛvələnt/ *adj* common: *Lung diseases used to be prevalent among miners.*

prevent /prɪˈvɛnt/ *v* to stop someone doing something or something happening: *He prevented me from going.* **preˈvention** *n.*

> **prevent** is used with **from**: *The high wall prevented them from seeing the garden.*

preˈventable *adj* that can be prevented: *Many people die from preventable diseases.*
preˈventive or **preˈventative** *adj* intended to stop crime or disease *etc* from happening or occurring: *preventive medicine.*

preview /ˈpriːvjuː/ *n* a viewing of a play, film *etc* before it is open to the public.

previous /ˈpriːvɪəs/ *adj* earlier in time or order: *on a previous occasion*; *the previous owner of the house.* **ˈpreviously** *adv.*

prey /preɪ/, *plural* **prey**, *n* animals that are hunted by other animals for food: *The lion tore at its prey.*
beast of prey *n* an animal, for example the lion, that kills and eats others.
bird of prey *n* a bird, for example the eagle, that kills and eats small birds and animals.
prey on or **prey upon** to attack as prey: *Hawks prey upon smaller birds.*

> **prey** is a noun or a verb: a bird of **prey** (not **pray**); to **prey on** (not **pray on**) smaller creatures.

prey on your mind to worry: *The argument preyed on her mind for the rest of the evening.*

price /praɪs/ *n* **1** the amount of money for which a thing is bought or sold: *The price of the book was £10.* **2** what must be given up or suffered in order to gain something: *Loss of freedom is often the price of success.* — *v* to mark a price on something: *I haven't priced these articles yet.*

> to ask the **price** (not **cost**) of something. See also **cost**.

ˈpriceless *adj* too valuable to have a price: *priceless jewels.*
ˈpricey *adj* expensive.
at a price at a high price: *We can get dinner at this hotel — at a price.*
at any price even if the cost is very high: *We are determined to succeed at any price.*
not at any price never; in no circumstances: *They decided not to tell the truth at any price.*

prick /prɪk/ *v* to pierce slightly with a sharp point: *She pricked her finger on a pin*; *He pricked a hole in the paper.* — *n* **1** a pain caused by pricking: *You'll just feel a slight prick in your arm.* **2** a tiny hole made by a sharp point: *a pin-prick.*
prick up its ears to raise the ears in excitement, attention *etc*: *The dog pricked up its ears at the sound of the doorbell.*

prickle /ˈprɪkəl/ *n* **1** a sharp point growing on a plant or animal: *A hedgehog is covered with prickles.* **2** a feeling of being pricked: *a* *prickle of fear.* — *v* to have a feeling of pricking.

'**prickly** *adj* covered with prickles: *Holly is a prickly plant.*

pride /praɪd/ *n* **1** pleasure that you take in what you have done or in people, things *etc* you are concerned with: *She looked with pride at her handsome sons.* **2** a feeling of self-respect: *His pride was hurt by her criticism.* **3** a group of lions.

pride and joy the person or thing that someone is proud of: *He was his parents' pride and joy.*

pride of the finest thing in a certain group *etc*: *The pride of our collection is this painting.*

pride of place the most important place: *They gave pride of place at the exhibition to a Chinese vase.*

pride yourself on to think highly of a skill or quality that you have: *She prides herself on being able to speak three foreign languages.*

take pride in to feel pride about something: *He took great pride in his achievements.*

priest /priːst/ *n* **1** a clergyman in the Christian Church, especially the Roman Catholic and Anglican churches. **2** an official in other religions: *a Buddhist priest.*

'**priesthood** *n* **1** priests in general: *the Catholic priesthood.* **2** the office or position of a priest: *He was called to the priesthood.*

prim /prɪm/ *adj* too formal and correct: *a prim manner; a prim old lady.* '**primly** *adv.* '**primness** *n.*

primary /'praɪmərɪ/ *adj* first; most important: *His primary concern was for his children's safety.* **primarily** /'praɪmɛrɪlɪ/ *adv.*

primary colours those colours from which all others can be made: *Red, blue and yellow are primary colours.*

primary school a school for children below the age of 11.

primate /'praɪmeɪt/ *n* a member of the highest class of animals: *Human beings, apes and monkeys are primates.*

prime /praɪm/ *adj* **1** first or most important: *a matter of prime importance.* **2** best: *in prime condition.* — *n* the time of greatest health and strength: *the prime of life.* — *v* to give someone information in advance: *He had been well primed and had answers ready for all their questions.*

prime minister the chief minister of a government.

prime number a number that cannot be divided exactly, except by itself and 1, for example 3, 5, 7, 31.

primer /'praɪmə(r)/ *n* a book that gives basic information about a subject.

primitive /'prɪmɪtɪv/ *adj* **1** belonging to the earliest times: *primitive stone tools.* **2** simple or rough: *He made a primitive boat out of some pieces of wood.*

prince /prɪns/ *n* **1** a male member of a royal family, especially a son or grandson of a king or queen: *Prince Charles.* **2** the ruler of a small state, for example Monaco.

princess /'prɪnsɛs/ *n* **1** a female member of a royal family, especially a daughter or granddaughter of a king or queen: *Princess Anne.* **2** the wife or widow of a prince.

principal /'prɪnsɪpəl/ *adj* most important: *Shipbuilding was one of Britain's principal industries.* — *n* **1** the head of a school, college or university. **2** the amount of money in a bank *etc* on which interest is paid.

> the **principal** (not **principle**) dancer of the company.
> the **principal** (not **principle**) of the college.

principally /'prɪnsɪplɪ/ *adv* mostly; mainly: *It's principally young people who buy clothes from this shop.*

principle /'prɪnsɪpəl/ *n* **1** a general truth, rule or law: *the principle of gravity.* **2** the theory by which a machine *etc* works: *the principle of the jet engine.*

'**principles** *n* your own personal rules of behaviour: *It is against my principles to borrow money.*

in principle in general but not necessarily in detail: *The workers agree with the management in principle, but would like further discussions.*

on principle because of your moral beliefs: *I disagree with divorce on principle.*

> high moral **principles** (not **principals**).

print /prɪnt/ *n* **1** a mark made by pressure: *a footprint; a fingerprint.* **2** printed lettering: *I can't read the print in this book.* **3** a design or picture produced by printing: *There are several framed prints on the wall.* **4** a photograph made from a negative. — *v* **1** to mark letters *etc* on paper by using a printing press *etc*: *The invitations will be printed on white paper.* **2** to publish a book, article *etc* in printed form: *His new novel will be printed next month.* **3** to produce a photographic image on paper: *He develops and prints his* *own photographs.* **4** to write, using capital letters, or unjoined small letters: *Please print your name and address.* **5** to put a design on cloth or paper *etc*: *a printed silk shirt.*

'**printer** *n* **1** a person or business that prints books, newspapers *etc.* **2** a machine that prints data from a computer.

'**printing** *n* the work of a printer.

'**printing press** a machine for printing.

out of print no longer available from the publisher: *That book has been out of print for years.*

print out to produce a printed copy of data from a computer: *The files are being printed out now.* '**printout** *n.*

prior /praɪə(r)/ *adj* earlier; previous: *He suddenly left, without any prior warning*; *I can't come — I have a prior engagement.*

pri'ority *n* **1** the right to go first: *An ambulance must have priority over other traffic.* **2** something that must be done first: *Our priority is to feed the hungry.*

prise /praɪz/ *v* to loosen something using force: *He prised open the lid with a knife.*

prism /ˈprɪzm/ *n* **1** a solid shape whose sides are parallel and whose two ends are the same shape and size. **2** a glass object of this shape, which breaks up a beam of white light into the colours of the rainbow.

prison /ˈprɪzən/ *n* a building in which criminals are kept: *He was sent to prison*; *He is in prison.*

'**prisoner** *n* anyone who has been captured and is held against their will as a criminal *etc*: *The prisoners escaped from jail.*

prisoner of war, *plural* **prisoners of war**, a member of the armed forces captured in a war.

take prisoner, **keep prisoner** to capture and hold someone against their will: *Many soldiers were taken prisoner*; *She was kept prisoner in a locked room.*

privacy /ˈprɪvəsɪ/ *n* being away from other people's sight or interest: *You can do what you like in the privacy of your own home, but you must behave well in public.*

private /ˈpraɪvət/ *adj* **1** for or belonging to one person or a group, not to the general public: *The headmaster lives in a private apartment in the school*; *This information is to be kept strictly private*; *You shouldn't listen to private conversations.* **2** owned by a person or group of people and not by the state or government: *private education*; *a private hospital.* **3** to do with your personal life and not with your job: *He never discusses his private life in the office.* — *n* a soldier with the lowest army rank. '**privately** *adv.*

in private with no-one else listening or watching: *May I speak to you in private?*

privilege /ˈprɪvɪlɪdʒ/ *n* a favour or right given to only one person, or to a few people: *Senior students are usually allowed certain privileges.* '**privileged** *adj.*

prize /praɪz/ *n* **1** a reward for good work *etc*: *He was awarded a lot of prizes at school.* **2** something won in a competition *etc*: *I've won first prize!* — *v* to value highly: *He prized my friendship above everything else.*

pro[1] /proʊ/ short for **professional**: *a tennis pro.*

pro[2] /proʊ/: **pros and cons** the arguments for and against: *Let's hear all the pros and cons before we make a decision.*

pro- /proʊ/ in favour of something: *pro-British.*

probability /prɒbəˈbɪlɪtɪ/ *n* **1** how likely it is that something will happen: *There is little probability that you will catch the disease in this country.* **2** something that is probable or likely: *The probability is that the murderer washed his hands in the kitchen.*

probable /ˈprɒbəbəl/ *adj* expected to happen or to be true; likely: *the probable result*; *A disaster of that sort is possible but not probable.*

> The opposite of **probable** is **improbable**. See also **possible**.

'**probably** *adv*: *I'll probably telephone you this evening.*

probation /prəˈbeɪʃən/ *n* **1** a period of time during which people who have committed a crime are allowed to go free on condition that they behave well, and go regularly to see a social worker called a **probation officer**: *He was put on probation for two years.* **2** a period of time during which a person is carefully watched to see that they are able to do their job properly: *After leaving college teachers are on probation for a year.*

probe /proʊb/ *n* **1** a long thin instrument used by doctors to examine a wound *etc.* **2** an investigation: *A police probe into illegal activities.* — *v* **1** to investigate: *He probed into her private life.* **2** to examine something with a probe: *The doctor probed the wound*; *He probed about in the hole with a stick.*

problem /ˈprɒbləm/ *n* **1** a difficulty; a matter

about which it is difficult to decide what to do: *Life is full of problems.* **2** a question to be answered or solved: *mathematical problems.* **proble'matic** or **proble'matical** *adj.*

procedure /prə'siːdʒə(r)/ *n* the order or method of doing something: *They followed the usual procedures.*

proceed /prə'siːd/ *v* **1** to go on; to continue: *They proceeded along the road*; *They proceeded with their work.* **2** to set about doing a job *etc*: *I want to make a cupboard, but I don't know how to proceed.* **3** to begin; to do something: *They proceeded to ask a lot of questions.*

pro'ceedings *n plural* **1** things that happen or take place on a particular occasion, for example at a meeting: *All the parents came to the meeting, and the proceedings lasted for five hours.* **2** legal action that is taken against someone: *The landlord started proceedings against his tenants because they hadn't paid the rent.*

proceeds /'prəʊsiːdz/ *n* money or profit made from a sale *etc*: *They gave the proceeds of the sale to charity.*

process /'prəʊses/ *n* **1** a method or way of manufacturing things: *We are using a new process to make glass.* **2** a series of events that produce change or development: *The process of growing up can be difficult for a child.* — *v* to deal with something; to put something through a process: *Have your photographs been processed?*; *The information is being processed by computer.*

'processed *adj* treated in a special way: *processed cheese.*

in the process of in the middle of; during: *He is in the process of moving house*; *These goods were damaged in the process of manufacture.*

procession /prə'seʃən/ *n* a line of people, vehicles *etc* moving forward in order: *The procession moved slowly through the streets.*

proclaim /prə'kleɪm/ *v* to announce or state publicly: *He was proclaimed the winner.*

proclamation /prɒklə'meɪʃən/ *n* an official public announcement about something important: *the proclamation of Lithuania's independence.*

procure /prə'kjʊə(r)/ *v* to obtain or get something.

prod /prɒd/ *v* **1** to push with something pointed; to poke: *He prodded her arm with his finger.* **2** to urge; to encourage: *She prodded him into action.* — *n*: *She gave him a prod with her elbow.*

prodigal /'prɒdɪgəl/ *adj* spending too much money; using too much of something; wasteful: *He was prodigal with the money he inherited from his parents.*

prodigious /prə'dɪdʒəs/ *adj* enormous: *prodigious wealth.*

prodigy /'prɒdɪdʒɪ/ *n* something strange and wonderful: *A very clever child is sometimes called a child prodigy; prodigies of nature.*

produce *v* /prə'djuːs/ **1** to bring out: *She produced a letter from her pocket.* **2** to give birth to a baby animal: *A cow produces one or two calves a year.* **3** to cause: *His joke produced a shriek of laughter from the children.* **4** to make; to manufacture: *The factory produces furniture.* **5** to grow: *A few farmers produce enough food for the whole population.* **6** to arrange for a play or film *etc* to be shown to the public: *He has produced both operas and films.* — *n* /'prɒdjuːs/ something that is produced, especially crops, eggs, milk *etc* from farms: *farm produce.*

producer *n* **1** a person who organizes the business side of putting on plays *etc* and making films. **2** a person, company or country that grows or makes something: *France is a major producer of wine.*

product /'prɒdʌkt/ *n* **1** a result: *The plan was the product of hours of thought.* **2** something manufactured: *The firm manufactures metal products.* **3** the result of multiplying one number by another: *The product of 9 and 2 is 18.*

pro'duction *n* **1** the process of producing something: *car-production; mass production.* **2** the amount produced, especially of manufactured goods: *The new methods increased production.* **3** a particular version of a play *etc*: *a new production of 'Romeo and Juliet'.*

pro'ductive *adj* producing a lot: *productive land; Our discussion was not very productive.*

produc'tivity *n* the rate at which goods are produced, or work is done: *The company must increase productivity to make a profit.*

profess /prə'fes/ *v* **1** to declare openly. **2** to claim; to pretend: *He professed to be an expert.*

pro'fession *n* **1** an occupation or job that needs special knowledge, such as medicine, law, teaching *etc*. **2** the people who have such an occupation: *the legal profession.*

pro'fessional *adj* **1** belonging to a profession: *professional skill.* **2** having a very high standard: *a very professional performance.* **3** done for money: *My brother*

professor

is a professional footballer but I'm just an amateur. — *n* (sometimes shortened to **pro**) a person who is professional: *a golf professional; a golf pro*.

pro'fessionalism *n* great skill and care taken when doing a job: *The school play was acted with considerable professionalism by the pupils*.

pro'fessionally *adv*: *Lawyers must be professionally qualified; She plays tennis professionally*.

professor /prə'fɛsə(r)/ *n* a university teacher who is the head of a department: *He is a professor of English at Leeds; Professor Jones*.

> **professor** ends in **-or**.

proficient /prə'fɪʃənt/ *adj* skilled; expert: *He is proficient in several languages*. **proficiency** *n*: *a certificate of proficiency in German*.

profile /'proʊfaɪl/ *n* a side view, especially of a face, head *etc*: *She has a beautiful profile*. **keep a low profile** to behave so that people do not notice you: *The princess kept a low profile at her friend's wedding*.

profit /'prɒfɪt/ *n* **1** money which is gained in business *etc*, for example from selling something for more than was paid for it: *I made a profit of £8000 on my house; He sold it at a huge profit*. **2** advantage; benefit: *A great deal of profit can be had from travelling abroad*. — *v* to gain profit from something: *The business profited from its exports; He profited by his opponent's mistakes*.

> **profited** and **profiting** are spelt with one **t**.

'profitable *adj* giving profit: *The deal was quite profitable; a profitable experience*. **'profitably** *adv*.

profound /prə'faʊnd/ *adj* **1** deep; very great: *In the fairytale, the princess fell into a profound sleep; She sat in profound thought; They lived in profound happiness*. **2** showing great knowledge or understanding: *His remarks were very profound*. **pro'foundly** *adv*.

profuse /prə'fjuːs/ *adj* plentiful: *profuse thanks*. **pro'fusely** *adv*.

progeny /'prɒdʒɪnɪ/ *n* children or descendants: *He has been married three times and has numerous progeny*.

prognosis /prɒg'noʊsɪs/, *plural* **prognoses** /prɒg'noʊsiːz/, *n* a prediction about the future, especially a doctor's prediction on the course of a patient's illness and their chances of recovery: *The prognosis is not good for this patient*.

programme /'proʊgræm/ *n* **1** a show or item that is broadcast on television or radio: *We always watch gardening programmes*. **2** a plan of events; a scheme: *What's the programme for this morning?; a programme of lectures; a programme of reforms*. **3** the leaflet that gives information about a performance of a play *etc*: *According to the programme, the show begins at 8.00*. — *v* to program.

'program *n* a set of data, instructions *etc* put into a computer. — *v* to give information, instructions *etc* to a computer *etc*, so that it can do a particular job: *She programmed the video to record the film*.

'programmer *n* a person who prepares a program for a computer.

progress *n* /'proʊgrɛs/ **1** movement forward; advance: *the progress of events*. **2** improvement: *The students are making good progress*. — *v* /prə'grɛs/ **1** to go forward: *We had progressed only a few miles when the car broke down*. **2** to improve: *Your English is progressing*. **pro'gression** *n*.

pro'gressive *adj* **1** developing and advancing by stages: *a progressive illness*. **2** using or encouraging new methods: *progressive education; The new headmaster is very progressive*. **pro'gressively** *adv*. **pro'gressiveness** *n*.

in progress happening; taking place: *There is a meeting in progress*.

prohibit /prə'hɪbɪt/ *v* to forbid: *Smoking is prohibited*. **prohibition** /proʊhɪ'bɪʃən/ *n*.

prohibitive /prə'hɪbɪtɪv/ *adj* too expensive: *They wanted diamonds but the cost was prohibitive*.

project *n* /'prɒdʒɛkt/ **1** a plan or scheme: *a building project*. **2** a piece of study or research: *I am doing a project on Italian art*. — *v* /prə'dʒɛkt/ **1** to plan or suggest for the future: *the Prime Minister's projected trip to Europe*. **2** to make lights or images appear on a surface: *The diagrams were projected on the wall where everyone could see them clearly*. **3** to throw outwards, forwards or upwards: *The missile was projected into space*. **4** to stick out: *A sharp rock projected from the sea*. **5** to show or represent yourself in a certain way: *He tried to project himself as kind and thoughtful*. **pro'jection** *n*.

pro'jector *n* a machine for projecting pictures or films on to a screen.

proliferate /prə'lɪfəreɪt/ v to increase in number quickly: *The types of computer available in the shops have proliferated in the past two years.* **prolifer'ation** n.

prolific /prə'lɪfɪk/ adj producing a lot of new work: *a very prolific author.*

prologue /'prəʊlɒg/ n a speech or piece of writing that introduces a play or book: *Shakespeare wrote prologues to some of his plays.*

prolong /prə'lɒŋ/ v to make longer: *Please do not prolong the discussion unnecessarily.*

pro'longed adj continuing for a long time: *her prolonged absence from school.*

promenade /prɒmə'nɑːd/ n (often shortened to **prom**) a road for the public to walk along, usually beside the sea: *They went for a walk along the promenade.*

prominent /'prɒmɪnənt/ adj 1 standing out: *prominent front teeth.* 2 easily seen: *The tower is a prominent landmark.* 3 famous: *a prominent politician.* **'prominence** n.

'prominently adv: *This ticket should be displayed prominently in a car window.*

promise /'prɒmɪs/ v 1 to say that you will, or will not, do something etc: *I promise that I won't be late; I promise not to be late; I won't be late, I promise!* 2 to say that you will give a gift, help etc: *He promised me a new dress.* — n 1 something promised: *He made a promise; I'll go with you — that's a promise!* 2 a sign of future success: *She shows great promise in her work.* 3 to show signs of being successful, good etc: *It promises to be a lovely day.*

'promising adj showing signs of future success: *She's a promising pianist; Her work is promising.*

promote /prə'məʊt/ v 1 to raise someone to a higher rank or position: *He was promoted to head teacher.* 2 to encourage; to help the progress of something: *He worked hard to promote this scheme.* 3 to encourage the buying of goods etc: *We are promoting a new brand of soap-powder.* **pro'moter** n. **pro'motion** n.

> The opposite of **promote** (a person) is **demote**.

prompt[1] /prɒmpt/ adj immediate; punctual: *a prompt reply; I'm surprised that she's late. She's usually so prompt.* — adv exactly: *The film will start at 8 o'clock prompt.* **'promptly** adv.

prompt[2] /prɒmpt/ v 1 to cause someone to do something: *Hearing her play prompted me to have piano lessons too.* 2 to help someone to remember what they must say next: *My job was to prompt the actors if they forgot their lines.*

prone /prəʊn/ adj 1 lying face downwards: *in a prone position.* 2 likely to experience etc: *He is prone to illness.*

prong /prɒŋ/ n a spike of a fork.

pronged adj: *a two-pronged fork.*

pronoun /'prəʊnaʊn/ n a word used instead of a noun: *'He', 'it', and 'who' are pronouns.*

pronounce /prə'naʊns/ v to speak words or sounds, especially in a certain way: *He pronounced my name wrongly; The 'b' in 'lamb' and the 'k' in 'knob' are not pronounced.*

pro'nounced adj noticeable: *Her English accent is very pronounced when she speaks French.*

pronunci'ation n: *She had difficulty with the pronunciation of his name.*

> **pronounce** is spelt with **-ou-**.
> **pronunciation** is spelt with **-u-**.

proof /pruːf/ n evidence, information etc that shows definitely that something is true: *We still have no proof that he is innocent.*

-proof protected against something; able to resist something: *a waterproof covering.*

prop /prɒp/ n a support: *The ceiling was held up with wooden props.* — v to lean something against something else: *He propped his bicycle against the wall.*

prop up to support something in an upright position, or stop it from falling: *We had to prop up the roof; He propped himself up against the wall.*

propaganda /prɒpə'gændə/ n opinions, ideas etc that are spread by a political group or an organization in order to influence people: *This leaflet contains nothing but propaganda — why can't they give us facts?*

propagate /'prɒpəgeɪt/ v 1 to spread news etc. 2 to make plants produce seeds; to breed animals. **propa'gation** n.

propel /prə'pɛl/ v to drive forward, especially mechanically: *The boat is propelled by a diesel engine.*

pro'peller n a device made of several blades, that turns round very fast and is used to drive a ship or an aircraft.

proper /'prɒpə(r)/ adj 1 right; correct: *The proper equipment makes the whole operation quicker and safer; You should have done your* *school-work at the proper time — it's too late to start now.* **2** complete; thorough: *Have you made a proper search?* **3** respectable; well-mannered: *It isn't considered proper to talk with your mouth full of food.*

'**properly** *adv* **1** correctly: *She can't pronounce his name properly.* **2** completely: *I didn't have time to read the book properly.*

proper noun or **proper name** a noun or name that names a particular person, thing or place: *'John' and 'New York' are proper nouns.*

property /'prɒpəti/ *n* **1** something that you own: *These books are my property.* **2** land or buildings that you own: *He has property in Scotland.* **3** a quality: *Hardness is a property of diamonds.*

prophecy /'prɒfəsi/ *n* **1** the telling of what is going to happen in the future. **2** something that is prophesied: *He made many prophecies about the future.*

prophesy /'prɒfɪsaɪ/ *v* to tell what will happen in the future: *She prophesied that they would lead a happy life.*

> **prophecy** is a noun: *Her* **prophecy** (not **prophesy**) *came true.*
> **prophesy** is a verb: *to* **prophesy** (not **prophecy**) *the future.*

prophet /'prɒfɪt/ *n* **1** a person who claims to be able to prophesy the future. **2** a person who tells people what God wants, intends *etc*: *the prophet Isaiah.* **prophetic** /prə'fɛtɪk/ *adj.* **pro'phetically** *adv.*

'**prophetess** *n* a female prophet.

proportion /prə'pɔːʃən/ *n* **1** a part of a total amount: *Only a small proportion of the class passed the exam.* **2** the relation in size, number *etc* of one thing to another: *The proportion of girls to boys in our school is three to two.* **3** the size and measurements of something: *The hospital is a building of huge proportions.* **pro'portional** *adj.* **pro'portionally** *adv.*

pro'portionate *adj* being in correct proportion: *Should your wages be proportionate to the amount of work you do?* **pro'portionately** *adv.*

in proportion having the correct relationship between its parts: *Your drawing isn't in proportion — the dog is almost as large as the cow.*

in proportion to 1 compared with: *She has long legs in proportion to her height.* **2** growing at the same rate: *My salary has not increased in proportion to the cost of living.*

out of proportion too big, small *etc* in relation to other things: *He worries too much about details and gets them right out of proportion.*

proposal /prə'poʊzəl/ *n* **1** something proposed or suggested; a plan: *proposals for peace.* **2** an offer of marriage: *She received three proposals.*

propose /prə'poʊz/ *v* **1** to suggest: *I proposed my friend for the job; Who proposed this scheme?* **2** to intend: *He proposes to build a new house.* **3** to make an offer of marriage: *He proposed to me last night and I accepted him.* **proposition** /prɒpə'zɪʃən/ *n.*

proprietor /prə'praɪətə(r)/ *n* an owner, especially of a shop, hotel *etc.*

pro'prietress *n* a female owner.

prosaic /proʊ'zeɪɪk/ *adj* ordinary or dull: *a prosaic speech.*

prose /proʊz/ *n* writing that is not in verse; ordinary written or spoken language.

prosecute /'prɒsɪkjuːt/ *v* to accuse someone of a crime and bring a legal action against them: *He was prosecuted for careless driving; The sign in the shop said 'Shoplifters will be prosecuted'.* **prose'cution** *n.*

prospect /'prɒspɛkt/ *n.* **1** a view of something in the future: *He didn't like the prospect of trying to find a job.* **2** a chance for future development or promotion: *a job with good prospects.*

pros'pective *adj* hoping, expecting or likely to be: *a prospective buyer for a house.*

prospectus /prə'spɛktəs/, *plural* **prospectuses**, *n* a booklet issued by a university or college, giving details of the courses you can study there: *He read about the accommodation available at the university in its prospectus.*

prosper /'prɒspə(r)/ *v* to do well; to succeed: *His business is prospering.*

pros'perity *n* success; wealth: *We wish you happiness and prosperity.*

'**prosperous** *adj* successful, especially in business: *a prosperous businessman.* '**prosperously** *adv.*

prostitute /'prɒstɪtjuːt/ *n* a person, especially a woman, who has sexual intercourse for money. **prosti'tution** *n.*

prostrate *adj* /'prɒstreɪt/ **1** lying flat, especially face downwards. **2** exhausted; overwhelmed; completely overcome: *She was prostrate with grief.* — *v* /prɒ'streɪt/ to throw yourself flat on the floor to show how humble you are: *They prostrated themselves before the emperor.*

protagonist /prəˈtagənɪst/ *n* **1** an important character in a play, novel or film *etc*: *She is the protagonist in this drama.* **2** a supporter: *He is one of the main protagonists of the government.*

protect /prəˈtɛkt/ *v* to guard or defend from danger; to keep safe: *She protected the children from every danger; He wore a fur jacket to protect himself against the cold.*

pro'tected *adj* protected by law from being shot *etc*: *Elephants are protected animals.*

pro'tection *n* **1** protecting or being protected: *He ran to his mother for protection; This kind of lock will give extra protection against burglary.* **2** something that protects: *The trees were a good protection against the wind.*

pro'tective *adj* **1** giving protection: *protective clothing.* **2** wanting to keep someone safe: *Parents are naturally protective towards their children.*

pro'tector *n* a person or thing that protects.

protein /ˈprəʊtiːn/ *n* any of a large number of substances present in eggs, fish, meat *etc*.

protest *v* /prəˈtɛst/ **1** to show that you are strongly against something: *The demonstrators were protesting against the closing of the school.* **2** to declare definitely: *She protested that she was innocent.* — *n* /ˈprəʊtɛst/ a strong statement against something; an objection: *He made no protest when he was arrested and taken to prison.* — *adj*: *His supporters are organizing a protest march to get him freed.* **pro'tester** *n*.

under protest unwillingly: *I went to the meeting, but only under protest.*

Protestant /ˈprɒtɪstənt/ *n* a member of any of the Christian churches that separated from the Roman Catholic church at or after the time of the Reformation. **'Protestantism** *n*.

protocol /ˈprəʊtəkɒl/ *n* the correct way to act in formal situations, or when acting as a diplomat: *What is the protocol when speaking to the Queen?*

prototype /ˈprəʊtətaɪp/ *n* the first model that is made of a new design that later models will be developed from.

protractor /prəˈtraktə(r)/ *n* an instrument for drawing and measuring angles on paper.

protrude /prəˈtruːd/ *v* to stick out; to project: *His teeth protrude.*

proud /praʊd/ *adj* **1** feeling pleased because of something you have done or because of people, things *etc* you are concerned with: *He was proud of his new house; She was proud of her son's success; He was proud to be a member of the school team.* **2** having too good an opinion of yourself: *She was too proud to talk to us.* **3** wishing to be independent: *She was too proud to accept help.* **'proudly** *adv*.

prove /pruːv/ *v* **1** to show that something is true or correct: *This fact proves his guilt; He was proved guilty; Can you prove your theory?* **2** to turn out to be: *His theory proved to be correct; This tool proved very useful.* **proven** /ˈpruːvən/ *adj* proved.

> The noun from **prove** is **proof**.

proverb /ˈprɒvɜːb/ *n* a well-known saying that gives good advice or expresses a supposed truth: *Two common proverbs are 'Many hands make light work' and 'Don't count your chickens before they're hatched!'*

provide /prəˈvaɪd/ *v* **1** to give; to supply: *He provided the wine for the meal; He provided them with a bed for the night.* **2** to have enough money to supply what is necessary: *He is unable to provide for his family.*

pro'vided or **pro'viding** *conjunction* if; on condition: *We can buy it provided we have enough money.*

providential /prɒvɪˈdɛnʃəl/ *adj* lucky: *Your coming here today was quite providential.*

province /ˈprɒvɪns/ *n* a division of a country, empire *etc*: *Britain was once a Roman province.* **pro'vincial** *adj*.

provision /prəˈvɪʒən/ *n* the providing of something: *The government are responsible for the provision of education for all children.* — *v* to supply, especially an army, with food.

pro'visional *adj* only for the present time; that may be changed: *a provisional offer; a provisional driving license.* **pro'visionally** *adv*.

pro'visions *n* food: *The campers got their provisions at the village shop.*

make provision for to provide what is necessary for: *You should make provision for your old age.*

provocation /prɒvəˈkeɪʃən/ *n* a deliberate attempt to make someone angry: *She refused to react to his provocation.* **pro'vocative** *adj*.

provoke /prəˈvəʊk/ *v* **1** to make someone angry: *Are you trying to provoke me?* **2** to cause: *His words provoked laughter.* **3** to cause a person *etc* to react in an angry way: *His bad behaviour provoked her into shouting at him.*

prow /praʊ/ *n* the front part of a ship; the bow.

prowess /ˈpraʊɪs/ *n* skill; ability: *athletic prowess.*

prowl /praʊl/ *v* to move about carefully in order to steal, attack, catch *etc*: *Tigers were prowling in the jungle.* **ˈprowler** *n*.
on the prowl prowling: *Thieves are always on the prowl.*

proximity /prɒkˈsɪmɪtɪ/ *n* nearness: *Their house is in close proximity to ours.*

proxy /ˈprɒksɪ/ *n* a person legally allowed to act or vote for you: *If she's in hospital she should vote by proxy.*

prudent /ˈpruːdənt/ *adj* wise and careful: *a prudent person.* **ˈprudently** *adv.* **ˈprudence** *n.*

prune[1] /pruːn/ *v* to trim a tree *etc* by cutting off some twigs and branches: *Prune the shrubs in winter.*

prune[2] /pruːn/ *n* a dried plum.

pry /praɪ/ *v* to try to find out about something that is a secret, especially other people's affairs: *He is always prying into my business.*

psalm /sɑːm/ *n* a song from the Book of Psalms in the Bible.

pseudonym /ˈsjuːdənɪm/ or /ˈsuːdənɪm/ *n* a false name used by an author: *He wrote under a pseudonym.*

psychiatrist /saɪˈkaɪətrɪst/ *n* a doctor who treats mental illness.
psychiatry /saɪˈkaɪətrɪ/ *n* the treatment of mental illness. **psychiatric** /saɪkɪˈatrɪk/ *adj.*

psychic /ˈsaɪkɪk/ *adj* 1 (also **ˈpsychical**) having to do with the mind and not the body: *a psychic illness.* 2 having strange powers of the mind, such as being able to know other people's thoughts: *She often knows things about people without being told — she must be psychic.* — *n* a person who has psychic powers.

psychoanalysis /saɪkoʊəˈnalɪsɪs/ *n* the treatment of patients with mental or emotional problems which involves asking them about their past life to try and discover what may be causing their illness: *Psychoanalysis helped him to understand why he was depressed.* **psychoˈanalyse** /saɪkoʊˈanəlaɪz/ *v.* **psychoˈanalyst** *n.*

psychology /saɪˈkɒlədʒɪ/ *n* 1 the study or science of the human mind. 2 the particular type of mind that a person or group of people has: *gang psychology.* **psychological** /saɪkəˈlɒdʒɪkəl/ *adj.* **psychoˈlogically** *adv.*
psyˈchologist *n* a person who is trained in psychology.

psychopath /ˈsaɪkoʊpaθ/ *n* a person with a serious personality problem which causes them to be violent and aggressive: *This murder was the work of a psychopath.*

psychotherapy /saɪkoʊˈθɛrəpɪ/ *n* the treatment of mental illness using psychological methods rather than drugs.

pub /pʌb/ *n* a place where alcoholic drinks may be bought and drunk.

puberty /ˈpjuːbətɪ/ *n* the time when a child's body becomes mature.

public /ˈpʌblɪk/ *adj* having to do with, or belonging to, all the people of a town, nation *etc*: *a public library; a public meeting; The public announcements are on the back page of the newspaper; This information should be made public and not kept secret any longer.* **ˈpublicly** *adv.*

public holiday a day on which all shops, offices and factories are closed for a holiday.

public spirit a desire to do things for the good of the community. **public-ˈspirited** *adj.*

public transport the bus and train services provided by a state or community for the public.

in public in front of other people: *They are always quarrelling in public.*

the public people in general: *This swimming pool is open to the public every day.*

> **the public** is singular: *The public has a right to know the truth.*

publication /pʌblɪˈkeɪʃən/ *n* 1 the publishing of a book *etc*; the announcing of something publicly: *the publication of a new novel; the publication of the facts.* 2 something that has been published, such as a book or magazine.

publicity /pʌˈblɪsɪtɪ/ *n* 1 advertising: *There is a lot of publicity about the dangers of smoking.* 2 the state of being widely known: *Film stars usually like publicity.*

publicize /ˈpʌblɪsaɪz/ *v* to make something widely known.

publish /ˈpʌblɪʃ/ *v* to prepare, print and produce a book *etc* for sale: *His new novel is being published this month.*

'publisher *n* a person or company that publishes books, magazines *etc*.

'publishing *n* the business of a publisher.

pucker /'pʌkə(r)/ *v* to crease or wrinkle: *Your forehead puckers when you frown.*

pudding /'pʊdɪŋ/ *n* **1** any of several kinds of soft sweet foods made with eggs, flour, milk *etc*: *sponge pudding*; *rice pudding*. **2** the sweet course of a meal; dessert: *What's for pudding?*

puddle /'pʌdəl/ *n* a small pool of water *etc*: *It had been raining, and there were puddles in the road.*

puff /pʌf/ *n* **1** a small blast of air, wind *etc*; a gust: *A puff of wind moved the branches.* **2** any of various kinds of soft, round, light objects: *a powder puff*. — *v* **1** to blow with short puffs: *Stop puffing cigarette smoke into my face!*; *He puffed at his pipe.* **2** to breathe quickly, after running *etc*: *He was puffing as he climbed the stairs.*

puffed *adj* breathing quickly: *I'm puffed after running so fast!*

'puffy *adj* swollen: *a puffy face*.

puff out or **puff up** to swell up or grow fatter; to make something do this: *The bird puffed out its feathers*; *Her eye puffed up after the wasp stung her.*

pull /pʊl/ *v* **1** to move something, especially towards yourself, by using force: *He pulled the chair towards the fire*; *She pulled at the door but couldn't open it*; *Help me to pull my boots off*; *This railway engine can pull twelve carriages.* **2** to row: *He pulled towards the shore.* **3** to steer or move in a certain direction: *The car pulled in at the garage*; *I pulled into the side of the road*; *The train pulled out of the station*; *He pulled off the road.* **4** to injure a muscle *etc* by using too much force: *I've pulled a muscle in my leg.* — *n* **1** the action of pulling: *I felt a pull at my sleeve.* **2** a pulling force: *magnetic pull*.

pull apart or **pull to pieces** to destroy something completely by pulling or tearing: *He pulled the flower to pieces.*

pull away to move back suddenly in surprise *etc*: *She pulled away from him and screamed.*

pull down to destroy a building deliberately: *The church has been pulled down.*

pull a face or **pull faces** to make strange expressions with your face: *The children were pulling faces at each other*; *He pulled a face when he smelt the fish.*

pull off 1 to succeed or manage something: *The boss was proud that they had pulled the deal off.* **2** to remove a piece of clothing quickly: *They pulled off their jackets and ran into the classroom.*

pull on to put on a piece of clothing hastily: *She pulled on a sweater.*

pull out to withdraw from an agreement *etc*: *The company has pulled out of all its European contracts.*

pull through to get better; to help someone get better: *He is very ill, but he'll pull through*; *The doctor pulled him through.*

pull together to work together for the same purpose: *We all pulled together and the job became much easier.*

pull yourself together to get your emotional feelings under control and behave calmly: *He tried hard to pull himself together and deal with the situation.*

pull up to stop: *The car pulled up at the traffic lights.*

pulley /'pʊlɪ/ *n* a wheel over which a rope *etc* can pass in order to lift heavy objects.

pullover /'pʊloʊvə(r)/ *n* a knitted garment for the top part of your body; a sweater.

pulp /pʌlp/ *n* **1** the soft, fleshy part of a fruit. **2** a soft mass: *Paper is made from wood-pulp.*

'pulpy *adj* like pulp.

pulpit /'pʊlpɪt/ *n* a raised box or platform in church, where the priest or minister stands when he is preaching.

See **stage**.

pulsate /pʌl'seɪt/ *v* to move with a strong, regular rhythm or beat: *loud, pulsating music.*

pulse /pʌls/ *n* the regular beating of your heart which can be checked by feeling the artery on your wrist: *The doctor took her pulse.*

puma /'pjuːmə/ *n* a wild animal like a large cat, found in America.

pump /pʌmp/ *n* **1** a machine for making water *etc* rise from under the ground: *Every village used to have a pump from which everyone drew their water.* **2** a machine or device for forcing liquid, air or gas into, or out of, something: *a bicycle pump.* — *v* to raise or force with a pump: *Oil is being pumped out of the ground.*

pump up to inflate tyres *etc* with a pump.

pumpkin /'pʌmpkɪn/ *n* a large, round, thick-skinned yellow fruit, eaten as food.

pun /pʌn/ *n* a joke that is based on words that have the same sound but a different meaning: *An example of a pun is 'A news-*

paper is black and white and read all over' — when you hear 'read' you think of 'red'.

punch[1] /pʌntʃ/ *n* a hot drink made of spirits or wine, water and sugar *etc.*

punch[2] /pʌntʃ/ *v* to hit with your fist: *She punched him on the nose.* — *n*: *He gave him a punch.*

'punchline *n* the important last bit of a funny story or joke.

punch[3] /pʌntʃ/ *n* a tool or device for making holes in leather, paper *etc.* — *v* to make holes in something with a punch: *The inspector punched our tickets.*

punctual /'pʌŋtʃʊəl/ *adj* arriving *etc* on time; not late: *Please be punctual for your appointment*; *She's a very punctual person.* **punctu'ality** *n.* **'punctually** *adv.*

punctuate /'pʌŋktʃʊeɪt/ *v* **1** to divide up sentences by commas, full stops, colons *etc.* **2** to interrupt something many times: *Our conversation was punctuated by her silly giggles.* **punctu'ation** *n.*

punctuation mark any of the symbols used for punctuating, such as a comma, full stop, question mark *etc.*

puncture /'pʌŋktʃə(r)/ *v* to make a small hole in something, especially a tyre: *Some glass on the road punctured my new tyre.* — *n* a hole, especially in a tyre: *My car has had two punctures this week.*

pungent /'pʌndʒənt/ *adj* sharp and strong: *a pungent smell.* **'pungently** *adv.*

punish /'pʌnɪʃ/ *v* to make someone suffer for a crime or fault: *He was punished for stealing the money*; *The teacher punishes disobedience.*

'punishable *adj* that you can be punished for: *In those days, many crimes were punishable by death.*

'punishing *adj* making you weak and exhausted: *He had set himself a punishing schedule.*

'punishment *n*: *Punishment follows crime*; *The teacher gave her some extra work to do as a punishment for being lazy.*

punk /pʌŋk/ *n* **1** a style of dressing and behaving in the 1970s and 1980s that was meant to shock people and was intended as a kind of protest against society. **2** (also **punk rock**) rock music that is played in a loud and aggressive way. **3** a young person who likes punk music, dresses in a very strange or shocking way, or dyes their hair a strange colour.

punt /pʌnt/ *n* an open boat with a flat bottom and square ends that is moved by someone standing on the end and pushing against the bottom of the river *etc* with a long pole. — *v* to travel in a punt: *They punted up the river.*

punt

puny /'pju:nɪ/ *adj* small and weak: *He was ashamed of his puny muscles.*

pup /pʌp/ *n* **1** a baby dog: *There were six pups in the litter.* **2** the baby of certain other animals: *a seal pup.*

pupa /'pju:pə/, *plural* **pupae** /'pju:pi:/, *n* the tightly wrapped-up form that an insect takes when it is changing from a larva to its perfect form, for example from a caterpillar to a butterfly.

pupil[1] /'pju:pɪl/ *n* a person who is being taught: *The school has 2000 pupils*; *How many pupils does the piano teacher have?*

pupil[2] /'pju:pɪl/ *n* the round opening in the middle of your eye through which the light passes.

puppet /'pʌpət/ *n* a doll that can be moved by wires, or fitted over your hand and worked by your fingers.

'puppet-show *n* a play *etc* performed by puppets.

puppy /'pʌpɪ/ *n* a baby dog.

purchase /'pɜ:tʃəs/ *v* to buy: *I purchased a new car.* — *n* **1** anything that has been bought: *She carried her purchases home in a bag.* **2** the buying of something: *The purchase of a car should never be a hasty matter.*

'purchaser *n* a buyer.

pure /pjʊə(r)/ *adj* **1** not mixed with anything else: *pure gold.* **2** clean: *pure water.* **3** complete; absolute: *a pure accident.* **'purely** *adv.* **'pureness** *n.*

purge /pɜ:dʒ/ *v* to make something clean by clearing it of everything that is bad, not wanted *etc*: *He was trying to purge his life of some of the things that caused him worry and distress.* — *n.*

purgative /'pɜ:gətɪv/ *n* a medicine which clears waste matter out of the body.

purify /'pjʊərɪfaɪ/ *v* to make something pure: *to purify water.* **purifi'cation** *n.*

puritanical /pjʊərɪ'tanɪkəl/ *adj* with very strict

moral and religious principles: *a puritanical attitude towards alcohol.*

purity /'pjʊərətɪ/ *n* pureness: *The purity of the mountain air.*

purple /'pɜːpl/ *n* a dark colour made by mixing blue and red.

purpose /'pɜːpəs/ *n* **1** the reason for doing something: *What is the purpose of your visit to Britain?* **2** what something is used for: *The purpose of this button is to stop the machine in an emergency.*

'purposeful *adj* having a definite purpose; determined: *He walked in with a purposeful look on his face.* **'purposefully** *adv.*

'purposely *adv* deliberately; intentionally; not by accident: *You trod on my toe purposely*; *He banged the door purposely to get my attention.*

on purpose purposely: *Did you break the cup on purpose?*

purr /pɜː(r)/ *v* to make the low, murmuring sound of a cat when it is pleased. — *n* a sound like this.

purse /pɜːs/ *n* a small bag for carrying money: *I looked in my purse for some change.* — *v* to close your lips tightly: *She pursed her lips in anger.*

pursue /pə'sjuː/ *v* **1** to follow someone, especially in order to catch them; to chase: *They pursued the thief through the town.* **2** to continue with something; to find out more about something: *She wanted more freedom to pursue her many interests.*

pursuit /pə'sjuːt/ *n* the action of pursuing: *The thief ran down the street with a policeman in pursuit.*

pus /pʌs/ *n* a thick, yellowish liquid that forms in infected wounds *etc.*

push /pʊʃ/ *v* **1** to press against something, in order to move it: *He pushed the door open*; *She pushed him away*; *He pushed against the door with his shoulder*; *Stop pushing!*; *I had a good view of the race till someone pushed in front of me.* **2** to try to make someone do something: *She pushed him into asking his boss for more money.* — *n*: *She gave him a push and he fell over.*

'push-button *adj* operated by pressing a button: *a push-button telephone.*

'push-chair *n* a small folding chair on wheels used for pushing a young child around.

'pushover *n* **1** someone from whom you can easily get what you want: *He's a real pushover when it comes to borrowing money.* **2** something that is easy to do or win: *He's so clever, these exams will be a pushover for him.*

'pushy *adj* behaving in a forceful and bossy way: *You need to be pushy to succeed in show business.*

at a push if really necessary: *I could lend you the money at a push, but I would have almost nothing left.*

push around to treat roughly: *He pushes his younger brother around.*

push in to take a place further forward in a queue than you should.

push off 1 to go away: *I wish you'd push off!* **2** to push against something with your hands *etc*, to help you move, leap *etc*: *He got into the boat and pushed off using a pole.*

push on to continue: *Push on with your work.*

push over to push someone so that they fall: *He pushed me over.*

push through to force others to accept: *The government pushed the law through parliament.*

puss /pʊs/ or **pussy** /'pʊsɪ/ *n* a cat.

put /pʊt/ *v* **1** to place something in a certain position or situation: *He put the plate in the cupboard*; *Did you put any sugar in my coffee?*; *He put his arm around her*; *I'm putting a new lock on the door*; *You've put me in a bad temper.* **2** to present a suggestion, question *etc*: *I put several questions to him*; *She put her ideas before the committee.* **3** to express in words: *He put his refusal very politely*; *Children sometimes have such a funny way of putting things!* **4** to write something: *Having started the letter, she couldn't think what to put*; *What did you put for question 8?*

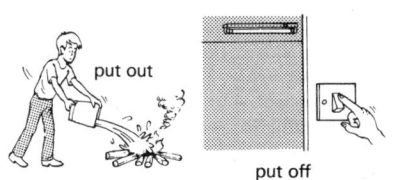

put out

put off

put; **put**; **put**: *She put the cups on the table*; *He has put his shoes outside the door.*

put across or **put over** to express something clearly: *You put your point across very well.*

put aside 1 to lay down; to stop doing something: *She put aside her needlework.* **2** to save for the future: *He tries to put aside a little money each month.*

put away to return something to its proper place: *She put her clothes away in the drawer.*

put back 1 to return something to the place you got it from: *Did you put my keys back?* **2** to postpone or delay something: *The meeting has been put back until next Tuesday.*

put by to save for future use: *He had put money by for an emergency like this.*

put down 1 to lower: *You can put your hands down!* **2** to set down something that you are holding: *Put that knife down immediately!* **3** to bring a rebellion *etc* under control. **4** to kill an animal painlessly when it is old or very ill. **5** to make someone feel stupid: *She seemed to enjoy putting her children down in public.*

put down to to believe that one thing is caused by another: *Parents are putting their children's bad behaviour down to bad teaching at school.*

put your feet up to take a rest.

put forward to suggest: *Your name has been put forward for secretary.*

put in 1 to get something fitted in your house *etc*: *We're having a new shower put in.* **2** to do a certain amount of work *etc*: *He put in an hour's training today.*

put off 1 to switch off a light *etc*: *Please put the light off!* **2** to delay: *He put off leaving till Thursday.* **3** to stop someone concentrating: *Stop humming — you're putting me off.* **4** to make someone dislike or not want something: *Don't talk about hospitals just now, you'll put me off my dinner.*

put on 1 to switch on a light *etc*: *Put the light on!* **2** to dress yourself in a piece of clothing: *Which shoes are you going to put on?* **3** to increase: *The car put on speed; I've put on weight.* **4** to behave in a way that is not natural to you: *She put on a funny accent to read the story; He's not really angry — he's just putting it on.*

See **take off.**

put out 1 to hold out your hand *etc*: *He put out his hand to steady her.* **2** to switch off a light *etc*: *Please put out the lights.* **3** to stop a fire burning: *The fire brigade soon put out the fire.* **4** to give someone trouble or extra work: *Are you sure you can do this? I don't want to put you out.* **5** to annoy someone: *I was really put out because the weather was so bad.*

The job of the fire brigade is to **put out** (not **put off**) fires.

put through 1 to connect someone on the telephone: *The operator put me through to the wrong department.* **2** to make someone suffer an unpleasant experience: *She put him through a very tough examination.*

put together to construct: *The vase broke, but I managed to put it together again.*

put up 1 to raise: *Put up your hand if you know the answer!* **2** to build: *They're putting up some new houses.* **3** to fix something up on a wall *etc*: *He put the picture up.* **4** to increase: *I see food prices have been put up again.* **5** to give someone accommodation in your house: *Could you put me up for a few nights?*

put up with to bear patiently: *I cannot put up with all this noise.*

putt /pʌt/ *v* to hit a golf ball gently forward along the ground near a hole.

putty /'pʌtɪ/ *n* a cement-like paste used to fill in holes and cracks in wood and to fix windows in frames: *Dentists use a type of putty to take impressions of teeth.*

puzzle /'pʌzəl/ *v* **1** to present someone with a problem that is difficult to solve or with a situation *etc* that is difficult to understand; to confuse: *The question puzzled them; I was puzzled by her sudden disappearance; What puzzles me is how he got here so soon.* **2** to think long and carefully about a problem *etc*: *I puzzled over the sum.* — *n* **1** a problem that causes a lot of thought: *Her behaviour was a puzzle to him.* **2** a game to test your thinking, knowledge or skill: *a jigsaw puzzle; a crossword puzzle.*

'puzzling *adj* difficult to understand: *a puzzling remark.*

puzzle out to understand something; to find the answer to a problem by thinking hard about it: *It took some time to puzzle out what language the lady was speaking.*

pygmy or **pigmy** /'pɪgmɪ/ *n* a member of an African race of very small people.

pyjamas or **pajamas** /pə'dʒɑːməz/ *n* a suit for sleeping, consisting of trousers and a jacket: *Where are my pyjamas?; Whose is this pair of pyjamas?; two pairs of pyjamas.*

pyjamas takes a plural verb, but **a pair of pyjamas** is singular.

pylon /ˈpaɪlən/ *n* a tall steel tower for supporting electric power cables.

pyramid /ˈpɪrəmɪd/ *n* **1** a solid shape with flat sides in the shape of a triangle, that comes to a point at the top. **2** an ancient tomb built in this shape in Egypt.

pyre /paɪə(r)/ *n* a pile of wood on which a dead body is burned: *a funeral pyre*.

python /ˈpaɪθən/ *n* a large snake that twists around its prey and crushes it.

Q

quack /kwak/ *n* the cry of a duck. — *v* to make this sound: *The ducks quacked noisily as they swam across the pond.*

quad /kwɒd/ short for **quadrangle** or **quadruplet**.

quadrangle /ˈkwɒdraŋɡəl/ *n* a square courtyard surrounded by buildings, especially in a school, college *etc*.

quadrilateral /kwɒdrɪˈlatərəl/ *n* a flat shape with four straight sides.

quadruped /ˈkwɒdrʊpɛd/ *n* an animal with four legs: *Cows, goats and sheep are all quadrupeds.*

quadruple /kwɒdˈruːpəl/ *adj* **1** four times as much or as many. **2** made up of four parts *etc*. — *v* to make or become four times as great.

quadruplet /ˈkwɒdrʊplət/ *n* one of four children born at the same time to one mother (shortened to **quad**).

See also **triplet, quintuplet**.

quaint /kweɪnt/ *adj* odd; old-fashioned: *quaint customs*. **'quaintly** *adv*. **'quaintness** *n*.

quake /kweɪk/ *v* to shake: *The ground quaked under their feet.* — *n* an earthquake.

qualification /kwɒlɪfɪˈkeɪʃən/ *n* a skill that you have, or an exam that you have passed that makes you suitable to do a job *etc*: *What qualifications do you need for this job?*

qualify /ˈkwɒlɪfaɪ/ *v* **1** to make or become suitable for something: *Even if you have spent a year in England, that does not qualify you to teach English*; *She is too young to qualify for a place in the team.* **2** to show that you are suitable for a job *etc* especially by passing a test: *I hope to qualify as a doctor.*
'qualified *adj*: *a qualified engineer.*

quality /ˈkwɒlɪtɪ/ *n* **1** how good something is: *We produce several different qualities of paper*; *In this firm, we look for quality rather than quantity.* **2** something that you notice about a thing or person; a characteristic that someone or something has: *Kindness is a human quality that everyone admires.*

qualm /kwɑːm/ *n* a sudden worry: *They had no qualms about taking time off.*

quandary /ˈkwɒndərɪ/ *n* a situation in which you cannot decide what to do: *He is in a quandary as to what he should do next.*

quantity /ˈkwɒntɪtɪ/ *n* an amount, especially a large amount: *What quantity of paper do you need?*; *I buy these goods in quantity*; *a small quantity of cement; large quantities of tinned food.*

quarantine /ˈkwɒrəntiːn/ *n* the keeping away from the public of people or animals that might be infected with a disease: *to be in quarantine for chickenpox.* — *v* to put a person or animal in quarantine.

quarrel /ˈkwɒrəl/ *n* an angry disagreement or argument: *I've had a quarrel with my girlfriend.* — *v* to have an angry argument with someone: *I've quarrelled with my girlfriend*; *My girlfriend and I have quarrelled.*

> **quarrelled** and **quarrelling** are spelt with two **l**s;
> **quarrel** and **quarrelsome** have one **l**.

'quarrelsome *adj* quarrelling a lot: *quarrelsome children*. **'quarrelsomeness** *n*.

quarry /ˈkwɒrɪ/ *n* a place, usually a very large hole in the ground, from which stone is taken for building *etc*. — *v* to dig stone in a quarry.

quarter /ˈkwɔːtə(r)/ *n* **1** one of four equal parts of something: *There are four of us, so we'll cut the cake into quarters*; *It's quarter past four*; *In the first quarter of the year his firm made a profit*; *an hour and a quarter; two and a quarter hours.* **2** a district or part of a town: *He works in the business quarter of the city.* **3** a direction: *People were arriving at the conference from all quarters.* — *v* **1** to divide into four equal parts: *to quarter a melon.* **2** to give soldiers *etc* somewhere to stay: *The soldiers were quartered all over the town.*

'quarterly *adj* happening, published *etc* once every three months: *a quarterly journal*; *quarterly payments.* — *adv* once every three months: *We pay our electricity bill quarterly.* — *n* a magazine *etc* which is published once every three months.

'quarters *n* a place to stay, especially for soldiers.

quarter-'final *n* the third-last round in a competition.

at close quarters close together: *The soldiers were fighting with the enemy at close quarters.*

quartet /kwɔːˈtɛt/ *n* **1** a group of four singers

or musicians. **2** a piece of music composed for a group of four to play or sing.

quartz /kwɔːts/ *n* a hard substance found in rocks in the form of crystals that can be used in electronic clocks and watches. — *adj*: *a quartz watch*.

quaver /ˈkweɪvə(r)/ *v* to sound shaky; to tremble: *His voice quavered with fright as he spoke*. — *n*: *He tried to sound brave but there was a quaver in his voice*.

quay /kiː/ *n* a stone-built landing-place, where boats are loaded and unloaded: *The boat is moored at the quay*.

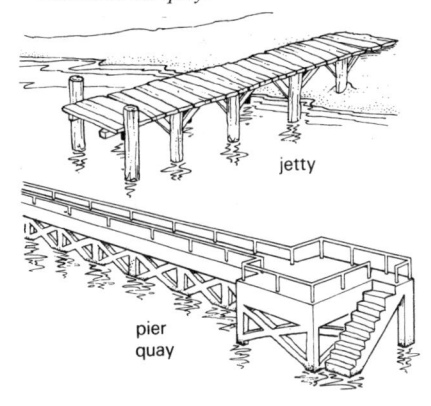

jetty

pier
quay

queasy /ˈkwiːzɪ/ *adj* feeling as if you are about to be sick: *The motion of the boat made her feel queasy*.

queen /kwiːn/ *n* **1** a woman who rules a country: *the Queen of England; Queen Elizabeth II*. **2** the wife of a king: *The king and his queen were both present*. **3** a woman who is regarded as outstanding in some way: *a beauty queen; a movie queen*. **4** a playing-card with a picture of a queen on it: *I have two aces and a queen*. **5** an important chess-piece. **6** the egg-laying female of certain kinds of insect, especially bees, ants and wasps.

queer /kwɪə(r)/ *adj* odd; strange: *queer behaviour*.

quell /kwɛl/ *v* **1** to put an end to a rebellion *etc* by force: *to quell a riot*. **2** to calm: *to quell someone's fears*.

quench /kwɛntʃ/ *v* **1** to drink enough to take away your thirst: *I had a glass of lemonade to quench my thirst*. **2** to put out a fire: *The firemen were unable to quench the fire*.

query /ˈkwɪərɪ/ *n* a question: *In answer to your query about hotel reservations I am sorry to tell you that we have no vacancies*. — *v* to express doubt about a statement *etc*: *I think the waiter has added up the bill wrongly — you should query it*.

See **inquire, inquiry**.

quest /kwɛst/ *n* a search: *the quest for gold*.

question /ˈkwɛstʃən/ *n* **1** something that is said, written *etc* that asks for an answer from someone: *The question is, do we really need a new computer?* **2** a problem or matter for discussion: *There is the question of how much to pay him*. **3** a problem in a school exercise, exam *etc*: *We had to answer four questions in three hours*. **4** a suggestion; a possibility: *There is no question of our dismissing him*. — *v* **1** to ask a person questions: *I'll question him about what he was doing last night*. **2** to doubt: *He questioned her right to use the money*.

'questionable *adj* that may not be good or proper: *Her motives seem questionable*.

question mark a mark (?) used in writing to indicate a question.

'question-master *n* the person who asks the questions in a quiz *etc*.

questionnaire /kwɛstʃəˈnɛə(r)/ *n* a written list of questions to be answered by a large number of people to provide information for a report *etc*.

in question being discussed or referred to: *Where were you on the night in question?*

no question of no possibility of: *There is no question of the shop closing down*.

out of the question impossible; not allowed: *It is quite out of the question for you to go out tonight*.

queue /kjuː/ *n* a line of people waiting for something: *a queue for the football match; a bus queue*. — *v* to stand in a queue: *We had to queue to get into the cinema*.

queue up to stand in a queue: *We queued up for tickets*.

quibble /ˈkwɪbəl/ *v* to argue over small or unimportant details: *He quibbled over the amount of money a new shirt would cost him*. — *n* a minor objection or criticism: *I don't have any major comments to make, but just one or two quibbles*.

quick /kwɪk/ *adj* **1** done *etc* in a short time: *a quick trip into town*. **2** moving with speed: *He's a very quick walker; I made a grab at the dog, but it was too quick for me*. **3** doing something without delay; prompt: *He is always quick to help; a quick answer; He's very quick at arithmetic*. — *adv* quickly:

quick-frozen food. **'quickly** *adv.* **'quickness** *n.*

'quicken *n* to make or become quicker: *He quickened his pace.*

'quicksands *n* loose, wet sand that sucks down anyone who stands on it.

'quicksilver *n* mercury.

quick-'tempered *adj* easily made angry.

quiet /'kwaɪət/ *adj* **1** making little or no noise: *Tell the children to be quiet*; *It's very quiet out in the country*; *a quiet person.* **2** free from worry, excitement *etc*: *I live a very quiet life.* **3** not busy: *We'll have a quiet afternoon watching television.* — *n* a quiet state or time: *in the quiet of the night*; *All I want is peace and quiet.* — *v* to quieten.

> **quiet**, adjective: *She has a quiet voice*; *Keep quiet.*
> **quite**, adverb: *This book is quite good.*

'quietly *adv.* **'quietness** *n.*

'quieten *v* to make or become quiet: *I expect you to quieten down when I come into the classroom, children!*

keep quiet about something to keep something secret: *I'd like you to keep quiet about the child's father being in prison.*

on the quiet secretly: *He had been using the company's computer on the quiet.*

quill /kwɪl/ *n* a large feather, especially one made into a pen.

quilt /kwɪlt/ *n* a bedcover filled with feathers *etc.*

'quilted *adj* made of two layers of material with padding between them: *a quilted jacket.*

quin /kwɪn/ *n* short for **quintuplet.**

quinine /'kwɪniːn/ *n* a drug used against malaria.

quintet /kwɪn'tɛt/ *n* **1** a group of five singers or musicians. **2** a piece of music composed for a group of five to sing or play.

quintuplet /'kwɪntʊplət/ *n* one of five children born at the same time to one mother (shortened to **quin**).

> See also **triplet, quadruplet.**

quirk /kwɜːk/ *n* **1** something strange or unusual in a person's behaviour *etc*: *Throwing biscuit crumbs over his shoulder is just one of his little quirks.* **2** a strange happening: *By a quirk of fate, she met him again years later.*

quit /kwɪt/ *v* **1** to stop or give up something: *I'm going to quit teaching.* **2** to leave: *They have been ordered to quit the house by next week.*

quite /kwaɪt/ *adv* **1** completely: *This task is quite impossible.* **2** fairly; rather: *It's quite warm today*; *He's quite a good artist*; *I quite like the idea.* — used to show that you agree: *'I think he is being unfair to her.' 'Quite.'*

> See also **quiet.**

quits /'kwɪts/ even; when neither person owes the other anything: *If you pay for the damage to my car then we'll be quits.*

quiver[1] /'kwɪvə(r)/ *v* to tremble; to shake: *Her lip quivered and her eyes filled with tears.* — *n* a quivering sound, movement *etc.*

quiver[2] /'kwɪvə(r)/ *n* a long, narrow case for carrying arrows in.

quiz /kwɪz/, *plural* **quizzes**, *n* a game or competition in which knowledge is tested by asking questions: *a television quiz.*

'quizzical *adj* seeming to ask a question: *a quizzical look.*

quota /'kwoʊtə/ *n* the part or share given to or received by each member of a group *etc.*

quotation /kwoʊ'teɪʃən/ *n* **1** something quoted: *a quotation from Shakespeare.* **2** a price mentioned for a job *etc.*

quotation marks marks (" " or ' ') used to show that a person's words are being repeated exactly; inverted commas: *He said 'I'm going out.'*

quote /kwoʊt/ *v* **1** to repeat the exact words of a person as they were said or written: *The President's speech was quoted on the television news.* **2** to name a price: *He quoted a price for repairing the bicycle.*

R

rabbi /'rabaɪ/ *n* a Jewish priest or teacher of the law.

rabbit /'rabɪt/ *n* a small long-eared animal, found living wild in fields or sometimes kept as a pet.

> A rabbit **squeals**.
> A male rabbit is a **buck**.
> A female rabbit is a **doe**.
> A tame rabbit lives in a **hutch**.
> A wild rabbit lives in a **burrow** or **warren**.

rabble /'rabəl/ *n* a noisy disorderly crowd: *The protestors were dismissed by the minister as a small and unrepresentative rabble.*

rabies /'reɪbiːz/ *n* a disease that causes madness in dogs and other animals.

raccoon or **racoon** /rə'kuːn/ *n* a small, furry animal with a striped, bushy tail.

race[1] /reɪs/ *n* a competition to find who or which is the fastest: *a horse race.* — *v* **1** to run in a race; to put into a race: *I'm racing my horse on Saturday; The horse is racing against five others.* **2** to go *etc* quickly: *He raced along the road on his bike.*

race[2] /reɪs/ *n* a group of people with the same ancestors and certain characteristics that make them different from other groups: *the African races; the European race.* — *adj*: *Good race relations are important within a city where there are groups of people of different nationalities.*

the human race all human beings.

racecourse /'reɪskɔːs/ *n* a course over which horse races are run.

racehorse /'reɪshɔːs/ *n* a horse bred and used for racing.

racetrack /'reɪstrak/ *n* a course over which races are run by cars, dogs, athletes *etc*.

racial /'reɪʃəl/ *adj* having to do with different human races: *racial characteristics; racial hatred.*

'racialism *n* racism.

'racialist *n*.

racing /'reɪsɪŋ/ *n* the sport of racing animals or vehicles: *horse-racing; motor-racing.*

'racing-car *n* a car specially designed and built for racing.

racism /'reɪsɪzm/ *n* **1** the belief that some races are better than others. **2** prejudice against someone because of their race. **'racist** *n*: *I suspect him of being a racist* — *adj*: *racist attitudes.*

rack[1] /rak/ *n* a frame or shelf for holding objects such as letters, plates, luggage *etc*: *Put these tools back in the rack; Put your bag in the luggage-rack.*

rack[2] /rak/: **rack your brains** to think hard.

racket[1] or **racquet** /'rakɪt/ *n* a kind of bat used for hitting the ball in tennis, badminton *etc*: *a squash-racket.*

racket[2] /'rakɪt/ **1** a loud noise or disturbance: *Who's making that racket?* **2** an illegal scheme for making money: *They were running some kind of racket.*

racoon another spelling of **raccoon**.

racquet another spelling of **racket**[1].

radar /'reɪdɑː(r)/ *n* a method of showing the direction and distance of an object by means of radio waves that bounce off the object and return to their source.

radiant /'reɪdɪənt/ *adj* **1** showing great joy: *a radiant smile.* **2** sending out rays of heat, light *etc*. **'radiance** *n*. **'radiantly** *adv*.

radiate /'reɪdɪeɪt/ *v* **1** to send out rays of light, heat *etc*; to come out from a source of light, heat *etc*: *Heat and light radiate from the sun; A fire radiates heat.* **2** to spread out from a centre: *All the roads radiate from the market square.*

radi'ation *n* rays of light, heat *etc* or of any radioactive substance.

'radiator *n* **1** a device for heating a room. **2** a device in a car that helps to cool the engine.

radical /'radɪkəl/ *adj* **1** very basic; fundamental: *The bridge will have to be knocked down because there is a radical fault in its design; Britain's strategy will need radical revision.* **2** wanting great and important changes: *He has radical ideas on education.* — *n* someone who wants great and important changes. **'radically** *adv*.

radio /'reɪdɪoʊ/, plural **radios**, *n* a device for the sending and receiving of human speech, music *etc*: *a pocket radio; The concert is being broadcast on radio; I heard about it on the radio.* — *adj*: *a radio programme; radio waves.* — *v* to send a message by radio: *An urgent message was radioed to us this evening.*

radioactive /ˌreɪdɪoʊ'aktɪv/ *adj* giving off powerful rays that are very harmful and dangerous: *Uranium is a radioactive metal that is used to produce nuclear energy*; *It is very difficult to get rid of radioactive waste from nuclear power stations.* **radioac'tivity** *n.*

radio-controlled /reɪdɪoʊ kənˈtroʊld/ *adj* operated by radio signals: *a radio-controlled model car.*

radiography /reɪdɪˈɒgrəfɪ/ *n* the act or process of taking X-rays: *She works in the hospital's radiography department.* **radi'ographer** *n.*

radio telescope /reɪdɪoʊ ˈtɛlɪskoʊp/ a telescope that picks up radio waves from stars and planets in space.

radish /ˈradɪʃ/ *n* a plant with a sharp-tasting root, eaten raw in salads.

radium /ˈreɪdɪəm/ *n* a radioactive element used to treat cancer: *She was given radium therapy for the tumour.*

radius /ˈreɪdɪəs/ *n* **1** (*plural* **'radiuses**) the area within a certain distance from a central point: *They searched within a radius of one mile from the school.* **2** (*plural* **radii** /ˈreɪdɪaɪ/) a straight line from the centre of a circle to its edge.

raffia /ˈrafɪə/ *n* a material used for weaving mats *etc*, got from palm-tree leaves.

raffle /ˈrafəl/ *n* a way of raising money by selling numbered tickets, a few of which will win prizes: *I won this doll in a raffle.* — *adj*: *raffle tickets.*

raft /rɑːft/ *n* a number of logs, planks *etc* fastened together and used as a boat.

rafter /ˈrɑːftə(r)/ *n* one of the long pieces of wood that support a roof.

rag /rag/ *n* a torn piece of cloth: *I'll polish my bike with this rag.*

rags *n* old, torn clothes: *The beggar was dressed in rags.*

rage /reɪdʒ/ *n* violent anger: *He flew into a rage*; *He shouted with rage.* — *v* **1** to shout in great anger: *He raged at his secretary.* **2** to blow with great force: *The storm raged all night.* **3** to continue with great violence: *The battle raged for two whole days.*

'raging *adj* violent; very bad: *raging toothache*; *a raging storm.*

all the rage very much in fashion.

ragged /ˈragɪd/ *adj* **1** dressed in old, torn clothing: *a ragged beggar.* **2** torn: *ragged clothes.* **3** rough or uneven: *a ragged edge.* **'raggedly** *adv.* **'raggedness** *n.*

raid /reɪd/ *n* **1** a sudden armed attack against an enemy: *The soldiers made a raid on the harbour.* **2** an unexpected visit by the police, for example to catch a criminal or to search for illegal drugs: *The police carried out a raid on the home of a drug-dealer.* **3** the entering of a place in order to steal something: *A total of £50 000 was stolen in the bank raid.* — *v*: *The police raided the gambling club*; *The robbers raided a jewellery shop.*

rail /reɪl/ *n* **1** a bar of metal, wood *etc* used in fences *etc* or for hanging things on: *Don't lean over the rail*; *a curtain-rail*; *a towel-rail.* **2** a long bar of steel that forms the track on which trains *etc* run: *The engine and two carriages had come off the rails.*

'railing *n* a fence or barrier of metal or wooden bars: *They've put railings up all round the park.*

'railway or **'railroad** *n* a track with two parallel steel rails on which trains run: *They're building a new railway.* — *adj*: *a railway station.*

by rail on the railway: *goods sent by rail.*

rain /reɪn/ *n* water falling from the clouds in drops: *We've had a lot of rain today*; *I enjoy walking in the rain.* — *v*: *I think it will rain today*; *Is it raining?*

> **drizzle** is very fine, light rain: *continuous drizzle*; it is used as a verb: *You don't need an umbrella — it's only drizzling.*
> A **shower** is a short period of rain: *a light shower*; *a heavy shower.*
> A **rainstorm** or **downpour** is a period of very heavy rain.
> A **thunderstorm** is a storm with thunder and lightning and usually heavy rain.

rainbow /ˈreɪnboʊ/ *n* the coloured arch sometimes seen in the sky opposite the sun when rain is falling.

'raincoat *n* a coat worn to keep out the rain.

'raindrop *n* a single drop of rain.

'rainfall *n* the amount of rain that falls in a certain place in a certain time.

'rainforest *n* a thick tropical forest in an area where there is a lot of rain: *Many rainforests have been destroyed in recent years.*

'rain-gauge *n* an instrument for measuring rainfall.

'rainstorm *n* a period of very heavy rain.

'rainy *adj* having many showers of rain: *a rainy day*; *the rainy season*; *rainy weather.*

rain cats and dogs to rain very hard.

rain off to prevent something from happening because of rain: *The football match was rained off after the first half.*

raise /reɪz/ *v* **1** to move or lift something to a

high position: *Raise your right hand*; *Raise the flag*; *The truck raised a cloud of dust as it passed.* **2** to make higher: *We'll raise that wall about 20 centimetres.* **3** to grow crops or breed animals for food: *We don't raise pigs on this farm.* **4** to bring up a child: *She has raised a large family.* **5** to state a question, objection *etc* which you wish to have discussed: *Has anyone in the audience any points they would like to raise?* **6** to collect; to gather: *We'll try to raise money to repair the swimming-pool.* **7** to cause: *His joke raised a laugh.* — *n* an increase in wages or salary: *I'm going to ask the boss for a raise.*

> **raise** means to lift something: *Raise* (not *rise*) *your hand*.
> **rise** means to stand up or go up: *Smoke rises* (not *raises*) *from the chimney*.

raise someone's hopes to make someone hopeful.
raise someone's spirits to make someone cheerful.
raise the roof to make a lot of noise.
raisin /'reɪzən/ *n* a dried grape: *She put raisins and sultanas in the cake.*
rajah /'rɑːdʒə/ *n* an Indian prince.
rake /reɪk/ *n* a tool, like a large comb with a long handle, used for smoothing earth, gathering hay and leaves together *etc*. — *v* to smooth or gather with a rake: *I'll rake these grass-cuttings up later.*
rake up to talk about unpleasant things that happened, that people would prefer to forget: *I asked him not to rake up the past.*
rally /'ralɪ/ *v* **1** to come or bring together: *The general tried to rally his troops after the defeat*; *The supporters rallied to save the club from collapse.* **2** to recover health or strength: *She rallied from her illness.* — *n* **1** a large gathering of people for some purpose: *a Scout's rally.* **2** a meeting, usually of cars or motorcycles, for a competition, race *etc*. **3** the number of times the ball is hit between points in a game like tennis: *That was the longest rally of the match so far.*
rally round to come together for a joint effort, especially of support: *When John's business was in difficulty, his friends all rallied round to help him.*
ram /ram/ *n* **1** a male sheep. **2** something heavy, especially part of a machine, used for ramming: *a battering ram.* — *v* **1** to run into something and cause damage to it: *His car rammed into the car in front of it.* **2** to push with great force: *We rammed the post into the ground.*
Ramadan /'raməadan/ *n* the ninth month of the Muslim year, when Muslims fast between sunrise and sunset: *His family always fasts during Ramadan.*
ramble /'rambəl/ *v* **1** to go for a walk, usually in the countryside: *Thomas was rambling in the woods somewhere.* **2** to speak in a confused way. — *n* a walk taken for pleasure.
'**rambler** *n*.
ramp /ramp/ *n* a sloping surface: *The car drove up the ramp from the quay to the ship.*
rampage /ram'peɪdʒ/ *v* to rush about angrily, violently or in excitement: *The elephants rampaged through the jungle.*
go on the rampage to rampage, causing damage and destruction.
rampant /'rampənt/ *adj* very common; out of control: *rampant weeds*; *rampant crime*.
rampart /'rampɑːt/ *n* a wall for defence.
ramshackle /'ramʃakəl/ *adj* in very bad condition: *a ramshackle building in need of repair.*
ran *see* **run**.
ranch /rɑːntʃ/ *n* a farm, especially one in America for rearing cattle or horses.
rancid /'ransɪd/ *adj* tasting or smelling bad: *rancid butter.*
rancour /'raŋkə(r)/ *n* a feeling of bitterness or hatred that lasts a long time: *There has always been a feeling of rancour between them.*
random /'randəm/ *adj* done *etc* without any plan or system: *a random selection.* '**randomly** *adv*.
at random without any plan or system: *Choose a number at random.*
rang *see* **ring**².
range /reɪndʒ/ *n* **1** a selection; a variety: *a wide range of books for sale*; *He has a very wide range of interests.* **2** the distance over which an object can be sent or thrown; the distance over which a sound can be heard *etc*: *What is the range of this missile?*; *We are within range of their guns.* **3** the amount between certain limits: *I'm hoping for a salary within the range £10 000 to £14 000.* **4** a row; a ridge: *a mountain range.* — *v* **1** to put things in rows: *The two armies were ranged on opposite sides of the valley.* **2** to vary between certain limits: *inflation rates across Europe range from 3% to 12%.*
'**ranger** *n* a person who looks after a forest or park.
rank /raŋk/ *n* **1** a line or row: *a soldier in the*

ransack

front rank; *a taxi-rank*. **2** a person's position according to importance *etc*: *He was promoted to the rank of sergeant*; *a police officer of very high rank*; *Doctors belong to the higher ranks of society*. — *v* to place or be placed according to importance *etc*: *Apes rank above dogs in intelligence*.

rank and file 1 ordinary people. **2** ordinary soldiers, not officers.

ransack /'ransak/ *v* **1** to search thoroughly: *She ransacked the whole house for her keys.* **2** to take goods from places by force: *The army ransacked the conquered city.*

ransom /'ransəm/ *n* a sum of money *etc* paid for the freeing of a prisoner. — *v* to pay money *etc* to free someone.

hold to ransom to keep someone as a prisoner until a ransom is paid: *Their son was held to ransom for three days.*

rant /rant/ *v* to talk in a loud, angry way: *He ranted on and on for hours.*

rap /rap/ *n* a quick knock; a sharp tap: *He heard a rap on the door.* — *v* to hit sharply: *He rapped on the table and called for silence.*

rap out to say sharply: *He rapped out a command.*

rape /reɪp/ *v* to force a person to have sexual intercourse against their will. — *n* the crime of doing this. **'rapist** *n*.

rapid /'rapɪd/ *adj* quick; fast: *rapid progress*; *a rapid heart-beat*. **'rapidly** *adv*. **ra'pidity** *n*.

'rapids *n* a place in a river where the water flows very fast, usually over and between dangerous rocks.

rapture /'raptʃə(r)/ *n* great delight.

rare /rɛə(r)/ *adj* **1** not found very often; unusual: *a rare flower*; *An eclipse of the sun is a rare event*. **2** not cooked for very long: *a rare steak*.

'rarely *adv* not often: *I rarely go to bed before midnight*.

> **rarely** means the same as **seldom**: *The baby rarely (or seldom) cries*.
> **scarcely** means the same as **hardly**. See **scarcely**.

raring /'rɛərɪŋ/: **raring to go** eager to start.

rarity /'rɛərɪtɪ/ *n* **1** being rare: *Their rarity has given them a special value*. **2** something that is rare: *This stamp is a rarity*.

rascal /'rɑːskəl/ *n* a naughty person, especially a child: *a cheeky little rascal*; *That shop is run by a pack of rascals*.

rash[1] /raʃ/ *adj* foolishly hasty; not thinking carefully before acting: *a rash person*; *It was rash of you to leave your present job without first finding another*. **'rashly** *adv*. **'rashness** *n*.

rash[2] /raʃ/ *n* a large number of red spots on the skin: *That child has a rash — is it measles?*

rasher /'raʃə(r)/ *n* a thin slice of bacon or ham.

rasp /rɑːsp/ *v* to make a harsh, scraping sound: *'Where's your commonsense?' he rasped*. — *n* a harsh, scraping sound: *the rasp of a file on wood*.

raspberry /'rɑːzbərɪ/ *n* a small, soft, red berry: *raspberry jam*.

rat /rat/ *n* a small animal with a long tail, like a mouse but larger.

rat race the continual competition for success at work, and wealth: *He decided to leave the rat race and go on a round-the-world cruise for a year*.

rate /reɪt/ *n* **1** the number of occasions within a certain period of time when something happens: *There is a high accident rate in the factory*. **2** the number or amount of something in relation to a total: *There was a failure rate of one pupil in ten in the exam*. **3** the speed with which something happens or is done: *He works at a very fast rate*. **4** the level of pay, cost *etc* for a particular job *etc*: *What is the rate of pay for this job?* — *v* to value; to regard: *I don't rate this book very highly*.

at any rate used before making what you have just said clearer or more accurate: *I don't think they saw the joke — at any rate, they didn't laugh*.

rather /'rɑːðə(r)/ *adv* **1** to a certain extent; slightly; a little: *He's rather nice*; *That's a rather silly question*; *She's rather a pretty girl*. **2** more willingly; preferably: *I'd rather do it now than later*; *Can we do it now rather than tomorrow?*; *Wouldn't you rather have the red one than the blue one?* **3** more exactly; more correctly: *He agreed, or rather he didn't disagree*; *You might say he was foolish rather than wicked*.

ratify /'ratɪfaɪ/ *v* to agree formally to accept:

All of the countries have now ratified the treaty. **ratifi'cation** *n.*

ratio /'reɪʃɪəʊ/, plural **ratios**, *n* the proportion of one thing compared to another: *There is a ratio of two girls to one boy in this class.*

ration /'raʃən/ *n* a measured amount of food *etc* allowed during a particular period of time: *The soldiers were each given a ration of food for the day.* — *v* to allow only a certain amount of food *etc* to a person or animal during a particular period of time: *During the oil shortage, petrol was rationed.*

rational /'raʃənəl/ *adj* **1** able to think, reason and judge *etc*: *Man is a rational animal.* **2** sensible; reasonable: *There must be a rational explanation for those strange noises.*

> The opposite of **rational** is **irrational**.

rattle /'ratəl/ *v* to make a series of short, sharp noises by knocking together: *The cups rattled as he carried the tray in.* — *n* **1** a rattling noise: *the rattle of cups.* **2** a child's toy that makes a noise of this sort: *The baby waved its rattle.*

'rattlesnake *n* a poisonous American snake with bony rings in its tail which rattle.

rattle off to say something quickly without having to think: *He rattled off his classmates' names for the teacher.*

raucous /'rɔːkəs/ *adj* rough, harsh and usually loud: *a raucous laugh.*

ravage /'ravɪdʒ/ *v* to plunder and destroy land *etc.*

rave /reɪv/ *v* **1** to talk wildly as if you are mad. **2** to talk very eagerly: *He's raving about this new record he's heard.*

raven /'reɪvən/ *n* a large black bird of the crow family.

raven

ravenous /'ravənəs/ *adj* very hungry: *The children were ravenous after playing football all afternoon.* **'ravenously** *adv.*

ravine /rə'viːn/ *n* deep narrow valley.

ravishing /'ravɪʃɪŋ/ *adj* beautiful: *She looks ravishing tonight.*

raw /rɔː/ *adj* **1** not cooked: *raw meat.* **2** in the natural state, before going through a manufacturing process: *raw cotton; What raw materials are used to make plastic?*

ray /reɪ/ *n* **1** a narrow beam of light, heat *etc*: *the sun's rays; X-rays; a ray of light.* **2** a small amount: *a ray of hope.*

rayon /'reɪɒn/ *n* a kind of artificial silk.

raze /reɪz/ *v* to destroy a city *etc* completely.

razor /'reɪzə(r)/ *n* an instrument with a sharp blade or electrically-powered cutters used for shaving hair from your skin.

reach /riːtʃ/ *v* **1** to arrive at a place: *We'll never reach London before dark; The noise reached our ears; Have they reached an agreement yet?* **2** to touch or get hold of something: *My keys have fallen down this hole and I can't reach them.* **3** to stretch out your hand in order to touch or get hold of something: *He reached across the table for another cake; She reached out and took the book.* **4** to make contact with someone: *If anything happens you can always reach me by phone.* **5** to extend: *The school playingfields reach from here to the river.* — *n* **1** a distance that can be travelled easily: *My house is within reach of London.* **2** the distance you can stretch your arm: *I keep medicines on the top shelf, out of the children's reach; My keys are down that hole, just out of reach.*

> **reach** is followed by the destination: *They reached Venice at noon.*
> **arrive** is used with **at** or **in**.
> See **arrive**.

react /rɪ'akt/ *v* to behave in a certain way as a result of something: *How did he react when you called him a fool?; He reacted angrily to the criticism; Hydrogen reacts with oxygen to form water.*

re'action *n* **1** the way a person reacts to something: *What was his reaction to your remarks?* **2** a process of change that occurs when two or more substances are put together: *a chemical reaction between iron and acid.*

re'actionary *adj* against change and progress and in favour of a return to a former system: *a politician with reactionary views.* — *n.*

re'actor *n* an apparatus in which nuclear energy is produced.

read /riːd/ *v* **1** to look at and understand words or other signs: *The children are learning to read and write French and English; I like reading adventure stories; Read as much as* *you can*; *to read music.* **2** to learn something by reading: *I read in the paper today that the government is going to increase taxes.* **3** to read aloud, usually to someone else: *I always read my daughter a story before she goes to bed*; *Parents ought to read more to their children.* **4** to study a subject at a university: *She is reading mathematics at London University.* **5** to look at what is recorded on an instrument *etc*; to record an amount, temperature *etc*: *The thermometer read 34° Celsius*; *The nurse read the thermometer.* **6** to be worded; to say: *His letter reads as follows: 'Dear Sir,...'.* — *n* an interesting and enjoyable author or book: *I'm looking for a good read to take on holiday.*

> read; read /rɛd/; read /rɛd/: *She read the story aloud*; *Have you read any good books lately?*

'**readable** *adj* **1** pleasant to read: *a readable book.* **2** able to be read: *Your writing is scarcely readable.*

'**reader** *n* **1** a person who reads a lot of books, magazines *etc*: *He's a keen reader.* **2** a person who reads a particular newspaper, magazine *etc*: *The editor asked readers to write to him with their opinions.* **3** a reading-book: *an English reader.*

read between the lines to understand something, for example in a letter, that is not actually written there.

read into to see some extra meaning in something that is said or done: *You're reading too much into his refusal.*

read on to continue to read: *He paused for a few moments, and then read on.*

read out to read aloud: *Read out the answers to the questions.*

read over, **read through** to read from beginning to end: *I'll read through your composition, and let you know if I find any mistakes.*

read up to learn about a subject by reading books about it: *to read up a subject.*

readily /'rɛdɪlɪ/ *adv* **1** willingly: *I'll readily help you.* **2** without difficulty: *I can readily answer all your questions.*

reading /'riːdɪŋ/ *n* **1** the ability to read: *Billie is very good at reading.* **2** the figure, measurement, temperature *etc* shown on an instrument *etc*: *The reading on the thermometer was 40°.*

readjust /riːə'dʒʌst/ *v* to get used to something again: *He found it difficult to readjust to home life after months in prison.* **read'justment** *n*.

ready /'rɛdɪ/ *adj* **1** prepared; able to be used *etc* immediately or when needed; able to do something immediately or when necessary: *I've packed our cases, so we're ready to leave*; *Is tea ready yet?*; *Your coat has been cleaned and is ready to be collected.* **2** willing: *I'm always ready to help.* **3** quick: *You're too ready to find faults in other people*; *He always has a ready answer.* **4** likely; about to do something: *My head feels as if it's ready to burst.* '**readiness** *n*.

ready-'made or **ready-to-'wear** *adjs* made in standard sizes, and for sale to anyone rather than made for one particular person: *a ready-made suit*; *ready-to-wear clothes.*

real /rɪəl/ *adj* **1** actually existing: *There's a real monster in that cave.* **2** not artificial; genuine: *real leather*; *Is that diamond real?* **3** actual: *He may own the factory, but it's his manager who is the real boss.* **4** great: *a real surprise*; *a real problem.*

'**realism** *n* the style of art that aims to show things as they really are.

'**realist** *n* someone who sees a situation as it really is and deals with it in a practical way: *He is a realist and knows that he has to work hard in order to pass his exams.*

rea'listic *adj* **1** showing or seeing things as they really are: *a realistic painting*; *You won't get all your clothes into that case — be realistic!* **2** not real, but appearing to be real: *realistic sound effects.* **realistically** /rɪə'lɪstɪklɪ/ *adv*.

reality /rɪ'alɪtɪ/ *n* that which is real and not imaginary: *We were glad to get back to reality after hearing the ghost story.*

in reality really; actually: *John said he liked the food, but in reality it was terrible.*

realize /'rɪəlaɪz/ *v* **1** to know; to understand: *I realize that I can't have everything I want*; *I realized my mistake.* **2** to make real; to make something come true: *He realized his ambition to become an astronaut.* **reali'zation** *n*.

really /'rɪəlɪ/ *adv* **1** in fact; actually: *He looks stupid but he's really very clever.* **2** very: *That's a really nice dress!* **3** used to express surprise *etc*: *'Mr Davis is going to be the next manager.' 'Oh, really?'*; *Really! You mustn't be so rude!*

realm /rɛlm/ *n* **1** a kingdom. **2** an area of activity, interest *etc*: *She's well-known in the realm of sport.*

reap /riːp/ v to cut and gather: *The farmer is reaping the wheat.*
'reaper n a person or machine that reaps.
reappear /riːəˈpɪə(r)/ v to appear again: *The boy disappeared behind the wall, and reappeared a few yards away.* **reapˈpearance** n.

> to **reappear** (not **reappear again**).

rear¹ /rɪə(r)/ n **1** the back part of something: *There is a bathroom at the rear of the house.* **2** your bottom: *He sits on his rear all day doing nothing.* — adj positioned behind: *the rear wheels of the car.*
rear-view mirror a mirror on a vehicle's windscreen which allows the driver to see traffic behind them: *She looked into her rear-view mirror before turning right.*
bring up the rear to be the last one in a line of people moving together.
rear² /rɪə(r)/ v **1** to feed and care for a family, animals *etc* while they grow up: *She has reared six children; He rears cattle.* **2** to rise up on the hind legs: *The horse reared in fright as the car passed.* **3** to raise: *The snake reared its head.*
rear up to rear: *the horse reared up.*
rearrange /riːəˈreɪndʒ/ v to arrange differently: *We'll rearrange the chairs.* **rearˈrangement** n.
reason /ˈriːzən/ n **1** the cause of, or explanation for, an event or happening: *What is the reason for this noise?; What is your reason for going to London?; The reason I am going is that I want to.* **2** the power of your mind to think, form opinions *etc*: *Only humans have the power of reason — animals have not.* — v **1** to be able to think, form opinions *etc*: *Humans have the ability to reason.* **2** to argue; to work out after some thought: *She reasoned that if he had caught the 6.30 p.m. train, he would be home by 8.00.*

> A **reason** explains why you do something: *What was your reason for dismissing him?*
> A **cause** makes something happen: *Greed is often a cause of war.*

'reasonable adj **1** sensible: *a reasonable suggestion.* **2** willing to listen to argument; acting with good sense: *You can't expect me to do all this work — be reasonable!.* **3** fair; correct; acceptable: *Is £10 a reasonable price for this book?* **4** satisfactory; as much as you might expect or want: *There were a reasonable number of people at the meeting.*
'reasonably adv: *He behaved very reasonably; The car is reasonably priced; The meeting was reasonably well attended.*
'reasoning n the process of thinking that helps you to reach a decision or conclusion: *What made you change your mind? Explain your reasoning step by step.*
lose your reason to become insane; to go mad.
reason with to argue with someone; to persuade someone to be more sensible: *We reasoned with Jim for hours, but he still refused to talk to her.*
reassemble /riːəˈsɛmbəl/ v **1** to put things together after taking them apart: *The mechanic took the engine to pieces, then reassembled it.* **2** to come together again: *The pupils thought about the problem separately, and reassembled to discuss it together.*
reassure /riːəˈʃʊə(r)/ v to take away your doubts or fears about something: *I reassured him that everyone liked his poem.*
reasˈsurance n **1** the reassuring of someone: *I'm only asking for a little reassurance.* **2** something you say *etc* to reassure someone: *In spite of the doctor's reassurances, she was still worried.*
reasˈsuring adj: *the doctor's reassuring remarks.* **reasˈsuringly** adv.
rebate /ˈriːbeɪt/ n a return of part of a sum of money paid: *He was given a tax rebate.*
rebel n /ˈrɛbəl/ **1** someone who fights against people in authority, for example a government: *The rebels killed many soldiers.* **2** someone who does not accept the rules of normal behaviour *etc*: *My son is a bit of a rebel.* — adj: *rebel troops.* — v /rɪˈbɛl/ to fight against people in authority: *The people rebelled against the king.*

> The noun **'rebel** has the accent on the first half of the word; the verb **reˈbel** has the accent on the second half.

rebellion /rɪˈbɛljən/ n **1** an open or armed fight against a government *etc*. **2** a refusal to obey orders or to accept rules *etc*.
reˈbellious v rebelling or likely to rebel: *rebellious troops.* **reˈbelliously** adv. **reˈbelliousness** n.
rebound /rɪˈbaʊnd/ v **1** to bounce or spring back: *The ball rebounded off the wall.* **2** to have a bad effect on the person performing the action: *The lies he told rebounded on him in the end.*

on the rebound /ˈriːbaʊnd/ while still recovering from an emotional shock, especially the end of a love affair: *She agreed to marry him on the rebound.*

rebuff /rɪˈbʌf/ *v* to reject or refuse unkindly: *He rebuffed her offer of help.* — *n*: *My offer met with a rebuff.*

rebuke /rɪˈbjuːk/ *v* to speak severely to someone because they have done wrong; to scold: *The boy was rebuked by his teacher for cheating.* — *n*: *She got a rebuke from her mother for coming home late.*

recall /rɪˈkɔːl/ *v* **1** to order someone to return: *He had been recalled to hospital.* **2** to remember: *I don't recall when I last saw him.* — *n* **1** an order to return: *the recall of soldiers to duty.* **2** /ˈriːkɔːl/ the ability to remember.

See **remember**.

recap /ˈriːkap/ *v* to mention something again to remind people of it: *Let's recap the main points that we've covered so far.*

recapture /riːˈkaptʃə(r)/ *v* to capture again: *The soldiers recaptured the city*; *The prisoners were recaptured.* — *n*: *The recapture of the town.*

recede /rɪˈsiːd/ *v* to move back: *The floods receded*; *His hair is receding from his forehead.*

receipt /rɪˈsiːt/ *n* **1** the receiving of something: *Please sign this form to acknowledge receipt of the money.* **2** a note saying that money *etc* has been received: *I paid the bill and he gave me a receipt.*

receive /rɪˈsiːv/ *v* **1** to get or be given: *He received a letter*; *They received a good education.* **2** to welcome or greet someone: *They received their guests warmly.* **3** to respond to something that you are told *etc*: *The news was received in silence.*

receive is spelt with **-ei-**.

reˈceiver *n* **1** the part of a telephone that you hold to your ear. **2** an apparatus for receiving radio or television signals. **3** a stereo amplifier with a built-in radio.

recent /ˈriːsənt/ *adj* happening, done *etc* not long ago: *Things have changed in recent weeks*; *recent events.*
ˈrecently *adv*: *He came to see me recently.*

receptacle /rɪˈsɛptɪkəl/ *n* something that is made to put or keep things in; a container: *A dustbin is a receptacle for rubbish.*

reception /rɪˈsɛpʃən/ *n* **1** the receiving of something: *His speech got a good reception.* **2** a formal party: *a wedding reception.* **3** the quality of radio or television signals: *Radio reception is poor in this area.* **4** the part of a hotel, hospital *etc* where visitors enter and are attended to.

reˈceptionist *n* someone in a hotel, office *etc* whose job is to answer the telephone, attend to guests *etc.*

receptive /rɪˈsɛptɪv/ *adj* willing to listen to and accept suggestions and new ideas: *We like to think we are receptive to suggestions from our students.*

recess /rɪˈsɛs/ *n* **1** a part of a room set back from the main part: *We can put the dining-table in the recess.* **2** a period of free time between classes.

recession /rɪˈsɛʃən/ *n* a period when there is a fall in the amount of trade a country does, and a rise in poverty and the number of people who are unemployed: *This country has been in a recession for the past four years*; *a world recession.*

recipe /ˈrɛsɪpɪ/ *n* a set of instructions on how to prepare and cook something: *a recipe for curry.* — *adj*: *a recipe book.*

recipient /rɪˈsɪpɪənt/ *n* someone who receives something: *the recipient of a letter.*

reciprocal /rɪˈsɪprəkəl/ *adj* given by two people, countries *etc*, to each other: *After the end of the war, the two countries made a reciprocal agreement to return all their prisoners.* **reˈciprocally** *adv.*

recital /rɪˈsaɪtəl/ *n* **1** a public performance of music or songs: *a recital of Schubert's songs.* **2** the reciting of something.

recitation /rɛsɪˈteɪʃən/ *n* a poem *etc* which is recited: *a recitation from Shakespeare.*

recite /rɪˈsaɪt/ *v* to repeat aloud from memory: *to recite a poem.*

reckless /ˈrɛkləs/ *adj* very careless; done without any thought of the outcome: *a reckless driver*; *reckless driving.* **ˈrecklessly** *adv.* **ˈrecklessness** *n.*

reckon /ˈrɛkən/ *v* **1** to consider: *He is reckoned to be the best pianist in Britain.* **2** to suppose: *'Is this the house?' 'I reckon so.'* **3** to calculate: *I reckon this will only take a few minutes.*

ˈreckoning *n* calculation; counting: *By my reckoning, we must be about eight kilometres from the town.*

reckon on to expect: *I didn't reckon on the meeting taking so long.*

reckon with to have to deal with: *If you get caught, you'll have the police to reckon with.*

reclaim /rɪˈkleɪm/ *v* **1** to ask for something that you own, that has been found by someone else: *A purse has been found and can be reclaimed at the manager's office.* **2** to make land *etc* suitable to be used for something: *They have built dams and reclaimed farming land from the sea.* **recla'mation** *n*.

recline /rɪ'klaɪn/ *v* to lie back or lie down: *She was reclining on the sofa.*

recluse /rɪ'kluːs/ *n* a person who lives alone and chooses not to see other people: *He has been a recluse since his wife died.* **re'clusive** *adj*.

recognition /rɛkəg'nɪʃən/ *n* the recognizing of someone or something: *They gave the boy a medal in recognition of his courage.*

recognize /'rɛkəgnaɪz/ *v* **1** to see, hear *etc* someone or something *etc* and know who or what they are, because you have seen or heard them before: *I recognized his handwriting*; *I recognized him by his voice.* **2** to admit: *Everyone recognized his skill.* **recog'nizable** *adj*.

recoil /rɪ'kɔɪl/ *v* to move quickly back or away from something or someone because of fear or horror: *He recoiled from the dentist's drill*; *She recoiled at the sight of the dead animal.*

recollect /rɛkə'lɛkt/ *v* to remember: *I can't recollect exactly what he said.*

See **remember**.

recol'lection *n* **1** the power of remembering. **2** something that is remembered: *My book is called 'Recollections of Childhood'.*

recommend /rɛkə'mɛnd/ *v* **1** to advise: *The doctor recommended a long holiday.* **2** to suggest as being particularly good, suitable *etc*: *He recommended her for the job.*

recommend has one **c** and two **m**s.

recommen'dation *n* **1** the recommending of someone or something: *I gave her the job on his recommendation.* **2** something recommended: *The recommendations of the committee.*

reconcile /'rɛkənsaɪl/ *v* **1** to make people become friendly again, for example after they have quarrelled: *Why won't you be reconciled with him?* **2** to bring two or more different aims *etc* into agreement: *The workers want high wages and the bosses want high profits — it's almost impossible to reconcile these two aims.* **3** to make someone accept something: *Her mother didn't want the marriage to take place but she is reconciled to it now.* **reconcili'ation** *n*.

recondition /riːkən'dɪʃən/ *v* to put something in good condition again by cleaning, repairing *etc*.
recon'ditioned *adj*: *a reconditioned television set.*

reconsider /riːkən'sɪdə(r)/ *v* to think about something again and possibly change your opinion, decision *etc*: *Please reconsider your decision to leave the firm.* **reconside'ration** *n*.

reconstruct /riːkən'strʌkt/ *v* to get a picture or idea of something or how something happened by using all the details that are known: *The police reconstructed the crime using the evidence of three witnesses.* **recon'struction** *n*.

record *n* /'rɛkɔːd/ **1** a written report of facts, events *etc*: *historical records*; *I wish to keep a record of everything that is said at this meeting.* **2** a round flat piece of plastic on which music *etc* is recorded: *a record of Beethoven's Sixth Symphony.* **3** the best perfomance so far; something that has never yet been beaten: *He holds the record for the 1000 metres.* **4** the collected facts from the past that are known about someone or something: *This school has a very poor record of success in exams*; *He has a criminal record.* — *adj* /'rɛkɔːd/ better than all previous ones: *a record score.* — *v* /rɪ'kɔːd/ **1** to write a description of something so that it can be read in the future: *The decisions will be recorded in the minutes of the meeting.* **2** to put something on a record or tape so that it can be listened to or watched in the future: *I've recorded the whole concert.* **3** to show a figure *etc* as a reading: *The thermometer recorded 35°C yesterday.*

re'corder *n* **1** a musical wind instrument. **2** an instrument for recording on to tape.

re'cording *n* something recorded on tape, a record *etc*: *This is a recording of Beethoven's Fifth Symphony.*

'record-player *n* a machine that plays records.

in record time very quickly.

set the record straight to tell the truth about something to correct a misunderstanding

recount /rɪ'kaʊnt/ *v* to tell: *He recounted his adventures.*

recover /rɪ'kʌvə(r)/ *v* **1** to become well again; to return to good health *etc*: *He is recovering from a serious illness.* **2** to get back: *The police have recovered the stolen jewels.*

re'covery *n*: *The patient made a good recov-*

...ery after his illness; the recovery of stolen property.

recreation /rɛkrɪ'eɪʃən/ *n* a pleasant activity that you do in your spare time: *I have little time for recreation*; *amusements and recreations*. **recre'ational** *adj*.

recrimination /rɪkrɪmɪ'neɪʃən/ *n* an accusation that you make against a person who has already accused you of something: *There will be recriminations if you accuse him wrongly of theft.*

recruit /rɪ'kruːt/ *n* **1** someone who has just joined the army, air force *etc*. **2** someone who has just joined a club *etc*: *The drama group had two new recruits.* — *v* to get people to join the army, or a club *etc*: *to recruit troops*; *to recruit new members*. **re'cruitment** *n*.

rectangle /'rɛktaŋɡəl/ *n* a flat, four-sided shape with opposite sides equal and all its angles right angles. **rec'tangular** *adj*.

rectify /'rɛktɪfaɪ/ *v* to correct a mistake *etc*: *We shall rectify the error as soon as possible.*

recuperate /rɪ'kuːpəreɪt/ *v* to get better from an illness; to recover. **recuper'ation** *n*.

recur /rɪ'kɜː(r)/ *v* to happen again: *His illness has recurred.*

recurrence /rɪ'kʌrəns/ *n*: *a recurrence of his illness.*

recurrent /rɪ'kʌrənt/ *adj*: *a recurrent illness.*

recycle /riː'saɪkəl/ *v* to put a used substance through a special process so that it can be used again: *Waste paper can be recycled to make brown wrapping paper.*

red /rɛd/ *n* **1** the colour of blood. **2** a colour between red and brown, used about hair, fur *etc*. — *adj*: *red cheeks*; *red lips*; *Her eyes were red with crying*; *A fox has red fur*. **'redness** *n*.

'redden *v* **1** to make or become red: *to redden your lips with lipstick*. **2** to blush: *She reddened as she realized her mistake.*

'reddish *adj* a kind of red colour: *The leaves are thin and reddish underneath.*

Red Indian a North American Indian.

in the red to have spent more money than you have: *The company was thousands of pounds in the red.*

redeem /rɪ'diːm/ *v* **1** to make up for the faults of someone or something: *He was very lazy, but his kindness redeemed him in her opinion.* **2** in religion, to save someone from being punished by God for their sins.

red-handed /rɛd'handɪd/: **catch someone red-handed** to catch someone while they are doing something wrong: *His mother caught him red-handed stealing money from her purse.*

red-hot /rɛd'hɒt/ *adj* glowing red with heat: *red-hot steel.*

re-do /riː'duː/ *v* to do again.

re-do; re-did /riː'dɪd/; **re-done** /riː'dʌn/.

red tape /rɛd'teɪp/ *n* official rules and procedures that seem unnecessary and cause problems and delays.

reduce /rɪ'djuːs/ *v* **1** to make less, smaller *etc*; to decrease: *The shop reduced its prices*; *The train reduced speed*. **2** to lose weight by dieting: *You will have to reduce if you want to get into that dress.* **3** to put into a bad state: *The bombs reduced the city to ruins.* **re'ducible** *adj*.

reduction /rɪ'dʌkʃən/ *n*: *price reductions.*

redundant /rɪ'dʌndənt/ *adj* **1** having lost your job because there isn't enough work left for you to do: *350 men have been made redundant at the shipyard*; *There were angry protests from the redundant workers*. **2** no longer needed; unnecessary: *The old typewriter is now redundant because we have a word-processor.* **re'dundancy** *n*.

reed /riːd/ *n* **1** a tall, stiff stalk of grass growing on wet or marshy ground: *reeds along a riverbank*. **2** a thin piece of cane or metal in certain wind instruments.

reef /riːf/ *n* a line of rocks *etc* just above or below the surface of the sea: *The ship got stuck on a reef.*

reek /riːk/ *v* to smell strongly of something unpleasant: *He reeks of cigarette smoke.* — *n*: *There was a reek of tobacco smoke in the café.*

reel /riːl/ *n* **1** a wheel-shaped or cylinder-shaped object of wood, metal *etc* on which thread, film, fishing-lines *etc* can be wound: *a reel of cotton*; *He changed the reel in the projector*. **2** a lively Scottish, Irish or American dance: *The fiddler played a reel*; *to dance a reel.* — *v* to stagger; to sway; to whirl: *The drunk man reeled along the road*; *My brain was reeling with all the information that he gave me.*

reel off to repeat quickly and easily, without pausing: *He reeled off the list of names.*

re-elect /riːə'lɛkt/ *v* to elect again: *She has been re-elected President.* **re-e'lection** *n*.

re-enter /riː'ɛntə(r)/ *v* to enter again: *The spaceship will re-enter the Earth's atmosphere tomorrow.* **re-entry** /riː'ɛntrɪ/ *n*.

to **re-enter** a room (not **re-enter** a room **again**).

refer /rɪˈfɜː(r)/ *v* **1** to talk or write about something; to mention: *He doesn't like anyone referring to his wooden leg.* **2** to concern; to mean: *What were you referring to when you said that?* **3** to pass on to someone else for a decision *etc*: *The case was referred to a higher law-court.* **4** to use a reference book to find out something: *Refer to a dictionary whenever you can't spell a word.*

referred and **referring** are spelt with **-rr-**.

referee /rɛfəˈriː/ *n* **1** a person who supervises boxing matches and football matches *etc*: *The referee sent two of the players off the field.* **2** someone who is willing to provide a note about your character, ability *etc*, for example when you apply for a new job. — *v* to act as a referee for a match: *to referee a football match.*

reference /ˈrɛfərəns/ *n* **1** a mention: *He made several references to her latest book.* **2** a note about your character, ability *etc*: *Our new secretary had excellent references from her previous employer.* **3** a note in a book *etc* showing where a particular piece of information comes from, or where you can find further information. **4** the act of referring. **5** a reference book.

reference book a book that you look at occasionally for information, for example a dictionary or encyclopaedia.

with reference to about; concerning: *I am writing with reference to your letter of 30 March.*

reference is spelt with **-r-**.

referendum /rɛfəˈrɛndəm/ *n* a vote in which all the people of a country or region are asked to vote for or against an important proposal: *In 1975 the British government held a national referendum on whether or not to stay in the European Community.*

refill *v* /riːˈfɪl/ to fill something again: *He refilled his glass.* — *n* /ˈriːfɪl/ **1** a full container that replaces an empty one: *She put a refill in her pen.* **2** another filling: *He stopped for a refill at the petrol station.*

refine /rɪˈfaɪn/ *v* **1** to make something pure by taking out dirt, waste substances *etc*: *Oil is refined before it is used.* **2** to improve: *We have refined our methods since the work began.*

re'fined *adj* **1** that has been refined: *refined sugar.* **2** having good manners and being very formal: *a very refined young man.*

re'finement *n* slight changes that you make to improve something.

re'finery *n* a place where sugar or oil *etc* is refined: *an oil refinery.*

reflect /rɪˈflɛkt/ *v* **1** to send back light, heat *etc*: *The white sand reflected the sun's heat.* **2** to give an image of something: *She was reflected in the mirror; The lake reflected the mountains.* **3** to express or demonstrate something: *It was an interview that reflected his true political beliefs.* **4** to think carefully: *Give me a minute to reflect.*

re'flecting *adj* able to reflect: *a reflecting surface.*

re'flection *n* **1** the process of sending back light, heat *etc*. **2** an image: *She looked at her reflection in the water.* **3** a thing that expresses or shows something: *His unhappiness is a reflection of his mistakes in life.* **2** thought: *After reflection, I felt I had made the wrong decision.*

re'flector *n* something that reflects light, heat *etc*.

re'flective *adj* thinking deeply: *She had a reflective expression.*

reflex /ˈriːflɛks/ *n* **1** an automatic movement of a part of your body. **2** the ability to react immediately to something sudden and unexpected: *You need good reflexes to drive a car very fast.* — *adj*: *The movement of your leg when your knee is tapped is a reflex action.*

reform /rɪˈfɔːm/ *v* **1** to improve; to remove the faults from something: *to reform the education system.* **2** to give up bad habits, improve your behaviour *etc*: *Alan had tried to reform, but was still a criminal; It's time you reformed your ways.* — *n* the improving of something; an improvement: *Many reforms in education are needed.* **reformation** /rɛfəˈmeɪʃn/ *n*. **re'formed** *adj*.

refrain[1] /rɪˈfreɪn/ *n* a line of words or music repeated regularly in a song; a chorus.

refrain[2] /rɪˈfreɪn/ *v* not to do; to avoid: *Please refrain from smoking.*

refrain is followed by **from**: *Refrain from running in the corridor.*

refresh /rɪˈfrɛʃ/ *v* to give someone new strength and energy; to make someone feel

refrigerator

less hot, tired *etc*: *This glass of cool lemonade will refresh you.*
re'freshing *adj* **1** giving new strength and energy; having a cooling and relaxing effect: *a refreshing drink of cold water.* **2** pleasing and unusual: *It is refreshing to hear a politician speak so honestly.* **re'freshingly** *adv.*
re'freshments *n* food and drink: *Light refreshments are available in the other room.*
refresh someone's memory to remind someone of the facts and details of something.

refrigerator /rɪˈfrɪdʒəreɪtə(r)/ *n* a device like a box or cupboard that keeps food cold (often shortened to **fridge**): *Milk should be kept in the refrigerator.*
re'frigerate *v* to keep food cold: *Meat should be refrigerated.* **refrige'ration** *n.*

refuel /riːˈfjuːəl/ *v* to put more fuel into a car, plane *etc*: *The driver stopped to refuel.*

refuge /ˈrɛfjuːdʒ/ *n* a place that gives shelter or protection from danger, trouble *etc*: *The escaped prisoner found refuge in a church.*
refugee /rɛfjʊˈdʒiː/ *n* someone who seeks shelter, especially in another country, from war, disaster *etc*: *Refugees were pouring into the city.* — *adj*: *a refugee camp.*

refund *v* /riːˈfʌnd/ to pay back: *They refunded the money at once.* — *n* /ˈriːfʌnd/ the paying back of money: *They demanded a refund.*

refurbish /riːˈfɜːbɪʃ/ *v* to clean, decorate and make more modern: *These flats are going to be completely refurbished.* **re'furbishment** *n.*

refusal /rɪˈfjuːzəl/ *n* the act of refusing: *I was surprised at his refusal to help me.*

refuse[1] /rɪˈfjuːz/ *v* **1** not to do what you have been asked, or are expected, to do: *He refused to help me; She refused to believe what I said; When I asked him to leave, he refused.* **2** not to accept: *He refused my offer of help; They refused our invitation; She refused the money.* **3** not to give permission *etc*: *I was refused permission to take a day off.*

refuse[2] /ˈrɛfjuːs/ *n* rubbish.

> **'refuse**, meaning rubbish, has its accent on the first half of the word.

regain /rɪˈɡeɪn/ *v* to get back again: *The champion was beaten in January but regained the title in March.*

regal /ˈriːɡəl/ *adj* like, or suitable for, a king or queen: *She has a regal appearance; regal robes.* **'regally** *adv.*

regalia /rɪˈɡeɪlɪə/ *n* the traditional clothes, ornaments and jewellery which are worn as a sign of authority by a judge, king or queen *etc* on important occasions: *The mayor wore his full regalia.*

regard /rɪˈɡɑːd/ *v* **1** to consider to be: *I regard Jim as a friend.* **2** to think of someone or something as being very good, important *etc*; to respect: *He is very highly regarded by his friends.* **3** to think of something with a particular feeling: *I regard war with horror.* **4** to look at someone or something: *He regarded me over the top of his glasses.* — *n* **1** thought; attention: *He drove without regard for her safety or his own.* **2** sympathy; care; consideration: *He shows no regard for other people.* **3** good opinion; respect: *I hold him in high regard.*

re'garding *prep* about; concerning: *Have you any suggestions regarding this project?*
re'gardless *adj, adv* not thinking or caring about costs, problems, dangers *etc*: *There may be difficulties but I shall carry on regardless.*
re'gards *n* greetings; good wishes: *Give my regards to your mother.*
as regards as far as something is concerned: *As regards the meeting, I am unable to attend.*
with regard to about; concerning: *I have no complaints with regard to his work.*

> **with regards** is sometimes used in ending a letter.

> **with regard to** means 'about'.

regent /ˈriːdʒənt/ *n* a person who governs a country while the king or queen is a child or ill: *Her uncle, the prince regent, ruled until her twenty-first birthday.*

regime /reɪˈʒiːm/ *n* a system of government or a particular government: *a country ruled by a corrupt regime; the Communist regime.*

regiment /ˈrɛdʒɪmənt/ *n* a group of soldiers commanded by a colonel. **regi'mental** *adj.*

region /ˈriːdʒən/ *n* **1** a part of a country, the world *etc*: *Do you know this region well?; in tropical regions.* **2** an area of the body: *in the region of the heart.*
'regional *adj*: *regional dress; regional customs.* **'regionally** *adv.*
in the region of about; around; near: *The cost will be in the region of £200 000.*

register /ˈrɛdʒɪstə(r)/ *n* a book containing a written list, record *etc*: *a school attendance register.* — *v* **1** to write something in a register: *to register the birth of a baby.* **2** to write your name, or have your name written, in a register *etc*: *They registered at the Hilton Hotel.* **3** to show a figure, amount *etc*: *The thermometer registered 25° Celsius.* **regis'tration** *n.*

registration number the set of numbers and letters on the front and back of a vehicle that identify it.

regret /rɪˈgrɛt/ *v* to be sorry about: *I regret my foolish behaviour; I regret to inform you that your application for the job was unsuccessful.* — *n* a feeling of sorrow, or of having done something wrong: *I have no regrets about what I did; I heard the news of his death with deep regret.*

> **regretted** and **regretting** are spelt with two **t**s.

re'gretful *adj* feeling regret: *She felt regretful that she could not see her father before he died.*
re'gretfully *adv* with regret: *Regretfully, we have had to refuse your offer.*
re'grettable *adj*: *a regrettable mistake.*
re'grettably *adv.*

> **regrettable** is spelt with two **t**s.

regular /ˈrɛgjʊlə(r)/ *adj* **1** usual: *Saturday is his regular shopping day.* **2** equal in distance or measurement: *They placed guards at regular intervals round the camp.* **3** even: *Is his pulse regular?* **4** doing the same things at the same time each day *etc*: *a man of regular habits.* **5** frequent: *He's a regular visitor.* **6** permanent; lasting: *He's looking for a regular job.* **7** symmetrical: *A square is a regular figure.* **8** of ordinary size: *I don't want the large size of packet — just give me the regular one.* — *n* someone who regularly goes to the same shop, *etc* as a customer. **regu'larity** *n.*

> The opposite of **regular** is **irregular**.

'regularly *adv*: *He comes here regularly.*
regulate /ˈrɛgjʊleɪt/ *v* **1** to control: *Traffic lights are used to regulate traffic.* **2** to adjust a piece of machinery *etc* so that it works at a certain rate *etc*: *Can you regulate this watch so that it keeps time accurately?*
regu'lation *n* a rule or instruction: *These regulations must be obeyed.* — *adj* made *etc* according to official rules: *envelopes of regulation size.*
rehabilitate /riːəˈbɪlɪteɪt/ *v* **1** to help someone who has been ill or in prison to adapt to a normal life: *She helps rehabilitate elderly people who have been in hospital for a long while.* **2** to accept again someone who has been rejected or criticized for their political beliefs: *an artist whose work was rehabilitated after a thirty year ban by the Soviet regime.* **rehabili'tation** *n* .

rehearsal /rɪˈhɜːsəl/ *n* the rehearsing of a play or performance: *I want the whole cast of the play at tonight's rehearsal.*
dress rehearsal a final rehearsal, wearing costumes.

rehearse /rɪˈhɜːs/ *v* to practise something before performing in front of an audience: *You must rehearse the scene again.*

reign /reɪn/ *n* the time during which a king or queen rules: *in the reign of Queen Victoria.* — *v* **1** to rule, as a king or queen: *The king reigned for forty years.* **2** to be present or exist: *Silence reigned at last.*

> to **reign** (not **rein**) over a kingdom.

reimburse /riːɪmˈbɜːs/ *v* to pay a person money to cover what they have spent on something: *They reimbursed her train fare.*

reincarnation /riːɪŋkɑːˈneɪʃən/ *n* **1** the belief that your soul will be born again in a different body after your death: *Buddhists believe in reincarnation.* **2** a person whose soul has been born again in a different body: *The Dalai Lama is a reincarnation.*

reindeer /ˈreɪndɪə(r)/, *plural* **reindeer**, *n* a large deer of Northern Europe, Asia and America.

reinforce /riːɪnˈfɔːs/ *v* to make something stronger: *This bridge needs to be reinforced.*
rein'forcement *n.*
reinforcements *n* troops added to an army *etc* in order to strengthen it: *The general called for reinforcements.*

reins /reɪnz/ *n* **1** two straps attached to a bridle for guiding a horse. **2** straps fitted round a very small child so that it can be prevented from straying.

> to hold the horse's **reins** (not **reigns**).

rein in to stop or restrain a horse by pulling on the reins.

reinstate /riːɪnˈsteɪt/ *v* to give someone back their previous job or position: *His supporters want him reinstated as Chairman.*

reject *v* /rɪˈdʒɛkt/ to refuse to accept: *She rejected his offer of help.* — *n* /ˈriːdʒɛkt/ something that is rejected because it is faulty *etc.* **re'jection** *n.*

rejoice /rɪ'dʒɔɪs/ v to feel or show great happiness: *They rejoiced at the victory.*

re'joicing n celebration: *There was great rejoicing at the news of John's success.*

relapse v /rɪ'læps/ **1** to become ill again after a period of better health: *The operation made her feel better for a time but she soon relapsed.* **2** to begin to act badly again after a period of better behaviour: *He gave up smoking and started taking more exercise but he soon relapsed into his bad habits.* — n /rɪ'læps/ or /'riːlæps/ a return to bad health or illness after a period of better health: *He suffered a relapse.*

relate /rɪ'leɪt/ v **1** to tell a story *etc*: *He related all that had happened to him.* **2** to be about, concerned or connected with something: *Have you any information relating to the effects of this drug?*

re'lated adj belonging to the same family: *I'm related to him — he's my brother.*

> to be **related to** (not **related with**) someone.

relation /rɪ'leɪʃən/ n **1** someone who belongs to your family either by birth or because of marriage: *uncles, aunts, cousins and other relations.* **2** a connection between facts, events *etc*. **3** (**relations**) contact and communications between people, countries *etc*: *to establish friendly relations.*

re'lationship n **1** the friendship, contact, communications *etc* that exist between people: *He finds it very difficult to form lasting relationships.* **2** the fact that, or the way in which, things are connected: *Is there any relationship between crime and poverty?* **3** being related by birth or because of marriage: *'What is the relationship between you two?' 'We're cousins.'*

in relation to compared with: *At 65, he's quite young in relation to previous Presidents.*

relative /'relətɪv/ n a relation: *All his relatives attended the funeral.* — adj compared with something else, or with a situation in the past *etc*: *the relative speeds of a car and a train; She used to be rich but now lives in relative poverty.*

'relatively adv quite; fairly: *He seems relatively happy now.*

relax /rɪ'læks/ v **1** to make or become less stiff or tight; to make or become less worried *etc*; to rest completely: *The doctor gave him a drug to make him relax; Relax your shoulders; He relaxed his grip on the rope for a second and it was dragged out of his hand.* **2** to make or become less strict: *The rules were relaxed because of the Queen's visit.*

relax'ation n: *I play golf for relaxation.*

relay v /rɪ'leɪ/ to receive and pass on a message, news *etc* by telegraph, radio, television *etc.* — n /'riːleɪ/ the sending of news *etc* by these devices.

relay race a race between teams, in which runners are spaced out along the whole track, and the second runner can start only when the first runner reaches him, and so on.

release /rɪ'liːs/ v **1** to set free; to allow to leave: *He was released from prison yesterday.* **2** to stop holding *etc*; to allow to move, fall *etc*: *He released his hold on the rope.* **3** to move a fastening, brake *etc* that prevents something from moving *etc*: *He released the brake and drove off.* **4** to allow news *etc* to be given to the public: *The list of winners has just been released.* — n: *After his release, the prisoner went home.*

relegate /'relɪgeɪt/ v to put someone or something down to a lower grade or less important position: *The local football team has been relegated to the Second Division.*

relent /rɪ'lent/ v to become less severe or unkind; to agree after refusing at first: *At first she wouldn't let them go to the cinema, but in the end she relented.*

re'lentless adj without pity; not allowing anything to keep you from what you are doing or trying to do: *The police fight a relentless battle against crime.* **re'lentlessly** adv. **re'lentlessness** n.

relevant /'reləvənt/ adj having some connection with what is being discussed *etc*: *Your remarks are interesting but not relevant to the present discussion.* **'relevance** n.

> The opposite of **relevant** is **irrelevant**.

reliable /rɪ'laɪəbəl/ adj **1** able to be depended on or trusted: *Get Lucy to help you — she's very reliable.* **2** likely to be true: *Is this information reliable?* **relia'bility** n. **re'liably** adv.

> The opposite of **reliable** is **unreliable**.

reliance /rɪ'laɪəns/ n dependence on something: *a child's reliance on its parents.*

reliant /rɪ'laɪənt/ adj dependent on someone or something: *The baby is totally reliant on its parents for food, warmth and love.*

relic /'relɪk/ n **1** something left from a past

time: *relics of an ancient civilization.* **2** something connected with a dead person, especially a saint.

relief /rɪ'li:f/ *n* **1** a lessening or stopping of pain, worry *etc*: *He gave a sigh of relief when he had finished his exam; It was a relief to find that nothing had been stolen.* **2** help given to people in need of it: *to send relief to starving people.* **3** someone who takes over a job from someone else after a period of time: *The bus-driver was waiting for his relief.* — *adj*: *A relief fund has been started for the victims of the flood; a relief driver.*

relieve /rɪ'li:v/ *v* **1** to lessen or stop pain, worry *etc*: *The doctor gave him some drugs to relieve the pain; to relieve the hardship of the refugees.* **2** to take over a job or task from someone: *You guard the door first, and I'll relieve you in two hours.* **3** to dismiss someone from their job: *He was relieved of his duties.* **4** to take something heavy, difficult *etc* from someone: *May I relieve you of that heavy case?; He relieved me of the task of writing the letter.*

re'lieved *adj* no longer anxious or worried: *I was relieved to hear you had arrived safely.*

religion /rɪ'lɪdʒən/ *n* **1** a belief in, or the worship of, a god or gods. **2** a particular system of belief or worship: *Christianity and Islam are two different religions.*

re'ligious *adj* **1** concerned with religion: *religious education; a religious leader.* **2** believing in a religion: *a religious man.* **re'ligiously** *adv.* **re'ligiousness** *n.*

relinquish /rɪ'lɪŋkwɪʃ/ *v* to give up: *The king was forced to relinquish control of the country; We shall have to relinquish our plans for a new hall.*

relish /'relɪʃ/ *v* to enjoy greatly: *He relishes his food.* — *n* pleasure; enjoyment: *He ate the food with great relish; I have no relish for such a boring task.*

relive /ri:'lɪv/ *v* to experience something again, especially in your imagination: *I have relived that moment many times.*

reluctant /rɪ'lʌktənt/ *adj* unwilling: *Sue was reluctant to go to school.* **re'luctance** *n.* **re'luctantly** *adv.*

rely /rɪ'laɪ/ *v*: **rely on 1** to depend on: *I am relying on you to help me.* **2** to trust someone to do something; to be certain that something will happen: *We can rely on Mary to keep a secret; John should get here soon, but we can't rely on it.*

remain /rɪ'meɪn/ *v* **1** to be left: *Little remained of the house after the fire.* **2** to stay; not to leave: *I shall remain here.* **3** to continue to be: *The problem remains unsolved.*

to **remain** or **stay** behind when the rest have gone.
to **stay** (not **remain**) with someone for a holiday.

re'mainder *n* the amount or number that is left when the rest has gone, been done or taken away *etc*: *The remainder of the work will be done tomorrow; If you divide 10 by 3, what is the remainder?*

re'mains *n* what is left after part has been taken away, eaten, destroyed *etc*: *The remains of the picnic were lying all over the grass.*

remains has no singular form.

remand /rɪ'mɑ:nd/: **on remand** having appeared in court and be waiting for trial, either in prison or at home on bail: *Some prisoners spend months in prison on remand before their trial.*

remark /rɪ'mɑ:k/ *n* a comment; something said: *The chairman made a few remarks, then introduced the speaker.* — *v* to say; to comment: *He remarked on the time; 'It's late,' he remarked; He remarked that it was late.*

re'markable *adj* unusual; worth mentioning; extraordinary: *What a remarkable thing to happen; She's a remarkable person.*

re'markably *adv*: *Their replies were remarkably similar.*

remedial /rɪ'mi:dɪəl/ *adj* intended to help or cure: *She does remedial work with the less clever children; remedial exercises.*

remedy /'remədɪ/ *n* a cure for an illness or something bad: *I know a good remedy for toothache.* — *v* to put right: *These mistakes can be remedied.*

remember /rɪ'membə(r)/ *v* **1** to keep something in your mind, or to bring it back into your mind after forgetting it for a time: *I remember you — we met three years ago; I remember watching the first men landing on the moon; Remember to telephone me tonight; I don't remember where I hid it.* **2** to pass on good wishes from one person to another: *Please remember me to your mother.*

remind

> **recall** and **recollect** mean the same as **remember**: *I cannot remember* (or *recall* or *recollect*) *her name*.
> **remember** also means to keep in your mind: *Remember to switch off the television*; *Remember that he's only three*.
> **remind** means to make someone remember: *He reminded me of my appointment*.
>
> I remember **meeting** (not **to have met**) him.

re'membrance *n* remembering or reminding: *The pupils gave their teacher a photograph in remembrance of his work with them.*

remind /rɪ'maɪnd/ *v* **1** to tell someone that they ought to do, remember *etc* something: *Remind me to post that letter*; *She reminded me of my promise.* **2** to make someone remember or think of someone or something: *She reminds me of her sister*; *This food reminds me of my schooldays.*

> See **remember**.

re'minder *n* something that reminds you to do something: *Leave the bill on the table as a reminder that I still have to pay it.*

reminisce /rɛmɪ'nɪs/ *v* to talk or write about things that you remember from your past: *The old lady enjoyed reminiscing about her youth.*

reminiscence /rɛmɪ'nɪsəns/ *n* something that you remember from your past, and tell people about: *The children listened attentively to their grandfather's reminiscences about his childhood.*

remi'niscent *adj* **1** reminding you of someone or something, because of some similarity: *Her voice was reminiscent of her grandmother's*; *The drink had a taste reminiscent of mangos.* **2** talking or thinking about the past: *He was in a reminiscent mood.*

remiss /rɪ'mɪs/ *adj* careless or having failed to do something which you should have done: *It was very remiss of me not to invite him to my party.*

remnant /'rɛmnənt/ *n* a small piece, amount or a small number that is left over from a larger piece, amount or number: *The shop is selling remnants of cloth at half price.*

remonstrate /'rɛmənstreɪt/ *v* to protest to someone or argue with them: *He remonstrated with the manager about the poor quality of the food in the restaurant.*

remorse /rɪ'mɔːs/ *n* regret for something bad you have done; pity: *The murderer seemed to feel no remorse.* **re'morseful** *adj.* **re'morsefully** *adv.*

re'morseless *adj* cruel; having no pity: *a remorseless tyrant.*

remote /rɪ'məʊt/ *adj* **1** far away in time or place; far from any other village, town *etc*: *a remote village in New South Wales*; *a farmhouse remote from the city.* **2** distantly related: *a remote cousin.* **3** very small or slight: *a remote chance of success.* **4** unfriendly: *She seemed rather remote.* **re'motely** *adv.* **re'moteness** *n.*

remote control the control of a switch, model or machine *etc* from a distance using radio or electrical signals: *The model ship is guided by remote control.*

removable /rɪ'muːvəbəl/ *adj* able to be separated or removed: *a removable collar.*

removal /rɪ'muːvəl/ *n* **1** the removing of something: *the removal of a stain.* **2** moving house; moving furniture to a new house: *Our removal takes place on Monday*; *furniture removal.*

remove /rɪ'muːv/ *v* **1** to take away: *Will someone please remove all this rubbish!*; *I can't remove this stain from my shirt.* **2** to take off a piece of clothing: *Please remove your hat.* **3** to move to a new house *etc*: *He has removed to London.*

> to **move** (not **remove**) house.

render /'rɛndə(r)/ *v* **1** to cause someone or something to become; to make: *His rude remark rendered her speechless with astonishment.* **2** an old word for give: *She was quick to render assistance to the injured man.*

rendezvous /'rɒndeɪvuː/ or /'rɒndɪvuː/, *plural* **rendezvous** /'rɒndeɪvuːz/, *n* an arrangement, or a place, for meeting someone: *We had arranged a rendezvous for 10.30 a.m.*; *Our rendezvous was the coffee-bar.*

renegade /'rɛnəgeɪd/ *n* a person who leaves the political or religious group to which they belong and joins an enemy or rival group: *a renegade from the other political party*; *a renegade priest.*

renew /rɪ'njuː/ *v* **1** to begin, do *etc* again: *He renewed his efforts to escape.* **2** to pay for a licence *etc* to be continued: *My television licence has to be renewed in October.* **3** to make something new or fresh: *I've renewed all the cushion covers.* **re'newable** *adj.* **re'newal** *n.*

> to **renew** your licence (not **renew** your licence **again**).

renounce /rɪ'naʊns/ v to say you will no longer do, be involved in or believe in something: *The terrorists must renounce violence before we can discuss peace.* **renunciation** /rɪnʌnsɪ'eɪʃən/ n.

renovate /'rɛnəveɪt/ v to make as good as new again: *to renovate an old building.* **reno'vation** n.

renown /rɪ'naʊn/ n fame.

re'nowned adj famous: *a renowned actress.*

a **renowned** (not **renown**) musician.

rent /rɛnt/ n money paid, usually regularly, for the use of a house, shop, land etc that belongs to someone else: *The rent for this flat is £50 a week.* — v to pay or receive rent for the use of a house, shop, land etc: *We rent this flat from Mr Smith; Mr Smith rents this flat to us.*

See also **let**.

'rental n **1** money paid as rent. **2** the act of renting.

rent out to allow people to use a house etc that you own in exchange for money.

renunciation see **renounce**.

repaid see **repay**.

repair /rɪ'pɛə(r)/ v **1** to mend; to put back into good condition: *to repair a torn jacket.* **2** to put right; to make up for: *Nothing can repair the harm done by his cruelty.* — n **1** the repairing of something damaged or broken: *I put my car into the garage for repairs; The bridge is under repair.* **2** a condition; a state: *The road is in bad repair; The house is in a good state of repair.*

re'pairable adj able to be mended.

re'pairman n a man who repairs things.

in good repair, in bad repair in good or bad condition

reparable /'rɛpərəbəl/ adj able to be put right.

repay /rɪ'peɪ/ v to pay back: *When are you going to repay the money you borrowed?; I must find a way of repaying his kindness; How can I repay him for his kindness?* **re'payment** n.

re'pay; repaid /rɪ'peɪd/; **re'paid**.

repeal /rɪ'piːl/ v to make a law etc no longer valid: *Parliament voted to repeal the law on capital punishment.* — n the act of repealing a law etc: *He campaigned for the repeal of the law.*

repeat /rɪ'piːt/ v **1** to say or do again: *Would you repeat those instructions, please?* **2** to tell someone something that you have been told by someone else: *Please do not repeat what I've just told you.* **3** to recite something you have learnt by heart: *to repeat a poem.* — n something that is repeated: *I'm tired of seeing all these repeats on television.* — adj: *a repeat performance.*

to **repeat** the lesson (not **repeat** the lesson **again**).

re'peated adj said, done etc many times: *In spite of repeated warnings, he went on smoking.*

re'peatedly adv many times: *I've asked him repeatedly to tidy his room.*

repeat yourself to repeat what you have already said: *Listen carefully because I don't want to have to repeat myself.*

repel /rɪ'pɛl/ v **1** to resist or fight an enemy successfully: *to repel invaders.* **2** to cause a feeling of disgust: *She was repelled by his dirty appearance.* **3** to force something to move away: *Oil repels water.*

repellant /rɪ'pɛlənt/ n a chemical substance used to keep something away: *a mosquito repellant.* — adj causing a strong feeling of disgust: *The thought of an afternoon with him was deeply repellant to me.*

repent /rɪ'pɛnt/ v **1** to be sorry for your past sins. **2** to wish that you had not done something: *He repented of his selfish behaviour.* **re'pentance** n. **re'pentant** adj.

repercussion /riːpə'kʌʃən/ n a usually bad and unexpected result or effect: *I didn't realize that the decision would have so many serious repercussions.*

repertoire /'rɛpətwɑː(r)/ n a list of songs, plays or operas etc that a performer or singer can perform: *His repertoire includes all of the baritone parts in Mozart's operas.*

repetition /rɛpə'tɪʃən/ n the repeating of something: *After many repetitions, he got the words right.*

repetitive /rɪ'pɛtɪtɪv/ adj doing or saying the same thing too often: *a repetitive job.*

replace /rɪ'pleɪs/ v **1** to put something new in place of something old or damaged: *I must replace that broken lock; He replaced the cup he broke with a new one.* **2** to take someone's place: *She has replaced him as manager.* **3** to put something back where it was: *Please replace the books on the shelves.* **re'placeable** adj.

See **substitute**.

re'placement n: *I broke your cup — here's a replacement.*

replay *v* /riːˈpleɪ/ **1** to play a sports match *etc* again: *The semi-final will be replayed next week*. **2** to play again something that has been recorded: *press this button to replay the tape*. — *n* /ˈriːpleɪ/ **1** a sports match that is played again. **2** an incident in a sports match *etc* that is shown again on television, immediately after it first happened: *You must watch the action replay to see where exactly the ball landed*.

replica /ˈrɛplɪkə/ *n* an exact copy, especially of a work of art: *The real statue is in New York — this one is only a replica*.

reply /rɪˈplaɪ/ *v* to answer: *'I don't know,' he replied*; *Should I reply to his letter?* — *n* an answer: *I'll write a reply to his letter*; *What did he say in reply to your question?*

to **reply to** a letter (not **reply** a letter).

report /rɪˈpɔːt/ *n* **1** a description of what has been said, seen, done *etc*: *a school report*; *a police report on the accident*. **2** a loud noise, especially of a gun being fired. — *v* **1** to give a description of what has been said, seen, done *etc*: *A serious accident has been reported*; *His speech was reported in the newspaper*. **2** to make a complaint about someone to someone in authority: *The boy was reported to the headmaster for being rude to a teacher*. **3** to tell someone in authority about something: *He reported the theft to the police*. **4** to announce that you are present and ready for work *etc*: *The boys were ordered to report to the police-station every Saturday afternoon*; *Report to me when you return*; *How many policemen reported for duty?*

reˈporter *n* someone who writes articles and reports for a newspaper: *Reporters and photographers rushed to the scene of the fire*.

repose /rɪˈpəʊz/ *n* rest; calm; peacefulness.

represent /rɛprɪˈzɛnt/ *v* **1** to speak or act on behalf of others: *You have been chosen to represent us at the conference*. **2** to stand for something: *This black dot on the map represents the fort*. **3** to be a good example of; to show: *What he said represents the feelings of many people*. **represenˈtation** *n*.

repreˈsentative *adj* typical: *We need opinions from a representative group of people*. — *n* **1** someone who represents a business; a travelling salesman: *Our representative will call on you this afternoon*. **2** a person who represents a person or group of people: *A Member of Parliament is the representative of the people who elect him*.

repress /rɪˈprɛs/ *v* to hold back; to stop: *He repressed his tears*; *She repressed a desire to hit the naughty boy*. **reˈpression** *n*. **reˈpressive** *adj*.

reprieve /rɪˈpriːv/ *v* to pardon a criminal or to delay the punishment: *The murderer was sentenced to death, but later reprieved*. — *n* **1** an order that reprieves a criminal: *The murderer was granted a reprieve*. **2** a delay before something very bad happens: *The workers have had a reprieve — the factory is not going to close down next month after all*.

reprimand /ˈrɛprɪmɑːnd/ *v* to speak angrily or severely to someone because they have done wrong; to scold: *The head-teacher reprimanded the boy for his behaviour*. — *n*: *He was given a severe reprimand*.

reprisal /rɪˈpraɪzəl/ *n* something bad that you do to someone who has done something bad to you: *The attack was a reprisal for the enemy's attack the previous day*.

reproach /rɪˈprəʊtʃ/ *v* to scold in a gentle way; to rebuke: *She reproached me for not telling her about my problems*. — *n*: *a look of reproach*.

reˈproachful *adj* showing or expressing reproach: *a reproachful look*. **reˈproachfully** *adv*.

reproduce /riːprəˈdjuːs/ *v* **1** to make a copy of; to produce again; to copy: *to reproduce documents*; *Jim could reproduce the teacher's voice exactly*. **2** to produce babies, seeds *etc*: *How do fish reproduce?*

reproduction /riːprəˈdʌkʃən/ *n* **1** the process of reproducing: *He is studying reproduction in rabbits*. **2** a copy: *These paintings are all reproductions*.

reproductive /riːprəˈdʌktɪv/ *adj* concerned with reproduction: *the reproductive organs of a rabbit*.

reproof /rɪˈpruːf/ *n* a scolding; a rebuke: *He got a reproof from the teacher for being lazy*; *She gave them a stern glance of reproof*.

reprove /rɪˈpruːv/ *v* to scold: *The teacher reproved the boys for coming late to school*.

reptile /ˈrɛptaɪl/ *n* a cold-blooded animal of the group to which snakes, lizards, crocodiles *etc* belong. **reptilian** /rɛpˈtɪlɪən/ *adj*.

republic /rɪˈpʌblɪk/ *n* a country that is governed by representatives elected by the people, and has no king or queen: *the Republic of Ireland*.

repudiate /rɪˈpjuːdɪeɪt/ *v* to refuse to accept; to refuse to accept; to reject: *She repudiated everything the politician said*.

reptiles

cobra

alligator

crocodile

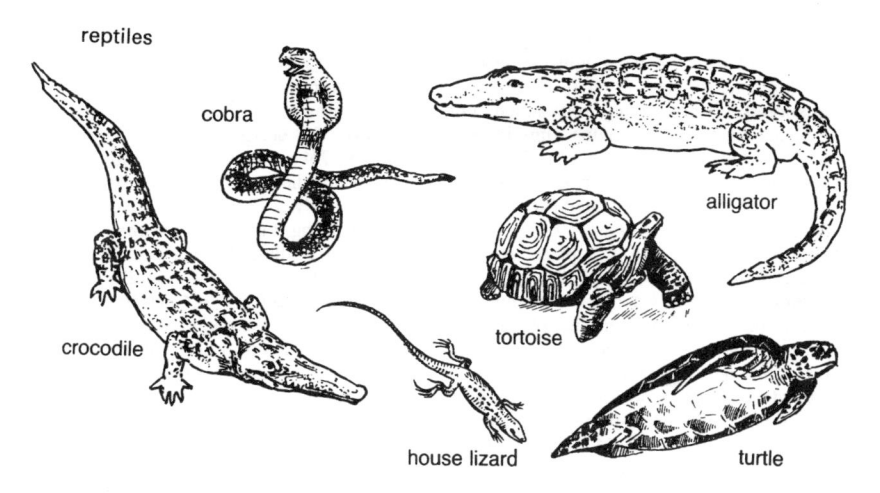

tortoise

house lizard

turtle

repulse /rɪˈpʌls/ v **1** to reject; to refuse in an unfriendly way: *He repulsed their offers of friendship.* **2** to fight an enemy and force them to retreat: *The army repulsed the invading forces.* — n: *The invaders suffered a repulse after crossing the border.*

reˈpulsive adj horrible; disgusting: *What a repulsive smell!* **reˈpulsively** adv. **reˈpulsiveness** n.

reputable /ˈrɛpjʊtəbəl/ adj having a good reputation: *a reputable firm.*

reputation /rɛpjʊˈteɪʃən/ n the opinion that people have about someone or something: *That firm has a bad reputation; He has made a reputation for himself as an expert in computers.*

reputed /rɪˈpjuːtɪd/ adj having a particular reputation: *He is reputed to be very wealthy.* **reˈputedly** adv.

request /rɪˈkwɛst/ n **1** a polite demand: *I did that at his request.* **2** something asked for: *The next record I will play is a request.* — v to ask politely: *People using this library are requested not to talk.*

by request because you are asked to: *I'm singing this next song by request.*

on request when requested: *Buses stop here only on request.*

require /rɪˈkwaɪə(r)/ v **1** to need: *Is there anything you require?* **2** to ask or order someone to do something: *You are required by law to send your children to school.*

reˈquirement n something that is needed, asked for, ordered *etc*: *Our firm will be able to supply all your requirements.*

rescue /ˈrɛskjuː/ v to save: *The lifeboat was sent out to rescue the sailors from the sinking ship.* — n: *After his rescue, the climber was taken to hospital; They came quickly to our rescue.* **ˈrescuer** n.

research n /rɪˈsɜːtʃ/ or /ˈriːsɜːtʃ/ a close and careful study to find out new facts or information: *He is working on cancer research.* — adj: *a research student.* — v /rɪˈsɜːtʃ/: *What subject are you researching?* **reˈsearcher** n.

resemblance /rɪˈzɛmbləns/ n a likeness: *I can see some resemblance between him and his father.*

resemble /rɪˈzɛmbəl/ v to be like; to look like: *He doesn't resemble either of his parents.*

resent /rɪˈzɛnt/ v to feel annoyed about something because you think it is unfair, insulting *etc*: *I resent his interference in my affairs.* **reˈsentment** n.

reˈsentful adj feeling annoyed in this way: *She feels resentful that her sister married before she did.* **reˈsentfully** adv.

reservation /rɛzəˈveɪʃən/ n **1** the reserving of something: *the reservation of a room; to make a reservation at a restaurant; a hotel reservation.* **2** a doubt.

reserve /rɪˈzɜːv/ v **1** to ask for something to be kept for the use of a particular person: *The restaurant is usually busy, so I'll phone up today and reserve a table.* **2** to keep something for the use of a particular person or group of people *etc*: *These seats are reserved for the committee members.* — n **1** something that is kept for use when needed: *The farmer kept a reserve of food in case he was cut off by floods.* **2** a piece of land used for a special purpose: *a wild-life reserve; a* *nature reserve.* **3** the habit of not saying very much, not showing what you are feeling, thinking *etc*; shyness.

re'served *adj* not saying very much; not showing what you are feeling, thinking *etc*: *a reserved manner.*

reservoir /'rɛzəvwɑː(r)/ *n* a place, usually a man-made lake, where water for drinking *etc* is stored.

reside /rɪ'zaɪd/ *v* to live in a place: *He now resides in a suburb of Stockholm.*

residence /'rɛzɪdəns/ *n* **1** a person's home; the grand house of someone important: *the Prime Minister's residence.* **2** living in a place: *during his residence in Spain.*

resident /'rɛzɪdənt/ *n* someone who lives or has their home in a particular place: *a resident of London.* — *adj* **1** living in a place: *He is now resident in Taiwan.* **2** living in the place where you work: *a resident caretaker.*
resi'dential *adj* containing houses rather than offices, shops *etc*: *This district is mainly residential.*

residue /'rɛzɪdjuː/ *n* something that is left over: *the residue of a meal.* **residual** /rɪ'zɪdjʊəl/ *adj.*

resign /rɪ'zaɪn/ *v* **1** to leave a job *etc*: *He resigned from his post.* **2** to make yourself accept something with patience and calmness: *He has resigned himself to the possibility that he may never walk again.*
resignation /rɛzɪg'neɪʃən/ *n.*

resilient /rɪ'zɪlɪənt/ *adj* able to recover quickly from bad luck, illness *etc*: *The company was so strong and resilient it was virtually unaffected by the recession.* **re'silience** *n.*

resin /'rɛzɪn/ *n* a sticky substance produced by certain trees, such as pines and firs, used in making plastics: *a factory which produces synthetic resin.*

resist /rɪ'zɪst/ *v* **1** to fight against: *to resist an attack; It's hard to resist temptation.* **2** to be able to stop yourself doing, taking *etc* something: *I couldn't resist laughing at his dirty face; I can't resist strawberries.* **3** to be unaffected or undamaged by something: *a metal that resists acids.*
re'sistance *n* **1** fighting against something: *The rebel army met with strong resistance from government troops; resistance to temptation; resistance to disease.* **2** the force that one object, substance *etc* exerts against the movement of another object *etc.*
re'sistant *adj*: *This breed of cattle is resistant to disease.*

resolute /'rɛzəluːt/ *adj* determined; not willing to give up: *a resolute attitude; She remained resolute in spite of difficulties.*

resolution /rɛzə'luːʃən/ *n* **1** a firm decision to do something: *He made a resolution to get up early.* **2** a decision made by a group of people: *They passed a resolution to ban smoking.* **3** the quality of being resolute.

resolve /rɪ'sɒlv/ *v* **1** to make a firm decision to do something: *I've resolved to work harder.* **2** to pass a resolution: *They resolved to ban smoking.* **3** to get rid of a problem *etc*: *to resolve a difficulty.* — *n* **1** determination to do what you have decided to do: *He showed great resolve.* **2** a firm decision: *It is his firm resolve to become a doctor.*
re'solved *adj* determined: *I am resolved to go and nothing will stop me.*

resonant /'rɛzənənt/ *adj* **1** echoing, or producing echoing sounds: *Many big churches are very resonant inside.* **2** with a ringing quality which makes it deep, strong: *a resonant voice.* **'resonance** *n.*

resort /rɪ'zɔːt/ *v* to use something as a way of solving a problem: *He resorted to threats when they refused to give him money.* — *n* a place visited by many people, especially for holidays: *Brighton is a popular resort.*

as a last resort or **in the last resort** only because all other ways have failed: *We could ask our parents to lend us the money as a last resort.*

resound /rɪ'zaʊnd/ *v* **1** to ring or echo: *The audience's cheers resounded through the building; Her fame resounded through the town.* **2** to be filled with sound: *The hall resounded with the sound of her footsteps.*
re'sounding *adj* **1** ringing and echoing: *resounding cheers.* **2** very great or clear: *a resounding victory.*

resource /rɪ'zɔːs/ *n* **1** (**resources**) something that gives help, support *etc* when needed; a supply; a means: *We have used up all our resources; We haven't the resources at this school for teaching handicapped children.* **2** (**resources**) the wealth of a country, or the supply of materials *etc* which bring this wealth: *This country is rich in natural resources.* **3** the ability to find ways of solving difficulties: *He is full of resource.*
re'sourceful *adj* good at finding ways of solving difficulties, problems *etc.* **re'sourcefully** *adv.* **re'sourcefulness** *n.*

respect /rɪ'spɛkt/ *n* **1** admiration; good opinion: *He is held in great respect by everyone.* **2** consideration; thoughtfulness; willingness to obey *etc*: *He shows no respect for* *his parents.* **3** a particular detail, feature *etc*: *John is very like Chris in some respects.* — *v* **1** to admire someone: *I respect you for what you did.* **2** to show consideration for someone *etc*; to be willing to obey someone: *You ought to respect your teacher; You should respect other people's feelings.*

re'spectable *adj* **1** having a good reputation or character: *a respectable family.* 2 correct; acceptable: *respectable behaviour.* **3** good enough, or suitable, to wear: *You can't go out in those torn trousers — they're not respectable.* **4** large, good *etc* enough; fairly large, good *etc*: *Four goals is a respectable score.* **re'spectably** *adv.* **respecta'bility** *n.*
re'spectful *adj*: *respectful pupils.* **re'spectfully** *adv.* **re'spectfulness** *n.*

re'specting *prep* about: *Joan said nothing respecting her new job.*

re'spective *adj* belonging to each person or thing; own: *Peter and George went to their respective homes.*

re'spectively *adv* referring to each person or thing in order: *Peter, James and John were first, second and third respectively.*

re'spects *n* greetings: *He sends his respects to you.*

pay your respects to visit someone out of politeness: *I can't stay long but I must just pay my respects to your mother.*

with respect to about; concerning: *With respect to your request, we regret that we are unable to assist you in this matter.*

respiration /rɛspəˈreɪʃən/ *n* breathing: *The process of breathing in and out is called respiration.*

'respirator *n* **1** a kind of mask that someone, such as a fireman or soldier, wears over the mouth and nose in order to be able to breathe when in a smoke-filled room or when surrounded by poisonous gas. **2** a device that is used to help very ill or injured people to breathe when they cannot breathe naturally.

'respiratory *adj* having to do with breathing: *the human respiratory system.*

respite /ˈrɛspaɪt or /ˈrɛspɪt/ *n* a short period of rest from something difficult or unpleasant: *The pain continued without respite for about two hours.*

respond /rɪˈspɒnd/ *v* **1** to answer: *He didn't respond to my question.* **2** to show a good reaction: *His illness did not respond to treatment by drugs.*

response /rɪˈspɒns/ *n* a reply; a reaction: *Our letters have met with no response.*

responsibility /rɪspɒnsɪˈbɪlɪtɪ/ *n* **1** something that someone has to look after, do *etc*: *He takes his responsibilities very seriously.* **2** having important duties: *a position of responsibility.* **3** being the cause of something: *The police have no doubt about his responsibility for the accident.*

re'sponsible *adj* **1** having a duty to see that something is done *etc*: *We'll make one person responsible for buying the food.* **2** having many duties: *The job of manager is a very responsible post.* **3** being the cause of something: *Who is responsible for the stain on the carpet?* **4** able to be trusted; sensible: *We need a responsible person for this job.*

re'sponsibly *adv* in a sensible way: *Do try to behave responsibly.*

responsive /rɪˈspɒnsɪv/ *adj* reacting quickly in a suitable and positive way: *The disease is responsive to treatment.* **re'sponsively** *adv.* **re'sponsiveness** *n.*

rest[1] /rɛst/ *n* **1** a break after or between periods of work; a period of freedom from worries or work *etc*: *Digging the garden is hard work — let's stop for a rest; Let's have a rest; Take a rest; I need a rest from all these problems — I'm going to take a week's holiday.* **2** sleep: *He needs a good night's rest.* **3** something which holds or supports something: *a bookrest.* **4** a state of not moving: *The machine is at rest.* — *v* **1** to stop working *etc* in order to get new strength: *Stop and rest a minute; Stop reading and rest your eyes; Let's rest our legs.* **2** to sleep; to lie quietly: *Mother is resting at the moment.* **3** to lean against something: *Her head rested on his shoulder.* **4** to stay fixed: *Her gaze rested on the jewels.* **5** to be calm *etc*: *I will never rest until I know he is happy.* **6** to depend on something: *Our hopes now rest on him, since all else has failed.* **7** to belong to: *The choice rests with you.*

come to rest to stop moving: *The ball came to rest under a tree.*

rest[2] /rɛst/: **the rest 1** what is left when part of something is taken away, finished *etc*: *the rest of the meal.* **2** all the other people, things *etc*: *Jack went home, but the rest of us went to the cinema.*

restaurant /ˈrɛstərɒnt/ *n* a place where meals may be bought and eaten.

> The pronunciation of **restaurant** is /ˈrɛstərɒnt/.

restful /ˈrɛstfəl/ *adj* **1** bringing rest: *a restful* *holiday.* **2** making you feel calm: *Some people find blue a restful colour.* **3** peaceful; calm: *The patient seems more restful now.* **'restfully** *adv.* **'restfulness** *n.*

restless /'rɛstləs/ *adj* **1** always moving; showing signs of worry, boredom, impatience *etc*: *a restless child; He's been doing the same job for years now and he's beginning to get restless.* **2** without sleep: *a restless night.* **'restlessly** *adv.* **'restlessness** *n.*

restore /rɪ'stɔː(r)/ *v* **1** to repair something so that it looks as it used to. **2** to bring back to a normal or healthy state: *The patient was soon restored to health.* **3** to bring or give back: *to restore law and order; The police restored the stolen cars to their owners.* **resto'ration** *n.*

restrain /rɪ'streɪn/ *v* to prevent someone from doing something; to control: *He was so angry he could hardly restrain himself; He had to be restrained from hitting the man; He restrained his anger with difficulty.*

restraint /rɪ'streɪnt/ *n* **1** a control that prevents you from doing something: *There are certain legal restraints which limit our freedom.* **2** being able to keep your anger in control: *She showed a lot of restraint not to fight back.*

restrict /rɪ'strɪkt/ *v* to limit: *Use of the television is restricted to senior pupils; Living in a city restricts a child's freedom.*

re'striction *n*: *There are certain restrictions on what you may wear to school.*

result /rɪ'zʌlt/ *n* **1** anything that is due to something already done: *His deafness is the result of a car accident; He went deaf as a result of an accident; He tried a new method, with excellent results.* **2** the answer to a sum *etc*: *Add all these figures and tell me the result.* **3** the final score: *What was the result of Saturday's match?* **4** the list of people who have been successful in a competition; the list of subjects a person has passed or failed in an examination *etc*: *He had very good exam results; The results will be published next week.* — *v* **1** to be caused by something: *We will pay for any damage that results from our experiments.* **2** to have as a result: *The match resulted in a draw.*

resume /rɪ'zjuːm/ *v* to begin again after stopping: *We'll resume the meeting after tea.* **resumption** /rɪ'zʌmpʃən/ *n.*

resurgence /rɪ'sɜːdʒəns/ *n* a return to action, growth, importance or influence *etc* after a period of quietness: *There has been a resurgence in nationalistic feelings in parts of Europe during the past two years.*

resurrect /rɛzə'rɛkt/ *v* to bring something back into use or existence after it has been unused or forgotten for some time: *They have resurrected the old idea of building a supermarket here.*

resur'rection *n* the process of being brought back to life again after death.

resuscitate /rɪ'sʌsɪteɪt/ *v* to bring or come back to consciousness: *The lifeguard managed to resuscitate her even though she had been under the water for several minutes.* **resusci'tation** *n.*

retail /'riːteɪl/ *v* to sell goods to a customer in a shop *etc*, not to a businessman *etc* who is going to sell them again. — *adj* having to do with the sale of goods in shops *etc*: *a retail price.*

'retailer *n* a shopkeeper.

retain /rɪ'teɪn/ *v* **1** to remember: *He finds it difficult to retain information.* **2** to keep: *These plates don't retain heat very well.* **retention** *n.*

retaliate /rɪ'tælieɪt/ *v* to do something bad to someone in return for something bad they have done to you: *Peter kicked Sarah, and she retaliated by pulling his hair.* **retali'ation** *n.*

retard /rɪ'tɑːd/ *v* to make slower: *The train's progress was retarded by snow; The baby's development was retarded by an accident.*

re'tarded *adj* slow in learning: *a retarded child.*

retention *see* **retain**.

rethink /riː'θɪŋk/ *v* to think of ways to change something: *The government is having to rethink its economic policy.*

> **re'think; rethought** /riː'θɔːt/; **re'thought**

reticent /'rɛtɪsənt/ *adj* not willing to say very much about oneself or ones feelings: *She is always very reticent with people she hasn't known very long.*

retina /'rɛtɪnə/, *plural* **retinas** or **retinae** /'rɛtɪniː/, *n* the lining at the back of the eye which receives the image from the lens and passes it on to the brain.

retire /rɪ'taɪə(r)/ *v* **1** stop working when you reach a particular age: *He retired at the age of 65.* **2** to go away: *to retire to bed; to retire to your own room.*

re'tired *adj* having stopped working: *a retired teacher.*

re'tirement *n* retiring from work; being

retired from work: *It is not long till his retirement*; *She's enjoying her retirement.*

re'tiring *adj* shy: *a retiring person.*

retort /rɪ'tɔːt/ *v* to make a quick and clever or angry reply: *'You're too old,' she said. 'You're not so young yourself,' he retorted.* — *n* a reply of this type.

retrace /rɪ'treɪs/: **retrace your steps** to go back over the route that you have come along: *He lost his keys somewhere on his way home, and had to retrace his steps until he found them.*

retract /rɪ'trakt/ *v* to say that you did not mean something that you said before: *The minister retracted his comments when he was interviewed this morning.*

retreat /rɪ'triːt/ *v* **1** to move back or away from a battle, usually because the enemy is winning: *Our army was forced to retreat.* **2** to withdraw; to take yourself away: *He retreated to his room.* — *n* **1** the action of retreating: *After their retreat, the enemy troops left the area.* **2** a quiet, private place: *They spent the weekend at their mountain retreat.*

retribution /rɛtrɪ'bjuːʃən/ *n* the punishment someone deserves: *The public is demanding retribution for recent terrorist attacks.*

retrieve /rɪ'triːv/ *v* to get back something that was lost *etc*: *My hat blew away, but I managed to retrieve it*; *Our team retrieved its lead in the second half.* **re'trieval** *n*.

re'triever *n* a dog trained to find and bring back birds and animals that have been shot.

retrospective /rɛtrə'spɛktɪv/ *adj* applying to the past as well as to the present and future: *a retrospective law.*

return /rɪ'tɜːn/ *v* **1** to come back; to go back: *He returned to London from Paris yesterday*; *The pain has returned*; *We'll return to this subject later in the lesson.* **2** to give, send or put something back where it came from: *He returned the book to its shelf*; *Please return my umbrella.* **3** to do something to someone that they have done to you: *She hit him and he returned the blow.* **4** in tennis *etc*, to hit a ball back to your opponent: *She returned his serve.* — *n* **1** returning; home-coming: *They were looking forward to their son's return from his holiday abroad*; *On our return, we found the house had been burgled.* **2** a return ticket: *Do you want a single or return?* — *adj*: *a return journey.*

to **return** (not **return back**) someone's book.

return ticket a ticket allowing you to travel to a place and back again.

by return of post by the next post: *Please send me your reply by return of post.*

in return for as an exchange for something: *He sent me flowers in return for my help.*

many happy returns an expression of good wishes said to you on your birthday: *He visited his mother on her birthday to wish her many happy returns.*

reunion /riː'juːnjən/ *n* a meeting of people who have not met for some time: *We attended a reunion of former pupils of our school.*

reunite /riːjuː'naɪt/ *v* to bring or come together after being separated: *The children were reunited with their parents.*

rev /rɛv/: **rev up** to make an engine run faster, especially when the car *etc* is not moving: *I was woken by the sound of a car revving up in the street outside.*

reveal /rɪ'viːl/ *v* **1** to make something known: *All their secrets have been revealed.* **2** to show; to allow to be seen: *The curtains opened to reveal an empty stage.* **re'vealing** *adj*.

revel /'rɛvəl/: **revel in** to enjoy something very much: *The children revelled in all the excitement.*

revelation /rɛvə'leɪʃən/ *n* the revealing of a secret *etc*; a discovery of facts: *amazing revelations.*

revenge /rɪ'vɛndʒ/ *n* harm done to someone in return for harm that they have done to you: *I'll get my revenge on you somehow*; *Jim took his revenge on Susan for laughing at him by hiding a frog in her desk*; *In revenge, she stole his pen*; *She did it out of revenge.* — *v* to get your revenge: *He revenged himself on his enemies*; *I'll soon be revenged on you all.*

See **avenge**.

revenue /'rɛvɪnjuː/ *n* the money that a government receives: *Most of the government's revenue comes from income tax.*

reverberate /rɪ'vɜːbəreɪt/ *v* **1** to echo, repeat or reflect many times: *The sound of banging reverberated through the room.* **2** to be heard continually: *The scandal reverberated through the town.* **3** to have an effect which lasts a long time: *The consequences of his decision will reverberate for years.*

revere /rɪ'vɪə(r)/ *v* to respect greatly: *The students all revered their teacher.*

'reverence *n* great respect: *He was held in reverence by those who worked for him.*

'**Reverend** *n* a title given to a clergyman, usually written **Rev.**: *the Rev. John Brown*.
'**reverent** *adj* showing reverence: *to give reverent thanks to God*. '**reverently** *adv*.

The opposite of **reverent** is **irreverent**.

reversal /rɪˈvɜːsəl/ *n* the changing of something to its opposite: *the reversal of a decision*.
reverse /rɪˈvɜːs/ *v* **1** to move backwards: *He reversed the car into the garage*. **2** to put into the opposite position, order *etc*; to make one thing change places with another: *He reversed the order of the events on the programme*. **3** to change something to the exact opposite: *to reverse a decision*. — *n* **1** the opposite: *'Are you hungry?' 'Quite the reverse — I've eaten far too much!'* **2** a defeat; a piece of bad luck. **3** a backwards direction; the gear in a car that makes it go backwards: *He put the car into reverse*. **4** the back of a coin, medal *etc*: *the reverse of a coin*. — *adj*: *I hold the reverse opinion to yours*; *She put the car into reverse gear*; *the reverse side of a coin*.
re'versible *adj* **1** able to be reversed: *permanent damage that isn't reversible*. **2** able to be worn with either side out: *Is that raincoat reversible?*

the opposite of **reversible** is **irreversible**.

revert /rɪˈvɜːt/ *v* to go back to a previous state or position: *The land will revert to its natural state if it is not farmed*.
review /rɪˈvjuː/ *n* **1** the act of examining something to decide if any changes are necessary: *The whole system is under review*. **2** a report about a book, play *etc* giving an opinion of it. — *v* **1** to consider again: *We shall review the situation in a month's time*. **2** to write a review of a book *etc*: *The book was reviewed in yesterday's newspaper*.
re'viewer *n* a person who reviews books *etc*.
revise /rɪˈvaɪz/ *v* **1** to correct faults and make improvements in a book *etc*: *This dictionary has been completely revised*. **2** to study your previous work, notes *etc* in preparation for an examination *etc*: *You'd better start revising your English for your exam*. **3** to change: *to revise your opinion*. **revision** *n*.
revive /rɪˈvaɪv/ *v* **1** to come, or bring, back to consciousness, strength, health *etc*: *They attempted to revive the woman who had fainted*; *She soon revived*; *The flowers revived in water*; *to revive someone's hopes*. **2** to come or bring back to use *etc*: *This old custom has recently been revived*. **re'vival** *n*.
revoke /rɪˈvəʊk/ *v* to make no longer valid or to cancel: *The ruling did not revoke the teacher's independent authority to administer punishment*.
revolt /rɪˈvəʊlt/ *v* **1** to rebel against a government *etc*: *The army revolted against the king*. **2** to disgust: *His habits revolt me*; *I was revolted by the film about the war*. — *n* rebellion: *The peasants rose in revolt*; *The government have crushed the revolt*.
re'volting *adj* causing a feeling of disgust: *revolting food*.
revolution /ˌrɛvəˈluːʃən/ *n* **1** a complete circle or turn round a central point, made, for example, by a record turning on a record-player, or the Earth moving on its axis or round the Sun. **2** a successful, and usually violent attempt by a group of people within a country to change or overthrow its political system: *The French Revolution of 1789 put an end to the monarchy in France*. **3** a great change in ideas, methods *etc*: *Computers have caused a revolution in the way many people work*.
revo'lutionary *adj* **1** completely new and different: *He discovered a revolutionary process for recording sound*. **2** attempting to cause a political revolution: *He was sent to prison for revolutionary activities*. — *n* a person who takes part in, or tries to cause, a revolution: *The dictator imprisoned the revolutionaries*.
revo'lutionize *v* to cause great changes in ideas, methods *etc*: *This new machinery will revolutionize the paper-making industry*.
revolve /rɪˈvɒlv/ *v* to move, roll or turn in a complete circle around a central point: *A wheel revolves on its axle*; *The Moon revolves round the Earth*; *The Earth revolves about the Sun and also revolves on its axis*.
re'volver *n* a pistol.
re'volving *adj*: *revolving doors*.
revulsion /rɪˈvʌlʃən/ *n* a feeling of disgust.
reward /rɪˈwɔːd/ *n* **1** something given in return for work done, good behaviour *etc*: *They gave him a plant as a reward for his kindness*. **2** a sum of money offered for finding a criminal, or lost property *etc*: *A reward of £100 has been offered to the person who finds the diamond brooch*. — *v* to give a reward to someone for something: *He was rewarded for his services*; *His services were rewarded*.

See **award**.

re'warding *adj* giving satisfaction: *I'm looking for a more rewarding job.*

rewind /rɪ'waɪnd/ *v* to make a tape or film *etc* go backwards: *Now rewind the tape and check your answers.*

> **re'wind**; **rewound** /rɪ'waʊnd/; **re'wound**: *I rewound the film carefully and removed it from my camera*; *Make sure the tape has been fully rewound before you start to listen.*

rewrite /rɪ'raɪt/ *v* to write something again in a different or better way: *I had to rewrite my introduction several times before I was satisfied with it.*

> **re'write**; **rewrote** /rɪ'roʊt/; **rewritten** /rɪ'rɪtən/: *We rewrote the words of the song for a joke*; *The play has been completely rewritten since its first performance.*

rhetoric /'rɛtərɪk/ *n* speech or writing that is intended simply to impress people.

rhetorical question a question that does not require an answer from the reader or listener.

rheumatism /'ruːmətɪzm/ *n* a kind of disease that causes pain in your joints and muscles: *The old lady has rheumatism in her legs and finds it difficult to walk.*

rhino /'raɪnoʊ/, *plural* **rhinos**, *n* short for **rhinoceros**.

rhinoceros /raɪ'nɒsərəs/ *n* a large thick-skinned animal with one or two horns on its nose.

rhombus /'rɒmbəs/ *n* a flat shape with four equal sides, that is not a square.

rhyme /raɪm/ *n* **1** a short poem: *a book of rhymes for children.* **2** a word which is like another in its final sound: *Beef and leaf are rhymes.* **3** verse or poetry using words that rhyme at the ends of the lines: *To amuse the teacher he wrote his composition in rhyme.* — *v* to be rhymes: *Beef rhymes with leaf.*

rhythm /'rɪðəm/ *n* **1** a regular, repeated pattern of sounds in music, poetry *etc*: *Just listen to the rhythm of those drums.* **2** a regular, repeated pattern of movements: *The rowers lost their rhythm.* **3** an ability to sing, move *etc* with rhythm: *That girl has got rhythm.*
'rhythmic or **'rhythmical** *adj* done with rhythm: *rhythmic movement*; *The dancing was very rhythmical.* **'rhythmically** *adv*.

rib /rɪb/ *n* **1** any one of the bones that curve round and forward from your backbone, enclosing your heart and lungs. **2** anything that is similar in shape *etc*: *an umbrella rib*; *the ribs of a boat.*

ribbon /'rɪbən/ *n* a long narrow strip of material used in decorating clothes, tying hair *etc*: *a blue ribbon*; *four metres of red ribbon.*

rice /raɪs/ *n* a plant whose seeds are used as food: *risotto and other rice-based dishes.*

> **rice** is never used in the plural.

rich /rɪtʃ/ *adj* **1** wealthy; having a lot of money, possessions *etc*: *a rich man.* **2** having a lot of something: *This part of the country is rich in coal.* **3** valuable: *a rich reward.* **4** containing a lot of fat, eggs, spices *etc*: *a rich sauce.* **5** very beautiful and expensive: *rich materials.* **'richly** *adv*. **'richness** *n*.
'riches *n* lots of money; wealth: *His riches do not make him a happy man.*

> **riches** means wealth; it has no singular form.
> **the rich** means rich people; the opposite is **the poor**.

rickety /'rɪkəti/ *adj* not well made; likely to collapse; shaky: *This chair is rather rickety.*

rickshaw /'rɪkʃɔː/ *n* a small two-wheeled carriage pulled by a man.

rid *v* to free someone *etc* from something: *We must try to rid the town of rats.*

> **rid; rid; rid**: *He rid himself of his worries*; *She has rid herself of her problems.*

be rid of, **get rid of** to remove; to free yourself from: *I thought I'd never get rid of these weeds.*

good riddance /'rɪdəns/ words you use when you are happy to have got rid of something: *I've thrown out all those old books, and good riddance to the lot of them!*

ridden *see* **ride**.

riddle /'rɪdəl/ *n* a puzzle that describes an object, person *etc* in a mysterious way: *The answer to the riddle 'What flies for ever, and never rests?' is 'the wind'.*

ride /raɪd/ *v* **1** to travel in a car, train or bus: *to ride on a bus.* **2** to travel on and control a horse or bicycle: *Can you ride a bicycle?*; *Which horse is he riding in this race?*; *My daughter goes riding at the riding school every Saturday.* — *n*: *He likes to go for a long bicycle ride on a Sunday afternoon*; *I went for a ride on my horse*; *Would you like* *a ride in my new car?*; *May I have a ride on your bike?*

> **ride; rode** /rood/; **ridden** /'rɪdən/: *John rode five miles on his bicycle*; *He has ridden a horse for several years now.*

'**rider** *n*: *a horse-rider*; *The rider of the motor-cycle was hurt.*

ridge /rɪdʒ/ *n* **1** a long narrow raised piece of ground *etc*: *A plough makes furrows and ridges in the soil.* **2** a long narrow row of hills. **3** the top edge of something where two sloping surfaces meet: *a roof-ridge.*

ridicule /'rɪdɪkjuːl/ *v* to laugh at; to mock: *It's easy to ridicule what can be seen as an old-fashioned attitude.* — *n* laughter at someone or something; mockery: *Despite the ridicule of his neighbours, he continued to build a spaceship in his garden.*

ridiculous /rɪ'dɪkjʊləs/ *adj* very silly; deserving to be laughed at: *You look ridiculous in that hat!* **ri'diculously** *adv*. **ri'diculousness** *n*.

rife /raɪf/ *adj* (used about bad things) very common: *Disease is rife in the refugee camps.*

rifle /'raɪfəl/ *n* a gun with a long barrel, fired from the shoulder. — *v* to search through something: *The thief rifled through the drawers.*

> See **gun**.

rift /rɪft/ *n* **1** a split or crack: *The sun shone briefly through a rift in the clouds.* **2** a bad quarrel between people that makes them stop being friends: *A pact which healed the rift between the two sections of the community.*

rig /rɪg/ *v* **1** to fit a ship with ropes and sails. **2** to dishonestly control or arrange how something happens so that it benefits you: *There were suggestions that the election had been rigged by the winning party.* — *n* **1** an oil-rig. **2** any special equipment, tools *etc* for some purpose. **3** the arrangement of sails *etc* of a sailing-ship.

'**rigging** *n* the ropes *etc* which control a ship's masts and sails.

rig up to build quickly: *They rigged up a shelter.*

right /raɪt/ *adj* **1** on the side of your body that usually has the more skilful hand; to the side of you that is toward the east when you are facing north: *When I'm writing, I hold my pen in my right hand.* **2** correct: *Is that the right answer to the question?*; *Did you get the sum right?*; *Put all the toys back in their right places.* **3** morally correct; good: *It's not right to let thieves keep what they have stolen.* **4** suitable: *He's not the right man for this job.* **4** normal: *Her voice didn't sound quite right on the phone.* — *n* **1** something you ought to be allowed to have, do *etc*: *Everyone has the right to a fair trial*; *You must fight for your rights*; *You have no right to say that.* **2** that which is correct or good: *Who's in the right in this argument?* **3** the right side, part or direction: *Turn to the right*; *Take the second road on the right.* — *adv* **1** exactly: *He was standing right here.* **2** immediately: *I'll go right after lunch.* **3** close: *He was standing right beside me.* **4** completely; all the way: *The bullet went right through his arm.* **5** to the right: *Turn right.* **6** correctly: *Have I done this sum right?* — *v* **1** to bring back to the correct position: *The boat tipped over, but righted itself again.* **2** to correct something that is bad: *to right a wrong.* — used to mean I understand, I'll do what you say *etc*: *'I want you to type some letters for me.' 'Right, I'll do them now.'*

> The opposite of **right**, meaning the side of the body, is **left**.
> The opposite of **right**, meaning correct, is **wrong**.

right angle an angle of 90°, like any of the four angles in a square.

righteous /'raɪtʃəs/ *adj* good: *a righteous man.* '**righteously** *adv*. '**righteousness** *n*.

'**rightful** *adj* proper; having a right to something: *He is the rightful owner of the house.* '**rightfully** *adv*: *The house is rightfully mine.*

'**right-hand** *adj* at the right; to the right: *the top right-hand drawer of my desk*; *Take the right-hand turning.*

right-'handed *adj* using the right hand more easily than the left: *Most people are right-handed.*

'**rightly** *adv* justly: *He was rightly punished for his cruelty.*

right wing the group of people in a political party who have the most conservative views.
right-wing *adj*: *Some right-wing members disagree with this policy.*

> See also **left wing**.

by rights used to suggest what should be the case, although it isn't: *By rights she ought to be sent to prison.*

get right to do something correctly: *Did you get that sum right?*

go right to happen just as you want; to be successful: *Nothing ever goes right for him.*

in the right legally or morally right: *You were in the right and I was in the wrong so I apologize.*

in your own right through your own ability or qualifications, rather than through other people's: *Her husband is famous but she's very talented in her own right.*

not in your right mind, not right in the head mad: *He can't be in his right mind, making stupid suggestions like that!*

put right 1 to repair: *There is something wrong with this kettle — can you put it right?* **2** to change something that is wrong: *You've made a mistake in that sum — you'd better put it right; My watch is slow — I'll have to put it right.* **3** to make someone healthy again: *That medicine will soon put you right.*

right away or **right now** immediately: *You can start right away.*

right of way 1 the right to continue along a road when other traffic must stop: *Who has right of way at this junction?* **2** a public road or path going across private land.

serve someone right to be the punishment deserved by someone: *If you fall and hurt yourself, it'll serve you right for climbing up there when I told you not to.*

within your rights not breaking the law: *You are quite within your rights if you want to make a complaint.*

rigid /'rɪdʒɪd/ *adj* **1** completely stiff; not able to be bent easily: *An iron bar is rigid.* **2** very strict, and not likely to change: *subject to rigid control by central government.* **'rigidly** *adv.*

'rigidness, ri'gidity *ns.*

rigorous /'rɪgərəs/ *adj* **1** strict or harsh: *rigorous discipline.* **2** strictly accurate: *He always pays rigorous attention to detail.* **'rigorously** *adv.*

rim /rɪm/ *n* an edge or border: *the rim of a cup.*

'rimless *adj* without a rim: *rimless spectacles.*

rimmed *adj*: *horn-rimmed spectacles; Her eyes were red-rimmed from crying.*

rind /raɪnd/ *n* a thick, hard outer layer or covering, especially the outer surface of cheese or bacon, or the peel of fruit: *bacon-rind; lemon-rind.*

ring[1] /rɪŋ/ *n* **1** a small circle of gold *etc* that you wear round your finger: *a wedding ring; She wears a diamond ring.* **2** a circle of metal, wood *etc* for any of various purposes: *a scarf-ring; a key-ring; The trap-door had a ring attached for lifting it.* **3** anything that is like a circle in shape: *The children formed a ring round their teacher; The hot teapot left a ring on the polished table.* **4** an enclosed space for boxing matches, circus performances *etc*: *the circus-ring; The crowd cheered as the boxer entered the ring.* — *v* to form a ring round something; to put, draw *etc* a ring round something: *The teacher ringed the mistakes in Joe's composition with a red pen.*

ring[2] /rɪŋ/ *v* **1** to sound: *The doorbell rang; He rang the doorbell; The telephone rang.* **2** to telephone someone: *I'll ring you tonight; He rang his mother up.* **3** to ring a bell, for example in a hotel, to tell someone to come, to bring something *etc*: *She rang for the maid.* **4** to make a high sound like a bell: *The glass rang as she hit it with a metal spoon.* **5** to make a loud, clear sound: *His voice rang through the house; A shot rang out.* — *n* **1** the sound of ringing: *There was a ring at the door.* **2** a telephone call: *I'll give you a ring.*

> **ring; rang** /raŋ/; **rung** /rʌŋ/: *She rang the bell; He has just rung me.*

ring a bell to stir your memory slightly: *His name rings a bell, but I can't remember where I've heard it.*

ring back to telephone someone who has telephoned: *If he is busy at the moment, he can ring me back; He'll ring back tomorrow.*

ring true to sound true: *His story does not ring true.*

ringleader /'rɪŋli:də(r)/ *n* someone who leads others into doing something wrong: *The teacher punished the ringleader.*

ringlet /'rɪŋlɛt/ *n* a long curl of hair.

ringmaster /'rɪŋmɑːstə(r)/ *n* a person who is in charge of performances in a circus ring.

rink /rɪŋk/ *n* **1** an area of ice, for ice-skating, ice hockey *etc*. **2** a smooth floor for roller-skating.

rinse /rɪns/ *v* **1** to wash clothes *etc* in clean water to remove soap *etc*: *After washing the towels, rinse them out.* **2** to clean a cup, your mouth *etc* by filling it with clean water *etc* and then emptying the water out: *The dentist asked me to rinse my mouth out.* — *n* the action of rinsing: *Give the cup a rinse.*

riot /'raɪət/ *n* a noisy disturbance made by a large group of people: *The protest march*

developed into a riot. — *v* to take part in a riot: *The protesters were rioting in the street.*
'rioter *n*.

rip /rɪp/ *v* to tear: *He ripped his shirt on a branch; His shirt ripped; The roof of the car was ripped off in the crash; to rip up floorboards; He ripped open the envelope.* — *n* a tear or hole: *There's a rip in my shirt.*

rip off 1 to remove quickly and often violently: *She ripped the sticking-plaster off his leg.* **2** to cheat or steal from, usually by charging too much: *He always tries to rip his clients off.* **rip-off** *n*.

ripe /raɪp/ *adj* ready to be gathered in or eaten: *ripe corn; ripe apples.* **'ripeness** *n*.
'ripen *v* to make or become ripe: *The sun ripened the corn; The corn ripened in the sun.*

ripple /'rɪpəl/ *n* a little wave or movement on the surface of the water *etc*: *He threw the stone into the pond, and watched the ripples spread across the water.* — *v* to move gently: *The boat glided through the rippling water.*

rise /raɪz/ *v* **1** to become greater, larger, higher *etc*; to increase: *Food prices are still rising; His temperature rose; If the river rises much more, there will be a flood; Bread rises when it is baked.* **2** to move upwards: *Smoke was rising from the chimney; The birds rose into the air.* **3** to get up from bed: *He rises every morning at six o'clock.* **4** to stand up: *The children all rose when the headmaster came in.* **5** to appear above the horizon: *The sun rises in the east and sets in the west.* **6** to slope upwards: *The hills rose in front of us.* **7** to rebel: *The people rose in revolt against the dictator.* **8** to move to a higher rank, a more important position *etc*: *He rose to the rank of colonel.* **9** to begin: *The river Rhône rises in the Alps.* **10** to start to blow hard: *Don't go out in the boat — the wind has risen.* **11** to be built: *Office blocks are rising all over the town.* **12** to come back to life: *Jesus has risen.* — *n* **1** the act of rising: *a rise in prices; He had a rapid rise to power; the rise of Mao Tse-tung.* **2** an increase in salary or wages: *She asked her boss for a rise.* **3** a slope or hill: *The house is just beyond the next rise.*

> **rise; rose** /rəʊz/; **risen:** *He rose from his seat; The sun has risen.*
> The sun **rises in** (not **rises up from**) the east.
> See also **raise**.

'rising *n* the action of rising: *the rising of the sun.* — *adj*: *the rising sun; rising prices.*

give rise to to cause: *This plan has given rise to various problems.*

risk /rɪsk/ *n* danger; possible loss or injury: *He thinks we shouldn't go ahead with the plan because of the risks involved.* — *v* to put something in danger; to leave something to chance: *He would risk his life for his friend; He risked all his money on betting on that horse; He was willing to risk death to save his friend; I'd better leave early as I don't want to risk being late for the play.*
'risky *adj* possibly causing or bringing loss, injury *etc*: *It was a risky strategy, but it worked.*

at risk in danger; likely to suffer loss, injury *etc*: *You mustn't place your family at risk.*

at the risk of with the possibility of loss, injury, trouble *etc*: *He saved the little girl at the risk of his own life; At the risk of shocking you, I must tell you the horrible truth.*

run the risk or **take the risk** to do something which involves a risk: *I took the risk of buying you a ticket for the match — I hope you can come; He didn't want to run the risk of losing his money.*

take risks or **take a risk** to do something which might cause loss, injury *etc*.

rite /raɪt/ *n* a fixed, formal action *etc*, especially one used in a religious ceremony: *The priest performed the usual rites; marriage rites.*

ritual /'rɪtʃʊəl/ *n* **1** a ceremony with a set of fixed actions and words: *Every religion has its own rituals.* **2** a set of actions that people regularly perform in a particular situation: *First thing in the morning, she goes through the ritual of washing her face, cleaning her teeth and brushing her hair.* — *adj* happening as part of a ritual: *a ritual washing of the hands.*

rival /'raɪvəl/ *n* a person or thing that competes with another: *For students of English, this dictionary is without a rival; The two brothers are rivals for the first prize.* — *adj*: *rival teams.* — *v* to be, or try to be, as good as someone or something else: *She could not hope to rival her sister's achievements; Nothing rivals football for excitement and entertainment.*

> **rivalled** and **rivalling** are spelt with 2 **l**s.

'rivalry *n* the state of being rivals: *the rivalry between business companies.*

river /'rɪvə(r)/ *n* a large stream of water flowing across land: *The Thames is a river; the River Thames; the Hudson River.*

'river-bed *n* the ground over which a river runs.

'riverside *n* the ground along or near the side of a river: *He has a bungalow on the riverside.*

rivet /'rɪvɪt/ *n* a bolt for fastening plates of metal together. — *v* **1** to fasten with rivets: *They riveted the sheets of metal together.* **2** to fix firmly: *His eyes were riveted on the television.*

road /rəʊd/ *n* **1** a way with a hard level surface for people, vehicles *etc* to travel on: *This road takes you past the school; Are we on the right road for Brisbane?* **2** used in the names of roads or streets: *His address is 24 School Road.* **3** a way that leads to something: *He's on the road to disaster.*

See **street** and **route**.

'roadblock *n* a barrier put across a road in order to stop or slow down traffic: *The police set up a roadblock.*

'roadside *n* the ground beside a road: *Flowers were growing by the roadside.*

'roadway *n* the part of a road on which cars *etc* travel: *Don't walk on the roadway.*

'roadworks *n* the building or repairing of a road.

by road by car or truck, not by train: *The goods will be sent by road.*

on the road travelling: *We've been on the road since 7 o'clock this morning.*

roam /rəʊm/ *v* to walk about without any fixed plan or purpose; to wander: *He roamed from town to town.*

roar /rɔː(r)/ *v* **1** to give a loud deep cry; to shout: *The lions roared; The general roared his commands.* **2** to laugh loudly: *The audience roared with laughter at the man's jokes.* **3** to make a loud deep sound: *The thunder roared.* **4** to move fast with a loud deep sound: *He roared past on his motorbike.* — *n*: *a roar of laughter; the lion's roars; the roar of traffic.*

'roaring *adj* very good; very great: *The show was a roaring success.*

roast /rəʊst/ *v* to cook or be cooked in an oven, or over a fire *etc*: *to roast a chicken over the fire; The beef was roasting in the oven.* — *adj* roasted: *roast beef.* — *n* meat that has been roasted or is for roasting: *She bought a roast for dinner.*

'roasting *adj* very hot: *It's roasting outside.*

rob /rɒb/ *v* to steal from a person, place *etc*: *He robbed a bank; I've been robbed!*

'robber *n*: *The bank robbers got away with nearly £50 000.*

'robbery *n*: *Robbery is a serious crime*; *He was charged with four robberies.*

to **rob** a bank or a person.
to **steal** a watch, pencil, money *etc*.

robe /rəʊb/ *n* **1 (robes)** long loose clothing: *Many Arabs still wear robes; a judge's robes.* **2** a loose garment: *a bath-robe; a beach-robe.*

robin /'rɒbɪn/ *n* a small bird with a red breast.

robot /'rəʊbɒt/ *n* a machine that works like a human being.

robust /rəʊ'bʌst/ *adj* strong; healthy: *a robust child.*

rock¹ /rɒk/ *n* **1** a large lump or mass of stone: *The ship struck a rock and sank; He built his house on solid rock.* **2** a large stone: *The climber was killed by a falling rock.* **3** a hard sweet made in the shape of a stick.

rock² /rɒk/ *v* **1** to swing gently backwards and forwards or from side to side: *The mother rocked the cradle.* **2** to shake or move violently: *The earthquake rocked the building.*

rock³ /rɒk/ *n* music with a strong beat, often played on electric instruments: *a rock guitarist; She likes rock.* — *adj*: *a rock band.*

'rockery /'rɒkərɪ/ *n* a part of a garden that is built of rocks and soil, where small plants and flowers are grown.

rocket /'rɒkɪt/ *n* **1** a tube containing materials which, when set on fire, give off a jet of gas which drives the tube forward. This kind of device can be used as a firework, for signalling, or for launching a spacecraft. **2** a spacecraft launched in this way: *The Americans have sent a rocket to Mars.* — *v* to rise or increase very quickly: *Bread prices have rocketed.*

rocking-chair /'rɒkɪŋ tʃeə(r)/ *n* a chair that rocks backwards and forwards.

rocking-horse /'rɒkɪŋ hɔːs/ *n* a toy horse that rocks backwards and forwards.

rocky¹ /'rɒkɪ/ *adj* full of rocks: *a rocky coastline.*

rocky² /'rɒkɪ/ *adj* not firm; not steady.

rod /rɒd/ *n* a long thin stick or piece of wood, metal *etc*: *a fishing-rod; a measuring-rod.*

rode *see* **ride**.

rodent /'rəʊdənt/ *n* any of several animals with large front teeth for gnawing, for example squirrels, beavers, rats *etc*.

rodeo /'rəʊdɪəʊ/ or /'rəʊdeɪəʊ/, *plural* **rodeos**, *n* a show or contest of riding *etc* by cowboys.

roe[1] /rəʊ/ *n* the eggs of fish: *cod roe*.
roe[2] /rəʊ/ or **roe deer** /'rəʊdɪə(r)/ *n* a small deer found in Europe and Asia.
rogue /rəʊg/ *n* **1** a dishonest person: *I wouldn't buy a car from a rogue like him.* **2** a mischievous person: *She's a little rogue sometimes.*
role or **rôle** /rəʊl/ *n* **1** a part played by an actor or actress in a play *etc*: *He is playing the rôle of King Lear.* **2** the part played, or job done, by someone: *He played a central role in founding the group.*
roll[1] /rəʊl/ *n* **1** material, for example paper, rolled or wound round a tube *etc*: *a roll of kitchen foil; a toilet-roll.* **2** bread shaped into a small round mass that can be sliced and filled with meat, cheese *etc*: *a cheese roll.* **3** the action of rolling: *Our dog loves a roll on the grass.* **4** a long low sound: *a roll of thunder; a roll of drums.* — *v* **1** to move by turning like a wheel or ball: *The coin rolled under the table; He rolled the ball towards the puppy; The ball rolled away.* **2** to move on wheels, rollers *etc*: *The children rolled the cart up the hill, then let it roll back down again.* **3** to fold up a carpet *etc* into the shape of a tube: *to roll the carpet back.* **4** to turn over: *The dog rolled on to its back; Stop rolling about on that dirty floor!* **5** to shape clay *etc* into a ball by turning it about between your hands: *He rolled the clay into a ball.* **6** to make something flat by rolling something heavy over it: *to roll out pastry.* **7** to rock from side to side while travelling forwards: *The storm made the ship roll.* **8** to make a series of low sounds: *The thunder rolled; The drums rolled.*

roll up 1 to fold up something into a roll: *He rolled up his sleeves.* **2** to arrive: *John rolled up ten minutes late.*
roll[2] /rəʊl/ *n* a list of names, for example of pupils in a school *etc*.

'**roll-call** *n* the calling of names from a list, to find out if anyone is missing, in a school class *etc*.
roller /'rəʊlə(r)/ *n* **1** something shaped like a tube, often used for flattening: *a garden roller; a road-roller.* **2** a small tube-shaped object on which hair is wound to curl it. **3** a long large wave on the sea.
rollercoaster /'rəʊləkəʊstə(r)/ *n* a fairground entertainment in which you ride on a very high, fast railway with bends and curves in it.
roller-skate /'rəʊləskeɪt/ *n* a skate with wheels instead of a blade: *a pair of roller-skates.* — *v* to move on roller-skates.
rolling-pin /'rəʊlɪŋpɪn/ *n* a roller of wood *etc* for flattening out dough.
Roman /'rəʊmən/ *adj* connected with Rome, especially ancient Rome: *Roman coins.* — *n* a person belonging to Rome.

Roman alphabet the alphabet in which Western European languages such as English are written.
Roman Catholic a member of the Christian church that recognizes the Pope as its head. — *adj*: *the Roman Catholic Church.*
Roman numerals I, II, III *etc*, as opposed to the Arabic numerals 1, 2, 3 *etc*.
romance /'rəʊmæns/ or /rə'mæns/ *n* **1** the relationship between people who are in love: *It was a beautiful romance, but it didn't last.* **2** a story about a relationship like this: *She writes romances.*

romantic *adj* **1** about people who are in love: *a romantic novel.* **2** having to do with love; causing feelings of love: *romantic music; a romantic mood.* **romantically** /rəʊ'mæntɪklɪ/ or /rə'mæntɪklɪ/ *adv*.
ro'manticize *v* to make something seem happier, more exciting or interesting than it really is.
romp /rɒmp/ *v* to play in a lively way: *The children and their dog were romping about on the grass.* — *n*: *The children had a romp in the grass.*
roof /ru:f/, *plural* **roofs**, *n* the top covering of a building *etc*: *a flat roof; the roof of a car.* — *v* to put a roof on a building: *to roof a new house.*

roof rack a metal frame on the roof of a car for carrying luggage *etc*.
rook /rʊk/ *n* **1** a large black bird of the crow family. **2** a chess-piece (also called a **castle**).
room /ru:m/ *n* **1** one part of a house or building: *This house has six rooms; a bedroom; a dining-room.* **2** space: *The bed takes up a lot of room; There's no room for a piano; We'll move the bookcase to make room for the television.*

See **place**.

-roomed: *a four-roomed house.*
'**room-mate** *n* another student *etc* with whom you share a room in a hostel *etc*.
room service the serving of food and drinks to a hotel guest in their room: *He rang for room service and ordered a cup of coffee.*
'**roomy** *adj* having plenty of space: *roomy cupboards.*

roost /ru:st/ *n* a branch *etc* on which a bird rests at night.

'rooster *n* a farmyard cock.

root[1] /ru:t/ *n* **1** the part of a plant that grows under the ground and draws food and water from the soil: *Trees often have deep roots.* **2** the base of something growing in the body: *the roots of your hair; The root of this tooth is infected.* **3** cause; origin: *Love of money is the root of all evil; We must get at the root of the trouble.* **4** family history and background: *He left his roots and moved to the city.* — *v* to grow roots: *These plants aren't rooting very well.*

root beer a kind of non-alcoholic drink made from the roots of certain plants.

root crop plants with roots that are grown for food, such as carrots or turnips.

root out 1 to pull up or tear out by the roots: *The gardener began to root out the weeds.* **2** to get rid of something completely: *We must do our best to root out poverty.*

take root to grow strong roots: *The plants took root and grew well.*

root[2] /ru:t/ *v* to poke about; to search about: *The pigs were rooting about for food.*

rope /roʊp/ *n* a thick cord, made by twisting together lengths of hemp, nylon *etc*: *He tied the two vehicles together with a rope; a skipping rope.* — *v* to tie with a rope: *He roped the cases to the roof of the car.*

rope-'ladder *n* a ladder made with wooden rungs linked together with rope.

rope in to include: *We roped Julie in to help with the concert.*

rope off to separate or divide with a rope: *The police roped off the part of the street where the bomb exploded.*

rosary /'roʊzərɪ/ *n* a group of prayers counted on a string of beads, used by Roman Catholics.

rose[1] see **rise**.

rose[2] /roʊz/ *n* **1** a brightly-coloured flower, often with a sweet scent, growing on a bush with sharp thorns. **2** a pink colour.

rosette /roʊ'zɛt/ *n* a circular badge made of coloured ribbon: *He wore a green rosette to show that he was supporting the team which was playing in the green shirts.*

roster /'rɒstə(r)/ *n* a rota.

rostrum /'rɒstrəm/ *n* a platform for a speaker or the conductor of an orchestra to stand on: *The audience clapped as the conductor mounted the rostrum.*

See **stage**.

rosy /'roʊzɪ/ *adj* **1** rose-coloured; pink: *rosy cheeks.* **2** bright; hopeful: *His future looks rosy.*

rot /rɒt/ *v* to make or become bad or decayed: *The fruit is rotting on the ground; Water rots wood.* — *n* **1** decay: *The floorboards are affected by rot.* **2** nonsense: *Don't talk rot!*

rota /'roʊtə/, *plural* **rotas**, *n* a list of jobs or duties and the names of the people who take turns doing them: *She kept a rota of the children's chores in the kitchen.*

rotary /'roʊtərɪ/ *adj* turning like a wheel: *a rotary movement.*

rotate /roʊ'teɪt/ *v* **1** to turn like a wheel: *He rotated the handle; The earth rotates.* **2** to change or happen in a particular order: *The Presidency rotates among members of the major groups.* **ro'tation** *n*.

rotor /'roʊtə(r)/ *n* the set of blades on top of a helicopter that go round very fast.

rotten /'rɒtən/ *adj* **1** having gone bad; decayed: *rotten vegetables; rotten wood.* **2** bad; mean: *It was a rotten thing to do.* **'rottenness** *n*.

rough /rʌf/ *adj* **1** not smooth: *Her skin felt rough.* **2** not even: *a rough path.* **3** harsh; not gentle: *a rough voice.* **4** noisy and violent: *rough behaviour.* **5** stormy: *The sea was rough; rough weather.* **6** not exact; not careful: *a rough drawing; a rough estimate.* **'roughly** *adv.* **'roughness** *n*.

'roughen *v* to make or become rough: *The wind roughened the sea.*

rough it to live without the comforts you are used to: *You can stay at my house if you don't mind roughing it.*

sleep rough to sleep outdoors because you have no home.

roulette /ru:'lɛt/ *n* a game of chance, played with a ball on a revolving wheel.

round /raʊnd/ *adj* shaped like a circle or ball: *a round hole; a round stone; This plate isn't quite round.* — *adv* **1** in the opposite direction: *He turned round.* **2** in a circle: *They all stood round and listened; A wheel goes round.* **3** from one person to another: *They passed the letter round; The news went round.* **4** to a particular place, usually a person's home: *Are you coming round tonight?; We'll go round to Peter's.* — *prep* **1** on all sides of something: *There was a wall round the garden; He looked round the room.* **2** passing all sides of something and returning to the starting-place: *They ran round the tree.* **3** changing direction at a corner *etc*: *He came round the corner.* **4** in or to all parts of a town *etc*: *The news spread all round the* town. — *n* **1** a complete circuit: *a round of golf.* **2** a regular journey: *a postman's round.* **3** a burst of cheering, shooting *etc*: *They gave him a round of applause*; *The soldier fired several rounds.* **4** a part of a competition *etc*: *The winners of the first round will go through to the next.* — *v* to go round: *The car rounded the corner.*

'rounded *adj* curved: *a rounded arch.*

'roundabout *n* **1** a moving, circular platform with toy horses *etc* on which children ride at a fair. **2** a circular piece of ground where several roads meet, and round which traffic must travel. — *adj* not direct: *a roundabout route.*

round trip 1 a journey to a place and back again. **2** a trip to several places and back, taking a circular route.

round about 1 surrounding: *She sat with her children round about her.* **2** near: *There are not many houses round about.* **3** nearly; approximately: *There must have been round about a thousand people there.*

round up to collect together: *The farmer rounded up the sheep.*

rouse /raʊs/ *v* **1** to wake up: *She blinked her eyes, as if roused out of a coma.* **2** to excite: *Her interest was roused by what he said.*

'rousing *adj* exciting: *a rousing speech.*

rout /raʊt/ *v* to defeat completely: *The enemy army was routed in the battle.* — *n*: *The battle ended with the rout of the enemy.*

route /ruːt/ *n* **1** a way of getting somewhere; a road: *Our route took us through the mountains.* **2** a way of achieving something: *Hard work is a certain route to success.*

A **route** is a way of getting somewhere using particular roads: *We drove to school by a new route* (not *road*) *this morning.*

routine /ruːˈtiːn/ *n* a regular, fixed way of doing things: *your daily routine.* — *adj* regular; ordinary: *routine work.* **rou'tinely** *adv.*

rove /roʊv/ *v* to wander; to roam: *He roved through the streets.* **'rover** *n.*

row[1] /roʊ/ *n* a line: *two rows of houses*; *They were sitting in a row*; *They sat in the front row in the theatre.*

in a row one after the other with no breaks or changes in between: *They've won eight games in a row.*

row[2] /raʊ/ *n* **1** a noisy quarrel: *They had a terrible row.* **2** a continuous loud noise: *They heard a row in the street.* — *v* to quarrel noisily: *They had never rowed with each other before.*

row, meaning a noise or a quarrel, is pronounced to rhyme with *cow*.

row[3] /roʊ/ *v* **1** to move a boat through the water using oars: *Can you row a boat?*; *He rowed up the river.* **2** to take someone or something in a rowing-boat: *He rowed them across the lake.*

'rower *n* a person who rows.

'rowing-boat or **'row-boat** *n* a boat which is moved by oars.

rowdy /ˈraʊdɪ/ *adj* noisy and rough: *The crowds of football supporters were often crude and rowdy.*

royal /ˈrɔɪəl/ *adj* having to do with, or belonging to, a king, queen *etc*: *the royal family.*

'royalty *n* **1** a payment made to a writer, singer, musician *etc* for every book, record *etc* sold. **2** the state of being royal, or royal people in general.

rub /rʌb/ *v* to move one thing against another: *He rubbed his eyes*; *The horse rubbed its head against my shoulder*; *The back of my shoe is rubbing against my heel.* — *n*: *He gave the teapot a rub with a polishing cloth.*

rub it in to keep reminding someone about something unpleasant that they want to forget.

rub off on to be transferred from one person to another: *Some of her enthusiasm must have rubbed off on you.*

rub out to remove a mark, writing *etc* with a rubber; to erase.

rub up to polish: *She rubbed up the silver.*

rubber /ˈrʌbə(r)/ *n* **1** a strong elastic substance: *Tyres are made of rubber.* **2** a piece of rubber used to rub out pencil marks *etc.* — *adj*: *a pair of rubber boots.*

rubber band a thin circle of rubber used for holding things together.

'rubbery *adj* like rubber.

rubbish /ˈrʌbɪʃ/ *n* **1** things that have been thrown away, or that should be thrown away: *Our rubbish is taken away twice a week.* **2** nonsense: *Don't talk rubbish!*

rubble /ˈrʌbəl/ *n* small pieces of stone, brick *etc.*

ruby /ˈruːbɪ/ *n* a deep-red precious stone: *a ring set with rubies.* — *adj*: *a ruby necklace.*

rucksack /ˈrʌksak/ *n* a bag that you carry on your back.

rudder /ˈrʌdə(r)/ *n* a flat piece of wood, metal *etc* fixed to the back of a boat for steering.

ruddy /ˈrʌdɪ/ *adj* red; rosy: *ruddy cheeks.*

rude /ruːd/ *adj* **1** not polite; showing bad manners: *rude behaviour.* **2** not decent; vulgar: *His mother told him not to use such rude words.* **'rudely** *adv.* **'rudeness** *n.*

rudiments /'ruːdɪmənts/ *n* the first or basic rules, facts or skills of a subject: *The students are taught the rudiments of film and television production.*

rueful /'ruːfəl/ *adj* showing or feeling sorrow: *a rueful face.*

ruffian /'rʌfɪən/ *n* a violent, brutal person: *He was attacked by a gang of ruffians.*

ruffle /'rʌfəl/ *v* to make something untidy, especially hair, feathers *etc*: *The wind ruffled her hair; The bird ruffled its feathers.*

rug /rʌɡ/ *n* **1** a mat for the floor; a small carpet. **2** a thick blanket.

Rugby or **rugby** /'rʌɡbɪ/ *n* a game like football, using an egg-shaped ball that may be carried (also called **'rugger**).

rugged /'rʌɡɪd/ *adj* **1** rough; rocky: *rugged mountains.* **2** strong; tough: *He was a tall man with rugged features.* **'ruggedly** *adv.* **'ruggedness** *n.*

rugger /'rʌɡə(r)/ another name for **Rugby**.

ruin /'ruːɪn/ *n* **1** collapse; destruction; decay: *the ruin of a city.* **2** a cause of ruin: *Drink was his ruin.* **3** complete loss of money: *The company is facing ruin.* — *v* to destroy: *The scandal ruined his career.* **rui'nation** *n.*

'ruined *adj* destroyed; completely spoilt: *ruined houses.*

'ruins *n* destroyed and decayed buildings: *the ruins of the castle.*

in ruins in a ruined state: *The town lay in ruins.*

rule /ruːl/ *n* **1** government: *This city was once under foreign rule.* **2** a regulation; an order: *school rules.* **3** a general standard that guides your actions: *I make it a rule never to be late for appointments.* **4** a marked strip of wood, metal *etc* for measuring: *He measured the windows with a 100-centimetre rule.* — *v* **1** to govern: *The king ruled wisely.* **2** to decide: *The judge ruled that the witness should be allowed to speak.* **3** to draw a straight line: *He ruled a line across the page.*

ruled *adj* having straight lines drawn across: *ruled paper.*

'ruler *n* **1** a person who governs: *the ruler of the state.* **2** a long narrow piece of wood, plastic *etc* for drawing straight lines: *I can't draw straight lines without a ruler.*

'ruling *adj* governing: *the ruling party.* — *n* a decision: *The judge gave his ruling.*

as a rule usually: *I don't go out in the evening as a rule.*

rule out to leave out: *We mustn't rule out the possibility of bad weather.*

rum /rʌm/ *n* an alcoholic drink made from sugar cane: *a bottle of rum.*

rumble /'rʌmbəl/ *v* to make a low grumbling sound: *Thunder rumbled in the distance.* — *n*: *the rumble of thunder.*

rummage /'rʌmɪdʒ/ *v* to search by turning things out or over: *He rummaged in the drawer for a clean shirt.* — *n* a thorough search.

rumour /'ruːmə(r)/ *n* news passed from person to person, that may not be true: *I heard a rumour that you had got a new job; Don't listen to rumour — find out the truth.*

'rumoured *adj* said to be true (but not necessarily so): *It's rumoured that he's leaving his job.*

rump /rʌmp/ *n* **1** the rear end of an animal: *He slapped the donkey on its rump to make it move.* **2** (also **rump steak**) beef that is cut from the rear end of a cow.

run /rʌn/ *v* **1** to move quickly, faster than walking: *He ran down the road.* **2** to move smoothly: *Trains run on rails.* **3** to flow: *Rivers run to the sea; The tap is running.* **4** to work; to operate: *The engine is running; He ran the motor to see if it was working.* **5** to organize; to manage: *He runs the business very efficiently.* **6** to travel regularly: *The buses run every half hour; The train is running late this evening.* **7** to last or continue; to go on: *The play ran for six weeks.* **8** to come out; to spread: *When I washed my new dress the colour ran.* — *n* **1** a period of running: *He went for a run before breakfast.* **2** a trip; a drive: *We went for a run in the country.* **3** a period: *He's had a run of bad luck.*

> **run; ran** /ran/; **run**: *She ran home; He has run the business for two years.*

'runaway *n* a person, animal *etc* that runs away: *The police caught the two runaways.* — *adj* **1** out of control: *a runaway train.* **2** happening very easily: *a runaway success.*

run-'down *adj* **1** tired; exhausted: *He feels run-down.* **2** in very bad condition: *a run-down area of the city.*

'run-in *n* a quarrel or argument: *He had another run-in with his boss at work today.*

run-of-the-'mill *adj* ordinary; not special: *My job is very run-of-the-mill.*

run-up *n* the period of time immediately

rung

before an event: *the run-up to an election.*

in the running having a chance of success: *She's in the running for the job of director.*

on the run escaping; running away: *He's on the run from the police.*

run across to meet unexpectedly: *I ran across an old friend.*

run after to chase: *The dog ran after a cat.*

run along to go away: *Run along now, children!*

run away to escape: *He ran away from school.*

run away with 1 to steal: *He ran away with all her money.* **2** to go too fast for you to control: *The horse ran away with him.*

run down 1 to stop working: *My watch has run down — it needs rewinding.* **2** to knock down: *I was run down by a bus.* **3** to criticize: *You should stop running yourself down!*

run for it to try to escape: *Quick — run for it!*

run into 1 to meet unexpectedly: *I ran into her in the street.* **2** to crash into something: *The car ran into a lamp-post.*

run off to make copies of something, especially using a machine: *I'll run off a few more copies of the text for our visitors.*

run out 1 to come to an end: *The food has run out.* **2** to have no more: *We've run out of money.*

run through to discuss or read quickly: *She ran through her main points again before finishing the class.*

run over 1 to knock down or drive over: *Don't let the dog out of the garden or he'll get run over.* **2** to repeat for practice: *Let's run over the plan again.*

rung[1] /rʌŋ/ *n* a step on a ladder: *a missing rung.*

rung[2] *see* **ring**.

runner /'rʌnə(r)/ *n* **1** a person or horse that runs: *There are five runners in this race.* **2** the long narrow part on which a sledge *etc* moves. **3** a long stem of a plant, such as a strawberry plant, which puts down roots.

runner-'up *n* a person, thing *etc* that is second in a race or competition: *My friend won the prize and I was the runner-up.*

See **champion**.

running /'rʌnɪŋ/ *n* **1** the sport of running. **2** managing, organizing or operating a business *etc*: *She looks after the day-to-day running of the nursing home.* — *adj* **1** for running: *running shoes.* **2** continuous: *a running commentary on the football match.* — *adv* one after another; continuously: *We travelled for four days running.*

in the running, out of the running having or not having a chance of winning: *He had a bad start, but he's still in the running for third place.*

runny /'rʌnɪ/ *adj* liquid or watery: *runny honey.*

runway /'rʌnweɪ/ *n* a wide path from which aircraft take off, and on which they land: *The plane landed on the runway.*

rupture /'rʌptʃə(r)/ *n* a tearing; a breaking. — *v* to break or tear.

rural /'rʊərəl/ *adj* having to do with the countryside: *a rural area.*

> The opposite of **rural** is **urban**.

ruse /ruːz/ *n* a clever trick or plan to deceive someone.

rush[1] /rʌʃ/ *v* **1** to hurry; to go quickly: *He rushed into the room.* **2** to take someone quickly: *She rushed him to the doctor.* — *n* **1** a sudden quick movement: *They made a rush for the door.* **2** a hurry: *I'm in a dreadful rush.*

rush hour a period when there is a lot of traffic on the roads, usually when people are going to or leaving work.

rush[2] /rʌʃ/ *n* a tall, grass-like plant that grows in or near water.

rusk /rʌsk/ *n* a dry biscuit, like hard toast: *Rusks are good for babies to bite on when their teeth start growing.*

rust /rʌst/ *n* the reddish-brown substance that forms on iron and steel: *The car was covered with rust.* — *v* to become covered with rust: *There's a lot of old metal rusting in the garden.*

> **rust** is never used in the plural: *There is a lot of rust on the car.*

rustic /'rʌstɪk/ *adj* **1** having to do with the countryside; simple: *rustic life.* **2** roughly made: *a rustic fence; a rustic bench.*

rustle /'rʌsəl/ *v* to make a soft, whispering or crackling sound: *The leaves rustled.* — *n*: *There was a rustle of papers as the students finished their exam.*

rustle up to prepare something quickly using whatever materials are available: *Shall I rustle up some lunch?*

rusty /'rʌstɪ/ *adj* **1** covered with rust: *a rusty old bicycle.* **2** not as good as it used to be: *My French was so rusty that I couldn't understand much.*

rut /rʌt/ *n* a deep track made by a wheel *etc*

in soft ground: *The road was full of ruts.*
in a rut fixed in a boring routine: *I feel I'm in a rut and must change my job.*
ruthless /'ruːθləs/ *adj* cruel; without pity: *a ruthless attack*; *a ruthless tyrant*. **'ruthlessly** *adv*. **'ruthlessness** *n*.

rutted /'rʌtɪd/ *adj* having ruts: *a deeply-rutted path.*

rye /raɪ/ *n* a kind of cereal. — *adj*: *rye bread*; *rye flour*.

S

Sabbath /'sabəθ/ *n* the day of the week regularly set aside for religious services and rest: among Jews, Saturday; among most Christians, Sunday.

sabotage /'sabətɑːʒ/ *v* to destroy or damage machinery, vehicles *etc* as a protest, or during a war: *The railway lines had been sabotaged by the enemy.* — *n*: *The machinery in the factory had been so badly damaged that the police were sure it was a case of sabotage.*

saboteur /sabə'tɜː(r)/ *n* a person who commits sabotage: *The bridge was blown up by saboteurs.*

sac /sak/ *n* a small, bag-like part of an animal or plant: *Cobras have sacs filled with poison inside their heads.*

saccharin /'sakərɪn/ *n* a very sweet chemical that can be used instead of sugar.

sachet /'saʃeɪ/ *n* a small packet of something: *a sachet of shampoo.*

sack[1] /sak/ *n* a large bag made of rough cloth, strong paper or plastic: *The potatoes were put into sacks.*

sack[2] /sak/ *v* to dismiss someone from a job: *One of the workmen was sacked for drunkenness.*

get the sack to be sacked.

sacred /'seɪkrɪd/ *adj* holy; connected with religion or with God: *Temples, mosques, churches and synagogues are all sacred buildings.*

sacrifice /'sakrɪfaɪs/ *n* **1** the offering of something to a god: *A lamb was offered in sacrifice.* **2** the thing that is offered in this way. **3** something you give up in order to gain something more important or to benefit another person: *His parents made sacrifices to pay for his education.* — *v* **1** to offer as a sacrifice: *He sacrificed a sheep in the temple.* **2** to give away *etc* for the sake of something or someone else: *He sacrificed his life trying to save the children from the burning house.* **sacri'ficial** *adj*.

sad /sad/ *adj* unhappy: *He is very sad about his cat's death*; *Mary occasionally felt sad that she had left it all behind*; *a sad face.* **'sadly** *adv*. **'sadness** *n*.

'sadden *v* to make someone feel sad: *The headmistress said she was saddened by reports of pupils' bad behaviour.*

saddle /'sadəl/ *n* a seat for a rider: *The bicycle saddle is too high.* — *v* to put a saddle on a horse.

saddle with to give someone an unpleasant task or responsibility that they don't want: *The others went shopping and I was saddled with looking after the children.*

sadism /'seɪdɪzm/ *n* getting pleasure from hurting other people or animals. **sadist** /'seɪdɪst/ *n*.

sadistic /sə'dɪstɪk/ *adj*: *sadistic cruelty.*

safari /sə'fɑːri/ *n* an expedition or tour, especially in Africa, for hunting animals: *We often went out on safari.*

safe /seɪf/ *adj* **1** protected; free from danger *etc*: *The children are safe from danger in the garden*; *You should keep your money in a safe place.* **2** not hurt or harmed: *The missing child has been found safe and well.* **3** not causing harm: *These pills are safe for children.* **4** able to be trusted: *a safe driver.* — *n* a heavy metal box or chest in which money and valuable things are kept: *There is a small safe hidden behind the picture on the wall.*

> to keep your money in a **safe** (not **save**) place.

'safeguard *n* anything that gives protection: *A good lock on your door is a safeguard against burglary.* — *v* to protect: *Put a good lock on your door to safeguard your property.*

'safely *adv* without harm or risk: *He got home safely.*

'safety *n* being safe: *I worry about the children's safety on these busy roads.*

safety belt a fixed belt in a car or aircraft used to keep a passenger from being thrown out of their seat in an accident, crash *etc*.

safety net 1 a large net placed under someone who is performing high above the ground. **2** something that might protect people from money difficulties.

safety pin a pin that has a cover over its point when it is closed.

on the safe side being very careful; not taking any risks: *There should be plenty of space but you should buy your tickets early to be on the safe side.*

safe and sound not injured or harmed:

They came home safe and sound after a terrible journey.

saffron /'safrən/ *n* a bright yellow powder obtained from a type of crocus, used to add flavour and colour to food: *Add some saffron to the rice.*

sag /sag/ *v* to bend or hang down, especially in the middle: *She sagged into her chair and sobbed.*

saga /'sɑːgə/ *n* a very long story.

sage /seɪdʒ/ *n* a wise man. — *adj* wise: *sage advice.*

sago /'seɪgoʊ/ *n* a substance from inside the trunk of certain palm trees, used in cooking.

said *see* **say**.

sail /seɪl/ *n* 1 a sheet of strong cloth spread to catch the wind, by which a ship is driven forward. 2 a journey in a ship: *He went for a sail in his yacht.* — *v* 1 to move or steer across water: *The ship sailed away; He sailed the yacht to the island.* 2 to travel in a ship: *I've never sailed in an ocean liner.* 3 to begin a voyage: *The ship sails today; My aunt sailed today for New York.* 4 to move steadily and easily: *Clouds sailed across the sky; He sailed through his exams.*

'sailing *n*: *Sailing is the sport I enjoy most.*

sailing boat a boat that uses a sail or sails.

'sailor *n* a member of a ship's crew whose job is helping to sail a ship: *a loyal crew of sailors.*

sail through to pass an examination or test easily: *He sailed through his final exams.*

saint /seɪnt/ or /sənt/ *n* a title given especially by the Roman Catholic Church to a very good or holy person after their death (shortened to **St** /sənt/ in names of places): *Saint Peter and all the saints; St John's School.*

'saintly *adj* very holy or very good: *He led a saintly life.*

sake /seɪk/: **for the sake of someone** or **something 1** in order to benefit: *He bought a house in the country for the sake of his wife's health.* 2 because of a desire for something: *For the sake of peace, he said he agreed with her.*

salad /'saləd/ *n* a dish of mixed raw vegetables.

salary /'salərɪ/ *n* a fixed, regular, usually monthly, payment for work: *Overall, salary levels have almost doubled in a year.*

sale /seɪl/ *n* 1 the giving of something to someone in exchange for money: *the sale of a house; Sales of cars have increased.* 2 in a shop *etc*, an offer of goods at reduced prices for a short time: *I bought my dress in a sale.*

'salesman, *plural* **salesmen**, **'saleswoman**, *plural* **saleswomen**, **'salesperson**, *plural* **salespeople** *ns* a person who sells, or shows goods to customers in a shop *etc*.

for sale intended to be sold: *Have you any pictures for sale?*

on sale available for buying, especially in a shop: *His book goes on sale next week.*

saliva /sə'laɪvə/ *n* the liquid that forms in your mouth.

sallow /'saloʊ/ *adj* pale, not pink-cheeked.

salmon /'samən/, *plural* **'salmon**, *n* a large edible fish with pink flesh.

salon /'salɒn/ *n* a place where hairdressing *etc* is done: *a beauty salon; a hairdressing salon.*

saloon /sə'luːn/ *n* 1 a car with seats for at least four people: *Most cars are saloons.* 2 a bar where alcoholic drinks are sold. 3 a large room on a passenger ship: *the dining-saloon.*

salt /sɒlt/ *n* 1 a white substance used for flavouring food: *The soup needs more salt.* 2 any other substance formed, like salt, from a metal and an acid. — *adj* 1 containing salt: *salt water.* 2 preserved in salt: *salt pork.* — *v* to put salt on or in something: *Have you salted the potatoes?*

'salted *adj* containing, or preserved with, salt: *salted butter; salted beef.*

'saltwater *adj* living or growing in the sea: *saltwater fish.*

'salty *adj* containing, or tasting of, salt: *Tears are salty.*

salute /sə'luːt/ *v* 1 to raise your hand to your forehead to show respect: *They saluted their commanding officer.* 2 to honour by firing large guns: *They saluted the Queen by firing one hundred guns.* — *n* the action of saluting: *The officer gave a salute.*

salvage /'salvɪdʒ/ *v* to save something from loss or ruin in a fire, shipwreck *etc*: *He salvaged his books from the burning house.* — *n* 1 the salvaging of something. 2 property *etc* that has been salvaged: *Was there any salvage from the wreck?*

salvation /sal'veɪʃən/ *n* 1 the saving of someone from death or danger. 2 in religion, the freeing of a person from sin, or the saving of someone's soul.

same /seɪm/ *adj* 1 alike; very similar: *The houses in this road are all the same; You have the same eyes as your brother.* 2 not different: *My friend and I are the same age; He went to the same school as I did.* 3 not changed: *It was the same every year, wasn't it?* — *pron* the same thing: *He sat down and* we all did the same. — *adv* in the same way: *I dislike boxing and I feel the same about wrestling.*

all the same nevertheless: *I'm sure I locked the door, but, all the same, I'll go and check.*

at the same time 1 together; all together: *I can't whistle and sing at the same time.* **2** however; on the other hand: *It's a good idea, but at the same time, it's risky.*

the same again used when requesting or ordering the same drink *etc* as before: *May I have the same again, please?*

sample /'sɑːmpəl/ *n* a part taken from something to show the quality of the rest of it: *samples of the artist's work.* — *v* to try a sample of something: *He sampled my cake.*

sanatorium /sanə'tɔːrɪəm/, *plural* **sanatoriums** or **sanatoria**, *n* a hospital for patients recovering from illnesses which last a long time: *a sanatorium for people with tuberculosis.*

sanction /'saŋkʃən/ *n* **1** official permission: *He gave the plan his sanction.* **2** action taken to encourage or force someone to do what others want them to do: *Several countries threatened to impose sanctions on his country unless he allowed elections to be held.* — *v* to approve of officially: *He sanctioned the plan.*

sanctuary /'saŋktjʊərɪ/ *n* **1** a place where someone is safe from arrest or violence; the safety that such a place gives: *In earlier times a criminal could use a church as a sanctuary; Most countries won't give sanctuary to people who hijack aeroplanes.* **2** an area of land where wild birds or wild animals are protected: *You can't visit the island because it is a bird sanctuary.*

sand /sand/ *n* **1** tiny grains of crushed rocks, shells *etc*, found on beaches *etc*. **2** an area of sand, especially on a beach: *We lay on the sand.*

sandal /'sandəl/ *n* a light shoe made of a sole with straps to hold it on to the foot.

sandbag /'sandbag/ *n* a sack filled with sand that is used to build walls as a protection against floods, gunfire *etc*.

sandcastle /'sandkɑːsəl/ *n* a pile of sand that looks like a castle, made by children playing on the beach.

sandpaper /'sandpeɪpə(r)/ *n* paper with sand glued to it, used for smoothing and polishing.

sandwich /'sanwɪdʒ/ *n* two slices of bread with food between: *ham sandwiches.* — *v* to place or press between two objects *etc*: *His car was sandwiched between two lorries.*

sandy /'sandɪ/ *adj* **1** filled or covered with sand: *a sandy beach.* **2** of a colour between blond and red: *He has sandy hair.*

sane /seɪn/ *adj* **1** not mad: *in a perfectly sane state of mind.* **2** sensible: *a very sane person.*

the opposite of **sane** is **insane**.

sang *see* **sing**.

sanitary /'sanɪtərɪ/ or /'sanətrɪ/ *adj* **1** concerned with the protection of health through cleanliness and hygiene: *A sanitary inspector came to look at the drains.* **2** clean; free from dirt and germs: *The public health measures required to help achieve more sanitary urban areas.*

sanitation /sanɪ'teɪʃən/ *n* the arrangements for protecting health, especially drainage.

sanity /'sanɪtɪ/ *n* the condition of being sane: *I am concerned about his sanity.*

sank *see* **sink**.

sap /sap/ *n* the liquid in trees, plants *etc*: *The sap flowed out when he broke the stem of the flower.* — *v* to drain or exhaust over a period of time: *The long climb had sapped the cyclists' strength and slowed them down to walking pace.*

sapling /'saplɪŋ/ *n* a young tree.

sapphire /'safaɪə(r)/ *n* a dark-blue precious stone. — *adj*: *a sapphire ring.*

sarcasm /'sɑːkazm/ *n* unkindness in speaking to someone or about them; unkind remarks, made by saying the opposite of what is really meant: *'That was clever, wasn't it?'* she said with heavy sarcasm.

sar'castic *adj*: *a sarcastic person; sarcastic remarks.* **sar'castically** *adv*.

sardine /sɑː'diːn/ *n* a small fish like a herring, often packed in oil in small tins.

sari /'sɑːrɪ/ *n* a traditional kind of dress worn by Hindu women that consists of a single long piece of fabric wrapped round the body.

sash /saʃ/ *n* a broad band of cloth worn round the waist, or over one shoulder: *a white dress with a red sash at the waist.*

sat *see* **sit**.

Satan /'seɪtən/ *n* the Devil; the spirit of evil. **satanic** /sə'tanɪk/ *adj*.

satchel /'satʃəl/ *n* a small bag for schoolbooks *etc*, that you carry on your back.

satellite /'satəlaɪt/ *n* **1** a smaller body that moves round a planet: *The Moon is a satellite of the Earth.* **2** a man-made object fired into space to travel round the Earth: *an orbiting telecommunications satellite.*

satellite dish a round dish-shaped aerial used for receiving television programmes that are broadcast by means of a satellite.

satin /'satɪn/ *n* a closely woven silk with a shiny surface. — *adj: a satin dress.*

satire /'sataɪə(r)/ *n* **1** a kind of humour that attacks the bad and stupid things that go on in the world by making you laugh at them: *Political satire is common in television shows.* **2** a play, book *etc* that uses satire to make you laugh at something stupid or bad: *The book is a satire on dictatorship.*

satirical /sə'tɪrɪkəl/ *adj: a satirical remark.*

satisfaction /satɪs'fakʃən/ *n* **1** the satisfying of someone or their needs *etc*: *the satisfaction of desires.* **2** pleasure; contentment: *Your success gives me great satisfaction.*

satisfactory /satɪs'faktərɪ/ *adj* **1** good enough to satisfy: *Your work is not satisfactory.* **2** fairly good: *The condition of the sick man is satisfactory.* **satis'factorily** *adv.*

satisfied /'satɪsfaɪd/ *adj* pleased: *I'm not satisfied with your work.*

satisfy /'satɪsfaɪ/ *v* **1** to give a person enough of what they want or need to take away hunger, curiosity *etc*: *The apple didn't satisfy my hunger.* **2** to please: *He is not satisfied with his job; She is very difficult to satisfy.* **3** to convince: *The police were satisfied that he was telling the truth.*

satisfying /'satɪsfaɪɪŋ/ *adj: The story had a satisfying ending.*

> **satisfactory** means fairly good, or just good enough; it can also mean pleasing: *satisfactory work; a satisfactory result.*
> **satisfying** means giving you pleasure or satisfaction: *a satisfying meal.*
> **satisfied** means pleased: *a satisfied customer.* The opposite is **dissatisfied.**

satsuma /sat'suːmə/ *n* a small fruit similar to an orange.

saturate /'satʒʊreɪt/ *v* to make something very wet: *Saturate the earth round the plants.* **satu'ration** *n.*

Saturday /'satədɪ/ *n* the seventh day of the week, the day following Friday.

sauce /sɔːs/ *n* a liquid that is poured over food in order to add flavour: *tomato sauce.*
'saucepan *n* a deep pan usually with a long handle.

saucer /'sɔːsə(r)/ *n* a small shallow dish for placing under a cup.

sauna /'sɔːnə/ *n* **1** a hot steam bath: *She had a refreshing sauna after her game of squash.* **2** a room or building where you can have a sauna.

saunter /'sɔːntə(r)/ *v* to walk or stroll about without hurry: *He sauntered through the park.* — *n* a walk or stroll.

sausage /'sɒsɪdʒ/ *n* a food made of minced meat, fat, spices and bread, in the shape of a tube.

savage /'savɪdʒ/ *adj* **1** wild: *a savage beast.* **2** fierce and cruel: *savage behaviour.* **3** not civilized: *savage tribes.* — *v* to attack: *He was savaged by a tiger.* — *n* a savage person: *a tribe of savages.* **'savagely** *adv.* **'savageness, savagery** /'savɪdʒrɪ/ *ns.*

save /seɪv/ *v* **1** to rescue; to bring out of danger: *He saved his friend from drowning; The house was burnt but he saved the pictures.* **2** to keep money *etc* for future use: *He's saving up to buy a bicycle; They're saving for a house.* **3** to avoid or prevent something: *Frozen foods save a lot of trouble; I'll telephone and that will save me writing a letter.* **4** in football *etc*, to prevent the opposing team from scoring a goal: *The goalkeeper saved six goals.* — *n: The goalkeeper made a great save.* — *prep* except: *All the children save John had gone home.*

> to **save** (not **safe**) up to buy a bicycle.

'saver *n: The telephone is a great time-saver.*
'saving *n* an amount of time or money *etc* that you do not have to use or spend: *He made a saving of £20 by not taking a taxi.*
'savings *n* money saved up: *He keeps his savings in the bank.*

saviour /'seɪvjə(r)/ *n* **1** a person who rescues someone or something from evil, danger *etc*: *He was the saviour of his country.* **2** (**Saviour**) Jesus Christ, who saves people from sin.

savoury /'seɪvərɪ/ *adj* having a salty or sharp taste or smell; not sweet: *a savoury omelette.*

saw[1] *see* **see**.

saw[2] /sɔː/ *n* a tool for cutting with a long metal blade that has teeth along its edge: *He used a saw to cut through the branch.* — *v* to cut with a saw: *He sawed the log in two.*

> **saw; sawed; sawn:** *She sawed up the log; Have you sawn the wood?*

'sawdust *n* dust made by sawing.
'sawmill *n* a place in which wood is mechanically sawn.

saxophone /'saksəfoʊn/ *n* a musical instrument with a curved metal tube, played by blowing.

say /seɪ/ *v* **1** to speak: *What did you say?*; *She said 'Yes.'* **2** to state; to declare: *She said she had enjoyed meeting me*; *She is said to be very beautiful*. **3** to repeat: *to say your prayers*. **4** to guess: *I can't say when he'll return*. **5** to give information: *A sign said the road was closed*; *My watch has stopped — what does yours say?*; *This book says that learning languages is easy*. — *n* a chance or right to express an opinion: *You've already had your say — now listen to me*; *We have no say in how the money will be spent*.

> **say**; **said** /sɛd/; **said**: *She said 'No.'*; *What was said at the meeting?*

'saying *n* something often said, especially a proverb.

go without saying to be so obvious that it does not need to be said: *It goes without saying that we will provide all your meals*.

let's say or **say** approximately; about: *You'll arrive there in, say, three hours*.

that is to say in other words; I mean: *He was here last Thursday, that's to say the 4th of June*.

scab /skab/ *n* a crust formed over a sore or wound. **'scabby** *adj*.

scabbard /'skabəd/ *n* a case for a sword, worn on a belt.

scaffolding /'skafəldɪŋ/ *n* the metal poles and wooden planks used by men who are repairing the outside of a building, or building something new.

scald /skɔːld/ *v* to burn your skin with hot liquid or steam: *He scalded his hand with boiling water*. — *n* a burn caused by hot liquid or steam.

'scalding *adj*: *scalding hot water*.

scale[1] /skeɪl/ *n* **1** a set of regularly spaced marks made on something, for example a thermometer or a ruler, for use as a measure; a system of numbers, measurements *etc*: *the Celsius scale*. **2** a series or system of increasing values: *a wage scale*. **3** in music, a group of notes going up or down in order: *The boy practised his scales on the piano*. **4** the size of measurements on a map *etc* compared with the real size of the country *etc* shown by it: *In a map drawn to the scale 1:50 000 one centimetre represents half a kilometre*. **5** the size of an activity: *These toys are being manufactured on a large scale*.

scale[2] /skeɪl/ *v* to climb a ladder, cliff *etc*.

scale[3] /skeɪl/ *n* any of the small thin plates or flakes that cover the skin of fishes, reptiles *etc*: *A herring's scales are silver in colour*.

scales /skeɪlz/ *n* a machine for weighing: *He weighed the flour on the kitchen scales*.

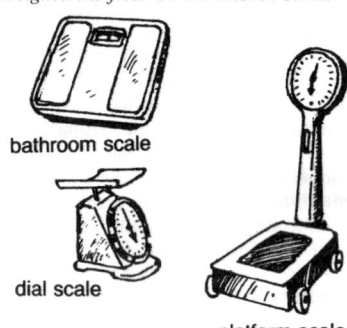

bathroom scale

dial scale

scales

platform scale

scallop /'skɒləp/ or /'skaləp/ *n* an edible water animal like an oyster, with a pair of fan-shaped shells.

scalp /skalp/ *n* the skin of the part of your head that is covered by hair: *Rub the shampoo well into your scalp*.

scalpel /'skalpəl/ *n* a small, very sharp knife used by doctors in surgical operations.

scaly /'skeɪlɪ/ *adj* covered with scales: *A dragon is a scaly creature*.

scamper /'skampə(r)/ *v* to run quickly and lightly: *His horse went scampering up the hill to win by five lengths*.

scan /skan/ *v* **1** to examine carefully: *He scanned the horizon for any sign of a ship*. **2** to look at quickly but not in detail: *She scanned the newspaper for news of the murder*. **3** to examine the inside of something using a special machine: *The machine scans the whole body and produces a picture on the screen*. — *n*: *The scan showed that the unborn baby was healthy*.

'scanner *n* a machine which examines the body closely and carefully using X-rays or a laser beam: *The hospital has raised funds to buy a new brain scanner*.

scandal /'skandəl/ *n* **1** the talk and discussion that follow an event that people consider shocking or shameful: *When their daughter ran away from home, they kept the matter secret in order to avoid a scandal*. **2** something very bad; something that makes you very angry: *the scandal of drug-dealing*; *The state of the roads here is a scandal*. **3** unkind talk about other people: *You should neither* *listen to nor pass on gossip and scandal about other people*

'scandalize *v* to cause someone to feel shocked or offended: *The whole town was scandalized by her behaviour.*

'scandalous *adj* **1** shocking; shameful: *He lost his job because of his scandalous behaviour.* **2** making you very angry: *It's scandalous that we should all be punished for his mistake.* **'scandalously** *adv.*

scant /skant/ *adj* very little; not very much: *She only paid scant attention to what her friends thought.*

'scanty *adj* hardly enough; small in size or amount: *They were given such scanty portions of food that they still felt hungry afterwards.*

'scantily *adv*: *The children were dirty and very scantily dressed.*

scapegoat /'skeɪpgoʊt/ *n* a person who is blamed or punished for the mistakes of others: *The manager of the football team was made a scapegoat for the team's failure, and was forced to resign.*

scar /skɑː(r)/ *n* the mark that is left by a wound *etc*: *There was a scar on her arm where the dog had bitten her.* — *v*: *He recovered from the accident but his face was badly scarred.*

scarce /skɛəs/ *adj* not many; not enough: *Food is scarce because of the drought.*

'scarcely *adv* only just; not quite: *Speak louder please — I can scarcely hear you*; *They have scarcely enough money to live on.*

> **scarcely** means the same as **hardly**: *I can scarcely (or hardly) hear you*; it does not mean the same as **rarely**. See **rarely**.

scarcity /'skɛəsɪtɪ/ *n* a lack; a shortage: *a scarcity of jobs.*

scare /skɛə(r)/ *v* to frighten: *You'll scare the baby if you shout*; *His warning scared them into working harder.* — *n* **1** a feeling of fear: *The noise gave me a scare.* **2** a situation that makes a lot of people afraid: *a bomb scare.*

'scarecrow *n* a figure like a man, dressed in old clothes, put up in a field to scare away birds and stop them eating the seeds *etc*.

scared /'skɛəd/ *adj* frightened: *I'm scared of spiders.*

scare away or **scare off** to make someone or something go away or stay away because of fear: *The birds were scared away by the dog.*

scarf /skɑːf/, *plural* **scarves** or **scarfs**, *n* a long strip of material to wear round your neck.

scarlet /'skɑːlət/ *n* a bright red colour. — *adj*: *scarlet poppies*; *She blushed scarlet.*

scarves /skɑːvz/ *plural* of **scarf**.

scathing /'skeɪðɪŋ/ *adj* very critical: *a scathing remark.*

scatter /'skatə(r)/ *v* **1** to send or go in different directions: *The sudden noise scattered the birds*; *The crowds scattered when the bomb exploded.* **2** to throw loosely in different directions: *The load from the overturned lorry was scattered over the road.*

'scattered *adj* occasional; not close together: *Scattered showers are forecast for this morning*; *The few houses in the valley are very scattered.*

scavenge /'skavɪndʒ/ *v* to search amongst rubbish for food or useful things. **'scavenger** *n*.

scenario /sɪ'nɑːrɪoʊ/ *n* **1** a description of what happens in a play or film. **2** one way that a situation might develop in the future: *He described the likely scenario if we didn't follow his advice.*

scene /siːn/ *n* **1** the place of a real or imagined event: *The scene of the story is a village in New South Wales.* **2** an incident *etc* that is seen or remembered: *He remembered scenes from his childhood.* **3** a show of anger: *I was very angry but I didn't want to make a scene.* **4** the view that you see in front of you: *The sheep grazing on the hillside made a peaceful scene.* **5** one division of a play *etc*: *The hero dies in the last scene.*

scenery /'siːnərɪ/ *n* **1** the painted background for a play *etc* on a stage. **2** the general appearance of a landscape *etc*: *They enjoyed the beautiful scenery of Tasmania.*

> **scenery** is never used in the plural.

scenic /'siːnɪk/ *adj* **1** having to do with scenery: *clever scenic effects in the film.* **2** surrounded by beautiful scenery: *a scenic route.*

scent /sɛnt/ *v* **1** to discover by the sense of smell: *The dog scented a cat.* **2** to suspect: *As soon as he came into the room he scented trouble.* **3** to give a pleasant smell to something: *The roses scented the air.* — *n* **1** a pleasant smell: *This rose has a delightful scent.* **2** a smell that can be followed: *The dogs picked up the man's scent and then lost it again.*

'scented *adj* sweet-smelling: *scented soap.*

sceptic /'skɛptɪk/ *n* a person who will not

sceptre

believe something; a doubter: *I don't think it's surprising that there are a few sceptics around.*
'sceptical *adj*: *Some people think apples clean your teeth, but I'm sceptical about that.*
scepticism /'skɛptəsɪzm/ *n* a doubting attitude: *The new drug is still regarded with scepticism by many doctors.*
sceptre /'sɛptə(r)/ *n* the rod carried by a king or queen as a sign of power.
schedule /'ʃɛdju:l/ or /'skɛdju:l/ *n* the time set or fixed for doing something *etc*; a timetable: *Here is a work schedule for next month.* — *v* to plan the time of an event *etc*: *The meeting is scheduled for 9.00 a.m. tomorrow.*
scheme /ski:m/ *n* **1** a plan; an arrangement; a way of doing something: *a colour scheme for the room*; *There are various schemes for improving the roads.* **2** a dishonest plan: *His scheme to steal the money was discovered.* — *v* to plot: *He was punished for scheming against the President.*
scholar /'skɒlə(r)/ *n* **1** a person of great knowledge and learning: *a fine classical scholar.* **2** a student who has been awarded a scholarship.
'scholarly *adj* having or showing knowledge: *a scholarly person*; *a scholarly book.*
'scholarship *n* **1** knowledge and learning: *a man of great scholarship.* **2** money given to good students so that they may go on with further studies: *She was awarded a scholarship.*
school[1] /sku:l/ *n* a large number of fish, whales or other water animals that swim together.
school[2] /sku:l/ *n* **1** a place for teaching children: *She goes to school*; *He's not at university — he's still at school.* **2** the time that you spend at school: *After school we usually have homework to do.* **3** the pupils and teachers of a school: *The whole school assembled in the hall to hear the headmistress speak.* **4** a place where you can be instructed in a skill: *a riding school*; *a driving school.*

See **go**.

school age /'sku:l eɪdʒ/ *n* the age when a child must go to school: *children of school age.*
schoolbag /'sku:lbag/ *n* a bag for carrying books *etc* to and from school.
schoolboy /'sku:lbɔɪ/, **schoolgirl** /'sku:lɡɜ:l/ *ns* a boy or girl who goes to school.
schoolchild /'sku:ltʃaɪld/, plural **school-**
children /'sku:ltʃɪldrən/, *n* a child who goes to school.
schooldays /'sku:ldeɪz/ *n* the time during someone's life when they go to school: *Did you enjoy your schooldays?*
schoolfellow /'sku:lfɛloʊ/ *n* a person who is at the same school as you are.
schooling /'sku:lɪŋ/ *n* the education or instruction that you receive at school: *She only had five years of formal schooling.*
school-leaver /'sku:l li:və(r)/ *n* a person who has just left school.
schoolmaster /'sku:lmɑ:stə(r)/ *n* a man who teaches in school.
schoolmate /'sku:lmeɪt/ *n* a schoolfellow, especially a friend.
schoolmistress /'sku:lmɪstrɪs/ *n* a woman who teaches in school.
school of thought /sku:l əv'θɔ:t/ *n* beliefs shared by a specific group of people: *There are various schools of thought on this point.*
schoolteacher /'sku:lti:tʃə(r)/ *n* a person who teaches in a school.
schooner /'sku:nə(r)/ *n* a fast sailing ship with two or more masts.
science /'saɪəns/ *n* **1** knowledge gained by observation and experiment. **2** a branch of knowledge such as biology, chemistry, physics *etc*. **3** these subjects considered as a group: *My daughter prefers science to languages.*
scien'tific *adj* having to do with sciences: *scientific discoveries*; *scientific methods.*
scien'tifically *adv.*
'scientist *n* a person who studies one or more branches of science.
science fiction stories dealing with future times on Earth or in space.
scissors /'sɪzəz/ *n* a cutting instrument with two blades: *Where are my scissors?*; *Whose is this pair of scissors?*

scissors always takes a plural verb, but **a pair of scissors** is singular.

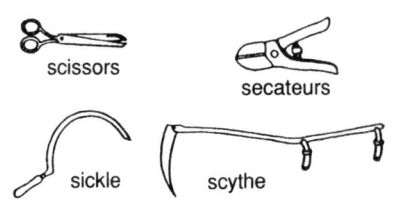

scissors

secateurs

sickle

scythe

scoff /skɒf/ *v* to express scorn: *She scoffed at my poem.*

scold /skoʊld/ v to criticize or blame loudly and angrily: *She scolded the child for coming home so late.*
　'**scolding** n: *I got a scolding for doing careless work.*

scone /skɒn/ or /skoʊn/ n a small, round, flat cake made from flour and fat: *We had scones with butter and jam for tea.*

scoop /skuːp/ n **1** a spoon-like tool, used for lifting, serving *etc*: *a grain scoop; an ice-cream scoop.* **2** an important or exciting news story that one newspaper *etc* publishes before the others can. — v to move with, or as if with, a scoop: *He scooped the crumbs together with his fingers.*
　scoop out to remove with a digging action or using a spoon-like tool: *Remove the stone from the fruit and scoop out the flesh.*

scooter /ˈskuːtə(r)/ n **1** a small motor-cycle. **2** a child's vehicle made of a foot-board with two small wheels and a handlebar, that is moved along by pushing one foot against the ground.

scope /skoʊp/ n **1** opportunity; chance; possibility: *There's plenty of scope for improvement in your work, children!* **2** extent: *It's beyond the scope of our realistic imagination.*

scorch /skɔːtʃ/ v to burn slightly: *She scorched her dress with the iron; That material scorches easily.*
　'**scorching** adj very hot: *a scorching day.*

score /skɔː(r)/ n **1** the number of points, goals *etc* gained in a game, competition *etc*: *The cricket score is 59 for 3.* **2** the written form of a piece of music. — v **1** to gain goals *etc* in a game: *He scored two goals before half-time.* **2** to put a line through a word, name *etc* to remove it; to cross something out: *Please could you score my name off the list?; Is that word meant to be scored out?*
　'**scoreboard** n a large board on which the score is shown.
　'**scorer** n **1** a person who scores points, goals *etc*: *Our team scored two goals — Smith and Brown were the scorers.* **2** the person whose job is to write down the score during a match.
　scores very many: *She received scores of letters about her radio programme.*
　on that score about that: *He seems to be working hard at school so we are not worried on that score.*

scorn /skɔːn/ n a very low opinion of someone or something; contempt; disgust: *He looked at my drawing with scorn.* — v to show scorn for someone or something: *They scorned my suggestion; I scorn cowards.*
　'**scornful** adj feeling scorn; expressing scorn: *a scornful remark; He was rather scornful about your book; She was scornful of his cowardly behaviour.* '**scornfully** adv. '**scornfulness** n.

scorpion /ˈskɔːpɪən/ n an animal of the spider family, that has a tail with a sting.

scot-free /skɒtˈfriː/ adj not hurt; not punished: *I shall find out who broke the window — I'm determined that the person who did it shall not escape scot-free.*

scoundrel /ˈskaʊndrəl/ n a very wicked person.

scour /ˈskaʊə(r)/ v **1** to clean something by rubbing or scrubbing it hard: *She scoured the dirty saucepan.* **2** to make a thorough search of an area *etc* looking for a thing or person: *She scoured the whole room for her lost contact lens.*

scourge /skɜːdʒ/ n a cause of great suffering to many people: *Vaccination has freed us from the scourge of smallpox.*

scout /skaʊt/ n **1** a person, aircraft *etc* sent out to bring in information or to spy: *The scouts reported that enemy troops were nearby.* **2** (**Scout**) a member of the Scout Movement, an organization for boys. — v to go out and collect information; to spy: *A party was sent ahead to scout.*

scowl /skaʊl/ v to look in a bad-tempered or angry way: *He scowled at the children.* — n an angry expression on the face: *His face was set in a perpetual scowl*

Scrabble[1] ® /ˈskræbəl/ n a kind of word-building game.

scrabble[2] /ˈskræbəl/ v to move your fingers around trying to find or get hold of something: *He was on his knees in the sand, scrabbling about for his glasses.*

scramble /ˈskræmbəl/ v **1** to crawl or climb quickly, using arms and legs: *They scrambled up the slope; He scrambled over the rocks.* **2** to move hastily: *He scrambled to his feet.* **3** to rush, or struggle with others, to get something: *The boys scrambled for the ball.* — n a rush or struggle: *There was a scramble for the best seats.*
　scrambled eggs eggs mixed with milk and salt and then cooked in a pan with butter.

scrap /skræp/ n **1** a small piece: *a scrap of paper.* **2** a piece of food left over after a meal: *They gave the scraps to the dog.* **3** waste articles that are only valuable for the material they contain: *The old car was sold* *as scrap.* — *adj*: *scrap metal.* — *v* to throw away: *They scrapped the old television set.*

'**scrapbook** *n* a book with blank pages on which to stick pictures *etc*: *The actor kept a scrapbook of newspaper cuttings about his career.*

scrap heap a large pile of rubbish.

scrape /skreɪp/ *v* **1** to rub against something sharp or rough, usually causing damage: *He drove too close to the wall and scraped his car.* **2** to clean, or remove, by rubbing with something sharp: *He scraped his boots clean*; *He scraped the paint off the door.* **3** to make a harsh noise by rubbing: *Stop scraping your feet!* **4** to make a hole *etc* by scratching: *The dog scraped a hole in the sand.* — *n* **1** the action or sound of scraping. **2** a mark or slight wound made by scraping: *a scrape on the knee.* **3** a situation that may lead to punishment: *Tom is always getting into scrapes.*

'**scraper** *n* a tool or instrument for scraping, especially one for scraping paint and wallpaper off walls *etc*.

scrape through to pass a test *etc*, but only just: *He scraped through his exams.*

scrape together to collect something with great difficulty: *If we can scrape together enough money, we'll replace the roof next year.*

scrappy /'skrapɪ/ *adj* consisting of bits and pieces: *a scrappy meal.*

scratch /skratʃ/ *v* **1** to mark or hurt by moving something sharp across a surface: *The cat scratched my hand*; *How did you scratch your leg?*; *I scratched myself on a rose bush.* **2** to rub your skin with your fingernails to stop itching: *You should try not to scratch insect bites.* **3** to make marks by scratching: *He scratched his name on the rock with a sharp stone.* — *n* a mark, injury or sound made by scratching: *Her arm was covered in scratches*; *The dog gave a scratch at the door to ask to be let in.*

start from scratch to start something from the very beginning: *He now has a very successful business, but he started from scratch.*

up to scratch good enough: *His work isn't really up to scratch these days — I wonder what's wrong with him?*

scrawl /skrɔːl/ *v* to write untidily or hastily: *I scrawled a hasty note to her.* — *n* untidy handwriting: *a hasty scrawl.*

scream /skriːm/ *v* **1** to shout or cry very loudly: *He was screaming with pain*; *'Look out!' she screamed*; *We screamed with laughter.* **2** to make a loud, shrill noise: *The sirens screamed.* — *n* a loud, shrill cry or noise.

screech /skriːtʃ/ *v* to make a harsh, shrill cry, shout or noise: *She screeched a warning at him*; *The car screeched to a halt.* — *n* a loud, shrill cry or noise: *screeches of laughter*; *a screech of brakes.*

screen /skriːn/ *n* **1** a flat, movable, covered frame that you use for privacy, for decoration, or for protection from cold or heat: *Screens were put round the patient's bed*; *a fire-screen.* **2** anything that you use as a screen: *He hid behind the screen of bushes.* **3** the surface on which films or television pictures appear: *a television screen*; *a cinema screen.* — *v* **1** to hide or protect: *The tall grass screened him from view.* **2** to test people to make sure they haven't got a particular disease: *Adults should be regularly screened for cancer.* **3** to show something on television or at the cinema: *His latest film will be screened in the autumn.*

'**screenplay** *n* the text of a film.

screw /skruː/ *n* a kind of nail that is driven into something by a firm twisting action: *I need four strong screws for fixing the cupboard to the wall.* — *v* **1** to fix with a screw: *He screwed the handle to the door.* **2** to fix with a twisting movement: *Make sure that the hook is fully screwed in.*

'**screwdriver** *n* a tool for turning screws.

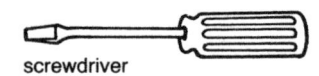

screwdriver

screw up to crumple: *She screwed up the letter.*

screw up your courage to try to become brave enough to do a dangerous or unpleasant thing.

scribble /'skrɪbəl/ *v* **1** to write quickly or carelessly: *He scribbled a message.* **2** to make meaningless marks with a pencil *etc*: *The children were punished for scribbling on the wall.* — *n* **1** untidy, careless handwriting. **2** a mark *etc* made by scribbling.

script /skrɪpt/ *n* **1** the text of a play, talk *etc*: *Have the actors all got their scripts?* **2** a system of writing: *Chinese script*; *Arabic script.*

'**scriptwriter** *n* a person who writes scripts for films or for television or radio programmes.

scripture /'skrɪptʃə(r)/ *n* **1** the sacred writings

of a religion: *Buddhist and Hindu scriptures.* **2 (Scripture)** the Bible.

scroll /skrəʊl/ *n* a roll of paper with writing on it. — *v* to move text up or down on a computer screen so that you can look at other parts of the same file.

scrotum /'skrəʊtəm/ *n* the pocket of skin that contains the testicles.

scrounge /skraʊndʒ/ *v* to get what you want by begging for it from someone: *He's always scrounging; Do you mind if I scrounge a few sheets of paper?*

scrub¹ /skrʌb/ *v* to rub hard in order to clean: *She's scrubbing the floor; She scrubbed the mess off the carpet.* — *n*: *I'll give the floor a scrub; Your hands need a good scrub.*

scrub² /skrʌb/ *n* low bushes and trees that grow in an area of poor soil.

scruff /skrʌf/: **by the scruff of the neck** by the collar or by the skin on the back of the neck: *The man took his son by the scruff of the neck and asked him where he had been.*

scruffy /'skrʌfɪ/ *adj* dirty and untidy: *scruffy clothes; a scruffy room.*

scruples /'skru:pəlz/ *n* moral principles that prevent you from doing anything that you believe is wrong: *He had no scruples about taking money from his mother.*

scrupulous /'skru:pjələs/ *adj* careful in attending to small details; careful not to do anything wrong; absolutely honest: *He is scrupulous in dealing with the accounts.* **'scrupulously** *adv*.

scrutinize /'skru:tɪnaɪz/ *v* to look at very closely and carefully: *She scrutinized the signature on the letter.* **'scrutiny** *n*.

scuba-diving /'sku:bədaɪvɪŋ/ *n* the activity of swimming under water, with cylinders of compressed air on your back for breathing.

scuff /skʌf/ *v* to make scratches on a polished or smooth surface by rubbing with something hard: *He has scuffed the toes of his new boots.*

scuffle /'skʌfəl/ *n* a fight: *The two men quarrelled and then there was a scuffle.*

sculptor /'skʌlptə(r)/ *n* an artist who carves or models in stone, clay, wood *etc*. **'sculptress** *n* a female sculptor.

sculpture /'skʌlptʃə(r)/ *n* **1** the art of modelling or carving figures, shapes *etc*: *He went to art school to study painting and sculpture.* **2** work done by sculptors: *ancient Greek sculpture; They've put up a new sculpture outside the library.*

scum /skʌm/ *n* dirty foam on the surface of a liquid: *The pond was covered with scum.*

scurry /'skʌrɪ/ *v* to run quickly: *The mouse scurried into its hole.* — *n*: *There was a scurry of feet as the children rushed to their desks.*

scuttle¹ /'skʌtəl/ *v* to run with short, quick steps: *I poked the spider and it scuttled away.*

scuttle² /'skʌtəl/ *n* a metal container for storing coal beside a fire in a house.

scythe /saɪð/ *n* a tool with a long, curved blade for cutting tall grass *etc*. — *v* to cut grass *etc* with a scythe.

sea /si:/ *n* **1** the mass of salt water covering most of the Earth's surface: *I enjoy swimming in the sea; The sea is very deep here.* **2** a particular area of sea: *the Baltic Sea; These fish are found in tropical seas.* — *adj*: *sea monsters.*

'seabed *n* the bottom or floor of the sea: *creatures that live on the seabed.*

seafaring /'si:fɛərɪŋ/ *adj* living a sailor's life: *a seafaring man.*

'seafood *n* fish or shellfish from the sea.

'seafront *n* a promenade; part of a town where the buildings face the sea.

'sea-going *adj* designed and equipped for travelling far from the coast: *a sea-going yacht.*

'seagull *n* a large white sea bird.

'seahorse *n* a small fish with a head shaped like the head of a horse, and a curved tail.

sea level the level of the surface of the sea used as a base from which the height of land can be measured: *300 metres above sea level.*

at sea 1 on a ship and away from land: *He has been at sea for months.* **2** puzzled: *Can you help me with this problem? I'm a bit at sea.*

go to sea to become a sailor: *He wants to go to sea.*

seal¹ /si:l/ *n* **1** a piece of wax stamped with a design, attached to a document to show that it is genuine and legal. **2** a piece of wax used to seal a parcel. **3** something that joins tightly or closes up completely: *There was a rubber seal round the lid of the jar.* — *v* **1** to put a seal on a document *etc*: *The document was signed and sealed.* **2** to close completely: *He licked and sealed the envelope; All the air is removed from a can of food before it is sealed.* **3** to decide or settle something: *to seal an agreement.*

seal off to form a barrier or ring around an area so that nothing or nobody can enter or leave it: *The police sealed the area off so that the gang could not escape.*

seal[2] /siːl/ *n* any of several kinds of sea animal, some having fur, living partly on land.

sea-lion /ˈsiːlaɪən/ *n* a large type of seal.

seam /siːm/ *n* **1** the line formed by the sewing together of two pieces of cloth *etc*. **2** the line where two things meet or join: *Water was coming in through the seams of the boat.* — *v* to sew a seam in a garment: *I've pinned the skirt together but I haven't seamed it yet.*

seaman /ˈsiːmən/, *plural* **seamen** /ˈsiːmɛn/, *n* a sailor.

sear /sɪə(r)/ *v* to scorch: *The iron was too hot and it seared the delicate fabric.*

search /sɜːtʃ/ *v* **1** to look for something carefully: *I've been searching for that book for weeks; He searched the whole house but couldn't find his watch; Have you searched through your pockets thoroughly?* **2** to look all over a person for weapons, stolen goods, drugs *etc*: *He was taken to the police station, searched and questioned.* — *n*: *She made a thorough search for the missing necklace.* **ˈsearcher** *n*.

> We are **searching** or **looking** (not **finding**) for the lost dog.

ˈsearching *adj* trying to find out the truth: *a searching question; a searching look*.

ˈsearchlight *n* a strong light that can be turned in any direction, used to see enemy aeroplanes in the sky *etc*.

search party a group of people looking for someone who is lost: *A search party was sent out to look for the missing climbers.*

search warrant an official document giving the police permission to search a building.

in search of searching for someone or something: *We went in search of a restaurant.*

seashell /ˈsiːʃɛl/ *n* the shell of a sea creature.

seashore /ˈsiːʃɔː(r)/ *n* the land close to the sea; the beach.

seasick /ˈsiːsɪk/ *adj* ill because of the motion of a ship at sea: *Were you seasick on the voyage?* **ˈseasickness** *n*.

seaside /ˈsiːsaɪd/ *n* a place beside the sea: *We like to go to the seaside in the summer.*

> **seashore** means beach: *They walked along the seashore collecting shells.*
> **seaside** means a place beside the sea: *'Are you going to the seaside this summer?' 'Yes, we're going to Blackpool.'*

season /ˈsiːzən/ *n* **1** one of the main divisions of the year: *The four seasons are spring, summer, autumn and winter; The monsoon brings the rainy season.* **2** the usual or suitable time for something: *the football season.* — *v* to add salt, pepper *etc* to food: *She seasoned the meat with plenty of pepper.*

ˈseasonal *adj* done at a particular time of year only: *seasonal sports.*

ˈseasoned *adj* having a lot of experience in a particular activity: *a seasoned traveller.*

ˈseasoning *n* something used to season food: *Salt and pepper are used as seasonings.*

season ticket a ticket that can be used repeatedly during a certain period: *a three-month season ticket.*

in season available for buying and eating: *That fruit is not in season just now.*

out of season not in season.

seat /siːt/ *n* **1** an object for sitting on; a chair *etc*: *Are there enough seats for everyone?* **2** the part of a chair *etc* on which you sit: *The seat of this chair is broken.* **3** the part of a garment that covers your bottom: *He had a hole in the seat of his trousers.* **4** a place in which a person has a right to sit: *I bought two seats for the play; a seat in Parliament.* — *v* **1** to give someone a seat: *I seated myself at my desk; She was seated in the armchair.* **2** to have seats for a certain number of people: *Our table seats eight.*

seat belt a safety belt fitted to a seat in a car or aeroplane to hold passengers in their seats in an accident: *Was she wearing her seat belt?*

ˈseating *n* the supply or arrangement of seats: *a seating plan.*

take a seat to sit down: *Please take a seat!*

seaweed /ˈsiːwiːd/ *n* plants growing in the sea.

secateurs /ˈsɛkətɜːz/ *n plural* a tool like a pair of strong scissors that is used for cutting the stems of plants: *The gardener used a pair of secateurs to prune the rose bushes.*

secluded /sɪˈkluːdɪd/ *adj* far away from people *etc*: *Monks live secluded lives; a secluded cottage.*

seclusion /sɪˈkluːʒən/ *n*.

second[1] /ˈsɛkənd/ *n* **1** the sixtieth part of a minute: *He ran the race in three minutes and forty seconds.* **2** a short time: *I'll be there in a second.*

second[2] /ˈsɛkənd/ *adj* **1** next after the first in time, place *etc*: *February is the second month of the year; She finished the race in second place.* **2** less good; less important *etc*: *She's a member of the school's second swimming team.* — *adv* next after the first: *He came second in the race.* — *n* **1** a second person, thing *etc*: *You're the second to arrive*; *The second of the two suggestions was the more sensible.* **2** something that is damaged or faulty and therefore sold at a reduced price: *This vase is a second.* — *v* to support someone else's proposal at a meeting so that a vote can be taken.

'**secondary** *adj* **1** coming after, and at a higher level than, primary: *a secondary school*; *secondary education*. **2** less important: *a matter of secondary importance.*

'**secondly** *adv*: *I have two reasons for not buying the house — first, it's too big, and secondly it's too far from town.*

second-'best *adj* next after the best; not as good as the best: *She wore her second-best dress.* — *n*: *He is the second best in his class at maths.*

second-'class *adj* **1** not of the very best quality: *a second-class restaurant*. **2** for travelling in a less comfortable part of a train *etc*: *a second-class ticket.* — *adv*: *I'll be travelling second-class.*

second floor 1 in British English, the floor of a building that is two floors above the ground floor. **2** in American English, the floor that is above the ground floor of a building.

second-'hand *adj* **1** previously used by someone else: *second-hand clothes.* **2** not received directly from the person concerned, but from someone else: *He didn't tell me himself, I heard it second-hand.*

second nature a habit which is fixed so firmly that it seems to be part of a person's character: *Driving fast is second nature to him.*

second-'rate *adj* not of the best quality: *The play was pretty second-rate.*

second thoughts a change of opinion: *I'm having second thoughts about selling the piano.*

every second day, week *etc* every other day, week *etc*: *The classroom is cleaned every second day.*

second to none better than every other of the same kind: *As a portrait painter, he is second to none.*

secret /'siːkrət/ *adj* hidden from other people; not known to other people: *a secret agreement*; *He kept his illness secret from everybody.* — *n* something which is, or must be kept, secret: *The date of their marriage is a secret.* '**secrecy** *n*.

secret agent a spy.

secret service a government department dealing with spying *etc*.

in secret secretly: *This must all be done in secret.*

keep a secret not to tell something secret to anyone else.

secretarial /ˌsɛkrəˈtɛərɪəl/ *adj* having to do with secretaries or their duties: *secretarial work*; *She is training at a secretarial college.*

secretary /ˈsɛkrətərɪ/ *n* **1** a person employed to write letters, keep records and make business arrangements *etc* for another person: *He dictated a letter to his secretary.* **2** a person who deals with the official business of an organization *etc*: *The secretary read out the minutes of the society's last meeting.*

secrete /sɪˈkriːt/ *v* **1** to produce a liquid: *Your skin secretes sweat when you feel hot.* **2** to hide something in a secret place: *A large quantity of cash had been secreted behind the bookcase.* **seˈcretion** *n*.

secretive /ˈsiːkrətɪv/ *adj* inclined to hide your thoughts and activities from other people: *He's rather a secretive person.*

secretly /ˈsiːkrətlɪ/ *adv* without other people knowing: *He secretly copied her telephone number into his notebook.*

sect /sɛkt/ *n* especially in religion, a group of people with strong beliefs, that has split from a larger group. **sectarian** /sɛkˈtɛərɪən/ *adj*.

section /ˈsɛkʃən/ *n* **1** a part; a division: *The book is divided into five sections*; *She works in the accounts section of the business.* **2** a view of the inside of anything when it is cut right through: *a section of the stem of a flower.* '**sectional** *adj*.

sector /ˈsɛktə(r)/ *n* **1** a section of a circle. **2** a part of a large area or group of people: *The committee has representatives from all sectors of the community.* **3** a part of the business activities of a country: *the public sector.*

secular /ˈsɛkjʊlə(r)/ *adj* not spiritual or religious: *He paints both secular and religious pictures.*

secure /sɪˈkjʊə(r)/ *adj* **1** safe; free from danger, loss *etc*: *Is your house secure against burglary?* **2** fastened; fixed; strong; firm: *Is the lock secure?*; *Is that door secure?* **3** definite; not likely to be lost: *He has a secure job.* — *v* **1** to make something safe: *Keep your jewellery in the bank to secure it against theft.* **2** to fasten: *He secured the boat with a rope.* **seˈcurely** *adv*.

sedate

> The opposite of **secure** is **insecure**.

se'curity *n* **1** safety: *A happy home gives children a feeling of security.* **2** arrangements that prevent people breaking in, or escaping: *This alarm system will give the factory some security; There has to be tight security at a prison.*

sedate[1] /sɪ'deɪt/ *adj* calm; full of dignity: *The headmistress was a tall, sedate lady.*

sedate[2] /sɪ'deɪt/ *v* to give someone a drug to calm them down: *The doctor sedated the patient with some pills.*

se'dation *n*: *The doctor put her under sedation.*

sedative /'sɛdətɪv/ *n* a drug that has a calming effect.

sedentary /'sɛdəntərɪ/ *adj* sitting down most of the time: *a sedentary job.*

sediment /'sɛdɪmənt/ *n* the material that settles at the bottom of a liquid, for example the mud that collects at the bottom of a river.

seduce /sɪ'dju:s/ *v* **1** to persuade someone to have sexual intercourse : *He tries to seduce all the girls.* **2** to tempt into doing something wrong: *She was seduced into crime by a friend.* **se'duction** *n.*

seductive /sɪ'dʌktɪv/ *adj* **1** sexually attractive and charming: *a seductive smile.* **2** tempting: *a very seductive offer.*

see /si:/ *v* **1** to have sight: *After six years of blindness, he found he could see.* **2** to notice with your eyes: *I can see her in the garden.* **3** to look at something; to watch: *Did you see that play on television?* **4** to understand: *I see what you mean.* **5** to find out: *I'll see what I can do for you.* **6** to meet: *I'll see you at the usual time.* **7** to go with someone; to take someone somewhere: *I'll see you home.*

> **see; saw** /sɔː/; **seen** /siːn/: *She saw you yesterday; I have seen this film before.*
> See **watch**.

I'll see or **we'll see** used to avoid giving a definite answer: *'Can I go swimming tomorrow?' 'We'll see.'*

see about to deal with something: *I'll see about this tomorrow.*

seeing that considering that: *Seeing that he's ill, he's unlikely to come.*

see off to go with someone who is starting on a journey to the place they are leaving from: *He saw me off at the station.*

see through not to be deceived by a person, trick *etc*: *We soon saw through him and his little plan.*

see to to attend to someone or something: *I must see to the baby; I'll go and see to the dinner.*

see you or **see you around** used for saying goodbye to someone you have not arranged to meet again.

see you later used to say goodbye to someone you will meet again soon.

you see used to draw someone's attention to what you are trying to explain: *You see her problem is that she's really very lonely.*

seed /siːd/ *n* the part of a tree, plant *etc* from which a new plant may be grown: *sunflower seeds; grass seed.*

'seedless *adj* having no seeds: *seedless grapes.*

'seedling *n* a young plant just grown from a seed.

'seedbed *n* ground prepared for growing seeds.

seedy /'siːdɪ/ *adj* dirty; in bad condition; not respectable: *a seedy little shop in a back street.*

seeing /'siːɪŋ/ or **seeing as** or **seeing that** because: *We thought we'd come to see you, seeing we were in the area; Seeing as we've paid for the tickets, we should go even if we don't really feel like it.*

seek /siːk/ *v* to try to find: *to seek a cure for cancer; to seek a solution to a problem.*

> **seek; sought** /sɔːt/; **sought**: *He sought his doctor's advice; They have sought for a solution for many years.*

seem /siːm/ *v* to appear to be, or to do, something: *Thin people always seem to be taller than they really are; She seems kind; He seemed to hesitate for a minute.*

'seeming *adj* apparent; what appears to be: *He said, with seeming embarrassment, that he would have to leave immediately.* **'seemingly** *adv.*

seen *see* **see**.

seep /siːp/ *v* to flow slowly through a small opening or leak: *Blood seeped out through the bandage round his head.*

seesaw /'siːsɔː/ *n* a long, flat piece of wood, metal *etc*, balanced on a central support so that one end of it goes up as the other goes down: *The boy fell off the seesaw in the park.* — *v* to move up and down like a seesaw.

seethe /siːð/ *v* **1** to be very crowded with people, insects *etc* that are moving about:

The beach was seething with people. **2** to be very angry: *He was seething when he lost the tennis match.*

'seething *adj: a seething mass of ants.*

segment /'sɛgmənt/ *n* a part or section: *He divided the orange into segments.*

segregate /'sɛgrɪgeɪt/ *v* to keep people, groups *etc* apart from each other: *At football matches, the supporters of the two teams are segregated.* **segre'gation** *n.*

seize /siːz/ *v* **1** to take suddenly; to grab; to grasp: *She seized the gun from him*; *He seized her by the arm*; *Seize your opportunities while you can.* **2** to take possession of something; to confiscate: *The police seized the drugs.*

> seize is spelt with -ei- (not -ie-).

seizure /'siːʒə(r)/ *n* the seizing of something: *seizure of property.*

seize on to accept with enthusiasm: *I suggested a cycling holiday, and he seized on the idea.*

seize up to stop moving easily and working: *The car's engine has seized up*; *My knees have seized up with too much bending.*

seldom /'sɛldəm/ *adv* rarely; not often: *I've seldom heard such nonsense.*

> See **rarely**.

select /sə'lɛkt/ *v* to choose from among a number: *She selected a blue dress from the wardrobe*; *You have been selected to do the job.* — *adj* picked or chosen carefully: *He invited a select group of friends to the party.* **se'lection** *n* **1** the selecting of things or people: *The singing-teacher made a selection of children for the choir.* **2** a collection or group of things that have been selected: *a selection of fruit.* **3** a range of things to choose from: *There is a large selection of holidays that we can afford in this brochure.* **se'lective** *adj* choosing carefully: *Be very selective in your television-watching.*

self /sɛlf/, *plural* **selves** /sɛlvz/, *n* your own body, personality and desires: *You can't help thinking of your own self first.*

self-assurance /sɛlfə'ʃʊərəns/ *n* confidence. **self-as'sured** *adj.*

self-catering /sɛlf'keɪtərɪŋ/ *adj* in which the guest provides and prepares their own food: *self-catering accommodation for students*; *She goes on self-catering holidays so she does not have to eat hotel food.*

self-centred /sɛlf'sɛntəd/ *adj* interested only in your own affairs; selfish.

self-confessed /sɛlfkən'fɛst/ *adj* openly admitting that you have a particular fault or bad habit: *He's a self-confessed layabout.*

self-confidence /sɛlf'kɒnfɪdəns/ *n* belief in your own powers: *You need plenty of self-confidence to be a good airline pilot.* **self-'confident** *adj.*

self-conscious /sɛlf'kɒnʃəs/ *adj* too easily becoming shy in the presence of others: *She'll never be a good teacher — she's too self-conscious.* **self-'consciously** *adv.* **self-'consciousness** *n.*

self-contained /sɛlfkɒn'teɪnd/ *adj* complete and separate; not sharing a kitchen, bathroom *etc* with other people: *The old lady has a self-contained flat in her son's house.*

self-control /sɛlfkən'trəʊl/ *n* control of yourself, your feelings *etc*: *He behaved with great self-control although he was very angry.*

self-defence /sɛlfdɪ'fɛns/ *n* defence of your own body, property *etc* against attack: *He killed his attacker in self-defence.*

self-employed /sɛlfɪm'plɔɪd/ *adj* working for yourself; not employed by someone else.

self-esteem /sɛlfɪ'stiːm/ *n* your good opinion of yourself: *His self-esteem suffered when he failed the exam.*

self-evident /sɛlf'ɛvɪdənt/ *adj* clear; not needing proof or explanation.

self-explanatory /sɛlfɪk'splænətərɪ/ *adj* easily understood; needing no further explanation: *The diagram is self-explanatory.*

self-indulgent /sɛlfɪn'dʌldʒənt/ *adj* allowing yourself to have things that you want or enjoy. **self-in'dulgence** *n.*

self-interest /sɛlf'ɪntrɛst/ *n* consideration only for your own aims and advantages: *He acted out of self-interest.*

selfish /'sɛlfɪʃ/ *adj* caring only for your own pleasure or advantage: *a selfish person*; *selfish behaviour.* **'selfishly** *adv.* **'selfishness** *n.*

selfless /'sɛlfləs/ *adj* thinking of other people's needs or wants before your own: *a selfless act.*

self-made /sɛlf'meɪd/ *adj* having become rich or successful by your own efforts: *a self-made millionaire.*

self-pity /sɛlf'pɪtɪ/ *n* pity for yourself: *He's full of self-pity since he lost his job and makes no attempt to try and find another one.*

self-portrait /sɛlf'pɔːtrət/ *n* a portrait that you make of yourself: *to paint a self-portrait.*

self-reliant /sɛlfrɪ'laɪənt/ *adj* independent; not needing help from other people.

self-respect /sɛlfrɪ'spɛkt/ *n* respect for yourself and concern for your reputation: *Well-*

known people should have more self-respect than to take part in television advertising.
self-res'pecting adj: No self-respecting oil tycoon has fewer than two helicopters.

self-righteous /sɛlfˈraɪtʃəs/ adj too convinced of your own goodness, and too critical of other people's faults: 'Some people are always late for school, but I never am', he said in a self-righteous voice. **self-'righteously** adv. **self-'righteousness** n.

self-sacrifice /sɛlfˈsakrɪfaɪs/ n the giving up of your own desires in order to help others: With great self-sacrifice she gave up her holiday to look after her sick aunt.

self-satisfied /sɛlfˈsatɪsfaɪd/ adj too easily pleased with yourself and your achievements.

self-service /sɛlfˈsɜːvɪs/ n an arrangement by which customers themselves collect the goods that they want to buy. — adj: a self-service restaurant.

self-sufficient /sɛlfsəˈfɪʃənt/ adj able to make or get everything that is needed without the help of others: The island is self-sufficient in food; a self-sufficient community. **self-suf'ficiency** n.

sell /sɛl/ v **1** to give something in exchange for money: He sold her a car; I've got some books to sell. **2** to have for sale: This shop sells tools. **3** to be sold: His book sold well.

> **sell; sold** /soʊld/; **sold**: She sold her old car; We have sold our house.

'sell-by date the last date on which an item may be displayed for sale: All the biscuits were sold before their sell-by date.
seller n a person or business that sells: a book-seller.
sell off to sell quickly and cheaply: They're selling off their old stock.
sell out to sell all of something: We've sold out of copies of The Times today; Seats for the concert are sold out; The concert is sold out. **'sell-out** n.
sell up to sell your house, business etc.

sellotape ® /ˈsɛləteɪp/ n a type of clear tape with glue on one side, for sticking paper or cardboard etc: She wrapped the parcel in brown paper and fastened it with sellotape. — v to fasten with sellotape: She sellotaped the picture to the door.

selves plural of **self**.

semen /ˈsiːmən/ n the liquid containing sperms that is produced by the male sexual organs.

semester /sɪˈmɛstə(r)/ n one of the two periods into which the school or university year is divided in some countries: He left college after his first semester.

semicircle /ˈsɛmɪsɜːkəl/ n a half circle: The chairs were arranged in a semicircle round the speaker.

semicolon /sɛmɪˈkoʊlɒn/ n the punctuation mark (;).

semiconductor /sɛmɪkənˈdʌktə(r)/ n a substance such as silicon, that can conduct electricity at high temperatures or when it is slightly impure, and can be used in electronic devices.

semi-conscious /sɛmɪˈkɒnʃəs/ adj partly conscious.

semi-detached /sɛmɪdɪˈtatʃt/ adj joined to another house on one side but separate on the other: a semi-detached bungalow.

semifinal /sɛmɪˈfaɪnəl/ n a match, round etc immediately before the final: She reached the semi-finals of the competition.
semi'finalist n a person, team etc competing in a semi-final.

seminar /ˈsɛmɪnɑː(r)/ n a class in a university or college in which a small number of students discuss or study a topic with a teacher.

Senate /ˈsɛnət/ n the senior council in the government of the United States, Canada, Australia and many other countries.

send /sɛnd/ v **1** to order someone to go somewhere: She sent the boy to the headmaster. **2** to post; to get something carried to someone: Send me a postcard; to send a telegram; The headmaster sent all the parents a note. **3** to put someone into a particular state: His jokes sent her into fits of laughter. **4** to throw, push, kick etc: His kick sent the ball straight into the goal.

> **send; sent** /sɛnt/; **sent**: She sent me a parcel; The boy has been sent home.

'sender n a person who sends a letter etc.
send for 1 to ask someone to come: The woman became so ill that her son was sent for; to send for a doctor. **2** to order something: I'll send for a taxi; She sent away for the paint-box that she saw advertised in the paper.
send in to offer or submit something for a competition etc: He sent in three drawings for the competition.
send off to join with others in saying goodbye to someone at the place from which they are leaving on a journey: A

crowd gathered at the station to send the football team off. **'send-off** n.

send out 1 to distribute: *A notice has been sent out to all employees.* **2** to produce: *This plant is sending out some new shoots.*

send up to laugh at or ridicule someone by imitating them: *He made his friends laugh by sending up their teacher.*

senile /'si:naɪl/ *adj* mentally or physically weak because of old age: *He is nearly senile and is finding it harder and harder to look after himself.* **se'nility** n.

senior /'si:nɪə(r)/ *adj* **1** older in years or higher in rank: *John is senior to me by two years; He is two years my senior; senior army officers.* **2 (Senior)** used for the father of someone who has the same name (often written **Snr**, **Sr** or **Sen.**): *John Jones Senior.* — *n* someone who is older or higher in rank: *The teacher asked a senior to look after the new pupil.* **seni'ority** n.

senior citizen a person who has passed retirement age.

sensation /sɛn'seɪʃən/ *n* **1** the ability to feel through the sense of touch: *Cold can cause a loss of sensation in the fingers and toes.* **2** a feeling: *a sensation of faintness.* **3** a general feeling, or a cause, of excitement: *His arrest was the sensation of the week.*

sen'sational *adj* **1** causing great excitement *etc*: *a sensational piece of news.* **2** very good: *The film was sensational.* **3** intended to create feelings of excitement *etc*: *That magazine is too sensational for me.* **sen'sationally** *adv*.

sense /sɛns/ *n* **1** one of the five powers — hearing, taste, sight, smell and touch — by which a person or animal feels or notices. **2** an ability to understand something: *a good musical sense; She has no sense of humour; Where's your sense of fairness?* **3** good judgement: *You can rely on him — he has plenty of sense.* **4** a meaning of a word: *The word 'right' has several different senses.* — *v* to feel; to realize: *He sensed that she was angry with him, although she didn't say anything.*

'senseless *adj* **1** unconscious: *The blow knocked him senseless.* **2** foolish: *What a senseless thing to do!*

'senses *n* a person's normal state of mind: *When he came to his senses, he was lying in a hospital bed.*

in a sense partly; in one way: *You're right in a sense, but you've forgotten several important points.*

make sense 1 to have an understandable meaning: *This sentence doesn't make sense.* **2** to be sensible or wise: *Wouldn't it make sense to wait here a little longer?*

make sense of to understand: *Can you make sense of this sentence?*

sensible /'sɛnsɪbəl/ *adj* wise; having good judgement: *She's a sensible, reliable person; a sensible suggestion.*

'sensibly *adv*: *He sensibly brought his umbrella in case it rained.*

sensitive /'sɛnsɪtɪv/ *adj* **1** easily getting affected by something; easily damaged: *She has sensitive skin.* **2** reacting to something: *Photographs are made on film that is sensitive to light.* **3** easily feeling hurt or offended: *He's very sensitive — you must try not to hurt his feelings.* **'sensitively** *adv*. **sensi'tivity** n.

sensor /'sɛnsə(r)/ *n* an instrument which can detect and give a signal of things such as light, heat and movement: *The building has a good security system with sensors which can detect the presence of people.*

sensual /'sɛnʃʊəl/ *adj* having, showing or suggesting a liking for physical, especially sexual, pleasure: *a sensual dancer.*

sensu'ality *n*: *Her sensuality showed in the way she walked.*

sensuous /'sɛnʃʊəs/ *adj* giving pleasure to the senses: *the sensuous feeling of warm sand under your feet.* **'sensuously** *adv*.

sent *see* **send**.

sentence /'sɛntəns/ *n* **1** a number of words forming a complete statement: *'I want it' and 'Give it to me!' are sentences.* **2** a punishment imposed by a law-court: *a sentence of three years' imprisonment; He is under sentence of death.* — *v* to condemn a person to a particular punishment: *He was sentenced to life imprisonment.*

sentiment /'sɛntɪmənt/ *n* tender feelings; emotion: *a song full of patriotic sentiment.*

senti'mental *adj* **1** too full of tender feeling: *a sentimental person; a sentimental film about a little boy and a donkey.* **2** having to do with your emotions or feelings: *The ring has sentimental value, as my husband gave it to me.* **senti'mentally** *adv*. **sentimen'tality** n.

sentry /'sɛntrɪ/ *n* a soldier or other person on guard at an entrance *etc*, to stop anyone who has no right to enter: *The entrance was guarded by two sentries.*

separable /'sɛpərəbəl/ *adj* able to be separated.

> The opposite of **separable** is **inseparable**.

separate *v* /'sɛpəreɪt/ **1** to set apart; to keep apart: *He separated the money into two piles; The Atlantic Ocean separates America from Europe; A policeman tried to separate the men who were fighting; One chicken seemed to have got separated from the rest.* **2** to go in different directions: *We all walked along together and separated at the crossroads.* **3** to start living apart from each other by choice: *Her parents have separated.* — *adj* /'sɛpərət/ **1** divided; not joined: *He sawed the wood into four separate pieces; The garage is separate from the house.* **2** different: *This happened on two separate occasions.*

> **separate** is spelt with -ar- (not -er-).

'separately *adv*: *We have two different problems here — we must consider them separately; Jane and Elizabeth didn't come here together — they arrived separately; Cook the stuffing separately from the turkey.*

'separates *n* garments such as jerseys, skirts, trousers, blouses and shirts, rather than dresses or suits.

sepa'ration *n* **1** being separated: *They were together again after a separation of three years.* **2** an arrangement by which a husband and wife remain married but live separately.

separate out to separate: *Separate out the blue pieces and the red pieces.*

September /sɛp'tɛmbə(r)/ *n* the ninth month of the year, the month following August.

septic /'sɛptɪk/ *adj* full of pus; infected with germs: *A wound should be cleaned to stop it going septic; a septic finger.*

sequel /'siːkwəl/ *n* **1** a story that continues an earlier story: *She has just written a sequel to her popular book about a boy called Adrian Mole.* **2** a result: *There was an unpleasant sequel to that event.*

sequence /'siːkwəns/ *n* a series of events *etc* following one another in a particular order: *He described the sequence of events leading to his dismissal from the firm.*

serenade /sɛrə'neɪd/ *n* a song or piece of music performed at night especially outside the house of someone you love.

serene /sə'riːn/ *adj* calm: *a serene face; serene weather.* **se'renely** *adv*. **serenity** /sə'rɛnɪtɪ/ *n*.

sergeant /'sɑːdʒənt/ *n* **1** an officer of low rank in the British army or air force. **2** a police officer senior to an ordinary policeman.

serial /'sɪərɪəl/ *n* a story that is published or broadcast one part at a time: *Have you been reading that serial in the magazine?; I missed the last part of the serial on television.*

'serialize *v* to publish or broadcast a story as a serial: *to serialize a book.* **seriali'zation** *n*.

serial number a set of numbers marked on something to identify it and distinguish it from others of the same type.

series /'sɪərɪz/, *plural* **'series**, *n* **1** a number of similar things done one after another: *a series of scientific discoveries.* **2** a set of programmes: *Are you watching the television series on Britain's castles?* **3** a set of books: *a series of school text-books.*

> **a series** takes a singular verb: *The series of programmes begins next Tuesday.*

serious /'sɪərɪəs/ *adj* **1** grave; solemn: *a quiet, serious boy; You're looking very serious.* **2** earnest; sincere: *Is he serious about wanting to be a doctor?* **3** intended to make you think hard: *He reads very serious books.* **4** causing worry; dangerous: *a serious head injury; The situation is becoming serious.* **'seriousness** *n*.

'seriously *adv*: *Is he seriously thinking of being an actor?; She is seriously ill.*

take something or **someone seriously** to treat a thing or person as important: *Don't take him seriously — he's often joking.*

sermon /'sɜːmən/ *n* a serious talk, especially one given in church discussing a passage in the Bible.

serpent /'sɜːpənt/ *n* a snake.

serrated /sə'reɪtɪd/ *adj* having V-shaped points along the edge: *a serrated knife.*

servant /'sɜːvənt/ *n* **1** a person who is employed by someone to help to run their house *etc*. **2** a person employed by the government in the running of the country *etc*: *civil servants.*

serve /sɜːv/ *v* **1** to work for someone as a servant: *He served his master for forty years.* **2** to distribute food *etc*: *She served the soup to the guests; The waiter served me with a glass of wine.* **3** to supply goods to a customer in a shop: *Which shop assistant served you?* **4** to be suitable for a purpose: *This upturned bucket will serve as a seat.* **5** to perform your duty, for example as a member of the armed forces: *He served his country as a soldier for twenty years.* **6** to undergo a prison sentence; to have to stay in prison as a punishment for a crime: *He served six years for armed robbery.* **7** in tennis and similar games, to start the play by throwing up the ball *etc* and hitting it:

Is it your turn to serve? — *n*: *She hit a good serve.*

'**server** *n* the person who serves the ball in tennis *etc*.

'**servers** *n* a pair of instruments like a large spoon and fork for serving out salad *etc*: *a pair of salad-servers.*

it serves you *etc* **right** you *etc* deserve your misfortune *etc*: *He has done no work so it will serve him right if he fails his exam.*

serve out to distribute to each of a number of people: *She served out the pudding.*

serve up to start serving a meal.

service /'sɜːvɪs/ *n* **1** the serving of customers in a hotel, shop *etc*: *You get very slow service in that shop.* **2** (usually **services**) work that helps people; work that you do for your employer *etc*: *He was rewarded for his services to refugees; He has given faithful service to the firm for many years.* **3** a check made of all parts of a car, machine *etc* to make sure that it is working properly: *Bring your car in for a service.* **4** regular public transport: *There is a good train service into the city.* **5** a religious ceremony: *He attends a church service every Sunday; the marriage service.* **6** in tennis and similar games, the serving of the ball: *He has a strong service.* **7** a department of public or government work: *the Civil Service.* **8** employment in the army, navy or air force: *military service.* — *v* to check a car, machine *etc* thoroughly to make sure that it works properly.

'**serviceable** *adj* **1** useful; able to be used: *This old typewriter is no longer serviceable.* **2** strong; lasting well: *serviceable shoes.*

service charge a charge added to a hotel or restaurant bill to cover the cost of the waiter *etc*: *The service charge is usually ten per cent of the bill.*

service station a petrol station at which you can get your car checked or repaired.

serviette /sɜːvɪ'ɛt/ *n* a table napkin: *a paper serviette.*

serving /'sɜːvɪŋ/ *n* a portion of food that is served to you; a helping: *This recipe will be enough for four servings.*

session /'sɛʃən/ *n* **1** a meeting, or period of meetings, of a court, council, parliament *etc*: *The judge will sum up the case at tomorrow's court session.* **2** a period of time spent on a particular activity: *a filming session.* **3** a school year or one part of this: *the summer session.*

in session holding a meeting; doing its official business; not on holiday: *Visitors are not allowed when the committee is in session.*

set /sɛt/ *v* **1** to put; to place: *She set the tray down on the table.* **2** to put plates, knives, forks *etc* on a table for a meal: *Please would you set the table for me?* **3** to give a person a task *etc* to do: *The witch set the prince three tasks; The teacher set a test for her pupils.* **4** to disappear below the horizon: *It gets cooler when the sun sets.* **5** to become firm and solid: *Has the concrete set?; How long will it take for the jelly to set?* **6** to adjust: *He set his alarm-clock for 7.00 a.m.; The bomb was set to go off at 2.45 a.m.* **7** to arrange hair in waves or curls. **8** to fix something into the surface of something else, for example jewels in a ring: *The gold ring was set with rubies.* **9** to arrange: *Has a date been set for the competition yet?* **10** to put broken bones into the correct position for healing: *The doctor set his broken arm.* **11** to write music for words to be sung to: *A composer set the words of the poem to music.* — *n* **1** a group of things used or belonging together: *a set of tools.* **2** an apparatus for receiving radio or television programmes *etc*: *a television set; a radio set.* **3** the fixing of your hair in a particular style when you wash it: *a shampoo and set.* **4** scenery for a play; the part of a studio where a film is being made. **5** a group of six or more games in tennis: *She won the first set and lost the next two.*

> **set; set; set**: *He set the table; The sun has set.*
> The sun sets **in** (not **to**) the west.

'**set-square** *n* a triangular instrument with one right angle, used in geometrical drawing *etc*.

set-'to, *plural* **set-'tos**, *n* a fight or quarrel: *The two boys had a set-to in the street.*

all set ready: *We were all set to leave when the phone rang.*

set about to begin: *How will you set about this task?*

set against opposed to: *She's set against moving house again.*

set aside to keep something for a special purpose: *He set aside some cash for use at the weekend.*

set back to delay the progress of someone or something: *Her illness set her back in her school-work.* '**setback** *n*.

set down to stop and let passengers out: *The bus set us down outside the post-office.*

settee

set in to come and remain for some time: *The rain started at midday and seemed to have set in for the afternoon.*

set off 1 to start a journey: *We set off to go to the beach.* **2** to explode; to make something go off: *His father allowed him to set off some of the fireworks*; *Opening the front door sets the burglar alarm off.*

set on or **set upon 1** to attack: *The gang set upon him in the dark.* **2** determined to do something: *He seems set on leaving his job.*

set out 1 to start a journey: *He set out to explore the countryside.* **2** to intend to do something: *He deliberately set out to make me look stupid.*

set up 1 to establish: *When was the organization set up?* **2** to arrange; to construct: *He set up the apparatus for the experiment.*

settee /sɛˈtiː/ *n* a sofa.

setting /ˈsɛtɪŋ/ *n* **1** background: *The castle is the perfect setting for a mystery story.* **2** one of the positions on the controls of a machine *etc*: *The photo is too dark because the camera was on the wrong setting.*

settle /ˈsɛtəl/ *v* **1** to put into a comfortable place or position: *I settled myself in the armchair.* **2** to come to rest: *Dust had settled on the books.* **3** to calm: *I gave him a pill to settle his nerves.* **4** to go and live: *Many people from Scotland settled in New Zealand.* **5** to reach a decision about something: *Have you settled the date for his visit?* **6** to come to an agreement about something; to solve: *The dispute between the manager and the employees is still not settled.* **7** to pay a bill: *to settle your accounts.*

'settlement *n* **1** an agreement: *The two sides have at last reached a settlement.* **2** a small community: *a farming settlement.*

'settler *n* a person who settles in a country that is being newly populated: *the early settlers on the east coast of America.*

settle down 1 to become quiet, calm and peaceful: *He waited for the audience to settle down before he spoke.* **2** to begin to concentrate on something: *He settled down to his schoolwork.* **3** to live a quieter life by staying in the same place or getting married.

settle for to agree on something less than you originally wanted: *There are several jobs I'd like to do but I'll settle for anything in the beginning.*

settle in to become used to new surroundings: *You'll soon settle in!*

settle on to choose: *Which car did you settle on?*

settle up to pay a bill: *He asked the waiter for the bill, and settled up.*

seven /ˈsɛvən/ *n* **1** the number 7. **2** the age of 7. — *adj* **1** 7 in number. **2** aged 7.

'seventh *n* one of seven equal parts. — *n, adj* the next after the sixth.

seventeen /sɛvənˈtiːn/ *n* **1** the number 17. **2** the age of 17. — *adj* **1** 17 in number. **2** aged 17.

seventy /ˈsɛvəntɪ/ *n* **1** the number 70. **2** the age of 70. — *adj* **1** 70 in number. **2** aged 70.

sever /ˈsɛvə(r)/ *v* to break off: *His arm was severed in the accident.*

several /ˈsɛvərəl/ or /ˈsɛvrəl/ *adj* more than one or two, but not a great many: *Several weeks passed before he got a reply to his letter.* — *pron* some; a few: *Several of the teachers are ill.*

severe /səˈvɪə(r)/ *adj* **1** very bad; serious: *a severe shortage of food*; *a severe illness*; *Our team suffered a severe defeat.* **2** strict; harsh: *a severe mother*; *a severe scolding.* **se'verely** *adv.* **se'verity** *n.*

sew /soʊ/ *v* to make, stitch or attach something with thread, using a needle: *She sewed the pieces together*; *Have you sewn my button on yet?*

> **sew; sewed; sewn**: *He sewed the badge on to his jacket*; *I've sewn your button on again.*
> to **sew** (not **sow**) a button on.

sew up to close up by sewing; to mend: *I've sewn up the hole in your sock.*

sewage /ˈsuːɪdʒ/ *n* waste matter carried away in sewers.

sewer[1] /soʊə(r)/ *n* an underground pipe or channel for carrying away water *etc* from drains.

sewer[2] /soʊə(r)/ *n* someone who sews: *You're a neat sewer.*

sewing /ˈsoʊɪŋ/ *n* **1** the activity of sewing: *I was taught sewing at school.* **2** work to be sewn: *She picked up a pile of sewing.*

'sewing-machine *n* a machine for sewing.

sex /sɛks/ *n* either of the two classes, male and female, into which human beings and animals are divided according to the part they play in producing babies: *Jeans are worn by people of both sexes*; *What sex is the puppy?*

'sexism *n* contempt shown to the members of one sex, usually women, by members of the other: *She accused her boss of sexism because he refused to promote any women.*

'sexist *n*: *All of his women employees believe he is a sexist.* — *adj*: *a sexist attitude.*

sexual /ˈsɛkʃʊəl/ *adj* concerned with the production of babies: *the sexual organs.* **'sexually** *adv*.

sexual intercourse the sexual activity between a man and woman that is necessary for the producing of babies.

'sexy *adj* attractive to the opposite sex; making you think about the opposite sex etc.

shabby /ˈʃabɪ/ *adj* **1** old and worn out: *shabby curtains*; *shabby clothes*. **2** wearing old or dirty clothes: *a shabby old man*. **'shabbily** *adv*. **'shabbiness** *n*.

shack /ʃak/ *n* a roughly-built hut: *a wooden shack.*

shackles /ˈʃakəlz/ *n* a pair of iron rings joined by a chain that are put on a prisoner's wrists, ankles *etc*, to stop him moving very far.

'shackle *v* to put shackles on someone.

shade /ʃeɪd/ *n* **1** slight darkness caused by the blocking of light: *I prefer to sit in the shade rather than in the sun.* **2** the dark parts of a picture: *the light and shade in a portrait.* **3** something used as a screen or shelter from light or heat: *to put up a sunshade*; *a lampshade.* **4** a variety of colour; a slight difference: *a pretty shade of green.* — *v* **1** to shelter from light; to screen a light to reduce its brightness: *to shade a bulb*; *He put up his hand to shade his eyes.* **2** to make a part of a drawing *etc* darker: *You should shade the side of the face more in your drawing.*

shades *n* sunglasses.

shadow /ˈʃadoʊ/ *n* **1** an area of shade on the ground *etc* caused by an object blocking the light: *We were in the shadow of the building.* **2** (**the shadows**) darkness; shade: *I didn't notice you standing there in the shadows.* **3** a dark patch: *You look tired — there are shadows under your eyes.* **4** a very slight amount: *There's not a shadow of doubt that he stole the money.* — *v* **1** to hide in shadow: *A broad hat shadowed her face.* **2** to follow someone in order to spy on them: *We shadowed him for a week.*

'shadowy *adj* **1** full of shadows: *shadowy corners.* **2** dark; difficult to see properly: *A shadowy figure went past.*

shady /ˈʃeɪdɪ/ *adj* **1** sheltered; giving shelter from heat or light: *a shady tree*; *a shady corner of the garden.* **2** dishonest: *a shady business.* **'shadiness** *n*.

shaft /ʃɑːft/ *n* **1** the long straight part or handle of a tool, weapon *etc*: *the shaft of a golf-club.* **2** one of two poles on a cart *etc* to which a horse *etc* is harnessed: *The horse stood patiently between the shafts.* **3** a long, narrow space, for example for a lift in a building: *a liftshaft*; *a mineshaft.* **4** a ray of light: *a shaft of sunlight.*

shaggy /ˈʃagɪ/ *adj* covered with rough hair or fur; rough and untidy: *The dog had a shaggy coat*; *a shaggy dog.* **'shagginess** *n*.

shake /ʃeɪk/ *v* **1** to tremble; to move to and fro violently: *She shook the bottle*; *The explosion shook the building*; *I was shaking from head to toe.* **2** to shock; to weaken: *He was shaken by the accident*; *My confidence in him has been shaken.* — *n* **1** the action of shaking: *He gave the bottle a shake.* **2** a drink made by whisking the ingredients together: *a chocolate milk-shake.*

> shake; shook /ʃʊk/; **'shaken**: *She shook hands with him*; *Have you shaken the bottle properly?*

'shaky *adj* **1** weak; trembling with age, illness *etc*: *a shaky voice*; *shaky handwriting.* **2** unsteady; likely to collapse: *That bookcase looks a bit shaky.* **3** not very good: *My arithmetic has always been very shaky.* **'shakily** *adv*. **'shakiness** *n*.

shake hands or **shake someone's hand** to grasp someone's hand in greeting.

shake your head to turn your head from side to side to mean 'No': *'Are you coming?' I asked. She shook her head.*

shake off to get rid of something: *I can't seem to shake this cold off.*

shake up to reorganize something thoroughly. **'shake-up** *n*.

shall /ʃal/ *v* **1** used to form future tenses of other verbs when the subject is **I** or **we**: *We shall be leaving tomorrow*; *I'll have arrived by this time tomorrow*; *Shall I ever see you again?*

> See the note at **will**[2].

2 used to show your intention: *I shan't be late tonight.* **3** used when you are making up your mind or asking for advice or instructions: *Shall I tell him, or shan't I?*; *Shall we go now?* **4** used as a form of command: *You shall go if I say you must.*

I shall or **I'll** /aɪl/;
We shall or **we'll** /wiːl/;
shall not or **shan't** /ʃɑːnt/: *I'll miss you when you've gone*; *We shan't wait for a bus — we'll walk.*

shallow /ˈʃaloʊ/ *adj* not deep: *shallow water*; *a shallow pit*. **'shallowness** *n*.

sham /ʃam/ *n* something that is only pretended: *The whole trial was a sham.* — *adj* pretended; false: *a sham fight*; *Are those diamonds real or sham?* — *v* to pretend: *He shammed sleep*; *He shammed dead*; *I think she's only shamming.*

shamble /ˈʃambəl/ *v* to walk slowly without lifting your feet properly: *The old man shambled along.*

shambles /ˈʃambəlz/ *n* a great mess and confusion: *Her room is a shambles*; *The meeting was a complete shambles and nothing was decided.*

shame /ʃeɪm/ *n* **1** an unpleasant feeling of guilt, foolishness or failure: *I was full of shame at my rudeness*; *He felt no shame at his behaviour.* **2** dishonour; disgrace: *The news that he had stolen money brought shame on his whole family.* **3** a pity: *What a shame that he didn't get the job!* — *v* to make someone feel ashamed.
'shameful *adj* disgraceful: *shameful behaviour*. **'shamefully** *adv*.
'shameless *adj* feeling no shame; causing no shame: *a shameless liar*; *a shameless lie*. **'shamelessly** *adv*.
put to shame to make someone feel ashamed of their own efforts *etc*: *Your lovely drawing puts me* (or *mine*) *to shame.*
to my shame: *To my shame, my daughter always beats me at chess.*

shampoo /ʃamˈpuː/ *n* **1** a soapy liquid for washing your hair. **2** a liquid *etc* used for cleaning other things, such as cars, carpets, armchairs *etc*. **3** a wash with shampoo: *I had a shampoo and set at the hairdresser's.* — *v* to wash with shampoo: *She shampoos her hair every day.*

shank /ʃank/ *n* the long straight part of a nail, screw *etc*.

shan't short for **shall not**.

shanty /ˈʃantɪ/ *n* a roughly-built hut or shack.

shape /ʃeɪp/ *n* **1** the form or outline of anything: *People are all different shapes and sizes*; *The house is built in the shape of a letter L*. **2** condition; state: *I must start training so as to get into good shape for the match.* — *v* **1** to make something into a certain shape; to form; to model: *She shaped the dough into three separate loaves.* **2** to influence strongly: *This event shaped his whole life.* **3** to develop: *The team is shaping well.*
-shaped: *A rugby ball is egg-shaped.*
'shapeless *adj* lacking shape: *a shapeless coat*. **'shapelessness** *n*.
'shapely *adj* having a pleasing shape: *a shapely body*. **'shapeliness** *n*.
out of shape 1 not in its proper shape: *I sat on my hat and it's rather out of shape.* **2** not as fit and healthy as you can be: *I realized how out of shape I was when we started to run.*
take shape to develop into a definite form: *My garden is gradually taking shape.*

share /ʃɛə(r)/ *n* **1** one of the parts of something that is divided among several people *etc*: *We all had a share of the cake*; *We each paid our share of the bill.* **2** the part played by a person in something done by several people *etc*: *I had no share in the decision.* **3** a fixed sum of money invested in a business company by a **'shareholder**. — *v* **1** to divide something among a number of people: *We shared out the money among us.* **2** to have or use something together with other people; to allow someone to use something of yours: *The students share a sitting-room*; *The little boy hated sharing his toys with other children.* **3** to pay part of a bill with someone else: *He wouldn't let her share the cost of the taxi.* **4** to tell someone about something: *She wanted to share the good news with her friends.*
share out to share among several people: *We shared out the food.*

shark /ʃɑːk/ *n* a type of large, fierce, flesh-eating fish.

sharp /ʃɑːp/ *adj* **1** having a thin edge that can cut, or a point that can pierce: *a sharp knife*. **2** clear; distinct: *These photographs are nice and sharp*; *sharp details*. **3** sudden; quick: *a sharp left turn.* **4** keen, acute or intense: *He gets a sharp pain after eating.* **5** angry; severe: *'Be quiet, children!' she said in a sharp voice.* **6** good at hearing; good at seeing: *Dogs have sharp ears*; *What sharp eyes you have!* **7** shrill; sudden: *a sharp cry.* **8** higher than the correct musical note: *The last note sounded sharp to me.* — *adv* **1** punctually: *Come at six o'clock sharp.* **2** with a change of direction: *Turn sharp left here.* **3** slightly higher than the correct musical pitch: *She always sings sharp.* — *n* a sign (♯) in music, that makes a note higher by another half note. **'sharpness** *n*.

'sharpen *v* to make or grow sharp: *He sharpened his pencil.*

'sharpener *n* a tool for sharpening: *a pencil-sharpener.*

'sharply *adv*: *a sharply-pointed piece of glass; The road turned sharply to the left; He spoke sharply to her for being late again.*

sharp-'witted *adj* able to think quickly and well; clever: *a sharp-witted boy.*

look sharp to be quick; to hurry: *Bring me the books and look sharp!*

shatter /'ʃatə(r)/ *v* **1** to break violently into small pieces: *The stone shattered the window; The window shattered.* **2** to upset greatly: *She was shattered by the news of his death.* **'shattered** *adj*.

shave /ʃeɪv/ *v* **1** to cut away hair with a razor: *He shaves only once a week; Bill has shaved his beard off; Many monks shave their heads.* **2** to scrape; to cut away: *I'll have to shave some wood off the edge of the door.* — *n*: *I need a wash and a shave.*

'shaven *adj* shaved: *Many monks have shaven heads.*

'shaver *n* an electrical tool for shaving hair.

'shavings *n* very thin strips of wood *etc*: *The glasses were packed in wood shavings.*

shawl /ʃɔːl/ *n* a garment for covering your shoulders, or your head and shoulders: *The old lady wore a woollen shawl round her shoulders.*

> See **cape**.

she /ʃiː/ *pron* (used as the subject of a verb) a female person or animal: *When the girl saw us, she asked the time.* — *n* a female person or animal: *Is a cow a he or a she?* **she-** female: *a she-wolf.*

sheaf /ʃiːf/, *plural* **sheaves** /ʃiːvz/, *n* a bundle: *a sheaf of corn; She was carrying a sheaf of papers.*

shear /ʃɪə(r)/ *v* **1** to clip or cut wool from a sheep. **2** to cut hair off: *All her curls have been shorn off; He has been shorn of all his curls.* **3** to cut: *The heavy blade sheared through the metal sheet.*

> **shear**; **sheared**; **shorn** /ʃɔːn/ or **sheared**: *He sheared the sheep; The sheep have been shorn (or sheared).*

shears /ʃɪəz/ *n* a cutting-tool with two blades, like a large pair of scissors: *These shears are blunt; Here is a sharper pair of shears.*

> **shears** takes a plural verb, but **a pair of shears** is singular.

sheath /ʃiːv/, *plural* **sheaths** /ʃiːðz/, *n* **1** a case for a sword or blade. **2** a long close-fitting covering: *The rocket is encased in a metal sheath.*

sheathe /ʃiːð/ *v* to put into a sheath: *He sheathed his sword.*

sheaves plural of **sheaf**.

shed[1] /ʃɛd/ *n* a roughly-built building for working in, or for storage: *a wooden shed; a garden shed.*

shed[2] /ʃɛd/ *v* **1** to send out light *etc*: *The torch shed a bright light on the path ahead.* **2** to cast off clothing, skin, leaves *etc*: *Many trees shed their leaves in autumn.* **3** to produce tears or blood: *Don't waste time shedding tears over your mistake — just don't make the same mistake again!; If only the countries of the world could settle their quarrels without shedding blood!*

> **shed**; **shed**; **shed**: *The moon shed a silver light on the sea; The trees had shed their leaves.*

she'd /ʃiːd/ short for **she had** or **she would**.

sheen /ʃiːn/ *n* shine; shininess.

sheep /ʃiːp/, *plural* **sheep**, *n* a kind of animal related to the goat, whose flesh is used as food and from whose wool clothing is made: *a flock of sheep.*

> A sheep **bleats**.
> A baby sheep is a **lamb**.
> A male sheep is a **ram**.
> A female sheep is a **ewe**.
> Sheep are looked after by a **shepherd**.

'sheepdog *n* a dog trained to work with sheep.

'sheepish *adj* foolish; ashamed: *a sheepish expression.* **'sheepishly** *adv*.

'sheepskin *n* leather made from the skin of a sheep, usually with the wool left on it: *a sheepskin coat.*

sheer /ʃɪə(r)/ *adj* **1** absolute: *It all happened by sheer chance.* **2** very steep: *a sheer drop to the sea.* — *adv*: *The land rises sheer out of the sea.*

sheet /ʃiːt/ *n* **1** a broad piece of cloth for a bed: *She put clean sheets on all the beds.* **2** a large, thin, flat piece of some material: *a sheet of paper; a sheet of glass.*

sheik or **sheikh** /ʃeɪk/ *n* an Arab chief.

shelf /ʃɛlf/, *plural* **shelves** /ʃɛlvz/, *n* a long narrow board for laying things on, fixed to a wall *etc*: *We'll have to put up some more shelves for all these books.*

shell /ʃɛl/ *n* **1** the hard outer covering of several kinds of sea or land animals, or of an egg, nut *etc*: *an eggshell; A tortoise can pull its head and legs under its shell.* **2** the framework or outer shape of a building: *After the fire, all that was left of the building was its shell.* **3** a metal case filled with explosives and fired from a large gun *etc*: *A shell exploded right beside him.* — *v* **1** to remove a vegetable *etc* from its shell or pod: *You have to shell peas before eating them.* **2** to fire explosive shells at troops *etc*: *to shell the enemy troops.*

'**shellfish**, *plural* **shellfish**, *n* any of several kinds of sea animal covered with a shell such as an oyster, crab *etc*.

'**shell-shock** *n* a nervous illness caused by the frightening conditions of war: *Many soldiers came back from the front suffering from shell-shock.*

come out of your shell to become less shy.

she'll /ʃiːl/ short for **she will**.

shelter /'ʃɛltə(r)/ *n* **1** a place where you are protected from the weather *etc*: *We gave the old man shelter for the night in our house; When the rain started, we took shelter under a tree.* **2** a building that gives protection: *At some bus stops there are bus shelters for people to wait in.* — *v* **1** to go into a place of shelter: *They had sheltered from a rain storm.* **2** to give protection: *The garden was sheltered by a row of tall trees.*

'**sheltered** *adj* **1** protected from the wind and rain: *They anchored the boat in a sheltered bay.* **2** protected from unpleasant things in life: *She had a very sheltered upbringing.*

shelve /ʃɛlv/ *v* **1** to slope downwards: *The seabed shelves steeply just here.* **2** to postpone a plan *etc*: *The project has been shelved for a year.*

shelves plural of **shelf**.

shelving /'ʃɛlvɪŋ/ *n* shelves or material for building shelves: *The supermarket shelving has been rearranged.*

shepherd /'ʃɛpəd/ *n* a person who looks after sheep: *The shepherd and his dog gathered the sheep in.* — *v* to guide a group of people to a place: *Tourists were being shepherded from room to room.*

'**shepherdess** *n* a female shepherd.

sherbet /'ʃɜːbət/ *n* a sweet powder that is mixed with water to make a fizzy drink, or is eaten as a sweet: *The little girl bought a packet of orange sherbet.*

sheriff /'ʃɛrɪf/ *n* in the USA, the chief law officer of a county, concerned with keeping order.

she's /ʃiːz/ short for **she is**, **she has**.

shield /ʃiːld/ *n* **1** a broad piece of metal, wood *etc* that soldiers in earlier times carried as a protection against weapons. **2** something that protects: *This steel plate acts as a heat shield.* **3** a trophy shaped like a shield: *My son won the shield for the high jump in the school sports.* — *v* to protect: *Motor-cyclists wear goggles to shield their eyes from dust; He put up his hand to shield his eyes from the sun.*

shift /ʃɪft/ *v* **1** to move; to change the position of something: *to shift furniture.* **2** to change direction: *The wind has shifted to the west.* **3** to transfer: *She shifted the blame on to me.* **4** to get rid of something; to remove: *This cleaning liquid shifts stains.* — *n* **1** a group of people who begin work on a job when another group stops work: *Cleaning the machinery is the job of the night-shift.* **2** the length of time, or the period of time during which this group works: *The men work an eight-hour shift; The evening shift begins at 17.00 hours.* **3** a change of position or direction: *There has been a shift in public opinion.*

'**shifty** *adj* dishonest: *His eyes have a shifty expression.*

shimmer /'ʃɪmə(r)/ *v* to shine with a quivering light: *The moonlight shimmered on the lake.*

shin /ʃɪn/ *n* the front part of your leg below the knee.

shine /ʃaɪn/ *v* **1** to give out light; to direct light towards someone or something: *The light shone from the window; The policeman shone his torch; He shone a torch on the lock.* **2** to be bright: *He polished the silver cup until it shone.* **3** to polish: *He tries to make a living by shining shoes.* **4** to be very good at something: *She shines at most sports.* — *n* **1** brightness; the state of being well polished: *He likes a good shine on his shoes.* **2** the polishing of something: *I'll just give my shoes a shine.*

> **shine; shone** /ʃɒn/; **shone**: *The sun shone all day; He got a fright when the torch was shone in his eyes.*
> But: *He shined my shoes for me; I've shined 20 pairs of shoes today.*

shingle /'ʃɪŋɡəl/ *n* the pebbles on a beach:

There's too much shingle and not enough sand on this beach.

shingles /'ʃɪŋgəlz/ *n* a kind of infectious disease causing a rash of painful blisters.

shining /'ʃaɪnɪŋ/ *adj* very bright and clear; producing or reflecting light; polished: *a shining star*; *The windows were clean and shining.*

shiny /'ʃaɪnɪ/ *adj* polished; reflecting light; glossy: *This paper has a shiny surface*; *clean, shiny shoes.*

ship /ʃɪp/ *n* **1** a large boat: *We could see a ship on the horizon*; *a fleet of ships.* **2** a vehicle that travels through the sky: *an airship*; *a spaceship.* — *v* to send goods by ship: *The books were shipped to Australia.*

> See **in**.

'shipbuilder *n* a person whose business is the construction of ships: *a firm of shipbuilders.* **'shipbuilding** *n*.

'shipment *n* **1** a load of goods sent by sea: *a shipment of wine from Portugal.* **2** the sending of goods by sea.

'shipper *n* a person who arranges for goods to be shipped: *a firm of shippers.*

'shipping *n* **1** transport by ship. **2** ships: *There is always a lot of shipping in the harbour.*

'shipwreck *n* **1** the accidental sinking or destruction of a ship: *There were many shipwrecks on the rocky coast.* **2** a wrecked ship: *an old shipwreck lying on the shore.* — *v*: *We were shipwrecked off the coast of Africa.*

'shipyard *n* a place where ships are built or repaired.

shirk /ʃɜːk/ *v* to avoid something that you shouldn't try to avoid: *to shirk work*; *to shirk the truth.* **'shirker** *n*.

shirt /ʃɜːt/ *n* a loose-fitting garment that you wear on the upper part of your body: *a short-sleeved shirt*; *She wore black jeans and a white cotton shirt.*

shit /ʃɪt/ *n* an impolite word for the solid waste matter from your bowels.

shiver /'ʃɪvə(r)/ *v* to tremble with cold, fear etc. — *n*: *She gave a little shiver as she put her toe in the water.*

'shivery *adj*: *The thought of ghosts gave her a shivery feeling*; *She felt shivery after her swim.*

shoal /ʃəʊl/ *n* a great number of fish swimming together in one place: *a shoal of herring.*

shock /ʃɒk/ *n* **1** a violent disturbance to your feelings: *The news of the accident gave us all a shock.* **2** the effect on your body of an electric current passing through it (usually called an **electric shock**): *He got a slight electric shock when he touched the wire.* **3** a sudden bump coming with great force: *the shock of an earthquake.* **4** an unhealthy condition of the body caused by a bad shock: *He is suffering from shock as a result of his accident*; *The doctor treated him for shock.* — *v* to upset; to horrify: *Everyone was shocked by his death.*

'shocking *adj* very bad: *shocking news*; *shocking behaviour.*

'shockingly *adv*: *The dress was shockingly expensive.*

shod /ʃɒd/ *adj* **1** with a shoe or shoes on. **2** with a hard metal tip or cover: *a steel-shod walking-stick.*

shoddy /'ʃɒdɪ/ *adj* badly made; poor in quality: *shoddy furniture*; *shoddy work.*

shoe /ʃuː/ *n* **1** an outer covering for your foot: *a new pair of shoes.* **2** a curved piece of iron nailed to the hoof of a horse (also called a **'horseshoe**). — *v* to put a shoe or shoes on a horse.

> **shoe**; **shod** /ʃɒd/ or **shoed** /ʃuːd/; **shod** or **shoed**: *The blacksmith shoed the horse*; *The horse has been shod.*

'shoelace *n* a cord for fastening a shoe.

'shoemaker *n* a person who makes, repairs or sells shoes.

shoestring /'ʃuːstrɪŋ/: **on a shoestring** using very little money: *The film was made on a shoestring.*

shone *see* **shine**.

shoo /ʃuː/ a word you shout when chasing an animal *etc* away. — *v*: *She shooed the pigeons away.*

shook *see* **shake**.

shoot /ʃuːt/ *v* **1** to fire bullets, arrows *etc* from a gun, bow *etc*: *The enemy were shooting at us*; *He shot an arrow through the air.* **2** to hit or kill with a bullet, arrow *etc*: *He went out to shoot pigeons*; *The prisoner was told he would be shot at dawn*; *The police shot him in the leg.* **3** to move swiftly: *He shot out of the room*; *The pain shot up his leg.* **4** to take moving pictures for a film: *That film was shot in Spain*; *We will start shooting next week.* **5** to kick or hit a ball *etc* at a goal in order to try to score: *Shoot!* — *n* a new growth on a plant: *The deer were eating the young shoots on the trees.*

shoot; **shot** /ʃɒt/; **shot**: *She shot the tiger*; *Help! I've been shot.*

'**shooting-star** *n* another name for a meteor.

shoot down 1 to hit a plane with a shell *etc* and cause it to crash. **2** to kill a person with a gun.

shoot up to grow; to increase rapidly: *Arthur has shot up since I last saw him*; *Prices have shot up.*

shop /ʃɒp/ *n* **1** a place where goods are sold: *a baker's shop*. **2** a place where any kind of industry is carried on; a workshop. — *v* to visit shops for the purpose of buying goods: *We shop on Saturdays*; *She goes shopping once a week.*

shop assistant a person employed in a shop to serve customers.

'**shopkeeper** *n* a person who owns and runs a shop.

'**shoplifter** *n* a person who steals goods from a shop. '**shoplifting** *n*.

'**shopper** *n* **1** a person who is shopping: *The street was full of shoppers*. **2** a large bag used when shopping.

'**shopping** *n* **1** the activity of buying goods in shops: *Have you a lot of shopping to do?* **2** the goods you have bought: *He helped her carry her shopping home.* — *adj*: *a shopping list*; *a shopping-basket*; *a shopping-bag.*

shopping centre a place, often a very large building, where there are a large number of different shops.

shop around to compare the price and quality of goods in various shops before deciding to buy: *It's worth shopping around — you may get a bargain.*

shore /ʃɔː(r)/ *n* the land along the edge of the sea or of any large area of water: *a walk along the shore*; *When the ship reached Gibraltar the passengers were allowed on shore.*

shorn see **shear**.

short /ʃɔːt/ *adj* **1** not long: *You look nice with your hair short*; *Do you think my dress is too short?* **2** not tall; smaller than usual: *a short man*. **3** not lasting long; brief: *a short film*; *in a very short time.* **4** not as much as it should be: *When I checked my change, I found it was 72 pence short.* **5** not having enough: *Most of us are short of money these days.* **6** crisp: *short pastry*. — *adv* suddenly: *He stopped short when he saw me.* '**shortness** *n*.

See **low** and **tall**.

'**shortage** *n* a lack; not enough of something: *a shortage of water.*

'**shortbread** *n* a crumbly biscuit that is made from flour, butter and sugar: *Would you like some shortbread with your tea?*

'**shortcake** *n* a soft kind of shortbread.

short circuit /ʃɔːt ˈsɜːkɪt/ a bad electrical connection that causes a machine to stop working properly. — *v* (**short-circuit**).

'**shortcoming** *n* a fault.

'**short cut** a quick way between two places: *I'm in a hurry — I'll take a short cut across the field.*

'**shorten** *v* to make or become shorter: *The dress is too long — we'll have to shorten it.*

'**shortening** *n* the fat used for making pastry.

'**shorthand** *n* a method of writing rapidly, using strokes, dots *etc* to represent sounds.

'**shortlist** *n* a list of the best people for a job *etc*, selected from a larger number of people.

short-lived /ʃɔːtˈlɪvd/ *adj* living or lasting only for a short time: *short-lived insects.*

'**shortly** *adv* soon: *He will be here shortly*; *Shortly after that, the police arrived.*

shorts *n* short trousers for men or women: *Where are my running shorts?*; *a clean pair of shorts.*

shorts takes a plural verb, but **a pair of shorts** is singular.

short-'sighted *adj* seeing clearly only things that are near: *I don't recognize people at a distance because I'm short-sighted.* **short-'sightedness** *n*.

short-'tempered *adj* easily made angry: *My father is very short-tempered in the mornings.*

short-'term *adj* only lasting for a short period of time.

cut short to interrupt; to leave something unfinished: *She had to cut her holiday short when she heard the news.*

fall short not to reach a certain target: *The money collected fell short of the amount required.*

for short as a shortening: *His name is Victor, but he's called Vic for short.*

go short not to get enough of something: *As children, we often went short of food.*

in short in a few words: *In short, you all need to work harder!*

run short of not to have enough: *We're running short of money.*

short and sweet: *His reply was short and sweet: 'Get out!'*

short for an abbreviation of: *'Phone' is short for 'telephone'*; *What is 'Ltd' short for?*

shot[1] /ʃɒt/ *n* **1** the firing of a bullet *etc*: *He fired one shot.* **2** the sound of a gun being fired: *He heard a shot.* **3** a throw, hit, turn *etc* in a game or competition: *It's your shot*; *Can I have a shot?*; *He played some good shots in that tennis match*; *Good shot!* **4** an attempt: *I don't know if I can do that, but I'll have a shot at it.* **5** a photograph or a scene in a film: *That's a lovely shot of the dog.* **6** someone who uses a gun: *He's a good shot.* **7** an injection: *a shot of pain killer.* **8** a heavy metal ball which is thrown as a sport.

'shotgun *n* a type of rifle.

like a shot very eagerly: *He accepted my invitation like a shot.*

a shot in the dark a guess.

shot[2] *see* **shoot**.

should /ʃʊd/ *v* **1** past tense of **shall**: *I thought I should never see you again*; *We wondered whether we'd ever get home.* **2** used to say what ought to be done *etc*: *You should hold your knife in your right hand*; *You shouldn't have said that, should you?* **3** used to say what is likely to happen *etc*: *If you leave now, you should arrive there by six o'clock.* **4** used after certain expressions of sorrow, surprise *etc*: *I'm surprised that you should dislike travelling so much.* **5** used after **if** in some sentences: *If anything should happen to me, I want you to remember everything I have told you today.* **6** used with **I** or **we** to express a wish: *We should like to thank you for your help*; *I'd love to see the Great Wall of China.* **7** used to describe an event that is rather surprising: *I was just about to get on the bus when who should come along but John, the very person I was going to visit.*

> **I should** or **I'd** /aɪd/;
> **we should** or **we'd** /wiːd/;
> **should not** or **shouldn't** /'ʃʊdənt/: *I said I'd be home by midnight*; *We shouldn't waste food, should we?*

shoulder /'ʃəʊdə(r)/ *n* **1** the part of your body between your neck and the upper part of your arm: *He was carrying the child on his shoulders.* **2** something that looks like a shoulder: *the shoulder of the hill.* — *v* **1** to lift something on to your shoulder: *He shouldered his pack and set off on his walk.* **2** to bear; to face: *He must shoulder his* responsibilities. **3** to make your way by pushing with your shoulder: *He shouldered his way through the crowd.*

shoulder bag a bag with a long strap that you wear over one shoulder.

shoulder blade the broad flat bone at the back of your shoulder.

shoulder to shoulder close together; side by side; *We'll fight shoulder to shoulder.*

shouldn't short for **should not**.

shout /ʃaʊt/ *n* a loud cry; a call: *He heard a shout*; *A shout went up from the crowd when he scored a goal.* — *v* to say something very loudly: *He shouted the message across the river*; *I'm not deaf — there's no need to shout*; *There seemed to be a voice shouting from the loudspeaker.*

shout down to shout loudly so that another person cannot be heard: *The angry workers shouted the manager down.*

shove /ʃʌv/ *v* to push roughly: *I shoved the papers into a drawer*; *I'm sorry I bumped into you — somebody shoved me*; *Stop shoving!* — *n* a rough push: *He gave the table a shove.*

shovel /'ʃʌvəl/ *n* a tool like a spade, with a short handle, used for scooping up and moving coal, gravel *etc.* — *v* to move with a shovel: *He shovelled snow from the path.*

> **shovelling** and **shovelled** are spelt with two **l**s.

show /ʃəʊ/ *v* **1** to let something be seen: *Show me your new dress*; *Please show your membership card when you come to the club*; *His work is showing signs of improvement.* **2** to be able to be seen: *The tear in your dress hardly shows.* **3** to present or display something for the public to look at: *They are showing a new film*; *Which film is showing at the cinema?*; *His paintings are being shown at the art gallery.* **4** to point out; to point to: *He showed me which road to take*; *Show me the man you saw yesterday.* **5** to guide: *Please show this lady to the door*; *They showed him round the factory.* **6** to demonstrate: *Will you show me how to do it?* **7** to prove: *That just shows how stupid he is.* — *n* **1** an entertainment, exhibition, performance *etc*: *a horse-show*; *a flower show*; *a TV show.* **2** the showing of some quality; an appearance; an impression: *There was no show of support for his suggestion*; *Good quality is more important than outward show.*

show; showed; shown /ʃoʊn/: *She showed me her drawing*; *The film was shown on television.*

> to go **to the cinema** (not **for a show**).

show business entertainment on stage, television *etc*, especially shows, comedy *etc*.

'showcase *n* a glass case in a museum *etc*, for displaying objects in.

'showdown *n* a fight or argument which settles a dispute that has lasted a long time: *It's time you had a showdown with him.*

for show only intended to impress people: *The books were only for show — nobody ever read them.*

good show! that's good!

on show being displayed: *There are over five hundred paintings on show here.*

show off 1 to display something for people to admire: *He showed off his new car.* **2** to try to impress other people by doing or saying things that you think they will admire: *Stop showing off!*

'show-off *n*: *What a show-off Willie is!*

show up 1 to reveal the faults of something: *Mary's drawing was so good that it showed mine up.* **2** to arrive as arranged: *He said he'd be there by six but he didn't show up.* **3** to make someone feel ashamed or embarrassed: *He showed the whole family up by arguing in public.*

shower /'ʃaʊə(r)/ *n* **1** a short fall of rain: *I got caught in a shower on my way here.* **2** anything resembling a fall of rain: *a shower of bullets.* **3** a bath in which water is sprayed down on you from above: *I'm going to take a shower*; *We're having a shower fitted in the bathroom.* — *v* **1** to pour down in large quantities; to give: *to shower someone with compliments.* **2** to bathe in a shower: *He showered and dressed.*

> See **rain**.

'showerproof *adj* waterproof, but only in a small amount of rain: *That coat is only showerproof and will not keep you dry in a storm.*

'showery *adj* raining occasionally: *showery weather.*

showing /'ʃoʊɪŋ/ *n* **1** an exhibition or display: *a showing of his recent paintings.* **2** a screening or performance: *Is there another showing later today?* **3** a display of behaviour that indicates what a person is like: *On this showing, he certainly won't get the job.*

showjumping /'ʃoʊdʒʌmpɪŋ/ *n* a competition in which people ride horses over fences.

showman /'ʃoʊmən/ *n* a person who produces shows and entertainments.

'showmanship *n* the ability to display things in an entertaining way: *Showmanship is important to a magician.*

shown *see* **show**.

showroom /'ʃoʊruːm/ *n* a room where objects for sale are displayed for people to see: *a car showroom.*

showy /'ʃoʊɪ/ *adj* too bright in colour *etc*; too easily noticed: *He wears rather showy clothes.*

shrank *see* **shrink**.

shrapnel /'ʃrapnəl/ *n* small pieces of metal from an exploding bomb *etc*: *The soldier was injured by shrapnel*; *a shrapnel wound.*

shred /ʃrɛd/ *n* **1** a long, narrow torn strip: *His shirt was torn to shreds*; *a tiny shred of material.* **2** a very small amount of something: *The police don't have a shred of evidence against me.* — *v* to cut or tear into shreds: *to shred paper.*

'shredder *n* a machine that shreds pieces of paper very finely in order to make it impossible to read them.

shrew /ʃruː/ *n* a small, brown animal like a mouse with a long, pointed nose and very sharp teeth.

shrewd /ʃruːd/ *adj* showing good judgement; wise: *a shrewd man*; *a shrewd choice.*

'shrewdly *adv*. **'shrewdness** *n*.

shriek /ʃriːk/ *v* to scream; to shout: *She shrieked whenever she saw a spider*; *We were shrieking with laughter.* — *n*: *She gave a shriek as she felt someone grab her arm*; *shrieks of laughter.*

shrill /ʃrɪl/ *adj* high and clear: *the shrill voice of a child.* **'shrilly** /'ʃrɪl-lɪ/ *adv*. **'shrillness** *n*.

shrimp /ʃrɪmp/ *n* **1** a small long-tailed shellfish. **2** an unkind word for a small person.

shrine /ʃraɪn/ *n* a sacred place: *Many people visited the shrine where the saint lay buried.*

shrink /ʃrɪŋk/ *v* **1** to become smaller because of washing *etc*: *My jersey shrank in the wash.* **2** to move back in fear: *She shrank back from the fierce dog.* **3** to want to avoid something: *She shrank from telling him the bad news.*

> **shrink; shrank** /ʃraŋk/; **shrunk** /ʃrʌŋk/: *The jersey shrank when I washed it*; *Have these socks shrunk?*

shrivel /'ʃrɪvəl/ *v* to make or become dried

up, wrinkled and withered: *The flowers shrivelled up in the heat.*

shroud /ʃraʊd/ *n* **1** a cloth wrapped around a dead body. **2** something that covers: *The mountain-top was hidden in a shroud of mist.* — *v* to cover; to hide: *Her death was shrouded in mystery.*

shrub /ʃrʌb/ *n* a small bush; a large plant.
  'shrubbery *n* an area where shrubs grow.

shrug /ʃrʌg/ *v* to show doubt, lack of interest *etc* by raising your shoulders: *When I asked him if he knew what had happened, he just shrugged his shoulders.* — *n*: *She gave a shrug of disbelief.*
  shrug off 1 to get rid of easily: *He always manages to shrug off colds.* **2** to dismiss as not important or serious: *She shrugged off the criticism of her new book.*

shrunk *see* **shrink**.

shrunken /'ʃrʌŋkən/ *adj* shrunk; having become very thin: *People become shrunken with age.*

shudder /'ʃʌdə(r)/ *v* to tremble from fear, disgust, cold *etc.* — *n*: *He gave a shudder of horror.*

shuffle /'ʃʌfəl/ *v* **1** to move your feet along the ground *etc* without lifting them: *The old man shuffled along the street.* **2** to mix playing-cards: *It's your turn to shuffle.* — *n*: *He gave the cards a shuffle.*

shun /ʃʌn/ *v* to avoid; to keep away from.

shunt /ʃʌnt/ *v* **1** to move a train or railway carriage from one track to another. **2** to move things or people from place to place: *I've been shunted around from one department to another all day.*

shut /ʃʌt/ *v* **1** to move a door, window, lid *etc* so as to cover the opening; to move a drawer, book *etc* so that it is no longer open; to close: *Shut that door, please!*; *Shut your eyes and don't look*; *The door shut with a bang*; *Shut your books, children!* **2** to close and lock a building *etc* at the end of the day *etc*; to be closed: *The shops all shut at half past five.* **3** to stop using a building *etc*: *The factory is going to be shut.* **4** to stop someone *etc* from getting through a door by shutting it: *The dog was shut inside the house.* — *adj* closed: *Is the door shut or open?*

> **shut; shut; shut**: *She shut the window; I've shut the door.*

shut away to hide or lock something in a place where nobody sees it.

shut down to be closed for a long time or for ever: *Another nuclear power station is to be shut down.*

shut off 1 to stop an engine working, a liquid flowing *etc*: *I'll need to shut the gas off before I repair the stove.* **2** to keep away: *He shut himself off from the rest of the world.*

shut out 1 to prevent a thing or person from getting in: *We had been shut out of our own house!* **2** to stop yourself from thinking about something: *She tried to shut the memory out.*

shut up 1 to stop speaking: *Tell them to shut up!*; *That'll shut him up!* **2** to close and lock: *It's time to shut up the shop.*

shutter /'ʃʌtə(r)/ *n* **1** a wooden cover for a window: *He closed the shutters.* **2** the moving cover over the lens of a camera, which opens when a photograph is taken.

shuttle /'ʃʌtəl/ *n* **1** in weaving, a device for carrying the thread backwards and forwards across the other threads. **2** a device for making loops in the lower thread in a sewing-machine. **3** an air, train or other transport service that operates backwards and forwards between two places: *an airline shuttle between London and Edinburgh*; *A space shuttle travels between space stations.*
  'shuttlecock *n* a cork ball with feathers fixed round it, used in the game of badminton.

shy /ʃaɪ/ *adj* **1** feeling nervous in the presence of others, especially strangers; not wanting to attract attention: *She is too shy to go to parties*; *He's shy of strangers.* **2** easily frightened; timid: *Deer are very shy animals.* — *v* to turn suddenly aside in fear: *The horse shied at the strangers.* **'shyly** *adv.* **'shyness** *n.*

> **shy; 'shyer** or **'shier; 'shyest** or **'shiest**: *He's a shy boy, but his sister is shyer, and his brother is the shyest of the three.*

shy away from to avoid doing or accepting because you are afraid or worried: *She shied away from telling him the bad news because she knew it would upset him.*

sibling /'sɪblɪŋ/ *n* a brother or sister: *He has three siblings — two sisters and one brother.*

sick /sɪk/ *adj* **1** vomiting; needing to vomit: *He has been sick three times today*; *I feel sick*; *If you get car-sick you probably get air-sick and sea-sick as well.* **2** ill: *The doctor told me that my husband is very sick.* **3** very tired of something: *I'm sick of doing this*;

I'm sick and tired of hearing about it! — *n* **1** vomit. **2** (**the sick**) people who are ill.

See also **ill**.

'sicken *v* **1** to become sick. **2** to disgust: *The thought of that crime sickens me.* **'sickening** *adj* .

make someone sick to disgust or make you very angry: *The way she always complains makes me sick!*

sickle /'sɪkəl/ *n* a tool with a curved blade for cutting grain *etc*.

sickly /'sɪklɪ/ *adj* often becoming ill; unhealthy: *a sickly child.*

sickness /'sɪknɪs/ *n* illness; disease: *There is a lot of sickness in the refugee camp.*

side /saɪd/ *n* **1** an edge: *Flowers were growing at the side of the field*; *He lives on the same side of the street as I do.* **2** a surface of something: *A cube has six sides.* **3** one of two surfaces that are not the top, bottom, front or back: *There is a label on the side of the wardrobe.* **4** either surface of a piece of paper, cloth *etc*: *Don't waste paper — write on both sides!* **5** the right or left part of the body: *I've got a pain in my right side.* **6** a part of a town *etc*: *He lives on the north side of the town.* **7** a slope of a hill: *a mountain-side.* **8** a team playing a match *etc*: *Which side is winning?* **9** one of the people or groups involved in an argument or quarrel: *Whose side are you on?* — *v* to support one person against another in an argument: *My brothers always side with each other against me when we quarrel.*

'sideboard *n* a large piece of furniture with shelves and drawers, for holding dishes and glasses: *She keeps her best plates in the sideboard in the sitting-room.*

-sided: *a four-sided figure.*

side effect an additional, usually bad, effect of a drug *etc*: *These pills have some unpleasant side effects.*

'sideline *n* **1** a business *etc* carried on in addition to your main job: *He's a mechanic, but he drives a taxi as a sideline.* **2** one of the lines around the edge of a football field *etc*.

'sidelines *n plural* the position or point of view of someone who is not actually taking part in a sport, argument *etc*: *She made some suggestions from the sidelines*; *He likes standing on the sidelines and not having to make decisions.*

'sidelong *adv, adj* from or to one side, not directly: *a sidelong glance.*

'side-road or **'side-street** *n* a small, minor road or street: *The man ran down the side-road and disappeared.*

'sidetrack *v* to distract someone into doing or talking about something else.

'sidewalk *n* a pavement; a footpath.

'sideways *adj, adv* to or towards one side: *He moved sideways*; *a sideways movement.*

side by side beside one another; close together: *They walked along the street side by side.*

side with to support one of the opposing sides in an argument *etc*: *Don't side with him against us!*

take sides to join in on one side or the other in an argument *etc*: *Everybody in the class took sides in the argument.*

siding /'saɪdɪŋ/ *n* a short railway line beside the main one where wagons, carriages and engines are kept while not in use.

sidle /'saɪdəl/ *v* to move quietly sideways, so as not to attract attention: *He sidled out of the room.*

siege /siːdʒ/ *n* an attempt to capture a fort or town by keeping it surrounded with armed forces until it surrenders: *The town is under siege.*

siege is spelt with **-ie-** (not **-ei-**).

siesta /sɪ'ɛstə/ *n* a short sleep or rest that people in hot countries take in the afternoon.

sieve /sɪv/ *n* a container with a bottom full of very small holes, used to separate liquids from solids or small, fine pieces from larger ones *etc*: *He poured the soup through a sieve to remove all the lumps.* — *v*: *She sieved the flour.*

sift /sɪft/ *v* **1** to sieve: *Sift the flour before making the cake.* **2** to separate things out and examine them carefully: *I had to sift through a lot of data before I found what I was looking for.*

sigh /saɪ/ *v* to take a long, deep breath and breathe out noisily, to express tiredness, relief and several other feelings: *She sighed with boredom.* — *n*: *She gave a sigh of relief.*
heave a sigh to sigh.

sight /saɪt/ *n* **1** the power of seeing: *The blind man had lost his sight in the war.* **2** the distance within which something can be seen: *The boat was within sight of land*; *The end of this job is in sight.* **3** something worth seeing: *to see the sights of London.* **4** a view:

A strange sight met our eyes. **5** something that looks ridiculous, shocking *etc*: *You look a sight in those awful clothes!* **6** a device on a gun *etc* that guides your eye when you aim. — *v* to get a view of something; to see suddenly: *The captain sighted the coast as dawn broke.*

-sighted having certain kinds of eye-sight: *a long-sighted person.*

'sighting *n* an occasion when something is seen: *The man the police are looking for has been sighted twice in the city.*

'sight-seeing *n* visiting the famous and interesting buildings and places in a city *etc*: *We spent the day sight-seeing in London.* **'sightseer** /ˈsaɪtsiːə(r)/ *n*.

at first sight when first seen or examined: *At first sight, she appeared to be very old, but she really wasn't.*

at sight or **on sight** as soon as someone or something is seen: *The soldiers were told to shoot the enemy on sight.*

catch sight of to see: *He caught sight of her in the crowd.*

in sight expected to happen soon: *There seemed to be no end in sight.*

lose sight of to stop being able to see: *She lost sight of him in the crowd.*

sign /saɪn/ *n* **1** a mark used to mean something; a symbol: *+ is the sign for addition.* **2** a notice that gives information to the public: *The sign above the shop-door said 'Hamid & Sons, grocers'; a road-sign.* **3** a movement that is intended to tell someone something: *He made a sign to me to keep still.* **4** something that is evidence of something else: *There were no signs of life at the house, so he thought they were away.* **5** something that shows what is coming: *Clouds are often a sign of rain.* — *v* **1** to write your name on a document *etc*: *Sign at the bottom, please; He signed his name on the document.* **2** to make a movement that tells someone something: *She signed to me to say nothing.*

sign in or **sign out** to officially record your arriving or leaving a place by writing your name in a book.

sign up 1 to agree formally to do something: *He has signed up to join the army; I've signed up for a French language course.* **2** to get someone to sign a contract: *The team has signed up two new players in a month.*

signal /ˈsɪgnəl/ *n* **1** a sign, for example a movement of the hand, a light, a sound *etc*, giving a command, warning or other message: *He gave the signal to advance.* **2** a device that uses coloured lights to tell you when to stop or go: *a railway signal; traffic signals.* **3** the sound received or sent out by a radio set *etc*. — *v*: *The policeman signalled the driver to stop; to signal a message; She signalled to him across the room.*

'signalman *n* **1** a person who works railway signals. **2** a person who sends signals: *He is a signalman in the army.*

signature /ˈsɪgnətʃə(r)/ *n* a signed name: *His signature is on the cheque.*

signboard /ˈsaɪnbɔːd/ *n* a board with a notice on it: *The signboard said 'House for Sale'.*

significance /sɪgˈnɪfɪkəns/ *n* meaning; importance: *a matter of great significance.*

significant /sɪgˈnɪfɪkənt/ *adj* full of meaning; important. **sigˈnificantly** *adv*.

signify /ˈsɪgnɪfaɪ/ *v* **1** to mean: *A frown signifies disapproval.* **2** to show: *He signified his approval with a nod.*

sign language /ˈsaɪn læŋwɪdʒ/ *n* a system of hand gestures used as a language by deaf people.

signpost /ˈsaɪnpoʊst/ *n* a post with a sign on it showing the direction and distance of places: *We passed a signpost that said 'London 40 kilometres'.*

silence /ˈsaɪləns/ *n* a time when there is no sound: *A sudden silence followed his remark.* — *v* to make silent: *The arrival of the teacher silenced the class.* — a cry used to tell people to be quiet: *'Silence, children!'*

silencer /ˈsaɪlənsə(r)/ *n* a part of a gun or engine exhaust that reduces the noise it makes.

silent /ˈsaɪlənt/ *adj* without noise; without sound; very quiet: *The house was empty and silent; The tiger moved through the grass with silent tread.* **'silently** *adv*.

in silence without saying anything: *The children listened in silence to the story.*

silhouette /sɪluːˈɛt/ *n* a dark image showing only the outline of a person, like a shadow: *We could see his silhouette against the curtain.*

silhou'etted *adj* appearing as a dark shape against a light background: *The trees were silhouetted against the silver sky.*

silicon /ˈsɪlɪkən/ *n* a substance that occurs as grey crystals or brown powder, and is used as a semiconductor in electronic devices.

silicon chip a tiny piece of silicon used in computers *etc*.

silk /sɪlk/ *n* **1** very fine, soft threads made by silkworms. **2** thread, cloth *etc* made from this: *The dress was made of silk.* — *adj*: *a silk dress.*

'silkworm *n* a type of caterpillar that makes silk.

'silky *adj* soft, fine and rather shiny like silk: *silky hair; silky fur.*

sill /sɪl/ *n* a ledge of wood, stone *etc* at the bottom of a window: *a window-sill.*

silly /'sɪlɪ/ *adj* foolish; not sensible: *Don't be so silly!; silly children.* **'silliness** *n*.

silt /sɪlt/ *n* fine sand and mud left behind by flowing water.

silver /'sɪlvə(r)/ *n* **1** a precious, shiny grey metal that is used in jewellery, ornaments *etc*: *The tray was made of solid silver.* **2** things made of silver, especially knives, forks, spoons *etc*: *Burglars broke into the house and stole all our silver.* — *adj* **1** made of, of the colour of, or looking like, silver: *a silver brooch; silver stars; silver paint.* **2** twenty-fifth: *a silver wedding anniversary.*

silver foil, **silver paper** a common type of wrapping material, made of metal, with a silvery appearance: *The sweets were wrapped in silver paper.*

silver medal in competitions, the medal awarded as second prize.

'silvery *adj* like silver, especially in colour: *the silvery moon.*

similar /'sɪmɪlə(r)/ *adj* like something else; alike: *My house is similar to yours; Our jobs are similar.* **similarity** /sɪmɪ'larɪtɪ/ *n*.

'similarly *adv* in the same, or a similar, way.

simile /'sɪmɪlɪ/ *n* any phrase in which one thing is described as being like another: *The phrase 'eyes sparkling like diamonds' is a simile.*

simmer /'sɪmə(r)/ *v* to cook gently; to boil very gently: *The stew simmered on the stove.*

simmer down to stop being angry and become calm again: *She was so angry she thought a long walk would help her simmer down.*

simple /'sɪmpəl/ *adj* **1** not difficult; easy: *a simple task.* **2** not complicated: *a simple design.* **3** without luxury: *He leads a very simple life.* **4** plain: *the simple truth.* **5** full of trust: *the simple mind of a child.* **'simpleness** *n*.

simple-'minded *adj* stupid.

simplicity /sɪm'plɪsɪtɪ/ *n* the quality of simpleness: *a task of the utmost simplicity.*

simplify /'sɪmplɪfaɪ/ *v* to make something simpler: *This sentence is too long and complicated — can you simplify it?* **simplifi'cation** *n*. **'simplified** *adj*.

sim'plistic *adj* too simple and straightforward: *He gave a simplistic explanation which did not reflect the complicated situation.*

'simply *adv* **1** only: *I was simply trying to help.* **2** absolutely: *simply beautiful.* **3** in a simple manner: *She was always very simply dressed.*

simulate /'sɪmjʊleɪt/ *v* **1** to pretend: *He simulated illness in order not to have to go to school.* **2** to make something appear to be real: *This machine simulates the flight of an aeroplane.* **simu'lation** *n*.

'simulated *adj* artificial; not real: *simulated leather; a simulated accident.*

'simulator *n* a device that simulates particular conditions: *The astronauts had to spend a lot of time in the space simulator to get used to weightlessness.*

simultaneous /sɪməl'teɪnɪəs/ *adj* happening, or done, at exactly the same time: *When you go to a play in a foreign language, you can sometimes get a device that gives you a simultaneous translation.* **simul'taneously** *adv*.

sin /sɪn/ *n* wickedness; a wicked act, especially one that breaks a religious law: *It is a sin to envy the possessions of other people; Lying and cheating are both sins.* — *v* to do wrong; to commit a sin: *People ask God to forgive them when they have sinned.*

since /sɪns/ *conjunction* **1** from the time that: *Since I left school, I have been working as a shop assistant.* **2** at a time after: *I've had flu since I last saw you.* **3** because: *Since you are so unwilling to help, I shall have to do the job myself.* — *adv* **1** from that time onwards: *She broke her leg last year and has been limping ever since.* **2** at a later time: *I didn't like him then, but we have since become friends.* — *prep* **1** from the time of something in the past until the present time: *She has been very unhappy ever since her quarrel with her boyfriend.* **2** at a time between something in the past and the present time: *I've changed my address since last year.*

> Do not use **ago** with **since**: *It is months since I last saw Jim*, or *I last saw Jim months ago* (not *It is months ago since I last saw Jim*). *It was months ago that I last saw Jim* is correct.
> See also **for**.

sincere /sɪn'sɪə(r)/ *adj* **1** true; genuine: *sincere love; sincere friends.* **2** not trying to pretend or deceive: *a sincere person*. **sin'cerity** *n*.

> The opposite of **sincere** is **insincere**.

sin'cerely *adv*: *I sincerely hope that you will succeed*.

yours sincerely a phrase used to end formal letters which begin 'Dear Mr.' or 'Dear Mrs.' *etc*, addressing a person by name.

> See **faithfully**.

sinew /'sɪnjuː/ *n* a strong cord that joins a muscle to a bone.

sinful /'sɪnfʊl/ *adj* wicked. **'sinfully** *adv*. **'sinfulness** *n*.

sing /sɪŋ/ *v* to make musical sounds with your voice: *He sings very well*; *She sang a Scottish song*; *I could hear the birds singing*.

> **sing**; **sang** /saŋ/; **sung** /sʌŋ/: *She sang while she worked*; *This song should be sung to the harp*.

'singer *n* a person who sings: *Are you a good singer?*; *He is training to be an opera singer*; *a choir of 40 singers*.

'singing *n*: *She's going to study singing when she leaves school*. — *adj*: *a singing lesson*; *a singing-teacher*.

singe /sɪndʒ/ *v* to burn slightly; to scorch: *She singed her dress by ironing it with too hot an iron*.

> **'singeing** meaning 'burning slightly' is spelt with an **e**.

single /'sɪŋɡəl/ *adj* **1** one only: *The spider hung on a single thread*. **2** for one person only: *a single bed*. **3** not married: *a single person*. **4** for, or in, one direction only: *a single fare*; *a single journey*; *Is your ticket single or return?* — *n* a one-way ticket: *Do you want a single or return?* **'singleness** *n*.

single-'handed *adj*, *adv* working *etc* by yourself, without help: *He runs the restaurant single-handed*.

single-'minded *adj* having only one clear aim or purpose: *You must be completely single-minded if you want to succeed in business nowadays*.

single parent a mother or father bringing up a child or children alone.

'singles *n* a tennis match *etc* in which there is one player on each side.

'singly *adv* one by one; separately: *They all arrived together, but they left singly*.

single out to pick out for special treatment: *He was singled out to receive special thanks for his work*.

singular /'sɪŋɡjʊlə(r)/ *n* the form of a word which expresses only one: *'Foot' is the singular of 'feet'*; *Is this noun in the singular or plural?* — *adj* **1** referring to one only: *a singular verb*. **2** a rather old-fashioned word for unusual or remarkable: *She was a woman of singular beauty*.

'singularly *adv* unusually; to a remarkable degree: *I found him to be a singularly unpleasant character*.

sinister /'sɪnɪstə(r)/ *adj* suggesting, or warning of, evil: *sinister happenings*; *His disappearance is very sinister*.

sink /sɪŋk/ *v* **1** to go down below the surface of water; to make a ship *etc* do this: *The ship sank in deep water*; *The battleship was sunk by a torpedo*. **2** to go down; to get lower: *The sun sank slowly behind the hills*; *Her voice sank to a whisper*. **3** to go deeply into something: *Rain sinks into the soil*. **4** to become sad: *My heart sinks when I think of the difficulties ahead*. — *n* a basin with a drain and a water supply connected to it: *He washed the dishes in the sink*.

> **sink**; **sank** /saŋk/; **sunk** /sʌŋk/: *The ship sank*; *The stone had sunk to the bottom of the lake*.

sink in 1 to become absorbed: *We tried to wipe the wine up before it sank into the carpet*. **2** to be fully realized or understood: *The news didn't really sink in until I read it in the paper*.

sinner /'sɪnə(r)/ *n* a person who sins.

sinus /'saɪnəs/ *n* one of the spaces in the bones of the face near the nose: *Your sinuses may get blocked when you have a bad cold*.

sip /sɪp/ *v* to drink in very small mouthfuls. — *n* a very small mouthful: *She took a sip of the medicine*.

siphon or **syphon** /'saɪfən/ *n* **1** a bent pipe or tube for moving liquid from one container into another, lower, container: *He used a siphon to remove the petrol from the tank*. **2** a bottle which makes the liquid in it fizzy as it is let out: *He got some soda-water from the siphon*.

siphon off to draw liquid from a container: *He siphoned off the petrol from the tank*.

sir /sɜː(r)/ *n* **1** a polite word you use for addressing a man: *Excuse me, sir!*; *He started his letter 'Dear Sirs,'*. **2** used as the

siren

title of a knight or a nobleman: *Sir Thomas Raffles*.

siren /'saɪərən/ *n* a device that gives out a loud shrill noise as a signal or a warning: *a factory siren*.

sister /'sɪstə(r)/ *n* **1** a female relation who has the same parents as you do: *I have a brother and two sisters*. **2** a senior nurse: *She's a sister on Ward 5*. **3** a member of a nunnery *etc*; a nun: *The sisters prayed together*.

'**sister-in-law**, *plural* '**sisters-in-law**, *n* **1** the sister of your husband or wife. **2** your brother's wife.

'**sisterly** *adj* of or like a sister: *sisterly love*.

sit /sɪt/ *v* **1** to rest on your bottom; to be seated: *He likes sitting on the floor; She was sitting on a bench in the middle of the corridor*. **2** to lie; to be in, or put in, a certain position: *The parcel is sitting on the table; She sat the baby on the floor*. **3** to be an official member of a committee *etc*: *He sat on several committees*. **4** to perch: *An owl was sitting on the branch*. **5** to take an examination: *to sit an English exam*. **6** to have your picture painted or your photograph taken: *She is sitting for a portrait*.

> **sit**; **sat** /sat/; **sat**: *We sat in silence*; *He had sat there for three hours*.

sit about or **sit around** to do nothing except sit, usually because there's nothing else to do: *I hate sitting around doing nothing*.

sit back to rest: *He sat back in his armchair and read the newspaper*.

sit down to take a seat; to get into a sitting position: *Let's sit down over here*; *Do sit down!*

sit out 1 to stay patiently in a difficult situation until the end: *We didn't enjoy the concert but we sat it out because our friends did*. **2** not to join in with a part of an event: *We sat out the fast dances because it was so hot in the hall*.

sit up 1 to rise to a sitting position: *Can the patient sit up?* **2** not to go to bed although it is very late: *We sat up all night discussing the situation*.

site /saɪt/ *n* a place where a building, town *etc* is, was, or is to be, built: *a building-site; The site for the new factory has not been chosen yet*.

sit-in /'sɪtɪn/ *n* a protest in which people occupy a building for a long time: *The students campaigning for higher grants staged a sit-in in the library*.

sitting /'sɪtɪŋ/ *n* **1** one of the times when a particular meal is served in the same place to a different group of people: *There are two sittings for dinner: at seven o'clock and at nine*. **2** a session; a time when an official group meets.

sitting-room /'sɪtɪŋruːm/ *n* the room in a house that is used for sitting in *etc*: *She took the guests into the sitting-room*.

situated /'sɪtʃʊeɪtɪd/ *adj* to be in a particular place: *The new school is situated on the north side of town*.

situation /sɪtʃʊ'eɪʃən/ *n* **1** circumstances: *an awkward situation*. **2** a job: *She found a situation as a secretary*.

six /sɪks/ *n* **1** the number 6. **2** the age of 6. — *adj* **1** 6 in number. **2** aged 6.

at sixes and sevens in confusion: *We've been at sixes and sevens since we moved house*.

sixth *n* one of six equal parts. — *n, adj* the next after the fifth.

sixteen /sɪk'stiːn/ *n* **1** the number 16. **2** the age of 16. — *adj* **1** 16 in number. **2** aged 16.

sixty /'sɪkstɪ/ *n* **1** the number 60. **2** the age of 60. — *adj* **1** 60 in number. **2** aged 60.

size /saɪz/ *n* **1** largeness: *an area the size of a football pitch*. **2** a particular measurement in clothes, shoes *etc*: *I take size 5 in shoes*.

'**sizeable** *adj* fairly large: *Sarah had a sizeable bruise on her knee after falling downstairs*.

size up to study something carefully in order to form an opinion about it: *I looked at the man for a long time, trying to size him up*.

sizzle /'sɪzəl/ *v* to make a hissing sound: *The steak sizzled in the frying-pan*.

skate /skeɪt/ *n* **1** a boot with a steel blade fixed to it for moving on ice *etc*. **2** a roller-skate. — *v* to move on skates: *Can you skate?; to go skating on the river*. '**skater** *n*.

'**skateboard** *n* a narrow board with four small wheels, that you stand on and ride about on.

roller-skate   ice-skate

skateboard

'skateboarding *n* the activity of riding on a skateboard: *The boys do a lot of skateboarding in the park.*

'skating *n* the sport or activity of moving around on ice wearing skates.

'skating-rink *n* an area of ice designed for skating on.

skate round or **skate over** to avoid facing or considering: *She skated over the problems.*

skeleton /'skɛlɪtən/ *n* **1** the bony framework of an animal or person: *The archaeologists dug up the skeleton of a dinosaur.* **2** any framework or outline: *the steel skeleton of a building.*

sketch /skɛtʃ/ *n* **1** a rough plan; a quick drawing: *Make a quick sketch of the classroom.* **2** a short account without many details: *The book began with a sketch of the author's life.* **3** a short comedy scene in a show on stage or on television. — *v*: *They went out with their pencils and paper and sketched the church.*

'sketch-book *n* a book for doing sketches in.

'sketchy *adj* not thorough: *My knowledge of chemistry is rather sketchy.*

skewer /'skjuːə(r)/ *n* a long metal pin for roasting meat on.

ski /skiː/, *plural* **skis**, *n* one of a pair of long narrow strips of wood *etc* that are attached to your feet for gliding over snow, water *etc.* — *v* to move on skis: *Can you ski?*; *to go skiing in the mountains.* — *adj*: *a ski instructor*; *ski boots.*

> **ski; skiing; skied** /skiːd/; **skied**: *I went skiing at Christmas*; *He skied down the slope.*

skid /skɪd/ *v* to slide accidentally sideways: *The back wheel of his bike skidded and he fell off.* — *n*: *I had a nasty skid on a patch of ice.*

skier /'skiːə(r)/ *n* someone who skies: *He's a good skier.* **'skiing** *n*.

skilful /'skɪlfəl/ *adj* having, or showing, skill: *a skilful surgeon.* **'skilfully** *adv.* **'skilfulness** *n*.

> **skilful** is spelt with **-l-** (not **-ll-**).

skill /skɪl/ *n* **1** cleverness at doing something: *This job requires a lot of skill.* **2** a job or activity that requires training and practice; an art: *Children quickly master the skills of reading and writing.*

skilled *adj* **1** having skill, especially skill gained by training: *a skilled craftsman*; *She is skilled at all types of dressmaking.* **2** requiring skill: *a skilled job.*

skim /skɪm/ *v* **1** to remove floating matter, for example cream, from the surface of a liquid: *Skim the fat off the gravy.* **2** to move lightly and quickly over a surface: *The bird skimmed across the water.* **3** to read quickly, missing out parts: *She skimmed through the book.*

skimmed milk milk from which the cream has been removed.

skimp /skɪmp/ *v* to provide or use too little of something: *Many old people skimp on food and heating to save money.*

'skimpy *adj* brief or too small and not covering very much; *She wore a skimpy swimsuit.*

skin /skɪn/ *n* **1** the natural outer covering of an animal or person: *She felt the cool breeze on her skin*; *A snake can shed its skin.* **2** a thin outer layer on fruit *etc*: *a tomato-skin.* **3** a thin film or layer that forms on a liquid: *Boiled milk often has a skin on it.* — *v* to remove the skin from: *He skinned and cooked the rabbit.*

skin-'deep *adj* affecting the surface only and not really important: *Beauty is only skin-deep.*

'skin-diver *n* someone who does skin-diving.

'skin-diving *n* the activity of swimming under water without a special diving suit, using only light breathing equipment.

skin-'tight *adj* fitting very tightly: *His jeans were skin-tight.*

by the skin of your teeth only just: *We escaped by the skin of our teeth.*

skinny /'skɪnɪ/ *adj* very thin: *You must eat more — you're very skinny.*

skip /skɪp/ *v* **1** to go along with a hop on each foot in turn: *The little girl skipped up the path.* **2** to jump over a rope that you turn under your feet and over your head. **3** to miss out: *Skip Chapter 2.* **4** not to attend something that you should attend: *The boys were punished for skipping their French class.* — *n* a hop on one foot in skipping.

skipper /'skɪpə(r)/ *n* the captain of a ship, an aeroplane, or a team. — *v*: *Who skippered the team?*

skipping-rope /'skɪpɪŋroʊp/ *n* a rope, often with handles attached to either end, that is used for skipping.

skirmish /'skɜːmɪʃ/ *n* a brief battle or argument: *He was killed in a skirmish between* *the protesters and the police*; *a skirmish in parliament over the new law.*

skirt /skɜːt/ *n* **1** a garment, worn by women, that hangs from the waist: *Was she wearing trousers or a skirt?* **2** the lower part of a dress, coat *etc*: *a dress with a narrow skirt.* — *v* to go around the edge of something: *Fields skirted the motorway.*

skirt around or **skirt round** to avoid something; *The manager skirted round the subject of a pay increase.*

skit /skɪt/ *n* a short act on stage, or piece of writing, that makes fun of something: *The skit on the policeman was the funniest part of the show.*

skittle /'skɪtəl/ *n* a bottle-shaped object that you try to knock down with a ball.

'skittles *n* a game in which the players try to knock down a number of skittles all at once with a ball.

skulk /skʌlk/ *v* to wait, hidden from view, to avoid meeting people: *He was discovered skulking in the bushes.*

skull /skʌl/ *n* the bony case that contains your brain.

skunk /skʌŋk/ *n* a small animal, found in North America, that defends itself by giving out a bad-smelling liquid.

sky /skaɪ/ *n* the part of space above the earth, where you can see the sun, moon *etc*; the heavens: *The sky was blue and cloudless; The skies were grey all week.*

'sky-diver *n* someone who does sky-diving.
'sky-diving *n* the activity of jumping from an aircraft and performing tricks in the air before your parachute opens.
sky-'high *adj, adv* very high: *sky-high prices; The car was blown sky-high by the explosion.*
'skyline *n* the outline of buildings, hills *etc* seen against the sky: *the New York skyline.*
'skyscraper *n* a high building of very many storeys.

slab /slab/ *n* a thick slice; a thick flat piece: *concrete slabs; a slab of cake.*

slack /slak/ *adj* **1** loose; not tightly stretched: *Leave the rope slack.* **2** not carefully or properly done: *The robbers were looking for signs of slack security.* **3** lazy; not hard-working. **'slackly** *adv.* **'slackness** *n.*

slacken /'slakən/ *v* to make or become looser: *She felt his grip on her arm slacken.*

slacks /slaks/ *n* loose, casual trousers.

slain *see* **slay**.

slalom /'slɑːləm/ *n* a race in and out of obstacles on a twisting course, usually on skis or in canoes.

slam /slam/ *v* to shut violently, making a loud noise: *He slammed the door.* — *n*: *The door closed with a slam.*

slander /'slɑːndə(r)/ *n* a spoken statement which tells lies about someone: *Slander could damage a person's good reputation.* — *v.*

slang /slaŋ/ *n* informal words or phrases that you use in conversation, especially with people of your own age, but not when you are writing or being polite: *school slang; 'Mug' is slang for 'face'.*

slant /slɑːnt/ *v* to slope: *The house is very old and all the floors and ceilings slant a little.* — *n*: *Your writing has a backward slant.*
'slanting *adj*: *slanting writing.*

slap /slap/ *v* **1** to give someone a blow with the palm of your hand or anything flat: *She slapped his face.* **2** to put something onto a surface quickly and carelessly: *She ran upstairs and slapped on some make-up.* — *n*: *Tim got a slap from his mother for being rude.*

slapdash /'slapdaʃ/ *adj* quickly and carelessly done: *His work has become rather slapdash recently.*

slapstick /'slapstɪk/ *n* a kind of comedy that uses actions, not words, to make you laugh: *Slapstick is the kind of comedy in which people throw messy pies at each other's faces, and trip each other up.*

slash /slaʃ/ *v* **1** to make long cuts in something: *Her attacker slashed her arm with a razor.* **2** to strike violently: *He slashed at the snake with a stick.* **3** to greatly reduce something suddenly: *The workforce had been slashed from 410 000 to 300 000.* — *n*: *There was a long slash in her dress; He gave the snake a slash with his stick.*

slat /slat/ *n* a thin strip of wood or metal: *The door is made of narrow slats.*

slate /sleɪt/ *n* an easily split kind of stone, blue or grey in colour; a shaped piece of this, used to make roofs: *Slates fell off the roof in the wind.*

slaughter /'slɔːtə(r)/ *n* **1** the killing of people or animals in large numbers: *Many people protested at the slaughter of seals.* **2** the killing of animals for food: *Methods of slaughter must be humane.* — *v* **1** to kill animals for food: *Thousands of cattle are slaughtered here every year.* **2** to kill in a cruel manner, especially in large numbers: *The soldiers slaughtered the villagers.*

'slaughter-house *n* a place where animals are killed for food; an abattoir.

slave /sleɪv/ *n* someone who works for and belongs to someone else: *In the 19th century many Africans were sold as slaves in the United States.* — *v* to work very hard: *I've been slaving away all day while you've been sitting watching television.* **'slavery** *n*.

slay /sleɪ/ *v* to kill.

> **slay; slew** /sluː/; **slain** /sleɪn/: *Jack slew the giant*; *The dragon was slain by St George.*

sleazy /'sliːzɪ/ *adj* dirty, neglected and seeming to be dishonest: *a sleazy part of town.*

sledge /slɛdʒ/ *v* a vehicle made for sliding upon snow. — *v* to ride on a sledge: *The children went sledging in the snow.*

sleek /sliːk/ *adj* smooth and shining: *sleek hair.*

sleep /sliːp/ *v* to rest with your eyes closed, in a state of natural unconsciousness: *Goodnight — sleep well!*; *I can't sleep — I'm not tired.* — *n*: *It is important for children to get plenty of sleep*; *I had a nice long sleep this afternoon*; *I had only four hours' sleep last night.*

> **sleep; slept** /slɛpt/; **slept**: *I slept well last night*; *John has slept in that room all his life.*

'sleeper *n* **1** a person who is asleep: *Nothing occurred to disturb the sleepers.* **2** a compartment you sleep in, on a railway train: *I'd like to book a sleeper on the London train.*

sleeping bag a large warm bag for sleeping in, used by campers, mountaineers *etc*.

sleeping pill or **sleeping tablet** a pill that can be taken to make you sleep.

'sleepless *adj* without sleep: *He spent a sleepless night worrying about the exam.*

'sleepwalk *v* to walk about while you are asleep: *She was sleepwalking again last night.* **'sleepwalker** *n*.

'sleepy *adj* **1** wanting to sleep; drowsy: *I feel very sleepy after that long walk.* **2** dull; not bright and alert: *She always has a sleepy expression.* **3** very quiet; lacking excitement: *a sleepy town.* **'sleepily** *adv*. **'sleepiness** *n*.

get to sleep to succeed in going to sleep.

go to sleep 1 to start sleeping: *It was late when the children finally went to sleep.* **2** to become numb: *My legs went to sleep because I had been kneeling on the floor for so long.*

put to sleep 1 to make someone unconscious with an anaesthetic: *The doctor will give you an injection to put you to sleep.* **2** to kill an animal painlessly: *As my cat was so old and ill, he had to be put to sleep.*

sleep in to sleep longer than you usually do: *Sorry I'm late — I slept in.*

sleep like a log or **sleep like a top** to sleep very well: *After my hard day's work I slept like a log.*

sleet /sliːt/ *n* rain mixed with snow or hail: *It was getting colder and the rain was beginning to turn to sleet.*

sleeve /sliːv/ *n* **1** the part of a garment that covers your arm: *He tore the sleeve of his jacket.* **2** a stiff envelope for a gramophone record.

-sleeved: *a long-sleeved dress.*

'sleeveless *adj* without sleeves: *a sleeveless dress.*

have or **keep something up your sleeve** to keep something secret for possible use at a later time: *I'm keeping this idea up my sleeve.*

sleigh /sleɪ/ *n* a large sledge, pulled by a horse.

sleight /slaɪt/: **sleight of hand** skill in moving your hands quickly to trick or deceive people: *Conjurors rely on sleight of hand to perform tricks.*

slender /'slɛndə(r)/ *adj* **1** thin; slim; narrow: *She is tall and slender*; *a tree with a slender trunk.* **2** slight; small: *His chances of winning are extremely slender.*

slept *see* **sleep**.

slew *see* **slay**.

slice /slaɪs/ *n* a thin broad piece of meat, bread *etc*; a slab or a triangular section cut from a cake: *How many slices of meat would you like?*; *She cut herself a large slice of cake.* — *v* **1** to cut into slices: *He sliced the cucumber.* **2** to cut with a sharp blade or knife: *Alan sliced off the end of the packet.* **sliced** *adj* cut into slices: *a sliced loaf.*

slick /slɪk/ *adj* **1** done well and efficiently without seeming to involve much effort: *a slick performance.* **2** clever at persuading people but perhaps not completely honest: *a slick salesman.* — *n* a broad band of oil floating on the surface of the sea *etc*: *An oil-slick is floating towards the coast.*

slide /slaɪd/ *v* **1** to move over a surface fast and smoothly; to slip: *The coin slid under the chair*; *He slid the coin across the table to me*; *Children must not slide in the school corridors.* **2** to move downwards or get worse: *sliding standards*; *He slid back into his old bad habits.*— *n* **1** the action of sliding: *to have a slide on the ice.* **2** a playground

slight

apparatus with a smooth sloping surface, for children to slide down. **3** a small glass plate on which specimens are placed when they are viewed under a microscope. **4** a small transparent photograph for projecting on to a screen *etc*: *The lecture was illustrated with slides.*

> **slide; slid** /slɪd/; **slid**: *He slid down the icy slope*; *The book had slid across the floor.*

sliding door a door that slides across an opening rather than swinging on a hinge.

slight /slaɪt/ *adj* **1** small; not great; not very bad: *a slight breeze*; *We have a slight problem*; *She has a slight cold*; *There has been a slight improvement in your work.* **2** slim and light: *He looked too slight to be a boxer.*

'slightest *adj* least possible; any at all: *I haven't the slightest idea where he is*; *The slightest difficulty seems to upset her.*

'slightly *adv*: *I'm still slightly worried about it.*

in the slightest at all: *You haven't upset me in the slightest*; *That doesn't worry me in the slightest.*

not in the slightest not at all: *It doesn't matter in the slightest*; *'Do you care?' 'Not in the slightest.'*

slily another spelling of **slyly**.

slim /slɪm/ *adj* **1** thin: *Taking exercise is one way of keeping slim.* **2** not good; slight: *There's still a slim chance that we'll find the child alive.* — *v* to try to become slimmer, for example by eating less: *I mustn't eat cakes — I'm trying to slim.* **'slimness** *n*.

slime /slaɪm/ *n* thin, slippery mud or other matter that is soft, sticky and half-liquid: *There was a layer of slime at the bottom of the pond.* **'slimy** *adj*. **'sliminess** *n*.

sling /slɪŋ/ *n* a bandage hanging from your neck or shoulders to support an injured arm: *He had his broken arm in a sling.* — *v* **1** to throw violently: *Jim slung my bag through the open window.* **2** to support, hang or swing by means of a strap, sling *etc*: *He had a camera slung round his neck.*

> **sling; slung** /slʌŋ/; **slung**: *He slung his rucksack on to his back*; *His coat was slung over his shoulder.*

slingshot /'slɪŋʃɒt/ *n* a catapult.

slink /slɪŋk/ *v* to go quietly or secretly: *He slunk into the kitchen and stole a cake.*

> **slink; slunk** /slʌŋk/; **slunk**: *He slunk out of sight*; *The snake had slunk into the bushes.*

slip¹ /slɪp/ *n* a small piece of paper: *She wrote down his telephone number on a slip of paper.*

slip² /slɪp/ *v* **1** to slide accidentally and lose your balance: *I slipped and fell on the ice.* **2** to slide, or drop, out of the right position or out of control: *The plate slipped out of my grasp.* **3** to move quietly, especially without being noticed: *She slipped out of the room.* **4** to put something with a quick, light movement: *She slipped the letter back in its envelope.* — *n* **1** an act of slipping: *One slip and you could be dead, so be careful.* **2** a small mistake: *Everyone makes the occasional slip.* **3** a petticoat.

'slipper *n* a loose, soft kind of shoe for wearing indoors.

'slippery *adj* so smooth as to cause slipping: *The path is slippery — watch out!* **'slipperiness** *n*.

'slipstream *n* a fast stream of air behind a moving vehicle such as a car or aircraft.

give someone the slip to escape: *The bank robbers gave the policemen the slip.*

let slip to tell a secret *etc* without meaning to: *He let slip that it was his birthday that day.*

slip into to put on clothes quickly: *She slipped into her nightdress.*

slip off 1 to take clothes off quickly: *Slip off your shoe.* **2** to move away quietly: *We'll slip off when no-one's looking.*

slip on to put clothes on quickly: *She slipped on her jacket.*

slip up to make a mistake.

slip your mind to be forgotten: *I'm afraid I completely forgot you were coming — it just slipped my mind.*

slipshod /'slɪpʃɒd/ *adj* careless and untidy: *slipshod work.*

slit /slɪt/ *v* to make a long cut in something: *He slit the animal's throat*; *She slit the envelope open with a knife.* — *n* a long cut; a narrow opening: *a slit in the material.*

> **slit; slit; slit**: *Alice slit the material with scissors*; *The envelope had been slit open.*

slither /'slɪðə(r)/ *v* to slide; to slip: *The dog was slithering about on the mud.*

sliver /'slɪvə(r)/ *n* a long thin piece cut or broken from something: *She cut slivers of cheese.*

slob /slɒb/ *n* a lazy, untidy and rude person:

He has become a slob since he was sacked.

slog /slɒg/ *v* **1** to hit someone or something hard: *She slogged him with her handbag*; *He slogged the golf-ball into the air.* **2** to work very hard: *He has been slogging all week for his exams.* **3** to walk with a lot of effort: *We slogged up the steep hill.* — *n*: *Working for exams is a hard slog*; *We were really tired after the long, hard slog up the hill*; *He gave the ball a slog.*

slogan /ˈsloʊgən/ *n* an easily-remembered and often-repeated phrase that is used in advertising *etc*.

slop /slɒp/ *v* to splash, spill, or move around violently in a container: *The water was slopping about in the bucket.*

slope /sloʊp/ *n* **1** a direction that is neither level nor upright; an upward or downward slant: *The floor is on a slight slope.* **2** the side of a hill: *The house stands on a gentle slope.* — *v*: *The field slopes towards the road.*
'sloping *adj*: *a sloping roof.*

sloppy /ˈslɒpɪ/ *adj* **1** half-liquid: *sloppy food.* **2** careless: *sloppy work.*

slosh /slɒʃ/ *v* **1** to splash about in a container: *We could hear the petrol sloshing about in the tank.* **2** to put liquid somewhere in a careless and untidy way: *He sloshed some water on his face.*

slot /slɒt/ *n* a small narrow opening, especially one to receive coins: *I put the correct money in the slot, but the machine didn't start.* — *v* to fit something into a small space: *He slotted the tape into the recorder.*

slot machine a machine that is operated by putting a coin into a slot.

slouch /slaʊtʃ/ *v* to move, stand or sit with your shoulders rounded and your head hanging forward: *He was slouching in a chair.*

slovenly /ˈslʌvənlɪ/ *adj* careless, dirty and lazy.

slow /sloʊ/ *adj* **1** not fast; not moving quickly; taking a long time: *a slow train*; *The service at that restaurant is very slow*; *He was very slow to offer help.* **2** showing a time earlier than the real time; behind in time: *My watch is five minutes slow.* **3** not clever; not quick at learning: *He's slow at arithmetic.* — *v* to make, or become slower: *The car slowed to turn the corner*; *He slowed the car.* **'slowness** *n*.

'slowly *adv*: *He slowly opened his eyes.*

slow down, slow up to make or become slower: *The police were warning drivers to slow down*; *The fog was slowing up the traffic.*
in slow motion slower than the speed of real life: *The winning goal was shown again in slow motion.*

sludge /slʌdʒ/ *n* thick, soft mud or something like this.

slug /slʌg/ *n* a creature like a snail, but without a shell.

'sluggish *adj* lazy, working or moving more slowly than usual: *She got out of bed feeling tired and sluggish.*

slum /slʌm/ *n* a part of a town *etc* where the conditions are dirty and overcrowded and the buildings in a bad state: *That new block of flats is rapidly turning into a slum.* — *adj*: *a slum dwelling.*

slumber /ˈslʌmbə(r)/ *v* to sleep: *The children were slumbering peacefully.* — *n*: *She was in a deep slumber.*

slump /slʌmp/ *v* to fall or sink suddenly and heavily: *He slumped wearily into a chair.* — *n* a period when a country's economy is doing very badly.

slung *see* **sling**.

slunk *see* **slink**.

slur /slɜː(r)/ *v* to pronounce in a way which is not clear: *He slurred his words because he was drunk.* — *n* an insult which could damage someone's good reputation: *She got angry when people cast slurs on her character.*

slurp /slɜːp/ *v* to drink very noisily: *He was slurping the soup up as quickly as he could.*

slush /slʌʃ/ *n* partly melted snow on the ground.

sly /slaɪ/ *adj* cunning; deceitful: *sly behaviour.*
'slyly or **'slily** *adv*. **'slyness** *n*.

smack /smak/ *v* to strike smartly and loudly; to slap: *She smacked the child's hand.* — *n*: *He gave the child a hard smack*; *He could hear the smack of the waves against the side of the ship.* — *adv* directly and with force: *He ran smack into the door.*

smack of to seem to have a particular, usually unpleasant, quality: *Her remarks about our new car smacked of jealousy.*

small /smɔːl/ *adj* **1** little; not large; not important: *She was holding a small boy by the hand*; *There's only a small amount of sugar left*; *He runs a small advertising business*; *There were a few small mistakes in your work.* **2** not capital: *The teacher showed the children how to write a capital G and a small g.*

See also **young**.

small change coins of small value.
small hours the period after midnight: *I was*

woken in the small hours by a dog barking.

smallpox /'smɔːlpɒks/ *n* a serious disease in which there is a bad rash of large, pus-filled spots that leave scars.

small print the information or conditions of a legal document or contract, which you might not notice unless you read it very carefully: *Don't sign anything until you've read all the small print.*

small talk polite conversation about unimportant things, for example, at a party.

smart /smɑːt/ *adj* **1** neat and well-dressed; fashionable: *You're looking very smart today*; *a smart suit.* **2** clever and quick in thought and action: *We need a smart boy to help in the shop.* **3** brisk; sharp: *She gave him a smart slap on the cheek.* — *v* to have a sharp stinging feeling: *The thick smoke made his eyes smart*; *His cheek was smarting where she had slapped him.*

'**smarten** *v* to make or become smarter: *He has smartened up a lot in appearance lately*; *Smarten yourself up before you go and see the headmaster.*

'**smartly** *adv*: *She is always smartly dressed.*

'**smartness** *n*.

smash /smæʃ/ *v* **1** to break in pieces; to be ruined: *The plate dropped on the floor and smashed into little pieces*; *This unexpected news had smashed all his hopes*; *He smashed up his car in an accident.* **2** to strike with great force; to crash: *The car smashed into a lamp-post.* — *n* **1** the sound of a breakage; a crash: *I heard a smash in the kitchen.* **2** an accident; a crash: *There has been a bad car smash.* **3** a strong blow: *He gave his opponent a smash on the jaw.* **4** in tennis *etc*, a hard downward shot.

'**smashing** *adj* marvellous; splendid: *What a smashing idea!*; *a smashing new bike.*

smear /smɪə(r)/ *v* **1** to spread something sticky or oily over a surface: *The little boy smeared jam on the chair.* **2** to rub; to smudge: *He brushed against the newly painted notice and smeared the lettering.* — *n*: *There's a dirty smear on your face.*

smell /smɛl/ *n* **1** the power of being aware of things through your nose: *Dogs have a good sense of smell.* **2** the thing that is noticed by using this power: *a pleasant smell*; *There's a strong smell of gas.* **3** the using of this power: *These roses have a lovely perfume — come and have a smell.* — *v* **1** to notice through your nose: *I thought I smelt burning.* **2** to give off a smell: *The roses smelt beautiful*; *My hands smell of onions.* **3** to examine something using your sense of smell: *Let me smell those flowers.* **4** to give off a bad smell: *His feet smell.*

> **smell**; **smelt** /smɛlt/ or **smelled**; **smelt** or **smelled**: *He said he smelt gas*; *We had already smelt the gas.*

-smelling: *a nasty-smelling liquid*; *sweet-smelling flowers.*

'**smelly** *adj* having a bad smell: *smelly fish.*

'**smelliness** *n*.

smell out to find by smelling: *We buried the dog's bone, but he smelt it out again.*

smelt¹ /smɛlt/ *v* to melt ore in order to separate metal from waste.

smelt² *see* **smell**.

smile /smaɪl/ *v* to show pleasure, amusement *etc* by turning up the corners of your mouth: *He smiled warmly at her as he shook hands*; *They all smiled politely at the joke.* — *n*: *'How do you do?' he said with a smile*; *the happy smiles of the children.*

'**smiling** *adj*: *a happy, smiling face.*

all smiles very happy: *The children were all smiles when the headmistress promised them a day's holiday.*

smirk /smɜːk/ *v* to smile in a self-satisfied or silly way. — *n*.

smock /smɒk/ *n* a loose garment worn over clothes to protect them: *Artists often wear smocks to protect their clothes from paint.*

smog /smɒg/ *n* smoke mixed with fog that hangs over some busy industrial areas: *Smog makes it difficult to breathe properly.*

smoke /sməʊk/ *n* **1** the cloudlike gases and bits of soot given off by something that is burning: *Smoke was coming out of the chimney*; *He puffed cigarette smoke into my face.* **2** the smoking of a cigarette *etc*: *He went outside for a smoke.* — *v* **1** to give off smoke: *The factory chimney was smoking.* **2** to draw in and puff out the smoke from a cigarette *etc*: *I don't smoke*; *He smokes cigars*; *He smokes a pipe.* **3** to preserve ham, fish *etc* by hanging it in smoke.

smoked *adj* preserved by having been hung in smoke: *smoked fish.*

'**smokeless** *adj* burning without smoke: *smokeless fuel.*

'**smoker** *n* someone who smokes cigarettes *etc*: *When did you become a smoker?*

> A person who doesn't smoke is called a **non-smoker**.

'**smoking** *n* the habit of smoking cigarettes

etc: *Smoking may damage your health.*
'smoky *adj* **1** filled with smoke: *The atmosphere in the room was thick and smoky.* **2** like smoke in appearance *etc*: *smoky glass.* **'smokiness** *n.*

go up in smoke to be destroyed by fire: *The house went up in smoke.*

smooth /smu:ð/ *adj* **1** having an even surface; not rough: *Her skin is as smooth as satin.* **2** without lumps: *Make the mixture into a smooth paste.* **3** without breaks, stops or jerks: *Did you have a smooth flight from New York?* **4** without problems or difficulties: *a smooth journey.* — *v* **1** to make something smooth or flat: *She tried to smooth the creases out.* **2** to rub a liquid substance *etc* gently over a surface: *Smooth the cleansing liquid over your face and neck*; *Smooth the ointment into your skin.*
'smoothly *adv*: *The plane landed smoothly*; *The meeting went very smoothly.*
'smoothness *n.*

smother /'smʌðə(r)/ *v* **1** to kill or die from lack of air; to suffocate: *It's better not to give the baby a pillow as he may get smothered by it.* **2** to prevent a fire from burning by covering it thickly: *He threw sand on the fire to smother it.*

smoulder /'smoʊldə(r)/ *v* to burn slowly, without a flame.

smudge /smʌdʒ/ *n* a smear; a rubbed mark: *There's a smudge of paint on your nose.* — *v*: *Her writing was smudged and untidy.* **'smudgy** *adj.*

smug /smʌg/ *adj* feeling or looking very pleased with yourself: *You didn't get all your sums right, so there's no need to look smug, even if you did do better than Paul.* **'smugly** *adv.* **'smugness** *n.*

smuggle /'smʌgəl/ *v* to bring goods into or send them out from a country illegally, or without paying duty: *He was caught smuggling drugs through the Customs.* **'smuggler** *n.*
'smuggling *n*: *the laws against smuggling*; *drug-smuggling.*

smut /smʌt/ *n* **1** a small piece of dirt or soot that leaves a dark mark on something. **2** talk that is disgusting, especially in a sexual way.

snack /snak/ *n* a light, hasty meal or a small item of food eaten between meals: *I usually have a snack at lunchtime.* — *adj*: *a snack lunch.*

snack bar a café or counter where you can buy light meals or sandwiches.

snag /snag/ *n* a small difficulty; a problem: *We did not realize at first how many snags there were in our plan.* — *v* to catch or tear clothing on something sharp or rough: *Don't snag your tights on the roses as you pass.*

snail /sneɪl/ *n* a small animal with a soft body and a shell, that moves slowly along the ground: *Snails leave a silvery trail as they move along.*

at a snail's pace very slowly.

snake /sneɪk/ *n* a legless reptile with a long body, that moves along the ground with a twisting movement. Some snakes have a poisonous bite: *He was bitten by a snake and nearly died.* — *v* to move like a snake: *He snaked his way through the narrow tunnel.*

A snake **hisses**.

'snake-charmer *n* a person who can handle snakes and make them perform dancing movements.

snap /snap/ *v* **1** to make a biting movement; to grasp with the teeth: *The dog snapped at his ankles*; *The dog snapped up the piece of meat and ran away.* **2** to break with a sudden sharp noise: *He snapped the stick in half*; *The handle of the cup snapped off.* **3** to make a sudden sharp noise in moving *etc*: *The lid snapped shut*; *Can you snap your fingers?* **4** to speak in a sharp, angry way: *'Be quiet'* he snapped. **5** to take a photograph of something: *He snapped the children playing in the garden.* — *n* **1** the noise of snapping: *There was a loud snap as his pencil broke.* **2** a photograph; a snapshot: *He wanted to show us his holiday snaps.* — *adj* done quickly and suddenly without careful thought: *a snap decision.*

'snappy *adj* bad-tempered; inclined to speak angrily: *He is always rather snappy on a Monday morning.* **'snappily** *adv.* **'snappiness** *n.*

'snapshot *n* a photograph, especially one taken quickly: *That's a good snapshot of the children.*

snap up to buy something without hesitating, probably because it is unusually cheap: *The goods in the sale were all snapped up in the first hour.*

snare /snɛə(r)/ *n* a trap for catching an animal. — *v* to catch with a snare: *He snared a couple of rabbits.*

snarl /snɑ:l/ *v* to growl angrily, showing the teeth: *The dog snarled at the burglar.* — *n*: *The dog gave an angry snarl.*

snatch /snatʃ/ *v* **1** to try to seize or grab suddenly: *The monkey snatched the biscuit out of my hand.* **2** to take quickly, when you have time or the opportunity: *She managed to snatch an hour's sleep.* — *n* **1** an attempt to seize: *The thief made a snatch at her handbag.* **2** a short piece of music, conversation *etc*: *a snatch of conversation.*

sneak /sniːk/ *v* to go somewhere quietly and secretly, especially for a dishonest purpose: *He must have sneaked into my room when no-one was looking and stolen the money.* — *n* a mean, deceitful person, especially someone who tells the teacher or someone in authority about what you have done wrong.

  'sneakers *n* rubber-soled running shoes.
  'sneaking *adj* not certain or definite but probably true: *I had a sneaking feeling that we were being watched.*
  sneak up on to approach someone quietly, especially in order to surprise them

sneer /snɪə(r)/ *v* **1** to raise your top lip at one side in a kind of smile that expresses scorn. **2** to express your scorn for something: *He sneered at my drawing.* — *n* **1** a sneering expression on your face. **2** a scornful remark.

sneeze /sniːz/ *v* to blow out air suddenly and noisily through your nose: *The pepper made him sneeze.* — *n*: *He felt a sneeze coming.*

snide /snaɪd/ *adj* critical or disapproving.

sniff /snɪf/ *v* **1** to draw in air through your nose with a slight noise. **2** to do this when trying to smell something: *He sniffed suddenly, wondering if he could smell smoke.* — *n*: *She gave the cheese a sniff.*

  'sniffle *v* to sniff repeatedly, especially because you have a cold or are crying.
  sniff out to discover by using the sense of smell: *The police used dogs to sniff out the explosives.*

snigger /ˈsnɪɡə(r)/ *v* to laugh quietly in an unpleasant manner, for example at someone else's bad luck: *When the teacher dropped her glasses, several of the children sniggered*; *What are you sniggering at?* — *n*.

snip /snɪp/ *v* to cut sharply, especially with a single quick action, with scissors *etc*: *I snipped off two inches of thread.* — *n* a cut with scissors: *With a snip of her scissors she cut a hole in the cloth.*

snipe /snaɪp/ *v* **1** to shoot at someone from a hidden position: *The bank robbers sniped at the police from behind a wall.* **2** to attack someone with words: *Politicians are often sniped at in newspapers.*

sniper /ˈsnaɪpə(r)/ *n* a person who shoots at people from a hidden position.

snippet /ˈsnɪpɪt/ *n* a small amount of: *a snippet of information.*

snivel /ˈsnɪvəl/ *v* to complain tearfully: *The child snivelled all the way home because he was tired.*

snob /snɒb/ *n* someone who admires people of high rank or class, and despises those in a lower class *etc* than themselves. **'snobbery** *n*.
  'snobbish *adj*: *She always had a snobbish desire to live in an area of expensive housing.* **'snobbishly** *adv*. **'snobbishness** *n*.

snooker /ˈsnuːkə(r)/ *n* a game played on a large table by two players, who use long thin sticks called cues, to hit a white ball and knock coloured balls into pockets at the sides of the table: *Let's have a game of snooker*; *a snooker match.*

snoop /snuːp/ *v* to investigate things that do not concern you: *She's always snooping into other people's business.*

snooty /ˈsnuːtɪ/ *adj* behaving rudely because you think you are better than other people

snooze /snuːz/ *v* to sleep lightly: *His grandfather was snoozing in his armchair.* — *n*: *He's having a snooze.*

snore /snɔː(r)/ *v* to make a noise like a snort while sleeping, when you breathe in: *Do I snore when I'm asleep?* — *n*: *He gave a loud snore and turned over in bed.*

snorkel /ˈsnɔːkəl/ *n* a tube fixed to a submarine, or used by an underwater swimmer, with one end sticking out above the water to let in air. — *v* to swim under water using a snorkel: *Let's go snorkelling.*

snort /snɔːt/ *v* **1** to force air noisily through your nostrils, breathing either in or out: *The horses snorted impatiently.* **2** to make a similar noise, showing disapproval, anger, contempt, amusement *etc*: *She snorted at his silly idea.* — *n*: *a snort of impatience*; *She gave a snort of laughter.*

snout /snaʊt/ *n* the projecting mouth and nose part of certain animals, especially of a pig.

snow /snəʊ/ *n* frozen water vapour that falls to the ground in soft white flakes: *About 15 centimetres of snow had fallen overnight.* — *v*: *It's snowing heavily*; *It snowed during the night*; *Has it stopped snowing?*

  'snowball *n* snow pressed into a hard ball for throwing. — *v* to grow or develop quickly: *They started selling by mail order and the business just snowballed from there.*

'snowdrift *n* snow that has been blown together by the wind to form a deep pile.

'snowdrop *n* a small white flower.

snowed in unable to leave a place because of heavy snow.

snowed under with more work than you can deal with.

'snowfall *n* **1** a fall or shower of snow that settles on the ground: *There was a heavy snowfall last night.* **2** the amount of snow that falls in a certain place: *The snowfall last year was much higher than average.*

'snowflake *n* one of the soft, light flakes composed of groups of crystals, in which snow falls: *A few large snowflakes began to fall from the sky.*

'snowman *n* a figure of a person made out of snow.

'snowplough *n* a vehicle that is used to clear snow from roads or railways.

'snowstorm *n* a heavy fall of snow.

snow-'white *adj* white like snow.

'snowy *adj* **1** full of, or producing a lot of, snow: *The weather has been very snowy recently.* **2** white like snow: *the old man's snowy hair.*

snub /snʌb/ *v* to treat someone rudely; to insult someone on purpose: *She snubbed him by taking no notice of him.* — *n*: *He considered it a snub when she didn't come to his party.*

snuffle /'snʌfəl/ *v* to make sniffing noises, or breathe noisily, when you have a cold.

snug /snʌg/ *adj* warm; comfortable; sheltered from the cold: *The house is small but snug; We were snug from head to toe in our rubber suits.*

'snuggle *v* to curl your body up for warmth *etc*: *She snuggled up to her mother and went to sleep.*

'snugly *adv* **1** comfortably; warmly: *The girl had a scarf wrapped snugly round her neck.* **2** fitting closely, comfortably and neatly: *The bookcase fits snugly between the television and the door.*

so /soʊ/ *adv* **1** to this extent; to such an extent: *'The snake was about so long,' he said, holding his hands about a metre apart; Don't get so worried!; She was so pleased with his work in school that she bought him a new bicycle; He departed without so much as a goodbye; You've been so kind to me!; Thank you so much!* **2** in this way; in that way: *He wants everything to be left just so; It so happens that I have to go to an important meeting tonight.* **3** as already indicated: *'Are you really leaving your job?' 'Yes, I've already told you so'; If you needed money you should have said so; 'Is she arriving tomorrow?' 'Yes, I hope so'; If you haven't read the notice, please do so now; 'Is that so?' 'Yes, it's really so'; 'Was your father angry?' 'Yes, even more so than I was expecting — in fact, so much so that he refused to speak to me all day!* **4** also: *'I hope we'll meet again.' 'So do I.'; She has a lot of money and so has her husband.* **5** indeed: *'You said you were going shopping today.' 'So I did, but I've changed my mind.'; 'You'll need this book tomorrow, won't you?' 'So I shall.'* — *conjunction* therefore: *John had a bad cold, so I took him to the doctor; 'So you think you'd like this job, then?' 'Yes.'; And so they got married and lived happily ever after.*

and so on or **and so forth** and more of the same kind of thing: *He told me to work harder, and so on.*

or so used to show that a period or amount *etc* is not exact: *It'll take a day or so to sort things out.*

so as to in order to: *He sat at the front so as to be able to hear.*

so far, so good all is well up to this point: *So far, so good — we've checked the equipment, and everything's ready.*

so that 1 in order that: *I'll wash this dress so that you can wear it tomorrow.* **2** with the result that: *He got up very late, so that he was late for work.*

soak /soʊk/ *v* **1** to put something into a liquid and leave it there: *She soaked the clothes overnight in soapy water.* **2** to make very wet: *That shower has completely soaked me.* **3** to flow into, and be absorbed by, a material *etc*: *The blood has soaked through the bandage.*

soaked *adj* extremely wet: *She got soaked in the rain.*

'soaking or **soaking wet** *adj* very wet: *She took off her soaking clothes; My hair's soaking wet.*

soak up to absorb: *This paper towel will soak up the spilt tea.*

so-and-so /'soʊənsoʊ/ *n* **1** a person whose name you do not know or cannot remember: *She said everyone seemed to be ill — so-and-so had a cold and so-and-so felt sick — she was the only healthy person there.* **2** an unpleasant person: *Sometimes my* *grandfather can be an old so-and-so.*

soap /soʊp/ *n* a substance used in washing: *He found a bar of soap and began to wash his hands.* — *v* to rub with soap: *She soaped the baby all over.*

  soap opera a radio or television series about the daily life and problems of a particular group of people.

'soapy *adj*: *soapy water.*

soar /sɔː(r)/ *v* to fly high; to rise high and quickly: *Seagulls soared above the cliffs; Prices have soared recently.*

sob /sɒb/ *v* to weep noisily: *I could hear her sobbing in her bedroom.* — *n*: *I could hear her sobs coming from the bedroom.*

sober /'soʊbə(r)/ *adj* **1** serious: *a sober mood.* **2** not bright: *She wore a sober grey dress.* **3** not drunk: *Don't give me a drink — I've got to drive home so I want to stay sober.*

  'sobering *adj* making you think about things more seriously: *a sobering thought.*

  'soberly *adv.*

  sober up to recover from the effects of alcohol: *Have a cup of coffee to sober you up a bit.*

so-called /soʊ'kɔːld/ *adj* wrongly called; not true: *Your so-called friends have gone to the cinema without you!*

soccer /'sɒkə(r)/ *n* football played according to certain rules.

sociable /'soʊʃəbəl/ *adj* fond of the company of others; friendly: *He's a cheerful, sociable man.*

> See **social**.

social /'soʊʃəl/ *adj* **1** having to do with the life of people in a community: *social problems; People tend to get divided into upper and lower social classes.* **2** living in communities: *Ants are social insects.* **3** having to do with meeting and being friendly with other people: *a social club.* **'socially** *adv.*

> **sociable** means friendly: *Sociable people enjoy the company of others.*
> **social** means having to do with living with other people in a community: *It is important for old people to have an active social life.*

  social science the study of the way people in societies and communities behave, including economics, politics and sociology.

  social work work in a service provided by the government for the care of people in need.

socialism /'soʊʃəlɪzəm/ *n* a system of government under which a country's wealth, such as its land or industries, is owned by the state, not by individual people.

'socialist *adj* having to do with socialism: *a socialist republic.* — *n* a person who believes in socialism.

society /sə'saɪətɪ/ *n* **1** people in general: *Bad drivers are a danger to society.* **2** a particular section of the people of the world or a country: *middle-class society.* **3** an association; a club: *a model railway society.* **4** company; companionship: *I enjoy the society of young people.*

sociology /soʊsɪ'ɒlədʒɪ/ *n* the study of human behaviour in society. **soci'ologist** *n*.

sock /sɒk/ *n* a woollen, cotton or nylon covering for the foot and ankle: *I need a new pair of socks; Are these socks yours?*

  pull your socks up to make an effort to do better than you have been doing recently: *If he doesn't pull his socks up, he'll fail his exams.*

socket /'sɒkɪt/ *n* a specially shaped hole or set of holes into which something is fitted: *We need a new electric socket for the television.*

soda /'soʊdə/ *n* **1** a substance that is used for washing; another substance used in baking. **2** soda-water.

  'soda-water *n* water through which the gas carbon dioxide has been passed, making it fizzy.

sodden /'sɒdən/ *adj* very wet: *It had rained so much the ground was sodden.*

sodium /'soʊdɪəm/ *n* a silver-white element found in many common substances including salt (**sodium chloride**).

sofa /'soʊfə/ *n* a long soft seat with a back and arms; a couch.

> See **bench**.

soft /sɒft/ *adj* **1** not hard; not firm: *a soft cushion.* **2** pleasantly smooth to feel: *The dog has a soft, silky coat.* **3** not loud: *a soft voice.* **4** not bright or harsh: *a soft pink.* **5** not severe or strict enough: *Is society too soft on criminals?* **6** not alcoholic: *At the party they were serving soft drinks as well as wine and spirits.* **'softly** *adv.* **'softness** *n*.

soft-'boiled *adj* slightly boiled, so that the yolk is still soft: *She likes her eggs soft-boiled.*

  soft drink a cold drink that does not contain any alcohol: *Lemonade and fruit juices are soft drinks.*

soften /'sɒfən/ *v* to make or become soft or

softer, less strong, or less painful: *When she lost her job his kind words softened the blow for her.*

soft-'hearted *adj* kind; generous.

soft-'spoken *adj* having a quiet, gentle-sounding voice.

'software *n* computer programs.

soggy /'sɒgɪ/ *adj* very wet and soft: *Water makes paper soggy.*

soil[1] /sɔɪl/ *n* the upper layer of the earth, in which plants grow: *to plant seeds in the soil.*

soil[2] /sɔɪl/ *v* to dirty: *Don't soil your dress with these dusty books!*

solace /'sɒləs/ *n* comfort when you are sad: *She found some solace in writing poetry; His religion was a great solace to him.*

solar /'soʊlə(r)/ *adj* having to do with, powered by, or influenced by, the sun: *the solar year; a solar heating system.*

solar system the Sun or any star and the planets that move round it.

sold *see* **sell**.

soldier /'soʊldʒə(r)/ *n* a member of an army: *Philip wants to be a soldier when he grows up.*

sole[1] /soʊl/ *n* **1** the underside of your foot. **2** the underside of a boot or shoe.

sole[2] /soʊl/, *plural* **sole** or **soles**, *n* a small, flat, edible fish.

sole[3] /soʊl/ *adj* **1** only; single: *To be successful is his sole purpose in life.* **2** not shared; belonging to one person or group only: *She has sole right to the house.*

'solely *adv* only: *She was solely responsible for the accident.*

solemn /'sɒləm/ *adj* **1** serious; earnest: *He looked very solemn as he announced the bad news.* **2** stately; dignified: *a solemn procession.* **'solemnly** *adv.* **'solemnness** *n.*

solemnity /sə'lɛmnɪtɪ/ *n* being solemn: *the solemnity of the occasion.*

solicit /sə'lɪsɪt/ *v* to ask for advice, help or money from someone: *Ministers are soliciting support from other governments.*

solicitor /sə'lɪsɪtə(r)/ *n* a lawyer who gives legal advice to people, for example if they want to buy a house, or write their wills, or are arrested by the police.

solid /'sɒlɪd/ *adj* **1** not easily changing shape; not in the form of liquid or gas: *Water becomes solid when it freezes; solid substances.* **2** not hollow: *The tyres of the earliest cars were solid.* **3** firm: *That's a solid piece of furniture; His argument is based on good solid facts.* **4** completely made of one substance: *This bracelet is made of solid gold; We dug till we reached solid rock.* **5** without gaps: *The policemen formed themselves into a solid line.* **6** having height, length and thickness: *A cube is a solid figure.* **7** following one another without a pause: *I've been working for six solid hours.* — *n* **1** a substance that is solid: *Butter is a solid but milk is a liquid.* **2** a shape that has height, length and thickness.

solidarity /sɒlɪ'darɪtɪ/ *n* support and agreement between people in a group or between groups of people: *workers' solidarity.*

solidify /sə'lɪdɪfaɪ/ *v* to make or become solid.

so'lidity, 'solidness *ns.*

'solidly *adv* **1** firmly; strongly: *solidly-built houses.* **2** continuously: *I worked solidly from 8.30 a.m. till lunchtime.*

soliloquy /sə'lɪləkwɪ/ *n* a speech made to yourself, especially in a play: *The audience knew what the character was thinking from his soliloquies.*

solitary /'sɒlɪtərɪ/ *adj* alone; lonely; without companions: *a solitary traveller; She lives a solitary life.*

solitary confinement keeping a person completely alone in prison.

solitude /'sɒlɪtjuːd/ *n* the state of being alone: *He likes solitude; He lives in solitude.*

solo /'soʊloʊ/ *n* a performance by a single person especially of a musical piece, for voice, instrument *etc*: *She sang a solo; He played a solo on the violin.* — *adj*: *a solo flight in an aeroplane.* — *adv*: *to fly solo.*

'soloist *n* someone who plays, sings *etc* a solo.

soluble /'sɒljʊbəl/ *adj* **1** that can be dissolved in water: *She prefers soluble aspirin to the tablet form.* **2** having an answer: *They still believe that the situation is soluble.*

solution /sə'luːʃən/ *n* **1** an answer to a problem, difficulty or puzzle: *the solution to a crossword.* **2** the discovery of an answer to a problem *etc*. **3** a liquid with something dissolved in it: *a solution of salt and water.*

solve /sɒlv/ *v* **1** to discover the answer to a problem *etc*: *The mathematics teacher gave the children some problems to solve.* **2** to clear up or explain a mystery, crime *etc*: *That crime has never been solved.*

solvent /'sɒlvənt/ *n* having enough money to pay all your debts: *He has managed to keep the company solvent despite economic problems.*

sombre /'sɒmbə(r)/ *adj* **1** dark and gloomy: *She was dressed in sombre black; The fur-*

niture was heavy and sombre. **2** serious; sad: *He looked sombre and never smiled; She was in a sombre mood.* **'sombrely** *adv.*

some /sʌm/ *pron, adj* **1** an indefinite amount or number: *I can see some people walking across the field; You'll need some money if you're going shopping; Some of the ink was spilt on the desk.* **2** a certain, or small, amount or number: *'Has she any experience of the work?' 'Yes, she has some.'; Some people like the idea and some don't.* **3** certain: *He's quite kind in some ways.* — *adj* an unnamed thing, person *etc*: *Jim is visiting some relative of his.*

> **some; more; most:** *I ate some ice-cream, but Jill ate more, and David ate most of all.*

> **some; any:**
> use **any** with **not**: *I have some money in the bank, but my brother hasn't any money; I don't have any food to spare — ask Diana for some.*

somebody /'sʌmbədɪ/ *pron* someone.
some day or **someday** /'sʌmdeɪ/ *adv* sometime in the future: *I'll beat him some day.*
somehow /'sʌmhaʊ/ *adv* in some way: *I'll get there somehow.*
someone /'sʌmwʌn/ *pron* **1** a person not known or not named: *There's someone at the door — would you answer it?; We all know someone who needs help.* **2** a person of importance: *He thinks he is someone.*
someplace /'sʌmpleɪs/ *adv* somewhere.
somersault /'sʌməsɔːlt/ *n* a leap or roll in which you turn with your feet going over your head: *She performed a somersault.* — *v*: *He somersaulted off the diving-board.*
something /'sʌmθɪŋ/ *pron* **1** a thing not known or not stated: *Would you like something to eat?* **2** a thing of importance: *There's something in what you say.*

> **or something** used to show that you are not sure about what you have just said: *She's called Jenny or Janet or something.*

> **something like** similar to: *It was a bird something like a seagull.*

sometime /'sʌmtaɪm/ *adv* at an unknown time: *We'll go there sometime next week.*

> *They went away sometime* (without **-s**) *in July;*
> but: *Sometimes* (with **-s**) *she gets very lonely.*

sometimes /'sʌmtaɪmz/ *adv* occasionally: *Sometimes he seems very forgetful.*

See **sometime**.

somewhat /'sʌmwɒt/ *adv* rather; a little: *He is somewhat sad; The news puzzled me somewhat.*
somewhere /'sʌmweə(r)/ *adv* **1** in or to some place not known or not named: *They live somewhere in London; They're going somewhere in Thailand for their holidays.* **2** used when giving an approximate amount or time: *aged somewhere between 45 and 50; It was built somewhere around 1825.*
son /sʌn/ *n* a male child.
'son-in-law, *plural* **'sons-in-law**, *n* a daughter's husband.
sonata /sə'nɑːtə/ *n* a piece of classical music for a solo instrument: *a piano sonata.*
song /sɒŋ/ *n* **1** a musical composition for singing: *He wrote this song for his wife.* **2** the activity of singing: *He burst into song; bird-song.*
sonic /'sɒnɪk/ *adj* having to do with sound: *A sonic boom is the sudden loud noise that you hear when an aircraft is travelling faster than the speed of sound.*
soon /suːn/ *adv* **1** in a short time from now: *I hope he arrives soon; They'll be here sooner than you think.* **2** early: *It's too soon to tell.* **3** willingly: *I'd just as soon do the job myself if you can't do it; I would sooner stand than sit.*

> **as soon as** when: *You may have a biscuit as soon as we get home.*

> **no sooner ... than**: *No sooner had he arrived than he was told he must leave again.*

> **sooner or later** sometime; eventually: *He'll come home sooner or later.*

> **the sooner the better** as quickly as possible: *'When shall I tell him?' 'The sooner the better!'*

soot /sʊt/ *n* the black powder left after the burning of coal *etc*. **'sooty** *adj.*
soothe /suːð/ *v* **1** to calm, comfort or quieten someone: *She was so upset that it took half an hour to soothe her.* **2** to ease pain *etc*: *The medicine soothed the child's toothache.* **'soothing** *adj*. **'soothingly** *adv.*
sophisticated /sə'fɪstɪkeɪtɪd/ *adj* **1** knowing a lot about the world and about what is fashionable to do and to wear: *a sophisticated young girl.* **2** complicated: *sophisticated machinery.* **sophisti'cation** *n.*
soporific /sɒpə'rɪfɪk/ *adj* making you feel sleepy or bored: *I find the heat soporific.*
soppy /'sɒpɪ/ *adj* sentimental in a silly way: *I*

didn't like that soppy film about the prince and the beautiful poor girl.

soprano /sə'prɑːnoʊ/, *plural* **so'pranos**, *n* the highest singing voice for a woman or young boy.

sorcery /'sɔːsəri/ *n* witchcraft; magic, especially of an evil kind.

    'sorcerer *n* a man who uses sorcery.

    'sorceress *n* a female sorcerer.

sordid /'sɔːdɪd/ *adj* **1** dirty; unpleasant: *The room was in a sordid mess.* **2** dishonest; unworthy: *sordid behaviour.* **'sordidly** *adv.* **'sordidness** *n.*

sore /sɔː(r)/ *adj* **1** painful: *I have a sore leg.* **2** suffering pain: *I am still a bit sore after my operation.* — *n* a painful, infected spot on the skin: *His hands were covered with horrible sores.* **'soreness** *n.*

See **pain**.

    'sorely *adv* badly: *I miss him sorely.*

    sore point a subject that is likely to upset or irritate someone when mentioned.

sorrow /'sɒroʊ/ *n* grief; something that causes grief: *He felt great sorrow when his mother died*; *Her son's wickedness was a great sorrow to her.*

    'sorrowful *adj* full of sorrow: *sorrowful people*; *a sorrowful expression.* **'sorrowfully** *adv.* **'sorrowfulness** *n.*

sorry /'sɒri/ *adj* **1** used when apologizing or expressing regret: *I'm sorry that I forgot to return your book*; *Did I give you a fright? I'm sorry.* **2** apologetic; full of regret: *I think he's really sorry for his bad temper.* **3** unsatisfactory; bad: *a sorry state of affairs.* — a word used when you apologize, or when you ask someone to repeat what they have just said: *Did I tread on your toe? Sorry!*; *Sorry, what did you say?*

    be sorry for or **feel sorry for** to pity: *I'm sorry for the poor woman*; *I felt sorry for Anne when she was punished.*

sort /sɔːt/ *n* a class, type or kind: *I like all sorts of books*; *She was wearing a sort of crown.* — *v* to separate into classes or groups, putting each thing in its place: *She sorted the buttons into large ones and small ones.*

    sort of slightly: *I feel sort of worried about him.*

    sort out 1 to separate one lot or type of things from a general mixture: *Sort out which clothes you want to take on holiday.* **2** to correct, improve, solve *etc*: *You must sort out your business affairs.*

SOS /ɛsoʊ'ɛs/ *n* a signal calling for help or rescue: *Send an SOS to the mainland to tell them that we are sinking!*

so-so /'soʊsoʊ/ *adj* not very good: *Your work is so-so.*

sought *see* **seek**.

soul /soʊl/ *n* **1** your spirit; the non-physical part of someone, that is often thought to continue in existence after they die: *People often discuss whether animals and plants have souls.* **2** a person: *She's a wonderful old soul.* **3** a perfect example: *She's the soul of kindness.*

    'soulful *adj* having or expressing deep feelings, especially of sadness: *The baby animals had large soulful eyes.*

    'soulless *adj* **1** without kind or noble feelings: *a soulless person.* **2** dull; boring: *a soulless job.*

    'soul-destroying *adj* dull; boring: *a soul-destroying task.*

sound[1] /saʊnd/ *adj* **1** strong; in good condition: *The foundations of the house are not very sound*; *He's 87, but he's still sound in mind and body.* **2** deep: *sound sleep*; *She's a very sound sleeper.* **3** full; thorough: *a sound training.* **4** accurate: *a sound piece of work.* **5** sensible: *His advice is always very sound.* **'soundly** *adv.* **'soundness** *n.*

    sound asleep sleeping deeply: *The baby is sound asleep.*

sound[2] /saʊnd/ *n* **1** the impressions sent to your brain by your sense of hearing: *Deaf people live in a world without sound.* **2** something that you hear: *Odd sounds were coming from the kitchen.* **3** the impression given by a piece of news, a description *etc*: *I didn't like the sound of her hairstyle at all!* — *adj*: *sound waves.* — *v* **1** to make a sound; to make something make a sound: *Sound the bell!*; *The bell sounded.* **2** to signal something by means of a bell, bugle, drum *etc*: *Sound the retreat!*; *Sound the alarm!* **3** to make a particular impression; to seem; to appear: *Your singing sounded very good*; *That sounds like a train.* **4** to pronounce: *In the word 'lamb' the letter b is not sounded.* **'soundless** *adj.* **'soundlessly** *adv.*

See **horn**.

sound[3] /saʊnd/ *v* to measure the depth of water *etc.*

    sound out to try to find out someone's opinion *etc*: *I'll sound out the headmaster on your suggestion.*

sound effects /'saʊnd ɪfɛkts/ sounds other

than speech or music, used in films, radio etc.

sounding /ˈsaʊndɪŋ/ n measurement of depth of water etc: He took a sounding.

soundproof /ˈsaʊndpruːf/ adj not allowing sound to pass in, out, or through: The walls are soundproof. — v to make walls, a room etc soundproof.

'soundtrack n a recording of the music from a film or programme: The soundtrack from the television series is available on record.

soup /suːp/ n a liquid food made from meat, vegetables etc: She made some chicken soup.

sour /saʊə(r)/ adj 1 having a taste of the same sort as that of lemon juice or vinegar: Unripe apples are sour; These plums taste sour; Milk goes sour if you keep it too long. 2 bad-tempered: She was looking very sour this morning. — v to make or become sour.
'sourly adv. **'sourness** n.

source /sɔːs/ n 1 the place, person, circumstance, thing etc from which anything begins or comes: They have discovered the source of the trouble. 2 the spring from which a river flows: the source of the Nile.

south /saʊθ/ n 1 the direction to your right when you face the rising sun; any part of the earth lying in that direction: He stood facing towards the south; She lives in the south of France. 2 (often written S) one of the four main points of the compass. — adj 1 in the south: She works on the south coast. 2 from the direction of the south: a south wind. — adv towards the south: The road leading south from the crossroads.

See **north**.

'southbound adj travelling or leading towards the south: southbound traffic; the southbound carriageway of a motorway.

south-'east, south-'west ns the direction midway between south and east, or south and west: a mountain in the south-west of the country. — adjs: a south-east wind. — advs: to travel south-west.

south'easterly adj 1 coming from the south-east. 2 towards the south-east.

south-'eastern, south-'western adj of the south-eastern or south-west: They climbed the mountain from its south-western side.

southerly /ˈsʌðəli/ adj 1 coming from the south: a southerly wind. 2 looking, lying etc towards the south: in a southerly direction.

southern /ˈsʌðən/ adj belonging to the south: Australia is in the southern hemisphere.

'southward adj, adv towards the south: in a southward direction; moving southward.

'southwards adv towards the south: We are moving southwards.

the South Pole the southern end of the earth's axis.

souvenir /suːvəˈnɪə(r)/ n something you buy, keep or are given to remind you of a place or occasion: He kept a large sea-shell in his room as a souvenir of his holiday.

sovereign /ˈsɒvrɪn/ n a king or queen. — adj self-governing: a sovereign state.
'sovereignty n the independent power that a country has to govern itself.

sow[1] /saʊ/ v to scatter seeds over, or put seeds into, the ground: Sow the seeds from spring to early summer; I sowed carrots in this part of the garden; This field has been sown with wheat.

to **sow** (not **sew**) seed.
sow; sowed; sown: I sowed flowers in the garden; We've sown wheat this year.

sow[2] /saʊ/ n a female pig.

soya bean /ˈsɔɪə biːn/ or **soybean** /ˈsɔɪbiːn/ n a type of bean used as a substitute for meat etc.

soy sauce a salty brown sauce made from soya beans.

space /speɪs/ n 1 a gap; an empty place: I couldn't find a space for my car. 2 room; the area available for use: Have you enough space to turn round?; Is there space for one more person? 3 the region outside the Earth's atmosphere, in which all stars and other planets etc are situated: travellers through space. — v to leave gaps between one thing and the next: He spaced the rows of potatoes so that they were half a metre apart; Space your words out more when you write — they're too close together.

See **place**.

'space-age adj extremely up-to-date and advanced: space-age travel.

'spacecraft n a vehicle for travelling in space.

'spaceman n someone who travels in space; an astronaut.

'spaceship n a spacecraft.

'spacesuit n a suit worn by a spaceman.

'spacing n the distance left between objects, written words etc, when they are set out.

spacious /ˈspeɪʃəs/ adj having plenty of room;

large: *Their dining-room is very spacious.* **'spaciously** *adv.* **'spaciousness** *n.*

spade¹ /speɪd/ *n* a tool with a broad blade and a handle, used for digging.

spade² /speɪd/ *n* one of the playing-cards of the suit spades, which have black shapes like this ♠ on them.

spaghetti /spəˈgɛti/ *n* an Italian food consisting of long pieces of pasta.

span /span/ *n* **1** the length between the supporting pillars of a bridge or arch: *The first span of the bridge is one hundred metres long.* **2** the full time for which anything lasts: *Seventy or eighty years is the normal span of a human life.* — *v* to stretch across: *A bridge spans the river.*

spaniel /ˈspanjəl/ *n* a breed of dog with large ears which hang down.

spank /spaŋk/ *v* to strike someone with the palm of your hand, especially on their bottom, as a punishment: *The child was spanked for his disobedience.* — *n*: *His mother gave him a spank on the bottom.* **'spanking** *n*: *He got a spanking from his mother.*

spanner /ˈspanə(r)/ *n* a tool used for tightening or loosening nuts, bolts *etc*.

spare /spɛə(r)/ *v* **1** to manage without: *No-one can be spared from this office.* **2** to set aside for a purpose: *I can't spare the time for a holiday.* **3** to treat someone with mercy: *'Spare us!' they begged.* **4** to avoid causing someone grief, trouble *etc*: *Break the news gently in order to spare her as much pain as possible.* **5** to avoid: *He spared no expense in helping us.* — *adj* **1** extra; not actually being used: *We haven't a spare bedroom for guests in our house*; *Most cars carry a spare tyre.* **2** free for leisure *etc*: *What do you do in your spare time?* — *n* a spare part for a car *etc*: *They sell spares at that garage.* **'sparing** *adj* careful or economical. **'sparingly** *adv.*

spare part a part for a machine *etc*, used to replace an identical part if it breaks *etc*.

to spare extra: *I'll go to an exhibition if I have time to spare.*

spark /spɑːk/ *n* **1** a tiny red-hot piece thrown off by something burning, or when two very hard surfaces are struck together: *Sparks were being thrown into the air from the burning building.* **2** a trace; a small amount: *The children showed no spark of enthusiasm when the teacher suggested an arithmetic test.* — *v* **1** to give off sparks. **2** to start; to cause: *Her remark sparked off a serious quarrel.*

sparkle /ˈspɑːkəl/ *v* to glitter, as if throwing off tiny sparks: *The snow sparkled in the sunlight.* — *n*: *the sparkle of diamonds*; *There was a sparkle in her eyes.* **'sparkling** *adj.*

sparkling wine wine which is slightly fizzy: *Champagne is an expensive type of sparkling wine.*

sparrow /ˈsparoʊ/ *n* a small brown bird.

sparse /spɑːs/ *adj* poor and thin; not plentiful: *sparse trees*; *sparse grass.* **'sparsely** *adv.*

spartan /ˈspɑːtən/ *adj* very basic, without any luxuries at all: *spartan living conditions.*

spasm /ˈspazm/ *n* **1** a sudden jerking movement of the muscles which you cannot control: *The muscles in his leg were in spasm.* **2** a strong short occurrence or burst: *a spasm of pain.*

spastic /ˈspastɪk/ *adj* suffering from brain damage that causes severe difficulties in controlling muscles. — *n* a person who is spastic.

spat *see* **spit**.

spate /speɪt/ *n* a sudden large number or amount: *The police say there has been a spate of similar incidents lately.*

spatial /ˈspeɪʃəl/ *adj* to do with the size or position of something.

spatter /ˈspatə(r)/ *v* to splash in small drops or patches: *The paint spattered all over the wall as the tin fell to the ground.*

spawn /spɔːn/ *n* the eggs of fish, frogs *etc*: *In the spring, the pond is full of frog-spawn.*

speak /spiːk/ *v* **1** to say words; to talk: *His throat is so sore that he can't speak*; *He spoke a few words to us*; *May I speak to you for a moment?*; *We spoke for hours about the problem.* **2** to be able to talk in a particular language: *She speaks Russian.* **3** to tell your thoughts, the truth *etc*: *I always speak my mind.* **4** to make a speech; to talk to an audience: *The Prime Minister spoke on television about unemployment.*

> **speak**; **spoke**; **'spoken**: *He spoke to her yesterday*; *I've already spoken to him about that.*

'speaker *n* **1** someone who speaks. **2** the device in a radio, record-player *etc* that converts the electrical impulses into sounds (also called a **loudspeaker**): *Our record-player needs a new speaker.*

generally speaking in general: *Generally speaking, men are stronger than women.*

on speaking terms friendly again after an

argument: *We can't ask them to come together because they're not on speaking terms at the moment.*

so to speak used to show that you are using a colourful expression that is not meant literally: *I knew she'd be angry, but when she heard the truth she went up the wall, so to speak.*

speak for to express the opinion of another person: *I'm not at all happy about this but I can't speak for anyone else.*

speak for itself to have an obvious meaning: *You can see what's happened — the results speak for themselves.*

speak out to say boldly what you think: *The time has come to speak out.*

speak up to speak louder: *Speak up! We can't hear you.*

spear /spɪə(r)/ *n* a long-handled weapon. — *v* to pierce or kill with a spear: *He went out in a boat and speared some fish.*

'spearhead *n* **1** the pointed tip of a spear. **2** the leading person or group that begins an attack. — *v* to lead an attack: *The campaign was spearheaded in the early 1960s.*

spearmint /'spɪəmɪnt/ *n* a type of leaf with a fresh-tasting flavour.

special /'spɛʃəl/ *adj* **1** out of the ordinary; unusual; exceptional: *a special occasion; a special friend.* **2** for a particular purpose: *a special tool for drilling holes; There will be a special train to take people to the football match.* — *n* something that is produced or organized for a particular purpose, for example an extra train service or an extra edition of a newspaper.

'specialist *n* someone who makes a very deep study of a particular subject: *Dr Brown is a heart specialist.*

speciality /spɛʃɪ'alɪtɪ/, or **specialty** /'spɛʃəltɪ/ *n* **1** a subject about which you have special knowledge: *His speciality is physics.* **2** something that you make or do particularly well: *Dictionaries are a specialty of this firm.*

'specialize *v* to give your attention to a particular subject: *He specializes in computers.* **specializ'ation** *n*.

'specialized *adj* having a specific purpose: *specialized equipment.*

'specially *adv* with one particular purpose: *I picked these flowers specially for you.*

> **specially** means for a special purpose: *I bought this hat specially for the wedding.*
> **especially** means particularly: *I like these photos, especially the one of you.*

species /'spiːʃiːz/, *plural* **'species**, *n* **1** a group of animals *etc* whose members are so similar or closely related as to be able to breed together: *There are several species of zebra.* **2** a kind; a sort: *What species of vehicle is this?*

specific /spɪ'sɪfɪk/ *adj* **1** giving all the details clearly: *specific instructions.* **2** particular; exactly stated or described: *Each of the bodily organs has its own specific function.*
spe'cifically *adv*: *This dictionary is intended specifically for learners of English.*

specify /'spɛsɪfaɪ/ *v* **1** to mention particularly: *He specified the main illnesses that are caused by poverty.* **2** to order specially: *She ordered a cake from the baker and specified green icing.*

specimen /'spɛsɪmɪn/ *n* something used as a sample: *We looked at specimens of different types of rock under the microscope.*

speck /spɛk/ *n* **1** a small spot or stain: *a speck of ink.* **2** a tiny piece: *a speck of dust.*

speckle /'spɛkəl/ *n* a little coloured spot: *The eggs were pale blue with dark green speckles.*

specs /spɛks/ *n* spectacles.

spectacle /'spɛktəkəl/ *n* a sight: *The royal wedding was a great spectacle.*

spectacles /'spɛktəkəlz/ *n* a pair of framed lenses that you wear to help your eyesight; glasses: *Where are my spectacles?; That's the second pair of spectacles I've lost this week.*

> **spectacles** takes a plural verb, but **a pair of spectacles** is singular.

spectacular /spɛk'takjʊlə(r)/ *adj* splendid; impressive: *a spectacular performance.*
spec'tacularly *adv.*

spectator /spɛk'teɪtə(r)/ *n* someone who watches an event: *Fifty thousand spectators came to the match.*

> See **audience**.

spectre /'spɛktə(r)/ *n* **1** a ghost: *He thought he could see spectres flying through the air.* **2** something that causes fear because it might happen in the future: *The spectre of war was hanging over the country at that time.*

spectrum /'spɛktrəm/, *plural* **spectra** /'spɛktrə/ or **'spectrums**, *n* **1** all the different colours that are produced when light goes through a prism or a drop of water: *The colours of the rainbow form the spectrum.* **2** all the different forms of something: *Actors can express the whole spectrum of feelings in the way they speak.*

speculate /ˈspɛkjʊleɪt/ v to guess. **specuˈlation** n.

sped see **speed**.

speech /spiːtʃ/ n **1** saying words; the ability to say words: *Speech is the chief means of communication between people*. **2** the words that you say; the way you speak: *Your speech is too full of slang words*; *The old man's speech was very slow*. **3** a talk given to an audience: *parliamentary speeches*.

ˈspeechless adj unable to speak, because of surprise, shock *etc*: *He looked at her in speechless amazement*. **ˈspeechlessly** adv.

speed /spiːd/ n **1** rate of moving: *to move along at a slow speed*; *The car was travelling at high speed*. **2** quickness: *Speed is essential in this job*. — v **1** to move or progress quickly; to hurry. **2** to drive faster than is allowed by law: *The policeman said that I had been speeding*.

> **speed; sped** /spɛd/ **or ˈspeeded; sped or ˈspeeded**: *Ben sped from the blocks with his usual electric start*; *The car speeded along the motorway*; *I tried to catch him, but he had sped out of the room*.

ˈspeedboat n a small, fast boat with a powerful engine.

ˈspeeding n the offence of driving faster than the speed limit: *He was fined for speeding*.

speedometer /spɪˈdɒmɪtə(r)/ n an instrument on a car *etc* showing how fast you are travelling.

ˈspeedy adj quick: *a speedy answer*. **ˈspeedily** adv. **ˈspeediness** n.

speed limit a limit, set by law, to how fast you may drive on any particular road.

speed up 1 to increase speed: *The car speeded up as it left the town*. **2** to quicken the rate of something: *Work on this project has had to be speeded up*.

> **speed up; speeded up; speeded up**.

spell¹ /spɛl/ n **1** a set of words that is supposed to have magical power: *The witch recited a spell and turned herself into a swan*. **2** a strong influence: *He was completely under her spell*.

spell² /spɛl/ n **1** a turn at work: *Shortly afterwards I did another spell at the machine*. **2** a period of time during which something lasts: *a spell of bad health*. **3** a short time: *We stayed in the country for a spell and then came home*.

spell³ /spɛl/ v **1** to say or write in order the letters of a word: *I asked him to spell his name for me*; *How do you spell 'gauge'?* **2** to form a word: *C-a-t spells 'cat'*. **3** to be able to spell words correctly: *I can't spell!*

> **spell; spelt or spelled; spelt or spelled**: *He spelt my name correctly*; *My name has been spelt wrong again!*

ˈspelling n: *Her spelling is terrible*; *The teacher gave the children a spelling test*.

spell out 1 to explain something clearly and in detail: *He spelt out his plan for the committee and they took a vote on it*. **2** to write or say the letters that form a word: *When I'm speaking on the telephone, I usually ask people to spell their names out*.

spend /spɛnd/ v **1** to use up or pay out money: *He spends more than he earns*. **2** to pass time: *I spent a week in Spain this summer*.

> **spend; spent** /spɛnt/; **spent**: *He spent his last 50p on chocolate*; *We've spent good money on your education*.

ˈspendthrift n a person who spends his money carelessly.

sperm /spɜːm/ n **1** the fluid in a male animal that fertilizes the female egg. **2** (*plural* **sperms** or **sperm**) one of the fertilizing cells in this fluid.

sphere /sfɪə(r)/ n a solid object that is the shape of a ball: *The earth is a sphere*.

spherical /ˈsfɛrɪkəl/ adj completely round, like a ball: *The world is not flat, but spherical*.

Sphinx /sfɪŋks/ n the huge stone statue of a creature with a human head and a lion's body, that stands near the pyramids at Gisa in Egypt.

spice /spaɪs/ n **1** any of several strong-smelling, sharp-tasting substances used to flavour food: *We added cinnamon and other spices to the dish*. **2** something that adds interest and enjoyment to life: *I need some spice in my life!* — v.

spiced adj containing spices: *spiced dishes*. **ˈspicy** adj tasting of spices: *a spicy cake*. **ˈspiciness** n.

spick and span /spɪkənˈspan/ neat, clean and tidy: *The whole house looks spick and span*.

spider /ˈspaɪdə(r)/ n a small creature with eight legs and no wings, that spins a web.

spike /spaɪk/ n a hard, thin, pointed object: *The fence had long spikes on top*. **spiked** adj.

'spiky *adj* having spikes: *the spiky coat of a hedgehog.*

spill /spɪl/ *v* to pour out accidentally: *He spilt milk on the floor*; *Vegetables spilt out of the burst bag.*

> **spill; spilt** or **spilled; spilt** or **spilled**: *She spilt tea over her dress*; *I've spilt the milk.*

spill the beans to give away information that was supposed to remain secret.

spin /spɪn/ *v* **1** to turn round rapidly: *She spun round in surprise*; *He spun a coin on the table.* **2** to form threads from wool, cotton *etc* by pulling it out and twisting it: *The old woman was spinning wool.* — *n*: *The car ran into a patch of ice and went into a spin.*

> **spin; spun** /spʌn/; **spun**: *The spider spun a web*; *It had spun its web in the corner of the window.*

spin out to cause to last longer than is normal: *He spun out his speech for an extra five minutes.*

spinach /'spɪnɪtʃ/ *n* a plant whose young leaves are eaten as a vegetable.

spinal /'spaɪnəl/ *adj* having to do with your spine: *a spinal injury.*

spindle /'spɪndəl/ *n* a pin on which something turns, for example the shaft of a knob on a radio *etc.*

spin-dry /spɪn'draɪ/ *v* to remove most of the water from wet clothes by spinning them around very fast in a special machine called a **spin drier** or **spin dryer**.

spine /spaɪn/ *n* **1** the line of linked bones running down the back of humans and many animals; the backbone: *She damaged her spine when she fell.* **2** the narrow back part of a book: *The title was written on the spine.* **3** a thin, stiff, pointed part growing on an animal or a plant: *the spines of a porcupine.*

'spineless *adj* without courage or character: *He's too spineless to stand up for himself!*

spinner /'spɪnə(r)/ *n* someone who spins.

spin-off /'spɪnɒf/ *n* something useful that happens or is formed during the making of something else, without being planned: *There have been a lot of spin-offs from space research.*

spinster /'spɪnstə(r)/ *n* a woman who has never married.

spiny /'spaɪnɪ/ *adj* covered with spines: *a spiny cactus.*

spiral /'spaɪərəl/ *adj* coiled; winding round like a spring: *a spiral staircase*; *a spiral shell.* — *n*: *She wound the piece of wire round and round her finger so that it formed a spiral.* **'spirally** *adv.*

spire /spaɪə(r)/ *n* a tall, pointed tower.

> See **steeple**.

spirit /'spɪrɪt/ *n* **1** your personality and the things you believe in; your soul, which some people believe remains alive when your body dies: *Our great leader may be dead, but his spirit still lives on*; *Evil spirits have taken possession of him.* **2** liveliness; courage: *He acted with spirit.* **3** a feeling; a sense: *Have you no spirit of fairness?* **3** the general feeling or atmosphere created by several people at once: *team spirit*; *Everyone entered into the party spirit.* **4** the real meaning or intention of something: *We should remember the spirit as well as the letter of the law.*

'spirited *adj* full of courage or liveliness: *a spirited speech.* **'spiritedly** *adv.*

-spirited having a particular kind of mood or attitude; *high-spirited children.*

'spirits *n* **1** your mood: *He's in good spirits.* **2** strong alcoholic drinks like whisky, brandy *etc*: *He never drinks spirits.*

spiritual /'spɪrɪtʃʊəl/ *adj* concerned with your spirit or soul, or your religious beliefs. **'spiritually** *adv.*

spirit away or **spirit off** to take away secretly and suddenly.

spit /spɪt/ *n* the liquid that forms in your mouth; saliva. — *v* **1** to throw out spit from your mouth: *He spat on the floor*; *In her anger, she spat at him.* **2** to throw out: *The fire spat out sparks.*

> **spit; spat** /spæt/; **spat**: *He spat out the cherry stone*; *The dog was tired of being spat at by the cat.*

spite /spaɪt/ *n* a desire to hurt or offend someone: *He hid her book out of spite.* — *v* to try to hurt, upset or annoy someone: *To spite me, she went out with my old boyfriend.* **'spiteful** *adj*: *a spiteful remark*; *a spiteful person.* **'spitefully** *adv.* **'spitefulness** *n.*

in spite of 1 taking no notice of something: *He went out in spite of his father's orders that he must stay at home.* **2** although something has happened, is a fact *etc*: *In spite of all the rain that had fallen, the ground was still very dry.*

> Write **in spite of** (not **inspite of**).

spittle /ˈspɪtəl/ *n* the liquid that forms in your mouth; spit; saliva.

splash /splaʃ/ *v* **1** to make something wet with drops of liquid, mud *etc*: *A passing car splashed my coat with water.* **2** to fly about in drops: *Water splashed everywhere.* **3** to move with splashes; to make splashes: *The children were splashing about in the sea*; *We splashed through the puddles.* — *n* **1** a scattering of drops of liquid; the noise made by this: *He fell into the river with a loud splash.* **2** a mark made by splashing: *There was a splash of mud on her dress.* **3** a bright patch: *a splash of colour.*

'splashdown *n* the landing of a spacecraft in the sea at the end of a space flight.

splash out to spend more money than you would normally spend on something: *We splashed out on something new for everyone in the family.*

splatter /ˈsplatə(r)/ *v* to splash with, or in small drops: *She splattered paint on the walls*; *She splattered the walls with the paint*; *The rain splattered the door.*

splay /spleɪ/ *v* to spread wide; to open wide: *the splayed fingers of one hand*; *The birds splayed their wings in the sunshine.*

splendid /ˈsplɛndɪd/ *adj* **1** brilliant; magnificent; very rich and grand: *He looked splendid in his robes.* **2** very good or fine: *This is a splendid essay, Catherine!* **'splendidly** *adv*.

splendour /ˈsplɛndə(r)/ *n* grand beauty; magnificence; brilliance: *the splendour of the snow-covered mountains.*

splice /splaɪs/ *v* to join two pieces together neatly by the ends: *He spliced the ropes by weaving their threads together.*

splint /splɪnt/ *n* a piece of wood *etc* used to keep a broken arm or leg in a fixed position while it heals.

'splinter *n* a small sharp broken piece of wood *etc*: *She got a splinter in her finger from the rough wooden plank.* — *v* to split into splinters: *The door splintered under the heavy blow.*

split /splɪt/ *v* **1** to break or tear apart: *to split firewood*; *My skirt has split down the side.* **2** to divide: *The dispute split the workers into two opposing groups.* — *n* a crack, tear or break: *There is a split in your jacket.*

> split; split; split: *She split the chocolate in half; They've split the work into two parts.*

splitting headache a very bad headache.

split up to end a close relationship by separating from each other: *She has split up with her boyfriend.*

splutter /ˈsplʌtə(r)/ *v* to make spitting sounds, for example as you talk because of excitement or anger: *She spluttered with anger.* — *n*.

spoil /spɔɪl/ *v* **1** to damage; to ruin; to make something bad or useless: *If you touch that flower you'll spoil it.* **2** to give children *etc* too much of what they want and make their characters worse by doing so: *Don't give Jane so many presents — you mustn't spoil her.*

> spoil; spoilt /spɔɪlt/ or spoiled; spoilt or spoiled: *He spoilt the dinner by burning it*; *You've spoilt my drawing!*

spoilt *adj*: *He's a very spoilt child!*

'spoilsport *n* a person who spoils, or refuses to join in, the fun of others.

spoke[1] /spəʊk/ *n* one of the ribs or bars from the centre to the rim of the wheel of a bicycle, cart *etc*.

spoke[2], **spoken** *see* **speak**.

spokesman /ˈspəʊksmən/, **spokeswoman** /ˈspəʊkswʊmən/ or **spokesperson** /ˈspəʊkspɜːsən/ *n* a person who speaks on behalf of a group of people.

sponge /spʌndʒ/ *n* **1** a sea animal, or its soft skeleton, which has many holes and is able to suck up and hold water. **2** a piece of this skeleton, used for washing your body; an artificial substitute for this. **3** a light kind of cake or pudding. **4** a wipe with a sponge: *Give the baby's face a sponge.* — *v* to wipe or clean with a sponge: *She sponged the child's face.*

sponge bag a small waterproof bag for keeping soap and toothpaste *etc* in.

sponge cake a light cake made with flour, fat, eggs and sugar.

spongy /ˈspʌndʒɪ/ *adj* soft and springy; holding water like a sponge: *spongy ground.*

sponge on or **sponge off** to get money or food *etc* from someone without doing or giving anything in return.

sponsor /ˈspɒnsə(r)/ *n* **1** to pay some or all the money that is needed for a particular event or project, often as a form of advertising: *The company sponsored several football matches.* **2** to promise someone that you will pay a certain sum of money to a charity if he or she completes a particular task: *Are you willing to sponsor me on a 24-mile walk for the Leprosy Fund?* — *n* a

spontaneous /spɒn'teɪnɪəs/ *adj* **1** of your own free will: *a spontaneous offer of help.* **2** natural; not forced: *a spontaneous smile.* **spon'taneously** *adv.* **spontaneity** /spɒntə'neɪɪtɪ/ *n.*

spooky /'spu:kɪ/ *adj* frightening: *I don't walk through the woods at night because they're so spooky.*

spool /spu:l/ *n* a cylindrical holder on to which thread or photographic film *etc* is wound.

spoon /spu:n/ *n* an instrument shaped like a shallow bowl with a handle for lifting food to your mouth, or for stirring tea, coffee *etc*: *a teaspoon; a soupspoon.* — *v* to lift or scoop up with a spoon: *She spooned food into the baby's mouth.*

'spoonful *n* the amount held by a spoon: *three spoonfuls of sugar.*

> The plural of **spoonful** is **spoonfuls** (not spoonsful).

'spoon-feed *v* **1** to feed a baby *etc* with a spoon. **2** to teach or treat people in a way that does not allow them to think for themselves.

> **'spoon-feed; 'spoon-fed; 'spoon-fed.**

sporadic /spə'rædɪk/ *adj* happening from time to time at irregular intervals: *sporadic gunfire.* **spo'radically** *adv.*

spore /spɔː(r)/ *n* a cell, produced by bacteria and some plants, which grows into a new individual: *Fungi produce spores.*

sport /spɔːt/ *n* **1** games or competitions involving physical activity: *She's very keen on sport of all kinds.* **2** a particular game or amusement of this kind: *Football is my favourite sport; hunting, shooting, fishing and other sports.* **3** a good-natured, kind person: *He's a good sport to agree to help us!*

'sporting *adj* **1** having to do with sports: *That tennis match was one of the best sporting events of the year; the sporting world.* **2** kind; friendly; helpful: *It was very sporting of him to let me use his bicycle when mine had a puncture; a sporting gesture.* **'sportingly** *adv.*

sports *adj* designed, or suitable, for sports: *a sports centre; sports equipment.*

'sportsman *n* **1** someone who takes part in sports: *He is a very keen sportsman.* **2** someone who is fair and generous in sport: *He's a real sportsman — he doesn't seem to care if he wins or loses.*

'sportsmanlike *adj* behaving honestly and fairly when playing sports.

'sportsmanship *n* a sportsmanlike attitude.

'sportswear *n* clothing designed for playing sports in.

'sportswoman *n* a girl or woman who takes part in sport.

spot /spɒt/ *n* **1** a small mark or stain: *She was trying to remove a spot of grease from her skirt.* **2** a small, round mark of a different colour from its background: *His tie was blue with white spots.* **3** a pimple or red mark on your skin: *She had chicken-pox and was covered in spots.* **4** a place or small area, especially the exact place where something happened *etc*: *The girls showed the policeman the spot where they had seen the stolen car.* **5** a small amount: *May I borrow a spot of sugar?* — *v* **1** to catch sight of someone or something: *She spotted him at the very back of the crowd.* **2** to recognize or pick out: *Can you spot the mistake in this picture?*

spot check an inspection or test which is made without previous warning: *The police are carrying out spot checks on vehicle road licences.*

'spotless *adj* very clean: *a spotless kitchen.*

'spotlight *n* a circle of light that is thrown on to a small area, for example on a stage; the lamp that projects this beam. — *v* **1** to light with a spotlight. **2** to show something up clearly; to draw attention to something: *to spotlight a difficulty.*

> **'spotlight; 'spotlit** or **'spotlighted; 'spotlit** or **'spotlighted.**

'spotted *adj*: *Her dress was spotted with paint; a spotted tie.*

'spotty *adj* covered with spots: *a spotty face.*

in a spot in trouble: *Can you help me? — I'm in a spot!*

on the spot 1 at once: *She liked the dress so much that she bought it on the spot.* **2** in the exact place where something is happening; in the place where you are needed: *It was a good thing you were on the spot when he had his heart attack.* — *adj* **1**: *an on-the-spot decision.* **2**: *our on-the-spot reporter.*

put someone on the spot to put someone in a difficult position where they must answer or act when they would rather not: *His question put me on the spot.*

spot on very accurate: *His description of Mary was spot on!*

spouse /spaʊs/ *n* a husband or wife.

spout /spaʊt/ *v* to be forced out in a jet; to burst out: *Water spouted from the hole in the pipe.* — *n* **1** the part of a kettle, teapot, jug, waterpipe *etc* through which the liquid it contains is poured out. **2** a strong flow of water *etc*; a jet.

sprain /spreɪn/ *v* to twist a joint, especially your ankle or wrist so as to injure the muscles *etc* round it: *She sprained her ankle yesterday.* — *n*: *'Is your ankle broken?' 'No, I think it's only a sprain.'*

sprang *see* **spring**.

sprawl /sprɔːl/ *v* **1** to sit, lie or fall with your arms and legs spread out: *Several tired-looking people were sprawling in armchairs.* **2** to spread over a wide area in an irregular way.

'**sprawling** *adj*: *the huge, sprawling city of Los Angeles.*

spray /spreɪ/ *n* **1** a mist or jet of small flying drops of water *etc*: *The perfume came out of the bottle in a fine spray.* **2** a device with many small holes for producing a mist or jet like this: *Mary took a perfume spray from her handbag.* **3** a liquid for spraying: *She bought a can of hair-spray to keep her hairstyle in place.* — *v* to pour out in a mist or jet: *The water sprayed all over everyone*; *She sprayed water over the flowers*; *He sprayed the roses with insecticide.*

spread /sprɛd/ *v* **1** to cover a surface: *She spread honey on her bread*; *She spread the bread with jam.* **2** to reach a wider area; to affect a larger number of people *etc*; to distribute widely: *The news spread through the village very quickly*; *Spread the good news!* **3** to distribute over an area, period of time *etc*: *The exams were spread over a period of ten days.* — *n* **1** the process of reaching a wider area, affecting more people *etc*: *the spread of information by television*; *the spread of crime.* **2** a food to be spread on bread *etc*: *Have some chicken spread.*

> **spread; spread; spread**: *The disease spread quickly*; *The books were spread out on the table.*

spread out 1 to extend; to stretch out: *The fields spread out in front of him*; *He spread the map out on the table.* **2** to distribute: *The meetings of the club are spread out over the whole year.* **3** to scatter: *She spread the leaflets out on the table*; *They spread out and began to search the whole hillside.*

sprig /sprɪg/ *n* a small piece of a plant; a twig.

> See **branch**.

sprightly /'spraɪtlɪ/ *adj* lively and moving quickly: *a sprightly old lady.*

spring /sprɪŋ/ *v* **1** to jump, leap or move swiftly, usually upwards: *She sprang into the boat*; *Do you spring out of bed in the morning?* **2** to develop from; to be the result of: *His nervousness springs from shyness.* — *n* **1** a coil of wire or a similar device that can be pressed down but returns to its original shape when released: *a watch-spring*; *the springs in a chair.* **2** the season of the year when plants begin to grow, March to May in cooler northern regions: *Spring is my favourite season.* **3** a leap or sudden movement: *The lion made a sudden spring at its prey.* **4** the ability to spring back again after being stretched, squashed *etc*: *There's not a lot of spring in this old trampoline.* **5** the ability to leap or jump well: *A dancer needs plenty of spring.* **6** a small stream flowing out from the ground.

> **spring; sprang** /spraŋ/; **sprung** /sprʌŋ/: *He sprang out of the chair*; *New buildings have sprung up since I was last here.*

'**springboard** *n* **1** a type of diving-board that bends under your weight, so that you can spring off it. **2** a board on which gymnasts jump before vaulting.

spring cleaning thorough cleaning of a house *etc* in spring.

spring roll a roll of thin pastry filled with vegetables and meat and cooked in oil.

'**springtime** *n* the season of spring.

springy /'sprɪŋɪ/ *adj*: *This is a nice springy mattress*; *thick, springy grass*; *to walk with springy steps.*

spring on to tell someone something that is not expected: *This meeting was sprung on me yesterday and I'm afraid I'm really not very well prepared for it.*

spring up to develop or appear suddenly: *New buildings are springing up everywhere.*

sprinkle /'sprɪŋkəl/ *v* to scatter something over something else in small drops or bits: *He sprinkled salt over his food*; *He sprinkled the roses with water.*

'**sprinkler** *n* an apparatus for sprinkling something, for instance water over a lawn.

sprint /sprɪnt/ *n* a run or running race performed at high speed over a short distance: *Who won the 100 metres sprint?* — *v* to run at full speed especially in a race: *He sprinted the last few hundred metres.*

'**sprinter** *n* a person who is good at running short distances very fast.

sprout /spraʊt/ *v* **1** to develop leaves, shoots *etc*: *The trees are sprouting new leaves.* **2** to develop horns, produce feathers *etc*: *The young birds are sprouting their first feathers.* — *n* a new shoot: *bean sprouts.*

sprout up to grow: *That fruit bush has sprouted up fast; Jennifer has sprouted up a lot since I last saw her.*

spruce /spruːs/ *adj* neat and smart: *You're looking very spruce today.*

spruce up to smarten: *I'll go and spruce up before going out.*

sprung *see* **spring**.

spun *see* **spin**.

spur /spɜː(r)/ *n* **1** a small instrument with a sharp point or points that riders wear on their heels and dig into the horse's sides to make it go faster. **2** anything that urges a person to make greater efforts: *He was driven on by the spur of ambition.*

spur on to urge a horse to go faster, using spurs; to urge a person to make greater efforts: *He spurred his horse on; The thought of the prize spurred her on.*

on the spur of the moment suddenly; without planning: *I was passing your house and decided to visit you on the spur of the moment.*

spurn /spɜːn/ *v* to reject scornfully: *He spurned her offers of help.*

spurt /spɜːt/ *v* to spout: *Blood spurted from the wound.* — *n* a sudden burst: *a spurt of blood; a spurt of energy.*

spy /spaɪ/ *n* a secret agent or person employed to gather information secretly, especially about the military affairs of other countries: *She was arrested as a spy.* — *v* **1** to be a spy: *He had been spying for the Russians for many years.* **2** to see or notice: *She spied a human figure on the mountainside.*

> **spy**; '**spying**; **spied**; **spied**: *She was spying for the enemy; He spied a strange bird.*

'**spyhole** *n* a hole through which you can look without being seen.

spy on to watch a person *etc* secretly: *The police had been spying on the gang for several months.*

squabble /ˈskwɒbəl/ *v* to quarrel: *The children are always squabbling over their toys.* — *n* a noisy quarrel.

squad /skwɒd/ *n* a small group of soldiers, workmen *etc* working together; a team: *The men were divided into squads to perform different duties; a squad of workmen.*

squadron /ˈskwɒdrən/ *n* a division of a regiment, a section of a fleet, or a group of aeroplanes.

squalid /ˈskwɒlɪd/ *adj* very dirty; filthy: *The houses are squalid and overcrowded.*

squalor /ˈskwɒlə(r)/ *n*: *They lived in squalor.*

squander /ˈskwɒndə(r)/ *v* to waste: *He squandered all his money on gambling; She is squandering her time watching television when she should be studying.*

square /skweə(r)/ *n* **1** a four-sided flat shape with all sides equal in length and all the angles right angles. **2** something with this shape. **3** an open place in a town, with the buildings round it. **4** the resulting number when a number is multiplied by itself: 3×3, or 3^2, equals 9, so 9 is the square of 3. — *adj* **1** having the shape of a square or right angle: *I need a square piece of paper; He has a square chin.* **2** measuring a particular amount on all four sides: *This piece of wood is two metres square.* **3** equal; not owing any money: *Here's the £10 you lent me — does that make us square now?* — *adv* firmly and directly: *She hit him square on the point of the chin.* — *v* **1** to give a square shape to something; to make something square. **2** to multiply a number by itself: *Two squared is four.* **3** to agree; to match or fit: *His evidence doesn't square with the facts.*

squared *adj* marked out in squares: *squared paper.*

square meal a good, satisfying meal.

square root a number that gives another particular number when it is multiplied by itself: *The square root of nine is three.*

squash /skwɒʃ/ *v* to press, squeeze or crush: *He tried to squash too many clothes into his case; The tomatoes got squashed at the bottom of the shopping-bag.* — *n* **1** a crowd; a crowding together of people *etc*: *There was a great squash in the doorway.* **2** a drink containing the juice of crushed fruit: *Have some orange squash!* **3** a type of game played in a walled court with rackets and a rubber ball.

squat /skwɒt/ *v* to sit down on your heels or in a crouching position: *The beggar squatted all day in the market place.* — *adj* short and fat: *He has a squat body.*

squawk /skwɔːk/ v to give a loud, harsh cry: *The hen squawked and ran away.* — n: *The goose gave a squawk when it saw the fox.*

squeak /skwiːk/ n a shrill cry or sound: *the squeaks of the mice; The door gave a squeak as she opened it.* — v: *The hinge is squeaking.* **'squeaky** adj: *squeaky shoes.*

squeal /skwiːl/ n a long, shrill cry: *The children welcomed their father home with squeals of delight.* — v: *This puppy squealed with pain.*

squeamish /'skwiːmɪʃ/ adj easily shocked and made to feel sick: *She is squeamish about blood.*

squeeze /skwiːz/ v **1** to press something tightly: *He squeezed her hand lovingly; He squeezed the clay into a ball.* **2** to force someone or something into a narrow space: *The dog squeezed itself into the hole; We were all squeezed into the back seat of the car.* **3** to force something, for example liquid, out of something by pressing: *to squeeze oranges.* — n: *Give the lemon a squeeze; He gave her hand a squeeze; We all got into the car, but it was a squeeze; Would you like a squeeze of lemon on your fish?*
'squeezer n an instrument for squeezing: *a lemon squeezer.*
squeeze up to move closer together: *Could you all squeeze up on the bench and make room for me?*

squelch /skwɛltʃ/ n the sucking sound made by movement in a thick, sticky substance such as mud: *the squelch of boots in the wet sand.* — v to make this sound: *She squelched along in the mud.*

squid /skwɪd/, plural **squid** or **squids**, n a sea creature with ten tentacles.

squiggle n a short, wavy written line: *His signature looks like a big squiggle to me.*

squint /skwɪnt/ n a fault in the eyes that makes them turn inward: *The baby has a squint.* — v **1** to have a squint: *The baby squints; You squint when you try to look at your nose.* **2** to look through half-closed eyes: *She squinted in the sudden bright light.*

squirm /skwɜːm/ v to twist your body; to wriggle: *He lay squirming on the ground with pain.*

squirrel /'skwɪrəl/ n a small red-brown or grey animal with a large bushy tail, that can sit on its back legs and use its front paws to feed itself.

squirt /skwɜːt/ v to shoot out in a narrow spray or jet: *The elephant squirted water over itself; Water squirted from the hose.*

St, **St.**, short for **Saint** or **Street**, in names of places.

stab /stab/ v to wound or pierce with a pointed instrument or weapon: *He stabbed her with a dagger; He had been stabbed in the chest; stabbed through the heart.* — n **1** an act of stabbing: *He had received a stab in the chest.* **2** causing a stabbing feeling: *a stab of pain.*
'stabwound n a wound caused by stabbing.

stabilize /'steɪbɪlaɪz/ v to make something firm or steady: *He put a strip of board under the cupboard to stabilize it.*

stable[1] /'steɪbəl/ adj **1** firm and steady; well-balanced: *This chair isn't very stable.* **2** firmly established; likely to last: *a stable government.* **3** sensible: *She has a stable personality.* **sta'bility** n.

stable[2] /'steɪbəl/ n **1** a building in which horses are kept. **2 (stables)** an establishment where horses are kept for hiring *etc*: *He runs the riding stables.*

stack /stak/ n **1** a large, neatly shaped pile, of hay, straw, wood *etc*: *a haystack.* **2** a set of shelves for books in a library *etc*. — v to arrange things in a large, neat, pile: *Stack the files up against the wall.*
stacked adj with large numbers of things arranged in piles: *Her desk was stacked with papers.*

stadium /'steɪdɪəm/ n a large sports-ground or racecourse with seats for spectators: *The athletics competitions were held in the new stadium.*

staff[1] /stɑːf/ n a group of people employed in running a business, school *etc*: *The school has a large teaching staff; The staff are annoyed about the changes; Two members of staff are leaving the school at the end of term.* — v to supply with staff: *Most of our offices are staffed by volunteers.*

> **staff** can take a singular or plural verb.

'staffroom n a sitting-room for the staff of a school: *A meeting will be held in the staffroom.*

staff[2] /stɑːf/, plural **staves**, n a stick; a pole.

stag /stag/ n a male deer.

stage[1] /steɪdʒ/ n a raised platform for performing or acting on, in a theatre, hall *etc*. — v **1** to prepare and produce a play *etc* in a theatre: *This play was first staged in 1928.* **2** to organize an event *etc*: *The protesters are planning to stage a demonstration.*

Figure labels: stage, rostrum, pulpit

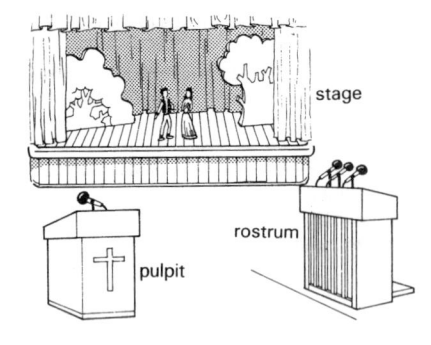

'stage-manage *v* **1** to organize the scenery and lights *etc* for a play. **2** to organize an event *etc* in order to create an effect: *The wedding was stage-managed by her mother.*
stage manager the person who organizes the scenery and lights *etc* for a play.

stage² /steɪdʒ/ *n* **1** a period or step in the development of something; a particular moment: *The plan is in its early stages*; *We know that several people survived the plane-crash, but at this stage, we don't know how many survivors there are.* **2** part of a journey: *The first stage of our journey will be the flight to Frankfurt.* **3** a section of a bus route.

stagger /'stagə(r)/ *v* **1** to sway, move or walk unsteadily: *The drunk man staggered along the road.* **2** to astonish: *I was staggered to hear that he had died.* **3** to arrange people's hours of work, holidays *etc* so that they do not begin and end at the same times.
'staggering *adj* astonishing: *staggering news.*

stagnant /'stagnənt/ *adj* **1** standing still, not flowing, therefore dirty and unhealthy: *Stagnant water*; *a stagnant pool.* **2** dull; making no progress: *Trade is stagnant at present.*
stagnate /stag'neɪt/ *v* to be or become stagnant: *I feel that I'm stagnating in this job and I should move on.* **stag'nation** *n*.

staid /steɪd/ *adj* serious and often a bit dull: *Her clothes are always very staid.*

stain /steɪn/ *v* **1** to leave a mark, especially a permanent one, on a garment *etc*: *The coffee I spilt has stained my trousers.* **2** to become marked in this way: *Silk stains easily.* **3** to dye or colour wood: *The wooden chairs had been stained brown.* — *n* a dirty mark on cloth *etc* that is difficult or impossible to remove: *His overall was covered with paint-stains.*

stained glass a glass panel made of pieces of glass of different colours put together to form a picture: *There are some very famous stained glass windows in the church.*

stainless steel a metal that is a mixture of steel and chromium and does not rust.

stair /steə(r)/ *n* **1** a set of steps inside a building, going from one floor to another: *We need a new carpet for the stair.* **2** one of these steps: *a flight of stairs*; *He fell down the stairs.*
'staircase or **'stairway** *n* a flight of stairs: *A dark narrow staircase led up to the top floor.*

stake¹ /steɪk/ *n* a strong stick or post, especially a pointed one used as a support or as part of a fence.

stake² /steɪk/ *n* a sum of money that you risk in betting. — *v* to bet: *I'm going to stake £5 on that horse.*
at stake 1 to be won or lost: *A great deal of money is at stake.* **2** in great danger: *Our children's future is at stake.*
stake a claim to state that you have a right to have something.

stalactite /'staləktaɪt/ *n* a spike of limestone hanging from the roof of a cave *etc* formed by the dripping of water containing lime.

stalagmite /'staləgmaɪt/ *n* a spike of limestone rising from the floor of a cave, formed by water dripping from the roof.

stale /steɪl/ *adj* not fresh; dry and tasteless: *stale bread.*
'stalemate *n* a position in a game of chess or a dispute in which neither side can win: *The discussions ended in a stalemate*; *There is no way to break the stalemate between them.*

stalk¹ /stɔːk/ *n* the stem of a plant or of a leaf, flower or fruit: *If the stalk is damaged, the plant may die.*

stalk² /stɔːk/ *v* **1** to walk stiffly and proudly: *He stalked out of the room in anger.* **2** to spread dangerously through a place: *Disease and famine stalk the country.* **3** in hunting, to move gradually as close as possible to an animal, trying to remain hidden: *to stalk deer.*

stall¹ /stɔːl/ *n* **1** a compartment in a cowshed *etc*: *cattle stalls.* **2** a small shop or a counter on which goods are displayed for sale: *He bought a newspaper at the bookstall in the station*; *The market-place was full of traders' stalls.*

stalls *n* in a theatre, the seats on the ground floor: *I always sit in the stalls.*

stall² /stɔːl/ *v* **1** to stop suddenly because of lack of power: *The car stalled when I was halfway up the hill.* **2** to delay or avoid taking some action: *I can't get a direct answer — he keeps stalling.*

stallion /'staljən/ *n* a fully-grown male horse.

stalwart /'stɔːlwət/ *adj* strong and reliable: *He's one of our most stalwart supporters.*

stamen /'steɪmən/ *n* the delicate stalk inside a flower, that produces pollen.

stamina /'stamɪnə/ *n* strength that helps you to go on exercising or working for a long time: *Long-distance runners need plenty of stamina.*

stammer /'stamə(r)/ *n* the fault in speaking of being unable to produce certain sounds easily: *'You m-m-must m-m-meet m-m-my m-m-mother' is an example of a stammer*; *That child has a bad stammer.* — *v* to speak with a stammer; to speak in a similar way because of fright, nervousness *etc*: *He stammered an apology.*

stamp /stamp/ *v* **1** to bring your foot down with force on the ground: *He stamped his foot with rage*; *She stamped on the insect.* **2** to print or mark: *He stamped the date at the top of his letter*; *The oranges were all stamped with the exporter's name.* **3** to stick a postage stamp on a letter *etc*: *I've addressed the envelope but I haven't stamped it.* — *n* **1** stamping your foot: *'Give it to me!' she shouted with a stamp of her foot.* **2** the instrument used to stamp a design *etc* on a surface: *He put the date on the bill with a rubber-stamp.* **3** a postage stamp: *He stuck the stamps on the parcel*; *He collects foreign stamps.* **4** a design *etc* made by stamping: *All the goods had the manufacturer's stamp on them.*

stamp out to put an end to something; to get rid of something: *to stamp out a wicked custom*; *to stamp out a rebellion.*

stampede /stam'piːd/ *n* a sudden wild rush of animals *etc*: *a stampede of buffaloes*; *The school bell rang for lunch and there was a stampede for the door.* — *v* to rush in a stampede: *The noise made the elephants stampede.*

stance /stɑːns/ *n* **1** a position or manner of standing: *an upright stance.* **2** an attitude: *She has adopted a tough stance towards them.*

stand /stand/ *v* **1** to be in an upright position, not sitting or lying: *His leg was so painful that he could hardly stand*; *After the storm, few trees were left standing*; *One felt as if one was standing on the deck of a ship.* **2** to rise to your feet: *He pushed back his chair and stood up*; *Stand up when your teacher comes into the room.* **3** to remain without moving: *The train stood for an hour outside Newcastle.* **4** to remain unchanged: *This law still stands.* **5** to be in a particular place: *There is now a factory where our house once stood.* **6** to be in a particular state: *As things stand, we can do nothing to help.* **7** to put in a particular position, especially upright: *He picked up the fallen chair and stood it beside the table.* **8** to undergo; to bear: *He will stand trial for murder*; *I can't stand her rudeness any longer.* **9** to have an opinion about something: *Where do you stand on this issue?* **10** to be a candidate in an election: *Who is standing for President?* **11** to buy a drink or meal for someone: *I stood him lunch because he'd been so helpful.* — *n* **1** a position in which you stand ready to fight *etc*: *The guard took up his stand at the gate.* **2** an object for holding or supporting something: *a coat-stand*; *The sculpture had been removed from its stand for cleaning.* **3** a stall where goods are displayed for sale or advertisement. **4** a large structure beside a football pitch, *etc* with rows of seats for spectators: *The stand was crowded.*

> **stand**; **stood** /stʊd/; **stood**: *A stranger stood at the door*; *He had stood there all day.*

'stand-by, *plural* **'stand-bys**, *n* **1** readiness for action: *Two fire-engines went directly to the fire, and a third was on stand-by.* **2** something that can be used in an emergency *etc*: *Fruit is a good stand-by when children get hungry between meals.*

'standing *n* position or reputation: *He has a very high standing in the town.*

'standing-room *n* space for standing only, not sitting: *There was standing-room only on the bus.*

make a stand to fight to defend yourself or your opinion strongly: *Environmental groups are making a stand against the proposals.*

make someone's hair stand on end to frighten someone: *The horrible scream made his hair stand on end.*

stand aside to move to one side so as to get out of someone's way: *He stood aside to let me past.*

stand back to move backwards or away: *A crowd gathered round the injured man, but a* *policeman ordered everyone to stand back.*

stand by 1 to watch something happening without doing anything: *I couldn't just stand by while he was hitting the child.* **2** to be ready to act: *The police are standing by in case of trouble.* **3** to support; to stay loyal to someone: *She stood by him throughout his trial.*

stand down to withdraw from a contest *etc*.

stand fast or **stand firm** to refuse to give in.

stand for 1 to be a shortening of something: *HQ stands for headquarters.* **2** to represent: *I like to think that our school stands for all that is best in education.* **3** to accept; to tolerate: *I won't stand for this bad behaviour.*

stand in to take someone's place for a short time or perform their duties for them: *Could you stand in for me at the meeting?* **'stand-in** *n*.

stand on your own two feet to manage your own affairs without help.

stand out to be noticeable: *She stood out as one of the cleverest girls in the school.*

stand up not to keep an appointment: *It was very unkind of her to stand him up when he'd already bought the tickets.*

stand up for to support or defend someone *etc*: *She stood up for him when the others laughed at him.*

stand up to 1 to defend yourself against someone; to fight back: *He stood up to the bigger boys who tried to bully him.* **2** to last, in spite of something: *These chairs have stood up to very hard use.*

take a stand to say publicly what you think although it may be unpopular: *The management has taken a firm stand on working hours.*

standard /'standəd/ *n* **1** something used as a basis of measurement: *The kilogram is the international standard of weight.* **2** a basis for judging quality; a level of excellence you aim at, require or reach: *You can't judge a child's drawing by the same standards as you would judge that of a trained artist*; *high standards of behaviour*; *Her dancing did not reach the standard required for entry into the ballet school.* — *adj* normal; usual: *The Post Office likes the public to use a standard size of envelope.*

'standardize *v* to make or keep products *etc* of one size, shape *etc* for the sake of convenience. **standardi'zation** *n*.

below standard not as good as is required.
up to standard as good as is required.

standpoint /'standpɔɪnt/ *n* a point of view: *What is his standpoint on this issue?*

standstill /'standstɪl/: **be at**, **come to** or **reach a standstill** to remain without moving; to stop, halt *etc*: *The traffic was at a standstill.*

stank *see* **stink**.

stanza /'stanzə/ *n* a verse in a poem.

staple[1] /'steɪpəl/ *n* a chief product of trade or industry. — *adj* chief; main: *Rice is their staple food.*

staple[2] /'steɪpəl/ *n* **1** a U-shaped type of nail. **2** a U-shaped piece of wire that is driven through sheets of paper *etc* to fasten them together. — *v*: *The papers had been stapled together.*

'stapler *n* an instrument for stapling papers.

star *n* **1** any of the fixed bodies in the sky, which are really distant suns: *The Sun is a star, and the Earth is one of its planets.* **2** any of the bodies in the sky appearing as points of light: *The sky was full of stars.* **3** a shape with a number of points, usually five or six. **4** a leading actor or actress; a well-known performer: *a film star*; *a television star*; *a football star.* — *v* **1** to play a leading part in a play, film *etc*: *She has starred in two films.* **2** to have a certain actor *etc* as its leading performer: *The film starred Elvis Presley.*

see stars to see flashes of light as a result of a hard blow on your head.

thank your lucky stars to be grateful for your good luck.

starboard /'stɑːbəd/ *n* the right side of a ship or aircraft, when you are looking towards the bow or front.

See **port**.

starch /stɑːtʃ/ *n* **1** a white food substance found especially in flour, potatoes *etc*: *Bread contains starch.* **2** a powder prepared from this, used for stiffening clothes. — *v*: *to starch a dress.*

starched *adj* stiff with starch: *a starched collar.*

stardom /'stɑːdəm/ *n* the state of being a famous actor or performer: *Vivien Leigh shot to stardom in the film 'Gone with the Wind'.*

stare /steə(r)/ *v* to look hard for a long time: *They stared at her strange clothes in amazement*; *Jonathan stared from the window at the unfamiliar landscape*; *Don't stare — it's rude!* — *n*: *He gave me a long stare.*

starfish /'stɑːfɪʃ/ *n* a small sea animal with five pointed arms.

stark /stɑːk/ *adj* **1** bare and plain in an unattractive way: *a stark landscape.* **2** complete: *a stark contrast.* — *adv* completely: *stark naked.*

starlight /'stɑːlaɪt/ *n* light from the stars.

starling /'stɑːlɪŋ/ *n* a small bird with dark, shiny feathers.

starlit /'stɑːlɪt/ *adj* bright with stars: *a starlit night.*

starry /'stɑːrɪ/ *adj* full of stars; shining like stars: *a starry night; starry eyes.*

start[1] /stɑːt/ *v* to jump or jerk suddenly because of fright, surprise *etc*: *The sudden noise made me start.* — *n*: *He gave a start of surprise; What a start the news gave me!*

start[2] /stɑːt/ *v* **1** to begin a journey: *We shall have to start at 5.30 a.m. in order to get to the boat in time.* **2** to begin: *He starts working at six o'clock every morning; In writing we start from the top left hand side; She started to cry; She starts her new job next week; Haven't you started your meal yet?; What time does the play start?* **3** to begin to work; to make something begin to work: *I can't start the car; The car won't start; The clock stopped but I started it again.* **4** to establish something; to get something going: *One of the students decided to start a college magazine.* — *n* **1** the beginning of something: *The runners lined up at the start; He stayed in the lead after a good start; I shall have to make a start on that work.* **2** in a race, chase *etc*, the advantage of beginning before or further forward than others: *The youngest child in the race got a start of five metres; The driver of the stolen car already had twenty minutes' start before the police began to chase him.*

'starter *n* **1** the first part of a meal: *We had tomato soup as a starter.* **2** a device in a car *etc* for starting the engine. **3** a person, horse *etc* that actually runs in a race: *There were only five starters because several horses were withdrawn from the race.* **4** a person who gives the signal for a race to start.

'starting-point *n* the point from which something begins.

for a start used to introduce the first or most important of several things: *You can't possibly know what he's like — you've never met him for a start!*

get off to a good or **bad start** to do well or badly in the early stages of an activity: *My day got off to a bad start when I cut myself shaving.*

start off 1 to begin a journey: *It's time we started off.* **2** to begin; to establish something or someone; to get someone or something going: *The meeting started off with the chairman's speech of welcome; His father started him off as a bookseller by lending him money to buy a shop.*

start on to begin dealing with a particular task: *I'm going to start on the gardening in the morning.*

start out 1 to begin a journey; to start off: *We shall have to start out at dawn.* **2** to begin your life or career *etc* in a particular way: *He started out as a delivery boy and worked his way up to management level.*

start over to make a second, fresh start: *Can we forget what's happened and start over?*

startle /'stɑːtəl/ *v* to give someone a shock or surprise: *The sound startled me.*

'startling *adj* unusual or unexpected and therefore shocking: *The report includes some startling statistics.*

starvation /stɑːˈveɪʃən/ extreme hunger; not having enough food to keep you alive: *n*: *They died of starvation.*

starve /stɑːv/ *v* **1** to die, or suffer, from hunger: *In the drought, many people and animals starved; You'll starve to death if you don't eat.* **2** to give no food, or not enough food, to someone: *They were accused of starving their prisoners.* **3** to be very hungry: *Can't we have supper now? I'm starving.*

be starved of not to get enough of something that is necessary: *The project was starved of money; The child was starved of love.*

state[1] /steɪt/ *n* **1** the condition in which a thing or person is: *the bad state of the roads; The room was in an untidy state; He inquired about her state of health; He was not in a fit state to run in the race.* **2** a country considered as a political community: *The Prime Minister visits the Queen once a week to discuss affairs of state; The care of sick and elderly people is partly the job of the state.* **3** a part of a country that has its own government: *The speed limit in America varies from state to state.* — *adj*: *The railways are under state control.*

in a state nervous or very anxious: *She gets into such a state before an exam!*

state of affairs a situation, especially a bad one: *This state of affairs cannot continue.*

state[2] /steɪt/ *v* to say or announce clearly, carefully and definitely: *You have not yet stated your intentions.*

stately /'steɪtlɪ/ *adj* noble, dignified and impressive: *She is tall and stately*; *a stately home*.

statement /'steɪtmənt/ *n* **1** the stating of something; something that is stated: *The Prime Minister will make a statement tomorrow on the new education plans*. **2** a written statement of how much money a person has, owes *etc*: *a bank statement*.

statesman /'steɪtsmən/ *n* an important political leader whom people respect.

static /'statɪk/ *adj* not moving; not changing: *The latest weather report says that the area of high pressure will remain static for the next few days*. — *n* (also **static electricity**) tiny electric sparks that are caused by rubbing two things together: *You get static when you comb your hair with a plastic comb*.

station /'steɪʃən/ *n* **1** a place with a ticket office, waiting rooms *etc*, where trains, buses or coaches stop to allow passengers to get on or off: *a bus station*; *She arrived at the station in good time for her train*. **2** a local headquarters or centre: *How many fire-engines are kept at the fire station?*; *a radio station*; *Where is the police station?*; *military stations*; *naval stations*. **3** a post; a position of duty: *The watchman remained at his station all night*. — *v* to place in a position of duty: *He stationed himself at the corner of the road to keep watch*; *The regiment is stationed abroad*.

stationary /'steɪʃənərɪ/ *adj* standing still; not moving: *a stationary vehicle*; *The car remained stationary*.

> a **stationary** (not **stationery**) car.

stationer /'steɪʃənə(r)/ *n* a person who sells stationery.
'**stationery** *n* paper, envelopes, pens and other articles used in writing *etc*.

> to buy **stationery** (not **stationary**) at the bookshop.
> **stationery** is never used in the plural: *pencils, pens and other pieces of stationery*.

statistics /stə'tɪstɪks/ **1** *n plural* figures that give you information about something: *The latest statistics on education show that there are more students at universities and colleges than ever before*. **2** *n* the study of such figures: *He is studying statistics*.

statue /'statʃuː/ *n* a figure of a person or animal made of bronze, stone, wood *etc*: *A statue of Nelson stands at the top of Nelson's Column*; *The children stood as still as statues*.

stature /'statʃə(r)/ *n* **1** height of body: *a man of great stature*. **2** importance or greatness: *a musician of international stature*.

status /'steɪtəs/ *n* **1** your position in society, especially as seen by other people: *Does a doctor have a higher status than a teacher?* **2** the position of a person as a member of a group, that gives him or her certain rights: *He has the status of a British citizen*.
status quo /steɪtəs 'kwoʊ/ the situation as it is now: *Our members have voted to maintain the status quo*.
status symbol something that you have that shows that you are wealthy or that you have high social status.

statute /'statjuːt/ *n* a law or rule: *There are several statutes governing road use*.
'**statutory** *adj* required or fixed by law: *a statutory right*.

staunch /stɔːntʃ/ *adj* firm and loyal: *a staunch supporter*.

stave /steɪv/: **stave off** to delay or stop something happening immediately: *They had a couple of biscuits each to stave off their hunger*.

staves plural of **staff**².

stay /steɪ/ *v* **1** to remain in a place for a time: *We stayed three nights at that hotel in Paris*; *Aunt Mary is coming to stay with us for a fortnight*; *Would you like to stay for supper?*; *Stay and watch that television programme*. **2** to remain in a particular position, place or condition: *The doctor told her to stay in bed*; *He never stays long in any job*; *Stay away from the office till your cold is better*; *Why won't these socks stay up?*; *Stay where you are — don't move!*; *In 1900, people didn't realize that motor cars were here to stay*. — *n*: *We had an overnight stay in London*.

> See **remain**.

stay behind to remain in a place after others have left it: *They all left the office at five o'clock, but he stayed behind to finish some work*.
staying power stamina: *She has great staying power when it comes to her work*.
stay in to remain at home: *I'm staying in tonight to watch television*.
stay on to remain at a place of study or work longer than usual: *We had to stay on*

at school an extra term to study for the exam.

stay out to remain out of doors: *The children mustn't stay out after 9 p.m.*

stay put to remain where placed: *Once a baby can crawl, he won't stay put for long.*

stay up not to go to bed: *The children wanted to stay up and watch television.*

steadfast /'stɛdfɑːst/ *adj* firm; never changing: *a steadfast friend.* **'steadfastly** *adv.* **'steadfastness** *n.*

steady /'stɛdɪ/ *adj* **1** firm; not shaky: *The table isn't steady; You need a steady hand to be a surgeon.* **2** regular; even: *a steady temperature; He was walking at a steady pace.* **3** never changing: *steady faith.* — *v* to make or become steady: *He stumbled but managed to steady himself.* **'steadiness** *n.*

'steadily *adv*: *His work is improving steadily.*

steak /steɪk/ *n* a slice of meat, especially beef, or fish, for frying: *a piece of steak; two cod steaks.*

steal /stiːl/ *v* **1** to take another person's property, especially secretly, without permission: *Thieves broke into the house and stole money and jewellery; He was sent away from the school because he had been stealing.* **2** to do something quickly or secretly: *He stole a glance at her.* **3** to move quietly: *He stole quietly out of the room.*

> **steal; stole** /stoʊl/; **'stolen**: *Joe stole Sally's purse; My watch has been stolen.* See also **rob**.

stealth /stɛlθ/ *n* behaviour that is secret or quiet.

stealthy /'stɛlθɪ/ *adj* done secretly or quietly, so as not to attract people's attention: *He took a stealthy glance at his watch; I heard stealthy footsteps coming along the passage.* **'stealthily** *adv.*

steam /stiːm/ *n* **1** a gas or vapour that rises from hot or boiling water *etc*: *A cloud of steam was coming out of the kettle; Steam rose from the wet earth in the hot sun.* **2** power obtained from steam under pressure: *The machinery is driven by steam; Diesel fuel has replaced steam on the railways.* — *adj*: *steam power; steam engines.* — *v* **1** to give out steam: *A kettle was steaming on the stove.* **2** to move by means of steam: *The ship steamed across the bay.* **3** to cook by steam: *The pudding should be steamed for four hours.*

'steamboat or **'steamship** *n* a ship driven by steam.

steam engine a moving engine for pulling a train, or a fixed engine, driven by steam.

'steamer *n* a steamship.

steam roller a type of vehicle driven by steam, with wide and heavy wheels for flattening the surface of newly-made roads *etc*.

steamed-'up *adj* angry or very worried about something.

'steamy *adj* full of steam: *The air was steamy in the launderette.*

full steam ahead at the greatest speed possible.

let off steam to behave in a way that releases energy or anger that has built up inside you: *After the argument she felt that she wanted to scream to let off steam.*

run out of steam to have no more energy.

steam up to become covered with steam: *My glasses steamed up when I left the cool building.*

steel /stiːl/ *n* a very hard metal that is a mixture of iron and carbon, used for making tools *etc*: *tools of the finest steel.* — *adj*: *steel knives.*

'steelworks *n* a factory where steel is made.

steel yourself to prepare yourself for something unpleasant: *He steeled himself to see her again; Steel yourself for a shock.*

steep /stiːp/ *adj* rising sharply: *The hill was too steep for me to cycle up; a steep path; a steep climb.* **'steeply** *adv.* **'steepness** *n.*

steeped /stiːpt/ *adj* full of; having a lot of: *The old town is steeped in history.*

steeple /'stiːpəl/ *n* a high tower on a church *etc.*

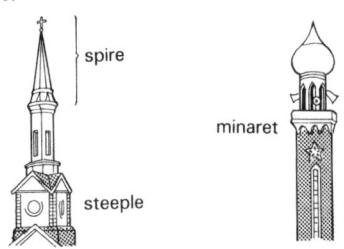

spire

steeple

minaret

steer /stɪə(r)/ *v* to control the course of a ship, car *etc*: *He steered the car through the narrow streets; I steered out of the harbour; She managed to steer the conversation towards the subject of her birthday.*

'steering-wheel *n* the wheel in a car for steering it, or the wheel on a ship that is turned to control the rudder.

stem /stɛm/ *n* **1** the part of a plant that grows upward from the root; the part from which a leaf, flower or fruit grows; a stalk: *Poppies have long, hairy, twisting stems.* **2** the narrow part of various objects, for instance of a wine-glass, between the bowl and the base: *the stem of a wine-glass*; *The stem of his favourite pipe broke.* **3** the upright piece of wood or metal at the bow of a ship: *As the ship struck the rock, she shook from stem to stern.* — *v* **1** to be caused by: *Hate sometimes stems from envy.* **2** to stop or slow something down: *He used his scarf to stem the flow of blood.*

See **branch**.

stench /stɛntʃ/ *n* a strong, bad smell: *the stench of stale tobacco smoke.*

stencil /ˈstɛnsɪl/ *n* a piece of paper, metal or plastic with a design cut out of it, which can be put on to a piece of paper and coloured or painted over to reproduce the design: *She used stencils to do the lettering on the poster.*

step /stɛp/ *n* **1** one movement of the foot in walking, running, dancing *etc*: *He took a step forward*; *She was walking with hasty steps.* **2** the sound made by someone walking *etc*: *I heard steps approaching*; *noisy footsteps.* **3** a particular movement with the feet, for example in dancing: *The dance has some complicated steps.* **4** a flat surface on which you put your foot when going up or coming down a stair, ladder *etc*: *A flight of steps led down to the cellar*; *Mind the step!*; *She was sitting on the doorstep.* **5** a stage in progress, development *etc*: *Mankind made a big step forward with the invention of the wheel*; *His present job is a step up from his previous one.* **6** an action; a move towards achieving an aim *etc*: *That would be a sensible step to take*; *I shall take steps to prevent this happening again.* — *v* to take a step; to walk: *He opened the door and stepped out*; *She stepped quickly along the road.*

'stepladder *n* a short ladder with two sides that support it.

stepping stone a stone in the water that you can step on to cross a river *etc*.

in step with the same foot going forward at the same time: *Soldiers are trained to march in step*; *Keep in step!*

out of step not in step: *One of the marching soldiers was out of step.*

step aside to move to one side: *He stepped aside to let me pass.*

step by step gradually: *He improved step by step.*

step down to resign from a position of authority: *The president stepped down after two years because of illness.*

step in to become involved in a situation, usually in order to help.

step out to walk with long, vigorous steps.

step up to increase: *The police are stepping up their efforts to fight crime.*

watch your step to be careful, especially over your own behaviour.

take steps to take the necessary action in order to achieve something: *We need to take urgent steps to stop pollution.*

watch your step 1 to walk carefully. **2** to behave carefully.

step- /stɛp/ a relationship not by blood but by another marriage.

'step-child *n* a step-son or step-daughter.

'step-father *n* a man who is married to your mother, but isn't your own father.

'step-mother *n* a woman who is married to your father, but isn't your own mother.

'step-sister, 'step-brother *ns* a daughter or son of your step-father or step-mother.

'step-son, 'step-daughter, 'step-child *ns* a son or daughter from your wife's or husband's previous marriage.

stereo /ˈstɛrɪoʊ/, *plural* **stereos**, *n* a record-player which plays the sound through two speakers. — *adj*: stereo sound.

stereotype /ˈstɛrɪətaɪp/ *n* a general idea, image or phrase which has come to represent a particular type of person or thing: *He is the stereotype of a bank manager.*

sterile /ˈstɛraɪl/ *adj* **1** unable to produce crops, seeds or babies: *sterile soil*; *Starvation makes women sterile.* **2** free from germs; completely clean: *A doctor's instruments must be sterile.* **steˈrility** *n*.

'sterilize *v* **1** to make a woman or a female animal sterile by means of a surgical operation. **2** to make something completely free of germs by boiling it in water: *to sterilize medical instruments.* **steriliˈzation** *n*.

sterling /ˈstɜːlɪŋ/ *n* the money used in Great Britain: *He changed his lira into sterling.* — *adj* of good quality: *He has done some sterling work.*

stern[1] /stɜːn/ *adj* harsh; severe; strict: *The teacher looked rather stern*; *She had a stern voice.* **'sternly** *adv*. **'sternness** *n*.

stern[2] /stɜːn/ *n* the back part of a ship.

steroid /ˈstɪərɔɪd/ or /ˈstɛrɔɪd/ *n* one of several chemicals found in the body, including hormones, some of which can be taken to improve the size of muscles: *Some athletes take steroids illegally to try to improve their performance.*

stethoscope /ˈstɛθəskoʊp/ *n* an instrument with which a doctor can listen to the beats of your heart.

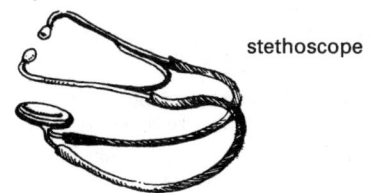

stethoscope

stew /stjuː/ *v* to cook meat, fruit *etc* by slowly boiling it: *She stewed the apples; The meat was stewing in the pan.* — *n* a dish of stewed meat *etc*: *I've made some beef stew.*

steward /ˈstjuːəd/ *n* **1** a passengers' attendant, especially on a ship. **2** a person who helps to arrange, and is an official at, races, entertainments *etc*. **3** a person who supervises the supply of food and stores in a club, on a ship *etc*.

steward'ess *n* a woman who is a passengers' attendant, especially on an aeroplane: *an air stewardess.*

stick¹ /stɪk/ *v* **1** to push something sharp or pointed into or through something: *She stuck a pin through the papers to hold them together; Stop sticking your elbow into me!* **2** to be pushed into or through something: *Two arrows were sticking in his back.* **3** to fasten or be fastened by glue *etc*: *He licked the flap of the envelope and stuck it down; These labels don't stick very well; He stuck the broken vase together again; His brothers used to call him Bonzo and the name has stuck.* **4** to make or become fixed and unable to move or progress: *The car stuck in the mud; The cupboard door has stuck; I'll help you with your arithmetic if you're stuck.*

> **stick; stuck** /stʌk/; **stuck**: *He stuck the stamp on the envelope; Can you help me?* — *I'm stuck.*

'sticker *n* a label or sign with a design, message *etc*, for sticking on a car window *etc*: *The car sticker said 'Blood donors needed'.*

stick around to remain in a place: *I'll stick around after the party to help you tidy up.*

stick at to continue to do something even when it is difficult: *He never sticks at anything for long.*

stick by to stay loyal to someone or something: *His friends stuck by him when he was in trouble.*

stick out 1 to project; to put out: *His front teeth stick out; He stuck out his tongue.* **2** to be noticeable: *Her red hair sticks out in a crowd.*

stick to not to give up; not to abandon: *We've decided to stick to our previous plan; If you stick to me, I'll stick to you.*

stick together 1 to fasten together; to be fastened together: *We'll stick the pieces together; The rice is sticking together.* **2** to remain loyal to each other: *They've stuck together all these years.*

stick up for to defend or support: *She always sticks up for her sister at school.*

stick² /stɪk/ *n* **1** a branch or twig from a tree: *They were sent to find sticks for firewood.* **2** a long, thin piece of wood *etc* shaped for a special purpose: *She always walks with a stick nowadays; a walking-stick; a hockey-stick; a drumstick; candlesticks.* **3** a long piece: *a stick of rhubarb.*

get hold of the wrong end of the stick to misunderstand something.

sticky /ˈstɪkɪ/ *adj* **1** designed to stick to another surface: *to mend a book with sticky tape.* **2** likely to stick to other things: *sticky sweets.* **3** difficult: *a sticky situation.*

come to a sticky end to have an unpleasant fate or death.

stiff /stɪf/ *adj* **1** very firm; not easily bent or folded; rigid: *He has walked with a stiff leg since he injured his knee; stiff cardboard.* **2** moving with difficulty, pain *etc*: *I can't turn the key — the lock is stiff; I woke up with a stiff neck; I was stiff all over after my long cycle-ride.* **3** difficult to do: *a stiff examination.* **4** strong: *a stiff breeze.* **'stiffly** *adv.* **'stiffness** *n.*

'stiffen *v* to make or become stiff: *You can stiffen cotton with starch; He stiffened with fright when he heard the unexpected sound.*

bore someone stiff to make someone desperately bored: *The children were bored stiff by the teacher's lesson.*

scare someone stiff to frighten someone very badly: *His driving scares me stiff.*

stifle /ˈstaɪfəl/ *v* **1** to prevent someone from breathing; to be prevented from breathing; to suffocate: *He was stifled to death when smoke filled his bedroom; I'm stifling in this heat.* **2** to put out flames; to extinguish.

'stifling *adj* very hot: *stifling heat.*

stigma /'stɪgmə/ *n* a bad reputation that something has because people think it is disgraceful in some way: *He finds it hard to bear the stigma of being unemployed.*

stiletto /stɪ'letoʊ/, *plural* **stilettos**, *n* a shoe with a high, thin heel: *She never wears stilettos.*

still[1] /stɪl/ *adj* without movement or noise: *The city seems very still in the early morning; Please keep still while I brush your hair!; still water; still weather.* — *adv: Sit still!; Stand still!* — *n* a photograph of a scene from a film. **'stillness** *n.*

still[2] /stɪl/ *adv* **1** up to and including the present time: *Are you still working for the same firm?; By Saturday he still hadn't replied to my letter.* **2** nevertheless; in spite of that: *Although the doctor told him to rest, he still went on working; This picture is not valuable — still, I like it.* **3** even: *He seemed very ill in the afternoon and in the evening looked still worse.*

> Use **still** when something is going on and has not stopped: *Are the children still up? They should be in bed by now.*
> Use **yet** when you expect something to happen: *Have the children gone to bed yet?*

stilted /'stɪltɪd/ *adj* unnatural or formal: *He spoke in rather stilted English.*

stilts /stɪlts/ *n* **1** a pair of poles with supports for the feet, on which you can stand and walk about. **2** tall poles fixed under a house *etc* to support it if it is built on a steep hillside *etc.*

stimulant /'stɪmjʊlənt/ *n* a drug or medicine that makes you feel more active.

stimulate /'stɪmjʊleɪt/ *v* to rouse or encourage someone: *After listening to the violin concert, he felt stimulated to practise the violin again.* **stimu'lation** *n.*

'stimulating *adj* very interesting: *a stimulating discussion.*

stimulus /'stɪmjʊləs/, *plural* **stimuli** /'stɪmjʊlaɪ/ *n* **1** something that encourages you to do something: *Many people think that children need the stimulus of exams to make them work better at school.* **2** something that makes a person, animal or plant do something: *Light is the stimulus that causes a flower to open.*

sting /stɪŋ/ *n* **1** a part of some plants, insects *etc*, for example nettles and wasps, that can prick your skin and inject an irritating or poisonous fluid into the wound: *Bees leave their stings behind in the wound, but wasps don't.* **2** the piercing of the skin with this part; the wound, pain or swelling caused by it: *Some spiders give a poisonous sting; You can soothe a wasp sting by putting vinegar on it.* — *v* **1** to injure with a sting: *The child was badly stung by nettles; Do those insects sting?* **2** to smart; to be painful: *The salt water made his eyes sting.*

> **sting; stung** /stʌŋ/; **stung**: *A bee stung him on the finger; I've been stung!*

stingy /'stɪndʒɪ/ *adj* mean; not generous. **'stingily** *adv.* **'stinginess** *n.*

stink /stɪŋk/ *v* to have a very bad smell: *That fish stinks; The house stinks of cats.* — *n* a very bad smell: *What a stink!*

> **stink; stank** /staŋk/; **stunk** /stʌŋk/: *The rotting fish stank; If the dead mouse hadn't stunk so much, I wouldn't have been able to find it.*

stint /stɪnt/ *n* a fixed amount of time or work to be done: *She hasn't done her stint of the cooking yet.*

stipulate /'stɪpjʊleɪt/ *v* to state as a necessary condition: *The contract stipulates that you must work at least forty hours each week.* **stipu'lation** *n.*

stir /stɜː(r)/ *v* **1** to mix a liquid *etc* with a continuous circular movement of a spoon *etc*: *He put sugar and milk into his tea and stirred it; She stirred the sugar into the mixture.* **2** to move, either gently or vigorously: *The breeze stirred her hair; He stirred in his sleep; Come on — stir yourselves!* — *n* a fuss; a disturbance: *The news caused a stir.*

stirring /'stɜːrɪŋ/ *adj* exciting: *a stirring tale.*
stir up to cause trouble *etc*: *He was trying to stir up trouble at the factory.*

stirrups /'stɪrəps/ *n plural* a pair of metal loops hanging on straps from a horse's saddle, that you put your feet in when riding a horse.

stitch /stɪtʃ/ *n* **1** a loop made in thread, wool *etc* by a needle in sewing or knitting: *She sewed the hem with small, neat stitches; Bother! I've dropped a stitch.* **2** a type of stitch forming a particular pattern in sewing, knitting *etc*: *The cloth was edged in blanket stitch; The jersey was knitted in stocking stitch.* **3** a piece of thread *etc* used to join the edges of a wound: *When he cut his head he needed twelve stitches.* **4** a sharp pain in the side of your body especially while you are running. — *v* to sew or put stitches into something: *She stitched the two pieces together*; *I stitched the button on to my coat*; *I'll stitch this button on again.*

'stitching *n*: *The stitching is very untidy.*

in stitches laughing a lot: *His stories kept us in stitches.*

stitch up: *The doctor stitched up the wound.*

stock /stɒk/ *n* **1** a store of goods in a shop, warehouse *etc*: *Buy while stocks last!* **2** a supply of something: *We bought a large stock of food for the camping trip.* **3** farm animals; livestock: *He would like to purchase more stock.* **4** a share in the capital of a company: *to invest in stocks and shares.* **5** the handle of a whip, rifle *etc.* **6** liquid in which meat or vegetables have been cooked, used to make soups and sauces *etc*: *chicken stock.* — *adj* common; usual: *stock sizes of shoes.* — *v* **1** to keep a supply of something for sale: *Does this shop stock writing-paper?* **2** to supply a shop, farm *etc* with goods, animals *etc*: *He cannot afford to stock his farm any longer.*

'stockbroker *n* a person who buys and sells shares in companies on behalf of investors: *Her stockbroker handles all of her business investments.*

stock exchange a market for buying and selling shares in businesses.

stock market a stock exchange, or the business carried out there: *Prices have fallen on the stock market.*

'stockpile *n* a large reserve supply: *She keeps a stockpile of sugar in her cupboard.* — *v* to buy or collect a stockpile of something: *She has been stockpiling sugar.*

'stocktaking *n* the process of counting all the goods in a shop or factory at a particular time.

in stock available for sale: *The tools you ordered are now in stock.*

out of stock not available for sale: *The pens you want are out of stock.*

stock up to build up a supply of something: *The boys stocked up with chocolate and lemonade for their walk.*

take stock to think carefully about every aspect of a situation, usually before deciding what to do next: *She says she will work for another five years and then take stock.*

stockade /stɒ'keɪd/ *n* a fence of strong posts put up round a camp, settlement *etc* for defence.

stocking /'stɒkɪŋ/ *n* one of a pair of close-fitting coverings for the legs and feet, reaching to or above the knee: *Most women prefer tights to stockings nowadays.*

stock-still /stɒk'stɪl/ *adv* completely still; without moving at all: *He stood stock-still.*

stocky /'stɒkɪ/ *adj* short, stout and strong: *a stocky little boy.* **'stockily** *adv.* **'stockiness** *n.*

stoic /'stoʊɪk/ or **stoical** /'stoʊɪkəl/ *adj* enduring pain or difficulties without complaining: *He sat listening patiently with a stoical expression on his face.* **'stoically** *adv.* **stoicism** /'stoʊɪsɪzm/ *n.*

stoke /stoʊk/ *v* **1** to put coal or other fuel on: *She stoked the fire with wood.* **2** to make a dispute, argument *etc* worse: *This news will stoke the conflict.*

stole, stolen *see* **steal**.

stomach /'stʌmək/ *n* **1** the bag-like organ in the body into which food passes when swallowed, and where it is digested. **2** the part of the body between the chest and thighs; the belly: *a pain in the stomach.* — *v* to be able to bear or put up with something: *I can't stomach television programmes that show real operations.*

'stomach-ache *n* a pain in the belly.

stomp /stɒmp/ *v* to stamp; to tread heavily.

stone /stoʊn/ *n* **1** the material of which rocks are composed: *In early times, men made tools out of stone*; *Stalactites are formed from limestone*; *The house is built of stone, not brick.* **2** a piece of this: *He threw a stone at the dog.* **3** a piece of this shaped for a special purpose: *paving stones*; *a grindstone.* **4** a gem; a jewel: *diamonds, rubies and other stones.* **5** the hard shell containing the nut or seed in some fruits such as peaches and cherries: *a cherry-stone.* **6** a unit of weight equal to 14 pounds or 6.35 kilograms. — *v* **1** to remove the stones from fruit: *to stone cherries.* **2** to throw stones at someone.

stone-'cold *adj* completely cold: *Your soup has gone stone-cold.*

stone-'dead *adj* completely dead.

stone-'deaf *adj* completely deaf: *'Can he hear anything at all?' 'No, he's stone-deaf.'*

'stony *adj* **1** full of, or covered with, stones: *a stony path*; *a stony beach.* **2** hard and cold in manner: *He gave me a stony stare.*

a stone's throw a very short distance: *They live only a stone's throw away from here.*

stood *see* **stand**.

stool /stu:l/ *n* a seat without a back: *a piano-stool.*

stoop /stu:p/ *v* **1** to bend your body forward

and downward: *The doorway was so low that he had to stoop his head to go through it*; *She stooped down to talk to the child.* **2** to do something that you would normally consider bad or wrong: *I couldn't believe that she had stooped to lying to me.* — *n* a stooping position of the body, shoulders *etc*: *Many people develop a stoop as they grow older.*

stooped *adj*: *stooped shoulders.*

stop /stɒp/ *v* **1** to cease moving; to make something cease moving; to halt: *He stopped the car and got out*; *This train does not stop at Birmingham*; *He stopped to look at the map*; *He signalled with his hand to stop the bus.* **2** to prevent someone *etc* from doing something: *We must stop him going*; *Can't you stop him working so hard?*; *I was going to say something rude but stopped myself just in time.* **3** to cease: *That girl just can't stop talking*; *The rain has stopped*; *It has stopped raining.* **4** to block; to close up: *He stopped his ears with his hands when she started to shout at him.* **5** to stay: *Will you be stopping long at the hotel?* — *n* **1** the act of stopping: *We made only two stops on our journey*; *Work came to a stop for the day.* **2** a place for a bus *etc* to stop: *a bus stop.* **3** in punctuation, a full stop: *You need a stop at the end of the sentence.* **4** a device, for example a wedge *etc*, for keeping something in a fixed position: *a door-stop.*

> **stop to do something** means to pause in order to do something: *We stopped to look at the map.*
> **stop doing something** means to cease doing what you are doing: *Stop shouting!*

'stopgap *n* a person or thing that fills a gap in an emergency: *He was made headmaster as a stopgap till a new man could be appointed.*

'stoppage *n* refusing to work; a strike: *The company lost millions because of the month-long stoppage.*

'stopper *n* an object, for example a cork, that is put into the neck of a bottle, jar, hole *etc* to close it.

'stopping *n* a filling in a tooth: *One of my stoppings has come out.*

stop-'press *n* the most recent news, put into a specially reserved space in a newspaper after the printing has been started.

'stopwatch *n* a watch with a hand that can be stopped and started, used in timing a race *etc.*

put a stop to to prevent something from continuing: *We must put a stop to this waste.*

stop at nothing to be willing to do anything, however dishonest *etc*, in order to get something: *He'll stop at nothing to get what he wants.*

stop off to make a halt on a journey *etc*: *We stopped off at Edinburgh to see the castle.*

stop over to make a stay of a night or more: *We're planning to stop over in Amsterdam.* **'stopover** *n*.

stop up to block: *Some rubbish got into the drain and stopped it up.*

storage /'stɔːrɪdʒ/ *n* the storing of something: *When he went abroad, he had to put his furniture into storage in a warehouse.*

store /stɔː(r)/ *n* **1** a supply of goods *etc* from which things are taken when required: *They took a store of dried and canned food on the expedition*; *Who is in charge of stores for the trip?* **2** a large collected amount: *These books contain a great store of knowledge.* **3** a shop: *The post office here is also the village store*; *a department store.* — *v* **1** to put something into a place for keeping: *We stored our furniture in the attic while the tenants used our house.* **2** to stock a place *etc* with goods *etc*: *The museum is stored with interesting exhibits.*

'storehouse or **'storeroom** *n* a building or room where goods *etc* are stored: *There is a storeroom behind the shop.*

in store 1 kept or reserved for future use: *I keep plenty of tinned food in store for emergencies.* **2** coming in the future: *There's trouble in store for her!*

set store by to value something: *She sets great store by his advice.*

store up to collect and keep: *I don't know why she stores up all those old magazines.*

storey /'stɔːrɪ/, *plural* **'storeys**, *n* one of the floors or levels in a building: *an apartment block of 17 storeys.*

-storeyed: *A two-storeyed house is one with a ground floor and one floor above it.*

stork /stɔːk/ *n* a wading bird with a long beak, neck and legs.

storm /stɔːm/ *n* **1** very bad weather with strong wind, lightning, thunder, heavy rain *etc*: *a rainstorm*; *a thunderstorm*; *a storm at sea*; *The roof was damaged by the storm.* **2** a violent outbreak of feeling *etc*: *a storm of anger*; *a storm of applause.* — *v* **1** to shout very loudly and angrily: *He stormed at her.* **2** to move in an angry manner: *He stormed out of the room.* **3** to attack a building *etc* with great force, and capture it: *They stormed the castle.*

See **rain** and **wind**.

'stormy *adj* **1** having a lot of strong wind, heavy rain *etc*: *a stormy day; stormy weather; a stormy voyage.* **2** full of anger: *in a stormy mood; a stormy discussion.*

story /'stɔːrɪ/ *n* an account of an event *etc*, real or imaginary: *the story of the disaster; the story of his life; What sort of stories do boys aged 10 like?; adventure stories; love stories; murder stories; a story-book; He's a good story-teller.*

stout /staʊt/ *adj* **1** strong and thick: *a stout stick.* **2** brave: *stout resistance; stout opposition.* **3** fat: *He's getting stout.*

stove /stoʊv/ *n* **1** an apparatus using coal, gas, electricity *etc*, used for cooking: *a gas stove; Put the saucepan on the stove.* **2** an apparatus for heating a room.

stow /stoʊ/ *v* to pack neatly; to put away: *The sailor stowed his belongings in his locker; She stowed her jewellery away in a locked drawer.*

stow away to hide yourself on a ship, aircraft *etc* before its departure, in order to travel on it without paying the fare: *He stowed away on a cargo ship for New York.* — *n* (**'stowaway**) a person who stows away: *They found a stowaway on the ship.*

straddle /'stradəl/ *v* to stand or sit with one leg or part on either side of: *The bridge straddles the river.*

straggle /'stragəl/ *v* **1** to grow or spread untidily: *His beard straggled over his chest.* **2** to walk too slowly to keep up with the other walkers or marchers: *Some of the younger children were straggling behind.*

'straggler *n* a person who walks too slowly during a march *etc* and gets left behind.

'straggly *adj*: *straggly hair.* **'straggliness** *n*.

straight /streɪt/ *adj* **1** not bent; not curved; not curling: *a straight line; straight hair.* **2** honest; frank: *Give me a straight answer!* **3** lying in the proper position; not crooked: *Your tie isn't straight.* **4** correct; tidy; sorted out: *I'll never get this house straight!; Now let's get the facts straight!* **5** not smiling or laughing: *You should keep a straight face while you tell a joke.* — *adv* **1** in a straight line; directly: *His route went straight across the desert; The dress fell straight from her shoulders; Keep straight on.* **2** immediately; without any delay: *He went straight home after the meeting.* **3** honestly; fairly: *You're not playing straight.* **'straightness** *n*.

'straighten *v* to make or become straight: *He straightened his tie; The road curved and then straightened; The path straightened out when it reached the river; He bent over and then straightened up; We must try to straighten out this muddle.*

straight'forward *adj* **1** without difficulties or complications; simple: *a straightforward task.* **2** frank; honest: *a nice straightforward boy.*

straight talking frank discussion: *The time has come for some straight talking.*

go straight to start to lead an honest life: *He promised to go straight when he got out of prison.*

straight away or **straight off** immediately: *Do it straight away!*

straight out frankly: *I just told him straight out that I didn't believe him.*

strain /streɪn/ *v* **1** to use to the greatest possible extent: *He strained his ears to hear the whisper.* **2** to make a great effort: *They strained at the door, trying to pull it open; He strained to reach the rope.* **3** to injure a muscle *etc* through too much use: *He has strained a muscle in his leg; You'll strain your eyes by reading in such a poor light.* **4** to stretch too far; to put too much pressure on something: *The constant interruptions were straining his patience.* **5** to separate solid matter from liquid: *to strain the tea; to strain off the water from the vegetables.* — *n* **1** force or weight put on something: *Can nylon ropes take more strain than the old kind of rope?* **2** the bad effect on your mind and body of too much work, worry *etc*: *to suffer from strain.* **3** an injury to a muscle *etc* caused by straining it: *muscular strain.* **4** too great a demand: *These constant delays are a strain on our patience.*

strained *adj* not natural; done with effort: *a strained smile.*

'strainer *n* a sieve for separating solids from liquids: *a tea-strainer.*

strait /streɪt/ *n* a narrow strip of sea between two pieces of land: *the Straits of Gibraltar; the Bering Strait.*

See **isthmus**.

straitjacket /'streɪtdʒakɪt/ *n* a type of strong jacket which prevents a person from moving their arms.

straitlaced /streɪt'leɪst/ *adj* strict and severe

in attitude or behaviour: *My mother is very straitlaced and doesn't approve of me going out at night.*

strand /strand/ *n* a thin thread, for example one of those twisted together to form rope, string, knitting-wool *etc*; a thin lock of hair: *She pushed the strands of hair back from her face.*

'stranded *adj* left helpless: *He was left stranded in Nepal without money or passport.*

be stranded to get stuck on rocks *etc*: *The ship was stranded on rocks.*

strange /streɪndʒ/ *adj* **1** not known, not seen *etc* before; foreign: *What would you do if you found a strange man in your house?*; *Are you good at finding your way about in a strange country?* **2** unusual; odd: *She had a strange look on her face*; *a strange noise.*
'strangely *adv.* **'strangeness** *n.*

'stranger *n* **1** a person whom you have not met before: *Children are often warned not to talk to strangers*; *I've met her once before, so she's not a complete stranger to me.* **2** someone who is in a place for the first time and does not know it well: *I can't tell you where the post office is — I'm a stranger here myself.*

strangle /'straŋɡəl/ *v* to kill someone by gripping or squeezing their neck tightly: *He strangled her with a nylon stocking*; *This top button is nearly strangling me!* **strangulation** /straŋɡjʊ'leɪʃən/ *n.*

strap /strap/ *n* a narrow strip of leather, cloth *etc* used to fasten things, hold things, hang things on *etc*: *I need a new strap for my camera*; *a watch-strap*; *luggage straps.* — *v* **1** to beat someone on the hand with a leather strap: *He was strapped for being rude to the teacher.* **2** to fasten with a strap *etc*: *The two pieces of luggage were strapped together*; *He strapped on his new watch.*

'strapping *adj* large and strong: *a big strapping girl.*

strap up to fasten or bind with a strap, bandage *etc*: *His injured knee was washed and strapped up.*

strategy /'stratədʒɪ/ *n* the art of planning or carrying out a plan *etc*: *military strategy.* **strategic** /strə'tiːdʒɪk/ *adj.* **stra'tegically** *adv.*

stratum /'strɑːtəm/, *plural* **strata** /'strɑːtə/, *n* **1** a layer of rock in the earth's crust: *This stratum of rock was formed hundreds of years ago.* **2** a group of people of a particular level or social class: *He belongs to the upper stratum of society.*

straw /strɔː/ *n* **1** the dry, cut stalks of corn *etc*: *The cows need fresh straw.* **2** a single stalk of corn: *There's a straw in your hair.* **3** a paper or plastic tube for sucking up a drink: *He was sipping orange juice through a straw.*

the last straw or **the final straw** the last in a series of problems which makes you feel that you cannot tolerate the situation any more.

strawberry /'strɔːbərɪ/ *n* a small juicy red fruit. — *adj*: *strawberry ice-cream.*

stray /streɪ/ *v* to wander, especially from the right path, place *etc*: *The shepherd went to search for some sheep that had strayed.* — *n* a cat or dog that has strayed and has no home. — *adj* **1** wandering or lost: *stray cats and dogs.* **2** occasional; scattered: *The sky was clear except for one or two stray clouds.*

streak /striːk/ *n* **1** a long mark or stripe: *a streak of lightning.* **2** a trace of some quality in a person's character *etc*: *She has a streak of selfishness.* — *v* **1**: *The child's face was streaked with tears*; *Her dark hair was streaked with grey.* **2** to move very fast: *The runner streaked round the racetrack.*
'streaky *adj.*

streaked *adj* marked with a streak or streaks: *His face was streaked with blood.*

stream /striːm/ *n* **1** a small river: *He managed to jump across the stream.* **2** a flow of something: *A stream of water was pouring down the gutter*; *Streams of people were coming out of the cinema*; *He got into the wrong stream of traffic.* **3** the current of a river *etc*: *He was swimming against the stream.* **4** in schools, one of the classes into which children of the same age are divided according to ability. — *v* **1** to flow: *Tears streamed down her face*; *Workers streamed out of the factory gates*; *Her hair streamed out in the wind.* **2** to divide schoolchildren into classes according to ability: *Many people disapprove of streaming in schools.*

'streamer *n* a long narrow banner; a narrow paper ribbon: *The aeroplane was trailing a streamer that read 'Come to the Festival'.*

streamline /'striːmlaɪn/ *v* **1** to make a vehicle *etc* long and smooth so that it will move easily through air or water. **2** to make a business *etc* more efficient, especially by making it simpler: *The company streamlined its production methods.*

'streamlined *adj* **1** shaped so as to be able to move faster: *a streamlined racing-car.* **2**

made more efficient: *a modern, streamlined kitchen.*

street /striːt/ *n* a road with houses, shops *etc* on one or both sides, in a town or village (often written **St** in names of roads): *the main shopping street; I met her in the street; Her address is 12 High St.*

> A **street** is in a busy part of a town or village, with houses, shops *etc* usually on both sides.
> A **road** is a way made for vehicles to travel on, and leads from one place to another.

street directory a booklet giving an index and plans of a city's streets.

streets ahead much more advanced; much better: *The new product is streets ahead of the competition.*

up your street exactly right for you because of your likes and abilities: *You will enjoy the course — it's right up your street.*

strength /strenθ/ *n* **1** the quality of being strong: *He got his strength back slowly after his illness.* **2** the good things about a person: *Her greatest strength is her sense of humour.*
'strengthen *v* to make or become strong: *He did exercises to strengthen his muscles; The wind strengthened.*

on the strength of as a result of; directly because of: *On the strength of these calculations, we shall be happy to do business with you.*

strenuous /'strɛnjʊəs/ *adj* requiring effort or energy: *a strenuous climb; a strenuous effort.*
'strenuously *adv*.

stress /strɛs/ *n* **1** the effect of too much worry, work *etc*; strain: *the stresses of modern life; Her headaches may be caused by stress.* **2** special emphasis that is put on something that is particularly important: *The General laid particular stress on the need for secrecy.* **3** force or emphasis placed, in speaking, on particular syllables or words: *In the word 'window' we put stress on the first syllable.* **4** a physical force that may bend or break something: *metal that bends under stress.* — *v* **1** to emphasize a syllable: *Stress the last syllable in 'violin'.* **2** to emphasize something you are saying: *He stressed the need for speed.*

'stressful *adj* causing you to feel mental stress: *Being a hospital doctor can be a very stressful job.*

lay stress on or **put stress on** to emphasize: *He laid stress on the point about hard work.*

> to **stress** (not **stress on**) a point.
> to **lay stress on** a point is correct.

stretch /strɛtʃ/ *v* **1** to make or become longer or wider especially by pulling: *She stretched the piece of elastic to its fullest extent; This material stretches; The dog yawned and stretched itself; He stretched up as far as he could, but still could not reach the shelf.* **2** to reach; to extend: *The Great Barrier Reef stretches some 2000 kilometres from northeast Australia past Queensland's undeveloped coast.* — *n* **1** the action of stretching: *He got out of bed and had a good stretch.* **2** an extent, in distance or time: *This is a bad stretch of road; a stretch of twenty years.*
'stretcher *n* a light folding bed with handles for carrying a sick or wounded person: *The injured man was carried to an ambulance on a stretcher.*

> See **bed**.

at a stretch continuously: *I can't work for more than three hours at a stretch.*

stretch your legs to go for a walk for the sake of exercise: *I need to stretch my legs.*

stretch out to straighten; to extend: *She stretched out a hand for the child to hold; He stretched himself out on the bed.*

strew /struː/ *v* to scatter: *Rubbish was strewn about on the ground; The ground was strewn with rubbish.*

> **strew; strewed; strewn**: *He strewed his clothes around; She has strewn bits of paper all over the floor.*

stricken /'strɪkən/ *adj* badly affected by something: *stricken with grief.*

strict /strɪkt/ *adj* **1** severe; stern; insisting on obedience: *This class needs a strict teacher; His parents were very strict with him; The school rules are too strict; strict orders.* **2** exact: *the strict truth.* **'strictness** *n*. **'strictly** *adv.*

strictly speaking if we must be completely accurate, act according to rules *etc*: *Strictly speaking, he should be punished for this.*

stride /straɪd/ *v* to walk with long steps: *He strode along the path; He strode off in anger.* — *n* a long step: *He walked with long strides.*

> **stride; strode** /stroʊd/; **'stridden**: *She strode along the path; He had stridden off.*

get into your stride to begin to work well or effectively: *I don't want to stop now — I'm just getting into my stride.*

make great strides to progress well: *He's making great strides in his piano-playing.*

strident /'straɪdənt/ *adj* loud and harsh: *a strident voice.*

strife /straɪf/ *n* fighting or quarrelling: *There was a lot of strife within the political party.*

strike /straɪk/ *v* **1** to hit; to knock: *He struck me in the face with his fist; Why did you strike him?; The stone struck me a blow on the head; His head struck the table as he fell; The tower of the church was struck by lightning.* **2** to attack: *The enemy troops struck at dawn.* **3** to produce sparks or a flame by rubbing: *He struck a match.* **4** to stop work as a protest, or to try to force employers to give better pay *etc*: *The men decided to strike for higher wages.* **5** to make a strong clear sound: *He struck a note on the piano; The clock struck twelve.* **6** to impress: *I was struck by the resemblance between the two men; How does the plan strike you?* **7** to come into your mind: *A thought struck me.* **8** to manufacture coins: *This coin was struck in 1979.* **9** to go in a certain direction: *He left the path and struck off across the fields.* **10** to lower or take down tents, flags *etc*. **11** to discover gold or oil in the earth or under water: *Three years passed before they struck gold for the first time.* — *n* **1** the stopping of work as a protest: *The miners' strike lasted for three months.* **2** a military attack, especially from the air.

> **strike; struck** /strʌk/; **struck**: *She struck a match; The building was struck by lightning.*

'striker *n* **1** a worker who strikes. **2** in football, a forward player.

'striking *adj* noticeable; impressive: *She is tall and striking; She wears striking clothes.*

'strikingly *adv*: *a strikingly attractive face.*

strike a bargain to make a deal or agreement with someone.

strike at to aim a blow at a person *etc*: *He struck at the dog with his stick.*

strike down to hit or knock a person down: *He was struck down by a car.*

strike out 1 to erase or cross out a word *etc*: *He read the essay and struck out a word here and there.* **2** to start fighting: *He strikes out with his fists whenever he's angry.*

strike up 1 to begin to play a tune *etc*: *The band struck up a cheerful tune.* **2** to begin a friendship, conversation *etc*: *to strike up an acquaintance with someone.*

within striking distance quite near: *Both sides believe they are within striking distance of a lasting agreement.*

string /strɪŋ/ *n* **1** long narrow cord made of threads twisted together, for tying, fastening *etc*: *a piece of string to tie a parcel; a ball of string; a puppet's strings; apron-strings.* **2** one of the pieces of wire, gut *etc* on which you play the notes on a violin *etc*: *There are four strings on a violin.* **3** a series or group of things threaded on a cord *etc*: *a string of beads.* **4** a series of things of the same type: *a string of disasters.* — *v* **1** to put beads *etc* on a string *etc*: *The pearls were sent to a jeweller to be strung.* **2** to put a string or strings on a bow or stringed instrument. **3** to remove strings from vegetables *etc*. **4** to tie and hang with string *etc*: *The farmer strung up the dead crows on the fence.*

> **string; strung** /strʌŋ/; **strung**: *She strung her guitar; He has strung his bow.*

string bean the long, edible green or yellow pod of certain beans.

stringed instruments musical instruments that have strings, such as violins, violas, cellos, guitars *etc*.

strings *n* the stringed instruments in an orchestra: *The conductor said the strings were too loud.*

string out to stretch into a long line: *The runners were strung out along the course.*

with no strings attached or **without strings** with no special conditions: *We apologize and will send you a refund with no strings attached.*

stringent /'strɪndʒənt/ *adj* severe: *The laws against theft should be more stringent.* **'stringently** *adv*.

strip /strɪp/ *v* **1** to remove the covering of something: *He stripped the old varnish off the wall.* **2** to undress: *She stripped the child and put him in the bath; He stripped and dived into the water; to strip off your clothes.* **3** to remove the contents of a house *etc*: *They stripped the house of all its furnishings.* **4** to take away something from someone: *The officer was stripped of his rank.* — *n* **1**

a long narrow piece of something: *a strip of paper*; *a strip of grass*. **2** a strip cartoon. **3** a footballer's shirt, shorts and socks.

strip cartoon a line of drawings, in a newspaper or comic paper, telling a story.

stripe /straɪp/ *n* a band of colour *etc*: *The wallpaper was grey with broad green stripes*; *A zebra has black and white stripes*.

striped *adj* having stripes: *a striped shirt*; *blue-and-white-striped curtains*.

'stripy *adj*: *A tiger has a stripy coat*.

strive /straɪv/ *v* to try very hard; to struggle: *He always strives to please his teacher*.

> **strive**; **strove** /stroʊv/; **'striven**: *He strove to win the prize*; *She has striven for success for many years*.

strode *see* **stride**.

stroke[1] /stroʊk/ *n* **1** the action of hitting; the blow given: *He felled the tree with one stroke of the axe*; *the stroke of a whip*. **2** a sudden occurrence of something: *a stroke of lightning*; *What a stroke of luck to find that money!* **3** the sound made by a clock striking the hour: *She arrived on the stroke of ten*. **4** a mark made in one direction by a pen, pencil, paintbrush *etc*: *short, even pencil strokes*. **5** a movement of the arms and legs in swimming, or a particular method of swimming: *He swam with slow, strong strokes*; *Can you do backstroke?*; *She's good at breaststroke*. **6** a sudden attack in the brain that can leave a person unable to move or speak.

at a stroke with a single effort; all at once: *We can't solve all these problems at a stroke*.

stroke[2] /stroʊk/ *v* to keep rubbing gently in one direction, especially as a sign of affection: *He stroked the cat*; *The dog loves being stroked*; *She stroked the child's hair*. — *n*: *He gave the dog a stroke*.

stroll /stroʊl/ *v* to walk without hurry; to wander: *He strolled along the street*. — *n* a gentle walk: *I went for a stroll round the town*.

strong /strɒŋ/ *adj* **1** firm; powerful; not weak: *strong furniture*; *a strong castle*; *a strong wind*; *She's a strong swimmer*; *He has a very strong will*; *He is not strong enough to lift that heavy table*. **2** very noticeable; very intense: *a strong colour*; *a strong smell*; *a strong flavour*; *I took a strong dislike to him*. **3** made with a strong taste or flavour: *strong tea*. **'strongly** *adv*.

> to be **strong in** (not **at**) mathematics, but **good at** (not **in**) mathematics.

going strong continuing in a healthy condition: *Is the company still going strong?*; *He's 95 and still going strong*.

'stronghold *n* a fort, fortress or castle *etc*.

strong language swearing; abuse.

strong-'minded *adj* determined.

strong point something you are very good at: *Arithmetic isn't one of my strong points*.

strove *see* **strive**.

struck *see* **strike**.

structure /'strʌktʃə(r)/ *n* **1** the way in which something is arranged or organized: *the structure of a human body*. **2** a building; something that is built or constructed: *A bridge is a structure for taking a road across a river etc*. — *v* to organize or arrange: *You should structure your essay so that the points follow on logically*. **'structural** *adj*.

struggle /'strʌɡəl/ *v* **1** to twist and fight to escape: *The child struggled in his arms*. **2** to make great efforts; to try hard: *All his life he has been struggling against injustice*. **3** to move with difficulty: *He struggled out of the hole*. — *n* the action of struggling; a fight: *The struggle for independence was long and hard*.

struggle on to manage to survive or progress with difficulty: *They struggled on through the storm*; *I had a headache all day but managed to struggle on until 5 o'clock*.

strum /strʌm/ *v* to play with sweeping movements of the fingers: *She strummed her guitar*; *He strummed a tune*.

strung *see* **string**.

strut /strʌt/ *v* to walk in a stiff, proud way: *She was strutting along the street in her new dress, looking very pleased with herself*; *The cock strutted round the farmyard*.

stub /stʌb/ *n* **1** the short remaining end of a cigarette, pencil or other long thin object: *There were ten cigarette stubs in the ashtray*. **2** the small part of a cheque or ticket that you keep after tearing off the larger part. — *v* to hurt your toe by striking it against something hard: *She stubbed her toe on the table leg*.

stub out *v* to put out a cigarette or cigar by pressing it against something hard: *He stubbed out his cigarette in the ashtray*.

stubble /'stʌbəl/ *n* **1** the short stalks of corn left standing in the fields when corn has been cut. **2** short coarse hairs that grow on a man's face when he has not shaved for a few days: *A grey stubble covered his chin.*

stubborn /'stʌbən/ *adj* unwilling to give way, obey *etc*: *He's as stubborn as a donkey.* **'stubbornly** *adv*. **'stubbornness** *n*.

stubby /'stʌbɪ/ *adj* short and thick: *He has stubby fingers.*

stuck *see* **stick**¹.

stud /stʌd/ *n* a knob or nail with a large head, used as a fastener, for decoration, or on the soles of boots or shoes: *The studs on the bottom of football boots help to stop the player slipping in the mud.*

student /'stju:dənt/ *n* **1** a person studying for a degree at a university *etc*: *university students; a medical student.* **2** a boy or girl at school.

studied /'stʌdɪd/ *adj* carefully practised or planned to create a particular impression: *After a pause he gave a studied answer.*

studio /'stju:dɪoʊ/, *plural* **'studios**, *n* **1** the workroom of an artist or photographer. **2** a place in which cinema films are made: *This film was made at Ramrod Studios.* **3** a room from which radio or television programmes are broadcast: *a television studio.*

studious /'stju:dɪəs/ *adj* spending much time in careful studying: *a studious girl.* **'studiously** *adv*. **'studiousness** *n*.

study /'stʌdɪ/ *v* **1** to gain knowledge of a subject by reading *etc*; to spend time learning a subject: *What subject is he studying?; He is studying French literature; He is studying for a degree in mathematics; She's studying to be a teacher.* **2** to look at something carefully: *He studied the railway timetable; Give yourself time to study the problem in detail.* — *n* **1** reading and learning about something: *He spends all his evenings in study; She has made a study of the habits of bees.* **2** a room in a house *etc*, in which to study, read, write *etc*: *The headmaster wants to speak to you in his study.*

> to **study** (not **study about**) history.
> to **learn** is to get to know something and memorize it: *Did you learn French at school?*
> to **study** is to spend time learning, or learning about, a subject: *He's studying algebra in the library; I'm studying European history.*

stuff¹ /stʌf/ *n* **1** material; substance: *What is that black oily stuff on the beach?; The doctor gave me some good stuff for removing warts.* **2** unimportant things, objects *etc*: *We'll have to get rid of all this stuff when we move house.*

know your stuff to have a lot of skill and knowledge in your particular job or subject.

stuff² /stʌf/ *v* **1** to pack or fill tightly: *His drawer was stuffed with papers; She stuffed the fridge with food; The children have been stuffing themselves with ice-cream.* **2** to fill a turkey, chicken *etc* with stuffing before cooking. **3** to fill the skin of a dead animal or bird so that it keeps the appearance it had when alive: *They stuffed the golden eagle.*

'stuffing *n* **1** material used for stuffing toy animals *etc*: *The teddy-bear had lost its stuffing.* **2** a mixture used in cooking for stuffing meat, vegetables *etc*.

stuff up to block: *He stuffed the hole up with some newspaper.*

stuffy /'stʌfɪ/ *adj* too warm; without any fresh air: *Why do you sit in this stuffy room all day?* **'stuffiness** *n*.

stumble /'stʌmbəl/ *v* **1** to strike your foot against something and nearly fall: *He stumbled over the edge of the carpet.* **2** to walk with difficulty, nearly falling over: *He stumbled along the track in the dark.* **3** to make mistakes, or hesitate, in speaking, reading aloud *etc*: *He stumbled over the difficult words as he read aloud in class.*

stumbling block an obstacle or difficulty: *It is an excellent scheme but the stumbling block is the cost.*

stumble across or **stumble on** to find by chance: *I stumbled across this book today.*

stump /stʌmp/ *n* **1** the part of a tree left in the ground after the trunk has been cut down. **2** the part of a limb, tooth, pencil *etc* remaining after the main part has been cut or broken off, worn away *etc*. — *v* **1** to walk with heavy, stamping steps: *He stumped angrily out of the room.* **2** to puzzle: *I'm stumped!*

'stumpy *adj* short and thick like a stump: *The cat had a stumpy tail.*

stun /stʌn/ *v* **1** to make someone unconscious usually by a blow on the head: *The blow stunned him.* **2** to shock; to astonish: *I was stunned by the news of her death.*

stung *see* **sting**.

stunk *see* **stink**.

stunning /'stʌnɪŋ/ *adj* marvellous: *a stunning dress.*

stunt¹ /stʌnt/ *v* to prevent the full growth or development of a child *etc*: *It is thought that*

smoking by a pregnant mother may stunt the baby's growth.
'**stunted** *adj* not well-grown: *a stunted tree.*
stunt[2] /stʌnt/ *n* something daring and spectacular that is done to attract attention *etc*: *One of his stunts was to cross the Niagara Falls blindfold on a tightrope.*
'**stuntman** or '**stuntwoman** *n* a person who takes the place of an actor in film scenes involving athletic skill and danger.
stupendous /stjʊˈpɛndəs/ *adj* tremendous or amazing: *The number of stars in the sky is stupendous; It was a stupendous concert.*
stupid /ˈstjuːpɪd/ *adj* foolish; slow at understanding: *a stupid mistake; He isn't as stupid as he looks.* '**stupidly** *adv.* **stuˈpidity** *n.*
stupor /ˈstjuːpə(r)/ *n* a semi-conscious condition.
sturdy /ˈstɜːdɪ/ *adj* **1** strong and healthy: *He is small but sturdy.* **2** firm and well-made: *sturdy furniture.* '**sturdily** *adv.* '**sturdiness** *n.*
stutter /ˈstʌtə(r)/ *v* to stammer: *He stutters sometimes when he's excited; 'I've s-s-seen a gh-gh-ghost,' he stuttered.* — *n*: *He has a bad stutter.* '**stutterer** *n.*
sty /staɪ/ *n* **1** a building in which pigs are kept. **2** a painful swelling on the eyelid.
style /staɪl/ *n* **1** a manner of doing something, such as writing, speaking, painting, building *etc*: *I like the style of her writing; different styles of architecture.* **2** a fashion in clothes, hair *etc*: *the new style of shoe; Do you like my new hairstyle?* **3** elegance in dress, behaviour *etc*: *She certainly has style.* — *v* **1** to arrange hair in a certain way: *I'm going to have my hair cut and styled.* **2** to design in a certain style: *These clothes are styled for comfort.*
'**stylish** *adj* smart; elegant; fashionable: *stylish clothes.* '**stylishly** *adv.*
'**stylist** *n* **1** a person who designs styles in clothes *etc*. **2** a person who arranges hair in a style: *a hair-stylist.*
in style in a luxurious, elegant way: *He likes to do things in style.*
stylus /ˈstaɪləs/ *n* a needle for a record-player.
suave /swɑːv/ *adj* polite and charming, but often not sincere: *a suave young man.*
subconscious /sʌbˈkɒnʃəs/ *n* the part of the mind that you are not aware of but which influences your behaviour: *The cause of her depression is locked in her subconscious.* — *adj* influenced by or existing in the subconscious: *subconscious desires.* **subˈconsciously** *adv.*

subdivide /sʌbdɪˈvaɪd/ *v* to divide into smaller parts or divisions: *Each class of children is subdivided into groups according to reading ability.* **subdiˈvision** *n.*
subdue /səbˈdjuː/ *v* to overcome; to bring under control: *After months of fighting the rebels were subdued.*
subˈdued *adj* quiet; not bright; not lively: *subdued voices; He seems subdued today.*
subject *adj* /ˈsʌbdʒɛkt/ not independent; ruled by another country *etc*: *subject nations.* — *n* /ˈsʌbdʒɛkt/ **1** a person who is under the rule of a monarch; a member of a country that has a monarchy *etc*: *We are the subjects of the Queen; He is a British subject.* **2** someone or something that is talked about, written about *etc*: *We discussed the price of food and similar subjects; The teacher tried to think of a good subject for the children's composition; I've said all I can on that subject.* **3** a branch of study or learning in school, university *etc*: *He is taking exams in seven subjects; Mathematics is his best subject.* **4** in a sentence *etc*, the word representing the person or thing that usually does the action shown by the verb: *The cat sat on the mat; He hit her because she broke his toy; He was hit by the ball.* — *v* /səbˈdʒɛkt/ **1** to bring a person, country *etc* under control: *They have subjected all the neighbouring states to their rule.* **2** to make someone or something undergo something: *He was subjected to cruel treatment; These tyres are subjected to various tests before leaving the factory.*
subˈjective *adj* resulting from your own thoughts and feelings only; not objective: *a subjective opinion.* **subˈjectively** *adv.*
subject to 1 likely to suffer from something: *He is subject to colds.* **2** depending on: *These plans will be carried out next week, subject to your approval.*
sublime /səˈblaɪm/ *adj* of overwhelming greatness or beauty: *a sublime moment in her life.*
submarine /sʌbməˈriːn/ *n* a ship that can travel under the surface of the sea.
submerge /səbˈmɜːdʒ/ *v* to cover with water; to sink under water: *I watched the submarine submerging.* **subˈmergence** or **subˈmersion** *n.*
submission /səbˈmɪʃən/ *n* **1** the act of submitting. **2** being submissive; humbleness.
subˈmissive *adj* humble and obedient: *a submissive servant.*
submit /səbˈmɪt/ *v* **1** to yield to control; to allow yourself to be treated, usually in a

bad way, by another person *etc*: *I refuse to submit to his control*; *The rebels were ordered to submit*; *The prisoners had to submit to torture*. **2** to offer a plan, suggestion, proposal, entry *etc*: *Competitors for the painting competition must submit their entries by Friday*.

subnormal /sʌbˈnɔːməl/ *adj* having a very low level of intelligence.

subordinate /səˈbɔːdɪnət/ *adj* lower in rank or importance: *These questions are subordinate to the main problem*. — *n* a person with a less important rank or position: *He always tries to help his subordinates*. — *v* to treat something as being less important than another thing: *She had to subordinate her personal ambition to the needs of her family*.

subscribe /səbˈskraɪb/ *v* **1** to give money to a charity or other cause: *He subscribes to a lot of charities*; *We each subscribed £5 towards the present*. **2** to promise to receive and pay for a weekly, monthly *etc* magazine *etc*: *I've been subscribing to that magazine for four years*. **sub'scriber** *n*. **sub'scription** *n*.

subsequent /ˈsʌbsɪkwənt/ *adj* following; coming after: *The story describes the hero's capture by pirates, and his subsequent escape and journey home*. **'subsequently** *adv*.

subsequent to after: *The child became ill subsequent to eating the ice-cream*.

subservient /səbˈsɜːvɪənt/ *adj* **1** too ready to do what others want. **2** considered to be less important than another thing: *The needs of the individual must be subservient to those of the whole community*.

subside /səbˈsaɪd/ *v* **1** to sink lower: *When a building starts to subside, cracks usually appear in the walls*. **2** to become quieter: *They stayed anchored in harbour till the wind subsided*. **subsidence** /ˈsʌbsɪdəns/ or /səbˈsaɪdəns/ *n*.

subsidiary /səbˈsɪdɪərɪ/ *adj* of secondary or lesser importance: *She took two subsidiary subjects as well as her main subject for her university course*. — *n* a company controlled by another, larger company: *The company owns several subsidiaries in other countries*.

subsidize /ˈsʌbsɪdaɪz/ *v* to pay money to companies, farmers, artists *etc* in order to keep the price of their products or services low for the public: *The production of rice is subsidized by the government*.

'subsidized *adj*: *subsidized food*.

subsidy /ˈsʌbsɪdɪ/ *n*: *Which industries are supported by government subsidies?*

subsist /səbˈsɪst/ *v* to live on just enough food or money.

sub'sistence *n*: *to live at subsistence level*.

substance /ˈsʌbstəns/ *n* **1** a material: *Rubber is a tough, stretchy substance*. **2** the basic meaning; the most important idea of something: *The substance of her argument was that women are superior to men in all ways*. **3** importance; truth: *There was no substance to the story the newspapers printed*.

substantial /səbˈstanʃəl/ *adj* **1** solid; strong: *a substantial table*. **2** large: *a substantial sum of money*; *a substantial meal*. **sub'stantially** *adv*.

substitute /ˈsʌbstɪtjuːt/ *v* to put someone or something in the place of someone or something else; to take the place of someone else: *I substituted your name for mine on the list*; *Mrs Jones will be substituting for the headmaster this term*. — *n* a person or thing used or acting instead of another: *You could use lemons as a substitute for limes*; *She is not well enough to play in the tennis match, so we must find a substitute*. **substi'tution** *n*.

> When you **substitute** X **for** Y, you use X.
> When you **replace** X **with** Y, you use Y.

subterfuge /ˈsʌbtəfjuːdʒ/ *n* a trick or plan for avoiding difficulties or hiding something: *She used subterfuge to get him to do what she wanted*.

subtitle /ˈsʌbtaɪtəl/ *n* **1** a second title to a book. **2** in films, a translation of foreign speech appearing at the bottom of the screen: *I found it difficult to read the subtitles*.

subtle /ˈsʌtəl/ *adj* **1** faint or delicate in quality; difficult to describe or explain: *There is a subtle difference between 'unnecessary' and 'not necessary'*; *a subtle flavour*. **2** clever or cunning: *He has a subtle mind*. **subtlety** /ˈsʌtəltɪ/ *n*. **'subtly** *adv*.

subtract /sʌbˈtrakt/ *v* to take one number or quantity from another: *If you subtract 5 from 8, 3 is left*; *In their first year at school, most children learn to add and subtract*. **sub'traction** *n*.

suburb /ˈsʌbɜːb/ *n* an area of houses in the outer parts of a city, town *etc*: *Croydon is a suburb of London*; *They decided to move out to the suburbs*.

suburban /səˈbɜːbən/ *adj*: *suburban housing*.

suburbia /səˈbɜːbɪə/ *n* the suburbs of towns and cities.

subversive /səb'vɜːsɪv/ *adj* likely to destroy, weaken or overthrow a government: *He was arrested for publishing subversive books.* — *n* a subversive person.

  sub'vert *v* to try to weaken or destroy a government *etc*. **sub'version** *n*.

subway /'sʌbweɪ/ *n* **1** an underground passage for pedestrians, under a busy road: *Cross by the subway.* **2** an underground railway in a city: *Go by subway.*

succeed /sək'siːd/ *v* **1** to manage to do what you have been trying to do: *He succeeded in persuading her to marry him; He's happy to have succeeded in his chosen career; She tried three times to pass her driving-test, and at last succeeded.* **2** to follow next in order; to take the place of someone or something else: *He succeeded his father as manager of the firm; When your uncle dies, who will succeed to his property?; The cold summer was succeeded by a stormy autumn.*

> The opposite of **succeed**, meaning to be successful, is **fail**.

success /sək'sɛs/ *n* **1** the achievement of an aim: *I wish you success in your exams; He has achieved great success in his career.* **2** a person or thing that succeeds: *She's a great success as a teacher.*

> The opposite of **success** is **failure**.

  successful *adj* having success: *Were you successful in finding a new house?; a successful career.* **suc'cessfully** *adv*.

succession /sək'sɛʃən/ *n* **1** the right of succeeding to a throne, to a title *etc*: *The Princess is fifth in succession to the throne.* **2** a number of things following after one another: *a succession of bad harvests.*

  in succession one after another: *five wet days in succession.*

  successive /sək'sɛsɪv/ *adj* following one after the other: *He won three successive matches.* **suc'cessively** *adv*.

  successor /sək'sɛsə(r)/ *n* a person who follows, and takes the place of another: *Who will be appointed as the manager's successor?*

succinct /sək'sɪŋkt/ *adj* brief and precise: *Her account of what happened was clear and succinct.* **suc'cinctly** *adv*.

succulent /'sʌkjʊlənt/ *adj* juicy and delicious: *succulent peaches.*

succumb /sə'kʌm/ *v* to give in to: *She succumbed to temptation.*

such /sʌtʃ/ *adj* **1** of the same kind: *Animals that gnaw, such as mice, rats, rabbits and weasels are called rodents; I've seen several such buildings; I've never done such a thing before; doctors, dentists and such people.* **2** of that name: *She asked to see Mr Johnson but was told there was no such person there.* **3** so great; so bad, good *etc*: *She never used to have such a bad temper; He shut the window with such force that the glass broke; This is such a shock!; They have been such good friends to me!* — *pron*: *I have only a few photographs, but can show you such as I have.*

  as such in the exact meaning of the word: *He wasn't punished as such, but we'll watch him closely for a while.*

  'such-and-such *adj, pron* used to refer to any person or thing: *Let's suppose that you go into such-and-such a shop and ask for such-and-such.*

  such as used to introduce one or more examples: *a profession such as medicine or teaching; a summer such as we experienced last year.*

suck /sʌk/ *v* **1** to draw liquid *etc* into your mouth: *As soon as they are born, young animals learn to suck milk from their mothers; She sucked up the lemonade through a straw.* **2** to hold something between your lips or inside your mouth, as though drawing liquid from it: *to suck a sweet; He sucked the end of his pencil.* **3** to draw in: *The vacuum cleaner sucked up all the dirt from the carpet; A plant sucks up moisture from the soil.* — *n*: *She took a suck of her lollipop.*

  'sucker *n* **1** a person or thing that sucks: *Are these insects bloodsuckers?* **2** an organ of an animal, such as an octopus, by which it sticks to objects. **3** a rubber or plastic disc that can be pressed on to a surface and sticks there. **4** a side shoot coming from the root of a plant. **5** a person who is easily deceived.

suckle /'sʌkəl/ *v* to feed a baby with milk from the breasts or udder: *The cow suckled her calf.*

suction /'sʌkʃən/ *n* **1** the action of sucking. **2** the force that draws liquid up into a tube *etc*, or that makes a sucker *etc* stick to a surface.

sudden /'sʌdən/ *adj* happening *etc* quickly, without being expected: *a sudden attack; His decision to get married is rather sudden!; a sudden bend in the road.* **'suddenness** *n*.

  'suddenly *adv*: *He suddenly woke up; Sud-*

denly he realized that she had a gun.
all of a sudden suddenly: *All of a sudden the lights went out.*

suds /sʌdz/ *n plural* soap bubbles: *You get a lot of suds from a small quantity of washing powder.*

sue /suː/ *v* **1** to start a law case against someone, usually in order to get money from them: *The man who was injured in the car crash is suing the other driver for £50 000 damages.* **2** to ask for something: *His wife is suing for divorce.*

suede /sweɪd/ *n* leather from a sheep or lamb *etc* with a soft surface like velvet. — *adj*: *suede shoes.*

suffer /ˈsʌfə(r)/ *v* **1** to feel pain, misery *etc*: *He suffered terrible pain from his injuries*; *The crash killed him instantly — he didn't suffer at all.* **2** to be punished: *I'll make you suffer for the harm you have done me.* **3** to experience: *The army suffered enormous losses.* **4** to be neglected: *I like to see you enjoying yourself, but you mustn't let your work suffer.* **5** to have something wrong with you; to have often: *Depression is almost impossible to describe to those who have not suffered from it*; *She suffers from headaches.* **ˈsufferer** *n*.

ˈsuffering *n* pain; misery: *The shortage of food caused widespread suffering*; *She keeps complaining about her sufferings.*

sufficient /səˈfɪʃənt/ *adj* enough: *We haven't sufficient food to feed all these people*; *Will £10 be sufficient for your needs?* **sufˈficiency** *n.* **sufˈficiently** *adv.*

> The opposite of **sufficient** is **insufficient**.

suffix /ˈsʌfɪks/ *n* a letter or group of letters that is added to the end of a word to change its meaning or use: *The suffix 's' must be added to the noun 'monkey' to form the plural 'monkeys'.*

suffocate /ˈsʌfəkeɪt/ *v* to kill or die through lack of air or because breathing is prevented: *A baby may suffocate if it sleeps with a pillow*; *The smoke was suffocating him.* **suffoˈcation** *n.*

sugar /ˈʃʊɡə(r)/ *n* the sweet substance that is obtained from sugar-cane, or from the juice of certain other plants: *Do you take sugar in your coffee?* — *v* to sweeten, or cover, with sugar.

ˈsugar-cane *n* a tall grass from the juice of which sugar is obtained.

sugar-ˈcoated *adj* covered with icing: *sugar-coated biscuits.*

sugar lump a small cube of sugar.

sugar tongs an instrument for lifting sugar lumps: *a pair of sugar tongs.*

ˈsugary *adj* very sweet.

suggest /səˈdʒest/ *v* **1** to mention or propose an idea *etc*: *He suggested a different plan*; *I suggest doing it this way*; *She suggested to me two suitable people for this job*; *I suggest that we have lunch now.* **2** to hint; to say in an indirect way: *Are you suggesting that I'm too old for the job?*

suggestion /səˈdʒestʃən/ *n* **1** the suggesting of something. **2** something that is suggested; a proposal or idea: *Has anyone any other suggestions to make?*; *What a clever suggestion!* **3** a slight trace: *There was a suggestion of boredom in his tone.*

sugˈgestive *adj* leading you to think about something: *The colours in the painting were suggestive of deep sadness.*

suicide /ˈsuːɪsaɪd/ *n* the deliberate killing of yourself; the taking of your own life: *to commit suicide.*

suit /suːt/ *n* **1** a set of clothes made to be worn together, for example a jacket and trousers for a man, or a jacket and skirt or trousers for a woman. **2** a garment for a particular purpose: *a bathing-suit*; *a diving-suit.* **3** a case in a law-court: *He won his suit.* **4** one of the four sets of playing-cards — spades, hearts, diamonds, clubs. — *v* **1** to be convenient for someone; to be agreeable: *The arrangements did not suit us*; *The climate suits me very well.* **2** to look right for someone: *Long hair suits her*; *That dress doesn't suit her.* **3** to make something fitting or suitable: *He suited his speech to his audience.*

suit yourself to do what you want to do.

suitable /ˈsuːtəbəl/ *adj* **1** right for a purpose or occasion: *Those shoes are not suitable for walking in the country*; *Many people applied for the job but not one of them was suitable.* **2** convenient: *We must find a suitable day for our meeting.* **suitaˈbility** *n.*

ˈsuitably *adv*: *You're not suitably dressed for a wedding.*

suitcase /ˈsuːtkeɪs/ *n* a case with flat sides, to put your clothes in when you are travelling.

suite /swiːt/ *n* a number of things forming a set: *a suite of furniture*; *He has composed a suite of music for the film.*

suited /ˈsuːtɪd/ *adj* suitable; fit: *He's particularly suited to this kind of work.*

suitor /'suːtə(r)/ *n* a man who wants to marry a woman: *She had several suitors.*

sulk /sʌlk/ *v* to show anger by being silent: *He's sulking because his mother won't let him have an ice-cream.*
 'sulky *adj*: *She's in a sulky mood; a sulky girl.* **'sulkily** *adv.* **'sulkiness** *n.*

sullen /'sʌlən/ *adj* silent and angry: *a sullen young man; a sullen expression.* **'sullenly** *adv.* **'sullenness** *n.*

sulphur /'sʌlfə(r)/ *n* a light yellow element that burns with a blue flame and an unpleasant smell, used to make matches and gunpowder.

sultana /sʌl'tɑːnə/ *n* a small, seedless raisin.

sultry /'sʌltrɪ/ *adj* hot but cloudy, and likely to become stormy: *sultry weather.* **'sultriness** *n.*

sum /sʌm/ *n* **1** the total made by two or more things or numbers added together: *The sum of 12, 24, 7 and 11 is 54.* **2** a quantity of money: *It will cost an enormous sum to repair the swimming-pool.* **3** a problem in arithmetic: *My children are better at sums than I am.*
 sum up 1 to give the main points of something: *He summed up the discussion.* **2** to form an opinion about a situation *etc*: *She can usually sum up a situation in a couple of minutes.*

summarize /'sʌməraɪz/ *v* to make a summary of a story *etc*: *He summarized the arguments.*
 'summary *n* a shortened form of a statement, story *etc* giving only the main points: *A summary of his speech was printed in the newspaper.*

summer /'sʌmə(r)/ *n* the warmest season of the year, June till September in northern regions: *I went to Italy last summer.* — *adj*: *summer holidays.*
 'summertime *n* the season of summer.

summit /'sʌmɪt/ *n* **1** the highest point: *They reached the summit of the mountain at midday.* **2** a conference between heads of governments.

See **mountain**.

summon /'sʌmən/ *v* to order someone to come: *He was summoned to appear in court; The headmaster summoned her to his room.*
 summons /'sʌmənz/ *n* an order to appear in court; an order to come and see someone: *The driver who caused the car crash received a summons from the court; She went to the headmaster's office as soon as she got his summons.*

 summon up to make a great effort to have enough strength or courage *etc* to do something: *I couldn't summon up the courage to tell him.*

sumptuous /'sʌmptʃʊəs/ *adj* expensive and splendid: *a sumptuous meal.*

sun /sʌn/ *n* **1** the round body in the sky that gives light and heat to the earth: *The sun is nearly 150 million kilometres away from the earth.* **2** any of the fixed stars: *Do other suns have planets revolving round them?* **3** light and heat from the sun; sunshine: *We sat in the sun; In Britain they don't get enough sun; The sun has faded the curtains.* — *v* to sit or lie in the sunshine: *He's sunning himself in the garden.*

sunbathe /'sʌnbeɪθ/ *v* to lie or sit in the sun, especially wearing few clothes, in order to get a suntan.

sunbeam /'sʌnbiːm/ *n* a ray of the sun.

sunburn /'sʌnbɜːn/ *n* **1** a red colour of the skin caused by being out in hot sun too long. **2** suntan.

sunburned /'sʌnbɜːnd/ or **sunburnt** /'sʌnbɜːnt/ *adj*: *sunburnt faces.*

sundae /'sʌndeɪ/ *n* a portion of ice-cream served with fruit, syrup *etc*: *a fruit sundae.*

Sunday /'sʌndɪ/ *n* the first day of the week, the day following Saturday, kept for rest and worship among Christians.
 Sunday best the smart garments that you wear for special occasions.
 Sunday school a school attended by children on Sundays for religious instruction.
 a month of Sundays a very long time.

sundial /'sʌndaɪəl/ *n* a device, in a garden *etc*, for telling the time from the shadow of a rod or plate cast on its surface by the sun.

sundry /'sʌndrɪ/ *adj* various; assorted: *The stall was selling cakes, biscuits and other sundry snacks.*
 all and sundry everybody: *The invitation is open to all and sundry.*

sunflower /'sʌnflaʊə(r)/ *n* a large yellow flower with petals like rays of the sun, from the seeds of which we get oil.

sung *see* **sing**.

sunglasses /'sʌnglɑːsɪz/ *n* glasses of dark-coloured glass or plastic to protect your eyes in bright sunlight.

sunk, sunken *see* **sink**.

sunken /'sʌŋkən/ *adj* **1** below the water. **2** surrounded by dark shadows: *Her eyes appeared sunken after her illness.* **3** at a lower level than the surrounding area: *a sunken bath.*

sunless /'sʌnlıs/ *adj* without sun; without sunlight: *a sunless day; a sunless room.*

sunlight /'sʌnlaıt/ *n* the light of the sun.

sunlit /'sʌnlıt/ *adj* lit up by the sun: *a sunlit room.*

sunny /'sʌnı/ *adj* **1** filled with sunshine: *sunny weather.* **2** cheerful and happy: *a sunny smile.*

sunrise /'sʌnraız/ *n* the rising of the sun in the morning, or the time of this: *We get up at sunrise.*

sunset /'sʌnsɛt/ *n* the setting of the sun in the evening, or the time of this.

sunshine /'sʌnʃaın/ *n* the light of the sun: *The children were playing in the sunshine.*

sunstroke /'sʌnstroʊk/ *n* an illness caused by being in the hot sun for too long.

suntan /'sʌntan/ *n* a brown colour of the skin: *I'm trying to get a suntan.* **'suntanned** *adj.*

super /'suːpə(r)/ or /'sjuːpə(r)/ *adj* extremely good, nice *etc*: *a super new dress.*

superb /sʊ'pɜːb/ *adj* magnificent; excellent: *a superb view.* **su'perbly** *adv.*

supercilious /suːpə'sılıəs/ *adj* showing that you think you are better than other people: *a supercilious smile.*

superficial /suːpə'fıʃəl/ *adj* **1** affecting the surface only: *The wound is only superficial.* **2** not thorough: *superficial knowledge.* **super'ficially** *adv.*

superfluous /sʊ'pɜːfluəs/ *adj* more than is needed or wanted: *Your advice is superfluous.*

superhuman /suːpə'hjuːmən/ *adj* beyond what is human: *a man of superhuman strength.*

superimpose /suːpərım'poʊz/ *v* to put on top of something: *She superimposed two shades of paint to get the effect she wanted.*

superintend /suːpərın'tɛnd/ *v* to supervise: *She superintended the children; He superintended the job.*

superintendent /suːpərın'tɛndənt/ *n* **1** a senior police officer. **2** a person who supervises a building, project or department.

superior /sʊ'pıərıə(r)/ *adj* higher in rank, better or greater: *Is a captain superior to a commander in the navy?; With his superior strength he managed to overwhelm his opponent.* — *n* a person who is better than, or higher in rank than, another or others. **superi'ority** *n.*

> to be **superior to** (not **than**) something. The opposite of **superior** is **inferior**.

superlative /sʊ'pɜːlətıv/ *adj* the word used for adjectives and adverbs that are used in comparisons to describe something or someone that goes beyond all the others, like these underlined words: *He is the best man for this job; the worst moment of my life; Jane tried the hardest; He arrived most quickly.*

superman /'suːpəmən/ *n* an imagined man of the future with amazing powers.

supermarket /'suːpəmɑːkıt/ *n* a large, self-service store selling food and other goods.

supernatural /suːpə'natʃərəl/ *adj* beyond what is natural or physically possible: *supernatural happenings; a creature of supernatural strength.*

supersede /suːpə'siːd/ *v* to take the place of something older or less modern: *These large computers have been superseded by much smaller personal computers.*

supersonic /suːpə'sɒnık/ *adj* faster than the speed of sound: *These aircraft can travel at supersonic speeds; Concorde is a supersonic aeroplane.*

superstar /'suːpəstɑː(r)/ *n* a very famous person, especially in films, popular music or sport.

superstition /suːpə'stıʃən/ *n* **1** belief in magic, witchcraft and other strange powers. **2** an example of this kind of belief: *There is an old superstition that those who marry in May will have bad luck.*

super'stitious *adj*: *superstitious beliefs; She is very superstitious.*

superstructure /'suːpəstrʌktʃə(r)/ *n* **1** that part of a ship which is above the main deck. **2** that part of a building which is above the foundations.

supertanker /'suːpətaŋkə(r)/ *n* a very large ship for transporting oil.

supervise /'suːpəvaız/ *v* to direct; to control; to be in charge of: *to supervise the workers on a building site; to supervise the building of a road; Who supervises this department?* **super'vision** *n.* **'supervisor** *n.*

> **supervisor** is spelt **-or** (not **-er**).

supper /'sʌpə(r)/ *n* a meal taken in the evening: *Would you like some supper?; She has invited me to supper.*

supplant /sə'plɑːnt/ *v* to take the place of: *She is trying hard to supplant him at work.*

supple /'sʌpəl/ *adj* able to bend and stretch easily: *Take exercise if you want to keep supple.* **'suppleness** *n.*

supplement /'sʌplımənt/ *n* **1** an addition that is made to something to make it better or more complete: *The supplement to the dictionary contains hundreds of new words.* **2** an extra part of a newspaper that is published in addition to the main part: *A colour supplement is a coloured magazine that you get free with some newspapers.* — *v* to increase or improve something by adding something else: *He supplements his wages by working as a gardener.*

supplementary /ˌsʌplɪˈmentərɪ/ *adj*: *A supplementary volume to the dictionary has just been published.*

supply /səˈplaɪ/ *v* to give; to provide: *Extra paper will be supplied by the teacher if it is needed; The town is supplied with water from a reservoir in the hills; The shop was unable to supply what she wanted.* — *n* **1** the supplying of something. **2** an amount or quantity that is supplied; a stock or store: *a supply of food; Who will be responsible for the expedition's supplies?; Fresh supplies will be arriving soon.*

> to **supply** someone **with** something (not **supply** someone something).

su'pplier *n* a person or company that supplies something.

in short supply scarce: *Bread is in short supply.*

support /səˈpɔːt/ *v* **1** to carry the weight of someone or something; to hold upright, in place *etc*: *That chair won't support him; It won't support his weight; He limped home, supported by a friend on either side.* **2** to help; to encourage: *He has always supported our cause; His family supported him in his decision.* **3** to supply your family *etc* with food and clothes *etc*: *He has a wife and four children to support.* **4** to show that something is true or accurate: *What evidence is there to support your theory?* **5** to be in favour of one particular person or team in a competition: *Which football team do you support?* — *n* **1** the supporting of something: *The plan was cancelled because of lack of support; Her job is the family's only means of support; I would like to say a word or two in support of his proposal.* **2** something that supports a bridge, roof, arch *etc*; a pillar, column *etc*: *One of the supports of the bridge collapsed.*

sup'porter *n* someone who supports a person, cause, team *etc*: *football supporters.*

sup'portive *adj* giving help or sympathy: *She's a very supportive friend.*

suppose /səˈpəʊz/ *v* **1** to believe; to guess: *Who do you suppose telephoned today?; 'I suppose you'll be going to the meeting?' 'Yes, I suppose so'; 'No, I don't suppose so'; Do you suppose she'll win?; 'That can't be true, can it?' 'No, I suppose not'.* **2** to consider as a possibility: *Let's suppose we each had 100 francs to spend; Suppose the train's late — what shall we do?* **3** used to make a suggestion or give an order in a polite way: *Suppose we have lunch now!; Suppose you make us a cup of tea!*

supposedly /səˈpəʊzɪdlɪ/ *adv* used to show that you doubt the truth of what you are saying: *He's supposedly one of the best doctors in the country.*

sup'posing if: *Supposing she doesn't come, what shall we do?*

supposition /ˌsʌpəˈzɪʃən/ *n* something thought to be true: *That's pure supposition with no basis in fact; The supposition was that the princess had gone into hiding.*

supposed to 1 believed to; thought to: *He's supposed to be the best doctor in the town.* **2** expected to: *You're supposed to make your own bed every morning.*

suppress /səˈpres/ *v* **1** to defeat: *to suppress a rebellion.* **2** to keep back; to stop: *She suppressed a laugh; to suppress information.* **sup'pression** *n*.

supreme /sʊˈpriːm/ *adj* **1** the highest or most powerful: *the supreme ruler.* **2** the greatest possible: *supreme courage.* **su'premely** *adv*.

supremacy /sʊˈprɛməsɪ/ *n* that state of being the most powerful: *The war decided the question of military supremacy.*

sure /ʃʊə(r)/ *adj* **1** having no doubt: *I'm sure that I gave him the book; I'm not sure what her address is; 'There's a bus at two o'clock.' 'Are you quite sure?'; I thought her idea was good, but now I'm not so sure; I'll help you — you can be sure of that!* **2** certain to do or get something: *He's sure to win; You're sure of a good dinner if you stay at that hotel.* **3** reliable; dependable: *a sure way to cure hiccups; a safe, sure method.* — *adv* certainly; of course: *Sure I'll help you!; 'Would you like to come?' 'Sure!'*

'surely *adv* **1** used in questions, exclamations *etc* to show what you consider probable: *Surely she's finished her work by now!; You don't believe what she said, surely?* **2** without doubt; certainly: *Slowly but surely we're achieving our aim.*

be sure to don't forget to do something: *Be sure to switch off the television.*

for sure definitely; certainly: *We don't know for sure that he's coming.*

make sure to act so that, or check that, something is sure: *Arrive early at the cinema to make sure of getting a seat!*; *I think he's coming today but I'll telephone to make sure.*

sure enough: *I thought she'd be angry, and sure enough she was.*

sure of yourself confident.

surf /sɜːf/ *n* the foam made as waves break on rocks or on the shore: *The children were playing in the white surf.* — *v* to ride on waves towards the shore, standing or lying on a surfboard.

surface /'sɜːfɪs/ *n* **1** the outside or top layer of anything: *Two-thirds of the earth's surface is covered with water*; *This road has a very uneven surface.* **2** a person's outward appearance or apparent character: *On the surface she seems an unfriendly person, but she's really very kind.* — *v* **1** to cover a surface with something: *They are surfacing this road with tarmac at last.* **2** to come to the surface of a liquid: *The submarine surfaced next to the ship.* **3** to appear again: *The old arguments quickly surfaced again.*

surface mail mail sent by ship, train *etc* and not by aeroplane.

surfeit /'sɜːfɪt/ *n* an excess: *There has been a surfeit of sport on television recently.*

surfer /'sɜːfə(r)/ *n* a person who surfs.

surfing /'sɜːfɪŋ/ *n* the sport of riding on a surfboard.

surfboard /'sɜːfbɔːd/ *n* a board on which a person can ride on the surf towards the shore.

surge /sɜːdʒ/ *v* to move forward with great force: *The waves surged over the rocks.* — *n* a surging movement, or a sudden rush: *The stone hit his head and he felt a surge of pain*; *a sudden surge of anger.*

surgeon /'sɜːdʒən/ *n* a doctor who treats injuries or diseases by operations in which the body sometimes has to be cut open.

'surgery *n* **1** the work of a surgeon: *to specialize in surgery.* **2** a doctor's or dentist's room in which they examine patients.

'surgical *adj* of or relating to surgery: *surgical techniques.* **'surgically** *adv*.

surly /'sɜːlɪ/ *adj* rude or sharp in speech or behaviour: *He spoke in a surly voice.*

surmount /sə'maʊnt/ *v* to overcome: *He has surmounted all his problems.*

surname /'sɜːneɪm/ *n* a person's family name: *Smith is a common British surname.*

surpass /sə'pɑːs/ *v* to be, or do, better, or more than: *His work surpassed my expectations.*

surplus /'sɜːpləs/ *n* an amount left over when whatever is needed has been taken: *This country produces a surplus of grain.* — *adj*: *surplus grain.*

The opposite of **surplus** is **deficit**.

surprise /sə'praɪz/ *n* something sudden or unexpected; the feeling caused by this: *The news caused some surprise*; *Your letter was a pleasant surprise*; *He stared at her in surprise*; *To my surprise the door was unlocked.* — *adj*: *a surprise visit.* — *v* **1** to cause someone surprise: *The news surprised me.* **2** to come upon someone without warning: *They surprised the enemy from the rear.*

sur'prised *adj* feeling surprise: *I'm surprised he's not here*; *You behaved badly — I'm surprised at you!*; *I wouldn't be surprised if he won.*

sur'prising *adj* likely to cause surprise: *surprising news*; *It is not surprising that he won.*

sur'prisingly *adv*.

take by surprise 1 to come to, or catch, someone unexpectedly: *The news took me by surprise.* **2** to capture a fort *etc* by a sudden, unexpected attack.

surreal /sə'rɪəl/ *adj* having a strange unreal quality, like a dream: *a surreal painting.*

surrender /sə'rendə(r)/ *v* to give up: *The general refused to surrender to the enemy*; *He surrendered his claim to the throne*; *You must surrender your old passport when applying for a new one.* — *n*: *The army was forced into surrender*; *the surrender of the fort to the enemy.*

surreptitious /sʌrəp'tɪʃəs/ *adj* done secretly: *She paid a surreptitious visit to her doctor.*

surrep'titiously *adv*.

surrogate /'sʌrəgət/ *adj* acting as a substitute for another person or thing. — *n*.

surround /sə'raʊnd/ *v* **1** to be, or come, all round: *Britain is surrounded by sea*; *Enemy troops surrounded the town.* **2** to put round: *He surrounded the castle with a high wall.*

sur'rounding *adj* lying or being all round: *the village and its surrounding scenery.*

sur'roundings *n* **1** the scenery *etc* that is round a place: *a pleasant hotel in delightful surroundings.* **2** the conditions *etc* in which a person, animal *etc* lives: *He was happy to be at home again in his usual surroundings.*

surveillance /sə'veɪləns/ *n* a close watch on someone, especially by the police: *The* *suspect has been kept under surveillance for a week.*

survey *v* /səˈveɪ/ **1** to look at something: *He looked out of his window and surveyed his garden.* **2** to inspect carefully: *They surveyed the damage left by the earthquake.* **3** to measure and work out the shape of a piece of land *etc*, especially when you are planning new roads or buildings. — *n* /ˈsɜːveɪ/.

survive /səˈvaɪv/ *v* **1** to remain alive: *He didn't survive long after the accident.* **2** to live longer than someone else: *He died in 1940 but his wife survived him by another 20 years.*
sur'vival *n*.
sur'viving *adj* remaining alive.
sur'vivor *n* a person who survives a disaster.

susceptible /səˈsɛptɪbəl/ *adj* easily influenced, damaged or affected by something: *The child has always been susceptible to infections.*

suspect *v* /səˈspɛkt/ **1** to think a person *etc* guilty: *Whom do you suspect of the crime?*; *I suspect him of robbing the bank.* **2** to have doubts about something: *I suspected her motives.* **3** to think probable: *I suspect that she's trying to hide her true feelings.* — *n* /ˈsʌspɛkt/ a person who is thought guilty: *There are three possible suspects in this murder case.* — *adj* not able to be trusted: *I think his statement is suspect.*

> to **suspect that** means to think something is likely: *We suspect that he is the murderer.*
> to **doubt whether** means to think something is unlikely: *I doubt whether he is the murderer.*

suspend /səˈspɛnd/ *v* **1** to hang: *The meat was suspended from a hook.* **2** to keep something from falling or sinking: *Particles of dust are suspended in the air.* **3** to stop something for a while: *All business will be suspended until after the New Year celebrations.* **4** to stop someone for a certain length of time from doing their job, usually as a punishment: *The footballer was suspended from playing for three months.*
su'spenders *n* **1** a pair of elastic straps for holding up socks or stockings. **2** braces for holding up trousers.
su'spense *n* a state of uncertainty and anxiety: *We waited in suspense for the result of the competition.*
su'spension *n* **1** the suspending of something or someone: *He was punished by a two-month suspension from football.* **2** the system of springs *etc* that supports a motor vehicle, making it more comfortable to ride in.
suspension bridge a type of bridge that has its roadway suspended from cables supported by a tower at each end.

suspicion /səˈspɪʃən/ *n* the suspecting of someone or something; doubt; distrust: *They looked at each other with suspicion*; *I have a suspicion she is not telling the truth.*
under suspicion suspected of doing something wrong: *Until we find the truth, everyone is under suspicion.*
su'spicious *adj* **1** feeling or showing suspicion: *I'm always suspicious of people who won't look at me straight in the eyes*; *She gave him a suspicious glance.* **2** causing suspicion: *He died in suspicious circumstances.*
su'spiciously *adv*.

sustain /səˈsteɪn/ *v* **1** to give help or strength to someone: *The thought of seeing his family again sustained him throughout his long time in prison*; *She took a few sandwiches to sustain her during the journey.* **2** to suffer: *He sustained head injuries when he fell off the ladder.* **3** to bear: *The tree could hardly sustain the weight of its fruit.* **4** to keep something going: *He couldn't sustain the pace he had set at the beginning of the race.*
su'stained *adj* continued for a long time: *The pianist received sustained applause for her performance.*

swab /swɒb/ *n* **1** a small piece of cotton used to clean wounds: *She used a swab to apply the cream.* **2** a sample of fluid from the body taken for examination: *The doctor took a swab from her throat to check for infection.*

swagger /ˈswagə(r)/ *v* to walk as though very pleased with yourself: *I saw him swaggering along the street in his new suit.* — *n*.

swallow¹ /ˈswɒloʊ/ *v* **1** to make food or drink pass down your throat to your stomach: *Try to swallow the pill*; *His throat was so painful that he could hardly swallow.* **2** to accept a lie *etc* without question: *You'll never get her to swallow that story!* — *n* an act of swallowing.
swallow your pride to behave humbly, for example by making an apology.
swallow up to close around; to hide completely: *She was swallowed up in the crowd.*

swallow² /ˈswɒloʊ/ *n* a bird with long wings and a divided tail.

A swallow **twitters**.

swam *see* **swim**.

swamp /swɒmp/ *n* wet, marshy ground: *These trees grow best in swamps.* — *v* to cover deeply with water: *A great wave swamped the deck.*

'**swampy** *adj*: *The land is very swampy — it will have to be drained.*

swan /swɒn/ *n* a large, usually white, water bird with a long graceful neck.

swap another spelling of **swop**.

swarm /swɔːm/ *n* **1** a great number of insects or other small creatures moving together: *a swarm of ants; a swarm of bees.* **2** a great number; a crowd: *swarms of people.* — *v* **1** to move in great numbers: *The children swarmed out of the school.* **2** to follow the queen bee in a swarm: *The bees are swarming.*

swarthy /'swɔːðɪ/ *adj* with a dark complexion: *He is dark and swarthy.*

swat /swɒt/ *v* to crush a fly *etc* by slapping it with something flat: *He swatted the fly with a folded newspaper.*

sway /sweɪ/ *v* **1** to move from side to side, or up and down, with a swinging or rocking action: *The branches swayed gently in the breeze.* **2** to influence: *She's too easily swayed by her friends' opinions.* — *n* the motion of swaying: *the sway of the ship's deck.*

swear /sweə(r)/ *v* **1** to state or promise solemnly: *The witness must swear to tell the truth; Swear never to reveal the secret; I swear I'm innocent of this crime.* **2** to use the name of God and other sacred words, or dirty words, in anger or for emphasis; to curse: *Don't swear in front of the children!*

> **swear; swore** /swɔː(r)/; **sworn** /swɔːn/: *She swore to tell the truth; He has sworn an oath.*

'**swearword** *n* a rude or offensive word.

swear by to believe completely in the value or usefulness of something: *He has been taking vitamin tablets for years, and swears by them.*

swear in to accept someone's promise that they will accept the responsibility of their new position: *The President will be sworn in next week.*

sweat /swɛt/ *n* the moisture that comes out through the skin: *He was dripping with sweat after running so far in the heat.* — *v*: *Vigorous exercise makes you sweat.*

'**sweater** *n* a knitted pullover.

> See **cardigan**.

'**sweatshirt** *n* a cotton jersey worn for sport or casually.

'**sweaty** *adj* **1** wet with sweat. **2** causing you to sweat: *sweaty work.*

a cold sweat a state of shock, fear *etc*.

sweep /swiːp/ *v* **1** to clean a room *etc* using a brush or broom: *The room has been swept clean.* **2** to move with a brushing or rushing movement: *to sweep up rubbish; She swept the crumbs off the table with her hand; The wave swept him overboard; The wind nearly swept me off my feet.* **3** to move swiftly: *High winds sweep across the desert; The disease is sweeping through the country; She swept into my room without knocking on the door.* — *n* **1** the action of sweeping with a brush *etc*: *She gave the room a sweep.* **2** a sweeping movement: *He indicated the damage with a sweep of his hand.* **3** a person who cleans chimneys.

> **sweep; swept** /swɛpt/; **swept**: *He swept up the crumbs; She has swept the floor.*

'**sweeper** *n* a person or thing that sweeps: *a road-sweeper; a carpet-sweeper.*

'**sweeping** *adj* **1** large and having a wide effect: *The government introduced sweeping changes in education.* **2** too general and possibly not considered carefully enough: *a sweeping criticism.*

at a sweep in a single action or move; all at once: *He sacked half of his employees at a sweep.*

sweep out to sweep a room *etc* thoroughly: *to sweep the classroom out.*

sweet /swiːt/ *adj* **1** tasting like sugar; not sour, salty or bitter: *as sweet as honey.* **2** pleasant; fragrant: *the sweet smell of flowers.* **3** delightful to hear: *the sweet song of the nightingale.* **4** attractive; charming; nice: *What a sweet little baby!; a sweet smile; You look sweet in that dress; Isobel has a sweet nature.* — *n* **1** a small piece of sweet food, such as chocolate, toffee *etc*: *a packet of sweets; Have a sweet.* **2** a dish or course of sweet food at the end of a meal; a pudding or dessert: *The waiter served the sweet.* '**sweetness** *n*.

'**sweetcorn** *n* yellow grains of maize that are eaten as a vegetable when they are young and sweet.

'**sweeten** *v* to make or become sweet: *to sweeten food with sugar.*

'**sweetener** *n* a substance used to sweeten food or drink instead of sugar: *artificial sweeteners.*

'**sweetheart** *n* **1** a boyfriend or girlfriend. **2**

used as a name for someone you love; darling: *Goodbye, sweetheart!*

'sweetly *adv* in an attractive, charming, kindly manner: *She smiled very sweetly.*

sweet potato a tropical climbing plant with an edible yellow root.

sweet tooth a fondness for sweet foods: *She never refuses chocolate — she has a very sweet tooth.*

swell /swɛl/ *v* to make or become larger, greater or thicker: *The insect-bite made her finger swell up; The continual rain had swollen the river; I invited her to join us in order to swell the number of people on the trip.* — *adj* very good: *a swell idea; That's swell!* — *n* the up and down movement of the sea when there are no breaking waves.

> **swell; swelled; swollen** /'swoʊlən/: *His ankle swelled; The river is swollen with rain.*

'swelling *n* a swollen area on the body: *She had a swelling on her arm where the wasp had stung her.*

swelter /'swɛltə(r)/ *v* to be uncomfortably hot: *I'm sweltering in this heat!; It's sweltering today.*

swept *see* **sweep**.

swerve /swɜːv/ *v* to turn away suddenly from a line or course: *The car driver swerved to avoid the dog.* — *n*: *The bus gave a sudden swerve and rocked the passengers in their seats.*

swift[1] /swɪft/ *adj* fast; quick: *a swift horse; a swift-footed animal.* **'swiftly** *adv*. **'swiftness** *n*.

swift

swift[2] /swɪft/ *n* a bird rather like a swallow.

swig /swɪg/ *v* to drink in large gulps, usually from a bottle: *He stopped running for a moment to swig some of the water he was carrying.* — *n*.

swill /swɪl/ *v* **1** to clean something by pouring a lot of water over it; to rinse: *He swilled out the dirty cups.* **2** to drink a lot of something, especially an alcoholic drink: *He sat in the bar swilling beer.* — *n* (also **pigswill**) waste food in water that is given to pigs to eat.

swim /swɪm/ *v* **1** to move through water using arms and legs or fins, tails *etc*: *The children aren't allowed to go sailing until they've learnt to swim; I'm going swimming; They watched the fish swimming about in the aquarium; She attempted to swim the river but had to give up half-way across.* **2** to seem to be going round and round as a result of dizziness: *My head's swimming.* — *n*: *We went for a swim in the lake.*

> **swim; swam** /swam/; **swum** /swʌm/: *He swam across the river; We have swum three lengths of the swimming-pool.*

'swimmer *n*: *He's a strong swimmer.*

'swimming-bath or **'swimming-pool** *n* an indoor or outdoor pool for swimming in.

'swimming-trunks *n* short pants worn by boys and men for swimming.

'swimsuit or **'swimming-costume** *n* a garment worn by girls or women for swimming.

swindle /'swɪndəl/ *v* to cheat someone, especially out of money: *That shopkeeper has swindled me out of £2!; He swindled a hundred pounds out of her.* — *n*: *What a swindle — I paid £50 for this watch and it doesn't work!*

'swindler *n* a person who swindles others.

swine /swaɪn/ *n* **1** an old word for a pig. **2** a rude word for someone who behaves badly towards others: *He left me to pay the bill, the swine!*

swing /swɪŋ/ *v* **1** to move from side to side, or forwards and backwards from a fixed point: *You swing your arms when you walk; The children were swinging on a rope hanging from a tree; The door swung open; He swung the load on to his shoulder.* **2** to walk with a stride: *He swung along the road.* **3** to turn suddenly: *He swung round and stared at them.* **4** to try to hit someone: *He swung at me with a baseball bat.* — *n* **1** a go or turn at swinging: *He was having a swing on the rope.* **2** a swinging movement: *the swing of a pendulum.* **3** a strong dancing rhythm: *The music should be played with a swing.* **4** a seat for swinging, hung on ropes or chains from a supporting frame *etc*.

> **swing; swung** /swʌŋ/; **swung**: *The door swung open; The goal has swung the game in our favour.*

'swinging *adj* fashionable and exciting: *the swinging city of London.*

swing door a door that swings open in both directions.

in full swing going ahead, or continuing, busily: *The work was in full swing.*

swipe /swaɪp/ *v* to hit something hard, with a strong swing of your arm: *She swiped the tennis ball into the air; He swiped at the fly on his leg but missed it.* — *n*: *She gave the boy a swipe across the face.*

swirl /swɜːl/ *v* to move quickly, with a whirling motion: *The leaves swirled along the ground.* — *n*: *The dancers came on stage in a swirl of colour.*

swish /swɪʃ/ *v* to move or cause to move with a rustling sound: *Her long skirt swished as she danced; He swished open the curtains.*

switch /swɪtʃ/ *n* **1** a small device for turning an electric current on or off: *The switch is down when the power is on and up when it's off; He couldn't find the light-switch.* **2** a change: *After several switches of direction they found themselves on the right road.* **3** a thin stick. — *v* to change; to turn: *He switched the lever to the 'off' position; Let's switch over to another programme; Having considered that problem, they switched their attention to other matters.*

'switchboard *n* a board with lots of switches for making connections by telephone, for instance in a large office or hotel: *He rang the company and asked the lady at the switchboard to connect him with the manager.*

switch on, switch off to turn on or turn off an electric current, light *etc*: *He switched on the light; Switch off the electricity before going on holiday.*

> to **switch on** (not **open**) the light.
> to **switch off** (not **shut**) the light.

swivel /'swɪvəl/ *v* to turn round quickly; to spin: *He swivelled round when he heard a strange noise behind him; She swivelled her chair round to face the desk.*

swollen /'swəʊlən/ *adj* increased in size because of swelling: *He had a swollen ankle after falling downstairs; a swollen stream.* See also **swell**.

swollen-'headed *adj* too pleased with yourself; conceited: *He's very swollen-headed about his success.*

swoon /swuːn/ *v* to lose consciousness; to faint: *The girls were so excited when the pop-singer appeared on stage that they nearly swooned.*

swoop /swuːp/ *v* to rush or fly downwards: *The owl swooped down on its prey.* — *n*.

swop or **swap** /swɒp/ *v* to exchange one thing for another: *He swopped his ball with another boy for a pistol; They swopped books with each other.* — *n* an exchange: *a fair swop.*

sword /sɔːd/ *n* a weapon with a long blade that is sharp on one or both edges: *He drew his sword and killed the man.*

'swordfish *n* a large fish with a long, pointed upper jaw.

swore see **swear**.

sworn /swɔːn/ *adj* **1** having sworn always to remain a friend, enemy *etc*: *They are sworn enemies.* **2** made by someone who has sworn to tell the truth: *The prisoner made a sworn statement.* See also **swear**.

swot /swɒt/ *v* to study hard and seriously: *She has been swotting for her exams.* — *n* a person who studies too hard: *His friends think he is a swot because he has been working hard for his exams.*

swot up to study very hard: *She has been swotting up her French.*

swum see **swim**.

swung see **swing**.

syllable /'sɪləbəl/ *n* a word or part of a word that is a single sound: *'Cheese' has one syllable, 'but-ter' has two and 'mar-ga-rine' has three.*

syllabus /'sɪləbəs/ *n* a list of subjects that students have to study at school or university.

symbol /'sɪmbəl/ *n* a thing that represents or stands for something: *The cross is a symbol of Christianity; The dove is a symbol of peace; The sign ÷ is the symbol for division.*

sym'bolic *adj*: *In the Christian religion, bread and wine are symbolic of Christ's body and blood.* **sym'bolically** *adv*.

'symbolism *n* the use of symbols to represent things: *The painting is full of symbolism.*

'symbolize *v* to be a symbol of something: *A ring symbolizes everlasting love.*

symmetric /sɪ'mɛtrɪk/ or **symmetrical** /sɪ'mɛtrɪkəl/ *adj* having symmetry: *The two sides of a person's face are never completely symmetrical.*

sym'metrically *adv*: *Coloured squares arranged symmetrically on the wall.*

symmetry /'sɪmətrɪ/ *n* the state in which two parts, on either side of a dividing line, are equal in size, shape and position.

sympathetic /sɪmpə'θɛtɪk/ *adj* **1** showing or feeling sympathy: *She was very sympathetic when I failed my exam; a sympathetic smile.* **2** to agree with or support an idea or cause *etc*. **sympa'thetically** *adv*.

sympathize /ˈsɪmpəθaɪz/ v to show or feel sympathy for someone or their opinions: *I find it difficult to sympathize with him when he complains so much.*

ˈsympathizer n a person who supports or approves of an idea or cause, but may not take any direct action: *He was known to be a Communist sympathizer.*

sympathy /ˈsɪmpəθɪ/ n the sharing of the feelings or attitudes of others: *When her husband died, she received many letters of sympathy*; *Are you in sympathy with the strikers?*

symphony /ˈsɪmfənɪ/ n a long piece of music for an orchestra. **symˈphonic** *adj.*

symptom /ˈsɪmptəm/ n something that goes with a particular illness: *A cold, fever and headache are the usual symptoms of flu.*

synagogue /ˈsɪnəgɒg/ n a Jewish place of worship.

synchronize /ˈsɪŋkrənaɪz/ v **1** to happen, or make something happen, at the same time as something else: *In foreign films, the movements of the actors' lips are often not synchronized with the sounds of their words*; *The voices and lip-movements don't synchronize.* **2** to adjust watches so that they say the same time: *The bank-robbers synchronized watches.* **synchroniˈzation** *n.*

syndrome /ˈsɪndroʊm/ n a set of symptoms which are the sign of a particular illness: *There is a new blood test to detect babies suffering from this syndrome before birth.*

synonym /ˈsɪnənɪm/ n a word which means the same, or nearly the same, as another: *'Happy' and 'pleased' are synonyms.* **synˈonymous** *adj.*

syntax /ˈsɪntaks/ n the grammatical rules which govern the position words may have in a sentence and how they relate to each other: *He finds English syntax difficult to understand.*

synthesis /ˈsɪnθəsɪs/, *plural* **syntheses** /ˈsɪnθəsiːz/, n **1** the forming of a product by combining various different chemical substances: *Plastic is produced by synthesis.* **2** a combination: *His latest proposal is a synthesis of old and new ideas.* **ˈsynthesize** *v.*

ˈsynthesizer n an electronic musical instrument that can make a wide range of different sounds.

synˈthetic *adj* artificial; produced by a chemical process; not natural: *Nylon is a synthetic material.* — n a synthetic material: *In a hot climate natural materials are more comfortable to wear than synthetics.*

syringe /sɪˈrɪndʒ/ n an instrument for sucking up and squirting out liquids, used, with a needle fitted to it, for giving injections or taking blood out of the body.

syrup /ˈsɪrəp/ n water, or the juice of fruits, boiled with sugar and made thick and sticky.

ˈsyrupy *adj* like syrup.

system /ˈsɪstəm/ n **1** an arrangement of many parts that work together: *a railway system*; *the solar system*; *the human digestive system.* **2** a way of organizing something according to certain ideas *etc*: *a system of education.* **3** a plan; a method: *There's a new system for serving meals to the pupils.* **systeˈmatic** *adj.* **systeˈmatically** *adv.*

get something out of your system to get rid of a feeling by expressing it openly: *Have a good cry and get it all out of your system.*

T

tab /tab/ *n* a small piece of some material attached to something, standing up so that it can be seen, held, pulled *etc*: *You open the packet by pulling the tab*; *Hang your jacket up by the tab*.

keep tabs on to watch a thing or person closely so that you know exactly where they are and what they are doing.

tabby /'tabɪ/ *n* a striped cat, especially a female one.

table /'teɪbəl/ *n* **1** a piece of furniture with a flat surface on legs: *Put the plates on the table*. **2** a statement of facts or figures arranged in columns *etc*: *The results of the experiment can be seen in table 5.*

'tablecloth *n* a cloth for covering a table.

'tablespoon *n* a large spoon.

'tablespoonful *n*: *two tablespoonfuls of sugar.*

> The plural of **tablespoonful** is **tablespoonfuls** (not **tablespoonsful**).

table tennis a game played on a table with small bats and a light ball.

lay or **set the table** to put a tablecloth, plates, knives, forks *etc* on a table for a meal.

tablet /'tablət/ *n* **1** a pill: *Take these tablets for your headache*. **2** a flat piece or bar of soap *etc*. **3** a flat surface on which words are engraved *etc*: *They put up a marble tablet in memory of the poet.*

tabloid /'tablɔɪd/ *n* a newspaper printed on small pages, often with short articles and lots of pictures.

taboo /tə'buː/, *plural* **taboos**, *n* anything which is forbidden for social or religious reasons: *Alcohol is a taboo for Muslims*. — *adj*: *a taboo subject.*

tabulate /'tabjʊleɪt/ *v* to arrange in columns or a table: *He tabulated all the results.*

tacit /'tasɪt/ *adj* understood, but not actually stated: *There is a tacit agreement in the office that we don't smoke here*. **'tacitly** *adv*.

taciturn /'tasɪtɜːn/ *adj* saying little, quiet: *He has a taciturn nature.*

tack /tak/ *n* **1** a short nail with a broad flat head: *a carpet-tack*. **2** in sewing, a large, temporary stitch used to hold pieces of material in position for you to machine them together. **3** a course of action: *If this doesn't work we shall have to try a different tack.* — *v* to fasten with tacks: *I tacked the carpet down*; *She tacked the pieces of material together.*

tack on to add an extra part to something: *I tacked a couple of extra visits onto my trip to see all the major sights in the city.*

tackle /'takəl/ *v* **1** to try to grasp or seize someone: *The policeman tackled the thief*. **2** to deal with a difficulty: *We still have several problems to tackle.* — *n* **1** equipment: *fishing tackle*; *riding tackle*. **2** a system for lifting heavy weights: *lifting tackle*. **3** the ropes and rigging of a boat. **4** an act of tackling someone: *a skilful tackle by the fastest rugby player in the country.*

tacky /'takɪ/ *adj* **1** cheap and badly made: *tacky souvenirs for tourists*. **2** not quite dry; sticky: *The paint is still tacky so you mustn't touch it yet.*

tact /takt/ *n* care and skill in your behaviour towards people, in order to avoid hurting or offending them: *He showed tact in dealing with the less clever children.*

'tactful *adj*: *A tactful teacher praises the slower children whenever possible*. **'tactfully** *adv*.

tactics /'taktɪks/ *n plural* **1** the things that you do in order to win or get what you want: *The politicans planned their tactics for the election*. **2** the ways of arranging troops, warships *etc* during a battle, in order to win: *The generals discussed their tactics.*

'tactical *adj* **1** to do with tactics: *The general was famous for his tactical skill*. **2** planned to get the best possible result: *It was the correct tactical decision, although it seemed foolish at first*. **'tactically** *adv*.

tactless /'taktləs/ *adj* lacking tact, thoughtless: *A tactless remark can cause much unhappiness*. **'tactlessly** *adv*.

tadpole /'tadpoʊl/ *n* a young frog or toad in its first stage as a round black head with a tail.

tag /tag/ *n* a label: *a price-tag*; *a name-tag*. — *v*: *to tag a label on to something.*

tag along to go with someone, especially without being invited: *My little sister always wants to tag along when I go to the park.*

tail /teɪl/ *n* **1** the part of an animal, bird or fish that sticks out behind the rest of its body: *The dog wagged its tail*; *A fish swims* *by moving its tail.* **2** anything that has a similar position: *the tail of an aeroplane*. — *v* to follow closely: *The detectives tailed the thief to the station.*

> A dog wags its **tail** (not **tale**).

tails *n, adv* the side of a coin that does not have the head on it: *He tossed the coin and it came down tails.*

tail-'end *n* the very end or last part: *the tail-end of the procession.*

tail off to become gradually less, slower or weaker: *The noise of the engine tailed off as the car went into the distance.*

tailor /'teɪlə(r)/ *n* a person who cuts and makes suits, overcoats *etc*: *He has his clothes made by a tailor.* — *v* **1** to make clothes so that they fit well: *She wore a smart, tailored jacket.* **2** to design something for a particular purpose: *We tailor courses to suit the students' particular needs.*

tailor-'made *adj* made by a tailor to fit a person exactly: *a tailor-made dress.*

tainted /'teɪntɪd/ *adj* spoiled from contact with, or affected by, something bad or evil: *Her good reputation has been tainted by the scandal.*

take /teɪk/ *v* **1** to reach out for something and grasp, hold, lift, pull it *etc*: *He took my hand*; *He took the book down from the shelf*; *He opened the drawer and took out a gun*; *I've had a tooth taken out.* **2** to carry or lead to another place: *I took the books back to the library*; *The police took him away*; *I took the dog out for a walk.* **3** to do some action: *I think I'll take a walk*; *Will you take a look?*; *to take a shower.* **4** to get, receive, buy, rent *etc*: *I'm taking French lessons*; *I'll take three kilos of strawberries*; *We took a house in London.* **5** to accept: *He took my advice*; *I won't take that insult from you!*; *I'm afraid we can't take back goods if you don't show us your receipt.* **6** to need; to require: *How long does it take you to get home?*; *It takes time to do a difficult job like this.* **7** to travel by bus *etc*: *I'm taking the next train to London*; *I took a taxi.* **8** to photograph: *She took a picture of the scenery.* **9** to make a note, record *etc*: *He took a note of her telephone number*; *The nurse took the patient's temperature.* **10** to remove, use *etc* with or without permission: *Someone's taken my coat*; *He took all my money.* **11** to consider: *Take John, for example.* **12** to win: *He took the first prize.* **13** to make less or smaller by a certain amount; to subtract: *Take four from ten, and that leaves six.* **14** to eat or drink: *Take these pills*; *Do you take sugar in your tea?* **15** to be in charge of; to lead; to run: *Will you take the class for me this evening?* **16** to have enough space for something: *I don't think the car will take any more luggage.* **17** to react to something in a certain way: *He took the news calmly.* **18** to feel: *He took pleasure in his work.* **19** to go down or turn into a road: *Take the second road on the left.* **20** to do a test, examination *etc*: *I'm taking my driving test tomorrow.* **21** to think; to suppose: *I take it you'll be wanting a birthday cake?* **22** to capture: *The city was taken by the enemy on the next day.*

> **take**; **took** /tʊk/; **'taken**: *She took the books home*; *He has taken the job.*
> See also **bring**.

'take-away *n* **1** food prepared and bought in a restaurant but taken away and eaten somewhere else: *I'll go and buy a take-away.* **2** a restaurant that sells take-aways. — *adj*: *a take-away meal*; *a take-away Indian restaurant.*

take after to be or look like a parent or relation: *She takes after her father.*

take a lot out of you to make you very tired: *All this worry has taken a lot out of her.*

take apart to separate into different pieces: *We had to take the cupboard apart to get it through the door.*

take away to remove: *Nobody can take your memories away from you*; *If you don't take these chocolates away I shall eat them all.*

take back 1 to return something to the place it came from: *I'm taking my books back to the library.* **2** to admit that something you said was wrong: *I quite like him now — I take back all those things I said about him.*

take down 1 to make a note of something: *He took down her name and address.* **2** to remove a building *etc* bit by bit: *We took the tent down as soon as it was daylight.*

take for to make the mistake of thinking that someone is someone or something they are not: *I took you for your brother*; *Do you take me for a fool?*

take in 1 to give someone shelter: *He had nowhere to go, so I took him in.* **2** to understand and remember: *I didn't take in what* he said. **3** to deceive or cheat: *He took me in with his story.*

take off 1 to remove clothes *etc*: *He took off his coat.* **2** not to work during a period of time: *I'm taking tomorrow morning off.* **3** to imitate unkindly: *Tom is good at taking the teacher off.* **4** to become successful or very popular: *The scheme took off much faster than we had expected.* **5** to leave the ground: *The plane took off for Rome at 9.30 a.m.* **'take-off** *n.*

> The opposite of **put on** your coat is **take off** (not **take out**) your coat.

take on 1 to agree to do work *etc*: *He took on the job.* **2** to allow passengers to get on or in: *The bus stops here to take on passengers.*

take out 1 to get something from the place it is in: *She opened her purse and took out a coin.* **2** to remove a part of the body: *The dentist says I've got to have a tooth taken out.* **3** to invite someone to go with you and to pay for them: *He took her out for a meal after the show.*

take out on to behave badly towards someone because you are angry or upset about something else: *I'm sorry you lost the match, but please don't take it out on me!*

take over 1 to do something after someone else stops doing it: *He retired last year, and I took over his job from him.* **2** to take control of a business company *etc*: *When was this company taken over by Breakages Ltd?* **'take-over** *n.*

take to 1 to feel or begin to feel a liking for someone: *We took to your new friends immediately.* **2** to begin doing something regularly: *She's taken to wearing a hat all the time.*

take up 1 to use space, time *etc*: *I won't take up much of your time*; *How much space will the chest of drawers take up?* **2** to begin a hobby, pastime *etc*: *He has taken up the violin.* **3** to pick up: *He took up the book and began to read it.* **4** to discuss something that is worrying you with a person in authority: *I shall have to take this up with the transport department.*

take up on 1 to accept an offer *etc*: *Thanks for the invitation — I'll take you up on that sometime.* **2** to say that you disagree with something someone says or to ask them to explain it further: *Can I take you up on that last point?*

takings /'teɪkɪŋz/ *n plural* the amount of money taken in a shop, at a cinema, zoo *etc*: *After closing the shop, the shopkeeper took the day's takings to the bank.*

talcum powder /'talkəm paʊdə(r)/ *n* fine, usually perfumed powder (often shortened to **talc**): *She put some talc on the baby after she had bathed him.*

tale /teɪl/ *n* **1** a story: *He told me the tale of his travels.* **2** a lie: *He told me he had a lot of money, but that was just a tale.*

> to read the children a fairy **tale** (not **tail**).

talent /'talənt/ *n* a special ability or skill: *a talent for drawing.*

'talented *adj* naturally clever or skilful: *a talented pianist.*

talk /tɔːk/ *v* to speak; to have a conversation: *They talked to each other for a long time*; *What did they talk about?*; *I'm teaching my parrot to talk*; *You must stop talking when the teacher comes into the classroom*; *How old are babies when they learn to talk?* — *n* **1** a conversation or discussion: *Robert and I had a long talk about the film.* **2** a lecture: *The doctor gave the school a talk on health.* **3** useless discussion: *There's too much talk and not enough action.*

'talkative *adj* talking a lot: *a talkative person.*

talk back to answer rudely: *Don't talk back to me!*

talk big to talk as if you are very important; to boast.

talk down to to speak to someone as if they are not as important or clever as you are: *Children dislike being talked down to.*

talk someone into doing something or **talk someone out of doing something** to persuade someone to do something, or persuade someone not to do something.

talk over to discuss: *We talked over the whole idea.*

talk round to persuade: *I managed to talk her round.*

talk sense or **talk nonsense** to say sensible, or ridiculous, things: *I do wish you would talk sense*; *Don't talk nonsense.*

tall /tɔːl/ *adj* **1** higher than normal: *a tall man.* **2** having a particular height: *John is only four feet tall.* **'tallness** *n.*

a tall story a story which is hard to believe.

> **tall** is used especially of people, and of other narrow upright objects; the opposite of **tall** is **short**: *a tall girl; a tall tree; a tall building; Is she tall or short?*
> **high** is used of objects that are a long way off the ground, or reach a great height; the opposite of **high** is **low**: *a high shelf; a high diving-board; a high mountain; a high wall.*

tally /'talɪ/ *n* an account: *He kept a tally of all the work he did.* — *v* to agree or match: *Their stories tally; His story tallies with mine.*

tambourine /tambə'riːn/ *n* a shallow, one-sided drum with tinkling metal discs in the rim, held in the hand and shaken or beaten.

tambourine

tame /teɪm/ *adj* used to living with people; not wild or dangerous: *He kept a tame bear as a pet.* — *v* to make tame: *It is impossible to tame some animals.* **'tameness** *n*.

> The opposite of **tame** is **wild**.

tamper /'tampə(r)/ *v* to meddle: *Don't tamper with the engine.*

tan /tan/ *v* **1** to make an animal's skin into leather by treating it with certain substances. **2** to make skin brown: *She was tanned by the sun.* — *n* **1** a light brown colour. **2** suntanned skin: *He came back from holiday with a tan.*

tandem /'tandəm/ *n* a long bicycle for two people with two seats and two sets of pedals.

tangent /'tandʒənt/ *n* a straight line that touches a curve but does not cut through it.

go off at a tangent to begin to think or talk about something completely different.

tangerine /tandʒə'riːn/ *n* a kind of small orange that has a sweet taste and is easily peeled.

tangible /'tandʒɪbəl/ *adj* able to be felt or seen, real: *The changes had no tangible effects.*

tangle /'taŋgəl/ *n* an untidy, messy state: *The child's hair was in a tangle.* — *v* to make or become tangled: *Don't tangle my wool when I'm knitting.*

'tangled *adj*: *tangled hair.*

tank /taŋk/ *n* **1** a large container for liquids or gas: *a hot-water tank.* **2** a heavy steel-covered vehicle armed with guns.

'tanker *n* a ship or lorry for carrying oil *etc.*

'tankard *n* a large metal mug: *He drank his beer from a tankard.*

tanned /'tand/ *adj* made brown by the sun: *a tanned face.*

tantalize /'tantəlaɪz/ *v* to make someone want something that they cannot have: *He tantalized his sister by showing her his ice-cream and then eating it all himself; The tantalizing smells from the restaurant made me feel hungry.*

tantamount /'tantəmaʊnt/: **tantamount to** having the same effect or result as: *His refusal to appear in court to answer the charges is tantamount to an admission of guilt.*

tantrum /'tantrəm/ *n* a fit of extreme rage, with shouting and stamping: *She's having a tantrum again.*

tap[1] /tap/ *n* a quick touch; a light knock: *I heard a tap at the door.* — *v*: *He tapped at the window; She tapped me on the shoulder.*

tap[2] /tap/ *n* any of several kinds of device, usually with a handle and valve that can be shut or opened, for controlling the flow of liquid or gas: *Turn the tap off!* — *v* to attach a device to someone's telephone wires in order to be able to listen to their telephone conversations: *My phone is being tapped.*

tape /teɪp/ *n* **1** a narrow strip or band of cloth used for tying *etc*: *bundles of letters tied with tape.* **2** a narrow strip, of paper, plastic, metal *etc*, with many different purposes: *adhesive tape; insulating tape; I recorded the concert on tape.* — *v* **1** to fasten or stick with tape. **2** to record on tape: *He taped the concert.*

tape deck the part of a hi-fi that you play and record tapes on.

'tape-measure or **'measuring-tape** *n* a length of tape, marked with centimetres, metres *etc* for measuring.

tape recorder a machine that records sounds on magnetic tape and reproduces them when required.

tape recording a recording of something on tape.

taper /'teɪpə(r)/ *n* a long, thin candle. — *v* to make or become narrower at one end: *The leaves taper off to a point.*

'tapering *adj*: *tapering fingers.*

tapestry /'tapɪstrɪ/ *n* a piece of cloth with a picture or design sewn or woven into it:

Two large tapestries hung on the wall.

tar /tɑː(r)/ *n* any of several kinds of thick, black, sticky material obtained from wood, coal *etc* and used in roadmaking *etc*. — *v* to cover with tar: *The road has just been tarred.*

target /'tɑːgɪt/ *n* **1** a marked board or other object aimed at in shooting, darts *etc*: *His shots hit the target every time.* **2** any object at which shots, bombs *etc* are directed: *Their target was the royal palace.* **3** a result you are trying to achieve: *Our target is to raise £10 000 by the end of the year.* — *v* to aim something: *Our advertisements are carefully targeted at particular age-groups.*

tariff /'tarɪf/ *n* **1** a list of prices or charges: *a hotel tariff.* **2** a tax to be paid on particular goods imported or exported: *Each of the two countries agreed to cut tariffs on goods imported from the other.*

tarmac /'tɑːmak/ *n* **1** a mixture of small stones and tar that is used to make road surfaces *etc*: *a tarmac road.* **2** a piece of ground with a tarmac surface, such as a road or runway at an airport: *The plane was standing on the tarmac.*

tarnish /'tɑːnɪʃ/ *v* **1** to become dull and stained: *Objects made of silver, copper or brass tarnish easily.* **2** to damage: *The politician's reputation was tarnished by the scandal.* **'tarnished** *adj.*

tarpaulin /tɑːˈpɔːlɪn/ *n* a sheet of strong, waterproof material: *The goods on the truck were covered by a tarpaulin.*

tart /tɑːt/ *n* a pie containing fruit or jam: *an apple tart.*

tartan /ɑ*}ˈtɑːtən/ *n* a woollen cloth with a coloured checked pattern, usually from Scotland: *Her skirt was made of tartan.*

task /tɑːsk/ *n* a piece of work; a duty that must be done: *household tasks.*

tassel /'tasəl/ *n* a hanging bunch of threads, used as a decoration on a uniform, hat, shawl *etc*, or on a cushion *etc*. **'tasselled** *adj.*

taste /teɪst/ *v* **1** to recognize the flavour of something: *I can taste ginger in this cake.* **2** to test or find out the flavour or quality of food *etc* by eating or drinking a little of it: *Please taste this and tell me if it is too sweet.* **3** to have a particular flavour: *Someone brought me a cup of hot tea; it tasted good*; *This milk tastes sour*; *The sauce tastes of garlic.* **4** to eat food, especially with enjoyment: *I haven't tasted such a delicious curry for ages.* — *n* **1** one of the five senses, the sense by which we are aware of flavour: *the sense of taste*; *A lemon is bitter to the taste.* **2** flavour: *This wine has an unusual taste.* **3** a small quantity of food *etc* for tasting: *Do have a taste of this cake!* **4** a liking: *a taste for music*; *a strange taste in books*; *expensive tastes.*

'tasteful *adj* attractive and showing good judgement: *The furniture was simple but tasteful.* **'tastefully** *adv.*

'tasteless *adj* **1** lacking flavour: *tasteless food.* **2** unattractive; not showing good judgement: *She owns a lot of tasteless jewellery.* **3** offensive or vulgar.

-tasting having a particular kind of taste: *a sweet-tasting liquid.*

'tasty *adj* having a good flavour: *tasty food.* **'tastiness** *n.*

in bad taste offensive; likely to upset people: *a joke in very bad taste.*

tattered /'tatəd/ *adj* torn: *a tattered book.*

tatters /'tatəz/ *n* torn and ragged pieces: *His clothes were in tatters.*

tattoo[1] /təˈtuː/ *v* to make coloured patterns or pictures on part of a person's body by pricking the skin and putting in dyes: *The design was tattooed on his arm.* — *n*: *His arms were covered with tattoos.* **tat'tooed** *adj.*

tattoo[2] /təˈtuː/ *n* **1** a rhythm that you beat on a drum, or with your fingers on a table *etc*: *He beat a little tattoo with his fingers.* **2** an outdoor military show with music *etc*: *The Edinburgh Tattoo is held every August in front of the Castle.*

tatty /'tatɪ/ *adj* shabby and untidy: *The beggar was wearing tatty old clothes.*

taught *see* **teach**.

taunt /tɔːnt/ *v* to say unkind or cruel things to someone in order to annoy them; to tease someone in a cruel way: *The children at school taunted him because of his big ears.* — *n*: *He was upset by their taunts.*

taut /tɔːt/ *adj* pulled or stretched tight: *The rope needs to be taut.*

tavern /'tavən/ *n* an old-fashioned word for a pub.

tawny /'tɔːnɪ/ *adj* yellowish-brown in colour: *The dog had tawny hair.*

tax /taks/ *n* **1** a charge made by the government on a person's income or on the price of goods *etc* to help pay for the running of the state: *income tax*; *a tax on tobacco.* **2** a strain: *The continual noise was a tax on her nerves.* — *v* **1** to make a person pay tax; to put a tax on goods *etc*: *He is taxed on his* *income*; *Alcohol is taxed.* **2** to put a strain on: *Don't tax your strength!*

tax'ation *n* **1** the system of collecting taxes. **2** the amount of money that people have to pay as tax.

taxi /'tæksɪ/ *n* a car that can be hired with its driver, especially for short journeys: *I took a taxi from the hotel to the station.* — *v* to move slowly along the ground before beginning to speed up for take-off: *The plane taxied along the runway.*

> **'taxi** (verb); **'taxis** or **'taxies**; **'taxiing** or **'taxying**; **'taxied**.

taxi rank a place where taxis stand waiting to be hired: *There is a taxi rank at the railway station.*

taxing /'tæksɪŋ/ *adj* difficult; requiring a lot of effort: *a taxing job.*

tea /tiː/ *n* **1** a plant grown in Asia or its dried and prepared leaves: *I bought half a kilo of tea.* **2** a drink made by adding boiling water to these leaves: *Have a cup of tea!* **3** a cup of tea: *Two teas, please!* **4** a small meal in the afternoon or a larger one in the early evening, at which tea is often drunk: *She invited him to tea.*

'tea-bag *n* a small bag made of very thin paper, containing tea.

teach /tiːtʃ/ *v* to instruct or train: *Do you enjoy teaching children?*; *I've been teaching for five years*; *She teaches English*; *Mrs Fernandez teaches the violin*; *Experience has taught him nothing.*

'teacher *n* a person who teaches, especially in a school.

'teaching *n* **1** the work of a teacher: *Teaching is a satisfying job.* **2** guidance; instruction; something that is taught: *the teachings of Christ*; *the teaching of the Christian Church.* — *adj*: *the teaching staff of this school.*

> **teach**; **taught** /tɔːt/; **taught**: *She taught French last year*; *I've taught at this school for a long time.*

teak /tiːk/ *n* **1** a tree that grows in Asia. **2** its very hard wood: *The table is made of teak.* — *adj*: *teak furniture.*

tea leaves /'tiːliːvz/ the dried leaves of the tea plant that are used for making tea.

team /tiːm/ *n* **1** a group of people forming a side in a game: *a football team.* **2** a group of people working together: *a team of doctors.* **3** two or more animals working together, pulling a plough *etc*: *a team of horses.*

team up to join with others to do something together: *They teamed up with another family to rent a house for the holidays.*

'teamwork *n* co-operation between people who work together: *Our success is based on good teamwork between the management and the workers.*

tea-party /'tiːpɑːtɪ/ *n* an afternoon party at which tea *etc* is served: *She has been invited to a tea-party.*

teapot /'tiːpɒt/ *n* a pot with a spout used for making and pouring tea.

tear[1] /tɪə(r)/ *n* a drop of liquid coming from your eyes when you cry, either because of some strong feeling, especially sadness, or because something, for example smoke or onions, has irritated them: *tears of joy*; *tears of laughter*; *Tears were flowing down my face*; *The pain brought tears to his eyes.*

'teardrop *n* a single tear: *The doll had a teardrop painted on her cheek.*

'tearful *adj*: *She was very tearful*; *a tearful farewell*; *tearful faces.* **'tearfully** *adv.* **'tearfulness** *n.*

tear gas a type of gas which blinds people temporarily by stinging their eyes and making them cry: *The police fired tear gas into the crowd.*

'tear-stained *adj* streaked with tears: *a tear-stained face.*

in tears crying; weeping: *She was in tears over the broken doll.*

tear[2] /teə(r)/ *v* **1** to make a split or hole in something with a sudden pulling action; to remove something by this sort of action: *He tore the photograph into pieces*; *You've torn a hole in your jacket*; *I tore the picture out of the magazine.* **2** to become torn: *Newspapers tear easily.* **3** to rush: *He tore along the road.* — *n* a hole or split made by tearing: *There's a tear in my dress.*

tear apart to pull something into pieces: *He was so angry, he tore the book apart.*

tear away to force someone to stop doing something: *Can you tear yourself away from your computer for a few minutes?*

torn between one thing and another having a very difficult choice to make between two things: *He was torn between obedience to his parents and loyalty to his friends.*

tear down to bring a building *etc* to the ground: *The statue that had stood in the square for years was torn down in minutes.*

tear up to tear into pieces: *She tore up the letter.*

tear; tore /tɔː(r)/; **torn** /tɔːn/: *John tore his trousers on the fence; Jim had torn the newspaper into small pieces.*

'tearaway *n* a wild, badly behaved young person: *He used to be a tearaway but he has become kind and polite since he got a job.*

tease /tiːz/ *v* **1** to annoy or irritate on purpose: *He's teasing the cat.* **2** to annoy or laugh at someone playfully: *His school-friends tease him about his size.* — *n* someone who enjoys teasing others: *He's a tease!* **'teasing** *adj.* **'teasingly** *adv.*

'teaser *n* a puzzle or difficult problem: *This question is a teaser.*

tea-set /'tiːsɛt/ or **tea-service** /'tiːsɜːvɪs/ *n* a set of cups, saucers and plates, and sometimes a teapot and milk-jug.

teaspoon /'tiːspuːn/ *n* **1** a small spoon for use with a teacup: *I need a teaspoon to stir my tea.* **2** a teaspoonful: *a teaspoon of salt.* **'teaspoonful** *n*: *two teaspoonfuls of salt.*

The plural of **teaspoonful** is **teaspoonfuls** (not **teaspoonsful**).

teat /tiːt/ *n* the part of a female animal's breast or udder through which milk passes to the baby; a nipple.

technical /'tɛknɪkəl/ *adj* having to do with science, or with scientific, mechanical and industrial skills: *a technical college; technical drawing; Myopia is the technical term for short-sightedness.* **'technically** *adv.*

techni'cality *n* one of the details involved in a particular process or subject: *I don't know anything about the technicalities of computing.*

technician /tɛk'nɪʃən/ *n* a person specialized or skilled in a practical art: *She trained as a dental technician; laboratory technicians.*

technique /tɛk'niːk/ *n* the way in which something is, or should be, practised: *They admired the pianist's faultless technique.*

technology /tɛk'nɒlədʒɪ/ *n* the study of science applied to practical purposes: *a college of science and technology.* **techno'logical** *adj.* **tech'nologist** *n.*

teddy /'tɛdɪ/ *n* a child's stuffed toy bear (also called a **'teddy-bear**).

tedious /'tiːdɪəs/ *adj* boring; continuing for a long time: *a tedious lesson.* **'tediously** *adv.* **'tediousness** *n.*

teem /tiːm/ *v* **1** to be very full of people or animals that are moving about: *On Saturdays the supermarket teems with shoppers; The pond was teeming with fish.* **2** to rain heavily: *It teemed with rain all night; The rain was teeming down.* **'teeming** *adj.*

teenage /'tiːneɪdʒ/ *adj* of, or in, the teens; belonging to people in their teens: *teenage children; teenage clothes; teenage behaviour.* **'teenager** *n* someone who is in their teens.

teens /tiːnz/ *n* **1** the years of your life between the ages of thirteen and nineteen: *She's in her teens.* **2** the numbers from thirteen to nineteen.

tee shirt /'tiːʃɜːt/ a light shirt of knitted cotton *etc*, usually with short sleeves (also spelt **T-shirt**).

teeth the plural of **tooth**.

teethe /tiːð/ *v* to grow your first teeth: *The baby keeps crying because he is teething.*

teething troubles the problems and difficulties that occur when a system or machine *etc* is new.

teetotal /tiː'toʊtəl/ *adj* never drinking alcoholic drinks: *The whole family is teetotal.*

tee'totaller *n* a person who never drinks alcoholic drinks.

telecast /'tɛlɪkɑːst/ *n* a television broadcast. — *v* to broadcast on television.

telecommunications /tɛlɪkəmjuːnɪ'keɪʃənz/ *n* the science of sending messages or information by telephone, telegraph, radio, computer *etc*.

telegram /'tɛlɪgram/ *n* a message sent by telegraph: *He received a telegram wishing him a happy birthday.*

telegraph /'tɛlɪgrɑːf/ *n* a system of sending messages using either wires and electricity or radio: *Send this message by telegraph.* — *v*: *He telegraphed the time of his arrival; He telegraphed to say when he would arrive.*

telepathy /tɪ'lɛpəθɪ/ *n* the communication of thoughts or ideas directly from one person's mind to another person's mind: *He knew exactly what I was thinking — it must have been telepathy.* **tele'pathic** *adj.*

telephone /'tɛlɪfoʊn/, often shortened to **phone**, *n* an instrument for speaking to someone from a distance, using either an electric current which passes along a wire, or radio waves: *I spoke to her yesterday on the telephone; I'll let you know by telephone what time I'm arriving.* — *adj*: *a telephone operator; a telephone number.* — *v*: *I'll telephone you tomorrow; He said he would telephone his time of arrival; Please would you* *telephone for a taxi?*; *Can you telephone Australia from England?*

> to **telephone** (not **telephone to**) someone.

te'lephonist *n* a person who operates a telephone switchboard in a telephone exchange.

telephone booth or **telephone box** a small room or compartment containing a telephone for public use.

telephone directory a book containing a list of the names, addresses and telephone numbers of all the people with telephones in a particular area: *Look them up in the telephone directory.*

telephone exchange the building where telephone lines are connected when you make telephone calls.

telephone number the number you dial in order to speak to someone on the telephone.

telephoto lens /tɛlɪfoʊtoʊ'lɛnz/ a camera lens which produces large images of distant or small objects.

telescope /'tɛlɪskoʊp/ *n* a kind of tube containing lenses through which distant objects appear closer: *He looked at the ship through his telescope.* — *v* to push or be pushed together so that one part slides inside another, like the parts of a closing telescope: *The crash telescoped the railway coaches.*

teletext /'tɛlɪtɛkst/ *n* a service which provides news and information that can be seen in written form on television.

televise /'tɛlɪvaɪz/ *v* to send a picture by television: *The football match was televised.*

television /'tɛlɪvɪʒən/, often shortened to **TV** /tiːviː/, *n* the sending of pictures from a distance, and the showing of them on a screen; an apparatus (also called a **television set**) with a screen for receiving these pictures: *When was television invented?*; *Do you often watch television?*; *I saw the film on television*; *Our television set is broken*; *We've got two televisions.*

> to **watch** (not **see**) television.

telex /'tɛlɛks/ *n* **1** a machine which you type a message into and which then sends that message to be printed out by another machine at a distance: *We use the office telex to send messages abroad.* **2** a message sent by such a machine: *I sent him a telex with the information.*

tell /tɛl/ *v* **1** to inform: *I told her I had had a sort of breakdown*; *Peter told me the news, and then told it all to Janet*; *Can you tell me what time the next train leaves?*; *Philip, tell me how you spell 'beautiful'.* **2** to order; to command; to suggest; to warn: *I told him to go away.* **3** to utter: *to tell lies*; *to tell the truth*; *to tell a story.* **4** to distinguish; to see a difference; to know or decide: *Can you tell the difference between the twins?*; *I can't tell one from the other*; *You can tell if the meat is cooked by the colour.* **5** to give away a secret: *You mustn't tell or we'll get into trouble.*

> **tell**; **told** /toʊld/; **told**: *He told me the news*; *You should have told me before.*

'telling *adj* effective; significant: *He made several telling remarks that evening.*

tell off to scold: *The teacher told me off for not doing my homework.* **telling-'off** *n*: *He gave me a good telling-off.*

'telltale *adj* showing or suggesting something that is secret or hidden: *I saw the telltale tears in her eyes.* **'tell-tale** *n* a person who tells tales.

tell tales to give someone in authority information about someone who has done wrong: *You mustn't tell tales.*

tell the time to know what time it is by looking at a clock *etc* or by any other means: *He can tell the time from the position of the sun*; *Could you tell me the time, please?*

you never can tell it is possible: *It might rain — you never can tell.*

'teller *n* **1** a bank employee who receives money from and pays it out to the bank's clients. **2** a person who counts the votes at an election.

temper /'tɛmpə(r)/ *n* **1** a mood: *He's in a bad temper.* **2** a tendency to become unpleasant when angry: *He has a terrible temper.* **3** an angry state: *She's in a temper.*

-tempered: *good-tempered*; *bad-tempered*; *sweet-tempered.*

keep your temper not to lose your temper: *He was very annoyed but he kept his temper.*
lose your temper to show anger: *He lost his temper and shouted at me.*

temperament /'tɛmpərəmənt/ *n* the way you feel and behave: *a person of nervous temperament.*

tempera'mental *adj* easily getting upset or excited.

temperate /'tɛmpərət/ *adj* neither very hot nor very cold: *The British climate is temperate.*

temperature /'tɛmprətʃə(r)/ *n* **1** a degree of cold or heat: *The food must be kept at a low temperature.* **2** a level of body heat that is higher than normal; a fever: *She had a temperature and wasn't feeling well.*
take someone's temperature to measure someone's body heat, using a thermometer.

temple[1] /'tɛmpəl/ *n* a building in which people worship: *a Hindu temple.*

temple[2] /'tɛmpəl/ *n* either of the flat parts of your head at the side of your forehead: *The stone hit him on the temple.*

tempo /'tɛmpoʊ/, *plural* **tempos** or **tempi** /'tɛmpiː/, *n* **1** the speed at which a piece of music is played: *a typical waltz tempo.* **2** a rate or speed: *the tempo of life.*

temporary /'tɛmpərəri/ *adj* lasting, acting, used *etc* for a short time only: *a temporary job*; *He made a temporary repair.* **'temporarily** *adv.* **'temporariness** *n.*

tempt /tɛmpt/ *v* to make someone want to do something especially something wrong: *He was tempted to steal the purse when he saw it lying on the table*; *The sight of the blue sea and the golden sand tempted them into the water for a swim.*
temp'tation *n* the tempting of someone; something that tempts you: *He knew cigarettes were bad for him, but he found it hard to resist the temptation to smoke*; *We are all surrounded by temptations.*
'tempting *adj* attractive: *That cake looks tempting.* **'temptingly** *adv.*

ten /tɛn/ *n* **1** the number 10. **2** the age of 10. — *adj* **1** 10 in number. **2** aged 10.
tens *n* the two-figure numbers, from 10 to 99.
tenth /tɛnθ/ *n* one of ten equal parts. — *n, adj* the next after the ninth.

tenacious /tɪ'neɪʃəs/ *adj* determined or obstinate: *She is very tenacious and will not give up looking for a job until she has found one.* **tenacity** /tɪ'næsɪti/ *n.*

tenant /'tɛnənt/ *n* someone who pays rent to you for the use of a house, building, land *etc* that you own: *A tenant can complain to an authority if the rent that his landlord charges is too high.*

tend[1] /tɛnd/ *v* to keep something in good condition; to look after someone who is ill: *He's in the garden tending his roses*; *She tended her sick mother all weekend.*

tend[2] /tɛnd/ *v* to be likely to do something; to do something frequently: *Plants tend to die in hot weather*; *He tends to get angry too easily.*

tendency *n* likelihood; inclination: *He has a tendency to forget things.*

tender[1] /'tɛndə(r)/ *adj* **1** soft; not hard; not tough: *This meat is nice and tender.* **2** sore; painful when touched: *His injured leg is still tender.* **3** loving; gentle: *She had a tender heart.* **'tenderness** *n.* **'tenderly** *adv.*
tender-'hearted *adj* kind; easily made to feel pity. **tender-'heartedness** *n.*

tender[2] /'tɛndə(r)/ *v* to offer or present something as a suggestion: *The minister was forced to tender his resignation*; *Two more companies have tendered for the building contract.* — *n.*

tendon /'tɛndən/ *n* a cord of strong tissue that joins a muscle to a bone: *She strained a tendon in her ankle playing tennis.*

tendril /'tɛndrɪl/ *n* a thin, curling part of a climbing plant that attaches itself to a support: *The tendrils of the vine twisted round the fence.*

tennis /'tɛnɪs/ *n* a game for two or four players who use rackets to hit a ball to each other over a net. — *adj*: *a tennis match.*

tenor /'tɛnə(r)/ *n* the highest singing voice for a man.

tense[1] /tɛns/ *n* a form of a verb that shows the time of its action in relation to the time of speaking: *a verb in the past tense*; *the present tense*; *the future tense.*

tense[2] /tɛns/ *adj* **1** anxious; full of anxiety; nervous: *The crowd was tense with excitement*; *a tense situation.* **2** tightly stretched: *All the muscles in her neck felt tense.* — *v* to make or become tight: *He tensed his muscles.* **'tensely** *adv.*

> **tense**, adjective, has no **d** in it: *The children were tense with expectation.*

tension /'tɛnʃən/ *n* **1** the condition of being pulled or stretched tight. **2** mental strain; anxiety: *She is suffering from tension*; *the tensions of modern life.*

tent /tɛnt/ *n* a movable shelter made of canvas or another material: *We went camping and slept in a tent*; *Where shall we pitch our tent?*

tentacle /'tɛntɪkəl/ *n* a long, thin, arm-like or horn-like part of an animal, used to feel, grasp *etc*: *An octopus has eight tentacles.*

tentative /'tɛntətɪv/ *adj* **1** cautious and careful: *She took a tentative step towards him.* **2** not completed or finalized: *tentative arrangements.* **'tentatively** *adv.*

tenterhooks /'tɛntəhʊks/: **on tenterhooks** nervous, anxious or worried: *I've been on*

tenterhooks all day waiting to hear if she's had her baby.
tenuous /ˈtɛnjʊəs/ *adj* slight or weak: *His excuse sounded tenuous.*
tenure /ˈtɛnjə(r)/ or /ˈtɛnjʊə(r)/ *n* the length of time a person holds a position or property: *He made several important changes during his brief tenure as chairman.*
tepid /ˈtɛpɪd/ *adj* slightly warm: *I don't like drinking tepid water — I prefer it cold.*
term /tɜːm/ *n* **1** a limited period of time: *a term of imprisonment; a term of office.* **2** a division of a school or university year: *the autumn term.* **3** a word; an expression: *Myopia is a medical term for short-sightedness.* — *v* to name; to call: *Pictures that try to represent feelings or ideas rather than real objects are termed 'abstract'.*
terms *n* **1** the conditions of an agreement: *The directors of the firm and the employees had a meeting to arrange terms for a new pay settlement.* **2** a way of looking at a subject: *I'd enjoy the job, but in terms of my career, it wouldn't be a very good move.* **3** a relationship between people: *They are on friendly terms.*
in the long or **short term** to do with the near future or extending over a longer period of time: *We can expect large profits in the long term, but we must have short-term cuts first.*
terminal /ˈtɜːmɪnəl/ *n* **1** a building containing the arrival and departure areas for passengers at an airport; a building in the centre of a city or town where passengers can buy tickets for air travel *etc* and can be transported by bus *etc* to an airport: *an air terminal.* **2** a large station at either end of a railway line; a station for long-distance buses: *a bus terminal.* **3** computer equipment (usually a keyboard and screen) which allows you to use a central computer. — *adj* causing death: *a terminal illness.* **'terminally** *adv.*
terminate /ˈtɜːmɪneɪt/ *v* to bring or come to an end or limit: *The teacher terminated the lesson five minutes early; to terminate a conversation.* **termi'nation** *n.*
terminology /ˌtɜːmɪˈnɒlədʒɪ/ *n* the words and phrases used in a particular subject: *computer terminology.*
terminus /ˈtɜːmɪnəs/, *plural* **terminuses** or **termini** /ˈtɜːmɪnaɪ/, *n* the end of a railway or bus route: *I get off at the bus terminus.*
termite /ˈtɜːmaɪt/ *n* a pale-coloured, wood-eating insect, like an ant.

terrace /ˈtɛrɪs/ *n* **1** one of a number of flat strips of ground, cut like large steps into the side of a hillside: *Vines are grown on terraces on the hillside.* **2** an open paved area next to a house or hotel, where people sit, eat *etc*: *On hot evenings, we often have dinner outside on the terrace.* **3** a row of houses joined to each other by their side walls. **4** a street with rows of terraced houses; a word used in the names of certain streets: *She lives in Gladstone Terrace.*
'terraced *adj*: *terraced rice fields.*
terraced house *n* one of a row of houses joined to each other by their side walls.
terrain /təˈreɪn/ *n* an area of land, especially with regard to its features: *mountainous terrain.*
terrapin /ˈtɛrəpɪn/ *n* a small turtle that lives on land and in fresh water: *He keeps two terrapins as pets.*
terrible /ˈtɛrɪbəl/ *adj* **1** very bad: *That music is terrible!* **2** causing great pain, suffering *etc*: *It was a terrible disaster.* **3** causing great fear or horror: *The noise of the guns was terrible.*
'terribly *adv* **1** very: *She is terribly clever.* **2** very badly: *Does your leg hurt terribly?*
terrier /ˈtɛrɪə(r)/ *n* any of several breeds of small dog.
terrific /təˈrɪfɪk/ *adj* **1** marvellous; wonderful: *a terrific party.* **2** very great, powerful *etc*: *Joan gave Alan a terrific slap.* **ter'rifically** *adv.*
terrify /ˈtɛrɪfaɪ/ *v* to frighten someone very much: *She was terrified by the thunder.* **'terrifying** *adj.*
territorial /ˌtɛrɪˈtɔːrɪəl/ *adj* having to do with national territory: *territorial boundaries.*
territory /ˈtɛrɪtərɪ/ *n* **1** a stretch of land; a region: *They explored the territory around the North Pole.* **2** the land under the control of a ruler or state: *British territory.*
terror /ˈtɛrə(r)/ *n* very great fear; something that causes this: *John's terror increased as the door swung slowly open; I have a terror of spiders; the terrors of war.*
'terrorist *n* someone who tries to frighten people or governments into doing what he wants by using violence or threats: *The plane was hijacked by terrorists.* — *adj*: *terrorist activities.* **'terrorism** *n.*
'terrorize *v* **1** to frighten very much: *A lion escaped from the zoo and terrorized the whole town.* **2** to frighten someone into doing what you want by threatening them. **terrori'zation** *n.*

'terror-stricken *adj* feeling very great fear: *The children were terror-stricken.*

terse /tɜːs/ *adj* brief and rather rude: *She wrote a terse reply to his letter.*

test /tɛst/ *n* **1** a set of questions or exercises to find out your ability, knowledge *etc*; a short examination: *an arithmetic test.* **2** something done to find out whether something is in good condition *etc*: *a blood test.* **3** an event, situation *etc* that shows how good something is: *The frightening experience was a test of his courage.* **4** a way to find out if something exists or is present: *She was given a test for cancer.* — *v*: *The students were tested on their French; They tested the new aircraft; Have you ever had your blood tested?; to test someone for cancer.*

> A **test** is a short examination: *to come top in the arithmetic test.*
> A **text** is the written or printed words of something: *They read the text of the play.*

testament /'tɛstəmənt/ *n* something that proves that another thing is true: *The quality of her work is a testament to her talent.*

testicle /'tɛstɪkəl/ *n* one of the two glands in the male body in which sperm is produced.

testify /'tɛstɪfaɪ/ *v* to provide information or evidence, especially in a court of law; to be a witness in a legal case: *She testified that her husband had been at home on the night of the murder.*

testimonial /tɛstɪ'moʊnɪəl/ *n* a written statement about someone's character, skills and abilities: *He asked his previous employer for a testimonial when he applied for the new job.*

testimony /'tɛstɪmənɪ/ *n* the statement made by a witness in a court of law: *The jury listened carefully to her testimony.*

tetanus /'tɛtə'nəs/ *n* a disease that causes muscles, especially in the jaw, to go stiff.

tether /'tɛðə(r)/ *n* a rope for tying an animal to a post *etc*. — *v*: *He tethered the goat to the post.*

text /tɛkst/ *n* in a book, the written or printed words: *The illustrations have to be fitted into the text after the text is printed.*

> See **test**.

'textbook *n* a book containing information on a particular subject, used by students in schools, *etc*: *a biology textbook used in secondary schools.*

textile /'tɛkstaɪl/ *n* a cloth or fabric made by weaving: *woollen textiles.* — *adj*: *the textile industry.*

texture /'tɛkstʃə(r)/ *n* **1** the way something feels when touched *etc*: *the texture of wood, stone, skin etc.* **2** the way that a piece of cloth is woven: *the loose texture of this material.*

than /ðən/ or /ðæn/ *conjunction* a word used in comparisons: *It is easier than I thought; I sing better than he does; The sky was clearer than it had been for a week.*

> He is stronger **than** (not then) **I am** or **than me**.

> She likes dancing better than **I** (like dancing) or better than **I do**.
> She likes you better than (she likes) **me**.

thank /θæŋk/ *v* to express gratitude to someone for something they have given you or done for you: *He thanked me for the present.*

'thankful *adj* grateful; relieved and happy: *He was thankful that the journey was over; a thankful sigh.* **'thankfully** *adv*. **'thankfulness** *n*.

'thankless *adj* for which no-one is grateful: *Collecting taxes is a thankless task.* **'thanklessly** *adv*.

thanks *n* expression of gratitude: *Please give her my thanks for all her kindness.* — used in expressing gratitude; thank you: *Thanks very much for your present; Thanks a lot!; No, thanks; Yes, thanks.*

> There is no singular form of **thanks**.

'Thanksgiving *n* a public holiday in America and Canada.

thank God, thank goodness or **thank heavens** used to express relief about something: *Thank heavens she escaped in time; Thank goodness for weekends — I need a rest!*

thanks to because of: *Thanks to Alan's bad behaviour, the whole class had to stay in at lunchtime.*

thank you I thank you: *Thank you very much for your help; No, thank you.*

that /ðæt/ or /ðət/, *plural* **those** /ðəʊz/, *adj* used to refer to a person, thing *etc* that is some distance away from you, or has already been mentioned *etc*: *Don't take this book — take that one; Who is that man over there?; At that time, I was living in Japan; When are you going to return those books I* *lent you?* — *pron* **1** used to refer to a thing, person *etc* that is some distance away from you, or has already been mentioned *etc*: *What is that you've got in your hand?*; *Who is that?*; *That is the Prime Minister*; *Those were my instructions.* **2** used in a clause that describes or distinguishes someone or something. Note that you can leave 'that' out, if it is the object of the clause: *Where is the parcel that arrived this morning?*; *Here is the book (that) you wanted*; *Who is the man (that) you were talking to?* — *conjunction* **1** (often left out) used after verbs like **know**, **say**, **tell** *etc*: *He told me (that) she was ill*; *I know (that) you didn't do it*; *I was surprised (that) he had gone.* **2** used in wishes *etc*: *Oh, that the holidays would come!*

like that in that way: *Don't hold it like that — you'll break it!*

that is or **that is to say** used to explain more clearly something that you have just said: *I once painted this house, that is, I painted a picture of it.*

that's that there is no more to be said or done: *I'm not going and that's that.*

thatch /θatʃ/ *n* straw, rushes *etc* used as a roofing material for houses. — *v* to cover the roof of a house with thatch.

thatched *adj*: *thatched cottages.*

that'd /ðatɪd/ short for **that had** or **that would**.

that'll /ðatəl/ short for **that will**.

that's /ðats/ short for **that is** or **that has**.

thaw /θɔː/ *v* **1** to melt; to make or become liquid: *The snow thawed quickly.* **2** to defrost: *Frozen food must be thawed before cooking.* — *n* the melting of ice and snow at the end of winter; the change of weather that causes this: *The thaw has come early this year.*

the /ðə/, /ðɪ/ or /ðiː/ *adj* **1** used to refer to a person, thing *etc* mentioned previously, described in a following phrase, or already known: *Where is the book I put on the table?*; *My mug is the tall blue one*; *Switch the light off!* **2** used with a singular noun to mean any of the people, things *etc* of the same kind: *The horse is a beautiful animal*; *Always give your name when you answer the telephone*; *You play the piano very well.* **3** used before an adjective to make a usually plural noun: *Take care of the sick and elderly.* **4** used in titles and names or to refer to someone or something when there is only one: *the Duke of Edinburgh*; *the Indian Ocean*. **5** used after a preposition with words referring to a unit of quantity, time *etc*: *In this job we are paid by the hour*; *to buy fruit by the kilo.* **6** used with superlative adjectives and adverbs: *He is the kindest man I know*; *Who can run the fastest?* **7** used with comparative adjectives to show that someone or something *etc* is better, worse *etc* because of something: *He has had a week's holiday and looks the better for it.*

> **the** is pronounced /ðiː/ before words beginning with **a, e, i, o, u**, and **h** when **h** is not sounded: *the apples*; *the umbrella*; *the hour*.
> **the** is pronounced /ðə/ before all other letters, and **u** when its sound is /juː/: *the book*; *the house*; *the university*.

the..., the... used to show the connection or relationship between two actions, states, processes *etc*: *The harder you work, the more you earn.*

theatre /'θɪətə(r)/ *n* **1** a place where plays, operas *etc* are publicly performed. **2** plays in general; any theatre: *Are you going to the theatre tonight?* **3** a room in a hospital where surgical operations are performed.

the'atrical *adj* **1** to do with theatres, plays or acting. **2** artificial behaviour, done for people to take notice of: *He gave us a theatrical wave and walked out of the room.*

theft /θɛft/ *n* stealing: *He was jailed for theft.*

their /ðɛə(r)/ *adj* **1** belonging to them: *This is their car.* **2** used instead of **his** or **her** where a person of unknown sex is referred to: *When you see someone in trouble, do you go to their aid?* **3** used instead of **his or her** when people of both sexes are referred to: *Has everyone got their books ready?*

> See **there**.

theirs /ðɛəz/ *pron* something *etc* belonging to them: *These books are theirs*; *He is a friend of theirs*; *Is this their house? No, theirs is on the corner.*

them /ðɛm/ or /ðəm/ *pron* (used as the object of a verb or preposition) **1** people, animals, things *etc*: *Let's invite them to dinner*; *What will you do with them?* **2** used instead of **him**, **him or her** *etc* where a person of unknown sex or people of both sexes are referred to: *If anyone touches that, I'll hit them.*

them'selves *pron* **1** used as the object of a verb or preposition when people, animals *etc* are both the subject and the object: *They hurt themselves*; *Those who have committed* themselves to the tradition model of education. **2** used to emphasize **they**, **them** or the names of people, animals *etc*: *They themselves did nothing wrong*; *The English themselves don't speak English very well.* **3** without help *etc*: *They decided to do it themselves.*

theme /θi:m/ *n* the subject of a discussion, essay *etc*: *The theme for tonight's talk is education.*

then /ðɛn/ *adv* **1** at that time, in the past or future: *I was at school then*; *If you're coming next week, I'll see you then*; *Sometimes my legs went weak — then I had to steady myself against a wall.* **2** (used with prepositions) that time: *John should be here by then*; *I'll be home before then*; *Goodbye till then.* **3** after that: *I had a drink, and then I went home.* **4** in that case: *He might not give us the money and then what should we do?* **5** often used at the end of sentences in which you ask for an explanation, opinion *etc*, or in which you show surprise *etc*: *What do you think of that, then?* — *conjunction* in that case; as a result: *If you're tired, then you must rest.*

> Let's visit the museum and **then** (not **than**) the zoo.

thence /ðɛns/ *adv* an old-fashioned word meaning from the place that was just mentioned: *We travelled overland to San Francisco and thence we continued west by ship.*

theology /θɪˈɒlədʒɪ/ *n* **1** the study of God and religion: *She has a degree in theology.* **2** a particular system of religious belief: *Muslim theology.* **theoˈlogical** *adj*.

theoretical /θɪəˈrɛtɪkəl/ *adj* based on theory and ideas rather than practical knowledge or experience: *theoretical physics.*

theoˈretically *adv* possible but not absolutely certain to happen in reality: *He should be here by ten o'clock theoretically.*

theory /ˈθɪərɪ/ *n* **1** an idea or explanation that has not yet been proved to be correct: *John had a theory about the origin of fire*; *There are many theories about the origin of life.* **2** the main ideas in an art, science *etc* as opposed to the practice of actually doing it: *A musician has to study both the theory and practice of music*; *This helps students relate theory to practice.*

in theory as an idea; according to the facts: *The journey takes three hours in theory, but four in practice, because there are always delays at the roadworks.*

therapeutic /θɛrəˈpju:tɪk/ *adj* **1** of or relating to the healing of diseases: *Some herbs have therapeutic effects.* **2** making you feel relaxed: *Laughter can be very therapeutic.*

therapy /ˈθɛrəpɪ/ *n* the treatment of diseases without the use of surgery, and often without drugs: *She tried a course of water therapy for her skin problems.* **ˈtherapist** *n*.

there /ðɛə(r)/ *adv* **1** at, in, or to that place: *He lives there*; *Don't go there.* **2** used to begin sentences in which you announce a fact *etc*: *There has been an accident at the factory*; *There seems to be something wrong.* **3** at that point: *Don't stop there — tell me what happened next!* **4** used to draw attention to someone or something: *There she goes now!*; *There it is!* — used in various other ways: *There, now — things aren't as bad as they seem*; *There! That's that job done*; *There! I said you would hurt yourself, and now you have!*

> **there** means in that place; **their** means belonging to **them**: *Tell them to hang their coats over there.*

ˈthereabouts *adv* about there; about that: *a hundred or thereabouts*; *at three o'clock or thereabouts*; *She lives in York, or thereabouts.*

thereˈafter *adv* after that.

thereˈby *adv* in that way.

therefore /ˈðɛəfɔ:(r)/ *adv* for that reason: *Tony works hard, and therefore has a good chance of winning the prize.*

there's /ðɛəz/ short for **there is**.

there you are 1 used when giving something to someone: *'May I borrow your pen please?' 'There you are.'* **2** used to finish an explanation of a situation: *Things could be better, but there you are.* **3** used to point out that you were right about something: *There you are — I knew you could do it!*

thermal *adj* **1** of or relating to heat: *thermal energy.* **2** designed to keep the body warm: *thermal underclothes.* — *n* a current of warm air used by birds and gliders to move upwards: *Hang-gliders need to know how to use thermals if they are to stay in the air.*

thermometer /θəˈmɒmɪtə(r)/ *n* an instrument used for measuring temperature, especially your body temperature: *The nurse took his temperature with a thermometer.*

thermostat /ˈθɜ:məstat/ *n* a device that automatically controls the temperature of a room or of water in a boiler, by switching the heating system on or off.

thesaurus /θɪˈsɔːrəs/, *plural* **thesauruses**, *n* a book which lists words according to sense: *She used her thesaurus to find words with related meanings.*

these plural of **this**.

thesis /ˈθiːsɪs/, *plural* **theses** /ˈθiːsiːz/ *n* a long written report based on original research, and often done as part of a university degree: *She spent four years writing her thesis.*

they /ðeɪ/ *pron* (used as the subject of a verb) **1** people, animals or things: *If you're looking for the children, they are in the garden.* **2** used instead of **he** or **she** when a person of unknown sex is referred to: *'There's someone on the telephone.' 'What do they want?'* **3** used instead of **he or she** when people of both sexes are being referred to: *If anyone does that, they are to be severely punished.*

they'd /ðeɪd/ short for **they had** or **they would**.

they'll /ðeɪl/ short for **they will**.

they're /ðeə(r)/ or /ˈdeɪə(r)/ short for **they are**.

they've /ðeɪv/ short for **they have**.

thick /θɪk/ *adj* **1** having a fairly large distance between opposite sides; not thin: *a thick book*; *thick walls*; *thick glass.* **2** having a certain distance between opposite sides: *The glass is a centimetre thick.* **3** containing solid matter; not flowing easily when poured: *thick soup.* **4** dense: *a thick forest; thick hair.* **5** difficult to see through: *thick fog.* **6** full of, covered with *etc*: *The room was thick with dust; The air was thick with smoke.* **7** not clear: *a thick accent; His voice was thick with emotion.* **8** an unkind word meaning not intelligent. — *n* the thickest part: *in the thick of the forest.* **'thickly** *adv*. **'thickness** *n*.

'thicken *v* to make or become thick or thicker: *I thickened the sauce by adding some flour; The fog thickened and we could no longer see the road.*

in the thick of something very busy with something: *We were in the thick of our holiday preparations when I broke my leg.*

through thick and thin no matter what happens; at all times: *He has been my friend through thick and thin.*

thicket /ˈθɪkɪt/ *n* a group of trees or bushes growing closely together: *He hid in a thicket.*

thick-skinned /θɪkˈskɪnd/ *adj* not easily hurt or offended: *You won't upset her — she's very thick-skinned.*

thief /θiːf/, *plural* **thieves** /θiːvz/, *n* a person who steals: *The thief got away with all my money; a gang of thieves.*

thigh /θaɪ/ *n* the part of your leg between your knee and hip.

thimble /ˈθɪmbəl/ *n* a cap to protect your finger and push the needle with when you are sewing.

thin /θɪn/ *adj* **1** having a short distance between opposite sides; not thick: *thin paper; The walls of these houses are too thin.* **2** having not much flesh; not fat: *She looks very thin in that dress.* **3** not containing any solid matter; lacking in taste; containing a lot of water or too much water: *thin soup.* **4** not dense or crowded; not thick: *His hair is getting rather thin; a thin audience.* **5** not believable: *a thin excuse.* — *v* to make or become thin or thinner: *The crowd thinned after the parade was over.* **'thinly** *adv*. **'thinness** *n*.

thin air nowhere: *He disappeared into thin air.*

thing /θɪŋ/ *n* **1** an object; something that is not living: *What do you use that thing for?* **2** any fact, quality, idea *etc* that you can think of or refer to: *Music is a wonderful thing; I hope I haven't done the wrong thing; That was a stupid thing to do.* **3** something that is suitable, fashionable or popular: *The thing with the teenagers around here is to have a car.*

things *n* **1** clothes and other possessions: *Take all your wet things off; Which cupboard shall I put my things in?* **2** life in general; the circumstances in your life: *Things are not that simple.*

a good thing lucky: *It's a good thing she wasn't alone when she fell.*

for one thing used to introduce one of the reasons for something: *She won't want to wear that — for one thing, she hates anything black.*

have a thing about to have a strong liking or disliking for: *I've got a thing about opera.*

the thing is ... the important fact or question is; the problem is: *The thing is, is he going to help us?*

think /θɪŋk/ *v* **1** to have or form ideas in your mind: *Can babies think?; I was thinking about my mother.* **2** to have or form opinions in your mind; to believe: *He thinks the world is flat; What do you think of his poem?; What do you think of his suggestion?; He thought me very stupid.* **3** to plan: *I must think what to do; I was thinking of going to London next week.* **4** to imagine or expect: *He seemed to* think he had no business being alive; I never thought this job could take so long. **5** to remember or understand: *Let me think what her name is*; *I couldn't think what he meant.* — *n*: *Go and have a think about it before you make up your mind.*

> **think**; **thought** /θɔːt/; **thought**: *I thought you were going to help me*; *They hadn't thought of the difficulties.*

'**thinker** *n* a person who thinks deeply; a wise man: *Gandhi was one of the world's great thinkers.*

'**thinking** *n* **1** the act of using your mind to think: *You must do some serious thinking before you decide on a career.* **2** your opinion or judgement: *What's your thinking on this?* — *adj* intelligent; interested in important and serious issues: *a magazine for thinking people.*

think better of something to change your mind and decide not to do something: *We were going to move house but we thought better of it.*

think well of or **think highly of** to have a good opinion of someone or something: *The teacher thinks very well of James*; *She thought highly of him.*

not think much of to have a very low opinion of someone or something: *He didn't think much of what I had done.*

think of 1 to remember to do something; to keep in your mind; to consider: *You always think of everything!*; *Have you thought of the cost?* **2** to remember: *I've met him before, but I can't think of his name!* **3** to be willing to do something: *I would never think of being rude to her.*

think out to plan; to work out in your mind: *He thought out the whole plan.*

think over to think carefully about something: *He thought it over, and decided not to go.*

think twice to hesitate before doing something; to decide not to do something: *I would think twice about going, if I were you.*

think up to invent: *He thought up a new game.*

thin-skinned /θɪn'skɪnd/ *adj* easily getting offended or feeling hurt: *Be careful what you say to him — he's very thin-skinned.*

third /θɜːd/ *n* one of three equal parts. — *n, adj* the next after the second. — *adv* in the third position: *John came first in the race, and I came third.*

'**thirdly** *adv*: *First, I haven't enough money, secondly, I'm too old, and thirdly, it's raining.*

third party a third person who is not directly involved in an action, contract *etc*: *Was there a third party present when you and she agreed to the sale?*

thirst /θɜːst/ *n* **1** the dryness you have in your mouth and throat when you need a drink: *I have a terrible thirst.* **2** a strong desire for something: *a thirst for knowledge.* — *v* to have a great desire for: *He's thirsting for revenge.*

'**thirsty** *adj* **1** suffering from thirst: *I'm so thirsty — I must have a drink.* **2** causing a thirst: *Digging the garden is thirsty work.* '**thirstily** *adv*. '**thirstiness** *n*.

thirteen /θɜː'tiːn/ *n* **1** the number 13. **2** the age of 13. — *adj* **1** 13 in number. **2** aged 13.

thirty /'θɜːtɪ/ *n* **1** the number 30. **2** the age of 30. — *adj* **1** 30 in number. **2** aged 30.

this /ðɪs/, *plural* **these** /ðiːz/, *adj* used to refer to a person, thing *etc* nearby, or belonging to the present, or just being mentioned: *This book is better than that one*; *I prefer these trousers*; *Jobs are hard to find these days*; *Come here this minute!* — *pron*: *Read this — you'll like it*; *This is my friend John Smith*; *I didn't think swimming would be as easy as this*; *This is the moment I've been waiting for.*

like this in this way: *It would be quicker if you did it like this.*

this and that various events, activities or subjects: *'What were you talking about?' 'Oh, just this and that.'*

thistle /'θɪsəl/ *n* a plant with prickly leaves and purple flowers.

thorn /θɔːn/ *n* a hard, sharp point sticking out from the stem of certain plants: *Roses have thorns.*

'**thorny** *adj* **1** covered with thorns: *a thorny branch.* **2** difficult; causing trouble *etc*: *a thorny problem.*

thorough /'θʌrə/ or /'θʌroʊ/ *adj* **1** very careful; attending to every detail: *He's a thorough worker.* **2** done with a high level of care, attention to detail *etc*: *His work is very thorough.* **3** complete; absolute: *a thorough waste of time.*

thoroughbred /'θʌrəbrɛd/ or /'θʌroʊbrɛd/ *n* a horse bred from pedigree parents, usually for racing: *She breeds and trains thoroughbreds.*

thoroughfare /'θʌrəfɛə(r)/ or /'θʌroʊfɛə(r)/ *n* a public road or street: *Don't park your car on a busy thoroughfare.*

thoroughgoing /θʌrə'goʊɪŋ/ *adj* very thorough, complete: *The government wanted to introduce thoroughgoing changes to the country's health service.*

thoroughly /'θʌrəlɪ/ *adv* **1** with great care; attending to every detail: *She doesn't do her job very thoroughly.* **2** completely; very: *Cleaning the house is a thoroughly boring job.*

thoroughness /'θʌrənɪs/ *n* care; attention to detail.

those plural of **that**.

though /ðoʊ/ *conjunction* in spite of the fact that; although: *He went out, though I told him not to; He went for a walk even though it was raining.* — *adv* however: *I wish I hadn't done it, though.*

as though as if: *You sound as though you've got a cold; It looked as though luck had deserted them.*

thought[1] *see* **think**.

thought[2] /θɔːt/ *n* **1** an idea: *I had a sudden thought.* **2** consideration: *After a great deal of thought we decided to emigrate to America.* **3** general opinion: *scientific thought.*

'thoughtful *adj* **1** thinking deeply: *You look thoughtful; a thoughtful mood.* **2** thinking of other people; considerate: *It was very thoughtful of you to buy her a present.* **'thoughtfully** *adv*. **'thoughtfulness** *n*.

'thoughtless *adj* not thinking about other people; inconsiderate: *thoughtless words.* **'thoughtlessly** *adv*. **'thoughtlessness** *n*.

-thought-out: *a well-thought-out essay.*

thousand /'θaʊzənd/, *plural* **'thousand** or **'thousands**, *n* **1** the number 1000: *one thousand; several thousand.* **2** a thousand pounds or dollars: *The car cost twelve thousand.* — *adj* 1000 in number.

> You use **thousand** (not **thousands**) after a number: *three thousand children.*

'thousandth *n* one of a thousand equal parts. — *n, adj* the last of a thousand people, things *etc*.

thousands of 1 several thousand: *He's got thousands of pounds in the bank.* **2** lots of: *I've read thousands of books.*

thrash /θraʃ/ *v* **1** to spank: *The child was soundly thrashed.* **2** to move about violently: *The wounded animal thrashed about on the ground.* **3** to defeat easily: *Our team was thrashed 18-nil.*

> to **thrash** (not **thresh**) someone for being naughty.

'thrashing *n*: *He needs a thrashing!*

thrash out to discuss a problem *etc* thoroughly and to come to an agreement about it: *The committee thrashed it out for three hours before coming to this decision.*

thread /θrɛd/ *n* **1** a thin strand of cotton, wool, silk *etc* especially when used for sewing: *a needle and some thread.* **2** the spiral ridge around a screw: *This screw has a worn thread.* **3** the connection between the various details of a story *etc*: *I've lost the thread of what he's saying.* — *v* **1** to pass a thread through: *I cannot thread this needle.* **2** to make your way through: *She threaded her way through the crowd.*

'threadbare *adj* old; worn thin: *He wears his old threadbare shorts to do the gardening.*

threat /θrɛt/ *n* **1** a warning that you are going to hurt or punish someone: *The teacher carried out his threat to punish the children.* **2** a sign of something dangerous or unpleasant which may be, or is, about to happen: *a threat of rain; the threat of war.* **3** a source of danger: *The Tirpitz was a major threat to Allied shipping.*

'threaten *v* **1** to make a threat: *She threatened to kill herself; He threatened me with violence.* **2** to be about to come: *A storm is threatening.* **'threatening** *adj*. **'threateningly** *adv*.

three /θriː/ *n* **1** the number 3. **2** the age of 3. — *adj* **1** 3 in number. **2** aged 3.

three-di'mensional *adj* having three dimensions — height, length and thickness (often shortened to **3-D** in talking about films *etc*): *A cube is a three-dimensional shape; 3-D photography.*

three-'quarter *adj* not quite full-length: *a three-quarter-length coat.*

three quarters: *I've dug three quarters of the garden — I'll dig the last quarter tomorrow.*

three quarters of an hour 45 minutes: *I'll be home in three quarters of an hour.*

thresh /θrɛʃ/ *v* to beat the stalks of corn in order to extract the grain.

> to **thresh** (not **thrash**) corn.

threshold /'θrɛʃhoʊld/ *n* **1** a doorway forming the entrance to a house *etc*: *He paused on the threshold and then entered.* **2** beginning: *She is on the threshold of a brilliant career.*

threw *see* **throw**.

thrift /θrɪft/ *n* the ability to save money *etc*; economy: *Thrift is important when you're running a household.* **'thrifty** *adj.* **'thriftily** *adv.* **'thriftiness** *n.*

thrill /θrɪl/ *v* to excite; to feel excitement: *She was thrilled by the invitation.* — *n* excitement; something that causes this: *the thrill of going abroad*; *It was a great thrill to win the first prize.*
'thriller *n* an exciting novel, film or play: *He gave me a thriller to read.*
'thrilling *adj* exciting.

thrive /θraɪv/ *v* to grow strong and healthy: *Children thrive on good food*; *The business is thriving.*
'thriving *adj* successful: *a thriving industry.*

throat /θrəʊt/ *n* **1** the back part of your mouth: *She has a sore throat.* **2** the front part of the neck: *She wore a silver brooch at her throat.*
'throaty *adj* deep; hoarse: *a throaty laugh.*
'throatily *adv.* **'throatiness** *n.*

throb /θrɒb/ *v* **1** to beat: *Her heart throbbed with excitement.* **2** to beat regularly like the heart: *The engine was throbbing gently.* **3** to beat regularly with pain; to be very painful: *My toe is throbbing.* — *n*: *the throb of the engine.*

throne /θrəʊn/ *n* the ceremonial chair of a king, queen, emperor *etc*, pope or bishop.

throng /θrɒŋ/ *n* a crowd: *Throngs of people gathered to see the Queen.* — *v* to crowd or fill: *People thronged the streets to see the President.*

throttle /'θrɒtəl/ *v* to kill by choking or strangling: *The scarf was too tight round her neck and she felt as if she was being throttled.* — *n* a pedal which controls a vehicle's speed by controlling the amount of fuel going into the engine: *She pressed down on the throttle and the car shot away.*

through /θruː/ *prep* **1** into something from one direction and out of it in the other: *The water flows through a pipe*; *He walked through the door.* **2** from side to side or end to end of something: *He walked through the town.* **3** from the beginning to the end of: *She read through the magazine.* **4** because of: *He lost his job through his own stupidity.* **5** by way of; with the help of: *He got the job through a friend.* **6** from ... to: *I go to work Monday through Friday.* — *adv*: *He opened the window and climbed through*; *I drove through to the other side of the town*; *Your shirt is wet through.* — *adj* taking you all the way without a change of train: *There isn't a through train to Perth — you'll have to change.*
be through with to be finished with a thing or person: *As far as I am concerned, you and I are through.*

throughout /θruːˈaʊt/ *prep* **1** in all parts of an area: *The police are seeking her throughout the country.* **2** from start to finish of something: *She complained throughout the journey.* — *adv* in every part: *The house was furnished throughout.*

throw /θrəʊ/ *v* **1** to send something through the air with force; to hurl; to fling: *He threw the ball to her*; *Then he threw his rake down.* **2** to make the rider fall off: *My horse threw me.* **3** to confuse: *Her remark threw me for a moment.* — *n*: *That was a good throw!*

> **throw; threw** /θruː/; **thrown** /θrəʊn/: *He threw the book across the room*; *Well thrown!*

throw away 1 to get rid of: *Why don't you throw away these old clothes?* **2** to waste: *We throw away thousands of pounds a year on things we don't need.*

throw in to include as a gift: *When I bought his car he threw in the radio and a box of tools.*

throw off 1 to get rid of: *She finally managed to throw off her cold.* **2** to take off quickly: *He threw off his coat.*

throw open to open suddenly and wide: *He threw open the door and walked in.*

throw out to get rid of: *I must throw out these old newspapers*; *You'll be thrown out of the school if you go on behaving badly.*

throw up a slang expression for to vomit: *She had too much to eat, and threw up on the way home.*

thru *see* **through**.

thrush /θrʌʃ/ *n* a bird with brown feathers and a spotted chest.

thrust /θrʌst/ *v* to push suddenly and violently: *He thrust his spade into the ground*; *She thrust forward through the crowd*; *She thrust her arm through his.* — *n* **1** a sudden or violent movement forward: *He made several thrusts with his sword.* **2** the most important idea or part of something: *He tried to explain the main thrust of his research to us.*

> **thrust; thrust; thrust**: *He thrust his arm through hers*; *Her belongings were thrust into a cupboard.*

thud /θʌd/ *n* a dull sound like that of something heavy falling to the ground: *He dropped the book with a thud.*

thug /θʌg/ *n* a violent or rough man: *He was attacked by thugs.*

thumb /θʌm/ *n* the short thick finger of the hand, set at a different angle from the other four. — *v* to turn over the pages of a book with your thumb and fingers: *She was thumbing through the dictionary.*

'**thumb-nail** *n* the nail on your thumb.

'**thumbprint** *n* a mark made by pressing your thumb on to a surface.

thumbs-'up *n* a sign expressing a wish for good luck, success *etc*: *He gave me the thumbs-up.*

thump /θʌmp/ *n* a heavy blow or hit: *They heard a thump on the door; A book fell off the shelf and gave him a thump on the head.* — *v*: *She thumped him with her fists; Their boots thumping up and down as they marched, the soldiers approached the lone figure.*

thunder /'θʌndə(r)/ *n* **1** the deep rumbling sound heard in the sky after a flash of lightning: *a clap or peal of thunder; a thunderstorm.* **2** a loud rumbling: *the thunder of horses' hooves.* — *v* **1** to rumble *etc*: *It rained and thundered all night.* **2** to make a noise like thunder: *The children thundered up the stairs.*

'**thunderbolt** *n* **1** a flash of lightning immediately followed by thunder. **2** a sudden great surprise: *The news of her father's arrest came as a complete thunderbolt.*

'**thunderous** *adj* very loud, like thunder: *The aeroplane made a thunderous noise as it passed overhead; thunderous applause.* '**thunderously** *adv*.

'**thunderstorm** *n* a storm with thunder and lightning and usually heavy rain.

See **rain**.

Thursday /'θɜːzdɪ/ *n* the fifth day of the week, the day following Wednesday.

thus /ðʌs/ *adv* in this or that way; therefore: *She offered to type his work out for him, and thus he was able to finish the job quickly.*

thwart /θwɔːt/ *v* to stop; to hinder; to prevent someone from doing something: *All his attempts to get rich were thwarted; The police managed to thwart the plot against the king; When you have a good plan, you don't like to be thwarted.*

tiara /tɪˈɑːrə/ *n* a jewelled ornament for your head, similar to a crown.

tick[1] /tɪk/ *n* **1** a regular sound, especially that of a watch, clock *etc*. **2** a moment: *Wait a tick!* — *v*: *Your watch ticks very loudly.*

tick[2] /tɪk/ *n* a mark (√) used to show that something is correct, has been noted *etc*. — *v* to put this mark beside an item or name on a list *etc*: *She ticked everything off on the list.*

tick someone off or **give someone a ticking-off** to scold someone: *The teacher gave me a ticking-off for being late.*

tick away or **tick by** to pass: *The hours ticked by and he still hadn't arrived.*

tick over to continue to operate at a slow rate: *We've got just enough work to keep the office ticking over until next year.*

tick[3] /tɪk/ *n* a type of small, blood-sucking insect: *Our dog has ticks.*

ticket /'tɪkɪt/ *n* **1** a piece of card or paper that gives you a right, for example to travel on a vehicle, enter a theatre *etc*: *a bus-ticket; a cinema-ticket.* **2** a label, especially giving the price on clothing for sale: *Don't forget to remove the ticket.*

tickle /'tɪkəl/ *v* **1** to touch a particular part of someone's skin lightly, making them laugh: *to tickle someone's feet; to tickle someone under the arms.* **2** to feel as if it is being touched in this way; to itch: *My nose tickles.* **3** to amuse: *The funny story tickled him.* — *n*: *She gave his toes a tickle; I've got a tickle in my throat that keeps making me cough.*

'**ticklish** *adj* **1** easily made to laugh when tickled: *Are you ticklish?* **2** not easy to manage; difficult: *a ticklish problem.*

tickled pink very pleased.

tidal /'taɪdəl/ *adj* having to do with the tide; affected by the tide: *a tidal river.*

tidal wave an enormous wave caused by an earthquake *etc*.

tide /taɪd/ *n* the regular movement of the sea in and out, happening twice a day: *It's high tide; When is low tide?; The tide is coming in; The tide is going out.*

tide someone over to help someone to get through a difficult period: *I borrowed some money to tide me over until I could get to the bank.*

tidy /'taɪdɪ/ *adj* **1** in good order; neat: *a tidy room; I'm usually a tidy person; Her hair never looks tidy.* **2** fairly big: *a tidy sum of money.* — *v* to put in good order; to make neat: *He tidied his papers; She was tidying the room up when her mother arrived.* '**tidily** *adv*. '**tidiness** *n*.

tidy away to put something away neatly: *She tidied the clothes away in the cupboard.*

tie /taɪ/ *v* **1** to fasten with a string, rope *etc*: *He tied the horse to a tree*; *The parcel was tied with string*; *I don't like this job — I hate being tied to a desk.* **2** to fasten by knotting; to make a knot or bow in: *He tied his shoelaces*; *The belt of this dress ties at the front.* **3** to score the same number of points *etc* in a game, competition *etc*: *Three people tied for first place.* — *n* **1** a strip of material worn tied round your neck under the collar of a shirt: *He wore a shirt and tie.* **2** something that joins: *the ties of friendship.* **3** an equal score or result in a game, competition *etc*; a draw. **4** a game or match to be played.

> tie; **'tying**; tied; tied: *He's tying his tie*; *You haven't tied your shoe-laces.*

tied up 1 busy: *I can't discuss this matter just now — I'm tied up with other things.* **2** connected with something: *I believe he's tied up with films.*

tie down to limit someone's freedom: *Her work tied her down.*

tie in with to be connected with; to fit in with: *The lecture will fit in with an exhibition of paintings to be shown at the same time.*

tie up to keep someone in a place by tying rope *etc* around them.

tier /tɪə(r)/ *n* a row of seats: *They sat in the first tier.*

tiff /tɪf/ *n* a slight quarrel: *She's had a tiff with her boyfriend.*

tiger /'taɪɡə(r)/ *n* a large wild animal of the cat family, with a striped coat.

> A tiger **roars** or **growls**.
> A baby tiger is a **cub**.
> A female tiger is a **'tigress**.
> A tiger lives in a **lair**.

tight /taɪt/ *adj* **1** fitting very closely: *I couldn't open the box because the lid was too tight*; *My trousers are too tight.* **2** not loose: *He made sure that the knot was tight.* **3** strict and very careful: *She keeps tight control over her temper.* **4** not allowing much time or room: *We'll have to keep to a very tight schedule if we are to finish the work in time*; *a tight space.* — *adv* **1** closely: *Hold me tight*; *a tight-fitting dress.* **2** with no extra room or space: *The room was packed tight with people.* **'tightness** *n.*

-tight sealed so as to keep something in or out: *airtight*; *watertight.*

'tighten *v* **1** to make or become tight or tighter: *to tighten your belt*; *to tighten your grip.* **2** to become stricter: *The laws concerning the sale of alcohol have been tightened up.*

'tightly *adv*: *She held his hand tightly*; *a tightly-packed suitcase.*

'tightrope *n* a tightly-stretched rope or wire on which acrobats balance.

tights *n* a close-fitting garment that covers your feet, legs and body to the waist: *She bought three pairs of tights*; *Are these your tights?*

> **tights** always takes a plural verb, but **a pair of tights** is singular.

tigress /'taɪɡrɪs/ *n* a female tiger.

tile /taɪl/ *n* **1** a piece of baked clay used in covering roofs, walls, floors *etc*: *Some of the tiles were blown off the roof during the storm.* **2** a piece of plastic material used for covering floors *etc.* — *v* to cover a roof, floor *etc* with tiles: *We had to have the roof tiled.*

tiled *adj* covered with tiles.

till¹ /tɪl/ *prep* up to a particular time: *I'll wait till six o'clock.* — *conjunction* up to the time when or the place where: *Go on till you reach the station.*

till² /tɪl/ *n* the drawer where money is kept in a shop *etc.*

tilt /tɪlt/ *v* to go or put something into a sloping or slanting position: *He tilted his chair backwards*; *The lamp tilted and fell.* — *n* a slant; a slanting position: *The table is at a slight tilt.*

timber /'tɪmbə(r)/ *n* **1** wood, especially for building: *The house is built of timber.* **2** trees suitable for building *etc*: *a hundred acres of good timber.* **3** a wooden beam used in the building of a house, ship *etc.*

time /taɪm/ *n* **1** the hour of the day: *What time is it?*; *to tell the time.* **2** the passing of days, years, events *etc*: *time and space*; *Time will tell whether we've made a good decision.* **3** a point or period connected with a particular event: *at the time of his wedding*; *breakfast-time.* **4** the quantity of minutes, hours, days *etc*, spent in, or available for, a particular activity *etc*: *This won't take much time to do*; *I enjoyed the time I spent in Paris*; *At the end of the exam, the supervisor called 'Your time is up!'* **5** a suitable moment or period: *Now is the time to ask him.* **6** one of a number of occasions: *He's been to France four times.* **7** a period or occasion and the experience you associate with it: *He* *went through an unhappy time when she died; We had some good times together.* **8** the speed at which a piece of music should be played: *in slow time.* — *v* **1** to measure the time taken by a happening, event *etc* or by a person, in doing something: *He timed the journey; to time a runner.* **2** to choose a particular time for doing something: *You timed your arrival perfectly — I was just going to cut this cake.*

time bomb a bomb that has been set to explode at a particular time.

'timeless *adj* not affected by time passing.

time limit a fixed length of time during which you must do and finish something: *The examination has a time limit of three hours.*

'timely *adj* coming at the right moment: *Your arrival was most timely.* **'timeliness** *n*.

'timer *n* an instrument that measures time.

times *n* **1** a period: *We live in difficult times.* **2** in mathematics, used to mean multiplied by: *Four times two is eight.*

'timetable *n* a list of the times of trains, school classes *etc*.

'timing *n* **1** the measuring of the amount of time taken. **2** the art of speaking and acting at the moment when you can achieve the best effect: *Actors must have a good sense of timing.*

all in good time soon enough; be patient: *'I haven't had my pocket-money yet.' 'All in good time.'*

all the time continually: *He's so bad-tempered all the time.*

at a time on each occasion: *She was often abroad for weeks at a time.*

at one time at a particular moment or period in the past: *At one time, he used to have a beard.*

at times occasionally; sometimes: *He's sad at times.*

before your time existing or happening before you were born: *The Beatles were a bit before my time.*

behind the times old-fashioned.

behind time late: *Hurry up! We're behind time already!*

for the time being meanwhile: *I am staying at home for the time being.*

from time to time occasionally; sometimes: *From time to time he brings me a present.*

have no time for someone to dislike or disapprove of someone: *I've little time for people who won't try.*

in good time early enough; well before the arranged time: *We arrived in good time for the concert.*

in time 1 early enough: *The police intervened just in time to prevent serious injury; Are we in time to catch the train?* **2** at the same speed or rhythm: *They marched in time with the music.*

> **in time** means early enough: *I'll be home in time for tea.*
> **on time** means at the arranged or expected time; punctual; punctually: *Please be on time for work in the mornings.*

no time or **no time at all** a very short time indeed: *The journey took no time at all; They finished in no time.*

on time at the right time; punctual; punctually: *The train arrived on time; He was on time for his appointment.*

> See **in time**.

save time to avoid spending time: *Take my car instead of walking, if you want to save time.*

take your time to do something as slowly as you wish.

time after time or **time and again** or **time and time again** often; repeatedly; many times.

waste time to spend time unnecessarily: *Don't waste time discussing unimportant details.*

timid /'tɪmɪd/ *adj* easily frightened; nervous; shy: *A mouse is a timid creature.* **'timidly** *adv.* **ti'midity** *n*.

timpani /'tɪmpənɪ/ *n plural* another word for kettledrums.

tin /tɪn/ *n* **1** a silvery white metal: *Is that box made of tin or steel?* **2** a sealed container for preserved food, made of thin sheets of iron covered with tin or another metal (also called a **can**): *a tin of fruit.* **3** a container of the same material for cake, biscuits *etc*: *a biscuit-tin.* — *adj*: *a tin can; a tin plate.*

'tinfoil *n* very thin sheets of tin or another metal used for wrapping *etc*: *to wrap sandwiches in tinfoil.*

tinge /tɪndʒ/ *n* a slight trace of colour: *The material was white but had a blue tinge.*

tinged *adj* having a slight amount of something: *The occasion was tinged with sadness because their son couldn't be there.*

tingle /'tɪŋɡəl/ *v* to have a prickling feeling: *My fingers were tingling with cold.*

tinker /'tɪŋkə(r)/ *v* to try to repair or improve

something, usually without having the necessary skills: *He enjoys tinkering around with old motorcycles*; *Who's been tinkering with the television?*

tinkle /'tɪŋkəl/ *v* to make a sound of, or like, the ringing of small bells: *The doorbell tinkled.* — *n*: *I heard the tinkle of breaking glass.*

tinned /'tɪnd/ *adj* sealed in a tin for preservation *etc*: *tinned foods.*

tin-opener /'tɪnoʊpənə(r)/ *n* a tool for opening tins of food.

tinsel /'tɪnsəl/ *n* strings of sparkling, glittering material used for decorating a room *etc* for a festival or celebration. **'tinselly** *adj.*

tint /tɪnt/ *n* a shade of a colour. — *v* to colour or dye slightly: *She had her hair tinted red.*

tiny /'taɪnɪ/ *adj* very small: *a tiny insect.*

tip[1] /tɪp/ *n* the small or thin end, point or top of something: *the tips of my fingers.*

on the tip of your tongue almost said or remembered, but not quite: *It was on the tip of her tongue to tell him the truth, but for some reason she didn't*; *His name was on the tip of my tongue while he was talking to me but I didn't manage to remember it.*

tip[2] /tɪp/ *v* **1** to make something slant: *The boat tipped to one side.* **2** to empty something from a container, or remove something from a surface, with this kind of movement: *He tipped the water out of the bucket.* **3** to dump rubbish: *People have been tipping their rubbish in this field.* — *n* **1** a place where rubbish is thrown: *a rubbish tip.* **2** a very untidy place: *His bedroom is always a tip.*

tip over to knock over; to fall over; to overturn: *He tipped the lamp over*; *She put the jug on the edge of the table and it tipped over.*

tip[3] /tɪp/ *n* a gift of money given to a waiter *etc*, for personal service: *I gave him a generous tip.* — *v* to give a gift of this sort to someone: *She tipped the hairdresser.*

tip[4] /tɪp/ *n* a piece of useful information; a hint: *He gave me some good tips about gardening.*

tip off to warn: *The police had been tipped off about the burglary that had been planned.* **'tip-off** *n.*

tipped /tɪpt/ *adj* with a tip: *filter-tipped cigarettes*; *a white-tipped tail*; *an arrow tipped with poison.*

tipsy /'tɪpsɪ/ *adj* slightly drunk.

tiptoe /'tɪptoʊ/ *v* to walk on your toes, usually in order to be quiet: *He tiptoed past her bedroom door.*

walk or **stand** *etc* **on tiptoe** to walk, stand *etc* on your toes: *He stood on tiptoe to reach the shelf.*

tip-top /tɪp'tɒp/ *adj* excellent: *The horse is in tip-top condition.*

tire[1] another spelling of **tyre**.

tire[2] /taɪə(r)/ *v* **1** to make, or become, exhausted and in need of rest; to weary: *Walking tired her*; *She tires easily.* **2** to become bored with something: *She never tired of watching the children play.*

tired *adj* **1** wearied; exhausted: *She was too tired to continue.* **2** no longer interested; bored: *I'm tired of answering stupid questions!* **'tiredness** *n.*

'tireless *adj* never becoming weary or exhausted; never resting: *a tireless worker*; *tireless energy.* **'tirelessly** *adv.*

'tiresome *adj* troublesome; annoying.

'tiring *adj* causing tiredness: *I've had a tiring day*; *The journey was very tiring.*

tire out to tire or exhaust completely: *The hard work tired her out.*

tissue /'tɪʃuː/ or /'tɪsjuː/ *n* **1** one of the kinds of substance of which your body is made: *the tissues of the body*; *muscular tissue.* **2** a piece of thin soft paper used for wiping your nose *etc*: *He bought a box of tissues for his cold.*

tissue paper very thin paper, used for packing, wrapping *etc.*

tit /tɪt/: **tit for tat** hurting or injuring someone in return for being hurt by them: *He tore my dress, so I spilt ink on his suit. That's tit for tat.*

titbit /'tɪtbɪt/ *n* a tasty little piece of food: *He gave the dog a titbit.*

titchy /'tɪtʃɪ/ *adj* very small: *She offered me a titchy piece of cake.*

title /'taɪtəl/ *n* **1** the name of a book, play, painting, piece of music *etc*: *The title of the painting is 'A Winter Evening'.* **2** a word put before your name to show rank, honour, occupation *etc*: *Sir John*; *Lord Henry*; *Captain Smith*; *Professor Brown*; *Dr (Doctor) Mary Bevan.* **3** the position of champion in sport: *He will defend his title in the next match.*

'titled *adj* having a title that shows noble rank: *a titled lady.*

titular /'tɪtʃʊlə(r)/ *adj* having the title of an office but none of its duties: *He is only a titular professor.*

titter /'tɪtə(r)/ *v* to laugh in a silly, nervous or embarrassed way. — *n.*

to /tuː/ or /tə/ *prep* **1** towards; in the direction

of: *I cycled to the station*; *The book fell to the floor.* **2** so as to attend: *I went to the concert*; *I don't want to go to school.* **3** as far as: *His story is a lie from beginning to end.* **4** until: *Did you stay to the end of the concert?* **5** used in expressing various connections and relationships between actions, people and things: *He sent the book to us*; *You're the only person I can talk to*; *Please be kinder to your sister*; *Listen to me!*; *Did you reply to his letter?*; *Where's the key to this door?*; *He sang to his guitar.* **6** into a particular state or condition: *She tore the letter to pieces.* **7** used in expressing comparison: *He's junior to me*; *We won the match by 5 goals to 2.* **8** showing the purpose or effect of an action *etc*: *He came quickly to my assistance*; *To my horror, he took a gun out of his pocket.* **9** used with a verb to express various meanings: *I want to go!*; *He asked me to come*; *He worked hard to earn a lot of money*; *These buildings were designed to resist earthquakes*; *He asked her to stay but she didn't want to.* — *adv* /tuː/ into a closed or almost closed position: *He pulled the door to.*

to and fro /froʊ/ backwards and forwards: *They ran to and fro in the street.*

toad /toʊd/ *n* an animal like a large frog.

> A toad **croaks**.
> A baby toad is a **tadpole**.

toadstool /'toʊdstuːl/ *n* a fungus that looks like a mushroom but is poisonous: *He ate a toadstool thinking it was a mushroom and almost died.*

toast[1] /toʊst/ *v* to drink in honour of someone or something: *We toasted the bride and bridegroom*; *Let us toast the new ship.* — *n*: *Let's drink a toast to our friends!*

toast[2] /toʊst/ *v* to make bread *etc* brown in front of a fire, under a grill *etc*: *We toasted slices of bread for tea.* — *n* bread that has been toasted: *He always has two pieces of toast for breakfast.*

'**toasted** *adj*: *toasted cheese*; *How well do you like your bread toasted?*

'**toaster** *n* an electric machine for toasting bread.

toast rack *n* a small stand in which slices of toast can be served.

tobacco /tə'bakoʊ/ *n* a plant that has leaves that are dried and used for smoking in pipes, cigarettes, cigars *etc*: *Tobacco may be bad for your health.*

to'bacconist *n* a person who sells tobacco, cigarettes *etc*.

toboggan /tə'bɒgən/ *n* a vehicle like a long, low seat made for sliding over snow. — *v* to ride a toboggan: *The children tobogganed down the hill*; *We went tobogganing.*

today /tə'deɪ/ *adv* **1** on this day: *I'm not going to school today.* **2** at the present time: *Life is easier today than it was a hundred years ago.* — *n*: *Today is Friday*; *Here is today's newspaper*; *People of today want more holidays and less work.*

toddle /'tɒdəl/ *v* to walk unsteadily when you first learn to walk: *The baby has begun to toddle.*

'**toddler** *n* a very young child who has just learnt to walk.

toe /toʊ/ *n* **1** one of the five finger-like end parts of your foot: *These tight shoes hurt my toes.* **2** the front part of a shoe, sock *etc*: *There's a hole in the toe of my sock.*

'**toenail** *n* the nail that grows on your toes: *to cut your toenails.*

toe the line to act according to the rules.

toffee /'tɒfɪ/ *n* a sticky sweet made of sugar and butter.

together /tə'gɛðə(r)/ *adv* **1** with someone or something else; in company: *They travelled together.* **2** at the same time: *They all arrived together.* **3** so as to be joined or united: *He nailed the pieces of wood together.* **4** acting with one or more other people: *Together we persuaded him.*

to'getherness *n* a feeling of closeness and understanding between people.

together with in company with; in addition to: *My knowledge, together with his money, should be very useful.*

toil /tɔɪl/ *v* **1** to work hard and long: *He toiled all day in the fields.* **2** to move with great difficulty: *He toiled along the road with all his luggage.* — *n* hard work: *He slept well after his hours of toil.*

toilet /'tɔɪlət/ *n* a lavatory: *Do you want to go to the toilet?*; *Where is the ladies' toilet?* — *adj*: *a toilet seat.*

toilet paper thin paper that you use to clean your body after going to the toilet.

'**toiletries** *n plural* the things that you use for washing yourself, cleaning your teeth, taking care of your skin *etc*, such as soap, shampoo and toothpaste: *Most supermarkets sell toiletries.*

toilet roll a roll of toilet paper.

token /'toʊkən/ *n* **1** a sign; a symbol: *Wear this ring as a token of our friendship.* **2** a piece of paper that is worth a certain amount of money that you can spend on a certain product or in a certain shop: *I was given a £20 book token.* **3** a piece of metal or plastic that can be used instead of a coin, for example in a slot machine. — *adj* small, but representing something larger or more serious: *The workers were given a small pay rise as a token of the management's good intentions.*

told *see* **tell**.

tolerable /ˈtɒlərəbəl/ *adj* **1** able to be borne or endured: *The heat was barely tolerable.* **2** quite good: *The food was tolerable.*

tolerance /ˈtɒlərəns/ *n* **1** the ability to be fair and understanding to people whose ways, opinions *etc* are different from your own. **2** the ability to bear something: *tolerance of pain.*

tolerant /ˈtɒlərənt/ *adj* showing tolerance: *I really am a very tolerant person, but I can't bear his rudeness much longer; Try and be tolerant towards other people; Be tolerant of other people's faults.* **'tolerantly** *adv.*

tolerate /ˈtɒləreɪt/ *v* to bear or endure; to put up with: *I couldn't tolerate his rudeness.* **tole'ration** *n.*

toll[1] /toʊl/ *v* to ring slowly: *The bell tolled solemnly.*

toll[2] /toʊl/ *n* **1** the number of people killed or injured by something: *The death toll from the earthquake has risen to 2000.* **2** a tax charged for crossing a bridge, driving on certain roads *etc*: *All cars pay a toll of £1.* — *adj*: *a toll bridge.*

take a toll or **take its toll** to begin to have a bad effect; to cause hardship or suffering: *The hard work was beginning to take its toll on all of us.*

tomato /təˈmɑːtoʊ/, *plural* **to'matoes**, *n* a juicy vegetable, used in salads, sauces *etc*: *We had a salad of lettuce, tomatoes and cucumbers.* — *adj*: *tomato sauce.*

tomb /tuːm/ *n* a grave: *He was buried in the family tomb.*

'tombstone *n* a gravestone.

tomboy /ˈtɒmbɔɪ/ *n* a girl who likes rough games and activities: *She's a real tomboy!*

tombstone /ˈtuːmstoʊn/ *n* an ornamental stone placed over a grave.

tomcat /ˈtɒmkat/ *n* a male cat.

tomorrow /təˈmɒroʊ/ *adv* **1** on the day after today: *The members of the team will be announced tomorrow.* **2** in the future: *Tomorrow we die.* — *n*: *Tomorrow is Saturday; tomorrow's world.*

ton /tʌn/ *n* a unit of weight equal to 2240 pounds (or, in America, 2000 pounds) or 0.016 tonnes.

tons *n* a lot: *I've got tons of letters to write.*

tone /toʊn/ *n* **1** the quality of a sound, especially a voice: *He spoke in a gentle tone; He told me about the film in a tone of disapproval; That violin has a very good tone.* **2** a shade of colour: *various tones of green.* **3** firmness of body or muscle: *Your muscles lack tone — you need exercise.* — *v* to fit in well; to blend: *The brown sofa tones well with the walls.*

tone-'deaf *adj* not able to hear or sing the difference between notes in music.

tone down to make or become softer, less harsh *etc*: *The red paint is too bright — we'll have to tone it down.*

tongs /tɒŋz/ *n* an instrument for holding and lifting objects: *Where are the sugar-tongs?; a pair of tongs.*

> **tongs** takes a plural verb but **a pair of tongs** is singular.

tongue /tʌŋ/ *n* **1** the fleshy organ inside your mouth, that you use for tasting, swallowing, speaking *etc*: *The doctor looked at her tongue.* **2** the tongue of an animal used as food. **3** something with the same shape as a tongue: *a tongue of flame.* **4** a language: *English is his mother-tongue; your native tongue; a foreign tongue.*

'tongue-tied *adj* too shy, embarrassed or nervous to speak.

tongue twister a phrase or sentence that is difficult to say quickly and correctly.

tongue in cheek said as a joke; not meant seriously: *I'm sure his answer was given tongue in cheek; She obviously had her tongue in her cheek when she wrote this letter.*

tonic /ˈtɒnɪk/ *n* medicine that gives strength or energy: *The doctor prescribed a tonic.*

tonic water a clear, bitter-tasting fizzy drink.

tonight /təˈnaɪt/ *adv* on the night of this present day: *I'm going home early tonight.* — *n*: *Here is tonight's weather forecast.*

tonne /tʌn/ *n* a unit of weight equal to 1000 kilograms.

tonsil /ˈtɒnsɪl/ *n* either one of a pair of lumps of tissue at the back of the throat: *He had to have his tonsils out.*

tonsillitis /tɒnsɪˈlaɪtɪs/ *n* an illness caused by an infection in the tonsils.

too /tuː/ *adv* **1** more than is required, desirable or suitable: *He's too fat to run far; This sum* is too difficult for me; *Your essay is too long.* **2** also; as well: *Jim went home early, and John did too.*

not too not very: *He's not too well; I'm not too good at arithmetic.*

took *see* **take**.

tool /tu:l/ *n* an instrument for doing work: *hammers, saws and other tools; Advertising is a powerful tool.*

toot /tu:t/ *n* a quick blast of a trumpet, car-horn *etc.* — *v*: *He tooted the horn.*

See **horn**.

tooth /tu:θ/, plural **teeth** /ti:θ/, *n* **1** any of the hard, bone-like objects that grow in your mouth, that you use for biting and chewing: *I broke a tooth on a peach stone.* **2** something that looks or acts like a tooth: *the teeth of a comb.*

'toothache *n* a pain in a tooth: *I've got terrible toothache.*

'toothbrush *n* a brush for cleaning your teeth.

toothed *adj*: *A gear is a toothed wheel; a sharp-toothed animal.*

'toothless *adj* without teeth: *a toothless old man.*

'toothpaste *n* a paste used to clean your teeth.

'toothpick *n* a small piece of wood for picking out food from between your teeth.

a sweet tooth a liking for sweet food: *I've always had a sweet tooth.*

top[1] /tɒp/ *n* **1** the highest part of anything: *the top of the hill; the top of your head; The book is on the top shelf.* **2** the position of the cleverest in a class *etc*: *He's at the top of the class.* **3** the upper surface: *the table-top.* **4** a lid: *I've lost the top of this jar; a bottle-top.* **5** a woman's garment for the upper half of the body; a blouse, sweater *etc*: *I bought a new skirt and top.* — *adj* having gained the best marks in a school class *etc*: *She's top of the class again.* — *v* **1** to cover on the top: *She topped the cake with cream.* **2** to rise above: *Our exports have topped £100 000.* **3** to remove the top of something, especially to remove the remains of the stalk from fruit: *to top strawberries.*

'top-heavy *adj* heavier at the top than at the bottom and therefore likely to fall over.

'topmost *adj* right at the top: *in the topmost branches of the tree.*

at the top of your voice very loudly: *They were shouting at the top of their voices.*

from top to bottom completely: *They've painted the house from top to bottom.*

on top of 1 on the top surface of: *Your bags are on top of the wardrobe.* **2** in addition to: *She broke her leg and then on top of that, she lost her job.*

on top of the world very well and happy: *She's on top of the world — she's just got engaged to be married.* **3** overwhelming; depressing: *Don't let all that paperwork get on top of you.*

over the top stronger or more extreme than necessary.

top up to refill a half-empty container: *Let me top up your glass.*

top[2] *n* a kind of toy that spins.

sleep like a top to sleep very well: *The child slept like a top after a day on the beach.*

topaz /'toʊpaz/ *n* a yellowish brown precious stone: *a topaz necklace.*

topic /'tɒpɪk/ *n* something spoken or written about; a subject: *They discussed the weather and other topics.*

'topical *adj* interesting and important at the present time: *a topical subject.* **'topically** *adv*.

topping /'tɒpɪŋ/ *n* something that forms a covering on top of food *etc*: *strawberry ice-cream with chocolate topping.*

topple /'tɒpəl/ *v* to fall; to make something fall: *The child toppled over; He toppled the pile of books.*

top-secret /tɒp'si:krət/ *adj* very secret: *top-secret information.*

topsyturvy /tɒpsɪ'tɜ:vɪ/ *adj, adv* upside down; in confusion: *Everything was turned topsy-turvy.*

torch /tɔ:tʃ/ *n* **1** a small light that you can carry about with you, worked by an electric battery: *He shone his torch into her face.* **2** a piece of wood *etc* set on fire and carried as a light.

tore *see* **tear**[2].

torment *n* /'tɔ:mɛnt/ **1** very great pain, suffering, worry *etc*: *He was in torment.* **2** something that causes this: *Her shyness was a torment to her.* — *v* /tɔ:'mɛnt/ to cause pain, suffering, worry *etc* to someone: *She was tormented with toothache.*

torn *see* **tear**[2].

tornado /tɔ:'neɪdoʊ/, plural **tor'nadoes**, *n* a violent whirlwind that can cause great damage: *The village was destroyed by a tornado.*

See **hurricane**.

torpedo /tɔː'piːdoʊ/, *plural* **tor'pedoes**, *n* an underwater weapon for firing at ships: *The ship was struck by an enemy torpedo.* — *v*: *The ship was torpedoed.*

torrent /'tɒrənt/ *n* a rushing stream: *The rain fell in torrents; a torrent of abuse.*

tor'rential *adj* like a torrent: *torrential rain; The rain was torrential.*

torso /'tɔːsoʊ/, *plural* **torsos**, *n* the main part of the human body without the arms, legs and head: *a statue of a man's torso.*

tortoise /'tɔːtəs/ *n* a four-footed, slow-moving animal covered with a hard shell.

tortuous /'tɔːtjʊəs/ *adj* **1** full of twists and turns: *They followed a tortuous road up the mountain.* **2** difficult to follow: *a tortuous piece of prose.*

torture /'tɔːtʃə(r)/ *v* **1** to treat someone cruelly and cause them pain, as a punishment, or in order to make them confess something, give information *etc*: *to torture prisoners.* **2** to cause someone a lot of pain or misery: *She was tortured by jealousy.* — *n* **1** the torturing of people: *The king would not permit torture.* **2** something causing great suffering: *the torture of toothache.*

toss /tɒs/ *v* **1** to throw into or through the air: *She tossed the ball into the air.* **2** to throw yourself restlessly from side to side: *She tossed about all night, unable to sleep.* **3** to be thrown about: *The boat tossed wildly in the rough sea.* **4** to throw a coin into the air and decide something according to which side falls uppermost: *They tossed a coin to decide which of them should go first.* — *n* an act of tossing.

toss up to toss a coin to decide a matter: *We tossed up whether to go to the play or the ballet.*

tot /tɒt/ *n* a small child: *a tiny tot.*

tot up to add numbers together: *Just a moment while I tot up the bill.*

total /'toʊtəl/ *adj* whole; complete: *What was the total cost of the holiday?; The car was a total wreck.* — *n* the whole amount of various sums added together: *The total came to £10.* — *v* to add up to: *The doctor's fees totalled £20.*

'totally *adv* completely: *two totally different things; Mary gave totally the wrong answer.*
total up to add up: *He totalled up the money he had earned at the end of the week.*

totem /'toʊtəm/ *n*: **totem pole** a tall wooden column on which animals, birds and plants are carved: *Totem poles are often carved by North American Indians.*

totter /'tɒtə(r)/ *v* to move unsteadily as if you are about to fall: *The building tottered and collapsed; He tottered down the road.*

touch /tʌtʃ/ *v* **1** to come into contact, or make contact with something else: *Their shoulders touched; He touched the water with his foot.* **2** to feel with your hand: *He touched her cheek.* **3** to make someone feel pity, sympathy *etc*: *I was touched by her generosity.* **4** to be concerned with; to have anything to do with: *I wouldn't touch a job like that.* **5** to be as good as someone at doing something: *Nobody could touch him as a comedian — he was simply funnier than everyone else.* — *n* **1** the action of touching; the feeling of being touched: *I felt a touch on my shoulder.* **2** one of the five senses, the sense by which we feel things: *the sense of touch; Her skin was cold to the touch.* **3** a mark or stroke *etc* to improve the appearance of something: *Sue put the finishing touches to her make-up.* **4** a small amount of something: *I noticed a touch of sarcasm in her voice.*

'touching *adj* causing pity, sympathy or deep feeling: *a touching story.*

'touchingly *adv*: *He spoke touchingly about the children he had left behind.*

'touchy *adj* easily annoyed or offended: *You're very touchy today.* **'touchily** *adv*. **'touchiness** *n*.

in touch in communication: *I have kept in touch with my school-friends.*

lose touch to stop communicating with someone: *I used to see him quite often but we have lost touch now.*

out of touch 1 not in communication with someone: *We've been out of touch for a few months.* **2** not sympathetic towards something; not understanding something: *Older people sometimes seem out of touch with the modern world.*

touch down to land: *The plane should touch down at 2 o'clock.*

touch off to make something explode: *A spark touched off the gunpowder; The fight was touched off by John's insult to Bob.*

touch on or **touch upon** to mention something briefly while dealing with another subject.

tough /tʌf/ *adj* **1** strong; not easily broken, worn out *etc*: *Plastic is a tough material.* **2** difficult to chew: *This meat is rather tough.* **3** strong; able to bear hardship, illness *etc*: *Mary is tough enough to get over the disappointment.* **4** rough and violent: *tough lads; It's a tough neighbourhood.* **5** difficult to deal with; difficult to beat: *a tough problem*; *The competition was really tough.* — *n* a rough person; a bully: *He's a young tough!* **'toughness** *n*.

'toughen *v* to make or become tough.

get tough with someone to deal very firmly with someone, or use force, to get them to do what you want: *When he started to argue, I got tough with him.*

tour /tʊə(r)/ *n* **1** a journey to several places and back: *They went on a tour of Italy.* **2** a visit around a particular place: *He took us on a tour of the house and gardens.* **3** an official period of time of work, usually abroad: *He did a tour of duty in Fiji.* — *v* to go on a tour around: *to tour Europe.*

'tourism *n* the industry dealing with tourists: *Tourism is an important part of our economy.*

'tourist *n* someone who travels for pleasure: *London is usually full of tourists.* — *adj*: *the tourist industry.*

tournament /'tʊənəmənt/ *n* a competition in which many players compete in many separate games: *I'm playing in the next tennis tournament.*

tow /toʊ/ *v* to pull something with a rope, chain or cable: *The tugboat towed the ship out of the harbour*; *The car had to be towed to the garage.* — *n*: *The car broke down and a lorry gave us a tow to the nearest garage.*

in tow accompanying; following along: *She arrived at the party with her whole family in tow.*

towards /tə'wɔːdz/ or **toward** /tə'wɔːd/ *prep* **1** moving, facing *etc* in the direction of someone or something: *He walked toward the door*; *She turned towards him.* **2** in relation to: *I feel quite friendly towards him.* **3** as a help to: *Here's £3 towards the cost of the journey.* **4** near: *Towards night-time, the weather worsened.*

towel /'taʊəl/ *n* a piece of absorbent cloth or paper for drying yourself, your hands, dishes *etc*: *a bath-towel*; *a hand-towel*; *Pass me a paper towel — I've spilt the milk.*

tower /'taʊə(r)/ *n* **1** a tall narrow building; a castle: *the Tower of London.* **2** a tall narrow part of a castle or other building: *a church-tower.* — *v* to rise high: *The mountains towered above them*; *The headmaster towered over the child.*

tower block a very tall building where people live or work.

'towering *adj* **1** very high: *towering cliffs.* **2** very violent or angry: *He was in a towering rage.*

town /taʊn/ *n* **1** a group of houses, shops, schools *etc*, that is bigger than a village but smaller than a city: *I'm going into town to buy a dress.* **2** the people who live in a group of houses *etc* of this sort: *The whole town came to see the play.* **3** towns in general as opposed to the countryside: *Do you live in the country or the town?*

town hall the building in which the official business of a town is done.

'townsfolk, **'townspeople** *ns* the people living in a town.

go to town to do something very thoroughly and with great enthusiasm or to spend a lot of money on it: *She really went to town over the wedding — only the best was good enough for her.*

toxic /'tɒksɪk/ *adj* poisonous: *toxic substances.*

toxin /'tɒksɪn/ *n* a poison produced naturally by plants, animals or bacteria: *The water had been polluted by toxins.*

toy /tɔɪ/ *n* an object made for a child to play with: *He got lots of toys for his birthday.* — *adj*: *a toy dog*; *toy soldiers.* — *v* to play with something in an idle way: *He wasn't hungry and sat toying with his food.*

trace /treɪs/ *n* **1** a mark or sign left by something: *There were traces of egg on Alan's tie*; *There's still no trace of the missing child.* **2** a small amount: *Traces of poison were found in the cup.* — *v* **1** to follow or discover by means of clues, evidence *etc*: *The police have traced him to London*; *The source of the infection has not yet been traced.* **2** to make a copy of a picture *etc* by putting transparent paper over it and drawing the outline *etc*: *to trace a map.*

'tracing *n* a copy made by tracing: *I made a tracing of the diagram.*

track /trak/ *n* **1** a mark left: *They followed the lion's tracks.* **2** a path or rough road: *a mountain track.* **3** a course on which runners, cyclists *etc* race: *a running track.* **4** a railway line. **5** one of the songs or pieces of music recorded on a CD, tape or record. — *adj*: *the marathon and other track events.* — *v* to follow someone or something by the marks, footprints *etc* that they have left: *They tracked the wolf to its lair.*

track record all the successes and failures that a person or organization has had: *He has an excellent track record and we think he's the right man for the job.*

'tracksuit *n* a warm suit worn by athletes

tractor

etc especially before and after exercising.

keep track of to keep yourself informed about something: *I've kept track of your career over the years.*

lose track of not to keep yourself informed about something: *He lost track of the argument.*

on the right or **wrong track** having the right or wrong sort of idea about something: *They haven't got the answer yet but they're on the right track.*

track down to search for and find someone or something: *I managed to track down an old copy of the book.*

tractor /'træktə(r)/ *n* a motor vehicle for pulling agricultural machinery.

trade /treɪd/ *n* **1** the buying and selling of goods: *Japan does a lot of trade with Britain.* **2** a business, occupation or job: *He's in the jewellery trade.* — *v* **1** to buy and sell: *They made a lot of money by trading; They trade in fruit and vegetables.* **2** to exchange: *I traded my watch for a bicycle.*

'trader *n* someone who trades: *She bought some fruit from a street trader.*

'trademark or **'tradename** *n* a mark or name belonging to a particular company that is put on goods made by the company.

'tradesman *n* a person who buys and sells goods.

trade union an organization of workers who do the same type of work, formed to protect them and improve their pay and working conditions.

trade in to give an old thing as part of the cost of a new one: *He traded his car in for a newer model.*

tradition /trə'dɪʃən/ *n* **1** customs, beliefs, stories *etc*: *These songs have been preserved by tradition.* **2** a custom, belief, story *etc* that is passed on. **tra'ditional** *adj*. **tra'ditionally** *adv*.

traffic /'træfɪk/ *n* vehicles, aircraft, ships *etc* moving about: *There's a lot of traffic on the roads.* — *v* to buy and sell illegally: *He was convicted of drug trafficking.*

> **traffic** is never used in the plural: *There's too much traffic on the roads.*

traffic island a small pavement in the middle of a road, for you to stand on on your way across.

traffic jam a situation in which large numbers of road vehicles are prevented from moving freely.

traffic lights lights of changing colours for controlling traffic at road crossings *etc*: *Turn left at the traffic lights.*

tragedy /'trædʒədɪ/ *n* **1** a drama about unfortunate events with a sad outcome: *'Hamlet' is one of Shakespeare's tragedies.* **2** an unfortunate or sad event: *His early death was a great tragedy for his family.*

> The opposite of **tragedy** is **comedy**.

tragic /'trædʒɪk/ *adj* **1** sad; unfortunate: *I heard of the tragic death of her son.* **2** having to do with tragedy: *Hamlet is a tragic hero.* **'tragically** *adv*.

trail /treɪl/ *v* **1** to drag, or be dragged, along loosely: *Sarah's skirt trailed along the ground.* **2** to walk slowly and wearily: *He trailed down the road.* **3** to follow the track of someone or something: *John trailed the spy to her home.* **4** to be behind in a competition or to have a lower score than the other competitors: *She's trailing by one game to four.* — *n* **1** a track: *The bear's trail was easy for the hunters to follow.* **2** a path through a forest or other wild area: *a mountain trail.* **3** a line, or series of marks, left by something as it passes: *There was a trail of blood across the floor.*

'trailer *n* **1** a vehicle pulled behind a motorcar *etc*: *We carry our luggage in a trailer.* **2** a series of short pieces taken from a film or television programme as an advertisement for it.

train[1] /treɪn/ *n* **1** a railway engine with its carriages or trucks: *I caught the train to London.* **2** a part of a long dress or robe that trails behind: *The bride wore a dress with a train.* **3** a connected series: *Then began a train of events which ended in disaster.* **4** a line of animals carrying people or baggage: *a mule train; a baggage train.*

> See **in**.

train[2] /treɪn/ *v* **1** to prepare, be prepared, or prepare yourself, through instruction, practice, exercise *etc*, for a sport, job, profession *etc*: *I was trained as a teacher; The racehorse was trained by my uncle.* **2** to teach a child or animal to behave well. **3** to point a gun or camera at someone: *He realized that the cameras were trained right on him.*

trained *adj*: *She's a trained nurse; a well-trained dog.*

trai'nee *n* someone who is being trained: *He's a trainee with an industrial firm.* — *adj*: *a trainee teacher.*

trainer *n* someone who prepares people or animals for sport, a race *etc*.

training *n* **1** preparation for a sport: *He has gone into training for the race.* **2** the learning of a job: *It takes many years of training to be a doctor.*

trait /treɪt/ *n* a particular quality of a person's character: *Patience is one of his good traits.*

traitor /'treɪtə(r)/ *n* someone who changes to the enemy's side or gives away information to the enemy: *He was a traitor to his country.*

trajectory /trə'dʒɛktərɪ/ *n* the path that a moving object follows, especially the curve of an object moving through the air: *They followed the missile's trajectory through their binoculars.*

tram /træm/ *n* a long car running on rails and usually driven by electric power, for carrying passengers, especially along the streets of a town.

tramp /træmp/ *v* **1** to walk with heavy footsteps: *He tramped up the stairs.* **2** to walk for a long distance: *She loves tramping over the hills.* — *n* **1** someone with no fixed home or job, who travels around on foot and lives by begging: *He gave his old coat to a tramp.* **2** a long walk. **3** the sound of heavy footsteps.

trample /'træmpəl/ *v* to tread heavily on something: *The horses trampled the grass.*

trampoline /'træmpəli:n/ *n* a frame across which a piece of canvas *etc* is stretched, attached by springs, for gymnasts *etc* to jump on: *Children love jumping on trampolines.*

trance /trɑ:ns/ *n* a sleep-like state in which you don't notice what is happening around you.

tranquil /'træŋkwɪl/ *adj* quiet; peaceful: *Life in the country is usually more tranquil than life in the town.* **'tranquilly** *adv.* **tran'quillity** *n.*

tranquillizer /'træŋkwɪlaɪzə(r)/ *n* a drug, especially a pill, that makes people feel calm and sleepy: *The doctor gave her a tranquillizer to calm her down after the shock of the accident.*

transaction /træn'zækʃən/ *n* a piece of business, such as the buying and selling of something: *The manager gave a report on the important business transactions that had taken place during the year.*

transcend /træn'sɛnd/ *v* to be more important or better than: *Loyalty to your country should transcend loyalty to the company you work for.*

transcript /'trænskrɪpt/ *n* a written copy of something spoken: *The newspaper published a transcript of their conversation.*

transfer *v* /træns'fɜ:(r)/ **1** to remove something to another place: *He transferred the letter from his briefcase to his pocket.* **2** to move to another place, job, vehicle *etc*: *They're transferring me to the Bangkok office; I'm transferring to a job in Hong Kong; You will have to transfer to the Kweilin train.* — *n* /'trænsfɜ:(r)/ **1** the transferring of something: *He arranged the transfer of his bank account without difficulty.* **2** a design that can be transferred from one surface to another, for example from paper to cloth as a guide for embroidery.

transferable /træns'fɜ:rəbəl/ *adj* able to be transferred from one place or person to another; able to be used by another person: *This ticket is not transferable.*

transform /træns'fɔ:m/ *v* to change completely: *He transformed the old kitchen into a beautiful sitting-room; A witch had transformed him into a frog.* **transfor'mation** *n.*

transfusion /træns'fju:ʒən/ *n* the process of injecting blood into someone who is very ill or has lost a lot of blood in an accident: *The patient was given a blood transfusion during the operation.*

transient /'trænzɪənt/ *adj* passing quickly, temporary: *Life sometimes seems very transient.*

transistor /træn'zɪstə(r)/ *n* **1** a small electronic device that controls the flow of an electric current. **2** a portable radio that uses these devices: *She took her transistor everywhere with her.*

transit /'trænzɪt/ *n* the carrying of goods or passengers from one place to another: *The company is responsible for the transit of goods from London to Amsterdam.*

in transit in the process of travelling from one place to another: *All of the passengers who are in transit are requested to wait for their next flights in the airport lounge.*

transition /træn'zɪʃən/ *n* a change from one place, state *etc* to another: *The transition from child to adult can be difficult.*

tran'sitional *adj*: *a transitional stage; a transitional period.*

'transitory *adj* lasting only for a short time: *Her good mood was only transitory.*

transitive /'trænzɪtɪv/ *adj* having a direct object, such as *watch* in the sentence *I can't watch TV and work at the same time.*

See **intransitive**.

translate /træns'leɪt/ *v* to put something said

translucent

or written into another language: *John was able to translate the tourist's question from French into English.*

> to **translate into** (not **in**) another language.

translation /trans'leɪʃən/ *n*: *He bought a French translation of 'Alice in Wonderland' in a bookshop*; *The translation of poetry is always a difficult job.*

trans'lator *n* a person who translates.

translucent /tranz'luːsənt/ *adj* allowing light to pass through, but not transparent: *translucent silk.* **trans'lucence, trans'lucency** *ns.*

transmission /tranz'mɪʃən/ *n* **1** the transmitting of something: *the transmission of disease*; *the transmission of messages.* **2** a radio or television broadcast.

transmit /tranz'mɪt/ *v* **1** to pass on: *He transmitted the message*; *Insects can transmit disease.* **2** to send out radio or television signals: *The programme will be transmitted at 5.00 p.m.*

trans'mitter *n* an apparatus for transmitting; a person who transmits: *a radio transmitter.*

transparent /tran'spærənt/ *adj* able to be seen through: *The box has a transparent lid.* **trans'parently** *adv.*

trans'parency *n* a small transparent photograph in a frame for projecting on to a screen; a slide.

transpire /tran'spaɪə(r)/ *v* to become known: *It transpired that he had been lying all the time.*

transplant *n* /'transplɑːnt/ an operation in which a part of one person's body is removed and put into the body of another person who is very ill: *His mother gave one of her kidneys because he needed a kidney transplant.* — *v* /trans'plɑːnt/ **1** to perform a transplant: *Surgeons are able to transplant most organs.* **2** to plant a growing plant in another place: *He transplanted the rosebushes from the back garden into the front garden.*

transport *v* /tran'spɔːt/ to carry goods, passengers *etc* from one place to another: *The goods were transported by air.* — *n* /'transpɔːt/ the transporting of things or people: *The transport of goods by sea and air*; *road transport*; *My husband is using my car, so I have no means of transport.*

transpor'tation *n* transport.

trap /trap/ *n* **1** a device for catching animals: *He set a trap to catch the bear*; *a mousetrap.* **2** a plan or trick for taking a person by surprise: *He fell straight into the trap.* — *v* to catch in a trap or by a trick: *He lives by trapping animals and selling their fur*; *She trapped him into admitting that he had made a mistake.*

'trap-door *n* a small door, or opening, in a floor or ceiling: *A trap-door in the ceiling led to the attic.*

trapeze /trə'piːz/ *n* a horizontal bar hung on two ropes, on which gymnasts or acrobats perform.

trappings /'trapɪŋz/ *n* the items like clothes and money *etc* that go with a particular occasion, ceremony or position: *He enjoyed the trappings of power, like a chauffeur-driven car and a personal bodyguard.*

trash /traʃ/ *n* rubbish: *Find a bin to put all this trash in*; *Those sweets are no better than trash.* **'trashy** *adj.*

'trashcan *n* a dustbin.

trauma /'trɔːmə/ *n* an emotional shock which may have effects which last a long time: *The divorce was a trauma for everyone concerned.* **trau'matic** *adj.*

travel /'travəl/ *v* **1** to go from place to place; to journey: *I travelled to Scotland by train.* **2** to move: *Light travels in a straight line.* **3** to visit places, especially foreign countries: *He has travelled a great deal.* — *n*: *They say that travel improves your mind*; *Travel to and from work can be very tiring.*

'traveller *n* a person who travels: *a weary traveller.*

travel agency a shop where you can make arrangements and buy tickets for holidays and journeys.

travel agent a person who works in or owns a travel agency.

traveller's cheque a cheque you can change into foreign money when you are abroad: *to cash a traveller's cheque.*

> **travelled**, **traveller** and **travelling** are spelt with two ls.

trawler /'trɔːlə(r)/ *n* a boat that is used to catch fish by dragging a large, bag-like net across the bottom of the sea.

tray /treɪ/ *n* a flat piece of wood, metal *etc* with a low edge, for carrying dishes *etc*: *She brought in the tea on a tray*; *a tea-tray.*

treacherous /'trɛtʃərəs/ *adj* **1** betraying; likely to betray: *a treacherous person.* **2** dangerous: *The roads are treacherous in winter.* **'treacherously** *adv.*

'treachery *n* the betraying of someone; disloyalty: *His treachery led to the capture and imprisonment of his friend.*

treacle /'tri:kəl/ *n* a sweet, thick, dark, sticky liquid that is produced from sugar: *Some cakes are made with treacle.*

tread /trɛd/ *v* **1** to place your feet on something: *Please don't tread on the grass.* **2** to walk along or over something: *He trod the streets looking for a job.* **3** to crush with your feet: *We watched them treading the grapes.* — *n* **1** a way of walking: *I heard his heavy tread.* **2** the pattern of grooves in the surface of a tyre: *The tread has been worn away.* **3** the part of a step or stair on which you put your foot.

> **tread; trod** /trɒd/; **trodden** /'trɒdən/: *He trod on her toes; The path was well trodden.*

treason /'tri:zən/ *n* the crime of betraying your own country, for instance by helping a foreign power to conquer it, or by giving secret information about it to its enemies: *He was convicted of treason and sent to prison for life.*

treasure /'trɛʒə(r)/ *n* **1** a store of money, gold, jewels *etc*: *The place where the treasure was buried was marked on the map.* **2** something very valuable: *Our babysitter is a real treasure!* — *v* to value something; to think of something as very valuable: *I treasure the hours I spend in the country.*

'treasured *adj* regarded as precious; valued: *The photograph of her son is her most treasured possession.*

'treasurer *n* the person who is responsible for the money and accounts of a club or organization.

treasury *n* the government department responsible for a country's finances.

treat /tri:t/ *v* **1** to deal with, or behave towards a thing or person, in a certain manner: *She treated her dog very kindly.* **2** to try to cure a person or a disease, injury *etc*: *The doctor treated her for earache; How would you treat a broken leg?* **3** to put something through a process: *The woodwork has been treated with a new chemical.* **4** to buy a meal, present *etc* for someone: *I'll treat you to lunch.* — *n* something that is provided specially to give you pleasure, for example an outing: *He took them to the theatre as a treat.*

'treatment *n*: *This chair seems to have received rough treatment; This patient requires urgent treatment; What is the right treatment for this disease?*

treatise /'tri:tɪs/ *n* a formal piece of writing about a particular subject: *Her treatise is on the relationship between poverty and disease.*

treaty /'tri:tɪ/ *n* an agreement between states or governments: *The two presidents signed a peace treaty at the end of the war.*

treble[1] /'trɛbəl/ *adj, adv* three times as much, many *etc*: *Food costs treble what it cost two years ago; Her marks were treble those of Paul.* — *v* to make, or become, three times as much: *He trebled his earnings.* **'trebly** *adv.*

treble[2] /'trɛbəl/ *n* **1** the high singing voice of a young boy. **2** the range of notes played with the right hand on the piano.

tree /tri:/ *n* the largest kind of plant, with a thick, firm, wooden stem, and branches: *We have three apple trees growing in our garden.*

trek /trɛk/ *v* to make a long, hard journey. — *n*: *a trek through the mountains.*

trellis /'trɛlɪs/ *n* a frame made of strips of wood, that is used to support climbing plants *etc*: *The roses grew up a trellis.*

tremble /'trɛmbəl/ *v* to shake with cold, fear, weakness *etc*: *She trembled with cold.*

tremendous /trɪ'mɛndəs/ *adj* **1** very large; very great: *The response to our appeal was tremendous.* **2** very good: *That's tremendous news!*

tre'mendously *adv* very: *This book is tremendously interesting.*

tremor /'trɛmə(r)/ *n* a shaking; a quivering: *A slight earthquake is called an earth tremor.*

trench /trɛntʃ/ *n* a long narrow ditch dug in the ground especially as a protection for soldiers against gunfire: *The soldiers returned to the trenches.*

trend /trɛnd/ *n* **1** a fashion: *She follows all the latest trends in clothing.* **2** the direction of progress: *The trend in education is towards more helpful teaching methods.*

'trendy *adj* following the latest fashions: *a trendy club.*

set a trend to start a new fashion.

trepidation /trɛpɪ'deɪʃən/ *n* fear or nervousness: *She entered the room with trepidation.*

trespass /'trɛspəs/ *v* to enter private land *etc* illegally: *You are trespassing on my land.* — *n* the act of trespassing. **'trespasser** *n*.

trestle /'trɛsəl/ *n* a wooden support with various purposes, used for example to form the legs of a temporary table.

trial /'traɪəl/ *n* **1** a test: *Give the new car a trial.*

2 a legal process by which a person is judged in a court of law: *Their trial will be held next week.* **3** a source of trouble or anxiety: *My son is a great trial to me.*

trial run a test to make sure something works properly before it is actually needed.

on trial 1 being tried in a court of law: *She's on trial for murder.* **2** undergoing tests: *The new computer is on trial.*

trial and error trying different ways or things until you find the best one: *He learned to cook by trial and error.*

triangle /ˈtraɪæŋgəl/ *n* **1** a flat shape with three sides and three angles. **2** a musical instrument consisting of a metal bar bent into a triangular shape, that you strike with a small hammer.

tri'angular *adj* in the shape of a triangle: *a triangular road-sign.*

tribal /ˈtraɪbəl/ *adj* having to do with tribes: *tribal customs.*

tribe /traɪb/ *n* **1** a race of people, or a family, who are all descended from the same ancestor: *the tribes of Israel.* **2** a group of families, especially of a primitive or wandering people, ruled by a chief: *the desert tribes of Africa.*

'tribesman *n* a man who belongs to a tribe: *an African tribesman.*

tribunal /traɪˈbjuːnəl/ *n* a special court which deals with particular cases or problems: *She took her case against her employee to an industrial tribunal.*

tributary /ˈtrɪbjʊtərɪ/ *n* a stream or river that flows into a larger river.

tribute /ˈtrɪbjuːt/ *n* something said, given or done to express praise or thanks: *One must pay tribute to her dedication; Many tributes of flowers were laid on the actor's grave; This monument was erected as a tribute to the president.*

trick /trɪk/ *n* **1** something that is done to cheat or deceive someone, or make them appear stupid and cause laughter: *The children loved to play tricks on their teacher.* **2** a clever or skilful action done to amuse people: *The magician performed some clever tricks.* **3** a special, usually clever way of doing something: *The cupboard door sticks but there is a trick to opening it easily.* — *adj* intended to deceive you and give you a false impression: *trick photography.* — *v* to deceive or cheat you, especially to make you do something you don't want to do: *He realized he had been tricked into agreeing;* *They tricked her out of her share of the money.*

'trickery *n* cheating; deception: *I suspect that there's some trickery going on.*

trickle /ˈtrɪkəl/ *v* to flow in small amounts: *Tears trickled down Gerry's face.* — *n* a small amount: *a trickle of water; At first there was only a trickle of people but soon a crowd arrived.*

trickster /ˈtrɪkstə(r)/ *n* a cheat.

tricky /ˈtrɪkɪ/ *adj* difficult: *a tricky problem; a tricky person to deal with.* **'trickily** *adv*.

tricycle /ˈtraɪsɪkəl/ *n* a cycle with three wheels.

trifle /ˈtraɪfəl/ *n* **1** anything of very little value: *When you are very rich, £1000 is a mere trifle.* **2** a sweet pudding made of spongecake, fruit, cream *etc*.

'trifling *adj* unimportant: *a trifling amount of money.*

trigger /ˈtrɪgə(r)/ *n* a small lever on a gun, which is pulled to make the gun fire. — *v* to be the cause of some event, especially a major one: *Quite a small happening can trigger off a war.*

trilogy /ˈtrɪlədʒɪ/ *n* a group of three related plays, novels, poems or operas *etc*: *Her books on the history of Venice form a trilogy.*

trim /trɪm/ *v* **1** to cut the edges or ends of something in order to make it shorter or neat: *He's trimming the hedge; She had her hair trimmed.* **2** to decorate a dress *etc*: *She trimmed the sleeves with lace.* **3** to arrange the sails of a boat *etc* suitably for the weather conditions. — *n* a haircut: *She went to the hairdresser's for a trim.* — *adj* **1** neat and tidy: *a trim appearance.* **2** slim; not fat. **'trimly** *adv*. **'trimness** *n*.

'trimming *n* something added as a decoration: *lace trimming.*

'trimmings *n* extra things that you add to something to improve its appearance or taste *etc*: *a roast turkey dinner with all the trimmings.*

trinket /ˈtrɪŋkɪt/ *n* a small ornament or piece of jewellery: *That shop sells postcards and trinkets.*

trio /ˈtriːoʊ/ *n* a group of three, especially a group of three musicians: *A trio was playing in the hotel lounge.*

trip /trɪp/ *v* **1** to catch your foot and stumble or fall; to make someone do this: *She tripped over the carpet and fell; He tried to trip her up by sticking his foot out in front of her.* **2** to walk with short, light steps: *She tripped happily along the road.* — *n* a journey; a tour: *She went on a trip to Paris.*

triple /ˈtrɪpəl/ *adj* three times as much as usual: *He received triple wages for all his extra work.* — *v* to make or become three times as much, big *etc*; to treble: *He tripled his income*; *His income tripled in ten years.*

triplet /ˈtrɪplət/ *n* one of three children or animals born to the same mother at the same time: *She's just had triplets.*

See **quadruplet** and **quintuplet**.

tripod /ˈtraɪpɒd/ *n* a stand with three legs for supporting a camera: *He used a tripod when taking photographs at night.*

trite /traɪt/ *adj* having no meaning because repeated or used too often: *The film is full of trite ideas about love.*

triumph /ˈtraɪəmf/ *n* **1** a great victory or success: *The battle ended in a triumph for the Romans.* **2** a state of happiness, celebration, pride *etc* after a success: *The winners went home in triumph.* — *v* to win a victory: *The Romans triumphed over their enemies.*

triˈumphant *adj*: *The triumphant team were welcomed home*; *Triumphant crowds welcomed the winners home*; *He gave a triumphant shout when he found the book he had lost.* **triˈumphantly** *adv*.

trivia /ˈtrɪvɪə/ *n* unimportant matters or details: *I haven't time to worry about such trivia.*

ˈtrivial *adj* of very little importance: *trivial details*; *trivial remarks.* **ˈtrivially** *adv*.

triviˈality *n* **1** something that is trivial: *Don't worry about trivialities.* **2** unimportance; silliness.

ˈtrivialize *v* to make something seem unimportant: *She feels her position in the company is trivialized.*

trod, trodden *see* **tread**.

troll /trɒl/ *n* an imaginary creature of humanlike form, a dwarf or a giant.

trolley /ˈtrɒlɪ/ *n* **1** a type of small cart for carrying things *etc*: *At the supermarket, she filled her trolley with groceries.* **2** a small cart used for serving tea, food *etc*: *She brought the tea in on a trolley.*

ˈtrolley-bus *n* a bus that is driven by power from an overhead wire to which it is connected.

trombone /trɒmˈboʊn/ *n* a brass musical instrument.

tromˈbonist *n* a person who plays the trombone.

troop /truːp/ *n* **1** a group of ordinary soldiers. **2** a crowd or collection of people or animals: *A troop of visitors arrived.* — *v* to go in a group: *They all trooped into the headmaster's room.*

trophy /ˈtroʊfɪ/ *n* **1** a prize for winning in a sport *etc*: *He won a silver trophy for shooting.* **2** something you keep to remind you of a success *etc*: *He shot the tiger and brought back its skin as a trophy.*

tropical /ˈtrɒpɪkəl/ *adj* belonging to the tropics or very hot countries: *a tropical climate*; *tropical plants.* **ˈtropically** *adv*.

tropics /ˈtrɒpɪks/ *n* the hot regions north and south of the equator: *The ship is heading for the tropics.*

trot /trɒt/ *v* **1** to move with fairly fast, bouncy steps, faster than a walk but slower than a gallop: *The horse trotted down the road.* **2** to run with little steps: *The child trotted along beside his mother.* — *n* the pace of trotting: *The horsemen rode at a trot.*

on the trot one after another without a break: *He missed three meetings on the trot.*

trotter /ˈtrɒtə(r)/ *n* a pig's foot.

See **foot**.

trouble /ˈtrʌbəl/ *n* worry, difficulty, anxiety or extra work; something that causes these things: *I had a lot of trouble finding the book you wanted*; *Her injured ankle is causing her trouble again*; *What a trouble children are sometimes!* — *v* **1** to cause someone worry or sadness: *She was troubled by the news of her sister's illness.* **2** used as part of a very polite request: *May I trouble you to close the window?* **3** to make an effort: *He didn't even trouble to tell me what had happened.*

ˈtroubled *adj* **1** worried; anxious: *His face wore a troubled expression.* **2** disturbed; not peaceful: *troubled sleep.*

ˈtroublemaker *n* a person who continually, and usually deliberately, causes worry, difficulty or disturbance to other people: *Beware of Miriam — she is a real troublemaker.*

ˈtroublesome *adj* causing worry or difficulty: *troublesome children.*

go to a lot of trouble to put a lot of work or effort into something: *I went to a lot of trouble to give them a good time.*

in trouble 1 having serious problems: *The company is in financial trouble.* **2** in a situation where you have done something wrong and are likely to be punished: *She's in trouble for not doing her homework.*

take trouble to do something with great care: *She had taken a lot of trouble over the meal.*

take the trouble to make an effort to do something: *He didn't even take the trouble to answer the letter.*

trough /trɒf/ *n* a long, low, open container for animals' food or water.

trousers /ˈtraʊzəz/ *n* an outer garment for the lower part of your body, covering each leg separately: *He wore a pair of black trousers; Where are George's maroon trousers?; This pair of trousers needs a wash.*

> **trousers** takes a plural verb, but **a pair of trousers** is singular.

trout /traʊt/, *plural* **trout**, *n* an edible freshwater fish of the salmon family.

trowel /ˈtraʊəl/ *n* **1** a tool like a small shovel, used in gardening: *Bob prepared the flowerbed with a trowel.* **2** a tool with a flat blade, for spreading mortar, plaster *etc*.

truant /ˈtruːənt/ *n* someone who stays away from school without permission: *The truants were found in the sweet-shop and sent back to school.* **ˈtruancy** *n*.

play truant to be a truant: *He was always playing truant from school.*

truce /truːs/ *n* a rest from fighting that is agreed to by both sides: *The two countries agreed on a fortnight's truce; They called a truce while they discussed the possibility of ending the war.*

truck /trʌk/ *n* **1** a railway vehicle for carrying goods. **2** a lorry: *Joe's father drives a truck.*

trudge /trʌdʒ/ *v* to walk with slow, tired or heavy steps: *She trudged up the hill carrying the baby.* — *n*: *a long trudge through the snow.*

true /truː/ *adj* **1** telling something that really happened; not invented; agreeing with fact; not wrong: *a true statement of the facts; Is it true that Jennifer stole the ring?* **2** accurate: *His book gives a true picture of life in South Africa.* **3** faithful; loyal: *He has been a true friend to me.* **4** properly called a particular thing: *A spider is not a true insect.*

ˈtruly *adv* **1** really: *I truly believe that this decision is the right one.* **2** really; sincerely; dearly: *He loved her truly.*

come true to actually happen: *The whole experience was like a dream come true.*

trumped-up /ˈtrʌmptʌp/ *adj* false or invented: *There were several trumped-up charges against him.*

trumpet /ˈtrʌmpɪt/ *n* **1** a brass musical wind instrument. **2** the noise an elephant makes: *The elephant gave a loud trumpet.* — *v*: *The elephant trumpeted.*

blow your own trumpet to boast; to praise yourself: *He really isn't very clever but he is always blowing his own trumpet.*

trumps /trʌmps/ *n* the suit of cards that has a higher value than the other three suits in a particular card game.

truncheon /ˈtrʌnʃən/ *n* a short, thick, heavy stick carried by police officers; a baton.

trundle /ˈtrʌndəl/ *v* to roll slowly and heavily along on wheels: *The huge lorry trundled along the road; He trundled his barrow through the streets.*

trunk /trʌŋk/ *n* **1** the main stem of a tree: *a tree-trunk.* **2** a large box or chest for packing or keeping clothes *etc* in: *He packed his trunk and sent it to Canada by sea.* **3** an elephant's long nose. **4** your body, not including your arms and legs: *He has a short, powerful trunk, and muscular limbs.* **5** the boot of a car: *Put your luggage in the trunk.*

trunk call a telephone call to a place at a distance: *He made a trunk call from London to Glasgow.*

trunks *n* short trousers or pants worn by boys or men, especially the kind used for swimming: *bathing-trunks.*

truss /trʌs/ *v* to tie tightly: *She trussed the chicken and put it in the oven; The burglars trussed up the guards.*

trust /trʌst/ *v* **1** to have confidence or faith; to believe: *She trusted in him.* **2** to give something to someone, believing that it will be used well and sensibly: *I can't trust him with my car.* **3** to hope: *I trust that you will have a good journey.* — *n* **1** belief or confidence in the power, reality, truth, goodness *etc* of a person or thing: *I have a lot of trust in your ability; Put your trust in God.* **2** charge; care; responsibility: *The child was placed in my trust.* **3** responsibility given to a person by someone who believes that they will manage it well: *He holds a position of trust in the firm.*

ˈtrusting *adj* believing that other people are honest; having trust in other people.

ˈtrustworthy *adj* able to be trusted: *Is your friend trustworthy?* **ˈtrustworthiness** *n*.

on trust without checking or having proof: *She decided to take what he was saying on trust as he had never lied to her before.*

trust you to... it is typical of you to do such a silly thing: *Trust you to be late for your own wedding!*

truth /tru:θ/ *n* **1** the state of being true: *I am certain of the truth of his story*. **2** the true facts: *Tell the truth about what you were doing last night*. **3** a generally accepted fact about something: *scientific truths*.

'truthful *adj* **1** telling the truth: *She's a truthful child*. **2** true: *a truthful account of what happened*. **'truthfully** *adv*. **'truthfulness** *n*.

to tell you the truth really; actually: *To tell you the truth I forgot it was your birthday last week*.

try /traɪ/ *v* **1** to attempt; to make an effort: *He tried to answer the questions*; *Let's try and climb that tree!*; *I had tried to warn her of the conditions we might expect*; *The Party was at least trying to seem reasonable*. **2** to test; to make an experiment in order to find out whether something will be successful, satisfactory *etc*: *She tried washing her hair with a new shampoo*; *Have you tried this new washing-powder?*; *Try one of these sweets!* **3** to judge someone in a court of law: *The prisoners were tried for murder*. **4** to strain: *You are trying my patience*. — *n* an attempt; an effort: *Have a try at this question — it's not too difficult*.

> **try; 'trying; tried; tried**: *She's trying to skate*; *She tried again*; *Have you tried skating?*

'trying *adj* difficult; annoying; causing strain, anxiety or impatience: *Having to stay such a long time in hospital must be very trying*; *It has been a trying week in the office*; *She's a very trying woman!*

try on to put on clothes *etc* to see if they fit: *She tried on a hat in the shop*.

try out to test something by using it: *We are trying out new teaching methods*.

T-shirt another spelling of **tee shirt**.

tub /tʌb/ *n* **1** a round container for holding water, washing clothes *etc*. **2** a bath: *He was sitting in the tub*. **3** a small round container in which certain foods are sold; a small carton: *a tub of ice-cream*.

tuba /'tju:bə/ *n* a large brass musical wind instrument.

tuberculosis /tju:bɜ:kjʊ'ləʊsɪs/ *n* an infectious disease affecting the lungs: *Tuberculosis is common in some parts of the world*.

tubby /'tʌbɪ/ *adj* rather plump: *She used to be tubby as a child, but she's quite slim now*.

tube /tju:b/ *n* **1** a long, narrow cylinder-shaped object; a pipe: *The water flowed through a rubber tube*. **2** an underground railway in London: *I go to work on the tube*. **3** a long narrow container for a soft substance, made of soft metal or plastic, which you squeeze to get out the contents: *a tube of toothpaste*.

tuber /'tju:bə(r)/ *n* a swelling on the stem or root of a plant: *Potatoes are the tubers of the potato plant*.

tubing /'tju:bɪŋ/ *n* a long length of rubber or metal *etc* in the shape of a tube.

tuck /tʌk/ *n* **1** a fold sewn into a piece of material: *Her dress had tucks down the front*. **2** sweets, cakes *etc*. — *v* to push *etc*: *He tucked his shirt into his trousers*; *She tucked her hand into his*.

tuck in or **into 1** to gather bedclothes *etc* closely round someone: *I said goodnight and tucked him in*; *She tucked him into bed*. **2** to eat greedily or with enjoyment: *Emma tucked into her chocolates*; *Come on — sit down and tuck in!*

Tuesday /'tju:zdɪ/ *n* the third day of the week, the day following Monday.

tuft /tʌft/ *n* a small bunch; a clump: *tufts of grass*.

tug /tʌg/ *v* to pull sharply and strongly: *He tugged at the door but it wouldn't open*; *She took his hand and tugged him out of the room*. — *n* a strong, sharp pull: *He gave the rope a tug*.

'tug-boat *n* a small boat with a very powerful engine, for towing larger ships.

tug-of-'war *n* a competition in which two people or teams pull at opposite ends of a rope, trying to pull their opponents over a centre line.

tuition /tju:'ɪʃən/ *n* teaching, especially to individual pupils: *She gives piano tuition*.

tulip /'tju:lɪp/ *n* a plant with brightly-coloured cup-shaped flowers, grown from a bulb.

tumble /'tʌmbəl/ *v* to fall, especially in a helpless or confused way: *She tumbled down the stairs*. — *n* a fall: *She had a tumble on the stairs*.

tumble drier or **tumble dryer** a machine for drying clothes: *She put the washing in the tumble dryer because it was raining*.

'tumbler *n* a large drinking glass.

'tumblerful *n*: *He drank two tumblerfuls of water*.

tummy /'tʌmɪ/ *n* a child's word for stomach, really meaning the belly: *I've a pain in my tummy*. — *adj*: *tummy-ache*.

tumour /'tju:mə(r)/ *n* a kind of lump that is growing on or in the body: *The surgeon removed a tumour from her lung*; *a brain tumour*.

tumult /'tju:mʌlt/ *n* a great noise, especially

made by a crowd: *He could hear a great tumult in the street.*
tu'multuous *adj*: *The crowd gave him a tumultuous welcome*; *tumultuous applause.*
tu'multuously *adv.*

tuna /'tju:nə/, *plural* **'tuna** or **'tunas**, *n* a large edible seafish of the mackerel family (also called **tunny**).

tune /tju:n/ *n* musical notes put together in a pleasing order; a melody: *He played a tune on the violin.* — *v* **1** to adjust a musical instrument, or its strings *etc* to the correct pitch: *The orchestra tuned their instruments.* **2** to adjust a radio *etc* so that it receives a particular station: *The radio was tuned to a Japanese station.* **3** to adjust an engine to make it run properly.
'tuneful *adj* having a pleasing tune: *That song is very tuneful.*
'tuneless *adj* having no tune; unmusical: *The child was singing in a tuneless voice.*
in tune 1 adjusted so as to give the correct note, or so as to be in harmony with another instrument; in harmony with other voices: *Is the violin in tune with the piano?*; *Are your instruments in tune?*; *Someone in the choir isn't singing in tune.* **2** agreeing with or understanding other people: *His ideas are not in tune with the rest of the committee and we are finding this a problem.*
out of tune not in tune.
tune in to tune a radio to a particular station or programme: *We usually tune in to the news.*
tune up to tune instruments: *The orchestra was tuning up.*

tunic /'tju:nɪk/ *n* **1** a soldier's or policeman's jacket. **2** a loose garment worn in ancient Greece and Rome. **3** a similar type of modern garment.

tunnel /'tʌnəl/ *n* an underground passage, especially one cut through a hill or under a river: *The road goes through a tunnel under the river.* — *v* to make a tunnel: *They escaped from prison by tunnelling under the walls.*

tunny /'tʌnɪ/ *n* another name for **tuna**.

turban /'tɜ:bən/ *n* a long piece of cloth worn wound round the head, especially by men in parts of north Africa and southern Asia.

turbulent /'tɜ:bjʊlənt/ *adj* **1** very rough: *The boat sank in turbulent seas.* **2** very confused: *the turbulent years of the war.* **'turbulently** *adv.* **'turbulence** *n.*

turf /tɜ:f/, *plural* **turfs** or **turves** /tɜ:vz/, *n* grass and the earth it grows out of; a square piece cut from this: *They cut away several turfs to make a place for the camp-fire*; *He walked across the springy turf.* — *v* **1** to cover with turfs: *We are going to turf over one of the flower-beds.* **2** to throw: *We turfed him out of the house.*

turkey /'tɜ:kɪ/ *n* a large farmyard bird, eaten at Christmas and other festivals.

turmoil /'tɜ:mɔɪl/ *n* a state of wild confused movement; disorder: *The house is in a turmoil — I must tidy it*; *His mind was in turmoil.*

turn /tɜ:n/ *v* **1** to move round or over; to go round; to revolve: *He turned the handle*; *The handle turned*; *to turn the pages of a book*; *Turn to Chapter 9.* **2** to face or go in another direction: *She turned and disappeared down a short flight of stairs.* **3** to change direction: *The road turned to the left.* **4** to aim or point: *Turn your feet out when you dance.* **5** to direct: *He turned his attention to his work.* **6** to go round: *They turned the corner.* **7** to change; to become: *You can't turn lead into gold*; *The snow was beginning to turn to rain*; *She turned her hair pink with her new hairspray*; *Her hair's turned white.* — *n* **1** the action of turning: *He gave the handle a turn.* **2** your chance or duty to do something: *It's your turn to choose a record*; *Whose turn is it to wash up?*

turn on the light
turn on the radio
turn on the tap
turn on the TV
turn on the gas

'turning *n* a place where one road leads away from another: *Take the second turning on the right.*

'turning-point *n* a place where, or time when, an important change happens: *the turning-point in his life.*

do someone a good turn to do something helpful for someone: *He did me several good turns.*

in turn or **by turns** one after another, in regular order: *They answered the teacher's questions in turn.*

out of turn not in the correct order: *He answered a question out of turn.*

take a turn for the better, take a turn for the worse to become better or worse: *Her health has taken a turn for the worse.*

take turns to do something one after the other, not at the same time: *They took turns to look after the baby.*

turn a blind eye to pretend not to see or notice something: *Because he works so hard, his boss turns a blind eye when he comes in late.*

turn against to dislike or disapprove of someone or something that you liked before: *He turned against his friends.*

turn away to move away; to send away: *He turned away in disgust*; *The police turned away the crowds.*

turn back to go back in the opposite direction: *He began to climb the mountain but turned back when it began to snow.*

turn down 1 to say 'no' to; to refuse: *He turned down her request.* **2** to reduce the noise *etc* produced by something: *Please turn the television down — it's far too loud.*

turn in to hand over a person or thing to someone in authority: *They turned the escaped prisoner in to the police.*

turn loose to set free: *He turned the horse loose in the field.*

turn off 1 to stop water, gas or electricity flowing: *I've turned off the electricity at the main switch*; *I turned off the tap*; *He turned off the light*; *Have you turned the oven off?* **2** to take a road that leads away from the one you are on: *You turn off the High Street just before the bridge.*

'turn-off *n*: *Her farm is at the end of this turn-off.*

See **put out**.

turn on 1 to make water, gas or electricity start to flow: *He turned on the gas*; *I turned on the tap*; *He turned the radio on.* **2** to attack: *The dog turned on him.*

turn out 1 to send away; to make someone leave: *His mother got so tired of his bad behaviour that she turned him out of the house.* **2** to make or produce: *I have a week to turn out my report.* **3** to empty; to clear: *I turned out the cupboard.* **4** to turn off: *Turn out the light!* **5** to happen; to prove to be: *He turned out to be right*; *It turned out that he was right.* **6** to come out in a crowd: *A large crowd turned out to see the procession.*

'turnout *n*: *The turnout was poor because of the bad weather.*

turn over 1 to give something up: *He turned the money over to the police.* **2** to turn a page on to its other side: *She turned over a page or two.*

turn up 1 to appear; to arrive: *He turned up at our house.* **2** to be found: *Don't worry — the watch will turn up again.* **3** to increase the sound *etc* produced by something: *Turn up the radio — I want to hear the news.*

turnip /'tɜ:nɪp/ *n* a plant with a large round edible root: *a field of turnips.*

turnover /'tɜ:nəʊvə(r)/ *n* **1** the total value of goods a company sells in a period of time: *Our annual turnover is now more than a million pounds.* **2** the rate at which workers leave a company and are replaced by new ones.

turnstile /'tɜ:nstaɪl/ *n* a revolving gate with metal bars that allows only one person to pass at a time, usually after paying an entrance fee: *There is a turnstile at the entrance to the football ground.*

turntable /'tɜ:nteɪbəl/ *n* the flat, round part of a record player where the record lies while it is being played.

turpentine /'tɜ:pəntaɪn/ *n* a liquid obtained from certain trees, used for cleaning paint off brushes.

turquoise /'tɜ:kwɔɪz/ *n* **1** a greenish-blue precious stone: *The ring was set with a turquoise.* **2** a greenish-blue colour. — *adj*: *a pale turquoise dress.*

turret /'tʌrɪt/ *n* a small tower on a castle or other building.

turtle /'tɜ:təl/ *n* a kind of large tortoise, especially one living in water.

turves plural of **turf**.

tusk /tʌsk/ *n* one of a pair of large curved teeth which project from the mouth of certain animals, for instance the elephant and the walrus.

See **fang**.

tussle /'tʌsəl/ *n* an energetic struggle or fight, especially between two people who both want something: *There was a tussle over the house so in the end it was sold and the money was split between them.*

tutor /'tju:tə(r)/ *n* **1** a teacher of a group of students in a university *etc.* **2** a teacher employed to teach a child at home: *His parents employed a tutor for him instead of sending him to school.* — *v* to teach: *He tutored the child in mathematics.*

tu'torial *n* a lesson given by a university or college lecturer to a small group of students: *The department does most of its teaching in tutorials; a tutorial group.*

tutu /'tu:tu:/ *n* a female ballet-dancer's short stiff skirt.

tuxedo /tʌk'si:dou/ *n* a dinner jacket.

twang /twaŋ/ *n* a sound of, or like, a tightly-stretched string being pulled and let go, or breaking: *The string broke with a sharp twang.* — *v*: *She twanged the strings of the guitar.*

tweak /twi:k/ *n* a sharp pull or twist: *She gave his nose a tweak.* — *v* to pull or twist sharply: *She tweaked his nose.*

tweed /twi:d/ *n* a thick, rough woollen material, usually with coloured flecks in it: *a jacket made from tweed; a tweed suit.*

tweezers /'twi:zəz/ *n plural* a small tool for pulling out hairs or gripping small objects: *She used a pair of tweezers to pluck her eyebrows; I need some tweezers to get the splinter out of your finger.*

twelve /twɛlv/ *n* **1** the number 12. **2** the age of 12. — *adj* **1** 12 in number. **2** aged 12.

twelfth /twɛlfθ/ *n* one of twelve equal parts. — *n, adj* the next after the eleventh.

twenty /'twɛnti/ *n* **1** the number 20. **2** the age of 20. — *adj* **1** 20 in number. **2** aged 20.

twice /twaɪs/ *adv* **1** two times: *I've been to London twice; Twice he seriously wounded men in duels.* **2** two times the amount of something: *She has twice his courage.* **3** two times as good *etc* as someone or something: *Don't be frightened of him — you're twice the man he is.*

twiddle /'twɪdəl/ *v* to twist something round and round: *He twiddled the knob on the radio.*

twig /twɪg/ *n* a small branch of a tree.

See **branch**.

twilight /'twaɪlaɪt/ *n* the time of the dim light just before the sun sets.

twin /twɪn/ *n* one of two children or animals born to the same mother at the same time: *She gave birth to twins.* — *adj*: *They have twin daughters; Bill and Ben are twin brothers; I have a twin sister.*

twine /twaɪn/ *n* a strong kind of string made of twisted threads: *He tied the parcel with twine.* — *v* to twist: *The ivy twined round the tree.*

twinge /twɪndʒ/ *n* a sudden sharp pain: *He felt a twinge of pain in his foot; She felt a twinge of regret as she left her old house for good.*

twinkle /'twɪŋkəl/ *v* **1** to shine with a small, slightly unsteady light: *The stars twinkled in the sky.* **2** to shine with amusement: *His eyes twinkled with mischief.* — *n*: *The headmistress spoke sternly to the children who had played the trick, but there was a twinkle in her eye all the same.*

twirl /twɜ:l/ *v* to turn round and round; to spin: *She twirled her hair round her finger.* — *n*: *She did a twirl on one foot.*

twist /twɪst/ *v* **1** to turn round: *He twisted the knob.* **2** to bend this way and that way: *The road twisted through the mountains.* **3** to wind around or together: *The dog's lead got twisted round a lamp-post; He twisted the pieces of string to make a rope.* **4** to force something out of the correct shape or position: *I've twisted my ankle.* **5** to change the meaning of what someone has said: *Journalists twist everything you say.* — *n* **1** the action of twisting: *He gave her arm a twist.* **2** a twisted piece of something: *She added a twist of lemon to his drink.* **3** a bend: *The road was full of twists and turns.* **4** something unexpected: *The story had a strange twist at the end.*

'twisted *adj*: *a twisted branch.*

twist someone's arm to force or to try hard to persuade someone to do something.

twitch /twɪtʃ/ *v* **1** to move jerkily: *His hands were twitching.* **2** to give something a little pull or jerk: *He twitched her sleeve.* — *n* a twitching movement.

twitter /'twɪtə(r)/ *n* a light, chirping sound, made by birds: *He could hear the twitter of sparrows.* — *v*: *The swallows twittered overhead.*

two /tu:/ *n* **1** the number 2. **2** the age of 2. — *adj* **1** 2 in number. **2** aged two.

two-'faced *adj* deceitful: *a two-faced person.*

twosome /'tu:səm/ *n* two people; a couple: *They usually travel in a twosome.*

two-'way *adj* able to operate in two ways; moving in two directions: *two-way traffic; a two-way radio.*

in two in two pieces: *The magazine was torn in two.*

See **divide**.

tycoon /taɪ'ku:n/ *n* a rich and powerful businessman: *an oil tycoon.*

tying see **tie**.

type[1] /taɪp/ *n* **1** a kind; a sort; a variety: *What type of house would you prefer to live in?*;

hood is a type of hat. **2** a person of a particular kind: *Harriet wasn't the nervy type.*

type² /taɪp/ *v* to write something using a typewriter: *Can you type?* — *n* the style and size of printing used in books and newspapers *etc*: *The words were printed in heavy type.*

'typewriter *n* a machine with keys for printing letters on a piece of paper: *an electric typewriter.*

'typewriting *n* writing produced by a typewriter.

'typewritten *adj* typed: *a typewritten letter.*

typhoid /'taɪfɔɪd/ *n* an infectious disease producing fever and diarrhoea, caused by bacteria in water: *Typhoid can be fatal.*

typhoon /taɪ'fuːn/ *n* a violent storm occurring in the East: *They were caught in a typhoon in the China seas.*

See **hurricane**.

typical /'tɪpɪkəl/ *adj* having the usual qualities and characteristics: *He is a typical Englishman.* **'typically** *adv.*

typify /'tɪpɪfaɪ/ *v* to be a typical mark or example of something: *His behaviour typifies the attitudes of his generation.*

typing /'taɪpɪŋ/ *n* **1** the art of using a typewriter; work produced on a typewriter: *He's learning typing and shorthand.* **2** work that has been or must be typed: *five pages of typing.*

typist /'taɪpɪst/ *n* a person whose job is to type.

tyrant /'taɪrənt/ *n* a cruel and unjust ruler: *The people suffered many years of misery under foreign tyrants.* **ty'rannical** *adj.* **ty'rannically** *adv.* **tyranny** /'tɪrəni/ *n.*

tyre or **tire** /taɪə(r)/ *n* a thick, rubber, air-filled ring around the edge of the wheel of a car, bicycle *etc*: *The tyres of this car need pumping up.*

U

udder /'ʌdə(r)/ n the bag-like part of a cow, goat etc that hangs between her legs and produces milk for her babies.

ugh! /ʌg/ a word used to express disgust: *Ugh! The cat has been sick!*

ugly /'ʌglɪ/ adj **1** unpleasant to look at; not attractive; not good-looking: *an ugly face.* **2** unpleasant, nasty; dangerous: *ugly black clouds*; *The crowd was in an ugly mood.* **'ugliness** n.

ulcer /'ʌlsə(r)/ n a kind of sore on the skin or inside the body.

ulterior /ʌl'tɪərɪə(r)/ adj hidden, kept secret: *She has ulterior motives for wanting to help.*

ultimate /'ʌltɪmət/ adj last; final: *an ultimate warning*; *an ultimate goal in life.*
'ultimately adv in the end: *We hope ultimately to be able to buy a house of our own.*
the ultimate the greatest or best in a particular way: *This new car is the ultimate in speed and comfort.*

ultimatum /ʌltɪ'meɪtəm/, plural **ultimatums** or **ultimata**, n a final warning that hostile action will be taken unless certain conditions are met: *She issued an ultimatum to her husband that unless her demands were met, she would divorce him.*

ultra- /ʌltrə/ prefix extremely: *an ultra-modern computing system.*

ultrasound /'ʌltrəsaʊnd/ n sound waves which cannot be heard by the human ear, used for examining things happening inside the body: *The doctor used ultrasound to measure the size of the baby in her womb.*

ultraviolet /ʌltrə'vaɪələt/ adj invisible to the human eye and having the effect of tanning the skin: *ultraviolet radiation from the sun.*

umbrella /ʌm'brɛlə/ n an apparatus for protecting you from the rain, made of a folding covered framework attached to a stick with a handle.

umpire /'ʌmpaɪə(r)/ n a person who supervises a game, makes sure that it is played according to the rules, and decides doubtful points: *Tennis players usually have to accept the umpire's decision.* — v to act as umpire: *Have you umpired a tennis match before?*

unable /ʌn'eɪbəl/ adj without enough strength, power, skill, time, information etc to be able to do something: *He was unable to sleep*; *I shall be unable to meet you for lunch today.*

unable to understand, but **incapable of understanding**.

unacceptable /ʌnək'sɛptəbəl/ adj that you cannot accept or allow: *This kind of behaviour is unacceptable.* **unac'ceptably** adv.

unaccompanied /ʌnə'kʌmpənɪd/ adj alone; without another person: *unaccompanied children*; *unaccompanied singing.*

unaffected /ʌnə'fɛktɪd/ adj **1** not upset; not affected: *The child seemed unaffected by his father's death*; *It has been raining heavily, but this evening's football arrangements are unaffected.* **2** natural; genuine: *unaffected behaviour.*

unafraid /ʌnə'freɪd/ adj not afraid.

unaided /ʌn'eɪdɪd/ adj on your own; without any help: *The baby was too young to feed herself unaided.*

unanimous /juː'nænɪməs/ adj with everyone agreeing: *The whole school was unanimous in its approval of the headmaster's plan*; *a unanimous decision.* **u'nanimously** adv.

unarmed /ʌn'ɑːmd/ adj without weapons or any other means of defence: *The gangster shot an unarmed policeman*; *Judo is a type of unarmed fighting.*

unashamed /ʌnə'ʃeɪmd/ adj showing no shame or embarrassment.
unashamedly /ʌnə'ʃeɪmədlɪ/ adv: *She was weeping unashamedly.*

unassuming /ʌnə'sjuːmɪŋ/ adj modest and quiet: *a shy and unassuming young man.*

unattached /ʌnə'tatʃt/ adj not connected with anyone or anything else.

unattended /ʌnə'tɛndɪd/ adj not being looked after: *Passengers are asked not to leave luggage unattended.*

unauthorized /ʌn'ɔːθəraɪzd/ adj not having the permission of the people in authority: *She was dismissed by her boss for unauthorized use of the firm's equipment.*

unavoidable /ʌnə'vɔɪdəbəl/ adj that cannot be avoided or prevented: *The accident was unavoidable.*
una'voidably adv: *They were unavoidably delayed.*

unaware /ʌnə'wɛə(r)/ adj not aware; not knowing: *He was so quiet that I was unaware of his presence in the room.*

take someone unawares to surprise or startle someone: *He came into the room so quietly that he took me unawares.*

unbalanced /ʌnˈbalənst/ *adj* **1** slightly mad; not thinking sensibly. **2** not fair to all sides of an argument: *The article did not give a balanced version of the story.*

unbearable /ʌnˈbɛərəbəl/ *adj* too painful, or too unpleasant *etc* to bear: *This toothache is almost unbearable*; *What an unbearable boy he is!*
un'bearably *adv*: *unbearably painful*; *unbearably rude.*

unbeatable /ʌnˈbiːtəbəl/ *adj* very good; the best: *Our sale offers unbeatable value for money.*

unbelievable /ʌnbɪˈliːvəbəl/ *adv* too bad, good *etc* to be believed: *unbelievable stupidity*; *Her good luck is unbelievable!* **unbe'lievably** *adv.*

unborn /ʌnˈbɔːn/ *adj* not yet born; still in the mother's womb: *The unborn baby gets nourishment from its mother's body.*

unbroken /ʌnˈbroʊkən/ *adj* having no breaks or gaps: *an unbroken run of luck.*

unbuckle /ʌnˈbʌkəl/ *v* to undo the buckle of a belt, strap *etc*: *He unbuckled his belt.*

unbutton /ʌnˈbʌtən/ *v* to unfasten the buttons of a garment: *She unbuttoned her coat.*

uncalled-for /ʌnˈkɔːldfɔː(r)/ *adj* unnecessary and usually rather rude: *Some of the remarks he made at the meeting were quite uncalled-for.*

uncanny /ʌnˈkanɪ/ *adj* strange or mysterious: *She had the uncanny talent for knowing exactly what I was thinking.*

uncertain /ʌnˈsɜːtən/ *adj* **1** not sure; not definitely knowing: *I'm uncertain of my future plans*; *The government is uncertain what is the best thing to do.* **2** not definitely known; not settled: *My plans are still uncertain.*
un'certainly *adv.*
un'certainty *n* **1** the state of being uncertain. **2** something that is not certain: *Life is full of uncertainties.*

uncharacteristic /ʌnkarɪkˈtərɪstɪk/ *adj* not typical or usual. **uncharacter'istically** *adv.*

uncharitable /ʌnˈtʃarɪtəbəl/ *adj* unkind and unfair. **un'charitably** *adv.*

uncle /ˈʌŋkəl/ *n* the brother of your father or mother, or the husband of your aunt: *He's my uncle*; *Hallo, Uncle Jim!*

unclear /ʌnˈklɪə(r)/ *adj* not clear, confusing or confused: *His meaning is unclear.*

uncoil /ʌnˈkɔɪl/ *v* to straighten from a coiled position: *The snake uncoiled itself.*

uncomfortable /ʌnˈkʌmftəbəl/ *adj* **1** not comfortable: *That's a very uncomfortable chair*; *Don't you get uncomfortable sitting on the floor?* **2** embarrassed; shy: *I always feel uncomfortable in a room full of strangers.*
un'comfortably *adv.*

uncommon /ʌnˈkɒmən/ *adj* rare; unusual: *This type of animal is becoming very uncommon.*
un'commonly *adv* very; unusually: *an uncommonly clever person.*

uncommunicative /ʌnkəˈmjuːnɪkətɪv/ *adj* refusing to talk or tell what you are thinking: *Something seems to be worrying him — he's become very uncommunicative lately.*

uncompromising /ʌnˈkɒmprəmaɪzɪŋ/ *adj* refusing to change or alter a belief: *Her attitude is hard and uncompromising.*

unconcerned /ʌnkənˈsɜːnd/ *adj* not worried or interested.

unconditional /ʌnkənˈdɪʃənəl/ *adj* with no conditions attached: *His offer of money is unconditional.* **uncon'ditionally** *adv.*

unconscious /ʌnˈkɒnʃəs/ *adj* **1** stunned; not conscious, usually because of a bad illness or an accident: *She was unconscious for three days after her car-crash.* **2** not aware; not intended; not deliberate: *He was unconscious of having said anything rude*; *Her rudeness is quite unconscious.* — *n* the deepest level of your mind, the workings of which go on without you being aware of them. **un'consciously** *adv*. **un'consciousness** *n.*

uncontrollable /ʌnkənˈtroʊləbəl/ *adj* that you cannot control: *She suddenly had an uncontrollable urge to kick something.* **uncon'trollably** *adv.*

unconventional /ʌnkənˈvɛnʃənəl/ *adj* unusual; different from other people: *an unconventional lifestyle.* **uncon'ventionally** *adv.*

uncooperative /ʌnkoʊˈɒpərətɪv/ *adj* refusing to be helpful.

uncountable /ʌnˈkaʊntəbəl/ *adj* **1** not able to be numbered. **2** not able to have a plural: *Weather is an uncountable noun.*

uncover /ʌnˈkʌvə(r)/ *v* to remove the cover from something; to reveal something: *His criminal activities were finally uncovered.*

undaunted /ʌnˈdɔːntɪd/ *adj* fearless; not discouraged: *He was undaunted by his failure.*

undecided /ʌndɪˈsaɪdɪd/ *adj* **1** not having made up your mind: *She was undecided as to whether she should go or not.* **2** not decided: *The date of the meeting is still undecided.*

undeniable /ʌndɪˈnaɪəbəl/ *adj* clearly true or certain: *She may not be very clever but her beauty is undeniable.* **undeˈniably** *adv.*

under /ˈʌndə(r)/ *prep* **1** beneath; lower than; covered by: *Your pencil is under the chair; Strange plants grow under the sea; She hid the letter under her pillow.* **2** less than: *Children under five should not cross the street alone; You can do the job in under an hour.* **3** in your charge; obeying your orders: *She has 50 workers under her.* **4** used to express various relations: *The fort was under attack; The business improved under the new management; The matter is under consideration.* — *adv*: *The swimmer surfaced and went under again; children aged seven and under.*

> You put a saucer **under** (not **below**) a cup; the opposite of **under** is **over**.

> You look down from a hill at the fields **below** (not **under**) you; the opposite of **below** is **above**.

under- **1** beneath, as in **underline**. **2** too little, as in **underpay**. **3** lower in rank: *the under-manager.* **4** less in age than: *a nursery for under-fives.*

underclothes /ˈʌndəkloʊðz/ *n* clothes worn next to your skin, under your outer clothes. **ˈunderclothing** *n* underclothes.

undercover /ʌndəˈkʌvə(r)/ *adj* working in secret; done in secret: *He is an undercover agent for the Americans.*

underdog /ˈʌndədɒg/ *n* a person who is in a weak position: *I always feel I should support the underdog in a match or competition.*

underestimate /ʌndərˈɛstɪmeɪt/ *v* to make too low an estimate of the value or importance of: *Don't underestimate his abilities.*

underfoot /ʌndəˈfʊt/ *adv* under your feet: *The ground was wet underfoot.*

undergarment /ˈʌndəgɑːmənt/ *n* an article of clothing worn under the outer clothes.

undergo /ʌndəˈgoʊ/ *v* **1** to experience: *The villagers underwent terrible hardships during the war.* **2** to go through a process: *The car is undergoing repairs; She has been undergoing medical treatment.*

> **underˈgo**; **underwent** /ʌndəˈwɛnt/; **undergone** /ʌndəˈgɒn/.

undergraduate /ʌndəˈgrædjʊət/ *n* a university student who has not yet passed the final examinations.

underground *adj* /ˈʌndəgraʊnd/ below the surface of the ground: *an underground railway; underground streams.* — *adv* /ʌndəˈgraʊnd/ **1** under the surface of the ground: *Rabbits live underground.* **2** into hiding: *He will go underground if the police start looking for him.* — *n* /ˈʌndəgraʊnd/ an underground railway (also called a **subway**): *She hates travelling by the underground; I'll come on the underground.*

undergrowth /ˈʌndəgroʊθ/ *n* low bushes or large plants growing among trees: *She tripped over in the thick undergrowth.*

underhand /ʌndəˈhand/ *adj* dishonest: *The other competitors complained that he had used underhand methods to win the competition.*

underlie /ʌndəˈlaɪ/ *v* to be the basis or cause of something: *The desire to be liked underlies most of his behaviour.* **underˈlying** *adj.*

> **underˈlie**; **underˈlay** /ʌndəˈleɪ/; **underlain** /ʌndəˈleɪn/.

underline /ʌndəˈlaɪn/ *v* **1** to draw a line under something: *He wrote down the title of his essay and underlined it.* **2** to emphasize the importance of something: *In his speech he underlined several points.*

undermine /ʌndəˈmaɪn/ *v* to weaken: *Continuous hard work had undermined his health.*

underneath /ʌndəˈniːθ/ *prep* under; beneath: *She was standing underneath the light; Have you looked underneath the bed?* — *adv*: *Molly had the top bunk and Milly had the one underneath.* — *n* the part or side beneath: *Have you ever seen the underneath of a bus?*

underpants /ˈʌndəpants/ *n* a man's or boy's short undergarment worn over the bottom: *a clean pair of underpants; Are these your underpants?*

underpass /ˈʌndəpɑːs/ *n* a road or path that passes under another road, railway *etc.*

underprivileged /ʌndəˈprɪvɪlɪdʒd/ *adj* having less money, opportunities *etc* than most other people in society.

underrate /ʌndəˈreɪt/ *v* to think that a thing or person is less clever or important *etc* than they really are: *Don't underrate him — he has a lot of powerful friends.*

underside /ˈʌndəsaɪd/ *n* the part or side lying beneath.

understand /ʌndəˈstand/ *v* **1** to see the meaning of something: *I can't understand this question; I don't understand why he* was so angry; *I can understand Japanese, although I don't speak it well; Speak slowly to foreigners so that they'll understand you.* **2** to know someone or something thoroughly: *She is a good teacher — she really understands children; I don't understand computers.* **3** to learn or realize something: *At first I didn't understand how ill she was; I understood that you were planning to leave today.*

> **under'stand; understood** /ʌndə'stʊd/; **under'stood**: *We understood that he was coming; I don't think I've understood you correctly.*

under'standable *adj* able to be understood or explained: *His anger is quite understandable.*

under'standably *adv*: *She was understandably upset.*

under'standing *adj* good at knowing how other people feel: *an understanding person; Try to be more understanding!* — *n* **1** the power of thinking clearly: *a man of great understanding.* **2** the ability to understand another person's feelings: *His kindness and understanding were a great comfort to her.* **3** an agreement: *The two men have reached an understanding after their disagreement.*

make yourself understood to make your meaning or intentions clear: *He tried speaking French to them, but couldn't make himself understood.*

understatement /ʌndə'steɪtmənt/ *n* a statement which expresses less than the truth about something: *To say he's foolish is an understatement — he's really quite mad.*

understudy /ʌndə'stʌdɪ/ *n* a person who can take the place of a particular actor or actress if necessary.

undertake /ʌndə'teɪk/ *v* **1** to accept a duty, task *etc*: *He undertook the job willingly.* **2** to promise: *I undertake to complete the work in a fortnight.*

> **under'take; undertook** /ʌndə'tʊk/; **under'taken.**

undertaker /'ʌndəteɪkə(r)/ *n* a person who organizes funerals.

undertaking /'ʌndəteɪkɪŋ/ *n* **1** a task; a piece of work: *I didn't realize what a large undertaking this job would be.* **2** a promise: *He made an undertaking that he would pay the money back.*

undertone /'ʌndətoʊn/ *n* a low, quiet voice.

undervalue /ʌndə'væljuː/ *v* to treat someone or something as less valuable or important than they really are.

underwater /ʌndə'wɔːtə(r)/ *adj*: *underwater exploration; an underwater camera.* — *adv*: *to swim underwater.*

underwear /'ʌndəwɛə(r)/ *n* underclothes: *She washed her skirt, blouse and underwear.*

underwent *see* **undergo**.

underworld /'ʌndəwɜːld/ *n* **1** a group of people in a city that live by committing crimes: *A member of the underworld told the police where the murderer was hiding.* **2** in mythology, a place people go to when they die.

undesirable /ʌndɪ'zaɪərəbəl/ *adj* **1** not wanted: *These pills can have some undesirable effects.* **2** unpleasant; nasty: *My son has made some undesirable friends; undesirable behaviour.*

undid *see* **undo**.

undignified /ʌn'dɪgnɪfaɪd/ *adj* clumsy; making you look foolish: *She landed at the bottom of the stairs in a very undignified position.*

undivided /ʌndɪ'vaɪdɪd/ *adj* full; completely concentrated: *Please give the matter your undivided attention.*

undo /ʌn'duː/ *v* **1** to unfasten; to untie: *Can you undo the knot in this string?; He undid his jacket.* **2** to reverse, cancel or remove the effect of something: *The evil that he did can never be undone.*

> **un'do; undid** /ʌn'dɪd/; **undone** /ʌn'dʌn/.

undoing /ʌn'duːɪŋ/ *n* the cause of ruin or disaster: *His laziness was his undoing.*

undone *adj* **1** not done; not finished: *I don't like going to bed leaving work undone.* **2** not fastened: *One of my shoelaces has come undone.*

undoubted /ʌn'daʊtɪd/ *adj* certain; clear; obvious: *his undoubted talents.*

un'doubtedly *adv* without doubt; certainly: *You are undoubtedly correct.*

undress /ʌn'drɛs/ *v* to take clothes off: *She undressed the child; Undress yourself and get into bed; I undressed and went to bed.*

un'dressed *adj* not wearing any or many clothes.

undue /ʌn'djuː/ *adj* too great; more than is necessary: *undue caution.*

un'duly *adv*: *to be unduly severe.*

unearth /ʌn'ɜːθ/ *v* to discover something or remove it from where it is put away: *to unearth new facts; I've unearthed this old hat for you to wear at the fancy-dress party.*

unearthly /ʌn'ɜːθlɪ/ *adj* **1** strange and a bit

frightening: *The children heard unearthly groans coming from the cave.* **2** very unreasonable: *He rang her at the unearthly hour of 5 a.m.*

unease /ʌn'iːz/ *n* uneasiness.

uneasy /ʌn'iːzɪ/ *adj* anxious; worried; shy; embarrassed: *When her son did not return, she grew uneasy; I feel uneasy in the company of strangers.* **un'easiness** *n*.
un'easily *adv*: *He glanced uneasily at his watch.*

unemployed /ˌʌnɪm'plɔɪd/ *adj* without a job: *He has been unemployed for three months.* — *n* people who are unemployed.
unem'ployment *n* **1** the state of being unemployed: *If the factory is closed, many men will face unemployment.* **2** the numbers of people without work: *Unemployment has reached record figures this year.*

unending /ʌn'ɛndɪŋ/ *adj* never finishing; continuous: *For some people, life is just an unending struggle for survival.*

unequal /ʌn'iːkwəl/ *adj* not equal in quantity, quality *etc*: *They got unequal shares of the money.* **un'equally** *adv*.

uneven /ʌn'iːvən/ *adj* **1** not even: *The road surface here is very uneven.* **2** not all of the same standard: *His work is very uneven.* **un'evenly** *adv*. **un'evenness** *n*.

unexpected /ˌʌnɪk'spɛktɪd/ *adj* not expected; sudden: *his unexpected death.* **unex'pectedly** *adv*.

unfailing /ʌn'feɪlɪŋ/ *adj* constant: *We admired her unfailing courage.*
un'failingly *adv* always: *He is unfailingly polite.*

unfair /ʌn'fɛə(r)/ *adj* not fair; not just: *unfair treatment.* **un'fairly** *adv*. **un'fairness** *n*.

unfaithful /ʌn'feɪθfʊl/ *adj* not loyal. **un'faithfulness** *n*.

unfamiliar /ˌʌnfə'mɪlɪə(r)/ *adj* not known to you; not knowing something well: *He felt nervous about walking along unfamiliar streets; I am unfamiliar with this neighbourhood.*

unfashionable /ʌn'faʃənəbəl/ *adj* not fashionable or popular: *In many countries it's unfashionable to smoke nowadays.*

unfasten /ʌn'fɑːsən/ *v* to undo something that is fastened: *He unfastened his jacket.*

unfit /ʌn'fɪt/ *adj* **1** not good enough; not in a suitable state: *This water is unfit for drinking; He has been ill and is quite unfit to travel.* **2** not as strong and healthy as is possible: *You become unfit if you don't take regular exercise.* **un'fitness** *n*.

unfold /ʌn'fəʊld/ *v* **1** to open and spread out a map, newspaper *etc*: *He sat down and unfolded his newspaper.* **2** to make or become known: *She gradually unfolded her plan to them; The story gradually unfolded.*

unforeseen /ˌʌnfɔː'siːn/ *adj* not known about before it happens, not predicted: *The plan was upset by unforeseen developments.*

unforgettable /ˌʌnfə'gɛtəbəl/ *adj* never able to be forgotten: *an unforgettable experience.*

unforgivable /ˌʌnfə'gɪvəbəl/ *adj* so bad that it cannot be forgiven: *That's an unforgivable way to treat someone.*

unfortunate /ʌn'fɔːtʃənət/ *adj* **1** unlucky: *He has been very unfortunate.* **2** regrettable: *an unfortunate mistake.*
un'fortunately *adv*: *I'd like to help but unfortunately I can't.*

unfounded /ʌn'faʊndɪd/ *adj* not based on facts; not true: *The rumours are completely unfounded.*

unfriendly /ʌn'frɛndlɪ/ *adj* unpleasant or impolite: *I hope you didn't think I was being unfriendly when I didn't answer you.*

ungainly /ʌn'geɪnlɪ/ *adj* awkward; clumsy.

ungrateful /ʌn'greɪtfʊl/ *adj* not giving thanks for kindness *etc*: *It will look very ungrateful if you don't write and thank him.*

unguarded /ʌn'gɑːdɪd/ *adj* **1** not protected or guarded: *She turned around, leaving her handbag unguarded.* **2** careless; saying more than you wanted to: *He admitted the truth in an unguarded moment.*

unhappy /ʌn'hapɪ/ *adj* **1** not happy; sad: *He had an unhappy childhood.* **2** unfortunate; unlucky: *An unhappy chance brought me face to face with the headmaster, just as I was leaving early.* **3** not satisfied: *I'm not very happy with your work.* **un'happily** *adv*. **un'happiness** *n*.

unhealthy /ʌn'hɛlθɪ/ *adj* not healthy: *He is fat and unhealthy; an unhealthy climate.* **un'healthily** *adv*. **un'healthiness** *n*.

unheard-of /ʌn'hɜːd ɒv/ *adj* surprising or shocking because it has not happened before: *Not long ago, it was unheard-of for women to do this kind of work.*

unhygienic /ˌʌnhaɪ'dʒiːnɪk/ *adj* not hygienic, dirty: *The restaurant was forced to close because the kitchens were unhygienic.*

unicorn /'juːnɪkɔːn/ *n* in fairy tales *etc*, an animal like a white horse with one straight horn on its forehead.

unidentified /ˌʌnaɪ'dɛntɪfaɪd/ *adj* not identified; not recognized: *an unidentified body.*
unidentified flying object an object in the

uniform /'juːnɪfɔːm/ *n* special clothes worn by all members of an organization, for instance soldiers, children at a particular school *etc*: *The policemen were in uniform*; *The pupils like their new uniforms.* — *adj* the same everywhere, or in every case; not varying: *The sky was a uniform grey.* **'uniformly** *adv*. **'uniformed** *adj* wearing a uniform: *a uniformed police officer*.

uni'formity *n* the state in which everything or person is exactly the same: *the uniformity of modern architecture*.

unify /'juːnɪfaɪ/ *v* to join several things together to form a single whole: *The country used to consist of several small states and was unified only recently.* **unifi'cation** *n*.

unilateral /juːnɪ'lætərəl/ *adj* involving, affecting or done by only one person in a group: *The country cannot take unilateral action but must act with its allies.* **uni'laterally** *adv*.

unimportant /ˌʌnɪm'pɔːtənt/ *adj* not important or significant: *The changes he has suggested are unimportant*.

uninhabitable /ˌʌnɪn'hæbɪtəbəl/ *adj* impossible for people to live in: *The floods made the houses uninhabitable for a while*.

uninhabited /ˌʌnɪn'hæbɪtɪd/ *adj* where nobody lives: *an uninhabited desert island*.

unintelligible /ˌʌnɪn'tɛlɪdʒəbəl/ *adj* impossible to understand: *I'm afraid I found his explanation completely unintelligible*.

uninterested /ʌn'ɪntrɪstɪd/ *adj* lacking interest; showing no enthusiasm: *I told him the news but he seemed uninterested*.

> **uninterested** means lacking interest: *uninterested pupils*.
> **disinterested** means not favouring one side; being fair to both sides: *a disinterested judgement*.

uninterrupted /ˌʌnɪntə'rʌptɪd/ *adj* **1** continuing without a pause: *four hours of uninterrupted rain.* **2** not blocked by anything: *We have an uninterrupted view of the sea*.

uninvited /ˌʌnɪn'vaɪtɪd/ *adj* not invited; not wanted: *uninvited guests*; *uninvited interference*.

union /'juːnjən/ *n* the joining together of things or people; a combination; a partnership: *Their marriage was a perfect union*.

Union Jack the national flag of the United Kingdom.

unique /juː'niːk/ *adj* being the only one of its kind; having no equal: *His style is unique.*

> *a* **unique** (not **very unique**) opportunity; **very** is not needed.

unisex /'juːnɪsɛks/ *adj* in a style that can be worn by both men and women: *unisex clothes*; *a unisex hairstyle*.

unison /'juːnɪsən/ *n* **1** the same musical note, or series of notes, produced by several voices singing, or instruments playing, together: *They sang in unison.* **2** agreement: *They acted in unison*.

unit /'juːnɪt/ *n* **1** a single thing *etc* within a group: *The building is divided into twelve different apartments or living units.* **2** a quantity that is used as a standard: *The dollar is the standard unit of currency in America.* **3** the smallest whole number, 1, or any number between 1 and 9.

unite /juː'naɪt/ *v* to join together; to make or become one: *England and Scotland were united under one parliament in 1707*; *He was united with his friends again*; *Let us unite against the common enemy*.

u'nited *adj* **1** joined politically: *the United States of America.* **2** joined together by love or friendship: *a united family.* **3** joint; shared: *a united effort*.

unity /'juːnɪtɪ/ *n* the state of being united or in agreement: *When will men learn to live in unity with each other?*

universe /'juːnɪvɜːs/ *n* everything — earth, planets, sun, stars *etc* — that exists anywhere: *Somewhere in the universe there might be another world like ours*.

uni'versal *adj* affecting, including *etc* the whole of the world or all people: *English may become a universal language that everyone can learn and use.* **uni'versally** *adv*.

university /juːnɪ'vɜːsɪtɪ/ *n* a place of learning where a large number of subjects are taught up to a high standard: *Many pupils go to university after they leave school*.

unjust /ʌn'dʒʌst/ *adj* not just; unfair: *an unjust punishment*.

unkind /ʌn'kaɪnd/ *adj* not kind; cruel: *You were very unkind to her*; *It was unkind of you to tease her.* **un'kindness** *n*.

unknowingly /ʌn'nəʊɪŋlɪ/ *adv* without realizing: *She unknowingly gave the patient the wrong medicine*.

unknown /ʌn'nəʊn/ *adj* **1** not known: *This news has come from an unknown source.* **2** not famous; not well-known: *an unknown actor*.

the unknown anything that people do not know about: *a fear of the unknown*.

unleaded petrol /ʌnlɛdɪd 'pɛtrəl/ petrol with very little lead in it.

unless /ʌn'lɛs/ *conjunction* **1** if not: *Don't come unless I telephone.* **2** except when: *The directors have a meeting on Friday, unless there is nothing to discuss.*

unlike /ʌn'laɪk/ *prep* **1** different from: *I never saw twins who were so unlike each other.* **2** not usual for someone; not characteristic of someone: *It is unlike Mary to be so silly.*

unlikely /ʌn'laɪklɪ/ *adj* not likely or probable: *an unlikely explanation*; *She's unlikely to arrive before 7.00 p.m.*; *It is unlikely that she will come.*

unlimited /ʌn'lɪmɪtɪd/ *adj* as much as you want or can use: *This ticket allows unlimited travel on all train services for two months.*

unload /ʌn'loʊd/ *v* to remove cargo from a ship, vehicle *etc*: *The men were unloading the ship.*

unlock /ʌn'lɒk/ *v* to open something that is locked: *Unlock this door, please!*

unlucky /ʌn'lʌkɪ/ *adj* not lucky; not fortunate: *I am unlucky — I never win at cards.*
un'luckily *adv* unfortunately: *Unluckily, he has hurt his hand and cannot play the piano.*

unmarried /ʌn'marɪd/ *adj* not married.

unmistakable /ʌnmɪ'steɪkəbəl/ *adj* very clear; impossible to misunderstand: *His meaning was unmistakable.*

unmoved /ʌn'muːvd/ *adj* not affected; not upset: *He was unmoved by her tears.*

unnatural /ʌn'natʃərəl/ *adj* not natural; strange; queer: *an unnatural silence.* **un'naturally** *adv.*

unnecessary /ʌn'nɛsəsərɪ/ *adj* **1** not necessary: *It is unnecessary to waken him yet.* **2** that could have been avoided: *Your mistake caused a lot of unnecessary work in the office.* **unneces'sarily** *adv.*

unnoticed /ʌn'noʊtɪsd/ *adj* not seen by anyone: *He managed to slip into the room unnoticed.*

unobtrusive /ʌnɒb'truːsɪv/ *adj* not noticeable: *We tried to be as unobtrusive as possible.* **unob'trusively** *adv.*

unoccupied /ʌn'ɒkjʊpaɪd/ *adj* not lived in, empty: *These flats have been unoccupied for years.*

unofficial /ʌnə'fɪʃəl/ *adj* not yet having official approval: *Unofficial reports say that several people have been badly injured.* **unof'ficially** *adv.*

unpack /ʌn'pak/ *v* to take out things that are packed: *He unpacked his clothes*; *Have you unpacked yet?*; *I've unpacked my case.*

unpaid /ʌn'peɪd/ *adj* **1** not receiving money for work that is done: *an unpaid assistant.* **2** done without payment: *unpaid overtime.* **3** not yet paid: *unpaid bills.*

unpleasant /ʌn'plɛzənt/ *adj* not pleasant; nasty: *an unpleasant smell.* **un'pleasantly** *adv.*

unpopular /ʌn'pɒpjʊlə(r)/ *adj* not popular or liked: *He has always been unpopular.*

unprecedented /ʌn'prɛsɪdɛntɪd/ *adj* never having happened before: *The Queen talked with unprecedented frankness about her life.*

unqualified /ʌn'kwɒlɪfaɪd/ *adj* **1** not having any qualifications or knowledge for something: *I'm unqualified to advise you I'm afraid.* **2** absolute; complete: *The performance was an unqualified success.*

unquestionable /ʌn'kwɛstʃənəbəl/ *adj* not able to be doubted; completely certain: *unquestionable proof.*
un'questionably *adv* certainly: *Unquestionably, he deserves to be punished.*
un'questioning *adj* with no doubt or disagreement: *unquestioning obedience*; *unquestioning belief.*

unravel /ʌn'ravəl/ *v* **1** to take the knots out of thread, string *etc*: *She could not unravel the tangled thread.* **2** to undo knitting. **3** to solve: *to unravel a mystery.*

unreal /ʌn'rɪəl/ *adj* not actually existing: *He lives in an unreal world imagined by himself.* **unre'ality** *n.*

unreasonable /ʌn'riːzənəbəl/ *adj* not sensible; asking too much: *It is unreasonable to expect children to work so hard*; *That butcher charges unreasonable prices.*

unrefined /ʌnrɪ'faɪnd/ *adj* in a raw or natural state: *unrefined sugar.*

unrelenting /ʌnrɪ'lɛntɪŋ/ *adj* going on and on without stopping or losing power or strength: *The rain was unrelenting.*

unreliable /ʌnrɪ'laɪəbəl/ *adj* not to be relied on or trusted: *My old car is getting very unreliable.*

unrest /ʌn'rɛst/ *n* trouble and discontent among the people: *There was unrest all over the country when the government introduced higher taxes.*

unrivalled /ʌn'raɪvəld/ *adj* far better than anything else: *The museum contains an unrivalled collection of Greek vases.*

unroll /ʌn'roʊl/ *v* to open so that it is flat: *She unrolled the carpet on the floor.*

unruly /ʌn'ruːlɪ/ *adj* badly behaved; not easily controlled: *an unruly boy*; *unruly behaviour.* **un'ruliness** *n.*

unsatisfactory /ˌʌnsatɪsˈfaktərɪ/ *adj* not good enough: *Your work is unsatisfactory, Anna — you must try harder.*

See **dissatisfied**.

unscathed /ʌnˈskeɪðd/ *adj* without being harmed or injured: *They escaped from the burning building unscathed.*

unscrew /ʌnˈskruː/ *v* to remove or loosen something by taking out screws; to loosen something with a twisting action: *He unscrewed the cupboard door.*

unsightly /ʌnˈsaɪtlɪ/ *adj* ugly: *Those new buildings are very unsightly.*

unstable /ʌnˈsteɪbəl/ *adj* **1** likely to move, fall over or change suddenly: *an unstable political situation.* **2** likely to have sudden changes of mood.

unsuccessful /ˌʌnsəkˈsɛsfʊl/ *adj* not successful: *She tried to find him but was unsuccessful.*

unsuitable /ʌnˈsuːtəbəl/ *adj* not suitable or right: *Those shoes are unsuitable for school.*

unsure /ʌnˈʃʊə(r)/ *adj* **1** not certain or decided: *I was unsure about the correct postal address.* **2** not having confidence about yourself: *She was still a little unsure of herself in American society.*

unsuspecting /ˌʌnsəˈspɛktɪŋ/ *adj* not aware of something that is about to happen; not aware of danger: *The murderer walked quietly up behind his unsuspecting victim.*

untangle /ʌnˈtaŋɡəl/ *v* to free something from a tangle; to disentangle: *I'm trying to untangle this string.*

unthinkable /ʌnˈθɪŋkəbəl/ *adj* too bad, unusual *etc* to be considered: *It would be unthinkable to ask him to tell a lie.*

unthinking /ʌnˈθɪŋkɪŋ/ *adj* not thinking carefully enough before acting. **un'thinkingly** *adv.*

untidy /ʌnˈtaɪdɪ/ *adj* **1** not tidy; in a mess: *His room is always very untidy.* **2** not keeping things tidy or arranged neatly: *an untidy person.*

untie /ʌnˈtaɪ/ *v* to loosen; to unfasten: *He untied the string from the parcel.*

until /ʌnˈtɪl/ *prep* up till a particular time: *He was here until one o'clock.* — *conjunction* up to the time when, or place where: *Walk straight on until you come to the hospital; I won't know his opinion until I get a letter from him.*

until is spelt with one l.

until means up till: *He will be here until one o'clock.*
by means at or just before a particular time: *He will be here by one o'clock.*

untiring /ʌnˈtaɪərɪŋ/ *adj* never stopping; never giving up: *his untiring efforts; her untiring energy.* **un'tiringly** *adv.*

untold /ʌnˈtoʊld/ *adj* **1** not told; not revealed: *The horrible story is better left untold; Her secret remained untold.* **2** too great to be counted, measured *etc*: *There are an untold number of stars in the universe; The king lived in untold wealth while his people died of hunger.*

untoward /ˌʌntəˈwɔːd/ *adj* not favourable or convenient: *untoward events.*

untrue /ʌnˈtruː/ *adj* not true; false: *an untrue statement.*

un'truth *n* a lie.

un'truthful *adj* lying; dishonest: *She was being untruthful when she said she didn't care.*

untwist /ʌnˈtwɪst/ *v* to straighten from a twisted position: *He untwisted the wire.*

unused *adj* **1** /ʌnˈjuːsəd/ not familiar with something because you haven't done it much before: *He was unused to having to cook his own meals.* **2** /ʌnˈjuːzəd/ not having been used: *an unused stamp.*

unusual /ʌnˈjuːʒʊəl/ *adj* not usual; rare: *It is unusual for him to arrive late; He has an unusual job.* **un'usually** *adv.*

unwanted /ʌnˈwɒntəd/ *adj*: *unwanted interference.*

unwarranted /ʌnˈwɒrəntəd/ *adj* not deserved or reasonable: *She felt his anger was unwarranted because she had already apologized once.*

unwary /ʌnˈwɛərɪ/ *adj* not cautious: *If you are unwary he will cheat you.* **un'warily** *adv.* **un'wariness** *n.*

unwelcome /ʌnˈwɛlkəm/ *adj* received unwillingly or with disappointment: *unwelcome news; unwelcome guests; I felt unwelcome in her house.*

unwell /ʌnˈwɛl/ *adj* not in good health: *He felt unwell this morning.*

unwieldy /ʌnˈwiːldɪ/ *adj* large and awkward to carry or manage: *This suitcase is too unwieldy for me.*

unwilling /ʌnˈwɪlɪŋ/ *adj* not willing; reluctant: *He's unwilling to accept the money.* **un'willingly** *adv.* **un'willingness** *n.*

unwind /ʌnˈwaɪnd/ *v* **1** to undo or come out of a wound position: *He unwound the bandage* *from his ankle; The snake unwound itself.* **2** to relax: *She found the best way to unwind after work was to take a hot bath.*

> **un'wind; unwound** /ʌn'waʊnd/; **un'wound.**

unwitting /ʌn'wɪtɪŋ/ *adj* not realizing something; not aware of what is really happening: *She was the unwitting carrier of stolen goods.* **un'wittingly** *adv.*

unworthy /ʌn'wɜːðɪ/ *adj* **1** very bad; shameful: *That was an unworthy way to behave.* **2** not deserving: *He's unworthy to be chosen for such an important job.* **3** less good than should be expected from someone: *Such bad behaviour is unworthy of him.* **un'worthily** *adv.* **un'worthiness** *n.*

unwound *see* **unwind.**

unwrap /ʌn'ræp/ *v* to open something wrapped: *He unwrapped the gift.*

unzip /ʌn'zɪp/ *v* to undo the zip of a dress *etc.*

up /ʌp/ *adv* **1** to, or at, a higher position; into an upright position: *Is the elevator going up?; She looked up at him; The price of coffee is up again; Stand up; He got up from his chair.* **2** out of bed; not in bed: *What time do you get up?; He stayed up all night; Jack's up already.* **3** towards, and as far as, the place where you *etc* are: *A taxi drove up and we got in; She walked quickly up to the front door.* **4** louder: *Turn the radio up; Speak up!* **5** used with many verbs to express various meanings: *Hurry up!; You'll end up in hospital if you don't drive more carefully; She locked the house up; I've used up all the paper; She tore the letter up.* — *prep* **1** to or at a higher level on something: *He went up the mountain; She's up the ladder; to go up the stairs; to climb up a tree.* **2** along: *They walked up the street; Their house is up the road.*

up to 1 busy with: *What is he up to now?* **2** able to do: *He isn't quite up to the job.* **3** reaching the standard of: *This work isn't up to your best.* **4** having to be decided, chosen *etc* by a particular person: *It's up to you to decide; The final choice is up to him.* **5** as far, or as much, as: *He counted up to 100; from Egyptian times up to the present day.*

upbringing /'ʌpbrɪŋɪŋ/ *n* the process of bringing up a child: *He had a stern upbringing.*

update /ʌp'deɪt/ *v* **1** to add the latest information: *Could someone update me on what's been happening here?* **2** to make something more modern: *An updated version of this software will soon be available.* **'update** *n.*

upheaval /ʌp'hiːvəl/ *n* a great change or disturbance: *Moving house always causes upheaval; There were political upheavals after the election of the new government.*

uphill /ʌp'hɪl/ *adv* up a slope: *We travelled uphill for several hours.* — *adj* **1** sloping upwards: *an uphill journey.* **2** difficult: *This will be an uphill struggle.*

uphold /ʌp'hoʊld/ *v* to support: *His family upholds him in his campaign.*

> **up'hold; upheld** /ʌp'hɛld/; **up'held.**

upholster /ʌp'hoʊlstə(r)/ *v* to fit seats with springs, stuffing, covers *etc*: *He upholstered the chair.* **up'holstered** *adj.*

up'holstery *n* **1** the business or process of upholstering. **2** the springs, coverings *etc* of a seat: *car upholstery.*

upkeep /'ʌpkiːp/ *n* the keeping of a house, car *etc* in a good condition; the cost of this.

uplifting /ʌp'lɪftɪŋ/ *adj* making you feel happier or more hopeful: *The minister made an uplifting speech.*

upon /ə'pɒn/ *prep* on: *He sat upon the floor; Please place it upon the table.*

upper /'ʌpə(r)/ *adj* higher: *the upper floors of the building; He has a scar on his upper lip.* — *n* the part of a shoe above the sole: *The uppers are made of leather and the soles are made of nylon.*

'uppermost *adj* highest: *in the uppermost room of the castle.* — *adv*: *Thoughts of her father were uppermost in her mind.*

the upper hand an advantage: *Our team managed to get the upper hand in the end.*

upright /'ʌpraɪt/ *adj* **1** standing straight up; erect; vertical: *a row of upright posts.* **2** just and honest: *an upright, honourable man.* — *adv* vertically: *He placed the books upright in the bookcase; She stood upright.* — *n* an upright post *etc* supporting a construction: *When building the fence, place the uprights two metres apart.*

uprising /'ʌpraɪzɪŋ/ *n* a fight against a government *etc*; a rebellion: *There was an armed uprising against the dictator.*

uproar /'ʌprɔː(r)/ *n* an outbreak of noise, shouting *etc*: *The whole town was in an uproar after the football team's victory.*

up'roarious *adj* very noisy, especially with much laughter: *an uproarious welcome.* **up'roariously** *adv.*

uproot /ʌp'ruːt/ *v* to pull a plant *etc* out of the earth together with its roots: *to uproot weeds.*

upset *v* /ʌp'sɛt/ **1** to overturn; to knock over:

He upset a glass of wine over the table. **2** to disturb; to put out of order: *His illness has upset all our arrangements.* **3** to make someone sad, unhappy *etc*: *His friend's death upset him very much.* — *adj* /ʌpˈsɛt/ disturbed; unhappy: *Is he very upset about failing his exam?* — *n* /ˈʌpsɛt/ a disturbance: *He has a stomach upset; I couldn't bear the upset of moving house again.*

up'set; up'set; up'set.

upshot /ˈʌpʃɒt/ *n* the final outcome or result of a discussion *etc*: *The upshot of it all was that the decision was reversed.*

upside down /ˌʌpsaɪdˈdaʊn/ **1** with the top part underneath: *The plate was lying upside down on the floor.* **2** into a state of confusion: *The burglars turned the house upside down.*

upstairs /ʌpˈstɛəz/ *adv* on or to an upper floor: *His room is upstairs; She went upstairs to her bedroom.* — *n* the upper floor: *The ground floor needs painting, but the upstairs is nice.* — *adj: an upstairs sitting-room.*

upstream /ʌpˈstriːm/ *adv* towards the source of a river, stream *etc*: *Salmon swim upstream to lay their eggs.*

upsurge /ˈʌpsɜːdʒ/ *n* a sudden rise or increased amount: *There has been a sudden upsurge in homelessness.*

uptake /ˈʌpteɪk/: **quick on the uptake** quick to understand or realize something: *He isn't very quick on the uptake but he works well when he's sure of what to do.*

up-to-date /ˌʌptəˈdeɪt/ *adj* **1** new: *up-to-date technology.* **2** having the latest information: *Doctors have to keep themselves up-to-date with developments in medicine.*

upturn /ˈʌptɜːn/ *n* an increase or improvement: *a sharp upturn in the economy.*

upward /ˈʌpwəd/ *adj* going up; directed up: *They took the upward path; an upward glance.*

'**upwards** *adv* towards a higher position: *He was lying on the floor face upwards; The path led upwards.*

upwards of greater than: *We had upwards of 200 replies.*

uranium /jʊˈreɪnɪəm/ *n* a radioactive metal that is used as a nuclear fuel.

urban /ˈɜːbən/ *adj* having to do with a city or town: *He dislikes urban life; urban traffic.*

The opposite of **urban** is **rural**.

urchin /ˈɜːtʃɪn/ *n* a mischievous, dirty or ragged, child: *She was chased by a crowd of urchins.*

urge /ɜːdʒ/ *v* **1** to beg; to ask earnestly: *He urged her to drive carefully; 'Come with me,' he urged.* **2** to recommend; to insist on something: *She urged caution.* — *n* a strong desire: *I felt an urge to hit him.*

urge on to try to persuade a person *etc* to go on: *He urged his followers on.*

urgent /ˈɜːdʒənt/ *adj* needing immediate attention: *There is an urgent message for the doctor.* '**urgently** *adv.* '**urgency** *n.*

urine /ˈjʊərɪn/ *n* the waste fluid passed out of the bodies of humans and animals from the bladder.

'**urinary** *adj: a urinary infection.*

'**urinate** *v* to pass urine from the bladder.

urn /ɜːn/ *n* **1** a tall vase, especially one for holding the ashes of a dead person. **2** a large metal container with a tap, in which tea or coffee is made, for example in a canteen: *a tea-urn.*

us /ʌs/ *pron* used as the object of a verb or preposition; the word you use for yourself along with one or more other people: *She told us to be quiet; A plane flew over us.*

usable /ˈjuːzəbəl/ *adj* that can be used: *Are any of these clothes usable?*

usage /ˈjuːzɪdʒ/ *n* **1** treatment: *These chairs have had a lot of rough usage.* **2** the way in which the words of a language are used; the way a particular word is used.

use[1] /juːz/ *v* **1** to employ something for a purpose: *What did you use to open the can?; Use your common sense!* **2** to consume: *We're using far too much electricity.*

used /juːzd/ *adj* not new: *used cars.*

used /juːzt/ **to 1** accustomed to: *She isn't used to such hard work.* **2** was or were in the habit of doing something: *I used to swim every day; She used not to be so forgetful; We drove past the place where I used to work*

'**user** *n* a person who uses a particular product, machine or service: *users of public transport.*

user-'friendly *adj* simple to use or understand: *Modern computers need to be user-friendly.*

use up to use something until no more is left: *Has the milk all been used up?*

use[2] /juːs/ **1** *n* the using of something: *The use of force in this case cannot be justified; This telephone number is for use in emergencies.* **2** the purpose for which something may be used: *This little knife has plenty of uses; I have no further use for these clothes.* **3** value; advantage: *Is this coat of any use to you?; It's no use offering to help when it's too late.*

4 the power of using: *She lost the use of her right arm as a result of the accident.* **5** permission to use something: *He let me have the use of his car while he was away.*

'useful *adj* helpful or serving a purpose well: *a useful tool; She made herself useful by doing the washing for her mother.*

'usefully *adv* in a useful way: *He spent the day usefully in repairing the car.*

'usefulness *n.*

'useless *adv* having no use; having no point or purpose: *Why don't you throw away those useless things?; We can't do it — it's useless to try.*

it's no use it's impossible: *He tried in vain to do it, then said 'It's no use.'*

come into use to begin to be used.

come in useful to be helpful in a particular situation: *The extra bed will come in useful when we have visitors.*

go out of use to stop being used.

make use of or **put to good use** to use something for a particular purpose: *He makes use of his training; He puts his training to good use in that job.*

usher /'ʌʃə(r)/ *n* a person who shows people to their seats in a theatre *etc.* — *v* to lead: *The waiter ushered him to a table.*

usherette /ʌʃə'rɛt/ *n* a female usher.

usual /'juːʒʊəl/ *adj* done, happening *etc* most often; customary: *Are you going home by the usual route?; There are more people here than usual; This kind of behaviour is quite usual in children of that age; As usual, he was late.*

'usually *adv* on most occasions: *We are usually at home in the evenings; Usually we finish work at 5 o'clock.*

usurp /jʊ'zɜːp/ *v* to take power or authority illegally: *He usurped the throne.*

utensil /jʊ'tɛnsɪl/ *n* an instrument, tool *etc* used in everyday life: *pots and pans and other kitchen utensils.*

utility /jʊ'tɪlɪtɪ/ *n* **1** usefulness: *Some kitchen tools have very little utility.* **2** a useful public service, for example the supply of water, gas, electricity *etc.*

utilize /'juːtɪlaɪz/ *v* to use something in an effective way: *The extra money is being utilized to buy books for the school library; Old newspapers can be utilized for making recycled paper.* **utili'zation** *n.*

utmost /'ʌtmoʊst/ *adj* greatest possible: *Take the utmost care!*

do your utmost to make the greatest possible effort: *She has done her utmost to help him.*

utter[1] /'ʌtə(r)/ *adj* complete; total: *There was utter silence; utter darkness.* **'utterly** *adv.*

utter[2] /'ʌtə(r)/ *v* to produce a sound from your mouth: *She uttered a sigh of relief; She didn't utter a single word.*

U-turn /'juːtɜːn/ *n* a turn in the shape of a **U**, made by a driver *etc* in order to go back the way he has just come.

V

v short for **versus**.

V- /viː/ shaped like a V: *a V-necked pullover*.

vacancy /ˈveɪkənsɪ/ *n* a job or place that has not been filled: *We have a vacancy for a typist*.

vacant /ˈveɪkənt/ *adj* **1** empty; not occupied: *a vacant chair*; *Are there any rooms vacant in this hotel?* **2** showing no intelligence or interest: *a vacant stare*.
ˈvacantly *adv*: *He stared vacantly out of the window*.

vacation /vəˈkeɪʃən/ *n* a holiday: *a summer vacation*.

on vacation not working; having a holiday: *She has gone to Italy on vacation*.

vaccinate /ˈvaksɪneɪt/ *v* to protect someone against a disease by putting the germs of a related disease (called a **vaccine** /ˈvaksiːn/) into their blood: *Has your child been vaccinated against smallpox?* **vacciˈnation** *n*.

vacuum /ˈvakjʊəm/ *n* a space from which all air or other gas has been removed. — *v* to clean with a vacuum cleaner: *She vacuumed the carpet*.
vacuum cleaner a machine that cleans carpets *etc* by sucking dust into itself.
vacuum flask a container that keeps drinks hot or cold.

vagina /vəˈdʒaɪnə/ *n* the opening in a woman's body that comes from her womb, through which a baby passes when it is born.

vagrant /ˈveɪɡrənt/ *n* a person who has no home or job and spends their life wandering about the streets: *The city opened two more hostels for vagrants*.

vague /veɪɡ/ *adj* **1** not clear; not definite: *Through the fog we saw the vague outline of a ship*; *I have only a vague idea of how this machine works*. **2** forgetful; absent-minded; not precise: *He is always very vague when making arrangements*. **ˈvaguely** *adv*. **ˈvagueness** *n*.

vain /veɪn/ *adj* **1** having too much pride in your appearance, achievements *etc*: *She's very vain about her good looks*. **2** not successful; useless: *He made a vain attempt to reach the drowning woman*. **3** empty; meaningless: *vain threats*; *vain promises*. **ˈvainly** *adv*.

in vain without success: *He tried in vain to open the locked door*.

vale /veɪl/ *n* a valley.

valentine /ˈvaləntaɪn/ *n* a sweetheart chosen on St Valentine's Day, February 14, or a card that you send to your sweetheart on this day. — *adj*: *a valentine card*.

valet /ˈvaleɪ/ or /ˈvalɪt/ *n* a manservant who looks after his master's clothes *etc*.

valiant /ˈvalɪənt/ *adj* brave: *valiant deeds*.

valid /ˈvalɪd/ *adj* **1** reasonable; acceptable: *a valid excuse*. **2** legally effective: *a valid passport*. **vaˈlidity** *n*.

valley /ˈvalɪ/ *n* an area of low land between hills or mountains, often with a river running through it.

See **mountain**.

valour /ˈvalə(r)/ *n* courage, especially in battle.

valuable /ˈvaljʊəbəl/ *adj* **1** having high value: *a valuable painting*. **2** very useful: *a valuable piece of information*.
ˈvaluables *n* things of special value: *jewellery and other valuables*.

valuation /valjʊˈeɪʃən/ *n* a judgement of how much money something is worth.

value /ˈvaljuː/ *n* **1** importance; usefulness: *His special knowledge was of great value to us*. **2** price: *What is the value of that stamp?* **3** fairness of exchange for your money: *You get good value for money at this supermarket!* **4** a principle or belief that influences your behaviour: *the changing values of our modern society*. — *v* **1** to suggest a suitable price for something: *This painting has been valued at £50 000*. **2** to regard something as good or important: *They had ceased to value what had first so attracted them to each other*.
ˈvalued *adj* regarded as precious: *What is your most valued possession?*
ˈvalueless *adj* having no value; worthless: *The necklace is completely valueless*.

valve /valv/ *n* a device that opens and closes a pipe or tube: *the valve in a bicycle tyre*.

vampire /ˈvampaɪə(r)/ *n* a dead person who is imagined to rise from the grave at night and suck the blood of people.

van /van/ *n* **1** a motor vehicle for carrying goods. **2** a luggage or goods compartment on a train.

vandal /ˈvandəl/ *n* a person who deliberately damages or destroys public buildings or other property: *Vandals have damaged this telephone box.* **'vandalism** *n.*

'vandalize *v* to deliberately damage property for no purpose: *The bus stop was vandalized at some time over the weekend.*

vanilla /vəˈnɪlə/ *n* a pod from a type of orchid, used to flavour food: *She put vanilla in her cake.*

vanish /ˈvænɪʃ/ *v* to become no longer visible; to disappear, especially suddenly: *The ship vanished over the horizon.*

vanity /ˈvænɪtɪ/ *n* too much pride in your appearance, achievements *etc*: *Vanity is his chief fault.*

vaporize /ˈveɪpəraɪz/ *v* to change into vapour.

vapour /ˈveɪpə(r)/ *v* **1** the gas-like form into which a substance can be changed by heating: *water vapour.* **2** mist or smoke in the air.

variable /ˈveərɪəbəl/ *adj* varying or that may be varied: *The winds here tend to be variable; These windows are available in variable designs.* **variaˈbility** *n.*

variant /ˈveərɪənt/ *n* a different form of something: *There are several variants to the end of this story.*

variation /veərɪˈeɪʃən/ *n* **1** the extent to which something varies; a difference: *In the desert there are great variations in temperature.* **2** in music, a development of a theme.

varied /ˈveərɪd/ *adj* full of variety: *He has had a varied career.*

variety /vəˈraɪətɪ/ *n* **1** the quality of being of many different kinds or of changing often: *There's great variety of experience in this job.* **2** a mixed collection: *The children got a variety of toys on their birthdays.* **3** a kind: *They grow fourteen different varieties of rose.* **4** mixed theatrical entertainment including dances, songs, short sketches *etc.* — *adj*: *a variety show.*

various /ˈveərɪəs/ *adj* **1** different: *His reasons for leaving were many and various.* **2** several: *Various people have told me about you.* **'variously** *adv.*

varnish /ˈvɑːnɪʃ/ *n* a sticky liquid that you paint on to wood *etc* to give it a glossy surface. — *v*: *Don't sit on that chair — I've just varnished it.*

vary /ˈveərɪ/ *v* to make, be or become different: *These apples vary in size from small to medium; His work never varies.*

vase /vɑːz/ *n* a jar or jug used as an ornament or for holding cut flowers.

vast /vɑːst/ *adj* very large; immense: *He inherited a vast fortune.* **'vastly** *adv.* **'vastness** *n.*

vat /væt/ *n* a large barrel or tank for holding liquids such as beer.

vault /vɔːlt/ *n* **1** a leap, especially one in which you use your hands or a pole to push off with. **2** a strong underground room in a bank *etc*. **3** an arched roof or ceiling especially in a church. — *v* to leap: *He vaulted over the fence.*

vaunt /vɔːnt/ *v* to boast about: *She vaunted her new car.*

veal /viːl/ *n* the flesh of a calf, used as food.

veer /vɪə(r)/ *v* to change direction suddenly: *The car veered across the road and hit the wall; The driver was forced to veer sharply.*

vegetable /ˈvɛdʒɪtəbəl/ *n* **1** a plant or part of a plant used as food: *We grow potatoes, beans and other vegetables.* — *adj*: *vegetable oil.* **2** a plant: *Grass is a vegetable, gold is a mineral and a human being is an animal.*

vegetarian /vɛdʒɪˈtɛərɪən/ *n* a person who does not eat meat or fish. — *adj*: *a vegetarian dish.*

vegetation /vɛdʒɪˈteɪʃən/ *n* plants in general; plants of a particular region or type: *There is hardly any vegetation in a desert; tropical vegetation.*

vehement /ˈviːəmənt/ *adj* strongly or forcefully expressed: *vehement denials.* **'vehemently** *adv.*

vehicle /ˈviːɪkəl/ *n* a means of transport on land, especially on wheels, such as a car, bus, bicycle *etc.*

veil /veɪl/ *n* a piece of thin cloth worn over your face or head to hide or cover it: *Some women wear veils for religious reasons, to prevent strangers from seeing their faces.* — *v* to cover with a veil: *She veiled her face.* **veiled** *adj*: *a veiled lady; The bride was veiled.*

vein /veɪn/ *n* **1** any of the tubes that carry the blood back to your heart from the rest of your body. **2** a similar-looking line on a leaf. **3** a particular style or manner of writing or speaking: *His speech started with a joke but was basically in a serious vein.*

velocity /vəˈlɒsɪtɪ/ *n* speed: *He went hunting with high velocity bullets in his rifle.*

velvet /ˈvɛlvɪt/ *n* a cloth made from silk *etc* with a soft, thick surface: *Her dress was made of velvet.* — *adj*: *a velvet jacket.* **'velvety** *adj* soft, like velvet.

vendetta /vɛnˈdɛtə/ *n* a bitter quarrel between families: *The vendetta between them started*

when her great-great uncle killed his great-great grandfather.
vendor /'vɛndə(r)/ *n* a person who sells something.
veneer /və'nɪə(r)/ *n* a thin top layer which makes something look more attractive than it really is.
venerable /'vɛnərəbəl/ *adj* greatly respected because old and wise: *a venerable old priest.*
venerate /'vɛnəreɪt/ *v* to think of with great respect: *His tomb has been venerated for centuries.*
venereal /və'nɪərɪəl/: **venereal disease** *n* a disease that is passed on by sexual intercourse (often shortened to **VD** /viː'diː/).
vengeance /'vɛndʒəns/ *n* harm done in return for injury received; revenge.
  with a vengeance in an intensive manner: *It had begun to snow with a vengeance; She was polishing the table with a vengeance.*
venison /'vɛnɪsən/ *n* the flesh of deer, used as food: *roast venison.*
venom /'vɛnəm/ *n* **1** the poison that some snakes, spiders and scorpions produce in order to kill their prey. **2** the wish to harm other people; great hatred: *There was a lot of venom in his remarks.*
  'venomous *adj* **1** poisonous: *A cobra is a venomous snake.* **2** full of hatred: *a venomous speech.*
vent /vɛnt/ *n* a hole to allow air, smoke *etc* to pass out or in: *an air-vent.* — *v* to get rid of your anger *etc* by expressing it in a violent way: *He was angry with himself and vented his rage on his son by beating him.*
  give vent to to vent: *He gave vent to his anger in a furious letter to the newspaper.*
ventilate /'vɛntɪleɪt/ *v* to make a room *etc* fresher and cooler by letting fresh air into it: *Kitchens must be properly ventilated.* **venti'lation** *n*.
  'ventilator *n* a device for ventilating a room *etc.*
ventriloquist /vɛn'trɪləkwɪst/ *n* a person who can speak without moving their mouth, so that it seems as if another person is talking: *In the television show, the ventriloquist pretended to have a conversation with a puppet.*
venture /'vɛntʃə(r)/ *n* an undertaking or scheme that usually involves risk: *a business venture.* — *v* **1** to dare to go: *Every day the child ventured further into the forest.* **2** to dare to do something: *He ventured to kiss her hand; I ventured to remark that her skirt was too short.* **3** to risk: *He decided to venture all his money on the scheme.*

venue /'vɛnjuː/ *n* a place where an event takes place: *The venue for the match hasn't been announced yet.*
veranda or **verandah** /və'randə/ *n* a kind of long porch extending along the side of a house.

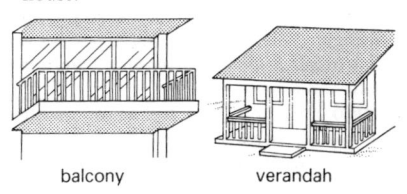

balcony   verandah

verb /vɜːb/ *n* the word or phrase that tells what a person or thing does: *I saw him; He ran away from me; I have a feeling; What is this?*
  'verbal *adj* **1** spoken, not written; having to do with spoken words: *a verbal agreement.* **2** having to with verbs. **'verbally** *adv.*
verdict /'vɜːdɪkt/ *n* **1** the decision of a jury at the end of a trial: *The jury brought in a verdict of guilty.* **2** a decision or judgement.
verge /vɜːdʒ/ *n* a border, especially a grass edge to a road *etc.* — *v* to be close to: *He is verging on old age.*
  on the verge of just about to start: *She was on the verge of tears.*
verify /'vɛrɪfaɪ/ *v* to confirm that something is true; to check that something is true or correct: *Can you verify her statement?; The detective verified the story of the stolen diamonds.* **'verifiable** *adj.* **verifi'cation** *n.*
vermin /'vɜːmɪn/ *n* all types of wild animal that carry disease or destroy plants and food.
versatile /'vɜːsətaɪl/ *adj* **1** able to turn easily from one task, activity or occupation to another: *a versatile entertainer; He will easily get another job — he is so versatile.* **2** useful for many purposes: *a versatile tool.* **versa'tility** *n.*
verse /vɜːs/ *n* **1** a number of lines of poetry, grouped together and forming a separate unit within the poem, song, hymn *etc*: *This song has three verses.* **2** a short section in a chapter of the Bible. **3** poetry, as opposed to prose: *He expressed his ideas in verse.*
version /'vɜːʃən/ *n* an account from one point of view: *The boy gave his version of what had occurred.*
versus /'vɜːsəs/ *prep* against (often shortened to **v**): *the England v Wales rugby match.*
vertebra /'vɜːtɪbrə/, *plural* **vertebrae**

vertical

/'vɜːtɪbriː/, *n* any of the pieces of bone which form the spine: *She bruised several of her vertebrae when she fell from the horse.*

vertebrate /'vɜːtəbrət/ or /'vɜːtəbreɪt/ *n* a creature with a spine, such as animals, birds and fish: *An octopus is not a vertebrate.*

vertical /'vɜːtɪkəl/ *adj* standing straight up; upright: *You lie in a horizontal position and you stand in a vertical position.* **'vertically** *adv*.

vertigo /'vɜːtɪɡoʊ/ *n* a feeling of dizziness caused by heights: *She suffers from vertigo so don't let her go near the edge of the cliff.*

verve /vɜːv/ *n* great liveliness or enthusiasm: *His performance lacked verve.*

very /'vɛrɪ/ *adv* **1** extremely: *He's very clever; You came very quickly.* **2** absolutely: *The very first thing you must do is ring the police; She has a car of her very own.* — *adj* **1** exactly the thing, person *etc* mentioned: *You're the very man I want to see; At that very minute the door opened.* **2** extreme: *at the very end of the day; at the very top of the tree.* **3** mere: *The very suggestion of a sea voyage makes her feel sick.*

not very not: *I'm not very good at swimming; I'm not feeling very well.*

very well used to express agreement to a request *etc*: *'Please be home before midnight.' 'Very well.'*

vessel /'vɛsəl/ *n* **1** a container, usually for liquid: *a glass vessel containing acid.* **2** a ship: *a grain-carrying vessel.*

vest /vɛst/ *n* **1** an undergarment for the top half of your body: *He was dressed only in a vest and underpants.* **2** a waistcoat: *jacket, vest and trousers.*

vestibule /'vɛstɪbjuːl/ *n* a small entrance hall: *There were several doors opening out of the vestibule.*

vestige /'vɛstɪdʒ/ *n* a trace, slight amount or hint: *After the explosion, not a vestige of the building was left.*

vet[1] /vɛt/ *n* short for **veterinary surgeon**.

vet[2] /vɛt/ *v* to examine a thing or person carefully before accepting them: *Every newspaper article was vetted before it was published.*

veteran /'vɛtərən/ *n* **1** someone who has served as a soldier, especially during a war: *a war veteran.* **2** someone who has had experience in a particular job, sport *etc* for a long time: *He is a veteran politician; This tennis championship is for veterans only.*

veterinary /'vɛtərɪnərɪ/ *adj* having to do with the treatment of diseases in animals: *veterinary medicine.*

veterinary surgeon a doctor for animals (often shortened to **vet**).

veto /'viːtoʊ/ *v* to forbid something; to refuse to agree to something: *The president vetoed the minister's proposal.* — *n* (*plural* **vetoes**) the right to forbid something: *The leader used his veto against the proposed changes.*

vex /vɛks/ *v* to make someone angry; to irritate someone: *His rude behaviour vexed her; She felt very vexed that she hadn't been invited to his party.*

via /vɪə/ or /vaɪə/ *prep* by way of: *We went to America via Japan.*

viable /'vaɪəbəl/ *adj* having a reasonable chance of being successful: *Does my idea sound viable to you?; This is unlikely to be a viable option.* **via'bility** *n*.

viaduct /'vaɪədʌkt/ *n* a long bridge carrying a road or railway over a valley *etc*.

vibrant /'vaɪbrənt/ *adj* very lively, bright or exciting: *The dancers were dressed in vibrant colours.*

vibrate /vaɪ'breɪt/ *v* to shake, tremble, or move rapidly to and fro: *Every sound that we hear is making part of our ear vibrate; The engine is vibrating.* **vi'bration** *n*.

vicar /'vɪkə(r)/ *n* a clergyman of the Church of England.

'vicarage *n* the house of a vicar.

vice /vaɪs/ *n* **1** a serious moral fault: *Continual lying is a vice.* **2** a bad habit: *Smoking is not one of my vices.* **3** a tool that holds the object you are working on so that it doesn't move.

vice- /vaɪs/ next in rank to; acting as deputy for: *the vice-president of the United States.*

vice versa /vaɪs'vɜːsə/ or /vaɪsə'vɜːsə/ the other way round: *Dogs often chase cats but not usually vice versa.*

vicinity /vɪ'sɪnɪtɪ/ *n* an area surrounding a particular place: *There are no parks in this vicinity; They live somewhere in the vicinity of the theatre.*

vicious /'vɪʃəs/ *adj* evil; cruel; likely to attack you: *Keep back from that dog — it's vicious.* **'viciously** *adv*. **'viciousness** *n*.

vicious circle a situation in which a problem creates other problems which in turn make the first problem appear again.

victim /'vɪktɪm/ *n* a person who suffers death or harm as a result of someone else's action or a disaster *etc*: *a murder victim; Food is being sent to the victims of the disaster.*

victimize /'vɪktɪmaɪz/ *v* to treat unfairly: *They*

felt they were being victimized because of the colour of their skin.

victor /'vɪktə(r)/ *n* the person who wins a battle or other contest.

vic'torious *adj* winning: *the victorious army.*

'victory *n* success in a battle, struggle or contest: *Our team has had two defeats and eight victories; to win a victory over a handicap.*

video /'vɪdɪoʊ/ *adj* having to do with television pictures. — *n* (*plural* **videos**) **1** the broadcasting of television pictures. **2** a videotape. **3** a video recorder. — *v* to record on to a video recorder or videotape: *He videoed the television programme.*

video camera a camera which records moving images and sound on tape: *She filmed the children playing using her video recorder.*

video game an electronic game played using a television or computer screen: *Her son spends hours playing video games.*

video recorder a cassette recorder that records sound and vision.

'videotape *n* recording tape carrying pictures and sound.

vie /vaɪ/ *v* to compete with someone: *The two pupils vied with one another for the first prize.*

vie; **'vying** /vaɪɪŋ/; **vied**; **vied**: *The twins are always vying with each other; They vied with each other for the prize.*

view /vjuː/ *n* **1** an outlook on to, or picture of, a scene: *Your house has a fine view of the hills; He painted a view of the harbour.* **2** an opinion: *Tell me your views on this subject.* **3** an opportunity to see or inspect something: *We were given a private view of the exhibition before it was opened to the public.* — *v* to look at something: *She viewed the scene with astonishment.*

'viewer *n* **1** a person who watches television: *This programme has five million viewers.* **2** a device with a magnifying lens, and often with a light for looking at photographic slides.

'viewpoint *n* a point of view: *I am looking at the matter from a different viewpoint.*

in view of something because of something: *In view of the bad weather we decided not to go out.*

point of view a way of looking at a subject, matter *etc*: *You must consider everyone's point of view before deciding.*

with a view to with a particular aim or intention: *They bought the boat with a view to using it for their holidays.*

vigil /'vɪdʒɪl/ *n* a period of staying awake, especially as part of a religious ceremony or festival, or to watch over someone who is ill: *Many Christians keep the Easter vigil.*

vigilant /'vɪdʒɪlənt/ *adj* watchful or ready for danger. **'vigilance** *n*.

vigour /'vɪgə(r)/ *n* strength and energy: *He began his new job with enthusiasm and vigour.*

'vigorous *adj*: *a vigorous dance.* **'vigorously** *adv*.

vigour is spelt **-our**.
vigorous is spelt **-or-**.

vile /vaɪl/ *adj* horrible; disgusting: *That was a vile thing to say!; The blue cheese tasted vile.*

villa /'vɪlə/ *n* a house, especially in the country or suburbs; a house used for holidays at the seaside.

village /'vɪlɪdʒ/ *n* **1** a group of houses *etc* that is smaller than a town: *They live in a little village.* **2** the people who live there: *The whole village turned out to see the celebrations.*

'villager *n* a person who lives in a village.

villain /'vɪlən/ *n* a person who is wicked or has a very bad character: *the villain of the story.*

vinaigrette /vɪnɪ'grɛt/ *n* a mixture of oil and vinegar used as a salad dressing.

vindicate /'vɪndɪkeɪt/ *v* to prove to be correct or without blame: *Recent events have vindicated his decision to start his own business.* **vindi'cation** *n*.

vindictive /vɪn'dɪktɪv/ *adj* feeling or showing spite or hatred: *He keeps sending me vindictive letters.*

vine /vaɪn/ *n* **1** a climbing plant which bears grapes: *In the winter months the vines were taken down from their supporting wires.* **2** any climbing plant.

vineyard /'vɪnjəd/ *n* an area which is planted with grape vines.

vinegar /'vɪnɪgə(r)/ *n* a sour liquid made from wine, beer *etc*, used in seasoning or preparing food: *Mix some oil and vinegar as a dressing for the salad.*

vintage /'vɪntɪdʒ/ *n* the grape harvest of a particular year and the good quality wine made from it: *That was a good vintage for wines from Bordeaux.* — *adj*: *vintage champagne.*

vinyl /'vaɪnɪl/ *n* a strong kind of plastic: *We*

viola

have a blue vinyl floor-covering in our bathroom.

viola /vɪ'oʊlə/ *n* a kind of large violin.

violate /'vaɪəleɪt/ *v* **1** to break a promise, law or rule: *The footballer was suspended for violating the rules.* **2** to break into a sacred place: *Thieves have violated the emperor's tomb.* **3** to disturb: *The loud music is violating the peace of the countryside.* **vio'lation** *n*.

violence /'vaɪələns/ *n* great roughness and force, especially causing destruction, injury or damage: *Try not to use violence against children; She was terrified by the violence of the storm.*

violent /'vaɪələnt/ *adj* **1** having, using, or showing, great force: *There was a violent storm at sea; a violent earthquake; He has a violent temper; She gave him a violent blow.* **2** caused by force: *a violent death.* **'violently** *adv.*

violet /'vaɪələt/ *n* **1** a small purple flower. **2** a purple colour.

violin /ˌvaɪə'lɪn/ *n* a musical instrument with four strings, played with a bow: *She played the violin in the school orchestra.* **vio'linist** *n*.

violin　　viola

violoncello　　double bass

viper /'vaɪpə(r)/ *n* a small poisonous snake found in Europe.

virgin /'vɜːdʒɪn/ *n* a person, especially a woman, who has had no sexual intercourse.

virile /'vɪraɪl/ *adj* having all the traditional male qualities such as strength and the ability to produce children: *virile young actors.* **vi'rility** *n*.

virtual /'vɜːtʃʊəl/ *adj* not actual, but having the effect of being actual: *The princess influenced all the king's decisions, so that she was the virtual ruler of the country.*

'virtually *adv* more or less; almost: *My work is virtually finished.*

virtue /'vɜːtʃuː/ or /'vɜːtjuː/ *n* **1** a good moral quality: *Honesty is a virtue.* **2** a good quality: *The house is small, but it has the virtue of being easy to clean.* **3** goodness of character etc: *She is a person of great virtue.* **'virtuous** *adj.*

virtuoso /ˌvɜːtʃʊ'oʊsoʊ/, *plural* **virtu'osos**, *n* a highly skilled musician: *He is a virtuoso on the piano; a virtuoso musician.*

virulent /'vɪrʊlənt/ *adj* having a harmful effect very quickly: *a virulent disease.*

virus /'vaɪrəs/ *n* **1** any of various kinds of germs that are smaller than bacteria: *Viruses can cause influenza, mumps, chickenpox and many other infectious diseases.* **2** a piece of computer code put into a program to destroy data and cause errors. **'viral** *adj.*

visa /'viːzə/ *n* an official permit to visit a country: *You'll need a visa if you want to visit Russia.*

visible /'vɪzəbəl/ *adj* able to be seen: *The house is visible through the trees; The scar on her face is scarcely visible now.* **visi'bility** *n.* **'visibly** *adv.*

The opposite of **visible** is **invisible**.

vision /'vɪʒən/ *n* **1** something seen in the imagination or in a dream. **2** the ability to see or plan into the future: *Politicians should be men of vision.* **3** the ability to see: *He is slowly losing his vision.* **4** the picture on a television screen: *The vision is very poor on that television set.*

visit /'vɪzɪt/ *v* **1** to go to see a person or place: *We visited my parents at the weekend; They visited the Taj Mahal while they were in India.* **2** to stay in a place or with a person for a time: *My mother visits us each summer; Many birds visit Britain only during the summer months.* — *n*: *We went on a visit to my aunt's.*

'visitor *n* a person who visits: *We're having visitors next week.*

pay a visit to visit: *She paid her aunt a visit; we paid a visit to the library.*

visor /'vaɪzə(r)/ *n* **1** the moveable part of a helmet that covers the face: *The knight pulled down his visor before the battle began.* **2** a moveable flap that can be folded down in front of the windscreen of a car *etc*

visual /'vɪʒʊəl/ *adj* having to do with seeing: *She has a very good visual memory — she can always remember what people look like*; *The bright green light produced strange visual effects.* **'visually** *adv.*

visual aids *n plural* pictures, slides, films or models that are used to help you understand or learn something: *Biology teachers use a lot of visual aids.*

'visualize *v* to form a clear picture of something or someone in your mind: *It is impossible to visualize the size of the universe*; *I know his name, but I can't visualize him.*

vital /'vaɪtəl/ *adj* **1** essential; very important: *Speed is vital to the success of our plan*; *It is vital that we arrive at the hospital soon.* **2** lively and energetic: *a vital person.* **'vitally** *adv.*

vi'tality *n* liveliness and energy: *a girl of great vitality.*

vitamin /'vɪtəmɪn/ *n* any of a group of substances necessary for healthy life, different ones occurring in different natural things such as raw fruit, vegetables, fish, meat *etc*: *Vitamin C is found in fruit and vegetables.*

vivacious /vɪ'veɪʃəs/ *adj* lively and attractive: *She has a vivacious personality.*

vivid /'vɪvɪd/ *adj* **1** brilliant; very bright: *The door was painted a vivid yellow*; *The trees were vivid in their autumn colours.* **2** clear: *I have many vivid memories of that holiday*; *a vivid description.* **3** active; lively: *She has a vivid imagination.* **'vividly** *adv.* **'vividness** *n.*

vixen /'vɪksən/ *n* a female fox: *The vixen was followed by her cubs.*

vocabulary /və'kabjʊlərɪ/ *n* **1** words in general: *This book contains some difficult vocabulary.* **2** words known and used by one person, or within a particular trade or profession: *He has a vocabulary of about 20 000 words*; *Each of the sciences has its own special vocabulary.* **3** a list of words in alphabetical order with meanings.

vocal /'voʊkəl/ *adj* **1** having to do with your voice, or with speaking or singing: *Your voice is produced by your vocal organs.* **2** eager to express your opinion: *He's always very vocal at meetings.*

'vocalist *n* a singer: *a female vocalist.*

vocal cords folds of tissue in your throat that produce the sounds used in speech, singing *etc* when vibrated.

vocation /voʊ'keɪʃən/ *n* **1** a feeling of having a special duty to do a particular kind of work, especially medical work, teaching, or caring for people in some way. **2** an occupation or profession of this kind. **vo'cational** *adj.*

vodka /'vɒdkə/ *n* a strong, colourless, alcoholic drink.

voice /vɔɪs/ *n* **1** the sounds that come from your mouth when you speak or sing: *He has a very deep voice*; *He spoke in a loud voice.* **2** your voice as a means of expression; your opinion: *The voice of the people must not be ignored.* — *v* **1** to express feelings *etc*: *He voiced his anger.* **2** to pronounce a letter *etc* with a sound in your throat as well as with your breath: *'Th' should be voiced in 'this' but not in 'think'.* **voiced** *adj.* **'voiceless** *adj.*

lose your voice to be unable to speak because of having a cold, sore throat *etc*: *When I had flu I lost my voice for three days.*

raise your voice to speak more loudly than normal, especially in anger: *I don't want to have to raise my voice to you again.*

void /vɔɪd/ *adj* not valid, having no official authority: *The agreement is now void.* — *n* an empty space: *Her husband's death left a void in her life.*

volatile /'vɒlətaɪl/ *adj* **1** quickly becoming upset or angry: *a volatile child.* **2** likely to change quickly and suddenly: *a volatile situation in which anything could happen.*

volcanic /vɒl'kanɪk/ *adj* having to do with volcanoes; produced by volcanoes: *a volcanic eruption*; *volcanic rock.*

volcano /vɒl'keɪnoʊ/, *plural* **vol'canoes**, *n* a hill or mountain with an opening at the top through which molten rock, ashes *etc* are thrown up from inside the earth: *The village was destroyed when the volcano erupted.*

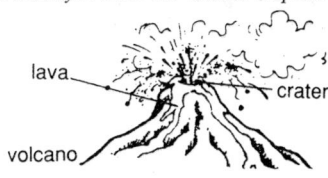

volley /'vɒlɪ/ *n* **1** in tennis, the hitting of a ball before it bounces. **2** a burst of firing *etc*: *a volley of shots.* — *v*: *She volleyed the ball back across the net.*

'volleyball *n* a game in which you hit the ball over a high net with your hand.

volt /voʊlt/ *n* a unit for measuring the strength of an electric current.

'voltage *n* an electrical force that is measured in volts.

volume /'vɒljuːm/ *n* **1** a book: *This library contains over a million volumes.* **2** one of a series of books: *Where is Volume 15 of the encyclopedia?* **3** the amount of space occupied by something; the amount of space inside a container: *What is the volume of the petrol tank?* **4** amount: *A large volume of work remains to be done.* **5** the loudness of the sound coming from a radio, television *etc*: *Turn up the volume on the radio.*

voluntary /'vɒləntərɪ/ *adj* **1** done by choice, not by accident or because you are asked or forced to: *a voluntary act.* **2** without payment: *She does a lot of voluntary work.* **'voluntarily** *adv.*

volunteer /vɒlən'tɪə(r)/ *v* **1** to offer to do something of your own free will: *He volunteered to act as messenger*; *She volunteered for a dangerous job.* **2** to offer an opinion *etc*: *Two or three people volunteered suggestions.* — *n* someone who offers to do something of their own free will: *The charitable organizations depend on the help of volunteers.*

voluptuous /və'lʌptʃʊəs/ *adj* sexually attractive, especially in having large breasts and hips: *a voluptuous female dancer.*

vomit /'vɒmɪt/ *v* to throw out the contents of your stomach through your mouth; to be sick: *The movement of the ship made her feel like vomiting.* — *n* food *etc* that has been vomited.

vote /vəʊt/ *n* **1** the choice you make between candidates at an election, or between the two sides in a debate: *to give your vote to a candidate.* **2** the action of voting: *A vote was taken to decide the matter.* **3** the right to vote: *In Britain, the vote was given to women over twenty-one in 1928*; *Nowadays everyone over eighteen has a vote.* — *v* to give your vote: *She voted for the Conservative candidate*; *I always vote Labour*; *I shall vote against the Government's new education plans.*

'voter *n* a person who votes or has the right to vote.

vouch /vaʊtʃ/ *v* **1** to say that you are sure that something is fact or truth: *Will you vouch for the truth of the statement?* **2** to say that you are sure of the goodness and honesty of someone: *My friends will vouch for me.*

voucher /vaʊtʃə(r)/ *n* a piece of paper that you can use like money in certain shops, restaurants *etc*: *My granny has sent me a £20 voucher so that I can buy myself some cassettes*; *a luncheon voucher.*

vow /vaʊ/ *n* a solemn promise, especially one made to God: *The monks have taken a vow of silence*; *marriage vows.* — *v* to make a vow: *He vowed that he would die rather than surrender.*

vowel /'vaʊəl/ *n* in English and many other languages, the letters *a, e, i, o, u.*

voyage /'vɔɪdʒ/ *n* a long journey, especially by sea: *The voyage to America used to take many weeks.* — *v* to make a voyage: *They voyaged for many months.*

'voyager *n* a person who goes on a voyage.

vulgar /'vʌlgə(r)/ *adj* not decent; not polite; ill-mannered: *vulgar behaviour.* **'vulgarly** *adv.* **vul'garity** *n.*

vulnerable /'vʌlnərəbəl/ *adj* not protected against attack; likely to be hurt or damaged: *Small animals are vulnerable to attack from birds of prey.* **vulnera'bility** *n.*

vulture /'vʌltʃə(r)/ *n* a large bird of prey that lives chiefly on the flesh of dead animals.

vying *see* **vie.**

W

wad /wɒd/ *n* **1** a mass of loose material pressed into a solid piece: *He blocked the hole in the wall with a wad of newspaper*; *She put a wad of cottonwool over the cut on his hand to stop it bleeding*. **2** a large bundle: *He took a wad of £100 notes from his wallet*.

waddle /'wɒdəl/ *v* to take short steps and move from side to side in walking: *The ducks waddled across the road*.

wade /weɪd/ *v* to walk through water, mud *etc*: *He waded across the river*; *We can wade the stream at its narrowest point*.

wafer /'weɪfə(r)/ *n* a very thin biscuit, often eaten with ice-cream: *an ice-cream wafer*; *a wafer biscuit*.

'**wafer-thin** *adj* extremely thin: *wafer-thin sandwiches*.

waffle[1] /'wɒfəl/ *v* to write or talk at length but expressing very little: *He waffled on about his plans but nobody was listening*. — *n*: *His speech was just a lot of waffle*. — *n*.

waffle[2] /'wɒfəl/ *n* a potato pancake with a grid-like pattern: *They had waffles and eggs for breakfast*.

waft /wɒft/ *v* to float or drift gently: *The sounds of the music wafted through the air*.

wag /waɡ/ *v* to move from side to side: *The dog wagged its tail*; *He wagged his head in time to the music*.

wage[1] /weɪdʒ/ *v* to carry on a war *etc*: *The North waged war against the South*.

wage[2] /weɪdʒ/ *n* (usually **wages**) payment for work: *His wages are less than £100 a week*.

> **wages** takes a plural verb: *His wages are too low.*

waggle /'waɡəl/ *v* to move from side to side: *His beard waggled as he ate*.

wagon or **waggon** /'waɡən/ *n* **1** a four-wheeled vehicle for carrying heavy loads: *a hay wagon*. **2** an open railway container for goods: *a goods wagon*.

waif /weɪf/ *n* a child without a home or family.

wail /weɪl/ *v* to cry loudly; to make a long sound like a cry: *The little boy was wailing over his broken toy*; *The sirens wailed*. — *n*: *I heard the wail of a police siren*.

waist /weɪst/ *n* **1** the narrow part of the human body between the ribs and hips: *She has a very small waist*. **2** the part of a garment that goes round your waist: *This skirt is too loose in the waist*.

waistcoat /'weɪstkəʊt/ *n* a short, sleeveless garment, especially for a man, buttoned up the front, that is worn under a jacket: *a three-piece suit consists of trousers, jacket and waistcoat*.

'**waistline** *n* **1** the shape or size that you are around the waist: *His waistline is not as small as it used to be*. **2** the part of a piece of clothing that fits in the area of the waist: *She dresses in clothes that have a high waistline*.

wait /weɪt/ *v* **1** to stay where you are, until someone or something comes: *We have been waiting for the bus for half an hour*; *I am waiting for her to arrive*; *Wait for me!*; *Wait two minutes while I go inside*. **2** to expect: *I'm just waiting for that pile of dishes to fall!* **3** to serve dishes, drinks *etc*: *She employed four women to wait on the guests*; *You must learn how to wait at table*. — *n* a delay: *There was a long wait before they could get on the train*.

'**waiter** *n* a man who serves people with food in a restaurant *etc*.

waiting list a list of people who want something that is not yet available or possible: *Please put my name on the waiting list*.

'**waiting-room** *n* a room in which people may wait at a station, doctor's surgery *etc*.

'**waitress** *n* a woman who serves people with food in a restaurant *etc*.

wait about or **wait around** to remain in the same place, doing nothing, waiting for someone or something in particular: *I don't want to have to wait about at the airport*.

wait and see to wait patiently without getting anxious: *We don't know if the medicine will help — we must just wait and see*.

wait up to stay out of bed at night, waiting for someone to arrive or return: *I'll be late back — don't wait up for me*.

waive /weɪv/ *v* **1** not to insist that a rule be obeyed: *The judge waived the rule about not speaking in court*. **2** not to insist on your right to something: *She waived her right to object*.

wake[1] /weɪk/ *v* to stop sleeping; to stop someone sleeping: *Wake up — you're late!*; *Go and wake the others, will you?*

wake; **woke** /woʊk/; **woken** /'woʊkən/: *She woke up early*; *The noise has woken the baby*.

'**wakeful** *adj* not feeling tired and not sleeping very much: *Some babies are very wakeful at night*.

'**waken** *v* to wake: *What time are you going to waken him?*; *I wakened early this morning*.

wake up to to become aware of something: *He suddenly woke up to the danger he was in*.

wake[2] /weɪk/ *n* the line of disturbed water or air left behind a moving ship or aircraft.

in the wake of following or happening after, as a result of: *Disease nearly always follows in the wake of floods*.

walk /wɔːk/ *v* **1** to move on foot: *He walked across the room and sat down*; *How long will it take to walk to the station?*; *She walks her dog in the park every morning*. **2** to travel on foot for pleasure: *We're going walking in the hills for our holidays*. **3** to go on foot along a street *etc*: *It's dangerous to walk the streets of New York alone after dark*. — *n* **1** a journey on foot: *to go for a walk*; *to take a walk*; *It's a long walk to the station*. **2** a manner of walking: *I recognized her walk*. **3** a route for walking: *There are many pleasant walks in this area*.

'**walker** *n* a person who goes walking for pleasure.

walkie-'talkie *n* a radio set that you carry round with you for sending and receiving messages: *The soldiers spoke to each other on the walkie-talkie*.

'**walking-stick** *n* a stick you use to help you walk: *The old lady has been using a walking-stick since she hurt her leg*.

'**walkover** *n* an easy victory: *The match was a walkover for his team*.

'**walkway** *n* a path *etc* for pedestrians only.

walk off with 1 to win easily: *He walked off with all the prizes at the school sports*. **2** to steal: *The thieves have walked off with my best silver and china*.

walk of life your position in society: *We have members from all walks of life who all get on well with each other*.

walk on air to feel extremely happy.

walk out to leave suddenly and angrily: *The discussion was so ridiculous I walked out*.

wall /wɔːl/ *n* **1** an object built of stone, brick *etc*, used to enclose something or separate one area from another: *There's a wall round the garden*; *The Great Wall of China*; *a garden wall*. **2** any of the sides of a building or room: *One wall of the room is yellow — the rest are white*. — *v* to enclose something with a wall: *We've walled in the playground to prevent the children getting out*.

walled *adj*: *a walled city*.

have your back to the wall to be in a desperate situation.

up the wall crazy: *This problem is driving me up the wall!*

wall-to-wall covering the whole floor of a room: *wall-to-wall carpet*.

wallet /'wɒlɪt/ *n* **1** a small case made of soft leather, plastic *etc*, carried in the pocket and used for holding paper money, personal papers *etc*. **2** a similar case for holding other things: *a plastic wallet containing a set of small tools*.

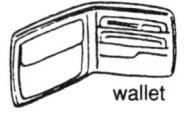

purse
wallet

wallop /'wɒləp/ *v* to hit or beat severely: *He threatened to wallop his son if he didn't go to bed immediately*.

wallow /'wɒloʊ/ *v* to roll about with enjoyment: *The pig wallowed in the dirt*.

wallpaper /'wɔːlpeɪpə(r)/ *n* paper that is used to decorate the walls of a room: *The new wallpaper made the room look much bigger*. — *v*: *He has finally finished wallpapering the bedroom*.

walnut /'wɔːlnʌt/ *n* **1** a tree whose wood is used for making furniture *etc*. **2** the nut produced by this tree. — *adj*: *a walnut table*.

walrus /'wɔːlrəs/, *plural* **'walruses** or **walrus**, *n* a large sea animal with huge tusks, related to the seal.

waltz /wɔːlts/ or /wɔːls/ *n* **1** an old-fashioned dance to music with three beats in every bar: *She did not know how to do a waltz*. **2** the music for such a dance: *He is famous for his waltzes*. — *v*.

wan /wɒn/ *adj* pale and sickly-looking: *She still looks wan after her illness*. '**wanly** *adv*. '**wanness** *n*.

wand /wɒnd/ *n* a long slender rod used as the symbol of magic power by magicians, fairies *etc*: *In the story, the fairy waved her magic wand and the frog became a prince*.

wander /'wɒndə(r)/ *v* **1** to go from place to place with no definite purpose: *I'd like to spend a holiday wandering through France*; *The mother wandered the streets looking for* her child. **2** to go astray; to stray away from home or from the proper place: *Our dog often wanders off*; *My attention was wandering*. **'wanderer** *n*.

> to **wander** (not **wonder**) through the countryside.

wane /weɪn/ *v* **1** to appear to become smaller as less of it is visible: *The moon is waning*. **2** to become less strong or powerful: *Support for the party was waning fast*.

wangle /'wæŋgəl/ *v* to obtain something by trickery or clever management: *He got us seats for the concert — I don't know how he wangled it*.

want /wɒnt/ *v* **1** to wish to have or do something; to desire: *Do you want a cigarette?*; *She wants to know where he is*; *I don't want to go near them*; *Do you want to talk about it?*; *She knew that if he wanted he could have killed her*. **2** to need: *This wall wants a coat of paint*. **3** to lack: *This house wants none of the usual modern features but I do not like it*. — *n* **1** something you desire: *The child has a long list of wants*. **2** poverty: *They have lived in want for many years*. **3** a lack: *There's no want of opportunities these days*. **'wanted** *adj* **1** being searched for by the police: *He is a wanted man*; *He is wanted for murder*. **2** needed; cared for: *Old people must be made to feel wanted*.

war /wɔː(r)/ *n* an armed struggle between nations: *The larger army will win the war*; *to declare war on another country*; *the horrors of war*. — *adj*: *war crimes*. — *v* to fight: *The two countries have been warring with each other for ten years*.

> See **battle**.

warble /'wɔːbəl/ *v* to sing in a trembling voice, as some birds do.
'warbler *n* any of several kinds of small singing bird.

ward /wɔːd/ *n* **1** a room with beds for patients in a hospital: *He is in Ward 2 at the hospital*. **2** someone who is under the legal control and care of a person who is not their parent, or of a court: *She was made a ward of court so that she could not marry until she was eighteen*.

ward off to keep something away; to fight something successfully: *He smoked a pipe to ward off mosquitos*; *The troops warded off the attack by the enemy*.

war-dance /'wɔːdɑːns/ *n* a dance performed by people of tribal societies before going to war.

warden /'wɔːdən/ *n* **1** the person in charge of an old people's home, a students' hostel *etc*: *The warden has reported that two students are missing from the hostel*. **2** a person who controls parking and the movement of traffic in an area: *If the traffic warden sees your car parked there you will be fined*. **3** a person who guards a game reserve.

warder /'wɔːdə(r)/ *n* a person who guards prisoners in jail.

wardrobe /'wɔːdrəʊb/ *n* **1** a cupboard in which clothes may be hung: *Hang your suit in the wardrobe*. **2** a supply of clothing: *She bought a complete new wardrobe in Paris*.

warehouse /'weəhaʊs/ *n* a building in which goods are stored: *a furniture warehouse*.

warfare /'wɔːfeə(r)/ *n* fighting, as in a war: *Nuclear weapons are not used in conventional warfare*.

warhead /'wɔːhed/ *n* the front part of a missile, that contains the explosives.

warily, wariness *see* **wary**.

warlike /'wɔːlaɪk/ *adj* fond of fighting: *a warlike nation*.

warm /wɔːm/ *adj* **1** fairly, or pleasantly hot: *Are you warm enough, or shall I close the window?*; *a warm summer's day*. **2** protecting you from the cold: *a warm jumper*. **3** welcoming, friendly *etc*: *a warm welcome*; *a warm smile*. — *v* to make or become warm: *He warmed his hands in front of the fire*; *Have a cup of tea to warm you up*; *The room will soon warm up*. **'warmly** *adv*. **'warmness** *n*.

'warmth *n* the state of being warm: *The warmth of the fire*; *The warmth of her smile made me feel welcome*.

warm'hearted *adj* kind: *a warmhearted old lady*. **warm'heartedness** *n*.

warm to 1 to become more interested in or enthusiastic about something: *He refused completely at first but now he seems to be warming to the idea*. **2** to begin to like someone more.

warm up to prepare for something by practising gently: *Players should always warm up before a match*.

warmongering /'wɔːmʌŋgərɪŋ/ *n* behaviour which encourages people to be enthusiastic supporters of war: *This decisive action put an end to his warmongering*.

warn /wɔːn/ *v* **1** to tell someone in advance about a danger *etc*: *Black clouds warned us of the approaching storm*; *They warned her* *that she would be ill if she didn't rest.* **2** to advise someone against doing something: *I was warned against speeding by the policeman*; *They warned him not to be late.*

'warning *n* an event, or something said or done, that warns: *He gave her a warning against driving too fast*; *His heart attack will be a warning to him not to work so hard*; *The earthquake came without warning.* — *adj*: *She received a warning message.* **'warningly** *adv*.

warp¹ /wɔːp/ *v* to make or become twisted out of shape: *The door has been warped by all the rain we've had lately.* — *n* the shape into which something is twisted by warping: *The rain has given this door a permanent warp.* **warped** *adj*.

warp² /wɔːp/ *n* the set of threads that are stretched from top to bottom of a loom during weaving; the threads going across the loom are the **weft**.

warpath /'wɔːpɑːθ/ *n* the march or route to war or a quarrel: *She's very angry and is on the warpath after him.*

warrant /'wɒrənt/ *v* to be a good reason or excuse for something: *A slight cold does not warrant your staying off work.* — *n* something that gives authority, especially a legal document giving the police the authority to search someone's house, arrest someone *etc*: *The police have a warrant for his arrest.*

warren /'wɒrən/ *n* an underground home dug by rabbits, with a large number of burrows linked by tunnels.

warrior /'wɒrɪə(r)/ *n* a soldier or skilled fighting man: *The chief of the tribe called his warriors together.*

warship /'wɔːʃɪp/ *n* a ship used for fighting battles at sea.

wart /wɔːt/ *n* a small hard lump on the skin.

wartime /'wɔːtaɪm/ *n* a period during which a war is going on: *Sugar was difficult to get in wartime.*

wary /'weərɪ/ *adj* cautious: *a wary animal*; *Be wary of lending money to him.* **'warily** *adv*. **'wariness** *n*.

was /wɒz/ *see* **be**.

wash /wɒʃ/ *v* **1** to clean with water and soap *etc*: *How often do you wash your hair?*; *You wash the dishes and I'll dry*; *You should wash yourself at least once a day*; *We can wash in the stream.* **2** to be able to be washed without being damaged: *This fabric doesn't wash very well.* **3** to flow against, over *etc*: *The waves washed against the ship.* **4** to sweep away *etc* by means of water: *The floods have washed away hundreds of houses.* — *n* **1** an act of washing: *He's just gone to have a wash.* **2** things to be washed or being washed: *Your sweater is in the wash.* **3** a liquid with which you wash something: *a mouthwash.* **4** a thin coat of water-colour paint *etc*: *The background of the picture was a pale blue wash.* **5** the waves caused by a moving boat *etc*: *The rowing-boat was tossing about in the wash from the ship's propellers.*

'washable *adj* able to be washed without being damaged: *Is this dress washable?*

'washbasin or **washhand basin** a basin in which to wash your face and hands: *We are having a new washhand basin fitted in the bathroom.*

'washing *n* **1**: *I don't mind washing, but I hate ironing.* **2** clothes washed or to be washed: *I'll hang the washing out to dry*; *I must deal with this huge pile of washing.*

washed-'out *adj* **1** tired: *I feel washed-out today.* **2** faded as a result of washing: *She wore a pair of old, washed-out jeans.*

washing machine an electric machine for washing clothes.

washing powder a powder that you add to water to help to wash clothes.

washing-'up *n* dishes to be cleaned after a meal *etc*: *I'll help you with the washing-up.*

'washout *n* a failure: *The demonstration was a complete washout.*

'washroom *n* a lavatory.

wash out 1 to remove a dirty mark with soap and water: *That coffee stain hasn't washed out of my dress.* **2** to wash the inside of something thoroughly.

wash up 1 in British English, to wash dishes *etc* after a meal: *I'll help you wash up.* **2** in American English, to wash your face and hands: *I'll go and get washed up before dinner.* **3** to bring up on to the shore: *A lot of rubbish has been washed up on the beach.*

wasn't /'wɒzənt/ short for **was not**.

wasp /wɒsp/ *n* a winged insect that has a sting and a slender yellow-and-black-striped body.

wastage /'weɪstɪdʒ/ *n* loss by wasting; the amount wasted: *Of the total amount, roughly 20% was wastage.*

waste /weɪst/ *v* to use more than is necessary of something, or not to use something in a useful way: *We waste a lot of food*; *You're wasting my time with all these stupid* *questions.* — *n* **1** useless material that is to be got rid of: *industrial waste from the factories.* **2** the wasting of something: *That was a waste of an opportunity.* **3** a huge area of land that is not or cannot be used: *the Arctic wastes.* — *adj*: *waste land.*

'wasted *adj* not necessary or successful: *It was a wasted visit — she was too busy to see us.*

'wasteful *adj* involving or causing waste: *Throwing away that bread is wasteful.* 'wastefully *adv.* 'wastefulness *n.*

waste away to lose weight, strength and health *etc*: *He is wasting away because he has a terrible disease.*

go to waste to be thrown away unused or allowed to go bad: *I can't bear to see good food go to waste!*

watch /wɒtʃ/ *n* **1** a kind of small clock that you wear on your wrist: *He wears a gold watch; a wrist-watch.* **2** a period of standing guard during the night: *I'll take the watch from two o'clock till six.* **3** in the navy *etc*, a group of officers and men who are on duty for a number of hours. — *v* **1** to look at someone or something: *He was watching her carefully; He is watching television.* **2** to look out for someone or something: *They've gone to watch for the ship coming in; Could you watch for the postman?* **3** to be careful about someone or something: *Watch that you don't fall off that wall!; Watch him! He's dangerous.* **4** to guard or take care of someone: *Watch the prisoner and make sure he doesn't escape; Please watch the baby while I go shopping; The hen is watching over her chicks.* **5** to wait for a chance: *Watch your chance, and then run.* 'watcher *n.*

to **watch** (not **see**) television.

'watchful *adj* alert and cautious: *watchful eyes; If you are watchful you will not be robbed.* 'watchfully *adv.* 'watchfulness *n.*

'watchdog *n* **1** a dog that guards someone's property *etc*: *We leave a watchdog in our office at night to scare away thieves.* **2** a person or group whose job is to protect something, such as people's rights.

'watchman *n* a man employed to guard a building *etc* against thieves, especially at night: *The bank-robbers shot the watchman.*

'watchword *n* a motto or slogan used by members of a group of people: *'Be prepared' is the Scouts' watchword.*

keep watch to be on guard: *He kept watch while the other soldiers slept.*

watch your step to be careful what you do or say: *The boss is in a bad mood, so watch your step and don't say anything wrong!*

watch out to be careful: *Watch out for the cars!; Watch out! The police are coming!*

watch over to guard or look after someone: *She watched over the child until he was better.*

water /'wɔːtə(r)/ *n* a clear liquid without taste or smell when pure: *She drank two glasses of water; Each bedroom in the hotel is supplied with hot and cold running water; The water's too cold to go swimming; transport by land and water.* — *v* **1** to supply plants *etc* with water: *He watered the flowers.* **2** to produce saliva: *His mouth watered at the sight of all the food.* **3** to fill with tears: *The dense smoke made his eyes water.*

'water-closet *n* a lavatory (often shortened to **WC**).

'watercolour *n* **1** a paint that is thinned with water instead of oil. **2** a painting done with watercolours.

'waterfall *n* a natural fall of water from a height such as a rock or a cliff.

See **rapids**.

'waterfront *n* a part of a town *etc* that faces the sea or a lake: *He lives on the waterfront.*

watering can a container with a spout, used for watering plants.

water level the level of the suface of a mass of water: *The water level in the reservoir is sinking.*

'waterlogged *adj* so wet that it cannot soak up any more water: *The ground was waterlogged after the storm.*

'watermelon *n* a melon with green skin and red flesh.

'waterproof *adj* not allowing water to soak through: *waterproof material.* — *n* a coat made of waterproof material: *She was wearing a waterproof.* — *v* to make material waterproof.

'water-skiing *n* the sport of skiing on water, towed by a motor-boat. 'water-ski *v.*

'watertight *adj* made in such a way that water cannot pass through.

water vapour water in the form of a gas, produced by evaporation.

'waterway *n* a channel, such as a canal or river, along which ships can sail.

'watery *adj* **1** like water: *watery soup.* **2** full of water, tears *etc*: *watery eyes.* **3** pale: *a watery blue; a watery sky.*

get into deep water to get into a difficult or dangerous situation.

hold water to be convincing: *His explanation won't hold water.*

water down to add water to something: *This milk has been watered down.*

watt /wɒt/ *n* a unit of power.

wave /weɪv/ *n* **1** a moving ridge, on the surface of water: *rolling waves; a boat tossing on the waves.* **2** a vibration travelling through the air: *radio waves; sound waves; light waves.* **3** a curl in hair: *Are those waves natural?* **4** a rise; an increase: *a wave of violence; The pain came in waves.* **5** the action of waving: *She recognized me, and gave me a wave.* — *v* **1** to move backwards and forwards: *The flags waved gently in the breeze.* **2** to curl or perm hair: *She's had her hair waved; Her hair waves naturally.* **3** to make a gesture *etc* with your hand, or something held in your hand, especially as a greeting: *She waved to me across the street; Everyone was waving handkerchiefs in farewell.*

'**waveband** *n* a range of wavelengths used to transmit radio programmes.

'**wavelength** *n* **1** the distance from any given point on one radio wave to the corresponding point on the next. **2** the length of the radio wave used by a particular broadcasting station.

on the same wavelength able to understand someone because you have similar ideas and opinions.

wave aside to decide that a difficulty *etc* is not important enough to consider.

waver /'weɪvə(r)/ *v* to be unsteady or uncertain: *He wavered between accepting and refusing.*

wavy /'weɪvɪ/ *adj* full of waves: *Her hair is wavy but her sister's hair is straight.*

wax[1] /waks/ *v* to appear to grow in size as more of it becomes visible: *The moon is waxing.*

wax[2] /waks/ *n* **1** the sticky, fatty substance of which bees make their cells. **2** the sticky, yellowish substance that forms in your ears. **3** a manufactured, fatty substance used in polishing, to give a good shine: *furniture wax.* **4** a substance used in making candles, models *etc*, that melts when heated.— *v* to polish or rub with wax.

waxed *adj* having a coating of wax: *waxed paper.*

'**waxen** or '**waxy** *adj* like wax.

'**waxwork** *n* a lifelike model, usually of someone famous, made of wax.

'**waxworks** *n* a museum of wax models.

way /weɪ/ *n* **1** an opening; a passageway: *This is the way out; There's no way through.* **2** a route, direction *etc*: *Which way shall we go?; Which is the way to Princes Street?; He drove past on his way to the visitors' car park; Will you be able to find your way to my house?; She limped back the way she had come; The errand took me out of my way; a motorway; a railway.* **3** used in the names of roads: *His address is 21 Melville Way.* **4** a distance: *It's a long way to the school; The nearest shops are only a short way away.* **5** a method; a manner: *Which is the easiest way to cook rice?; It was a good way to work up an appetite; He's got a funny way of talking; This is the quickest way to chop onions.* **6** an aspect of something: *In some ways this job is quite difficult; In a way I feel sorry for him.* **7** a habit: *He has some rather nasty ways.* **8** used with many verbs to give the idea of progressing or moving: *He pushed his way through the crowd; They soon ate their way through the food.* — *adv* by a long distance or time: *The winner finished the race way ahead of the other competitors; It's way past your bedtime.*

'**wayside** *n* the side of the road, path *etc*: *We can stop by the wayside and have a picnic.*

be on your way or **get on your way** to start or continue a journey *etc*: *I must be on my way now.*

by the way used in mentioning another subject: *By the way, did you know he was getting married?*

get your own way or **have your own way** to do, get *etc* what you want: *You can't always have your own way.*

give way 1 to collapse: *The bridge may give way at any time.* **2** to agree to something that you did not at first agree with: *She finally gave way to the children and bought them ice-creams.*

go out of your way to do more than is really necessary: *He went out of his way to help us.*

have it your own way to get your own way: *Oh, have it your own way — I'm tired of arguing.*

in a big way or **in a small way** used to describe the size or importance of an activity: *The company are planning to go into production in a big way.*

in the way blocking someone's progress, or occupying space that is needed by someone:

Don't leave your bicycle where it will get in the way of pedestrians; *Will I be in your way if I work at this table?*
lose your way to stop knowing where you are: *I lost my way through the city.*
make your way 1 to go: *They made their way towards the centre of the town.* **2** to be successful: *He has made his way in life.*
make way to stand aside and leave room: *The crowd parted to make way for the ambulance.*
no way definitely not.
out of the way not in the way: *'Get out of my way!' he said rudely.*
under way already begun; already making progress: *Peace talks are now under way.*
wayward /'weiwəd/ *adj* behaving badly; obstinate; disobedient: *a wayward child.*
we /wiː/ or /wɪ/ *pron* (used as the subject of a verb) the word you use for yourself, along with one or more other people: *We are going home tomorrow.*
weak /wiːk/ *adj* **1** not strong; feeble: *Her illness has made her very weak*; He has a weak heart. **2** not strong in character: *I'm very weak when it comes to giving up cigarettes.* **3** not good at a subject *etc*: *He is weak in mathematics.* **4** diluted; not strong: *weak tea.* **5** not good; not convincing: *a weak excuse.* **6** not very funny: *a weak joke.*
'weakly *adv.*

> to be **weak in** (not **at**) mathematics, but **bad** or **poor at** (not **in**) mathematics. See **good** and **strong**.

'weaken *v* to make or become weak: *The patient has weakened*; *The strain of the last few days has weakened him.*
'weakness *n* **1** the state of being weak. **2** a fault: *weaknesses of character*; *Smoking is one of my weaknesses.*
have a weakness for to have a liking for something: *She has a weakness for chocolate biscuits.*
wealth /wεlθ/ *n* **1** riches: *He is a man of great wealth.* **2** a great quantity: *a wealth of information.*
'wealthy *adj* having a lot of money and possessions; rich.
wean /wiːn/ *v* to teach a baby to take food other than its mother's milk: *Her baby is already one year old but she hasn't started to wean him yet.*
weapon /'wεpən/ *n* an instrument used for fighting: *Rifles, arrows, atom bombs and tanks are all weapons*; *Surprise is our best weapon.*
wear /wεə(r)/ *v* **1** to be dressed in something; to carry something on part of your body: *She wore a white dress*; *Does she usually wear spectacles?* **2** to arrange your hair in a particular way: *She wears her hair in a ponytail.* **3** to have a particular expression: *She wore an angry expression.* **4** to become thinner *etc* because of use, rubbing *etc*: *This carpet has worn in several places*; *This sweater is wearing thin at the elbows.* **5** to make a hole *etc* by rubbing, use *etc*: *I've worn a hole in the elbow of my jacket.* **6** to last: *This material doesn't wear very well.* — *n* **1** wearing; use: *I use this suit for everyday wear.* **2** clothes: *sportswear*; *leisure wear.* **3** damage due to use (often called **wear and tear**): *The hall carpet is showing signs of wear.*

> **wear**; **wore** /wɔː(r)/; **worn** /wɔːn/: *She wore a new dress*; *I have never worn spectacles.*

> to **put on** (not **wear**) your coat when you go out.

wear away to make or become damaged, thinner, smoother *etc* through use, rubbing *etc*: *The steps have worn away in places.*
wear down 1 to make shorter or thinner through frequent use: *This pencil has worn down quickly.* **2** to persuade someone by asking them repeatedly.
wear off to become less: *The pain is wearing off.*
wear on to pass slowly: *As the year wore on, he began to realize that she would never return.*
wear out 1 to become unfit for further use: *My socks have worn out*; *I've worn out my socks.* **2** to make someone very tired: *Children really wear you out!*
wear thin to begin to sound silly or unconvincing as a result of being used too often: *Don't you think that joke is wearing a little thin?*
wearisome /'wɪərɪsəm/ *adj* tiring; making you weary: *a wearisome journey.*
weary /'wɪərɪ/ *adj* tired; exhausted: *a weary sigh*; *He looks weary*; *I am weary of his jokes.* — *v* to make or become tired: *The patient wearies easily*; *Don't weary the patient.* **'wearily** *adv.* **'weariness** *n.*
weasel /'wiːzəl/ *n* a small wild animal with

weather /ˈwɛðə(r)/ *n* conditions in the atmosphere surrounding you — heat or cold, wind, rain, snow *etc*: *The weather is too cold for me*; *A grant to help meet the cost of extra fuel used in cold weather*; *stormy weather*. — *adj*: *a weather report*; *the weather forecast*. — *v* **1** to change gradually through exposure to wind, rain *etc*: *smooth, weathered stone*. **2** to survive safely: *The ship weathered the storm although she was badly damaged*.

'**weatherbeaten** *adj* made rough and darker by the sun and wind: *The fishermen had weatherbeaten faces*.

make heavy weather of to make something seem more difficult than it really is.

under the weather not very well: *I'm feeling a bit under the weather today*.

> **weather** refers to climatic conditions: *fine weather*.
> See also **climate**.

> **whether** is a conjunction: *Do you know whether he is coming?*

weave /wiːv/ *v* **1** to pass threads over and under each other on a loom *etc* to make cloth: *to weave cloth*. **2** to make baskets *etc* by a similar process.

> **weave**; **wove** /woʊv/; **woven** /ˈwoʊvən/: *She wove a beautiful scarf*; *He has woven a basket*.

'**weaver** *n* a person who weaves cloth.

web /wɛb/ *n* **1** a net made by a spider *etc*: *A fly was caught in the spider's web*. **2** the skin between the toes of ducks, swans, frogs *etc*. **webbed** *adj* having the toes joined by a web: *Ducks have webbed feet*.

wed /wɛd/ *v* to marry.

'**wedding** *n* a marriage ceremony: *The wedding will take place on Saturday*. — *adj*: *a wedding-cake*; *a wedding-ring*.

> See **marriage**.

we'd /wiːd/ short for **we would**, **we should** or **we had**.

wedge /wɛdʒ/ *n* **1** a piece of wood or metal, thick at one end and sloping to a thin edge at the other, used in splitting wood *etc* or in fixing something tightly in place: *She put a wedge under the door to prevent it swinging shut*. **2** something similar in shape: *a wedge of cheese*. — *v* to fix firmly in a narrow gap: *He was so fat that he got wedged in the doorway*.

Wednesday /ˈwɛdənzdɪ/ or /ˈwɛnzdɪ/ *n* the fourth day of the week, the day following Tuesday.

wee /wiː/ *adj* little; small: *It's a wee bit difficult to explain*; *A wee boy ran across the road*.

weed /wiːd/ *n* any wild plant, especially when growing where it is not wanted: *The garden is full of weeds*. — *v* to take weeds out of the ground: *to weed the garden*.

weed out to remove people or things that you don't want in a group: *They weeded out the students who needed extra practice*.

'**weedy** *adj* thin and weak-looking: *He was a weedy little man with a beard*.

week /wiːk/ *n* **1** any period of seven days, especially from Sunday to Saturday: *It's three weeks since I saw her*. **2** the five days from Monday to Friday: *He can't go during the week, but he'll go on Saturday or Sunday*. **3** the amount of time spent working during a period of seven days: *He works a forty-eight-hour week*.

'**weekday** *n* any day except a Saturday or Sunday: *Our office is open on weekdays*.

week'end *n* Saturday and Sunday, or Friday evening to Sunday evening: *We spent a weekend in Paris*. — *adj*: *a weekend trip*.

'**weekly** *adj* happening once a week; published once a week: *a weekly magazine*. — *adv* once a week: *The newspaper is published weekly*.

weep /wiːp/ *v* to cry; to shed tears: *She wept when she heard the terrible news*.

> **weep**; **wept** /wɛpt/; **wept**: *He wept bitter tears*; *I could have wept for joy*.

weft /wɛft/ *n* the threads going across a loom.

> See **warp**[2].

weigh /weɪ/ *v* **1** to find out how heavy something is by placing it on a scale: *He weighed himself on the bathroom scales*; *You must have your luggage weighed at the airport*. **2** to have a certain heaviness: *This parcel weighs one kilo*; *How much does this box weigh?* **3** to be a heavy burden to someone: *She was weighed down with two large suitcases*.

'**weighing-machine** *n* a machine for weighing people, loads *etc*: *I weighed myself on the weighing-machine at the railway station*.

weight /weɪt/ *n* **1** the amount that a person or thing weighs: *His weight is 80 kg*. **2** a piece of metal *etc* of a standard weight: *a seven-pound weight*. **3** burden; load: *You have taken a weight off my mind*. **4** importance: *Her opinion carries a lot of weight*.

'**weightless** *adj* not kept on the ground by gravity, so flying about freely: *The astronauts were weightless inside the spacecraft*. '**weightlessness** *n*.

'**weightlifting** *n* the sport in which people lift heavy weights. '**weightlifter** *n*.

'**weighty** *adj* **1** important: *a weighty reason*. **2** heavy. '**weightily** *adv*. '**weightiness** *n*.

put on weight to get fatter.

weigh down 1 to be so heavy that progress is slower than usual: *It will take longer to get to the top if you're weighed down by a heavy rucksack*. **2** to make someone feel worried or sad: *She was weighed down by her family problems*.

weigh on to worry or depress.

weigh up to consider different possibilities in order to make the right decision: *He was weighing up his chances of success*.

weir /wɪə(r)/ *n* a shallow dam across a river: *It is dangerous to swim near the weir*.

weird /wɪəd/ *adj* odd; very strange: *a weird story*. '**weirdly** *adv*.

welcome /ˈwɛlkəm/ *adj* **1** received with gladness and happiness: *She will make you welcome*; *He is a welcome visitor at our house*; *The extra money was very welcome*; *The holiday made a welcome change*. **2** gladly permitted to do something: *She's very welcome to borrow my books*. — *n* the receiving of a visitor *etc*: *We were given a warm welcome*. — *v* to receive or greet with pleasure and gladness: *We were welcomed by our hosts*; *She will welcome the chance to see you again*. — used to express gladness at someone's arrival: *Welcome to Britain!*

> She is always a **welcome** (not **welcomed**) visitor; The host **welcomed** the guests.

'**welcoming** *adj*: *a welcoming smile*.

you're welcome! a polite expression used in reply to thanks: '*Thank you very much!*' — '*You're welcome!*'

weld /wɛld/ *v* to join pieces of metal by pressure, often using heat, electricity *etc*. — *n* a joint made by welding. '**welder** *n*.

welfare /ˈwɛlfɛə(r)/ *n* good health; well-being: *Who is looking after the child's welfare?*

well[1] /wɛl/ *n* **1** a shaft made in the earth from which to obtain water, oil, natural gas *etc*. **2** the space round which a staircase winds: *He fell down the stair-well*. — *v* to flow freely: *Tears welled up in her eyes*.

well[2] /wɛl/ *adj* **1** healthy: *I don't feel at all well*; *She doesn't look very well*; *She's been ill but she's quite well now*. **2** in a satisfactory state; all right: *All is well now*. — *adv* **1** in a good, successful, suitable *etc* way: *He's done well to become a millionaire at thirty*; *She plays the piano well*; *Mother and baby are doing well*; *How well did he do in the exam?* **2** rightly; with good reason: *You may well look ashamed — that was a cruel thing to do*; *You can't very well refuse to go*. **3** with praise: *He speaks well of you*. **4** thoroughly: *Examine the car well before you buy it*. **5** by a long way: *He is well over fifty*. — a word used **1** to express surprise *etc*: *Well! I'd never have believed it*. **2** when re-starting a conversation, starting an explanation *etc*: *Do you remember John Watson? Well, he's become a teacher*.

> **well; better; best**: *My aunt knows me well, my sister knows me better, but my mother knows me best*.
> See also **good**.
> to play the piano very **well** (not **good**).

well-'balanced *adj* **1** sensible. **2** containing a good variety of healthy foods: *We should all try to eat a well-balanced diet*.

well-be'haved *adj* behaving correctly: *well-behaved children*.

well-'being *n* welfare; happiness: *She is always very concerned about her mother's well-being*.

well-'dressed *adj* wearing smart clothes: *She was always neat and well-dressed*.

well-'earned *adj* that you deserve: *She was enjoying a well-earned rest after her exams*.

well-'fed *adj* having plenty of good food to eat.

well-'groomed *adj* smart and tidy in appearance.

well-in'formed *adj* knowing a lot about something.

well-'kept carefully looked after: *a well-kept garden*.

well-'known *adj* familiar; famous: *a well-known TV personality*.

well-'mannered *adj* polite.

well-'meaning *adj* trying to be helpful and kind.

well-'off *adj* **1** rich: *He is very well-off*; *a well-off young lady*. **2** fortunate: *You children do not know when you are well off*.

well-read /wɛl'rɛd/ *adj* having read many books *etc*.

well-to-'do *adj* having enough money to live comfortably: *a well-to-do family*.

well-'wisher *n* someone who wants you to be successful: *His dressing-room was filled with flowers from well-wishers*.

as well too: *If you will go, I'll go as well*.

as well as in addition to: *She works in a restaurant in the evenings as well as doing a full-time job during the day*.

> Sally as well as Jane **is** working at this restaurant.

very well fine; all right: *Have you finished? Very well, you may go now*.

well done! used in congratulating a person: *I hear you won the competition. Well done!*

well enough fairly well: *'Did you do well in your exam?' 'Well enough.'*

we'll /wiːl/ short for **we shall** or **we will**.

went /wɛnt/ *see* **go**.

wept *see* **weep**.

were /wɜː(r)/ *see* **be**.

we're /wɪə(r)/ short for **we are**.

weren't /wɜːnt/ short for **were not**.

west /wɛst/ *n* **1** the direction in which the sun sets or any part of the earth lying in that direction: *The wind is blowing from the west*; *Geelong is to the west of Melbourne*; *in the west of Britain*. **2** (often written **W**) one of the four main points of the compass. — *adj* **1** in the west: *She's in the west wing of the hospital*. **2** from the direction of the west: *a west wind*. — *adv* towards the west: *The cliffs face west*.

'westerly *adj* **1** coming from the west: *a westerly wind*. **2** towards the west: *moving in a westerly direction*.

'western *adj* belonging to the west: *Western customs*. — *n* a film or novel about cowboys in North America.

'westernize *v* to make a people or country more like those in the West.

'westward *adj*, *adv* towards the west: *in a westward direction*; *They travelled westward*.

'westwards *adv* towards the west: *We journeyed westwards for two weeks*.

the West Europe, North America and South America.

wet /wɛt/ *adj* **1** soaked in, or covered with, water or another liquid: *We got soaking wet when it began to rain*; *His shirt was wet through with sweat*; *wet hair*; *The car skidded on the wet road*. **2** rainy: *a wet day*; *wet weather*; *It was wet yesterday*. **3** not yet dry: *wet paint*. — *v* to make wet: *She wet her hair and put shampoo on it*; *The baby has wet the bed*. **'wetness** *n*.

> **wet**; **wet** or **'wetted**; **wet** or **wetted**: *He wet his hair*; *It's easier to iron the sheets if they have been wetted first*.

wet blanket a dreary companion; someone who keeps complaining.

wet through completely soaked.

we've /wiːv/ short for **we have**.

whack /wak/ *v* to strike someone or something very hard, making a loud sound: *His father whacked him for misbehaving*. — *n* a blow: *His father gave him a whack across the ear*.

whale /weɪl/ *n* a very large animal that lives in the sea: *There is a school of whales in the bay*.

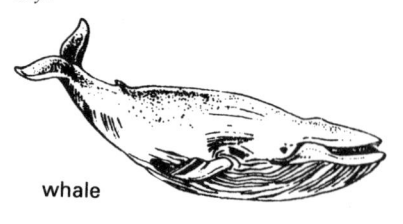

whale

'whaling *n* the hunting and killing of whales.

have a whale of a time to enjoy yourself very much: *They had a whale of a time at the party*.

wharf /wɔːf/, *plural* **wharfs** or **wharves**, *n* a platform alongside which ships are moored for loading and unloading.

what /wɒt/ *pron*, *adj* **1** used in questions especially about things: *What street is this?*; *What's your name?*; *What time is it?*; *What kind of bird is that?*; *What is he reading?*; *What did you say?*; *What is this cake made of?*; *'What do you want to be when you grow up?' 'A doctor.'*; *Tell me what you mean*; *I asked him what clothes I should wear*. **2** (also used as an *adv*) used in exclamations of surprise, anger *etc*: *What weather we're having!*; *What a fool he is!*; *What naughty children they are!*; *What a silly book this is!*; *What on earth is happening?* **3** the thing or things that: *Did you find what you wanted?*; *These tools are just what I need for this job*; *What that child needs is a good spanking!* **4** any things or amount that; whatever: *Please lend me what you can*.

what'ever *adj*, *pron* **1** any things or amount

that: *I'll lend you whatever books you need*; *You can choose whatever you want.* **2** no matter what: *You have to go on, whatever trouble you meet*; *Whatever else you do, don't do that!*; *Don't run away, whatever you do!*; *Whatever I say, it's always wrong.* — *adj* whatsoever; at all: *I had nothing whatever to do with the accident.* — *pron* (also spelt **what ever**) used in questions or exclamations to express surprise *etc*: *Whatever will he say when he hears this?*; *What ever are you doing?*

'**whatnot** *n* such things: *He told me all about his childhood and whatnot.*

whatso'ever *adj* at all: *That's nothing whatsoever to do with me.*

what about used to ask someone's opinion or plans about something, or to make suggestions: *What about your new book?*; *What about all this work?* — *We can't leave it till tomorrow*; *What about a cup of tea?*

> **How about** is often used for making suggestions: *How about going to the cinema tonight?*
>
> **What about** is often used when asking for someone's opinion or plans: *You can go out if you want, but what about your homework?*

what... for 1 why: *What did he do that for?* **2** for what purpose: *What is this switch for?*

what have you and similar things; and so on: *clothes, books and what have you.*

what if what will or would happen if: *What if he comes back and catches us?*

what... like used when you want information about someone or something: *'What does it look like?' 'It's small and square.'*; *'What's her mother like?' 'Oh, she's quite nice.'*; *We may go — it depends what the weather's like.*

what'll /'wɒtəl/ short for **what shall** or **what will**.

what's /wɒts/ short for **what is** or **what has**.

wheat /wi:t/ *n* a type of grain from which flour for making bread, cakes *etc* is obtained.

wheel /wi:l/ *n* **1** a circular frame or disc turning on a rod or axle, on which vehicles *etc* move along the ground: *A bicycle has two wheels, a tricycle three, and most cars four*; *a cartwheel.* **2** any of several things similar in shape and action: *a potter's wheel*; *a steering-wheel.* — *v* **1** to push a wheeled vehicle: *He wheeled his bicycle along the path.* **2** to turn quickly: *He wheeled round and slapped me.* **3** to fly in circles: *The seagulls wheeled about overhead.*

wheeled *adj*: *a wheeled vehicle*; *a four-wheeled vehicle.*

wheelbarrow /'wi:lbaroʊ/ *n* a small cart that you push, with one wheel at the front, and two legs and two handles at the back.

'**wheelchair** *n* a chair with wheels, used by invalids or those who cannot walk.

at the wheel in the driver's seat; driving: *My wife was at the wheel.*

wheeze /wi:z/ *v* to breathe with a rough gasping sound: *She's wheezing because she has a bad cold.*

when /wɛn/ *adv* at what time: *When did you arrive?*; *When will you see her again?*; *I asked him when the event had occurred*; *Tell me when to jump.* — *conjunction* **1** at or during the time at which: *It happened when I was abroad*; *When you see her, give her this message*; *When I've finished, I'll telephone you.* **2** in spite of the fact that; considering that: *Why do you walk when you have a car?*

whence /wɛns/ *adv* from what place; from where; because of what or which.

whenever /wɛn'ɛvə(r)/ *adv, conjunction* **1** at any time that: *Come and see me whenever you want to.* **2** at every time that: *I go to the theatre whenever I get the chance.*

where /wɛə(r)/ *adv* which place; to, from or in which place: *Where are you going?*; *Where are we going to?*; *We're told where to go and what to do*; *Do you know where we are?*; *Where does he get his ideas from?*; *Where did you buy that dress?*; *We asked where to find a good restaurant.* — *pron* to, from, or in which; the place to, from or in which; to or in the place to or in which: *It's nice going on holiday to a place where you've been before*; *This is the town where I was born*; *Is this the shop where you got your dress?*; *It's still where it was*; *I can't see him from where I am.*

'**whereabouts** *adv* near or in what place: *Whereabouts is it?*; *I don't know whereabouts it is.* — *n* the place where a person or thing is: *I don't know his whereabouts.*

where'as *conjunction* when in fact; but on the other hand: *He thought I was lying, whereas I was telling the truth.*

where'by *pron* by which: *We thought up a system whereby we made a lot of money without doing much work.*

wher'ever *pron* **1** no matter where: *I'll follow you wherever you may go*; *Wherever he is he will be thinking of you.* **2** to or in any place that: *Go wherever he tells you to go.* — *adv* (also spelt **where ever**) used in questions or exclamations to express surprise *etc*: *Wherever did she get that hat?*

where's /weəz/ short for **where is, where has**.

whet /wɛt/: **whet someone's appetite** to make someone want something more: *The photographs whetted their appetite for a similar trip.*

whether /'wɛðə(r)/ *conjunction* if: *I don't know whether it's possible.*

whether...or used to show a choice between two things: *He can't decide whether to go or not*; *She doesn't know whether or not to go*; *Whether you like the idea or not, I'm going ahead with it*; *Decide whether you're going or staying.*

See **weather**.

which /wɪtʃ/ *adj, pron* used in questions *etc* when asking someone to name something or someone from a particular group: *Which colour do you like best?*; *Which do you like best?*; *At which station should I change trains?*; *Which of the two girls do you like better?*; *Tell me which books you would like*; *Let me know which train you'll be arriving on*; *I can't decide which to choose.* — *pron* (able to be replaced by *that* except after a preposition; able to be left out except after a preposition or when it is the subject of the verb) the one that; the ones that: *This is the book which* (or *that*) *was on the table*; *This is the book which* (or *that*) *you wanted*; *This is the book you wanted*; *A nappy is a garment which* (or *that*) *is worn by babies*; *The chair which* (or *that*) *you are sitting on is broken*; *The chair you are sitting on is broken*; *This is not the book from which to learn about Russian history.* — *pron, adj* used, after a comma, to make a further remark about something: *My new car, which I paid several thousand pounds for, is not running well*; *He said he could speak Russian, which was untrue*; *My father may have to go into hospital, in which case he won't be going on holiday.*

which'ever *adj, pron* **1** any that, any one or ones that: *I'll take whichever books you don't want*; *Give me whichever you don't want*; *The prize will go to whichever of them writes the best essay.* **2** no matter which: *Whichever way I turned, I couldn't escape.*

which is which which is one and which is the other: *Mary and Susan are twins and I can't tell which is which.*

whiff /wɪf/ *n* a sudden puff of air, smoke, smell *etc*: *a whiff of petrol*; *a whiff of cigar smoke.*

while /waɪl/ *conjunction* (also **whilst** /waɪlst/) **1** during the time that: *I saw him while I was out walking.* **2** although: *While I sympathize, I can't really do very much to help.* — *n* a length of time: *It took me quite a while*; *It's a long while since we saw her.*

while away to pass time without boredom: *He whiled away the time by reading.*

worth your while worth your time and trouble: *It's not worth your while reading this book, because it isn't very good.*

whim /wɪm/ *n* a sudden desire; a change of mind: *I am tired of that child's whims.*

whimper /'wɪmpə(r)/ *v* to cry with a whining voice: *I heard a child whimpering.* — *n*: *The dog gave a little whimper.*

whine /waɪn/ *v* **1** to give a complaining cry or a cry of suffering: *The dog whines when it's left alone in the house.* **2** to make a similar noise: *I could hear the engine whine.* **3** to complain unnecessarily: *Stop whining about how difficult the job is!* — *n*: *the whine of an engine.*

whinny /'wɪnɪ/ *v* to make the cry of a horse: *The horse whinnied when it saw its master.*

whip /wɪp/ *n* a long cord or strip of leather attached to a handle, used for striking people as a punishment, driving horses *etc*: *He carries a whip but he would never use it on the horse.* — *v* **1** to strike with a whip: *He whipped the horse to make it go faster*; *The criminals were whipped.* **2** to beat eggs, cream *etc*. **3** to move fast especially with a twisting movement like a whip: *Suddenly he whipped round and saw me*; *He whipped out a revolver and shot her.*

whip up 1 to whip: *I'm whipping up eggs for the dessert.* **2** to produce quickly: *I'll whip up a meal in no time.* **3** to encourage a particular emotion among a group of people: *Let's try to whip up some enthusiasm for the new policies.*

whir or **whirr** /wɜː(r)/ *v* to move with a buzzing sound and a whirling action: *The propellers whirred and we took off.*

whirl /wɜːl/ *v* to move rapidly with a twisting or turning action: *She whirled round when I called her name*; *The wind whirled my hat away before I could grab it.* — *n* **1** an excited confusion: *a whirl of activity*; *My head's in a whirl — I can't believe it's all happening!* **2** a rapid turn.

'whirlpool *n* a strong circular current in a river or the sea.

'whirlwind *n* a violent circular current of wind with a whirling motion.
give it a whirl to intend to try something.

See **hurricane**.

whirr another spelling of **whir**.

whisk /wɪsk/ *v* **1** to sweep; to take rapidly: *He whisked the dirty dishes off the table*; *He whisked her off to the doctor*. **2** to beat eggs *etc* with a fork or whisk. — *n* a kitchen tool made of wire *etc*, for beating eggs, cream *etc*.

whisker /'wɪskə(r)/ *n* **1** (usually **whiskers**) hair growing down the sides of a man's face. **2** one of the long hairs between the nose and the mouth of a cat *etc*. **'whiskered**, **'whiskery** *adjs*.

See **beard**.

by a whisker only just: *The truck missed the child by a whisker*.

whisky /'wɪskɪ/ *n* an alcoholic drink made from grain, especially barley: *A lot of whisky is made in Scotland*.

whisper /'wɪspə(r)/ *v* **1** to speak very softly: *You'll have to whisper or he'll hear you*; *'Don't tell him,' she whispered*. **2** to make a soft sound in the wind: *The leaves whispered in the breeze*. — *n*: *They spoke in whispers*.

whistle /'wɪsəl/ *v* **1** to make a shrill sound by forcing your breath between the lips or teeth: *Can you whistle?*; *He whistled to attract my attention*; *He whistled a happy tune*. **2** to make a sound like this: *The electric kettle's whistling*; *The bullet whistled past his head*; *Listen to the wind whistling*. — *n* **1** the sound made by whistling: *I gave the dog a whistle and he came running*. **2** a musical pipe with high notes. **3** a device used by policemen, referees *etc* to make a whistling noise: *The referee blew his whistle at the end of the game*.

white /waɪt/ *adj* **1** having the colour of this paper. **2** having light-coloured skin; European in descent: *the first white man to explore Africa*. **3** pale because of fear, illness *etc*: *He went white with shock*. **4** with milk in it: *a white coffee, please*. — *n* **1** the colour of this paper. **2** a white-skinned person: *There is sometimes trouble between blacks and whites*. **3** the clear fluid in an egg, surrounding the yolk: *This recipe tells you to separate the yolks from the whites*. **4** the white part surrounding the coloured part of your eye: *the whites of your eyes*. **'whiteness** *n*.

white-'collar *adj* working in an office *etc*, rather than a factory: *white-collar workers*.
white lie a lie that is not a very bad one: *I'd rather tell my mother a white lie than tell her the truth and upset her*.

'whitewash *n* a mixture of lime and water for painting on to walls to make them white. — *v* to cover with whitewash. **'whitewashed** *adj*.

whizz /wɪz/ *v* to fly through the air with a hissing sound: *The arrow whizzed past his shoulder*.

who /huː/ *pron* (used as the subject of a verb) **1** what person or people: *Who is that woman in the green hat?*; *Who did that?*; *Who won?*; *Do you know who all these people are?* **2** (usually able to be replaced by **that**) the one that; the ones that: *The man who* (or *that*) *telephoned was a friend of yours*; *A doctor is a person who looks after people's health*. **3** used, after a comma, to make a further remark about a person or people: *His mother, who was tired out, gave him a smack*.

> In correct, formal English, **who** is used only as the subject of a verb; the form **whom** is used as the object of a verb or preposition: *The lady whom* (not *who*) *he had helped called to thank him*.

know who's who to know which people are important.
who'd /huːd/ short for **who would**, **who had**.
whoever /huːˈɛvə(r)/ *pron* **1** any person or people that: *Whoever gets the job will have a lot of work to do*. **2** no matter who: *Whoever rings, tell them I'm out*. **3** (also spelt **who ever**) used in questions to express surprise *etc*: *Whoever said that?*

whole /hoʊl/ *adj* **1** including everything or everyone; complete: *The whole class contributed money for the teacher's leaving present*; *a whole pineapple*. **2** not broken; in one piece: *She swallowed the biscuit whole*. — *n* **1** a single unit: *The different parts were joined to form a whole*. **2** the entire thing: *We spent the whole of one week sunbathing on the beach*; *The whole episode has been horrendous*.

whole'hearted *adj* sincere; keen: *wholehearted support*. **whole'heartedly** *adv*.

'wholemeal *n* flour made from the whole wheat grain or seed. — *adj*: *wholemeal bread*.

as a whole as a complete unit or group:

There are a few lazy children, but as a whole, the class works very hard.

on the whole taking everything into consideration: *Our trip was successful on the whole.*

wholesale /'həʊlseɪl/ *adj* buying goods on a large scale from a manufacturer and selling them to a shopkeeper: *a wholesale business.* — *adv*: *He buys the materials wholesale.*

'wholesaler *n* a person who buys and sells goods wholesale.

wholesome /'həʊlsəm/ *adj* healthy; good for your health: *Fresh fruit and vegetables are very wholesome*; *wholesome exercise.*

who'll /huːl/ short for **who will**.

wholly /'həʊlɪ/ *adv* completely; altogether: *I am not wholly certain.*

whom /huːm/ *pron* (used as the object of a verb or preposition, but in everyday speech sometimes replaced by **who**) **1** what person or people: *Whom* (or *who*) *do you want to see?*; *Whom* (or *who*) *did you give it to?*; *To whom shall I speak?* **2** (able to be left out or replaced by **that** except when following a preposition) the one that; the ones that: *The man whom* (or *that*) *you mentioned is here*; *The man you mentioned is here*; *Today I met some friends whom* (or *that*) *I hadn't seen for ages*; *I met some friends I hadn't seen for ages*; *This is the man to whom I gave it*; *This is the man whom* (or *who* or *that*) *I gave it to*; *This is the man I gave it to.* **3** used, after a comma, to make a further remark about a person or people: *My father, whom I'd like you to meet one day, is interested in your work.*

See **who**.

whoop /wuːp/ *n* a loud cry of delight, triumph *etc*: *a whoop of joy.* — *v*: *She gave a whoop of joy.*

whoops a word used when you make a mistake or have a slight accident: *Whoops! I nearly fell over the cat.*

who's /huːz/ short for **who is**, **who has**.

whose /huːz/ *adj*, *pron* **1** belonging to which person: *Whose is this jacket?*; *Whose jacket is this?*; *Whose is this?*; *Whose are these?*; *Whose car did you come back in?*; *In whose house did this incident happen?*; *Tell me whose pens these are.* **2** of whom: *Show me the boy whose father is a policeman.*

why /waɪ/ *adv* for which reason: *Why did you hit the child?*; *'I have to go to Surabaya on Friday.' 'Why?'*; *Why haven't you finished?*; *'I don't want to go swimming.' 'Why not?'*; *Tell me why you came here*; *She asked herself why she had to do this.* — *pron* for which: *Give me one good reason why I should help you!*

why not? can be used to express agreement: *'Let's go for a walk!' 'Why not?'*

wick /wɪk/ *n* the twisted threads of cotton *etc* in a candle, lamp *etc*, which draw up the oil or wax into the flame.

wicked /'wɪkɪd/ *adj* evil; sinful: *He is a wicked man*; *That was a wicked thing to do.* **'wickedly** *adv*. **'wickedness** *n*.

wicker /'wɪkə(r)/ *n* made of twigs, canes or rushes that are woven together: *a wicker basket*; *a wicker chair.*

wicket /'wɪkɪt/ *n* in cricket, a set of three upright wooden rods at which the bowler aims the ball.

'wicket-keeper *n* the fielder who stands immediately behind the wicket.

wide /waɪd/ *adj* **1** great in extent, especially from side to side: *wide streets.* **2** being a certain distance from one side to the other: *This material is three metres wide*; *How wide is it?* **3** great; large: *a wide experience of teaching.* — *adv* with a great distance from top to bottom or side to side: *He opened his eyes wide.* **'widely** *adv*. **'wideness** *n*.

'widen *v* to make or become wider: *They have widened the road*; *The lane widens here.*

wide-ranging /waɪd'reɪndʒɪŋ/ *adj* covering a large variety of subjects: *Our discussions were wide-ranging and productive.*

'widespread *adj* spread over a large area or among many people: *widespread hunger and disease.*

wide apart a great distance away from one another: *He held his hands wide apart.*

wide awake fully awake.

wide open fully open: *The door was wide open*; *Her eyes are wide open but she seems to be asleep.*

widow /'wɪdəʊ/ *n* a woman whose husband is dead: *My brother's widow has married again.* — *v*: *She was widowed in 1982 — her husband was killed in an air-crash.*

'widower *n* a man whose wife is dead.

width /wɪdθ/ *n* measurement from side to side; wideness: *What is the width of this material?*; *This fabric comes in three different widths.*

wield /wiːld/ *v* to use a tool, weapon *etc*: *to wield an axe.*

wife /waɪf/, *plural* **wives** /waɪvz/, *n* the woman to whom a man is married: *Come and meet my wife*; *He is looking for a wife.*

old wives' tale a bit of information or advice that is well-known but wrong.

wig /wɪɡ/ *n* an artificial covering of hair for the head: *Does she wear a wig?*

wiggle /ˈwɪɡəl/ *v* to waggle or wriggle: *She wiggled her hips.* — *n.*

'wiggly *adj* not straight; going up and down, from side to side *etc*: *a wiggly line.*

wigwam /ˈwɪɡwæm/ *n* a North American Indian tent made of skins *etc.*

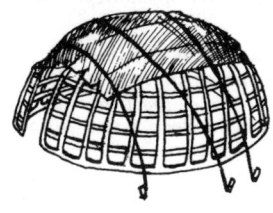

wigwam

wild /waɪld/ *adj* **1** not tame: *wolves and other wild animals.* **2** not cultivated: *wild flowers.* **3** not civilized; savage: *wild tribes.* **4** very stormy; violent: *a wild night at sea; a wild rage.* **5** mad; crazy: *He was wild with hunger; She was wild with anxiety.* **6** foolish: *a wild hope.* **7** not accurate; not reliable: *a wild guess.* **8** very angry. **'wildly** *adv.* **'wildness** *n.*

The opposite of **wild** is **tame**.

in the wild in its natural surroundings: *Young animals have to learn to look after themselves in the wild.*

wilderness /ˈwɪldənəs/ *n* a desert or wild area of a country *etc.*

wild-goose chase /waɪld ˈɡuːs tʃeɪs/ a search that takes you a long time and is unsuccessful.

wildlife /ˈwaɪldlaɪf/ *n* wild birds and animals: *We must protect wildlife.*

wilful /ˈwɪlfʊl/ *adj* **1** deliberate; intentional: *wilful damage.* **2** determined to do exactly what you like, not what other people suggest. **'wilfully** *adv.*

will[1] /wɪl/ *n* **1** the control you have over your actions and decisions; your own wishes; determination: *Do you believe in freedom of the will?; It was done against her will; He has no will of his own — he always does what the others want; Children often have strong wills; He has lost the will to live.* **2** a statement about what is to be done with your possessions *etc* after your death: *Have you made a will yet?* — *v* to try to make something happen using mental force or willpower: *She willed herself to keep on running.*

will[2] /wɪl/ *v* **1** used to form future tenses of other verbs: *He'll telephone you at six o'clock tonight; Will you be here again next week?; She will never make the same mistake again, will she?; They will have finished the work by tomorrow evening, won't they?*

The old grammar rule, that you use **shall** to form the simple future when the subject is *I* or *we*, is rarely obeyed now. **Will** is now much more common.

2 used in requests or commands: *Will you come into my office for a moment, please?; Will you please stop talking!* **3** used to offer something to someone: *Will you have a coffee?* **4** used to show willingness: *I'll do that for you if you like; I won't do it!* **5** used to state that something happens regularly, is quite normal *etc*: *Accidents will happen.* **6** used to say what you think is probable: *That will be my mother on the telephone.*

I will or **I'll** /aɪl/;
you will or **you'll** /juːl/;
he will or **he'll** /hiːl/;
she will or **she'll** /ʃiːl/;
it will or **it'll** /ˈɪtəl/;
we will or **we'll** /wiːl/;
they will or **they'll** /ðeɪl/;
will not or **won't** /wəʊnt/:
Will you or won't you do as I ask?; She'll ring you tomorrow; Boys will be boys, won't they?
See also **shall** and **would**.

-willed: *weak-willed people.*

'willing *adj* ready to agree to do something: *a willing helper; She's willing to help in any way she can.* **'willingly** *adv.* **'willingness** *n.*

at will whenever you want to: *He can waggle his ears at will.*

willow /ˈwɪləʊ/ *n* a tree with long, slender branches.

willpower /ˈwɪlpaʊə(r)/ *n* the determination to do something: *I don't have the willpower to stop smoking.*

wilt /wɪlt/ *v* to droop: *The plants are wilting because they haven't been watered.*

wily /ˈwaɪlɪ/ *adj* cunning; sly: *a wily fox; He is too wily for the police to catch him.* **'wiliness** *n.*

win /wɪn/ *v* **1** to obtain a victory in a contest; to succeed in coming first in a contest: *He won a fine victory in the election; Who is* *winning the war?*; *Who won the match?*; *He won the bet*; *She won the race*; *She won by five metres.* **2** to obtain a prize in a competition *etc*: *to win first prize*; *I won a fountain pen in the crossword competition.* **3** to obtain by your own efforts: *He won the teacher's approval.* — *n* a victory or success: *She's had two wins in four races.*

> **win**; **won** /wʌn/; **won**: *Who won the race?*; *Angela has won first prize.*

> to **beat** a person or a team: *I beat Robert in the spelling test*; *Team A beat Team B in the match.*
> to **win** a prize or a match *etc*: *He won the trophy*; *Team A won the competition.*

win over to succeed in gaining someone's support: *At first he refused to help us but we finally won him over.*
win the day to gain a victory; to be successful.
you can't win used when whatever you do will be wrong: *Whichever person I agree with, the other one will be offended — you can't win in a situation like this.*

wince /wɪns/ *v* to jerk with pain: *He winced as the dentist touched his broken tooth.*

winch /wɪntʃ/ *n* a cylinder with a rope or chain which winds up to lift or pull heavy loads. — *v* to move something using a winch.

wind¹ /wɪnd/ *n* **1** current of air: *The wind is strong today*; *There wasn't much wind yesterday*; *Cold winds blow across the desert.* **2** breath: *Climbing these stairs takes all the wind out of me.* **3** the gas that collects in your stomach and causes pain. — *v* to take someone's breath away: *The heavy blow winded him.* — *adj* played by being blown: *The flute is a wind instrument.*

> A **breeze** is a light wind: *cool breezes*; *a gentle breeze.*
> A **gale** is a very strong wind: *The gale forced the ships to take shelter in the harbour.*
> A **storm** is a period of bad weather with strong gales: *Many trees were blown down in the storm.*
> See also **hurricane**.

get wind of to hear about something: *You'll be punished if the headmaster gets wind of what you've done.*
like the wind very quickly: *The horse galloped away like the wind.*

wind² /waɪnd/ *v* **1** to wrap round in coils: *He wound the rope around his waist and began to climb.* **2** to make string, wool *etc* into a ball or coil: *to wind wool.* **3** to twist and turn: *The road winds up the mountain.* **4** to tighten the spring of a clock, watch *etc* by turning a knob, handle *etc*: *I forgot to wind my watch.*

> **wind**; **wound** /waʊnd/; **wound**: *She wound the wool*; *Have you wound the clock?*

wind up 1 to turn, twist or coil; to make into a ball or coil: *My ball of wool has unravelled — could you wind it up again?* **2** to wind a clock, watch *etc*: *She wound up the clock.* **3** to end: *I think it's time to wind the meeting up.* **4** to be somewhere at the end of a series of happenings: *He'll wind up in jail if he isn't careful.*

windfall /'wɪndfɔːl/ *n* **1** a piece of fruit that has fallen from a tree. **2** an unexpected gain, especially a sum of money: *He had a small windfall yesterday — he won £50 on the lottery.*

winding /'waɪndɪŋ/ *adj* full of bends *etc*: *a winding road.*

windmill /'wɪndmɪl/ *n* a tall building with a mill inside and long arms called **sails** on the outside, which are turned round by the wind.

window /'wɪndoʊ/ *n* an opening in the wall of a building that is fitted with a frame of wood, metal *etc* containing glass, that can be seen through and usually opened: *I saw her through the window*; *Open the window*; *Close the window*; *goods displayed in a shop window*; *Outside the window, dusk had fallen.*
'**windowsill** or **window ledge** *n* the narrow shelf along the bottom of a window.
window pane the piece of glass in a window.
window shopping *n* looking at things in shop windows, but not actually buying anything.

windpipe /'wɪndpaɪp/ *n* the tube through which you breathe air in and out.

windscreen /'wɪndskriːn/ *n* the front window of a vehicle, above the dashboard: *The windscreen was cracked by a flying stone.*
'**windscreen-wiper** *n* an arm that swings from side to side to clear the rain from a windscreen.

windsurfing /'wɪndsɜːfɪŋ/ *n* the sport of riding over the waves on a board with a sail.

windswept /'wɪndswept/ *adj* **1** that often has strong winds: *a windswept mountainside.* **2**

looking untidy because of a strong wind: *windswept hair*.

windy /'wɪndɪ/ *adj* having a lot of wind; exposed to wind: *a windy day*; *a windy hilltop*.

wine /waɪn/ *n* an alcoholic drink made from the juice of grapes or other fruit: *two bottles of wine*; *a wide range of fine wines*.

wing /wɪŋ/ *n* **1** one of the arm-like parts of a bird or bat that it uses in flying; one of the similar parts of an insect: *The eagle spread his wings and flew away*; *The bird cannot fly as it has an injured wing*; *These butterflies have red and brown wings*. **2** a similar part of an aeroplane: *the wings of a jet*. **3** a section built out to the side of a large house *etc*: *the west wing of the hospital*. **4** any of the corner parts of a motor vehicle: *The rear left wing of the car was damaged in the accident*. **5** a group in a political party who have particular opinions and beliefs: *right-wing attitudes*.

winged *adj* having wings: *a winged creature*.

take under your wing to take someone under your protection: *The older girl took the younger one under her wing and looked after her at school*.

wink /wɪŋk/ *v* **1** to shut and open an eye quickly in friendly greeting, or to show that something is a secret *etc*: *Gus winked at Jane when she arrived*; *Sarah winked at me as she said that she hadn't bought his present yet*. **2** to flicker and twinkle: *The city lights winked in the distance*. — *n*: *'Don't tell anyone I'm here', he said with a wink*.

winner /'wɪnə(r)/ *n* someone who wins; a victor.

winning /'wɪnɪŋ/ *adj* **1** victorious; successful: *the winning candidate*. **2** attractive; charming: *a winning smile*.

winning-post /'wɪnɪŋ pəʊst/ *n* in horse-racing, a post marking the place where the race finishes.

winter /'wɪntə(r)/ *n* the coldest season of the year, December till February in cooler northern regions: *We often have snow in winter*. — *adj*: *winter evenings*.

'wintertime *n* the season of winter.

'wintry *adj* typical of winter: *wintry weather*.

wipe /waɪp/ *v* **1** to clean or dry by rubbing with a cloth, paper *etc*: *Would you wipe the table for me?*; *Stop crying — wipe your eyes*. **2** to remove by rubbing with a cloth, paper *etc*: *The child wiped her tears away with her handkerchief*; *Wipe that writing off the blackboard*; *Please wipe up that spilt milk*. — *n*: *Give the table a wipe*.

wipe out 1 to clean the inside of something with a cloth *etc*: *She wiped the bowl out*. **2** to remove; to get rid of something: *He wiped out the memory of the dreadful journey*. **3** to destroy completely: *The entire family was wiped out in a car crash*.

wire /waɪə(r)/ *n* **1** metal drawn out into a long strand, as thick as string or as thin as thread: *We need some wire to connect the battery to the rest of the circuit*. **2** a single strand of this metal: *There must be a loose wire in my radio somewhere*. — *adj*: *a wire fence*. — *v* to fit a system of electric wires in a house *etc*: *The house has been wired up but the electricity hasn't been connected yet*.

wire-'netting *n* a material used in fencing *etc*.

'wiring *n* the wires that make up a building's electrical system: *The wiring is unsafe and must be renewed*.

wiry /'waɪərɪ/ *adj* slim but strong: *a wiry young man*.

wisdom /'wɪzdəm/ *n* knowledge and good sense: *Wisdom comes with experience*.

wisdom tooth any one of the four back teeth that come up after childhood, usually about the age of twenty.

wise /waɪz/ *adj* **1** having gained a great deal of knowledge from books or experience and able to use it well. **2** sensible: *You would be wise to do as he suggests*; *a wise decision*. **'wisely** *adv*.

> **wise** gives the idea of knowledge and experience: *The experienced businessman made a wise suggestion*.
> **clever** gives the idea of intelligence and smartness: *The quick-thinking boy made a clever suggestion*.

wish /wɪʃ/ *v* **1** to have a desire; to express a desire: *There's no point in wishing for a miracle*; *Touch the magic stone and wish*; *He wished that she would go away*; *I wish I had never met him*. **2** to require to do or have something: *Do you wish to sit down, sir?*; *We wished to share our story*; *I'll cancel the arrangement if you wish*. **3** to say that you hope for something for someone: *I wish you the very best of luck*. — *n* **1** a desire or longing, or the thing desired: *It's always been my wish to go to South America some day*. **2** an expression of a desire: *The fairy granted him three wishes*; *Did you make a wish?* **3** (usually **'wishes**) an expression of hope for success *etc* for someone: *He sends you his best wishes.*

wishful thinking what you would like to happen, rather than what is likely to happen.

'wishing-well *n* a well that is supposed to have the power of granting any wish you make when you are beside it.

wisp /wɪsp/ *n* thin strand: *a wisp of hair; a wisp of smoke.*

'wispy *adj*: *wispy hair.*

wistful /'wɪstfʊl/ *adj* thoughtful and rather sad; longing for something with little hope: *The dog looked into the butcher's window with a wistful expression on his face.* **'wistfully** *adv.* **'wistfulness** *n.*

wit /wɪt/ *n* **1** humour: *His plays are full of wit; I admire his wit.* **2** someone who can express ideas in a humorous way, tells jokes *etc*: *She's a great wit.* **3** common sense: *He did not have the wit to defend himself.*

at your wits' end completely confused; desperate.

keep or **have your wits about you** to be constantly prepared to deal with any difficulty.

witch /wɪtʃ/ *n* a woman who is supposed to have powers of magic, especially of an evil kind.

A man with magic powers is a **wizard**.

'witchcraft *n* magic performed by a witch.

with /wɪð/ or /wɪθ/ *prep* **1** in the company of; beside; among: *I was walking with my father; Do they enjoy playing with each other?; He used to play football with the Arsenal team; Put this book with the others.* **2** by means of; using: *Mend it with this glue; Cut it with a knife.* **3** used in expressing the idea of filling, covering *etc*: *Fill this jug with milk; He was covered with mud.* **4** used in describing disagreement and conflict: *They quarrelled with each other; He fought with my brother.* **5** used in descriptions of things: *a man with a limp; a girl with long hair; a stick with a handle; Treat this book with care.* **6** as the result of: *He was shaking with fear.* **7** in the care of: *Leave your case with the porter.* **8** in relation to; in the case of; concerning: *Be careful with that!; What's wrong with you?; What shall I do with these books?* **9** used in expressing a wish: *Down with school!*

withdraw /wɪð'drɔː/ *v* **1** to move back or away: *The general withdrew his troops; They withdrew from the competition.* **2** to take back something you have said: *She withdrew her remarks, and apologized; He has withdrawn the charges he made against her.* **with'drawal** *n.*

> **with'draw; withdrew** /wɪð'druː/; **withdrawn** /wɪð'drɔːn/.

with'drawn *adj* not friendly; very quiet.

wither /'wɪðə(r)/ *v* to fade, dry up, or decay: *The plants withered because they had no water; The heat has withered my plants.*

withering /'wɪðərɪŋ/ *adj* scornful: *a withering look.*

withhold /wɪð'hoʊld/ *v* to refuse to give: *to withhold permission.*

> **with'hold; withheld** /wɪð'hɛld/; **with'held**.

within /wɪ'ðɪn/ or /wɪ'θɪn/ *prep* **1** inside: *I could hear sounds from within the building.* **2** not breaking; not outside: *His actions were within the law.* **3** in no more than: *She'll be here within an hour.* — *adv* inside: *Car for sale. Apply within.*

without /wɪ'θaʊt/ or /wɪ'ðaʊt/ *prep* **1** in the absence of; not having: *They went without you; I could not live without him; We cannot survive without water.* **2** not: *He drove away without saying goodbye; You can't walk along this street without meeting someone you know.*

withstand /wɪð'stand/ *v* to oppose or resist successfully: *The city withstood the siege for eight months.*

> **with'stand; withstood** /wɪð'stʊd/; **with'stood**.

witness /'wɪtnəs/ *n* **1** someone who has seen or was present at an event *etc* and so has direct knowledge of it: *Someone must have seen the accident but the police can find no witnesses so far.* **2** a person who gives evidence, especially in a law court. — *v* to see something happening; to be present at an event: *This lady witnessed the accident at three o'clock this afternoon.*

-witted /'wɪtɪd/ *suffix* having a certain kind of intelligence: *quick-witted; a sharp-witted lad.*

witty /'wɪtɪ/ *adj* clever and amusing: *a witty person; witty remarks.* **'wittily** *adv.* **'wittiness** *n.*

wives /waɪvz/ plural of **wife**.

wizard /'wɪzəd/ *n* a man, especially in stories, who is said to have magic powers.

> See **witch**.

wobble /'wɒbəl/ v to rock unsteadily from side to side: *The bicycle wobbled and the child fell off.* — n a slight rocking, unsteady movement: *This table has a bit of a wobble.* **'wobbly** adj.

woe /woʊ/ n grief or misery: *He has many woes*; *He told a tale of woe.*
'woeful adj miserable; unhappy: *a woeful expression.* **'woefully** adv. **'woefulness** n.

wok /wɒk/ n a large, bowl-shaped pan used for cooking.

woke, woken see **wake**.

wolf /wʊlf/, plural **wolves** /wʊlvz/, n a wild animal of the dog family. — v to eat greedily: *He wolfed his breakfast and hurried out.*

> A wolf **howls**.
> A baby wolf is a **cub**.
> A wolf lives in a **lair**.
> Wolves hunt in **packs**.

woman /'wʊmən/, plural **women** /'wɪmɪn/, n **1** an adult human female: *His sisters are both grown women now*; *Some women will do anything in the name of beauty.* **2** a female domestic daily helper: *We have a woman who comes in to do the cleaning.* — adj: *a woman pilot.*
'womanly adj having qualities that are suitable to, or attractive in, women; feminine: *She's a kind, womanly person*; *womanly charm.*

womb /wu:m/ n the part of the body of a female mammal in which the babies grow until they are born.

won /wʌn/ see **win**.

wonder /'wʌndə(r)/ n **1** the feeling you have when you see something unexpected or extraordinary: *The glorious sunrise filled him with wonder.* **2** something strange, unexpected or extraordinary: *the Seven Wonders of the World*; *He goes swimming so often that it's a wonder he doesn't grow fins*; *The wonder of the discovery is that it was only made ten years ago.* — v **1** to be surprised: *Caroline is very fond of John — I shouldn't wonder if she married him.* **2** to feel curiosity: *Have you ever wondered why some people are left-handed?* **3** to feel a desire to know: *I wonder what the news is.*

> We **wonder** (not **wander**) at the huge number of stars.

'wonderful adj extraordinary; excellent; marvellous: *a wonderful opportunity*; *a wonderful present*; *She's a wonderful person.* **'wonderfully** adv.

'wonderingly adv with great curiosity and amazement: *The children gazed wonderingly at the puppets.*
'wonderland n a land or place full of wonderful things.
wondrous /'wʌndrəs/ adj wonderful.
no wonder it isn't surprising: *No wonder you like him — he spends all his money on you!*

won't /woʊnt/ short for **will not**.

woo /wu:/ v to seek someone as a wife: *He wooed the daughter of the king.* **'wooer** n.

wood /wʊd/ n **1** the material of which trees are composed: *My desk is made of wood*; *She gathered some wood for the fire.* **2** (often **woods**) a group of growing trees: *They went for a walk in the woods.* — adj: *The room is warmed by a wood fire.*
'woodcutter n a person whose job is cutting down trees.
'wooded adj covered with trees: *a wooded hillside.*
'wooden adj made of wood: *three wooden chairs.*
'woodland n land covered with woods: *a stretch of woodland.*
'woodwind n musical instruments that you play by blowing into, such as the clarinet, recorder and flute.
'woodwork n **1** carpentry: *He did woodwork at school.* **2** the parts of a building *etc* that are made of wood: *The woodwork in the house is rotting.*
'woody adj **1** covered with trees: *woody countryside.* **2** like wood: *a woody smell*; *a woody stem.*

woof /wʊf/ n the sound of a dog's bark.

wool /wʊl/ n the soft hair of sheep and some other animals, made into a long thread for knitting or into cloth for clothes *etc*: *I wear wool in winter*; *knitting-wool.* — adj: *a wool shawl.*
'woollen adj made of wool: *a woollen hat.*
'woollens n clothes made of wool: *Woollens should be washed by hand.*
'woolly adv made of, or like, wool: *a woolly jumper.* — n a garment, especially a jumper, knitted in wool: *winter woollies.*

word /wɜ:d/ n **1** the smallest unit of language. **2** a short conversation: *I'd like a word with you in my office.* **3** news: *When you get there, send word that you've arrived safely.* **4** a solemn promise: *He gave her his word that it would never happen again.* — v to choose words carefully to express your exact meaning: *a carefully worded statement.*

'wording *n* the words you choose to express your meaning: *It took us some time to get the wording of the invitation just right.*

word-'perfect *adj* able to repeat something from memory without any mistakes.

'word-processor *n* an electronic machine with a keyboard and a screen, that is used to type letters, documents *etc*.

break your word to fail to keep your promise.

by word of mouth by one person telling another in speech, not in writing: *She got the information by word of mouth.*

get a word in edgeways to have an opportunity to say something when someone else is talking: *I can never get a word in edgeways when my sisters are arguing.*

in a word to sum up briefly: *In a word, I don't like him.*

in other words used to say something in a different way: *He has problems with punctuation — in other words, he's always late.*

keep your word to keep your promise.

put in a good word for someone to say something good about a person to someone important: *He has promised to put in a good word for me to the manager.*

take someone at their word to believe someone without question and act according to their words.

take someone's word for it to trust that what someone says is true.

word for word in the exact words: *That's what he said, word for word.*

wore /wɔː(r)/ *see* **wear**.

work /wɜːk/ *n* **1** effort made in order to achieve or make something: *John has put a lot of work into the essay.* **2** employment: *I cannot find work.* **3** a task; the thing that you are working on: *Please clear your work off the table.* **4** a painting, book, play, piece of music *etc*: *the works of Shakespeare; This work was composed in 1816.* **5** what you produce as a result of your efforts: *His work has improved lately.* **6** your place of employment: *He left work at 5.30 p.m.; I don't think I'll go to work tomorrow.* — *v* **1** to do work: *You don't work hard enough; She works at the factory three days a week; I've been working on a new project.* **2** to make people do work: *He works his employees very hard.* **3** to be employed: *Are you working just now?* **4** to operate: *How does that machine work?* **6** to make your way slowly and carefully with effort or difficulty: *She worked her way up the rock face.*

'workable *adj* able to be carried out: *Your plan seems workable.*

'workbook *n* a student's exercise book with questions and spaces for answers.

'worker *n* **1** a person who is employed in an office, a factory *etc*: *office-workers; car-workers.* **2** a worker in a factory rather than an office *etc*. **3** someone who works: *He's a slow worker.*

'workforce *n* all the people working for a company, industry or country.

'workings *n* the way in which an organization or system operates: *She tried to explain the workings of the stock market to me.*

'workload *n* the amount of work you are given to do: *If you are not busy, I shall increase your workload.*

'workman *n* a man who does manual work: *the workmen on a building site.*

'workmanship *n* the skill of a workman; the skill with which something is made: *He admired the carpenter's workmanship; His new desk fell apart within a year, because the workmanship was so poor.*

'workout *n* a period of physical exercise.

works /wɜːkz/ *n* **1** a factory *etc*: *The steelworks are* (or *is*) *closed for the holidays.* **2** the mechanism of a watch, clock *etc*: *The works are all rusted.* **3** deeds, actions *etc*: *She has spent her life doing good works.*

'workshop *n* **1** a room or building where things are made or repaired: *He is a mechanic in a large metal workshop; a carpenter's workshop.* **2** a course of study or work for a group of people on a particular subject: *She is attending a poetry workshop; a dance workshop.*

'worktop or **work surface** *n* a flat surface in the kitchen on which you can prepare food: *easy-to-clean worktops.*

at work 1 working: *Susan's at work on a new book.* **2** at the office *etc* where you work: *Isn't Dorothy at work today?*

get or **set to work** to start work: *Could you get to work painting that ceiling?; I'll have to set to work on this mending this evening.*

go to work on to begin work on something: *We're thinking of going to work on an extension to the house.*

in working order operating correctly: *Your washing machine is in working order now.*

out of work having no employment: *He's been out of work for months.*

work of art a painting, sculpture *etc*.

work out 1 to solve; to calculate correctly: *I can't work out this puzzle*; *Work out how many hours there are in a year.* **2** to come to a satisfactory end: *Don't worry — it will all work out in the end.* **3** to do energetic physical exercises: *She's working out in the gym.*

work up 1 to excite or rouse gradually: *She worked herself up into a fury*; *Don't get so worked up!* **2** to raise; to build up: *I just can't work up any energy today.*

world /wɜːld/ *n* **1** the planet Earth: *every country of the world.* **2** the people who live on the planet Earth: *The whole world is waiting for a cure for cancer.* **3** any planet *etc*: *people from other worlds.* **4** a state of existence: *Do concentrate! You seem to be living in another world.* **5** an area of life or activity: *the insect world*; *the world of the businessman.* **6** a great deal: *The holiday did him the world of good.* **7** the lives and ways of ordinary people: *He's been a monk for so long that he knows nothing of the world.*

'worldly *adj* **1** to do with ordinary life on earth, not spiritual or eternal things: *She had no family to leave her worldly goods to.* **3** experienced and good at dealing with life and people.

'world-famous *adj* well-known throughout the world: *He is a world-famous orchestral conductor.*

world'wide *adj, adv* everywhere in the world: *a worldwide problem*; *Their products are sold worldwide.*

out of this world almost too good to be real: *The concert was out of this world.*

worm /wɜːm/ *n* a small creeping animal with a ringed body and no backbone; an earthworm. — *v* **1** to make your way slowly or secretly: *He wormed his way to the front of the crowd.* **2** to get information *etc* out of someone with difficulty: *It took me hours to worm the true story out of him.*

worn /wɔːn/ *adj* damaged by long use: *a badly-worn carpet.* See also **wear**.

worn out 1 too worn to be able to be used any more: *This jacket's worn out.* **2** very tired: *You look worn out.*

worry /'wʌrɪ/ *v* **1** to feel anxious; to make someone feel anxious: *His poor health worries me*; *His mother is worried about his education*; *There's no need to worry just because he's late.* **2** to annoy; to distract: *Don't worry me just now — I'm busy!* **3** to shake or tear with the teeth *etc* as a dog shakes and tears its prey *etc*. — *n* anxiety; a cause of anxiety: *Money is a constant worry to me*; *Try to forget your worries*; *Worry is bad for your health.*

'worried *adj: a worried look.*

worse /wɜːs/ *adj* **1** inferior; less good: *My exam results were bad but his were much worse than mine.* **2** not so well: *I feel worse today.* **3** more unpleasant: *Waiting for exam results is worse than sitting the exams.* — *adv* less well: *He behaves worse now than he did as a child.* — *pron* of two things or people, the one that is inferior: *the worse of the two alternatives.*

See **bad** and **badly**.

'worsen *v* to grow or make worse: *The situation has worsened.*

none the worse for not harmed by: *She seemed to be none the worse for her experience.*

worship /'wɜːʃɪp/ *v* **1** to honour greatly; to praise: *to worship God.* **2** to love or admire very greatly: *She worships her older brother.* — *n*: *A church is a place of worship*; *the worship of money.* **'worshipper** *n*.

worst /wɜːst/ *adj* worse than all the others: *That is the worst book I have ever read.* — *adv* worse than all the others: *Alan performed worst of all in the test.* — *pron* the thing, person *etc* that is worse than all the others: *the worst of the three*; *His behaviour is at its worst when he's with strangers*; *At the worst they can only make you pay a fine.*

See **bad** and **badly**.

at worst or **at the worst** from the worst point of view: *At worst we'll have to find a telephone and get help.*

get the worst of it to be defeated in a fight *etc*.

if the worst comes to the worst if the worst possible thing happens: *If the worst comes to the worst, you can sell your house.*

the worst of it is that the most unfortunate *etc* aspect of the situation is that: *The worst of it is that I've spent all my money.*

worth /wɜːθ/ *n* **1** value: *These books are of little worth*; *She sold 50 pounds' worth of tickets.* **2** the amount of something that takes or lasts for a particular period of time: *We've lost two weeks' worth of work.* **3** usefulness: *She has proved her worth as a member of the committee.* — *adj* **1** equal in value to: *This pen is worth five francs.* **2** good enough for: *His suggestion is worth*

considering; *The exhibition is worth a visit.* **'worthless** *adj* of no value: *worthless old coins.* **'worthlessly** *adv.* **'worthlessness** *n.*
worthy /'wɜːðɪ/ *adj* **1** good: *I willingly give money to a worthy cause.* **2** deserving something: *She is certainly worthy of the prize she has won.* **3** suitable for: *a performance worthy of a champion.* **4** important enough: *She was not thought worthy to be presented to the king.* **'worthily** *adv.* **'worthiness** *n.*
worth'while *adj* deserving attention, time and effort *etc*: *a worthwhile cause*; *It isn't worthwhile to ask him — he'll only refuse.*
worth someone's while useful, helpful or enjoyable: *It might be worth your while to ask for some help.*
would /wʊd/ *v* **1** the past tense of **will**: *He said he would be leaving at nine o'clock the next morning*; *I asked if he'd come and mend my television set*; *I asked him to do it, but he wouldn't*; *I thought you would have finished by now.* **2** used in speaking of things that are possible or probable; might: *If I asked her to the party, would she come?*; *I would have come to the party if you'd asked me*; *He'd be a good teacher, wouldn't he?* **3** used to express a preference, opinion, wish *etc* politely: *I would do it this way*; *It'd be a shame to lose the opportunity, wouldn't it?*; *She says she would like you to help her.* **4** used to express annoyance: *I've lost my car-keys — that would happen!* **5** used to talk about things that often happened in the past: *Wherever she was, she would always telephone me at six o'clock.*

> **I would** or **I'd** /aɪd/;
> **you would** or **you'd** /juːd/;
> **he would** or **he'd** /hiːd/;
> **she would** or **she'd** /ʃiːd/;
> **it would** or **it'd** /'ɪtəd/;
> **we would** or **we'd** /wiːd/;
> **they would** or **they'd** /ðeɪd/;
> **would not** or **wouldn't** /'wʊdənt/: *Who would have thought she'd win?*; *You'd like to go to the zoo, wouldn't you?*; *You wouldn't like to break your leg, would you?*
> Note: *They said they would* (not *will*) *arrive tomorrow.*

would you used to introduce a polite request to someone to do something: *Please would you close the door?*
'would-be *adj* trying or hoping to be or become: *a would-be film star.*
wound[1] /waʊnd/ *see* **wind**[2].

wound[2] /wuːnd/ *n* an injury: *The wound that he had received in the war still gave him pain occasionally*; *He died from a bullet-wound.* — *v* **1** to hurt; to injure: *He didn't kill the animal — he just wounded it*; *He was wounded in the battle.* **2** to hurt someone's feelings: *to wound someone's pride.*

> You are **wounded** in a battle *etc*, but **injured** in an accident.

'wounded *adj*: *wounded soldiers.*
wove, woven *see* **weave**.
wrangle /'raŋɡl/ *v* to argue noisily or bitterly: *The children are always wrangling with their mother about their bedtime.* — *n.*
wrap /rap/ *v* to roll or fold something round something or someone: *She wrapped the towel round herself*; *She wrapped the baby up in a warm shawl.* — *n* a warm covering to put over your shoulders.
'wrapper *n* a paper cover for a sweet, packet of cigarettes *etc*: *a sweet-wrapper.*
'wrapping *n* something used to pack something in: *She took the wrapping off the parcel.*
wrapping paper paper used to wrap presents.
wrap up to dress warmly: *You have to wrap up well if you visit England in winter*; *Wrap the child up well.*
wrapped up in to be deeply involved or interested in: *He was so wrapped up in his work that he didn't notice that she was ill.*
wrath /rɒθ/ *n* violent anger.
wreath /riːθ/, *plural* **wreaths** /riːðz/ or /riːθs/, *n* **1** a circular garland of flowers or leaves, placed at a grave, or put on someone's shoulders or head after their victory *etc*: *We put a wreath of flowers on her mother's grave.* **2** a curl of smoke, mist *etc*: *wreaths of smoke.*
wreck /rɛk/ *n* **1** a very badly damaged ship: *The divers found a wreck on the sea-bed.* **2** something in a very bad condition: *She shouldn't drive that car — it's a wreck!* **3** the destruction of a ship at sea: *The wreck of the Royal George.* — *v* to destroy or damage very badly: *The ship was wrecked on rocks in a storm*; *My son has wrecked my car*; *You have wrecked my plans.*
'wreckage *n* the remains of something wrecked: *After the accident, the wreckage was removed from the motorway.*
wrench /rɛntʃ/ *v* **1** to pull with a violent movement: *He wrenched the book out of my hand.* **2** to sprain: *to wrench your shoulder.* —

n **1** a violent pull or twist. **2** a painful parting or separation from someone: *It was a wrench to leave her, but he had to go.* **3** a strong tool for turning nuts, bolts *etc.*

wrestle /'rɛsəl/ *v* **1** to struggle with someone, especially as a sport. **2** to struggle with a problem *etc*: *I've been wrestling with the office accounts.*

'**wrestler** *n* a person who takes part in the sport of wrestling.

'**wrestling** *n* a sport in which people try to hold each other down on the ground: *a wrestling match.*

wretch /rɛtʃ/ *n* **1** a miserable, unhappy creature: *The poor wretch!* **2** a name used in annoyance or anger: *You wretch!*

wretched /'rɛtʃɪd/ *adj* **1** very poor or miserable: *She leads a wretched life.* **2** used in annoyance: *You wretched child!* '**wretchedly** *adv.* '**wretchedness** *n.*

wriggle /'rɪgəl/ *v* to twist to and fro: *The child kept wriggling in his seat; How are you going to wriggle out of this awkward situation?* — *n* a wriggling movement.

wring /rɪŋ/ *v* **1** to force water from material by twisting or by pressure: *He wrung the water from his wet shirt.* **2** to clasp and unclasp your hands in desperation, fear *etc.*

> **wring; wrung** /rʌŋ/; **wrung**: *John wrung out his window-cleaning cloth; I've wrung out most of the water.*

wrinkle /'rɪŋkəl/ *n* a small crease on your skin: *Her face is full of wrinkles.* — *v* to make or become full of wrinkles or creases: *The damp had wrinkled the pages.*

'**wrinkled** *adj* full of wrinkles: *a wrinkled face.*

wrist /rɪst/ *n* the part of your arm at the joint between hand and forearm: *I can't play tennis — I've hurt my wrist.*

'**wristwatch** *n* a watch worn on your wrist.

writ /rɪt/ *n* a legal document that orders you to do something: *He received a writ ordering him to appear in court as a witness.*

write /raɪt/ *v* **1** to make letters or words, especially with a pen or pencil on paper: *They wrote their names on a sheet of paper; Jack has learnt to read and write; Please write in ink.* **2** to compose the text of a book, poem *etc*: *She wrote a book on prehistoric monsters.* **3** to compose a letter and send it: *I'll write you a long letter about my holiday.*

> **write; wrote** /roʊt/; **written** /'rɪtən/: *He wrote to me last week; This book was written long ago.*

'**write-off** *n* a vehicle that has been so badly damaged that it is not worth repairing.

'**writer** *n* someone who writes, especially for a living: *Dickens was a famous English writer; the writer of this letter.*

'**writing** *n* **1** letters or other forms of script: *The Chinese form of writing; I can't read your writing.* **2** the art or activity of writing books *etc* as a job: *He never earned much money from writing.*

writing paper fine smooth paper for writing letters on.

'**writings** *n* the books, poems, *etc* of a particular writer: *the writings of Plato.*

'**written** *adj* in writing: *a written message.*

write back to send a letter to someone who has written to you.

write down : *She wrote down every word he said.*

write in to write a letter to a newspaper, television programme *etc*: *Several viewers have written in to say they enjoy our programme very much.*

write off **1** to write to an organization or company to order or ask for something: *I have written off for a price list.* **2** to accept or decide that a thing or person will not succeed: *I arrived so late that they had almost written me off.* **3** to accept that you are not going to get a particular amount of money back: *The company's debts had to be written off.*

write out to write the whole of something: *Write this exercise out in your neatest handwriting.*

write up to write a report or notes *etc* in a full, neat and final form: *We wrote up our lecture notes each evening.*

writhe /raɪð/ *v* to twist violently to and fro: *to writhe in agony; She writhed about when I tickled her.*

wrong /rɒŋ/ *adj* **1** incorrect: *The child gave the wrong answer; They would not have got his name wrong, he knew.* **2** mistaken: *I thought Singapore was south of the Equator, but I was quite wrong.* **3** not good; not right: *It was wrong to steal.* **4** not suitable: *He's the wrong man for the job.* **5** not right; not normal: *What's wrong with that child — why is she crying?* — *adv* incorrectly: *I think I may have spelt her name wrong.* — *n* that which is bad or evil: *He does not know right* *from wrong.* — *v* to insult; to hurt unjustly: *You wrong me by suggesting that I'm lying.*

The opposite of **wrong** is **right**.

'**wrongdoer** *n* a person who does wrong or illegal things: *The wrongdoers must be punished.* '**wrongdoing** *n*.

'**wrongful** *adj* not lawful; not fair: *wrongful dismissal from a job.* '**wrongfully** *adv*.

'**wrongly** *adv* **1** incorrectly: *The letter was wrongly addressed.* **2** unjustly: *I have been wrongly treated.*

do wrong: *You did wrong to punish him; You have done him wrong by punishing him unjustly.*

get wrong 1 to make a mistake: *I got that sum wrong.* **2** to misunderstand a person or situation: *You've got it all wrong — let me explain again; Don't get me wrong — I'm not angry with you.*

go wrong 1 to go badly: *Everything has gone wrong for her recently.* **2** to stop working properly: *The machine has gone wrong.* **3** to make a mistake: *Where did I go wrong in that sum?*

in the wrong guilty of a mistake or injustice: *Don't try to blame her — You're the one who's in the wrong!*

wrote *see* **write**.

wrung *see* **wring**.

wry /raɪ/ *adj* slightly mocking: *a wry smile.* '**wryly** *adv*.

X

xenophobia /zɛnə'foʊbɪə/ *n* a fear or hatred of foreign or strange people or things: *The government asked for a report on racism and xenophobia in education.*

Xerox /'zɛrɒks/ or /'zɪərɒks/ *n* the trademark of a kind of photocopying machine; a copy made by it. — *v*: *to Xerox a document.*

See **photocopy**.

Xmas /'krɪsməs/ a short way of writing Christmas.

X-ray /'ɛks reɪ/ *n* a photograph taken using special rays (**X-'rays**) that can pass through materials that light cannot pass through: *I'm going to hospital for an X-ray*; *We'll take an X-ray of your chest.* — *v*: *They X-rayed my arm to see if it was broken.*

xylophone /'zaɪləfoʊn/ *n* a musical instrument consisting of wooden or metal bars of various lengths attached to a frame, that produce different notes when struck by wooden hammers.

Y

yacht /jɒt/ *n* a boat or small ship built and used for racing or cruising: *We spent our holidays on a friend's yacht.*
'**yachting** *n* the pastime of sailing in a yacht.

yak /jak/, *plural* **yaks** or **yak**, *n* a long-haired ox, found in Tibet.

yam /jam/ *n* any of several kinds of potato-like tropical plants used as food.

yank /jaŋk/ *v* to pull something suddenly and violently: *She yanked the child out of the mud.* — *n*: *He gave the rope a yank.*

yap /jap/ *v* to give a high-pitched bark. — *n*: *The puppy gave a yap.*

yard[1] /jɑːd/ *n* an old unit of length equal to 0.914 metres (often written **yd**).

yard[2] /jɑːd/ *n* an enclosed area of ground beside a building: *Leave your bicycle in the yard*; *a school-yard*; *a courtyard.*

yarn /jɑːn/ *n* **1** wool, cotton *etc* spun into thread: *knitting-yarn*; *a length of yarn.* **2** a story that is exaggerated: *An old man told me a yarn about his youth.*

yashmak /ˈjaʃmak/ *n* a veil worn over the face below the eyes by some Muslim women: *Muslim women living in Europe don't always wear yashmaks.*

yawn /jɔːn/ *v* **1** to stretch your mouth wide and take a deep breath when you are tired or bored: *He yawned and fell asleep.* **2** to be wide open: *The mouth of the cave yawned in front of us.* — *n*: *She could not suppress a yawn of boredom.*
'**yawning** *adj* wide open: *a yawning gap.*

year /jɪə(r)/ *n* the period of time the earth takes to go once round the sun, 365 days, especially the 365 days from January 1 to December 31.

> A **decade** is a period of 10 years.
> A **century** is a period of 100 years.
> A **millennium** is a period of 1000 years.

'**yearly** *adj* happening *etc* every year: *We pay a yearly visit to my uncle.* — *adv* every year: *The festival is held yearly.*

-year-old *adj*: *a two-year-old girl.* — *n*: *She teaches a class of six-year-olds.*

years *n* a long time: *I've known her for years and years*; *They had to work for years and years to earn that money.*

all year round or **all year long** *etc* throughout the whole year: *The weather is so good here that you can swim all year round.*

yearn /jɜːn/ *v* to want something very much; to long: *to yearn for an end to the war.*
'**yearning** *n* a strong desire.

yeast /jiːst/ *n* a substance used to make bread swell before baking; used also to make beer.

yell /jɛl/ *n* a loud, shrill cry; a scream: *a yell of pain.* — *v*: *He yelled at her to be careful.*

yellow /ˈjɛloʊ/ *n* the colour of gold; the colour of the yolk of an egg: *Yellow is my favourite colour.* — *adj*: *a yellow dress.* — *v* to make or become yellow: *It was autumn and the leaves were beginning to yellow.*
'**yellowish** *adj* slightly yellow in colour.

yelp /jɛlp/ *v* to give a sharp, sudden cry: *The dog yelped with pain.* — *n*: *The dog gave a yelp of pain.*

yes /jɛs/ a word used to express agreement or consent: *Yes, that is true*; *Yes, you may go.*

yesterday /ˈjɛstədɪ/ *n* the day before today: *Yesterday was a tiring day.* — *adv*: *He went home yesterday.*

> We went to see a movie **last night** (not **yesterday night**);
> **yesterday morning** and **yesterday evening** are correct.

yet /jɛt/ *adv* **1** up till now: *He hasn't telephoned yet*; *We're not yet ready.* **2** used for emphasis: *He's made yet another mistake.* **3** even: *a yet more terrible experience.* — *conjunction* but; however: *He's pleasant enough, yet I don't like him.*

> See **still**.

as yet up to the present: *I haven't had a book published as yet.*

yeti /ˈjɛtɪ/ *n* an ape-like creature supposed to live in the Himalayas: *Some climbers believe they have seen the yeti's footprints in the snow.*

yield /jiːld/ *v* **1** to give up; to surrender: *He was forced to yield all his possessions to the state.* **2** to give way: *At last the door yielded*; *He yielded to his son's request*; *to yield to temptation.* **3** to produce *etc*: *How much milk does that herd of cattle yield?* — *n* the amount that is produced: *Natural fertilizers have been used to increase yields.*

yob /jɒb/ *n* a rough, aggressive and badly behaved boy or young man: *gangs of yobs.*

yoga /ˈjoʊgə/ *n* a system of exercise and meditation in which you stretch your body while doing breathing exercises: *She believes practising yoga helps keep her calm.*

yoghourt, yoghurt or **yogurt** /ˈjɒgət/ *n* a slightly sour-tasting, half-liquid food made from milk.

yogi /ˈjoʊgɪ/ *n* a person who has spent many years practising yoga: *She went to India to visit a yogi.*

yoke /joʊk/ *n* **1** a wooden frame placed over the necks of oxen to hold them together when they are pulling a cart *etc*. **2** a frame placed across someone's shoulders, for carrying buckets *etc*. **3** something that weighs people down, or prevents them being free: *the yoke of slavery.* **4** the part of a garment that fits over your shoulders and round your neck: *a black dress with a white yoke.* — *v* to join with a yoke: *He yoked the oxen to the plough.*

yolk /joʊk/ *n* the yellow part of an egg (also called the **'egg-yolk**).

you /juː/ *pron* **1** (used as the subject or object of a verb, or as the object of a preposition) the person or people you are speaking to: *You look well!; I asked you a question; Do you all understand?; Who came with you?* **2** used with a noun when calling someone something, especially something unpleasant: *You idiot!; You fools!* **3** people in general, including yourself: *You can go to prison for driving dangerously.*

you'd /juːd/ short for **you had, you would**.
you'll /juːl/ short for **you will**.

young /jʌŋ/ *adj* not old: *a young person; Young babies sleep a great deal; A young cow is called a calf.* — *n* baby animals or birds: *Most animals defend their young.*

He's **still too young** (not **small**) to take care of himself.

younger see **junior**.

'youngish *adj* quite young in age or appearance: *The clerk was a youngish man with red hair.*

'youngster *n* a young person: *A group of youngsters were playing football.*

the young young people in general.

your /jɔː(r)/ *adj* belonging to you: *your car.*
you're /jɔː(r)/ short for **you are**.
yours /jɔːz/ *pron* something belonging to you: *This book is not yours; Yours is on that shelf; Is he a friend of yours?*

yours faithfully, yours sincerely or **yours truly** expressions written before your signature at the end of a letter.

See also **faithfully** and **sincerely**.

yourself /jɔːˈsɛlf/, *plural* **yourselves** /jɔːˈsɛlvz/, *pron* **1** used as the object of a verb or preposition when the person or people you are speaking to is or are both the subject and object: *Why are you looking at yourselves in the mirror?; You can dry yourself with this towel.* **2** used to emphasize **you**: *You yourself can't do it, but you could ask someone else to do it.* **3** without help *etc*: *You can do it yourself!*

youth /juːθ/, *plural* **youths** /juːðz/, *n* **1** the early part of life: *Enjoy your youth!; He spent his youth in America.* **2** the state of being young: *the energy of youth.* **3** a boy between 15 and 20 years old: *He and two other youths were kicking a football about.* **4** young people: *the youth of today.*

youth club a place providing leisure activities for young people: *They went to a dance at the local youth club.*

'youthful *adj* **1** young: *The boy looked very youthful.* **2** active, young-looking *etc*: *Exercise will keep you youthful.* **3** having to do with youth: *youthful pleasures.* **'youthfully** *adv*. **'youthfulness** *n*.

youth hostel a place where people on walking and bicycling holidays etc can stay cheaply: *The whole family stayed in a youth hostel as they couldn't afford a hotel.*

you've /juːv/ short for **you have**.

yo-yo /ˈjoʊjoʊ/ *n* a toy consisting of two joined discs that you can make run up and down a string: *going up and down like a yo-yo.*

Z

zany /'zeɪnɪ/ *adj* crazy but fun: *a person with a zany sense of humour.*

zap /zap/ *v* **1** to kill, usually by shooting: *The video game lets you zap aliens.* **2** to erase from a computer screen: *She zapped the file.* **3** to change television channels using a remote control device.

zeal /ziːl/ *n* keenness; eagerness.
zealous /'zɛləs/ *adj*: *He is a zealous supporter of our cause.* **'zealously** *adv*.

zebra /'zɛbrə/ or /'ziːbrə/, *plural* **zebras, zebra**, *n* a striped animal of the horse family: *two zebras; a herd of zebra.*
zebra crossing a crossing-place for pedestrians in a street, marked in black and white stripes.

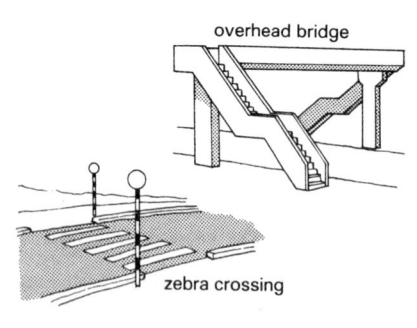

[Illustration: overhead bridge; zebra crossing]

zenith /'zɛnɪθ/ *n* **1** the point in the sky immediately above you: *The sun is at the zenith.* **2** the highest point: *His popularity has reached its zenith.*

zero /'zɪərəʊ/, *plural* **'zeros**, *n* **1** the number 0: *The figure 100 has two zeros in it.* **2** the point on a scale *etc* on which measurements are based: *The temperature was 5 degrees below zero.* **3** the exact time fixed for something to happen, for example an explosion, the launching of a spacecraft *etc*: *It is now 3 minutes to zero.*

zest /zɛst/ *n* keen enjoyment: *She joined in the games with zest.*

zigzag /'zɪɡzaɡ/ *adj* having sharp bends: *a zig-zag path through the woods.* — *v*: *The road zigzagged through the mountains.*

zinc /zɪŋk/ *n* a metal that is blue-white in colour.

zip[1] /zɪp/ *v* to move with a whizzing sound: *A bullet zipped past his head.*

zip[2] /zɪp/ *n* a device for fastening clothes *etc* consisting of two rows of metal or nylon teeth that fit into one another when a sliding tab is pulled along between them (also called a **'zipper** or a **zip fastener**). — *v* to fasten with a zip: *She zipped up her dress.*

zodiac /'zəʊdɪak/ *n* in astrology, an imaginary strip across the sky that is divided into twelve equal parts called the **signs of the zodiac**, each sign being named after a group of stars: *The twelfth sign of the zodiac is called Pisces, or the Fishes, and the sun is in this sign between February 19 and March 20.*

zone /zəʊn/ *n* an area; a region; a part of a town *etc* marked off for a special purpose: *a no-parking zone; a traffic-free zone.*

zoo /zuː/ *n* a place where wild animals are kept for the public to see, and for study, breeding *etc*.
zoology /zəʊ'ɒlədʒɪ/ *n* the scientific study of animals: *She studied zoology at university.*
zoo'logical *adj*.
zo'ologist *n* a person who studies or is an expert on zoology.

zoom /zuːm/ *v* to move fast with a loud humming or buzzing sound: *The motorbike zoomed past us; The plane zoomed across the sky.*
zoom lens a camera lens which can make an object appear larger or smaller: *He took several pictures of the ship with his zoom lens, some pictures showing the ship in the harbour, others showing the crew on deck.*
zoom in to bring something being photographed into close-up view: *The camera zoomed in on what the boy was writing.*

zuc'chini /zʊ'kiːnɪ/, *plural* **zuc'chini** or **zuc'chinis**, *n* a courgette.

APPENDIX

PREPOSITIONS

Prepositions are words you use to show position and movement with relation to objects and people.

Where is Paul? He's **on** the wall.

on, on to	The picture is **on** the wall.	The man is **on** television.
There's a mark **on** your skirt.	Is Sharon still **on** the telephone?	Sue goes to school **on** foot.
The others go **on** or **in** the bus.	The cup dropped **on** or **on to** the floor.	The candle is **on top of** the chest of drawers.
in, into, inside	The scarecrow is **in** the field.	Sally is **in** bed.
The teddy bear is **in** the shop window.	I saw the advert **in** the newspapers.	Sally is **in** or **at** school.
What is **inside** the chest?	The sweets were put **into** the jar.	Rosie is getting **into** the car.
out, outside	Who took a biscuit **out of** the tin?	The milk is **outside** the door.

606 APPENDIX

under		The mouse ran **under** the chair.	The saucer is **under** or **beneath** the cup.
below		Your ankle is **below** your knee.	The plane is flying **below** the clouds.
over		The sheep jumped **over** the fence.	Pete has a towel **over** his head.
above		There's a bee **above** your head.	The clock is **above** the fireplace.
through		The train came **through** the tunnel.	There's an arrow **through** your hat.
round		Mike walked **round** the tree.	The men sat **around** the fire.
at		Lorna is **at** the bus-stop.	Dad is sitting **at** the table.
between		The ball is **between** the doll and the brick.	The ball rolled **between** the posts.
among		The sweets were shared **among** the children.	Can you see the cow **among** the sheep?

off		The cat jumped **off** the chair.		Tony got **off** the train.	
against		The ladder is leaning **against** the wall.		Rangers are playing **against** Rovers.	
near		The horse is **near** the fence.		Don't go too **near** the edge!	
by		Our house is **by** the canal.		The family is travelling **by** car.	
behind		Phil is **behind** the door.		The bug crawled **behind** the picture.	
in front of		The bus is waiting **in front of** the hotel.		Don't run **in front of** the car!	
up		Jack and Jill climbed **up** the hill.	**past**		Ann is walking **past** the statue.
down		Steve is coming **down** the steps.	**along**		Ginny is walking **along** the stream.
beside		The jug is **beside** the bowl.	**towards**		The mouse is crawling **towards** the cheese.

BITS AND PIECES

drop	a **drop** of **water**	a **drop** of **rain**	a **drop** of **wine**
slice	a **slice** or **piece** of **cake**	a **slice** or **piece** of **bread**	a **slice** of **meat**
sheet	a **sheet** or **piece** of **paper**		a **sheet** of **glass**
bar	a **bar** of **chocolate** is divided into **pieces** of **chocolate**		a **bar** of **soap**
stick	a **stick** or **piece** of **chalk**		a **stick** of **chewing gum**
block	a **block** of **wood**		a **block** of **ice**
lump	**lumps** or **pieces** of **coal**		a **lump** of **sugar**

CONJUNCTIONS

Conjunctions are words you use to join sentences, words or phrases together. Their job is to be **'link-words'** between **similar and contrasting ideas or things:**

> Mum washes the clothes **and** the boys dirty them again.

In the above example, 'and' is joining two **sentences** together to make one sentence. Notice that there is a verb on each side of the 'link': 'washes' on the left, and 'dirty' on the right.

> Peter **and** Rita went for a walk in the rain.

In the above example, 'and' joins only two **words**, the names 'Peter' and 'Rita'. They are both the subject of the verb 'went'.

> I like buying clothes **and** going to parties.

In the above example, 'and' joins the two activities, 'buying clothes' and 'going to parties'. These are **phrases**, both following the verb 'like'.

> You can go to the match with me **or** you can go shopping with Mum.

In the above example, 'or' links two **sentences** that give alternative possibilities. Notice the verb 'can' on each side of the 'link'.

> I don't want to go to the match **or** go shopping.

In the above example, 'or' links the **phrases** 'go to the match' and 'go shopping'. The words 'I don't want to' apply to both these alternatives.

> Would you like fish **or** chicken for lunch?

In the above example, only the **words** 'fish' and 'chicken' are linked by 'or'. The words 'Would you like' apply to both these alternatives.

Notice that some conjunctions or 'link-words' can begin the sentence:

> **As** my grandmother was coming to stay, I cleaned the house.

> **After** you have washed the dishes, you can make the beds.

> **Once** you have made the beds, you can sweep the floor.

Here are some more conjunctions; notice that all these link **sentences**:

I like buying books, **but** I'm too lazy to read them.

Mary didn't write to Chris, **nor** did she telephone him.

Don't tell me **that** you've still got that old teddy-bear.

I'll scream **if** you don't stop playing that trombone.

Look **before** you leap!

I won't tell you my weight **unless** you tell me yours.

I'm not going to sweep the floor **because** I'm too tired.

Since you're so tired, you should go to bed early.

Mum enjoys watching television **while** she does the ironing.

Wipe your feet **when** you come through the door.

He took great care of his toys, **although** he was only three.

You are not to start eating **until** you have washed your hands.

APPENDIX 611

ISN'T IT

'Isn't it?' *isn't* the only **possible** question-tag. There are many more. You have to choose the right one. Think carefully about the subject and verb in the first part of the sentence, and make the question-tag match them. In the examples below the boxes contain **positive statements** and the balloons attached to them contain **negative tags**. These examples expect the answer **Yes**.

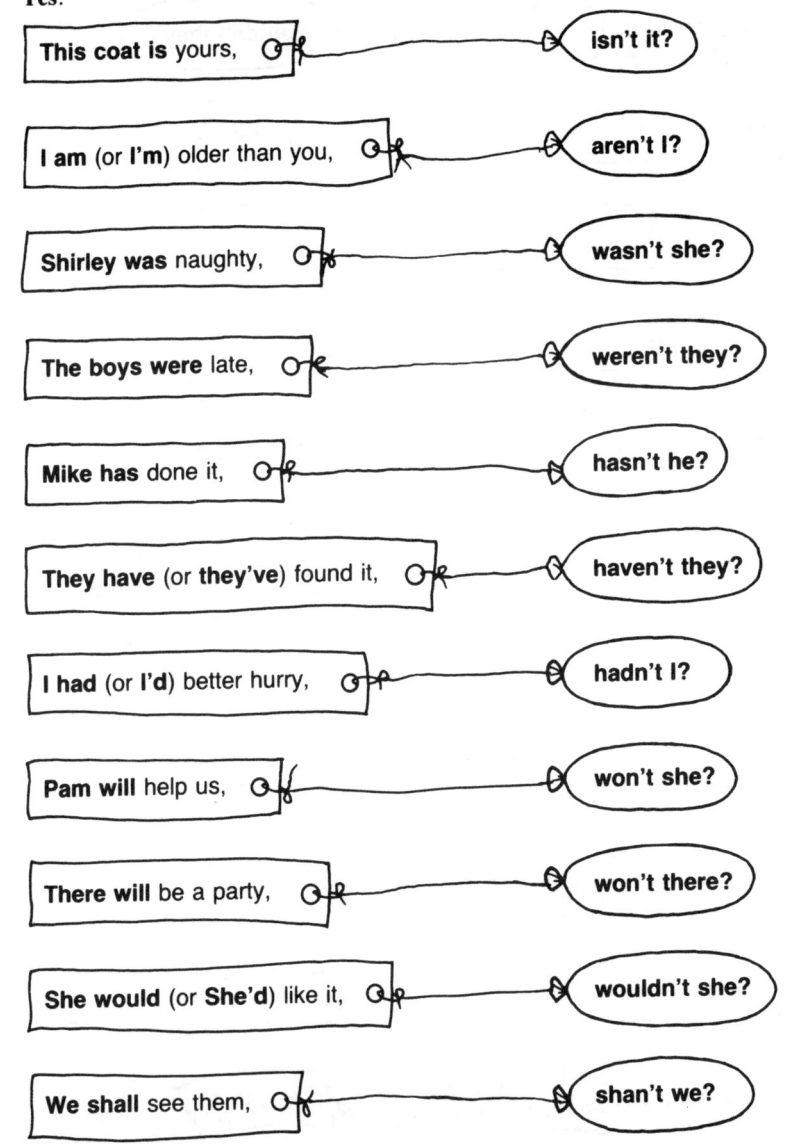

This coat **is** yours,	isn't it?
I am (or **I'm**) older than you,	aren't I?
Shirley was naughty,	wasn't she?
The boys were late,	weren't they?
Mike has done it,	hasn't he?
They have (or **they've**) found it,	haven't they?
I had (or **I'd**) better hurry,	hadn't I?
Pam will help us,	won't she?
There will be a party,	won't there?
She would (or **She'd**) like it,	wouldn't she?
We shall see them,	shan't we?

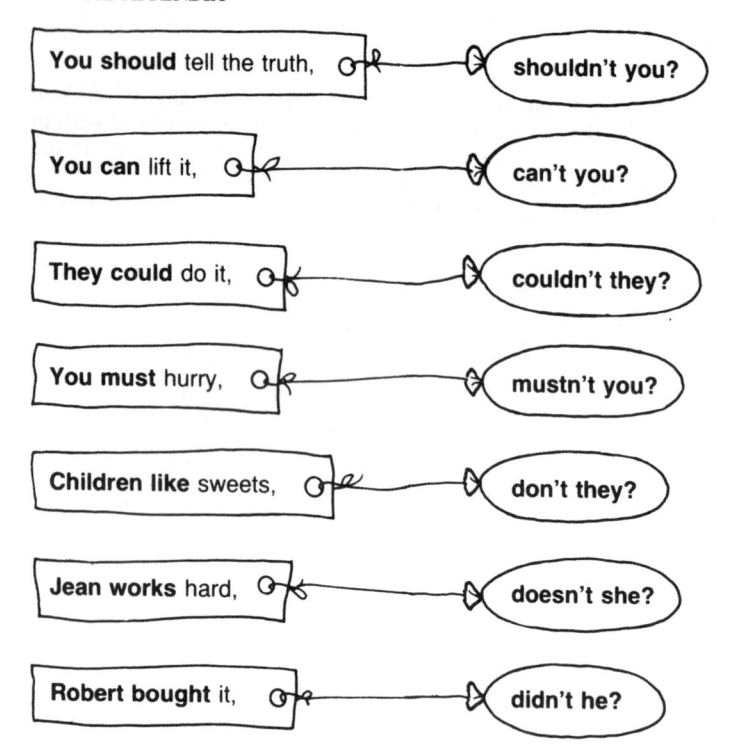

612 APPENDIX

You should tell the truth, — shouldn't you?

You can lift it, — can't you?

They could do it, — couldn't they?

You must hurry, — mustn't you?

Children like sweets, — don't they?

Jean works hard, — doesn't she?

Robert bought it, — didn't he?

In the examples below, the boxes contain **negative statements** and the labels attached to them contain **positive tags**. These examples expect the answer **No**.

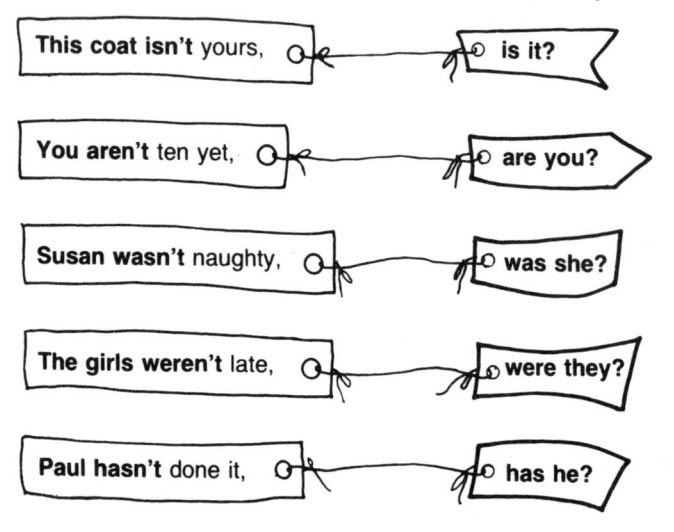

This coat isn't yours, — is it?

You aren't ten yet, — are you?

Susan wasn't naughty, — was she?

The girls weren't late, — were they?

Paul hasn't done it, — has he?

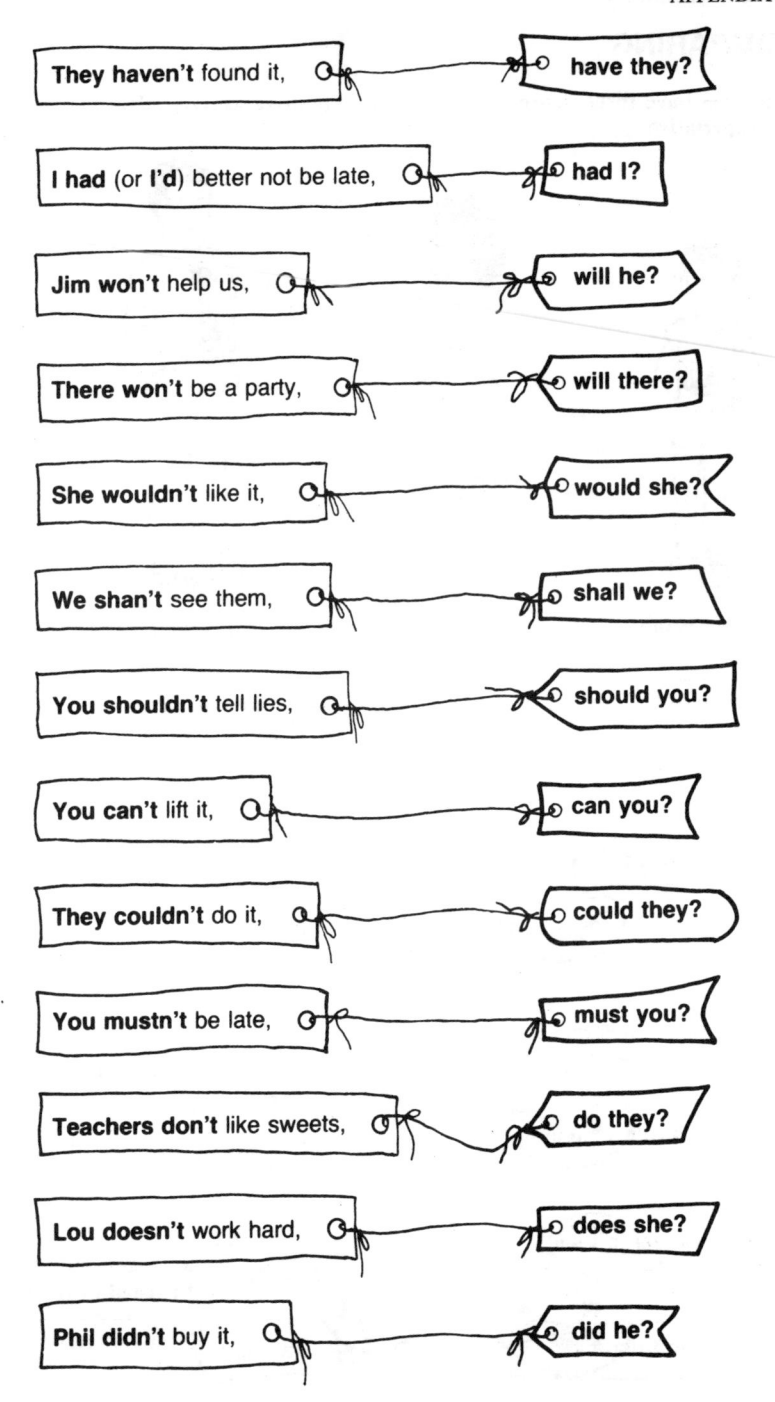

They **haven't** found it,	have they?
I had (or **I'd**) better not be late,	had I?
Jim **won't** help us,	will he?
There **won't** be a party,	will there?
She **wouldn't** like it,	would she?
We **shan't** see them,	shall we?
You **shouldn't** tell lies,	should you?
You **can't** lift it,	can you?
They **couldn't** do it,	could they?
You **mustn't** be late,	must you?
Teachers **don't** like sweets,	do they?
Lou **doesn't** work hard,	does she?
Phil **didn't** buy it,	did he?

COMPARING

Adjectives have three degrees of comparison: **positive**, **comparative** and **superlative**.

Tim is **tall**.

POSITIVE

Mum is **taller** than Tim.

COMPARATIVE

Dad is the **tallest** in the family.

SUPERLATIVE

This snake is **long** and **twisted**.

POSITIVE

This snake is **longer** and **more twisted** than the top one.

COMPARATIVE

This snake is the **longest** and **most twisted** of the three.

SUPERLATIVE

Remember that **adjectives** describe **people** and **things**.
With adjectives that have one syllable you form the **comparative** by adding
-er and the **superlative** by adding **-est**:

bright   bright*er*   bright*est*
warm   warm*er*   warm*est*

> **big**   big*ger*   big*gest*
> **fat**   fat*ter*   fat*test*
> Refer to the spelling rule on page 443.

With two-syllable adjectives ending in **-y** you change the **y** to **i** and use the **-er**
form for the comparative and the **-est** form for the superlative.

funny   funn*ier*   funn*iest*
happy   happ*ier*   happ*iest*

If the adjective has two or more syllables, you form the **comparative** by
adding **more** in front of it, and the **superlative** by adding **most** in front of it:

beautiful   *more* **beautiful**   *most* **beautiful**
careless   *more* **careless**   *most* **careless**
foolish   *more* **foolish**   *most* **foolish**

However, there are a number of other two-syllable adjectives that just use
the **-er** and **-est** forms. Here are some of them:

clever   clever*er*   clever*est*
common   common*er*   common*est*
narrow   narrow*er*   narrow*est*
polite   polit*er*   polit*est*
quiet   quiet*er*   quiet*est*
simple   simpl*er*   simpl*est*
stupid   stupid*er*   stupid*est*

The following positive, comparative and superlative adjectives don't obey
any rules. You just have to learn them:

bad	worse	worst
good	better	best
far	further, farther	furthest, farthest
little	less	least
many	more	most
much	more	most
some	more	most

You will find reminders in grey boxes to help you with
these adjectives when you look them up in the main part
of the dictionary.

Adverbs also have the **positive**, **comparative** and **superlative** degrees of comparison.

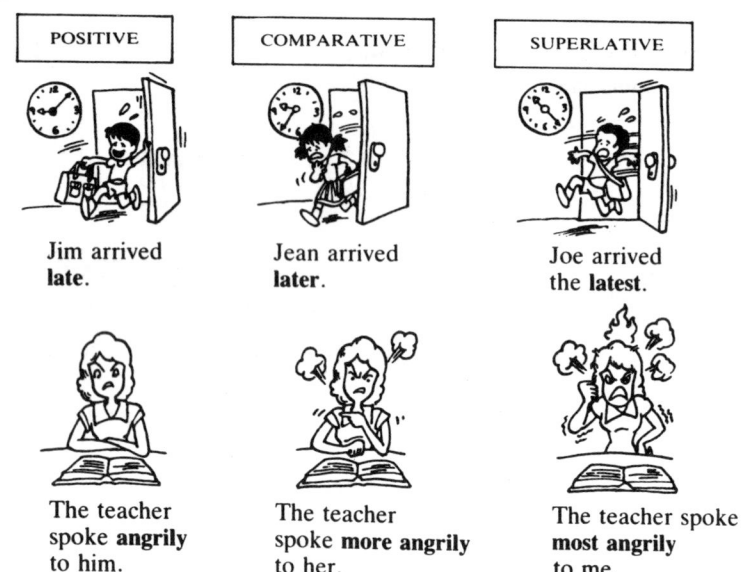

POSITIVE	COMPARATIVE	SUPERLATIVE
Jim arrived **late**.	Jean arrived **later**.	Joe arrived the **latest**.
The teacher spoke **angrily** to him.	The teacher spoke **more angrily** to her.	The teacher spoke **most angrily** to me.

Remember that **adverbs** describe **actions**, or things you **do**.
You form the **comparative** of most adverbs by putting **more** in front of them, and you form the **superlative** by putting **most** in front of them:

greedily	*more* **greedily**	*most* **greedily**
sweetly	*more* **sweetly**	*most* **sweetly**
warmly	*more* **warmly**	*most* **warmly**

Some short adverbs just use the **-er** form for the comparative and the **-est** form for the superlative:

long	**long**er	**long**est
near	**near**er	**near**est
hard	**hard**er	**hard**est
soon	**soon**er	**soon**est

The following adverbs don't obey normal rules in forming the comparative and superlative. You just have to learn them:

badly	worse	worst
well	better	best
far	further, farther	furthest, farthest
little	less	least
much	more	most

You will find reminders to help you with these adverbs when you look them up in the main part of the dictionary.

PUNCTUATION

Capitals come at the beginning of sentences. You use them for names, days and months and you write ' I ' as a capital.

> **M**y mother says **J**oe and **I** must visit the dentist on **T**uesday, 10th **S**eptember.

A **full stop** (**.**) comes at the end of a sentence and a **question mark** (**?**) comes after a question. An **exclamation mark** (**!**) follows commands and greetings and words that you shout out suddenly in surprise, anger or fear.

> Hallo**!** Fancy seeing you here**!** How are you**?**
> You're looking very well**.**

Full stops are used also in some short forms of words, names and titles.

M.P.	=	Member of Parliament	Dr.	=	Doctor
N.Z.	=	New Zealand	Ltd.	=	Limited
P.C.	=	Personal Computer	Rd.	=	Road

A **comma** (**,**) is used to separate things in a list. These may be nouns, phrases or adjectives describing a noun.

> He brought a ball, a spade, a cap and a bucket.

> Here is a very fat, lazy, spotted dog.

> My favourite activities are
> watching TV, cycling, playing with my dog and swimming.

Use a comma to mark a short pause in a sentence.

> When I got home from school, I changed into my jeans. My sister was in the kitchen, making the tea and singing to herself. I expected my brother to be in his room, but he had gone out. I decided I would have to do my homework, even the boring arithmetic.

Use commas round phrases or words that you put in to describe, explain or comment on something.

> I was anxious when I heard that Mr Black, **the headmaster of our school**, had called on my parents. He didn't come to talk about me, **I'm glad to say. However**, he did ask where I was. **Actually**, I'd gone to visit Peter, **a friend of mine**.

Use a comma before **please**, after **yes** and **no**, and before the name of the person who is being spoken to.

> Can you lend me a pencil, please?
> Yes, I can.
> No, you may not draw on the wall, George.

An **apostrophe** (') is used for possession, showing that one thing or person 'owns' another. The apostrophe comes after the whole 'owner' word – before the **s** with singular nouns and with plural nouns like **men**, **women** and **children** that do not end in s; after the **s** with other plural nouns.

the twins' bedroom

Bob's glasses

women's hats

You use an apostrophe also when you run two words together to make a short form, for example, when you write **won't** for **will not**. These forms are used especially when you are giving someone's actual words. The apostrophe shows where a letter or letters have been missed out.

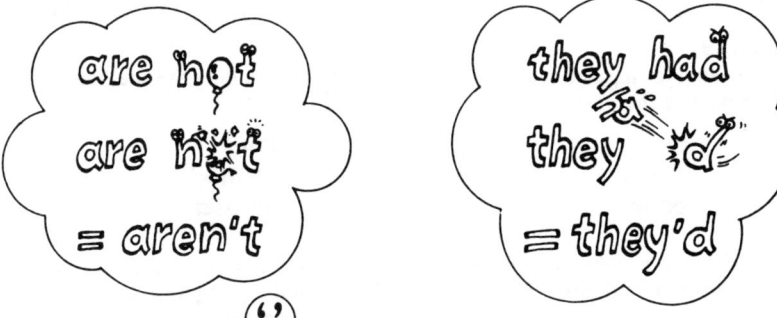

are not
are not
= aren't

they had
they 'd
= they'd

Quotation marks show the beginning and end of what is actually said by someone. You need a comma before the first quotation mark.

Paul said, 'Look at the rain!'
'Yes,' replied Maggie. 'There won't be any picnic today.'
'If we're very tidy,' suggested Joanna, 'we might be allowed a picnic in the sitting-room.'

'blah, blah, blah, blah, blah, blah,'

A **colon** gives the answer expected by the first part of the sentence.

You will need the following things : cardboard, glue and scissors.

A **semi-colon** can be used instead of conjunctions such as **and** and **but**.

Yesterday she felt very ill **but** she is better today.

Yesterday she felt very ill **;** she is better today.

SOME SPELLING RULES

Many words disobey the spelling rules, and many others are just difficult to spell. You will find notes in the main part of the dictionary to help you with some of the difficult spellings.

VERBS

You can add -ing and -ed to many verbs without changing the spelling of the first part of the verb:

fill	**fill**ing	**fill**ed
clean	**clean**ing	**clean**ed
echo	**echo**ing	**echo**ed

But if a verb is only one syllable long, with a single short vowel, and ends in a consonant, you double this final letter before adding -ing and -ed:

stop	**stopp**ing	**stopp**ed
bar	**barr**ing	**barr**ed
fan	**fann**ing	**fann**ed

If a verb has two or more syllables, and the last one has a single short vowel and ends in a consonant, you double this final letter if the stress comes on the last syllable:

pre'fer	**pre'ferr**ing	**pre'ferr**ed
ad'mit	**ad'mitt**ing	**ad'mitt**ed
e'quip	**e'quipp**ing	**e'quipp**ed

But if the stress is not on the last syllable, you don't double the final letter:

'enter	**'enter**ing	**'enter**ed
'gossip	**'gossip**ing	**'gossip**ed

If the last syllable has a short vowel and ends in -l, you double the l, no matter where the stress comes:

'signal	**'signall**ing	**'signall**ed
com'pel	**com'pell**ing	**com'pell**ed

If the verb ends in -c, you add a **k** before adding -ing or -ed:

picnic	**picnick**ing	**picnick**ed
panic	**panick**ing	**panick**ed

If the verb ends in -e, you remove the **e** before adding -ing, and instead of adding -ed, you just add -d:

stare	**star**ing	**star**ed
trace	**trac**ing	**trac**ed
issue	**issu**ing	**issu**ed
muffle	**muffl**ing	**muffl**ed

> But notice these verbs:
>
> | | | |
> |---|---|---|
> | **agree** | **agree**ing | **agree**d |
> | **dye** | **dye**ing | **dye**d |
> | **hoe** | **hoe**ing | **hoe**d |
> | **eye** | **eye**ing | **eye**d |
>
> You keep the **e** before **-ing**.

If the verb ends in **-y**, and there is no vowel before the **y**, you change the **y** to **i** before adding **-es** or **-ed**:

cry	**cry**ing	**cri**es	**cri**ed
hurry	**hurry**ing	**hurri**es	**hurri**ed

> If the verb has a vowel before the **y**, you keep the **y** when you add **-ing** and **-ed**:
>
> | | | |
> |---|---|---|
> | **stay** | **stay**ing | **stay**ed |
> | **survey** | **survey**ing | **survey**ed |
>
> but watch out for these:
>
> | | | |
> |---|---|---|
> | **lay** | **lay**ing | **lai**d |
> | **pay** | **pay**ing | **pai**d |
> | **say** | **say**ing | **sai**d |

If the verb ends in **-ie**, you change **ie** to **y** before adding **-ing**:

tie	**ty**ing	**tie**d
lie	**ly**ing	**lie**d

ADJECTIVES

You will find the rules for forming comparatives and superlatives in the section called **Comparing** on page 479. Notice the following spelling rules:

If an adjective ends in **-e**, you just add **-r** for the comparative and **-st** for the superlative:

ripe	**ripe**r	**ripe**st
polite	**polite**r	**polite**st
free	**free**r	**free**st

If the adjective is only one syllable long, with a single short vowel, and ends in a consonant, you double this final letter before adding **-er** and **-est**.

red	**redd**er	**redd**est
big	**bigg**er	**bigg**est

If the adjective has two syllables and ends in -y, you change the y to i before adding -er and -est:

angry	**angri**er	**angri**est
sunny	**sunni**er	**sunni**est

> But notice these one-syllable adjectives ending in -y:
>
> | | | |
> |---|---|---|
> | **dry** | *dri*er | *dri*est |
> | **sly** | *sly*er | *sly*est |
> | **shy** | **shi**er or **shy**er | **shi**est or **shy**est |

ADVERBS

You form most adverbs by adding -ly to the adjective:

usual	**usual**ly
chief	**chief**ly
stupid	**stupid**ly

> Notice that adjectives ending in -e keep the e before adding -ly, but these three drop it:
>
> | | |
> |---|---|
> | **true** | **tru**ly |
> | **due** | **du**ly |
> | **whole** | **whol**ly |

If the adjective ends in -ic, you add -ally to form the adverb:

basic	**basic**ally
frantic	**frantic**ally

> But the rule is broken by:
>
> | | |
> |---|---|
> | **public** | **public**ly |

If the adjective ends in -y, you change the y to i before adding -ly:

happy	**happi**ly
hungry	**hungri**ly

If the adjective ends in -le, you remove the e and add y:

simple	**simpl**y
double	**doubl**y

You often have a choice of spellings with adjectives ending in -y when it is pronounced ī:

dry	**dri**ly or **dry**ly
sly	**sli**ly or **sly**ly

IE OR EI?

Which way round do these letters come when the sound is *e* as in **he**? There is a rule that everybody learns, and it usually works:

> *i* before *e*,
> except after *c*.

This means that the order is **ie** except when a **c** comes first — then the order is **ei**. Have a look at these words:

chief	brief	conceit
siege	grief	deceive
achieve	thief	deceit
belief	ceiling	receive
relieve	conceive	receipt

> But the rule is broken by:
> **seize**   **neither**
> **weird**   **protein**
> **either**

SINGULAR and PLURAL

The plurals of most nouns are formed by adding **-s** to the singular form:

hut	huts
house	houses
donkey	donkeys

If the singular form of the noun ends in **-s, -ss, -x, -z, -sh** or **-ch** (when it is pronounced **ch** and not **k**), you form the plural by adding **-es**:

gas	gases
boss	bosses
box	boxes
quartz	quartzes
marsh	marshes
church	churches

> But notice the plural if **-ch** is pronounced **k**.
> You add only **-s** to form the plural:
> **stomach**   **stomachs**
> **monarch**   **monarchs**

If the noun ends in **-y**, and there is no vowel before the **y**, you change the **y** to **i** and add **-es**:

spy	spies
ally	allies
fairy	fairies
butterfly	butterflies

> But notice the plural of nouns that have a vowel before the **y**. You keep the **y** and add only -s to form the plural.
>
> | | |
> |---|---|
> | **play** | **play**s |
> | **chimney** | **chimney**s |

For most nouns ending in **-f** and **-fe** the plurals are formed by changing **-f** or **-fe** to **-ves**.

loaf	**loav**es
calf	**calv**es
thief	**thiev**es
knife	**kniv**es

> But there are some exceptions which add only -s to form the plural.
>
> | | |
> |---|---|
> | **belief** | **belief**s |
> | **chief** | **chief**s |
> | **cliff** | **cliff**s |
> | **proof** | **proof**s |
> | **roof** | **roof**s |
> | **safe** | **safe**s |

For most nouns ending in **-o**, you just add **-s** to form the plural.

piano	**piano**s
radio	**radio**s
yoyo	**yoyo**s
zoo	**zoo**s

> But certain nouns have plurals ending in **-oes**.
>
> | | |
> |---|---|
> | **potato**es | **hero**es |
> | **tomato**es | **veto**es |
> | **echo**es | **Negro**es |
> | **domino**es | **embargo**es |

Some nouns change the vowels to form the plural.

foot	f*ee*t
goose	g*ee*se
tooth	t*ee*th
man	m*e*n
mouse	m*i*ce

There is also a special plural formed by adding **-en**.

child	**childr**en
ox	**ox**en

COUNTABLE and UNCOUNTABLE

Countable nouns have a plural form:
books
people
flowers
eyes
children

A plural noun needs a verb in the plural:
His eyes are bright blue. All the people are sitting down.

When a countable noun is used in the singular, it needs a verb in the singular:
My right eye hurts.

Uncountable nouns have no plural form:
homework
furniture
news
rice
salt and pepper

An uncountable noun needs a verb in the singular:
Most of my homework is finished.
All this furniture is old and dirty.
There was rice on all the plates.

Some nouns can be **countable or uncountable**:

coffee	*I must buy some more coffee.*	*I'd like two coffees and one tea, please.*
hair	*Her hair is growing very long.*	*My aunt has lots of grey hairs.*
light	*A beam of light came through the door.*	*Don't forget to switch the lights off.*

A few nouns referring to **groups of people** can take both singular and plural verbs.

Both these sentences are correct:
The whole family is away on holiday.
How are your family?

Use a singular verb with these nouns when you are referring to the group as a whole:
3A is the top class.

Use a plural verb when you are thinking more about the individuals in the group:
The class are working on their individual projects.

Other examples of words like this are *group, team, committee, choir* and *audience*.

ARTICLES

a or **an**, **the** (ðiː) or **the** (ðə)

Use **a** or **the** (pronounced /ə/ and /ðə/) before a consonant sound.
Use **an** or **the** (pronounced /ən/ or /an/ and /ðɪ/ or /ðiː/) before a vowel sound.

a	book	*an*	orange
	person		umbrella
	uniform		hour
	one-legged man		honest girl

a/an or the

Use **the** before a noun when the person you're talking to knows which particular thing is being referred to because

- it has just been mentioned:
    She has a son and a daughter. The son is a teacher.
- it is connected with something that has been mentioned before:
    When I opened the door, the handle fell off.
- it is something that is unique:
    the sun ; the world.
- it is the only one you could possibly mean in the situation you are in:
    There's someone at the door.
    The President made a long speech.
- more information about it is in the same sentence:
    That's the man that stole my bike.
    Where's the key to room 21?
- it is a superlative (and therefore unique):
    She's the best swimmer in her class.
- it is with an ordinal number or *next, last* etc:
    I chose the second dish on the menu.
    You are the last person to arrive.

The should also be used when a singular noun refers to the idea of something, rather than a particular object:
   The telephone was invented in 1876.

Use **a** or **an** before a singular countable noun when the person you are talking to does not know which particular thing you are referring to:
   A dog walked into the room.
   I've got a good idea.

But do not use an article in this case, if the noun is uncountable or plural:
   There's some coffee over there.
   Some children were playing outside.

PRONOUNS

Pronouns are used instead of nouns to refer to people or things without naming them:

referring to the **subject** of a verb:

Who wants another ice cream?	*I do!*
I won the first prize!	*Did you?*
Where is my mother sitting?	*She's here!*
What is your address?	*It's in the book.*
That man's a private detective.	*Is he?*
Which children have already finished?	*We have!*
We're going to get married.	*You're joking!*
Why did the children run away?	*They were frightened.*

referring to the **object** of a verb:
    Look at me!
    I love you.
    The noise surprised her.
    A car passed him.
    Don't touch it!
    The headmaster told us off.
    I can't take you all.
    Would you put them in a vase?

referring to something that belongs to someone:
    Whose is this money?
    Could it be *yours*? No, it's not *mine*.
    But Themba dropped some money. It could be *his*.
    And Lindiwi lost her purse. It could be *hers*.

    Could it be *yours*? No it's not *ours*.
    But Themba and Lindiwi were searching for some money. It could be *theirs*.

in questions referring to the subject of the verb:

for actions:	*What* are you doing?
for things:	*What* is your name?
for people:	*Who* is talking?

in questions referring to the object of the verb:

for things:	*Which* book did you like best?
for people:	*Whom** or *who* did you meet?
	Whose pen are you using?

**Note:* When a preposition comes before this pronoun, you must use *whom*, but if you use a preposition at the end of the phrase, you can use *who*:
    From *whom* did you borrow the money?
    Who did you borrow the money *from*?

referring to a noun in another part of a sentence:
> for people, use **who** (subject), **whom** or **who** (object), **that** (subject or object) or **whose** (possessive):

Examples:
> *I know a woman who (or that) smokes a pipe.*
> *The girl whom (or who or that) I like best is leaving the school.*
>   (See note below.)
> *The man to whom she was speaking suddenly disappeared.*

or

> *The man who (or that) she was speaking to suddenly disappeared.*
>   (See note below.)
> *That's the man that (or who) helped me.*
> *The child whose father was a teacher knew all the answers.*

for things, use **which** or **that**:

Examples:
> *These are the tickets which (or that) we were given.*
> *The room in which we were staying had no windows.*
> *Where are the flowers which (or that) I picked for Granny?*
>   (See note below.)

Note: If they do not follow a preposition, **who**, **whom** or **which** can be replaced by **that** or missed out completely:
> *The room that (or which) we were staying in had no windows.*
> *The children who (or whom or that) Mrs. Nkosi usually teaches will join Standard 6 today.*

However, **who**, **which** or **that** should not be omitted if they are the subject of a verb:
> *That's the car which (or that) was parked there yesterday.*
> *There's the lady who (or that) drove me home.*

which and **who** can also be used to add further information about something or someone:
> *The film of 'Cry the Beloved Country', which was originally made in South Africa, has been shown all over the world.*
> *My teacher, who plays in a jazz band, is going to take us to a recording session.*

AUXILIARY VERBS: DO, HAVE, BE

Do, **have** and **be** help to make different forms of verbs in English:

do helps to make **questions** and **negative** verbs in **present** and **past** tenses.

For example:

	(negative)	(question)
I understand.	*I don't understand.*	*Do you understand.*
	He doesn't understand.	
She sat down.	*We didn't sit down.*	*Did you sit down?*

have helps to make the **perfect** tenses:

For example:
> *<u>Have</u> you <u>seen</u> my briefcase?*
> *<u>Has</u> he <u>gone</u>?*
> *I <u>haven't been</u> here for ages.*
> *They <u>had left</u> an hour before we arrived.*
> *<u>Will</u> you <u>have finished</u> by midnight?*

be helps to make **continuous** tenses:

For example:
> *Vincent <u>is studying</u> hard.*
> *<u>Are</u> you <u>enjoying</u> yourself?*
> *We <u>were watching</u> TV all evening.*
> *<u>Have</u> you <u>been waiting</u> long?*
> *They'<u>ll be leaving</u> soon.*

be also helps to make **passive** sentences:

For example:
> *Paper <u>is made</u> from wood.*
> *They <u>are being tested</u> on their vocabulary.*
> *The invitations <u>have not been sent out</u> yet.*
> *She <u>was asked</u> to give a speech.*
> *It'<u>ll be finished</u> soon.*

You can also use **do**, **have**, and **be** to make **short answers** to questions:

do:	*Does anyone know the answer?*	*Yes, I <u>do</u>!*
	Does this bus go into town?	*Of course it <u>doesn't</u>!*
	Who made this cake?	*Grace <u>did</u>.*
have:	*Have you read this book?*	*Yes, I <u>have</u>.*
	Has Lydia been invited?	*No, she <u>hasn't</u>.*
	Has the food gone already?	*Yes, but the drinks <u>haven't</u>.*
be:	*Are you still writing that letter?*	*Yes, I <u>am</u>.*
	Are they enjoying living in the city?	*Well, John <u>is</u> but Nomsa <u>isn't</u>.*
	'My parents are getting old and boring.'	*'Well, mine <u>aren't</u>!'*

VERB FORMS and TENSES

Use different forms of verbs to make different tenses:

For example:
> **drive** (present); **drove** (past); **driven** (perfect)
>
> *She <u>drives</u> to school every day.*
> *We <u>drove</u> through the gates just before they closed.*
> *Have you ever <u>driven</u> a bus?*

Use different tenses to express when something takes place:

TIME		***continuous tenses***
NOW, PRESENT	*I <u>understand</u>.* *He <u>agrees</u> with me.*	*She <u>is hoping</u> to go to university.*
Also for frequent actions	*I <u>write</u> a lot of letters.*	
THEN, PAST eg *yesterday* some time ago, last week, month etc	*I <u>went</u> home early yesterday.* *He <u>offered</u> to help me.*	*She <u>was sleeping</u> at midnight when I phoned her.*
FUTURE The time ahead, for which you make plans and decisions	*I'<u>ll</u> take you home.* *He'<u>ll</u> never <u>play</u> again.* *I'<u>m going to tell</u> you a story.* *He'<u>s going</u> to change his job.*	*She'<u>ll be flying</u> from New York tomorrow.* *She'<u>s going to be travelling</u> all the world.*
BEFORE NOW eg *ever, never, yet, for* or *since* a time	*I <u>have</u> never <u>spoken</u> to him.* *He <u>has been</u> here for hours.*	*She <u>has been reading</u> since early morning.*
BEFORE THEN (PAST)	*I <u>had been</u> there several times before.* *He <u>had</u> already <u>died</u>.*	*She <u>had been crying</u> for hours.*
BEFORE A TIME IN THE FUTURE eg *by* next week, month etc, *in* two days' time	*I <u>will have forgotten</u> this by tomorrow.* *He <u>will have finished</u> in an hour.*	*At 2 o'clock, she <u>will have been running</u> for exactly 30 minutes.*

MODAL VERBS

This is a small group of verbs that are used with other verbs. They are:
can, could, may, might, shall, should, will, would, must, ought to and **used to**.

They are followed by another verb:
I *can* swim.   You *must go* now.   I *used to live* in a flat.
Note: don't forget to include to with **ought to** and **used to**.

They do not need an 's' when used with **he, she** and **it**:
He can stay here tonight.
She may want to come.
It might rain tomorrow.

They are used to form questions without using **do/did**:
Can you swim?   Ought we to tell the police?
Note: put the subject of the verb between **ought** and **to**.

Note: used to can have a question form with **do/did**:
Did you used to have a green coat?

Their negative forms usually need only **not** or **n't** (without **do/did**):
You can't (or cannot) park there.
He shouldn't (or should not) work so hard.
We won't (or will not) wait any longer.
They oughn't (or ought not) to do that.

Note: Nowadays people say **didn't use to** instead of **used not to**:
I didn't use to like cheese, but I do now.

Impressão e acabamento
Cromosete
GRÁFICA E EDITORA LTDA.
Rua Uhland, 307 - Vila Ema
Cep: 03283-000 - São Paulo - SP
Tel/Fax: 011 6104-1176